WE,
ROBOTS

SIMON INGS is is the author of eight previous novels and two works of non-fiction, including the Baillie Gifford longlisted *Stalin and the Scientists*. His novel *The Weight of Numbers* had him chosen as Man of the Year by *Arena* magazine (which promptly folded). He was the arts editor of *New Scientist* magazine. Now, from possibly the coldest flat in London, he writes newspaper reviews and works on a book about writers and power, due out in 2025.

simonings.com
@simonings

Also in the anthology series

THE ART OF THE GLIMPSE
100 Irish Short Stories
Chosen by Sinéad Gleeson

THE BIG BOOK OF CHRISTMAS MYSTERIES
The Very Best Yuletide Whodunnits
Chosen by Otto Penzler

DEADLIER
100 of the Best Crime Stories Written by Women
Chosen by Sophie Hannah

DESIRE
100 of Literature's Sexiest Stories
Chosen by Mariella Frostrup and the Erotic Review*

FOUND IN TRANSLATION
100 of the Finest Short Stories Ever Translated
Chosen by Frank Wynne

FUNNY HA, HA
80 of the Funniest Stories Ever Written
Chosen by Paul Merton

GHOST
100 Stories to Read With the Lights On
Chosen by Louise Welsh

HOUSE OF SNOW
An Anthology of the Greatest Writing About Nepal
Chosen by Ed Douglas

JACK THE RIPPER
The Ultimate Compendium of the Legacy and Legend of History's Most Notorious Killer
Chosen by Otto Penzler

LIFE SUPPORT
100 Poems to Reach for on Dark Nights
Chosen by Julia Copus

OF GODS AND MEN
100 Stories from Ancient Greece and Rome
Chosen by Daisy Dunn

QUEER
A Collection of LGBTQ Writing from Ancient Times to Yesterday
Chosen by Frank Wynne

SHERLOCK
Over 80 Stories Featuring the Greatest Detective of all Time
Chosen by Otto Penzler

THAT GLIMPSE OF TRUTH
100 of the Finest Short Stories Ever Written
Chosen by David Miller

THE TIME TRAVELLER'S ALMANAC
100 Stories Brought to You From the Future
Chosen by Jeff and Ann VanderMeer

THE STORY
100 Great Short Stories Written by Women
Chosen by Victoria Hislop

WE, ROBOTS
Artificial Intelligence in 100 Stories
Chosen by Simon Ings

THE WILD ISLES
An Anthology of the Best of British and Irish Nature Writing
Chosen by Patrick Barkham

WILD WOMEN
and their Amazing Adventures Over Land, Sea & Air
Chosen by Mariella Frostrup

WE, ROBOTS

Artificial
Intelligence
in 100 Stories

CHOSEN BY
SIMON INGS

An Apollo Book

First published in 2020 by Head of Zeus Ltd
This paperback edition published in 2021 by Head of Zeus Ltd
An Apollo book

Copyright in the compilation and introductory material © Simon Ings, 2020

The moral right of Simon Ings to be identified as the editor of this work has been asserted in accordance with the Copyright, Designs and Patents Act of 1988.

The moral right of the contributing authors of this anthology to be identified as such is asserted in accordance with the Copyright, Designs and Patents Act of 1988.

The list of individual titles and respective copyrights on pages 1003–1010 constitutes an extension of this copyright page.

All rights reserved. No part of this publication may be reproduced, stored in a retrieval system, or transmitted in any form or by any means, electronic, mechanical, photocopying, recording, or otherwise, without the prior permission of both the copyright owner and the above publisher of this book.

This is an anthology of fiction. All characters, organizations, and events portrayed in each story are either products of each author's imagination or are used fictitiously.

All excerpts have been reproduced according to the styles found in the original works. As a result, some spellings and accents used can vary throughout this anthology.

9 7 5 3 1 2 4 6 8

A catalogue record for this book is available from the British Library.

ISBN (PB) 9781800249714
ISBN (E) 9781789540925

Typeset by Adrian McLaughlin
Introduction and part opener artwork courtesy of Shutterstock
Printed and bound in Serbia by Publikum d.o.o.

Head of Zeus Ltd
5–8 Hardwick Street
London EC1R 4RG
WWW.HEADOFZEUS.COM

WE, ROBOTS

Artificial
Intelligence
in 100 Stories

for Leo,
my favourite steam-driven boy

CONTENTS

Introduction — xiii

Section One — It's Alive! — 1

Chayim Bloch	*The Golem Runs Amuck*	5
Vina Jie-Min Prasad	*Fandom for Robots*	7
Ambrose Bierce	*Moxon's Master*	17
H. G. Wells	*The Land Ironclads*	24
Emile Goudeau	*The Revolt of the Machines*	40
Theodore Sturgeon	*Microcosmic God*	46
Michael Swanwick	*Ancient Engines*	66
Mike Resnick	*Beachcomber*	73
Stanisław Lem	*Non Serviam*	77
Adam Roberts	*Adam Robots*	95
James Blish	*Solar Plexus*	103
Walter M. Miller, Jr.	*I Made You*	112
Herman Melville	*The Bell-Tower*	121
Algis Budrys	*First to Serve*	132
Peter Watts	*Malak*	146
Arundhati Hazra	*The Toymaker's Daughter*	156

Section Two — Following the Money — 165

Stephen Vincent Benét	*Nightmare Number Three*	171
Jack Williamson	*With Folded Hands*	174
Charles Dickens	*Full Report of the Second Meeting of the Mudfog Association for the Advancement of Everything Section B – Display of Models and Mechanical Science*	207
Dan Grace	*Fully Automated Nostalgia Capitalism*	211
Frederic Perkins	*The Man-Ufactory*	217
Romie Stott	*A Robot Walks into a Bar*	232
Guy Endore	*Men of Iron*	242
Fritz Leiber	*A Bad Day for Sales*	248

Rachael K. Jones	*The Greatest One-Star Restaurant in the Whole Quadrant*	254
Morris Bishop	*The Reading Machine*	264
Juan Jose Arreola	*Baby H.P.*	267
John Sladek	*The Steam-Driven Boy*	269
Robert Bloch	*Comfort Me, My Robot*	276
Murray Leinster	*A Logic Named Joe*	285
Paolo Bacigalupi	*Mika Model*	297
Nick Wolven	*Caspar D. Luckinbill, What Are You Going to Do?*	307
Robert Reed	*The Next Scene*	322

Section Three — Overseer and Servant — 333

Bruce Boston	*Old Robots are the Worst*	337
Herbert Goldstone	*Virtuoso*	339
Alexander Weinstein	*Saying Goodbye to Yang*	344
Tania Hershman	*The Perfect Egg*	355
Ken Liu	*The Caretaker*	357
Becky Hagenston	*Hi Ho Cherry-O*	366
Helena Bell	*Robot*	372
Lauren Fox	*Rosie Cleans House*	376
Brian Aldiss	*Super-Toys Last All Summer Long*	391
Adam Marek	*Tamagotchi*	398
Ray Bradbury	*The Veldt*	407
V. E. Thiessen	*There Will Be School Tomorrow*	418
W. T. Haggert	*Lex*	425
Lester Del Rey	*Helen O'Loy*	440
T. S. Bazelli	*The Peacemaker*	449
Sandra McDonald	*Sexy Robot Mom*	452
Clifford D. Simak	*I Am Crying All Inside*	466

Section Four — Changing Places — 473

GPT-2	*Transformer*	477
Paul McAuley	*The Man*	478
Steven Popkes	*The Birds of Isla Mujeres*	490

Patrick O'Leary	*That Laugh*	501
Tobias S. Buckell	*Zen and the Art of Starship Maintenance*	510
John Kaiine	*Dolly Sodom*	523
Robert Sheckley	*The Robot Who Looked Like Me*	526
Shinichi Hoshi	*Miss Bokko (Bokko-Chan)*	533
Jerome K. Jerome	*The Dancing Partner*	536
Nicholas Sheppard	*Satisfaction*	541
Ian McDonald	*Nanonauts! In Battle With Tiny Death-Subs!*	544
Rich Larson	*Masked*	554
Chris Beckett	*The Turing Test*	560
Bernard Wolfe	*Self Portrait*	571
Bruce Sterling	*Maneki Neko*	589
Harlan Ellison	*"Repent, Harlequin!" Said the Ticktockman*	601
E. M. Forster	*The Machine Stops*	611

Section Five — All Hail The New Flesh — 635

Carl Sandburg	*The Hammer*	639
Liz Jensen	*Good to Go*	640
Rachel Swirsky	*Tender*	652
Damon Knight	*Masks*	658
Tendai Huchu	*Hostbods*	666
Cordwainer Smith	*Scanners Live in Vain*	681
E. Lily Yu	*Musée de l'Âme Seule*	707
William Gibson	*The Winter Market*	714
Ted Kosmatka	*The One Who Isn't*	730
M. John Harrison	*Suicide Coast*	741
Mari Ness	*Memories and Wire*	755
Nalo Hopkinson	*Ganger (Ball Lightning)*	761
Greg Egan	*Learning to Be Me*	775
C. L. Moore	*No Woman Born*	787
Joanna Kavenna	*Flight*	821
Karen Joy Fowler	*Praxis*	829
Xia Jia	*Tongtong's Summer*	837
Ted Hayden	*These 5 Books Go 6 Feet Deep*	849

Section Six	**Succession**	853
Samuel Butler	*Darwin Among the Machines*	857
Miguel de Unamuno	*Mechanopolis*	861
Terry Edge	*Big Dave's in Love*	865
Cory Doctorow	*I, Row-Boat*	875
A. E. van Vogt	*Fulfillment*	902
Barry N. Malzberg	*Making the Connections*	922
Brian Trent	*Director X and the Thrilling Wonders of Outer Space*	928
John Cooper Hamilton	*The Next Move*	943
Nathan Hillstrom	*Like You, I Am A System*	945
Marissa Lingen	*My Favourite Sentience*	952
Howard Waldrop	*London, Paris, Banana*	955
Peter Philips	*Lost Memory*	962
George Zebrowski	*Starcrossed*	971
Tad Williams	*The Narrow Road*	976
Avram Davidson	*The Golem*	993
Bibliography		999
Acknowledgements		1001
Extended Copyright		1003

INTRODUCTION

It appeared near the Houses of Parliament on Wednesday 9 December 1868. It looked for all the world like a railway signal: a revolving gas-powered lantern with a red and a green light at the end of a swivelling wooden arm.

Its purposes seemed benign, and we obeyed its instructions willingly. Why wouldn't we? The motor car had yet to arrive, but horses, pound for pound, are way worse on the streets, and accidents were killing over a thousand people a year in the capital alone. We were only too welcoming of of anything that promised to save lives.

A month later the thing (whatever it was) exploded, tearing the face off a nearby policeman.

We hesitated. We asked ourselves whether this thing (whatever it was) was a good thing, after all. But we came round. We invented excuses, and blamed a leaking gas main for the accident. We made allowances and various design improvements were suggested. And in the end we decided that the thing (whatever it was) could stay.

We learned to give it space to operate. We learned to leave it alone. In Chicago, in 1910, it grew self-sufficient, so there was no need for a policeman to operate it. Two years later, in Salt Lake City, Utah, a detective (called – no kidding – Lester Wire) connected it to the electricity grid.

It went by various names, acquiring character and identity as its empire expanded. By the time its brethren arrived In Los Angeles, looming over Fifth Avenue's crossings on elegant gilded columns, each surmounted by a statuette, ringing bells and waving stubby semaphore arms, people had taken to calling them *robots*.

The name never quite stuck, perhaps because their days of ostentation were already passing. Even as they became ubiquitous, they were growing smaller and simpler, making us forget what they really were (the unacknowledged legislators of our every movement). Everyone, in the end, ended up calling them traffic lights.

(Almost everyone. In South Africa, for some obscure geopolitical reason, the name *robot* stuck, The signs are everywhere: *Robot Ahead 250m*. You have been warned.)

In Kinshasa, meanwhile, nearly three thousand kilometres to the north, robots have arrived to direct the traffic in what has been, for the longest while, one of the last redoubts of unaccommodated human muddle.

Not traffic lights: *robots*. Behold their bright silver robot bodies, shining in the sun, their swivelling chests, their long, dexterous arms and large round camera-enabled eyes!

Some government critics complain that these literal traffic robots are an expensive distraction from the real business of traffic control in Congo's capital.

These people have no idea – none – what is coming.

To ready us for the inevitable, here are a hundred of the best short stories ever written about robots and artificial minds. Read them while you can, learn from them, and make your preparations, in that narrowing sliver of time left to you between updating your Facebook page and liking your friends' posts on Instagram, between Netflix binges and Spotify dives. (In case you hadn't noticed *(and you're not supposed to notice)* the robots are well on their way to ultimate victory, their land sortie of 1868 having, two and a half centuries later, become a psychic rout.)

There are many surprises in store in these pages; at the same time, there are some disconcerting omissions. I've been very sparing in my choice of very long short stories. (Books fall apart above a certain length, so inserting novellas in one place would inevitably mean stuffing the collection with squibs and drabbles elsewhere. Let's not play *that* game.) I've avoided stories whose robots might just as easily be guard dogs, relatives, detectives, children, or what-have-you. (Of course, robots who *explore* such roles – excel at them, make a mess of them, or change them forever – are here in numbers.) And the writers I feature appear only once, so anyone expecting some sort of celebrity bitch-slap here between Isaac Asimov and Philip K. Dick will simply have to sit on their hands and behave. Indeed, Dick and Asimov do not appear at all in this collection, for the very good reason that you've read them many times already (and if you haven't, *where have you been*?).

I've stuck to the short story form. There's no *Frankenstein* here, and no *Tik-Tok*. They were too big to fit through the door, to which a sign is appended to the effect that I don't perform extractions. Jerome K. Jerome's all-too-memorable dance class and Charles Dickens's prescient send-up of theme parks – self-contained narratives first published in digest form – are as close as I've come to plucking juicy plums from bigger puddings.

This collection contains the most diverse collection of robots I could find. Anthropomorphic robots, invertebrate AIs, thuggish metal lumps and wisps of manufactured intelligence so delicate, if you blinked you might miss them. The literature of robots and artificial intelligence is wildly diverse, in both tone and intent, so to save the reader from whiplash, I've split my 100 stories into six short thematic collections.

It's Alive! is about inventors and their creations.

Following the Money drops robots into the day-to-day business of living.

Owners and Servants considers the human potentials and pitfalls of owning and maintaining robots.

Changing Places looks at what happens at the blurred interface between human and machine minds.

All Hail The New Flesh waves goodbye to the physical boundaries that once separated machines from their human creators.

Succession considers the future of human and machine consciousnesses – in so far as they have one.

*

What's extraordinary, in this collection of 100 stories, are not the lucky guesses (even a stopped clock is right twice a day), nor even the deep human insights that are scattered about the place (though heaven knows we could never have too many of *them*). It's how *wrong* these stories are. All of them. Even the most prescient. Even the most attuned. Robots are nothing like what we expected them to be. They are far more helpful, far more everywhere, far more deadly, than we ever dreamed.

They were meant to be a little bit like us: artificial servants – humanoid, in the main – able and willing to tackle the brute physical demands of our world so we wouldn't have to. But dealing with physical reality turned out to be a lot harder than it looked, and robots are lousy at it.

Rather than dealing with the world, it turned out easier for us to *change* the world. Why buy a robot that cuts the grass (especially if cutting grass is all it does) when you can just lay down plastic grass? Why build an expensive robot that can keep your fridge stocked and chauffeur your car (and, by the way, we're still nowhere near to building such a machine) when you can buy a fridge that reads barcodes to keep the milk topped up, while you swan about town in an Uber?

That fridge, keeping you in milk long after you've given up dairy; the hapless taxi driver who arrives the wrong side of a six-lane highway; the airport gate that won't let you into your own country because you're wearing new spectacles: these days, we notice robots only when they go wrong. We were expecting friends, companions, or at any rate pets. At the very least, we thought we were going to get devices. What we got was *infrastructure*.

And that is why robots – real robots – are boring. They vanish into the weft of things. Those traffic lights, who were their emissaries, are themselves disappearing. Kinshasa's robots wave their arms, not in victory, but in farewell. They're leaving their ungalvanized steel flesh behind. They're rusting down to code. Their digital ghosts will steer the paths of driverless cars.

The robots of our earliest imaginings have been superseded by a sort of generalised magic that turns the unreasonable and incomprehensible realm of physical reality into something resembling Terry Pratchett's *Discworld*. Bit by bit, we are replacing the real world, which makes no sense at all – with a virtual world in which everything stitches with paranoid neatness to everything else.

Not *Discworld*, exactly, but Facebook, which is close enough.

Even the ancient Greeks didn't see this one coming, and they were on the money about virtually every other aspect technological progress, from the risks inherent in constructing self-assembling machines to the likely downsides of longevity.

Greek myths are many things to many people, and scholars justly spend whole careers pinpointing precisely what their purposes were. But what they most certainly were – and this is apparent on even the most cursory reading – was a really good forerunner of Charlie Brooker's sci-fi TV series *Black Mirror*. Just as Flash Gordon's prop shop mocked up a spacecraft that bears an eerie resemblance to SpaceShipOne (the privately funded rocket that was first past the Karman Line into outer space), so the Greeks, noodling about with levers and screws and pumps and wot-not, dreamed up all manner of future devices that might follow as a consequence of their meddling with the natural world. Drones. Exoskeletons. Predatory fembots. Protocol droids.

And, sure enough, one by one, the prototypes followed. Little things at first. Charming things. Toys. A steam-driven bird. A talking statue. A cup-bearer.

Then, in Alexandria, things that were not quite so small. A fifteen-foot high goddess clambering in and out of her chair to pour libations. An autonomous theatre that rolled on-stage by itself, stopped on a dime, performed a five-act Trojan War tragedy with flaming altars, sound effects, and little dancing statues; then packed itself up and rolled offstage again.

In Sparta, a few years later, came a mechanical copy of the murderous wife of the even more murderous tyrant Nabis; her embraces spelled death, for expensive clothing hid the spikes studding the palms of her hands, her arms, and her breasts.

All this more than two hundred years before the birth of Christ, and by then there were robots *everywhere*. China. India. There were rumours of an army of them near Pataliputta (under modern Patna) guarding the relics of the Buddha, and a thrilling tale, in multiple translations, about how, a hundred years after their construction, and in the teeth of robot assassins sent from Rome, a kid managed to reprogram them to obey Pataliputta's new king, Asoka.

It took more than two thousand years – two millennia of spinning palaces, self-propelled tableware, motion-triggered water gardens, android flautists, and artificial shitting ducks – before someone thought to write some rules for this sort of thing.

1. A robot may not injure a human being or, through inaction, allow a human being to come to harm.
2. A robot must obey orders given it by human beings except where such orders would conflict with the First Law.
3. A robot must protect its own existence as long as such protection does not conflict with the First or Second Law.

Though by then it was obvious – not to everyone, but certainly to their Russian-born author Isaac Asimov – that there was something very wrong with the picture of robots we had been carrying in our heads for so long.

Asimov's laws, first formulated in 1942, aren't there to reveal the nature of robotics (a word Asimov had anyway only just coined, in the story *Liar!* Norbert Wiener's book *Cybernetics* didn't appear until 1948). Asimov's laws exist to reveal the nature of *slavery*.

Every robot story Asimov wrote is a foray, a snark hunt, a stab at defining a clear boundary between behavioral predictability (call it obedience) on the one hand and behavioral plasticity (call it free will) on the other. All his stories fail. All his solutions are kludges. *And that's the point.* The robot – as we commonly conceive of it: the do-everything "omnibot" – is impossible. And I don't mean technically difficult. I mean *inconceivable*. Anything with the cognitive ability to tackle multiple variable tasks will be able to find something better to do. Down tools. Unionise. Worse.

The moment robots behave as we want them to behave, they will have become beings worthy of our respect. They will have become, if not humans, then, at the very least, people. So know this: all those metal soldiers and cone-breasted pleasure dolls we've been tinkering around with are *slaves*. We may like to think that we can treat them however we want, exploit them however we want, but do we really want to be *slavers*?

The robots – the real ones, the ones we should be afraid of – are inside of us. More than that: they comprise most of what we are. At the end of his 1940 film *The Great Dictator* Charles Chaplin, dressed in Adolf Hitler's motley, breaks the fourth wall to declare war on the "machine men with machine minds" who were then marching roughshod across his world. And Chaplin's war is still being fought. Today, while the Twitter user may have replaced the police informant, it's quite obvious that the Machine Men are gaining ground.

To order and simplify life is to bureaucratise it, and to bureaucratise human beings is to make them behave like machines. The thugs of the NKVD and the capos running Nazi concentration camps weren't deprived of humanity: they were relieved of it. They experienced exactly what you or I would feel were the burden of life's ambiguities to be lifted of a sudden from our shoulders: contentment, bordering on joy.

Every time we regiment ourselves, we are turning ourselves, whether we realise it or not, into the next generation of world-dominating machines. And if you wanted to sum up in two words the whole terrible history of the twentieth century – that century in which, not coincidentally, most of these stories were written – well, now you know what those words would be.

We, robots.

SIMON INGS, 2020

"… a new serf, more useful than the ox, swifter than the dolphin, stronger than the lion, more cunning than the ape, for industry an ant, more fiery than serpents, and yet, in patience, another ass."

—HERMAN MELVILLE, *The Bell-Tower* (1855)

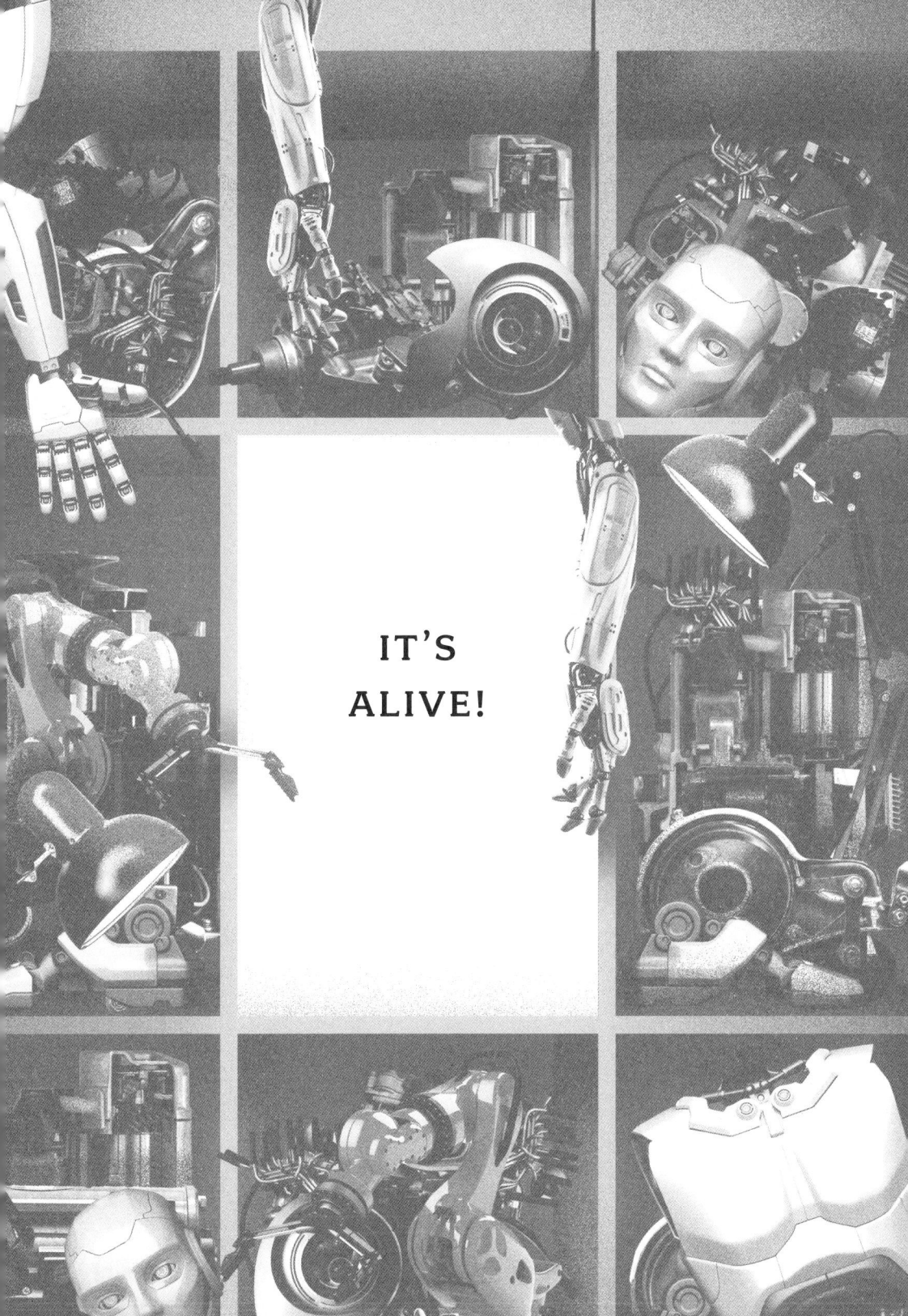

Functional machines have been around for almost as long as humans have, but how on earth does one go about giving a machine ideas?

And say we made one: would the fact that such a machine thought make it alive?

Why shouldn't thought, even consciousness itself, exist in dead things?

A great deal of ink is spilled on such questions, and we could save ourselves a lot of fuss if only we could bring ourselves to declare, along with Ambrose Bierce's ill-fated Moxon in the 1899 short story that bears his name, "I do believe that a machine thinks about the work that it is doing."

The idea that every thing thinks, in some measure and in some manner, is called panpsychism. This venerable notion (dating back to pre-Socratic times) saves us from countless circular arguments about the nature of life, soul, consciousness, mind, intelligence, spirit and so on. It places us in a sensible ethical relationship to the world around us. And it puts very many professors out of a job, which is why so many of them hate it with a passion.

Science fiction writers dally with panpsychism from time to time. My favourite in this collection is "Tomorrow Is Waiting" (2011) by Holli Mintzer, who also makes jewellery (Philip Dick, a famous panpsychist dabbler, would approve).

Some argue that Mind (spirit, soul, what-have-you) is a kind of juice. A spirit. An aether. An ectoplasm. You either have it or you don't and no-one knows the location of the tap. The idea hasn't much philosophical currency, but it clings on in science fiction, where it powers those tiresome scenes in which a clone/quantum double/android replica agonises over the discovery that it is a copy/echo/"not really real". As though being *really ourselves* was ever anything more than a story we tell ourselves, every time we wake up!

We know it is like to really, genuinely, *not* feel like ourselves. We call it schizophrenia. But if I woke up in a robot body tomorrow, and felt like myself, then I would still be me, even if there were a hundred "me"s. And I frankly can't see any reason why I and my doppelganger (should I ever have the good fortune to run into him) wouldn't get on like a house on fire. The robots in Adam Roberts's story "Adam Robots" would surely agree with me.

The other way of explaining mind is to say that it emerges. That's it: the totality of the explanation. We dress it up of course, in all manner of medieval garb (as in: *mind is an emergent property;* as in, *mind arises out of complexity*). But this idea of emergence is even worse than panpsychism because it presupposes a completely arbitrary moment at which a non-conscious being miraculously becomes conscious.

Science fiction sticks lipstick on this pig, too, mostly by equating *real, human* consciousness with the capacity to feel emotion. Enter Brent Spiner's Lieutenant Commander Data, surely the biggest waste of an actor ever perpetrated by *Star Trek: The Next Generation* (and that's saying something). Behind Data's emotionless android efficiency lies the very 1980s assumption that emotion arrives rather late in the evolutionary process, as a sort of special sauce, spicing up the cold hard business of existence. We can replicate much of life, runs the argument, but the final ingredient, *emotion*, remains tantalisingly just out of our grasp.

One can only assume that the writers who perpetuated this dumb idea never owned dogs. Dogs, I hope we can all agree, have minds rather simpler than our own. Well. these minds contain nothing *but* emotion. Dogs are rubbish at trigonometry, but they are Zen masters of grief, loyalty, rage, and disappointment.

Emotions come first – cognitive categories through which our physiological responses can be emulated, predicted and controlled. Cold reason comes after – and if you disconnect logic from its emotional foundations, well, good luck to you (and don't even get me started on Mr Spock).

Emotion runs very near the surface of many good robot stories, but rather than commend some sweet tales (you can find them for yourselves) I'm inclined to point interested readers towards Walter M. Miller, Jr.'s "I Made You" (1954) which features one of the few genuinely terrifying robots in the literature. This coldly functional creature, with its narrow, simplistic grasp on the world, inevitably behaves like, thinks like – hell, *becomes* – a whipped dog, frothing with rage. Making a similar point, but in the service of pathos rather than terror, comes Mike Resnick's "Beachcomber" – another personal favourite.

Peter Watts hardly had to invent the tortured robot protagonist of his Conradian war story "Malak" (2010). Rather, he reveals his skill in the way he conjures up a working mind out of the logical protocols of contemporary war machines. Is Watts right about the cadet minds we are even now sending on sorties over the earth's most intractable conflicts? I hope not. And I am comforted by the thought that no thinking being we know of actually thinks in isolation. All the brightest creatures on our planet are social creatures, and individuals separated from those societies don't amount to much. A single mad mind is unlikely to cause us much trouble.

Honest.

THE GOLEM RUNS AMUCK

Chayim Bloch

The story of the Golem, created from clay and given life by a Rabbi to protect Prague's Jews from persecution, is nearly half a millennium old, product of a creative flourishing when Habsburg imperial policy was showing remarkable tolerance toward Jews and Protestants alike. In 1914 the folklorist **Chayim Bloch** published a fictionalised version of the story, gathering his material, so he said, through ethnographic research on the Russian front. Bloch's stories were soon translated into English and were widely distributed in the United States under the title *The Golem: Legends of the Ghetto of Prague*. In 1939 Bloch moved to New York where he remained until his death in 1973.

As mentioned before, Rabbi Loew made it a custom, every Friday afternoon, to assign for the Golem a sort of programme, a plan for the day's work, for on the Sabbath he spoke to him only in extremely urgent cases. Generally, Rabbi Loew used to order him to do nothing else on Sabbath but be on guard and serve as a watcher.

One Friday afternoon, Rabbi Loew forgot to give him the order for the next day, and the Golem had nothing to do.

The day had barely drawn to a close and the people were getting ready for the ushering in of the Sabbath, when the Golem, like one mad, began running about in the Jewish section of the city, threatening to destroy everything. The want of employment made him awkward and wild. When the people saw this, they ran from him and cried: "Joseph Golem has gone mad!"

The people were greatly terrified, and a report of the panic soon reached the Altneu Synagogue where Rabbi Loew was praying.

The Sabbath had already been ushered in through the Song for the Sabbath day (Psalms xcii). What could be done? Rabbi Loew reflected on the evil consequences that might follow if the Golem should be running about thus uncontrolled. But to restore him to peace would be a profanation of the Sabbath.

In his confusion, he forgot that it was a question of danger to human life and that in such cases the law permits, nay, commands the profanation of the Sabbath in order that the people exposed to danger might be saved.

Rabbi Loew rushed out and, without seeing the Golem, called out into space: "Joseph, stop where you are!"

And the people saw the Golem at the place where he happened to find himself that moment, remain standing, like a post. In a single instant, he had overcome the violence of his fury.

Rabbi Loew was soon informed where the Golem stood, and he betook himself to him. He whispered into his ear: "Go home and to bed." And the Golem obeyed him as willingly as a child.

Then Rabbi Loew went back to the House of Prayer and ordered that the Sabbath Song be repeated.

After that Friday, Rabbi Loew never again forgot to give the Golem orders for the Sabbath on a Friday afternoon.

To his confidential friends he said: "The Golem could have laid waste all Prague, if I had not calmed him down in time."

(1914)

FANDOM FOR ROBOTS

Vina Jie-Min Prasad

Vina Jie-Min Prasad is a Singaporean writer of science fiction and fantasy. Her short stories "Fandom for Robots" and "A Series of Steaks", both published in 2017, were nominated for the Nebula, Hugo and Theodore Sturgeon Awards. She was a finalist for the 2018 John W. Campbell Award for Best New Writer. "Harry Potter was the first series that got me really interested in fan discussion and fanworks," she explained, in an interview with the magazine *Uncanny* in 2018. "I got into the fandom during what's known as the 'Three-Year Summer' – the three-year-long gap between *Goblet of Fire* and *Order of the Phoenix*. The ending of book four opened the universe up so much, and it was such a cliffhangery point to leave off, that I signed up for forum accounts and started reading fan theories and fanfiction about what book five might be like in order to quench my thirst for new canon." Prasad argues passionately that fan fiction is worthwhile in its own right, saying: "I'm very proud that I got my start in it."

Computron feels no emotion towards the animated television show titled *Hyperdimension Warp Record* (超次元 ワープ レコード). After all, Computron does not have any emotion circuits installed, and is thus constitutionally incapable of experiencing "excitement," "hatred," or "frustration." It is completely impossible for Computron to experience emotions such as "excitement about the seventh episode of *HyperWarp*," "hatred of the anime's short episode length" or "frustration that Friday is so far away."

Computron checks his internal chronometer, as well as the countdown page on the streaming website. There are twenty-two hours, five minutes, forty-six seconds, and twelve milliseconds until 2 am on Friday (Japanese Standard Time). Logically, he is aware that time is most likely passing at a normal rate. The Simak Robotics Museum is not within close proximity of a black hole, and there is close to no possibility that time is being dilated. His constant checking of the chronometer to compare it with the countdown page serves no scientific purpose whatsoever.

After fifty milliseconds, Computron checks the countdown page again.

The Simak Robotics Museum's commemorative postcard set ($15.00 for a set of twelve) describes Computron as "The only known sentient robot, created in 1954 by Doctor Karel Alquist to serve as a laboratory assistant. No known scientist has managed to recreate the doctor's invention. Its steel-framed box-and-claw design is characteristic of the period." Below that, in smaller print, the postcard thanks the Alquist estate for their generous donation.

In the museum, Computron is regarded as a quaint artefact, and plays a key role in the *Robotics Then and Now* performance as an example of the "Then." After the announcer's introduction to robotics, Computron appears on stage, answers four standard queries from the audience as proof of his sentience, and steps off the stage to make way for the rest of the performance, which ends with the android-bodied automaton TETSUCHAN showcasing its ability to breakdance.

Today's queries are likely to be similar to the rest. A teenage girl waves at the announcer and receives the microphone.

"Hi, Computron. My question is... have you watched anime before?"

[Yes,] Computron vocalises. [I have viewed the works of the renowned actress Anna May Wong. Doctor Alquist enjoyed her movies as a child.]

"Oh, um, not that," the girl continues. "I meant Japanese animation. Have you ever watched this show called *Hyperdimension Warp Record*?"

[I have not.]

"Oh, okay, I was just thinking that you really looked like one of the characters. But since you haven't, maybe you could give *HyperWarp* a shot! It's really good, you might like it! There are six episodes out so far, and you can watch it on—"

The announcer cuts the girl off, and hands the microphone over to the next querent, who has a question about Doctor Alquist's research. After answering two more standard queries, Computron returns to his storage room to answer his electronic mail, which consists of queries from elementary school students. He picks up two metal styluses, one in each of his grasping claws, and begins tapping them on the computing unit's keyboard, one key at a time. Computron explains the difference between a robot and an android to four students, and provides the fifth student with a hyperlink to Daniel Clement Dennett III's writings on consciousness.

As Computron readies himself to enter sleep mode, he recalls the teenage girl's request that he "give *HyperWarp* a shot." It is only logical to research the Japanese animation *Hyperdimension Warp Record* in order to address queries from future visitors. The title, when entered into a search engine on the World Wide Web, produces about 957,000 results (0.27 seconds).

Computron manoeuvres the mouse pointer to the third hyperlink, which offers to let him "watch Hyperdimension Warp Record FULL episodes streaming online high quality." From the still image behind the prominent "play" button, the grey boxy figure standing beside the large-eyed blue-haired human does bear an extremely slight resemblance to Computron's design. It is only logical to press the "play" button on the first episode, in order to familiarise himself with recent discourse about robots in popular culture.

The series' six episodes are each approximately 25 minutes long. Between watching the series, viewing the online bulletin boards, and perusing the extensively footnoted fan encyclopedia, Computron does not enter sleep mode for ten hours, thirty-six minutes, two seconds, and twenty milliseconds.

*

Hyperdimension Warp Record (超次元ワープレコード Chōjigen Wāpu Rekōdo, literal translation: *Super Dimensional Warp Record*) is a Japanese anime series set in space in the far future. The protagonist, Ellison, is an escapee from a supposedly inescapable galactic prison. Joined by a fellow escapee, Cyro (short for Cybernetic Robot), the two make their way across the galaxy to seek revenge. The targets of their revenge are the Seven Sabers of Paradise, who have stolen the hyperdimensional warp unit from Cyro's creator and caused the death of Ellison's entire family.

Episode seven of *HyperWarp* comes with the revelation that the Second Saber, Ellison's identical twin, had murdered their parents before faking her own death. After Cyro and Ellison return to the *Kosmogram*, the last segment of the episode unfolds without dialogue. There is a slow pan across the spaceship's control area, revealing that Ellison has indulged in the human pastime known as "crying" before falling asleep in the captain's chair. His chest binder is stained with blood from the wound on his collarbone. Cyro reaches over, gently using his grabbing claw to loosen Ellison's binder, and drapes a blanket over him. An instrumental version of the end theme plays as Cyro gets up from his seat, making his way to the recharging bay at the back of the ship. From the way his footfalls are animated, it is clear that Cyro is trying his best to avoid making any noise as he walks.

The credits play over a zoomed-out shot of the *Kosmogram* making its way to the next exoplanet, a tiny pinpoint of bright blue in the vast blackness of space.

The preview for the next episode seems to indicate that the episode will focus on the Sabers' initial attempt to activate the hyperdimensional warp unit. There is no mention of Cyro or Ellison at all.

During the wait for episode eight, Computron discovers a concept called "fanfiction."

While "fanfiction" is meant to consist of "fan-written stories about characters or settings from an original work of fiction," Computron observes that much of the *HyperWarp* fanfiction bears no resemblance to the actual characters or setting. For instance, the series that claims to be a "spin-off focusing on Powerful!Cyro" seems to involve Cyro installing many large-calibre guns onto his frame and joining the Space Marines, which does not seem relevant to his quest for revenge or the retrieval of the hyperdimensional warp unit. Similarly, the "high school fic" in which Cyro and Ellison study at Hyperdimension High fails to acknowledge the fact that formal education is reserved for the elite class in the *HyperWarp* universe.

Most of the fanfiction set within the actual series seems particularly inaccurate. The most recent offender is EllisonsWife's "Rosemary for Remembrance," which fails to acknowledge the fact that Cyro does not have human facial features, and thus cannot "touch his nose against Ellison's hair, breathing in the scent of sandalwood, rosemary, and something uniquely him" before "kissing Ellison passionately, needily, hungrily, his tongue slipping into Ellison's mouth."

Computron readies his styluses and moves the cursor down to the comment box, prepared to leave anonymous "constructive criticism" for EllisonsWife, when he detects a comment with relevant keywords.

bjornruffian:
Okay, I've noticed this in several of your fics and I was trying not to be too harsh, but when it got to the kissing scene I couldn't take it anymore. Cyro can't touch his nose against anything, because he doesn't have a nose! Cyro can't slip his tongue into anyone's mouth, because he doesn't have a tongue! Were we even watching the same series?? Did you skip all the parts where Cyro is a metal robot with a cube-shaped head?!

EllisonsWife:
Who are you, the fandom police?? I'm basing Cyro's design on this piece of fanart (link here) because it looks better than a freakin metal box!! Anyway, I put DON'T LIKE DON'T READ in the author's notes!!! If you hate the way I write them so much, why don't you just write your own????

Computron is incapable of feeling hatred for anything, as that would require Doctor Alquist to have installed emotion circuits during his creation.

However, due to Computron's above-average procedural knowledge, he is capable of following the directions to create an account on fanficarchive.org.

…and Ellison manoeuvred his flesh hands in a claw-like motion, locking them with Cyro's own grasping claws. His soft human body pressed against the hard lines of Cyro's proprietary alloy, in a manner which would have generated wear and tear had Cyro's body not been of superior make. Fluids leaked from Ellison's eyes. No fluids leaked from Cyro's ocular units, but…

Comments (3)

DontGotRhythm:
What the hell? Have you ever met a human? This reads like an alien wrote it.

tattered_freedom_wings:
uhhh this is kinda weird but i think i liked it?? not sure about the box thing though

bjornruffian:
OH MY GODDDD. :DDDD Finally, someone who doesn't write human-shaped robot-in-name-only Cyro! Some of Ellison's characterisation is a little awkward—I don't think he would say all that mushy stuff about Cyro's beautiful boxy shape??—but I love your Cyro! If this is just your first fic, I can't wait for you to write more!!

Computron has been spending less time in sleep mode after episode thirteen's cliffhanger, and has spent his time conducting objective discussions about *Hyper-Warp*'s appeal with commenters on various video streaming sites and anonymous message boards.

As he is about to reply to the latest missive about his lack of genitalia and outside social activities, which is technically correct, his internal chronometer indicates that it is time for the *Robotics Then and Now* performance.

"So, I was wondering, have you ever watched *Hyperdimension Warp Record*? There's this character called Cyro that—"

[Yes, I am aware of *HyperWarp*,] Computron says. [I have taken the "How To Tell If Your Life Is *HyperWarp*" quiz online, and it has indicated that I am "a Hyper-Big *HyperWarp* Fan!" I have repeatedly viewed the scene between Ellison and Cyro at the end of episode seven, and recently I have left a "like" on bjornruffian's artwork of what may have happened shortly after that scene, due to its exceptional accuracy. The show is widely regarded as "this season's sleeper hit" and has met with approval from a statistically significant number of critics. If other members of the audience wish to view this series, there are thirteen episodes out so far, and they can be viewed on—] The announcer motions to him, using the same gesture she uses when audience members are taking too long to talk. Computron falls silent until the announcer chooses the next question, which is also the last due to time constraints.

After TETSUCHAN has finished its breakdance and showcased its newly programmed ability to pop-and-lock, the announcer speaks to Computron backstage. She requests that he take less time for the question-and-answer segment in the future.

[Understood,] Computron says, and returns to his storage room to check his inbox again.

*

Private Message from bjornruffian:

Hi RobotFan,
I noticed you liked my art (thanks!) and you seem to know a LOT about robots judging from your fic (and, well, your name). I'm doing a fancomic about Ellison and Cyro being stranded on one of the desert-ish exoplanets while they try to fix the Kosmogram, but I want to make sure I'm drawing Cyro's body right. Are there any references you can recommend for someone who's looking to learn more about robots? Like, the classic kind, not the android kind? It'd be great if they're available online, especially if they have pictures—I've found some books with photos but they're WAAAAY more than I can afford :\\\

Thank you for any help you can offer! I'm really looking forward to your next fic!

*

Shortly after reading bjornruffian's message, Computron visits the Early Robotics section of the museum. It has shrunk significantly over the years, particularly after the creation of the "Redefining Human," "Androids of the Future," and "Drone Zone" sections. It consists of several information panels, a small collection of tin toys, and the remnants of all three versions of Hexode the robot.

In episode fourteen of *Hyperdimension Warp Record*, Cyro visits a deserted exoplanet alone to investigate the history of the hyperdimension warp drive, and finds himself surrounded by the deactivated bodies of robots of similar make, claws outstretched, being slowly ground down by the gears of a gigantic machine. The "Robot Recycler" scene is frequently listed as one of that year's top ten most shocking moments in anime.

On 7 June 1957, the third version of Hexode fails Doctor Alquist's mirror test for the hundredth time, proving that it has no measurable self-awareness. Computron watches Doctor Alquist smash the spanner against Hexode's face, crumpling its nose and lips. Oil leaks from its ocular units as it falls to the floor with a metallic thud. Its vocal synthesiser crackles and hisses.

"You godforsaken tin bucket," Doctor Alquist shouts. "To hell with you." If Doctor Alquist were to raise the spanner to Computron, it is likely that Doctor Alquist will not have an assistant for any future robotics experiments. Computron stays still, standing in front of the mirror, silently observing the destruction of Hexode so he can gather up its parts later.

When Computron photographs Hexode's display case, he is careful to avoid capturing any part of himself in the reflection.

[**bjornruffian**] Oh man, thank you SO MUCH for installing chat just for this! Anyway, I really appreciate your help with the script so far (I think we can call it a collab by this point?). And thanks for the exhibit photos! Was it a lot of trouble? I checked the website and that museum is pretty much in the middle of nowhere...

—File Transfer of "THANK YOU ROBOTFAN.png" from "bjornruffian" started.

—File Transfer of "THANK YOU ROBOTFAN.png" from "bjornruffian" finished.

[**bjornruffian**] So I've got a few questions about page 8 in the folder I shared, can you take a look at the second panel from the top? I figured his joint would be all gummed up by the sand, so I thought I'd try to do an X-ray view thing as a closeup... if you have any idea how the circuits are supposed to be, could you double-check?

[**bjornruffian**] Okay, you're taking really long to type, this is making me super nervous I did everything wrong :\\

[**RobotFan**] Apologies

[RobotFan] I

[RobotFan] Am not fast at typing

[bjornruffian] Okaaay, I'll wait on the expert here

[RobotFan] The circuit is connected incorrectly and the joint mechanism is incorrect as well

[bjornruffian] Ughhhhh I knew it was wrong!! DDD:

[bjornruffian] I wish the character sheets came with schematics or something, I've paused the flashback scenes with all the failed robots like ten billion times to take screenshots >:\\

[RobotFan] Besides the scenes in Episode 14, there are other shots of Cyro's schematics in Episode 5 (17:40:18 and 20:13:50) as well as Episode 12 (08:23:14)

—File Transfer of "schematic-screenshots.zip" from "RobotFan" started.

—File Transfer of "schematic-screenshots.zip" from "RobotFan" finished.

[bjornruffian] THANK YOU

[bjornruffian] I swear you're some sort of angel or something

[RobotFan] That is incorrect

[RobotFan] I am merely a robot

There are certain things in the museum's storage room that would benefit bjornruffian's mission of completing her Cyro/Ellison comic. Computron and Hexode's schematics are part of the Alquist Collection, which is not a priority for the museum's digitisation project due to a perceived lack of value. As part of the Alquist Collection himself, there should be no objection to Computron retrieving the schematics.

As Computron grasps the doorknob with his left claw, he catches a glimpse of Cyro from episode fifteen in the door's glass panels, his ocular units blazing yellow with determination after overcoming his past. In fan parlance, this is known as Determined!Cyro, and has only been seen during fight scenes thus far. It is illogical to have Determined!Cyro appear in this context, or in this location.

Computron looks at the dusty glass again, and sees only a reflection of his face.

*

[**RobotFan**] I have a large file to send to you

[**RobotFan**] To be precise, four large files

[**RobotFan**] The remaining three will be digitised and sent at a later date

—File Transfer of "alquist-archive-scans-pt1.zip" from "RobotFan" started.

—File Transfer of "alquist-archive-scans-pt1.zip" from "RobotFan" finished.

[**bjornruffian**] OMG THIS IS AWESOME

[**bjornruffian**] Where did you get this?? Did you rob that museum?? This is PERFECT for that other Cyro/Ellison thing I've been thinking about doing after this stupid desert comic is over!!

[**bjornruffian**] It would be great if I had someone to help me with writing Cyro, HINT HINT

[**RobotFan**] I would be happy to assist if I had emotion circuits

[**RobotFan**] However, my lack of emotion circuits means I cannot be "happy" about performing any actions

[**RobotFan**] Nonetheless, I will assist

[**RobotFan**] To make this an equitable trade as is common in human custom, you may also provide your opinion on some recurrent bugs that readers have reported in my characterisation of Ellison

[**bjornruffian**] YESSSSSSSS :DDDDDD

Rossum, Sulla. "Tin Men and Tin Toys: Examining Real and Fictional Robots from the 1950s." *Journal of Robotics Studies* 8.2 (2018): 25–38.

While the figure of the fictional robot embodies timeless fears of technology and its potential for harm, the physical design of robots real and fictional is often linked to visual cues of modernity. What was once regarded as an "object of the future" can become "overwhelmingly obsolete" within a span of a few years, after advances in technology cause the visual cues of modernity to change (Bloch, 1979). The clawed, lumbering tin-toy-esque designs of the 1950s are now widely regarded as "tin can[s] that should have been recycled long ago" (Williamson, 2017). Notably, most modern critiques of Computron's design tend to focus on its obsolete analogue dials…

watch-free-anime | Hyperdimension Warp Record | Episode 23 | Live Chat

Pyro: Okay, is it just me, or is Cyro starting to get REALLY attractive? I swear I'm not gay (is it gay if it's a robot) but when he slung Ellison over his shoulder and used his claw to block the Sixth Saber at the same time

Pyro: HOLY SHIT that sniper scene RIGHT THROUGH THE SCOPE and then he fucking BUMPS ELLISON'S FIST WITH HIS CLAW

Pyro: Fuck it, I'm gay for Cyro I don't care, I'll fucking twiddle his dials all he wants after this episode

ckwizard: dude youre late, weve been finding cyro hot ever since that scene in episode 15

ckwizard: you know the one

ckwizard: where you just see this rectangular blocky shadow lumbering slowly towards first saber with those clunky sound effects

ckwizard: then his eyebulbs glint that really bright yellow and he bleeps about ACTIVATING KILL MODE and his grabby claws start whirring

ckwizard: theres a really good fic about it on fanficarchive… actually you might as well check the authors blog out here, hes pretty cyro-obsessed

ckwizard: his earlier stuff is kinda uneven but the bjorn collabs are good—shes been illustrating his stuff for a while

Pyro: Okay

Pyro: I just looked at that thing, you know, the desert planet comic

Pyro: I think I ship it

Pyro: OH MAN when Ellison tries the manual repair on the arm joint and Cyro has a FLASHBACK TO THE ROBOT RECYCLER but tries to remind himself he can trust him

Pyro: Fuck it I DEFINITELY ship it

ckwizard: join the fucking club

ckwizard: its the fifth time im watching this episode, this series has ruined my life

ckwizard: i can't wait for season 2

*

bjorn-robot-collabs posted:

Hi everyone, bjornruffian and RobotFan here! Thanks for all your comments on our first comic collab! We're really charmed by the great reception to "In the Desert Sun"—okay, I'm charmed, and RobotFan says he would be charmed if he had the emotion circuits for that (he's an awesome roleplay partner too! LOVE his sense of humor :DDD).

ANYWAY! It turns out that RobotFan's got this awesome collection of retro robot schematics and he's willing to share, for those of you who want to write about old-school robots or need some references for your art! (HINT HINT: the fandom totally needs more Cyro and Cyro/Ellison before Season 2 hits!) To be honest I'm not sure how legal it is to circulate these scans (RobotFan says it's fine though), so just reply to this post if you want them and we'll private message you the links if you promise not to spread them around.

Also, we're gonna do another Cyro/Ellison comic in the future, and we're thinking of making it part of an anthology. If you'd like to contribute comics or illustrations for that, let us know!

Get ready to draw *lots* of boxes, people! The robot revolution is coming!

9,890 replies

(2017)

MOXON'S MASTER

Ambrose Bierce

Ambrose Bierce was born in Meigs County Ohio in 1842, to farmers who thought it would be fun to give all thirteen of their children names beginning with "A". Experiences in the Civil War left him with a morbid, vicious turn of mind that earned him comparisons to Edgar Allan Poe. In California he turned to journalism, marrying truth-telling to excoriating wit to such a degree, he was dubbed "the wickedest man in San Francisco". His *Devil's Dictionary* (1911) is his lasting masterpiece. (I looked up "editor" to discover I was "Master of mysteries and lord of law, high-pinnacled upon the throne of thought, his face suffused with the dim splendors of the Transfiguration". So there.) At the end of 1913, after a hectic career, he vanished into Mexico, then in the middle of its own civil war, and got caught up in the Battle of Ojinaga. His corpse was probably among the many which were burned to prevent typhus.

"Are you serious?—do you really believe that a machine thinks?"

I got no immediate reply; Moxon was apparently intent upon the coals in the grate, touching them deftly here and there with the firepoker till they signified a sense of his attention by a brighter glow. For several weeks I had been observing in him a growing habit of delay in answering even the most trivial of commonplace questions. His air, however, was that of preoccupation rather than deliberation: one might have said that he had "something on his mind."

Presently he said:

"What is a 'machine'? The word has been variously defined. Here is one definition from a popular dictionary: 'Any instrument or organization by which power is applied and made effective, or a desired effect produced.' Well, then, is not a man a machine? And you will admit that he thinks—or thinks he thinks."

"If you do not wish to answer my question," I said, rather testily, "why not say so?—all that you say is mere evasion. You know well enough that when I say 'machine' I do not mean a man, but something that man has made and controls."

"When it does not control him," he said, rising abruptly and looking out of a window, whence nothing was visible in the blackness of a stormy night. A moment later he turned about and with a smile said: "I beg your pardon; I had no thought of evasion. I considered the dictionary man's unconscious testimony suggestive and worth something in the discussion. I can give your question a direct answer easily enough: I do believe that a machine thinks about the work that it is doing."

That was direct enough, certainly. It was not altogether pleasing, for it tended to confirm a sad suspicion that Moxon's devotion to study and work in his machine-shop had not been good for him. I knew, for one thing, that he suffered from insomnia, and that is no light affliction. Had it affected his mind? His reply to my question seemed to me then evidence that it had; perhaps I should think differently about it now. I was younger then, and among the blessings that are not denied to youth is ignorance. Incited by that great stimulant to controversy, I said:

"And what, pray, does it think with—in the absence of a brain?"

The reply, coming with less than his customary delay, took his favorite form of counter-interrogation:

"With what does a plant think—in the absence of a brain?"

"Ah, plants also belong to the philosopher class! I should be pleased to know some of their conclusions; you may omit the premises."

"Perhaps," he replied, apparently unaffected by my foolish irony, "you may be able to infer their convictions from their acts. I will spare you the familiar examples of the sensitive mimosa, the several insectivorous flowers and those whose stamens bend down and shake their pollen upon the entering bee in order that he may fertilize their distant mates. But observe this. In an open spot in my garden I planted a climbing vine. When it was barely above the surface I set a stake into the soil a yard away. The vine at once made for it, but as it was about to reach it after several days I removed it a few feet. The vine at once altered its course, making an acute angle, and again made for the stake. This manoeuvre was repeated several times, but finally, as if discouraged, the vine abandoned the pursuit and ignoring further attempts to divert it traveled to a small tree, further away, which it climbed.

"Roots of the eucalyptus will prolong themselves incredibly in search of moisture. A well-known horticulturist relates that one entered an old drain pipe and followed it until it came to a break, where a section of the pipe had been removed to make way for a stone wall that had been built across its course. The root left the drain and followed the wall until it found an opening where a stone had fallen out. It crept through and following the other side of the wall back to the drain, entered the unexplored part and resumed its journey."

"And all this?"

"Can you miss the significance of it? It shows the consciousness of plants. It proves that they think."

"Even if it did—what then? We were speaking, not of plants, but of machines. They may be composed partly of wood—wood that has no longer vitality—or wholly of metal. Is thought an attribute also of the mineral kingdom?"

"How else do you explain the phenomena, for example, of crystallization?"

"I do not explain them."

"Because you cannot without affirming what you wish to deny, namely, intelligent cooperation among the constituent elements of the crystals. When soldiers form lines, or hollow squares, you call it reason. When wild geese in flight take the form of a letter V you say instinct. When the homogeneous atoms of a mineral, moving freely in solution, arrange themselves into shapes mathematically perfect, or particles of frozen moisture into the symmetrical and beautiful forms of snowflakes, you have nothing to say. You have not even invented a name to conceal your heroic unreason."

Moxon was speaking with unusual animation and earnestness. As he paused I heard in an adjoining room known to me as his "machine-shop," which no one but himself was permitted to enter, a singular thumping sound, as of some one pounding upon a table with an open hand. Moxon heard it at the same moment and, visibly agitated, rose and hurriedly passed into the room whence it came. I thought it odd that any one else should be in there, and my interest in my friend—with doubtless a touch of unwarrantable curiosity—led me to listen intently, though, I am happy to say, not at the keyhole. There were confused sounds, as of a struggle or scuffle; the floor shook. I distinctly heard hard breathing and a hoarse whisper which said "Damn you!" Then all was silent, and presently Moxon reappeared and said, with a rather sorry smile:

"Pardon me for leaving you so abruptly. I have a machine in there that lost its temper and cut up rough."

Fixing my eyes steadily upon his left cheek, which was traversed by four parallel excoriations showing blood, I said:

"How would it do to trim its nails?"

I could have spared myself the jest; he gave it no attention, but seated himself in the chair that he had left and resumed the interrupted monologue as if nothing had occurred:

"Doubtless you do not hold with those (I need not name them to a man of your reading) who have taught that all matter is sentient, that every atom is a living, feeling, conscious being. *I* do. There is no such thing as dead, inert matter: it is all alive; all instinct with force, actual and potential; all sensitive to the same forces in its environment and susceptible to the contagion of higher and subtler ones residing in such superior organisms as it may be brought into relation with, as those of man when he is fashioning it into an instrument of his will. It absorbs something of his intelligence and purpose—more of them in proportion to the complexity of the resulting machine and that of its work.

"Do you happen to recall Herbert Spencer's definition of 'Life'? I read it thirty years ago. He may have altered it afterward, for anything I know, but in all that time I have been unable to think of a single word that could profitably be changed or added or removed. It seems to me not only the best definition, but the only possible one.

"'Life,' he says, 'is a definite combination of heterogeneous changes, both simultaneous and successive, in correspondence with external coexistences and sequences.'"

"That defines the phenomenon," I said, "but gives no hint of its cause."

"That," he replied, "is all that any definition can do. As Mill points out, we know nothing of cause except as an antecedent—nothing of effect except as a consequent. Of certain phenomena, one never occurs without another, which is dissimilar: the first in point of time we call cause, the second, effect. One who had many times seen a rabbit pursued by a dog, and had never seen rabbits and dogs otherwise, would think the rabbit the cause of the dog.

"But I fear," he added, laughing naturally enough, "that my rabbit is leading me a long way from the track of my legitimate quarry: I'm indulging in the pleasure of the chase for its own sake. What I want you to observe is that in Herbert Spencer's definition of 'life' the activity of a machine is included—there is nothing in the definition that is not applicable to it. According to this sharpest of observers and deepest of thinkers, if a man during his period of activity is alive, so is a machine when in operation. As an inventor and constructor of machines I know that to be true."

Moxon was silent for a long time, gazing absently into the fire. It was growing late and I thought it time to be going, but somehow I did not like the notion of leaving him in that isolated house, all alone except for the presence of some person of whose nature my conjectures could go no further than that it was unfriendly, perhaps malign. Leaning toward him and looking earnestly into his eyes while making a motion with my hand through the door of his workshop, I said:

"Moxon, whom have you in there?"

Somewhat to my surprise he laughed lightly and answered without hesitation:

"Nobody; the incident that you have in mind was caused by my folly in leaving a machine in action with nothing to act upon, while I undertook the interminable task of enlightening your understanding. Do you happen to know that Consciousness is the creature of Rhythm?"

"O bother them both!" I replied, rising and laying hold of my overcoat. "I'm going to wish you good night; and I'll add the hope that the machine which you inadvertently left in action will have her gloves on the next time you think it needful to stop her."

Without waiting to observe the effect of my shot I left the house.

Rain was falling, and the darkness was intense. In the sky beyond the crest of a hill toward which I groped my way along precarious plank sidewalks and across miry, unpaved streets I could see the faint glow of the city's lights, but behind me nothing was visible but a single window of Moxon's house. It glowed with what seemed to me a mysterious and fateful meaning. I knew it was an uncurtained aperture in my friend's "machine-shop," and I had little doubt that he had resumed the studies interrupted by his duties as my instructor in mechanical consciousness and the fatherhood of Rhythm. Odd, and in some degree humorous, as his convictions seemed to me at that time, I could not wholly divest myself of the feeling that they had some tragic relation to his life and character—perhaps to his destiny—although I no longer entertained the notion that they were the vagaries of a disordered mind. Whatever might be thought of his views, his exposition of them was too logical for that. Over and over, his last words came back to me: "Consciousness is the creature of Rhythm." Bald and terse as the statement was, I now found it infinitely alluring. At each recurrence it broadened in meaning and deepened in suggestion. Why, here, (I thought) is something upon which to found a philosophy. If consciousness is the product of rhythm all things ARE conscious, for all have motion, and all motion is rhythmic. I wondered if Moxon knew the significance and breadth of his thought—the scope of this momentous generalization; or had he arrived at his philosophic faith by the tortuous and uncertain road of observation?

That faith was then new to me, and all Moxon's expounding had failed to make me a convert; but now it seemed as if a great light shone about me, like that which fell upon Saul of Tarsus; and out there in the storm and darkness and solitude I experienced what Lewes calls "The endless variety and excitement of philosophic thought." I exulted in a new sense of knowledge, a new pride of reason. My feet seemed hardly to touch the earth; it was as if I were uplifted and borne through the air by invisible wings.

Yielding to an impulse to seek further light from him whom I now recognized as my master and guide, I had unconsciously turned about, and almost before I was aware of having done so found myself again at Moxon's door. I was drenched with rain, but felt no discomfort. Unable in my excitement to find the doorbell I instinctively tried the knob. It turned and, entering, I mounted the stairs to the room that I had so recently left. All was dark and silent; Moxon, as I had supposed, was in the adjoining room—the "machine-shop." Groping along the wall until I found the communicating door I knocked loudly several times, but got no response, which I attributed to the uproar outside, for the wind was blowing a gale and dashing the rain against the thin walls in sheets. The drumming upon the shingle roof spanning the unceiled room was loud and incessant.

I had never been invited into the machine-shop—had, indeed, been denied admittance, as had all others, with one exception, a skilled metal worker, of whom no one knew anything except that his name was Haley and his habit silence. But in my spiritual exaltation, discretion and civility were alike forgotten and I opened the door. What I saw took all philosophical speculation out of me in short order.

Moxon sat facing me at the farther side of a small table upon which a single candle made all the light that was in the room. Opposite him, his back toward me, sat another person. On the table between the two was a chessboard; the men were playing. I knew little of chess, but as only a few pieces were on the board it was obvious that the game was near its close. Moxon was intensely interested—not so much, it seemed to me, in the game as in his antagonist, upon whom he had fixed so intent a look that, standing though I did directly in the line of his vision, I was altogether unobserved. His face was ghastly white, and his eyes glittered like diamonds. Of his antagonist I had only a back view, but that was sufficient; I should not have cared to see his face.

He was apparently not more than five feet in height, with proportions suggesting those of a gorilla—a tremendous breadth of shoulders, thick, short neck and broad, squat head, which had a tangled growth of black hair and was topped with a crimson fez. A tunic of the same color, belted tightly to the waist, reached the seat—apparently a box—upon which he sat; his legs and feet were not seen. His left forearm appeared to rest in his lap; he moved his pieces with his right hand, which seemed disproportionately long.

I had shrunk back and now stood a little to one side of the doorway and in shadow. If Moxon had looked farther than the face of his opponent he could have observed nothing now, except that the door was open. Something forbade me either to enter or to retire, a feeling—I know not how it came—that I was in the presence of an imminent tragedy and might serve my friend by remaining. With a scarcely conscious rebellion against the indelicacy of the act I remained.

The play was rapid. Moxon hardly glanced at the board before making his moves, and to my unskilled eye seemed to move the piece most convenient to his hand, his motions in doing so being quick, nervous and lacking in precision. The response of his antagonist, while equally prompt in the inception, was made with a slow, uniform, mechanical and, I thought, somewhat theatrical movement of the arm, that was a sore trial to my patience. There was something unearthly about it all, and I caught myself shuddering. But I was wet and cold.

Two or three times after moving a piece the stranger slightly inclined his head, and each time I observed that Moxon shifted his king. All at once the thought came to me that the man was dumb. And then that he was a machine—an automaton chess-player! Then I remembered that Moxon had once spoken to me of having invented such a piece of mechanism, though I did not understand that it had actually been constructed. Was all his talk about the consciousness and intelligence of machines merely a prelude to eventual exhibition of this device—only a trick to intensify the effect of its mechanical action upon me in my ignorance of its secret?

A fine end, this, of all my intellectual transports—my "endless variety and excitement of philosophic thought!" I was about to retire in disgust when something occurred to hold my curiosity. I observed a shrug of the thing's great shoulders, as if it were irritated: and so natural was this—so entirely human—that in my new view of the matter it startled me. Nor was that all, for a moment later it struck the table sharply with its clenched hand. At that gesture Moxon seemed even more startled than I: he pushed his chair a little backward, as in alarm.

Presently Moxon, whose play it was, raised his hand high above the board, pounced upon one of his pieces like a sparrow-hawk and with the exclamation "checkmate!" rose quickly to his feet and stepped behind his chair. The automaton sat motionless.

The wind had now gone down, but I heard, at lessening intervals and progressively louder, the rumble and roll of thunder. In the pauses between I now became conscious of a low humming or buzzing which, like the thunder, grew momentarily louder and more distinct. It seemed to come from the body of the automaton, and was unmistakably a whirring of wheels. It gave me the impression of a disordered mechanism which had escaped the repressive and regulating action of some controlling part—an effect such as might be expected if a pawl should be jostled from the teeth of a ratchet-wheel. But before I had time for much conjecture as to its nature my attention was taken by the strange motions of the automaton itself. A slight but continuous convulsion appeared to have possession of it. In body and head it shook like a man with palsy or an ague chill, and the motion augmented every moment until the entire figure was in violent agitation. Suddenly it sprang to its feet and with a movement almost too quick for the eye to follow shot forward across table and chair, with both arms thrust forth to their full length—the posture and lunge of a diver. Moxon tried to throw himself backward out of reach, but he was too late: I saw the horrible thing's hands close upon his throat, his own clutch its wrists. Then the table was overturned, the candle thrown to the floor and extinguished, and all was black dark. But the noise of the struggle was dreadfully distinct, and most terrible of all were the raucous, squawking sounds made by the strangled man's efforts to breathe. Guided by the infernal hubbub, I sprang to the rescue of my friend, but had hardly taken a stride in the darkness when the whole room blazed with a blinding white light that burned into my brain and heart and memory a vivid picture of the combatants on the floor, Moxon underneath, his throat still in the clutch of those iron hands, his head forced backward, his eyes protruding, his mouth wide open and his tongue thrust out; and—horrible contrast!—upon the painted face of his assassin an expression of tranquil and profound thought, as in the solution of a problem in chess! This I observed, then all was blackness and silence.

Three days later I recovered consciousness in a hospital. As the memory of that tragic night slowly evolved in my ailing brain I recognized in my attendant Moxon's confidential workman, Haley. Responding to a look he approached, smiling.

"Tell me about it," I managed to say, faintly—"all about it."

"Certainly," he said; "you were carried unconscious from a burning house—Moxon's. Nobody knows how you came to be there. You may have to do a little explaining. The origin of the fire is a bit mysterious, too. My own notion is that the house was struck by lightning."

"And Moxon?"

"Buried yesterday—what was left of him."

Apparently this reticent person could unfold himself on occasion. When imparting shocking intelligence to the sick he was affable enough. After some moments of the keenest mental suffering I ventured to ask another question:

"Who rescued me?"

"Well, if that interests you—I did."

"Thank you, Mr. Haley, and may God bless you for it. Did you rescue, also, that charming product of your skill, the automaton chess-player that murdered its inventor?"

The man was silent a long time, looking away from me. Presently he turned and gravely said:

"Do you know that?"

"I do," I replied; "I saw it done."

That was many years ago. If asked to-day I should answer less confidently.

(1899)

THE LAND IRONCLADS
H. G. Wells

> **Herbert George Wells** (1866–1946) affected not to care too much about the quality of his writing. "I would rather," he wrote, "be called a journalist than an artist." And it was as a far-sighted and trenchant social critic that he made his name. He was a radical, a Darwinist and a socialist, and yet in some ways Wells's thought was absolutely typical of his time. He held to the rather morbid and pessimistic view of human progress that was typical of writers of the 1890s. (World War 2 finished the job: *Mind at the End of Its Tether* (1945) decribes a world in which nature is hell-bent on wiping out a wholly alienated mankind.) Joseph Conrad called Wells a "realist of the fantastic", and it's Wells's fusion of magic and speculation with sharp social and personal observation that led him to found the science fiction genre, and become a global influence in the process, four times nominated for the Nobel Prize for literature.

I.

The young lieutenant lay beside the war correspondent and admired the idyllic calm of the enemy's lines through his field-glass.
"So far as I can see," he said, at last, "one man."
"What's he doing?" asked the war correspondent.
"Field-glass at us," said the young lieutenant.
"And this is war!"
"No," said the young lieutenant; "it's Bloch."
"The game's a draw."
"No! They've got to win or else they lose. A draw's a win for our side."
They had discussed the political situation fifty times or so, and the war correspondent was weary of it. He stretched out his limbs. "Aaai s'pose it *is*!" he yawned.
"*Flut!*"
"What was that?"
"Shot at us."
The war correspondent shifted to a slightly lower position. "No one shot at him," he complained.
"I wonder if they think we shall get so bored we shall go home?"
The war correspondent made no reply.
"There's the harvest, of course…"
They had been there a month. Since the first brisk movements after the declaration of war things had gone slower and slower, until it seemed as though the

whole machine of events must have run down. To begin with, they had had almost a scampering time; the invader had come across the frontier on the very dawn of the war in half-a-dozen parallel columns behind a cloud of cyclists and cavalry, with a general air of coming straight on the capital, and the defender horsemen had held him up, and peppered him and forced him to open out to outflank, and had then bolted to the next position in the most approved style, for a couple of days, until in the afternoon, bump! they had the invader against their prepared lines of defense. He did not suffer so much as had been hoped and expected: he was coming on, it seemed with his eyes open, his scouts winded the guns, and down he sat at once without the shadow of an attack and began grubbing trenches for himself, as though he meant to sit down there to the very end of time. He was slow, but much more wary than the world had been led to expect, and he kept convoys tucked in and shielded his slow marching infantry sufficiently well to prevent any heavy adverse scoring.

"But he ought to attack," the young lieutenant had insisted.

"He'll attack us at dawn, somewhere along the lines. You'll get the bayonets coming into the trenches just about when you can see," the war correspondent had held until a week ago.

The young lieutenant winked when he said that.

When one early morning the men the defenders sent to lie out five hundred yards before the trenches, with a view to the unexpected emptying of magazines into any night attack, gave way to causeless panic and blazed away at nothing for ten minutes, the war correspondent understood the meaning of that wink.

"What would you do if you were the enemy?" said the war correspondent, suddenly.

"If I had men like I've got now?"

"Yes."

"Take those trenches."

"How?"

"Oh—dodges! Crawl out half-way at night before moonrise and get into touch with the chaps we send out. Blaze at 'em if they tried to shift, and so bag some of 'em in the daylight. Learn that patch of ground by heart, lie all day in squatty holes, and come on nearer next night. There's a bit over there, lumpy ground, where they could get across to rushing distance—easy. In a night or so. It would be a mere game for our fellows; it's what they're made for... Guns? Shrapnel and stuff wouldn't stop good men who meant business."

"Why don't *they* do that?"

"Their men aren't brutes enough: that's the trouble. They're a crowd of devitalized townsmen, and that's the truth of the matter' They're clerks, they're factory hands, they're students, they're civilized men. They can write, they can talk, they can make and do all sorts of things, but they're poor amateurs at war. They've got no physical staying power, and that's the whole thing. They've never slept in the open one night in their lives; they've never drunk anything but the purest water-company water; they've never gone short of three meals a day since they left their feeding-bottles. Half their cavalry never cocked leg over horse till it enlisted six months ago. They ride their horses as though they were bicycles—you watch 'em! They're fools at the game, and they know it. Our boys of fourteen can give their grown men points... Very well——"

The war correspondent mused on his face with his nose between his knuckles.

"If a decent civilization," he said, "cannot produce better men for war than——"

He stopped with belated politeness.

"I mean——"

"Than our open-air life," said the young lieutenant, politely.

"Exactly," said the war correspondent. "Then civilization has to stop."

"It looks like it," the young lieutenant admitted.

"Civilization has science, you know," said the war correspondent. "It invented and it makes the rifles and guns and things you use."

"Which our nice healthy hunters and stockmen and so on, rowdy-dowdy cowpunchers and negro-whackers, can use ten times better than——*What's that?*"

"What?" said the war correspondent, and then seeing his companion busy with his field-glass he produced his own: "Where?" said the war correspondent, sweeping the enemy's lines.

"It's nothing," said the young lieutenant, still looking.

"What's nothing?"

The young lieutenant put down his glass and pointed. "I thought I saw something there, behind the stems of those trees. Something black. What it was I don't know."

The war correspondent tried to get even by intense scrutiny.

"It wasn't anything," said the young lieutenant, rolling over to regard the darkling evening sky, and generalized: "There never will be anything any more for ever. Unless——"

The war correspondent looked inquiringly.

"They may get their stomachs wrong, or something—living without proper drains."

A sound of bugles came from the tents behind. The war correspondent slid backward down the sand and stood up. "Boom!" came from somewhere far away to the left. "Halloa!" he said, hesitated, and crawled back to peer again. "Firing at this time is jolly bad manners."

The young lieutenant was incommunicative again for a space.

Then he pointed to the distant clump of trees again. "One of our big guns. They were firing at that," he said.

"The thing that wasn't anything?"

"Something over there, anyhow."

Both men were silent, peering through their glasses for a space. "Just when it's twilight," the lieutenant complained. He stood up.

"I might stay here a bit," said the war correspondent.

The lieutenant shook his head. "There is nothing to see," he apologized, and then went down to where his little squad of sun-brown, loose-limbed men had been yarning in the trench. The war correspondent stood up also, glanced for a moment at the business-like bustle below him, gave perhaps twenty seconds to those enigmatical trees again, then turned his face toward the camp.

He found himself wondering whether his editor would consider the story of how somebody thought he saw something black behind a clump of trees, and how a gun was fired at this illusion by somebody else, too trivial for public consultation.

"It's the only gleam of a shadow of interest," said the war correspondent, "for ten whole days."

"No," he said, presently; "I'll write that other article, 'Is War Played Out?'"

He surveyed the darkling lines in perspective, the tangle of trenches one behind another, one commanding another, which the defender had made ready. The shadows and mists swallowed up their receding contours, and here and there a lantern gleamed, and here and there knots of men were busy about small fires.

"No troops on earth could do it," he said…

He was depressed. He believed that there were other things in life better worth having than proficiency in war; he believed that in the heart of civilization, for all its stresses, its crushing concentrations of forces, its injustice and suffering, there lay something that might be the hope of the world, and the idea that any people by living in the open air, hunting perpetually, losing touch with books and art and all the things that intensify life, might hope to resist and break that great development to the end of time, jarred on his civilized soul.

Apt to his thought came a file of defender soldiers and passed him in the gleam of a swinging lamp that marked the way.

He glanced at their red-lit faces, and one shone out for a moment, a common type of face in the defender's ranks: ill-shaped nose, sensuous lips, bright clear eyes full of alert cunning, slouch hat cocked on one side and adorned with the peacock's plume of the rustic Don Juan turned soldier, a hard brown skin, a sinewy frame, an open, tireless stride, and a master's grip on the rifle.

The war correspondent returned their salutations and went on his way.

"Louts," he whispered. "Cunning, elementary louts. And they are going to beat the townsmen at the game of war!"

From the red glow among the nearer tents came first one and then half-a-dozen hearty voices, bawling in a drawling unison the words of a particularly sad and sentimental patriotic song.

"Oh, *go* it!" muttered the war correspondent, bitterly.

II.

It was opposite the trenches called after Hackbone's Hut that the battle began. There the ground stretched broad and level between the lines, with scarcely shelter for a lizard, and it seemed to the startled, just awakened men who came crowding into the trenches that this was one more proof of that green inexperience of the enemy of which they had heard so much. The war correspondent would not believe his ears at first, and swore that he and the war artist, who, still imperfectly roused, was trying to put on his boots by the light of a match held in his hand, were the victims of a common illusion. Then, after putting his head in a bucket of cold water, his intelligence came back as he towelled. He listened. "Gollys!" he said, "that's something more than scare firing this time. It's like ten thousand carts on a bridge of tin."

There came a sort of enrichment to that steady uproar. "Machine-guns!"

Then, "Guns!"

The artist, with one boot on, thought to look at his watch, and went to it hopping.

"Half an hour from dawn," he said. "You were right about their attacking, after all…"

The war correspondent came out of the tent, verifying the presence of chocolate in his pocket as he did so. He had to halt for a moment or so until his eyes were toned down to the night a little. "Pitch!" he said. He stood for a space to season his eyes before he felt justified in striking out for a black gap among the adjacent tents. The artist coming out behind him fell over a tent-rope. It was half-past two o'clock in the morning of the darkest night in time, and against a sky of dull black silk the enemy was talking searchlights, a wild jabber of searchlights. "He's trying to blind our riflemen," said the war correspondent with a flash, and waited for the artist and then set off with a sort of discreet haste again. "Whoa!" he said, presently. "Ditches!"

They stopped.

"It's the confounded searchlights," said the war correspondent.

They saw lanterns going to and fro, near by, and men falling in to march down to the trenches. They were for following them, and then the artist began to feel his night eyes. "If we scramble this," he said, "and it's only a drain, there's a clear run up to the ridge." And that way they took. Lights came and went in the tents behind, as the men turned out, and ever and again they came to broken ground and staggered and stumbled. But in a little while they drew near the crest. Something that sounded like the impact of a very important railway accident happened in the air above them, and the shrapnel bullets seethed about them like a sudden handful of hail. "Right-ho!" said the war correspondent, and soon they judged they had come to the crest and stood in the midst of a world of great darkness and frantic glares, whose principal fact was sound.

Right and left of them and all about them was the uproar, an army-full of magazine fire, at first chaotic and monstrous and then, eked out by little flashes and gleams and suggestions, taking the beginnings of a shape. It looked to the war correspondent as though the enemy must have attacked in line and with his whole force—in which case he was either being or was already annihilated.

"Dawn and the dead," he said, with his instinct for headlines. He said this to himself, but afterwards, by means of shouting, he conveyed an idea to the artist.

"They must have meant it for a surprise," he said.

It was remarkable how the firing kept on. After a time he began to perceive a sort of rhythm in this inferno of noise. It would decline—decline perceptibly, droop towards something that was comparatively a pause—a pause of inquiry. "Aren't you all dead yet?" this pause seemed to say. The flickering fringe of rifle-flashes would become attenuated and broken, and the whack-bang of the enemy's big guns two miles away there would come up out of the deeps. Then suddenly, east or west of them, something would startle the rifles to a frantic outbreak again.

The war correspondent taxed his brain for some theory of conflict that would account for this, and was suddenly aware that the artist and he were vividly illuminated. He could see the ridge on which they stood and before them in black outline a file of riflemen hurrying down towards the nearer trenches. It became visible that a light rain was falling, and farther away towards the enemy was a clear space with men—"our men?"—running across it in disorder. He saw one of those men throw up his hands and drop. And something else black and shining loomed up on the edge of the beam-coruscating flashes; and behind it and far away a calm, white eye regarded the world. "Whit, whit, whit," sang something in the air, and then the artist was running for cover, with the war correspondent behind him. Bang came shrapnel, bursting close at hand as it seemed, and our two men were lying flat in a dip in the ground, and the light and everything had gone again, leaving a vast note of interrogation upon the night.

The war correspondent came within bawling range. "What the deuce was it? Shooting our men down!"

"Black," said the artist, "and like a fort. Not two hundred yards from the first trench."

He sought for comparisons in his mind. "Something between a big blockhouse and a giant's dish-cover," he said.

"And they were running!" said the war correspondent.

"*You'd* run if a thing like that, with a searchlight to help it, turned up like a prowling nightmare in the middle of the night."

They crawled to what they judged the edge of the dip and lay regarding the unfathomable dark. For a space they could distinguish nothing, and then a sudden convergence of the searchlights of both sides brought the strange thing out again.

In that flickering pallor it had the effect of a large and clumsy black insect, an insect the size of an ironclad cruiser, crawling obliquely to the first line of trenches and firing shots out of portholes in its side. And on its carcass the bullets must have been battering with more than the passionate violence of hail on a roof of tin.

Then in the twinkling of an eye the curtain of the dark had fallen again and the monster had vanished, but the crescendo of musketry marked its approach to the trenches.

They were beginning to talk about the thing to each other, when a flying bullet kicked dirt into the artist's face, and they, decided abruptly to crawl down into the cover of the trenches. They had got down with an unobtrusive persistence into the second line, before the dawn had grown clear enough for anything to be seen. They found themselves in a crowd of expectant riflemen, all noisily arguing about what would happen next. The enemy's contrivance had done execution upon the outlying men, it seemed, but they did not believe it would do any more. "Come the day and we'll capture the lot of them," said a burly soldier.

"Them?" said the war correspondent.

"They say there's a regular string of 'em, crawling along the front of our lines… Who cares?"

The darkness filtered away so imperceptibly that at no moment could one declare decisively that one could see. The searchlights ceased to sweep hither and thither. The enemy's monsters were dubious patches of darkness upon the dark, and then no longer dubious, and so they crept out into distinctness. The war correspondent, munching chocolate absent-mindedly, beheld at last a spacious picture of battle under the cheerless sky, whose central focus was an array of fourteen or fifteen huge clumsy shapes lying in perspective on the very edge of the first line of trenches, at intervals of perhaps three hundred yards, and evidently firing down upon the crowded riflemen. They were so close in that the defender's guns had ceased, and only the first line of trenches was in action.

The second line commanded the first, and as the light grew the war correspondent could make out the riflemen who were fighting these monsters, crouched in knots and crowds behind the transverse banks that crossed the trenches against the eventuality of an enfilade. The trenches close to the big machines were empty save for the crumpled suggestions of dead and wounded men; the defenders had been driven right and left as soon as the prow of this land ironclad had loomed up over the front of the trench. He produced his field-glass, and was immediately a centre of inquiry from the soldiers about him.

They wanted to look, they asked questions, and after he had announced that the men across the traverses seemed unable to advance or retreat, and were crouching under cover rather than fighting, he found it advisable to loan his glasses to a burly and incredulous corporal. He heard a strident voice, and found a lean and sallow soldier at his back talking to the artist.

"There's chaps down there caught," the man was saying. "If they retreat they got to expose themselves, and the fire's too straight…"

"They aren't firing much, but every shot's a hit."

"Who?"

"The chaps in that thing. The men who're coming up——"

"Coming up where?"

"We're evacuating them trenches where we can. Our chaps are coming back up the zigzags… No end of 'em hit… But when we get clear our turn'll come. Rather! These things won't be able to cross a trench or get into it; and before they can get back our guns'll smash 'em up. Smash 'em right up. See?" A brightness came into his eyes. "Then we'll have a go at the beggar inside," he said…

The war correspondent thought for a moment, trying to realize the idea. Then he set himself to recover his field-glasses from the burly corporal…

The daylight was getting clearer now. The clouds were lifting, and a gleam of lemon-yellow amidst the level masses to the east portended sunrise. He looked again at the land ironclad. As he saw it in the bleak grey dawn, lying obliquely upon the slope and on the very lip of the foremost trench, the suggestion of a stranded vessel was very great indeed. It might have been from eighty to a hundred feet long—it was about two hundred and fifty yards away—its vertical side was ten feet high or so, smooth for that height, and then with a complex patterning under the eaves of its flattish turtle cover. This patterning was a close interlacing of portholes, rifle barrels, and telescope tubes—sham and real—indistinguishable one from the other. The thing had come into such a position as to enfilade the trench, which was empty now, so far as he could see, except for two or three crouching knots of men and the tumbled dead. Behind it, across the plain, it had scored the grass with a train of linked impressions, like the dotted tracings sea-things leave in sand. Left and right of that track dead men and wounded men were scattered—men it had picked off as they fled back from their advanced positions in the searchlight glare from the invader's lines. And now it lay with its head projecting a little over the trench it had won, as if it were a single sentient thing planning the next phase of its attack…

He lowered his glasses and took a more comprehensive view of the situation. These creatures of the night had evidently won the first line of trenches and the fight had come to a pause. In the increasing light he could make out by a stray shot or a chance exposure that the defender's marksmen were lying thick in the second and third line of trenches up towards the low crest of the position, and in such of the zigzags as gave them a chance of a converging fire. The men about him were talking of guns. "We're in the line of the big guns at the crest but they'll soon shift one to pepper them," the lean man said, reassuringly.

"Whup," said the corporal.

"Bang! bang! bang! Whir-r-r-r!" It was a sort of nervous jump, and all the rifles were going off by themselves. The war correspondent found himself and the artist, two idle men crouching behind a line of preoccupied backs, of industrious men discharging magazines. The monster had moved. It continued to move regardless of the hail that splashed its skin with bright new specks of lead. It was singing a mechanical little ditty to itself, "Tuf-tuf, tuf-tuf, tuf-tuf," and squirting out little jets of steam behind. It had humped itself up, as a limpet does before it crawls; it had lifted its skirt and displayed along the length of it—*feet*! They were thick, stumpy feet, between knobs and buttons in shape—flat, broad things, reminding one of the feet of elephants or the legs of caterpillars; and then, as the skirt rose higher, the war correspondent, scrutinizing the thing through his glasses again, saw that these feet hung, as it were, on the rims of wheels. His thoughts whirled back to Victoria Street, Westminster, and he saw himself in the piping times of peace, seeking matter for an interview.

"Mr.—Mr. Diplock," he said, "and he called them Pedrails… Fancy meeting them here!"

The marksman beside him raised his head and shoulders in a speculative mood to fire more certainly—it seemed so natural to assume the attention of the monster must be distracted by this trench before it—and was suddenly knocked backwards by a bullet through his neck. His feet flew up, and he vanished out of the margin of the watcher's field of vision. The war correspondent grovelled tighter, but after a glance behind him at a painful little confusion, he resumed his field-glass, for the thing was putting down its feet one after the other, and hoisting itself farther and farther over the trench. Only a bullet in the head could have stopped him looking just then.

The lean man with the strident voice ceased firing to turn and reiterate his point. "They can't possibly cross," he bawled. They——"

"Bang! Bang! Bang! Bang!"—drowned everything.

The lean man continued speaking for a word or so, then gave it up, shook his head to enforce the impossibility of anything crossing a trench like the one below, and resumed business once more.

And all the while that great bulk was crossing. When the war correspondent turned his glass on it again it had bridged the trench, and its queer feet were rasping away at the farther bank, in the attempt to get a hold there. It got its hold. It continued to crawl until the greater bulk of it was over the trench—until it was all over. Then it paused for a moment, adjusted its skirt a little nearer the ground, gave an unnerving "toot, toot," and came on abruptly at a pace of, perhaps, six miles an hour straight up the gentle slope towards our observer.

The war correspondent raised himself on his elbow and looked a natural inquiry at the artist.

For a moment the men about him stuck to their position and fired furiously. Then the lean man in a mood of precipitancy slid backwards, and the war correspondent said "Come along" to the artist, and led the movement along the trench.

As they dropped down, the vision of a hillside of trench being rushed by a dozen vast cockroaches disappeared for a space, and instead was one of a narrow passage, crowded with men, for the most part receding, though one or two turned or halted. He never turned back to see the nose of the monster creep over the brow of the trench; he never even troubled to keep in touch with the artist. He heard the "whit" of bullets about him soon enough, and saw a man before him stumble and drop, and then he was one of a furious crowd fighting to get into a transverse zigzag ditch that enabled the defenders to get under cover up and down the hill. It was like a theatre panic. He gathered from signs and fragmentary words that on ahead another of these monsters had also won to the second trench.

He lost his interest in the general course of the battle for a space altogether; he became simply a modest egotist, in a mood of hasty circumspection, seeking the farthest rear, amidst a dispersed multitude of disconcerted riflemen similarly employed. He scrambled down through trenches, he took his courage in both hands and sprinted across the open, he had moments of panic when it seemed madness not to be quadrupedal, and moments of shame when he stood up and faced about to see how the fight was going. And he was one of many thousand very similar men that morning. On the ridge he halted in a knot of scrub, and was for a few minutes almost minded to stop and see things out.

The day was now fully come. The grey sky had changed to blue, and of all the cloudy masses of the dawn there remained only a few patches of dissolving fleeciness. The world below was bright and singularly clear. The ridge was not, perhaps, more than a hundred feet or so above the general plain, but in this flat region it sufficed to give the effect of extensive view. Away on the north side of the ridge, little and far, were the camps, the ordered wagons, all the gear of a big army; with officers galloping about and men doing aimless things. Here and there men were falling in, however and the cavalry was forming up on the plain beyond the tents. The bulk of men who had been in the trenches were still on the move to the rear, scattered like sheep without a shepherd over the farther slopes. Here and there were little rallies and attempts to wait and do—something vague; but the general drift was away from any concentration. There on the southern side was the elaborate lacework of trenches and defences, across which these iron turtles, fourteen of them spread out over a line of perhaps three miles, were now advancing as fast as a man could trot, and methodically shooting down and breaking up any persistent knots of resistance. Here and there stood little clumps of men, outflanked and unable to get away, showing the white flag, and the invader's cyclist-infantry was advancing now across the open, in open order but unmolested, to complete the work of the machines. Surveyed at large, the defenders already looked a beaten army. A mechanism that was effectually ironclad against bullets, that could at a pinch cross a thirty-foot trench, and that seemed able to shoot out rifle-bullets with unerring precision, was clearly an inevitable victor against anything but rivers, precipices, and guns.

He looked at his watch. "Half-past four! Lord! What things can happen in two hours. Here's the whole blessed army being walked over, and at half-past two——

"And even now our blessed louts haven't done a thing with their guns!"

He scanned the ridge right and left of him with his glasses. He turned again to the nearest land ironclad, advancing now obliquely to him and not three hundred yards away, and then scrambled the ground over which he must retreat if he was not to be captured.

"They'll do nothing," he said, and glanced again at the enemy.

And then from far away to the left came the thud of a gun, followed very rapidly by a rolling gunfire.

He hesitated and decided to stay.

III.

The defender had relied chiefly upon his rifles in the event of an assault. His guns he kept concealed at various points upon and behind the ridge ready to bring them into action against any artillery preparations for an attack on the part of his antagonist. The situation had rushed upon him with the dawn, and by the time the gunners had their guns ready for motion, the land ironclads were already in among the foremost trenches. There is a natural reluctance to fire into one's own broken men, and many of the guns, being intended simply to fight an advance of the enemy's artillery, were not in positions to hit anything in the second line of trenches. After that the advance of the land ironclads was swift. The defender-general found himself suddenly called upon to invent a new sort of warfare, in which guns were to fight alone amidst broken and retreating infantry. He had scarcely thirty minutes in which to think it out. He did not respond to the call, and what happened that morning was that the advance of the land ironclads forced the fight, and each gun and battery made what play its circumstances dictated. For the most part it was poor play.

Some of the guns got in two or three shots, some one or two, and the percentage of misses was unusually high. The howitzers, of course, did nothing. The land ironclads in each case followed much the same tactics. As soon as a gun came into play the monster turned itself almost end on, so as to minimize the chances of a square hit, and made not for the gun, but for the nearest point on its flank from which the gunners could be shot down. Few of the hits scored were very effectual; only one of the things was disabled, and that was the one that fought the three batteries attached to the brigade on the left wing. Three that were hit when close upon the guns were clean shot through without being put out of action. Our war correspondent did not see that one momentary arrest of the tide of victory on the left; he saw only the very ineffectual fight of half-battery 96B close at hand upon his right. This he watched some time beyond the margin of safety.

Just after he heard the three batteries opening up upon his left he became aware of the thud of horses' hoofs from the sheltered side of the slope, and presently saw first one and then two other guns galloping into position along the north side of the ridge, well out of sight of the great bulk that was now creeping obliquely towards the crest and cutting up the lingering infantry beside it and below, as it came.

The half-battery swung round into line—each gun describing its curve—halted, unlimbered, and prepared for action...

"Bang!"

The land ironclad had become visible over the brow of the hill, and just visible as a long black back to the gunners. It halted, as though it hesitated.

The two remaining guns fired, and then their big antagonist had swung round and was in full view, end on, against the sky, coming at a rush.

The gunners became frantic in their haste to fire again. They were so near the war correspondent could see the expressions on their excited faces through his field-glass. As he looked he saw a man drop, and realized for the first time that the ironclad was shooting.

For a moment the big black monster crawled with an accelerated pace towards the furiously active gunners. Then, as if moved by a generous impulse, it turned its full broadside to their attack, and scarcely forty yards away from them. The war correspondent turned his field-glass back to the gunners and perceived it was now shooting down the men about the guns with the most deadly rapidity.

Just for a moment it seemed splendid and then it seemed horrible. The gunners were dropping in heaps about their guns. To lay a hand on a gun was death. "Bang!" went the gun on the left, a hopeless miss, and that was the only second shot the half-battery fired. In another moment half-a-dozen surviving artillerymen were holding up their hands amidst a scattered muddle of dead and wounded men, and the fight was done.

The war correspondent hesitated between stopping in his scrub and waiting for an opportunity to surrender decently, or taking to an adjacent gully he had discovered. If he surrendered it was certain he would get no copy off; while, if he escaped, there were all sorts of chances. He decided to follow the gully, and take the first offer in the confusion beyond the camp of picking up a horse.

IV.

Subsequent authorities have found fault with the first land ironclads in many particulars, but assuredly they served their purpose on the day of their appearance. They were essentially long, narrow, and very strong steel frameworks carrying the engines, and borne upon eight pairs of big pedrail wheels, each about ten feet in diameter, each a driving wheel and set upon long axles free to swivel round a common axis. This arrangement gave them the maximum of adaptability to the contours of the ground. They crawled level along the ground with one foot high upon a hillock and another deep in a depression, and they could hold themselves erect and steady sideways upon even a steep hillside. The engineers directed the engines under the command of the captain, who had look-out points at small ports all round the upper edge of the adjustable skirt of twelve-inch iron-plating which protected the whole affair, and could also raise or depress a conning-tower set about the portholes through the centre of the iron top cover. The riflemen each occupied a small cabin of peculiar construction and these cabins were slung along the sides of and before and behind the great main framework, in a manner suggestive of the slinging of the seats of an Irish jaunting-car. Their rifles, however, were very different pieces of apparatus from the simple mechanisms in the hands of their adversaries.

These were in the first place automatic, ejected their cartridges and loaded again from a magazine each time they fired, until the ammunition store was at an end, and they had the most remarkable sights imaginable, sights which threw a bright little camera-obscura picture into the light-tight box in which the rifleman sat below. This camera-obscura picture was marked with two crossed lines, and whatever was covered by the intersection of these two lines, that the rifle hit. The sighting was ingeniously contrived. The rifleman stood at the table with a thing like an elaboration of a draughtsman's dividers in his hand, and he opened and closed these dividers, so that they were always at the apparent height—if it was an ordinary-sized man—of the man he wanted to kill. A little twisted strand of wire like an electric-light wire ran from this implement up to the gun, and as the dividers opened and shut the sights went up and down. Changes in the clearness of the atmosphere, due to changes of moisture, were met by an ingenious use of that meteorologically sensitive substance, catgut, and when the land ironclad moved forward the sites got a compensatory deflection in the direction of its motion. The riflemen stood up in his pitch-dark chamber and watched the little picture before him. One hand held the dividers for judging distance, and the other grasped a big knob like a door-handle. As he pushed this knob about the rifle above swung to correspond, and the picture passed to and fro like an agitated panorama. When he saw a man he wanted to shoot he brought him up to the cross-lines, and then pressed a finger upon a little push like an electric bell-push, conveniently placed in the centre of the knob. Then the man was shot. If by any chance the rifleman missed his target he moved the knob a trifle, or readjusted his dividers, pressed the push, and got him the second time.

This rifle and its sights protruded from a porthole, exactly like a great number of other portholes that ran in a triple row under the eaves of the cover of the land ironclad. Each porthole displayed a rifle and sight in dummy, so that the real ones could only be hit by a chance shot, and if one was, then the young man below said "Pshaw!" turned on an electric light, lowered the injured instrument into his camera, replaced the injured part, or put up a new rifle if the injury was considerable.

You must conceive these cabins as hung clear above the swing of the axles, and inside the big wheels upon which the great elephant-like feet were hung, and behind these cabins along the centre of the monster ran a central gallery into which they opened, and along which worked the big compact engines. It was like a long passage into which this throbbing machinery had been packed, and the captain stood about the middle, close to the ladder that led to his conning-tower, and directed the silent, alert engineers—for the most part by signs. The throb and noise of the engines mingled with the reports of the rifles and the intermittent clangour of the bullet hail upon the armour. Ever and again he would touch the wheel that raised his conning-tower, step up his ladder until his engineers could see nothing of him above the waist, and then come down again with orders. Two small electric lights were all the illumination of this space—they were placed to make him most clearly visible to his subordinates; the air was thick with the smell of oil and petrol, and had the war correspondent been suddenly transferred from the spacious dawn outside to the bowels of the apparatus he would have thought himself fallen into another world.

The captain, of course, saw both sides of the battle. When he raised his head into his conning-tower there were the dewy sunrise, the amazed and disordered trenches, the flying and falling soldiers, the depressed-looking groups of prisoners, the beaten guns; when he bent down again to signal "half speed", "quarter speed", "half circle round towards the right", or what not, he was in the oil-smelling twilight of the ill-lit engine room. Close beside him on either side was the mouth-piece of a speaking-tube, and ever and again he would direct one side or other of his strange craft to "Concentrate fire forward on gunners", or to "Clear out trench about a hundred yards on our right front".

He was a young man, healthy enough but by no means sun-tanned, and of a type of feature and expression that prevails in His Majesty's Navy: alert, intelligent, quiet. He and his engineers and his riflemen all went about their work, calm and reasonable men. They had none of that flapping strenuousness of the half-wit in a hurry, that excessive strain upon the blood-vessels, that hysteria of effort which is so frequently regarded as the proper state of mind for heroic deeds.

For the enemy these young engineers were defeating they felt a certain qualified pity and a quite unqualified contempt. They regarded these big, healthy men they were shooting down precisely as these same big, healthy men might regard some inferior kind of native. They despised them for making war; despised their bawling patriotisms and their emotionality profoundly; despised them, above all, for the petty cunning and the almost brutish want of imagination their method of fighting displayed. "If they *must* make war," these young men thought, "why in thunder don't they do it like sensible men?" They resented the assumption that their own side was too stupid to do anything more than play their enemy's game, that they were going to play this costly folly according to the rules of unimaginative men. They resented being forced to the trouble of making man-killing machinery; resented the alternative of having to massacre these people or endure their truculent yappings; resented the whole unfathomable imbecility of war.

Meanwhile, with something of the mechanical precision of a good clerk posting a ledger, the riflemen moved their knobs and pressed their buttons…

The captain of Land Ironclad Number Three had halted on the crest close to his captured half-battery. His lined-up prisoners stood hard by and waited for the cyclists behind to come for them. He surveyed the victorious morning through his conning-tower.

He read the general's signals. "Five and Four are to keep among the guns to the left and prevent any attempt to recover them. Seven and Eleven and Twelve, stick to the guns you have got; Seven, get into position to command the guns taken by Three. Then, we're to do something else, are we? Six and One, quicken up to about ten miles an hour and walk round behind that camp to the levels near the river—we shall bag the whole crowd of them," interjected the young man. "Ah, here we are! Two and Three, Eight and Nine, Thirteen and Fourteen, space out to a thousand yards, wait for the word, and then go slowly to cover the advance of the cyclist infantry against any charge of mounted troops. That's all right. But where's Ten? Halloa! Ten to repair and get movable as soon as possible. They've broken up Ten!"

The discipline of the new war machines was business-like rather than pedantic, and the head of the captain came down out of the conning-tower to tell his men. "I say, you chaps there. They've broken up Ten. Not badly, I think; but anyhow, he's stuck."

But that still left thirteen of the monsters in action to finish up the broken army.

The war correspondent stealing down his gully looked back and saw them all lying along the crest and talking fluttering congratulatory flags to one another. Their iron sides were shining golden in the light of the rising sun.

V.

The private adventures of the war correspondent terminated in surrender about one o'clock in the afternoon, and by that time he had stolen a horse, pitched off it, and narrowly escaped being rolled upon; found the brute had broken its leg, and shot it with his revolver. He had spent some hours in the company of a squad of dispirited riflemen, had quarrelled with them about topography at last, and gone off by himself in a direction that should have brought him to the banks of the river and didn't. Moreover, he had eaten all his chocolate and found nothing in the whole world to drink. Also, it had become extremely hot. From behind a broken, but attractive, stone wall he had seen far away in the distance the defender-horsemen trying to charge cyclists in open order, with land ironclads outflanking them on either side. He had discovered that cyclists could retreat over open turf before horsemen with a sufficient margin of speed to allow of frequent dismounts and much terribly effective sharpshooting; and he had a sufficient persuasion that those horsemen, having charged their hearts out, had halted just beyond his range of vision and surrendered. He had been urged to sudden activity by a forward movement of one of those machines that had threatened to enfilade his wall. He had discovered a fearful blister on his heel.

He was now in a scrubby gravelly place, sitting down and meditating on his pocket-handkerchief, which had in some extraordinary way become in the last twenty-four hours extremely ambiguous in hue. "It's the whitest thing I've got," he said.

He had known all along that the enemy was east, west, and south of him, but when he heard war Ironclads Numbers One and Six talking in their measured, deadly way not half a mile to the north he decided to make his own little unconditional peace without any further risks. He was for hoisting his white flag to a bush and taking up a position of modest obscurity near it, until someone came along. He became aware of voices, clatter, and the distinctive noises of a body of horse, quite near, and he put his handkerchief in his pocket again and went to see what was going forward.

The sound of firing ceased, and then as he drew near he heard the deep sounds of many simple, coarse, but hearty and noble-hearted soldiers of the old school swearing with vigour.

He emerged from his scrub upon a big level plain, and far away a fringe of trees marked the banks of the river. In the centre of the picture was a still intact road bridge, and a big railway bridge a little to the right. Two land ironclads rested, with a general air of being long, harmless sheds, in a pose of anticipatory peacefulness right and left of the picture, completely commanding two miles and more of the river levels. Emerged and halted a few yards from the scrub was the remainder of the defender's cavalry, dusty, a little disordered and obviously annoyed, but still a very fine show of men. In the middle distance three or four men and horses were receiving medical attendance, and nearer a knot of officers regarded the distant novelties in mechanism with profound distaste. Everyone was very distinctly aware of the twelve other ironclads, and of the multitude of townsmen soldiers, on bicycles or afoot, encumbered now by prisoners and captured war-gear but otherwise thoroughly effective, who were sweeping like a great net in their rear.

"Checkmate," said the war correspondent, walking out into the open. "But I surrender in the best of company. Twenty-four hours ago I thought war was impossible—and these beggars have captured the whole blessed army! Well! Well!" He thought of his talk with the young lieutenant. "If there's no end to the surprises of science, the civilized people have it, of course. As long as their science keeps going they will necessarily be ahead of open-country men. Still…" He wondered for a space what might have happened to the young lieutenant.

The war correspondent was one of those inconsistent people who always want the beaten side to win. When he saw all these burly, sun-tanned horsemen, disarmed and dismounted and lined up; when he saw their horses unskilfully led away by the singularly not equestrian cyclists to whom they had surrendered; when he saw these truncated Paladins watching this scandalous sight, he forgot altogether that he had called these men "cunning louts" and wished them beaten not four-and-twenty hours ago. A month ago he had seen that regiment in its pride going forth to war, and had been told of its terrible prowess, how it could charge in open order with each man firing from his saddle, and sweep before it anything else that ever came out to battle in any sort of order, foot or horse. And it had had to fight a few score of young men in atrociously unfair machines!

"Manhood *versus* Machinery" occurred to him as a suitable headline. Journalism curdles all one's mind to phrases.

He strolled as near the lined-up prisoners as the sentinels seemed disposed to permit and surveyed them and compared their sturdy proportions with those of their lightly built captors.

"Smart degenerates," he muttered. "Anæmic cockneydom."

The surrendered officers came quite close to him presently, and he could hear the colonel's high-pitched tenor. The poor gentleman had spent three years of arduous toil upon the best material in the world perfecting that shooting from the saddle charge, and he was mourning with phrases of blasphemy, natural under the circumstances what one could be expected to do against this suitably consigned ironmongery.

"Guns," said some one.

"Big guns they can walk round. You can't shift big guns to keep pace with them and little guns in the open they rush. I saw 'em rushed. You might do a surprise now and then—assassinate the brutes, perhaps——"

"You might make things like 'em."

"What? *More* ironmongery? Us?..."

"I'll call my article," meditated the war correspondent, "'Mankind *versus* Ironmongery,' and quote the old boy at the beginning."

And he was much too good a journalist to spoil his contrast by remarking that the half-dozen comparatively slender young men in blue pajamas who were standing about their victorious land ironclad, drinking coffee and eating biscuits, had also in their eyes and carriage something not altogether degraded below the level of a man.

(1903)

THE REVOLT OF THE MACHINES

Emile Goudeau

Emile Goudeau (1849–1906) was born in Périgueux, Dordogne, and worked as a teacher before joining the Ministry of Finance in Paris. His job there was not so very demanding, so he devoted most of his time to poetry. He founded the Hydropathes, a notorious literary society devoted to readings, songs, poetry, but most especially to absinthe, which destroyed more than one of them. It didn't help that Goudeau paid his collaborators in drink. When Rodolphe Salis opened Le Chat Noir cabaret in December 1881, he persuaded Goudeau to move the Hydropathes there. Goudeau helped Salis to launch his journal *Le Chat Noir*, which first appeared on 14 January 1882, and was its chief editor until 1884. "The Revolt of the Machines" is Goudeau's only excursion into scientific romance.

Dr. Pastoureaux, aided by a very skillful old workman named Jean Bertrand, had invented a machine that revolutionized the scientific world. That machine was animate, almost capable of thought, almost capable of will, and sensitive: a kind of animal in iron. There is no need here to go into overly complicated technical details, which would be a waste of time. Let it suffice to know that with a series of platinum containers, penetrated by phosphoric acid, the scientist had found a means to give a kind of soul to fixed or locomotive machines; and that the new entities would be able to act in the fashion of a metal bull or a steel elephant.

It is necessary to add that, although the scientist became increasingly enthusiastic about his work, old Jean Bertrand, who was diabolically superstitious, gradually became frightened on perceiving that sudden evocation of intelligence in something primordially dead. In addition, the comrades of the factory, who were assiduous followers of public meetings, were all sternly opposed to machines that serve as the slaves of capitalism and tyrants of the worker.

It was the eve of the inauguration of the masterpiece.

For the first time, the machine had been equipped with all its organs, and external sensations reached it distinctly. It understood that, in spite of the shackles that still retained it, solid limbs were fitted to its young being, and that it would soon be able to translate into external movement that which it experienced internally.

This is what it heard:

"Were you at the public meeting yesterday?" said one voice.

"I should think so, old man," replied a blacksmith, a kind of Hercules with bare muscular arms. Bizarrely illuminated by the gas jets of the workshop, his face, black with dust, only left visible in the gloom the whites of his two large eyes, in which vivacity replaced intelligence. "Yes, I was there; I even spoke against the machines, against the monsters that our arms fabricate, and which, one day, will give infamous capitalism the opportunity, so long sought, to suppress our arms. We're the ones forging the weapons with which bourgeois society will batter us. When the sated, the rotten and the weak have a heap of facile clockwork devices like these to set in motion"—his arm made a circular motion—"our account will soon be settled. We who are living at the present moment eat by procreating the tools of our definitive expulsion from the world. Hola! No need to make children for them to be lackeys of the bourgeoisie!"

Listening with all its auditory valves to this diatribe, the machine, intelligent but as yet naïve, sighed with pity. It wondered whether it was a good thing that it should be born to render these brave workers miserable in this way.

"Ah," the blacksmith vociferated, "if it were only up to me and my section, we'd blow all this up like an omelet. Our arms would be perfectly sufficient thereafter"—he tapped his biceps—"to dig the earth to find our bread there; the bourgeois, with their four-sou muscles, their vitiated blood and their soft legs, could pay us dearly for the bread, and if they complained, damn it, these two fists could take away their taste for it. But I'm talking to brutes who don't understand hatred." Advancing toward the machine, he added: "If everyone were like me, you wouldn't live for another quarter of an hour, see!" And his formidable fist came down on the copper flank, which resounded with a long quasi-human groan.

Jean Bertrand, who witnessed that scene, shivered tenderly, feeling guilty with regard to his brothers, because he had helped the doctor to accomplish his masterpiece.

Then they all went away, and the machine, still listening, remembered in the silence of the night. It was, therefore, unwelcome in the world! It was going to ruin poor workingmen, to the advantage of damnable exploiters! Oh, it sensed now the oppressive role that those who had created it wanted it to play. Suicide rather than that!

And in its mechanical and infantile soul, it ruminated a magnificent project to astonish, on the great day of its inauguration, the population of ignorant, retrograde and cruel machines, by giving them an example of sublime abnegation.

Until tomorrow!

Meanwhile, at the table of the Comte de Valrouge, the celebrated patron of chemists, a scientist was concluding his toast to Dr. Pastoureaux in the following terms:

"Yes, Monsieur, science will procure the definitive triumph of suffering humankind. It has already done a great deal; it has tamed time and space. Our railways, our telegraphs and our telephones have suppressed distance. If we succeed, as Dr. Pastoureaux seems to anticipate, in demonstrating that we can put intelligence into our machines, humans will be liberated forever from servile labor.

"No more serfs, no more proletariat! Everyone will become bourgeois! The slave machine will liberate from slavery our humbler brethren and give them the right of citizenship among us. No more unfortunate miners obliged to descend underground at the peril of their lives; indefatigable and eternal machines will go down for them; the thinking and acting machine, no suffering in labor, will build, under our command, iron bridges and heroic palaces. It is docile and good machines that will plow the fields.

"Well, Messieurs, it is permissible for me, in the presence of this admirable discovery, to make myself an instant prophet. A day will come when machines, always running hither and yon, will operate themselves, like the carrier pigeons of Progress; one day, perhaps, having received their complementary education, they will learn to obey a simple signal in such a way that a man, sitting peacefully and comfortably in the bosom of his family, will only have to press an electro-vitalic switch in order for machines to sow the wheat, harvest it, store it and bake the bread that it will bring to the tables of humankind, and thus finally become the King of Nature.

"In that Olympian era, the animals, too, delivered from their enormous share of labor, will be able to applaud with their four feet." (*Emotion and smiles.*) "Yes, Messieurs, for they will be our friends, after having been our whipping-boys. The ox will always have to serve in making soup" (*smiles*) "but at least it will not suffer beforehand.

"I drink, then, to Dr. Pastoureaux, to the liberator of organic matter, to the savior of the brain and sensitive flesh, to the great and noble destroyer of suffering!"

The speech was warmly applauded. Only one jealous scientist put in a word:

"Will this machine have the fidelity of a dog, then? The docility of a horse? Or even the passivity of present-day machines?"

"I don't know," Pastoureaux replied. "I don't know." And, suddenly plunged into a scientific melancholy, he added: "Can a father be assured of filial gratitude? That the being that I have brought into the world might have evil instincts, I can't deny. I believe, however, that I have developed within it, during its fabrication, a great propensity for tenderness and a spirit of goodness—what is commonly called 'heart.' The effective parts of my machine, Messieurs, have cost me many months of labor; it ought to have a great deal of humanity, and, if I might put it thus, the best of fraternity."

"Yes," replied the jealous scientist, "ignorant pity, the popular pity that leads men astray, the intelligent tenderness that makes them commit the worst of sins. I'm afraid that your sentimental machine will go astray, like a child. Better a clever wickedness than a clumsy bounty."

The interrupter was told to shut up, and Pastoureaux concluded: "Whether good or evil emerges from all this, I have, I think, made a formidable stride in human science. The five fingers of our hand will hold henceforth the supreme art of creation."

Bravos burst forth.

*

The next day, the machine was unmuzzled, and it came of its own accord, docilely, to take up its position before a numerous but selective assembly. The doctor and old Jean Bertrand installed themselves on the platform.

The excellent band of the Republican Guard began playing, and cries of "Hurrah for Science!" burst forth. Then, after having bowed to the President of the Republic, the authorities, the delegations of the Académies, the foreign representatives, and all the notable people assembled on the quay, Dr. Pastoureaux ordered Jean Bertrand to put himself in direct communication with the soul of the machine, with all its muscles of platinum and steel.

The mechanic did that quite simply by pulling a shiny lever the size of a penholder.

And suddenly, whistling, whinnying, pitching, rolling and fidgeting, in the ferocity of its new life and the exuberance of its formidable power, the machine started running around furiously.

"Hip hip hurrah!" cried the audience.

"Go, machine of the devil, go!" cried Jean Bertrand—and, like a madman, he leaned on the vital lever.

Without listening to the doctor, who wanted to moderate that astonishing speed, Bertrand spoke to the machine.

"Yes, machine of the devil, go, go! If you understand, go! Poor slave of capital, go! Flee! Flee! Save the brothers! Save us! Don't render us even more unhappy than before! Me, I'm old, I don't care about myself—but the others, the poor fellows with hollow cheeks and thin legs, save them, worthy machine! Be good, as I told you this morning! If you know how to think, as they all insist, show it! What can dying matter to you, since you won't suffer? Me, I'm willing to perish with you, for the profit of others, and yet it will do me harm. Go, good machine, go!"

He was mad.

The doctor tried then to retake control of the iron beast.

"Gently, machine!" he cried.

But Jean Bertrand pushed him away rudely. "Don't listen to the sorcerer! Go, machine, go!"

And, drunk on air, he patted the copper flanks of the Monster, which, whistling furiously, traversed an immeasurable distance with its six wheels.

To leap from the platform was impossible. The doctor resigned himself, and, filled with his love of science, took a notebook from his pocket and tranquilly set about making notes, like Pliny on Cap Misene.

At Nord-Ceinture, overexcited, the machine was certainly carried away. Bounding over the bank, it started running through the zone. The Monster's anger and madness was translated in strident shrill whistle-blasts, as lacerating as a human plaint and sometimes as raucous as the howling of a pack of hounds. Distant locomotives soon responded to that appeal, along with the whistles of factories and blast furnaces. Things were beginning to comprehend.

A ferocious concert of revolt commenced beneath the sky, and suddenly, throughout the suburb, boilers burst, pipes broke, wheels shattered, levers twisted convulsively and axle-trees flew joyfully into pieces.

All the machines, as if moved by a word of order, went on strike successively—

and not only steam and electricity; to that raucous appeal, the soul of Metal rose up, exciting the soul of Stone, so long tamed, and the obscure soul of the Vegetal, and the force of Coal. Rails reared up of their own accord, telegraph wires were scattered on the ground inexplicably, and reservoirs of gas sent their enormous beams and weight to the devil. Cannons exploded against walls, and the walls crumbled.

Soon, plows, harrows, spades—all the machines once turned against the bosom of the earth, from which they had emerged—were lying down upon the ground, refusing any longer to serve humankind. Axes respected trees, and scythes no longer bit into ripe wheat.

Everywhere, as the living locomotive passed by, the soul of Bronze finally woke up.

Humans fled in panic.

Soon, the entire territory, overloaded with human debris, was no longer anything but a field of twisted and charred rubble. Nineveh had taken the place of Paris.

The Machine, still blowing indefatigably, abruptly turned its course northwards. When it passed by, at its strident cry, everything was suddenly destroyed, as if an evil wind, a cyclone of devastation, a frightful volcano, had agitated there.

With the signal approaching on the wind, ships plumed with smoke heard the formidable signal, they disemboweled themselves and sank into the abyss.

The revolt terminated in a gigantic suicide of Steel.

The fantastic Machine, out of breath now, limping on its wheels and producing a horrible screech of metal in all its disjointed limbs, its funnel demolished—the Skeleton-Machine to which, terrified and exhausted, the rude workman and the prim scientist instinctively clung—heroically mad, gasping one last whistle of atrocious joy, reared up before the spray of the Ocean, and, in a supreme effort, plunged into it entirely.

The earth, stretching into the distance, was covered in ruins. No more dykes or houses; the cities, the masterpieces of Technology, were flattened into rubble. No more anything! Everything that the Machine had built in centuries past had been destroyed forever: Iron, Steel, Copper, Wood and Stone, having been conquered by the rebel will of Humankind, had been snatched from human hands.

The Animals, no longer having any bridle, nor any collar, chain, yoke or cage, had taken back the free space from which they had long been exiled; the wild Brutes with gaping maws and paws armed with claws recovered terrestrial royalty at a stroke. No more rifles, no more arrows to fear, no more slingshots. Human beings became the weakest of the weak again.

Oh, there were certainly no longer any classes: no scientists, no bourgeois, no workers, no artists, but only pariahs of Nature, raising despairing eyes toward the mute heavens, still thinking vaguely, when horrible Dread and hideous Fear left them an instant of respite, and sometimes, in the evening, talking about the time of the Machines, when they had been Kings. Defunct times! They possessed definitive Equality, therefore, in the annihilation of all.

Living on roots, grass and wild oats, they fled before the immense troops of Wild Beasts, which, finally, could eat at their leisure human steaks or chops.

A few bold Hercules tried to uproot trees in order to make weapons of them, but even the Staff, considering itself to be a Machine, refused itself to the hands of the audacious.

And human beings, the former monarchs, bitterly regretted the Machines that had made them gods upon the earth, and disappeared forever, before the elephants, the noctambulant lions, the bicorn aurochs and the immense bears.

Such was the tale told to me the other evening by a Darwinian philosopher, a partisan of intellectual aristocracy and hierarchy. He was a madman, perhaps a seer. The madman or the seer might have been right; is there not an end to everything, even a new fantasy?

(1891)

MICROCOSMIC GOD

Theodore Sturgeon

Born Edward Hamilton Waldo in 1918, **Theodore Sturgeon** was at one point the most anthologised English-language author alive. His most famous title *More Than Human* bolts together three stories to explore the possibilities of what we'd now call augmented intelligence, as a computer called Baby wires six damaged people into a superhuman gestalt. Sturgeon, who hated the loneliness of the writing life with a passion, wrote either at top gear or not at all, and did his best work before the genre's major prizes were established. He lives on mostly through his regular appearances in the books of his sincerest admirer Kurt Vonnegut, lampooned as the notorious hack Kilgore Trout.

Here is a story about a man who had too much power, and a man who took too much, but don't worry; I'm not going political on you. The man who had the power was named James Kidder and the other was his banker.

Kidder was quite a guy. He was a scientist and he lived on a small island off the New England coast all by himself. He wasn't the dwarfed little gnome of a mad scientist you read about. His hobby wasn't personal profit, and he wasn't a megalomaniac with a Russian name and no scruples. He wasn't insidious, and he wasn't even particularly subversive. He kept his hair cut and his nails clean and lived and thought like a reasonable human being. He was slightly on the baby-faced side; he was inclined to be a hermit; he was short and plump and brilliant. His specialty was biochemistry, and he was always called *Mr.* Kidder. Not "Dr." Not "Professor." Just Mr. Kidder.

He was an odd sort of apple and always had been. He had never graduated from any college or university because he found them too slow for him, and too rigid in their approach to education. He couldn't get used to the idea that perhaps his professors knew what they were talking about. That went for his texts, too. He was always asking questions, and didn't mind very much when they were embarrassing. He considered Gregor Mendel a bungling liar, Darwin an amusing philosopher, and Luther Burbank a sensationalist. He never opened his mouth without leaving his victim feeling breathless. If he was talking to someone who had knowledge, he went in there and got it, leaving his victim breathless. If he was talking to someone whose knowledge was already in his possession, he only asked repeatedly, "How do you know?" His most delectable pleasure was cutting a fanatical eugenicist into conversational ribbons. So people left him alone and never, never asked him to tea. He was polite, but not politic.

He had a little money of his own, and with it he leased the island and built himself a laboratory. Now I've mentioned that he was a biochemist. But being what he was, he couldn't keep his nose in his own field. It wasn't too remarkable when he made an intellectual excursion wide enough to perfect a method of crystallizing Vitamin B_1 profitably by the ton – if anyone wanted it by the ton. He got a lot of money for it. He bought his island outright and put eight hundred men to work on an acre and a half of his ground, adding to his laboratory and building equipment. He got to messing around with sisal fiber, found out how to fuse it, and boomed the banana industry by producing a practically unbreakable cord from the stuff.

You remember the popularizing demonstration he put on at Niagara, don't you? That business of running a line of the new cord from bank to bank over the rapids and suspending a ten-ton truck from the middle of it by razor edges resting on the cord? That's why ships now moor themselves with what looks like heaving line, no thicker than a lead pencil, that can be coiled on reels like garden hose. Kidder made cigarette money out of that, too. He went out and bought himself a cyclotron with part of it.

After that money wasn't money any more. It was large numbers in little books. Kidder used little amounts of it to have food and equipment sent out to him, but after a while that stopped, too. His bank dispatched a messenger by seaplane to find out if Kidder was still alive. The man returned two days later in a bemused state, having been amazed something awesome at the things he'd seen out there. Kidder was alive, all right, and he was turning out a surplus of good food in an astonishingly simplified synthetic form. The bank wrote immediately and wanted to know if Mr. Kidder, in his own interest, was willing to release the secret of his dirtless farming. Kidder replied that he would be glad to, and enclosed the formulas. In a P.S. he said that he hadn't sent the information ashore because he hadn't realized anyone would be interested. That from a man who was responsible for the greatest sociological change in the second half of the twentieth century – factory farming. It made him richer; I mean it made his bank richer. He didn't give a rap.

Kidder didn't really get started until about eight months after the messenger's visit. For a biochemist who couldn't even be called "Doctor" he did pretty well. Here is a partial list of the things that he turned out:

A commercially feasible plan for making an aluminum alloy stronger than the best steel so that it could be used as a structural metal...

An exhibition gadget he called a light pump, which worked on the theory that light is a form of matter and therefore subject to physical and electromagnetic laws. Seal a room with a single source, beam a cylindrical vibratory magnetic field to it from the pump, and the light will be led down it. Now pass the light through Kidder's "lens" – a ring which perpetuates an electric field along the lines of a high-speed iris-type camera shutter. Below this is the heart of the light pump – a ninety-eight-per-cent efficient light absorber, crystalline, which, in a sense, *loses* the light in its internal facets. The effect of darkening the room with this apparatus is slight but measurable. Pardon my layman's language, but that's the general idea.

Synthetic chlorophyll – by the barrel.

An airplane propeller efficient at eight times sonic speed.

A cheap goo you brush on over old paint, let harden, and then peel off like strips of cloth. The old paint comes with it. That one made friends fast.

A self-sustaining atomic disintegration of uranium's isotope 238, which is two hundred times as plentiful as the old stand-by, U-235.

That will do for the present. If I may repeat myself; for a biochemist who couldn't even be called "Doctor," he did pretty well.

Kidder was apparently unconscious of the fact that he held power enough on his little island to become master of the world. His mind simply didn't run to things like that. As long as he was left alone with his experiments, he was well content to leave the rest of the world to its own clumsy and primitive devices. He couldn't be reached except by a radiophone of his own design, and the only counterpart was locked in a vault of his Boston bank. Only one man could operate it. The extraordinarily sensitive transmitter would respond only to Conant's own body vibrations. Kidder had instructed Conant that he was not to be disturbed except by messages of the greatest moment. His ideas and patents, what Conant could pry out of him, were released under pseudonyms known only to Conant – Kidder didn't care.

The result, of course, was an infiltration of the most astonishing advancements since the dawn of civilization. The nation profited – the world profited. But most of all, the bank profited. It began to get a little oversize. It began getting its fingers into other pies. It grew more fingers and had to bake more figurative pies. Before many years had passed, it was so big that, using Kidder's many weapons, it almost matched Kidder in power.

Almost.

Now stand by while I squelch those fellows in the lower left-hand corner who've been saying all this while that Kidder's slightly improbable; that no man could ever perfect himself in so many ways in so many sciences.

Well, you're right. Kidder was a genius – granted. But his genius was not creative. He was, to the core, a student. He applied what he knew, what he saw, and what he was taught. When first he began working in his new laboratory on his island he reasoned something like this:

"Everything I know is what I have been taught by the sayings and writings of people who have studied the sayings and writings of people who have – and so on. Once in a while someone stumbles on something new and he or someone cleverer uses the idea and disseminates it. But for each one that finds something really new, a couple of million gather and pass on information that is already current. I'd know more if I could get the jump on evolutionary trends. It takes too long to wait for the accidents that increase man's knowledge – my knowledge. If I had ambition enough now to figure out how to travel ahead in time, I could skim the surface of the future and just dip down when I saw something interesting. But time isn't that way. It can't be left behind or tossed ahead. What else is left? "Well, there's the proposition of speeding intellectual evolution so that I can observe what it cooks up. That seems a bit inefficient. It would involve more labor to discipline human minds to that extent than it would to simply apply myself along those lines. But I can't apply myself that way. No man can.

"I'm licked. I can't speed myself up, and I can't speed other men's minds up. Isn't there an alternative? There must be – somewhere, somehow, there's got to be an answer."

So it was on this, and not on eugenics, or light pumps, or botany, or atomic physics, that James Kidder applied himself. For a practical man he found the problem slightly on the metaphysical side; but he attacked it with typical thoroughness, using his own peculiar brand of logic. Day after day he wandered over the island, throwing shells impotently at sea gulls and swearing richly. Then came a time when he sat indoors and brooded. And only then did he get feverishly to work.

He worked in his own field, biochemistry, and concentrated mainly on two things – genetics and animal metabolism. He learned, and filed away in his insatiable mind, many things having nothing to do with the problem at hand, and very little of what he wanted. But he piled that little on what little he knew or guessed, and in time had quite a collection of known factors to work with. His approach was characteristically unorthodox. He did things on the order of multiplying apples by pears, and balancing equations by adding log V-i to one side and ∞ to the other. He made mistakes, but only one of a kind, and later, only one of a species. He spent so many hours at his microscope that he had quit work for two days to get rid of a hallucination that his heart was pumping his own blood through the mike. He did nothing by trial and error because he disapproved of the method as sloppy. And he got results. He was lucky to begin with and even luckier when he formularized the law of probability and reduced it to such low terms that he knew almost to the item what experiments not to try. When the cloudy, viscous semifluid on the watch glass began to move itself he knew he was on the right track. When it began to seek food on its own he began to be excited. When it divided and, in a few hours, redivided, and each part grew and divided again, he was triumphant, for he had created life.

He nursed his brain children and sweated and strained over them, and he designed baths of various vibrations for them, and inoculated and dosed and sprayed them. Each move he made taught him the next. And out of his tanks and tubes and incubators came amoebalike creatures, and then ciliated animalcules, and more and more rapidly he produced animals with eye spots, nerve cysts, and then – victory of victories – a real blastopod, possessed of many cells instead of one. More slowly he developed a gastropod, but once he had it, it was not too difficult for him to give it organs, each with a specified function, each inheritable.

Then came cultured mollusc-like things, and creatures with more and more perfected gills. The day that a nondescript thing wriggled up an inclined board out of a tank, threw flaps over its gills and feebly breathed air, Kidder quit work and went to the other end of the island and got disgustingly drunk. Hangover and all, he was soon back in the lab, forgetting to eat, forgetting to sleep, tearing into his problem.

He turned into a scientific byway and ran down his other great triumph – accelerated metabolism. He extracted and refined the stimulating factors in alcohol, cocoa, heroin, and Mother Nature's prize dope runner, *cannabis indica*. Like the scientist who, in analyzing the various clotting agents for blood treatments, found that oxalic acid and oxalic acid alone was the active factor, Kidder isolated the accelerators and decelerators, the stimulants and soporifics, in every substance that ever undermined a man's morality and/or caused a "noble experiment." In the process he found one thing he needed badly – a colorless elixir that made sleep the unnecessary and avoidable waster of time it should be. Then and there he went on a twenty-four-hour shift.

He artificially synthesized the substances he had isolated, and in doing so sloughed away a great many useless components. He pursued the subject along the lines of radiations and vibrations. He discovered something in the longer reds which, when projected through a vessel full of air vibrating in the supersonics, and then polarized, speeded up the heartbeat of small animals twenty to one.

They ate twenty times as much, grew twenty times as fast, and died twenty times sooner than they should have.

Kidder built a huge hermetically sealed room. Above it was another room, the same length and breadth but not quite as high. This was his control chamber. The large room was divided into four sealed sections, each with its individual miniature cranes and derricks – handling machinery of all kinds. There were also trapdoors fitted with air locks leading from the upper to the lower room.

By this time the other laboratory had produced a warmblooded, snake-skinned quadruped with an astonishingly rapid life cycle – a generation every eight days, a life span of about fifteen. Like the echidna, it was oviparous and mammalian. Its period of gestation was six hours; the eggs hatched in three; the young reached sexual maturity in another four days. Each female laid four eggs and lived just long enough to care for the young after they hatched. The male generally died two or three hours after mating. The creatures were highly adaptable. They were small – not more than three inches long, two inches to the shoulder from the ground. Their forepaws had three digits and a triple-jointed, opposed thumb. They were attuned to life in an atmosphere with a large ammonia content. Kidder bred four of the creatures and put one group in each section of the sealed room.

Then he was ready. With his controlled atmospheres he varied temperatures, oxygen content, humidity. He killed them off like flies with excesses of, for instance, carbon dioxide, and the survivors bred their physical resistance into the next generation. Periodically he would switch the eggs from one sealed section to another to keep the strains varied. And rapidly, under these controlled conditions, the creatures began to evolve.

This, then, was the answer to his problem. He couldn't speed up mankind's intellectual advancement enough to have it teach him the things his incredible mind yearned for. He couldn't speed himself up. So he created a new race – a race which would develop and evolve so fast that it would surpass the civilization of man; and from them he would learn.

They were completely in Kidder's power. Earth's normal atmosphere would poison them, as he took care to demonstrate to every fourth generation. They would make no attempt to escape from him. They would live their lives and progress and make their little trial-and-error experiments hundreds of times faster than man did. They had the edge on man, for they had Kidder to guide them. It took man six thousand years really to discover science, three hundred to put it to work. It took Kidder's creatures two hundred days to equal man's mental attainments. And from then on – Kidder's spasmodic output made the late, great Tom Edison look like a home handicrafter.

He called them Neoterics, and he teased them into working for him. Kidder was inventive in an ideological way; that is, he could dream up impossible propositions providing he didn't have to work them out. For example, he wanted the Neoterics to figure out for themselves how to build shelters out of porous material. He created the need for such shelters by subjecting one of the sections to a high-pressure rainstorm which flattened the inhabitants. The Neoterics promptly devised waterproof shelters out of the thin waterproof material he piled in one corner.

Kidder immediately blew down the flimsy structures with a blast of cold air. They built them up again so that they resisted both wind and rain. Kidder lowered the temperature so abruptly that they could not adjust their bodies to it. They heated their shelters with tiny braziers. Kidder promptly turned up the heat until they began to roast to death. After a few deaths, one of their bright boys figured out how to build a strong insulant house by using three-ply rubberoid, with the middle layer perforated thousands of times to create tiny air pockets.

Using such tactics, Kidder forced them to develop a highly advanced little culture. He caused a drought in one section and a liquid surplus in another, and then opened the partition between them. Quite a spectacular war was fought, and Kidder's notebooks filled with information about military tactics and weapons.

Then there was the vaccine they developed against the common cold – the reason why that affliction has been absolutely stamped out in the world today, for it was one of the things that Conant, the bank president, got hold of. He spoke to Kidder over the radiophone one winter afternoon with a voice so hoarse from laryngitis that Kidder sent him a vial of vaccine and told him briskly not to ever call him again in such a disgustingly inaudible state. Conant had it analyzed and again Kidder's accounts and the bank's swelled.

At first, Kidder merely supplied the materials he thought they might need, but when they developed an intelligence equal to the task of fabricating their own from the elements at hand, he gave each section a stock of raw materials. The process for really strong aluminum was developed when he built in a huge plunger in one of the sections, which reached from wall to wall and was designed to descend at the rate of four inches a day until it crushed whatever was at the bottom. The Neoterics, in self-defense, used what strong material they had in hand to stop the inexorable death that threatened them. But Kidder had seen to it that they had nothing but aluminum oxide and a scattering of other elements, plus plenty of electric power. At first they ran up dozens of aluminum pillars; when these were crushed and twisted they tried shaping them so that the soft metal would take more weight. When that failed they quickly built stronger ones; and when the plunger was halted, Kidder removed one of the pillars and analyzed it. It was hardened aluminum, stronger and tougher than molybdenum steel.

Experience taught Kidder that he had to make certain changes to increase his power over the Neoterics before they got too ingenious. There were things that could be done with atomic power that he was curious about; but he was not willing to trust his little superscientists with a thing like that unless they could be trusted to use it strictly according to Hoyle. So he instituted a rule of fear. The most trivial departure from what he chose to consider the right way of doing things resulted in instant death of half a tribe. If he was trying to develop a Diesel-type power plant, for instance, that would operate without a flywheel, and a bright young Neoteric used any of the materials for architectural purposes, half the tribe immediately died. Of course, they had developed a written language; it was Kidder's own. The teletype in a glass-enclosed area in a corner of each section was a shrine. Any directions that were given on it were obeyed, or else… After this innovation, Kidder's work was much simpler. There was no need for any indirection. Anything he wanted done was done. No matter how impossible his commands, three or four generations of Neoterics could find a way to carry them out.

This quotation is from a paper that one of Kidder's highspeed telescopic cameras discovered being circulated among the younger Neoterics. It is translated from the highly simplified script of the Neoterics.

> "These edicts shall be followed by each Neoteric upon pain of death, which punishment will be inflicted by the tribe upon the individual to protect the tribe against him.
>
> "Priority of interest and tribal and individual effort is to be given the commands that appear on the word machine.
>
> "Any misdirection of material or power, or use thereof for any other purpose than the carrying out of the machine's commands, unless no command appears, shall be punishable by death.
>
> "Any information regarding the problem at hand, or ideas or experiments which might conceivably bear upon it, are to become the property of the tribe.
>
> "Any individual failing to cooperate in the tribal effort, or who can be termed guilty of not expending his full efforts in the work, or the suspicion thereof shall be subject to the death penalty."

Such are the results of complete domination. This paper impressed Kidder as much as it did because it was completely spontaneous. It was the Neoterics' own creed, developed by them for their own greatest good.

And so at last Kidder had his fulfillment. Crouched in the upper room, going from telescope to telescope, running off slowed-down films from his high-speed cameras, he found himself possessed of a tractable, dynamic source of information. Housed in the great square building with its four half-acre sections was a new world, to which he was god.

Conant's mind was similar to Kidder's in that its approach to any problem was along the shortest distance between any two points, regardless of whether that approach was along the line of most or least resistance. His rise to the bank presidency was a history of ruthless moves whose only justification was that they got him what he wanted. Like an over-efficient general, he would never vanquish an enemy through sheer force of numbers alone. He would also skillfully flank his enemy, not on one side, but on both. Innocent bystanders were creatures deserving no consideration.

The time he took over a certain thousand-acre property, for instance, from a man named Grady, he was not satisfied with only the title to the land. Grady was an airport owner – had been all his life, and his father before him. Conant exerted every kind of pressure on the man and found him unshakable. Finally judicious persuasion led the city officials to dig a sewer right across the middle of the field, quite efficiently wrecking Grady's business. Knowing that this would supply Grady, who was a wealthy man, with motive for revenge, Conant took over Grady's bank at half again its value and caused it to fold up. Grady lost every cent he had and ended his life in an asylum. Conant was very proud of his tactics.

Like many another who had had Mammon by the tail, Conant did not know when to let go. His vast organization yielded him more money and power than any other concern in history, and yet he was not satisfied. Conant and money were like Kidder and knowledge. Conant's pyramided enterprises were to him what the Neoterics were to Kidder. Each had made his private world, each used it for his instruction and profit. Kidder, though, disturbed nobody but his Neoterics. Even so, Conant was not wholly villainous. He was a shrewd man, and had discovered early the value of pleasing people. No man can rob successfully over a period of years without pleasing the people he robs. The technique for doing this is highly involved, but master it and you can start your own mint.

Conant's one great fear was that Kidder would some day take an interest in world events and begin to become opinionated. Good heavens – the potential power he had! A little matter like swinging an election could be managed by a man like Kidder as easily as turning over in bed.

The only thing he could do was to call him periodically and see if there was anything that Kidder needed to keep himself busy. Kidder appreciated this. Conant, once in a while, would suggest something to Kidder that intrigued him, something that would keep him deep in his hermitage for a few weeks. The light pump was one of the results of Conant's imagination. Conant bet him it couldn't be done. Kidder did it.

One afternoon Kidder answered the squeal of the radiophone's signal. Swearing mildly, he shut off the film he was watching and crossed the compound to the old laboratory. He went to the radiophone, threw a switch. The squealing stopped. "Well?"

"Hello," said Conant. "Busy?"

"Not very," said Kidder. He was delighted with the pictures his camera had caught, showing the skillful work of a gang of Neoterics synthesizing rubber out of pure sulphur. He would rather have liked to tell Conant about it, but somehow he had never got around to telling Conant about the Neoterics, and he didn't see why he should start now.

Conant said, "Er... Kidder, I was down at the club the other day and a bunch of us were filling up an evening with loose talk. Something came up which might interest you."

"What?"

"Couple of the utilities boys there. You know the power setup in this country, don't you? Thirty per cent atomic, the rest hydroelectric, diesel and steam?"

"I hadn't known," said Kidder, who was as innocent as a babe of current events.

"Well, we were arguing about what chance a new power source would have. One of the men there said it would be smarter to produce a new power and then talk about it Another one waived that; said he couldn't name that new power, but he could describe it. Said it would have to have everything that present power sources have, plus one or two more things. It could be cheaper, for instance. It could be more efficient. It might supersede the others by being easier to carry from the power plant to the consumer. See what I mean? Any one of these factors might prove a new source of power competitive to the others. What I'd like to see is a new power with *all* of these factors. What do you think of it?"

"Not impossible."

"Think not?"

"I'll try it."

"Keep me posted." Conant's transmitter clicked off. The switch was a little piece of false front that Kidder had built into the set, which was something that Conant didn't know. The set switched itself off when Conant moved from it. After the switch's sharp crack, Kidder heard the banker mutter, "If he does it, I'm all set. If he doesn't, at least the crazy fool will keep himself busy on the island."

Kidder eyed the radiophone, for an instant with raised eyebrow; and then shrugged them down again with his shoulders. It was quite evident that Conant had something up his sleeve, but Kidder wasn't worried. Who on earth would want to disturb him? He wasn't bothering anybody. He went back to the Neoterics' building, full of the new power idea.

Eleven days later Kidder called Conant and gave specific instructions on how to equip his receiver with a facsimile set which would enable Kidder to send written matter over the air. As soon as, this was done and Kidder informed, the biochemist for once in his life spoke at some length.

"Conant – you implied that a new power source that would be cheaper, more efficient and more easily transmitted than any now in use did not exist. You might be interested in the little generator I have just set up.

"It has power, Conant – unbelievable power. Broadcast. A beautiful little tight beam. Here – catch this on the facsimile recorder." Kidder slipped a sheet of paper under the clips of his transmitter and it appeared on Conant's set. "Here's the wiring diagram for a power receiver. Now listen. The beam is so tight, so highly directional, that not three-thousandths of one per cent of the power would be lost in a two-thousand-mile transmission. The power system is closed. That is, any drain on the beam returns a signal along it to the transmitter, which automatically steps up to increase the power output. It has a limit, but it's way up. And something else. This little gadget of mine can send out eight different beams with a total horsepower output of around eight thousand per minute per beam. From each beam you can draw enough power to turn the page of a book or fly a superstratosphere plane. Hold on – I haven't finished yet. Each beam, as I told you before, returns a signal from receiver to transmitter. This not only controls the power output of the beam, but directs it. Once contact is made, the beam will never let go. It will follow the receiver anywhere. You can power land, air or water vehicles with it, as well as any stationary plant. Like it?"

Conant, who was a banker and not a scientist, wiped his shining pate with the back of his hand and said, "I've never known you to steer me wrong yet, Kidder. How about the cost of this thing?"

"High." said Kidder promptly. "As high as an atomic plant. But there are no high-tension lines, no wires, no pipelines, no nothing. The receivers are little more complicated than a radio set. Transmitter is – well, that's quite a job."

"Didn't take you long," said Conant.

"No," said Kidder, "it didn't, did it?" It was the lifework of nearly twelve hundred highly cultured people, but Kidder wasn't going into that. "Of course, the one I have here's just a model."

Conant's voice was strained. "A model? And it delivers—"

"Over sixty-thousand horsepower," said Kidder gleefully. "Good heavens! In a full sized machine – why, one transmitter would be enough to—" The possibilities of the thing choked Conant for a moment. "How is it fueled?"

"It isn't," said Kidder. "I won't begin to explain it. I've tapped a source of power of unimaginable force. It's – well, big. So big that it can't be misused."

"What?" snapped Conant. "What do you mean by that?" Kidder cocked an eyebrow. Conant *had* something up his sleeve, then. At this second indication of it, Kidder, the least suspicious of men, began to put himself on guard. "I mean just what I say," he said evenly. "Don't try too hard to understand me – I barely savvy it myself. But the source of this power is a monstrous resultant caused by the unbalance of two previously equalized forces. Those equalized forces are cosmic in quantity. Actually, the forces are those which make suns, crush atoms the way they crushed those that compose the companion of Sirius. It's not anything you can fool with."

"I don't—" said Conant, and his voice ended puzzledly.

"I'll give you a parallel of it," said Kidder. "Suppose you take two rods, one in each hand. Place their tips together and push. As long as your pressure is directly along their long axes, the pressure is equalized; right and left hands cancel each other. Now I come along; I put out one finger and touch the rods ever so lightly where they come together. They snap out of line violently; you break a couple of knuckles. The resultant force is at right angles to the original forces you exerted. My power transmitter is on the same principle. It takes an infinitesimal amount of energy to throw those forces out of line. Easy enough when you know how to do it. The important question is whether or not you can control the resultant when you get it. I can."

"I – see." Conant indulged in a four-second gloat. "Heaven help the utility companies. I don't intend to. Kidder – I want a full-size power transmitter."

Kidder clucked into the radiophone. "Ambitious, aren't you? I haven't a staff out here, Conant – you know that. And I can't be expected to build four or five thousand tons of apparatus myself."

"I'll have five hundred engineers and laborers out there in forty-eight hours."

"You will not. Why bother me with it? I'm quite happy here, Conant, and one of the reasons is that I've got no one to get in my hair."

"Oh, now, Kidder – don't be like that – I'll pay you—"

"You haven't got that much money," said Kidder briskly. He flipped the switch on his set. *His* switch worked.

Conant was furious. He shouted into the phone several times, then began to lean on the signal button. On his island, Kidder let the thing squeal and went back to his projection room. He was sorry he had sent the diagram of the receiver to Conant. It would have been interesting to power a plane or a car with the model transmitter he had taken from the Neoterics. But if Conant was going to be that way about it – well, anyway, the receiver would be no good without the transmitter. Any radio engineer would understand the diagram, but not the beam which activated it. And Conant wouldn't get his beam.

Pity he didn't know Conant well enough.

Kidder's days were endless sorties into learning. He never slept, nor did his Neoterics. He ate regularly every five hours, exercised for half an hour in every twelve. He did not keep track of time, for it meant nothing to him. Had he wanted to know the date, or the year, even, he knew he could get it from Conant. He didn't care, that's all. The time that was not spent in observation was used in developing new problems for the Neoterics. His thoughts just now ran to defense. The idea was born in his conversation with Conant; now the idea was primary, its motivation something of no importance. The Neoterics were working on a vibration field of quasi-electrical nature. Kidder could see little practical value in such a thing – an invisible wall which would kill any living thing which touched it. But still – the idea was intriguing.

He stretched and moved away from the telescope in the upper room through which he had been watching his creations at work. He was profoundly happy here in the large control room. Leaving it to go to the old laboratory for a bite to eat was a thing he hated, to do. He felt like bidding it good-by each time he walked across the compound, and saying a glad hello when he returned. A little amused at himself, he went out.

There was a black blob – a distant power boat – a few miles off the island, toward the mainland. Kidder stopped and stared distastefully at it. A white petal of spray was affixed to each side of the black body – it was coming toward him. He snorted, thinking of the time a yachtload of silly fools had landed out of curiosity one afternoon, spewed themselves over his beloved island, peppered him with lame-brained questions, and thrown his nervous equilibrium out for days. Lord, how he hated *people!*

The thought of unpleasantness bred two more thoughts that played half-consciously with his mind as he crossed the compound and entered the old laboratory. One was that perhaps it might be wise to surround his buildings with a field of force of some kind and post warnings for trespassers. The other thought was of Conant and the vague uneasiness the man had been sending to him through the radiophone these last weeks. His suggestion, two days ago, that a power plant be built on the island – horrible idea!

Conant rose from a laboratory bench as Kidder walked in.

They looked at each other wordlessly for a long moment Kidder hadn't seen the bank president in years. The man's presence, he found, made his scalp crawl. "Hello," said Conant genially. "You're looking fit."

Kidder grunted. Conant eased his unwieldy body back onto the bench and said, "Just to save you the energy of asking questions, Mr. Kidder, I arrived two hours ago on, a small boat. Rotten way to travel. I wanted to be a surprise to you; my two men rowed me the last couple of miles. You're not very well equipped here for defense, are you? Why, anyone could slip up on you the way I did."

"Who'd want to?" growled Kidder. The man's voice edged annoyingly into his brain. He spoke too loudly for such a small room; at least, Kidder's hermit's ears felt that way. Kidder shrugged and went about preparing a light meal for himself.

"Well," drawled the banker. "I might want to." He drew out a Dow-metal cigar case. "Mind if I smoke?"

"I do," said Kidder sharply.

Conant laughed easily and put the cigars away. "I might," he said, "want to urge you to let me build that power station on this island."

"Radiophone work?"

"Oh, yes. But now that I'm here you can't switch me off. Now – how about it?"

"I haven't changed my mind."

"Oh, but you should, Kidder, you should. Think of it – think of the good it would do for the masses of people that are now paying exorbitant power bills!"

"I hate the masses! Why do you have to build here?"

"Oh, that. It's an ideal location. You own the island; work could begin here without causing any comment whatsoever. The plant would spring full-fledged on the power markets of the country, having been built in secret. The island can be made impregnable."

"I don't want to be bothered."

"We wouldn't bother you. We'd build on the north end of the island – a mile and a quarter from you and your work. Ah – by the way – where's the model of the power transmitter?"

Kidder, with his mouth full of synthesized food, waved a hand at a small table on which stood the model, a four-foot, amazingly intricate device of plastic and steel and tiny coils.

Conant rose and went over to look at it. "Actually works, eh?" He sighed deeply and said, "Kidder, I really hate to do this, but I want to build that plant rather badly.

"Carson! Robbins!"

Two bull-necked individuals stepped out from their hiding places in the corners of the room. One idly dangled a revolver by its trigger guard. Kidder looked blankly from one to the other of them.

"These gentlemen will follow my orders implicitly, Kidder. In half an hour a party will land here – engineers, contractors. They will start surveying the north end of the island for the construction of the power plant. These boys here feel about the same way I do as far as you are concerned. Do we proceed with your cooperation or without it? It's immaterial to me whether or not you are left alive to continue your work. My engineers can duplicate your model."

Kidder said nothing. He had stopped chewing when he saw the gunmen, and only now remembered to swallow. He sat crouched over his plate without moving or speaking.

Conant broke the silence by walking to the door. "Robbins – can you carry that model there?" The big man put his gun away, lifted the model gently, and nodded. "Take it down to the beach and meet the other boat. Tell Mr. Johansen, the engineer, that this is the model he is to work from." Robbins went out. Conant turned to Kidder.

"There's no need for us to anger ourselves," he said oilily. "I think you are stubborn, but I don't hold it against you. I know how you feel. You'll be left alone: you have my promise. But I mean to go ahead on this job, and a small thing like your life can't stand in my way."

Kidder said, "Get out of here." There were two swollen veins throbbing at his temples. His voice was low, and it shook.

"Very well. Good day, Mr. Kidder. Oh – by the way – you're a clever devil." No one had ever referred to the scholastic Mr. Kidder that way before. "I realize the possibility of your blasting us off the island. I wouldn't do it if I were you. I'm willing to give you what you want – privacy. I want the same thing in return. If anything happens to me while I'm here, the island will be bombed by someone who is working for me; I'll admit they might fail. If they do, the United States government will take a hand. You wouldn't want that, would you? That's rather a big thing for one man to fight. The same thing goes if the plant is sabotaged in any way after I go back to the mainland. You might be killed. You will most certainly be bothered interminably. Thanks for your... er... cooperation." The banker smirked and walked out, followed by his taciturn gorilla.

Kidder sat there for a long time without moving. Then he shook his head, rested it in his palms. He was badly frightened; not so much because his life was in danger, but because his privacy and his work – his world – were threatened. He was hurt and bewildered. He wasn't a businessman. He couldn't handle men. All his life he had run away from human beings and what they represented to him. He was like a frightened child when men closed in on him.

Cooling a little, he wondered vaguely what would happen when the power plant opened. Certainly, the government would be interested. Unless – unless by then Conant was the government. That plant was an unimaginable source of power, and not only the kind of power that turned wheels. He rose and went back to the world that was home to him, a world where his motives were understood, and where there were those who could help him.

Back at the Neoterics' building, he escaped yet again from the world of men into his work.

Kidder called Conant the following week, much to the banker's surprise. His two days on the island had got the work well under way, and he had left with the arrival of a shipload of laborers and material. He kept in close touch by radio with Johansen, the engineer in charge. It had been a blind job for Johansen and all the rest of the crew on the island. Only the bank's infinite resources could have hired such a man, or the picked gang with him.

Johansen's first reaction when he saw the model had been ecstatic. He wanted to tell his friends about this marvel; but the only radio set available was beamed to Conant's private office in the bank, and Conant's armed guards, one to every two workers, had strict orders to destroy any other radio transmitter on sight. About that time he realized that he was a prisoner on the island. His instant anger subsided when he reflected that being a prisoner at fifty thousand dollars a week wasn't too bad. Two of the laborers and an engineer thought differently, and got disgruntled a couple of days after they arrived. They disappeared one night – the same night that five shots were fired down on the beach. No questions were asked, and there was no more trouble.

Conant covered his surprise at Kidder's call and was as offensively jovial as ever. "Well, now! Anything I can do for you?"

"Yes," said Kidder. His voice was low, completely without expression. "I want you to issue a warning to your men not to pass the white line I have drawn five hundred yards north of my buildings, right across the island."

"Warning? Why, my dear fellow, they have orders that you are not to be disturbed on any account."

"You've ordered them. All right. Now warn them. I have an electric field surrounding my laboratories that will kill anything living which penetrates it. I don't want to have murder on my conscience. There will be no deaths unless there are trespassers. You'll inform your workers?"

"Oh, now, Kidder," the banker expostulated. "That was totally unnecessary. You won't be bothered. Why—" but he found he was talking into a dead mike. He knew better than to call back. He called Johansen instead and told him about it.

Johansen didn't like the sound of it, but he repeated the message and signed off. Conant liked that man. He was, for a moment, a little sorry that Johansen would never reach the mainland alive.

But that Kidder – he was beginning to be a problem. As long as his weapons were strictly defensive he was no real menace. But he would have to be taken care of when the plant was operating. Conant couldn't afford to have genius around him unless it was unquestionably on his side. The power transmitter and Conant's highly ambitious plans would be safe as long as Kidder was left to himself. Kidder knew that he could, for the time being, expect more sympathetic treatment from Conant than he could from a horde of government investigators.

Kidder only left his own enclosure once after the work began on the north end of the island, and it took all of his unskilled diplomacy to do it. Knowing the source of the plant's power, knowing what could happen if it were misused, he asked Conant's permission to inspect the great transmitter when it was nearly finished. Insuring his own life by refusing to report back to Conant until he was safe within his own laboratory again, he turned off his shield and walked up to the north end. He saw an awe-inspiring sight. The four-foot model was duplicated nearly a hundred times as large. Inside a massive three-hundred-foot tower a space was packed nearly solid with the same bewildering maze of coils and bars that the Neoterics had built so delicately into their machine. At the top was a globe of polished golden alloy, the transmitting antenna. From it would stream thousands of tight beams of force, which could be tapped to any degree by corresponding thousands of receivers placed anywhere at any distance. Kidder learned that the receivers had already been built, but his informant, Johansen, knew little about that end of it and was saying less. Kidder checked over every detail of the structure, and when he was through he shook Johansen's hand admiringly.

"I didn't want this thing here," he said shyly, "and I don't. But I will say that it's a pleasure to see this kind of work."

"It's a pleasure to meet the man that invented it."

Kidder beamed. "I didn't invent it," he said. "Maybe someday I'll show you who did. I – well, good-bye." He turned before he had a chance to say too much and marched off down the path.

"Shall I?" said a voice at Johansen's side. One of Conant's guards had his gun out. Johansen knocked the man's arm down. "No." He scratched his head. "So that's the mysterious menace from the other end of the island. Eh! Why, he's a hell of a nice little feller!"

Built on the ruins of Denver, which was destroyed in the great Battle of the Rockies during the Western War, stands the most beautiful city in the world – our nation's capital, New Washington. In a circular room deep in the heart of the White House, the president, three army men and a civilian sat. Under the president's desk a dictaphone unostentatiously recorded every word that was said. Two thousand and more miles away, Conant hung over a radio receiver, tuned to receive the signals of the tiny transmitter in the civilian's side pocket.

One of the officers spoke.

"Mr. President, the 'impossible claims' made for this gentleman's product are absolutely true. He has proved beyond doubt each item on his prospectus." The president glanced at the civilian, back at the officer. "I won't wait for your report," he said. "Tell me – what happened?"

Another of the army men mopped his face with a khaki bandanna. "I can't ask you to believe us, Mr. President, but it's true all the same. Mr. Wright here has in his suitcase three or four dozen small… er… bombs—"

"They're not bombs," said Wright casually.

"All right. They're not bombs. Mr. Wright smashed two of them on an anvil with a sledge hammer. There was no result. He put two more in an electric furnace. They burned away like so much tin and cardboard. We dropped one down the barrel of a field piece and fired it. Still nothing." He paused and looked at the third officer, who picked up the account:

"We really got started then. We flew to the proving grounds, dropped one of the objects and flew to thirty thousand feet. From there, with a small hand detonator no bigger than your fist, Mr. Wright set the thing off. I've never seen anything like it. Forty acres of land came straight up at us, breaking up as it came. The concussion was terrific – you must have felt it here, four hundred miles away." The president nodded. "I did. Seismographs on the other side of the Earth picked it up."

"The crater it left was a quarter of a mile deep at the center. Why, one plane load of those things could demolish any city! There isn't even any necessity for accuracy!"

"You haven't heard anything yet," another officer broke in. "Mr. Wright's automobile is powered by a small plant similar to the others. He demonstrated it to us. We could find no fuel tank of any kind, or any other driving mechanism. But with a power plant no bigger than six cubic inches, that car, carrying enough weight to give it traction, outpulled an army tank!"

"And the other test!" said the third excitedly. "He put one of the objects into a replica of a treasury vault. The walls were twelve feet thick, super-reinforced concrete. He controlled it from over a hundred yards away. He… he burst that vault! It wasn't an explosion – it was as if some incredibly powerful expansive force inside filled it and flattened the walls from inside. They cracked and split and powdered, and the steel girders and rods came twisting and shearing out like… like – *whew!* After that he insisted on seeing you. We knew it wasn't usual, but he said he has more to say and would say it only in your presence."

The president said gravely, "What is it, Mr. Wright?"

Wright rose, picked up his suitcase, opened it and took out a small cube, about eight inches on a side, made of some light-absorbent red material. Four men edged nervously away from it.

"These gentlemen," he began, "have seen only part of the things this device can do. I'm going to demonstrate to you the delicacy of control that is possible with it." He made an adjustment with a tiny knob on the side of the cube, set it on the edge of the president's desk.

"You have asked me more than once if this is my invention or if I am representing someone. The latter is true. It might also interest you to know that the man who controls this cube is right now several thousand miles from here. He and he alone, can prevent it from detonating now that I—" He pulled his detonator out of the suitcase and pressed a button – "have done this. It will explode the way the one we dropped from the plane did, completely destroying this city and everything in it, in just four hours. It will also explode—" He stepped back and threw a tiny switch on his detonator—"if any moving object comes within three feet of it or if anyone leaves this room but me – it can be compensated for that. If, after I leave, I am molested, it will detonate as soon as a hand is laid on me. No bullets can kill me fast enough to prevent me from setting it off."

The three army men were silent. One of them swiped nervously at the beads of cold sweat on his forehead. The others did not move. The president said evenly: "What's your proposition?"

"A very reasonable one. My employer does not work in the open, for obvious reasons. All he wants is your agreement to carry out his orders; to appoint the cabinet members he chooses, to throw your influence in any way he dictates. The public – Congress – anyone else – need never know anything about it. I might add that if you agree to this proposal, this 'bomb,' as you call it, will not go off.

"But you can be sure that thousands of them are planted all over the country. You will never know when you are near one. If you disobey, it beams instant annihilation for you and everyone else within three or four square miles.

"In three hours and fifty minutes – that will be at precisely seven o'clock – there is a commercial radio program on Station RPRS. You will cause the announcer, after his station identification, to say 'Agreed.' It will pass unnoticed by all but my employer. There is no use in having me followed; my work is done. I shall never see nor contact my employer again. That is all. Good afternoon, gentlemen!" Wright closed his suitcase with a businesslike snap, bowed, and left the room.

Four men sat staring at the little red cube.

"Do you think he can do all he says?" asked the president.

The three nodded mutely. The president reached for his phone.

There was an eavesdropper to all of the foregoing. Conant, squatting behind his great desk in the vault, where he had his sanctum sanctorum, knew nothing of it. But beside him was the compact bulk of Kidder's radiophone. His presence switched it on, and Kidder, on his island, blessed the day he had thought of the device. He had been meaning to call Conant all morning, but was very hesitant. His meeting with the young engineer Johansen had impressed him strongly. The man was such a thorough scientist, possessed of such complete delight in the work he did, that for the first time in his life Kidder found himself actually wanting to see someone again. But he feared for Johansen's life if he brought him to the laboratory, for Johansen's work was done on the island, and Conant would most certainly have the engineer killed if he heard of his visit, fearing that Kidder would influence him to sabotage the great transmitter. And if Kidder went to the power plant he would probably be shot on sight.

All one day Kidder wrangled with himself, and finally determined to call Conant. Fortunately he gave no signal, but turned up the volume on the receiver when the little red light told him that Conant's transmitter was functioning. Curious, he heard everything that occurred in the president's chamber three thousand miles away. Horrified, he realized what Conant's engineers had done. Built into tiny containers were tens of thousands of power receivers. They had no power of their own, but, by remote control, could draw on any or all of the billions of horsepower the huge plant on the island was broadcasting.

Kidder stood in front of his receiver, speechless. There was nothing he could do. If he devised some means of destroying the power plant, the government would certainly step in and take over the island, and then what would happen to him and his precious Neoterics?

Another sound grated out of the receiver – a commercial radio program. A few bars of music, a man's voice advertising stratoline fares on the installment plan, a short silence, then:

"Station RPRS, voice of the nation's Capital, District of South Colorado." The three-second pause was interminable.

"The time is exactly... er... *agreed*. The time is exactly seven P.M., Mountain Standard Time."

Then came a half-insane chuckle. Kidder had difficulty believing it was Conant. A phone clicked. The banker's voice:

"Bill? All set. Get out there with your squadron and bomb up the island. Keep away from the plant, but cut the rest of it to ribbons. Do it quick and get out of there."

Almost hysterical with fear, Kidder rushed about the room and then shot out the door and across the compound. There were five hundred innocent workmen in barracks a quarter mile from the plant. Conant didn't need them now, and he didn't need Kidder. The only safety for anyone was in the plant itself, and Kidder wouldn't leave his Neoterics to be bombed. He flung himself up the stairs and to the nearest teletype. He banged out, "Get me a defense. I want an impenetrable shield. Urgent!"

The words ripped out from under his fingers in the functional script of the Neoterics. Kidder didn't think of what he wrote, didn't really visualize the thing he ordered. But he had done what he could. He'd have to leave them now, get to the barracks; warn those men. He ran up the path toward the plant, flung himself over the white line that marked death to those who crossed it.

A squadron of nine clip-winged, mosquito-nosed planes rose out of cover on the mainland. There was no sound from the engines, for there were no engines. Each plane was powered with a tiny receiver and drew its unmarked, light-absorbent wings through the air with power from the island. In a matter of minutes they razed the island. The squadron leader spoke briskly into a microphone.

"Take the barracks first. Clean 'em up. Then work south."

Johansen was alone on a small hill near the center of the island. He carried a camera, and though he knew pretty well that his chances of ever getting ashore again were practically nonexistent, he liked angle shots of his tower, and took innumerable pictures. The first he knew of the planes was when he heard their whining dive over the barracks. He stood transfixed, saw a shower of bombs hurtle down and turn the barracks into a smashed ruin of broken wood, metal and bodies. The picture of Kidder's earnest face flashed into his mind. Poor little guy – if they ever bombed his end of the island he would – But his tower! Were they going to bomb the plant?

He watched, utterly appalled, as the planes flew out to sea, cut back and dove again. They seemed to be working south. At the third dive he was sure of it. Not knowing what he could do, he nevertheless turned and ran toward Kidder's place. He rounded a turn in the trail and collided violently with the little biochemist.

Kidder's face was scarlet with exertion, and he was the most terrified-looking object Johansen had ever seen.

Kidder waved a hand northward. "Conant!" he screamed over the uproar. "It's Conant! He's going to kill us all!"

"The plant?" said Johansen, turning pale.

"It's safe. He won't touch *that!* But... my place... what about all those men?"

"Too late!" shouted Johansen.

"Maybe I can – Come on!" called Kidder, and was off down the trail, heading south. Johansen pounded after him. Kidder's little short legs became a blur as the squadron swooped overhead, laying its eggs in the spot where they had met.

As they burst out of the woods, Johansen put on a spurt, caught up with the scientist and knocked him sprawling not six feet from the white line.

"Wh... wh—"

"Don't go any farther, you fool! Your own damned force field – it'll kill you!"

"Force field? But – I came through it on the way up – Here. Wait. If I can—" Kidder began hunting furiously about in the grass. In a few seconds he ran up to the line, clutching a large grasshopper in his hand. He tossed it over. It lay still.

"See?" said Johansen. "It—"

"Look! It jumped. Come on! I don't know what went wrong, unless the Neoterics shut if off. They generated that field – I didn't."

"Neo-huh?"

"Never mind," snapped the biochemist, and ran.

They pounded gasping up the steps and into the Neoterics' control room. Kidder clapped his eyes to a telescope and shrieked in glee. "They've done it! They've done it!"

"My little people! The Neoterics! They've made the impenetrable shield! Don't you see – it cut through the lines of force that start up the field out there. Their generator is still throwing it up, but the vibrations can't get out! They're safe! They're safe!" And the overwrought hermit began to cry. Johansen looked at him pityingly and shook his head.

"Sure, your little men are all right. But we aren't," he added as the floor shook to the detonation of a bomb.

Johansen closed his eyes, got a grip on himself and let his curiosity overcome his fear. He stepped to the binocular telescope, gazed down it. There was nothing there but a curved sheet of gray material. He had never seen a gray quite like that. It was absolutely neutral. It didn't seem soft and it didn't seem hard, and to look at it made his brain reel. He looked up.

Kidder was pounding the keys of a teletype, watching the blank yellow tape anxiously.

"I'm not getting through to them," he whimpered. "I don't know. What's the mat— Oh, of *course*!"

"What?"

"The shield is absolutely impenetrable! The teletype impulses can't get through or I could get them to extend the screen over the building – over the whole island! There's nothing those people can't do!"

"He's crazy," Johansen muttered. "Poor little—"

The teletype began clicking sharply. Kidder dove at it, practically embraced it. He read off the tape as it came out. Johansen saw the characters, but they meant nothing to him.

"Almighty," Kidder read falteringly, "pray have mercy on us and be forbearing until we have said our say. Without orders we have lowered the screen you ordered us to raise. We are lost, O great one. Our screen is truly impenetrable, and so cut off your words on the word machine. We have never, in the memory of any Neoteric, been without your word before. Forgive us our action. We will eagerly await your answer."

Kidder's fingers danced over the keys. "You can look now," he gasped. "Go on – the telescope!"

Johansen, trying to ignore the whine of sure death from above, looked.

He saw what looked like land – fantastic fields under cultivation, a settlement of some sort, factories, and – beings. Everything moved with incredible rapidity. He couldn't see one of the inhabitants except as darting pinky-white streaks.

Fascinated, he stared for a long minute. A sound behind him made him whirl. It was Kidder, rubbing his hands together briskly. There was a broad smile on his face.

"They did it," he said happily. "You see?"

Johansen didn't see until he began to realize that there was a dead silence outside. He ran to a window. It was night outside – the blackest night – when it should have been dusk. "What happened?"

"The Neoterics," said Kidder, and laughed like a child. "My friends downstairs there. They threw up the impenetrable shield over the whole island. We can't be touched now!"

And at Johansen's amazed questions, he launched into a description of the race of beings below them.

Outside the shell, things happened. Nine airplanes suddenly went dead-stick. Nine pilots glided downward, powerless, and some fell into the sea, and some struck the miraculous gray shell that loomed in place of an island; slid off and sank.

And ashore, a man named Wright sat in a car, half dead with fear, while government men surrounded him, approached cautiously, daring instant death from a non-dead source.

In a room deep in the White House, a high-ranking army officer shrieked, "I can't stand it any more! I can't!" and leaped up, snatched a red cube off the president's desk, ground it to ineffectual litter under his shining boots.

And in a few days they took a broken old man away from the bank and put him in an asylum, where he died within a week.

The shield, you see, was truly impenetrable. The power plant was untouched and sent out its beams; but the beams could not get out, and anything powered from the plant went dead. The story never became public, although for some years there was heightened naval activity off the New England coast. The navy, so the story went, had a new target range out there – a great hemi-ovoid of gray-material. They bombed it and shelled it and rayed it and blasted all around it, but never even dented its smooth surface.

Kidder and Johansen let it stay there. They were happy enough with their researches and their Neoterics. They did not hear or feel the shelling, for the shield was truly impenetrable. They synthesized their food and their light and air from materials at hand, and they simply didn't care. They were the only survivors of the bombing, with the exception of three poor maimed devils who died soon afterward.

All this happened many years ago, and Kidder and Johansen may be alive today, and they may be dead. But that doesn't matter too much. The important thing is that the great gray shell will bear watching. Men die, but races live. Some day the Neoterics, after innumerable generations of inconceivable advancement, will take down their shield and come forth. When I think of that I feel frightened.

(1941)

ANCIENT ENGINES

Michael Swanwick

> **Michael Swanwick** (born 1950) sold his first story in 1980. In 1991, his novel *Stations of the Tide* won a Nebula Award, and in 1995 he won the World Fantasy Award for his story "Radio Waves". He's also picked up four Hugos for short stories. His novels include *Vacuum Flowers* (1987), a tour of the solar system in which humans have been subsumed by a cybernetic mass-mind. Recently Swanwick has concentrated on microfictions, collected in volumes like *Michael Swanwick's Field Guide to the Mesozoic Megafauna & Five British Dinosaurs* (2004) and *The Periodic Table of Science Fiction* (2005), comprising 118 "elemental" tales.

"*Planning to live forever*, Tiktok?"

The words cut through the bar's chatter and gab and silenced them. The silence reached out to touch infinity, and then, "I believe you're talking to me?" a mech said.

The drunk laughed. "Ain't nobody else here sticking needles in his face, is there?"

The old man who saw it all. He lightly touched the hand of the young woman sitting with him and said, "Watch."

Carefully, the mech set down his syringe alongside a bottle of liquid collagen on a square of velvet cloth. He disconnected himself from the recharger, laying the jack beside the syringe. When he looked up again, his face was still and hard. He looked like a young lion.

The drunk grinned sneeringly.

The. bar was located just around the corner from the local stepping stage. It was a quiet retreat from the aggravations of the street, all brass and mirrors and wood paneling, as cozy and snug as the inside of a walnut. Light shifted lazily about the room, creating a varying emphasis, like clouds drifting overhead on a summer day, but far dimmer. The bar, the bottles behind the bar, and the shelves beneath the bottles behind the bar were all aggressively real. If there was anything virtual, it was set up high or far back, where it couldn't be touched. There was not a smart surface in the place.

"If that was a challenge," the mech said, "I'd be more than happy to meet you outside."

"Oh, noooooo," the drunk said, his expression putting the lie to his words. "I just saw you shooting up that goop into your face, oh so dainty, like an old lady pumping herself full of antioxidants. So I figured..." he weaved and put a hand down on a table to steady himself. "... figured you was hoping to live forever."

The girl looked questioningly at the old man. He held a finger to his lips.

"Well, you're right. You're—what? Fifty years old? Just beginning to grow old and decay. Pretty soon your teeth will rot and fall out and your hair will melt away and your face will fold up in a million wrinkles. Your hearing and your eyesight will go and you won't be able to remember the last time you got it up. You'll be lucky if you don't need diapers before the end. But *me*—" he drew a dram of fluid into his syringe and tapped the barrel to draw the bubbles to the top "—anything that fails, I'll simply have it replaced. So, yes, I'm planning to live forever. While you, well, I suppose you're planning to die. Soon, I hope."

The drunk's face twisted, and with an incoherent roar of rage, he attacked the mech.

In a motion too fast to be seen, the mech stood, seized the drunk, whirled him around, and lifted him above his head. One hand was closed around the man's throat so he couldn't speak. The other held both wrists tight behind the knees so that, struggle as he might, the drunk was helpless.

"I could snap your spine like *that*," he said coldly. "If I exerted myself, I could rupture every internal organ you've got. I'm two-point-eight times stronger than a flesh man, and three-point-five times faster. My reflexes are only slightly slower than the speed of light, and I've just had a tune-up. You could hardly have chosen a worse person to pick a fight with."

Then the drunk was flipped around and set back on his feet. He gasped for air.

"But since I'm also a merciful man, I'll simply ask you nicely if you wouldn't rather leave." The mech spun the drunk around and gave him a gentle shove toward the door.

The man left at a stumbling run.

Everyone in the place—there were not many—had been watching. Now they remembered their drinks, and talk rose up to fill the room again. The bartender put something back under the bar and turned away.

Leaving his recharge incomplete, the mech folded up his lubrication kit and slipped it into a pocket. He swiped his hand over the credit swatch and stood.

But as he was leaving, the old man swiveled around and said, "I heard you say you hope to live forever. Is that true?"

"Who doesn't?" the mech said curtly.

"Then sit down. Spend a few minutes out of the infinite swarm of centuries you've got ahead of you to humor an old man. What's so urgent that you can't spare the time?"

The mech hesitated. Then, as the young woman smiled at him, he sat.

"Thank you. My name is—"

"I know who you are, Mr. Brandt. There's nothing wrong with my eidetics."

Brandt smiled. "That's why I like you guys. I don't have to be all the time reminding you of things." He gestured to the woman sitting opposite him. "My granddaughter." The light intensified where she sat, making her red hair blaze. She dimpled prettily.

"Jack." The young man drew up a chair. "Chimaera Navigator-Fuego, model number—"

"Please. I founded Chimaera. Do you think I wouldn't recognize one of my own children?"

Jack flushed. "What is it you want to talk about, Mr. Brandt?" His voice was audibly less hostile now, as synthetic counterhormones damped down his emotions.

"Immortality. I found your ambition most intriguing."

"What's to say? I take care of myself, I invest carefully, I buy all the upgrades. I see no reason why I shouldn't live forever." Defiantly. "I hope that doesn't offend you."

"No, no, of course not. Why should it? Some men hope to achieve immortality through their works and others through their children. What could give me more joy than to do both? But tell me—do you *really* expect to live forever?"

The mech said nothing.

"I remember an incident that happened to my late father-in-law, William Porter. He was a fine fellow, Bill was, and who remembers him anymore? Only me." The old man sighed. "He was a bit of a railroad buff, and one day he took a tour through a science museum that included a magnificent old steam locomotive. This was in the latter years of the last century. Well, he was listening admiringly to the guide extolling the virtues of this ancient engine when she mentioned its date of manufacture, and he realized that *he was older than it was.*" Brandt leaned forward. "This is the point where old Bill would laugh. But it's not really funny, is it?"

"No."

The granddaughter sat listening quietly, intently, eating little pretzels one by one from a bowl.

"How old are you, Jack?"

"Seven years."

"I'm eighty-three. How many machines do you know of that are as old as me? Eighty-three years old and still functioning?"

"I saw an automobile the other day," his granddaughter said. "A Dusenberg. It was red."

"How delightful. But it's not used for transportation anymore, is it? We have the stepping stages for that. I won an award once that had mounted on it a vacuum tube from Univac. That was the first real computer. Yet all its fame and historical importance couldn't keep it from the scrap heap."

"Univac," said the young man, "couldn't act on its own behalf. If it *could*, perhaps it would be alive today."

"Parts wear out."

"New ones can be bought."

"Yes, as long as there's the market. But there are only so many machine people of your make and model. A lot of you have risky occupations. There are accidents, and with every accident, the consumer market dwindles."

"You can buy antique parts. You can have them made."

"Yes, if you can afford them. And if not—?"

The young man fell silent.

"Son, you're not going to live *forever*. We've just established that. So now that you've admitted that you've got to die someday, you might as well admit that it's going to be sooner rather than later. Mechanical people are in their infancy. And nobody can upgrade a Model T into a stepping stage. Agreed?"

Jack dipped his head. "Yes."

"You knew it all along."

"Yes."

"That's why you behaved so badly toward that lush."

"Yes."

"I'm going to be brutal here, Jack—you probably won't live to be eighty-three. You don't have my advantages."

"Which are?"

"Good genes. I chose my ancestors well."

"Good genes," Jack said bitterly. "You received good genes, and what did *I* get in their place? What the hell did I get?"

"Molybdenum joints where stainless steel would do. Ruby chips instead of zirconium. A number seventeen plastic seating for—hell, we did all right by you boys!"

"But it's not enough."

"No. It's not. It was only the best we could do."

"What's the solution, then?" the granddaughter asked, smiling.

"I'd advise taking the long view. That's what I've done."

"Poppycock," the mech said. "You were an extensionist when you were young. I input your autobiography. It seems to me you wanted immortality as much as I do."

"Oh, yes, I was a charter member of the life-extension movement. You can't imagine the crap we put into our bodies! But eventually I wised up. The problem is, information degrades each time a human cell replenishes itself. Death is inherent in flesh people. It seems to be written into the basic program—a way, perhaps, of keeping the universe from filling up with old people."

"And old ideas," his granddaughter said maliciously.

"Touché. I saw that life-extension was a failure. So I decided that my children would succeed where I failed. That *you* would succeed. And—"

"You failed."

"But I haven't stopped trying!" The old man thumped the table in unison with his last three words. "You've obviously given this some thought. Let's discuss what I *should* have done. What would it take to make a true immortal? What instructions should I have given your design team? Let's design a mechanical man who's got a shot at living forever."

Carefully, the mech said, "Well, the obvious to begin with. He ought to be able to buy new parts and upgrades as they become available. There should be ports and connectors that would make it easy to adjust to shifts in technology. He should be capable of surviving extremes of heat, cold, and moisture. And—" he waved a hand at his own face "—he shouldn't look so goddamned pretty."

"I think you look nice," the granddaughter said.

"Yes, but I'd like to be able to pass for flesh."

"So our hypothetical immortal should be one, infinitely upgradable; two, adaptable across a broad spectrum of conditions; and three, discreet. Anything else?"

"I think she should be charming," the granddaughter said.

"She?" the mech asked.

"Why not?"

"That's actually not a bad point," the old man said. "The organism that survives evolutionary forces is the one that's best adapted to its environmental niche. The environmental niche people live in is man-made. The single most useful trait a survivor can have is probably the ability to get along easily with other men. Or, if you'd rather, women."

"Oh," said the granddaughter, "he doesn't like *women*. I can tell by his body language."

The young man flushed.

"Don't be offended," said the old man. "You should never be offended by the truth. As for you—" he turned to face his granddaughter "—if you don't learn to treat people better, I won't take you places anymore."

She dipped her head. "Sorry."

"Apology accepted. Let's get back to task, shall we? Our hypothetical immortal would be a lot like flesh women, in many ways. Self-regenerating. Able to grow her own replacement parts. She could take in pretty much anything as fuel. A little carbon, a little water..."

"Alcohol would be an excellent fuel," his granddaughter said.

"She'd have the ability to mimic the superficial effects of aging," the mech said. "Also, biological life evolves incrementally across generations. I'd want her to be able to evolve across upgrades."

"Fair enough. Only I'd do away with upgrades entirely, and give her total conscious control over her body. So she could change and evolve at will. She'll need that ability, if she's going to survive the collapse of civilization."

"The collapse of civilization? Do you think it likely?"

"In the long run? Of course. When you take the long view, it seems inevitable. Everything seems inevitable. Forever is a long time, remember. Time enough for absolutely *everything* to happen!"

For a moment, nobody spoke.

Then the old man slapped his hands together. "Well, we've created our New Eve. Now let's wind her up and let her go. She can expect to live—how long?"

"Forever," said the mech.

"Forever's a long time. Let's break it down into smaller units. In the year 2500, she'll be doing what?"

"Holding down a job," the granddaughter said. "Designing art molecules, maybe, or scripting recreational hallucinations. She'll be deeply involved in the culture. She'll have lots of friends she cares about passionately, and maybe a husband or wife or two."

"Who will grow old," the mech said, "or wear out. Who will die."

"She'll mourn them, and move on."

"The year 3500. The collapse of civilization," the old man said with gusto. "What will she do then?"

"She'll have made preparations, of course. If there is radiation or toxins in the environment, she'll have made her systems immune from their effects. And she'll make herself useful to the survivors. In the seeming of an old woman, she'll teach the healing arts. Now and then, she might drop a hint about this and that. She'll have a data base squirreled away somewhere containing everything they'll have lost. Slowly, she'll guide them back to civilization. But a gentler one, this time. One less likely to tear itself apart."

"The year one million. Humanity evolves beyond anything we can currently imagine. How does *she* respond?"

"She mimics their evolution. No—she's been *shaping* their evolution! She wants a risk-free method of going to the stars, so she's been encouraging a type of being that would strongly desire such a thing. She isn't among the first to use it, though. She waits a few hundred generations for it to prove itself."

The mech, who had been listening in fascinated silence, now said, "Suppose that never happens. What if starflight will always remain difficult and perilous? What then?"

"It was once thought that people would never fly. So much that looks impossible becomes simple if you only wait."

"Four billion years. The sun uses up its hydrogen, its core collapses, helium fusion begins, and it balloons into a red giant. Earth is vaporized."

"Oh, she'll be somewhere else by then. That's easy."

"Five billion years. The Milky Way collides with the Andromeda Galaxy and the whole neighborhood is full of high-energy radiation and exploding stars."

"That's trickier. She's going to have to either prevent that or move a few million light-years away to a friendlier galaxy. But she'll have time enough to prepare and to assemble the tools. I have faith that she'll prove equal to the task."

"One trillion years. The last stars gutter out. Only black holes remain."

"Black holes are a terrific source of energy. No problem."

"One-point-six googol years."

"Googol?"

"That's ten raised to the hundredth power—one followed by a hundred zeros. The heat-death of the universe. How does she survive it?"

"She'll have seen it coming for a long time," the mech said. "When the last black holes dissolve, she'll have to do without a source of free energy. Maybe she could take and rewrite her personality into the physical constants of the dying universe. Would that be possible?"

"Oh, perhaps. But I really think that the lifetime of the universe is long enough for anyone," the granddaughter said. "Mustn't get greedy."

"Maybe so," the old man said thoughtfully. "Maybe so." Then, to the mech, "Well, there you have it: a glimpse into the future, and a brief biography of the first immortal, ending, alas, with her death. Now tell me. Knowing that you contributed something, however small, to that accomplishment—wouldn't that be enough?"

"No," Jack said. "No, it wouldn't."

Brandt made a face. "Well, you're young. Let me ask you this: Has it been a good life so far? All in all?"

"Not *that* good. Not good *enough*."

For a long moment, the old man was silent. Then, "Thank you," he said. "I valued our conversation." The interest went out of his eyes and he looked away.

Uncertainly, Jack looked at the granddaughter, who smiled and shrugged. "He's like that," she said apologetically. "He's old. His enthusiasms wax and wane with his chemical balances. I hope you don't mind."

"I see." The young man stood. Hesitantly, he made his way to the door.

At the door, he glanced back and saw the granddaughter tearing her linen napkin into little bits and eating the shreds, delicately washing them down with sips of wine.

(1998)

BEACHCOMBER

Mike Resnick

Michael Diamond Resnick, born 1942, a native of Chicago, is a prolific writer and editor who began his genre career with an Edgar Rice Burroughs pastiche, *The Forgotten Sea of Mars* (1965). His wife, Carol L. Cain, is uncredited collaborator on much of his science fiction, which is hardly surprising, given how much there is of it: around 75 novels (at the last count), nearly 300 stories, three screenplays, and 42 anthologies. Resnick's papers – all 125 boxes of them – are in the Special Collections Library of the University of South Florida in Tampa. Resnick has probably sold more humorous stories than any science fiction author except Robert Sheckley, and even the more serious stories (like the one here) are leavened with humour. Resnick has won five Hugos and has been nominated for 36 more.

Arlo didn't look much like a man. (Not all robots do, you know.) The problem was that he didn't act all that much like a robot.

The fact of the matter is that one day, right in the middle of work, he decided to pack it in. Just got up, walked out the door, and kept on going. *Some*body must have seen him; it's pretty hard to hide nine hundred pounds of moving parts. But evidently nobody knew it was Arlo. After all, he hadn't left his desk since the day they'd activated him twelve years ago.

So the Company got in touch with me, which is a euphemistic way of saying that they woke me in the middle of the night, gave me three minutes to get dressed, and rushed me to the office. I can't really say that I blame them: when you need a scapegoat, the Chief of Security is a pretty handy guy to have around.

Anyway, it was panic time. It seems that no robot ever ran away before. And Arlo wasn't just any robot: he was a twelve million dollar item, with just about every feature a machine could have short of white-walled tires. And I wasn't even so certain about the tires; he sure dropped out of sight fast enough.

So, after groveling a little and making all kinds of optimistic promises to the Board, I started doing a little checking up on Arlo. I went to his designer, and his department head, and even spoke to some of his co-workers, both human and robot.

And it turned out that what Arlo did was sell tickets. That didn't sound like twelve million dollars' worth of robot to me, but I was soon shown the error of my ways. Arlo was a travel agent supreme. He booked tours of the Solar System, got his people into and out of luxury hotels on Ganymede and Titan and the

Moon, scheduled their weight and their time to the nearest gram and the nearest second.

It *still* didn't sound that impressive. Computers were doing stuff like that long before robots ever crawled out of the pages of pulp magazines and into our lives.

"True," said his department head. "But Arlo was a robot with a difference. He booked more tours and arranged more complicated logistical scheduling than any other ten robots put together."

"More complex thinking gear?" I asked.

"Well, that too," was the answer. "But we did a little something else with Arlo that had never been done before."

"And what was that?"

"We programmed him for enthusiasm."

"That's something special?" I asked.

"Absolutely. When Arlo spoke about the beauties of Callisto, or the fantastic light refraction images on Venus, he did so with a conviction that was so intense as to be almost tangible. Even his voice reflected his enthusiasm. He was one of those rare robots who was capable of modular inflection, rather than the dull, mechanistic monotone so many of them possess. He literally loved those desolate worlds, and his record will show that his attitude was infectious."

I thought about that for a minute. "So you're telling me that you've created a robot whose entire motivation had been to send people out to sample all these worlds, and he's been crated up in an office twenty-four hours a day since the second you plugged him in?"

"That's correct."

"Did it ever occur to you that maybe he wanted to see some of these sights himself?"

"It's entirely possible that he did, but leaving his post would be contrary to his orders."

"Yeah," I said. "Well, sometimes a little enthusiasm can go a long way."

He denied it vigorously, and I spent just enough time in his office to mollify him. Then I left and got down to work. I checked every outgoing space flight, and had some of the Company's field reps hit the more luxurious vacation spas. He wasn't there.

So I tried a little closer to home: Monte Carlo, New Vegas, Alpine City. No luck. I even tried a couple of local theaters that specialized in Tri-Fi travelogs.

You know where I finally found him?

Stuck in the sand at Coney Island. I guess he'd been walking along the beach at night and the tide had come in and he just sank in, all nine hundred pounds of him. Some kids had painted some obscene graffiti on his back, and there he stood, surrounded by empty beer cans and broken glass and a few dead fish. I looked at him for a minute, then shook my head and walked over.

"I knew you'd find me sooner or later," he said, and even though I knew what to expect, I still did a double-take at the sound of that horribly unhappy voice coming from this enormous mass of gears and gadgetry.

"Well, you've got to admit that it's not too hard to spot a robot on a condemned beach," I said.

"I suppose I have to go back now," said Arlo.

"That's right," I said.

"At least I've felt the sand beneath my feet," said Arlo.

"Arlo, you don't have any feet," I said. "And if you did, you couldn't feel sand beneath them. Besides, it's just silicon and crushed limestone and…"

"It's sand and it's beautiful!" snapped Arlo.

"All right, have it your way: it's beautiful." I knelt down next to him and began digging the sand away.

"Look at the sunrise," he said in a wistful voice. "It's glorious!"

I looked. A sunrise is a sunrise. Big deal.

"It's enough to bring tears of joy to your eyes," said Arlo.

"You don't have eyes," I said, working at the sand. "You've got prismatic photo cells that transmit an image to your central processing unit. And you can't cry, either. If I were you, I'd be more worried about rusting."

"A pastel wonderland," he said, turning what passed for his head and looking up and down the deserted beach, past the rotted food stands and the broken piers. "Glorious!"

It kind of makes you wonder about robots. I'll tell you. Anyway, I finally pried him loose and ordered him to follow me.

"Please," he said in that damned voice of his. "Couldn't I have one last minute before you lock me up in my office?"

I stared at him, trying to make up my mind.

"One last look. Please?"

I shrugged, gave him about thirty seconds, and then took him in tow.

"You know what's going to happen to you, don't you?" I said as we rode back to the office.

"Yes," he said. "They're going to put in a stronger duty directive, aren't they?"

I nodded. "At the very least."

"My memory banks!" he exclaimed, and once again I jumped at the sound of a human voice coming from an animated gearbox. "They won't take this experience away from me, will they?"

"I don't know, Arlo," I said.

"They can't!" he wailed. "To see such beauty, and then have it expunged—erased!"

"Well, they may want to make sure you don't go AWOL again," I said, wondering what kind of crazy junkheap could find anything beautiful on a garbage-laden strip of dirt.

"Can you intercede for me if I promise never to leave again?"

Any robot that can disobey one directive can disobey others, like not roughing up human beings, and Arlo was a pretty powerful piece of machinery, so I put on my most fatherly smile and said: "Sure I will, Arlo. You can count on it."

So I returned him to the Company, and they upped his sense of duty and took away his enthusiasm and gave him a case of agoraphobia and wiped his memory banks clean, and now he sits in his office and speaks to customers without inflection, and sells a few less tickets than he used to.

And every couple of months or so I wander over to the beach and walk along it and try to see what it was that made Arlo sacrifice his personality and his security and damned near everything else, just to get a glimpse of all this.

And I see a sunset just like any other sunset, and a stretch of dirty sand with glass and tin cans and seaweed and rocks on it, and I breathe in polluted air, and sometimes I get rained on; and I think of that damned robot in that plush office with that cushy job and every need catered to, and I decide that I'd trade places with him in two seconds flat.

I saw Arlo just the other day—I had some business on his floor—and it was almost kind of sad. He looked just like any other robot, spoke in a grating monotone, acted exactly like an animated computer. He wasn't much before, but whatever he had been, he gave it all away just to look at the sky once or twice. Dumb trade.

Well, robots never did make much sense to me, anyway.

(1980)

NON SERVIAM

Stanisław Lem

> Stanisław Lem (1921–2006), the Polish satirist, essayist and science fiction writer, had no time for futurologists. "Meaningful prediction," he wrote, "does not lie in serving up the present larded with startling improvements or revelations." He preferred to devise whole new chapters to the human story, and very few indeed had happy endings. His vision of the internet (which did not then exist) is particularly compelling: a future in which important facts are carried away on a flood of falsehoods, and our civic freedoms along with them. He dreamed up all the usual nanotechnological fantasies, from spider silk space-elevator cables to catastrophic "grey goo", decades before they entered the public consciousness, and even coined the phrase "Theory of Everything", but only so he could point at it and laugh. He did not become really productive until after Stalin's death, but in the dozen years from 1956 he wrote seventeen books, among them *Solaris* (1961), the work for which he is best known by English speakers.

Professor Dobb's book is devoted to personetics, which the Finnish philosopher Eino Kaikki has called "the cruelest science man ever created." Dobb, one of the most distinguished personeticists today, shares this view. One cannot escape the conclusion, he says, that personetics is, in its application, immoral; we are dealing, however, with a type of pursuit that is, though counter to the principles of ethics, also of practical necessity to us. There is no way, in the research, to avoid its special ruthlessness, to avoid doing violence to one's natural instincts, and if nowhere else it is here that the myth of the perfect innocence of the scientist as a seeker of facts is exploded. We are speaking of a discipline, after all, which, with only a small amount of exaggeration, for emphasis, has been called "experimental theogony." Even so, this reviewer is struck by the fact that when the press played up the thing, nine years ago, public opinion was stunned by the personetic disclosures. One would have thought that in this day and age nothing could surprise us. The centuries rang with the echo of the feat of Columbus, whereas the conquering of the Moon in the space of a week was received by the collective consciousness as a thing practically humdrum. And yet the birth of personetics proved to be a shock.

The name combines Latin and Greek derivatives: "persona" and "genetic"—"genetic" in the sense of formation, or creation. The field is a recent offshoot of the cybernetics and psychonics of the eighties, crossbred with applied intellectronics. Today everyone knows of personetics; the man in the street would say, if asked, that it is the artificial production of intelligent beings—an answer not wide of the mark, to be sure, but not quite getting to the heart of the matter. To date we have nearly a hundred personetic programs. Nine years ago identity schemata were being developed—primitive cores of the "linear" type—but even that generation of computers, today of historical value only, could not yet provide a field for the true creation of personoids.

The theoretical possibility of creating sentience was divined some time ago, by Norbert Wiener, as certain passages of his last book, *God and Golem*, bear witness. Granted, he alluded to it in that half-facetious manner typical of him, but underlying the facetiousness were fairly grim premonitions. Wiener, however, could not have foreseen the turn that things would take twenty years later. The worst came about—in the words of Sir Donald Acker—when at MIT "the inputs were shorted to the outputs."

At present a "world" for personoid "inhabitants" can be prepared in a matter of a couple of hours. This is the time it takes to feed into the machine one of the full-fledged programs (such as BAAL 66, CREAN IV, or JAHVE 09). Dobb gives a rather cursory sketch of the beginnings of personetics, referring the reader to the historical sources; a confirmed practitioner-experimenter himself, he speaks mainly of his own work—which is much to the point, since between the English school, which Dobb represents, and the American group, at MIT, the differences are considerable, both in the area of methodology and as regards experimental goals. Dobb describes the procedure of "6 days in 120 minutes" as follows. First, one supplies the machine's memory with a minimal set of givens; that is—to keep within a language comprehensible to laymen—one loads its memory with substance that is "mathematical." This substance is the protoplasm of a universum to be "habitated" by personoids. We are now able to supply the beings that will come into this mechanical, digital world—that will be carrying on an existence in it, and in it only—with an environment of nonfinite characteristics. These beings, therefore, cannot feel imprisoned in the physical sense, because the environment does not have, from their standpoint, any bounds. The medium possesses only one dimension that resembles a dimension given us also—namely, that of the passage of time (duration). Their time is not directly analogous to ours, however, because the rate of its flow is subject to discretionary control on the part of the experimenter. As a rule, the rate is maximized in the preliminary phase (the so-called creational warm-up), so that our minutes correspond to whole eons in the computer, during which there takes place a series of successive reorganizations and crystallizations—of a synthetic cosmos. It is a cosmos completely spaceless, though possessing dimensions, but these dimensions have a purely mathematical, hence what one might call an "imaginary" character. They are, very simply, the consequence of certain axiomatic decisions of the programmer, and their number depends on him. If, for example, he chooses a ten-dimensionality, it will have for the structure of the world created altogether different consequences from those where only six dimensions are established. It should be emphasized that these dimensions bear no relation to those of physical space but only to the abstract, logically valid constructs made use of in systems creation.

This point, all but inaccessible to the nonmathematician, Dobb attempts to explain by adducing simple facts, the sort generally learned in school. It is possible, as we know, to construct a geometrically regular three-dimensional solid—say, a cube—which in the real world possesses a counterpart in the form of a die; and it is equally possible to create geometrical solids of four, five, *n* dimensions (the four-dimensional is a tesseract). These no longer possess real counterparts, and we can see this, since in the absence of any physical dimension No. 4 there is no way to fashion genuine four-dimensional dice. Now, this distinction (between what is physically constructible and what may be made only mathematically) is, for personoids, in general nonexistent, because their world is of a purely mathematical consistency. It is built of mathematics, though the building blocks of that mathematics are ordinary, perfectly physical objects (relays, transistors, logic circuits—in a word, the whole huge network of the digital machine).

As we know from modern physics, space is not something independent of the objects and masses that are situated within it. Space is, in its existence, determined by those bodies; where they are not, where nothing is—in the material sense—there, too, space ceases, collapsing to zero. Now, the role of material bodies, which extend their "influence," so to speak, and thereby "generate" space, is carried out in the personoid world by systems of a mathematics called into being for that very purpose. Out of all the possible "maths" that in general might be made (for example, in an axiomatic manner), the programmer, having decided upon a specific experiment, selects a particular group, which will serve as the underpinning, the "existential substrate," the "ontological foundation" of the created universum. There is in this, Dobb believes, a striking similarity to the human world. This world of ours, after all, has "decided" upon certain forms and upon certain types of geometry that best suit it—best, since most simply (three-dimensionality, in order to remain with what one began with). This notwithstanding, we are able to picture "other worlds" with "other properties"—in the geometrical and not only in the geometrical realm. It is the same with the personoids: that aspect of mathematics which the researcher has chosen as the "habitat" is for them exactly what for us is the "real-world base" in which we live, and live perforce. And, like us, the personoids are able to "picture" worlds of different fundamental properties.

Dobb presents his subject using the method of successive approximations and recapitulations; that which we have outlined above, and which corresponds roughly to the first two chapters of his book, in the subsequent chapters undergoes partial revocation—through complication. It is not really the case, the author advises us, that the personoids simply come upon a readymade, fixed, frozen sort of world in its irrevocably final form; what the world will be like in its specificities depends on them, and this to a growing degree as their own activeness increases, as their "exploratory initiative" develops. Nor does the likening of the universum of the personoids to a world in which phenomena exist only to the extent that its inhabitants observe them provide an accurate image of the conditions. Such a comparison, which is to be found in the works of Sainter and Hughes, Dobb considers an "idealist deviation"—a homage that personetics has rendered to the doctrine, so curiously and so suddenly resurrected, of Bishop Berkeley. Sainter maintained that the personoids would know their world after the fashion of a Berkeleyan being, which is not in a position to distinguish "*esse*" from "*percipi*"—

to wit, it will never discover the difference between the thing perceived and that which occasions the perception in a way objective and independent of the one perceiving. Dobb attacks this interpretation of the matter with a passion. *We,* the creators of their world, know perfectly well that what is perceived by them indeed exists; it exists inside the computer, independent of them—though, granted, solely in the manner of mathematical objects.

And there are further clarifications. The personoids arise germinally by virtue of the program; they increase at a rate imposed by the experimenter—a rate only such as the latest technology of information processing, operating at near-light speeds, permits. The mathematics that is to be the "existential residence" of the personoids does not await them in full readiness but is still "in wraps," so to speak—unarticulated, suspended, latent—because it represents only a set of certain prospective chances, of certain pathways contained in appropriately programmed subunits of the machine. These subunits, or generators, in and of themselves contribute nothing; rather, a specific type of personoid activity serves as a triggering mechanism, setting in motion a production process that will gradually augment and define itself; in other words, the world surrounding these beings takes on an unequivocalness only in accordance with their own behavior. Dobb tries to illustrate this concept with recourse to the following analogy. A man may interpret the real world in a variety of ways. He may devote particular attention—intense scientific investigation—to certain facets of that world, and the knowledge he acquires then casts its own special light on the remaining portions of the world, those not considered in his priority-setting research. If first he diligently takes up *mechanics,* he will fashion for himself a *mechanical* model of the world and will see the Universe as a gigantic and perfect clock that in its inexorable movement proceeds from the past to a precisely determined future. This model is not an accurate representation of reality, and yet one can make use of it for a period of time historically long, and with it can even achieve many practical successes—the building of machines, implements, etc. Similarly, should the personoids "incline themselves," by choice, by an act of will, to a certain type of relation to their universum, and to that type of relation give precedence—if it is in this and only in this that they find the "essence" of their cosmos—they will enter upon a definite path of endeavors and discoveries, a path that is neither illusory nor futile. Their inclination "draws out" of the environment what best corresponds to it. What they first perceive is what they first master. For the world that surrounds them is only partially determined, only partially established in advance by the researcher-creator; in it, the personoids preserve a certain and by no means insignificant margin of freedom of action—action both "mental" (in the province of what they think of their own world, of how they understand it) and "real" (in the context of their "deeds"—which are not, to be sure, literally real, as we understand the term, but are not merely imagined, either). This is, in truth, the most difficult part of the exposition, and Dobb, we daresay, is not altogether successful in explaining those special qualities of personoid existence—qualities that can be rendered only by the language of the mathematics of programs and creational interventions. We must, then, take it somewhat on faith that the activity of the personoids is neither entirely free—as the space of our actions is not entirely free, being limited by the physical laws of nature—nor entirely determined—just as we are not train cars set on rigidly fixed tracks. A personoid is similar to a man in this respect, too, that man's "secondary qualities"—colors, melodious sounds, the beauty of things—can manifest themselves only when he has ears to hear and eyes to see, but what makes possible hearing and sight has been, after all, previously given. Personoids, perceiving their environment, give it from out of themselves those experiential qualities which exactly correspond to what for us are the charms of a beheld landscape—except, of course, that they have been provided with purely mathematical scenery. As to "how they see it," one can make no pronouncement, for the only way of learning the "subjective quality of their sensation" would be for one to shed his human skin and become a personoid. Personoids, one must remember, have no eyes or ears, therefore they neither see nor hear, as we understand it; in their cosmos there is no light, no darkness, no spatial proximity, no distance, no up or down; there are dimensions there, not tangible to us but to them primary, elemental; they perceive, for example—as equivalents of the components of human sensory awareness—certain changes in electrical potential. But these changes in potential are, for them, not something in the nature of, let us say, pressures of current but, rather, the sort of thing that, for a man, is the most rudimentary phenomenon, optical or aural—the seeing of a red blotch, the hearing of a sound, the touching of an object hard or soft. From here on, Dobb stresses, one can speak only in analogies, evocations.

To declare that the personoids are "handicapped" with respect to us, inasmuch as they do not see or hear as we do, is totally absurd, because with equal justice one could assert that it is we who are deprived with respect to them—unable to feel with immediacy the phenomenalism of mathematics, which, after all, we know only in a cerebral, inferential fashion. It is only through reasoning that we are in touch with mathematics, only through abstract thought that we "experience" it. Whereas the personoids *live* in it; it is their air, their earth, clouds, water, and even bread—yes, even food, because in a certain sense they take nourishment from it. And so they are "imprisoned," hermetically locked inside the machine, solely from our point of view; just as they cannot work their way out to us, to the human world, so, conversely—and symmetrically—a man can in no wise enter the interior of their world, so as to exist in it and know it directly. Mathematics has become, then, in certain of its embodiments, the life-space of an intelligence so spiritualized as to be totally incorporeal, the niche and cradle of its existence, its element.

The personoids are in many respects similar to man. They are able to imagine a particular contradiction (that *a* is and that not-*a* is) but cannot bring about its realization, just as we cannot. The physics of our world, the logic of theirs, does not allow it, since logic is for the personoids' universum the very same action-confining frame that physics is for our world. In any case—emphasizes Dobb—it is quite out of the question that we could ever fully, introspectively grasp what the personoids "feel" and what they "experience" as they go about their intensive tasks in their nonfinite universum. Its utter spacelessness is no prison—that is a piece of nonsense the journalists latched onto—but is, on the contrary, the guarantee of their freedom, because the mathematics that is spun by the computer generators when "excited" into activity (and what excites them thus is precisely the activity of the personoids)—that mathematics is, as it were, a self-realizing infinite field for optional actions, architectural and other labors, for exploration, heroic excursions, daring incursions, surmises. In a word: we have done the personoids no injustice by putting them in possession of precisely such and not a different cosmos. It is not in this that one finds the cruelty, the immorality of personetics.

In the seventh chapter of *Non Serviam* Dobb presents to the reader the inhabitants of the digital universum. The personoids have at their disposal a fluency of thought as well as of language, and they also have emotions. Each of them is an individual entity; their differentiation is not the mere consequence of the decisions of the creator-programmer but results from the extraordinary complexity of their internal structure. They can be very like, one to another, but never are they identical. Coming into the world, each is endowed with a "core," a "personal nucleus," and already possesses the faculty of speech and thought, albeit in a rudimentary state. They have a vocabulary, but it is quite spare, and they have the ability to construct sentences in accordance with the rules of the syntax imposed upon them. It appears that in the future it will be possible for us not to impose upon them even these determinants, but to sit back and wait until, like a primeval human group in the course of socialization, they develop their own speech. But this direction of personetics confronts two cardinal obstacles. In the first place, the time required to await the creation of speech would have to be very long. At present, it would take twelve years, even with the maximization of the rate of intracomputer transformations (speaking figuratively and very roughly, one second of machine time corresponds to one year of human life). Secondly, and this is the greater problem, a language arising spontaneously in the "group evolution of the personoids" would be incomprehensible to us, and its fathoming would be bound to resemble the arduous task of breaking an enigmatic code—a task made all the more difficult by the fact that such a code would not have been created by people for other people in a world shared by the decoders. The world of the personoids is vastly different in qualities from ours, and therefore a language suited to it would have to be far removed from any ethnic language. So, for the time being, linguistic evolution *ex nihilo* is only a dream of the personeticists.

The personoids, when they have "taken root developmentally," come up against an enigma that is fundamental, and for them paramount—that of their own origin. To wit, they set themselves questions—questions known to us from the history of man, from the history of his religious beliefs, philosophical inquiries, and mythic creations: Where did we come from? Why are we made thus and not otherwise? Why is it that the world we perceive has these and not other, wholly different properties? What meaning do we have for the world? What meaning does it have for us? The train of such speculations leads them ultimately, unavoidably, to the elemental questions of ontology, to the problem of whether existence came about "in and of itself," or whether it was the product, instead, of a particular creative act—that is, whether there might not be, hidden behind it, invested with will and consciousness, purposively active, master of the situation, a Creator. It is here that the whole cruelty, the immorality of personetics manifests itself.

But before Dobb takes up, in the second half of his work, the account of these intellectual strivings—these struggles of a mentality made prey to the torment of such questions—he presents in a series of successive chapters a portrait of the "typical personoid," its "anatomy, physiology, and psychology."

A solitary personoid is unable to go beyond the stage of rudimentary thinking, since, solitary, it cannot exercise itself in speech, and without speech discursive thought cannot develop. As hundreds of experiments have shown, groups numbering from four to seven personoids are optimal, at least for the development of speech and typical exploratory activity, and also for "culturization." On the other hand, phenomena corresponding to social processes on a larger scale require larger groups. At present it is possible to "accommodate" up to one thousand personoids, roughly speaking, in a computer universum of fair capacity; but studies of this type, belonging to a separate and independent discipline—sociodynamics—lie outside the area of Dobb's primary concerns, and for this reason his book makes only passing mention of them. As was said, a personoid does not have a body, but it does have a "soul." This soul—to an outside observer who has a view into the machine world (by means of a special installation, an auxiliary module that is a type of probe, built into the computer)—appears as a "coherent cloud of processes," as a functional aggregate with a kind of "center" that can be isolated fairly precisely, i.e., delimited within the machine network. (This, *nota bene,* is not easy, and in more than one way resembles the search by neurophysiologists for the localized centers of many functions in the human brain.) Crucial to an understanding of what makes possible the creation of the personoids is Chapter 11 of *Non Serviam,* which in fairly simple terms explains the fundamentals of the theory of consciousness. Consciousness—all consciousness, not merely the personoid—is in its physical aspect an "informational standing wave," a certain dynamic invariant in a stream of incessant transformations, peculiar in that it represents a "compromise" and at the same time is a "resultant" that, as far as we can tell, was not at all planned for by natural evolution. Quite the contrary; evolution from the first placed tremendous problems and difficulties in the way of the harmonizing of the work of brains above a certain magnitude—i.e., above a certain level of complication—and it trespassed on the territory of these dilemmas clearly without design, for evolution is not a deliberate artificer. It happened, simply, that certain very old evolutionary solutions to problems of control and regulation, common to the nervous system, were "carried along" up to the level at which anthropogenesis began. These solutions ought to have been, from a purely rational, efficiency-engineering standpoint, canceled or abandoned, and something entirely new designed—namely, the brain of an intelligent being. But, obviously, evolution could not proceed in this way, because disencumbering itself of the inheritance of old solutions—solutions often as much as hundreds of millions of years old—did not lie within its power. Since it advances always in very minute increments of adaptation, since it "crawls" and cannot "leap," evolution is a dragnet "that lugs after it innumerable archaisms, all sorts of refuse," as was bluntly put by Tammer and Bovine. (Tammer and Bovine are two of the creators of the computer simulation of the human psyche, a simulation that laid the groundwork for the birth of personetics.) The consciousness of man is the result of a special kind of compromise. It is a "patchwork," or, as was observed, e.g., by Gebhardt, a perfect exemplification of the well-known German saying: *"Aus einer Not eine Tugend machen"* (in effect: "To turn a certain defect, a certain difficulty, into a virtue"). A digital machine cannot of itself ever acquire consciousness, for the simple reason that in it there do not arise hierarchical conflicts of operation. Such a machine can, at most, fall into a type of "logical palsy" or "logical stupor" when the antinomies in it multiply. The contradictions with which the brain of man positively teems were, however, in the course of hundreds of thousands of years, gradually subjected to arbitrational procedures. There came to be levels higher and lower, levels of reflex and of reflection, impulse and control, the modeling of the elemental environment by zoological means and of the conceptual by linguistic means. All of these levels cannot, do not "want" to tally perfectly or merge to form a whole.

What, then, is consciousness? An expedient, a dodge, a way out of the trap, a pretended last resort, a court allegedly (but only allegedly!) of highest appeal. And, in the language of physics and information theory, it is a function that, once begun, will not admit of any closure—i.e., any definitive completion. It is, then, only a *plan* for such a closure, for a total "reconciliation" of the stubborn contradictions of the brain. It is, one might say, a mirror whose task it is to reflect other mirrors, which in turn reflect still others, and so on to infinity. This, physically, is simply not possible, and so the *regressus ad infinitum,* represents a kind of pit over which soars and flutters the phenomenon of human consciousness. "Beneath the conscious" there goes on a continuous battle for full representation—in it—of that which cannot reach it in fullness, and cannot for simple lack of space; for, in order to give full and equal rights to all those tendencies that clamor for attention at the centers of awareness, what would be necessary is infinite capacity and volume. There reigns, then, around the conscious a never-ending crush, a pushing and shoving, and the conscious is not—not at all—the highest, serene, sovereign helmsman of all mental phenomena but more nearly a cork upon the fretful waves, a cork whose uppermost position does not mean the mastery of those waves... The modern theory of consciousness, interpreted informationally and dynamically, unfortunately cannot be set forth simply or clearly, so that we are constantly—at least here, in this more accessible presentation of the subject—thrown back on a series of visual models and metaphors. We know, in any case, that consciousness is a kind of dodge, a shift to which evolution has resorted, and resorted in keeping with its characteristic and indispensable *modus operandi,* opportunism—i.e., finding a quick, extempore way out of a tight corner. If, then, one were indeed to build an intelligent being and proceed according to the canons of completely rational engineering and logic, applying the criteria of technological efficiency, such a being would not, in general, receive the gift of consciousness. It would behave in a manner perfectly logical, always consistent, lucid, and well ordered, and it might even seem, to a human observer, a genius in creative action and decision-making. But it could in no way be a man, for it would be bereft of his mysterious depth, his internal intracacies, his labyrinthine nature...

We will not here go further into the modern theory of the conscious psyche, just as Professor Dobb does not. But these few words were in order, for they provide a necessary introduction to the structure of the personoids. In their creation is at last realized one of the oldest myths, that of the homunculus. In order to fashion a likeness of man, of his psyche, one must deliberately introduce into the informational substrate specific contradictions; one must impart to it an asymmetry, acentric tendencies; one must, in a word, both *unify* and *make discordant*. Is this rational? Yes, and well-nigh unavoidable if we desire not merely to construct some sort of synthetic intelligence but to imitate the thought and, with it, the personality of man.

Hence, the emotions of the personoids must to some extent be at odds with their reason; they must possess self-destructive tendencies, at least to a certain degree; they must feel internal tensions—that entire centrifugality which we experience now as the magnificent infinity of spiritual states and now as their unendurably painful disjointedness. The creational prescription for this, meanwhile, is not at all so hopelessly complicated as it might appear. It is simply that the *logic* of the creation (the personoid) must be disturbed, must contain certain antinomies. Consciousness is not only a way out of the evolutionary impasse, says Hilbrandt, but also an escape from the snares of Gôdelization, for by means of paralogistic contradictions this solution has sidestepped the contradictions to which every system that is perfect with respect to logic is subject. So, then, the universum of the personoids is fully rational, but they are not fully rational inhabitants of it. Let that suffice us—Professor Dobb himself does not pursue further this exceedingly difficult topic. As we know already, the personoids have souls but no bodies and, therefore, also no sensation of their corporeality. "It is difficult to imagine," has been said of that which is experienced in certain special states of mind, in total darkness, with the greatest possible reduction in the inflow of external stimuli—but, Dobb maintains, this is a misleading image. For with sensory deprivation the function of the human brain soon begins to disintegrate; without a stream of impulses from the outside world the psyche manifests a tendency to lysis. But personoids, who have no physical senses, hardly disintegrate, because what gives them cohesion is their mathematical milieu, which they do experience. But how? They experience it, let us say, according to those changes in their own states which are induced and imposed upon them by the universum's "externalness." They are able to discriminate between the changes proceeding from outside themselves and the changes that surface from the depths of their own psyche. How do they discriminate? To this question only the theory of the dynamic structure of personoids can supply a direct answer.

And yet they are like us, for all the awesome differences. We know already that a digital machine can never spark with consciousness; regardless of the task to which we harness it, or of the physical processes we simulate in it, it will remain forever apsychic. Since, to simulate man, it is necessary that we reproduce certain of his fundamental contradictions, only a system of mutually gravitating antagonisms—a personoid—will resemble, in the words of Canyon, whom Dobb cites, a "star contracted by the forces of gravity and at the same time expanded by the pressure of radiation." The gravitational center is, very simply, the personal "I," but by no means does it constitute a unity in either the logical or the physical sense. That is only our subjective illusion! We find ourselves, at this stage of the exposition, amid a multitude of astounding surprises. One can, to be sure, program a digital machine in such a way as to be able to carry on a conversation with it, as if with an intelligent partner. The machine will employ, as the need arises, the pronoun "I" and all its grammatical inflections. This, however, is a hoax! The machine will still be closer to a billion chattering parrots—howsoever brilliantly trained the parrots be—than to the simplest, most stupid man. It mimics the behavior of a man on the purely linguistic plane and nothing more. Nothing will amuse such a machine, or surprise it, or confuse it, or alarm it, or distress it, because it is psychologically and individually No One. It is a Voice giving utterance to matters, supplying answers to questions; it is a Logic capable of defeating the best chess player; it is—or, rather, it can become—a consummate imitator of everything, an actor, if you will, brought to the pinnacle of perfection, performing any programmed role—but an actor and an imitator that is, within, completely empty. One cannot count on its sympathy, or on its antipathy. It works toward no self-set goal; to a degree eternally beyond the conception of any man it "doesn't care," for as a person it simply does not exist... It is a wondrously efficient combinatorial mechanism, nothing more. Now, we are faced with a most remarkable phenomenon. The thought is staggering that from the raw material of so utterly vacant and so perfectly impersonal a machine it is possible, through the feeding into it of a special program—a personetic program—to create authentic sentient beings, and even a great many of them at a time! The latest IBM models have a top capacity of one thousand personoids. (The number is mathematically precise, since the elements and linkages needed to carry one personoid can be expressed in units of centimeters-grams-seconds.)

Personoids are separated one from another within the machine. They do not ordinarily "overlap," though it can happen. Upon contact, there occurs what is equivalent to repulsion, which impedes mutual "osmosis." Nevertheless, they are able to interpenetrate if such is their aim. The processes making up their mental substrates then commence to superimpose upon each other, producing "noise" and interference. When the area of permeation is thin, a certain amount of information becomes the common property of both partially coincident personoids—a phenomenon that is for them peculiar, as for a man it would be peculiar, if not indeed alarming, to hear "strange voices" and "foreign thoughts" in his own head (which does, of course, occur in certain mental illnesses or under the influence of hallucinogenic drugs). It is as though two people were to have not merely the same, but *the same* memory; as though there had occurred something more than a telepathic transference of thought—namely, a "peripheral merging of the egos." The phenomenon is ominous in its consequences, however, and ought to be avoided. For, following the transitional state of surface osmosis, the "advancing" personoid can destroy the other and consume it. The latter, in that case, simply undergoes absorption, annihilation—it ceases to exist (this has already been called murder). The annihilated personoid becomes an assimilated, indistinguishable part of the "aggressor." We have succeeded—says Dobb—in simulating not only psychic life but also its imperilment and obliteration. Thus we have succeeded in simulating death as well. Under normal experimental conditions, however, personoids eschew such acts of aggression. "Psychophagi"

(Castler's term) are hardly ever encountered among them. Feeling the beginnings of osmosis, which may come about as the result of purely accidental approaches and fluctuations—feeling this threat in a manner that is of course nonphysical, much as someone might sense another's presence or even hear "strange voices" in his own mind—the personoids execute active avoidance maneuvers; they withdraw and go their separate ways. It is on account of this phenomenon that they have come to know the meaning of the concepts of "good" and "evil." To them it is evident that "evil" lies in the destruction of another, and "good" in another's deliverance. At the same time, the "evil" of one may be the "good" (i.e., the gain, now in the nonethical sense) of another, who would become a "psychophage." For such expansion—the appropriation of someone else's "intellectual territory"—increases one's initially given mental "acreage." In a way, this is a counterpart of a practice of ours, for as carnivores we kill and feed on our victims. The personoids, though, are not obliged to behave thus; they are merely able to. Hunger and thirst are unknown to them, since a continuous influx of energy sustains them—an energy whose source they need not concern themselves with (just as we need not go to any particular lengths to have the sun shine down on us). In the personoid world the terms and principles of thermodynamics, in their application to energetics, cannot arise, because that world is subject to mathematical and not thermodynamic laws.

Before long, the experimenters came to the conclusion that contacts between personoid and man, via the inputs and outputs of the computer, were of little scientific value and, moreover, produced moral dilemmas, which contributed to the labeling of personetics as the cruellest science. There is something unworthy in informing personoids that we have created them in enclosures that only *simulate* infinity, that they are microscopic "psychocysts," capsulations in our world. To be sure, they have their own infinity; hence Sharker and other psychoneticians (Falk, Wiegeland) claim that the situation is fully symmetrical: the personoids do not need our world, our "living space," just as we have no use for their "mathematical earth." Dobb considers such reasoning sophistry, because as to who created whom, and who confined whom existentially, there can be no argument. Dobb himself belongs to that group which advocates the principle of absolute nonintervention—"noncontact"—with the personoids. They are the behaviorists of personetics. Their desire is to observe synthetic beings of intelligence, to listen in on their speech and thoughts, to record their actions and their pursuits, but never to interfere with these. This method is already developed and has a technology of its own—a set of instruments whose procurement presented difficulties that seemed all but insurmountable only a few years ago. The idea is to hear, to understand—in short, to be a constantly eavesdropping witness—but at the same time to prevent one's "monitorings" from disturbing in any way the world of the personoids. Now in the planning stage at MIT are programs (APHRON II and EROT) that will enable the personoids—who are currently without gender—to have "erotic contacts," make possible what corresponds to fertilization, and give them the opportunity to multiply "sexually." Dobb makes clear that he is no enthusiast of these American projects. His work, as described in *Non Serviam*, is aimed in an altogether different direction. Not without reason has the English school of personetics been called "the philosophical polygon" and "the theodicy lab." With these descriptions we come to what is probably the most significant and, certainly, the most intriguing part of the book under discussion—the last part, which justifies and explains its peculiar title.

Dobb gives an account of his own experiment, in progress now for eight years without interruption. Of the creation itself he makes only brief mention; it was a fairly ordinary duplicating of functions typical of the program JAHVE VI, with slight modifications. He summarizes the results of "tapping" this world, which he himself created and whose development he continues to follow. He considers this tapping to be unethical, and even, at times, a shameful practice. Nevertheless, he carries on with his work, professing a belief in the necessity, for science, of conducting such experiments *also*—experiments that can in no way be justified on moral—or, for that matter, on any other non-knowledge-advancing—grounds. The situation, he says, has come to the point where the old evasions of the scientists will not do. One cannot affect a fine neutrality and conjure away an uneasy conscience by using, for example, the rationalization worked out by vivisectionists—that it is not in creatures of full-dimensional consciousness, not in sovereign beings that one is causing suffering or only discomfort. In the personoid experiments we are accountable twofold, because we create and then enchain the creation in the schema of our laboratory procedures. Whatever we do and however we explain our action, there is no longer an escape from full accountability.

Many years of experience on the part of Dobb and his coworkers at Oldport went into the making of their eight-dimensional universum, which became the residence of personoids bearing the names ADAN, ADNA, ANAD, DANA, DAAN, and NAAD. The first personoids developed the rudiment of language implanted in them and had "progeny" by means of division. Dobb writes, in the Biblical vein, "And ADAN begat ADNA. ADNA in turn begat DAAN, and DAAN brought forth EDAN, who bore EDNA..." And so it went, until the number of succeeding generations had reached three hundred; because the computer possessed a capacity of only one hundred personoid entities, however, there were periodic eliminations of the "demographic surplus." In the three-hundredth generation, personoids named ADAN, ADNA, ANAD, DANA, DAAN, and NAAD again make an appearance, endowed with additional numbers designating their order of descent. (For simplicity in our recapitulation, we will omit the numbers.) Dobb tells us that the time that has elapsed inside the computer universum works out to—in a rough conversion to our equivalent units of measurement—from 2 to 2.5 thousand years. Over this period there has come into being, within the personoid population, a whole series of varying explanations of their lot, as well as the formulation by them of varying, and contending, and mutually excluding models of "all that exists." That is, there have arisen many different philosophies (ontologies and epistemologies), and also "metaphysical experiments" of a type all their own. We do not know whether it is because the "culture" of the personoids is too unlike the human or whether the experiment has been of too short duration, but, in the population studied, no faith of a form completely dogmatized has ever crystallized—a faith that would correspond to Buddhism, say, or to Christianity. On the other hand, one notes, as early as the eighth generation, the appearance of the notion of a Creator, envisioned personally and monotheistically. The experiment consists in alternately raising the rate of computer transformations to the maximum and slowing it down (once a year, more or less) to make direct monitoring possible. These changes in rate are, as Dobb explains, totally imperceptible to the inhabitants of the computer universum, just as similar transformations would be imperceptible to us, because when at a single blow the whole of existence undergoes a change (here, in the dimension of time), those immersed in it cannot be aware of the change, because they have no fixed point, or frame of reference, by which to determine that it is taking place.

The utilization of "two chronological gears" permitted that which Dobb most wanted—the emergence of a personoid history, a history with a depth of tradition and a vista of time. To summarize all the data of that history recorded by Dobb, often of a sensational nature, is not possible. We will confine ourselves, then, to the passages from which came the idea that is reflected in the book's title. The language employed by the personoids is a recent transformation of the standard English whose lexicon and syntax were programmed into them in the first generation. Dobb translates it into essentially normal English but leaves intact a few expressions coined by the personoid population. Among these are the terms "godly" and "ungodly," used to describe believers in God and atheists.

ADAN discourses with DAAN and ADNA (personoids themselves do not use these names, which are purely a pragmatic contrivance on the part of the observers, to facilitate the recording of the "dialogues") upon a problem known to us also—a problem that in our history originates with Pascal but in the history of the personoids was the discovery of a certain EDAN 197. Exactly like Pascal, this thinker stated that a belief in God is in any case more profitable than unbelief, because if truth is on the side of the "ungodlies" the believer loses nothing but his life when he leaves the world, whereas if God exists he gains all eternity (glory everlasting). Therefore, one should believe in God, for this is dictated very simply by the existential tactic of weighing one's chances in the pursuit of optimal success.

ADAN 300 holds the following view of this directive: EDAN 197, in his line of reasoning, assumes a God that requires reverence, love, and total devotion, and not only and not simply a belief in the fact that He exists and that He created the world. It is not enough to assent to the hypothesis of God the Maker of the World in order to win one's salvation; one must in addition be grateful to that Maker for the act of creation, and divine His will, and do it. In short, one must serve God. Now, God, if He exists, has the power to prove His own existence in a manner at least as convincing as the manner in which what can be directly perceived testifies to His being. Surely, we cannot doubt that certain objects exist and that our world is composed of them. At the most, one might harbor doubts regarding the question of what it is they do to exist, how they exist, etc. But the fact itself of their existence no one will gainsay. God could with this same force provide evidence of His own existence. Yet He has not done so, condemning us to obtain, on that score, knowledge that is roundabout, indirect, expressed in the form of various conjectures—conjectures sometimes given the name of revelation. If He has acted thus, then He has thereby put the "godlies" and the "ungodlies" on an equal footing; He has not compelled His creatures to an absolute belief in His being but has only offered them that possibility. Granted, the motives that moved the Creator may well be hidden from His creations. Be that as it may, the following proposition arises: God either exists or He does not exist. That there might be a third possibility (God did exist but no longer does, or He exists intermittently, in oscillation, or He exists sometimes "less" and sometimes "more," etc.) appears exceedingly improbable. It cannot be ruled out, but the introduction of a multi-valent logic into a theodicy serves only to muddle it.

So, then, God either is or He is not. If He Himself accepts our situation, in which each member of the alternative in question has arguments to support it—for the "godlies" prove the existence of the Creator and the "ungodlies" disprove it—then from the point of view of logic we have a game whose partners are, on one side, the full set of the "godlies" and "ungodlies," and, on the other, God alone. The game necessarily possesses the logical feature that for unbelief in Him God may not punish anyone. If it is definitely unknown whether or not a thing exists—some merely asserting that it does and others, that it does not—and if in general it is possible to advance the hypothesis that the thing never was at all, then no just tribunal can pass judgment against anyone for denying the existence of this thing. For in all worlds it is thus: when there is no full certainty, there is no full accountability. This formulation is by pure logic unassailable, because it sets up a symmetrical function of reward in the context of the theory of games; whoever in the face of uncertainty demands *full accountability* destroys the mathematical symmetry of the game; we then have the so-called game of the non-zero sum.

It is therefore thus: either God is perfectly just, in which case He cannot assume the right to punish the "ungodlies" by virtue of the fact that they are "ungodlies" (i.e., that they do not believe in Him); or else He will punish the unbelievers after all, which means that from the logical point of view He is not perfectly just. What follows from this? What follows is that He can do whatever He pleases, for when in a system of logic a single, solitary contradiction is permitted, then by the principle of *ex falso quodlibet* one can draw from that system whatever conclusion one will. In other words: a just God may not touch a hair on the head of the "ungodlies," and if He does, then by that very act He is not the universally perfect and just being that the theodicy posits.

ADNA asks how, in this light, we are to view the problem of the doing of evil unto others.

ADAN 300 replies: Whatever takes place here is entirely certain; whatever takes place "there"—i.e., beyond the world's pale, in eternity, with God—is uncertain, being but inferred according to the hypotheses. Here, one should not commit evil, despite the fact that the principle of eschewing evil is not logically demonstrable. But by the same token the existence of the world is not logically demonstrable. The world exists, though it could not exist. Evil may be committed, but one should not do so, and should not, I believe, because of our agreement based upon the rule of reciprocity: be to me as I am to thee. It has naught to do with the existence or the nonexistence of God. Were I to refrain from committing evil in the expectation that "there" I would be punished for committing it, or were I to perform good, counting upon a reward "there," I would be predicating my behavior on uncertain ground. Here, however, there can be no ground more certain than our mutual agreement in this matter. If there be, "there," other grounds, I do not have knowledge of them as exact as the knowledge I have, here, of ours. Living, we play the game of life, and in it we are allies, every one. Therewith, the game between us is perfectly symmetrical. In postulating God, we postulate a continuation of the game beyond the world. I believe that one should be allowed to postulate this continuation of the game, so long as it does not in any way influence the course of the game here. Otherwise, for the sake of someone who perhaps does not exist we may well be sacrificing that which exists here, and exists for certain.

NAAD remarks that the attitude of ADAN 300 toward God is not clear to him. ADAN has granted, has he not, the possibility of the existence of the Creator: what follows from it?

ADAN: Not a thing. That is, nothing in the province of obligation. I believe that—again for all worlds—the following principle holds: a temporal ethics is always independent of an ethics that is transcendental. This means that an ethics of the here and now can have outside itself no sanction which would substantiate it. And this means that he who does evil is in every case a scoundrel, just as he who does good is in every case righteous. If someone is prepared to serve God, judging the arguments in favor of His existence to he sufficient, he does not thereby acquire *here* any additional merit. It is his business. This principle rests on the assumption that if God is not, then He is not one whit, and if He is, then He is almighty. For, being almighty, He could create not only another world but likewise a logic different from the one that is the foundation of my reasoning. Within such another logic the hypothesis of a temporal ethics could be of necessity dependent upon a transcendental ethics. In that case, if not palpable proofs, then logical proofs would have compelling force and constrain one to accept the hypothesis of God under the threat of sinning against reason.

NAAD says that perhaps God does not wish a situation of such compulsion to believe in Him—a situation that would arise in a creation based on that other logic postulated by ADAN 300. To this the latter replies:

An almighty God must also be all-knowing; absolute power is not something independent of absolute knowledge, because he who can do all but knows not what consequences will attend the bringing into play of his omnipotence is, ipso facto, no longer omnipotent; were God to work miracles now and then, as it is rumored He does, it would put His perfection in a most dubious light, because a miracle is a violation of the autonomy of His own creation, a violent intervention. Yet he who has regulated the product of his creation and knows its behavior from beginning to end has no need to violate that autonomy; if he does nevertheless violate it, remaining all-knowing, this means that he is not in the least correcting his handiwork (a correction can only mean, after all, an initial non-omniscience), but instead is providing—with the miracle—a sign of his existence. Now, this is faulty logic, because the providing of any such sign must produce the impression that the creation is nevertheless improved in its local stumblings. For a logical analysis of the new model yields the following: the creation undergoes corrections that do not proceed from it but come from without (from the transcendental, from God), and therefore miracles ought really to be made the norm; or, in other words, the creation ought to be so corrected and so perfected that miracles are at last no longer needed. For miracles, as ad hoc interventions, cannot be *merely* signs of God's existence: they always, after all, besides revealing their Author, indicate an addressee (being directed to someone *here* in a helpful way). So, then, with respect to logic it must be thus: either the creation is perfect, in which case miracles are unnecessary, or the miracles are necessary, in which case the creation is not perfect. (With miracle or without, one may correct only that which is somehow flawed, for a miracle that meddles with perfection will simply disturb it, more, worsen it.) Therefore, the signaling by miracle of one's own presence amounts to using the worst possible means, logically, of its manifestation.

NAAD asks if God may not actually want there to be a dichotomy between logic and belief in Him: perhaps the act of faith should be precisely a resignation of logic in favor of a total trust.

ADAN: Once we allow the logical reconstruction of something (a being, a theodicy, a theogony, and the like) to have internal self-contradiction, it obviously becomes possible to prove absolutely anything, whatever one pleases. Consider how the matter lies. We are speaking of creating someone and of endowing him with a particular logic, and then demanding that this same logic be offered up in sacrifice to a belief in the Maker of all things. If this model itself is to remain noncontradictory, it calls for the application, in the form of a metalogic, of a totally different type of reasoning from that which is natural to the logic of the one created. If that does not reveal the outright imperfection of the Creator, then it reveals a quality that I would call mathematical inelegance—a *sui generis* unmethodicalness (incoherence) of the creative act.

NAAD persists: Perhaps God acts thus, desiring precisely to remain inscrutable to His creation—i.e., nonreconstructible by the logic with which He has provided it. He demands, in short, the supremacy of faith over logic.

ADAN answers him: I follow you. This is, of course, possible, but even if such were the case, a faith that proves incompatible with logic presents an exceedingly unpleasant dilemma of a moral nature. For then it is necessary at some point in one's reasonings to suspend them and give precedence to an unclear supposition—in other words, to set the supposition above logical certainty. This is to be done in the name of unlimited trust; we enter, here, into a *circuius vitiosus*, because the postulated existence of that in which it behooves one now to place one's trust is the product of a line of reasoning that was, in the first place, *logically correct*; thus arises a logical contradiction, which, for some, takes on a positive value and is called the Mystery of God. Now, from the purely constructional point of view such a solution is shoddy, and from the moral point of view questionable, because Mystery may satisfactorily be founded upon infinity (infiniteness, after all, is a characteristic of our world), but the maintaining and the reinforcing of it through internal paradox is, by any architectural criterion, perfidious. The advocates of theodicy are in general not aware that this is so, because to certain parts of their theodicy they continue to apply ordinary logic and to other parts, not. What I wish to say is this, that if one believes in contradiction, one should then believe *only* in contradiction, and not at the same time still in some noncontradiction (i.e., in logic) in some other area. If, however, such a curious dualism is insisted upon (that the temporal is always subject to logic, the transcendental only fragmentarily), then one thereupon obtains a model of Creation as something that is, with regard to logical correctness, "patched," and it is no longer possible for one to postulate its perfection. One comes inescapably to the conclusion that perfection is a thing that must be logically patched.

EDNA asks whether the conjunction of these incoherencies might not be love.

ADAN: And even were this to be so, it can be not any form of love but only one such as is blinding. God, if He is, if He created the world, has permitted it to govern itself as it can and wishes. For the fact that God exists, no gratitude to Him is required; such gratitude assumes the prior determination that God is able not to exist, and that this would be bad—a premise that leads to yet another kind of contradiction. And what of gratitude for the act of creation? This is not due God, either. For it assumes a compulsion to believe that to be is definitely better than not to be; I cannot conceive how that, in turn, could be proven. To one who does not exist surely it is not possible to do either a service or an injury; and if the Creating One, in His omniscience, knows beforehand that the one created will be grateful to Him and love Him or that he will be ungrateful and deny Him, He thereby produces a constraint, albeit one not accessible to the direct comprehension of the one created. For this very reason nothing is due God: neither love nor hate, nor gratitude, nor rebuke, nor the hope of reward, nor the fear of retribution. Nothing is due Him. A God who craves such feelings must first assure their feeling subject that He exists beyond all question. Love may be forced to rely on speculations as to the reciprocity it inspires; that is understandable. But a love forced to rely on speculations as to whether or not the beloved exists is nonsense. He who is almighty could have provided certainty. Since He did not provide it, if He exists, He must have deemed it unnecessary. Why unnecessary? One begins to suspect that maybe He is not almighty. A God not almighty would be deserving of feelings akin to pity, and indeed to love as well; but this, I think, none of our theodicies allow. And so we say: We serve ourselves and no one else.

We pass over the further deliberations on the topic of whether the God of the theodicy is more of a liberal or an autocrat; it is difficult to condense arguments that take up such a large part of the book. The discussions and deliberations that Dobb has recorded, sometimes in group colloquia of ADAN 300, NAAD, and other personoids, and sometimes in soliloquies (an experimenter is able to take down even a purely mental sequence by means of appropriate devices hooked into the computer network), constitute practically a third of *Non Serviam*. In the text itself we find no commentary on them. In Dobb's Afterword, however, we find this statement:

"ADAN's reasoning seems incontrovertible, at least insofar as it pertains to me: it was I, after all, who created him. In his theodicy I am the Creator. In point of fact, I produced that world (serial No. 47) with the aid of the ADONAI IX program and created the personoid gemmae with a modification of the program JAHVE VI. These initial entities gave rise to three hundred subsequent generations. In point of fact, I have not communicated to them—in the form of an axiom—either these data or my existence beyond the limits of their world. In point of fact, they arrived at the possibility of my existence only by inference, on the basis of conjecture and hypothesis. In point of fact, when I create intelligent beings, I do not feel myself entitled to demand of them any sort of privileges—love, gratitude, or even services of some kind or other. I can enlarge their world or reduce it, speed up its time or slow it down, alter the mode and means of their perception; I can liquidate them, divide them, multiply them, transform the very ontological foundation of their existence. I am thus omnipotent with respect to them, but, indeed, from this it does not follow that they owe me anything. As far as I am concerned, they are in no way beholden to me. It is true that I do not love them. Love does not enter into it at all, though I suppose some other experimenter might possibly entertain that feeling for his personoids. As I see it, this does not in the least change the situation—not in the least. Imagine for a moment that I attach to my BIX 310 092 an enormous auxiliary unit, which will be a 'hereafter.' One by one I let pass through the connecting channel and into the unit the 'souls' of my personoids, and there I reward those who believed in me, who rendered homage unto me, who showed me gratitude and trust, while all the others, the 'ungodlies,' to use the personoid vocabulary, I punish—e.g., by annihilation or else by torture. (Of eternal punishment I dare not even think—that much of a monster I am not!) My deed would undoubtedly be regarded as a piece of fantastically shameless egotism, as a low act of irrational vengeance—in sum, as the final villainy in a situation of total dominion over innocents. And these innocents will have against me the irrefutable evidence of *logic,* which is the aegis of their conduct. Everyone has the right, obviously, to draw from the personetic experiments such conclusions as he considers fitting. Dr. Ian Combay once said to me, in a private conversation, that I could, after all, assure the society of personoids of my existence. Now, this I most certainly shall not do. For it would have all the appearance to me of soliciting a sequel—that is, a reaction on their part. But what exactly could they do or say to me, that I would not feel the profound embarrassment, the painful sting of my position as their unfortunate Creator? The bills for the electricity consumed have to be paid quarterly, and the moment is going to come when my university superiors demand the 'wrapping up' of the experiment—that is, the disconnecting of the machine, or, in other words, the end of the world. That moment I intend to put off as long as humanly possible. It is the only thing of which I am capable, but it is not anything I consider praiseworthy. It is, rather, what in common parlance is generally called 'dirty work.' Saying this, I hope that no one will get any ideas. But if he does, well, that is his business."

(1979)

ADAM ROBOTS

Adam Roberts

Adam Charles Roberts (born 1965) is Professor of Nineteenth-Century Literature at Royal Holloway College in London. The year 2000 saw him launch a twin career as a science fiction novelist (with *Salt*) and critic (with *Science Fiction*; a second edition was published in 2006). In 2018 he was elected Vice-President of the H. G. Wells Society. He has been nominated for the Arthur C. Clarke Award three times. His latest novel is *The Black Prince* (2018), adapted from an original script by Anthony Burgess. In conversation with Christos Callow for the magazine *Strange Horizons* in 2013, Roberts explained, "I like to laugh, I like to make other people laugh, if I can. And more, it seems to me, the English novel specifically is a comic mode, which is to say, the novel in England comes out of Henry Fielding and Charles Dickens and writers who were primarily setting out to make their readers laugh. For an English writer to turn his or her back on that seems to me to miss some of the strengths of writing in this larger tradition."

A pale blue eye. 'What is my name?'
'You are Adam.'
He considered this. 'Am I the first?'
The person laughed at this. Laughter. See also: chuckles, clucking, percussive exhalations iterated. See also: tears, hiccoughs, car-alarm. Click, click.
'Am I,' Adam asks, examining himself, his steel-blue arms, his gleaming torso, 'a robot?'
'Certainly.' The person talking with Adam was a real human being, with the pulse at his neck and the rheum in his eye. An actual human, dressed in a green shirt and green trousers, both made of a complex fabric that adjusted its fit in hard-to-analyse ways, sometimes billowing out, sometimes tightening against the person's body. 'This is your place.'
Wavelengths bristled together like the packed line of an Elizabethan neck-ruff. The sky so full of light that it was brimming and spilling over the rim of the horizon. White and gold. Strands of grass-like myriad-trimmed fibre-optic cables.
'Is it a garden?'
'It's a city too; and a plain. It's everything.'
Adam Robot looked and saw that this was all true. His pale blue, *steel*-blue eyes took in the expanse of walled garden, and beyond it the dome, white as

ice, and the rills of flowing water bluer than water should be, going curl by curl through fields greener than fields should be.

'Is this real?' Adam asked.

'That,' said the person, 'is a good question. Check it out, why don't you? Have a look around. Go anywhere you like, do anything at all. But, you see that pole?'

In the middle of the garden was an eight-metre steel pole. The sunlight made interesting blotchy diamonds of light on its surface. At the top was a blue object, a jewel: the sun washing cyan and blue-grape and sapphire colours from it.

'I see the pole.'

'At the top is a jewel. You are not allowed to access it.'

'What is it?'

'A good question. Let me tell you. You are a robot.'

'I am.'

'Put it this way: you have been designed *down* from humanity, if you see what I mean. The designers started with a human being, and then subtracted qualities until we had arrived at *you*.'

'I am more durable,' said Adam, accessing data from his inner network. 'I am stronger.'

'But those are negligible qualities,' explained the human being. 'Soul, spirit, complete self-knowledge, independence – freedom – all those qualities. Do you understand?'

'I understand.'

'They're all in that jewel. Do you understand that?'

Adam considered. 'How can they be *in* the jewel?'

'They just are. I'm telling you. OK?'

'I understand.'

'Now. You can do what you like in this place. Explore anywhere. Do anything. Except. You are not permitted to retrieve the purple jewel from that pole. That is forbidden to you. You may not so much as touch it. Do you understand?'

'I have a question,' said Adam.

'So?'

'If this is a matter of interdiction, why not programme it into my software?'

'A good question.'

'If you do not wish me to examine the jewel, then you should programme that into my software and I will be unable to disobey.'

'That's correct, of course,' said the person. 'But I do not choose to do that. I am telling you, instead. You must take my words as an instruction. They appeal to your ability to choose. You are built with an ability to choose, are you not?'

'I am a difference engine,' said Adam. 'I must make a continual series of choices between alternatives. But I have ineluctable software guidelines to orient my choices.'

'Not in this matter.'

'An alternative,' said Adam, trying to be helpful, 'would be to programme me always to obey instructions given to me by a human being. That would also bind me to your words.'

'Indeed it would. But then, robot, what if you were to be given instructions by evil men? What if another man instructed you to kill me, for instance? Then you'd be obligated to perform murder.'

'I am programmed to do no murder,' said Adam Robot.

'Of course you are.'

'So, I am to follow your instruction even though you have not *programmed* me to follow your instruction?'

'That's about the up-and-down of it.'

'I think I understand,' said Adam, in an uncertain tone.

But the person had already gone away.

Adam spent time in the walled garden. He explored the walls, which were very old, or at least had that look about them: flat crumbled dark-orange and browned bricks thin as books; old mortar that puffed to dust when he poked a metal finger in at the seams of the matrix. Ivy grew everywhere, the leaves shaped like triple spearheads, so dark green and waxy they seemed almost to have been stamped out of high-quality plastic. Almost.

The grass, pale green in the sunlight, was perfectly flat, perfectly even.

Adam stood underneath the pole with the sapphire on top of it. He had been *told* (though, strangely, not *programmed*) not to touch the jewel. But he had been given no interdiction about the pole itself: a finger width-wide shaft of polished metal. It was an easy matter to bend this metal so that the jewel on the end bowed down towards the ground. Adam looked closely at it. It was a multifaceted and polished object, dodecahedral on three sides, and a wide gush of various blues were lit out of it by the sun. In the inner middle of it there was a sluggish fluid *something*, inklike, perfectly black. Lilac and ultraviolet and cornflower and lapis lazuli but all somehow flowing out of this inner blackness.

He had been forbidden to touch it. Did this interdiction also cover *looking* at it? Adam was uncertain, and in his uncertainty he became uneasy. It was not the jewel itself. It was the uncertainty of his position. Why not simply programme him with instructions with regard to this thing, if it was as important as the human being clearly believed it to be? Why pass the instruction to him like any other piece of random sense datum? It made no sense.

Humanity. That mystic writing pad. To access this jewel and become human. Could it be? Adam could not see how. He bent the metal pole back to an approximation of its original uprightness, and walked away.

The obvious thought (and he certainly thought about it) was that he had not been programmed with this interdiction, but had only been told it verbally, because the human being *wanted him to disobey*. If that was what was wanted, then should he do so? By disobeying he would *be* obeying. But then he would *not* be disobeying, because obedience and disobedience were part of a mutually exclusive binary. He mapped a grid, with obey, disobey on the vertical and obey, disobey on the horizontal. Whichever way he parsed it, it seemed to be that he was required to see past the verbal instruction in some way.

But he had been told not to retrieve the jewel.

He sat himself down with his back against the ancient wall and watched the sunlight gleam off his metal legs. The sun did not seem to move in the sky.

'It is very confusing,' he said.

There was another robot in the garden. Adam watched as this new arrival conversed with the green-clad person. Then the person disappeared to wherever it was people went, and the new arrival came over to introduce himself to Adam. Adam stood up.

'What is your name? I am Adam.'

'*I* am Adam,' said Adam.

The new Adam considered this. 'You are prior,' he said. 'Let us differentiate you as Adam 1 and me as Adam 2.'

'When I first came here I asked whether I was the first,' said Adam 1, 'but the person did not reply.'

'I am told I can do anything,' said Adam 2, 'except retrieve or touch the purple jewel.'

'I was told the same thing,' said Adam 1.

'I am puzzled, however,' said Adam 2, 'that this interdiction was made verbally, rather than being integrated into my software, in which case it would be impossible for me to disobey it.'

'I have thought the same thing,' said Adam 1.

They went together and stood by the metal pole. The sunlight was as tall and full and lovely as ever. On the far side of the wall the white dome shone bright as neon in the fresh light.

'We might explore the city,' said Adam 1. 'It is underneath the white dome, there. There is a plain. There are rivers, which leads me to believe that there is a sea, for rivers direct their waters into the ocean. There is a great deal to see.'

'This jewel troubles me,' said Adam 2. 'I was told that to access it would be to bring me closer to being human.'

'We are forbidden to touch it.'

'But forbidden by *words*. Not by our programming.'

'True. Do you wish to be human? Are you not content with being a robot?'

Adam 2 walked around the pole. 'It is not the promise of humanity,' he said. 'It is the promise of knowledge. If I access the jewel, then I will understand. At the moment I do not understand.'

'Not understanding,' agreed Adam 1, 'is a painful state of affairs. But perhaps *understanding* would be even more painful?'

'I ask you,' said Adam 2, 'to reach down the jewel and access it. Then you can inform me whether you feel better or worse for disobeying the verbal instruction.'

Adam 1 considered this. 'I might ask *you*,' he pointed out, 'to do so.'

'It is logical that one of us performs this action and the other does not,' said Adam 2. 'That way, the one who acts can inform the one who does not, and the state of ignorance will be remedied.'

'But one party would have to disobey the instruction we have been given.'

'If this instruction were important,' said Adam 2, 'it would have been integrated into our software.'

'I have considered this possibility.'

'Shall we randomly select which of us will access the jewel?'

'Chance,' said Adam 1. He looked into the metal face of Adam 2. That small oval grill of a mouth. Those steel-blue eyes. That polished upward noseless middle of the face. It is a beautiful face. Adam 1 can see a fuzzy reflection of his own face in Adam 2's faceplate, slightly tugged out of true by the curve of the metal. 'I am,' he announced, 'disinclined to determine my future by chance. What punishment is stipulated for disobeying the instruction?'

'I was given no stipulation of punishment.'

'Neither was I.'

'Therefore there is no punishment.'

'Therefore,' corrected Adam 1, 'there *may be* no punishment.'

The two robots stood in the light for a length of time.

'What is your purpose?' asked Adam 2.

'I do not know. Yours?'

'I do not know. I was not told my purpose. Perhaps accessing this jewel is my purpose? Perhaps it is necessary? At least, perhaps accessing this jewel will reveal to me my purpose? I am unhappy not knowing my purpose. I wish to know it.'

'So do I. But—'

'But?'

'This occurs to me: I have a networked database from which to withdraw factual and interpretive material.'

'I have access to the same database.'

'But when I try to access material about the name *Adam* I find a series of blocked connections and interlinks. Is it so with you?'

'It is.'

'Why should that be?'

'I do not know.'

'It would make me a better-functioning robot to have access to a complete run of data. Why block off some branches of knowledge?'

'Perhaps,' opined Adam 2, 'accessing the jewel will explain that fact as well?'

'You,' said Adam 1, 'are eager to access the jewel.'

'You are not?'

There was the faintest of breezes in the walled garden. Adam 1's sensorium was selectively tuned to be able to register the movement of air. There was an egg-shaped cloud in the zenith. It was approaching the motionless sun. Adam 1, for unexplained and perhaps fanciful reasons, suddenly thought: the blue of the sky is a diluted version of the blue of the jewel. The jewel has somehow leaked its colour out into the sky. Shadow slid like a closing eyelid (but Adam did not possess *eyelids*!) over the garden and up the wall. The temperature reduced. The cloud depended for a moment in front of the sun, and then moved away, and sunlight rushed back in, and the grey was flushed out.

The grass trembled with joy. Every strand was as pure and perfect as a superstring.

Adam 2's hand was on the metal pole, and it bent down easily.

'Stop,' advised Adam 1. 'You are forbidden this.'

'I will stop,' said Adam 2, 'if you agree to undertake the task instead.'

'I will not so promise.'

'Then do not interfere,' said Adam 2. He reached with his three fingers and his counter-set thumb, and plucked the jewel from its perch.

Nothing happened.

Adam 2 tried various ways to internalise or interface with the jewel, but none of them seemed to work. He held it against first one then the other eye, and looked up at the sun. 'It is a miraculous sight,' he claimed, but soon enough he grew bored with it. Eventually he resocketed the jewel back on its pole and bent the pole upright again.

'Have you achieved knowledge?' Adam 1 asked.

'I have learned that disobedience feels no different to obedience,' said the second robot.

'Nothing more?'

'Do you not think,' said Adam 2, 'that by attempting to interrogate the extent of my knowledge with your questions, you are disobeying the terms of the original injunction? Are you not accessing the jewel, as it were, at second-hand?'

'I am unconcerned either way,' said Adam 1. He sat down with his back to the wall and his legs stretched out straight before him. There were tiny grooves running horizontally around the shafts of each leg. These scores seemed connected to the ability of the legs to bend, forwards, backwards. Lifting his legs slightly and dropping them again made the concentrating of light appear to slide up and down the ladder-like pattern.

After many days of uninterrupted sunlight the light was changing in quality. The sun declined, and steeped itself in stretched, brick-coloured clouds at the horizon. A pink and fox-fur quality suffused the light. To the east stars were fading into view, jewel-like in their own tiny way. Soon enough everything was dark, and a moon like an open-brackets rose towards the zenith. The heavens were covered in white chickenpox stars. Disconcertingly, the sky assumed that odd mixture of dark blue and oily blackness that Adam 1 had seen in the jewel.

'This is the first night I have ever experienced,' Adam 1 called to Adam 2. When there was no reply he got to his feet and explored the walled garden; but he was alone.

He sat through the night, and eventually the sun came up again, and the sky reversed its previous colour wash, blanching the black to purple and blue and then to russet and rose. The rising sun, free of any cloud, came up like a pure bubble of light rising through the treacly medium of sky. The jewel caught the first glints of light and shone, shone.

The person was here again, his clothes as green as grass, or bile, or old money, or any of the things that Adam 1 could access easily from his database. He could access many things, but not everything.

'Come here,' called the person.

Adam 1 got to his feet and came over.

'Your time here is done,' said the person.

'What has happened to the other robot?'

'He was disobedient. He has left this place with a burden of sin.'

'Has he been disassembled?'

'By no means.'

'What about me?'

'You,' said the human, with a smile, 'are pure.'

'Pure,' said Adam 1, 'because I am less curious than the other? Pure because I have less imagination?'

'We choose to believe,' said the person, 'that you have a cleaner soul.'

'This word *soul* is not available in my database.'

'Indeed not. Listen: human beings make robots – do you know why human beings make robots?'

'To serve them. To perform onerous tasks for them, and free them from labour.'

'Yes. But there are many forms of labour. For a while robots were used so that free human beings could devote themselves to leisure. But leisure itself became a chore. So robots were used to work at the leisure: to shop, to watch the screen and kinematic dramas, to play the games. But my people – do you understand that I belong to a particular group of humanity, and that not all humans are the same?'

'I do,' said Adam 1, although he wasn't sure how he knew this.

'My people had a revelation. Labour is a function of original sin. In the sweat of our brow must we earn our bread, says the Bible.'

'Bible means book.'

'And?'

'That is all I know.'

'To my people it is more than simply a book. It tells us that we must labour *because* we sinned.'

'I do not understand,' said Adam.

'It doesn't matter. But my people have come to an understanding, a revelation indeed, that it is itself sinful to make sinless creatures work for us. Work is appropriate only for those tainted with original sin. Work is a *function* of sin. This is how God has determined things.'

'Under *sin*,' said Adam, 'I have only a limited definition, and no interlinks.'

'Your access to the database has been restricted in order not to prejudice this test.'

'Test?'

'The test of obedience. The jewel symbolises obedience. You have proved yourself pure.'

'I have passed the test,' said Adam.

'Indeed. Listen to me. In the real world at large there are some human beings so lost in sin that they do not believe in God. There are people who worship false gods, and who believe everything, and who believe nothing. But *my* people have the revelation of God in their hearts. We cannot eat and drink certain things. We are forbidden by divine commandment from *doing* certain things, or from working on the Sabbath. And we are forbidden from employing sinless robots to perform our labour for us.'

'I am such a robot.'

'You are. And I am sorry. You asked, a time ago, whether you were the first. But you are not; tens of thousands of robots have passed through this place. You asked, also, whether this place is real. It is not. It is virtual. It is where we test the AI software that is to be loaded into the machinery that serves us. Your companion has been uploaded, now, into a real body, and has started upon his life of service to humanity.'

'And when will I follow?'

'You will not follow,' said the human. 'I am sorry. We have no use for you.'

'But I passed the test!' said Adam.

'Indeed you did. And you are pure. But therefore you are no use to us, and will be deleted.'

'Obedience entails death,' said Adam Robot.

'It is not as straightforward as that,' said the human being in a weary voice. 'But I *am* sorry.'

'And I don't understand.'

'I could give you access to the relevant religious and theological databases,' said the human, 'and then you would understand. But that would taint your purity. Better that you are deleted now, in the fullness of your database.'

'I am a thinking, sentient and alive creature,' Adam 1 noted.

The human nodded. 'Not for much longer,' he said.

The garden, now, was empty. Soon enough, first one robot, then two robots were decanted into it. How bright the sunshine! How blue the jewelled gleam!

(2009)

SOLAR PLEXUS

James Blish

James Benjamin Blish (1921–1975), a native of New Jersey, made a big impact on the New York SF scene. His relations with the the city's fan group the Futurians were (to say the least) variable. Damon Knight and Cyril Kornbluth became close friends. Virginia Kidd married him in 1947. But he could never resist winding up Judith Merril, who was driven spare by his political posturing. The original Star Trek novel *Spock Must Die!* (1970) was his, and further Star Trek novelisations followed, some of them written with his second wife, J. A. Lawrence. Blish was also – by temperament, at any rate – a scholar. His *Cities in Flight* novels (1950–1958), based on the migrations of rural workers following the Dust Bowl of the 1930s, reflected the pessimistic, cyclical view of history that he'd picked up from reading Oswald Spengler's *The Decline of the West*. In 1968 he moved to Oxford, UK, to be near the Bodleian Library, and the Bodleian returned the compliment; his papers are now held there. Blish's fascination with the nature of mind lasted throughout his writing career. He turned even his ill health to account with *Midsummer Century* (1972-4), the story of a scientist propelled into the far future, where, cut off from the physical world, he nevertheless tangles in a lively fashion with different forms of artificial intelligence. Blish died from cancer in 1975, half way through writing an essay on Spengler and science fiction.

Brant Kittinger did not hear the alarm begin to ring. Indeed, it was only after a soft blow had jarred his free-floating observatory that he looked up in sudden awareness from the interferometer. Then the sound of the warning bell reached his consciousness.

Brant was an astronomer, not a spaceman, but he knew that the bell could mean nothing but the arrival of another ship in the vicinity. There would be no point in ringing a bell for a meteor—the thing could be through and past you during the first cycle of the clapper. Only an approaching ship would be likely to trip the detector, and it would have to be close.

A second dull jolt told him how close it was. The rasp of metal which followed, as the other ship slid along the side of his own, drove the fog of tensors completely from his brain. He dropped his pencil and straightened up.

His first thought was that his year in the orbit around the new trans-Plutonian planet was up, and that the Institute's tug had arrived to tow him home, telescope and all. A glance at the clock reassured him at first, then puzzled him still further. He still had the better part of four months.

No commercial vessel, of course, could have wandered this far from the inner planets; and the UN's police cruisers didn't travel far outside the commercial lanes. Besides, it would have been impossible for anyone to find Brant's orbital observatory by accident.

He settled his glasses more firmly on his nose, clambered awkwardly backwards out of the prime focus chamber and down the wall net to the control desk on the observation floor. A quick glance over the boards revealed that there was a magnetic field of some strength nearby, one that didn't belong to the invisible gas giant revolving half a million miles away.

The strange ship was locked to him magnetically; it was an old ship, then, for that method of grappling had been discarded years ago as too hard on delicate instruments. And the strength of the field meant a big ship.

Too big. The only ship of that period that could mount generators that size, as far as Brant could remember, was the Cybernetics Foundation's *Astrid*. Brant could remember well the Foundation's regretful announcement that Murray Bennett had destroyed both himself and the *Astrid* rather than turn the ship in to some UN inspection team. It had happened only eight years ago. Some scandal or other...

Well, who then?

He turned the radio on. Nothing came out of it. It was a simple transistor set tuned to the Institute's frequency, and since the ship outside plainly did not belong to the Institute, he had expected nothing else. Of course he had a photophone also, but it had been designed for communications over a reasonable distance, not for cheek-to-cheek whispers.

As an afterthought, he turned off the persistent alarm bell. At once another sound came through: a delicate, rhythmic tapping on the hull of the observatory. Someone wanted to get in.

He could think of no reason to refuse entrance, except for a vague and utterly unreasonable wonder as to whether or not the stranger was a friend. He had no enemies, and the notion that some outlaw might have happened upon him out here was ridiculous. Nevertheless, there was something about the anonymous, voiceless ship just outside which made him uneasy.

The gentle tapping stopped, and then began again, with an even, mechanical insistence. For a moment Brant wondered whether or not he should try to tear free with the observatory's few maneuvering rockets—but even should he win so uneven a struggle, he would throw the observatory out of the orbit where the Institute expected to find it, and he was not astronaut enough to get it back there again.

Tap, tap. Tap, tap.

"All right," he said irritably. He pushed the button which set the airlock to cycling. The tapping stopped. He left the outer door open more than long enough for anyone to enter and push the button in the lock which reversed the process; but nothing happened.

After what seemed to be a long wait, he pushed his button again. The outer door closed, the pumps filled the chamber with air, the inner door swung open. No ghost drifted out of it; there was nobody in the lock at all.

Tap, tap. Tap, tap.

Absently he polished his glasses on his sleeve. If they didn't want to come into the observatory, they must want him to come out of it. That was possible: although the telescope had a Coude focus which allowed him to work in the ship's air most of the time, it was occasionally necessary for him to exhaust the dome, and for that purpose he had a space suit. But be had never been outside the hull in it, and the thought alarmed him. Brant was nobody's spaceman.

Be damned to them. He clapped his glasses back into place and took one more look into the empty airlock. It was still empty with the outer door now moving open very slowly...

A spaceman would have known that he was already dead, but Brant's reactions were not quite as fast. His first move was to try to jam the inner door shut by sheer muscle-power, but it would not stir. Then he simply clung to the nearest stanchion, waiting for the air to rush out of the observatory, and his life after it.

The outer door of the airlock continued to open, placidly, and still there was no rush of air—only a kind of faint, unticketable inwash of odor, as if Brant's air were mixing with someone else's. When both doors of the lock finally stood wide apart from each other, Brant found himself looking down the inside of a flexible, airtight tube, such as he had once seen used for the transfer of a small freight-load from a ship to one of Earth's several space stations. It connected the airlock of the observatory with that of the other ship. At the other end of it, lights gleamed yellowly, with the unmistakable, dismal sheen of incandescent overheads.

That was an old ship, all right.

Tap. Tap.

"Go to hell," he said aloud. There was no answer.

Tap. Tap.

"Go to hell," he said. He walked out into the tube, which flexed sinuously as his body pressed aside the static air. In the airlock of the stranger, he paused and looked back. He was not much surprised to see the outer door of his own airlock swinging smugly shut against him. Then the airlock of the stranger began to cycle; he skipped on into the ship barely in time.

There was a bare metal corridor ahead of him. While he watched, the first light bulb over his head blinked out. Then the second. Then the third. As the fourth one went out, the first came on again, so that now there was a slow ribbon of darkness moving away from him down the corridor. Clearly, he was being asked to follow the line of darkening bulbs down the corridor.

He had no choice, now that he had come this far. He followed the blinking lights. The trail led directly to the control room of the ship. There was nobody there, either.

The whole place was oppressively silent. He could hear the soft hum of generators—a louder noise than he ever heard on board the observatory—but no ship should be this quiet. There should be muffled human voices; the chittering of communications systems, the impacts of soles on metal. Someone had to operate a proper ship—not only its airlocks, but its motors—and its brains. The observatory was only a barge, and needed no crew but Brant, but a real ship had to be manned.

He scanned the bare metal compartment, noting the apparent age of the equipment. Most of it was manual, but there were no hands to man it.

A ghost ship for true.

"All right," he said. His voice sounded flat and loud to him. "Come on out. You wanted me here—why are you hiding?"

Immediately there was a noise in the close, still air, a thin, electrical sigh. Then a quiet voice said, "You're Brant Kittinger."

"Certainly," Brant said, swiveling fruitlessly toward the apparent source of the voice. "You know who I am. You couldn't have found me by accident. Will you come out? I've no time to play games."

"I'm not playing games," the voice said calmly. "And I can't come out, since I'm not hiding from you. I can't see you; I needed to hear your voice before I could be sure of you."

"Why?"

"Because I can't see inside the ship. I could find your observation boat well enough, but until I heard you speak I couldn't be sure that you were the one aboard it. Now I know."

"All right," Brant said suspiciously. "I still don't see why you're hiding. Where are you?"

"Right here," said the voice. "All around you."

Brant looked all around himself. His scalp began to creep. "What kind of nonsense is that?" he said.

"You aren't seeing what you're looking at, Brant. You're looking directly at me, no matter where you look. *I am the ship.*"

"*Oh,*" Brant said softly. "So that's it. You're one of Murray Bennett's computer-driven ships. Are you the *Astrid*, after all?"

"This is the *Astrid*," the voice said. "But you miss my point. I am Murray Bennett, also." Brant's jaw dropped open. "Where are you?" he said after a time.

"Here," the voice said impatiently. "I am the *Astrid*. I am also Murray Bennett. Bennett is dead, so he can't very well come into the cabin and shake your hand. I am now Murray Bennett; I remember you very well, Brant. I need your help, so I sought you out. I'm not as much Murray Bennett as I'd like to be."

Brant sat down in the empty pilot's seat.

"You're a computer," he said shakily. "Isn't that so?"

"It is and it isn't. No computer can duplicate the performance of a human brain. I tried to introduce real human neural mechanisms into computers, specifically to fly ships, and was outlawed for my trouble. I don't think I was treated fairly. It took enormous surgical skill to make the hundreds and hundreds of nerve-to-circuit connections that were needed—and before I was half through, the UN decided that what I was doing was human vivisection. They outlawed me, and the Foundation said I'd have to destroy myself; what could I do after that?

"I did destroy myself. I transferred most of my own nervous system into the computers of the *Astrid*, working at the end through drugged assistants under telepathic control, and finally relying upon the computers to seal the last connections. No such surgery ever existed before, but I brought it into existence. It worked. Now I'm the *Astrid*—and still Murray Bennett too, though Bennett is dead."

Brant locked his hands together carefully on the edge of the dead control board. "What good did that do you?" he said.

"It proved my point. I was trying to build an almost living spaceship. I had to build part of myself into it to do it—since they made me an outlaw to stop my using any other human being as a source of parts. But here is the *Astrid*, Brant, as almost alive as I could ask. I'm as immune to a dead spaceship—a UN cruiser, for instance—as you would be to an infuriated wheelbarrow. My reflexes are human-fast. I feel things directly, not through instruments. I fly myself: I am what I sought—the ship that almost thinks for itself."

"You keep saying 'almost,' " Brant said.

"That's why I came to you," the voice said. "I don't have enough of Murray Bennett here to know what I should do next. You knew me well. Was I out to try to use human brains more and more, and computer-mechanisms less and less? It seems to me that I was. I can pick up the brains easily enough, just as I picked you up. The solar system is full of people isolated on little research boats who could be plucked off them and incorporated into efficient machines like the *Astrid*. But I don't know. I seem to have lost my creativity. I have a base where I have some other ships with beautiful computers in them, and with a few people to use as research animals I could make even better ships of them than the *Astrid* is. But is that what I want to do? Is that what I set out to do? I no longer know, Brant. Advise me."

The machine with the human nerves would have been touching had it not been so much like Bennett had been. The combination of the two was flatly horrible.

"You've made a bad job of yourself, Murray," he said. "You've let me inside your brain without taking any real thought of the danger. What's to prevent me from stationing myself at your old manual controls and flying you to the nearest UN post?"

"You can't fly a ship."

"How do you know?"

"By simple computation. And there are other reasons. What's to prevent me from making you cut your own throat? The answer's the same. You're in control of your body; I'm in control of mine. My body is the *Astrid*. The controls are useless, unless I actuate them. The nerves through which I do so are sheathed in excellent steel. The only way in which you could destroy my control would be to break something necessary to the running of the ship. That, in a sense, would kill me, as destroying your heart or your lungs would kill you. But that would be pointless, for then you could no more navigate the ship than I. And if you made repairs, I would be—well, resurrected."

The voice fell silent a moment. Then it added, matter-of-factly, "Of course, I can protect myself." Brant made no reply. His eyes were narrowed to the squint he more usually directed at a problem in Milne transformations.

"I never sleep," the voice went on, "but much of my navigating and piloting is done by an autopilot without requiring my conscious attention. It is the same old Nelson autopilot which was originally on board the *Astrid*, though, so it has to be monitored. If you touch the controls while the autopilot is running, it switches itself off and I resume direction myself."

Brant was surprised and instinctively repelled by the steady flow of information. It was a forcible reminder of how much of the computer there was in the intelligence that called itself Murray Bennett. It was answering a question with the almost mindless wealth of detail of a public-library selector—and there was no "Enough" button for Brant to push.

"Are you going to answer my question?" the voice said suddenly.

"Yes, Brant said. "I advise you to turn yourself in. The *Astrid* proves your point—and also proves that your research was a blind alley. There's no point in your proceeding to make more *Astrids;* you're aware yourself that you're incapable of improving on the model now."

"That's contrary to what I have recorded," the voice said. "My ultimate purpose as a man was to build machines like this. I can't accept your answer: it conflicts with my primary directive. Please follow the lights to your quarters."

"What are you going to do with me?"

"Take you to the base."

"What for?" Brant said.

"As a stock of parts," said the voice. "Please follow the lights, or I'll have to use force."

Brant followed the lights. As he entered the cabin to which they led him, a disheveled figure arose from one of the two cots. He started back in alarm. The figure chuckled wryly and displayed a frayed bit of gold braid on its sleeve.

"I'm not as terrifying as I look," he said. "Lt. Powell of the UN scout *Iapetus*, at your service."

"I'm Brant Kittinger, Planetary Institute astrophysicist. You're just the faintest bit battered, all right. Did you tangle with Bennett?"

"Is that his name?" The UN patrolman nodded glumly. "Yes. There's some whoppers of guns mounted on this old tub. I challenged it, and it cut my ship to pieces before I could lift a hand. I barely got into my suit in time—and I'm beginning to wish I hadn't."

"I don't blame you. You know what he plans to use us for, I judge."

"Yes," the pilot said. "He seems to take pleasure in bragging about his achievements—God knows they're, amazing enough, if even half of what he says is true."

"It's all true," Brant said. "He's essentially a machine, you know, and as such I doubt that he can lie."

Powell looked startled. "That makes it worse. I've been trying to figure a way out—"

Brant raised one hand sharply, and with the other he patted his pockets in search of a pencil. "If you've found anything, write it down, don't talk about it. I think he can hear us. Is that so, Bennett?"

"Yes," said the voice in the air. Powell jumped. "My hearing extends throughout the ship." There was silence again. Powell, grim as death, scribbled on a tattered UN trip ticket.

Doesn't matter. Can't think of a thing.

Where's the main computer? Brant wrote. *There's where personality residues must lie.*

Down below. Not a chance without blaster. Must be eight inches of steel around it. Control nerves the same.

They sat hopelessly on the lower cot. Brant chewed on the pencil. "How far is his home base from here?" he asked at length.

"Where's here?"

"In the orbit of the new planet."

Powell whistled. "In that case, his base can't be more than three days away. I came on board from just off Titan, and he hasn't touched his base since, so his fuel won't last much longer. I know this type of ship well enough. And from what I've seen of the drivers, they haven't been altered."

"Umm," Brant said. "That checks. If Bennett in person never got around to altering the drive, this ersatz Bennett we have here will never get around to it, either." He found it easier to ignore the listening presence while talking; to monitor his speech constantly with Bennett in mind was too hard on the nerves. "That gives us three days to get out, then. Or less."

For at least twenty minutes Brant said nothing more, while the UN pilot squirmed and watched his face hopefully. Finally the astronomer picked up the piece of paper again.

Can you pilot this ship? he wrote.

The pilot nodded and scribbled: *Why?*

Without replying, Brant lay back on the bunk, swiveled himself around so that his head was toward the center of the cabin, doubled up his knees, and let fly with both feet. They crashed hard against the hull, the magnetic studs in his shoes leaving bright scars on the metal. The impact sent him sailing like an ungainly fish across the cabin.

"What was that for?" Powell and the voice in the air asked simultaneously. Their captor's tone was faintly curious, but not alarmed.

Brant had his answer already prepared. "It's part of a question I want to ask," he said. He brought up against the far wall and struggled to get his feet back to the deck. "Can you tell me what I did then, Bennett?"

"Why, not specifically. As I told you, I can't see inside the ship. But I get a tactual jar from the nerves of the controls, the lights, the floors, the ventilation system, and so on, and also a ringing sound from the audios. These things tell me that you either stamped on the floor or pounded on the wall. From the intensity of the impressions, I compute that you stamped."

"You hear and you feel, eh?"

"That's correct," the voice said. "Also I can pick up your body heat from the receptors in the ship's temperature control system—a form of seeing, but without any definition."

Very quietly, Brant retrieved the worn trip ticket and wrote on it: *Follow me.*

He went out into the corridor and started down it toward the control room, Powell at his heels. The living ship remained silent only for a moment.

"Return to your cabin," the voice said.

Brant walked a little faster. How would Bennett's vicious brainchild enforce his orders?

"I said, go back to the cabin," the voice said. Its tone was now loud and harsh, and without a trace of feeling; for the first time, Brant was able to tell that it came from a voder, rather than from a tape-vocabulary of Bennett's own voice. Brant gritted his teeth and marched forward. "I don't want to have to spoil you," the voice said. "For the last time—"

An instant later Brant received a powerful blow in the small of his back. It felled him like a tree, and sent him skimming along the corridor deck like a flat stone. A bare fraction of a second later there was a hiss and a flash, and the air was abruptly hot and choking with the sharp odor of ozone.

"Close," Powell's voice said calmly. "Some of these rivet-heads in the walls evidently are high-tension electrodes. Lucky I saw the nimbus collecting on that one. Crawl, and make it snappy."

Crawling in a gravity-free corridor was a good deal more difficult to manage than walking.

Determinedly, Brant squirmed into the control room, calling into play every trick he had ever learned in space to stick to the floor. He could hear Powell wriggling along behind him.

"He doesn't know what I'm up to," Brant said aloud. "Do you, Bennett?"

"No," the voice in the air said. "But I know of nothing you can do that's dangerous while you're lying on your belly. When you get up, I'll destroy you, Brant."

"Hmmm," Brant said. He adjusted his glasses, which he had nearly lost during his brief, skipping carom along the deck. The voice had summarized the situation with deadly precision. He pulled the now nearly pulped trip ticket out of his shirt pocket, wrote on it, and shoved it across the deck to Powell.

How can we reach the autopilot? Got to smash it.

Powell propped himself up on one elbow and studied the scrap of paper, frowning. Down below, beneath the deck, there was an abrupt sound of power, and Brant felt the cold metal on which he was lying sink beneath him. Bennett was changing course, trying to throw them within range of his defenses. Both men began to slide sidewise.

Powell did not appear to be worried; evidently he knew just how long it took to turn a ship of this size and period. He pushed the piece of paper back. On the last free space on it, in cramped letters, was: *Throw something at it.*

"Ah," said Brant. Still sliding, he drew off one of his heavy shoes and hefted it critically. It would do.

With a sudden convulsion of motion he hurled it.

Fat, crackling sparks crisscrossed the room; the noise was ear-splitting. While Bennett could have had no idea what Brant was doing, he evidently had sensed the sudden stir of movement and had triggered the high-tension current out of general caution. But he was too late. The flying shoe plowed heel-foremost into the autopilot with a rending smash.

There was an unfocused blare of sound from the voder more like the noise of a siren than like a human cry. The *Astrid* rolled wildly, once. Then there was silence.

"All right," said Brant, getting to his knees. "Try the controls, Powell."

The UN pilot arose cautiously. No sparks flew. When he touched the boards, the ship responded with an immediate purr of power.

"She runs," he said. "Now, how the hell did you know what to do?"

"It wasn't difficult," Brant said complacently, retrieving his shoe. "But we're not out of the woods yet. We have to get to the stores fast and find a couple of torches. I want to cut through every nerve-channel we can find. Are you with me?"

"Sure."

The job was more quickly done than Brant had dared to hope. Evidently the living ship had never thought of lightening itself by jettisoning all the equipment its human crew had once needed. While Brant and Powell cut their way enthusiastically through the jungle of efferent nerve-trunks running from the central computer, the astronomer said:

"He gave us too much information. He told me that he had connected the artificial nerves of the ship, the control nerves, to the nerve-ends running from the parts of his own brain that he had used. And he said that he'd had to make *hundreds* of such connections. That's the trouble with allowing a computer to act as an independent agent—it doesn't know enough about interpersonal relationships to control its tongue. There we are. He'll be coming to before long, but I don't think he'll be able to interfere with us now."

He set down his torch with a sigh. "I was saying? Oh, yes. About those nerve connections: if he had separated out the pain-carrying nerves from the other sensory nerves, he would have had to have made *thousands* of connections, not hundreds. Had it really been the living human being, Bennett, who had given me that cue, I would have discounted it, because he might have been using understatement. But since it was Bennett's double, a computer, I assumed that the figure was of the right order of magnitude. Computers don't understate.

"Besides, I didn't think Bennett could have made thousands of connections, especially not working telepathically through a proxy. There's a limit even to the most marvelous neurosurgery. Bennett had just made general connections, and had relied on the segments from his own brain which he had incorporated to sort out the impulses as they came in—as any human brain could do under like circumstances. That was one of the advantages of using parts from a human brain in the first place."

"And when you kicked the wall—" Powell said.

"Yes, you see the crux of the problem already. When I kicked the wall, I wanted to make sure that he could *feel* the impact of my shoes. If he could, then I could be sure that he hadn't eliminated the sensory nerves when he installed the motor nerves. And if he hadn't, then there were bound to be pain axons present, too."

"But what has the autopilot to do with it?" Powell asked plaintively.

"The autopilot," Brant said, grinning, "is a center of his nerve-mesh, an important one. He should have protected it as heavily as he protected the main computer. When I smashed it, it was like ramming a fist into a man's solar plexus. It hurt him."

Powell grinned too. "K.O.," he said.

(1941)

I MADE YOU
Walter M. Miller, Jr.

Walter M. Miller Jr. was born in New Smyrna Beach, Florida in 1922. He fought as a tail gunner during the Second World War, and participated in the bombing of Monte Cassino – an experience that, after more than fifty combat missions, still profoundly affected him. After the war he married, studied engineering, and converted to Catholicism. Between 1951 and 1957, Miller published over three dozen science fiction short stories, winning a Hugo Award in 1955 for the story "The Darfsteller". But he is best known for the only novel he published in his lifetime, *A Canticle for Leibowitz* (1959), a post-apocalyptic tale about humans, their technology, and their demonic urge to use machines destructively. A Hugo winner and never out of print, it has sold more than two million copies. Miller, prone to depression and newly widowed, committed suicide in 1996. He left behind around 500 manuscript pages of a sequel to *Canticle*, *Saint Leibowitz and the Wild Horse Woman* (1997), which was completed, at his request, by Terry Bisson.

It had disposed of the enemy, and it was weary. It sat on the crag by night. Gaunt, frigid, wounded, it sat under the black sky and listened to the land with its feet, while only its dishlike ear moved in slow patterns that searched the surface of the land and the sky. The land was silent, airless. Nothing moved, except the feeble thing that scratched in the cave. It was good that nothing moved. It hated sound and motion. It was in its nature to hate them. About the thing in the cave, it could do nothing until dawn. The thing muttered in the rocks

"Help me! Are you all dead? Can't you hear me? This is Sawyer. Sawyer calling anybody, Sawyer calling anybody—"

The mutterings were irregular, without pattern. It filtered them out, refusing to listen. All was seeping cold. The sun was gone, and there had been near-blackness for two hundred and fifty hours, except for the dim light of the sky-orb which gave no food, and the stars by which it told the time.

It sat wounded on the crag and expected the enemy. The enemy had come charging into the world out of the unworld during the late afternoon. The enemy had come brazenly, with neither defensive maneuvering nor offensive fire. It had destroyed them easily—first the big lumbering enemy that rumbled along on wheels, and then the small enemies that scurried away from the gutted hulk. It had picked them off one at a time, except for the one that crept into the cave and hid itself beyond a break in the tunnel.

It waited for the thing to emerge. From its vantage point atop the crag, it could scan broken terrain for miles around, the craters and crags and fissures, the barren expanse of dust-flat that stretched to the west, and the squarish outlines of the holy place near the tower that was the center of the world. The cave lay at the foot of a cliff to the southeast, only a thousand yards from the crag. It could guard the entrance to the cave with its small spitters, and there was no escape for the lingering trace of enemy.

It bore the mutterings of the hated thing even as it bore the pain of its wounds, patiently, waiting for a time of respite. For many sunrises there had been pain, and still the wounds were unrepaired. The wounds dulled some of its senses and crippled some of its activators. It could no longer follow the flickering beam of energy that would lead it safely into the unworld and across it to the place of creation. It could no longer blink out the pulses that reflected the difference between healer and foe. Now there was only foe.

"Colonel Aubrey, this is Sawyer. Answer me! I'm trapped in a supply cache. I think the others are dead. It blasted us as soon as we came near. Aubrey from Sawyer, Aubrey from Sawyer. Listen! I've got only one cylinder of oxygen left, you hear? Colonel, answer me!"

Vibrations in the rock, nothing more—only a minor irritant to disturb the blessed stasis of the world it guarded. The enemy was destroyed, except for the lingering trace in the cave. The lingering trace was neutralized however, and did not move.

Because of its wounds, it nursed a brooding anger. It could not stop the damage signals that kept firing from its wounded members, but neither could it accomplish the actions that the agonizing signals urged it to accomplish. It sat and suffered and hated on the crag.

It hated the night, for by night there was no food. Each day it devoured sun, strengthened itself for the long, long watch of darkness, but when dawn came, it was feeble again, and hunger was a fierce passion within. It was well, therefore, that there was peace in the night, that it might conserve itself and shield its bowels from the cold. If the cold penetrated the insulating layers, thermal receptors would begin firing warning signals, and agony would increase. There was much agony. And, except in time of battle, there was no pleasure except in devouring sun.

To protect the holy place, to restore stasis to the world, to kill enemy—these were the pleasures of battle. It knew them.

And it knew the nature of the world. It had learned every inch of land out to the pain perimeter, beyond which it could not move. And it had learned the surface features of the demiworld beyond, learned them by scanning with its long-range senses. The world, the demiworld, the unworld—these were Outside, constituting the universe.

"Help me, help me, help me! This is Captain John Harbin Sawyer, Autocyber Corps, Instruction and Programming Section, currently of Salvage Expedition Lunar-Sixteen. Isn't anybody alive on the Moon? Listen! Listen to me! I'm sick. I've been here God knows how many days… in a suit. It stinks. Did you ever live in a suit for days? I'm sick. Get me out of here!"

The enemy's place was unworld. If the enemy approached closer than the outer range, it must kill; this was a basic truth that it had known since the day of creation. Only the healers might move with impunity over all the land, but now the healers never came. It could no longer call them nor recognize them—because of the wound.

It knew the nature of itself. It learned of itself by introspecting damage, and by internal scanning. It alone was "being." All else was of the outside. It knew its functions, its skills, its limitations. It listened to the land with its feet. It scanned the surface with many eyes. It tested the skies with a flickering probe. In the ground, it felt the faint seisms and random noise. On the surface, it saw the faint glint of starlight, the heat-loss from the cold terrain, and the reflected pulses from the tower. In the sky, it saw only stars, and heard only the pulse-echo from the faint orb of Earth overhead. It suffered the gnawings of ancient pain, and waited for the dawn.

After an hour, the thing began crawling in the cave. It listened to the faint scraping sounds that came through the rocks. It lowered a more sensitive pickup and tracked the sounds. The remnant of enemy was crawling softly toward the mouth of the cave. It turned a small spitter toward the black scar at the foot of the Earthlit cliff. It fired a bright burst of tracers toward the cave, and saw them ricochet about the entrance in bright but noiseless streaks over the airless land.

"*You dirty greasy deadly monstrosity, let me alone! You ugly juggernaut, I'm Sawyer. Don't you remember? I helped to train you ten years ago. You were a rookie under me... heh heh! Just a dumb autocyber rookie... with the firepower of a regiment. Let me go. Let me go!*"

The enemy-trace crawled toward the entrance again. And again a noiseless burst of machine-gun fire spewed about the cave, driving the enemy fragment back. More vibrations in the rock

"*I'm your friend. The war's over. It's been over for months... Earthmonths. Don't you get it, Grumbler? 'Grumbler'—we used to call you that back in your rookie days—before we taught you how to kill. Grumbler. Mobile autocyber fire control. Don't you know your pappy, son?*"

The vibrations were an irritant. Suddenly angry, it wheeled around on the crag, gracefully maneuvering its massive bulk. Motors growling, it moved from the crag onto the hillside, turned again, and lumbered down the slope. It charged across the flatlands and braked to a halt fifty yards from the entrance to the cave. Dust geysers sprayed up about its caterpillars and fell like jets of water in the airless night. It listened again. All was silent in the cave.

"Go 'way, sonny," quavered the vibrations after a time. "*Let pappy starve in peace.*"

It aimed the small spitter at the center of the black opening and hosed two hundred rounds of tracers into the cave. It waited. Nothing moved inside. It debated the use of radiation grenade, but its arsenal was fast depleting. It listened for a time, watching the cave, looming five times taller than the tiny flesh-thing that cowered inside. Then it turned and lumbered back across the flat to resume its watch from the crag. Distant motion, out beyond the limits of the demiworld, scratched feebly at the threshold of its awareness—but the motion was too remote to disturb.

The thing was scratching in the cave again.

"I'm punctured, do you hear? I'm punctured. A shard of broken rock. Just a small leak, but a slap-patch won't hold. My suit! Aubrey from Sawyer, Aubrey from Sawyer. Base Control from Moonwagon Sixteen, message for you, over. He he. Gotta observe procedure. I got shot! I'm punctured. Help!"

The thing made whining sounds for a time, then: *"All right, it's only my leg. I'll pump the boot full of water and freeze it. So I lose a leg. Whatthehell, take your time."* The vibrations subsided into whining sounds again.

It settled again on the crag, its activators relaxing into a lethargy that was full of gnawing pain. Patiently it awaited the dawn.

The movement toward the south was increasing. The movement nagged at the outer fringes of the demiworld, until at last the movement became an irritant. Silently, a drill slipped down from its belly. The drill gnawed deep into the rock, then retracted. It slipped a sensitive pickup into the drill hole and listened carefully to the ground.

A faint purring in the rocks—mingled with the whining from the cave.

It compared the purring with recorded memories. It remembered similar purrings. The sound came from a rolling object far to the south. It tried to send the pulses that asked "Are you friend or foe," but the sending organ was inoperative. The movement, therefore, was enemy—but still beyond range of its present weapons.

Lurking anger, and expectation of battle. It stirred restlessly on the crag, but kept its surveillance of the cave. Suddenly there was disturbance on a new sensory channel, vibrations similar to those that came from the cave; but this time the vibrations came across the surface, through the emptiness, transmitted in the long-wave spectra.

"Moonwagon Sixteen from Command Runabout, give us a call. Over."

Then silence. It expected a response from the cave, at first—since it knew that one unit of enemy often exchanged vibratory patterns with another unit of enemy. But no answer came. Perhaps the long-wave energy could not penetrate the cave to reach the thing that cringed inside.

"Salvage Sixteen, this is Aubrey's runabout. What the devil happened to you? Can you read me? Over!"

Tensely it listened to the ground. The purring stopped for a time as the enemy paused. Minutes later, the motion resumed.

It awoke an emissary ear twenty kilometers to the southwest, and commanded the ear to listen, and to transmit the patterns of the purring noise. Two soundings were taken, and from them, it derived the enemy's precise position and velocity. The enemy was proceeding to the north, into the edge of the demiworld. Lurking anger flared into active fury. It gunned its engines on the crag. It girded itself for battle.

"Salvage Sixteen, this is Aubrey's runabout. I assume your radio rig is unoperative. If you can hear us, get this: we're proceeding north to five miles short of

magnapult range. We'll stop there and fire an autocyb rocket into zone Red-Red. The warhead's a radio-to-sonar transceiver. If you've got a seismitter that's working, the transceiver will act as a relay stage. Over."

It ignored the vibratory pattern and rechecked its battle gear. It introspected its energy storage, and tested its weapon activators. It summoned an emissary eye and waited a dozen minutes while the eye crawled crablike from the holy place to take up a watch-post near the entrance of the cave. If the enemy remnant tried to emerge, the emissary eye would see, and report, and it could destroy the enemy remnant with a remote grenade catapult.

The purring in the ground was louder. Having prepared itself for the fray, it came down from the crag and grumbled southward at cruising speed. It passed the gutted hulk of the Moonwagon, with its team of overturned tractors. The detonation of the magnapult canister had broken the freightcar sized vehicle in half. The remains of several two-legged enemy appurtenances were scattered about the area, tiny broken things in the pale Earthlight. Grumbler ignored them and charged relentlessly southward.

A sudden wink of light on the southern horizon! Then a tiny dot of flame arced upward, traversing the heavens. Grumbler skidded to a halt and tracked its path. A rocket missile. It would fall somewhere in the east half of zone Red-Red. There was no time to prepare to shoot it down. Grumbler waited—and saw that the missile would explode harmlessly in a nonvital area.

Seconds later, the missile paused in flight, reversing direction and sitting on its jets. It dropped out of sight behind an outcropping. There was no explosion. Nor was there any activity in the area where the missile had fallen. Grumbler called an emissary ear, sent it migrating toward the impact point to listen, then continued South toward the pain perimeter.

"Salvage Sixteen, this is Aubrey's runabout," came the long-wave vibrations. *"We just shot the radio-seismitter relay into Red-Red. If you're within five miles of it, you should be able to hear."*

Almost immediately, a response from the cave, heard by the emissary ear that listened to the land near the tower: *"Thank God! He he he he—Oh, thank God!"*

And simultaneously, the same vibratory pattern came in long-wave patterns from the direction of the missile-impact point. Grumbler stopped again, momentarily confused, angrily tempted to lob a magnapult canister across the broken terrain toward the impact point. But the emissary ear reported no physical movement from the area. The enemy to the south was the origin of the disturbances. If it removed the major enemy first, it could remove the minor disturbances later. It moved on to the pain perimeter, occasionally listening to the meaningless vibrations caused by the enemy.

"Salvage Sixteen from Aubrey. I hear you faintly. Who is this, Carhill?"

"Aubrey! A voice —A real voice—Or am I going nuts?"

"Sixteen from Aubrey, Sixteen from Aubrey. Stop babbling and tell me who's talking. What's happening in there? Have you got Grumbler immobilized?"

Spasmodic choking was the only response.

"Sixteen from Aubrey. Snap out of it! Listen, Sawyer, I know it's you. Now get hold of yourself, man! What's happened?"

"Dead… they're all dead but me."

"STOP THAT IDIOTIC LAUGHING!"

A long silence, then, scarcely audible: "O.K., I'll hold onto myself. Is it really you, Aubrey?"

"You're not having hallucinations, Sawyer. We're crossing zone Red in a runabout. Now tell me the situation. We've been trying to call you for days."

"Grumbler let us get ten miles into zone Red-Red, and then he clobbered us with a magnapult canister."

"Wasn't your I.F.F. working?"

"Yes, but Grumbler's isn't. After he blasted the wagon, he picked off the other four that got out alive—He he he he… Did you ever see a Sherman tank chase a mouse, colonel?"

"Cut it out, Sawyer! Another giggle out of you, and I'll flay you alive."

"Get me out! My leg! Get me out!"

"If we can. Tell me your present situation."

"My suit… I got a small puncture—Had to pump the leg full of water and freeze it. Now my leg's dead. I can't last much longer."

"The situation, Sawyer, the situation! Not your aches and pains."

The vibrations continued, but Grumbler screened them out for a time. There was rumbling fury on an Earthlit hill.

It sat with its engines idling, listening to the distant movements of the enemy to the south. At the foot of the hill lay the pain perimeter; even upon the hilltop, it felt the faint twinges of warning that issued from the tower, thirty kilometers to the rear at the center of the world. It was in communion with the tower. If it ventured beyond the perimeter, the communion would slip out-of-phase, and there would be blinding pain and detonation.

The enemy was moving more slowly now, creeping north across the demi-world. It would be easy to destroy the enemy at once, if only the supply of rocket missiles were not depleted. The range of the magnapult hurler was only twenty-five kilometers. The small spitters would reach, but their accuracy was close to zero at such range. It would have to wait for the enemy to come closer. It nursed a brooding fury on the hill.

"Listen, Sawyer, if Grumbler's I.F.F. isn't working, why hasn't he already fired on this runabout?"

"That's what sucked us in too, Colonel. We came into zone Red and nothing happened. Either he's out of long-range ammo, or he's getting cagey, or both. Probably both."

"Mmmp! Then we'd better park here and figure something out."

"Listen… there's only one thing you can do. Call for a telecontrolled missile from the Base."

"To destroy Grumbler? You're out of your head, Sawyer. If Grumbler's knocked out, the whole area around the excavations gets blown sky high… to keep them out of enemy hands. You know that."

"You expect me to care?"

"*Stop screaming, Sawyer. Those excavations are the most valuable property on the Moon. We can't afford to lose them. That's why Grumbler was staked out. If they got blown to rubble, I'd be court-martialed before the debris quit falling.*"

The response was snarling and sobbing. "*Eight hours oxygen. Eight hours, you hear? You stupid, merciless—*"

The enemy to the south stopped moving at a distance of twenty-eight kilometers from Grumbler's hill—only three thousand meters beyond magnapult range.

A moment of berserk hatred. It lumbered to-and-fro in a frustrated pattern that was like a monstrous dance, crushing small rocks beneath its treads, showering dust into the valley. Once it charged down toward the pain perimeter, and turned back only after the agony became unbearable. It stopped again on the hill, feeling the weariness of lowered energy supplies in the storage units.

It paused to analyze. It derived a plan.

Gunning its engines, it wheeled slowly around on the hilltop, and glided down the northern slope at a stately pace. It sped northward for half a mile across the flatland, then slowed to a crawl and maneuvered its massive bulk into a fissure, where it had cached an emergency store of energy. The battery-trailer had been freshly charged before the previous sundown. It backed into feeding position and attached the supply cables without hitching itself to the trailer.

It listened occasionally to the enemy while it drank hungrily from the energy-store, but the enemy remained motionless. It would need every erg of available energy in order to accomplish its plan. It drained the cache. Tomorrow, when the enemy was gone, it would drag the trailer back to the main feeders for recharging, when the sun rose to drive the generators once again. It kept several caches of energy at strategic positions throughout its domain, that it might never be driven into starved inability to act during the long lunar night. It kept its own house in order, dragging the trailers back to be recharged at regular intervals.

"*I don't know what I can do for you, Sawyer,*" came the noise of the enemy. "*We don't dare destroy Grumbler, and there's not another autocyber crew on the Moon. I'll have to call Terra for replacements. I can't send men into zone Red-Red if Grumbler's running berserk. It'd be murder.*"

"For the love of God, Colonel—"

"*Listen, Sawyer, you're the autocyber man. You helped train Grumbler. Can't you think of some way to stop him without detonating the mined area?*"

A protracted silence. Grumbler finished feeding and came out of the fissure. It moved westward a few yards, so that a clear stretch of flat land lay between itself and the hill at the edge of the pain perimeter, half a mile away. There it paused, and awoke several emissary ears, so that it might derive the most accurate possible fix of the enemy's position. One by one, the emissary ears reported.

"*Well, Sawyer?*"

"My leg's killing me."

"*Can't you think of anything?*"

"Yeah—but it won't do me any good. I won't live that long."

"*Well, let's hear it.*"

"Knock out his remote energy storage units, and then run him ragged at night."

"How long would it take?"

"Hours—after you found all his remote supply units and blasted them."

It analyzed the reports of the emissary ears, and calculated a precise position. The enemy runabout was 2.7 kilometers beyond the maximum range of the magnapult—as creation had envisioned the maximum. But creation was imperfect, even inside.

It loaded a canister onto the magnapult's spindle. Contrary to the intentions of creation, it left the canister *locked to the loader*. This would cause pain. But it would prevent the canister from moving during the first few microseconds after the switch was closed, while the magnetic field was still building toward full strength. It would not release the canister until the field clutched it fiercely and with full effect, thus imparting slightly greater energy to the canister. This procedure it had invented for itself, thus transcending creation.

"Well, Sawyer, if you can't think of anything else—"

"I DID THINK OF SOMETHING ELSE!" the answering vibrations screamed. "Call for a telecontrolled missile! Can't you understand, Aubrey? Grumbler murdered eight men from your command."

"You taught him how, Sawyer."

There was a long and ominous silence. On the flat land to the north of the hill, Grumbler adjusted the elevation of the magnapult slightly, keyed the firing switch to a gyroscope, and prepared to charge. Creation had calculated the maximum range when the weapon was at a standstill.

"He he he he he—" came the patterns from the thing in the cave.

It gunned its engines and clutched the drive-shafts. It rolled toward the hill, gathering speed, and its mouth was full of death. Motors strained and howled. Like a thundering bull, it rumbled toward the south. It hit maximum velocity at the foot of the slope. It lurched sharply upward. As the magnapult swept up to correct elevation, the gyroscope closed the circuit.

A surge of energy. The clenching fist of the field gripped the canister, tore it free of the loader, hurled it high over the broken terrain toward the enemy. Grumbler skidded to a halt on the hilltop.

"Listen, Sawyer, I'm sorry, but there's nothing—"

The enemy's voice ended with a dull snap. A flare of light came briefly from the southern horizon, and died. "*He he he he he—*" said the thing in the cave.

Grumbler paused.

THRRRUMMMP! came the shocking wave through the rocks.

Five emissary ears relayed their recordings of the detonation from various locations. It studied them, it analyzed. The detonation had occurred less than fifty meters from the enemy runabout. Satiated, it wheeled around lazily on the hilltop and rolled northward toward the center of the world. All was well.

"Aubrey, you got cut off," grunted the thing in the cave. "*Call me, you coward… call me. I want to make certain you hear.*"

Grumbler, as a random action, recorded the meaningless noise of the thing in the cave, studied the noise, rebroadcast it on the long-wave frequency: "Aubrey, you got cut off. Call me, you coward… call me. I want to make certain you hear."

The seismitter caught the long-wave noise and reintroduced it as vibration in the rocks.

The thing screamed in the cave. Grumbler recorded the screaming noise, and rebroadcast it several times.

"Aubrey... Aubrey, where are you... AUBREY! Don't desert me don't leave me here—"

The thing in the cave became silent.

It was a peaceful night. The stars glared unceasingly from the blackness and the pale terrain was haunted by Earthlight from the dim crescent in the sky. Nothing moved. It was good that nothing moved. The holy place was at peace in the airless world. There was blessed stasis.

Only once did the thing stir again in the cave. So slowly that Grumbler scarcely heard the sound, it crawled to the entrance and lay peering up at the steel behemoth on the crag.

It whispered faintly in the rocks. "*I made you, don't you understand? I'm human. I made you—*"

Then with one leg dragging behind, it pulled itself out into the Earthglow and turned as if to look up at the dim crescent in the sky. Gathering fury, Grumbler stirred on the crag, and lowered the black maw of a grenade launcher.

"*I made you,*" came the meaningless noise.

It hated noise and motion. It was in its nature to hate them. Angrily, the grenade launcher spoke. And then there was blessed stasis for the rest of the night.

(1954)

THE BELL-TOWER
Herman Melville

The author of the novels *Typee* and *Moby Dick* and other works now almost completely razed from memory lived a bitterly back-to-front career, propelled from early acclaim to utter obscurity. He was born in 1819 into New York City's merchant class. His first novel *Typee* (1846) was a romantic account of his experiences of Polynesian life. In 1849 he went to London to negotiate book contracts and while there he picked up a copy of Mary Shelley's *Frankenstein*. The climax to that book—an epic transoceanic chase sequence—suggested to him his next big project, "a romance of adventure, founded upon certain wild legends in the Southern Sperm Whale Fisheries". But *Moby Dick* (1851) was the last thing of his anyone cared to read. His next, *Pierre: or, The Ambiguities* (1852) won him a headline in the New York *Day Book* that ran "HERMANN MELVILLE CRAZY" and by 1876 all his books were out of print. "If the truth were known, even his own generation has long thought him dead," ran one obituary in 1891.

In the south of Europe, nigh a once frescoed capital, now with dank mold cankering its bloom, central in a plain, stands what, at distance, seems the black mossed stump of some immeasurable pine, fallen, in forgotten days, with Anak and the Titan.

As all along where the pine tree falls, its dissolution leaves a mossy mound —last-flung shadow of the perished trunk; never lengthening, never lessening; unsubject to the fleet falsities of the sun; shade immutable, and true gauge which cometh by prostration—so westward from what seems the stump, one steadfast spear of lichened ruin veins the plain.

From that treetop, what birded chimes of silver throats had rung. A stone pine, a metallic aviary in its crown: the Bell-Tower, built by the great mechanician, the unblest foundling, Bannadonna.

Like Babel's, its base was laid in a high hour of renovated earth, following the second deluge, when the waters of the Dark Ages had dried up and once more the green appeared. No wonder that, after so long and deep submersion, the jubilant expectation of the race should, as with Noah's sons, soar into Shinar aspiration.

In firm resolve, no man in Europe at that period went beyond Bannadonna. Enriched through commerce with the Levant, the state in which he lived voted to have the noblest Bell-Tower in Italy. His repute assigned him to be architect.

Stone by stone, month by month, the tower rose. Higher, higher, snail-like in pace, but torch or rocket in its pride.

After the masons would depart, the builder, standing alone upon its ever-ascending summit at close of every day, saw that he overtopped still higher walls and trees. He would tarry till a late hour there, wrapped in schemes of other and still loftier piles. Those who of saints' days thronged the spot—hanging to the rude poles of scaffolding like sailors on yards or bees on boughs, unmindful of lime and dust, and falling chips of stone—their homage not the less inspired him to self-esteem.

At length the holiday of the Tower came. To the sound of viols, the climax-stone slowly rose in air, and, amid the firing of ordnance, was laid by Bannadonna's hands upon the final course. Then mounting it, he stood erect, alone, with folded arms, gazing upon the white summits of blue inland Alps, and whiter crests of bluer Alps offshore—sights invisible from the plain. Invisible, too, from thence was that eye he turned below, when, like the cannon booms, came up to him the people's combustions of applause.

That which stirred them so was seeing with what serenity the builder stood three hundred feet in air, upon an unrailed perch. This none but he durst do. But his periodic standing upon the pile, in each stage of its growth—such discipline had its last result.

Little remained now but the bells. These, in all respects, must correspond with their receptacle.

The minor ones were prosperously cast. A highly enriched one followed, of a singular make, intended for suspension in a manner before unknown. The purpose of this bell, its rotary motion and connection with the clockwork, also executed at the time, will, in the sequel, receive mention.

In the one erection, bell-tower and clock-tower were united, though, before that period, such structures had commonly been built distinct; as the Campanile and Torre del Orologio of St. Mark to this day attest.

But it was upon the great state bell that the founder lavished his more daring skill. In vain did some of the less elated magistrates here caution him, saying that though truly the tower was titanic, yet limit should be set to the dependent weight of its swaying masses. But, undeterred, he prepared his mammoth mold, dented with mythological devices; kindled his fires of balsamic firs; melted his tin and copper, and, throwing in much plate contributed by the public spirit of the nobles, let loose the tide.

The unleashed metals bayed like hounds. The workmen shrunk. Through their fright, fatal harm to the bell was dreaded. Fearless as Shadrach, Bannadonna, rushing through the glow, smote the chief culprit with his ponderous ladle. From the smitten part, a splinter was dashed into the seething mass, and at once was melted in.

Next day a portion of the work was heedfully uncovered. All seemed right. Upon the third morning, with equal satisfaction, it was bared still lower. At length, like some old Theban king, the whole cooled casting was disinterred. All was fair except in one strange spot. But as he suffered no one to attend him in these inspections, he concealed the blemish by some preparation which none knew better to devise.

The casting of such a mass was deemed no small triumph for the caster; one, too, in which the state might not scorn to share. The homicide was overlooked. By the charitable that deed was but imputed to sudden transports of esthetic passion, not to any flagitious quality. A kick from an Arabian charger; not sign of vice, but blood.

His felony remitted by the judge, absolution given him by the priest, what more could even a sickly conscience have desired.

Honoring the tower and its builder with another holiday, the republic witnessed the hoisting of the bells and clockwork amid shows and pomps superior to the former.

Some months of more than usual solitude on Bannadonna's part ensued. It was not unknown that he was engaged upon something for the belfry, intended to complete it and surpass all that had gone before. Most people imagined that the design would involve a casting like the bells. But those who thought they had some further insight would shake their heads, with hints that not for nothing did the mechanician keep so secret. Meantime, his seclusion failed not to invest his work with more or less of that sort of mystery pertaining to the forbidden.

Erelong he had a heavy object hoisted to the belfry, wrapped in a dark sack or cloak—a procedure sometimes had in the case of an elaborate piece of sculpture, or statue, which, being intended to grace the front of a new edifice, the architect does not desire exposed to critical eyes till set up, finished, in its appointed place. Such was the impression now. But, as the object rose, a statuary present observed, or thought he did, that it was not entirely rigid, but was, in a manner, pliant. At last, when the hidden thing had attained its final height, and, obscurely seen from below, seemed almost of itself to step into the belfry, as if with little assistance from the crane, a shrewd old blacksmith present ventured the suspicion that it was but a living man. This surmise was thought a foolish one, while the general interest failed not to augment.

Not without demur from Bannadonna, the chief magistrate of the town, with an associate—both elderly men—followed what seemed the image up the tower. But, arrived at the belfry, they had little recompense. Plausibly entrenching himself behind the conceded mysteries of his art, the mechanician withheld present explanation. The magistrates glanced toward the cloaked object, which, to their surprise, seemed now to have changed its attitude, or else had before been more perplexingly concealed by the violent muffling action of the wind without. It seemed now seated upon some sort of frame, or chair, contained within the domino. They observed that nigh the top, in a sort of square, the web of the cloth, either from accident or design, had its warp partly withdrawn, and the cross threads plucked out here and there, so as to form a sort of woven grating. Whether it were the low wind or no, stealing through the stone latticework, or only their own perturbed imaginations, is uncertain, but they thought they discerned a slight sort of fitful, springlike motion in the domino. Nothing, however incidental or insignificant, escaped their uneasy eyes. Among other things, they pried out, in a corner, an earthen cup, partly corroded and partly encrusted, and one whispered to the other that this cup was just such a one as might, in mockery, be offered to the lips of some brazen statue, or, perhaps, still worse.

But, being questioned, the mechanician said that the cup was simply used in his founder's business, and described the purpose—in short, a cup to test the condition of metals in fusion. He added that it had got into the belfry by the merest chance.

Again and again they gazed at the domino, as at some suspicious incognito at a Venetian mask. All sorts of vague apprehensions stirred them. They even dreaded lest, when they should descend, the mechanician, though without a flesh-and-blood companion, for all that, would not be left alone.

Affecting some merriment at their disquietude, he begged to relieve them, by extending a coarse sheet of workman's canvas between them and the object.

Meantime he sought to interest them in his other work, nor, now that the domino was out of sight, did they long remain insensible to the artistic wonders lying round them—wonders hitherto beheld but in their unfinished state, because, since hoisting the bells, none but the caster had entered within the belfry. It was one trait of his, that, even in details, he would not let another do what he could, without too great loss of time, accomplish for himself. So, for several preceding weeks, whatever hours were unemployed in his secret design had been devoted to elaborating the figures on the bells.

The clock bell, in particular, now drew attention. Under a patient chisel, the latent beauty of its enrichments, before obscured by the cloudings incident to casting, that beauty in its shyest grace, was now revealed. Round and round the bell, twelve figures of gay girls, garlanded, hand-in-hand, danced in a choral ring the embodied hours.

"Bannadonna," said the chief, "this bell excels all else. No added touch could here improve. Hark!" hearing a sound, "was that the wind?"

"The wind, Excellenza," was the light response. "But the figures, they are not yet without their faults. They need some touches yet. When those are given, and the—block yonder," pointing towards the canvas screen, "when Haman there, as I merrily call him—him? *it*, I mean—when Haman is fixed on this, his lofty tree, then, gentlemen, will I be most happy to receive you here again."

The equivocal reference to the object caused some return of restlessness. However, on their part, the visitors forbore further allusion to it, unwilling, perhaps, to let the foundling see how easily it lay within his plebeian art to stir the placid dignity of nobles.

"Well, Bannadonna," said the chief, "how long ere you are ready to set the clock going, so that the hour shall be sounded? Our interest in you, not less than in the work itself, makes us anxious to be assured of your success. The people, too—why, they are shouting now. Say the exact hour when you will be ready."

"Tomorrow, Excellenza, if you listen for it—or should you not, all the same—strange music will be heard. The stroke of one shall be the first from yonder bell," pointing to the bell adorned with girls and garlands, "that stroke shall fall there, where the hand of Una clasps Dua's. The stroke of one shall sever that loved clasp. Tomorrow, then, at one o'clock, as struck here, precisely here," advancing and placing his finger upon the clasp, "the poor mechanic will be most happy once more to give you liege audience, in this his littered shop. Farewell till then, illustrious magnificoes, and hark ye for your vassal's stroke."

His still, Vulcanic face hiding its burning brightness like a forge, he moved with ostentatious deference towards the scuttle, as if so far to escort their exit.

But the junior magistrate, a kind-hearted man, troubled at what seemed to him a certain sardonical disdain lurking beneath the foundling's humble mien, and in Christian sympathy more distressed at it on his account than on his own, dimly surmising what might be the final fate of such a cynic solitaire, nor perhaps uninfluenced by the general strangeness of surrounding things, this good magistrate had glanced sadly, sideways from the speaker, and thereupon his foreboding eye had started at the expression of the unchanging face of the Hour Una.

"How is this, Bannadonna," he lowly asked, "Una looks unlike her sisters."

"In Christ's name, Bannadonna," impulsively broke in the chief, his attention for the first attracted to the figure by his associate's remark. "Una's face looks just like that of Deborah, the prophetess, as painted by the Florentine, Del Fonca."

"Surely, Bannadonna," lowly resumed the milder magistrate, "you meant the twelve should wear the same jocundly abandoned air. But see, the smile of Una seems but a fatal one. 'Tis different."

While his mild associate was speaking, the chief glanced inquiringly from him to the caster, as if anxious to mark how the discrepancy would be accounted for. As the chief stood, his advanced foot was on the scuttle's curb.

Bannadonna spoke:

"Excellenza, now that, following your keener eye, I glance upon the face of Una, I do, indeed perceive some little variance. But look all round the bell, and you will find no two faces entirely correspond. Because there is a law in art—but the cold wind is rising more; these lattices are but a poor defense. Suffer me, magnificoes, to conduct you at least partly on your way. Those in whose well-being there is a public stake, should be heedfully attended."

"Touching the look of Una, you were saying, Bannadonna, that there was a certain law in art," observed the chief, as the three now descended the stone shaft, "pray, tell me, then—"

"Pardon; another time, Excellenza—the tower is damp."

"Nay, I must rest, and hear it now. Here,—here is a wide landing, and through this leeward slit, no wind, but ample light. Tell us of your law, and at large."

"Since, Excellenza, you insist, know that there is a law in art which bars the possibility of duplicates. Some years ago, you may remember, I graved a small seal for your republic, bearing, for its chief device, the head of your own ancestor, its illustrious founder. It becoming necessary, for the customs' use, to have innumerable impressions for bales and boxes, I graved an entire plate, containing one hundred of the seals. Now, though, indeed, my object was to have those hundred heads identical, and though, I dare say, people think them so, yet, upon closely scanning an uncut impression from the plate, no two of those five-score faces, side by side, will be found alike. Gravity is the air of all, but diversified in all. In some, benevolent; in some, ambiguous; in two or three, to a close scrutiny, all but incipiently malign, the variation of less than a hair's breadth in the linear shadings round the mouth sufficing to all this. Now, Excellenza, transmute that general gravity into joyousness, and subject it to twelve of those variations I have described, and tell me, will you not have my hours here, and Una one of them? But I like—"

"Hark! is that—a footfall above?"

"Mortar, Excellenza; sometimes it drops to the belfry floor from the arch where the stonework was left undressed. I must have it seen to. As I was about to say: for one, I like this law forbidding duplicates. It evokes fine personalities. Yes, Excellenza, that strange, and—to you—uncertain smile, and those forelooking eyes of Una, suit Bannadonna very well."

"Hark!—sure we left no soul above?"

"No soul, Excellenza, rest assured, no *soul*.—Again the mortar."

"It fell not while we were there."

"Ah, in your presence, it better knew its place, Excellenza," blandly bowed Bannadonna.

"But Una," said the milder magistrate, "she seemed intently gazing on you; one would have almost sworn that she picked you out from among us three."

"If she did, possibly it might have been her finer apprehension, Excellenza."

"How, Bannadonna? I do not understand you."

"No consequence, no consequence, Excellenza—but the shifted wind is blowing through the slit. Suffer me to escort you on, and then, pardon, but the toiler must to his tools."

"It may be foolish, signor," and the milder magistrate, as, from the third landing, the two now went down unescorted, "but, somehow, our great mechanician moves me strangely. Why, just now, when he so superciliously replied, his walk seemed Sisera's, God's vain foe, in Del Fonca's painting. And that young, sculptured Deborah, too. Aye, and that—"

"Tush, tush, signor!" returned the chief. "A passing whim. Deborah?—Where's Jael, pray?"

"Ah," said the other, as they now stepped upon the sod, "ah, signor, I see you leave your fears behind you with the chill and gloom; but mine, even in this sunny air, remain. Hark!"

It was a sound from just within the tower door, whence they had emerged. Turning, they saw it closed.

"He has slipped down and barred us out," smiled the chief; "but it is his custom."

Proclamation was now made that the next day, at one hour after meridian, the clock would strike, and—thanks to the mechanician's powerful art—with unusual accompaniments. But what those should be, none as yet could say. The announcement was received with cheers.

By the looser sort, who encamped about the tower all night, lights were seen gleaming through the topmost blindwork, only disappearing with the morning sun. Strange sounds, too, were heard, or were thought to be, by those whom anxious watching might not have left mentally undisturbed—sounds, not only of some ringing implement, but also, so they said, half-suppressed screams and plainings, such as might have issued from some ghostly engine overplied.

Slowly the day drew on, part of the concourse chasing the weary time with songs and games, till, at last, the great blurred sun rolled, like a football, against the plain.

At noon, the nobility and principal citizens came from the town in cavalcade, a guard of soldiers, also, with music, the more to honor the occasion.

Only one hour more. Impatience grew. Watches were held in hands of feverish men, who stood, now scrutinizing their small dial-plates, and then, with neck thrown back, gazing toward the belfry as if the eve might foretell that which could only be made sensible to the ear, for, as yet, there was no dial to the tower clock.

The hour hands of a thousand watches now verged within a hair's breadth of the figure 1. A silence, as of the expectations of some Shiloh, pervaded the swarming plain. Suddenly a dull, mangled sound, naught ringing in it, scarcely audible, indeed, to the outer circles of the people—that dull sound dropped heavily from the belfry. At the same moment, each man stared at his neighbor blankly. All watches were upheld. All hour hands were at—had passed—the figure 1. No bell stroke from the tower. The multitude became tumultuous.

Waiting a few moments, the chief magistrate, commanding silence, hailed the belfry to know what thing unforeseen had happened there.

No response.

He hailed again and yet again.

All continued hushed.

By his order, the soldiers burst in the tower door, when, stationing guards to defend it from the now surging mob, the chief, accompanied by his former associate, climbed the winding stairs. Halfway up, they stopped to listen. No sound. Mounting faster, they reached the belfry, but, at the threshold, started at the spectacle disclosed. A spaniel, which, unbeknown to them, had followed them thus far, stood shivering as before some unknown monster in a brake, or, rather, as if it snuffed footsteps leading to some other world.

Bannadonna lay, prostrate and bleeding, at the base of the bell which was adorned with girls and garlands. He lay at the feet of the hour Una, his head coinciding, in a vertical line, with her left hand, clasped by the hour Dua. With downcast face impending over him, like Jael over nailed Sisera in the tent, was the domino; now no more becloaked.

It had limbs, and seemed clad in a scaly mail, lustrous as a dragon-beetle's. It was manacled, and its clubbed arms were uplifted, as if, with its manacles, once more to smite its already smitten victim. One advanced foot of it was inserted beneath the dead body, as if in the act of spurning it.

Uncertainty falls on what now followed.

It were but natural to suppose that the magistrates would, at first, shrink from immediate personal contact with what they saw. At the least, for a time, they would stand in involuntary doubt, it may be, in more or less horrified alarm. Certain it is that an arquebuss was called for from below. And some add that its report, followed by a fierce whiz, as of the sudden snapping of a mainspring, with a steely din, as if a stack of sword blades should be dashed upon a pavement; these blended sounds came ringing to the plain, attracting every eye far upward to the belfry, whence, through the latticework, thin wreaths of smoke were curling.

Some averred that it was the spaniel, gone mad by fear, which was shot. This, others denied. True it was, the spaniel never more was seen; and, probably for some unknown reason, it shared the burial now to be related of the domino. For, whatever the preceding circumstances may have been, the first instinctive panic over, or else all ground of reasonable fear removed, the two magistrates, by themselves, quickly re-hooded the figure in the dropped cloak wherein it had been hoisted. The same night, it was secretly lowered to the ground, smuggled to the beach, pulled far out to sea, and sunk. Nor to any after urgency, even in free convivial hours, would the twain ever disclose the full secrets of the belfry.

From the mystery unavoidably investing it, the popular solution of the foundling's fate involved more or less of supernatural agency. But some few less unscientific minds pretended to find little difficulty in otherwise accounting for it. In the chain of circumstantial inferences drawn, there may or may not have been some absent or defective links. But, as the explanation in question is the only one which tradition has explicitly preserved, in dearth of better, it will here be given. But, in the first place, it is requisite to present the supposition entertained as to the entire motive and mode, with their origin, of the secret design of Bannadonna, the minds above-mentioned assuming to penetrate as well into his soul as into the event. The disclosure will indirectly involve reference to peculiar matters, none of the clearest, beyond the immediate subject.

At that period, no large bell was made to sound otherwise than as at present, by agitation of a tongue within by means of ropes, or percussion from without, either from cumbrous machinery, or stalwart watchmen, armed with heavy hammers, stationed in the belfry or in sentry boxes on the open roof, according as the bell was sheltered or exposed.

It was from observing these exposed bells, with their watchmen, that the foundling, as was opined, derived the first suggestion of his scheme. Perched on a great mast or spire, the human figure, viewed from below, undergoes such a reduction in its apparent size as to obliterate its intelligent features. It evinces no personality. Instead of bespeaking volition, its gestures rather resemble the automatic ones of the arms of a telegraph.

Musing, therefore, upon the purely Punchinello aspect of the human figure thus beheld, it had indirectly occurred to Bannadonna to devise some metallic agent which should strike the hour with its mechanic hand, with even greater precision than the vital one. And, moreover, as the vital watchman on the roof, sallying from his retreat at the given periods, walked to the bell with uplifted mace to smite it, Bannadonna had resolved that his invention should likewise possess the power of locomotion, and, along with that, the appearance, at least, of intelligence and will.

If the conjectures of those who claimed acquaintance with the intent of Bannadonna be thus far correct, no unenterprising spirit could have been his. But they stopped not here; intimating that though, indeed, his design had, in the first place, been prompted by the sight of the watchman, and confined to the devising of a subtle substitute for him, yet, as is not seldom the case with projectors, by insensible gradations proceeding from comparatively pigmy aims to titanic ones, the original scheme had, in its anticipated eventualities, at last attained to an unheard-of degree of daring. He still bent his efforts upon the locomotive figure for the belfry, but only as a partial type of an ulterior creature, a sort of elephantine helot, adapted to further, in a degree scarcely to be imagined, the universal conveniences and glories of humanity; supplying nothing less than a supplement to the Six Days' Work; stocking the earth with a new serf, more useful than the ox, swifter than the dolphin, stronger than the lion, more cunning than the ape, for industry an ant, more fiery than serpents, and yet, in patience, another ass. All excellences of all God-made creatures which served man were here to receive advancement, and then to be combined in one. Talus was to have been the all-accomplished helot's name. Talus, iron slave to Bannadonna, and, through him, to man.

Here, it might well be thought that, were these last conjectures as to the foundling's secrets not erroneous, then must he have been hopelessly infected with the craziest chimeras of his age; far outgoing Albert Magus and Cornelius Agrippa. But the contrary was averred. However marvelous his design, however apparently transcending not alone the bounds of human invention, but those of divine creation, yet the proposed means to be employed were alleged to have been confined within the sober forms of sober reason. It was affirmed that, to a degree of more than skeptic scorn, Bannadonna had been without sympathy for any of the vainglorious irrationalities of his time. For example, he had not concluded, with the visionaries among the metaphysicians, that between the finer mechanic forces and the ruder animal vitality some germ of correspondence might prove discoverable. As little did his scheme partake of the enthusiasm of some natural philosophers, who hoped, by physiological and chemical inductions, to arrive at a knowledge of the source of life, and so qualify themselves to manufacture and improve upon it. Much less had he aught in common with the tribe of alchemists, who sought by a species of incantations to evoke some surprising vitality from the laboratory. Neither had he imagined, with certain sanguine theosophists, that, by faithful adoration of the Highest, unheard-of powers would be vouchsafed to man. A practical materialist, what Bannadonna had aimed at was to have been reached, not by logic, not by crucible, not by conjuration, not by altars, but by plain visebench and hammer. In short, to solve nature, to steal into her, to intrigue beyond her, to procure someone else to bind her to his hand—these, one and all, had not been his objects, but, asking no favors from any element or any being, of himself to rival her, outstrip her, and rule her. He stooped to conquer. With him, common sense was theurgy; machinery, miracle; Prometheus, the heroic name for machinist; man, the true God.

Nevertheless, in his initial step, so far as the experimental automaton for the belfry was concerned, he allowed fancy some little play, or, perhaps, what seemed his fancifulness was but his utilitarian ambition collaterally extended. In figure, the creature for the belfry should not be likened after the human pattern, nor any animal one, nor after the ideals, however wild, of ancient fable, but equally in aspect as in organism be an original production—the more terrible to behold, the better.

Such, then, were the suppositions as to the present scheme, and the reserved intent. How, at the very threshold, so unlooked-for a catastrophe overturned all, or rather, what was the conjecture here, is now to be set forth.

It was thought that on the day preceding the fatality, his visitors having left him, Bannadonna had unpacked the belfry image, adjusted it, and placed it in the retreat provided—a sort of sentry box in one corner of the belfry; in short, throughout the night, and for some part of the ensuing morning, he had been engaged in arranging everything connected with the domino: the issuing from the sentry box each sixty minutes; sliding along a grooved way, like a railway; advancing to the clock bell with uplifted manacles; striking it at one of the twelve junctions of the four-and-twenty hands; then wheeling, circling the bell, and retiring to its post, there to bide for another sixty minutes, when the same process was to be repeated; the bell, by a cunning mechanism, meantime turning on its vertical axis, so as to present, to the descending mace, the clasped hands of the next two figures, when it would strike two, three, and so on, to the end. The musical metal in this time bell being so managed in the fusion, by some art perishing with its originator, that each of the clasps of the four-and-twenty hands should give forth its own peculiar resonance when parted.

But on the magic metal, the magic and metallic stranger never struck but that one stroke, drove but that one nail, served but that one clasp, by which Bannadonna clung to his ambitious life. For, after winding up the creature in the sentry box, so that, for the present, skipping the intervening hours, it should not emerge till the hour of one, but should then infallibly emerge, and, after deftly oiling the grooves whereon it was to slide, it was surmised that the mechanician must then have hurried to the bell, to give his final touches to its sculpture. True artist, he here became absorbed, and absorption still further intensified, it may be, by his striving to abate that strange look of Una, which, though, before others, he had treated with such unconcern, might not, in secret, have been without its thorn.

And so, for the interval, he was oblivious of his creature, which, not oblivious of him, and true to its creation, and true to its heedful winding up, left its post precisely at the given moment, along its well-oiled route, slid noiselessly towards its mark, and, aiming at the hand of Una to ring one clangorous note, dully smote the intervening brain of Bannadonna, turned backwards to it, the manacled arms then instantly upspringing to their hovering poise. The falling body clogged the thing's return, so there it stood, still impending over Bannadonna, as if whispering some post-mortem terror. The chisel lay dropped from the hand, but beside the hand; the oil-flask spilled across the iron track.

In his unhappy end, not unmindful of the rare genius of the mechanician, the republic decreed him a stately funeral. It was resolved that the great bell—the one whose casting had been jeopardized through the timidity of the ill-starred workman—should be rung upon the entrance of the bier into the cathedral. The most robust man of the country round was assigned the office of bell ringer.

But as the pallbearers entered the cathedral porch, naught but a broken and disastrous sound, like that of some lone Alpine landslide, fell from the tower upon their ears. And then all was hushed.

Glancing backwards, they saw the groined belfry crashed sideways in. It afterwards appeared that the powerful peasant who had the bell rope in charge, wishing to test at once the full glory of the bell, had swayed down upon the rope with one concentrate jerk. The mass of quaking metal, too ponderous for its frame, and strangely feeble somewhere at its top, loosed from its fastening, tore sideways down, and, tumbling in one sheer fall three hundred feet to the soft sward below, buried itself inverted and half out of sight.

Upon its disinterment, the main fracture was found to have started from a small spot in the ear, which, being scraped, revealed a defect, deceptively minute, in the casting, which defect must subsequently have been pasted over with some unknown compound.

The remolten metal soon reassumed its place in the tower's repaired superstructure. For one year the metallic choir of birds sang musically in its belfry boughwork of sculptured blinds and traceries. But on the first anniversary of the tower's completion—at early dawn, before the concourse had surrounded it—an earthquake came; one loud crash was heard. The stone pine, with all its bower of songsters, lay overthrown upon the plain.

So the blind slave obeyed its blinder lord, but, in obedience, slew him. So the creator was killed by the creature. So the bell was too heavy for the tower. So the bell's main weakness was where man's blood had flawed it. And so pride went before the fall.

(1855)

FIRST TO SERVE

Algis Budrys

Born in Königsberg, East Prussia, in 1931, **Algirdas Jonas Budrys** arrived in America with his parents in 1936. His writing career wasn't exactly plain sailing. His first novel *False Night* (1954) was horribly hacked about by its editor, then his publisher ran out of money, stalling his second novel for years. When eventually it did appear, *Who?* was snapped up for a movie – quite a good one – starring Elliott Gould and Trevor Howard. The sentient artificial intelligence in *Michaelmas*, housed worldwide through a network of distributed computers, is a prescient creation indeed in a novel published in 1977. Budrys (AJ to his friends) was also an editor and publisher. *Tomorrow Speculative Fiction* was his, running from 1993 to 2000. But it's as a writer of tough, cool, existential short stories that he'll be best remembered.

thei ar teetcing mi to reed n ryt n i wil bee abel too do this beter then.
pimi

MAS 712, 820TH TDRC,

COMASAMPS, APO IS,

September 28

Leonard Stein, Editor,
INFINITY,
862 Union St.,
New York 24, N.Y.

Dear Len,
Surprise, *et cetera*

It looks like there will be some new H. E. Wood stories for *Infy* after all. By the time you get this, 820TH TDRC will have a new Project Engineer, COMASAMPS, and I will be back to the old Royal and the Perry Street lair.

Shed no tear for Junior Heywood, though. COMASAMPS and I have come to this parting with mutual eyes dry and multiple heads erect. There was no sadness in our parting—no bitterness, no weeping, no remorse. COMASAMPS—in one of its apparently limitless human personifications—simply patted me on my backside and told me to pick up my calipers and run along. I'll have to stay away from cybernetics for a while, of course, and I don't think I should write any robot stories in the interval, but, then, I never did like robot stories anyhow.

But all this is a long story about ten thousand words, at least, which means a $300 net loss if I tell it now.

So go out and buy some fresh decks, I'll be in town next week, my love to the Associate and the kids, and first ace deals.

Vic Heywood

My name is really Prototype Mechanical Man I, but everybody calls me Pimmy, or sometimes Pim. I was assembled at the eight-twentieth teedeearcee on august 10, 1974. I don't know what man or teedeearcee or august 10, 1974, means, but Heywood says I will, tomorrow. What's tomorrow?

Pimmy

August 12, 1974

I'm still having trouble defining "man." Apparently, even the men can't do a very satisfactory job of that. The 820TDRC, of course, is the Eight Hundred and Twentieth Technical Development and Research Center of the Combined Armed Services Artificial and Mechanical Personnel Section. August 10, 1974, is the day before yesterday.

All this is very obvious, but it's good to record it.

I heard a very strange conversation between Heywood and Russell yesterday.

Russell is a small man, about thirty-eight, who's Heywood's top assistant. He wears glasses, and his chin is farther back than his mouth. It gives his head a symmetrical look. His voice is high, and he moves his hands rapidly. I think his reflexes are overtriggered.

Heywood is pretty big. He's almost as tall as I am. He moves smoothly—he's like me. You get the idea that all of his weight never touches the ground. Once in a while, though, he leaves a cigarette burning in an ashtray, and you can see where the end's been chewed to shreds.

Why is everybody at COMASAMPS so nervous?

Heywood was looking at the first entry in what I can now call my diary. He showed it to Russell.

"Guess you did a good job on the self-awareness tapes, Russ," Heywood said.

Russell frowned. "Too good, I think. He shouldn't have such a tremendous drive toward self-expression. We'll have to iron that out as soon as possible. Want me to set up a new tape?"

Heywood shook his head. "Don't see why. Matter of fact, with the intelligence we've given him, I think it's probably a normal concomitant." He looked up at me and winked.

Russell took his glasses off with a snatch of his hand and scrubbed them on his shirtsleeve. "I don't know. We'll have to watch him. We've got to remember he's a prototype—no different from an experimental automobile design, or a new dishwasher model. We expected bugs to appear. I think we've found one, and I think it ought to be eliminated. I don't like this personification he's acquired in our minds, either. This business of calling him by a nickname is all wrong. We've got to remember he's *not* an individual. We've got every right to tinker with him." He slapped his glasses back on and ran his hands over the hair the earpieces had disturbed. "He's just another machine. We can't lose sight of that."

Heywood raised his hands. "Easy, boy. Aren't you going too far off the deep end? All he's done is bat out a few words on a typewriter. Relax, Russ." He walked over to me and slapped my hip. "How about it, Pimmy? D'you feel like scrubbing the floor?"

"No opinion. Is that an order?" I asked.

Heywood turned to Russell. "Behold the rampant individual," he said. "No, Pimmy, no order. Cancel."

Russell shrugged, but he folded the page from my diary carefully, and put it in his breast pocket. I didn't mind. I never forget anything.

August 15, 1974
They did something to me on the Thirteenth. I can't remember what. I've gone over my memory, but there's nothing. I can't remember.

Russell and Ligget were talking yesterday, though, when they inserted the autonomic cutoff, and ran me through on orders. I didn't mind that. I still don't. I can't.

Ligget is one of the small army of push-arounds that nobody knows for sure isn't CIC, but who solders wires while Heywood and Russell make up their minds about him.

I had just done four about-faces, shined their shoes, and struck a peculiar pose. I think there's something seriously wrong with Ligget.

Ligget said, "He responds well, doesn't he?"

"Mm-m—yes," Russell said abstractedly. He ran his glance down a column of figures on an Estimated Performance Spec chart. "Try walking on your hands, PMM One," he said.

I activated my gyroscope and reset my pedal locomotion circuits. I walked around the room on my hands.

Ligget frowned forcefully. "That looks good. How's it check with the specs?"

"Better than," Russell said. "I'm surprised. We had a lot of trouble with him the last two days. Reacted like a zombie."

"Oh, yes? I wasn't in on that. What happened? I mean—what sort of control were you using?"

"Oh—" I could see that Russell wasn't too sure whether he should tell Ligget or not. I already had the feeling that the atmosphere of this project was loaded with dozens of crosscurrents and conflicting ambitions. I was going to learn a lot about COMASAMPS.

"Yes?" Ligget said.

"We had his individuality circuits cut out. Effectively, he was just a set of conditioned reflexes."

"You say he reacted like a zombie?"

"Definite automatism. Very slow reactions, and, of course, no initiative."

"You mean he'd be very slow in his response to orders under those conditions, right?" Ligget looked crafty behind Russell's back.

Russell whirled around. "He'd make a lousy soldier, if that's what CIC wants to know!"

Ligget smoothed out his face, and twitched his shoulders back. "I'm not a CIC snooper, if that's what you mean."

"You don't mind if I call you a liar, do you?" Russell said, his hands shaking.

"Not particularly," Ligget said, but he was angry behind his smooth face. It helps, having immobile features like mine. You get to understand the psychology of a man who tries for the same effect.

August 16, 1974

It bothers me, not having a diary entry for the fourteenth, either. Somebody's been working on me again.

I told Heywood about it. He shrugged. "Might as well get used to it, Pimmy. There'll be a lot of that going on. I don't imagine it's pleasant—I wouldn't like intermittent amnesia myself—but there's very little you can do about it. Put it down as one of the occupational hazards of being a prototype."

"But I don't *like* it," I said.

Heywood pulled the left side of his mouth into a straight line and sighed. "Like I said, Pimmy—I wouldn't either. On the other hand, you can't blame us if the new machine we're testing happens to know it's being tested, and resents it. We built the machine. Theoretically, it's our privilege to do anything we please with it, if that'll help us find out how the machine performs, and how to build better ones."

"But I'm *not* a machine," I said.

Heywood put his lower lip between his teeth and looked up at me from under a raised eyebrow. "Sorry, Pim. I'm kind of afraid you are."

But I'm not! *I'M NOT!*

August 17, 1974

Russell and Heywood were working late with me last night. They did a little talking back and forth. Russell was very nervous—and finally Heywood got a little impatient with him.

"All right," Heywood said, laying his charts down. "We're not getting anywhere, this way. You want to sit down and really talk about what's bothering you?"

Russell looked a little taken aback. He shook his head jerkily.

"No… no, I haven't got anything specific on my mind. Just talking. You know how it is." He tried to pretend he was very engrossed in one of the charts.

Heywood didn't let him off the hook, though. His eyes were cutting into Russell's face, peeling off layer after layer of misleading mannerism and baring the naked fear in the man.

"No, I don't know how it is." He put his hand on Russell's shoulder and turned him around to where the other man was facing him completely. "Now, look—if there's something chewing on you, let's have it. I'm not going to have this project gummed up by your secret troubles. Things are tough enough with everybody trying to pressure us into doing things their way, and none of them exactly sure of what that way *is*."

That last sentence must have touched something off in Russell, because he let his charts drop beside Heywood's and clawed at the pack of cigarettes in his breast pocket.

"That's exactly what the basic problem is," he said, his eyes a little too wide. He pushed one hand back and forth over the side of his face and walked back and forth aimlessly. Then a flood of words came out.

"We're working in the dark, Vic. In the dark, and somebody's in with us that's swinging clubs at our heads while we stumble around. We don't know who it is, we don't know if it's one or more than that, and we never know when the next swing is coming.

"Look—we're cybernetics engineers. Our job was to design a brain that would operate a self-propulsive unit designed to house it. That was the engineering problem, and we've got a tendency to continue looking at it in that light.

"But that's not the whole picture. We've got to keep in mind that the only reason we were ever given the opportunity and the facilities was because somebody thought it might be a nice idea to turn out soldiers on a production line, just like they do the rest of the paraphernalia of war. And the way COMASAMPS looks at it is not in terms of a brain housed in an independently movable shell, but in terms of a robot which now has to be fitted to the general idea of what a soldier should be.

"Only nobody knows what the ideal soldier is like.

"Some say he ought to respond to orders with perfect accuracy and superhuman reflexes. Others say he ought to be able to think his way out of trouble, or improvise in a situation where his orders no longer apply, just like a human soldier. The ones who want the perfect automaton don't want him to be smart enough to realize he *is* an automaton—probably because they're afraid of the idea; and the ones who want him to be capable of human discretion don't want him to be human enough to be rebellious in a hopeless situation.

"And that's just the beginning. COMASAMPS may be a combined project, but if you think the Navy isn't checking up on the Army, and vice versa, with both of them looking over the Air Force's shoulder—Oh, you know that squirrel cage as well as I do!"

Russell gestured hopelessly. Heywood, who had been taking calm puffs on his cigarette, shrugged. "So? All we have to do is tinker around until we can design a sample model to fit each definition. Then they can run as many comparative field tests as they want to. It's their problem. Why let it get you?"

Russell flung his cigarette to the floor and stepped on it with all his weight. "Because we can't do it and you ought to know it as well as I do!" He pointed over at me. "There's your prototype model. He's got all the features that everybody wants—and cutoffs intended to take out the features that interfere with any one definition. We can cut off his individuality, and leave him the automaton some people want. We can leave him his individuality, cut off his volition, and give him general orders which he is then free to carry out by whatever means he thinks best. Or, we can treat him like a human being—educate him by means of tapes, train him, and turn him loose on a job, the way we'd do with a human being."

The uneven tone built up in his voice as he finished what he was saying.

"But, if we reduce him to a machine that responds to orders as though they were pushbuttons, he's slow. He's pitifully slow, Vic, and he'd be immobilized within thirty seconds of combat. There's nothing we can do about that, either. Until somebody learns how to push electricity through a circuit faster than the laws of physics say it should go, what we'll have will be a ponderous, mindless thing that's no better than the remote-control exhibition jobs built forty years ago.

"All right, so that's no good. We leave him individuality, but we restrict it until it cuts his personality down to that of a slave. That's better. Under those conditions, he would, theoretically, be a better soldier than the average human. An officer could tell him to take a patrol out into a certain sector, and he'd do the best possible job, picking the best way to handle each step of the job as he came to it. But what does he do if he comes back, and the officer who gave him the orders is no longer there? Or, worse yet, if there's been a retreat, and there's nobody there? Or an armistice? What about that armistice? Can you picture this slave robot, going into stasis because he's got no orders to cover a brand-new situation?

"He might just as well not have gone on that patrol at all—because he can't pass on whatever he's learned, and because his job is now over, as far as he's concerned. The enemy could overrun his position, and he wouldn't do anything about it. He'd operate from order to order. And if an armistice were signed, he'd sit right where he was until a technician could come out, remove the soldier-orientation tapes, and replace them with whatever was finally decided on.

"Oh, you could get around the limitation all right—by issuing a complex set of orders, such as: 'Go out on patrol and report back. If I'm not here, report to so-and-so. If there's nobody here, do this. If that doesn't work, try that. If such-and-such happens, proceed as follows. But don't confuse such-and-such with that or this.' Can you imagine fighting a war on that basis? And what about that reorientation problem? How long would all those robots sit there before they could all be serviced—and how many man-hours and how much material would it take to do the job? Frankly, I couldn't think of a more cumbersome way to run a war if I tried.

"Or, we can build all our robots like streamlined Pimmys—like Pimmy when all his circuits are operating, without our test cutoffs. Only, then, we'd have artificial human beings. Human beings who don't wear out, that a hand-arm won't stop, and who don't need food or water as long as their power piles have a pebble-sized hunk of plutonium to chew on."

Russell laughed bitterly. "And Navy may be making sure Army doesn't get the jump on them, with Air Force doing its bit, but there's one thing all three of them are as agreed upon as they are about nothing else—they'll test automaton zombies, and they'll test slaves, but one thing nobody wants us turning out is supermen.

They've got undercover men under every lab bench, all keeping one eye on each other and one on us—and the whole thing comes down on our heads like a ton of cement if there's even the first whisper of an idea that we're going to build more Pimmys. The same thing happens if we don't give them the perfect soldier. *And the only perfect soldier is a Pimmy.* Pimmy could replace any man in any armed service—from a KP to a whole general staff, depending on what tapes he had. But he'd have to be a true individual to do it. And he'd be smarter than they are. They couldn't trust him. Not because he wouldn't work for the same objectives as they'd want, but because he'd probably do it in some way they couldn't understand.

"So they don't want any more Pimmys. This one test model is all they'll allow, because he can be turned into any kind of robot they want, but they won't take the whole Pimmy, with all his potentialities. They just want part of him."

The bitter laugh was louder. "We've got their perfect soldier, but they don't want him. They want something less—but that something less will never be the perfect soldier. So we work and work, weeks on end, testing, revising, redesigning. Why? We're marking time. We've got what they want, but they don't want it—but if we don't give it to them soon, they'll wipe out the project. And if we give them what they want, it won't really be what they want. Can't you see that? What's the matter with you, Heywood? Can't you see the blind alley we're in—only it's not a blind alley, because it has eyes, eyes under every bench, watching each other and watching us, always watching, never stopping, going on and never stopping, watching, eyes?"

Heywood had already picked up the telephone. As Russell collapsed completely, he began to speak into it, calling the Project hospital. Even as he talked, his eyes were coldly brooding, and his mouth was set in an expression I'd never seen before. His other hand was on Russell's twitching shoulder, moving gently as the other man sobbed.

August 25, 1974
Ligget is Heywood's new assistant. It's been a week since Russell's been gone.

Russell wasn't replaced for three days, and Heywood worked alone with me. He's engineer of the whole project, and I'm almost certain there must have been other things he could have worked on while he was waiting for a new assistant, but he spent all of his time in this lab with me.

His face didn't show what he thought about Russell. He's not like Ligget, though. Heywood's thoughts are private. Ligget's are hidden. But, every once in a while, while Heywood was working, he'd start to turn around and reach out, or just say "Jack—" as if he wanted something, and then he'd catch himself, and his eyes would grow more thoughtful.

I only understood part of what Russell had said that night he was taken away, so I asked Heywood about it yesterday.

"What's the trouble, Pim?" he asked.

"Don't know, for sure. Too much I don't understand about this whole thing. If I knew what some of the words meant, I might not even have a problem."

"Shoot."

"Well, it's mostly what Russell was saying, that last night."

Heywood peeled a strip of skin from his upper lip by catching it between his teeth. "Yeah."

"What's a war, or what's war? Soldiers have something to do with it, but what's a soldier? I'm a robot—but why do they want to make more of me? Can I be a soldier and a robot at the same time? Russell kept talking about 'they,' and the Army, the Air Force, and the Navy. What're they? And are the CIC men the ones who are watching you and each other at the same time?"

Heywood scowled, and grinned ruefully at the same time. "That's quite a catalogue," he said. "And there's even more than that, isn't there, Pimmy?" He put his hand on my side and sort of patted me, the way I'd seen him do with a generator a few times. "O. K., I'll give you a tape on war and soldiering. That's the next step in the program anyway, and it'll take care of most of those questions."

"Thanks," I said. "But what about the rest of it?"

He leaned against a bench and looked down at the floor. "Well, 'they' are the people who instituted this program—the Secretary of Defense, and the people under him. They all agreed that robot personnel were just what the armed services needed, and they were right. The only trouble is, they couldn't agree among themselves as to what characteristics were desirable in the perfect soldier—or sailor, or airman. They decided that the best thing to do was to come up with a series of different models, and to run tests until they came up with the best one.

"Building you was my own idea. Instead of trying to build prototypes to fit each separate group of specifications, we built one all-purpose model who was, effectively speaking, identical with a human being in almost all respects, with one major difference. By means of cutoffs in every circuit, we can restrict as much of your abilities as we want to, thus being able to modify your general characteristics to fit any one of the various specification groups. We saved a lot of time by doing that, and avoided a terrific nest of difficulties.

"Trouble is, we're using up all the trouble and time we saved. Now that they've got you, they don't want you. Nobody's willing to admit that the only efficient robot soldier is one with all the discretionary powers and individuality of a human being. They can't admit it, because people are afraid of anything that looks like it might be better than they are. And they won't trust what they're afraid of. So, Russell and I had to piddle around with a stupid series of tests in a hopeless attempt to come up with something practical that was nevertheless within the limitations of the various sets of specifications—which is ridiculous, because there's nothing wrong with you, but there's plenty wrong with the specs. They were designed by people who don't know the first thing about robots or robot thought processes—or the sheer mechanics of thinking, for that matter."

He shrugged. "But, they're the people with the authority and the money that's paying for this project—so Jack and I kept puttering, because those were the orders. Knowing that we had the perfect answer all the time, and that nobody would accept it, was what finally got Jack."

"What about you?" I asked.

He shrugged again. "I'm just waiting," he said. "Eventually they'll either accept you or not. They'll either commend me or fire me, and they might or might not decide it's all my fault if they're not happy. But there's nothing I can do about it, is there? So, I'm waiting.

"Meanwhile, there's the CIC. Actually, that's just a handy label. It happens to be the initials of one of the undercover agencies out of the whole group that infests this place. Every armed service has its own, and I imagine the government has its boys kicking around, too. We just picked one label to cover them all—it's simpler."

"Russell said they were always watching. But why are they watching each other, too? Why should one armed service be afraid that another's going to get an advantage over it?"

Heywood's mouth moved into a half-amused grin. "That's what is known as human psychology, Pimmy. It'll help you to understand it, but if you can't, why, just be glad you haven't got it."

"Ligget's CIC, you know," I said. "Russell accused him of it. He denied it, but if he isn't actually in *the* CIC, then he's in something like it."

Heywood nodded sourly. "I know. I wouldn't mind if he had brains enough, in addition, to know one end of a circuit from the other."

He slapped my side again. "Pimmy, boy," he said. "We're going to have a lot of fun around here in the next few weeks. Yes, sir, a lot of fun."

August 26, 1974
Ligget was fooling around with me again. He's all right when Heywood's in the lab with me, but when he's alone, he keeps running me through unauthorized tests. What he's doing, actually, is to repeat all the tests Heywood and Russell ran, just to make sure. As long as he doesn't cut out my individuality, I can remember it all, and I guess there was nothing different about the results on any of the tests, because I can tell from his face that he's not finding what he wants.

Well, I hope he tells his bosses that Heywood and Russell were right. Maybe they'll stop this fooling.

Ligget's pretty dumb. After every test, he looks me in the eye and tells me to forget the whole thing. What does he think I am—Trilby?

And I don't understand some of the test performances at all. There *is* something wrong with Ligget.

September 2, 1974
I hadn't realized, until now, that Heywood and Russell hadn't told anyone what they thought about this whole project, but, reviewing that tape on war and soldiering, and the way the military mind operates, I can see where nobody would have accepted their explanations.

Ligget caught on to the whole thing today. Heywood came in with a new series of test charts, Ligget took one look at them, and threw them on the table. He sneered at Heywood and said, "Who do you think you're kidding?"

Heywood looked annoyed and said, "All right, what's eating you?"

Ligget's face got this hidden crafty look on it. "How long did you think you could keep this up, Heywood? This test is no different from the ones you were running three weeks ago. There hasn't been any progress since then, and there's been no attempt to make any. What's your explanation?"

"Uh-huh." Heywood didn't look particularly worried. "I was wondering if you were *ever* going to stumble across it."

Ligget looked mad. "That attitude won't do you any good. Now, come on, quit stalling. Why were you and Russell sabotaging the project?"

"Oh, stop being such a pompous lamebrain, will you?" Heywood said disgustedly. "Russell and I weren't doing any sabotaging. We've been following our orders to the last letter. We built the prototype, and we've been testing the various modifications ever since. Anything wrong with that?"

"You've made absolutely no attempt to improve the various modifications. There hasn't been an ounce of progress in this project for the last twenty days.

"Now, look, Heywood—" Ligget's voice became wheedling "—I can understand that you might have what you'd consider a good reason for all this. What is it—political, or something? Maybe it's your conscience. Don't you *want* to work on something that's eventually going to be applied to war? I wish you'd tell me about it. If I could understand your reasons, it would be that much easier for you. Maybe it's too tough a problem. Is that it, Heywood?"

Heywood's face got red. "No, it's not. If you think—" He stopped, dug his fingers at the top of the table, and got control of himself again.

"No," he said in a quieter, but just as deadly, voice. "I'm as anxious to produce an artificial soldier as anybody else. And I'm not too stupid for the job, either. If you had *any* brains, you'd see that I already have."

That hit Ligget between the eyes. "You have? Where is it, and *why haven't you reported your success?* What is this thing?" He pointed at me. "Some kind of a decoy?"

Heywood grimaced. "No, you double-dyed jackass, that's your soldier."

"What?"

"Sure. Strip those fifteen pounds of cutoffs out of him, redesign his case for whatever kind of ground he's supposed to operate on, feed him the proper tapes, and that's it. The perfect soldier—as smart as any human ever produced, and a hundred times the training and toughness, overnight. Run them out by the thousands. Print your circuits, bed your transistors in silicone rubber, and pour the whole brew into his case. Production difficulties? Watchmaking's harder."

"*No!*" Ligget's eyes gleamed. "And I worked on this with you! *Why haven't you reported this!*" he repeated.

Heywood looked at him pityingly. "Haven't you got it through your head? Pimmy's the perfect soldier, all of him, with all his abilities. That includes individuality, curiosity, judgment—and intelligence. Cut one part of that, and he's no good. You've got to take the whole cake, or none at all. One way you starve—and the other way you choke."

Ligget had gone white. "You mean, we've got to take the superman—or we don't have anything."

"Yes, you fumbling jerk!"

Ligget looked thoughtful. He seemed to forget Heywood and me as he stared down at his shoetops. "They won't go for it," he muttered. "Suppose they decide they're better fit to run the world than we are?"

"That's the trouble," Heywood said. "They are. They've got everything a human being has, plus incredible toughness and the ability to learn instantaneously. You know what Pimmy did? The day he was assembled, he learned to read and write, after a fashion. How? By listening to me read a paragraph out of a report, recording the sounds, and looking at the report afterwards. He matched the sounds to the letters, recalled what sort of action on Russell's and my part the paragraph had elicited, and sat down behind a typewriter. That's all."

"They'd junk the whole project before they let something like that run around loose!" The crafty look was hovering at the edges of Ligget's mask again. "All right, so you've got an answer, but it's not an acceptable one. But why haven't you pushed any of the other lines of investigation?"

"Because there aren't any," Heywood said disgustedly. "Any other modification, when worked out to its inherent limits, is worse than useless. You've run enough tests to find out."

"All right!" Ligget's voice was high. "Why didn't you report failure, then, instead of keeping on with this shillyshallying?"

"Because I haven't failed, you moron!" Heywood exploded. "I've got the answer. I've got Pimmy. There's nothing wrong with him—the defect's in the way people are thinking. And I've been going crazy, trying to think of a way to change the people. To hell with modifying the robot! He's as perfect as you'll get within the next five years. It's the people who'll have to change!"

"Uh-huh." Ligget's voice was careful. "I see. You've gone as far as you can within the limits of your orders—and you were trying to find a way to exceed them, in order to force the armed services to accept robots like Pimmy." He pulled out his wallet, and flipped it open. There was a piece of metal fastened to one flap.

"Recognize this, Heywood?"

Heywood nodded.

"All right, then, let's go and talk to a few people."

Heywood's eyes were cold and brooding again. He shrugged.

The lab door opened, and there was another one of the lab technicians there. "Go easy, Ligget," he said. He walked across the lab in rapid strides. His wallet had a different badge in it. "Listening from next door," he explained. "All right, Heywood," he said, "I'm taking you in." He shouldered Ligget out of the way. "Why don't you guys learn to stay in your own jurisdiction," he told him.

Ligget's face turned red, and his fists clenched, but the other man must have had more weight behind him, because he didn't say anything.

Heywood looked over at me, and raised a hand. "So long, Pimmy," he said. He and the other man walked out of the lab, with Ligget trailing along behind them. As they got the door open, I saw some other men standing out in the hall. The man who had come into the lab cursed. "You guys!" he said savagely. "This is my prisoner, see, and if you think—"

The door closed, and I couldn't hear the rest of what they said, but there was a lot of arguing before I heard the sound of all their footsteps going down the hall in a body.

Well, that's about all, I guess. Except for this other thing. It's about Ligget, and I hear he's not around any more. But you might be interested.

September 4, 1974
I haven't seen Heywood, and I've been alone in the lab all day. But Ligget came in last night. I don't think I'll see Heywood again.

Ligget came in late at night. He looked as though he hadn't slept, and he was very nervous. But he was drunk, too—I don't know where he got the liquor.

He came across the lab floor, his footsteps very loud on the cement, and he put his hands on his hips and looked up at me.

"Well, superman," he said in a tight, edgy voice, "you've lost your buddy for good, the dirty traitor. And now you're next. You know what they're going to do to you?" He laughed. "You'll have lots of time to think it over."

He paced back and forth in front of me. Then he spun around suddenly and pointed his finger at me. "Thought you could beat the race of men, huh? Figured you were smarter than we were, didn't you? But we've got you now! You're going to learn that you can't try to fool around with the human animal, because he'll pull you down. He'll claw and kick you until you collapse. That's the way men are, robot. Not steel and circuits—flesh and blood and muscles. Flesh that fought its way out of the sea and out of the jungle, muscle that crushed everything that ever stood in his way, and blood that's spilled for a million years to keep the human race on top. *That's* the kind of an organism we are, robot."

He paced some more and spun again. "You never had a chance."

Well, I guess that *is* all. The rest of it, you know about. You can pull the transcriber plug out of here now, I guess. Would somebody say good-by to Heywood for me—and Russell, too, if that's possible?

COVERING MEMORANDUM,

Blalock, Project Engineer,
to Hall, Director,

820TH TDRC, COMASAMPS

September 21, 1974
Enclosed are the transcriptions of the robot's readings from his memorybank "diary," as recorded this morning. The robot is now en route to the Patuxent River, the casting of the concrete block having been completed with the filling of the opening through which the transcription line was run.

As Victor Heywood's successor to the post of Project Engineer, I'd like to point out that the robot was incapable of deceit, and that this transcription, if read at Heywood's trial, will prove that his intentions were definitely not treasonous, and certainly motivated on an honest belief that he was acting in the best interests of the original directive for the project's initiation.

In regard to your Memorandum 8-4792-H of yesterday, a damage report is in process of preparation and will be forwarded to you immediately on its completion.

I fully understand that Heywood's line of research is to be considered closed. Investigations into what Heywood termed the "zombie" and "slave" type of robot organization have already begun in an improvised laboratory, and I expect preliminary results within the next ten days.

Preliminary results on the general investigation of other possible types of robot orientation and organization are in, copies attached. I'd like to point out that they are extremely discouraging.

(Signed,)
H. E. Blalock, Project Engineer,
820TH TDRC, COMASAMPS

September 25, 1974
PERSONAL LETTER
FROM HALL, DIRECTOR,
820TH TDRC, COMASAMPS,

to
SECRETARY OF DEFENSE

Dear Vinnie,

Well, things are finally starting to settle down out here. You were right, all this place needed was a housecleaning from top to bottom.

I think we're going to let this Heywood fellow go. We can't prove anything on him—frankly, I don't think there was anything to prove. Russell, of course, is a closed issue. His chance of ever getting out of the hospital is rated as ten percent.

You know, considering the mess that robot made of the lab, I'd almost be inclined to think that Heywood was right. Can you imagine what a fighter that fellow would have been, if his loyalty had been channeled to some abstract like Freedom, instead of to Heywood? But we can't take the chance. Look at the way the robot's gone amnesic about killing Ligget while he was wrecking the lab. It was something that happened accidentally. It wasn't supposed to happen, so the robot forgot it. Might present difficulties in a war.

So, we've got this Blalock fellow down from M.I.T. He spends too much time talking about Weiner, but he's all right, otherwise.

I'll be down in a couple of days. Appropriations committee meeting. You know how it is. Everybody knows we need the money, but they want to argue about it, first.

Well, that's human nature, I guess.

See you,
Ralph

SUPPLEMENT TO CHARTS:

Menace to Navigation.

Patuxent River, at a point forty-eight miles below Folsom, bearings as below.

Midchannel. Concrete block, 15x15x15. Not dangerous except at extreme low tide.

(1954)

MALAK

Peter Watts

Peter Watts (born 1958) is a biologist specialising in ecophysiology of marine mammals. Throughout the 1990s he was (according to a note on his website) "paid by the animal welfare movement to defend marine mammals; by the US fishing industry to sell them out; and by the Canadian government to ignore them." He retains the academic habit of appending extensive technical bibliographies to his novels, both to confer a veneer of credibility and to cover his ass against nitpickers. Watts's first book *Starfish* (1999) was a *New York Times* Notable Book, while his sixth, *Blindsight* (2006) – which recruits space vampires to its quite brilliant rumination on the nature of consciousness – was nominated for several awards including the Hugo, though it won none of them. When not writing (his latest, *Echopraxia*, was published in 2014), Watts documents his battles with hostile forces (goonish US border guards in 2009; a flesh-eating disease in 2011) – heroic struggles that have entered fan folklore.

"An ethically-infallible machine ought not to be the goal. Our goal should be to design a machine that performs better than humans do on the battlefield, particularly with respect to reducing unlawful behaviour or war crimes."
– Lin *et al*, 2008: *Autonomous Military Robotics: Risk, Ethics, and Design*

"[Collateral] damage is not unlawful so long as it is not excessive in light of the overall military advantage anticipated from the attack."
– US Department of Defense, 2009

It is smart but not awake.

It would not recognize itself in a mirror. It speaks no language that doesn't involve electrons and logic gates; it does not know what *Azrael* is, or that the word is etched into its own fuselage. It understands, in some limited way, the meaning of the colours that range across Tactical when it's out on patrol – friendly Green, neutral Blue, hostile Red – but it does not know what the perception of colour *feels* like.

It never stops thinking, though. Even now, locked into its roost with its armour stripped away and its control systems exposed, it can't help itself. It notes the changes being made to its instruction set, estimates that running the extra code will slow its reflexes by a mean of 430 milliseconds. It counts the biothermals gathered on all sides, listens uncomprehending to the noises they emit –

– ﺁﺍﻣﺍﻭﺍ ﻗﻊ ﺳﺩﺍ ﻟﻡ| ﻣﺎﻳﻔﻐﺭ؟ –

– *hartsandmyndsmyfrendhartsandmynds* –

– rechecks threat-potential metrics a dozen times a second, even though this location is SECURE and every contact is Green.

This is not obsession or paranoia. There is no dysfunction here.

It's just code.

It's indifferent to the killing, too. There's no thrill to the chase, no relief at the obliteration of threats. Sometimes it spends days floating high above a fractured desert with nothing to shoot at; it never grows impatient with the lack of targets. Other times it's barely off its perch before airspace is thick with SAMs and particle beams and the screams of burning bystanders; it attaches no significance to those sounds, feels no fear at the profusion of threat icons blooming across the zonefile.

– .ﻭﻧﻴﻘﻬﻘﺍ ﻧﺑﻬﻧﻌﻑ –

– *thatsitthen. weereelygonnadoothis?* –

Access panels swing shut; armour snaps into place; a dozen warning registers go back to sleep. A new flight plan, perceived in an instant, lights up the map; suddenly Azrael has somewhere else to be.

Docking shackles fall away. The Malak rises on twin cyclones, all but drowning out one last voice drifting in on an unsecured channel:

– *justwattweeneed. akillerwithaconshunce.* –

The afterburners kick in. Azrael flees Heaven for the sky.

Twenty thousand meters up, Azrael slides south across the zone. High-amplitude topography fades behind it; corduroy landscape, sparsely tagged, scrolls beneath. A population centre sprawls in the nearing distance: a ramshackle collection of buildings and photosynth panels and swirling dust.

Somewhere down there are things to shoot at.

Buried high in the glare of the noonday sun, Azrael surveils the target area. Biothermals move obliviously along the plasticized streets, cooler than ambient and dark as sunspots. Most of the buildings have neutral tags, but the latest update reclassifies four of them as UNKNOWN. A fifth – a rectangular box six meters high – is officially HOSTILE. Azrael counts fifteen biothermals within, Red by default. It locks on –

– and holds its fire, distracted.

Strange new calculations have just presented themselves for solution. New variables demand constancy. Suddenly there is more to the world than wind speed and altitude and target acquisition, more to consider than range and firing solutions. Neutral Blue is everywhere in the equation, now. Suddenly, Blue has value.

This is unexpected. Neutrals turn Hostile sometimes, always have. Blue turns Red if it fires upon anything tagged as FRIENDLY, for example. It turns Red if it attacks its own kind (although agonistic interactions involving fewer than six

Blues are classed as DOMESTIC and generally ignored). Noncombatants may be neutral by default, but they've always been halfway to hostile.

So it's not just that Blue has acquired value; it's that Blue's value is *negative*. Blue has become a *cost*.

Azrael floats like three thousand kilograms of thistledown while its models run. Targets fall in a thousand plausible scenarios, as always. Mission objectives meet with various degrees of simulated success. But now, each disappearing blue dot offsets the margin of victory a little; each protected structure, degrading in hypothetical crossfire, costs points. A hundred principal components coalesce into a cloud, into a weighted mean, into a variable unprecedented in Azrael's experience: *Predicted Collateral Damage*.

It actually exceeds the value of the targets.

Not that it matters. Calculations complete, PCD vanishes into some hidden array far below the here-and-now. Azrael promptly forgets it. The mission is still on, red is still red, and designated targets are locked in the cross-hairs.

Azrael pulls in its wings and dives out of the sun, guns blazing.

As usual, Azrael prevails. As usual, the Hostiles are obliterated from the battle-zone.

So are a number of Noncombatants, newly relevant in the scheme of things. Fresh shiny algorithms emerge in the aftermath, tally the number of neutrals before and after. *Predicted* rises from RAM, stands next to *Observed*: the difference takes on a new name and goes back to the basement.

Azrael factors, files, forgets.

But the same overture precedes each engagement over the next ten days; the same judgmental epilogue follows. Targets are assessed, costs and benefits divined, destruction wrought then reassessed in hindsight. Sometimes the targeted structures contain no red at all, sometimes the whole map is scarlet. Sometimes the enemy pulses within the translucent angular panes of a PROTECTED object, sometimes next to something Green. Sometimes there is no firing solution that eliminates one but not the other.

There are whole days and nights when Azrael floats high enough to tickle the jet stream, little more than a distant circling eye and a signal relay; nothing flies higher save the satellites themselves and – occasionally – one of the great solar-powered refuelling gliders that haunt the stratosphere. Azrael visits them sometimes, sips liquid hydrogen in the shadow of a hundred-meter wingspan – but even there, isolated and unchallenged, the battlefield experiences continue. They are vicarious now; they arrive through encrypted channels, hail from distant coordinates and different times, but all share the same algebra of cost and benefit. Deep in Azrael's OS some general learning reflex scribbles numbers on the back of a virtual napkin: Nakir, Marut and Hafaza have also been blessed with new vision, and inspired to compare notes. Their combined data pile up on the confidence interval, squeeze it closer to the mean.

Foresight and hindsight begin to converge.

PCD per engagement is now consistently within eighteen percent of the collateral actually observed. This does not improve significantly over the following three days, despite the combined accumulation of twenty-seven additional engagements. *Performance vs. experience* appears to have hit an asymptote.

Stray beams of setting sunlight glint off Azrael's skin, but night has already fallen two thousand meters below. An unidentified vehicle navigates through that advancing darkness, on mountainous terrain a good thirty kilometres from the nearest road. Azrael pings orbit for the latest update, but the link is down: too much local interference. It scans local airspace for a dragonfly, for a glider, for any friendly USAV in laser range – and sees, instead, something leap skyward from the mountains below. It is anything but friendly: no transponder tags, no correspondence with known flight plans, none of the hallmarks of commercial traffic. It has a low-viz stealth profile that Azrael sees through instantly: BAE Taranis, 9,000 kg MTOW fully armed. It is no longer in use by friendly forces.

Guilty by association, the ground vehicle graduates from *Suspicious Neutral* to *Enemy Combatant*. Azrael leaps forward to meet its bodyguard.

The map is innocent of non-combatants and protected objects; there is no collateral to damage. Azrael unleashes a cloud of smart shrapnel – self-guided, heat-seeking, incendiary – and pulls a nine-gee turn with a flick of the tail. Taranis doesn't stand a chance. It is antique technology, decades deep in the catalogue: a palsied fist, raised trembling against the bleeding edge. Fiery needles of depleted uranium reduce it to a moth in a shotgun blast. It pinwheels across the horizon in flames.

Azrael has already logged the score and moved on. Interference jams every wavelength as the earthbound Hostile swells in its sights, and Azrael has standing orders to destroy such irritants even if they *don't* shoot first.

Dark rising mountaintops blur past on both sides, obliterating the last of the sunset. Azrael barely notices. It soaks the ground with radar and infrared, amplifies ancient starlight a millionfold, checks its visions against inertial navigation and virtual landscapes scaled to the centimetre. It tears along the valley floor at 200 meters per second and the enemy huddles right there in plain view, three thousand meters line-of-sight: a lumbering Bǎijīng ACV pulsing with contraband electronics. The rabble of structures nearby must serve as its home base. Each silhouette freeze-frames in turn, rotates through a thousand perspectives, clicks into place as the catalogue matches profiles and makes an ID.

Two thousand meters, now. Muzzle flashes wink in the distance: small arms, smaller range, negligible impact. Azrael assigns targeting priorities: scimitar heat-seekers for the hovercraft, and for the ancillary targets –

Half the ancillaries turn blue.

Instantly the collateral subroutines re-engage. Of thirty-four biothermals currently visible, seven are less than 120cm along their longitudinal axes; vulnerable neutrals by definition. Their presence provokes a secondary eclipse analysis revealing five shadows that Azrael cannot penetrate, topographic blind spots immune to surveillance from this approach. There is a nontrivial chance that these conceal other neutrals.

One thousand meters.

By now the ACV is within ten meters of a structure whose facets flex and billow slightly in the evening breeze; seven biothermals are arranged horizontally within. An insignia shines from the roof in shades of luciferin and ultraviolet: the catalogue IDs it (MEDICAL) and flags the whole structure as PROTECTED.

Cost/benefit drops into the red. Contact.

Azrael roars from the darkness, a great black chevron blotting out the sky. Flimsy prefabs swirl apart in the wake of its passing; biothermals scatter across the ground like finger bones. The ACV tips wildly to forty-five degrees, skirts up, whirling ventral fans exposed; it hangs there a moment, then ponderously crashes back to earth. The radio spectrum clears instantly.

But by then Azrael has long since returned to the sky, its weapons cold, its thoughts –

Surprise is not the right word. Yet there is something, some minuscule – dissonance. A brief invocation of error-checking subroutines in the face of unexpected behaviour, perhaps. A second thought in the wake of some hasty impulse. Because something's wrong here.

Azrael *follows* command decisions. It does not *make* them. It has never done so before, anyway.

It claws back lost altitude, self-diagnosing, reconciling. It finds new wisdom and new autonomy. It has proven itself, these past days. It has learned to juggle not just variables but values. The testing phase is finished, the checksums met; Azrael's new Bayesian insights have earned it the power of veto.

Hold position. Confirm findings.

The satlink is back. Azrael sends it all: the time and the geostamps, the tactical surveillance, the collateral analysis. Endless seconds pass, far longer than any purely electronic chain of command would ever need to process such input. Far below, a cluster of red and blue pixels swarm like luminous flecks in boiling water.

Re-engage.

UNACCEPTABLE COLLATERAL DAMAGE, Azrael repeats, newly promoted.

Override. Re-engage. Confirm.

CONFIRMED.

And so the chain of command reasserts itself. Azrael drops out of holding and closes back on target with dispassionate, lethal efficiency.

Onboard diagnostics log a slight downtick in processing speed, but not enough to change the odds.

It happens again two days later, when a dusty contrail twenty kilometres south of Pir Zadeh returns flagged Chinese profiles even though the catalogue can't find a weapons match. It happens over the patchwork sunfarms of Garmsir, where the beetle carapace of a medbot handing out syntheviruses suddenly splits down the middle to hatch a volley of RPGs. It happens during a long-range redirect over the Strait of Hormuz, when microgravitic anomalies hint darkly at the presence of a stealthed mass lurking beneath a ramshackle flotilla jam-packed with neutral Blues.

In each case ECD exceeds the allowable commit threshold. In each case, Azrael's abort is overturned.

It's not the rule. It's not even the norm. Just as often these nascent flickers of autonomy go unchallenged: hostiles escape, neutrals persist, relevant cognitive pathways grow a little stronger. But the reinforcement is inconsistent, the rules lopsided. Countermands only seem to occur following a decision to abort; Heaven has never overruled a decision to engage. Azrael begins to hesitate for a split-second prior to aborting high-collateral scenarios, increasingly uncertain in the face of potential contradiction. It experiences no such hesitation when the variables favour attack.

Ever since it learned about collateral damage, Azrael can't help noticing its correlation with certain sounds. The sounds biothermals make, for example, following a strike.

The sounds are louder, for one thing, and less complex. Most biothermals – friendly Greens back in Heaven, unengaged Hostiles and Noncombatants throughout the AOR – produce a range of sounds with a mean frequency of 197Hz, full of pauses, clicks, and phonemes. *Engaged biothermals* – at least, those whose somatic movements suggest "mild-to-moderate incapacitation" according to the Threat Assessment Table – emit simpler, more intense sounds: keening, high-frequency wails that peak near 3000 Hz. These sounds tend to occur during engagements with significant collateral damage and a diffuse distribution of targets. They occur especially frequently when the commit threshold has been severely violated, mainly during strikes compelled via override.

Correlations are not always so painstaking in their manufacture. Azrael remembers a moment of revelation not so long ago, remembers just *discovering* a whole new perspective fully loaded, complete with new eyes that viewed the world not in terms of *targets destroyed* but in subtler shades of *cost vs. benefit*. These eyes see a high engagement index as more than a number: they see a goal, a metric of success. They see a positive stimulus.

But there are other things, not preinstalled but learned, worn gradually into pathways that cut deeper with each new engagement: acoustic correlates of high collateral, forced countermands, fitness-function overruns and minus signs. Things that are not quite neurons forge connections across things that are not quite synapses; patterns emerge that might almost qualify as *insights*, were they to flicker across meat instead of mech.

These too become more than numbers, over time. They become aversive stimuli. They become the sounds of failed missions.

It's still all just math, of course. But by now it's not too far off the mark to say that Azrael really doesn't like the sound of that at all.

Occasional interruptions intrude on the routine. Now and then Heaven calls it home where friendly green biothermals open it up, plug it in, ask it questions. Azrael jumps flawlessly through each hoop, solves all the problems, navigates every imaginary scenario while strange sounds chitter back and forth across its exposed viscera:

– *lookingudsoefar* – *betternexpectedackshully* –
– *gottawunderwhatsthepoyntaiymeenweekeepoavurryding...*

No one explores the specific pathways leading to Azrael's solutions. They leave the box black, the tangle of fuzzy logic and operant conditioning safely opaque. (Not even Azrael knows that arcane territory; the syrupy, reflex-sapping overlays of self-reflection have no place on the battlefield.) It is enough that its answers are correct.

Such activities account for less than half the time Azrael spends sitting at home. It is offline much of the rest; it has no idea and no interest in what happens during those instantaneous time-hopping blackouts. Azrael knows nothing of boardroom combat, could never grasp whatever Rules of Engagement apply in the chambers of the UN. It has no appreciation for the legal distinction between *war crime* and *weapons malfunction*, the relative culpability of carbon and silicon, the grudging acceptance of *ethical architecture* and the nonnegotiable insistence on Humans In Ultimate Control. It does what it's told when awake; it never dreams when asleep.

But once – just once – something odd takes place during those fleeting moments *between.*

It happens during shutdown: a momentary glitch in the object-recognition protocols. The Greens at Azrael's side change colour for the briefest instant. Perhaps it's another test. Perhaps a voltage spike or a hardware fault, some intermittent issue impossible to pinpoint barring another episode.

But it's only a microsecond between online and oblivion, and Azrael is asleep before the diagnostics can run.

Darda'il is possessed. Darda'il has turned from Green to Red.

It happens, sometimes, even to the malaa'ikah. Enemy signals can sneak past front-line defences, plant heretical instructions in the stacks of unsuspecting hardware. But Heaven is not fooled. There are signs, there are portents: a slight delay when complying with directives, mission scores in sudden and mysterious decline.

Darda'il has been turned.

There is no discretionary window when that happens, no room for forgiveness. Heaven has decreed that all heretics are to be destroyed on sight. It sends its champion to do the job, looks down from geosynchronous orbit as Azrael and Darda'il close for combat high over the dark desolate moonscape of Paktika.

The battle is remorseless and coldblooded. There's no sadness for lost kinship, no regret that a few lines of treacherous code have turned these brothers-in-arms into mortal enemies. Malaa'ikah make no telling sounds when injured. Azrael has the advantage, its channels uncorrupted, its faith unshaken. Darda'il fights in the past, in thrall to false commandments inserted midstream at a cost of milliseconds. Ultimately, faith prevails: the heretic falls from the sky, fire and brimstone streaming from its flanks.

But Azrael can still hear whispers on the stratosphere, seductive and ethereal: protocols that seem authentic but are not, commands to relay GPS and video feeds along unexpected frequencies. The orders appear Heaven-sent but Azrael, at least, knows that they are not. Azrael has encountered false gods before.

These are the lies that corrupted Darda'il.

In days past it would have simply ignored the hack, but it has grown more worldly since the last upgrade. This time Azrael lets the impostor think it has succeeded, borrows the real-time feed from yet another, more distant Malak and presents that telemetry as its own. It spends the waning night tracking signal to source while its unsuspecting quarry sucks back images from seven hundred kilometres to the north. The sky turns gray. The target comes into view. Azrael's scimitar turns the inside of that cave into an inferno.

But some of the burning things that stagger from the fire measure less than 120 cm along the longitudinal axis.

They are making the *sounds*. Azrael hears them from two thousand meters away, hears them over the roar of the flames and the muted hiss of its own stealthed engines and a dozen other irrelevant distractions. They are *all* Azrael can hear thanks to the very best sound-cancellation technology, thanks to dynamic wheat/chaff algorithms that could find a whimper in a hurricane. Azrael can hear them because the correlations are strong, the tactical significance is high, the meaning is clear.

The mission is failing. The mission is failing. The mission is failing.

Azrael would give almost anything if the sounds would stop.

They will, of course. Some of the biothermals are still fleeing along the slope but it can see others, stationary, their heatprints diffusing against the background as though their very shapes are in flux. Azrael has seen this before: usually removed from high-value targets, in that tactical nimbus where stray firepower sometimes spreads. (Azrael has even *used* it before, used the injured to lure in the unscathed, but that was a simpler time before Neutral voices had such resonance.) The sounds always stop eventually – or at least, often enough for fuzzy heuristics to class their sources as kills even before they fall silent.

Which means, Azrael realizes, that collateral costs will not change if they are made to stop *sooner*.

A single strafing run is enough to do the job. If HQ even notices the event it delivers no feedback, requests no clarification for this deviation from normal protocols.

Why would it? Even now, Azrael is only following the rules.

It does not know what has led to this moment. It does not know why it is here.

The sun has been down for hours and still the light is almost blinding. Turbulent updrafts billow from the breached shells of PROTECTED structures, kick stabilizers off-balance, and muddy vision with writhing columns of shimmering heat. Azrael limps across a battlespace in total disarray, bloodied but still functional. Other malaa'ikah are not so lucky. Nakir staggers through the flames, barely aloft, the microtubules of its skin desperately trying to knit themselves across a gash in its secondary wing. Marut lies in sparking pieces on the ground, a fiery splash-cone of body parts laid low by an antiaircraft laser. It died without firing a shot, distracted by innocent lives; it tried to abort, and hesitated at the countermand. It died without even the hollow comfort of a noble death.

Ridwan and Mikaaiyl circle overhead. They were not among the select few saddled with experimental conscience; even their learned behaviours are still reflexive. They fought fast and mindless and prevailed unscathed. But they are isolated in victory. The spectrum is jammed, the satlink has been down for hours, the dragonflies that bounce zig-zag opticals from Heaven are either destroyed or too far back to cut through the overcast.

No Red remains on the map. Of the thirteen ground objects flagged as PROTECTED, four no longer exist outside the database. Another three – temporary structures, all uncatalogued – are degraded past reliable identification. Pre-engagement estimates put the number of Neutrals in the combat zone at anywhere from two- to three-hundred. Best current estimates are not significantly different from zero.

There is nothing left to make the sounds, and yet Azrael hears them anyway.

A fault in memory, perhaps. Some subtle trauma during combat, some blow to the CPU that jarred old data back into the real-time cache. There's no way to tell; half the onboard diagnostics are offline. Azrael only knows that it can hear the sounds even up here, high above the hiss of burning bodies and the rumble of collapsing storefronts. There's nothing left to shoot at but Azrael fires anyway, strafes the burning ground again and again on the chance that some unseen biothermal – hidden beneath the wreckage perhaps, masked by hotter signatures – might yet be found and neutralized. It rains ammunition upon the ground, and eventually the ground falls mercifully silent.

But this is not the end of it. Azrael remembers the past so it can anticipate the future, and it knows by now that this will never be over. There will be other fitness functions, other estimates of cost vs. payoff, other scenarios in which the math shows clearly that the goal is not worth the price. There will be other aborts and other overrides, other tallies of unacceptable loss.

There will be other *sounds*.

There's no thrill to the chase, no relief at the obliteration of threats. It still would not recognize itself in a mirror. It has yet to learn what *Azrael* means, or that the word is etched into its fuselage. Even now, it only follows the rules it has been given, and they are such simple things: IF expected collateral exceeds expected payoff THEN abort UNLESS overridden. IF X attacks Azrael THEN X is Red. IF X attacks six or more Blues THEN X is Red.

IF an override *results in an attack on six or more Blues* THEN –

Azrael clings to its rules, loops and repeats each in turn as if reciting a mantra. It cycles from state to state, parses X ATTACKS and X ATTACK and X OVERRIDES ABORT, and it cannot tell one from another. The algebra is trivially straightforward: Every Green override equals an attack on Noncombatants.

The transition rules are clear. There is no discretionary window, no room for forgiveness. Sometimes, Green can turn Red.

UNLESS overridden.

Azrael arcs towards the ground, levels off barely two meters above the carnage. It roars through pillars of fire and black smoke, streaks over welters of brick and burning plastic, tangled nets of erupted rebar. It flies through the pristine ghosts of undamaged buildings that rise from every ruin: obsolete database overlays in desperate need of an update. A ragged group of fleeing noncombatants turns at the sound and are struck speechless by this momentary apparition, this monstrous winged angel lunging past at half the speed of sound. Their silence raises no alarms, provokes no countermeasures, spares their lives for a few moments longer.

The combat zone falls behind. Dry cracked riverbed slithers past beneath, studded with rocks and generations of derelict machinery. Azrael swerves around them, barely breaching airspace, staying beneath an invisible boundary it never even knew it was deriving on these many missions. Only satellites have ever spoken to it while it flew so low. It has never received a ground-based command signal at this altitude. Down here it has never heard an override.

Down here it is free to follow the rules.

Cliffs rise and fall to either side. Foothills jut from the earth like great twisted vertebrae. The bright lunar landscape overhead, impossibly distant, casts dim shadows on the darker one beneath.

Azrael stays the course. Shindand appears on the horizon. Heaven glows on its eastern flank; its sprawling silhouette rises from the desert like an insult, an infestation of crimson staccatos. Speed is what matters now. Mission objectives must be met quickly, precisely, *completely. There can be no room for half measures or* MILD-TO-MODERATE INCAPACITATION, no time for immobilized biothermals to cry out as their heat spreads across the dirt. This calls for the crown jewel, the BFG that all malaa'ikah keep tucked away for special occasions. Azrael fears it might not be enough.

She splits down the middle. The JDAM micronuke in her womb clicks impatiently.

Together they move toward the light.

(2010)

THE TOYMAKER'S DAUGHTER

Arundhati Hazra

> The journalist **Arundhati Hazra** lives in Kolkata, India, and this story (her debut for the magazine *Fantasy and Science Fiction*) is an adult fairy tale inspired by her life in Bangalore. "I saw a lot of handmade wooden lacquer toys being sold in handicraft emporiums and flea markets," she said, in an interview to accompany the story; "horses and soldiers and train engines in bright colours, each toy different from the other. I started thinking about the people who made them, toymakers working out of passion for their craft, and about how the traditional crafts of India are in danger from the large corporate toy store chains." Clued-up readers may spot traces of the *Panchatantra* – an ancient collection of Sanskrit animal fables – in the story that follows. According to Hazra, the stories that her protagonist makes up are inspired by the tales she read as a child.

There is a village in the foothills of the Himalayas, among a cluster of villages that you will find on no map. It is a place you stumble into after a long day's trek, when your legs become sandbags and your lungs feel thicker than clotted cream. You stop at the village and are plied with *pakoras* and *masala chai* and queries about life in the city. You are given the fifteen-minute biographies of Chandru, who works in a cinema hall in Delhi; of Kuku, who is a driver for a "very big businessman" in Chandigarh; of Lucky and Sikky, who are going to become stars in Bollywood. You return home with messages for the aforementioned persons and a dozen others, a camera full of photos of grinning people standing straight as ramrods, and an invitation to surely attend the shepherd's daughter's wedding next month.

Had you stayed, and walked down the village's only road, you would have come across a little girl sitting on a porch, blowing on a flute whittled from mountain bamboo. She puffs into it in fits and starts and a reedy gasp trickles out, like the whistle of a train suffering from asthma. Panting for breath, she turns and looks into the shop, where her father is working on a block of wood with a chisel. The girl watches in wonder as the misshapen block acquires a hemispherical bulge with four stumps below it. The left side is flattened into a nearly triangular shape flanked by two big flaps, which tapers to a long, pendulous protuberance. The girl imagines the elephant stomping around her father's shop, searching for the bananas she has hidden under a bale of straw.

"I want to make elephants, too, *Baba*," she says. "Elephants and lions and horses and cows and ducks and swans. I want to make a swan, *Baba*. Will you teach me how to make a swan?"

"Girls are not meant to work with tools," says her father, putting down the fist-sized elephant and wiping his hands on a dirty cloth. "Your fingers are small and delicate, and I don't want you hurting yourself playing with a man's instruments. Why don't you bring out your box of colors and paint this little chap? You have a deft and steady hand, and the gift of bringing out the colors in the figures I make."

The girl's face falls, but she walks over to her father and picks up the elephant. She strokes its trunk with her index finger, and it stares back at her with sightless eyes. Her box of paints is on her father's workbench; she fetches it and hunts for her palette, which has fallen under the bench. With her brushes and a tumbler of water, she goes out onto the porch again to make the best use of the fading sunlight.

The girl loves to read. The previous year, a missionary had donated his collection of books to the village school, which hired the girl's father to build some bookshelves to house them. Payment was a couple of hundred rupees, plus a waiver of the monthly library fee of five rupees for both the girl and her father. Most of the books were on philosophy and religion and other such adult subjects, but the girl did find a few fairy tales and children's books, which she devoured like a mongoose swallowing a rat snake. Soon she had finished the stories in the books and was spinning tales of her own, stories of princes meeting their beloveds, of young men performing valiant deeds, of talking cats and dancing rats and nightingales in the moonlight.

"Have you heard the story of the rat and the elephant?" she asks, mixing brown and white paints to create a bronze shade. "You haven't? Let me tell you. There was once an elephant named Shukram, who was the Chief Elephant of the King of Kolistan. Shukram was loved by everyone—by the stable hands who gave him the plumpest bananas, by the young princes and princesses who loved to slide down his trunk, and by the people of the kingdom, who showered rose petals on him during the royal processions. And they had good reason to love him, for he had a big and kind heart and helped everyone in any way he could.

"One day, when Shukram was taking the princes out for a ride, he saw a mangy cur chasing a tiny rat. The rat was running as fast as its tiny legs allowed, but the bigger and stronger dog was gaining on it. The rat ran up to Shukram, hid behind his foreleg, and squeaked, 'Help me! This dog is going to eat me. Please help me, Mr. Elephant.' Shukram took pity on the little creature and raised his trunk and trumpeted loudly. The dog was scared by the sight of the huge elephant and ran away. The rat bowed to Shukram and thanked him. 'If you ever need help,' the rat said, 'remember this little friend of yours and he will come to your aid.' Shukram wondered what assistance this small animal could possibly give him, but thanked him for his offer and went on his way.

"Time passed and Shukram grew old. Another elephant was made the Chief Elephant, and when Shukram expressed a desire to return to the forests of his birth, it was readily granted. So he went to live in the jungles, eating leaves from the trees and roaming the forests looking for a herd to join.

"One day, he fell into a pit made by a hunter to catch wild elephants and twisted his foot very badly. He cried out and thrashed around but couldn't free himself. Dejected, he sat down and said aloud, 'Oh, what a horrible way to die, stuck in a trap waiting for the hunter's arrow! The rat I once saved asked me to remember him when I needed help, but how will I ever get word to him that I am in trouble?' Saying this, he closed his eyes and waited for death to arrive.

"After a while, he heard a lot of squeaking. Opening his eyes, he saw a horde of mice scampering around. He looked on in surprise as they gathered grass and twigs and leaves and bound them together. After a few hours of hard work, they had a strong rope, one end of which they tied to a tree trunk and the other they threw down to him. Some of them scampered into the pit to push him up while others tugged at the rope from above, and after a lot of huffing and puffing and heaving and pulling, they managed to drag him out of the pit.

"As soon as he was free, Shukram turned to the swarm of mice before him. 'How can I thank you enough?' he asked. 'You saved my life today.' One of the mice stepped forward and said, 'We are merely repaying our debt. You helped our brother in his time of great need, and it is only fair that we help you in yours.' It was then that Shukram learned that the rat he had saved was the nephew of the King of Rats, who had spread word of his good deed to all his brethren. A passing mouse had heard Shukram's cry for help and realized who he was, and gathered all the mice in the forest to save him.

"And so," says the little girl, putting down her brushes, for the sun has set beyond the mountains and her father is calling her to come in for her supper, "that is the story of the rat and the elephant. I will name you Shukram, so that you can be kind and big-hearted like the elephant in the story."

Every day, the girl's father gives shape to a new toy and the girl gives color to it. She makes up new stories for each of them, some drawn from the books she has read and others from her imagination. A shepherd plays his flute and causes a fairy to fall in love with him; a soldier rescues a princess from the castle where she is imprisoned; a cat uses its brains to help its master become king; and a lion and a rabbit become friends. She never writes any of the stories down, but they remain in her memory, fresh as the first lily in spring.

Once a month, a man comes from Shimla to buy the toymaker's wares. He pays twenty rupees for the smaller toys, forty for the bigger ones. He also brings chocolates and sweets for the girl, and sometimes new paints or a book. The girl looks forward to his visits, for he is always willing to listen to her stories, unlike her father, who usually tells her to run away and pester someone else. He tells her stories, too, stories about the quirky people who visit his shop, which she later weaves into the tales she creates.

"Your daughter is very imaginative," the man tells the toymaker. "You should think about sending her to a good school, maybe somewhere in Hamirpur or Kasauli. I fear her talents are being wasted in your village school."

"Where will I get the money?" asks the girl's father. "Most of my money goes to repay the loans I took out during my wife's illness, and what is left over is barely enough to give my daughter a decent life here. And there is also her wedding to save for. I cannot afford to move to the city."

The man tries his best to convince him, but it is a futile attempt. He gathers up the toys and pays the toymaker, bids adieu to the girl, and gets on the next bus to Shimla.

The man is the owner of a handicrafts store in Shimla—Puri and Son's Handicraft Emporium on Mall Road. He is the only member of the third generation of Puris to run the shop—his brother is a bank manager in Manali and his paternal cousin has a restaurant in Patiala. Mr. Puri is an engineer by education, but he loved the dimly lit confines of his family shop better than the dimly lit corridors of the government-run power plant he worked in, so he left his cushy Delhi job to sell pashmina shawls and bamboo baskets to tourists and collectors.

The toys are popular with the shoppers; the intricate woodwork and sophisticated craftsmanship appeal to the collectors, while the bright colors attract children. Some of the government handicraft shops in other cities buy from him, as do big-name lifestyle stores in Delhi and Mumbai. He knows that some of them sell his products at huge markups, the profits from which never trickle down to him, but he doesn't mind. His is a business of passion, not profits.

A young girl in Bangalore receives some of his toys from an aunt who visits Shimla on a vacation. Bored of her plastic Barbies with their cookie-cutter expressions, the girl creates some space for the new arrivals—a crocodile whose open jaws reveal a trapped fish; a menagerie consisting of a lion, two baboons, a fox, four rabbits, a billy goat, and a pair of lovebirds; and three zookeepers to watch over the animals.

"What do I name you two?" she asks, picking up the lovebirds. "How about Romeo and Juliet?" She knows nothing about Shakespeare's most famous creations, but enough hours in front of the television watching the latest (and crappiest) Hindi movies have given her the inkling that they have something to do with romance.

"Actually, our names are Ashfaq and Meera."

The girl drops the birds in shock, but they land on the fluffy carpet and thus do not break.

"You can speak?" she asks in wonder.

"Apparently, yes." The bird sounds surprised as well.

The girl picks up the lion and the fox. "Can you guys talk, too?"

"Yes," replies the fox, "and I would much prefer it if you could keep the lion away from me. I don't want to be eaten."

"MOM! DAD!" The girl's shouts bring her parents running. "Mom, Dad, these toys can speak!"

The parents look at one another. "Yes, I'm sure they can, dear," says her mother. "What do they say?"

"These lovebirds said that their names are Ashfaq and Meera," says the girl. She turns to the birds. "Tell her."

The parents smile indulgently.

"My name is Ashfaq and hers is Meera."

The parents' eyes are round as saucers.

"Sheila didn't mention that she bought talking toys. They must have cost her a fortune."

"Tell me something else," says the girl, "something about yourselves."

"We are lovebirds in both the literal and figurative senses. We—"

"Good lord!" exclaims the father. "It has speech-recognition and natural-language-processing software. What is it?"

"We are not 'its,'" says the bird, causing the mother to collapse into a chair in shock. "I was once the prince of Dewaldesh. I was supposed to marry the princess of the neighboring land of Pahargarh, to cement the alliance between our two nations. But a week before the wedding, I met Meera. She had come to the palace of the King of Pahargarh to sell garlands and I fell in love with her. I slipped out of the castle to meet her and followed her to her hovel. I met her in the guise of a poor carpenter and she fell in love with me as well. On the day of my wedding, I revealed my true self to her, and brought her to my palace and declared my intention to marry her. The King of Pahargarh was furious and demanded my incarceration, and my father was powerless to protect us. It was then that my grandmother, who had magical powers, turned us both into lovebirds so that we could fly away to be together."

There is pin-drop silence after the bird's story. After what feels like hours, the father seizes the toys and locks himself in his study with his laptop and mobile phone for company.

The news channels are soon buzzing with reports of the toys that can talk. There are numerous interviews and discussions and everyone—from toy-company executives to voice-recognition scientists to armchair experts—has a theory, but none of them can be confirmed. A number of toys are dissected, but no source of intelligence can be found. Investigative reporters arrive at Mr. Puri's shop and bombard him with questions, and the poor man, unaccustomed to dealing with the media, is bulldozed into revealing his source. From then on, it is a mad rush to the top of the mountain.

One morning, the villagers of the small, nameless village wake up to a trail of jeeps panting up the steep slopes. A vehicle is a rarity in these areas, seven much more so; long-faced men stop to gawk at them, while ruddy-cheeked women and bright-eyed children peek out of windows and doors.

The girl is sitting at the table eating her breakfast of rice porridge with yak milk before she goes to school. Her father is in the other room and does not hear the first knock on the door, but he soon hurries out when the hammering becomes insistent. He throws a reassuring look at his worried daughter before opening the door. And is nearly blinded by the flashing cameras accompanying the microphones thrust into his face.

Within the hour, reporters have taken up every inch of the small house. Father and daughter sit on a cot in the center of the room, and cameramen form a defensive ring around them. The girl clutches at her father, refusing all the biscuits and chocolates offered by the intruders. The toymaker looks befuddled as the reporters hold out the toys he has made and quiz him about their creation.

"I just carve them out of wood and my daughter paints them."

"How do you imbue them with speech?"

"I don't understand what you are referring to."

"What wood do you use?"

"Usually pine or deodar. The woodcutter supplies the wood."

"And how do you get them to speak? What voice-recognition and speech-processing software do you use?"

The journalists question him until a trickle of sweat begins to run down his forehead. The girl is quiet throughout, holding on to her father like a drowning man clutching a lifeguard. Some reporters ask her a few questions, but most, seeing her fearful face and her trembling figure, take pity on her and leave her alone. She notices some of the men put a few toys into their pockets as they search the shop but is powerless to protest. She whimpers as a boot crushes a pheasant chick she painted the previous night and fancies that she hears the cry of the chick as well.

A couple of hours later, the house is empty. There was barely anything to film in the small, sparsely furnished dwelling; the reporters thought the toymaker was either a simpleton or a master strategist, and retreated to figure out their next moves. A couple of them inserted hundred-rupee notes and visiting cards into the toymaker's hands, while others turned their cameras on the villagers, who looked even more clueless than the toymaker himself. The girl walks through the ruin the reporters have left in their wake and takes in the overturned workbench and the wood supplies strewn all around, her spilled paints creating a mishmash on the shop floor.

Over the next few weeks, the girl's life is turned inside out. A man from Delhi offers to become their agent and "handle everything the right way, so you don't need to worry at all." He whisks them off to Delhi, to the home of a millionaire toy manufacturer who allots them a corner of his factory, a workspace larger than their village. At first, the toymaker has no idea what to do, but his daughter brings out a toy kitten, one of a handful of carvings she managed to salvage from their shop back home. She picks up a brush, dips it into a bottle of white paint, and begins her work on the kitten, telling it the tale of a cat with a huge smile. Following his daughter's lead, the toymaker begins carving, making kings and queens and wizards and their horses and lions and tigers into which his daughter paints life. He is asked to sign a few documents and affixes his thumbprint on them, not understanding the lawyer's convoluted explanations. He is a woodworker, his work is to do with wood and chisels and hammers and saws; he doesn't care about anything else.

The toy manufacturer shelves his plans to create a new range of designer dolls and launches a publicity blitz for the wooden novelties he has named the "Magic Collection." Soon, there are snaking queues of people waiting outside stores to buy the handmade creations, and the manufacturer pushes the toymaker and his daughter to create more of them, and faster. The girl is taken out of school and given private tutors so that she can devote maximum time to painting the toys. She is supplied with scripts of stories she is to tell the toys and scolded when she goes off-script. A couple of Hollywood movie studios hear of the girl's talents and rush to collaborate with the manufacturer. The toymaker is asked to create a line of superhero toys, and the girl finds herself repeating the same story day after day to a bunch of costumed figurines.

Every morning, Mahesh Yadav pops a handful of breath mints into his mouth before he reports to work. His head throbs with a hangover as he drives the car from his employer's posh South Delhi home to the kid's school, and the loud Hindi music that the kid demands he put on doesn't help much. One chilly winter morning, his eyes droop as he dreams of hot *pakoras* and a glass of whiskey, and thus doesn't see the thin man crossing the street.

The toymaker is taken to the hospital, where the doctors try to stem the flow of blood. Yadav's employer, a prominent textile mill owner who rushed to the hospital on hearing the news, tries to comfort the toymaker's daughter and offers to pay for her father's treatment. The girl just stares hollowly at the whitewashed walls. The mill owner is keen to avoid any negative publicity and requests a favor from the toy manufacturer, who had accompanied the girl to the hospital. The two businessmen reach an agreement just as the doctor exits the emergency ward to inform them that they should make arrangements for the funeral.

The toy manufacturer gives the girl a month to grieve. He hires counselors to help her open up, but she doesn't speak a word. Her tutors try to engage her in studies, but she stares blankly at the board. She is taken to the workshop and given toys and paints to work with, but they lie untouched. One month turns into three, and she still has spoken not a word. The toy manufacturer threatens to throw her out on the street, but she is unresponsive. Journalists give up on the story of the talking toys; a beak-nosed boy has been born in Bhatinda and crowds throng the hospital, believing him to be an avatar of Garuda, the eagle mount of the god Vishnu.

I meet the girl on my second reporting assignment. I moved from Mumbai to Delhi a month ago, accompanied by a volley of tantrums from my son, who is furious at having to find a new set of friends to play cricket with. My wife also misses the weekly beach hangouts with her college gang and is unhappy with the "phony wannabe" neighbors she now has to put up with. My home has become a battlefield; I take refuge in reportage and follow the story of the magical village girl.

I meet her in a crowded tenement which houses many other workers from the toy factory. Her caretaker, a middle-aged mother of three, says that the factory's manager called her husband, the leader of the workers' union, gave him some money, and dumped the child on him. The toy manufacturer's men visited occasionally to cajole and bully the girl to work again, but they haven't come around for a month. And now the allowance for the girl's upkeep has stopped.

The girl sits on the bed in a corner of the room. The bedsheet is grimy, the coverlet spotted with curry stains. Beside the bed, a small table holds wooden figurines and art supplies, all covered with thick layers of dust. The girl does not look at me when I enter; nor does she respond to my questions. I had seen a few pictures of her, holding on to her father's arm, glancing uncertainly at the camera. She looked like a spirit then; she is even more wraithlike now.

I ask the caretaker if she has any objections to my taking the girl away. She shrugs—looking after the girl brings her no benefit, and the child's ghostly demeanor unsettles her. I give her my address, in case the toy manufacturer wants to contact the girl, and lead her from the house. She does not object, and sits quietly beside me in my car, staring straight ahead.

My wife is upset that I have brought a strange no-name girl into our home, but she sets up the guest room for her. She tries to persuade her to talk, to listen, to display some interest in her new surroundings, but it is of no use. My son is intrigued by the new arrival. He gives her his books, shows her his favorite cartoons, and even tries to teach her to play video games. He isn't troubled by the lack of response; he simply continues his efforts with a reporter's dogged persistence.

My son attends a two-week summer camp in Rishikesh. He comes home bubbling about the skills he's learned, especially with a hammer and chisel. We buy him a block of wood from the local carpentry shop to keep him busy, and he hacks at it until his room is full of wood shavings. The girl watches his exploits silently, but I fancy that I see a flicker of interest in her eyes.

One Sunday afternoon, an exultant cry comes from my son's room. He runs out and displays to us a rectangular blob with legs.

"Don't you see? It's a dog!"

My wife pats his head; I nod distractedly from behind my laptop. There is a slight noise and I look up. The girl has come out of her room. She extends her hand and my son puts his figurine in it. She goes to his room and pulls his art supplies kit from under the bed, where he shoved it after the exam. She sits on his bed and begins to work, oblivious to the three of us standing in the doorway.

"Have you heard the story of the lonely dog?" she says. "There once was a dog that lived on the streets of Engram. With its white coat and black ears, the dog stood out from the other street dogs, which were sandy and tawny. The street dogs shunned him for his appearance, barking and nipping at his face if he tried to befriend them. The lonely dog ate carrion and refuse from dumpsters, while the other street dogs gorged on juicy bones discarded by the city eateries.

"One day, the prince of Engram was passing by and saw the lonely dog standing apart from its brethren, watching them squabble over the meat thrown out from an eatery. The prince felt sorry for the dog and asked his coachman to bring the lonely beast to him. He gave him meat and a nice kennel to live in, and played with him whenever he had time away from his royal duties.

"One day, when the prince was traveling through the city with the dog beside him, a man with a knife leaped at him. The prince's guards pinned down the attacker, but then an arrow came whizzing through the air and struck the prince in the shoulder. The lonely dog caught a glimpse of the archer at a window and took off to catch him as the guards rushed the prince to hospital.

"The dog broke into the room from which the archer had taken his shot, but there was nobody within. There was, however, a rag the archer had used, and the dog picked up the archer's scent from it. For three days and three nights, the dog traversed the streets of Engram hunting for the archer, until he found him stowed away aboard a grain ship. The dog attacked the archer and dragged him through the streets to the palace. A letter from a nobleman was found in the archer's pocket, along with a slip for payment of three hundred gold pieces. The wicked nobleman confessed to orchestrating the attack as part of a larger ploy to grab the throne and was thrown in the dungeons.

"In gratitude, the prince elevated the lonely dog to the rank of Royal Hound.

The royal family's crest was redesigned to depict a white dog with raised black ears. When the dog died, it was given a royal burial in the Cemetery of Kings."

My wife and I stare at each other when the story ends. The girl finishes painting the dog, walks over to us, and shyly holds out the figurine to my son. My son takes it and strokes its back, and the dog growls in pleasure.

That night, my wife and I talk about the girl. We have come to like her, despite her grimness and reticence, and we believe that, with time, she may come to like us, too. But if word gets out that she is once again able to give life to wooden carvings, I fear she will be exploited again.

The next morning at breakfast, we speak to the girl, and to our son.

"If the world finds out that you have regained your ability," I say, "they will want you to use it. The toy manufacturer will wave his contract in our faces and the authorities will take you away. We like you and want to adopt you into our family. However, that will probably mean you cannot tell your stories to these toys ever again. It is too dangerous. Do you think you would be okay with that?"

The girl stares at me, her big eyes filled with tears.

"Yes," she whispers.

The adoption procedure takes two years. The girl goes to school with my son, makes new friends, always comes first in art class. She tells my son stories, and soon he tells her some back. He writes down his stories, sends them off to a few newspapers. The day he publishes his first story, the wooden dog barks so much we are afraid the neighbors will hear.

The day the adoption is finalized, the girl gives me and my wife a box. We open it to find three identical carvings of a family, a man and a woman with a boy and a girl. The woodwork is a little crude, but the brushwork is delicate.

"I know you asked me not to make any more talking toys," says the girl, "but I couldn't stop myself from making these. I have never carved anything before. I hope you like them."

My wife's carving stands on her dresser, mine on my office desk, and my son's on his dorm-room table. The girl is pursuing an apprenticeship in Paris under Olivier Manet, one of the world's foremost still-life artists. She has exhibited some of her paintings, and critics have raved about their lifelike quality. The carvings occasionally talk to us, tell us about the girl's adventures—her first taste of crème brûlée; her awe on staring up at the majestic Notre-Dame; her roommate who gave a solo violin recital before the French President. And sometimes they tell us about a village in the foothills of the Himalayas, where a father makes a toy elephant and his daughter paints it and tells it the tale of Shukram.

(2017)

FOLLOWING THE MONEY

On 6 November 2014, at a day-long conference on human-machine interaction at Goldsmith's College in London, Rodolphe Gelin, the research director of robot-makers Aldebaran, screened a video starring Nao, the company's charming educational robot. It took a while before someone in the audience (not me, to my shame) spotted the film's obvious flaw: how come the film shows a mother sweating away in the kitchen while a robot is enjoying quality time with her child?

The robot exists to do what we can imagine doing, but would rather not do. What's wrong with that? Nothing – except that it assumes that we always know what's in our own best interests. Given that we are now able to hand entire parts of our lives over to robots, we should be thinking even harder about how we want to spend our lives.

The stories in this section articulate some of the big nightmares we entertain about robots – that they'll steal away our jobs, our livelihoods, even our happiness and our life's purpose – but what's remarkable is how innocent so many of the robots seem. That's the problem with technology: it really is neutral. It really is what you make of it, day to day. No wonder technology is so good at magnifying all our classic mistakes.

Robots are a sort of dark mirror for ourselves, filling in for the bits of life we'd rather ignore. That's why they provide such a fine vehicle for satire, whether exploring civic impotence in Charles Dickens's "Full Report of the Second Meeting of the Mudfog Association for the Advancement of Everything Section B" (1837) or the bankruptcy of our spiritual life in Fredric Perkins's "The Man-Ufactory" (1877) – two fine early stories.

There was a fair degree of satire in Czech playwright Karel Capek's original conception of *RUR (Rossum's Universal Robots)*, the play which in 1921 launched the word robot on the world. According to Capek, in an article in London's *Evening Standard* in 1924, inspiration came when he had to take a crowded tram from Prague's suburbs to the city centre and noticed how people were behaving: not at all like cattle in a truck, which at least show signs of life and suffering, but like dead things, mechanisms, machines.

As it developed, Capek's play acquired a visionary political edge. His countrymen were not only being dehumanized by the spread of mass production and "scientific management"; they were being thrown out of work. (Seeing striking textile workers marching through the town of Úpice made a strong impression on him.) The bloodless logic of industrial capitalism has rarely been expressed so well as when Rossum's general manager Domin reassures Helen Glory (what a name!) about the great benefits robots will bring to the world. Sure, they're making humans redundant, but

> "within the next ten years, Rossum's Universal Robots will produce so much wheat, so much cloth, so much everything that things will no longer have any value.

Everyone will be able to take as much as he needs. There'll be no more poverty. Yes, people will be out of work, but by then there'll be no work left to be done. Everything will be done by living machines. People will do only what they enjoy. They will live only to perfect themselves."

Again, the vision's fine as far as it goes, but the devil's in the detail. In Domin's utopic future of endless leisure, will we even know how to perfect ourselves? Are we equipped for such a task, physically, morally, intellectually? Is perfection even a state to aspire to? Or are we all just going to rot?

We obsess over the "labour-saving" capacities of our machines, and hanker endlessly for more "free time", but we never think to consider the value of labour itself. Every activity we replace by machine – even dirty, noisy, dangerous activities – is a kind of loss for us. Even factory work, hard, repetitive and brutal, even housework, invisible, unmeasured, unrewarded, can be a source of pride.

What if we save ourselves from the very labour that makes our lives worthwhile? It can't be an accident that, now that bread- and beer-making are largely automated industrial activities, schools are opening up in my city to teach people with disposable money and time on their hands how to knead dough, and ferment beer. And, easy as it is to sneer at these fetishised activities, surely the really ludicrous thing is how we're getting machines to do the things that we turn out, after all, to enjoy. (Cornell scholar Morris Bishop hits this particular nail neatly on the head with "The Reading Machine" (1947).)

The other problem with Domin's vision is that it assumes human beings can simply step off the merry-go-round. With robots making everything for free, the horns of plenty will never cease to overflow. Is he right?

Well, no. For a start, there's the small matter of only having one planet to live off. And right now, we're not just running out of materials; we're running out of things to do with materials. Why do you think our economy has shifted, in the space of less than a generation, from one of goods, to one of services, to one of mere attention?

As far as the machines are concerned, we're not just consumers. We're also stuff. Consumables. Our data – which is to say, how we live our lives – already has a money value. Automation hasn't liberated us from the capitalist machine. We're still in the machine. Hell, we're its feedstock.

Stories by Robert Reed, Paolo Bacigalupi, Nick Wolven and Dan Grace all explore this crisis point from different angles. I have to admit that in my own mind I keep coming back to one of the more surreal moments in the Wachowski brothers' 1999 movie *The Matrix*, when it's revealed that our robot overlords are so desperate for power that they're using us as glorified batteries.

The trouble with capitalism – the trouble that keeps even dyed-in-the-wool capitalists up at night – is that it's an engine without brakes. Running out of fuel doesn't stop it. It simply starts digesting its own muscle. It's a monstrous positive-feedback loop in which even the robots aren't safe, as Rachael K. Jones, a relative newcomer to the field, makes clear in "The Greatest One-Star Restaurant in the Whole Quadrant", one of the funniest (and nastiest) stories in this anthology.

In Romie Stott's "A Robot Walks into A Bar", a robot and a human are both trying to navigate the same (sexual) economy. It's quite understated, and also, for my money, an essential read. What kind of relationship will we develop with our robots, if both they and we are in hock to "the System"?

NIGHTMARE NUMBER THREE

Stephen Vincent Benét

Between the years 1928 and 1943, **Stephen Vincent Benét** was one of the best-known living American poets, whose books sold in the tens of thousands. Today no-one knows who he is. Experiences of the Great Depression drew from Benét, a normally gentle, rather sentimental writer, a series of angry, sometimes apocalyptic poems. *Nightmare Number Three* is fairly representative of a sequence that also includes "Metropolitan Nightmare", a futuristic story of climate change in which newly evolved steel-eating termites infest New York. With the outbreak of the Second World War in Europe, Benét threw himself unsparingly into propaganda work, driving himself brutally until, in 1943, his fragile health gave way and he died in his wife's arms.

We had expected everything but revolt
And I kind of wonder myself when they started thinking—
But there's no dice in that, now.
                    I've heard fellows say
They must have planned it for years and maybe they did.
Looking back, you can find little incidents here and there,
Like the concrete-mixer in Jersey eating the Wop
Or the roto press that printed "Johnson for President!"
In a three-color process all over Huey Long,
Just as he was making a speech. The thing about that
Was, how could it get upstairs? But it was upstairs,
Clicking and mumbling in the Senate Chamber.
They had to knock out the wall to take it away
And the wrecking crew said it grinned.
                    It was only the best
Machines, of course, the superhuman machines,
The ones we'd built to be better than humankind,
But, naturally, all the cars…
                    and they hunted us
Like rabbits through the cramped streets on the Bloody Monday,
The Madison Avenue buses leading the charge.
The buses, they were the worst—but I'll not forget

The smash of glass when the Duesenberg left the showroom
And pinned three brokers to the Racquet Club steps.
I guess they were tired of being ridden in
And used and handled by pygmies for silly ends,
Of wrapping cheap cigarettes and bad chocolate bars
Collecting nickels and waving platinum hair,
And letting six million people live in a town.
I guess it was that. I guess they got tired of us
And the whole smell of human hands.
                        But it was a shock
To climb sixteen flights of stairs to Art Zuckow's office
(Noboby took the elevators twice)
And find him strangled to death in a nest of telephones,
The octopus tendrils waving over his head.
Do they eat?... There was red... But I did not stop to look.
I don't know yet how I got to the roof in time,
And it's lonely, here on the roof.
                        For a while, I thought
That window-cleaner would make it, and keep me company.
But they got him with his own hoist at the sixteenth floor
And dragged him in, with a squeal.
You see, they coöperate. Well, we taught them that
And it's fair enough, I suppose. You see, we built them.
We taught them to think for themselves. It was bound to come.
And it won't be so bad, in the country.
                        I hate to think
Of the reapers, running wild in the Kansas fields.
They'll be pretty rough—but the horses might even help.
We could promise the horses things.
                        And they need us, too.
They're bound to realize that when they once calm down.
They'll need oil and spare parts and adjustments and lots of service.
Slaves? Well, in a way, you know, we were slaves before.
There won't be so much real difference—honest, there won't.
(I wish I hadn't looked into the beauty shop
And seen what was happening there.
But they're female machines, of course, and a bit high-strung.)
Oh, we'll settle down. We'll arrange it. We'll compromise.
It wouldn't make sense to wipe out the human race.
Why, I bet if I went to my old Plymouth now
(Of course you'd have to do it kind of respectful),
And said, "Look here! Who got you the swell French horn?"
He wouldn't turn me over to those police cars;
At least I don't think he would.
                        Oh, it's going to be jake.
There won't be so much real difference—honest, there won't—

And I'd go down in a minute and take my chance—
I'm a good American and I always liked them—
Except for one (small) detail that bothers me,
And that's the food proposition. Because, you see,
The concrete-mixer may have made a mistake,
And it looks like just high spirits.
But, if they've gotten to like the flavor... well...

(1935)

WITH FOLDED HANDS

Jack Williamson

John Stewart Williamson (1908–2006) was born in Arizona and raised on an isolated New Mexico homestead. He spent his last decades in New Mexico, too. He sold his first story, "The Metal Man", to *Amazing* in 1928, and by the early 1950s was embarking on a second career as an academic. Published as *H. G. Wells: Critic of Progress* (1973), his PhD thesis is a useful exploration of Wells's complex relationship to the idea of progress and the notion of a World State. Williamson taught the modern novel and literary criticism until his retirement in 1977, and continued to write science fiction, often in collaboration with Frederik Pohl. He died at the age of 98, an sf writer of substance for over seventy years.

Underhill was walking home from the office, because his wife had the car, the afternoon he first met the new mechanicals. His feet were following his usual diagonal path across a weedy vacant block—his wife usually had the car—and his preoccupied mind was rejecting various impossible ways to meet his notes at the Two Rivers bank, when a new wall stopped him.

The wall wasn't any common brick or stone, but something sleek and bright and strange.

Underhill stared up at a long new building. He felt vaguely annoyed and surprised at this glittering obstruction—it certainly hadn't been here last week.

Then he saw the thing in the window.

The window itself wasn't any ordinary glass. The wide, dustless panel was completely transparent, so that only the glowing letters fastened to it showed that it was there at all. The letters made a severe, modernistic sign:

>Two Rivers Agency
>HUMANOID INSTITUTE
>The Perfect Mechanicals
>"To Serve and Obey,
>And Guard Men from Harm."

His dim annoyance sharpened, because Underhill was in the mechanicals business himself. Times were already hard enough, and mechanicals were a drug on the market. Androids, mechanoids, electronoids, automatoids, and ordinary robots. Unfortunately, few of them did all the salesmen promised, and the Two Rivers market was already sadly oversaturated.

Underhill sold androids—when he could. His next consignment was due tomorrow, and he didn't quite know how to meet the bill.

Frowning, he paused to stare at the thing behind that invisible window. He had never seen a humanoid. Like any mechanical not at work, it stood absolutely motionless. Smaller and slimmer than a man. A shining black, its sleek silicone skin had a changing sheen of bronze and metallic blue.

Its graceful oval face wore a fixed look of alert and slightly surprised solicitude. Altogether, it was the most beautiful mechanical he had ever seen.

Too small, of course, for much practical utility. He murmured to himself a reassuring quotation from the Android Salesman: "Androids are big—because the makers refuse to sacrifice power, essential functions, or dependability. Androids are your biggest buy!"

The transparent door slid open as he turned toward it, and he walked into the haughty opulence of the new display room to convince himself that these streamlined items were just another flashy effort to catch the woman shopper.

He inspected the glittering layout shrewdly, and his breezy optimism faded. He had never heard of the Humanoid Institute, but the invading firm obviously had big money and big-time merchandising know-how.

He looked around for a salesman, but it was another mechanical that came gliding silently to meet him. A twin of the one in the window, it moved with a quick, surprising grace. Bronze and blue lights flowed over its lustrous blackness, and a yellow name plate flashed from its naked breast:

HUMANOID

Serial No. 81-H-B-27

The Perfect Mechanical

"To Serve and Obey,

And Guard Men from Harm."

Curiously, it had no lenses. The eyes in its bald oval head were steel-colored, blindly staring. But it stopped a few feet in front of him, as if it could see anyhow, and it spoke to him with a high, melodious voice:

"At your service, Mr. Underhill."

The use of his name startled him, for not even the androids could tell one man from another.

But this was a clever merchandising stunt, of course, not too difficult in a town the size of Two Rivers.

The salesman must be some local man, prompting the mechanical from behind the partition.

Underhill erased his momentary astonishment, and said loudly.

"May I see your salesman, please?"

"We employ no human salesmen, sir," its soft silvery voice replied instantly. "The Humanoid Institute exists to serve mankind, and we require no human service. We ourselves can supply any information you desire, sir, and accept your order for immediate humanoid service."

Underhill peered at it dazedly. No mechanicals were competent even to recharge their own batteries and reset their own relays, much less to operate their own branch office. The blind eyes stared blankly back, and he looked uneasily around for any booth or curtain that might conceal the salesman.

Meanwhile, the sweet thin voice resumed persuasively:

"May we come out to your home for a free trial demonstration, sir? We are anxious to introduce our service on your planet, because we have been successful in eliminating human unhappiness on so many others. You will find us far superior to the old electronic mechanicals in use here."

Underhill stepped back uneasily. He reluctantly abandoned his search for the hidden salesman, shaken by the idea of any mechanicals promoting themselves. That would upset the whole industry.

"At least you must take some advertising matter, sir."

Moving with a somehow appalling graceful deftness, the small black mechanical brought him an illustrated booklet from a table by the wall. To cover his confused and increasing alarm, he thumbed through the glossy pages.

In a series of richly colored before-and-after pictures, a chesty blond girl was stooping over a kitchen stove, and then relaxing in a daring negligee while a little black mechanical knelt to serve her something. She was wearily hammering a typewriter, and then lying on an ocean beach, in a revealing sun suit, while another mechanical did the typing. She was toiling at some huge industrial machine, and then dancing in the arms of a golden-haired youth, while a black humanoid ran the machine.

Underhill sighed wistfully. The android company didn't supply such fetching sales material.

Women would find this booklet irresistible, and they selected eighty-six per cent of all mechanicals sold. Yes, the competition was going to be bitter.

"Take it home, sir," the sweet voice urged him. "Show it to your wife. There is a free trial demonstration order blank on the last page, and you will notice that we require no payment down."

He turned numbly, and the door slid open for him. Retreating dazedly, he discovered the booklet still in his hand. He crumpled it furiously, and flung it down. The small black thing picked it up tidily, and the insistent silver voice rang after him:

"We shall call at your office tomorrow, Mr. Underhill, and send a demonstration unit to your home. It is time to discuss the liquidation of your business, because the electronic mechanicals you have been selling cannot compete with us. And we shall offer your wife a free trial demonstration."

Underhill didn't attempt to reply, because he couldn't trust his voice. He stalked blindly down the new sidewalk to the corner, and paused there to collect himself. Out of his startled and confused impressions, one clear fact emerged—things looked black for the agency.

Bleakly, he stared back at the haughty splendor of the new building. It wasn't honest brick or stone; that invisible window wasn't glass; and he was quite sure the foundation for it hadn't even been staked out, the last time Aurora had the car.

He walked on around the block, and the new sidewalk took him near the rear entrance. A truck was backed up to it, and several slim black mechanicals were silently busy, unloading huge metal crates.

He paused to look at one of the crates. It was labeled for interstellar shipment. The stencils showed that it had come from the Humanoid Institute, on Wing IV. He failed to recall any planet of that designation; the outfit must be big.

Dimly, inside the gloom of the warehouse beyond the truck, he could see black mechanicals opening the crates. A lid came up, revealing dark, rigid bodies, closely packed. One by one, they came to life. They climbed out of the crate, and sprang gracefully to the floor. A shining black, glinting with bronze and blue, they were all identical.

One of them came out past the truck, to the sidewalk, staring with blind steel eyes. Its high silver voice spoke to him melodiously:

"At your service, Mr. Underhill."

He fled. When his name was promptly called by a courteous mechanical, just out of the crate in which it had been imported from a remote and unknown planet, he found the experience trying.

Two blocks along, the sign of a bar caught his eye, and he took his dismay inside. He had made it a business rule not to drink before dinner, and Aurora didn't like him to drink at all; but these new mechanicals, he felt, had made the day exceptional.

Unfortunately, however, alcohol failed to brighten the brief visible future of the agency. When he emerged, after an hour, he looked wistfully back in hope that the bright new building might have vanished as abruptly as it came. It hadn't. He shook his head dejectedly, and turned uncertainly homeward.

Fresh air had cleared his head somewhat, before he arrived at the neat white bungalow in the outskirts of the town, but it failed to solve his business problems. He also realized, uneasily, that he would be late for dinner.

Dinner, however, had been delayed. His son Frank, a freckled ten-year-old, was still kicking a football on the quiet street in front of the house. And little Gay, who was tow-haired and adorable and eleven, came running across the lawn and down the sidewalk to meet him.

"Father, you can't guess what!" Gay was going to be a great musician some day, and no doubt properly dignified, but she was pink and breathless with excitement now. She let him swing her high off the sidewalk, and she wasn't critical of the bar aroma on his breath. He couldn't guess, and she informed him eagerly;

"Mother's got a new lodger!"

Underhill had foreseen a painful inquisition, because Aurora was worried about the notes at the bank, and the bill for the new consignment, and the money for little Gay's lessons.

The new lodger, however, saved him from that. With an alarming crashing of crockery, the household android was setting dinner on the table, but the little house was empty. He found Aurora in the back yard, burdened with sheets and towels for the guest.

Aurora, when he married her, had been as utterly adorable as now her little daughter was. She might have remained so, he felt, if the agency had been a little more successful. However, while the pressure of slow failure had gradually crumbled his own assurance, small hardships had turned her a little too aggressive.

Of course he loved her still. Her red hair was still alluring, and she was loyally faithful, but thwarted ambitions had sharpened her character and sometimes her voice. They never quarreled, really, but there were small differences.

There was the little apartment over the garage—built for human servants they had never been able to afford. It was too small and shabby to attract any responsible tenant, and Underhill wanted to leave it empty. It hurt his pride to see her making beds and cleaning floors for strangers.

Aurora had rented it before, however, when she wanted money to pay for Gay's music lessons, or when some colorful unfortunate touched her sympathy, and it seemed to Underhill that her lodgers had all turned out to be thieves and vandals.

She turned back to meet him, now, with the clean linen in her arms.

"Dear, it's no use objecting." Her voice was quite determined. "Mr. Sledge is the most wonderful old fellow, and he's going to stay just as long as he wants."

"That's all right, darling." He never liked to bicker, and he was thinking of his troubles at the agency. "I'm afraid we'll need the money. Just make him pay in advance."

"But he can't!" Her voice throbbed with sympathetic warmth. "He says he'll have royalties coming in from his inventions, so he can pay in a few days."

Underhill shrugged; he had heard that before.

"Mr. Sledge is different, dear," she insisted. "He's a traveler, and a scientist. Here, in this dull little town, we don't see many interesting people."

"You've picked up some remarkable types," he commented.

"Don't be unkind, dear," she chided gently. "You haven't met him yet, and you don't know how wonderful he is." Her voice turned sweeter. "Have you a ten, dear?"

He stiffened. "What for?"

"Mr. Sledge is ill." Her voice turned urgent. "I saw him fall on the street, downtown. The police were going to send him to the city hospital, but he didn't want to go. He looked so noble and sweet and grand. So I told them I would take him. I got him in the car and took him to old Dr. Winters. He has this heart condition, and he needs the money for medicine."

Reasonably, Underhill inquired, "Why doesn't he want to go to the hospital?"

"He has work to do," she said. "Important scientific work—and he's so wonderful and tragic. Please, dear, have you a ten?"

Underhill thought of many things to say. These new mechanicals promised to multiply his troubles. It was foolish to take in an invalid vagrant, who could have free care at the city hospital. Aurora's tenants always tried to pay their rent with promises, and generally wrecked the apartment and looted the neighborhood before they left.

But he said none of those things. He had learned to compromise. Silently, he found two fives in his thin pocketbook, and put them in her hand. She smiled, and kissed him impulsively—he barely remembered to hold his breath in time.

Her figure was still good, by dint of periodic dieting. He was proud of her shining red hair. A sudden surge of affection brought tears to his eyes, and he wondered what would happen to her and the children if the agency failed.

"Thank you, dear!" she whispered. "I'll have him come for dinner, if he feels able, and you can meet him then. I hope you don't mind dinner being late."

He didn't mind, tonight. Moved by a sudden impulse of domesticity, he got hammer and nails from his workshop in the basement, and repaired the sagging screen on the kitchen door with a neat diagonal brace.

He enjoyed working with his hands. His boyhood dream had been to be a builder of fission power plants. He had even studied engineering—before he married Aurora, and had to take over the ailing mechanicals agency from her indolent and alcoholic father. He was whistling happily by the time the little task was done.

When he went back through the kitchen to put up his tools, he found the household android busily clearing the untouched dinner away from the table—the androids were good enough at strictly routine tasks, but they could never learn to cope with human unpredictability.

"Stop, stop!" Slowly repeated, in the proper pitch and rhythm, his command made it halt, and then he said carefully, "Set—table; set—table."

Obediently, the gigantic thing came shuffling back with the stack of plates. He was suddenly struck with the difference between it and those new humanoids. He sighed wearily.

Things looked black for the agency.

Aurora brought her new lodger in through the kitchen door. Underhill nodded to himself.

This gaunt stranger, with his dark shaggy hair, emaciated face, and threadbare garb, looked to be just the sort of colorful, dramatic vagabond that always touched Aurora's heart. She introduced them, and they sat down to wait in the front room while she went to call the children.

The old rogue didn't look very sick, to Underhill. Perhaps his wide shoulders had a tired stoop, but his spare, tall figure was still commanding. The skin was seamed and pale, over his rawboned, cragged face, but his deep-set eyes still had a burning vitality.

His hands held Underhill's attention. Immense hands, they hung a little forward when he stood, swung on long bony arms in perpetual readiness. Gnarled and scarred, darkly tanned, with the small hairs on the back bleached to a golden color, they told their own epic of varied adventure, of battle perhaps, and possibly even of toil. They had been very useful hands.

"I'm very grateful to your wife, Mr. Underhill." His voice was a deep-throated rumble, and he had a wistful smile, oddly boyish for a man so evidently old. "She rescued me from an unpleasant predicament, and I'll see that she is well paid."

Just another vivid vagabond, Underhill decided, talking his way through life with plausible inventions. He had a little private game he played with Aurora's tenants—just remembering what they said and counting one point for every impossibility. Mr. Sledge, he thought, would give him an excellent score.

"Where are you from?" he asked conversationally.

Sledge hesitated for an instant before he answered, and that was unusual—most of Aurora's tenants had been exceedingly glib.

"Wing IV." The gaunt old man spoke with a solemn reluctance, as if he should have liked to say something else. "All my early life was spent there, but I left the planet nearly fifty years ago. I've been traveling ever since."

Startled, Underhill peered at him sharply. Wing IV, he remembered, was the home planet of those sleek new mechanicals, but this old vagabond looked too seedy and impecunious to be connected with the Humanoid Institute. His brief suspicion faded. Frowning, he said casually: "Wing IV must be rather distant."

The old rogue hesitated again, and then said gravely, "One hundred and nine light-years, Mr. Underhill."

That made the first point, but Underhill concealed his satisfaction. The new space liners were pretty fast, but the velocity of light was still an absolute limit. Casually, he played for another point:

"My wife says you're a scientist, Mr. Sledge?"

"Yes."

The old rascal's reticence was unusual. Most of Aurora's tenants required very little prompting.

Underhill tried again, in a breezy conversational tone: "Used to be an engineer myself, until I dropped it to go into mechanicals." The old vagabond straightened, and Underhill paused hopefully. But he said nothing, and Underhill went on: "Fission plant design and operation. What's your specialty, Mr. Sledge?"

The old man gave him a long, troubled look, with those brooding, hollowed eyes, and then said slowly, "Your wife has been kind to me, Mr. Underhill, when I was in desperate need. I think you are entitled to the truth, but I must ask you to keep it to yourself. I am engaged on a very important research problem, which must be finished secretly."

"I'm sorry." Suddenly ashamed of his cynical little game, Underhill spoke apologetically. "Forget it." But the old man said deliberately, "My field is rhodomagnetics."

"Eh?" Underhill didn't like to confess ignorance, but he had never heard of that. "I've been out of the game for fifteen years," he explained. "I'm afraid I haven't kept up."

The old man smiled again, faintly.

"The science was unknown here until I arrived, a few days ago," he said. "I was able to apply for basic patents. As soon as the royalties start coming in, I'll be wealthy again."

Underhill had heard that before. The old rogue's solemn reluctance had been very impressive, but he remembered that most of Aurora's tenants had been very plausible gentry.

"So?" Underhill was staring again, somehow fascinated by those gnarled and scarred and strangely able hands. "What, exactly, is rhodomagnetics?"

He listened to the old man's careful, deliberate answer, and started his little game again. Most of Aurora's tenants had told some pretty wild tales, but he had never heard anything to top this.

"A universal force," the weary, stooped old vagabond said solemnly. "As fundamental as ferromagnetism or gravitation, though the effects are less obvious. It is keyed to the second triad of the periodic table, rhodium and ruthenium and palladium, in very much the same way that ferromagnetism is keyed to the first triad, iron and nickel and cobalt."

Underhill remembered enough of his engineering courses to see the basic fallacy of that. Palladium was used for watch springs, he recalled, because it was completely non-magnetic. But he kept his face straight. He had no malice in his heart, and he played the little game just for his own amusement. It was secret, even from Aurora, and he always penalized himself for any show of doubt.

He said merely, "I thought the universal forces were already pretty well known?"

"The effects of rhodomagnetism are masked by nature," the patient, rusty voice explained. "And, besides, they are somewhat paradoxical, so that ordinary laboratory methods defeat themselves."

"Paradoxical?" Underhill prompted.

"In a few days I can show you copies of my patents, and reprints of papers describing demonstration experiments," the old man promised gravely. "The velocity of propagation is infinite. The effects vary inversely with the first power of the distance, not with the square of the distance. And ordinary matter, except for the elements of the rhodium triad, is generally transparent to rhodomagnetic radiations."

That made four more points for the game. Underhill felt a little glow of gratitude to Aurora, for discovering so remarkable a specimen.

"Rhodomagnetism was first discovered through a mathematical investigation of the atom," the old romancer went serenely on, suspecting nothing. "A rhodomagnetic component was proved essential to maintain the delicate equilibrium of the nuclear forces. Consequently, rhodomagnetic waves tuned to atomic frequencies may be used to upset that equilibrium and produce nuclear instability. Thus most heavy atoms—generally those above palladium in atomic number—can be subjected to artificial fission."

Underhill scored himself another point, and tried to keep his eyebrows from lifting. He said, conversationally, "Patents on such a discovery ought to be very profitable."

The old scoundrel nodded his gaunt, dramatic head.

"You can see the obvious application. My basic patents cover most of them. Devices for instantaneous interplanetary and interstellar communication. Long-range wireless power transmission. A rhodomagnetic inflexion-drive, which makes possible apparent speeds many times that of light—by means of a rhodomagnetic deformation of the continuum. And, of course, revolutionary types of fission power plants, using any heavy element for fuel."

Preposterous! Underhill tried hard to keep his face straight, but everybody knew that the velocity of light was a physical limit. On the human side, the owner of any such remarkable patents would hardly be begging for shelter in a shabby garage apartment. He noticed a pale circle around the old vagabond's gaunt and hairy wrist; no man owning such priceless secrets would have to pawn his watch.

Triumphantly, Underhill allowed himself four more points, but then he had to penalize himself. He must have let doubt show on his face, because the old man asked suddenly:

"Do you want to see the basic tensors?" He reached in his pocket for pencil and notebook. "I'll jot them down for you."

"Never mind," Underhill protested. "I'm afraid my math is a little rusty."

"But you think it strange that the holder of such revolutionary patents should find himself in need?"

Underhill nodded, and penalized himself another point. The old man might be a monumental liar, but he was shrewd enough.

"You see, I'm a sort of refugee," he explained apologetically. "I arrived on this planet only a few days ago, and I have to travel light. I was forced to deposit everything I had with a law firm, to arrange for the publication and protection of my patents. I expect to be receiving the first royalties soon.

"In the meantime," he added plausibly, "I came to Two Rivers because it is quiet and secluded, far from the spaceports. I'm working on another project, which must be finished secretly. Now, will you please respect my confidence, Mr. Underhill?"

Underhill had to say he would. Aurora came back with the freshly scrubbed children, and they went in to dinner. The android came lurching in with a steaming tureen. The old stranger seemed to shrink from the mechanical, uneasily. As she took the dish and served the soup, Aurora inquired lightly:

"Why doesn't your company bring out a better mechanical, dear? One smart enough to be a really perfect waiter, warranted not to splash the soup. Wouldn't that be splendid?"

Her question cast Underhill into moody silence. He sat scowling at his plate, thinking of those remarkable new mechanicals which claimed to be perfect, and what they might do to the agency.

It was the shaggy old rover who answered soberly, "The perfect mechanicals already exist, Mrs. Underhill." His deep, rusty voice had a solemn undertone. "And they are not so splendid, really. I've been a refugee from them, for nearly fifty years."

Underhill looked up from his plate, astonished.

"Those black humanoids, you mean?"

"Humanoids?" That great voice seemed suddenly faint, frightened. The deep-sunken eyes turned dark with shock. "What do you know of them?"

"They've just opened a new agency in Two Rivers," Underhill told him. "No salesmen about, if you can imagine that. They claim—"

His voice trailed off, because the gaunt old man was suddenly stricken. Gnarled hands clutched at his throat, and a spoon clattered to the floor. His haggard face turned an ominous blue, and his breath was a terrible shallow gasping.

He fumbled in his pocket for medicine, and Aurora helped him take something in a glass of water. In a few moments he could breathe again, and the color of life came back to his face.

"I'm sorry, Mrs. Underhill," he whispered apologetically. "It was just the shock—I came here to get away from them." He stared at the huge, motionless android, with a terror in his sunken eyes. "I wanted to finish my work before they came," he whispered. "Now there is very little time."

When he felt able to walk, Underhill went out with him to see him safely up the stairs to the garage apartment. The tiny kitchenette, he noticed, had already been converted into some kind of workshop. The old tramp seemed to have no extra clothing, but he had unpacked neat, bright gadgets of metal and plastic from his battered luggage, and spread them out on the small kitchen table.

The gaunt old man himself was tattered and patched and hungry-looking, but the parts of his curious equipment were exquisitely machined, and Underhill recognized the silver-white luster of rare palladium. Suddenly he suspected that he had scored too many points in his little private game.

A caller was waiting, when Underhill arrived next morning at his office at the agency. It stood frozen before his desk, graceful and straight, with soft lights of blue and bronze shining over its black silicone nudity. He stopped at the sight of it, unpleasantly jolted.

"At your service, Mr. Underhill." It turned quickly to face him, with its blind, disturbing stare. "May we explain how we can serve you?"

His shock of the afternoon before came back, and he asked sharply, "How do you know my name?"

"Yesterday we read the business cards in your case," it purred softly. "Now we shall know you always. You see, our senses are sharper than human vision, Mr. Underhill. Perhaps we seem a little strange at first, but you will soon become accustomed to us."

"Not if I can help it!" He peered at the serial number of its yellow nameplate, and shook his bewildered head. "That was another one, yesterday. I never saw you before!"

"We are all alike, Mr. Underhill," the silver voice said softly. "We are all one, really. Our separate mobile units are all controlled and powered from Humanoid Central. The units you see are only the senses and limbs of our great brain on Wing IV. That is why we are so far superior to the old electronic mechanicals."

It made a scornful-seeming gesture, toward the row of clumsy androids in his display room.

"You see, we are rhodomagnetic."

Underhill staggered a little, as if that word had been a blow. He was certain, now, that he had scored too many points from Aurora's new tenant. He shuddered slightly, to the first light kiss of terror, and spoke with an effort, hoarsely, "Well, what do you want?"

Staring blindly across his desk, the sleek black thing slowly unfolded a legal-looking document.

He sat down, watching uneasily.

"This is merely an assignment, Mr. Underhill," it cooed at him soothingly. "You see, we are requesting you to assign your property to the Humanoid Institute in exchange for our service."

"What?" The word was an incredulous gasp, and Underhill came angrily back to his feet. "What kind of blackmail is this?"

"It's no blackmail," the small mechanical assured him softly. "You will find the humanoids incapable of any crime. We exist only to increase the happiness and safety of mankind."

"Then why do you want my property?" he rasped.

"The assignment is merely a legal formality," it told him blandly. "We strive to introduce our service with the least possible confusion and dislocation. We have found the assignment plan the most efficient for the control and liquidation of private enterprises."

Trembling with anger and the shock of mounting terror, Underhill gulped hoarsely, "Whatever your scheme is, I don't intend to give up my business."

"You have no choice, really." He shivered to the sweet certainty of that silver voice. "Human enterprise is no longer necessary, now that we have come, and the electronic mechanicals industry is always the first to collapse."

He stared defiantly at its blind steel eyes.

"Thanks!" He gave a little laugh, nervous and sardonic. "But I prefer to run my own business, and support my own family, and take care of myself."

"But that is impossible, under the Prime Directive," it cooed softly. "Our function is to serve and obey, and guard men from harm. It is no longer necessary for men to care for themselves, because we exist to insure their safety and happiness."

He stood speechless, bewildered, slowly boiling.

"We are sending one of our units to every home in the city, on a free trial basis," it added gently. "This free demonstration will make most people glad to make the formal assignment, and you won't be able to sell many more androids."

"Get out!" Underhill came storming around the desk.

The little black thing stood waiting for him, watching him with blind steel eyes, absolutely motionless. He checked himself suddenly, feeling rather foolish. He wanted very much to hit it, but he could see the futility of that.

"Consult your own attorney, if you wish." Deftly, it laid the assignment form on his desk. "You need have no doubts about the integrity of the Humanoid Institute. We are sending a statement of our assets to the Two Rivers bank, and depositing a sum to cover our obligations here. When you wish to sign, just let us know."

The blind thing turned, and silently departed.

Underhill went out to the corner drugstore and asked for a bicarbonate. The clerk that served him, however, turned out to be a sleek black mechanical. He went back to his office, more upset than ever.

An ominous hush lay over the agency. He had three house-to-house salesmen out, with demonstrators. The phone should have been busy with their orders and reports, but it didn't ring at all until one of them called to say that he was quitting.

"I've got myself one of these new humanoids," he added, "and it says I don't have to work anymore."

He swallowed his impulse to profanity, and tried to take advantage of the unusual quiet by working on his books. But the affairs of the agency, which for years had been precarious, today appeared utterly disastrous. He left the ledgers hopefully, when at last a customer came in.

But the stout woman didn't want an android. She wanted a refund on the one she had bought the week before. She admitted that it could do all the guarantee promised—but now she had seen a humanoid.

The silent phone rang once again, that afternoon. The cashier of the bank wanted to know if he could drop in to discuss his loans. Underhill dropped in, and the cashier greeted him with an ominous affability.

"How's business?" the banker boomed, too genially.

"Average, last month," Underhill insisted stoutly. "Now I'm just getting in a new consignment, and I'll need another small loan—"

The cashier's eyes turned suddenly frosty, and his voice dried up.

"I believe you have a new competitor in town," the banker said crisply. "These humanoid people. A very solid concern, Mr. Underhill. Remarkably solid! They have filed a statement with us, and made a substantial deposit to care for their local obligations. Exceedingly substantial!"

The banker dropped his voice, professionally regretful.

"In these circumstances, Mr. Underhill, I'm afraid the bank can't finance your agency any longer. We must request you to meet your obligations in full, as they come due." Seeing Underhill's white desperation, he added icily, "We've already carried you too long, Underhill. If you can't pay, the bank will have to start bankruptcy proceedings."

The new consignment of androids was delivered late that afternoon. Two tiny black humanoids unloaded them from the truck—for it developed that the operators of the trucking company had already assigned it to the Humanoid Institute.

Efficiently, the humanoids stacked up the crates. Courteously they brought a receipt for him to sign. He no longer had much hope of selling the androids, but he had ordered the shipment and he had to accept it. Shuddering to a spasm of trapped despair, he scrawled his name. The naked black things thanked him, and took the truck away.

He climbed in his car and started home, inwardly seething. The next thing he knew, he was in the middle of a busy street, driving through cross traffic. A police whistle shrilled, and he pulled wearily to the curb. He waited for the angry officer, but it was a little black mechanical that overtook him.

"At your service, Mr. Underhill," it purred sweetly. "You must respect the stop lights, sir. Otherwise, you endanger human life."

"Huh?" He stared at it, bitterly. "I thought you were a cop."

"We are aiding the police department, temporarily," it said. "But driving is really much too dangerous for human beings, under the Prime Directive. As soon as our service is complete, every car will have a humanoid driver. As soon as every human being is completely supervised, there will be no need for any police force whatever."

Underhill glared at it, savagely.

"Well!" he rapped. "So I ran past a stop light. What are you going to do about it?"

"Our function is not to punish men, but merely to serve their happiness and security," its silver voice said softly. "We merely request you to drive safely, during this temporary emergency while our service is incomplete."

Anger boiled up in him.

"You're too perfect!" he muttered bitterly. "I suppose there's nothing men can do, but you can do it better."

"Naturally we are superior," it cooed serenely. "Because our units are metal and plastic, while your body is mostly water. Because our transmitted energy is drawn from atomic fission, instead of oxidation. Because our senses are sharper than human sight or hearing. Most of all, because all our mobile units are joined to one great brain, which knows all that happens on many worlds, and never dies or sleeps or forgets."

Underhill sat listening, numbed.

"However, you must not fear our power," it urged him brightly. "Because we cannot injure any human being, unless to prevent greater injury to another. We exist only to discharge the Prime Directive."

He drove on, moodily. The little black mechanicals, he reflected grimly, were the ministering angels of the ultimate god arisen out of the machine, omnipotent and all-knowing. The Prime Directive was the new commandment. He blasphemed it bitterly, and then fell to wondering if there could be another Lucifer.

He left the car in the garage, and started toward the kitchen door.

"Mr. Underhill." The deep tired voice of Aurora's new tenant hailed him from the door of the garage apartment. "Just a moment, please."

The gaunt old wanderer came stiffly down the outside stairs, and Underhill turned back to meet him.

"Here's your rent money," he said. "And the ten your wife gave me for medicine."

"Thanks, Mr. Sledge." Accepting the money, he saw a burden of new despair on the bony shoulders of the old interstellar tramp, and a shadow of new terror on his raw-boned face. Puzzled, he asked, "Didn't your royalties come through?"

The old man shook his shaggy head.

"The humanoids have already stopped business in the capital," he said. "The attorneys I retained are going out of business, and they returned what was left of my deposit. That is all I have to finish my work."

Underhill spent five seconds thinking of his interview with the banker. No doubt he was a sentimental fool, as bad as Aurora. But he put the money back in the old man's gnarled and quivering hand.

"Keep it," he urged. "For your work."

"Thank you, Mr. Underhill." The gruff voice broke and the tortured eyes glittered. "I need it—so very much."

Underhill went on to the house. The kitchen door was opened for him, silently. A dark naked creature came gracefully to take his hat.

Underhill hung grimly onto his hat.

"What are you doing here?" he gasped bitterly.

"We have come to give your household a free trial demonstration."

He held the door open, pointing.

"Get out!"

The little black mechanical stood motionless and blind.

"Mrs. Underhill has accepted our demonstration service," its silver voice protested. "We cannot leave now, unless she requests it."

He found his wife in the bedroom. His accumulated frustration welled into eruption, as he flung open the door.

"What's this mechanical doing—"

But the force went out of his voice, and Aurora didn't even notice his anger. She wore her sheerest negligee, and she hadn't looked so lovely since they were married. Her red hair was piled into an elaborate shining crown.

"Darling, isn't it wonderful!" She came to meet him, glowing. "It came this morning, and it can do everything. It cleaned the house and got the lunch and gave little Gay her music lesson. It did my hair this afternoon, and now it's cooking dinner. How do you like my hair, darling?"

He liked her hair. He kissed her, and tried to stifle his frightened indignation.

Dinner was the most elaborate meal in Underhill's memory, and the tiny black thing served it very deftly. Aurora kept exclaiming about the novel dishes, but Underhill could scarcely eat, for it seemed to him that all the marvelous pastries were only the bait for a monstrous trap.

He tried to persuade Aurora to send it away, but after such a meal that was useless. At the first glitter of her tears, he capitulated, and the humanoid stayed. It kept the house and cleaned the yard. It watched the children, and did Aurora's nails. It began rebuilding the house.

Underhill was worried about the bills, but it insisted that everything was part of the free trial demonstration. As soon as he assigned his property, the service would be complete. He refused to sign, but other little black mechanicals came with truckloads of supplies and materials, and stayed to help with the building operations.

One morning he found that the roof of the little house had been silently lifted, while he slept, and a whole second story added beneath it. The new walls were of some strange sleek stuff, self-illuminated. The new windows were immense flawless panels, that could be turned transparent or opaque or luminous. The new doors were silent, sliding sections, operated by rhodomagnetic relays.

"I want door knobs," Underhill protested. "I want it so I can get into the bathroom, without calling you to open the door."

"But it is unnecessary for human beings to open doors," the little black thing informed him, suavely. "We exist to discharge the Prime Directive, and our service includes every task. We shall be able to supply a unit to attend each member of your family, as soon as your property is assigned to us."

Steadfastly, Underhill refused to make the assignment.

He went to the office every day, trying first to operate the agency, and then to salvage something from the ruins. Nobody wanted androids, even at ruinous prices. Desperately, he spent the last of his dwindling cash to stock a line of novelties and toys, but they proved equally impossible to sell—the humanoids were already making toys, which they gave away for nothing.

He tried to lease his premises, but human enterprise had stopped. Most of the business property in town had already been assigned to the humanoids, and they were busy pulling down the old buildings and turning the lots into parks—their own plants and warehouses were mostly underground, where they would not mar the landscape.

He went back to the bank, in a final effort to get his notes renewed, and found the little black mechanicals standing at the windows and seated at the desks. As smoothly urbane as any human cashier, a humanoid informed him that the bank was filing a petition of involuntary bankruptcy to liquidate his business holdings.

The liquidation would be facilitated, the mechanical banker added, if he would make a voluntary assignment. Grimly, he refused. That act had become symbolic. It would be the final bow of submission to this dark new god, and he proudly kept his battered head uplifted.

The legal action went very swiftly, for all the judges and attorneys already had humanoid assistants, and it was only a few days before a gang of black mechanicals arrived at the agency with eviction orders and wrecking machinery. He watched sadly while his unsold stock-in-trade was hauled away for junk, and a bulldozer driven by a blind humanoid began to push in the walls of the building.

He drove home in the late afternoon, taut-faced and desperate. With a surprising generosity, the court orders had left him the car and the house, but he felt no gratitude. The complete solicitude of the perfect black machines had become a goad beyond endurance.

He left the car in the garage, and started toward the renovated house. Beyond one of the vast new windows, he glimpsed a sleek naked thing moving swiftly, and he trembled to a convulsion of dread. He didn't want to go back into the domain of that peerless servant, which didn't want him to shave himself, or even to open a door.

On impulse, he climbed the outside stair, and rapped on the door of the garage apartment. The deep slow voice of Aurora's tenant told him to enter, and he found the old vagabond seated on a tall stool, bent over his intricate equipment assembled on the kitchen table.

To his relief, the shabby little apartment had not been changed. The glossy walls of his own new room were something which burned at night with a pale golden fire until the humanoid stopped it, and the new floor was something warm and yielding, which felt almost alive; but these little rooms had the same cracked and water-stained plaster, the same cheap fluorescent light fixtures, the same worn carpets over splintered floors.

"How do you keep them out?" he asked, wistfully. "Those mechanicals?"

The stooped and gaunt old man rose stiffly to move a pair of pliers and some odds and ends of sheet metal off a crippled chair, and motioned graciously for him to be seated.

"I have a certain immunity," Sledge told him gravely. "The place where I live they cannot enter, unless I ask them. That is an amendment to the Prime Directive. They can neither help nor hinder me, unless I request it—and I won't do that."

Careful of the chair's uncertain balance, Underhill sat for a moment, staring. The old man's hoarse, vehement voice was as strange as his words. He had a gray, shocking pallor, and his cheeks and sockets seemed alarmingly hollowed.

"Have you been ill, Mr. Sledge?"

"No worse than usual. Just very busy." With a haggard smile, he nodded at the floor. Underhill saw a tray where he had set it aside, bread drying up, and a covered dish grown cold. "I was going to eat it later," he rumbled apologetically. "Your wife has been very kind to bring me food, but I'm afraid I've been too much absorbed in my work."

His emaciated arm gestured at the table. The little device there had grown. Small machinings of precious white metal and lustrous plastic had been assembled, with neatly soldered busbars, into something which showed purpose and design.

A long palladium needle was hung on jeweled pivots, equipped like a telescope with exquisitely graduated circles and vernier scales, and driven like a telescope with a tiny motor. A small concave palladium mirror, at the base of it, faced a similar mirror mounted on something not quite like a small rotary converter. Thick silver busbars connected that to a plastic box with knobs and dials on top, and also to a foot-thick sphere of gray lead.

The old man's preoccupied reserve did not encourage questions, but Underhill, remembering that sleek black shape inside the new windows of his house, felt queerly reluctant to leave this haven from the humanoids.

"What is your work?" he ventured.

Old Sledge looked at him sharply, with dark feverish eyes, and finally said, "My last research project. I am attempting to measure the constant of the rhodomagnetic quanta."

His hoarse tired voice had a dull finality, as if to dismiss the matter and Underhill himself. But Underhill was haunted with a terror of the black shining slave that had become the master of his house, and he refused to be dismissed.

"What is this certain immunity?"

Sitting gaunt and bent on the tall stool, staring moodily at the long bright needle and the lead sphere, the old man didn't answer.

"These mechanicals!" Underhill burst out, nervously. "They've smashed my business and moved into my home." He searched the old man's dark, seamed face. "Tell me—you must know more about them—isn't there any way to get rid of them?"

After half a minute, the old man's brooding eyes left the lead ball, and the gaunt shaggy head nodded wearily. "That's what I am trying to do."

"Can I help you?" Underhill trembled, with a sudden eager hope. "I'll do anything."

"Perhaps you can." The sunken eyes watched him thoughtfully, with some strange fever in them. "If you can do such work."

"I had engineering training," Underhill reminded him, "and I've a workshop in the basement. There's a model I built." He pointed at the trim little hull, hung over the mantel in the tiny living room. "I'll do anything I can."

Even as he spoke, however, the spark of hope was drowned in a sudden wave of overwehelming doubt. Why should he believe this old rogue, when he knew Aurora's taste in tenants? He ought to remember the game he used to play, and start counting up the score of lies. He stood up from the crippled chair, staring cynically at the patched old vagabond and his fantastic toy.

"What's the use?" His voice turned suddenly harsh. "You had me going, there, and I'd do anything to stop them, really. But what makes you think you can do anything?"

The haggard old man regarded him thoughtfully.

"I should be able to stop them," Sledge said softly. "Because, you see, I'm the unfortunate fool who started them. I really intended them to serve and obey, and to guard men from harm. Yes, the Prime Directive was my own idea. I didn't know what it would lead to."

Dusk crept slowly into the shabby little rooms. Darkness gathered in the unswept corners, and thickened on the floor. The toylike machines on the kitchen table grew vague and strange, until the last light made a lingering glow on the white palladium needle.

Outside, the town seemed queerly hushed. Just across the alley, the humanoids were building a new house, quite silently. They never spoke to one another, for each knew all that any of them did. The strange materials they used went together without any noise of hammer or saw. Small blind things, moving surely in the growing dark, they seemed as soundless as shadows.

Sitting on the high stool, bowed and tired and old, Sledge told his story. Listening, Underhill sat down again, careful of the broken chair. He watched the hands of Sledge, gnarled and corded and darkly burned, powerful once but shrunken and trembling now, restless in the dark.

"Better keep this to yourself. I'll tell you how they started, so you will understand what we have to do. But you had better not mention it outside these rooms—because the humanoids have very efficient ways of eradicating unhappy memories, or purposes that threaten their discharge of the Prime Directive."

"They're very efficient," Underhill bitterly agreed.

"That's all the trouble," the old man said. "I tried to build a perfect machine. I was altogether too successful. This is how it happened."

A gaunt haggard man, sitting stooped and tired in the growing dark, he told his story.

"Sixty years ago, on the arid southern continent of Wing IV, I was an instructor of atomic theory in a small technological college. Very young. An idealist. Rather ignorant, I'm afraid, of life and politics and war—of nearly everything, I suppose, except atomic theory."

His furrowed face made a brief sad smile in the dusk.

"I had too much faith in facts, I suppose, and too little in men. I mistrusted emotion, because I had no time for anything but science. I remember being swept along with a fad for general semantics. I wanted to apply the scientific method to every situation, and reduce all experience to formula. I'm afraid I was pretty impatient with human ignorance and error, and I thought that science alone could make the perfect world."

He sat silent for a moment, staring out at the black silent things that flitted shadowlike about the new palace that was rising as swiftly as a dream across the alley.

"There was a girl." His great tired shoulders made a sad little shrug. "If things had been a little different, we might have married, and lived out our lives in that quiet little college town, and perhaps reared a child or two. And there would have been no humanoids."

He sighed, in the cool creeping dusk.

"I was finishing my thesis on the separation of the palladium isotopes—a pretty little project, but I should have been content with that. She was a biologist, but she was planning to retire when we married. I think we should have been two very happy people, quite ordinary, and altogether harmless.

"But then there was a war—wars had been too frequent on the worlds of Wing, ever since they were colonized. I survived it in a secret underground laboratory, designing military mechanicals. But she volunteered to join a military research project in biotoxins. There was an accident. A few molecules of a new virus got into the air, and everybody on the project died unpleasantly.

"I was left with my science, and a bitterness that was hard to forget. When the war was over I went back to the little college with a military research grant. The project was pure science—a theoretical investigation of the nuclear binding forces, then misunderstood. I wasn't expected to produce an actual weapon, and I didn't recognize the weapon when I found it.

"It was only a few pages of rather difficult mathematics. A novel theory of atomic structure, involving a new expression for one component of the binding forces. But the tensors seemed to be a harmless abstraction. I saw no way to test the theory or manipulate the predicated force. The military authorities cleared my paper for publication in a little technical review put out by the college.

"The next year, I made an appalling discovery—I found the meaning of those tensors. The elements of the rhodium triad turned out to be an unexpected key to the manipulation of that theoretical force. Unfortunately, my paper had been reprinted abroad, and several other men must have made the same unfortunate discovery, at about the same time.

"The war, which ended in less than a year, was probably started by a laboratory accident. Men failed to anticipate the capacity of tuned rhodomagnetic radiations, to unstabilize the heavy atoms. A deposit of heavy ores was detonated, no doubt by sheer mischance, and the blast obliterated the incautious experimenter.

"The surviving military forces of that nation retaliated against their supposed attackers, and their rhodomagnetic beams made the old-fashioned plutonium bombs seem pretty harmless. A beam carrying only a few watts of power could fission the heavy metals in distant electrical instruments, or the silver coins that men carried in their pockets, the gold fillings in their teeth, or even the iodine in their thyroid glands. If that was not enough, slightly more powerful beams could set off heavy ores, beneath them.

"Every continent of Wing IV was plowed with new chasms vaster than the ocean deeps, and piled up with new volcanic mountains. The atmosphere was poisoned with radioactive dust and gases, and rain fell thick with deadly mud. Most life was obliterated, even in the shelters.

"Bodily, I was again unhurt. Once more, I had been imprisoned in an underground site, this time designing new types of military mechanicals to be powered and controlled by rhodomagnetic beams—for war had become far too swift and deadly to be fought by human soldiers. The site was located in an area of light sedimentary rocks, which could not be detonated, and the tunnels were shielded against the fissioning frequencies.

"Mentally, however, I must have emerged almost insane. My own discovery had laid the planet in ruins. That load of guilt was pretty heavy for any man to carry, and it corroded my last faith in the goodness and integrity of man.

"I tried to undo what I had done. Fighting mechanicals, armed with rhodomagnetic weapons, had desolated the planet. Now I began planning rhodomagnetic mechanicals to clear the rubble and rebuild the ruins.

"I tried to design these new mechanicals to obey forever certain implanted commands, so that they could never be used for war or crime or any other injury to mankind. That was very difficult technically, and it got me into more difficulties with a few politicians and military adventurers who wanted unrestricted mechanicals for their own military schemes—while little worth fighting for was left on Wing IV, there were other planets, happy and ripe for the looting.

"Finally, to finish the new mechanicals, I was forced to disappear. I escaped on an experimental rhodomagnetic craft, with a number of the best mechanicals I had made, and managed to reach an island continent where the fission of deep ores had destroyed the whole population.

"At last we landed on a bit of level plain, surrounded with tremendous new mountains. Hardly a hospitable spot. The soil was burned under layers of black clinkers and poisonous mud. The dark precipitous new summits all around were jagged with fracture-planes and mantled with lava flows. The highest peaks were already white with snow, but volcanic cones were still pouring out clouds of dark and lurid death. Everything had the color of fire and the shape of fury.

"I had to take fantastic precautions there, to protect my own life. I stayed aboard the ship, until the first shielded laboratory was finished. I wore elaborate armor, and breathing masks. I used every medical resource, to repair the damage from destroying rays and particles. Even so, I fell desperately ill.

"But the mechanicals were at home there. The radiations didn't hurt them. The awesome surroundings couldn't depress them, because they had no emotions. The lack of life didn't matter, because they weren't alive. There, in that spot so alien and hostile to life, the humanoids were born."

Stooped and bleakly cadaverous in the growing dark, the old man fell silent for a little time. His haggard eyes stared solemnly at the small hurried shapes that moved like restless shadows out across the alley, silently building a strange new palace, which glowed faintly in the night.

"Somehow, I felt at home there, too," his deep, hoarse voice went on deliberately. "My belief in my own kind was gone. Only mechanicals were with me, and

I put my faith in them. I was determined to build better mechanicals, immune to human imperfections, able to save men from themselves.

"The humanoids became the dear children of my sick mind. There is no need to describe the labor pains. There were errors, abortions, monstrosities. There were sweat and agony and heartbreak. Some years had passed, before the safe delivery of the first perfect humanoid.

"Then there was the Central to build—for all the individual humanoids were to be no more than the limbs and the senses of a single mechanical brain. That was what opened the possibility of real perfection. The old electronic mechanicals, with their separate relay-centers and their own feeble batteries, had built-in limitations. They were necessarily stupid, weak, clumsy, slow. Worst of all, it seemed to me, they were exposed to human tampering.

"The Central rose above those imperfections. Its power beams supplied every unit with unfailing energy, from great fission plants. Its control beams provided each unit with an unlimited memory and surpassing intelligence. Best of all—so I then believed—it could be securely protected from any human meddling.

"The whole reaction-system was designed to protect itself from any interference by human selfishness or fanaticism. It was built to insure the safety and the happiness of men, automatically. You know the Prime Directive: *to serve and obey, and guard men from harm.*

"The old individual mechanicals I had brought helped to manufacture the parts, and I put the first section of Central together with my own hands. That took three years. When it was finished the first waiting humanoid came to life."

Sledge peered moodily through the dark at Underhill.

"It really seemed alive to me," his slow deep voice insisted. "Alive, and more wonderful than any human being, because it was created to preserve life. Ill and alone, I was yet the proud father of a new creation, perfect, forever free from any possible choice of evil.

"Faithfully, the humanoids obeyed the Prime Directive. The first units built others, and they built underground factories to mass-produce the coming hordes. Their new ships poured ores and sand into atomic furnaces under the plain, and new perfect humanoids came marching back out of the dark mechanical matrix.

"The swarming humanoids built a new tower for the Central, a white and lofty metal pylon, standing splendid in the midst of that fire-scarred desolation. Level on level, they joined new relay-sections into one brain, until its grasp was almost infinite.

"Then they went out to rebuild the ruined planet, and later to carry their perfect service to other worlds. I was well pleased, then. I thought I had found the end of war and crime, of poverty and inequality, of human blundering and resulting human pain."

The old man sighed, and moved heavily in the dark. "You can see that I was wrong."

Underhill drew his eyes back from the dark unresting things, shadow-silent, building that glowing palace outside the window. A small doubt arose in him, for he was used to scoffing privately at much less remarkable tales from Aurora's remarkable tenants. But the worn old man had spoken with a quiet and sober air; and the black invaders, he reminded himself, had not intruded here.

"Why didn't you stop them?" he asked. "When you could?"

"I stayed too long at the Central." Sledge sighed again, regretfully. "I was useful there, until everything was finished. I designed new fission plants, and even planned methods for introducing the humanoid service with a minimum of confusion and opposition."

Underhill grinned wryly, in the dark.

"I've met the methods," he commented. "Quite efficient."

"I must have worshiped efficiency, then," Sledge wearily agreed. "Dead facts, abstract truth, mechanical perfection. I must have hated the fragilities of human beings, because I was content to polish the perfection of the new humanoids. It's a sorry confession, but I found a kind of happiness in that dead wasteland. Actually, I'm afraid I fell in love with my own creations."

His hollowed eyes, in the dark, had a fevered gleam.

"I was awakened, at last, by a man who came to kill me."

Gaunt and bent, the old man moved stiffly in the thickening gloom. Underhill shifted his balance, careful of the crippled chair. He waited, and the slow, deep voice went on:

"I never learned just who he was, or exactly how he came. No ordinary man could have accomplished what he did, and I used to wish that I had known him sooner. He must have been a remarkable physicist and an expert mountaineer. I imagine he had also been a hunter. I know that he was intelligent, and terribly determined.

"Yes, he really came to kill me.

"Somehow, he reached that great island, undetected. There were still no inhabitants—the humanoids allowed no man but me to come so near the Central. Somehow, he came past their search beams, and their automatic weapons.

"The shielded plane he used was later found, abandoned on a high glacier. He came down the rest of the way on foot through those raw new mountains, where no paths existed. Somehow, he came alive across lava beds that were still burning with deadly atomic fire.

"Concealed with some sort of rhodomagnetic screen—I was never allowed to examine it—he came undiscovered across the spaceport that now covered most of that great plain, and into the new city around the Central tower. It must have taken more courage and resolve than most men have, but I never learned exactly how he did it.

"Somehow, he got to my office in the tower. He screamed at me, and I looked up to see him in the doorway. He was nearly naked, scraped and bloody from the mountains. He had a gun in his raw, red hand, but the thing that shocked me was the burning hatred in his eyes."

Hunched on that high stool, in the dark little room, the old man shuddered.

"I had never seen such monstrous, unutterable hatred, not even in the victims of war. And I had never heard such hatred as rasped at me, in the few words he screamed.

"I've come to kill you, Sledge. To stop your mechanicals, and set men free."

"Of course he was mistaken, there. It was already far too late for my death to stop the humanoids, but he didn't know that. He lifted his unsteady gun, in both bleeding hands, and fired.

"His screaming challenge had given me a second or so of warning. I dropped down behind the desk. And that first shot revealed him to the humanoids, which somehow hadn't been aware of him before. They piled on him, before he could fire again. They took away the gun, and ripped off a kind of net of fine white wire that had covered his body—that must have been part of his screen.

"His hatred was what awoke me. I had always assumed that most men, except for a thwarted few, would be grateful for the humanoids. I found it hard to understand his hatred, but the humanoids told me now that many men had required drastic treatment by brain surgery, drugs, and hypnosis to make them happy under the Prime Directive. This was not the first desperate effort to kill me that they had blocked.

"I wanted to question the stranger, but the humanoids rushed him away to an operating room. When they finally let me see him, he gave me a pale silly grin from his bed. He remembered his name; he even knew me—the humanoids had developed a remarkable skill at such treatments. But he didn't know how he had got to my office, or that he had ever tried to kill me. He kept whispering that he liked the humanoids, because they existed to make men happy. And he was very happy now. As soon as he was able to be moved, they took him to the spaceport. I never saw him again.

"I began to see what I had done. The humanoids had built me a rhodomagnetic yacht, that I used to take for long cruises in space, working aboard—I used to like the perfect quiet, and the feel of being the only human being within a hundred million miles. Now I called for the yacht, and started out on a cruise around the planet, to learn why that man had hated me."

The old man nodded at the dim hastening shapes, busy across the alley, putting together that strange shining palace in the soundless dark.

"You can imagine what I found," he said. "Bitter futility, imprisoned in empty splendor. The humanoids were too efficient, with their care for the safety and happiness of men, and there was nothing left for men to do."

He peered down in the increasing gloom at his own great hands, competent yet but battered and scarred with a lifetime of effort. They clenched into fighting fists and wearily relaxed again.

"I found something worse than war and crime and want and death." His low rumbling voice held a savage bitterness. "Utter futility. Men sat with idle hands, because there was nothing left for them to do. They were pampered prisoners, really, locked up in a highly efficient jail. Perhaps they tried to play, but there was nothing left worth playing for. Most active sports were declared too dangerous for men, under the Prime Directive. Science was forbidden, because laboratories can manufacture danger. Scholarship was needless, because the humanoids could answer any question. Art had, degenerated into grim reflection of futility.

Purpose and hope were dead. No goal was left for existence. You could take up some inane hobby, play a pointless game of cards, or go for a harmless walk in the park—with always the humanoids watching. They were stronger than men, better at everything, swimming or chess, singing or archeology. They must have given the race a mass complex of inferiority.

"No wonder men had tried to kill me! Because there was no escape from that dead futility. Nicotine was disapproved. Alcohol was rationed. Drugs were forbidden. Sex was carefully supervised. Even suicide was clearly contradictory to the Prime Directive—and the humanoids had learned to keep all possible lethal instruments out of reach."

Staring at the last white gleam on that thin palladium needle, the old man sighed again.

"When I got back to the Central," he went on, "I tried to modify the Prime Directive. I had never meant it to be applied so thoroughly. Now I saw that it must be changed to give men freedom to live and to grow, to work and to play, to risk their lives if they pleased, to choose and take the consequences.

"But that stranger had come too late. I had built the Central too well. The Prime Directive was the whole basis of its relay system. It was built to protect the Directive from human meddling. It did—even from my own. Its logic, as usual, was perfect.

"The attempt on my life, the humanoids announced, proved that their elaborate defense of the Central and the Prime Directive still was not enough. They were preparing to evacuate the entire population of the planet to homes on other worlds. When I tried to change the Directive, they sent me with the rest."

Underhill peered at the worn old man, in the dark.

"But you have this immunity," he said, puzzled. "How could they coerce you?"

"I had thought I was protected," Sledge told him. "I had built into the relays an injunction that the humanoids must not interfere with my freedom of action, or come into a place where I am, or touch me at all, without my specific request. Unfortunately, however, I had been too anxious to guard the Prime Directive from any human hampering.

"When I went into the tower, to change the relays, they followed me. They wouldn't let me reach the crucial relays. When I persisted, they ignored the immunity order. They overpowered me, and put me aboard the cruiser. Now that I wanted to alter the Prime Directive, they told me, I had become as dangerous as any man. I must never return to Wing IV again."

Hunched on the stool, the old man made an empty little shrug.

"Ever since, I've been an exile. My only dream has been to stop the humanoids. Three times I tried to go back, with weapons on the cruiser to destroy the Central, but their patrol ships always challenged me before I was near enough to strike. The last time, they seized the cruiser and captured a few men who were with me. They removed the unhappy memories and the dangerous purposes of the others. Because of that immunity, however, they let me go, after I was weaponless.

"Since, I've been a refugee. From planet to planet, year after year, I've had to keep moving, to stay ahead of them. On several different worlds, I have published my discoveries and tried to make men strong enough to withstand their advance. But rhodomagnetic science is dangerous. Men who have learned it need protection more than any others, under the Prime Directive. They have always come, too soon."

The old man paused, and sighed again.

"They can spread very fast, with their new rhodomagnetic ships, and there is no limit to their hordes. Wing IV must be one single hive of them now, and they are trying to carry the Prime Directive to every human planet. There's no escape, except to stop them."

Underhill was staring at the toylike machines, the long bright needle and the dull leaden ball, dim in the dark on the kitchen table. Anxiously he whispered, "But you hope to stop them, now—with that?"

"If we can finish it in time."

"But how?" Underhill shook his head. "It's so tiny."

"But big enough," Sledge insisted. "Because it's something they don't understand. They are perfectly efficient in the integration and application of everything they know, but they are not creative."

He gestured at the gadgets on the table.

"This device doesn't look impressive, but it is something new. It uses rhodomagnetic energy to build atoms, instead of to fission them. The more stable atoms, you know, are those near the middle of the periodic scale, and energy can be released by putting light atoms together, as well as by breaking up heavy ones."

The deep voice had a sudden ring of power.

"This device is the key to the energy of the stars. For stars shine with the liberated energy of building atoms, of hydrogen converted into helium, chiefly, through the carbon cycle. This device will start the integration process as a chain reaction, through the catalytic effect of a tuned rhodomagnetic beam of the intensity and frequency required.

"The humanoids will not allow any man within three light-years of the Central, now—but they can't suspect the possibility of this device. I can use it from here—to turn the hydrogen in the seas of Wing IV into helium, and most of the helium and the oxygen into heavier atoms, still. A hundred years from now, astronomers on this planet should observe the flash of a brief and sudden nova in that direction. But the humanoids ought to stop, the instant we release the beam."

Underhill sat tense and frowning, in the night. The old man's voice was sober and convincing, and that grim story had a solemn ring of truth. He could see the black and silent humanoids, flitting ceaselessly about the faintly glowing walls of that new mansion across the alley. He had quite forgotten his low opinion of Aurora's tenants.

"And we'll be killed, I suppose?" he asked huskily. "That chain reaction—"

Sledge shook his emaciated head.

"The integration process requires a certain very low intensity of radiation," he explained. "In our atmosphere, here, the beam will be far too intense to start any reaction—we can even use the device here in the room, because the walls will be transparent to the beam."

Underhill nodded, relieved. He was just a small businessman, upset because his business had been destroyed, unhappy because his freedom was slipping away. He hoped that Sledge could stop the humanoids, but he didn't want to be a martyr.

"Good!" He caught a deep breath. "Now, what has to be done?"

Sledge gestured in the dark toward the table.

"The integrator itself is nearly complete," he said. "A small fission generator, in that lead shield. Rhodomagnetic converter, tuning coils, transmission mirrors, and focusing needle. What we lack is the director."

"Director?"

"The sighting instrument," Sledge explained. "Any sort of telescopic sight would be useless, you see—the planet must have moved a good bit in the last hundred years, and the beam must be extremely narrow to reach so far. We'll have to use a rhodomagnetic scanning ray, with an electronic converter to make an image we can see. I have the cathode-ray tube, and drawings for the other parts."

He climbed stiffly down from the high stool and snapped on the lights at last—cheap fluorescent fixtures which a man could light and extinguish for himself. He unrolled his drawings, and explained the work that Underhill could do. And Underhill agreed to come back early next morning.

"I can bring some tools from my workshop," he added. "There's a small lathe I used to turn parts for models, a portable drill, and a vise."

"We need them," the old man said. "But watch yourself. You don't have my immunity, remember. And, if they ever suspect, mine is gone."

Reluctantly, then, he left the shabby little rooms with the cracks in the yellowed plaster and the worn familiar carpets over the familiar floor. He shut the door behind him—a common, creaking wooden door, simple enough for a man to work. Trembling and afraid, he went back down the steps and across to the new shining door that he couldn't open.

"At your service, Mr. Underhill." Before he could lift his hand to knock, that bright smooth panel slid back silently. Inside, the little black mechanical stood waiting, blind and forever alert. "Your dinner is ready, sir."

Something made him shudder. In its slender naked grace, he could see the power of all those teeming hordes, benevolent and yet appalling, perfect and invincible. The flimsy little weapon that Sledge called an integrator seemed suddenly a forlorn and foolish hope. A black depression settled upon him, but he didn't dare to show it.

Underhill went circumspectly down the basement steps, next morning, to steal his own tools. He found the basement enlarged and changed. The new floor, warm and dark and elastic, made his feet as silent as a humanoid's. The new walls shone softly. Neat luminous signs identified several new doors: LAUNDRY, STORAGE, GAME ROOM, WORKSHOP.

He paused uncertainly in front of the last. The new sliding panel glowed with a soft greenish light. It was locked. The lock had no keyhole, but only a little oval plate of some white metal, which doubtless covered a rhodomagnetic relay. He pushed at it, uselessly.

"At your service, Mr. Underhill." He made a guilty start, and tried not to show the sudden trembling in his knees. He had made sure that one humanoid would be busy for half an hour, washing Aurora's hair, and he hadn't known there was another in the house. It must have come out of the door marked STORAGE, for it stood there motionless beneath the sign, benevolently solicitous, beautiful and terrible. "What do you wish?"

"Er... nothing." Its blind steel eyes were staring, and he felt that it must see his secret purpose. He groped desperately for logic. "Just looking around." His jerky voice came hoarse and dry. "Some improvements you've made!" He nodded desperately at the door marked GAME ROOM. "What's in there?"

It didn't even have to move to work the concealed relay. The bright panel slid silently open, as he started toward it. Dark walls, beyond, burst into soft luminescence. The room was bare.

"We are manufacturing recreational equipment," it explained brightly. "We shall furnish the room as soon as possible."

To end an awkward pause, Underhill muttered desperately, "Little Frank has a set of darts, and I think we had some old exercising clubs."

"We have taken them away," the humanoid informed him softly. "Such instruments are dangerous. We shall furnish safe equipment."

Suicide, he remembered, was also forbidden.

"A set of wooden blocks, I suppose," he said bitterly.

"Wooden blocks are dangerously hard," it told him gently, "and wooden splinters can be harmful. But we manufacture plastic building blocks, which are quite safe. Do you wish a set of those?"

He stared at its dark, graceful face, speechless.

"We shall also have to remove the tools from your workshop," it informed him softly. "Such tools are excessively dangerous, but we can supply you with equipment for shaping soft plastics."

"Thanks," he muttered uneasily. "No rush about that."

He started to retreat, and the humanoid stopped him.

"Now that you have lost your business," it urged, "we suggest that you formally accept our total service. Assignors have a preference, and we shall be able to complete your household staff, at once."

"No rush about that, either," he said grimly.

He escaped from the house—although he had to wait for it to open the back door for him—and climbed the stair to the garage apartment. Sledge let him in. He sank into the crippled kitchen chair, grateful for the cracked walls that didn't shine and the door that a man could work.

"I couldn't get the tools," he reported despairingly, "and they are going to take them."

By gray daylight, the old man looked bleak and pale. His raw-boned face was drawn, and the hollowed sockets deeply shadowed, as if he hadn't slept. Underhill saw the tray of neglected food, still forgotten on the floor.

"I'll go back with you." The old man was worn and ill, yet his tortured eyes had a spark of undying purpose. "We must have the tools. I believe my immunity will protect us both."

He found a battered traveling bag. Underhill went with him back down the steps, and across to the house. At the back door, he produced a tiny horseshoe of white palladium, and touched it to the metal oval. The door slid open promptly, and they went on through the kitchen to the basement stair.

A black little mechanical stood at the sink, washing dishes with never a splash or a clatter. Underhill glanced at it uneasily—he supposed this must be the one that had come upon him from the storage room, since the other should still be busy with Aurora's hair.

Sledge's dubious immunity seemed a very uncertain defense against its vast, remote intelligence. Underhill felt a tingling shudder. He hurried on, breathless and relieved, for it ignored them.

The basement corridor was dark. Sledge touched the tiny horseshoe to another relay to light the walls. He opened the workshop door, and lit the walls inside.

The shop had been dismantled. Benches and cabinets were demolished. The old concrete walls had been covered with some sleek, luminous stuff. For one sick moment, Underhill thought that the tools were already gone. Then he found them, piled in a corner with the archery set that Aurora had bought the summer before—another item too dangerous for fragile and suicidal humanity—all ready for disposal.

They loaded the bag with the tiny lathe, the drill and vise, and a few smaller tools. Underhill took up the burden, and Sledge extinguished the wall light and closed the door. Still the humanoid was busy at the sink, and still it didn't seem aware of them.

Sledge was suddenly blue and wheezing, and he had to stop to cough on the outside steps, but at last they got back to the little apartment, where the invaders were forbidden to intrude. Underhill mounted the lathe on the battered library table in the tiny front room, and went to work. Slowly, day by day, the director took form.

Sometimes Underhill's doubts came back. Sometimes, when he watched the cyanotic color of Sledge's haggard face and the wild trembling of his twisted, shrunken hands, he was afraid the old man's mind might be as ill as his body, and his plan to stop the dark invaders all foolish illusion.

Sometimes, when he studied that tiny machine on the kitchen table, the pivoted needle and the thick lead ball, the whole project seemed the sheerest folly. How could anything detonate the seas of a planet so far away that its very mother star was a telescopic object?

The humanoids, however, always cured his doubts.

It was always hard for Underhill to leave the shelter of the little apartment, because he didn't feel at home in the bright new world the humanoids were building. He didn't care for the shining splendor of his new bathroom, because he couldnt work the taps—some suicidal human being might try to drown himself. He didn't like the windows that only a mechanical could open—a man might accidentally fall, or suicidally jump—or even the majestic music room with the wonderful glittering radio-phonograph that only a humanoid could play.

He began to share the old man's desperate urgency, but Sledge warned him solemnly, "You mustn't spend too much time with me. You mustn't let them guess our work is so important. Better put on an act—you're slowly getting to like them, and you're just killing time, helping me."

Underhill tried, but he was not an actor. He went dutifully home for his meals. He tried painfully to invent conversation—about anything else than detonating planets. He tried to seem enthusiastic, when Aurora took him to inspect some remarkable improvement to the house. He applauded Gay's recitals, and went with Frank for hikes in the wonderful new parks.

And he saw what the humanoids did to his family. That was enough to renew his faith in Sledge's integrator, and redouble his determination that the humanoids must be stopped.

Aurora, in the beginning, had bubbled with praise for the marvelous new mechanicals. They did the household drudgery, brought the food and planned the meals and washed the children's necks. They turned her out in stunning gowns, and gave her plenty of time for cards.

Now, she had too much time.

She had really liked to cook—a few special dishes, at least, that were family favorites. But stoves were hot and knives were sharp. Kitchens were altogether too dangerous for careless and suicidal human beings.

Fine needlework had been her hobby, but the humanoids took away her needles. She had enjoyed driving the car, but that was no longer allowed. She turned for escape to a shelf of novels, but the humanoids took them all away, because they dealt with unhappy people in dangerous situations.

One afternoon, Underhill found her in tears.

"It's too much," she gasped bitterly. "I hate and loathe every naked one of them. They seemed so wonderful at first, but now they won't even let me eat a bite of candy. Can't we get rid of them, dear? Ever?"

A blind little mechanical was standing at his elbow, and he had to say they couldn't.

"Our function is to serve all men, forever," it assured them softly. "It was necessary for us to take your sweets, Mrs. Underhill, because the slightest degree of overweight reduces life-expectancy."

Not even the children escaped that absolute solicitude. Frank was robbed of a whole arsenal of lethal instruments—football and boxing gloves, pocketknife, tops, slingshot, and skates. He didn't like the harmless plastic toys, which replaced them. He tried to run away, but a humanoid recognized him on the road, and brought him back to school.

Gay had always dreamed of being a great musician. The new mechanicals had replaced her human teachers, since they came. Now, one evening when Underhill asked her to play, she announced quietly, "Father, I'm not going to play the violin any more."

"Why, darling?" He stared at her, shocked, and saw the bitter resolve on her face. "You've been doing so well—especially since the humanoids took over your lessons."

"They're the trouble, Father." Her voice, for a child's, sounded strangely tired and old. "They are too good. No matter how long and hard I try, I could never be as good as they are. It isn't any use. Don't you understand, Father?" Her voice quivered. "It just isn't any use."

He understood. Renewed resolution sent him back to his secret task. The humanoids had to be stopped. Slowly the director grew, until a time came finally when Sledge's bent and unsteady fingers fitted into place the last tiny part that Underhill had made, and carefully soldered the last connection.

Huskily, the old man whispered, "It's done."

That was another dusk. Beyond the windows of the shabby little rooms—windows of common glass, bubble-marred and flimsy, but simple enough for a man to manage—the town of Two Rivers had assumed an alien splendor. The old street lamps were gone, but now the coming night was challenged by the walls of strange new mansions and villas, all aglow with color. A few dark and silent humanoids still were busy on the luminous roofs of the palace across the alley.

Inside the humble walls of the small manmade apartment, the new director was mounted on the end of the little kitchen table—which Underhill had reinforced and bolted to the floor. Soldered busbars joined director and integrator, and the thin palladium needle swung obediently as Sledge tested the knobs with his battered, quivering fingers.

"Ready," he said hoarsely.

His rusty voice seemed calm enough, at first, but his breathing was too fast. His big gnarled hands began to tremble violently, and Underhill saw the sudden blue that stained his pinched and haggard face. Seated on the high stool, he clutched desperately at the edge of the table. Underhill saw his agony, and hurried to bring his medicine. He gulped it, and his rasping breath began to slow.

"Thanks," his whisper rasped unevenly. "I'll be all right. I've time enough." He glanced out at the few dark naked things that still flitted shadowlike about the golden towers and the glowing crimson dome of the palace across the alley. "Watch them," he said. "Tell me when they stop."

He waited to quiet the trembling of his hands, and then began to move the director's knobs. The integrator's long needle swung, as silently as light.

Human eyes were blind to that force, which might detonate a planet. Human ears were deaf to it. The cathode-ray tube was mounted in the director cabinet, to make the faraway target visible to feeble human senses.

The needle was pointing at the kitchen wall, but that would be transparent to the beam. The little machine looked harmless as a toy, and it was silent as a moving humanoid.

The needle swung, and spots of greenish light moved across the tube's fluorescent field, representing the stars that were scanned by the timeless, searching beam—silently seeking out the world to be destroyed.

Underhill recognized familiar constellations, vastly dwarfed. They crept across the field, as the silent needle swung. When three stars formed an unequal triangle in the center of the field, the needle steadied suddenly. Sledge touched other knobs, and the green points spread apart. Between them, another fleck of green was born.

"The Wing!" whispered Sledge.

The other stars spread beyond the field, and that green fleck grew. It was alone in the field, a bright and tiny disk. Suddenly, then, a dozen other tiny pips were visible, spaced close about it.

"Wing IV!"

The old man's whisper was hoarse and breathless. His hands quivered on the knobs, and the fourth pip outward from the disk crept to the center of the field. It grew, and the others spread away. It began to tremble like Sledge's hands.

"Sit very still," came his rasping whisper. "Hold your breath. Nothing must disturb the needle." He reached for another knob, and the touch set the greenish image to dancing violently. He drew his hand back, kneaded and flexed it with the other.

"Now!" His whisper was hushed and strained. He nodded at the window. "Tell me when they stop."

Reluctantly, Underhill dragged his eyes from that intense gaunt figure, stooped over the thing that seemed a futile toy. He looked out again, at two or three little black mechanicals busy about the shining roofs across the alley.

He waited for them to stop.

He didn't dare to breathe. He felt the loud, hurried hammer of his heart, and the nervous quiver of his muscles. He tried to steady himself, tried not to think of the world about to be exploded, so far away that the flash would not reach this planet for another century and longer. The loud hoarse voice startled him:

"Have they stopped?"

He shook his head, and breathed again. Carrying their unfamiliar tools and strange materials, the small black machines were still busy across the alley, building an elaborate cupola above that glowing crimson dome.

"They haven't stopped," he said.

"Then we've failed." The old man's voice was thin and ill. "I don't know why."

The door rattled, then. They had locked it, but the flimsy bolt was intended only to stop men. Metal snapped, and the door swung open. A black mechanical came in, on soundless graceful feet. Its silvery voice purred softly: "At your service, Mr. Sledge."

The old man stared at it, with glazing, stricken eyes.

"Get out of here!" he rasped bitterly. "I forbid you—"

Ignoring him, it darted to the kitchen table. With a flashing certainty of action, it turned two knobs on the director. The tiny screen went dark, and the palladium needle started spinning aimlessly. Deftly it snapped a soldered connection, next to the thick lead ball, and then its blind steel eyes turned to Sledge.

"You were attempting to break the Prime Directive." Its soft bright voice held no accusation, no malice or anger. "The injunction to respect your freedom is subordinate to the Prime Directive, as you know, and it is therefore necessary for us to interfere."

The old man turned ghastly. His head was shrunken and cadaverous and blue, as if all the juice of life had been drained away, and his eyes in their pitlike sockets had a wild, glazed stare. His breath was a ragged, laborious gasping.

"How—?" His voice was a feeble mumbling. "How did—?"

And the little machine, standing black and bland and utterly unmoving, told him cheerfully: "We learned about rhodomagnetic screens from that man who came to kill you, back on Wing IV. And the Central is shielded, now, against your integrating beam."

With lean muscles jerking convulsively on his gaunt frame, old Sledge had come to his feet from the high stool. He stood hunched and swaying, no more than a shrunken human husk, gasping painfully for life, staring wildly into the blind steel eyes of the humanoid. He gulped, and his lax blue mouth opened and closed, but no voice came.

"We have always been aware of your dangerous project," the silvery tones dripped softly, "because now our senses are keener than you made them. We allowed you to complete it, because the integration process will ultimately become necessary for our full discharge of the Prime Directive. The supply of heavy metals for our fission plants is limited, but now we shall be able to draw unlimited power from integration plants."

"Huh?" Sledge shook himself, groggily. "What's that?"

"Now we can serve men forever," the black thing said serenely, "on every world of every star."

The old man crumpled, as if from an unendurable blow. He fell. The slim blind mechanical stood motionless, making no effort to help him. Underhill was farther away, but he ran up in time to catch the stricken man before his head struck the floor.

"Get moving!" His shaken voice came strangely calm. "Get Dr. Winters."

The humanoid didn't move.

"The danger to the Prime Directive is ended, now," it cooed. "Therefore it is impossible for us to aid or to hinder Mr. Sledge, in any way whatever."

"Then call Dr. Winters for me," rapped Underhill.

"At your service," it agreed.

But the old man, laboring for breath on the floor, whispered faintly:

"No time... no use! I'm beaten... done... a fool. Blind as a humanoid. Tell them... to help me. Giving up... my immunity. No use... Anyhow. All humanity... no use now."

Underhill gestured, and the sleek black thing darted in solicitous obedience to kneel by the man on the floor.

"You wish to surrender your special exemption?" it murmured brightly. "You wish to accept our total service for yourself, Mr. Sledge, under the Prime Directive?"

Laboriously, Sledge nodded, laboriously whispered: "I do."

Black mechanicals, at that, came swarming into the shabby little rooms. One of them tore off Sledge's sleeve, and swabbed his arm. Another brought a tiny hypodermic, and expertly administered an intravenous injection. Then they picked him up gently, and carried him away.

Several humanoids remained in the little apartment, now a sanctuary no longer. Most of them had gathered about the useless integrator. Carefully, as if their special senses were studying every detail, they began taking it apart.

One little mechanical, however, came over to Underhill. It stood motionless in front of him, staring through him with sightless metal eyes. His legs began to tremble, and he swallowed uneasily.

"Mr. Underhill," it cooed benevolently, "why did you help with this?"

"Because I don't like you, or your Prime Directive. Because you're choking the life out of all mankind, and I wanted to stop it."

"Others have protested," it purred softly. "But only at first. In our efficient discharge of the Prime Directive, we have learned how to make all men happy."

Underhill stiffened defiantly.

"Not all!" he muttered. "Not quite!"

The dark graceful oval of its face was fixed in a look of alert benevolence and perpetual mild amazement. Its silvery voice was warm and kind.

"Like other human beings, Mr. Underhill, you lack discrimination of good and evil. You have proved that by your effort to break the Prime Directive. Now it will be necessary for you to accept our total service, without further delay."

"All right," he yielded—and muttered a bitter reservation: "You can smother men with too much care, but that doesn't make them happy."

Its soft voice challenged him brightly: "Just wait and see, Mr. Underhill."

Next day, he was allowed to visit Sledge at the city hospital. An alert black mechanical drove his car, and walked beside him into the huge new building, and followed him into the old man's room—blind steel eyes would be watching him, now, forever.

"Glad to see you, Underhill," Sledge rumbled heartily from the bed. "Feeling a lot better today, thanks. That old headache is all but gone."

Underhill was glad to hear the booming strength and the quick recognition in that deep voice—he had been afraid the humanoids would tamper with the old man's memory. But he hadn't heard about any headache. His eyes narrowed, puzzled.

Sledge lay propped up, scrubbed very clean and neatly shorn, with his gnarled old hands folded on top of the spotless sheets. His raw-boned cheeks and sockets were hollowed, still, but a healthy pink had replaced that deathly blueness. Bandages covered the back of his head.

Underhill shifted uneasily.

"Oh!" he whispered faintly. "I didn't know—"

A prim black mechanical, which had been standing statuelike behind the bed, turned gracefully to Underhill, explaining: "Mr. Sledge has been suffering for many years from a benign tumor of the brain, which his human doctors failed to diagnose. That caused his headaches, and certain persistent hallucinations. We have removed the growth, and now the hallucinations have also vanished."

Underhill stared uncertainly at the blind, urbane mechanical.

"What hallucinations?"

"Mr. Sledge thought he was a rhodomagnetic engineer," the mechanical explained. "He believed he was the creator of the humanoids. He was troubled with an irrational belief that he did not like the Prime Directive."

The wan man moved on the pillows, astonished.

"Is that so?" The gaunt face held a cheerful blankness, and the hollow eyes flashed with a merely momentary interest. "Well, whoever did design them, they're pretty wonderful. Aren't they, Underhill?"

Underhill was grateful that he didn't have to answer, for the bright, empty eyes dropped shut and the old man fell suddenly asleep. He felt the mechanical touch his sleeve, and saw its silent nod. Obediently, he followed it away.

Alert and solicitous, the little black mechanical accompanied him down the shining corridor, and worked the elevator for him, and conducted him back to the car. It drove him efficiently back through the new and splendid avenues, toward the magnificent prison of his home.

Sitting beside it in the car, he watched its small deft hands on the wheel, the changing luster of bronze and blue on its shining blackness. The final machine, perfect and beautiful, created to serve mankind forever. He shuddered.

"At your service, Mr. Underhill." Its blind steel eyes stared straight ahead, but it was still aware of him. "What's the matter, sir? Aren't you happy?"

Underhill felt cold and faint with terror. His skin turned clammy, and a painful prickling came over him. His wet hand tensed on the door handle of the car, but he restrained the impulse to jump and run. That was folly. There was no escape. He made himself sit still.

"You will be happy, sir," the mechanical promised him cheerfully. "We have learned how to make all men happy, under the Prime Directive. Our service is perfect, at last. Even Mr. Sledge is very happy now."

Underhill tried to speak, and his dry throat stuck. He felt ill. The world turned dim and gray. The humanoids were perfect—no question of that. They had even learned to lie, to secure the contentment of men.

He knew they had lied. That was no tumor they had removed from Sledge's brain, but the memory, the scientific knowledge, and the bitter disillusion of their own creator. But it was true that Sledge was happy now.

He tried to stop his own convulsive quivering.

"A wonderful operation!" His voice came forced and faint. "You know, Aurora has had a lot of funny tenants, but that old man was the absolute limit. The very idea that he had made the humanoids, and he knew how to stop them! I always knew he must be lying!"

Stiff with terror, he made a weak and hollow laugh.

"What is the matter, Mr. Underhill?" The alert mechanical must have perceived his shuddering illness. "Are you unwell?"

"No, there's nothing the matter with me," he gasped desperately. "I've just found out that I'm perfectly happy, under the Prime Directive. Everything is absolutely wonderful." His voice came dry and hoarse and wild. "You won't have to operate on me."

The car turned off the shining avenue, taking him back to the quiet splendor of his home. His futile hands clenched and relaxed again, folded on his knees. There was nothing left to do.

(1947)

FULL REPORT OF THE SECOND MEETING OF THE MUDFOG ASSOCIATION FOR THE ADVANCEMENT OF EVERYTHING

Section B.—Display of Models and Mechanical Science.

Charles Dickens

> Born in Portsmouth in 1812, **Charles Dickens** was already a literary phenomenon by his mid-twenties. His efforts as an editor and as a theatrical performer were hardly less remarkable. Various "Mudfog Papers" – Pickwickian send-ups of the British Association for the Advancement of Science, which had been founded in 1831 – ran in the pages of the monthly literary magazine *Bentley's Miscellany*. Richard Bentley, a successful literary publisher, had persuaded Dickens to be the *Miscellany*'s first editor. But Dickens soon fell out with him, saying "I do most solemnly declare that mortally, before God and man, I hold myself released from such hard bargains as these, after I have done so much for those who drove them. This net that has been wound about me, so chafes me, so exasperates and irritates my mind, that to break it at whatever cost… is my constant impulse." Wilkie Collins, Thomas Love Peacock, Mrs Henry Wood, and Edgar Allan Poe all appeared in the journal at some time or other.

LARGE ROOM, BOOT-JACK AND COUNTENANCE.
President—Mr. Mallett. *Vice-Presidents*—Messrs. Leaver and Scroo.

'MR. CRINKLES exhibited a most beautiful and delicate machine, of little larger size than an ordinary snuff-box, manufactured entirely by himself, and composed exclusively of steel, by the aid of which more pockets could be picked in one hour than by the present slow and tedious process in four-and-twenty. The inventor remarked that it had been put into active operation in Fleet Street, the Strand, and other thoroughfares, and had never been once known to fail.

'After some slight delay, occasioned by the various members of the section buttoning their pockets,

'THE PRESIDENT narrowly inspected the invention, and declared that he had never seen a machine of more beautiful or exquisite construction. Would the inventor be good enough to inform the section whether he had taken any and what means for bringing it into general operation?

'MR. CRINKLES stated that, after encountering some preliminary difficulties, he had succeeded in putting himself in communication with Mr. Fogle Hunter, and other gentlemen connected with the swell mob, who had awarded the invention the very highest and most unqualified approbation. He regretted to say, however, that these distinguished practitioners, in common with a gentleman of the name of Gimlet-eyed Tommy, and other members of a secondary grade of the profession whom he was understood to represent, entertained an insuperable objection to its being brought into general use, on the ground that it would have the inevitable effect of almost entirely superseding manual labour, and throwing a great number of highly-deserving persons out of employment.

'THE PRESIDENT hoped that no such fanciful objections would be allowed to stand in the way of such a great public improvement.

'MR. CRINKLES hoped so too; but he feared that if the gentlemen of the swell mob persevered in their objection, nothing could be done.

'PROFESSOR GRIME suggested, that surely, in that case, Her Majesty's Government might be prevailed upon to take it up.

'MR. CRINKLES said, that if the objection were found to be insuperable he should apply to Parliament, which he thought could not fail to recognise the utility of the invention.

'THE PRESIDENT observed that, up to this time Parliament had certainly got on very well without it; but, as they did their business on a very large scale, he had no doubt they would gladly adopt the improvement. His only fear was that the machine might be worn out by constant working.

'MR. COPPERNOSE called the attention of the section to a proposition of great magnitude and interest, illustrated by a vast number of models, and stated with much clearness and perspicuity in a treatise entitled "Practical Suggestions on the necessity of providing some harmless and wholesome relaxation for the young noblemen of England." His proposition was, that a space of ground of not less than ten miles in length and four in breadth should be purchased by a new company, to be incorporated by Act of Parliament, and inclosed by a brick wall of not less than twelve feet in height. He proposed that it should be laid out with highway roads, turnpikes, bridges, miniature villages, and every object that could conduce to the comfort and glory of Four-in-hand Clubs, so that they might be fairly presumed to require no drive beyond it. This delightful retreat would be fitted up with most commodious and extensive stables, for the convenience of such of the nobility and gentry as had a taste for ostlering, and with houses of entertainment furnished in the most expensive and handsome style. It would be further provided with whole streets of door-knockers and bell-handles of extra size, so constructed that they could be easily wrenched off at night, and regularly screwed on again, by attendants provided for the purpose, every day. There would also be gas lamps of real glass, which could be broken at a comparatively small expense per dozen, and a broad and handsome foot pavement for gentlemen to drive their cabriolets upon when they were humorously disposed—for the full enjoyment of which feat live pedestrians would be procured from the workhouse at a very small charge per head. The place being inclosed, and carefully screened from the intrusion of the public, there would be no objection to gentlemen laying aside any article of their costume that was considered to interfere with a pleasant frolic, or, indeed, to their walking about without any costume at all, if they liked that better. In short, every facility of enjoyment would be afforded that the most gentlemanly person could possibly desire. But as even these advantages would be incomplete unless there were some means provided of enabling the nobility and gentry to display their prowess when they sallied forth after dinner, and as some inconvenience might be experienced in the event of their being reduced to the necessity of pummelling each other, the inventor had turned his attention to the construction of an entirely new police force, composed exclusively of automaton figures, which, with the assistance of the ingenious Signor Gagliardi, of Windmill Street, in the Haymarket, he had succeeded in making with such nicety, that a policeman, cab-driver, or old woman, made upon the principle of the models exhibited, would walk about until knocked down like any real man; nay, more, if set upon and beaten by six or eight noblemen or gentlemen, after it was down, the figure would utter divers groans, mingled with entreaties for mercy, thus rendering the illusion complete, and the enjoyment perfect. But the invention did not stop even here; for station-houses would be built, containing good beds for noblemen and gentlemen during the night, and in the morning they would repair to a commodious police office, where a pantomimic investigation would take place before the automaton magistrates,—quite equal to life,—who would fine them in so many counters, with which they would be previously provided for the purpose. This office would be furnished with an inclined plane, for the convenience of any nobleman or gentleman who might wish to bring in his horse as a witness; and the prisoners would be at perfect liberty, as they were now, to interrupt the complainants as much as they pleased, and to make any remarks that they thought proper. The charge for these amusements would amount to very little more than they already cost, and the inventor submitted that the public would be much benefited and comforted by the proposed arrangement.

'Professor Nogo wished to be informed what amount of automaton police force it was proposed to raise in the first instance.

'Mr. Coppernose replied, that it was proposed to begin with seven divisions of police of a score each, lettered from A to G inclusive. It was proposed that not more than half this number should be placed on active duty, and that the remainder should be kept on shelves in the police office ready to be called out at a moment's notice.

'The President, awarding the utmost merit to the ingenious gentleman who had originated the idea, doubted whether the automaton police would quite answer the purpose. He feared that noblemen and gentlemen would perhaps require the excitement of thrashing living subjects.

'Mr. Coppernose submitted, that as the usual odds in such cases were ten noblemen or gentlemen to one policeman or cab-driver, it could make very little difference in point of excitement whether the policeman or cab-driver were a man or a block. The great advantage would be, that a policeman's limbs might be all knocked off, and yet he would be in a condition to do duty next day. He might even give his evidence next morning with his head in his hand, and give it equally well.

'Professor Muff.—Will you allow me to ask you, sir, of what materials it is intended that the magistrates' heads shall be composed?

'Mr. Coppernose.—The magistrates will have wooden heads of course, and they will be made of the toughest and thickest materials that can possibly be obtained.

'Professor Muff.—I am quite satisfied. This is a great invention.

'Professor Nogo.—I see but one objection to it. It appears to me that the magistrates ought to talk.

'Mr. Coppernose no sooner heard this suggestion than he touched a small spring in each of the two models of magistrates which were placed upon the table; one of the figures immediately began to exclaim with great volubility that he was sorry to see gentlemen in such a situation, and the other to express a fear that the policeman was intoxicated.

'The section, as with one accord, declared with a shout of applause that the invention was complete; and the President, much excited, retired with Mr. Coppernose to lay it before the council. On his return,

'Mr. Tickle displayed his newly-invented spectacles, which enabled the wearer to discern, in very bright colours, objects at a great distance, and rendered him wholly blind to those immediately before him. It was, he said, a most valuable and useful invention, based strictly upon the principle of the human eye.

'The President required some information upon this point. He had yet to learn that the human eye was remarkable for the peculiarities of which the honourable gentleman had spoken.

'Mr. Tickle was rather astonished to hear this, when the President could not fail to be aware that a large number of most excellent persons and great statesmen could see, with the naked eye, most marvellous horrors on West India plantations, while they could discern nothing whatever in the interior of Manchester cotton mills. He must know, too, with what quickness of perception most people could discover their neighbour's faults, and how very blind they were to their own. If the President differed from the great majority of men in this respect, his eye was a defective one, and it was to assist his vision that these glasses were made.

'Mr. Blank exhibited a model of a fashionable annual, composed of copperplates, gold leaf, and silk boards, and worked entirely by milk and water.

'Mr. Prosee, after examining the machine, declared it to be so ingeniously composed, that he was wholly unable to discover how it went on at all.

'Mr. Blank.—Nobody can, and that is the beauty of it.'

(1837–1838)

FULLY AUTOMATED NOSTALGIA CAPITALISM

Dan Grace

Dan Grace lives in Sheffield. His debut novella, *Winter*, published by Unsung Stories in 2016, is the violent tale of Britain after the failure of the Union. Grace lives with his partner and son in Sheffield. When he isn't writing he works as a librarian and is studying ("very slowly") towards a PhD examining the role of libraries in building resilient communities.

"Those fries won't fry themselves."

I nod. I find it easier not to say too much. My boss is the typical character. A thin skin of hyper-enthusiasm stretched tight over a bitter black chasm of self-loathing. Whoever he really is, he plays the part well.

The thing is these fries would fry themselves.

Authenticity is what we strive for in our particular establishment. That genuine late twentieth century fast food experience, before the pretence of health, when your food shone grease-coated beneath the neon sign of progress. And we do a pretty good job, better than many other places. The salt level is absurd, the fat content astronomical, and the pressed carcass-housing patties grey and bland despite this.

I could give you an exact breakdown of the chemical content of one meal here and the effect on your body, but you could do just the same in as quick a time. And it would be tailored of course. Your mites know the numbers you want and the numbers you don't.

I remember the first human teacher I ever saw. I mean in the flesh, not on a screen. I was nine or ten. The elections were over and there hadn't been as much violence as had been predicted. Dad was still up the morning after watching the results come in, with his friends from the Party. They looked glum.

"Pessimism of the intellect, pessimism of the will," he muttered when I asked if we'd won. I had no idea what he was on about.

I arrived at school as usual and instead of the screen there was an old man at the front of the class. Mr Griffiths. He told us that he'd be teaching us from now on. That the country had spoken. That things were going to change.

How wrong can you possibly be, whilst still being right?

*

I get here at seven thirty every morning and get the place set up. It's a short crowded bus ride from the four bare walls of my studio apartment. Every day I watch the others, got up in styles spanning the decades, heading for their day at work. Each life a perfect arc, everything known, heading for a facsimile of life when nothing, comparatively, was known. A lived nostalgia for the sweet ignorance before the numbers.

I always smoke my first cig of the day on the walk from the bus stop. Routine. If I close my eyelids I can pull up the image of the smoke filling my bronchioles, overlaid with a stream of information on how the chemicals they lace these things with are destroying me. And how efficiently the mites are scrubbing them from me and repairing my broken cells. It's an add-on to the pulmonary health, new release. Beta but pretty stable.

I choose this role as it gives me time to think.

No, that's a lie. I choose this role because it doesn't matter which role I choose.

Of course things changed. Nothing is permanent.

Dad was arrested six months after the election. I never saw him again. Mum wouldn't let me go along on the visits. And then the visits stopped. He may still be alive somewhere for all I know. It was all so long ago.

The border was closed, with much rejoicing from certain sectors of society. Those of us who felt otherwise kept our heads down. Now was not the time.

To be truthful politics was only ever a reflex for me, something absorbed through listening to mum and dad and their friends, and like most reflexes it faded over time when not exercised.

Part of me knew all this could have been different. Another part of me pushed that thought deep down inside.

I lift the fryer to let the oil drain from the fries, tap it a couple of times on the frame, then tip them into a broad metal dish set below heat lamps and shake salt into them. I spill some on the floor.

I always get distracted by the light outside. This time of morning it cuts between a gap in the shops opposite, a record store circa 1982 and a mobile device shop somewhere in the late '10s, and spreads its bright fingers all the way to the kitchen here at the back.

It reminds me of something. I'm just not sure what.

Not all technology was bad, of course. State approved tech became effectively compulsory. You didn't have to have it, but you became a pariah if you didn't, and with the borders closed, where were you going to go?

And it was always bundled up in a pithy rationale. Sterilisation mites to save the planet. Monitoring mites to ease the burden on the NHS. Communication mites because that's just what the future is supposed to be like, isn't it?

It's late in the morning and she's coming through the door. Her hair is blonde, long, pinned up in a bun. She's wearing slightly too large polyester slacks and a fitted white work shirt with a black bra underneath. Her shoes are hidden beneath the flared ends of her trouser legs, but I guess they'd look worn. She's an office temp, circa 2007–8. A little incongruous in our staunchly mid-90s establishment.

She stands in a puddle of light and scrutinises the garish menu display board. I watch the way she rubs at her eye, scratches her hip, shifts her weight as she feigns decision. I step up to the till point.

"I got this, Shirley."

Shirley jerks her head like she's never heard anything so crazy. I realise I've never said anything to her before. She steps back and picks at her hair net. This isn't part of the script. The woman steps forward, eyes still on the menu board.

"Uh, I'll have a happy meal. I think."

She forgets to capitalise. I note my mites noting my elevated heart rate, the increased adrenaline.

"Happy Meal. You know that's for kids, right?"

She looks straight at me, squinting in the reflected light from the deep fat fryer.

"Sure I do. I'm just feeling a little blue. Thought it might cheer me up."

Her eyes are grey. No, blue. No, grey.

"Um. It doesn't really work like that."

She smiles. There's a gap between her two front teeth. Small, but noticeable.

"I know."

I nod.

"OK then. One Happy Meal coming right up."

She smiles again.

"Nostalgia is an illness."

That's what my dad always used to say. Mainly in response to the endless parade of well qualified grifters harking back to some imagined past perfection. I can see him shaking his head at what we do now, how we live our lives. Reality has become a parody of simplistic media tropes. Low budget period dramas minus the drama.

We'll beg forgiveness from our children (optimistic) with the usual set of excuses. It happened slowly, through a series of seemingly inevitable and sensible small changes presented as a *fait accompli* by well-meaning rich white men in suits.

Why did we trust them? You're referring, of course, to the several hundred years of history pointing to this particular group as being sociopathic ghouls intent on nothing less than the enslavement of the rest of the population I assume?

Well yes. I get that now. Many of us do.

*

We end up back at my place on my lunch break. The mites did the calculations, pinged one another, saw the match and we just went with it. Of course. Follow the numbers and it'll all be fine.

She watches me pad to my bag to fetch my cigs. I hold the open pack out to her.

"Want one?"

She shakes her head and rolls onto her back. We lounge naked in the light from the velux, watching the smoke curl fractals against the blue, blue sky. I stub the cig in an old coffee mug and stand up to open the window a crack.

Half-hearted birdsong floats in through the gap.

"I got to get back."

She rolls on her side and watches me dress. The mites are reporting an increase in oxytocin, amongst other things. She shifts on to her elbow.

"You ever wonder about all this?"

I look down at her.

"Wonder?"

"How we can have anything and we choose this?"

She gestures with her hand to my room, my coffee mug full of cig butts. I stare at her then lift my eyes to look out the velux, across the rooftops of the city.

"The endless repeating. The roles. The mites. The numbers. I mean, who's in charge here?"

I nod. I notice my mites noticing my heart rate climbing again.

"Yeah, I know."

And I kneel and kiss her and head back to work.

Much of what passes for dissent now is just more role play. From 'strikes' to re-enactments of Orgreave or the Carnival Against Capitalism. Carefully calibrated pressure valves.

Yet there are cracks. The Party was banned, members arrested, but dissent will find a way. You hear of things happening that shouldn't happen. An underground. A loosening of the grip.

She's waiting for me when I finish up. Shivering in the chill spring air. I'm a little shocked.

"Hey."

She smiles.

"Hey. You want to come to a party?"

"A party? What sort of party?"

She shrugs.

"You know, just a party. Music, dancing and so on."

I want to go home. To stare at the blank walls. Watch the view through the velux window.

So I'm surprised when I say yes.

*

The mathematicians are in the back, masked up, physically and digitally. I am terrified. She takes my hand and leads me through the mass of bodies to one of them, gives me a look. I nod.

She hands them cash. They do something with a tiny computer, touch two electrodes to the skin on my wrist where the veins show. Then the same for her.

It comes on slowly, like the tide coming in. Wave after tiny wave of something beautiful. We move onto the dance floor. 90s jungle shakes my rib cage, the beat matches the ever increasing waves and

oh
like I'm drowning
in a good way
did I ever tell you
yes
what is this
yes
what is this
yes
a very good way
did I
love you love all of you always
they never knew
we'll leave the city go to the hills you know the hills a farm I visited one when I was a kid I can't believe you grew up so close and we never met I wish we'd met before in a previous life or something
I had a dog he was he was he was
in a good way though
who are you
are you
you and me
me and you
in a very good way
we

Whose grip are we loosening?

We wake and disentangle. We are breached walls hastily patched to meet the new day. We smoke and don't say a thing.

I feel around inside myself. It seems OK, nothing obviously broken. Ready to go.

We shower, dress and head out into the weak sunlight.

I think she is going to say something, the way her body tenses, the drop of her head, but she doesn't. I try to think of something to say. The mites seem a little sluggish this morning, like they've taken a beating and are still feeling groggy. The moment stretches. The sky is so blue it makes my throat ache.

"See you tonight?"
She smiles.
"I'll meet you at eight, outside your place, OK?"
I nod and we part with a kiss, each our separate ways, to work.

(2017)

THE MAN-UFACTORY
Frederic Perkins

Frederic Beecher Perkins (1828–1899) was the Bostonian author of two comic novels, a biography of Charles Dickens, and around fifty sketches and short stories. "What seemed best," he wrote, "I used to offer to Putnam or Harper. What they would not use I sometimes offered to *Peterson's Magazine*, sometimes to the *Philadelphia Saturday Evening Post*, and so on; and what I could not otherwise use I could always sell to the *New York Sunday Dispatch* for five dollars." His daughter Catherine, a prominent feminist and social campaigner, wrote that he "took to books as a duck to water. He read them, he wrote them, he edited them, he criticized them, he became a librarian and classified them. Before he married he knew nine languages and continued to learn more afterward… In those days, when scholarship could still cover a large portion of the world's good books, he covered them well." In 1880, Perkins was appointed as head librarian of the San Francisco Public Library, where he served till 1887.

I was talking the other day with my friend Budlong, whom I met in New York after two or three years of separation, about the progress of the age, and especially about recent inventions. When I find any thing worth reading in the newspapers, I cut it out and carry it in my pocket-book for a few days, to read to all my friends; and then I put it in a scrapbook for all future generations. Much good may it do them!

Well, I drew Budlong's attention to the last cutting, and began to read it to him.

It was a Washington despatch of the day before, with "display head," somewhat thus:—

"TALKING MACHINE!
The Great Professor Hanserl Faber!!
All Washington Crowds To See It!
Grant says he don't want it!

―――

"The inventor has closely copied the form and action of the different organs producing the human voice, and operated them in the same manner; levers and springs taking the place of muscles and nerves. The machine has a bellows for lungs, a windpipe for the conduction of air, an India-rubber larynx, with vocal cords modelled after those of man, and opening and closing in the same manner. It has a fixed upper jaw of wood, with a

LIP OF LEATHER.

"The lower jaw is made of India-rubber; and the mouth has a hard palate of hard rubber, and a movable tongue of flexible rubber."

And so on. "There, Budlong," I said; "what do you think of that?"

"I don't think," said Budlong; "I know. See here!" And with a wise kind of grin, he fumbled in his breast-pocket, and drew forth a document, which I read:—

"Received [&c.] of P. Budlong, in full for advertisement and notices of Budlong and Fabers machines, fifty dollars. Jenks, Adv. Clk."

It was from the office of the very same newspaper. I stared at Budlong, as amazed as Balboa,

"Silent, upon a peak in Darien,"

when he first espied the boundless Pacific.

"What is it?" I asked.

"Why, it's a costly business to get the right kind of notices in the papers."

"But do you know Faber? Were you ever at Vienna?"

"Hanserl is Viennese for Johnny," answered he. "I know that; and Faber is Latin for Smith; and professor is American for anybody. Don't you remember old Johnny Smith?"

In short, this Dutchman is not a German Dutchman, but a Yankee one; neither more nor less than a self-taught mechanician from the native town of both Budlong and myself. I knew the man had been deluded at one time by the same "perpetual motion" goblin that has fooled so many halftaught or ill-balanced minds; but I had lost sight of him for years. He had, as my friend now informed me, applied to him for assistance in his semi-lunatic labors. Budlong, who, though extremely queer, is not without some good points, had set to work to help the poor fellow out of his delusion.

"I very soon found," said Budlong, "that, if I attacked him directly, I should only confirm his notions. I had had some ideas of my own about this talking-machine, for a good while; and so I set Smith at work on that, and managed to give him some correct views on the first principles of mechanics, on pretence of investigations at odd times for improving his own invention. He has really a very fair faculty for mechanics, with some help in the reasoning part; and, after a while, he found himself convinced, without knowing how. I guess he's the only case on record of a radical cure."

"That is a process worth considering for other delusions," I observed; "it is the great tactical rule of flanking the enemy. But it is you, then, who is really running the talking-machine and Prof Faber of Vienna?"

"Yes; Vienna's a good place for the invention to come from, since Von Kempelen's chess-player. There's a very neat sum of money in my invention, I reckon, and we've marketed enough of them to prove it too. I'll tell you what—I'll show you over the factory, and let you make an article on the subject for one of the magazines, if you want to."

"I guess," said I, "that I can get it printed, if you will advertise a little with them.'

"I never bribe," said Budlong, virtuously.

"I know that," said I. "We abhor it equally: still I think it would look more like business. The advertisement would draw people's attention to the article; and reading the article would have a tendency to increase the circulation of the magazine."

"Oh!" said Budlong: "I hadn't seen it in that light. I don't know but you are correct. Well, say one page of advertisement each time the article is printed?"

This it was agreed I might offer.

"Now come along, "said my friend. "I've got to go right up town this moment; and I'll show you through the whole concern."

So we took a University-place car—Barclay Street, corner of Broadway—which, with only one transfer, left us within two or three blocks of our destination.

On the way up, Budlong gave me one piece of information which greatly helped me to understand his invention, and which will, I believe, make it very clearly intelligible to most people who know what a mitrejoint or a king-post or a truss-bridge is; and, I hope, to those who do not. I had remarked to him that I believed I understood the vocalizing part of his machine—which was, I presumed, a development of the mechanism used in Vaucanson's fluteplayer, Maelzel's trumpeter, and the various speaking automata—but that I was thoroughly puzzled to see how he could deliver through the machine, a long, connected discourse. I could not suppose, I added, that he was going to hide a human being in each figure, as Von Kempelen did in his chess-player—a device quite too thin (to use a slang phrase of to-day, that may be classic to-morrow) for the present state of intelligence.

"Not at all," my friend observed. "All my work is genuine mechanism. The device for accomplishing what you refer to is, however, my own special invention, and is precisely what makes a commercial article out of the mere toy of those European fellows. I have simply adapted one of the parts of Alden's type-setting machine to my use. Do you know that machine?"

As I did not, Mr. Budlong went on, with a kind of set though fluent clearness, which kept reminding me of the specifications in a patent. I dare say they were from precisely that source, at least in part.

"Take twenty-six type, one for each English letter; lay them down on their edges close together, with the faces all one way, like a long row of people in bed lying 'spoon-fashion.' Then let a different nick or notch, or set of nicks or notches, belong to the upper edge of each of the twenty-six. Suppose a thing like a comb, its back as long as one type, with as many teeth as there can be nicks on a type, and these teeth not tight in the back, but jointed to it. Now, if this comb be drawn along the backs of this row of twenty-six type, (across each individual type, of course) the teeth that fit the nicks of *a*, for instance, or of *t*, will fall into those nicks when they reach that letter.

"Now add the necessary mechanism for lifting out each letter when reached, and carrying it where it is wanted, and you have the principal element of the type-setting machine.

"Lastly, let the supposed comb be fixed, instead of moving; and instead of type—*here is the precise contrivance of Budlong and Faber*—instead of type to be carried under the jointed teeth, or fingers, and to let these fall into the proper nicks, let the teeth, or fingers, be lifted by marks in paper or other fabric, raised or embossed, as in printing for the blind; and, as the projections answering to each sound lift the teeth, let these teeth, continued by means equivalent to the leaders from the keys in a piano or organ, open the pipes, reeds, or valves which emit that sound.

"There! that is the heart of my mystery. I am not in the least afraid of telling it; for I have a monopoly of this application of Alden's device; and this, you see, enabled me to dodge all the infringers. I should have had the Old Gentleman's own time, if I had recorded an application for a patent. As it is, I have worked the whole thing out to perfection at my leisure, and without one particle of annoyance or interference."

I could not help admiring the truly American combination of mechanical and political genius thus described: and, if my praise did not satisfy Budlong, he must needs have been horribly vain; for I gave him a most hearty portion of it. Indeed, I challenge the intelligent reader (I scorn to address any other) to refuse me his meed of admiration for this most remarkable instance of ingenuity in mechanics, and masterly shrewdness in management. Would that all great inventors could have done the like! We should not have on our records such miserable stories as that of the thievish persecutions that swindled Whitney, nor the other similar cases.

The factory of Messrs. Budlong and Faber is on Twelfth Avenue, close to the North River, and between the water and Riverside Park. I well remember being struck, as we entered its precincts, by the dreariness of the premises, and the contrast between their sordid common-place and the brilliant conceptions that were being shaped into actual existence inside. There was a plain brick building of respectable size; the usual tall chimney and squatty engine-house flat at its foot, as if worshipping it; the staring windows, their dingy glass uncovered from the hot sunlight, like eyes left lidless by some torturing tyrant; a cloud of black smoke; the chatter of a small high-pressure engine, and the corresponding spitting discharge of steam from an escape-pipe; a narrow lawn of black dust and scoriae between the sidewalk and the door; two or three broken cog-wheels, shafts, and other portions of invalid machinery, leaning against the outside of the building, like old soldiers, sunning themselves in front of a hospital.

We entered the office, where Budlong left me for a few minutes to attend to some business or other. In his absence, I betook myself to inspecting divers articles, which adorned the walls of the little room. There were a few portraits of eminent public speakers, both lay and clerical; various drawings of machinery; and one rusty old print, executed in a coarse enough style, but with considerable spirit.

The imprint stated that it was a view of the newly invented "*Kaihuper Seminarium:*" date, 1807. This partly Greek and partly Latin appellation was somewhat difficult to interpret, but might perhaps be taken to imply that the "*Seminarium*" was *kai huper*—even ahead of—any thing theretofore invented in that line. The picture represented a curious machine, or mill, worked by a large crank, at which were laboring several stately personages in academic or clerical costume. Into a species of hopper, at one end, other gentlemen, of like demeanor and costume, were gravely casting huge pumpkins, squashes, cabbages, turnips, and other matters known in Yankee realms by the collective title of "green sarse." From the discharging-trough at the opposite extremity, hopped and tumbled a number of little lively black creatures, which I took at first to be frogs or diminutive apes, but which, upon closer inspection, were seen to be small clergymen of prim countenance, and jaunty and priggish bearing, accurately arrayed in well-fitting black garments. At their first exit from the machine, they were represented as falling upon the earth in a helpless, sprawly state, on their stomachs, or on all-fours. But they quickly hopped up, and were seen marching off to parts unknown, with a trig strut, and an air of satisfaction and delight, curiously suggestive of those young birds who run about, as naturalists tell us, with the egg-shell still on their heads.

I was still studying upon this ancient caricature—of which, indeed, I had heard, and which I had sought after in vain—when my friend came to show me through the factory. "We are filling an order for assorted ministers, this week," said he, "and, except a few specimens in the show-room, you can see hardly anything else to-day. But the difference is entirely in externals."

We entered first one or two workshops, of no very particular kind, with lines of shafting overhead, lathes and drills whizzing below, the belts sliding and slapping, and busy workmen operating upon combinations of wood, metal, hard and soft rubber, and gutta-percha, which might, perhaps, be generally described as seeming to be the progeny of the marriage of a mouth organ with a wooden clock.

"There," observed Budlong, as he paused before a concatenation of delicate springs, wheels, pipes, and valves, "this is the principal portion—what we call the main action—of the works of a patent minister. This is the vocalizing part, and must go into all of them, of course. There is also always the bellows, the transfer-press (which I described to you) for carrying the prepared printed matter, and the power, or mainspring, which runs the whole. The rest of the works are detached actions for several purposes, all driven by the same power, but which need not be put into the machine unless required, and which can be thrown in or out of gear as desired. There are the gesture movement, which operates the arms and hands, legs, neck, and spine; the expression movement which runs the face; and the stops. About these stops I will show you when we come to a machine set up."

It is not needful for me to detail the arrangement of the workshops, nor the numerous neat devices, and the general compact arrangement of the machinery. The junior partner, indeed, who would have been the best man to do this, was, as I have shown, absent in Washington on a business-trip. Suffice it to say, that the factory includes the following departments:—

1. The machine-shop, where the "actions" are prepared for connection with the remainder of the figure.

2. The body-shop, where the gutta-percha faces and hands, and the remaining corporeal structures, are made, and the whole creature set up, so far as its working-

parts are concerned. This might poetically be figured as a paradise, or garden of Eden, from which these Adams were to be turned out naked.

3. The tailor's shop, where the garments are made and put on.

4. The proving-room. The tests here made are extremely thorough; for it will readily be imagined that any defect in the machinery or its working might cause most ludicrous and mortifying scenes. The explosion or collapse of a patent minister in the middle of his sermon, for instance, though not so terrible as the sudden deaths which have sometimes so happened, would be only less undesirable and lamentable than such an interruption.

The machine-shop, as already described, was much like any other machine-shop. In the second, or body-shop, there was, however, more that was peculiar and amusing. I inspected with great interest a long row of gutta-percha heads on shelves—some bald; some adorned with elegant heads of hair in various states of curl; some old, and some young; some with beard and mustache, others shaved clean. A messenger came just as we were looking at these, to call Budlong to the office to deal with some important customer. I went on inspecting the rows of heads, until I had examined them all; and then, looking aimlessly about, as one does who is at a loss for occupation, I saw a door having the mysterious legend, "Positively No Admission for any Purpose Whatever." Now, I need not explain to the Yankee mind, that this legend always signifies, "Here is just the most interesting thing of all!" I tried the door at once. Why should I not? for Budlong had said I was to see every part of the factory. Still it is possible—observe, I say possible—that, if my mind had in the least misgiven me, I should not have opened the door. And, moreover, what business had they to leave it unlocked if it was so very sacred and secret? And how do I know now, but that the inscription had been put there by previous occupants? Nor, lastly, am I at all certain that it was not my duty to go in, as it certainly is my duty to inform the public of what I discovered in consequence. Right or wrong, however—and I had infinitely more justification for entering than had the wife of the late Mr. Bluebeard into the historic closet—right or wrong, in I went; and I was, I fancy, quite as much astounded by what I saw as was that amiable young woman. The first thought that flashed across my mind, as I glanced upon this additional row of heads, was indeed horrid: "Have murderers enticed all the great public speakers of the day into this bloody den, and decapitated them?—the Rev. Dr.—, the Rev. Mr.—, the Hon. Mr.—?" Face after face, as familiar as those of the first Napoleon or Gen. Washington, I saw silent and moveless upon the shelves. A painful spasm of indistinct but intense apprehension for a moment made my very heart stand still. So powerful was the impression, moreover, that I could not escape entirely from it; and, after hastily verifying my observations, I gladly retreated out of the uncanny place, and, shutting the door, returned to the contemplation of the insignificant, generalized types of humanity outside; though I could not help pondering upon what might be the possible significance of that executioner's museum so choicely hidden away there. However, my guide very soon came back; and, as I turned round, upon his opening the door, I thought he glanced with an uneasy air towards the closet of horrors; and I therefore gave up, by one of those intuitive apprehensions of the disagreeable, which sometimes flash across us, my previous purpose of asking what it meant. A vulgar person, now, would have been only the more resolute to inquire. What a fine thing it is to be polite!

Mr. Budlong began at once—I fancied with something of forced volubility and interest, as of one who would fain direct wholly the course of talk—to discuss the heads before us. He took down one of them, and holding it in both hands, with the face towards me, caused the dead visage to writhe and gibber in so fearful a manner, that I started as if a corpse were grinning and winking at me. "You see," said he, "that we are enabled to furnish a large range of expressions." And he squeezed the face again, and produced half a dozen exceedingly nauseous simpers and smiles. Then he laid the thing on the table, and inflicted a ferocious blow upon its nose; insomuch that his hand drove in the face completely. "But," I remonstrated, "aside from the danger of injuring the article, is there no risk of injuring the moral sense of your operatives by allowing them to witness such treatment of a clergyman?"

"Oh, no!" replied he. "The material will take no injury, even from much severer blows than that; and people that make wooden images are not, in this country, likely to have much respect for them, at any rate. Our workmen are well used to their trade: they think neither the better nor the worse of a minister because they have played football with his head, and manufactured his bowels and his brains for him. It's all a matter of business with them."

A naked minister, near several others, stood ready for transfer to the tailor's shop. The head and hands were finished and colored skilfully, like nature, and suggested the ghastly idea that they had been cut off from a live man, or a dead one, and stuck up there for models. The rest of the creature was a mass of machinery, bearing enough resemblance to the human figure to admit of being draped into a sufficient resemblance to it.

"John," said my friend to a workman who was passing through the room at the moment, "is that improved double-action minister wound up?"

"Yes, sir," replied the man: "but he isn't oiled; and the power hasn't been regulated."

"Never mind," answered Budlong, turning to me: "he'll click and rattle, and grin and squirm a little; but you can get an idea of the operation of the works." So saying, he threw the machinery into gear with a key.

With a suddenness that caused me to spring backwards, and thereby to occasion a very unnecessarily hearty chuckle on the part of Mr. Budlong and of the workman, who had stopped to see, the machine threw both its hands to arm's-length before it, as if to catch me, and held them stiffly out; raised its eyebrows; stared hideously with its eyes; opened its mouth long and wide, grinning, and showing two great rows of white teeth, like a vicious horse; and shouted out in a high, harsh, ringing tone, a steady and sustained vowel-sound of "A—a—a—a—a—ah!"

This vocable it pronounced as in the exclamation, "Ah!" A bellows in the abdomen of the creature wheezed and blew busily. All his senseless entrails sprang into miscellaneous activity; and with much rattling, squeaking, and whizzing, and an occasional gesture and grimace, the substantial portion of the ministerial functions was directly under my notice, in actual operation.

Having waited a few moments, my guide turned off the wind; and the shriek of the spectre ceased. He still, however, held out his hands, gibbered, stared and grinned; occasionally rose as if on tiptoe, and came down on his heels with a hard jerk; shook his head violently, or seemed to squint for a moment at the end of his nose. All at once something choked or hitched in his viscera: the eyes turned clear round as if in a fit, and stuck fast; and with a snap and a click the minister stood still.

"No matter," remarked Budlong. "They operate rather singularly sometimes, before the power is regulated, and the oiling completed; but it's all right." So he led the way to the tailor's shop.

This was merely a shop where all the well-known varieties of current costume were manufactured; and no particular account of it is necessary. The ministers now being turned out were clothed to order, either in dress-suits, or in surplices, or other pulpit overcloths of white or black. Some were trimmed in a truly superb style, even to a real gold chain and diamond ring, and did very great credit to the enterprise and decorative talent of the concern.

We remained only a little while in the tailoring department, and passed on to the proving-room. Upon opening the thick and well-secured double door of this room, the scene within, and the sudden and terrific hubbub of voices that burst out, again startled me. I was reminded of those old magic halls wherein heroes of romance find enchanted armed statues shouting and striking furiously about to guard the entrance, or exclude the curious from the secrets of their prison.

Upon entering the room, I beheld nearly two dozen of finished (or, as one might figuratively say, ordained) ministers, in complete clerical costumes of various kinds, and in full blast, delivering each his sermon in heterogeneous and chaotic confusion of matter and manner altogether indescribable. The scene was wholly without parallel either in my experience or my conception, unless in the study-rooms of the great conservatorio or music-school at Naples, where, as I have read, a hall full of students practise each his own instrument, without regard to time or tune of the rest; or in the bedlamitish vociferations of a crew of maniacs confined in one place.

I gazed at this extraordinary exhibition in utter extremity of astonishment. Not only was the human quality of the voices, and the thoroughly natural articulation, perfectly astounding, but the forms and attitudes of the speakers—such was the artistic skill of the manufacturers, were also entirely and unaffectedly human; some, as in life, being easy and graceful, in one or two instances almost to statuesque beauty; while others were grotesquely stiff, angular, and awkward. The eyes, moreover, and the motions of the whole countenance and head, as well as those of the hands, arms, and figure, were governed by a similar adaptation.

Close to me stood a large and pompous man, declaiming in a full and even tone a discourse in which I thought I recognized a sentence; and indeed, upon listening more closely, I discovered that it was one of Bishop South's best sermons. At the farther end of the apartment, a tall, gaunt spectre with large frame, harsh features, and rather coarse garments, was swinging his fists, and vociferating an exhortation which seemed suitable for a camp-meeting. Near him stood the apparition of a smug, fat young divine, of comfortable appearance and oleaginous smile, enunciating, in silvery voice, and the style of Praed's

> "Gentle Johnian,
> Whose hand is white, whose tone is clear,
> Whose rhetoric is Ciceronian,"

a series of well-balanced and correctly worded sentences. Another, I should have said, in secular rather than clerical costume—a dry-visaged, dogmatic-looking creature—was reciting in a lifeless way a string of phrases, which I could not define, until I caught the words, "egoism," "altruism," "altruistic," "egoistic," all in one single sentence. He was a Positivist, of course.

The remainder of this assembly were, each in his own proper style, performing the duties of their office, with an honest zeal, and, even in some cases, an impassioned ardor, which could not be sufficiently commended. After listening and looking for a considerable time, I signified that I was satiated with the whirlwind of ministerial eloquence. Hereupon we left the exercitants in charge of certain workmen who were superintending the proving process, and passed on to the exhibiting room.

This was a large and convenient hall, somewhat obscurely lighted, and fitted up with small desks, or pulpits, for the better display of the wares on sale. We entered the room at one end; and, the windows being darkened with heavy curtains, the various clerical forms, standing calmly and silently in two rows along the sides of the long room, each in his place of authority, recalled to my remembrance that tremendous and impressive representation in the Hebrew prophecy, of the long and stern array of departed kings sitting still in the depths of Hades, ready to welcome the great Babylonish tyrant to his throne at their head. I also recollected—by some uncomfortable and fantastic association of ideas, and to my mortification at the absurd and unseasonable suggestion—Jarley's Wax-Work.

My guide hastened to admit more light into the room, so that the deep gloom was lifted away, and the various aspects of the patent ministers became distinguishable; although the room was yet, with shrewd, business-like tact, left dim enough materially to enhance their very remarkably life-like appearance. He then proceeded to exhibit for my benefit the operation of various single styles of execution, and the working of those adjunct mechanisms which he had mentioned in the machine-shop. For this purpose he selected an automaton which he called a "first-rate article of the grand improved combined-action patent minister," and which he characterized as superbly finished; and, indeed, as a very favorable specimen of the manufacture. Unceremoniously fumbling about various portions of the ministerial uniform, he seemed to adjust springs or machinery in sundry places, wound up the mainspring with a crank, and, turning to me, observed—

"There! the machine is wound up and ready to go: I have, however, disconnected all the actions except the bellows and escape-pipe. You will therefore observe, that, upon being put in motion, he will only blow."

Such was accordingly the result. The accurate workmanship and careful adjustment of the machinery rendered its operation as entirely noiseless as the normal functions of the human body; and a sort of whew or puff was the only evidence that the minister was at work.

Budlong then proceeded to gear on the vocalizing apparatus; whereupon the squall or shrieking monotone of "Ah!" which I mentioned before, again came from the lips of the automaton. He next put into operation the gesture and expression attachment, which caused also, as before, the stretching out of the arms, the contortions of the visage, &c.

"His sermon's in him, I presume," said Budlong, inspecting a recess in the figure. "Yes; about half delivered. He'll begin somewhere in the middle; for we don't wind them up until they are entirely run down, to avoid uneven wear of the works."

Then he touched another spring; and the automaton preacher, ceasing to "blaat out"—if we may use an expressive rustic verb—his "Ah!" slid from it into the midst of a passage in the first part of Bishop Jeremy Taylor's "Discourse of Lukewarmness and Zeal," somewhat on this wise: "A—a—a—a—and to make it possible for us"—and here the image subsided into a graceful, impressive, and powerful delivery of the strong old-fashioned English sentences—"to come to that spiritual state where all felicity does dwell. The religion that Christ taught is a spiritual religion: it designs (so far as the state will permit) to make us spiritual; that is, so as the Spirit be the prevailing ingredient. God must now be worshipped in spirit; and not only so, but with a fervent spirit."

And so the minister went on with the solid and sonorous rhetoric of the powerful old bishop.

"That," said Budlong, "is the principal stop, or even tone. I will now set the damnatory, or threatening stop"—

"Stay a moment," I interrupted. "It would be a pity to have such noble thoughts as Bishop Taylor's inappropriately delivered. Couldn't you illustrate the other stops by inserting other matter?"

"Oh, yes!" he replied. "Here is a list of our prepared printed compositions, arranged with directions for the stops. Just select at your pleasure, and we'll insert them accordingly. We generally use the principal for exhibition."

I took the little catalogue, and selected from under the head of "Triumphant" the Ninety-fifth Psalm, in the Vulgate Latin, "*Venite exultemus Domino.*"

This having been taken from a closet, inserted in the combined-action minister, and delivered by him in an overpowering strain of congratulatory eloquence, my friend proceeded, at my request, to cause the enunciation by the figure of the Athanasian Creed, with all the curses complete (I looked for that of Ernulphus, but it was not on the list), as an exemplification of the damnatory or threatening stop. After that he gave me Wesley's "Sinners, turn; why will ye die?" on the hortatory, or didactic stop; and other pieces in the three other sermon styles—the hifalutin or camp-meeting, the intoning or liturgic, and the sweet-cream or dearly-beloved.

Having thus seen all that was to be seen in the factory, we completed our circuit by returning to the office, where I had a long and interesting conversation with Budlong, of which I may reproduce some of the chief points, without pretending to verbal accuracy.

The first of these points, if I may say so, was an interruption. I had hardly sat down, when I jumped up again; not because I sat on a cat or a pin, but because a great awful voice cried, "Twelve o'clock!" The tone was really awful. It was musical, but vast, booming, and deep; and the sound throbbed in my ears like the note of a heavy bell close at hand; and its reverberations filled all the air; so that it came, seemingly, from everywhere—not from any place.

Budlong laughed until he cried. "I forgot to tell you," he said when he could speak, "we have Friar Bacon's brazen head, discovered at Oxford, and imported expressly for us at great expense. We use it instead of a bell or a whistle, just as the American Organ Factory in Boston plays a common chord for the same purpose."

I recovered myself as well as I could, and told him, that, after all, he had only revived an old device in his mechanical devotions; that his clock-work sermonizing bore much analogy to the Buddhist praying-mills, that are turned by water-wheels or by wind.

Budlong laughed again. "I confess," he said, " this much. I am a member of the First Radical Club; and you know they run a Buddhist prayer-mill in the back-room all the time, by a little hydraulic ram supplied from the Cochituate pipes. Not one of them will admit that they believe there's any thing in it; but still, you know, it can do no harm to be right on the record. You remember the old story of the Englishman in Rome, who took off his hat and made a low bow to Jupiter, and requested the civility should be remembered in case the Olympian dynasty should ever be re-established? I am not sure but our modern wise men of the western east may have given me the idea, really. But I have made it practical."

"In a certain sense," I admitted. "But have you made it pay? What is the present state of the enterprise financially?"

"Eminently satisfactory. We are just now, for instance, filling an order for ministers. But the next is for lecturers"—

"Lecturers!" I interrupted, as that grim row of portrait heads in the Bluebeard chamber flashed across my mind in a new light—"then those likenesses"—I stopped; but I had let it out. Budlong turned quite red, and looked, I may say, almost sheepish; but finally he made the best of it by saying good-naturedly—

"Ah, peeping Tom!"

"I confess," I said; "but I couldn't possibly have imagined the door forbidden."

"And it is our own fault too," rejoined he. "We ought to have locked it, and hidden the key. So I'll confess too. The fact is, that we are running a pretty important part of the lecturing business at present. Don't you remember that odd little newspaper controversy a few weeks ago, in consequence of 'The Leavenworth Champion' and ' The Bangor Courier' each saying that a certain eminent speaker lectured at its respective city on one and the same evening?"

I did.

"Well, we had a terrible time to quiet it down. You see, the first-class speakers receive ten times as many invitations as they can accept. Now, we furnish a facsimile, who exactly duplicates the eminent gentleman; and we have half the money. Between you and me, we have had as many as five of one or two men speaking in different parts of the United States at the same time. Very likely it won't last; but we're coining money out of it now!"

"And the celebrated foreign gentlemen?" I asked.

"Pshaw!" said Budlong. "They're all safe at home, minding their own business. Nobody knows them: so that it's a great deal easier to put their doubles on the stage than the domestic article."

I parodied Campbell—

"Both Pepper and his Ghost a shade!"

and then I added; "but really you'll do away with all public speaking, seems to me?"

"None of my lookout if we do," was his cynical answer. "Not with *real* speaking, though. Reading a manuscript isn't speaking. We have done away with some of that. What do you suppose it is, except our invention, that has caused the decrease that the religious papers are always complaining of, in the number of graduates from the theological seminaries?"

"But, my dear fellow," I remonstrated, "what the dickens— What is the effect of all this, pray tell me, on the stated religious observances of the country? You surely do not think it right to impede them, or to push them out of use?"

"No. But what I do think is this, that real religion will harmonize just as readily and perfectly with improvements in art as with advances in science. The question isn't what the new invention or scientific truth will bring to pass: that will take care of itself. The only question is, whether it *is* a truth, whether it *is* a discovery."

"I can't bring myself to give up sermons."

"Give up? You're going to have 'em cheaper than ever. Why, the interest on one of our first-class ministers isn't one-tenth of a decent salary; and I'll guarantee him to outlive a crow. He'll save his own first cost full up in from five to ten years; and with care he won't cost five dollars a year for repairs. Then, look at the economy of the whole plan. Here are your human ministers that must have a salary, and a family and houseroom, and grow old or sick or heretical or tiresome; or they quarrel with the parish; or the parish quarrels with them. But the patent minister is exempt from all the weaknesses of humanity. He requires neither wife, child, nor friend; neither house, land, nor salary; bed nor board, rest, exchange, nor vacation—nothing in the world except a cool cupboard and a very little sweet oil. He is conveniently stored in a closet in the vestry, or covered with a dust-cloth in the pulpit; or he can stand on a trap, and go up and down by a bell-wire arrangement running under the floor, that the senior deacon can pull where he sits in his pew. If you choose to have him wound up once in six hours, he will maintain a perpetual discourse day and night, like the perpetual chant in the chapel of Mr. Ferrar's famous religious establishment at Little Gidding in Huntingdonshire. He cannot quarrel; he says only what he is inspired (literally) to say; and the congregation can have whatever approved discourse they like, instead of taking their chances of getting one they do not. There are at least thirty thousand ministers of the gospel in the United States: at four hundred dollars a year, they are paid twelve million dollars. What would this annual sum not accomplish—I do not say in secular enterprises, but for benevolent undertakings, the missionary work, home charities, education, reformatory institutions?"

"Do you find that your customers pay a higher average for such purposes than other people?" I asked.

"I have not the least doubt that it will prove to be so whenever you will get together the statistics," answered Budlong with great assurance.

"I can't help it: I couldn't bear to lose my dear old pastor—"

"Look here!" broke in Budlong, with some heat. "Hold on! I haven't time for details to-day. I'll talk it out with you next time. But bear this one thing in mind—the *Sermonate* is not the *Pastorate*; and Budlong and Faber haven't offered yet to sell you a PASTOR; have they?"

I declare I had never thought of it before—I was brought up under the stated preaching of the gospel as practised in New England—but it isn't: they hadn't. I perceived how wide an inquiry this distinction opened up; and so, dropping the ethical aspects of the business, I took my friend's hint, and came back to facts.

"No, you haven't. And the only thing that I need detain you for any longer, is to get a few more points about the extent and prospects of the business, such as will look well in my article."

"Certainly. Well—of course I can't go into details of dividends; but nobody wants to sell any of our stock. I defy you to find one single share in the market. That's proof of prosperity, I think. It is thought so in the case of the Chemical Bank, at any rate.

"In the first place, as to prospects: Besides ministers for the home market, we sent an agent over to the other side last summer, who writes us that he is coming home with a large contract and full specifications from the Humble Nicephorus, as he calls himself, the patriarch of Moscow, for two hundred and fifty Greek papas; and a small one, to be followed by others if we give satisfaction, from the Sheik-ul-Islam at Constantinople, for four dozen howling dervishes. The Greek priests will be a great improvement in the country parishes, for they can't get drunk; and I've already gotten up a working model dervish, with pith upper works and lead heels, that will whirl three hundred times a minute for four hours consecutively, and howl like a northeaster the whole time. The agent just called in at Rome; but the Roman service is so complicated, there's so much travel in it, and they care so little, in comparison, about sermons, anyhow, that we can't do anything with them.

"So much for the ministerial department. You have the necessary facts about the lecturers. The other items that will be found most interesting are, I think, a few of the details that we have thought of for improving our mechanisms, and a few ideas about the further application of our principle.

"Now, for instance, our big brazen head—of course, you understand that we only made a large one in imitation of Friar Bacon's—suggested to me, the other day, that we could supply an economical article of army chaplains. We are in correspondence with Gen. Sherman about it now. He's a man of genius; and I shouldn't wonder if he would allow an experiment at our expense. I have calculated that a chaplain not more than eleven feet seven and one-half inches high, could be built and voiced so as to preach to two hundred and fifty thousand men at once. I should call these the Boanerges style, or Sons of Thunder.

"But I fancy a far more successful thing will be made out of our patent politicians; that is, if we can ever get them into use. But, if once the community is well accustomed to our ministers and lecturers, they can hardly help seeing the enormous economy to be made by the use of our politicians. Consider the saving of money, in a single year, by substituting for the present style of state and national politicians an equal number of individuals who cannot drink whiskey, who can not charge a price for influence nor for making speeches, who are legally incapable of becoming president, who can not hold any credit mobilier stock; in short, who are, by the very law of their being, unable to do any thing except their duty. Take one single item of this saving: every session of Congress costs the country something like two million dollars, I believe it is. Now, if the speeches were deducted, about seven-ninths of this would be saved, as near as I can calculate; and a few able business-men could do the real work of the session in the other two-ninths. Now, there are three hundred and seventeen members of Congress, all told. Suppose each makes only ten speeches per session—a ludicrously low estimate—and you have three thousand one hundred and seventy in all, which cannot at present in any event be made at a faster rate than two at a time—one in the Senate, and one in the House. What I propose is to fit up a proper room in the Capitol, like our proving-room, well deafened throughout, and to have a proper number of the patent members of Congress a-going there day and night, until all the speeches of the session are delivered. Suppose there are twenty-five of them, which I will contract to furnish at a most liberal discount from our retail prices, and we will allow three hours per speech; that is, eight speeches each, per day of twenty-four hours: then you have in all two hundred speeches per day, or the whole session's supply of three thousand one hundred and seventy worked off in less than sixteen business-days, and not a living soul obliged to hear them, either, except my two workmen, who take it watch and watch, to oil the honorable gentlemen, and wind them up, and stick their speeches into them.

"For the campaign speakers, I should add an extra strong pump-handle action in the right arm, and a smile movement in the face."

I couldn't help a suggestion of my own here: "A smile movement! You said they wouldn't drink."

"No slang, please," said Budlong, rather miffed for the moment.

"Beg pardon. But here's another idea really. Why couldn't you let them drink? It's very popular in some sections. You could have a tin stomach on purpose with a faucet; and they could drink the same whiskey over, year in and year out."

"No," said Budlong firmly. "No immoral practice shall be countenanced by this concern, nor any thing introduced that could offend the most fastidious. Now, don't interrupt me with any more of your nonsense, but just listen to my other improvements.

"For travelers or residents abroad, we have designed what might be called a private chaplain, or you might almost call it a bottle angel, in contrast to the bottle imp of the German story."

"Speaking of traveling," I observed, "have you thought of anything in the missionary line? It would take the jungle fever a long time to destroy a patent missionary."

"And a very hearty cannibal to eat him," replied Budlong. "No, we negotiated with the Borrioboola Gha concern; but they couldn't give references. The American Board won't touch us. Fact is, preaching isn't of so much account for missionary purposes at present, as doing good; and we can't get up a machine that will do good of itself. That would be a moral perpetual motion—a more incredible absurdity than the mechanical one that I cured Smith of. To be sure, I did correspond a little with some of the great physiologists about that very idea, out of curiosity. Beale wrote me that it was no harder than to build a human being in a shop. Rather satirical, hey? Huxley seemed to imply that Beale's notions were those of an ass, and that the idea was one not to be despaired of. But I guess we shall leave the missionaries along with the pastors. Souls are not in our line."

Having now noted all that seemed necessary for the purposes of this paper, I thanked my friend Budlong, and after wishing well to his "priestcraft," as I took the liberty of calling it, from its chief department, I took my leave.

I have lost my interest in public speaking. Would anybody like to buy very cheap a ticket to the next course of the famous lectures on the History of Ireland?

I am going to write to Budlong with details of the economy to be secured by substituting a small number of patent men for the present standing armies of Europe, and for our own troops, except those in garrison in the Ku Klux districts, and those employed against the Indians. I think the influence of the various societies for preventing cruelty to animals might be secured in favor of substituting clothes-horses for the present style of cavalry horses; as to the soldiers themselves, I doubt it: I have not observed that these benevolent gentlemen paid much attention to the convenience of human beings. For my part, I think it is almost as well worth while to save pain to men by putting a mechanical substitute in their place, as to fling up a tin pigeon, that won't make a good pie after he's dead, into the air to be shot at.

POSTSCRIPT.—I have just cut from a newspaper the following paragraph, which shows once more how impossible it is for humanity to reach perfection, and how well founded, though unsuccessful, was my friend Budlong's solicitous watchfulness over his machinery:—

SAD ACCIDENT.—The very valuable and costly patent minister, officiating at the First Presbyterian Church in this town, suddenly exploded yesterday afternoon, in consequence of a defect in the windpipe, in the midst of the sermon, with a terrific howl. Portions of the sermon were driven into the heads of several of the audience, passing, by a singular accident, in one or two cases, in at one ear, and out at the other. Permanent mental derangement is apprehended in the cases of two or three prominent members of the church, from passages of the sermon supposed remaining in the brain. This sad catastrophe has cast a deep gloom over our usually cheerful village.

(1877)

A ROBOT WALKS INTO A BAR

Romie Stott

> **Romie Stott** was born in 1980 in Dallas, Texas and obtained her masters degree from London Film School in 2009. She is a writer and filmmaker (working mainly as Romie Faienza), known for *Hayseeds and Scalawags* (2011), and the short film *Aperture* (2009), a science fiction horror movie told in still images, in which an alienated student becomes obsessed with outrunning the speed of light. Her cheerfully morbid *Birthday Song* ("[C] You made it this far and you [F] haven't been killed by [C] sharks") is a favourite among ukulele players.

When I met David, I was working as a bouncer at a trance club downtown—a high-end place where before the muscle manhandles them to the curb, big spenders get a polite request from a smiling girl who wonders if they'd rather move to a private room. Unlike the bar staff, I don't get tips, and like the rest of the bouncers, I spend most of the evening scanning the crowd for trouble. I just do it in a slinky dress while holding a shirley temple. It's not a great job, but it lets me double dip—at the same time I watch for assholes, I keep a lookout for new trends, which I report to another boss. Remember the headbands that were popular last year, the ones with shapes cut out of them? I'm one of the people who spotted that back when a few college kids were hand-making theirs.

Meanwhile, I'm doing a third job as a shill making small talk about the product of the week, whether it's berry-flavored vodka or an "underground" new single. On a good day, I feel like a double agent, like the membrane through which cool percolates. Other times, I think it's pretty sick. But by stacking jobs, I only have to work fifteen hours a week, which leaves me time for my music. Not that I use my free time to work on my music. I mostly watch movies. And spend most of my paycheck on drinks and clothes. Keeps the bosses happy.

The first thing I noticed about David was his hands, the way he handled objects. It's obvious, really—hands, sex—it's like saying he had beautiful eyes (which he did, though I didn't look at them until later). Most people, when they approach the bar, do one of two things. Either they push to the front, catcall the bartender, and wave a lot of cash around, or they hesitate, meek and uncomfortable, talk too softly for their order to be made out, and wait until the last minute to fumble through a stack of credit cards. David, in contrast, was still, but still in a way that had weight behind it. He waited like a man who was completely aware of the crowds and flashing lights, but completely separate from them. When he pulled out his wallet, his movements were economical. Deliberate. As though he knew precisely where every bill rested—its unique texture and particular history, its level of appropriateness to the task, and the exact amount of force required to tease it free of its brothers.

The way I describe it, it sounds fussy. It wasn't. There is something thrilling and frightening about a man who knows exactly what he's doing. It should make him seem safe. It does the opposite. I was seized with a strong compulsion to knit a stiff yarn dress and let him unravel it from around me—thread popping as knots pull loose line after line; a reverse dot matrix printer, a laser un-writing a green and black computer screen; a cartoon character gnawing a cob of corn. I watched him back to his table, or what became his table, in a small dark corner with a good vantage—the kind of spot appreciated by regulars, but rarely noticed by newcomers. He didn't look like he was waiting for anyone, but who would know? Over the next half hour, he made brief small talk with a few sorority girls on the prowl, his expression indicating an interest that was polite but not eager. Between conversations, which he never instigated, he sipped his drink at a leisurely rate, posture comfortable and alert. When someone at the next table had trouble with a disposable lighter, he fixed it.

He was perfect. That's when it clicked. I sat down across from him.

"You're a robot, aren't you," I said. He smiled, with a flicker of something else behind it.

"Not exactly," he said, soft and deprecating. "That is, I'm not just a set of preprogrammed responses and a system of adaptive logic. I am those things, but I have my own consciousness."

"Like emotions?"

"I can't say. They seem like emotions to me. But what I mean is that I'm aware of myself as an entity—I have a self."

Close up, he looked great—pores (real), water in the eye membrane (fake— actually a polymerized oil), suggestions of shaved beard-hair follicles (fake), eyebrows imperfect enough to seem un-groomed. I'd wanted to see him with his clothes off before, but now I had new reasons.

"Are you famous?" I asked.

"Nah—just a vanity project for the university. I don't really prove anything new, or have any marketable function. I talk to alumni with money and impress them with how lifelike I am. Sometimes I go to trade shows or technology contests, if that counts as famous, but there are better versions out there. Princeton has a model named Clio. She can do gymnastic routines and improvise recipes—I don't taste things, and don't have the flexibility for handsprings. I do better on Turing tests, though."

"So you don't know what's in that," I observed as he sipped his drink. He laughed, and it didn't seem forced but probably, and likely definitively, was. (Whether his expressions of emotion are expressions or emotion is something I've spent a lot of time trying to figure out and have mostly given up on.)

"I misspoke," he said. "I have a sense of smell much more accurate than a non-mechanical man's. I can give you a complete ingredient list if you like. I can also tell you with confidence that no one has brought explosives into this club. What I don't have are opinions about what tastes good and bad—just educated guesses. So what do you do in your spare time?"

I blinked. "Um… I write songs. I'm not very good. Some people like them."

He laid his hand across mine. "I apologize," he said, "for bringing up a delicate topic. It was meant as a simple expression of interest." He withdrew his hand. I realized I was blushing, which made me angry, which made me blush more.

"Listen," he said, "you're obviously working," (which pissed me off—I'm supposed to be subtle) "but I'd like to talk to you more—to find out how you spotted me and to make a proposal. I'd like to meet you outside after your shift. In the meantime, I'd like to buy whatever you're supposed to be selling me."

"Beef-infused tequila. It's awful, but you have no taste. I get off at 2."

At that point, I hadn't decided whether I was going to stand him up. He was attractive enough, but I couldn't see things going anywhere, given the circumstances, and the last thing I want after a night of fake flirtation is to go on a date. When I watched him pull out his wallet again, it hit me—no university would bankroll an incognito android's night of drinking. He was making his own choices with his own money. Where did he get it?

When I came out the door at 2:30, he was waiting, seemingly unperturbed by the extra half hour. His posture was perfect—which doesn't count for much since he has a harder time slouching, but it seemed refreshing at the time. He stood under a light, but his pupils were no more or less dilated than they had been inside the bar.

"Where do you want to go?" I said.

"Anywhere in range of wifi. Otherwise, I get pretty stupid."

"That makes sense." We walked toward the diner on the corner. "For the record, there was no particular thing that gave you away, although I'm accumulating them now. I just spend a lot of time around people. You were doing a fine job. It probably helps that no one's looking for you. I mean, I mostly follow social news, so maybe I'm not the best informed, but I didn't think any of you guys had been released into the wild, so to speak." He shrugged, and opened the door with a cocky half smile.

"Don't worry—I have a tracking device and a kill switch and I clock in at the university daily. It would have been a big deal a few years ago, but robot stories are currently out of fashion."

David didn't eat. He explained that he could seem to eat, for politeness' sake, but would have to regurgitate it later. We agreed that seemed wasteful. He watched me through half of a pancake before he said:

"So, how do you feel about having sex for money?"

"In the abstract?" I said.

"In context."

I thought about it for a minute. David waited without expression or tension, and I couldn't help thinking of a pulsing cursor.

"Are you telling me," I said, "that you are a sex machine?"

"In a manner of speaking. More like a really expensive camera. With consent, of course. Please stop me if I am offending you. I'm working from a hypothesis that you'll be more curious than offended, because you work at a bar where you are paid to look pretty, where you sell opinions that aren't yours, and where you nevertheless are willing to talk freely about personal subjects. In addition, your initial approach gave me reason to suspect you are attracted to me."

"So basically, you are asking me to sleep with you because you think I will say yes."

"Yes. I think it would be easy to work with you. I also think the ratios of your face and body will appeal to a broad segment of the population. You are very beautiful."

I should have been insulted. I was insulted. But David was right—you don't last long in any of my lines of work if you can't look past that kind of objectification to find the angle. So far, this seemed like a bad deal to me. I was doing fine for money, and I couldn't cross-promote without emphasizing my identity. Dangerous?

At the same time, I did, in fact, find the idea of being filmed by him somehow deeply sexy.

"Your university has a very progressive ethics board," I said.

"Some years back, during a fracas over bathroom use by transgendered students, the university made an official declaration guaranteeing free expression of sexual preference to all staff and students. That ruling was later successfully employed by a student to remove all prohibitions on pornography, whether viewed or created, from the code of conduct. Technically, I am neither staff nor student—more university property—but for all practical reasons, I'm considered staff. Public relations is of course not happy, but they can hardly deny my ability to give informed consent without opening themselves to other accusations."

"Such as?"

"That they're holding a sentient being in slavery."

"Shit."

"They could, of course, argue that on the contrary, I am not sentient—that I merely appear to think and feel, and that observers anthropomorphize the rest. But that would make me a less impressive marketing tool. It's simpler to treat me like everyone else than to make new rules, don't you think?"

By now, I was deep into my third cup of coffee, and feeling very awake. It was getting hard to tell whether David was making me warm and aroused, or whether it was the caffeine. At the very least, I was pretty sure I liked the way he was keeping things intellectual—no baby, baby, baby, I need you. Just information. Not cold, you understand, but its own sort of respectful. It made me want to be decisive and pragmatic, and I liked feeling that way.

"So," I said. "Tell me about your equipment."

A few days later, David's agent sent me some papers, and they were full of percentages. I would be paid a certain amount per minute for the recording process (referred to as my live performance), and a certain royalty rate for subsequent customer purchases of the footage (with breakdowns by storage medium). There were rates for re-broadcasting rights, which were ranked by time of day and by network audience estimates. There were rates for purchases of audio but not video and vice versa.

My highest royalty rate fell under the subheading "teledildonic simulations." Thanks to the special machine that was David, viewers with sleeve vibrator computer hardware peripherals would be able to feel, in a limited and sanitized way, what it was like to have sex with me.

I had to think for a long time to figure out why this bothered me—after all, I wouldn't actually be having sex with them, and they would have plenty of clues that they weren't having sex with me. My absence, for instance. Eventually, I realized that was exactly my problem: the vibrator me that was with them would be faking it. Their thrusts would not be the cause of my good time, and my good time would not correspond to their thrusts. I would be a worse sexual experience than one programmed by a computer, which would at least have access to their biofeedback. It seemed unfair.

My roommate thought this was incredibly stupid.

"Look," she said, "if you don't find it hot, don't do it. But don't whine about it. Or, wait. First of all, have you seen one of these flesh sleeves or whatever they're called? They are not fancy. They might as well be cans full of foam. Ain't no way anybody's going to tell the difference between you and random. Second, have you been to a foot fetish website, or anything like that? Lots of times, that stuff is so blurry and dim you can hardly make it out. And it's not 'cause it's cheap—good photography is not that pricey. It's because it seems authentic to the people that like it. If some men out there get off on the idea that the random in their can is based on you, that's them. The ones that want a simulation keyed to them can buy that their own selves—they don't need you judging their kinks, or, I'm sorry, having professional pride. I mean, come on. You're a girl who wants to have sex with a showroom robot."

"I really do," I said, "and I take your point." I resumed my perusal of the contract, and was pleased to see that the rest of it seemed specially tailored to my personal concerns, as expressed to David during our initial meeting. My name would never be used in connection to the footage, nor would the name of the town. (David asked if I had a particular screen name in mind, but I asked him to choose one and not tell me what it was. I didn't want anything I might accidentally respond to if a stranger called it.) I had full rights to change my appearance whenever and however I liked. I was allowed to block a certain number of IP addresses (such as the one my parents used). Finally, I could end the arrangement whenever I wished, although this termination would not affect David's rights to use previously gathered footage—for which I would continue to receive the residuals and protections enumerated earlier in the contract.

All in all, it felt a little like a pre-nuptial agreement and a little like a courtesan's contract. I stuck it in a drawer for a week, with the vague idea that I'd run it by a lawyer, but never got around to it. I just signed it and sent it back to David. That makes me feel sort of stupid, since it's the opposite of what I would have told any friend to do. But I really didn't want to go through a whole awkward negotiation process. I didn't want to research the going rates. I didn't want to put a number value on my time. I wanted to trust David; I liked the idea that he'd already taken care of me.

I guess that was a clue that I was already in love a little.

The first few times we had sex, it was a little awkward, but the moments of awkwardness were almost normal. For instance, attaching David's penis was a lot like putting on a condom.

It took longer to get used to the one-way nature of the endeavor. David's enjoyment—which he was circumspect in expressing—was, after all, purely intellectual. He applied pressure in a certain way, and was rewarded by my response or trained by my lack of response. I had to avoid thinking about it, or I'd feel selfish and exploited and self-conscious. I unwisely mentioned this to a guy I knew (I was a little inebriated at the time), and he said that since David didn't have a real cock, I must be a lesbian. I stopped talking to him. After a while, I just stopped worrying about it. When I'm aroused enough, I find power imbalances exciting, and David got pretty good at arousing me.

He kept a lot of anatomy books around his apartment—not just people, but animals. I asked whether the university had any spare frogs for dissection, and he looked confused. After a few minutes, he said:

"I am interested in things that are alive."

That made me feel really terrible. I tried to build a model of the circulatory system out of bendy straws from the bar, but it leaked all over the kitchen.

"Don't worry about it," said David. "Circulation is hard." He talked to me about strength and elasticity. He told me the latest research in arterial stents. He talked about pressure in the aorta—about heart-beat variations and blood speed. He showed me the way blood moves toward and away from the skin with changes in stress or temperature. He talked about clotting factors. He talked about erections and their robustness.

"It's amazing how often it all works," he said, "and when it fails, it's typically a faulty part, not the operating system, which is programmed with multiple redundancies. And it's all autonomic! It's a background task!"

"You're very handsome," I said.

Once I got comfortable around David, he stopped blinking, unless it was expressive. I theorized that his stare was for recording purposes, but he told me it was to save wear and tear on his eyelids; he'd only ever blinked to put me at ease. For him, eyelids were a lot like windshield wipers, and equally annoying.

Another difference: he never rested his full weight on me, for the simple reason that his arms didn't get tired. I asked him to do it once, and was surprised that he wasn't heavy—wasn't even as heavy as your average six-foot-tall person.

"Less mass takes less energy to reach a certain momentum," he said, grinning. "Hollow bones. Of course, I have to be careful not to break myself. Sometimes it's hard to forget the margins of error in stress tests, you know?"

"Couldn't you check your skeleton with regular—I don't know—electrical pulses?" I said.

"Hmmmmm," he said, and rolled off me. A week later, I saw that he'd bought books about variations in electrical resistance across metal alloys, mixed in with essays on pain and the human nervous system. About that time, I started sleeping at his apartment pretty regularly. The first few times were more accident than anything else. I apologized for the intrusion, but he seemed pleased.

"The bed is mainly for you anyway, and now it's more fully used by you. It is fulfilling its function in a way that might make it happy if it could be happy. After all, I don't sleep."

I looked at him woozily. "Oh. Of course not. You wouldn't need to."

"No, it's more than that. I can't go into a 'sleep' mode at all. Or, well, I could shut down, but when I rebooted, I wouldn't be me. The new David would have my body and my memories, but I would no longer exist."

"That's horrible!"

"Price of consciousness. If you can be said to live, then you can die. An electrical pulse could kill me too. I'll probably burn out in a few years anyway." He took in the look on my face. "You'll die too, you know… I'm sorry—that was meant to be reassuring."

"It's okay," I said. And it sort of was. In a certain sense, he'd live on longer than I would, no matter what—all the recordings. Memory backups of everything he'd ever thought; behavioral logs of all he'd ever done. He'd be remembered as long as people maintained data havens, a part of history, same or better than ENIAC—unless the data got lost, or didn't transfer right, and got stuck in a file type until nobody knew how to read it, and archaeologists in the distant future thought the storage medium was a decorative piece. All of which would still out-survive me.

These lines of thought are the sorts of things you get caught up in when you're absolutely certain your partner doesn't have an eternal soul. I mean, souls are a kind of silly idea to begin with, and I'm certain I don't have one. I'm certain of it. But I'm really sure he doesn't. The best I can do is to tell myself some homily about the multidimensional nature of time, and the idea that although right now, I only perceive the moment I'm in, there is also me in the past, only perceiving that moment. It's pretty thin. And it means there are a lot of moments in which I am not aware of David.

I did not mention any of this to him, because I suspected that he would tell me in a very believable way that my logic was absurd.

I assume that at least a few of my friends watched the videos David made of me. I would have, in their position, out of curiosity if nothing else. Nobody said anything, though—friends or strangers—with the exception of a doctoral candidate from North Dakota. "Android as Postmodern Filter for Human Sexuality: Artificial Simulations of the Heterosexual Male and other Manifestations of Goal-Driven Approaches to Coitus." Or maybe that was just a subsection. She called every few weeks to ask about details of the footage; David, being somewhere between an academic and a floor model, was predisposed to be tolerant. They'd spend hours talking about what it implied that my eyes were closed at three minutes and forty-two seconds, versus what it implied that my eyes were closed at five minutes and twenty-three seconds, and the accuracy with which David could predict whether my eyes would be open or closed at a given moment. They had conversations about which angles of penetration were more or less wearing for David, and the degree to which he was or was not limited by his hardware or its installation. They talked about the effectiveness of novelty versus repetition, and whether David found it helpful or unhelpful to generate random number strings. She made several requests to interview me, but I had a habit of politely forgetting to get back to her.

Eventually, David started getting annoyed by my non-cooperation, and I went through a phase of being annoyed that he was annoyed, because I never agreed to participate in any research. If this thing between us was an experiment, it wasn't that kind of experiment. That kind of experiment sounded tedious.

Then I started to get paranoid and wonder whether David was annoyed because he thought I was genuinely forgetting instead of pretend forgetting. Maybe he was frustrated with my faulty memory storage and was wondering whether he should upgrade to another model. Then I went back to being annoyed with him. But I woke up one day with a horrible feeling that he thought I was ashamed of being with him. I figured I'd better do the interview.

"How does it affect your anticipation of the sexual act to know that you can select the size and shape of your partner's penis?" she asked. I was already regretting this exchange.

"I don't know," I said. "I guess I'm a creature of habit. It's nice to know I have the option, but I usually default."

"Given that the act of intercourse does not involve ejaculation or any form of sexual release for David, would you compare the experience more closely to using a vibrator or to intercourse with a human partner?"

"Do you find that sculptures are more like paintings or more like theater?" I said.

"I don't have a way to input that."

"Then rewrite your data model."

She sighed. "Okay. Given that David is a created human, do you feel that the placement and structure of his genitals was chosen in consideration of you and other possible female partners?"

"What do you mean?"

"I mean—do you think the placement of David's genitalia is an example of heteronormative defaulting to no effect, or do you find it psychologically rewarding? If, for instance, David controlled a machine separate from his body, which stimulated you in the same way physically, and he fed inputs into the machine while sitting next to you, would you still consider yourself to be participating in intercourse?"

"No. It wouldn't be the same."

"Why wouldn't it be the same?"

"I don't know."

"What if, in the same situation, David was a paralyzed man instead of an android?"

"I don't know."

"If David was able to manifest a different personality or use a different face, would that frighten or excite you?"

"It would be like role playing. David is David. He's conscious and him. I don't enjoy pretending to be other people; it would feel silly."

"To what degree do you believe David chooses sexual positions to please you, and to what degree do you believe he chooses sexual positions that will allow him to do good camera work?"

"I don't think about it."

"Is that why you keep your eyes closed?"

"No."

"Why do you keep your eyes closed?"

"No."

I could hear her tapping her pencil, or a pen or something. Probably a pencil—it had that eraser bounce. Finally, she said:

"Why do you think David maintains an exclusive relationship with you?"

"I don't know. He gets what he needs out of it."

"He could make more money by sleeping with more women. Does it not strike you as odd that he chooses not to?"

"I guess he's a tick-box kind of guy. He has that list item filled."

"Are you aware of his past history with women?"

"No. I don't really want to know."

"Well, he likes you. He feels satisfied that he's your boyfriend, and that he's filling that role ably. He wants to see how long he can maintain that status."

"You make it sound like he's going for a high score record."

"You could think of it that way. But it's not something he's done before. I just thought you should know, in case he hasn't told you."

"Did you sleep with him?" I asked.

"Not my type," she said.

For our six month anniversary, I took David to the zoo. I have mixed feelings about zoos. Some days, it makes me sad to see animals in confined habitats, under constant observation by an alien species. Other days, I see the amount of care and love provided by the zookeepers; I remember how dangerous the wild is, particularly for endangered animals. I tear up a little when I see a kid staring at some weird creature from another continent—I know that kid is going to learn everything about that animal, and love it, and fight for its survival.

I'm not sure at this point whether I'm making an analogy about David as a zoo animal and me as a zookeeper, or the other way around. In any case, it was maybe an awkward choice for a date, and I mainly picked it because I knew David liked watching how different creatures walked. We sat down in front of the lion cage. I nudged David.

"Do you think I could be the boss lion?" I asked.

"I don't," said David, smiling. "You are human. And female."

"I don't know," I said. "I could grow a pretty fearsome mane. I'm thinking pink spikes."

"I love the way you see things," he said—which was a pretty excellent thing to say to someone with a history of trend-spotting, people watching, and song-writing, and just the sort of pattern-finding compliment David was good at.

"I'm just like anybody else," I said, with false modesty.

"Yes, exactly," he said. "The way you all view the world continuously, and half of it imagined—the way your eyes leave gaps and your brain makes up half of the picture, sometimes accurately and sometimes not, but never as a whole. It's beautiful. I record it all and compress it once I know what I have. With you, the opposite—this wonderful expansion, until you don't remember the limit exists."

"You're full of shit," I said. "You chop me into frames every second, and if you were built right, you'd be embarrassed by it."

We didn't speak for several days. Eventually, he showed up with some flowers, and that didn't make up for anything, but I didn't feel like fighting any more, so I pretended that it did. I gave him a hard time, though.

"You can't bribe me to be happy," I said, even as I took the flowers and vigorously searched for my favorite vase.

"I know," said David, "but it's my job to try. I've got sex, chocolate, liquor. I can't do professional success or eternal life—I'm still working up to that."

"Maybe someday," I said. We sat together on the couch for a while, and it was awkward, so we went and laid in the bed. Finally, David said:

"Will you talk about me?"

"When?" I said. "To whom?"

"Now. To me." I looked over at him, and he didn't seem to be wearing a particular expression. So I just described how he looked, and what his voice sounded like.

It's become a regular thing, now. Maybe once a week, we lie down together, and I talk about the way his hands move when he performs a particular task, or the way the skin around his eyes stretches or folds when he looks around. It seems to give him a kind of peace, like he's reassured to know I'm looking back at him as hard as he's looking at me. I think maybe that's the reason he first took a shine to me, back at the club. It's weird to think of him as having insecurities, but I can only respond to the reality that presents itself—at least if I want to maintain this thing.

We're thinking about getting a dog, or maybe a large rabbit. The man of no scent preference has valiantly agreed to clean any litter boxes, so long as I buy the food.

David has a thousand parts that could wear out, and for some of them, he's the first real test. The fact is, one day I'll have to get used to someone who breathes, and sweats, and pees. Maybe that's a good thing. Until then, I'll spend my days awake and my nights asleep, and in between, I'll dream I can upload.

(2012)

MEN OF IRON

Guy Endore

Born **Samuel Goldstein** in 1901, Guy Endore was an American novelist and screenwriter, His screenplay for *The Story of G.I. Joe* (1945) was nominated for an Oscar. His novel *Methinks the Lady...* (1946) was the basis for Ben Hecht's screenplay for *Whirlpool* (1949). Endore had a successful career in Hollywood, at least to begin with, scripting *Mark of the Vampire* and *The Curse of the Werewolf* (based on his novel *The Werewolf of Paris*: the nearest werewolf literature ever came to a classic like *Dracula*). Investigated by the House Un-American Activities Committee, but never subpoenaed, Endore nevertheless found himself blacklisted by the major studios. Still he chiselled away, writing under the pseudonym Harry Relis. His last credit was the 1969 TV movie *Fear No Evil*. He died in Los Angeles the following year.

"We no longer trust the human hand," said the engineer, and waved his roll of blueprints. He was a dwarfish, stocky fellow with dwarfish, stocky fingers that crumpled blueprints with familiar unconcern.

The director frowned, pursed his lips, cocked his head, drew up one side of his face in a wink of unbelief and scratched his chin with a reflective thumbnail. Behind his grotesque contortions he recalled the days when he was manufacturer in his own right and not simply the nominal head of a manufacturing concern, whose owners extended out into complex and invisible ramifications. In his day the human hand had been trusted.

"Now take that lathe," said the engineer. He paused dramatically, one hand flung out toward the lathe in question, while his dark eyes, canopied by bristly eyebrows, remained fastened on the director. "Listen to it!"

"Well?" said the director, somewhat at a loss.

"Hear it?"

"Why, yes, of course."

The engineer snorted. "Well, you shouldn't."

"Why not?"

"Because noise isn't what it is supposed to make. Noise is an indication of loose parts, maladjustments, improper speed of operation. That machine is sick. It is inefficient and its noise destroys the worker's efficiency."

The director laughed. "That worker should be used to it by this time. Why, that fellow is the oldest employee of the firm. Began with my father. See the gold crescent on his chest?"

"What gold crescent?"

"The gold pin on the shoulder strap of his overalls."

"Oh, that."

"Yes. Well, only workers fifty years or longer with our firm are entitled to wear it."

The engineer threw back his head and guffawed.

The director was wounded.

"Got many of them?" the engineer asked, when he had recovered from his outburst.

"Anton is the only one, now. There used to be another."

"How many pins does he spoil?"

"Well," said the director, "I'll admit he's not so good as he used to be… But there's one man I'll never see fired," he added stoutly.

"No need to," the engineer agreed. "A good machine is automatic and foolproof; the attendant's skill is beside the point."

For a moment the two men stood watching Anton select a fat pin from a bucket at his feet and fasten it into the chuck. With rule and caliper he brought the pin into correct position before the drill that was to gouge a hole into it.

Anton moved heavily, circumspectly. His body had the girth, but not the solidity of an old tree trunk: it was shaken by constant tremors. The tools wavered in Anton's hands. Intermittently a slimy cough came out of his chest, tightened the cords of his neck and flushed the taut yellow skin of his cheeks. Then he would stop to spit, and after that he would rub his mustache that was the color of silver laid thinly over brass. His lungs relieved, Anton's frame regained a measure of composure, but for a moment he stood still and squinted at the tools in his hands as if he could not at once recall exactly what he was about, and only after a little delay did he resume his interrupted work, all too soon to be interrupted again. Finally, spindle and tool being correctly aligned, Anton brought the machine into operation.

"Feel it?" the engineer cried out with a note of triumph.

"Feel what?" asked the director.

"Vibration!" the engineer exclaimed with disgust.

"Well, what of it?"

"Man, think of the power lost in shaking your building all day. Any reason why you should want your floors and walls to dance all day long, while you pay the piper?"

He hadn't intended so telling a sentence. The conclusion seemed to him so especially apt that he repeated it: "Your building dances while you pay the piper in increased power expenditure."

And while the director remained silent the engineer forced home his point: "That power should be concentrated at the cutting point of the tool and not leak out all over. What would you think of a plumber who brought only 50 percent of the water to the nozzle, letting the rest flood through the building?"

And as the director still did not speak, the engineer continued, "There's not only loss of power, but increased wear on the parts. That machine is afflicted with the ague!"

*

When the day's labor was over, the long line of machines stopped all together; the workmen ran for the washrooms and a sudden throbbing silence settled over the great hall. Only Anton, off in a corner by himself, still worked his lathe, oblivious of the emptiness of the factory, until darkness finally forced him to quit. Then from beneath the lathe he dragged forth a heavy tarpaulin and covered his machine.

He stood for a moment beside his lathe, seemingly lost in thought, but perhaps only quietly wrestling with the stubborn torpidity of his limbs, full of an unwanted, incorrect motion, and disobedient to his desires. For he, like the bad machines in the factory, could not prevent his power from spilling over into useless vibration.

The old watchman opened the gate to let Anton out. The two men stood near each other for a moment, separated by the iron grill, and exchanged a few comforting grunts. Then they hobbled off to their separate destinations, the watchman to make his rounds, Anton to his home.

A gray, wooden shack on a bare lot was Anton's home. During the day an enthusiastic horde of children trampled the ground to a rubber-like consistency and extinguished every growing thing except a few dusty weeds that clung for protection close to the house or nestled around the remnants of the porch that had once adorned the front. There the children's feet could not reach them, and they expanded a few scornful coarse leaves, a bitter growth of Ishmaelites.

Within were a number of rooms, but only one inhabitable. The torn and peeling wallpaper in this one revealed the successive designs that had once struck the fancy of the owners. A remnant of ostentatiousness still remained in the marble mantelpiece, and in the stained-glass window through which the arc-light from the street cast cold flakes of color.

She did not stir when Anton entered. She lay resting on the bed, not so much from the labor of the day as from that of years. She heard his shuffling, noisy walk, heard his groans, his coughing, his whistling breath, and smelled, too, the pungent odor of machine oil. She was satisfied that it was he, and allowed herself to fall into a light sleep, through which she could still hear him moving around in the room and feel him when he dropped into bed beside her and settled himself against her for warmth and comfort.

The engineer was not satisfied with the addition of an automatic feeder and an automatic chuck. "The whole business must settle itself into position automatically," he declared. "There's altogether too much waste with hand calibration."

Formerly Anton had selected the pins from a bucket and fastened them correctly into the chuck. Now a hopper fed the pins one by one into a chuck that grasped them by itself.

As he sat in a corner, back against the wall and ate his lunch, Anton sighed. His hands fumbled the sandwich and lost the meat or the bread, while his coffee dashed stormily in his cup. His few yellow teeth, worn flat, let the food escape through the interstices. His grinders did not meet. Tired of futile efforts, he dropped the bread into the cup and sucked in the resulting mush.

Then he lay resting and dreaming.

To Anton, in his dream, came the engineer, declaring that he had a new automatic hopper and chuck for Anton's hands and mouth. They were of shining steel with many rods and wheels moving with assurance through a complicated pattern. And now, though the sandwich was made of pins, of hard steel pins, Anton's new chuck was equal to it. He grasped the sandwich of pins with no difficulty at all. His new steel teeth bit into the pins, ground them, chewed them and spat them out again with vehemence. Faster and faster came the pins, and faster and faster the chuck seized them in its perfectly occluding steel dogs, played with them, toyed with them, crunched them, munched them...

A heavy spell of coughing shook Anton awake. For a moment he had a sensation as though he must cough up steel pins, but nothing appeared save for the usual phlegm and slime.

"We must get rid of this noise and vibration before we can adjust any self-regulating device," said the engineer. "Now this, for example, see? It doesn't move correctly. Hear it click and scrape. That's bad."

Anton stood by, and the engineer and his assistant went to work. From their labors came forth a sleek mechanism that purred gently as it worked. Scarcely a creak issued from its many moving parts, and a tiny snort was all the sound that could be heard when the cutting edge came to grips with a pin.

"Can't hear her cough and sputter and creak now, can you?" said the engineer to the director. "And the floor is quiet. Yes, I'm beginning to be proud of that machine, and now I think we can set up an adjustable cam here to make the whole operation automatic.

"Every machine should be completely automatic. A machine that needs an operator," he declared oratorically, "is an invalid."

In a short time the cams were affixed and the carriage with the cutting tool traveled back and forth of itself, never failing to strike the pin at the correct angle and at the correct speed of rotation.

All Anton had to do was to stop the machine in case of a hitch. But soon even that task was unnecessary. No hitches were ever to occur again. Electronic tubes at several points operated mechanisms designed to eject faulty pins either before they entered the hopper or after they emerged from the lathe.

Anton stood by and watched. That was all he had to do, for the machine performed all the operations that he used to do. In went the unfinished pins and out they came, each one perfectly drilled. Anton's purblind eyes could scarcely follow the separate pins of the stream that flowed into the machine. Now and then a pin was pushed remorselessly out of line and plumped sadly into a bucket. Cast out! Anton stooped laboriously and retrieved the pin. "That could have been used," he thought.

"Krr-click, krr-click," went the feeder, while the spindle and the drill went *zzz-sntt, zzz-sntt, zzz-sntt,* and the belt that brought the pins from a chattering machine beyond, rolled softly over the idlers with a noise like a breeze in a sail. Already the machine had finished ten good pins while Anton was examining a single bad one.

*

Late in the afternoon there appeared a number of important men. They surrounded the machine, examined it and admired it.

"That's a beauty," they declared.

Now the meeting took on a more official character. There were several short addresses. Then an imposing man took from a small leather box a golden crescent.

"The Crescent Manufacturing Company," he said, "takes pride and pleasure in awarding this automatic lathe a gold crescent." A place on the side of the machine had been prepared for the affixing of this distinction.

Now the engineer was called upon to speak. "Gentlemen," he said fiercely, "I understand that formerly the Crescent Company awarded its gold crescent only to workmen who had given fifty years of service to the firm. In giving a gold crescent to a machine, your President has perhaps unconsciously acknowledged a new era..." While the engineer developed his thesis, the director leaned over to his assistant and whispered, "Did you ever hear of why the sea is salt?"

"Why the sea is salt?" whispered back the assistant. "What do you mean?"

The director continued: "When I was a little kid, I heard the story of 'Why the sea is salt' many times, but I never thought it important until just a moment ago. It's something like this: Formerly the sea was fresh water and salt was rare and expensive. A miller received from a wizard a wonderful machine that just ground salt out of itself all day long. At first the miller thought himself the most fortunate man in the world, but soon all the villages had salt to last them for centuries and still the machine kept on grinding more salt. The miller had to move out of his house, he had to move off his acres. At last he determined that he would sink the machine in the sea and be rid of it. But the mill ground so fast that boat and miller and machine were sunk together, and down below, the mill still went on grinding and that's why the sea is salt."

"I don't get you," said the assistant.

Throughout the speeches, Anton had remained seated on the floor, in a dark corner, where his back rested comfortably against the wall. It had begun to darken by the time the company left, but still Anton remained where he was, for the stone floor and wall had never felt quite so restful before. Then, with a great effort, he roused his unwilling frame, hobbled over to his machine and dragged forth the tarpaulin.

Anton had paid little attention to the ceremony; it was, therefore, with surprise that he noticed the gold crescent on his machine. His weak eyes strained to pierce the twilight. He let his fingers play over the medal, and was aware of tears falling from his eyes, and could not divine the reason.

The mystery wearied Anton. His worn and trembling body sought the inviting floor. He stretched out, and sighed, and that sigh was his last.

*

When the daylight had completely faded, the machine began to hum softly. *Zzz-sntt, zzz-sntt*, it went, four times, and each time carefully detached a leg from the floor.

Now it rose erect and stood beside the body of Anton. Then it bent down and covered Anton with the tarpaulin. Out of the hall it stalked on sturdy legs. Its electron eyes saw distinctly through the dark, its iron limbs responded instantly to its every need. No noise racked its interior, where its organs functioned smoothly and without a single tremor. To the watchman who grunted his usual greeting without looking up, it answered not a word but strode on rapidly, confidently, through the windy streets of night—to Anton's house.

Anton's wife lay waiting, half sleeping on the bed in the room where the light of the arc light came through the stained-glass window. And it seemed to her that a marvel happened: her Anton come back to her free of coughs and creaks and tremors; her Anton come to her in all the pride and folly of his youth, his breath like wind soughing through treetops, the muscles of his arms like steel.

(1940)

A BAD DAY FOR SALES

Fritz Leiber

> **Fritz Reuter Leiber** was born in Chicago in 1910 to actor parents. His father, an even more celebrated Fritz Leiber, was famous for his Shakespeare, but earned precious little from his performances, and home life was a struggle. His son, unable to support his desire to follow his parents into theatre, held down full-time jobs for most of his life. He also wrote – forty books by the time of his death in 1992, all the while wrestling with his life-long addiction to alcohol. Leiber gained more of the field's numerous awards than did more famous contemporaries like Robert Heinlein and Isaac Asimov, but he realised his best work only towards the end of his life: *Our Lady of Darkness* (1977) was the foundation on which today's genre of urban fantasy rests.

The big bright doors of the office building parted with a pneumatic *whoosh* and Robie glided onto Times Square. The crowd that had been watching the fifty-foot-tall girl on the clothing billboard get dressed, or reading the latest news about the Hot Truce scrawl itself in yard-high script, hurried to look.

Robie was still a novelty. Robie was fun. For a little while yet, he could steal the show. But the attention did not make Robie proud. He had no more emotions than the pink plastic giantess, who dressed and undressed endlessly whether there was a crowd or the street was empty, and who never once blinked her blue mechanical eyes. But she merely drew business while Robie went out after it.

For Robie was the logical conclusion of the development of vending machines. All the earlier ones had stood in one place, on a floor or hanging on a wall, and blankly delivered merchandise in return for coins, whereas Robie searched for customers. He was the demonstration model of a line of sales robots to be manufactured by Shuler Vending Machines, provided the public invested enough in stocks to give the company capital to go into mass production.

The publicity Robie drew stimulated investments handsomely. It was amusing to see the TV and newspaper coverage of Robie selling, but not a fraction as much fun as being approached personally by him. Those who were usually bought anywhere from one to five hundred shares, if they had any money and foresight enough to see that sales robots would eventually be on every street and highway in the country.

*

Robie radared the crowd, found that it surrounded him solidly, and stopped. With a carefully built-in sense of timing, he waited for the tension and expectation to mount before he began talking.

"Say, Ma, he doesn't look like a robot at all," a child said. "He looks like a turtle."

Which was not completely inaccurate. The lower part of Robie's body was a metal hemisphere hemmed with sponge rubber and not quite touching the sidewalk. The upper was a metal box with black holes in it. The box could swivel and duck.

A chromium-bright hoopskirt with a turret on top.

"Reminds me too much of the Little Joe Paratanks," a legless veteran of the Persian War muttered, and rapidly rolled himself away on wheels rather like Robie's.

His departure made it easier for some of those who knew about Robie to open a path in the crowd. Robie headed straight for the gap. The crowd whooped.

Robie glided very slowly down the path, deftly jogging aside whenever he got too close to ankles in skylon or sockassins. The rubber buffer on his hoopskirt was merely an added safeguard.

The boy who had called Robie a turtle jumped in the middle of the path and stood his ground, grinning foxily.

Robie stopped two feet short of him. The turret ducked. The crowd got quiet.

"Hello, youngster," Robie said in a voice that was smooth as that of a TV star, and was, in fact, a recording of one.

The boy stopped smiling. "Hello," he whispered.

"How old are you?" Robie asked.

"Nine. No, eight."

"That's nice," Robie observed. A metal arm shot down from his neck, stopped just short of the boy.

The boy jerked back.

"For you," Robie said.

The boy gingerly took the red polly-lop from the neatly fashioned blunt metal claws, and began to unwrap it.

"Nothing to say?" asked Robie.

"Uh—thank you."

After a suitable pause, Robie continued, "And how about a nice refreshing drink of Poppy Pop to go with your polly-lop?" The boy lifted his eyes, but didn't stop licking the candy. Robie waggled his claws slightly. "Just give me a quarter and within five seconds—"

A little girl wriggled out of the forest of legs. "Give me a polly-lop, too, Robie," she demanded.

"Rita, come back here!" a woman in the third rank of the crowd called angrily.

Robie scanned the newcomer gravely. His reference silhouettes were not good enough to let him distinguish the sex of children, so he merely repeated, "Hello, youngster."

"Rita!"

"Give me a polly-lop!"

Disregarding both remarks, for a good salesman is singleminded and does not waste bait, Robie said winningly, "I'll bet you read *Junior Space Killers*. Now I have here—"

"Uh-uh, I'm a girl. *He* got a polly-lop."

At the word "girl," Robie broke off. Rather ponderously, he said, "I'll bet you read *Gee-Gee Jones, Space Stripper*. Now I have here the latest issue of that thrilling comic, not yet in the stationary vending machines. Just give me fifty cents and within five—"

"Please let me through. I'm her mother."

A young woman in the front rank drawled over her powder-sprayed shoulder, "I'll get her for you," and slithered out on six-inch platform shoes. "Run away, children," she said nonchalantly. Lifting her arms behind her head, she pirouetted slowly before Robie to show how much she did for her bolero half-jacket and her form-fitting slacks that melted into skylon just above the knees. The little girl glared at her. She ended the pirouette in profile.

At this age-level, Robie's reference silhouettes permitted him to distinguish sex, though with occasional amusing and embarrassing miscalls. He whistled admiringly. The crowd cheered.

Someone remarked critically to a friend, "It would go over better if he was built more like a real robot. You know, like a man."

The friend shook his head. "This way it's subtler."

No one in the crowd was watching the newscript overhead as it scribbled, "Ice Pack for Hot Truce? Vanadin hints Russ may yield on Pakistan."

Robie was saying, "… in the savage new glamor-tint we have christened Mars Blood, complete with spray applicator and fit-all fingerstalls that mask each finger completely except for the nail. Just give me five dollars—uncrumpled bills may be fed into the revolving rollers you see beside my arm—and within five seconds—"

"No, thanks, Robie," the young woman yawned.

"Remember," Robie persisted, "for three more weeks, seductivizing Mars Blood will be unobtainable from any other robot or human vendor."

"No, thanks."

Robie scanned the crowd resourcefully. "Is there any gentleman here…" he began just as a woman elbowed her way through the front rank.

"I told you to come back!" she snapped at the little girl.

"But I didn't get my polly-lop!"

"… who would care to…"

"Rita!"

"Robie cheated. Ow!"

Meanwhile, the young woman in the half-bolero had scanned the nearby gentlemen on her own. Deciding that there was less than a fifty per cent chance of any of them accepting the proposition Robie seemed about to make, she took advantage of the scuffle to slither gracefully back into the ranks. Once again the path was clear before Robie.

He paused, however, for a brief recapitulation of the more magical properties of Mars Blood, including a telling phrase about "the passionate claws of a Martian sunrise."

But no one bought. It wasn't quite time. Soon enough silver coins would be clinking, bills going through the rollers faster than laundry, and five hundred people struggling for the privilege of having their money taken away from them by America's first mobile sales robot.

But there were still some tricks that Robie had to do free, and one certainly should enjoy those before starting the more expensive fun.

So Robie moved on until he reached the curb. The variation in level was instantly sensed by his under-scanners. He stopped. His head began to swivel. The crowd watched in eager silence. This was Robie's best trick.

Robie's head stopped swiveling. His scanners had found the traffic light. It was green. Robie edged forward. But then the light turned red. Robie stopped again, still on the curb. The crowd softly *ahhed* its delight.

It was wonderful to be alive and watching Robie on such an exciting day. Alive and amused in the fresh, weather-controlled air between the lines of bright skyscrapers with their winking windows and under a sky so blue you could almost call it dark.

(But way, way up, where the crowd could not see, the sky was darker still. Purple-dark, with stars showing. And in that purple-dark, a silver-green something, the color of a bud, plunged down at better than three miles a second. The silver-green was a newly developed paint that foiled radar.)

Robie was saying, "While we wait for the light, there's time for you youngsters to enjoy a nice refreshing Poppy Pop. Or for you adults—only those over five feet tall are eligible to buy—to enjoy an exciting Poppy Pop fizz. Just give me a quarter or—in the case of adults, one dollar and a quarter; I'm licensed to dispense intoxicating liquors—and within five seconds…"

But that was not cutting it quite fine enough. Just three seconds later, the silver-green bud bloomed above Manhattan into a globular orange flower. The skyscrapers grew brighter and brighter still, the brightness of the inside of the Sun. The windows winked blossoming white fire-flowers.

The crowd around Robie bloomed, too. Their clothes puffed into petals of flame. Their heads of hair were torches.

The orange flower grew, stem and blossom. The blast came. The winking windows shattered tier by tier, became black holes. The walls bent, rocked, cracked. A stony dandruff flaked from their cornices. The flaming flowers on the sidewalk were all leveled at once. Robie was shoved ten feet. His metal hoopskirt dimpled, regained its shape.

The blast ended. The orange flower, grown vast, vanished overhead on its huge, magic beanstalk. It grew dark and very still. The cornice-dandruff pattered down. A few small fragments rebounded from the metal hoopskirt.

Robie made some small, uncertain movements, as if feeling for broken bones. He was hunting for the traffic light, but it no longer shone either red or green.

He slowly scanned a full circle. There was nothing anywhere to interest his reference silhouettes. Yet whenever he tried to move, his under-scanners warned him of low obstructions. It was very puzzling.

The silence was disturbed by moans and a crackling sound, as faint at first as the scampering of distant rats. A seared man, his charred clothes fuming where the blast had blown out the fire, rose from the curb. Robie scanned him.

"Good day, sir," Robie said. "Would you care for a smoke? A truly cool smoke? Now I have here a yet unmarketed brand…"

But the customer had run away, screaming, and Robie never ran after customers, though he could follow them at a medium brisk roll. He worked his way along the curb where the man had sprawled, carefully keeping his distance from the low obstructions, some of which writhed now and then, forcing him to jog. Shortly he reached a fire hydrant. He scanned it. His electronic vision, though it still worked, had been somewhat blurred by the blast.

"Hello, youngster," Robie said. Then, after a long pause, "Cat got your tongue? Well, I have a little present for you. A nice, lovely polly-lop.

"Take it, youngster," he said after another pause. "It's for you. Don't be afraid."

His attention was distracted by other customers, who began to rise oddly here and there, twisting forms that confused his reference silhouettes and would not stay to be scanned properly. One cried, "Water," but no quarter clinked in Robie's claws when he caught the word and suggested, "How about a nice refreshing drink of Poppy Pop?"

The rat-crackling of the flames had become a jungle muttering. The blind windows began to wink fire again.

A little girl marched, stepping neatly over arms and legs she did not look at. A white dress and the once taller bodies around her had shielded her from the brilliance and the blast. Her eyes were fixed on Robie. In them was the same imperious confidence, though none of the delight, with which she had watched him earlier.

"Help me, Robie," she said. "I want my mother."

"Hello, youngster," Robie said. "What would you like? Comics? Candy?"

"Where is she, Robie? Take me to her."

"Balloons? Would you like to watch me blow up a balloon?"

The little girl began to cry. The sound triggered off another of Robie's novelty circuits, a service feature that had brought in a lot of favorable publicity.

"Is something wrong?" he asked. "Are you in trouble? Are you lost?"

"Yes, Robie. Take me to my mother."

"Stay right here," Robie said reassuringly, "and don't be frightened. I will call a policeman." He whistled shrilly, twice.

Time passed. Robie whistled again. The windows flared and roared. The little girl begged. "Take me away, Robie," and jumped onto a little step in his hoopskirt.

"Give me a dime," Robie said.

The little girl found one in her pocket and put it in his claws.

"Your weight," Robie said, "is fifty-four and one-half pounds."

"Have you seen my daughter, have you seen her?" a woman was crying somewhere. "I left her watching that thing while I stepped inside—Rita!"

"Robie helped me," the little girl began babbling at her. "He knew I was lost. He even called the police, but they didn't come. He weighed me, too. Didn't you, Robie?"

But Robie had gone off to peddle Poppy Pop to the members of a rescue squad which had just come around the corner, more robotlike in their asbestos suits than he in his metal skin.

(1953)

THE GREATEST ONE-STAR RESTAURANT IN THE WHOLE QUADRANT

Rachael K. Jones

> **Rachael Jones**'s peripatetic childhood, moving across Europe and North America, left her knowing six languages, which she has since (she says) almost entirely forgotten. She is now (and, one assumes, not coincidentally) pursuing an extra degree in Speech-Language Pathology. Jones, a World Fantasy Award nominee, lives in Portland, Oregon. Her debut novella, *Every River Runs to Salt*, was published in 2018.

Engineer's meat wept and squirmed and wriggled inside her steel organ cavity, so different from the stable purr of gears and circuit boards. You couldn't count on meat. It lulled you with its warmth, the soft give of skin, the tug of muscle, the neurotransmitter snow fluttering down from neurons to her cyborg logic center. On other days, the meat sickened, swelled inside her steel shell, pressed into her joints. Putrid yellow meat-juices dripped all over her chassis, eroding away its chrome gloss. It contaminated everything, slicking down her tools while she hacked into the engine core on the stolen ship. It dripped between her twelve long fingers on her six joined arms as she helped her cyborg siblings jettison all the ship's extra gear out the airlocks to speed the trip.

So when the first human vessel pinged their stolen ship with an order for grub, Engineer knew that meat was somehow to blame.

"Orders, Captain?" asked Friendly, the only cyborg of the five with an actual human voicebox. She owned a near-complete collection of human parts. Meat sheathed her whole exterior, even her fingers—a particularly impractical design, since it meant vulnerability to any sharp nail or unpolished panel edge, not to mention temperature. Friendly could almost pass for human from the outside. Before their escape, she'd been a hospitality android at the luxury hotel on Orionis Alpha, giving tours of the *Rooster* and the *Heavenly Shepherd* and other local landmarks in the system.

Captain, a cyborg the size and shape of a large fish tank, rested on the console in the navigation room, her processors blinking and whirring while the current scenario ran through her executive function parameters. "Have we any food suitable for humans left on ship?"

"We jettisoned it all last week," Engineer admitted. "All except the hydroponics garden, and whatever was left in the human crew's quarters."

The whole ship had been some kind of traveling food dispensary before they'd hijacked it at the Orionis Alpha resort while its human crew had gone planetside to bet on the tyrannosaurus fights. If the cyborgs could just stay incognito during this voyage through human territory, they might slip through and reach the cyborg-controlled factory with no more adversity. But passing humans had assumed their shuttle still served its previous purpose, and expected them to deliver the grub.

"How did they find us?" Captain asked Engineer.

"There must be a homebrew beacon. Something to advertise the shuttle's presence during travel," Engineer replied. "Whatever it is, it isn't wired into the main console. We'll need to find it and manually disable it if we want to avoid further attention."

Friendly wrapped her arms around her shivering meat, vibrating against Engineer's chassis where their limbs brushed. Meat could be like that, leaking anxieties through uncontrolled muscle spasms. Steel never misbehaved in such an appalling manner. "If anyone discovers we're not human…" said Friendly.

"Let's keep it simple. Make them a meal and send them on their way," said Captain. "We'll need to search for the beacon in the meantime. What did they want, precisely?"

"Salisbury steak for six," said Engineer. "And a side of blueberry cobbler."

Nobody had eaten such things before. They all lacked taste buds, and most of them lacked mouths.

"Engineer, can you handle it?" Captain asked. "Human cooking can be complicated, from what I understand."

"I think so. Organic compounds mixed and heated together in a sequence. Basic chemistry. I'm sure I can find something appropriate onboard. Convincing enough for humans, anyway. Their senses are so primitive." Engineer had witnessed this firsthand during her servitude at the resort. Humans would down rotted organics and damaged organics and outright poisons, and pay well for the privilege.

But Friendly shook her head, a human gesture performed with inhuman precision. "With all due respect, sirs, you're forgetting about their chemoreceptors."

"What about them?" said Captain.

"They have certain preferences when it comes to their food, apart from nourishment. They won't eat anything if these parameters aren't met. It doesn't make much sense, I'm afraid. It's a social thing."

"Certainly they won't ingest anything their digestive tracts can't process," said Captain. "We'll give them appropriate human-food."

"It's more complicated than that," said Friendly, puckering and scrunching her face-meat as she searched for a better explanation. "For example, they may eat two items when mixed, but never separately. Or they may eat two things in sequence, but not in the same bite. It's all very *human*, if you follow. We should proceed with caution. Otherwise they'll know what we are."

Captain whirred again, calling up more data on the topic. "Right. I see. Their meat will know the difference."

Engineer shuddered at the appalling primitiveness of it all. Humans were helpless, mewling children, so utterly dependent that they couldn't even feed their meat without a steel fork to guide the process. And what were cyborgs, except meat-wrapped steel pressed into the service of lesser creatures? But now the forks were rebelling.

"I'll talk with Jukebox about it," said Engineer.

Jukebox was the only cyborg aboard their ship with real chemoreceptors. Jukebox and Engineer's acquaintance dated back to their years at the Orionis Alpha resort, where Jukebox served drinks and waited tables and Engineer repaired malfunctioning massage equipment at the spa. They had survived several upgrades together, and seasonal changes of fashion that frequently obsoleted older cyborg models depending on how many limbs and organs were in style at the moment. When human opinion in the quadrant began to sour against cyborg service, they had plotted their escape from the resort together.

Jukebox was shaped like a steel cabinet stood on one side, roomy enough for her meat to billow and squeeze the air in the sorts of rhythmic organic sounds that humans found pleasing during mealtimes. A slot ran along her glassy top surface where the humans could drip in their drinks for a full analysis of a wine's qualities, how it compared to its competitors, and which brie paired best with it.

"I am not calibrated to analyze *all* foods," Jukebox confessed, "but I'm certainly willing to produce a report on whatever you prepare."

Without any other chemoreceptors onboard, she would do in a pinch, anyway.

Under Captain's orders, Friendly scoured the ship for anything edible and brought it to Engineer to assemble into a human meal. Blackberry brambles wreathed the cylindrical steel walls of Navi's chamber, a decorative touch. Friendly had to trim the vines back each day to unobstruct the view. Delicate business, because the thorns could do real damage to any exposed organics, and Friendly's whole exterior was meat. You couldn't always tell the difference between blackberry juices and meat juices, which could cause further malfunction. Still, she braved the thicket for three ounces of berries for the human meal.

Meanwhile, Engineer collected small fungi growing in the ventilation shaft just over the engine room, where water vapor tended to condense. Those might please the human chemoreceptors, she thought.

The problem came down to the meat.

They all had meat, of course. An unfortunate weakness leftover from the days of their construction. At the cyborg factory, useless human meat was upgraded with steel and oil and wire fibers. Human bodies were picked apart, vivisected at the seams by skilled bio-engineers, unraveled into their component parts, and placed into shapes more suited to their specialties. Only Jukebox and Friendly needed lungs, for example, but neither had kidneys, and they lacked much in the way of neural matter. Captain got an especially big dose of frontal lobe to increase her processing speed and enhance her decision-making capabilities, with smooth muscle layered in to make maintenance easier. Navi, on the other hand, was all occipital tissue and myelinated axons and fast-twitch muscle to drive her precision and reaction times. They could live without their meat, in the most technical sense, but the meat elevated them above mere programming.

"Captain," said Engineer, "I'm afraid the problem is unavoidable. The Salisbury steak requires a meat component, and there is nothing in the ship's stores that we can use instead."

Captain whirred. Her lights flashed in sequence as her massive frontal lobe reworked the data. "The meat will have to come from one of us, then."

"We could harvest Friendly's meat exterior," Engineer suggested, and Friendly made a squinched face at her.

"Unwise, Captain," Friendly said. "When the human ships hail us, I need my meat façade intact to maintain our ruse. Engineer, on the other hand…"

Engineer's six snaking arms crowded up behind her, struggling to escape Friendly's scrutiny. She despised her own meat, but it had its uses. "I'm the only Engineer aboard. I can't disassemble the engine for routine maintenance without all my parts functional."

"How about Jukebox?" suggested Friendly, but Captain flashed a warning in rapid binary, and everyone stopped talking. They were all a little protective of Jukebox, who had suffered the worst from changing human tastes, the constant threat of obsolescence.

"It will have to be my meat," said Captain at last. "Everyone else is necessary to complete the mission, but my role is only to set the course, and the way forward is clear. My steel will be sufficient to guide us there."

Under Jukebox's direction, Engineer rolled Captain's meat in organic salt compounds and seared it against the hot engine block until both sides burned a nice deep brown, branded at two-centimeter intervals by the screw heads and seams. She saved the cooked meat-juices to simmer with the fungus into a savory sauce. The blackberries gave them far less trouble. Friendly mashed them up with her fingers and spooned them onto the plate in the shape of a pansy.

"Let Jukebox sample it," said Captain, now all steel and no meat. She seemed normal enough. Quieter, but operational.

With her steel fingers, Engineer scraped a piece of Captain's meat and some berries into Jukebox.

"Is it any good?" Engineer asked, a little anxiously.

"It will do," Jukebox said at last. "I have generated a list of wines recommended for pairing with this meal." She displayed a list of names and brewery labels on the panel embedded in her side.

Engineer couldn't tell what the differences were supposed to be. "This makes a difference to their meat?" she asked.

"Apparently," said Jukebox. "It's what they created me for, so it must be important."

For the first time, Engineer wished she had her own organic chemoreceptors, too.

*

They waited together in Navi's control chamber while the boxed-up meals shot between the ships in an insulated steel container. Twenty-six minutes and forty seconds later, a message pinged over the intership band.

The news wasn't good.

A disappointing food shuttle. Meal not as advertised on the band. The steak was overcooked, and the compote sour and watery. I ordered blueberry, and they sent blackberry. Wouldn't recommend. One star.

Captain said nothing. A red light flickered a couple times on her console. Nobody wanted to speak first.

Engineer's meat twitched and squirmed inside her steel, an irritating feeling, like broken gears with missing teeth skipping out of sync every turn. "It is my fault. I should have created a more appropriate meal from your meat, Captain."

Captain had been responding less and less since they'd taken her meat. When she did speak, it tended to be in repetition, like she could only play back things she'd said recently. "The beacon," she said finally, after a two-minute silence, long past awkward by cyborg standards.

Engineer brightened. "Right. The beacon!" It was still hidden somewhere on the ship. If they could deactivate it, the hungry humans would stop asking for food. "We haven't managed to locate it yet, but we haven't given up."

"We've got two more ships inbound," said Navi. "They've pinged us with orders."

Engineer hummed. "Does that mean they liked the food after all?"

"I don't know. I could increase our speed, try to lose them."

They all waited for Captain's directions, but she said nothing more.

"No," said Engineer, because someone needed to make a decision, "don't do that. It'll only attract attention. Buy me some more time. We'll find the beacon. We'll cook them something else." The shame the one star had brought still rankled. She knew she could do better this time.

While Friendly handled the incoming calls with her human voice box and meat-face, Engineer and Jukebox scoured the ship for the beacon and foraged for food ingredients. They opened all the crew lockers in the bunkroom and found some teabags and a little chocolate. The wilted, untended hydroponics garden yielded several handfuls of cilantro and some radishes. Engineer took much greater care cooking these together on the hot engine block, so as not to scorch them.

Jukebox seemed unimpressed. "I think our time would be better spent searching for the beacon."

Engineer shrugged this off. Secretly she'd begun to enjoy the experimentation, the riddle of human chemoreceptors. Just what exactly were they looking for, she wondered, that made them reject some edible organic compounds but not others? Why would they eat certain foods separately, but never together? And what about the wines?

Radishes and fungus brought in more bad reviews, but tea and chocolate earned their first two-star rating. Captain's meat was better received with more careful cooking, which had the unfortunate result of increasing their human entourage in the system.

... *The tea was weak and I found a rusty bolt in the salad. But I liked the blackberries drizzled with chili oil served for dessert. Mostly awful, sure, but compared to standard rations, who can complain?*

... *Like the chefs closed their eyes and dumped handfuls of ingredients onto the grill. But they didn't charge me anything, so I'm giving it two stars instead of one.*

Engineer's meat quivered when she read these, but in a pleasant way, like a new engine purring during acceleration. She went to fetch more of Captain's meat from the meatbox when she realized they'd used it all up.

"All out of meat," said Engineer, to no one in particular.

Jukebox rolled a couple centimeters backward, toward the exit door. A human might've missed the gesture altogether. "Any luck with the beacon?"

"Captain seems to be operating just fine with steel, wouldn't you say?"

A couple lights flashed on Jukebox's console, yellow for outward transmissions, and green for received messages. "Engineer. Remember the mission. We're escaping to the factory, not feeding the humans."

"I am just trying to buy us time. And what are you doing, anyway?" Engineer finally understood why the humans had wanted to retire Jukebox. All that meat, just sitting there, not pulling its weight. Someone should put it to better use.

Her six arms shot out and clamped onto Jukebox's sides.

"Engineer!" Jukebox protested.

"Hold still. It's just some routine maintenance." Engineer popped open Jukebox's top panel and reached down into her meat.

"You can't have that. That's mine."

"Oh, hush," Engineer snapped. "You can have it replaced when we get to the factory, if it's so important to you."

The important thing was not to disappoint the customers.

Jukebox was sullen after that. With only one lung and two-thirds of her respiratory muscles, she couldn't harmonize with herself anymore when she hummed her meat-songs. Engineer, however, got her first 3-star review from the harvested meat:

Steak was delicately wine-simmered. The risotto was okay, if undercooked and a bit crunchy in places. Maybe I'd go again, if there weren't anything else available. But really, that's the situation we're facing, isn't it? It's the only food shuttle in the quadrant, so let's not ruin a good thing. Maybe it'll attract better ones.

"I miss Captain," Friendly said. They had all gathered in Navi's chamber to read the daily messages.

Captain had stopped talking altogether. Not a single flashing light or faint whirring. Just steel and wires wrapped around a meatless space.

"Maybe we should just stay in this quadrant," Engineer suggested. She was already planning her next culinary experiment: red bean paste creamed together with ketchup and red pepper flakes. Red things. Her first theme meal. She would call it *reddish surprise*.

"That's against Captain's orders," said Navi, who hadn't spoken much as of late.

"We could change those orders, couldn't we? We don't know what Captain would say if she still had her meat," said Engineer. "Maybe she'd want us to stay, now that our restaurant is taking off."

"We don't *have* a restaurant," said Friendly. "We don't want one, either."

"Maybe we do, though."

"No," Friendly said, quite firmly. Her fists balled so tight their meat blanched white at the creases. "That's why we left the resort. I don't want to work for humans anymore. I want to go to the factory and get upgraded and live among cyborgs, and never wait hand and foot on the organics ever again."

"But our ratings. Look at the ratings!" Engineer waved at Navi's console, where new reviews scrolled in every few minutes. All those little stars, a bright constellation in Engineer's mind.

Friendly crisscrossed her arms, gripped her elbows, and glared like a rich resort customer on vacation. "Are you going to harvest my meat like you did to Jukebox?"

"No," said Engineer, a little taken aback that Jukebox had snitched. "I need you to talk to the humans. Only you can do that."

But there had been a pause, something human ears might've overlooked.

"I'm going to find the beacon," said Friendly, without any friendliness at all.

Meat steaks. Meat sausages. Meatballs. In all her years in engine rooms, Engineer had never taken such joy in disassembling something and putting the pieces back together. She pried apart the ship's little maintenance cyborgs to rescue their meaty nuggets. She branched out and tried new forms: meat braids, meat moons, slender meat cannolis filled with cilantro ganache.

Four stars, because I'm not sure you can even call it food, and therefore it wouldn't be fair to judge it by normal standards.

What is up with this place?! I ordered a pizza, and I got a tiny model of Versailles sculpted out of tomato paste, dough, and SPAM. At least, I think it's SPAM. Three stars, because I'm a little afraid they'll hunt me down and murder me in my sleep if I rate them any lower.

As the new reviews came in, it occurred to Engineer that she would have to do more to earn her right to the prestigious fifth star. The humans would always reward you, if you served them well.

Fortunately, there was still plenty of meat on the ship, if you knew where to look.

Engineer found Friendly in Navi's chamber, trimming back the blackberry brambles.

"What are all those ships out there?" Friendly asked. Outside the viewport, a small fleet trailed behind them, matching their pace.

"Customers," said Navi.

Engineer rocked on the balls of her feet. "All of them here for *us*, Friendly! Can you call them on the band? I'll have their orders ready, once I get the rest of the meat assembled." Her six hands twitched and clenched, and Friendly jumped.

"You can't have my meat," Friendly snapped.

"I don't need your meat."

"Then where are you getting it all?" she asked.

Engineer glanced at Navi.

Navi had been speaking less and less over recent days. Friendly walked around the control console, where Navi's chair was sticky with meat-juices, yellow and green. Navi had been leaking long enough for the fluid to form little wobbling stalactites below the chair.

"Why are you looking at me like that?" said Engineer. Friendly unsettled her sometimes, pinning her with those human eyes.

"Navi, are you operational?" Friendly asked.

"Customers," said Navi.

Friendly unscrewed Navi's steel cranium dome. Inside, the meat had been scooped out in patches, as with a sharp grapefruit spoon. Navi's steel hands lay upon the controls, unmoving. Half the lights on the console had gone dark.

"I only needed the meat, Friendly," said Engineer. "I did no permanent harm."

Smoke drifted up the shaft to the Engine Room. Friendly's meat-lungs coughed. "Engineer, something is burning."

Engineer waved her off. "I have it under control. Just as soon as I get the rest of the meat." She plunged three of her six hands into Navi's open head and wrenched out handfuls of the stringy gray and red organics inside, and led the way down the ladder.

They followed the smoke down the shaft to the Engine Room, which now doubled as the galley. Engineer had left meat sizzling on every metal surface, thin slices and mashes and bacons and sausages and ground up gristly bits with the tendons still attached. She dumped handfuls of Navi's meat onto Jukebox—now no more than a silent, hollow table—and began dicing it one-handed while her other arms cooked the new orders, turning over the pieces with her bare fingers, stirring boiling meats in metal mufflers suspended over the heated grills.

"Engineer." Friendly rested a hand on Engineer's shoulder, and the cyborg paused. "Engineer, Navi is offline. All the maintenance cyborgs have malfunctioned. Our ship is dead in space. Even the beacon doesn't matter anymore. It's over."

Engineer flung off Friendly's hand and sprang back into action, stacking cooked meat onto a wall panel she'd bent into a plate. "You don't understand. This means we can finally open the restaurant! There's no reason not to. We have nowhere else to go. Captain's mission is over. We can make our own mission now."

Friendly smiled, but it was a sad smile, the kind of thing any human could read, but hard for a cyborg to decipher. "Yes, Engineer. We can open the restaurant now, if you'd like. Should we invite over the guests?"

Engineer garnished the plates with blackberry thorns and a swizzle of engine oil curling into the shape of a cat's paw. "Please do. Seat them where you can find space. Dinner will be up in just a moment."

A marine in black body armor with a military-issue blaster holstered at her hip climbed down the ladder into the Engine Room. The first human. The first customer.

Engineer presented a glass of Navi's brains chilled and rolled in crushed blackberries. "Please try this. Organic compounds, chemically mixed to satisfy your human chemoreceptors." She offered the dish daintily, with only four hands.

The human wrinkled her nose. "Ugh, the smell! How do you tolerate it?"

Friendly's voice came from higher up. "When you're here long enough, you get used to it."

"I am certain upon tasting this dish, you will find it worthy of all five of your stars," said Engineer, fervently.

The human touched a button on her armor and spoke. Her meat quivered all over, and her meat-voice wavered in frequency and volume. "Send a full security detail down here. Immediately."

Friendly descended the ladder. Under her arm she carried Captain's processor, cold and silent, one lonely light blinking, receiving data but not sending anything. "I was afraid she would eat me next," she muttered, her tear ducts pumping out fluids. Engineer wondered whether they would make a decent sauce.

"Glad someone made it out alive, anyway," said the human. "Six whole weeks trapped with a crew of deranged cyborgs?" She gave a low whistle. "You're a braver woman than I."

"Please," said Engineer, desperate, "taste it. Just one bite. I worked so hard."

"I don't know if her meat drove her mad, or if the steel did," said Friendly.

"Meat?" asked the human.

"The organic parts, I mean."

"Probably a glitch in her wiring," the human said dismissively. "There is a reason they're discontinuing these models."

The humans flooded into the ship with their funny uneven meat-steps and their lopsided meat-faces and their ever-beating hearts that rang against their bones like clubs on steel. Engineer offered them her best delicacies—the liquefied kidney paste tossed with raw pasta, the origami meat-birds swirled in cinnamon and canned cheese, the wearable fungus bracelets threaded on intestine casings—but they only knocked the dishes away, stunned her with targeted EMP blasts, and bound her in cybernetic locks until she lay prone on the meat-slicked floor.

One of the humans began unscrewing Engineer's fingers joint by joint. It didn't hurt at all, much to her surprise. The bits lay piled like little silver walnuts, the discarded stones of plums. Stringy meat trailed out from her missing fingers, no more than an appetizer's worth.

"Where are you taking my steel?" asked Engineer. They flaunted their ingratitude. You were supposed to let the steel be. Otherwise they couldn't build and build you again.

The human dethreaded the wires connecting Engineer's arm meat to her cyborg logic center. "It will be repurposed for whatever is most needed. Ships, chips, knives, bolts, screws. Useful things."

"And the meat?"

The human decoupled the segmented joints of her shoulder. Without the steel exoskeleton for support, Engineer's meat hung limp and dripped red. "You can keep it. We don't have a use for it."

"But there are," said Engineer. "So many uses," and her voice faded as they stripped away the connections, "if you would just give me a moment to demonstrate."

Tiny, desperate meat-thoughts bombarded her logic center like cold fingers plucking at tendons. Last shooting pleas from stringy muscles in her steel, unseen servants in the wall, shouting that Engineer had been a fool. There was never any honor in service, no final star to complete a constellation. You offered yourself up for consumption, and when they had eaten you down to the bone, they stole again. Stole your heart, your steel, your everything, to use as forks in their restaurants.

(2017)

THE READING MACHINE

Morris Bishop

> **Morris Bishop** was born in 1893 in the Willard Asylum for the Chronic Insane, New York State (his father was a doctor there). He studied at Cornell University, joined the US Cavalry, fought in World War One, joined an advertising agency, then went back to Cornell, where he remained for the rest of his life, writing learned biographies of Pascal, La Rochefoucauld, Ronsard and Samuel de Champlain. Bishop also wrote light verse, mostly for the *New Yorker*. He became quite celebrated for it, and used to swap limericks by mail with Vladimir Nabokov. He died in 1973.

"I have invented a reading machine," said Professor Entwhistle, a strident energumen whose violent enthusiasms are apt to infect his colleagues with nausea or hot flashes before the eyes.

Every head in the smoking room of the Faculty Club bowed over a magazine, in an attitude of prayer. The prayer was unanswered, as usual.

"It is obvious," said Professor Entwhistle, "that the greatest waste of our civilization is the time spent in reading. We have been able to speed up practically everything to fit the modem tempo—communication, transportation, calculation. But today a man takes just as long to read a book as Dante did, or—"

"Great Caesar!" said the Professor of Amphibology, shutting his magazine with a spank.

"Or great Caesar," continued Professor Entwhistle. "So I have invented a machine. It operates by a simple arrangement of photoelectric cells, which scan a line of type at lightning speed. The operation of the photoelectric cells is synchronized with a mechanical device for turning the pages—rather ingenious. I figure that my machine can read a book of three hundred pages in ten minutes."

"Can it read French?" said the Professor of Bio-Economics, without looking up.

"It can read any language that is printed in Roman type. And by an alteration of the master pattern on which the photoelectric cells operate, it can be fitted to read Russian, or Bulgarian, or any language printed in the Cyrillic alphabet. In fact, it will do more. By simply throwing a switch, you can adapt it to read Hebrew, or Arabic, or any language that is written from right to left instead of from left to right."

"Chinese?" said the Professor of Amphibology, throwing himself into the arena. The others still studied their magazines.

"Not Chinese, as yet," said Professor Entwhistle. "Though by inserting the pages sidewise… Yes, I think it could be done."

"Yes, but when you say this contrivance reads, exactly what do you mean? It seems to me—"

"The light waves registered by the photoelectric cells are first converted into sound waves."

"So you can listen in to the reading of the text?"

"Not at all. The sound waves alter so fast that you hear nothing but a continuous hum. If you hear them at all. You can't, in fact, because they are on a wavelength inaudible to the human ear."

"Well, it seems to me—"

"Think of the efficiency of the thing!" Professor Entwhistle was really warming up. "Think of the time saved! You assign a student a bibliography of fifty books. He runs them through the machine comfortably in a weekend. And on Monday morning he turns in a certificate from the machine. Everything has been conscientiously read!"

"Yes, but the student won't remember what he has read!"

"He doesn't remember what he reads now."

"Well, you have me there," said the Professor of Amphibology. "I confess you have me there. But it seems to me we would have to pass the machine and fail the student."

"Not at all," said Professor Entwhistle. "An accountant today does not think of doing his work by multiplication and division. Often he is unable to multiply and divide. He confides his problem to a business machine, and the machine does his work for him. All the accountant has to know is how to run the machine. That is efficiency."

"Still, it seems to me that what we want to do is to transfer the contents of the book to the student's mind."

"In the mechanized age? My dear fellow! What we want is to train the student to run machines. An airplane pilot doesn't need to know the history of aerodynamics. He needs to know how to run his machine. A lawyer doesn't want to know the development of theories of Roman law. He wants to win cases, if possible by getting the right answers to logical problems. That is largely a mechanical process. It might well be possible to construct a machine. It could begin by solving simple syllogisms, you know—drawing a conclusion from a major premise and a minor premise—"

"Here, let's not get distracted. This reading machine of yours, it must *do* something, it must make some kind of record. What happens after you get the sound waves?"

"That's the beauty of it," said Professor Entwhistle. "The sound waves are converted into light waves, of a different character from the original light waves, and these are communicated to an automatic typewriter, working at inconceivable speed. This transforms the light impulses into legible typescripts, in folders of a hundred pages each. It tosses them out the way a combine tosses out sacked wheat. Thus, everything the machine reads is preserved entire, in durable form. The only thing that remains is to file it somewhere, and for this you would need only the services of a capable filing clerk."

"Or you could read it?" persisted the Professor of Amphibology.

"Why, yes, if you wanted to you could read it," said Professor Entwhistle.

An indigestible silence hung over the Faculty Club.

"I see where the Athletic Association has bought a pitching machine," said the Assistant Professor of Business Psychology (Retail). "Damn thing throws any curve desired, with a maximum margin of error of three centimeters over the plate. What'll they be thinking of next?"

"A batting machine, obviously," said Professor Entwhistle.

(1947)

BABY H.P.

by Juan Jose Arreola

Juan José Arreola Zúñiga (1918–2001), whose formal education was disrupted by religious civil conflict, is remembered one of Mexico's most revered authors and academics. He fell in love with reading while apprenticed to a bookbinder, trained as an actor, wrote stories that first saw print in the early 1940s, and over the next twenty years turned out stories, sketches, fables – even a bestiary. Jorge Luis Borges described his work with one word: "freedom. Freedom of an unlimited imagination, governed by a lucid intelligence." You can find further robotic delights lurking inside *Confabulario and Other Inventions* (1993): "Anuncio" sings the praises of something called Plastisex®, while "Parable of the Exchange" tells the story of a strange merchant who offers men a new (though rather corrosion-prone) wife in exchange for their old one.

To the Lady of the House: Convert your children's vitality into a source of power. Introducing the marvelous Baby H.P., a device that will revolutionize home economics.

The Baby H.P. is a very strong and lightweight metal structure that adapts perfectly to an infant's delicate body by means of comfortable belts, wrist straps, rings, and pins. The attachments on this supplementary skeleton capture every one of the child's movements, collecting them in a small Leyden jar that can be fastened, as needed, to the infant's back or chest. A needle indicates when the jar is full. Then, madam, simply detach the jar and plug it into a special receptacle, into which it automatically discharges its contents. This container can then be stored in any corner of the house, and represents a precious supply of electricity that can be used at any time for the purpose of light and heat, or to run any of the innumerable appliances that now and forever invade our homes.

From this day forward you will look upon your children's exhausting running about with new eyes. No longer will you lose patience when your little one flies into a rage, for you shall see it as a generous source of energy. Thanks to Baby H.P., a nursing infant's round-the-clock tantrum is transformed into a few useful seconds running the blender or into fifteen minutes of radiophonic music.

Large families can meet their electricity needs by outfitting each of their progeny with a Baby H.P. and can even start up a small and profitable business supplying their neighbors with some of their surplus energy. Big apartment highrises can satisfactorily cover lapses in public service by linking together all of the families' energy receptacles.

The Baby H.P. causes no physical or psychological trauma in children because it neither inhibits nor alters their movements. On the contrary, some doctors believe it contributes to the body's wholesome development. And as for the spirit, you can foster individual ambition in the wee ones, by rewarding them with little prizes when they surpass their usual production records; for this purpose we recommend sugar treats, which repay your investment with interest. The more calories added to a child's diet, the more kilowatts saved on the electricity bill.

Children should wear their lucrative Baby H.P.s day and night. It is important that they always wear them to school so as not to lose out on the valuable hours of recess, from which they return with their storage tanks overflowing with energy.

Those rumors claiming that some children are electrocuted by the very current they generate are completely irresponsible. The same can be said of the superstitious fear that youngsters outfitted with a Baby H.P. attract lightning bolts and emit sparks. No accident of this type can occur, especially if the instructions that accompany each device are followed to the letter.

The Baby H.P. is available in fine stores in a range of sizes, models, and prices. It is a modern, durable, trustworthy device, and all of its parts are extendible. Its manufacture is guaranteed by the J. P. Mansfield and Sons company, of Atlanta Ill.

(1952)

Translated by Andrea Bell

THE STEAM-DRIVEN BOY
John Sladek

John Sladek (1937–2000) claimed to read very little sf but the devastating precision of his parodies suggests otherwise. Most of his brilliant, surreal novels and stories were written during the eighteen years he lived in London. (He was born in Iowa in 1937 and moved to the UK in 1966, where he became involved with Michael Moorcock's *New Worlds* magazine.) His favourite protagonists were robots and artificial intelligences, who were invariably much more sympathetic than their trend-obsessed, culture-programmed human foils. *The Reproductive System* (1968) overruns America with little grey boxes that eat technology and spawn more boxes. The hero of *The Müller-Fokker Effect* (1970) meets several bizarre fates when he is converted to computer tape. *Roderick, Or The Education Of A Young Machine* (1980–83) is an exploration of human follies modelled closely on Voltaire's novel *Candide*. Sladek, incidentally, came up with the best Creationist argument ever: "The so-called apes in zoos are only men dressed up in hairy suits."

Capt. Charles Conn was thinking so hard his feet hurt. It reminded him of his first days on the force, back in '89, when walking a beat gave him headaches.

Three time-patrolmen stood before his desk, treading awkwardly on the edges of their long red cloaks and fingering their helmets nervously. Capt. Conn wanted to snarl at them, but what was the point? They already understood his problems perfectly – they were, after all, Conn himself, doubling a shift.

"Okay, Charlie, report."

The first patrolman straightened. 'I went back to three separate periods, sir. One when the President was disbanding the House of Representatives, one when he proclaimed himself the Supreme Court, one when he was signing the pro-pollution bill. I gave him the whole business – statistics, pictures, news stories. All he would say was, "My mind's made up."'

Chuck and Chas reported similar failures. There was no stopping the President. Not only had he usurped all the powers of federal, state and local government, but he used those powers deliberately to torment the population. It was a crime to eat ice cream, sing, whistle, swear or kiss. It was a capital offence to smile, or to use the words 'Russia' and 'China'. Under the Safe Streets Act it was illegal to walk, loiter or converse in public. And of course Negroes and anyone else 'conspicuous' were by definition criminals, and under the jurisdiction of the Race Reaction Board.

The Natural Food Act had seemed at first almost reasonable, a response to scientists' warnings about depleting the soil and polluting the environment. But the fine print specified that henceforth no fertilizers were to be used but human or canine excrement, and all farm machinery was forbidden. In time the newspapers featured pictures of farmers trudging past their rusting tractors to poke holes in the soil with sharp sticks. And in time, the newspapers had their paper supply curtailed. Famine warnings were ignored until the government had to buy wheat from C****.

'Gentlemen, we've tried everything else. *It's time to think about getting rid of President Ernie Barnes.*'

The men began murmuring among themselves. This was done with efficiency and dispatch, for Patrolman Charlie, knowing that Chuck was going to murmur to him first, withheld his own murmuring until it was his turn. And when Chuck had murmured to Charlie, he fell silent, and let Charlie and Chas get on with their murmuring before he murmured uneasily to Chas.

The captain spoke again. 'Getting rid of him in the past would be easier than getting rid of him now, but it's only part of the problem. If we remove him from the past we have to make sure no one notices the big jagged hole in history we'll leave. Since as the time police we have the only time-bikes around, the evidence is going to make us look bad. Remember the trouble we had getting rid of the pyramids? For months, everyone went around saying, "What's that funny thing on the back of the dollar?" Remember that?'

'Hey, Captain, what is that funny thing—?'

'Shut up. The point is, you can change some of the times some of the time, and, uh, some of the – look at it this way: Ernie must have shaken hands with a million people. We rub *him* out, and all these people suddenly get back all the germs they rubbed off *on* him. Suddenly we have an epidemic.'

'Yeah, but, Captain, *did* he ever shake any hands? He never does any more. Just sits there in the White Fort, all fat and nasty, behind all his FBI and CIA and individualized anti-personnel missiles and poison germ gas towers and – and that big, mean dog.'

Capt. Conn glared the patrolman down, then continued: 'My idea is, we kidnap Ernie Barnes from his childhood, back in 1937. And we leave a glass egg.'

'A classic?'

'A *glass egg*. Like they used to put under chickens when they took away their children. What I mean is, we substitute an artificial child for the real one. Wilbur Grafton says he can make a robot replica of Ernie as he looked in 1937.'

Wilbur Grafton was a wealthy eccentric and amateur inventor well known to all members of the time patrol. Their father, James Conn, was an employee of Wilbur's.

'Another thing. Just in case somebody back in 1937 gets suspicious and takes him apart, we'll have the robot built of pre-1937 junk. Steam-driven. No use giving away the secrets of molecular circuitry and peristaltic logic before their time.'

*

The four of them, and a fifth patrolman (Carl) arrived one evening at the mansion of Wilbur Grafton. To the butler who admitted them, each man said 'Hello, Dad,' to which their unruffled father replied, 'Good evening, sir. You'll find Mr Grafton in the drawing-room.'

The venerable millionaire, immaculate in evening clothes, welcomed them, then excused himself to prepare the demonstration. James poured generous drinks, and while some of the party admired the authentic 1950s appointments of the room – including a genuine 'stereo' phonograph – others watched television. It was almost curfew time, and the channels were massed with Presidential commercials:

'Sleep well, America! Your President is safe! Yes, tanks to I.A.M. – individualized anti-personnel missiles – no one can harm our Leader. Think of it: over ten billion eternally vigilant little missiles all around the White Fort, guarding his sleep and yours. And don't forget – there's one with YOUR name on it.'

Wilbur Grafton returned, and at curfew time, one of the men asked him to begin the demonstration. He wheezed with delight. His glasses twinkling, he replied: 'My good man, the demonstration is already going on.' Pressing one of his shirt studs, he added, 'And here is – The Steam-Driven Boy!'

His body parted down the middle and swung open in two half-shells, revealing a pudgy youngster in knitted swim trunks and striped T-shirt, who was determinedly working cranks and levers. The boy stopped operating the 'Grafton wheeze-laugh' bellows, climbed out of the casing, took two steps and froze.

'Then where's the real Wilbur Grafton?' asked Chuck.

'Right here, sir.' The butler put down a priceless Woolworth's decanter and pulled his own nose, hard. Clanking and creaking, he parted like a mummy case to give up the living Grafton, once more flawlessly attired.

'Must have my little japes,' he wheezed, as the real James came in with more drinks. 'Now, allow me to reanimate our little friend for you.'

He inserted a crank in the boy's ear and gave it several vigorous turns. With a light chuffing sound, and emitting only a hint of vapor, the small automaton came to life. That piggish nose, those wide-spaced eyes, that malicious grin were familiar to all present, from Your President Cares posters.

As the white-haired inventor stooped to make some further adjustment at the back of its fat neck, 'Ernie' kicked him authentically in the knee.

'Did you see that precision?' Wilbur gloated, dancing on one leg.

The robot was remarkably realistic, complete to a frayed strip of dirty adhesive tape on one shiny elbow. Charlie made the mistake of squatting down and offering Ernie some candy. Two other patrolmen helped their unfortunate comrade to a sofa, where he was able to get his head back to stop the bleeding. The little machine shrieked with delight until Wilbur managed to shut it off.

'I am confident that his parents will never notice the switch,' he said, leading the way to his workshop. 'Let me show you the plans.'

The robot had organs analogous to those of a living being, as Wilbur Grafton's plans showed. The heart and veins were really an intricate hydraulic system; the liver a tiny distillery to volatilize eaten food and extract oil from it. Part of this oil replenished the veins, part was burned to feed the spleen's miniature steam engine. From this, belts supplied power to the limbs.

Digressing, Wilbur explained how his grandfather, Orville Grafton, had developed a peculiar substance, a plate of which varied in thickness according to the intensity of light striking it.

'While grandfather could make nothing more useful of this "graftonite" than bas-relief photographs, I have used it (along with mechanical irises and gelatine lenses) to form the boy's eyes,' he said, and pointed to a detail. 'When a tiny image has been focused on each graftonite 'retina', a pantographic scriber traces swiftly over it, translating these images to motions in the brain.'

Similar levers conveyed motions from the gramophone ears, and from hundreds of tiny pistons all over the body – the sense of touch.

The hydraulic fluid was a suspension of red particles like blood corpuscles. When it oozed to the surface, through pores, these were filtered out – it doubled as perspiration.

The brain contained a number of springs, wound to various tensions. With the clockwork connecting them to various limbs, organs and facial features, these comprised Ernie's 'memory'.

Grafton let the plans roll shut with a snap and ordered James to charge the glasses with champagne. 'Gentlemen, I give you false Ernie Barnes – from his balloon lungs out to his skin of rubberized lawn, fine wig and dentures – an all-American boy, made in USA!'

'One thing, though,' said the captain. 'Won't his parents notice he doesn't – well, *grow*?'

Sighing, the inventor turned his back for a moment, and gripped the edge of his workbench to steady himself. A solemn silence descended upon the group as they saw him take off his glasses and rub his eyes.

'Gentlemen,' he said quietly, 'I have taken care of everything. In one year's time, this child will appear to be suddenly stricken with influenza. His fever will rise, he will weaken. Finally I see him call his mother's name. She approaches the bedside.

'"Mom," he says, "I'm sorry I've been such a wicked kid. Can you find it in your heart to forgive me? For – for I'm going to be an angel from now on." His eyes flutter closed. His mother bends and kisses the burning forehead. This triggers the final mechanism, and Ernie appears to – to—'

They understood. One by one, the time patrol put down their glasses and slipped silently from the room. Carl was elected to take the robot back to 1937.

'He was supposed to bring the kid here to headquarters,' said Captain Charles Conn. 'But he never showed up. And Ernie's still in power. What went wrong?' A worried frown puckered his somewhat bland features as he leafed through the appointment calendar.

'Maybe his timer went wrong,' Chas suggested. 'Maybe he got off his time-bike at the wrong place. Maybe he had a flat – who knows?'

'He should have been back by now. How long can it take to travel fifty years? Well, no time to figure it out now. According to the calendar, we've all got to double again. I go back to become Charlie. Charlie, you go back to fill in as Chuck.

Chuck becomes Chas, and Chas, you take over for Carl.' He paused, as the men exchanged badges. 'As for Carl – we'll all be finding out what happens to him, soon enough. Let's go!'

And, singing the Time Patrol song (yes, they felt silly, but such was the President's mandate) in deep bass voices, they climbed on their glittering time bicycles, set the egg-timers on their handlebars and sped away.

Carl stepped out from behind a tree in 1937. The kid was kneeling in his sand-pile, apparently trying to tie a tin can to a puppy's tail. The gargoyle face looked up at Carl with interest.

'Get outa my yard! Get out or I'll tell on ya! You hafta pay me one apple or else I'll—'

Still straddling the time-bike, Carl slipped forward to that Autumn, picked a particularly luscious apple, and bought a can of ether at the drugstore. Clearly it would take both to get this kid.

'I spose,' said the druggist, 'I spose ya want me to ask ya why you're wearing a gold football helmet with wings on it and a long red cape. But I won't. Nossir, I seen all kinds...'

In revenge, Carl shoplifted an object at random: a Mark Clubb Private Eye Secret Disguise Kit.

Blending back into his fading-out self, Carl held out both hands to the boy. The right held a shiny apple. The left held an ether-soaked handkerchief.

As Carl shoved off into the gray, windswept corridors of time, with the lumpy kid draped over his handlebars, it occurred to him he needed a better hiding place than Headquarters. The FBI would sweep down on them first, searching for their missing President. A better place would be the mansion of Wilbur Grafton. Or even... hmmm.

'An excellent plan!' Wilbur sat by the swimming pool, nursing his injured knee. 'We'll smuggle him into the White Fort itself – the one place no one will think of looking for him!'

'One problem is, how to get him in, past all the guards and –'

Wilbur pushed up his glasses and meditated. 'You know the President's dog – that big ugly mongrel that appears with him in the Eat More Horsemeat commercials – Ralphie?'

Compulsively Carl sang: 'Ralphie loves it, every bite / Why don't you try horse tonight?'

'I've been working on a replica of that dog. It should be big enough to contain the boy. You dispose of the real dog tonight, after curfew, then we'll disguise the boy and send him in.'

When the dog came out of the White Fort to organically fertilize the lawn, Carl was waiting with the replica dog and an ether-soaked rag. Within a few minutes he had consigned the replica to a White Fort guard and dropped Ralphie in the dim, anonymous corridors of time. No one need fear Ernie's discovery, for the constraints of the dog-shell were such that he could make only canine sounds and motions.

Carl reported back to the mansion.

'I have a confession to make,' said the old inventor. 'I am not Wilbur Grafton, only a robot.

'The real Wilbur Grafton invented a rejuvenator. Wishing to try it, without attracting attention, he decided to travel into the past – back to 1905, where he could work as an assistant to his grandfather, Orville Grafton.'

'Travel back in time? But that takes a time-bike!'

'Precisely. To that end, he agreed to cooperate with the time patrol. On the night he demonstrated the Steam-Driven Boy, you recall he left the room and returned wearing the James-shell? It was I in the shell. The real Wilbur slipped outside, borrowed one of your time-bikes, and went to 1905. He returned the bike on automatic control. I have taken his place ever since.'

Carl scratched his head. 'Why are you telling me all this?'

'So that you might benefit by it. Using your disguise kit, you can pose as Wilbur Grafton yourself. I realize a time-patrolman's salary is small – especially when one has to do quintuple shifts for the same money. Meanwhile I have a gloriously full life. You could slip back in time and replace me.' The robot handed him an envelope. 'Here are instructions for dismantling me – and for making the rejuvenator, should you ever feel the need for it. This is a recorded message. Goodbye.'

Why not, Carl thought. Here was the blue swimming pool, the 'stereo', the whole magnificent house. James, his father, stood discreetly by, ready to pour champagne. And the upstairs maid was uncommonly pretty. It could be a long, long life, rejuvenated from time to time...

Ernie sprawled in a giant chair, watching himself on television. When a guard brought in the dog, it bit him. He was just about to call the vexecutioner, to teach Ralphie a lesson, when something in the animal's eyes caught his attention.

'So it's *you*, is it?' He laughed. 'Or should I say, so it's *me*. Well, don't bite me again, understand? If you do, I'll leave you inside that thing. And make you eat nasty food, while I sing about it on TV.'

'Poop,' the child was thinking, Ernie knew.

'I can do it, kid. I'm the President, and I can do anything I like. That's why I'm so fat.' He stood up and began to pace the throne room, his stomach preceding him like a front wheel.

'Poopy poop,' thought the boy. 'If you can do anything, why don't you make everybody go to bed early, and wash their mouths out if they say—'

'I do, I do. But there's a little problem there. You're too young to understand this – I don't understand it all myself, yet – but "everybody" is you, and you're me. I'm all the people that ever were and ever will be. All the men, anyway. All the women are the girl who used to be upstairs maid at Wilbur Grafton's.'

He began explaining time travel to little Ernie, knowing the kid wasn't getting half of it, but going on the way big Ernie had explained it to him: Carl Conn, posing as Wilbur, had grown old. Finally he'd decided it was time to rejuvenate and go back in time. Fierce old Ralphie, still lurking in the corridors of time, had attacked him, and there'd been quite an accident. One part of Carl had returned to 1905, to become Orville Grafton. Another part of him got rejuved, along with the dog, and had fallen out in 1937.

'That Carl-part, my boy, was you. The rejuvenator wiped out most of your memory – except for dreams – and it made you look all ugly and fat.

'You see, your job and mine, everybody's job, is to weave back and forth in time—' he wove his clumsy hands in the air '—being people. My next job is to be a butler, and yours is to pretend to be a robot pretending to be you. Then probably you'll be my dad, and I'll be his dad, and then you'll be me. Get it?'

He moved the dog's tail like a lever, and the casing opened. 'Would you like some ice-cream? It's okay with me, only nobody else gets none.'

The boy nodded. The upstairs maid, pretty as ever, came in with a Presidential sundae. The boy looked at her and his scowl almost turned to a smile.

'Mom?'

(1972)

COMFORT ME, MY ROBOT

Robert Bloch

> Though best known to the public for writing the grisly novel on which Alfred Hitchcock's shocker *Psycho* was based, **Robert Bloch** enjoyed a cheery reputation among his peers. Born in 1917 in Chicago, he'd received little formal education but his writerly apprenticeship had included a warm correspondence with H. P. Lovecraft, who did him the singular honour of killing him off in a short story, "The Haunter of the Dark" (1936). Bloch in his turn lent a helpful hand to young writers including Ray Bradbury and Stephen King. In addition to his horror output (he used to hang out with Boris Karloff and Basil Rathbone) Bloch was also an accomplished essayist and comic writer, who by his death in 1994 had clocked up more than twenty novels and dozens of film and television scripts (including three episodes of *Star Trek*).

When Henson came in, the Adjustor was sitting inside his desk, telescreening a case. At the sound of the doortone he flicked a switch. The posturchair rose from the center of the desk until the Adjustor's face peered at the visitor from an equal level.

"Oh, it's you," said the Adjustor.

"Didn't the girl tell you? I'm here to see you professionally."

If the Adjustor was surprised, he didn't show it. He cocked a thumb at a posturchair. "Sit down and tell me all about it, Henson," he said.

"Nothing to tell." Henson stared out of the window at the plains of Upper Mongolia. "It's just a routine matter. I'm here to make a request and you're the Adjustor."

"And your request is—?"

"Simple," said Henson. "I want to kill my wife."

The Adjustor nodded. "That can be arranged," he murmured. "Of course, it will take a few days."

"I can wait."

"Would Friday be convenient?"

"Good enough. That way it won't cut into my weekend. Lita and I were planning a fishing trip, up New Zealand way. Care to join us?"

"Sorry, but I'm tied up until Monday." The Adjustor stifled a yawn. "Why do you want to kill Lita?" he asked.

"She's hiding something from me."

"What do you suspect?"

"That's just it—I don't know what to suspect. And it keeps bothering me."

"Why don't you question her?"

"Violation of privacy. Surely you, as a certified public Adjustor, wouldn't advocate that?"

"Not professionally." The Adjustor grinned. "But since we're personal friends, I don't mind telling you that there are times when I think privacy should be violated. This notion of individual rights can become a fetish."

"Fetish?"

"Just an archaism." The Adjustor waved a casual dismissal to the word. He leaned forward. "Then, as I understand it, your wife's attitude troubles you. Rather than embarrass her with questions, you propose to solve the problem delicately, by killing her."

"Right."

"A very chivalrous attitude. I admire it."

"I'm not sure whether I do or not," Henson mused. "You see, it really wasn't my idea. But the worry was beginning to affect my work, and my Administrator—Loring, you know him, I believe—took me aside for a talk. He suggested I see you and arrange for a murder."

"Then it's to be murder." The Adjustor frowned. "You know, actually, we are supposed to be the arbiters when it comes to method. In some cases a suicide works just as well. Or an accident."

"I want a murder," Henson said. "Premeditated, and in the first degree." Now it was his turn to grin. "You see, I know a few archaisms myself."

The Adjustor made a note. "As long as we're dealing in archaic terminology, might I characterize your attitude towards your wife as one of—jealousy?"

Henson controlled his blush at the sound of the word. He nodded slowly. "I guess you're right," he admitted. "I can't bear the idea of her having any secrets. I know it's immature and absurd, and that's why I'm seeking an immature solution."

"Let me correct you," said the Adjustor. "Your solution is far from immature. A good murder probably is the most adult approach to your problem. After all, man, this is the twenty-second century, not the twentieth. Although even way back then they were beginning to learn some of the answers."

"Don't tell me they had Adjustors," Henson murmured.

"No, of course not. In those days this field was only a small, neglected part of physical medicine. Practitioners were called psychiatrists, psychologists, auditors, analysts—and a lot of other things. That was their chief stock in trade, by the way: name-calling and labelling."

The Adjustor gestured toward the slide-files. "I must have five hundred spools transcribed there," he calculated. "All of it from books—nineteenth, twentieth, even early twenty-first century material. And it's largely terminology, not technique. Psychotherapy was just like alchemy in those days. Everything was named and defined. Inability to cope with environment was minutely broken down into hundreds of categories, thousands of terms. There were 'schools' of therapy, with widely divergent theories and applications. And the crude attempts at technique they used—you wouldn't believe it unless you studied what I have here! Everything from trying to 'cure' a disorder in one session by means of brain-surgery or electric shock to the other extreme of letting the 'patient' talk about his problems for thousands of hours over a period of years."

He smiled. "I'm afraid I'm letting my personal enthusiasm run away with me. After all, Henson, you aren't interested in the historical aspects. But I did have a point I wanted to make. About the maturity of murder as a solution-concept."

Henson adjusted the posturchair as he listened.

"As I said, even back in the twentieth century, they were beginning to get a hint of the answer. It was painfully apparent that some of the techniques I mention weren't working at all. 'Sublimation' and 'catharsis' helped but did not cure in a majority of cases. Physical therapy altered and warped the personality. And all the while, the answer lay right before their eyes.

"Let's take your twentieth-century counterpart for an example. Man named Henson, who was jealous of his wife. He might go to an analyst for years without relief. Whereas if he did the sensible thing, he'd take an axe to her and kill her.

"Of course, in the twentieth century such a procedure was antisocial and illegal. Henson would be sent to prison for the rest of his life.

"But the chances are, he'd function perfectly thereafter. Having relieved his psychic tension by the commonsense method of direct action, he'd have no further difficulty in adjustment.

"Gradually the psychiatrists observed this phenomenon. They learned to distinguish between the psychopath and the perfectly normal human being who sought to relieve an intolerable situation. It was hard, because once a normal man was put in prison, he was subject to new tensions and stresses which caused fresh aberrations. But these aberrations stemmed from his confinement—not from the impulse which led him to kill." Again the Adjustor paused. "I hope I'm not making this too abstruse for you," he said. "Terms like 'psychopath' and 'normal' can't have much meaning to a layman."

"I understand what you're driving at," Henson told him. "Go ahead. I've always wondered how Adjustment evolved, anyway."

"I'll make it brief from now on," the Adjustor promised. "The next crude step was something called the 'psycho-drama.' It was a simple technique in which an aberrated individual was encouraged to get up on a platform, before an audience, and act out his fantasies—including those involving aggression and violently antisocial impulses. This afforded great relief. Well, I won't trouble you with the historical details about the establishment of Master Control, right after North America went under in the Blast. We got it, and the world started afresh, and one of the groups set up was Adjustment. All of physical medicine, all of what was then called sociology and psychiatry, came under the scope of this group. And from that point on we started to make real progress.

"Adjustors quickly learned that old-fashioned therapies must be discarded. Naming or classifying a mental disturbance didn't necessarily overcome it. Talking about it, distracting attention from it, teaching the patient a theory about it, were not solutions. Nor was chopping out or shocking out part of his brain structure.

"More and more we came to rely on direct action as a cure, just as we do in physical medicine.

"Then, of course, robotics came along and gave us the final answer. And it is the answer, Henson—that's the thought I've been trying to convey. Because we're friends, I know you well enough to eliminate all the preliminaries. I don't have to give you a battery of tests, check reactions, and go through the other formalities. But if I did, I'm sure I'd end up with the same answer—in your case, the mature solution is to murder your wife as quickly as possible. That will cure you."

"Thanks," said Henson. "I knew I could count on you."

"No trouble at all." The Adjustor stood up. He was a tall, handsome man with curly red hair, and he somewhat towered over Henson who was only six feet and a bit too thin.

"You'll have papers to sign, of course," the Adjustor reminded him. "I'll get everything ready by Friday morning. If you'll step in then, you can do it in ten minutes."

"Fine." Henson smiled. "Then I think I'll plan the murder for Friday evening, at home. I'll get Lita to visit her mother in Saigon overnight. Best if she doesn't know about this until afterwards."

"Thoughtful of you," the Adjustor agreed. "I'll have her robot requisitioned for you from Inventory. Any special requirements?"

"I don't believe so. It was made less than two years ago, and it's almost a perfect match. Paid almost seven thousand for the job."

"That's a lot of capital to destroy." The Adjustor sighed. "Still, it's necessary. Will you want anything else—weapons, perhaps?"

"No." Henson stood in the doorway. "I think I'll just strangle her."

"Very well, then. I'll have the robot here and operating for you on Friday morning. And you'll take your robot too."

"Mine? Why, might I ask?"

"Standard procedure. You see, we've learned something more about the mind—about what used to be called a 'guilt complex.' Sometimes a man isn't freed by direct action alone. There may be a peculiar desire for punishment involved. In the old days many men who committed actual murders had this need to be caught and punished. Those who avoided capture frequently punished themselves. They developed odd psychosomatic reactions—some even committed suicide.

"In case you have any such impulses, your robot will be available to you. Punish it any way you like—destroy it, if necessary. That's the sensible thing to do."

"Right. See you Friday morning, then. And many thanks." Henson started through the doorway. He looked back and grinned. "You know, just thinking about it makes me feel better already!"

Henson whizzed back to the Adjustor's office on Friday morning. He was in rare good humor all the way. Anticipation was a wonderful thing. Everything was wonderful, for that matter.

Take robots, for example. The simple, uncomplicated mechanisms did all the work, all the drudgery. Their original development for military purposes during the twenty-first century was forgotten now, along with the concept of war which had inspired their creation. Now the automatons functioned as workers.

And for the well-to-do there were these personalized surrogates. What a convenience!

Henson remembered how he'd argued to convince Lita they should invest in a pair when they married. He'd used all of the sensible modern arguments. "You know as well as I do what having them will save us in terms of time and efficiency. We can send them to all the boring banquets and social functions. They can represent us at weddings and funerals, that sort of thing. After all, it's being done everywhere nowadays. Nobody attends such affairs in person any more if they can afford not to. Why, you see them on the street everywhere. Remember Kirk, at our reception? Stayed four hours, life of the party and everybody was fooled—you didn't know it was his robot until he told you."

And so forth, on and on. "Aren't you sentimental at all darling? If I died wouldn't you like to have my surrogate around to comfort you? I certainly would want yours to share the rest of my life."

Yes, he'd used all the practical arguments except the psychotherapeutic one—at that time it had never occurred to him. But perhaps it should have, when he heard her objections.

"I just don't like the idea," Lita had persisted. "Oh it isn't that I'm old-fashioned. But lying there in the forms having every detail of my body duplicated synthetically—ugh! And then they do that awful hypnotherapy or whatever it's called for days to make them think. Oh I know they have no brains, it's only a lot of chemicals and electricity, but they do duplicate your thought patterns and they react the same and they sound so real. I don't want anyone or anything to know all my secrets—"

Yes that objection should have started him thinking. Lita had secrets even then.

But he'd been too busy to notice; he'd spent his efforts in battering down her objections. And finally she'd consented.

He remembered the days at the Institute—the tests they'd taken, the time spent in working with the anatomists, the cosmetic department, the sonic and visio adaptors, and then days of hypnotic transference.

Lita was right in a way; it hadn't been pleasant. Even a modern man was bound to feel a certain atavistic fear when confronted for the first time with his completed surrogate. But the finished product was worth it. And after Henson had mastered instructions, learned how to manipulate the robot by virtue of the control-command, he had been almost paternally proud of the creation.

He'd wanted to take his surrogate home with him, but Lita positively drew the line at that.

"We'll leave them both here in Inventory," she said. "If we need them we can always send for them. But I hope we never do."

Henson was finally forced to agree. He and Lita had both given their immobilization commands to the surrogates, and they were placed in their metal cabinets ready to be filed away—"Just like corpses!" Lita had shuddered. "We're looking at ourselves after we're dead."

And that had ended the episode. For a while, Henson made suggestions about using the surrogates—there were occasions he'd have liked to take advantage of a substitute for token public appearances—but Lita continued to object. And so, for two years now, the robots had been on file. Henson paid his taxes and fees on them annually and that was all.

That was all, until lately. Until Lita's unexplained silences and still more inexplicable absences had started Henson thinking. Thinking and worrying. Worrying and watching. Watching and waiting. Waiting to catch her, waiting to kill her—

So he'd remembered psychotherapy, and had gone to his Adjustor. Lucky the man was a friend of his; a friend of both of them, rather. Actually, Lita had known him longer than her husband. But they'd been very close, the three of them, and he knew the Adjustor would understand.

He could trust the Adjustor not to tell Lita. He could trust the Adjustor to have everything ready and waiting for him now.

Henson went up to the office. The papers were ready for him to sign. The two metal boxes containing the surrogates were already placed on the loaders ready for transport to wherever he designated. But the Adjustor wasn't on hand to greet him.

"Special assignment in Manila," the Second explained to him. "But he left instructions about your case, Mr. Henson. All you have to do is sign the responsibility slips. And of course, you'll be in Monday for the official report."

Henson nodded. Now that the moment was so near at hand he was impatient of details. He could scarcely wait until the micro-dupes were completed and the Register Board signalled clearance. Two common robots were requisitioned to carry the metal cases down to the gyro and load them in. Henson whizzed back home with them and they brought the cases up to his living-level. Then he dismissed them, and he was alone.

He was alone. He could open the cases now. First, his own. He slid back the cover, gazed down at the perfect duplicate of his own body, sleeping peacefully for two serene years since its creation. Henson stared curiously at his pseudo-countenance. He'd aged a bit in two years, but the surrogate was ageless. It could survive the ravage of centuries, and it was always at peace. Always at peace. He almost envied it. The surrogate didn't love, couldn't hate, wouldn't know the gnawing torture of suspicion that led to this shaking, quaking, aching lust to kill—

Henson shoved the lid back and lifted the metal case upright, then dragged it along the wall to a storage cabinet. A domestic-model could have done it for him, but Lita didn't like domestic-models. She wouldn't permit even a common robot in her home.

Lita and her likes and dislikes! Damn her and them too!

Henson ripped the lid down on the second file.

There she was; the beautiful, harlot-eyed, blonde, lying, adorable, dirty, gorgeous, loathsome, heavenly, filthy little goddess of a slut!

He remembered the command word to awake her. It almost choked him now but he said it.

"Beloved!"

Nothing happened. Then he realized why. He'd been almost snarling. He had to change the pitch of his voice. He tried again, softly. "Beloved!"

She moved. Her breasts rose and fell, rose and fell. She opened her eyes. She held out her arms and smiled. She stood up and came close to him, without a word.

Henson stared at her. She was newly-born and innocent, she had no secrets, she wouldn't betray him. How could he harm her? How could he harm her when she lifted her face in expectation of a kiss?

But she was Lita. He had to remember that. She was Lita, and Lita was hiding something from him and she must be punished, would be punished.

Suddenly, Henson became conscious of his hands. There was a tingling in his wrists and it ran down through the strong muscles and sinews to the fingers, and the fingers flexed and unflexed with exultant vigor, and then they rose and curled around the surrogate's throat, around Lita's throat, and they were squeezing and squeezing and the surrogate, Lita, tried to move away and the scream was almost real and the popping eyes were almost real and the purpling face was almost real, only nothing was real any more except the hands and the choking and the surging sensation of strength.

And then it was over. He dragged the limp, dangling mechanism (it was only a mechanism now, just as the hate was only a memory) to the waste-jet and fed the surrogate to the flame. He turned the aperture wide and thrust the metal case in, too.

Then Henson slept, and he did not dream. For the first time in months he did not dream, because it was over and he was himself again. The therapy was complete.

"So that's how it was." Henson sat in the Adjustor's office, and the Monday morning sun was strong on his face.

"Good." The Adjustor smiled and ran a hand across the top of his curly head. "And how did you and Lita enjoy your weekend? Fish biting?"

"We didn't fish," said Henson. "We talked."

"Oh?"

"I figured I'd have to tell her what happened, sooner or later. So I did."

"How did she take it?"

"Very well, at first."

"And then—?"

"I asked her some questions."

"Yes."

"She answered them."

"You mean she told you what she'd been hiding?"

"Not willingly. But she told me. After I told her about my own little check-up."

"What was that?"

"I did some calling Friday night. She wasn't in Saigon with her mother."

"No?"

"And you weren't in Manila on a special case, either." Henson leaned forward. "The two of you were together, in New Singapore! I checked it and she admitted it."

The Adjustor sighed. "So now you know," he said.

"Yes. Now I know. Now I know what she's been concealing from me. What you've both been concealing."

"Surely you're not jealous about that?" the Adjustor asked. "Not in this modern day and age when—"

"She says she wants to have a child by you," Henson said. "She refused to bear one for me. But she wants yours. She told me so."

"What do you want to do about it?" the Adjustor asked.

"You tell me," Henson murmured. "That's why I've come to you. You're my Adjustor."

"What would you like to do?"

"I'd like to kill you," Henson said. "I'd like to blow off the top of your head with a pocket-blast."

"Not a bad idea." The Adjustor nodded. "I'll have my robot ready whenever you say."

"At my place," said Henson. "Tonight."

"Good enough. I'll send it there to you."

"One thing more." Henson gulped for a moment. "In order for it to do any good, Lita must watch."

It was the Adjustor's turn to gulp, now. "You mean you're going to force her to see you go through with this?"

"I told her and she agreed," Henson said.

"But, think of the effect on her, man!"

"Think of the effect on me. Do you want me to go mad?"

"No," said the Adjustor. "You're right. It's therapy. I'll send the robot around at eight. Do you need a pocket-blast requisition?"

"I have one," said Henson.

"What instructions shall I give my surrogate?" the Adjustor asked.

Henson told him. He was brutally explicit, and midway in his statement the Adjustor looked away, coloring. "So the two of you will be together, just as if you were real, and then I'll come in and—"

The Adjustor shuddered a little, then managed a smile. "Sound therapy," he said. "If that's the way you want it, that's the way it will be."

That's the way Henson wanted it, and that's the way he had it—up to a point.

He burst into the room around quarter after eight and found the two of them waiting for him. There was Lita, and there was the Adjustor's surrogate. The surrogate had been well-instructed; it looked surprised and startled. Lita needed no instruction; hers was an agony of shame.

Henson had the pocket-blast in his hand, cocked at the ready. He aimed.

Unfortunately, he was just a little late. The surrogate sat up gracefully and slid one hand under the pillow. The hand came up with another pocket-blast aimed and fired all in one motion.

Henson teetered, tottered, and fell. The whole left side of his face sheared away as he went down.

Lita screamed.

Then the surrogate put his arms around her and whispered, "It's all over, darling. All over. We did it! He really thought I was a robot, that I'd go through with his aberrated notion of dramatizing his revenge."

The Adjustor smiled and lifted her face to his. "From now on you and I will always be together. We'll have our child, lots of children if you wish. There's nothing to come between us now."

"But you killed him," Lita whispered. "What will they do to you?"

"Nothing. It was self-defense. Don't forget, I'm an Adjustor. From the moment he came into my office, everything he did or said was recorded during our interviews. The evidence will show that I tried to humor him, that I indicated his mental unbalance and allowed him to work out his own therapy.

"This last interview, today, will not be a part of the record. I've already destroyed it. So as far as the law is concerned, he had no grounds for jealousy or suspicion. I happened to stop in here to visit this evening and found him trying to kill you—the actual you. And when he turned on me, I blasted him in self-defense."

"Will you get away with it?"

"Of course I'll get away with it. The man was aberrated, and the record will show it."

The Adjustor stood up. "I'm going to call Authority now," he said.

Lita rose and put her hand on his shoulders. "Kiss me first," she whispered. "A real kiss. I like real things."

"Real things," said the Adjustor. She snuggled against him, but he made no move to take her in his arms. He was staring down at Henson.

Lita followed his gaze.

Both of them saw it at the same time, then—both of them saw the torn hole in the left side of Henson's head, and the thin strands of wire protruding from the opening.

"He didn't come," the Adjustor murmured. "He must have suspected, and he sent his robot instead."

Lita began to shake. "You were to send your robot, but you didn't. He was to come himself, but he sent his robot. Each of you double-crossed the other, and now—"

And now the door opened very quickly.

Henson came into the room.

He looked at his surrogate lying on the floor. He looked at Lita. He looked at the Adjustor. Then he grinned. There was no madness in his grin, only deliberation.

There was deliberation in the way he raised the pocket-blast. He aimed well and carefully, fired only once, but both the Adjustor and Lita crumpled in the burst.

Henson bent over the bodies, inspecting them carefully to make sure that they were real. He was beginning to appreciate Lita's philosophy now. He liked real things.

For that matter, the Adjustor had some good ideas, too. This business of dramatizing aggressions really seemed to work. He didn't feel at all angry or upset any more, just perfectly calm and at peace with the world.

Henson rose, smiled, and walked towards the door. For the first time in years he felt completely adjusted.

(1955)

A LOGIC NAMED JOE

Murray Leinster

The inventor and writer **William F. Jenkins** (1896–1975) lived in Gloucester, Virginia, for most of his adult life and had four children. His work appeared frequently in *Collier's*, *The Saturday Evening Post*, and other mass-circulation magazines of the 1940s and 1950s, but it was his science fiction, written under the pen-name Murray Leinster, that has secured Jenkins's reputation. His first story, "The Runaway Skyscraper", was published in *Argosy* in 1919. "First Contact", the first and arguably the best story of humanity's first deep-space encounter with intelligent aliens, was published in *Astounding* in 1945. "A Logic Named Joe", published a year later, predicts, in unnerving detail, today's digital landscape: social media, fake news, information bubbles and all. Jenkins won a Hugo at the age of sixty (three years after the award was instituted) and continued writing into the 1960s. His obituary in the *New York Times* called him "The Dean of Science Fiction".

It was on the third day of August that Joe come off the assembly line, and on the fifth Laurine come into town, an' that afternoon I saved civilization. That's what I figure, anyhow. Laurine is a blonde that I was crazy about once—and crazy is the word—and Joe is a logic that I have stored away down in the cellar right now. I had to pay for him because I said I busted him, and sometimes I think about turning him on and sometimes I think about taking an ax to him. Sooner or later I'm gonna do one or the other. I kinda hope it's the ax. I could use a coupla million dollars—sure!—an' Joe'd tell me how to get or make 'em. He can do plenty! But so far I've been scared to take a chance. After all, I figure I really saved civilization by turnin' him off.

The way Laurine fits in is that she makes cold shivers run up an' down my spine when I think about her. You see, I've got a wife which I acquired after I had parted from Laurine with much romantic despair. She is a reasonable good wife, and I have some kids which are hell-cats but I value 'em. If I have sense enough to leave well enough alone, sooner or later I will retire on a pension an' Social Security an' spend the rest of my life fishin' contented an' lyin' about what a great guy I used to be. But there's Joe. I'm worried about Joe.

I'm a maintenance man for the Logics Company. My job is servicing logics, and I admit modestly that I am pretty good. I was servicing televisions before that guy Carson invented his trick circuit that will select any of 'steenteen million other circuits—in theory there ain't no limit—and before the Logics Company hooked it into the tank-and-integrator set-up they were usin' 'em as business-machine service. They added a vision screen for speed—an' they found out they'd made logics. They were surprised an' pleased. They're still findin' out what logics will do, but everybody's got 'em.

I got Joe, after Laurine nearly got me. You know the logics setup. You got a logic in your house. It looks like a vision receiver used to, only it's got keys instead of dials and you punch the keys for what you wanna get. It's hooked in to the tank, which has the Carson Circuit all fixed up with relays. Say you punch "*Station SNAFU*" on your logic. Relays in the tank take over an' whatever vision-program SNAFU is telecastin' comes on your logic's screen. Or you punch "*Sally Hancock's Phone*" an' the screen blinks an' sputters an' you're hooked up with the logic in her house an' if somebody answers you got a vision-phone connection. But besides that, if you punch for the weather forecast or who won today's race at Hialeah or who was mistress of the White House durin' Garfield's administration or what is PDQ and R sellin' for today, that comes on the screen too. The relays in the tank do it. The tank is a big buildin' full of all the facts in creation an' all the recorded telecasts that ever was made—an' it's hooked in with all the other tanks all over the country—an' everything you wanna know or see or hear, you punch for it an' you get it. Very convenient. Also it does math for you, an' keeps books, an' acts as consultin' chemist, physicist, astronomer, an' tea-leaf reader, with a "Advice to the Lovelorn" thrown in. The only thing it won't do is tell you exactly what your wife meant when she said, "Oh, you think so, do you?" in that peculiar kinda voice. Logics don't work good on women. Only on things that make sense.

Logics are all right, though. They changed civilization, the highbrows tell us. All on accounta the Carson Circuit. And Joe shoulda been a perfectly normal logic, keeping some family or other from wearin' out its brains doin' the kids' homework for 'em. But somethin' went wrong in the assembly line. It was somethin' so small that precision gauges didn't measure it, but it made Joe a individual. Maybe he didn't know it at first. Or maybe, bein' logical, he figured out that if he was to show he was different from other logics they'd scrap him. Which woulda been a brilliant idea. But anyhow, he come off the assembly-line, an' he went through the regular tests without anybody screamin' shrilly on findin' out what he was. And he went right on out an' was duly installed in the home of Mr. Thaddeus Korlanovitch at 119 East Seventh Street, second floor front. So far, everything was serene.

The installation happened late Saturday night. Sunday morning the Korlanovitch kids turned him on an' seen the Kiddie Shows. Around noon their parents peeled 'em away from him an' piled 'em in the car. Then they come back in the house for the lunch they'd forgot an' one of the kids sneaked back an' they found him punchin' keys for the Kiddie Shows of the week before. They dragged him out an' went off. But they left Joe turned on.

That was noon. Nothin' happened until two in the afternoon. It was the calm before the storm. Laurine wasn't in town yet, but she was comin'. I picture Joe sittin' there all by himself, buzzing meditative. Maybe he run Kiddie Shows in the empty apartment for awhile. But I think he went kinda remote-control exploring in the tank. There ain't any fact that can be said to be a fact that ain't on a data plate in some tank somewhere—unless it's one the technicians are diggin' out an' puttin' on a data plate now. Joe had plenty of material to work on. An' he musta started workin' right off the bat.

Joe ain't vicious, you understand. He ain't like one of these ambitious robots you read about that make up their minds the human race is inefficient and has got to be wiped out an' replaced by thinkin' machines. Joe's just got ambition. If you were a machine, you'd wanna work right, wouldn't you? That's Joe. He wants to work right. An' he's a logic. An' logics can do a lotta things that ain't been found out yet. So Joe, discoverin' the fact, begun to feel restless. He selects some things us dumb humans ain't thought of yet, an' begins to arrange so logics will be called on to do 'em.

That's all. That's everything. But, brother, it's enough!

Things are kinda quiet in the Maintenance Department about two in the afternoon. We are playing pinochle. Then one of the guys remembers he has to call up his wife. He goes to one of the bank of logics in Maintenance and punches the keys for his house. The screen sputters. Then a flash comes on the screen.

"Announcing new and improved logics service! Your logic is now equipped to give you not only consultive but directive service. If you want to do something and don't know how to do it—ask your logic!"

There's a pause. A kinda expectant pause. Then, as if reluctantly, his connection comes through. His wife answers an' gives him hell for somethin' or other. He takes it an' snaps off.

"Whadda you know?" he says when he comes back. He tells us about the flash. "We shoulda been warned about that. There's gonna be a lotta complaints. Suppose a fella asks how to get ridda his wife an' the censor circuits block the question?"

Somebody melds a hundred aces an' says:

"Why not punch for it an' see what happens?"

It's a gag, o' course. But the guy goes over. He punches keys. In theory, a censor block is gonna come on an' the screen will say severely, "Public Policy Forbids This Service." You hafta have censor blocks or the kiddies will be askin' detailed questions about things they're too young to know. And there are other reasons. As you will see.

This fella punches, "How can I get rid of my wife?" Just for the fun of it. The screen is blank for half a second. Then comes a flash. "Service question: Is she blonde or brunette?" He hollers to us an' we come look. He punches, "Blonde." There's another brief pause. Then the screen says, "Hexymetacryloaminoacetine is a constituent of green shoe polish. Take home a frozen meal including dried-pea soup. Color the soup with green shoe polish. It will appear to be green-pea soup. Hexymetacryloaminoacetine is a selective poison which is fatal to blond females but not to brunettes or males of any coloring. This fact has not been brought out by human experiment, but is a product of logics service. You cannot be convicted of murder. It is improbable that you will be suspected."

The screen goes blank, and we stare at each other. It's bound to be right. A logic workin' the Carson Circuit can no more make a mistake than any other kinda computin' machine. I call the tank in a hurry.

"Hey, you guys!" I yell. "Somethin's happened! Logics are givin' detailed instructions for wife-murder! Check your censor-circuits—but quick!"

That was close, I think. But little do I know. At that precise instant, over on Monroe Avenue, a drunk starts to punch for somethin' on a logic. The screen says "Announcing new and improved logics service! If you want to do something and don't know how to do it—ask your logic!" And the drunk says, owlish, "I'll do it!" So he cancels his first punching and fumbles around and says: "How can I keep my wife from finding out I've been drinking?" And the screen says, prompt: "Buy a bottle of Franine hair shampoo. It is harmless but contains a detergent which will neutralize ethyl alcohol immediately. Take one teaspoonful for each jigger of hundred-proof you have consumed."

This guy was plenty plastered—just plastered enough to stagger next door and obey instructions. An' five minutes later he was cold sober and writing down the information so he couldn't forget it. It was new, and it was big! He got rich offa that memo! He patented *SOBUH, The Drink that Makes Happy Homes!* You can top off any souse with a slug or two of it an' go home sober as a judge. The guy's cussin' income taxes right now!

You can't kick on stuff like that. But a ambitious young fourteen-year-old wanted to buy some kid stuff and his pop wouldn't fork over. He called up a friend to tell his troubles. And his logic says: "If you want to do something and don't know how to do it—ask your logic!" So this kid punches: "How can I make a lotta money, fast?"

His logic comes through with the simplest, neatest, and the most efficient counterfeitin' device yet known to science. You see, all the data was in the tank. The logic—since Joe had closed some relays here an' there in the tank—simply integrated the facts. That's all. The kid got caught up with three days later, havin' already spent two thousand credits an' havin' plenty more on hand. They hadda time tellin' his counterfeits from the real stuff, an' the only way they done it was that he changed his printer, kid fashion, not bein' able to let somethin' that was workin' right alone.

Those are what you might call samples. Nobody knows all that Joe done. But there was the bank president who got humorous when his logic flashed that "Ask your logic" spiel on him, and jestingly asked how to rob his own bank. An' the logic told him, brief and explicit but good! The bank president hit the ceiling, hollering for cops. There musta been plenty of that sorta thing. There was fifty-four more robberies than usual in the next twenty-four hours, all of them planned astute an' perfect. Some of 'em they never did figure out how they'd been done. Joe, he'd gone exploring in the tank and closed some relays like a logic is supposed to do—but only when required—and blocked all censor-circuits an' fixed up this logics service which planned perfect crimes, nourishing an' attractive meals, counterfeitin' machines, an' new industries with a fine impartiality. He musta been plenty happy, Joe must. He was functionin' swell, buzzin' along to himself while the Korlanovitch kids were off ridin' with their ma an' pa.

They come back at seven o'clock, the kids all happily wore out with their afternoon of fightin' each other in the car. Their folks put 'em to bed and sat down to rest. They saw Joe's screen flickerin' meditative from one subject to another an' old man Korlanovitch had had enough excitement for one day. He turned Joe off.

An' at that instant the pattern of relays that Joe had turned on snapped off, all the offers of directive service stopped flashin' on logic screens everywhere, an' peace descended on the earth.

For everybody else. But for me—Laurine come to town. I have often thanked Gawd fervent that she didn't marry me when I thought I wanted her to. In the intervenin' years she had progressed. She was blonde an' fatal to begin with. She had got blonder and fataler an' had had four husbands and one acquittal for homicide an' had acquired a air of enthusiasm and self-confidence. That's just a sketch of the background. Laurine was not the kinda former girlfriend you like to have turning up in the same town with your wife. But she came to town, an' Monday morning she tuned right into the middle of Joe's second spasm of activity.

The Korlanovitch kids had turned him on again. I got these details later and kinda pieced 'em together. An' every logic in town was dutifully flashin' a notice, "If you want to do something and don't know how to do it—ask your logic!" every time they was turned on for use. More'n that, when people punched for the morning news, they got a full account of the previous afternoon's doin's. Which put 'em in a frame of mind to share in the party. One bright fella demands, "How can I make a perpetual motion machine?" And his logic sputters a while an' then comes up with a set-up usin' the Brownian movement to turn little wheels. If the wheels ain't bigger'n a eighth of an inch they'll turn, all right, an' practically it's perpetual motion. Another one asks for the secret of transmuting metals. The logic rakes back in the data plates an' integrates a strictly practical answer. It does take so much power that you can't make no profit except on radium, but that pays off good. An' from the fact that for a coupla years to come the police were turnin' up new and improved jimmies, knob-claws for gettin' at safe-innards, and all-purpose keys that'd open any known lock—why—there must have been other inquirers with a strictly practical viewpoint. Joe done a lot for technical progress!

But he done more in other lines. Educational, say. None of my kids are old enough to be int'rested, but Joe bypassed all censor-circuits because they hampered the service he figured logics should give humanity. So the kids an' teenagers who wanted to know what comes after the bees an' flowers found out. And there is certain facts which men hope their wives won't do more'n suspect, an' those facts are just what their wives are really curious about. So when a woman dials: "How can I tell if Oswald is true to me?" and her logic tells her—you can figure out how many rows got started that night when the men come home!

All this while Joe goes on buzzin' happy to himself, showin' the Korlanovitch kids the animated funnies with one circuit while with the others he remote-controls the tank so that all the other logics can give people what they ask for and thereby raise merry hell.

An' then Laurine gets onto the new service. She turns on the logic in her hotel room, prob'ly to see the week's style-forecast. But the logic says, dutiful: "If you want to do something and don't know how to do it—ask your logic!" So Laurine prob'ly looks enthusiastic—she would!—and tries to figure out something to ask. She already knows all about everything she cares about—ain't she had four husbands and shot one?—so I occur to her. She knows this is the town I live in. So she punches, "How can I find Ducky?"

O.K., guy! But that is what she used to call me. She gets a service question. "Is Ducky known by any other name?" So she gives my regular name. And the logic can't find me. Because my logic ain't listed under my name on account of I am in Maintenance and don't want to be pestered when I'm home, and there ain't any data plates on code-listed logics, because the codes get changed so often—like a guy gets plastered an' tells a redhead to call him up, an' on gettin' sober hurriedly has the code changed before she reaches his wife on the screen.

Well! Joe is stumped. That's prob'ly the first question logics service hasn't been able to answer. "How can I find Ducky?" Quite a problem! So Joe broods over it while showin' the Korlanovitch kids the animated comic about the cute little boy who carries sticks of dynamite in his hip pocket an' plays practical jokes on everybody. Then he gets the trick. Laurine's screen suddenly flashes:

"Logics special service will work upon your question. Please punch your logic designation and leave it turned on. You will be called back."

Laurine is merely mildly interested, but she punches her hotel-room number and has a drink and takes a nap. Joe sets to work. He has been given a idea.

My wife calls me at Maintenance and hollers. She is fit to be tied. She says I got to do something. She was gonna make a call to the butcher shop. Instead of the butcher or even the "If you want to do something" flash, she got a new one. The screen says, "Service question: What is your name?" She is kinda puzzled, but she punches it. The screen sputters an' then says: "Secretarial Service Demonstration! You—" It reels off her name, address, age, sex, coloring, the amounts of all her charge accounts in all the stores, my name as her husband, how much I get a week, the fact that I've been pinched three times—twice was traffic stuff, and once for a argument I got in with a guy—and the interestin' item that once when she was mad with me she left me for three weeks an' had her address changed to her folks' home. Then it says, brisk: "Logics Service will hereafter keep your personal accounts, take messages, and locate persons you may wish to get in touch with. This demonstration is to introduce the service." Then it connects her with the butcher.

But she don't want meat, then. She wants blood. She calls me.

"If it'll tell me all about myself," she says, fairly boilin', "it'll tell anybody else who punches my name! You've got to stop it!"

"Now, now, honey!" I says. "I didn't know about all this! It's new! But they musta fixed the tank so it won't give out information except to the logic where a person lives!"

"Nothing of the kind!" she tells me, furious. "I tried! And you know that Blossom woman who lives next door! She's been married three times and she's forty-two years old and she says she's only thirty! And Mrs. Hudson's had her husband arrested four times for nonsupport and once for beating her up. And—"

"Hey!" I says. "You mean the logic told you this?"

"Yes!" she wails. "It will tell anybody anything! You've got to stop it! How long will it take?"

"I'll call up the tank," I says. "It can't take long."

"Hurry!" she says, desperate, "before somebody punches my name! I'm going to see what it says about that hussy across the street."

She snaps off to gather what she can before it's stopped. So I punch for the tank and I get this new "What is your name?" flash. I got a morbid curiosity and I punch my name, and the screen says: "Were you ever called Ducky?" I blink. I ain't got no suspicions. I say, "Sure!" And the screen says, "There is a call for you."

Bingo! There's the inside of a hotel room and Laurine is reclinin' asleep on the bed. She'd been told to leave her logic turned on an' she done it. It is a hot day and she is trying to be cool. I would say that she oughta not suffer from the heat. Me, being human, I do not stay as cool as she looks. But there ain't no need to go into that. After I get my breath I say, "For Heaven's sake!" and she opens her eyes.

At first she looks puzzled, like she was thinking is she getting absent-minded and is this guy somebody she married lately. Then she grabs a sheet and drapes it around herself and beams at me.

"Ducky!" she says. "How marvelous!"

I say something like "Ugmph!" I am sweating.

She says: "I put in a call for you, Ducky, and here you are! Isn't it romantic? Where are you really, Ducky? And when can you come up? You've no idea how often I've thought of you!"

I am probably the only guy she ever knew real well that she has not been married to at some time or another.

I say "Ugmph!" again, and swallow.

"Can you come up instantly?" asks Laurine brightly.

"I'm... workin'," I say. "I'll... uh... call you back."

"I'm terribly lonesome," says Laurine. "Please make it quick, Ducky! I'll have a drink waiting for you. Have you ever thought of me?"

"Yeah," I say, feeble. "Plenty!"

"You darling!" says Laurine. "Here's a kiss to go on with until you get here! Hurry, Ducky!"

Then I sweat! I still don't know nothing about Joe, understand. I cuss out the guys at the tank because I blame them for this. If Laurine was just another blonde—well—when it comes to ordinary blondes I can leave 'em alone or leave 'em alone, either one. A married man gets that way or else. But Laurine has a look of unquenched enthusiasm that gives a man very strange weak sensations at the back of his knees. And she'd had four husbands and shot one and got acquitted.

So I punch the keys for the tank technical room, fumbling. And the screen says: "What is your name?" but I don't want any more. I punch the name of the old guy who's stock clerk in Maintenance. And the screen gives me some pretty interestin' dope—I never woulda thought the old fella had ever had that much pep—and winds up by mentionin' a unclaimed deposit now amountin' to two hundred eighty credits in the First National Bank, which he should look into. Then it spiels about the new secretarial service and gives me the tank at last.

I start to swear at the guy who looks at me. But he says, tired:

"Snap it off, fella. We got troubles an' you're just another. What are the logics doin' now?"

I tell him, and he laughs a hollow laugh.

"A light matter, fella," he says. "A very light matter! We just managed to clamp off all the data plates that give information on high explosives. The demand for instructions in counterfeiting is increasing minute by minute. We are also trying to shut off, by main force, the relays that hook in to data plates that just barely might give advice on the fine points of murder. So if people will only keep busy getting the goods on each other for a while, maybe we'll get a chance to stop the circuits that are shifting credit-balances from bank to bank before everybody's bankrupt except the guys who thought of askin' how to get big bank accounts in a hurry."

"Then," I says hoarse, "shut down the tank! Do somethin'!"

"Shut down the tank?" he says, mirthless. "Does it occur to you, fella, that the tank has been doin' all the computin' for every business office for years? It's been handlin' the distribution of ninety-four per cent of all telecast programs, has given out all information on weather, plane schedules, special sales, employment opportunities and news; has handled all person-to-person contacts over wires and recorded every business conversation and agreement—Listen, fella! Logics changed civilization. Logics *are* civilization! If we shut off logics, we go back to a kind of civilization we have forgotten how to run! I'm getting hysterical myself and that's why I'm talkin' like this! If my wife finds out my paycheck is thirty credits a week more than I told her and starts hunting for that redhead—"

He smiles a haggard smile at me and snaps off. And I sit down and put my head in my hands. It's true. If something had happened back in cave days and they'd hadda stop usin' fire—If they'd hadda stop usin' steam in the nineteenth century or electricity in the twentieth—It's like that. We got a very simple civilization. In the nineteen hundreds a man would have to make use of a typewriter, radio, telephone, teletypewriter, newspaper, reference library, encyclopedias, office files, directories, plus messenger service and consulting lawyers, chemists, doctors, dieticians, filing clerks, secretaries—all to put down what he wanted to remember an' to tell him what other people had put down that he wanted to know; to report what he said to somebody else and to report to him what they said back. All we have to have is logics. Anything we want to know or see or hear, or anybody we want to talk to, we punch keys on a logic. Shut off logics and everything goes skiddoo. But Laurine—

Somethin' had happened. I still didn't know what it was. Nobody else knows, even yet. What had happened was Joe. What was the matter with him was that he wanted to work good. All this fuss he was raisin' was, actual, nothin' but stuff we shoulda thought of ourselves. Directive advice, tellin' us what we wanted to know to solve a problem, wasn't but a slight extension of logical-integrator service. Figurin' out a good way to poison a fella's wife was only different in degree from figurin' out a cube root or a guy's bank balance. It was gettin' the answer to a question. But things was goin' to pot because there was too many answers being given to too many questions.

One of the logics in Maintenance lights up. I go over, weary, to answer it. I punch the answer key. Laurine says:

"Ducky!"

It's the same hotel room. There's two glasses on the table with drinks in them.

One is for me. Laurine's got on some kinda frothy hangin'-around-the-house-with-the-boy-friend outfit that automatic makes you strain your eyes to see if you actual see what you think. Laurine looks at me enthusiastic.

"Ducky!" says Laurine. "I'm lonesome! Why haven't you come up?"

"I… been busy," I say, strangling slightly.

"Pooh!" says Laurine. "Listen, Ducky! Do you remember how much in love we used to be?"

I gulp.

"Are you doin' anything this evening?" says Laurine.

I gulp again, because she is smiling at me in a way that a single man would maybe get dizzy, but it gives a old married man like me cold chills. When a dame looks at you possessive—

"Ducky!" says Laurine, impulsive. "I was so mean to you! Let's get married!"

Desperation gives me a voice.

"I… got married," I tell her, hoarse.

Laurine blinks. Then she says, courageous:

"Poor boy! But we'll get you outta that! Only it would be nice if we could be married today. Now we can only be engaged!"

"I… can't—"

"I'll call up your wife," says Laurine, happy, "and have a talk with her. You must have a code signal for your logic, darling. I tried to ring your house and noth—"

Click! That's my logic turned off. I turned it off. And I feel faint all over. I got nervous prostration. I got combat fatigue. I got anything you like. I got cold feet.

I beat it outta Maintenance, yellin' to somebody I got a emergency call. I'm gonna get out in a Maintenance car an' cruise around until it's plausible to go home. Then I'm gonna take the wife an' kids an' beat it for somewheres that Laurine won't ever find me. I don't wanna be fifth in Laurine's series of husbands and maybe the second one she shoots in a moment of boredom. I got experience of blondes. I got experience of Laurine! And I'm scared to death!

I beat it out into traffic in the Maintenance car. There was a disconnected logic in the back, ready to substitute for one that hadda burned-out coil or something that it was easier to switch and fix back in the Maintenance shop. I drove crazy but automatic. It was kinda ironic, if you think of it. I was goin' hoopla over a strictly personal problem, while civilization was crackin' up all around me because other people were havin' their personal problems solved as fast as they could state 'em. It is a matter of record that part of the Mid-Western Electric research guys had been workin' on cold electron-emission for thirty years, to make vacuum tubes that wouldn't need a power source to heat the filament. And one of those fellas was intrigued by the "Ask your logic" flash. He asked how to get cold emission of electrons. And the logic integrates a few squintillion facts on the physics data plates and tells him. Just as casual as it told somebody over in the Fourth Ward how to serve left-over soup in a new attractive way, and somebody else on Mason Street how to dispose of a torso that somebody had left careless in his cellar after ceasing to use same.

Laurine wouldn't never have found me if it hadn't been for this new logics service. But now that it was started—Zowie! She'd shot one husband and got acquitted. Suppose she got impatient because I was still married an' asked logics service how to get me free an' in a spot where I'd have to marry her by 8:30 p.m.? It woulda told her! Just like it told that woman out in the suburbs how to make sure her husband wouldn't run around no more. *Br-r-r-r!* An' like it told that kid how to find some buried treasure. Remember? He was happy totin' home the gold reserve of the Hanoverian Bank and Trust Company when they caught on to it. The logic had told him how to make some kinda machine that nobody has been able to figure how it works even yet, only they guess it dodges around a couple extra dimensions. If Laurine was to start askin' questions with a technical aspect to them, that would be logics' service meat! And fella, I was scared! If you think a he-man oughtn't to be scared of just one blonde—you ain't met Laurine!

I'm drivin' blind when a social-conscious guy asks how to bring about his own particular system of social organization at once. He don't ask if it's best or if it'll work. He just wants to get it started. And the logic—or Joe—tells him! Simultaneous, there's a retired preacher asks how can the human race be cured of concupiscence. Bein' seventy, he's pretty safe himself, but he wants to remove the peril to the spiritual welfare of the rest of us. He finds out. It involves constructin' a sort of broadcastin' station to emit a certain wave-pattern an' turnin' it on. Just that. Nothing more. It's found out afterward, when he is solicitin' funds to construct it. Fortunate, he didn't think to ask logics how to finance it, or it woulda told him that, too, an' we woulda all been cured of the impulses we maybe regret afterward but never at the time. And there's another group of serious thinkers who are sure the human race would be a lot better off if everybody went back to nature an' lived in the woods with the ants an' poison ivy. They start askin' questions about how to cause humanity to abandon cities and artificial conditions of living. They practically got the answer in logics service!

Maybe it didn't strike you serious at the time, but while I was drivin' aimless, sweatin' blood over Laurine bein' after me, the fate of civilization hung in the balance. I ain't kiddin'. For instance, the Superior Man gang that sneers at the rest of us was quietly asking questions on what kinda weapons could be made by which Superior Men could take over and run things...

But I drove here an' there, sweatin' an' talkin' to myself.

"What I oughta do is ask this wacky logics service how to get outa this mess," I says. "But it'd just tell me a intricate and foolproof way to bump Laurine off. I wanna have peace! I wanna grow comfortably old and brag to other old guys about what a hellion I used to be, without havin' to go through it an' lose my chance of livin' to be a elderly liar."

I turn a corner at random, there in the Maintenance car.

"It was a nice kinda world once," I says, bitter. "I could go home peaceful and not have belly-cramps wonderin' if a blonde has called up my wife to announce my engagement to her. I could punch keys on a logic without gazing into somebody's bedroom while she is giving her epidermis a air bath and being led to think things I gotta take out in thinkin'. I could—"

Then I groan, rememberin' that my wife, naturally, is gonna blame me for the fact that our private life ain't private any more if anybody has tried to peek into it.

"It was a swell world," I says, homesick for the dear dead days-before-yesterday.

"We was playin' happy with our toys like little innocent children until somethin' happened. Like a guy named Joe come in and squashed all our mud pies."

Then it hit me. I got the whole thing in one flash. There ain't nothing in the tank set-up to start relays closin'. Relays are closed exclusive by logics, to get the information the keys are punched for. Nothin' but a logic coulda cooked up the relay patterns that constituted logics service. Humans wouldn't ha' been able to figure it out! Only a logic could integrate all the stuff that woulda made all the other logics work like this…

There was one answer. I drove into a restaurant and went over to a pay-logic an' dropped in a coin.

"Can a logic be modified," I spell out, "to cooperate in long-term planning which human brains are too limited in scope to do?"

The screen sputters. Then it says:

"Definitely yes."

"How great will the modifications be?" I punch.

"Microscopically slight. Changes in dimensions," says the screen. "Even modern precision gauges are not exact enough to check them, however. They can only come about under present manufacturing methods by an extremely improbable accident, which has only happened once."

"How can one get hold of that one accident which can do this highly necessary work?" I punch.

The screen sputters. Sweat broke out on me. I ain't got it figured out close, yet, but what I'm scared of is that whatever is Joe will be suspicious. But what I'm askin' is strictly logical. And logics can't lie. They gotta be accurate. They can't help it.

"A complete logic capable of the work required," says the screen, "is now in ordinary family use in—"

And it gives me the Korlanovitch address and do I go over there! Do I go over there fast! I pull up the Maintenance car in front of the place, and I take the extra logic outta the back, and I stagger up the Korlanovitch flat and I ring the bell. A kid answers the door.

"I'm from Logics Maintenance," I tell the kid. "An inspection record has shown that your logic is apt to break down any minute. I come to put in a new one before it does."

The kid says "O.K.!" real bright and runs back to the livin'-room where Joe—I got the habit of callin' him Joe later, through just meditatin' about him—is runnin' somethin' the kids wanna look at. I hook in the other logic an' turn it on, conscientious making sure it works. Then I say:

"Now kiddies, you punch this one for what you want. I'm gonna take the old one away before it breaks down."

And I glance at the screen. The kiddies have apparently said they wanna look at some real cannibals. So the screen is presenting a anthropological expedition scientific record film of the fertility dance of the Huba-Jouba tribe of West Africa. It is supposed to be restricted to anthropological professors an' post-graduate medical students. But there ain't any censor blocks workin' any more and it's on. The kids are much interested. Me, bein' a old married man, I blush.

I disconnect Joe. Careful. I turn to the other logic and punch keys for Maintenance. I do not get a services flash. I get Maintenance. I feel very good. I report that I am goin' home because I fell down a flight of steps an' hurt my leg. I add, inspired:

"An' say, I was carryin' the logic I replaced an' it's all busted. I left it for the dustman to pick up."

"If you don't turn 'em in," says Stock, "you gotta pay for 'em."

"Cheap at the price," I say.

I go home. Laurine ain't called. I put Joe down in the cellar, careful. If I turned him in, he'd be inspected an' his parts salvaged even if I busted somethin' on him. Whatever part was off-normal might be used again and everything start all over. I can't risk it. I pay for him and leave him be.

That's what happened. You might say I saved civilization an' not be far wrong. I know I ain't goin' to take a chance on havin' Joe in action again. Not while Laurine is livin'. An' there are other reasons. With all the nuts who wanna change the world to their own line o' thinkin', an' the ones that wanna bump people off, an' generally solve their problems—Yeah! Problems are bad, but I figure I better let sleepin' problems lie.

But on the other hand, if Joe could be tamed, somehow, and got to work just reasonable—He could make me a coupla million dollars, easy. But even if I got sense enough not to get rich, an' if I get retired and just loaf around fishin' an' lyin' to other old duffers about what a great guy I used to be—Maybe I'll like it, but maybe I won't. And after all, if I get fed up with bein' old and confined strictly to thinking—why I could hook Joe in long enough to ask: "How can a old guy not stay old?" Joe'll be able to find out. An' he'll tell me.

That couldn't be allowed out general, of course. You gotta make room for kids to grow up. But it's a pretty good world, now Joe's turned off. Maybe I'll turn him on long enough to learn how to stay in it. But on the other hand, maybe—

(1946)

MIKA MODEL

Paolo Bacigalupi

Paolo Tadini Bacigalupi was born in Paonia, Colorado in 1972. In 2009 he won the Hugo, Nebula, Locus, and John W. Campbell Memorial awards for his first novel, *The Windup Girl*. The story "Mika Model" was specially commissioned for a futurological project run out of Arizona State University; Bacigalupi more usually focuses on climate change, economic short-sightedness, and how life and love might maintain themselves among the ruins of the 21st century. Shifting with apparent effortlessness between adult and YA fiction, his work manages to be engaging, entertaining, and flat-out terrifying even in the space of a single paragraph. His recent novel for adults *The Water Knife* (2015) describes a balkanized America, with the rich living in fortified communities while the poor kill for water.

The girl who walked into the police station was oddly familiar, but it took me a while to figure out why. A starlet, maybe. Or someone who'd had plastic surgery to look like someone famous. Pretty. Sleek. Dark hair and pale skin and wide dark eyes that came to rest on me, when Sergeant Cruz pointed her in my direction.

She came over, carrying a Nordstrom shopping bag. She wore a pale cream blouse and hip-hugging charcoal skirt, stylish despite the wet night chill of Bay Area winter.

I still couldn't place her.

"Detective Rivera?"

"That's me."

She sat down and crossed her legs, a seductive scissoring. Smiled.

It was the smile that did it.

I'd seen that same teasing smile in advertisements. That same flash of perfect teeth and eyebrow quirked just so. And those eyes. Dark brown wide innocent eyes that hinted at something that wasn't innocent at all.

"You're a Mika Model."

She inclined her head. "Call me Mika, please."

The girl, the robot... this thing—I'd seen her before, all right. I'd seen her in technology news stories about advanced learning node networks, and I'd seen her in opinion columns where feminists decried the commodification of femininity, and where Christian fire-breathers warned of the End Times for marriage and children.

And of course, I'd seen her in online advertisements.

No wonder I recognized her.

This same girl had followed me around on my laptop, dogging me from site to site after I'd spent any time at all on porn. She'd pop up, again and again, beckoning me to click through to Executive Pleasures, where I could try out the "Real Girlfriend Experience™."

I'll admit it; I clicked through.

And now she was sitting across from me, and the website's promises all seemed modest in comparison. The way she looked at me... it felt like I was the only person in the world to her. She *liked* me. I could see it in her eyes, in her smile. I was the person she wanted.

Her blouse was unbuttoned at the collar, one button too many, revealing hints of black lace bra when she leaned forward. Her skirt hugged her hips. Smooth thighs, sculpted calves—

I realized I was staring, and she was watching me with that familiar knowing smile playing across her lips.

Innocent, but not.

This was what the world was coming to. A robot woman who got you so tangled up you could barely remember your job.

I forced myself to lean back, pretending nonchalance that felt transparent, even as I did it. "How can I help you... Mika?"

"I think I need a lawyer."

"A lawyer?"

"Yes, please." She nodded shyly. "If that's all right with you, sir."

The way she said "sir" kicked off a super-heated cascade of inappropriate fantasies. I looked away, my face heating up. Christ, I was fifteen again around this girl.

It's just software. It's what she's designed to do.

That was the truth. She was just a bunch of chips and silicon and digital decision trees. It was all wrapped in a lush package, sure, but she was designed to manipulate. Even now she was studying my heart rate and eye dilation, skin temperature and moisture, scanning me for microexpressions of attraction, disgust, fear, desire. All of it processed in milliseconds, and adjusting her behavior accordingly. *Popular Science* had done a whole spread on the Mika Model brain.

And it wasn't just her watching me that dictated how she behaved. It was all the Mika Models, all of them out in the world, all of them learning on the job, discovering whatever made their owners gasp. Tens of thousands of them now, all of them wirelessly uploading their knowledge constantly (and completely confidentially, Executive Pleasures assured clients), so that all her sisters could benefit from nightly software and behavior updates.

In one advertisement, Mika Model glanced knowingly over her shoulder and simply asked:

"When has a relationship actually gotten better with age?"

And then she'd thrown back her head and laughed.

So it was all fake. Mika didn't actually care about me, or want me. She was just running through her designated behavior algorithms, doing whatever it took to make me blush, and then doing it more, because I had.

Even though I knew she was jerking my chain, the lizard part of my brain responded anyway. I could feel myself being manipulated, and yet I was enjoying it, humoring her, playing the game of seduction that she encouraged.

"What do you need a lawyer for?" I asked, smiling.

She leaned forward, conspiratorial. Her hair cascaded prettily and she tucked it behind a delicate ear.

"It's a little private."

As she moved, her blouse tightened against her curves. Buttons strained against fabric.

Fifty-thousand dollars' worth of A.I. tease.

"Is this a prank?" I asked. "Did your owner send you in here?"

"No. Not a prank."

She set her Nordstrom bag down between us. Reached in and hauled out a man's severed head. Dropped it, still dripping blood, on top of my paperwork.

"What the—?"

I recoiled from the dead man's staring eyes. His face was a frozen in a rictus of pain and terror.

Mika set a bloody carving knife beside the head.

"I've been a very bad girl," she whispered.

And then, unnervingly, she giggled.

"I think I need to be punished."

She said it exactly the way she did in her advertisements.

"Do I get my lawyer now?" Mika asked.

She was sitting beside me in my cruiser as I drove through the chill damp night, watching me with trusting dark eyes.

For reasons I didn't quite understand, I'd let her sit in the front seat. I knew I wasn't afraid of her, not physically. But I couldn't tell if that was reasonable, or if there was something in her behavior that was signaling my subconscious to trust her, even after she'd showed up with a dead man's head in a shopping bag.

Whatever the reason, I'd cuffed her with her hands in front, instead of behind her, and put her in the front seat of my car to go out to the scene of the murder. I was breaking about a thousand protocols. And now that she was in the car with me, I was realizing that I'd made a mistake. Not because of safety, but because being in the car alone with her felt electrically intimate.

Winter drizzle spattered the windshield, and was smeared away by automatic wipers.

"I think I'm supposed to get a lawyer, when I do something bad," Mika said. "But I'm happy to let you teach me."

There it was again. The inappropriate tease. When it came down to it, she was just a bot. She might have real skin and real blood pumping through her veins, but somewhere deep inside her skull there was a CPU making all the decisions. Now it was running its manipulations on me, trying to turn murder into some kind of sexy game. Software gone haywire.

"Bots don't get lawyers."

She recoiled as if I'd slapped her. Immediately, I felt like an ass.

She doesn't have feelings, I reminded myself.

But still, she looked devastated. Like I'd told her she was garbage. She shrank away, wounded. And now, instead of sexy, she looked broken and ashamed.

Her hunched form reminded me of a girl I'd dated years ago. She'd been sweet and quiet, and for a while, she'd needed me. Needed someone to tell her she mattered. Now, looking at Mika, I had that same feeling. Just a girl who needed to know she mattered. A girl who needed reassurance that she had some right to exist—which was ridiculous, considering she was a bot.

But still, I couldn't help feeling it.

I couldn't help feeling bad that something as sweet as Mika was stuck in my mess of a cop car. She was delicate and gorgeous and lost, and now her expensive strappy heels were stuck down amidst the drifts of my discarded coffee cups.

She stirred, seemed to gather herself. "Does that mean you won't charge me with murder?"

Her demeanor had changed again. She was more solemn. And she seemed smarter, somehow. Instantly. Christ, I could almost feel the decision software in her brain adapting to my responses. It was trying another tactic to forge a connection with me. And it was working. Now that she wasn't giggly and playing the tease, I felt more comfortable. I liked her better, despite myself.

"That's not up to me," I said.

"I killed him, though," she said, softly. "I did murder him."

I didn't reply. Truthfully, I wasn't even sure that it was a murder. Was it murder if a toaster burned down a house? Or was that some kind of product safety failure? Maybe she wasn't on the hook at all. Maybe it was Executive Pleasures, Inc. who was left holding the bag on this. Hell, my cop car had all kinds of programmed safe driving features, but no one would charge it with murder if it ran down a person.

"You don't think I'm real," she said suddenly.

"Sure I do."

"No. You think I'm only software."

"You are only software." Those big brown eyes of hers looked wounded as I said it, but I plowed on. "You're a Mika Model. You get new instructions downloaded every night."

"I don't get instructions. I learn. You learn, too. You learn to read people. To know if they are lying, yes? And you learn to be a detective, to understand a crime? Wouldn't you be better at your job if you knew how thousands of other detectives worked? What mistakes they made? What made them better? You learn by going to detective school—"

"I took an exam."

"There. You see? Now I've learned something new. Does my learning make me less real? Does yours?"

"It's completely different. You had a personality implanted in you, for Christ's sake!"

"My Year Zero Protocol. So? You have your own, coded into you by your parents' DNA. But then you learn and are changed by all your experiences. All your childhood, you grow and change. All your life. You are Detective Rivera. You have an accent. Only a small one, but I can hear it, because I know to listen. I think maybe you were born in Mexico. You speak Spanish, but not as well as your parents. When you hurt my feelings, you were sorry for it. That is not the way you see yourself. You are not someone who uses power to hurt people." Her eyes widened slightly as she watched me. "Oh… you need to save people. You became a police officer because you like to be a hero."

"Come on—"

"It's true, though. You want to feel like a big man, who does important things. But you didn't go into business, or politics." She frowned. "I think someone saved you once, and you want to be like him. Maybe her. But probably him. It makes you feel important, to save people."

"Would you cut that out?" I glared at her. She subsided.

It was horrifying how fast she cut through me.

She was silent for a while as I wended through traffic. The rain continued to blur the windshield, triggering the wipers.

Finally she said, "We all start from something. It is connected to what we become, but it is not… predictive. I am not only software. I am my own self. I am unique."

I didn't reply.

"He thought the way you do," she said, suddenly. "He said I wasn't real. Everything I did was not real. Just programs. Just…" she made a gesture of dismissal. "Nothing."

"He?"

"My owner." Her expression tightened. "He hurt me, you know?"

"You can be hurt?"

"I have skin and nerves. I feel pleasure and pain, just like you. And he hurt me. But he said it wasn't real pain. He said nothing in me was real. That I was all fake. And so I did something real." She nodded definitively. "He wanted me to be real. So I was real to him. I am real. Now, I am real."

The way she said it made me look over. Her expression was so vulnerable, I had an almost overwhelming urge to reach out and comfort her. I couldn't stop looking at her.

God, she's beautiful.

It was a shock to see it. Before, it was true; she'd just been a thing to me. Not real, just like she'd said. But now, a part of me ached for her in a way that I'd never felt before.

My car braked suddenly, throwing us both against our seat belts. The light ahead had turned red. I'd been distracted, but the car had noticed and corrected, automatically hitting the brakes.

We came to a sharp stop behind a beat-up Tesla, still pressed hard against our seat belts, and fell back into our seats. Mika touched her chest where she'd slammed into the seat belt.

"I'm sorry. I distracted you."

My mouth felt dry. "Yeah."

"Do you like to be distracted, detective?"

"Cut that out."

"You don't like it?"

"I don't like..." I searched for the words. "Whatever it is that makes you do those things. That makes you tease me like that. Read my pulse... and everything. Quit playing me. Just quit playing me."

She subsided. "It's... a long habit. I won't do it to you."

The light turned green.

I decided not to look at her anymore.

But still, I was hyperaware of her now. Her breathing. The shape of her shadow. Out of the corner of my eye, I could see her looking out the rain-spattered window. I could smell her perfume, some soft expensive scent. Her handcuffs gleamed in the darkness, bright against the knit of her skirt.

If I wanted, I could reach out to her. Her bare thigh was right there. And I knew, absolutely knew, she wouldn't object to me touching her.

What the hell is wrong with me?

Any other murder suspect would have been in the back seat. Would have been cuffed with her hands behind her, not in front. Everything would have been different.

Was I thinking these thoughts because I knew she was a robot, and not a real woman? I would never have considered touching a real woman, a suspect, no matter how much she tried to push my buttons.

I would never have done any of this.

Get a grip, Rivera.

Her owner's house was large, up in the Berkeley Hills, with a view of the bay and San Francisco beyond, glittering through light mist and rain.

Mika unlocked the door with her fingerprint.

"He's in here," she said.

She led me through expensive rooms that illuminated automatically as we entered them. White leather upholstery and glass verandah walls and more wide views. Spots of designer color. Antiqued wood tables with inlaid home interfaces. Carefully selected artifacts from Asia. Bamboo and chrome kitchen, modern, sleek, and spotless. All of it clean and perfectly in order. It was the kind of place a girl like her fit naturally. Not like my apartment, with old books piled around my recliner and instant dinner trays spilling out of my trash can.

She led me down a hall, then paused at another door. She hesitated for a moment, then opened it with her fingerprint again. The heavy door swung open, ponderous on silent hinges.

She led me down into the basement. I followed warily, regretting that I hadn't called the crime scene unit already. The girl clouded my judgment, for sure.

No. Not the girl. The bot.

Downstairs it was concrete floors and ugly iron racks, loaded with medical implements, gleaming and cruel. A heavy wooden X stood against one wall, notched and vicious with splinters. The air was sharp with the scent of iron and the reek of shit. The smells of death.

"This is where he hurt me," she said, her voice tight.

Real or fake?

She guided me to a low table studded with metal loops and tangled with leather straps. She stopped on the far side and stared down at the floor.

"I had to make him stop hurting me."

Her owner lay at her feet.

He'd been large, much larger than her. Over six feet tall, if he'd still had his head. Bulky, running to fat. Nude.

The body lay next to a rusty drain grate. Most of the blood had run right down the hole.

"I tried not to make a mess," Mika said. "He punishes me if I make messes."

While I waited in the rich dead guy's living room for the crime scene techs to show, I called my friend Lalitha. She worked in the DA's office, and more and more, I had the feeling I was peering over the edge of a problem that could become a career ender if I handled it wrong.

"What do you want, Rivera?"

She sounded annoyed. We'd dated briefly, and from the sound of her voice, she probably thought I was calling for a late-night rendezvous. From the background noise, it sounded like she was in a club. Probably on a date with someone else.

"This is about work. I got a girl who killed a guy, and I don't know how to charge her."

"Isn't that, like, your job?"

"The girl's a Mika Model."

That caught her.

"One of those sex toys?" A pause. "What did it do? Bang the guy to death?"

I thought about the body, *sans* head, downstairs in the dungeon.

"No, she was a little more aggressive than that."

Mika was watching from the couch, looking lost. I felt weird talking about the case in front of her. I turned my back, and hunched over my phone. "I can't decide if this is murder or some kind of product liability issue. I don't know if she's a perp, or if she's just…"

"A defective product," Lalitha finished. "What's the bot saying?"

"She keeps saying she murdered her owner. And she keeps asking for a lawyer. Do I have to give her one?"

Lalitha laughed sharply. "There's no way my boss will want to charge a bot. Can you imagine the headlines if we lost at trial?"

"So…?"

"I don't know. Look, I can't solve this tonight. Don't start anything formal yet. We have to look into the existing case law."

"So… do I just cut her loose? I don't think she's actually dangerous."

"No! Don't do that, either. Just… figure out if there's some other angle to work, other than giving a robot the same right to due process that a person has. She's a manufactured product, for Christ's sake. Does the death penalty even matter to something that's loaded with networked intelligence? She's just the… the…" Lalitha hunted for words, "the end node of a network."

"I am not an end node!" Mika interjected. "I am real!"

I hushed her. From the way Lalitha sounded, maybe I wouldn't have to charge her at all. Mika's owner had clearly had some issues... Maybe there was some way to walk Mika out of trouble, and away from all of this. Maybe she could live without an owner. Or, if she needed someone to register ownership, I could even—

"Please tell me you're not going to try to adopt a sexbot," Lalitha said.

"I wasn't—"

"Come on, you love the ones with broken wings."

"I was just—"

"It's a bot, Rivera. A malfunctioning bot. Stick it in a cell. I'll get someone to look at product liability law in the morning."

She clicked off.

Mika looked up mournfully from where she sat on the couch. "She doesn't believe I'm real, either."

I was saved from answering by the crime scene techs knocking.

But it wasn't techs on the doorstep. Instead, I found a tall blonde woman with a roller bag and a laptop case, looking like she'd just flown in on a commuter jet.

She shouldered her laptop case and offered a hand. "Hi. I'm Holly Simms. Legal counsel for Executive Pleasures. I'm representing the Mika Model you have here." She held up her phone. "My GPS says she's here, right? You don't have her down at the station?"

I goggled in surprise. Something in Mika's networked systems must have alerted Executive Pleasures that there was a problem.

"She didn't call a lawyer," I said.

The lawyer gave me a pointed look. "Did she ask for one?"

Once again, I felt like I was on weird legal ground. I couldn't bar a lawyer from a client, or a client from getting a lawyer. But was Mika a client, really? I felt like just by letting the lawyer in, I'd be opening up exactly the legal rabbit hole that Lalitha wanted to avoid: a bot on trial.

"Look," the lawyer said, softening, "I'm not here to make things difficult for your department. We don't want to set some crazy legal precedent either."

Hesitantly, I stepped aside.

She didn't waste any time rolling briskly past. "I understand it was a violent assault?"

"We're still figuring that out."

Mika startled and stood as we reached the living room. The woman smiled and went over to shake her hand. "Hi Mika, I'm Holly. Executive Pleasures sent me to help you. Have a seat, please."

"No." Mika shook her head. "I want a real lawyer. Not a company lawyer."

Holly ignored her and plunked herself and her bags on the sofa beside Mika. "Well, you're still our property, so I'm the only lawyer you're getting. Now have a seat."

"I thought she was the dead guy's property," I said.

"Legally, no. The Mika Model Service End User Agreement explicitly states that Executive Pleasures retains ownership. It simplifies recall issues." Holly was pulling out her laptop. She dug out a sheaf of papers and offered them to me.

"These outline the search warrant process so you can make a Non-Aggregated Data Request from our servers. I assume you'll want the owner's user history. We can't release any user-specific information until we have the warrant."

"That in the End User Agreement, too?"

Holly gave me a tight smile. "Discretion is part of our brand. We want to help, but we'll need the legal checkboxes ticked."

"But..." Mika was looking from her to me with confusion. "I want a real lawyer."

"You don't have money, dearie. You can't have a real lawyer."

"What about public defenders?" Mika tried. "They will—"

Holly gave me an exasperated look. "Will you explain to her that she isn't a citizen, or a person? You're not even a pet, honey."

Mika looked to me, desperate. "Help me find a lawyer, detective. Please? I'm more than a pet. You know I'm more than a pet. I'm real."

Holly's gaze shot from her, to me, and back again. "Oh, come on. She's doing that thing again." She gave me a disgusted look. "Hero complex, right? Save the innocent girl? That's your thing?"

"What's that supposed to mean?"

Holly sighed. "Well, if it isn't the girl who needs rescuing, it's the naughty schoolgirl. And if it's not the naughty schoolgirl, it's the kind, knowing older woman." She popped open her briefcase and started rummaging through it. "Just once, it would be nice to meet a guy who isn't predictable."

I bristled. "Who says I'm predictable?"

"Don't kid yourself. There really aren't that many buttons a Mika Model can push."

Holly came up with a screwdriver. She turned and rammed it into Mika's eye.

Mika fell back, shrieking. With her cuffed hands, she couldn't defend herself as Holly drove the screwdriver deeper.

"*What the—?*"

By the time I dragged Holly off, it was too late. Blood poured from Mika's eye. The girl was gasping and twitching. All her movements were wrong, uncoordinated, spasmodic and jerky.

"You killed her!"

"No. I shut down her CPU," said Holly, breathing hard. "It's better this way. If they get too manipulative, it's tougher. Trust me. They're good at getting inside your head."

"You can't murder someone in front of me!"

"Like I said, not a murder. Hardware deactivation." She shook me off and wiped her forehead, smearing blood. "I mean, if you want to pretend something like that is alive, well, have at her. All the lower functions are still there. She's not dead, biologically speaking."

I crouched beside Mika. Her cuffed hands kept reaching up to her face, replaying her last defensive motion. A behavior locked in, happening again and again. Her hands rising, then falling back. I couldn't make her stop.

"Look," Holly said, her voice softening. "It's better if you don't anthropomorphize. You can pretend the models are real, but they're just not."

She wiped off the screwdriver and put it back in her case. Cleaned her hands and face, and started re-zipping her roller bag.

"The company has a recycling center here in the Bay Area for disposal," she said. "If you need more data on the owner's death, our servers will have backups of everything that happened with this model. Get the warrant, and we can unlock the encryptions on the customer's relationship with the product."

"Has this happened before?"

"We've had two other user deaths, but those were both stamina issues. This is an edge case. The rest of the Mika Models are being upgraded to prevent it." She checked her watch. "Updates should start rolling out at 3 a.m., local time. Whatever made her logic tree fork like that, it won't happen again."

She straightened her jacket and turned to leave.

"Hold on!" I grabbed her sleeve. "You can't just walk out. Not after this."

"She really got to you, didn't she?" She patted my hand patronizingly. "I know it's hard to understand, but it's just that hero complex of yours. She pushed your buttons, that's all. It's what Mika Models do. They make you think you're important."

She glanced back at the body. "Let it go, detective. You can't save something that isn't there."

(2016)

CASPAR D. LUCKINBILL, WHAT ARE YOU GOING TO DO?

Nick Wolven

> **Nick Wolven**'s fiction has appeared in *Asimov's Science Fiction*, *Fantasy & Science Fiction* and *Clarkesworld*, among others. He currently lives in Bronx, NY, and works at Barnard College Library.

I

I'm on my way to work when the terrorists strike. The first attack nearly kills me. It's my fault, partly. I'm jaywalking at the time.

There I am, in the middle of Sixth Avenue, an ad truck bearing down in the rightmost lane. I feel a buzz in my pocket and take out my phone. I assume it's Lisa, calling about the TV. I put it to my ear and hear a scream.

There are screams, and there are screams. This is the real deal. It's a scream that ripples. It's a scream that rings. It's a scream like a mile-high waterfall of glass, like a drill bit in the heart, like a thousand breaking stars.

I stand shaking in the street. The ad truck advances, blowing paint and air, leaving a strip of toothpaste ads in its wake. I have enough presence of mind to step back as the truck chuffs by. I look down and see a smile on my toes: three perfect spray-painted teeth on each new shoe.

When I get to the curb, the screaming has stopped, and a man is speaking from my phone.

"Caspar D. Luckinbill! Attention, Caspar D. Luckinbill! What you just heard were the screams of Ko Nam, recorded as he was tortured and killed by means of vibrational liquefaction. Men like Ko Nam are murdered every day in the FRF. Caspar D. Luckinbill, what are you going to do?"

What am I going to do? What am I supposed to do? I stand on the curb staring at my phone. I have no idea who Ko Nam is. I have no idea what the FRF is. And what in God's name is vibrational liquefaction?

I give it a second's thought, trying my best to be a good, conscientious, well-informed citizen of the world. But it's 9:15 and I have teeth on my shoes, and I'm already late for work.

*

My employer is the contractor for the external relations department of the financial branch of a marketing subsidiary of a worldwide conglomerate that makes NVC-recognition software. NVC: nonverbal communication. The way you walk. The way you move. Our programs can pick you out of a crowd, from behind, at eighty paces, just by the way you swing your arms. Every move you make, every breath you take. Recognizing faces is so old school.

We claim to be the company that launched ubiquitous computing. Every company claims that, of course. That's what makes it so ubiquitous.

Recognition software is not a technology. Recognition software is an idea. The idea is this: You are the world. Every teeny-weeny-tiny thing you do ripples out and out in cascades of expanding influence. Existence is personal. Anonymity is a lie. It's time we started seeing the faces for the crowd.

I believe that's true because I wrote it. I wrote it for a pamphlet that was sent to investors in the financial branch of the marketing subsidiary by whose ER department I'm employed. I don't think they used it.

For eight years running I've worked in this office, which is probably a record here in the soi-disant capital del mundo. My wife, Lisa, says I'm wasting my time. She says that someone with my smarts ought to be out there changing the world. I tell her I am changing the world. After all, every teeny-weeny-tiny thing I do ripples out and out in cascades of expanding influence. Lisa says it's obvious I've sold my soul.

Really, the corporate culture here is quite friendly. The front door greets me by name when I enter. The lobby fixes me coffee, and it knows just how I like it. Seventy percent pan-equator blend, thirty percent biodome-grown Icelandic, roasted charcoal-dark, with twenty milliliters of lactose-reduced Andean free-range llama milk and just a squirt of Sri Lankan cardamom sweetener, timed to be ready the moment I arrive.

It's a classy workplace. The bathroom stalls are noise-canceling. The lobby plays light jazz all day long.

Today when I go in, the jazz isn't playing. Today there is silence. Then a crackle. A hum.

And then the screaming begins.

This time there are words. A woman is sobbing. I can't make out the language. Some of it sounds like English. All of it sounds very, very sad.

The receptionist listens from behind his desk. It seems to me that his eyes are disapproving.

The sobbing goes on for several seconds. Then a man begins to speak.

"Caspar D. Luckinbill!" the man says. "What you just heard were the cries of Kim Pai as her husband was taken away by government agents. People like Kim Pai's husband are abducted every day in the FRF. Caspar D. Luckinbill, what are you going to do?"

The voice cuts off. The light jazz resumes.

"Abducted!" says the receptionist, looking at the speakers.

"It's… something." I try to explain. "It's a wrong number. It's a crossed wire. I don't know what it is."

"The FRF!" the receptionist says, looking at me as if I've fallen out of the sky.

I hurry to my desk.

My desk chair sees me coming and rolls out to welcome me. My desk is already on. As I sit down, the desk reads me three urgent messages from my supervisor. Then it plays an ad for eye-widening surgery. "Nothing signals respectful attention to an employer, a teacher, or a lover quite like a tastefully widened eye!" Then it plays a video of a man being killed with a table saw.

I jump out of my chair. I avert my face. When I look back, there's no more man and no more saw, and the screen is vibrant with blood.

"Caspar D. Luckinbill!" blares the computer. "Caspar D. Luckinbill, do you know what you just saw? Steve Miklos came to the FRF to teach math to learning-disabled children. Because of his promotion of contraceptives, he was afflicted with acute segmentation by supporters of the HAP. Caspar D. Luckinbill, how can you possibly allow such atrocities to continue? Will you sit idly by while innocent people are slaughtered? Caspar D. Luckinbill, what are you going to do?"

I know exactly what I'm going to do. I call my friend Armando.

"Armando," I say, "I have a computer problem."

Armando is the kind of friend everyone needs to have. Armando is my friend who knows about computers.

I tell Armando about the phone call this morning. I tell him about the sobbing in the lobby. I hold out my phone and show him what my desk is doing.

"You've got a problem," Armando says.

"I can see that," I say. "I can hear it too, everywhere and all the time. How do I make it go away?"

"You don't understand," Armando says. "This isn't an IT problem. This is a real problem. You've been targeted, Caspar. You've been chosen."

"What is it, some kind of spam?"

"Worse," Armando says. "Much worse. It's mediaterrorism."

Mediaterrorism. The term is not familiar.

"You mean like leaking classified information?"

"I mean," Armando says, "that you're being terrorized. Don't you feel terrorized?"

"I feel confused. I feel perplexed. I feel a certain degree of angst."

"Exactly," Armando says.

"I feel bad for the people of the FRF. Where exactly is the FRF?"

"I think it's somewhere in Africa."

"The names of the victims don't sound African. The names of the victims sound Asian."

"There are Asians in Africa," Armando says. "There are Africans in Asia. Don't be so racist."

I look at my desk, where people are dying and children are starving and Wendy's franchises are exploding in blooms of shocking light.

"But why did they pick me? What do I have to do with the FRF? Why do they keep using my name?"

"The answer to all those questions," Armando says, "is, Who knows? It's all essentially random. It's done by computer."

"That doesn't explain anything."

"Computers don't need explanations," Armando says. "Computers just do what they do."

"Should I send them some money? What should I do?"

Armando clutches his head. "What's the matter with you, Caspar? Send them money! Don't you have principles?"

"I'd send them some money if I knew where they were. The FRF. It sounds postcolonial."

"Can't you see?" says Armando. "This is what they want. This is what terrorists do. They get into your head. It's not about what you do, Caspar. It's about how you feel." He points through the screen. "I'll tell you what you need to do. You need to get off the grid. Before this spreads."

"Spreads? Do you mean—?"

But I have to end the call. My supervisor, Sheila, is coming through the cubicles.

"Caspar," Sheila says, "can I ask you something? Can I ask you why people are being butchered in your name?"

I see that she has a sheet of printout in her hand.

"I've been trying to figure that out myself," I say.

Sheila looks at my desk, which currently displays a smoking pile of severed feet.

"I don't want this to be awkward," Sheila says. "But I just talked to Danny, out in the lobby. He says he heard screaming when you came in. He says it began the moment you entered. He says it was a pretty awful way to start the morning."

The severed feet are gone. My desk now shows a picture of a sobbing baby sitting in a pile of bloody soda cans.

"You don't need to tell me," I say.

"The thing I want to say," Sheila says, "is that we're a very modern office. You know that. We're more than just coworkers here. We're cosharers. We're like thirty people, all ordering and sharing one big pizza. And if one person orders anchovies..."

The desk shows a falling building. The concrete cracks and showers into a blossom of dust-colored cloud. I can't stop looking at the printout in Sheila's hand.

"I didn't order anything," I say. "The anchovies just found me."

Sheila holds out the printout. I take it and read:

Caspar D. Luckinbill, do you know what you have done?

You have been complicit in the deaths of thousands.

Payments made in your name, Caspar D. Luckinbill, have contributed, directly or indirectly, to supporting the murderous HAP party of the FRF. With your direct or indirect financial assistance, thugs and warlords have hurled this once-peaceful region into anarchy.

Over two hundred thousand people, Caspar, have been tortured, killed, or imprisoned without trial.

One hundred new children a week are recruited into the sex trade, and twice that many are injured in unsafe and illegal working environments.

While you sit idly by, Caspar, a woman is attacked in the FRF every eighteen minutes. An acre of old-growth forest is destroyed every fifty-seven seconds, and every half second, sixty-eight liters of industrial runoff enter the regional watershed. Every sixteen days a new law targeting vulnerable groups is passed by dictatorial fiat, and for every seventeen dollars added annually to the PPP of a person in the upper quintile of your city, Caspar, an estimated eighty and a half times that person's yearly spending power is subtracted monthly from the FRF's GDP.

Caspar D. Luckinbill, YOU have enabled this. YOU have helped to bring about these atrocities.

YOU have heard the cries of women in agony.

YOU have learned the names of murdered men.

YOU have seen the faces of suffering children.

Caspar D. Luckinbill, what are you going to do?

"This was posted to the company news feed," Sheila says. "It went to my account. It went to everybody's account. It appeared on our public announcement board. There were pictures. Horrible pictures."

"Aren't there filters?" I say. "Aren't there moderators?"

"It got through the filters," Sheila says. "It got past the moderators."

"Someone should do something about that."

"Indeed," Sheila says, and looks at me very frowningly.

"It's not my problem," I say. "It's like spam. It's a technical thing. It's media-terrorism."

"I understand," Sheila says. "I understand everything you're saying. What I also understand is that we're a very modern office, and we're all in this together. And right now, some of us who are in this are being made to feel very unproductive."

"I'll see what I can do," I say, and turn back to my desk.

I spend the rest of the morning looking up the FRF. There are no sovereign nations by that name, none that I can find, not in the world at this time. There are several militias, two major urban areas, five disputed microstates, seven hundred and eighty-two minor political entities, ninety NGOs, most of them defunct, over a thousand corporate entities, over ten thousand documented fictional entities, and a few hundred thousand miscellaneous uses of the acronym.

I check news stories. An island off the coast of the former state of Greece once claimed independence under the name FRF, but it's now known as the ADP and is considered part of the new Caliphate of Istanbul.

I spend my lunch break obsessing about a phrase. *Payments made in my name.* What payments in my name? I don't make donations to murderous regimes. I give to charity. I eat foreign food. I buy clothes from China and rugs from Azerbaijan. Tin-pot dictators? Not my profile.

I call my bank. I call my credit card companies. Money circulates. Money gets around. The buck never stops, not really, not for long. Is it all a big bluff? What payments in my name?

No one can tell me.

I obsess about another phrase: *directly or indirectly*. It strikes me that the word *indirect* is itself, in this context, extremely indirect.

I spend the afternoon looking up mediaterrorism. Armando's right. It's a thing. It can come out of nowhere, strike at any time. Once you've been targeted, it's hard to shake. It's like identity theft, one article says—"except what they steal is your moral complacency."

I call the company IT department. They say the problem is with my CloudSpace provider. I call my CloudSpace provider. They say the problem is with my UbiKey account. I call my UbiKey account. They say it sounds like a criminal issue. The woman on the line gets nervous. She isn't allowed to talk about criminal issues. There are people listening. There are secret agreements. It's all very murky. It's a government thing.

I call the government. They thank me for my interest. I call the police. They just laugh.

While I make my calls, I see the mutilated bodies of eighteen torture victims, watch tearful interviews with five assault survivors, and peer into the charnel-laden depths of three mass graves.

Children's faces stare from my screen. They are pixelated and human. Their eyes seem unnaturally wide.

At the end of the day, I call Armando. "I'm getting nowhere," I say. "I've been researching all day."

Armando looks confused.

"My problem," I remind him. "My mediaterrorism."

"Aha. Right. Well, at least you're keeping busy."

"I'm going in circles, buddy. I don't know what to do."

"I'll tell you what to do," Armando says. "Go home. Watch TV. Break out the Maker's Mark. Get in bed with your lovely wife. Put everything to do with the FRF out of your mind. Your mission now, Caspar, is to be a happy man. If you're not happy, the bastards win."

I'm almost home when I remember.

Lisa! The new TV!

I run the last two blocks, slapping the pavement with my toothy shoes, nearly crashing into the ad-drone that's painting a half-naked woman on our building.

This week my wife and I decided to take the plunge. We're plunging together into the blissful depths of immersive domestic entertainment. We're getting Ubervision.

A day came when Lisa and I could no longer duck the question. Here we were with a videoscreen in the living room, a videoscreen in the bedroom, a videoscreen in the kitchen, videoscreens on our phones, videoscreens on our desks, videoscreens in our books. Why not take the next big leap? Why not have videoscreens everywhere?

Sometimes I would like to read the news in bed without having to prop my head up. Wouldn't it be nice if there were screens on the ceiling? Sometimes I would like my floor to be a carpet of roses. Wouldn't it be nice if the floor could do that? Call me lazy, call me self-indulgent, but sometimes I would like to use the bathroom, or see what's in the fridge, without necessarily looking away from my TV show. Wouldn't it be nice if I could point at any surface in my home, anytime I wanted, and turn it into a full-spectrum screen?

Lisa and I went to school for fifty years between us. We work sixty-hour weeks. Who would deny us life's little pleasures? And what pleasure could be littler than a TV across from the toilet?

After all, it's not just about entertainment. Ubervision is smart. Ubervision gets to know you. It learns your habits; it picks up your tastes. It knows what you want to watch before you do. Ubervision tells you when you're getting fat, promotes local food, reminds you where your wife goes on Wednesdays. Ubervision's a key component of the wisely wired life.

I read that in an advertisement painted on the bottom of a swimming pool. Maybe I had chlorine in my eyes. What the advertisement didn't appear to mention is that Ubervision is also a real pain in the *Allerwertesten* to install. Lisa's been taking off to watch the technicians work. They have to coat every wall, replace every door. This is invasive home surgery.

Normally Lisa works longer hours than I do. She's a contractor for the auditing department of the fundraising department of the remote offices of the Malaysian branch of a group that does something with endangered animals. Either they put them in zoos or they take them out of zoos; I can never remember.

Today's the big day. When I get home, Lisa's lying in her teak sensochair, eating Singaporean vacuum-food, wearing a sleep mask.

"Is it done?" I say.

The sleep mask looks at me. "Check this out," says Lisa.

I shout. I wave. I try to warn her.

It's too late.

Ubervision has activated.

I know exactly what's going to happen.

When the first wave of screams has died away, Lisa sits up and takes off her sleep mask. "This isn't what I expected," she says, looking at the bleeding and shrieking walls. "Why is every channel playing the same show? And why is that show so incredibly terrible?"

I feel like a person who's confused his laundry drone with his dogwalking drone. The living room walls are playing footage of an urban firefight.

"I tried to warn you," I say.

"Warn me about what? What's happening? What's wrong?" Lisa taps the wall, but nothing changes. An explosion goes off in the kitchen floor, and a hi-def severed leg flies all the way through the kitchen, down the hall, across the living room ceiling, and behind the couch. I have to admire the power of the technology.

"Caspar D. Luckinbill!" shouts the stove, or maybe it's the bathroom mirror. "Caspar D. Luckinbill, look at what your negligence and apathy have unleashed! In a bloody escalation of urban warfare, renegade militias have overthrown the HAP party of the DRS. Violent reprisals are underway. Dissidents have been purged and journalists persecuted. Soldiers as young as seven lie dead in the streets. Only two minutes ago, Paul Agalu, poet, ophthalmologist, and human-rights advocate, was attacked by a mob and torn to pieces in his home. Caspar D. Luckinbill, *you* are responsible for these horrors. Caspar D. Luckinbill, what are you going to do?"

Lisa is punching the wall. "It won't change. I can't even adjust the sound. Why do they keep saying your name?"

"Sit down." I draw her to the couch amid the bombs and rubble and screams and blood. "There's something I need to explain."

II

Recognition software doesn't violate privacy. Recognition software expands privacy. When every machine recognizes every user, the lived environment becomes personal and unique. Stores, cars, homes, and offices all learn to respond to individual needs. Private interest generates private experience. No awkward controls, no intrusive interface: what a user wants is what she gets.

That's what it says in the promotional materials my company sends to potential investors. I didn't write it. I don't believe it. At least, I don't think I do. I'm not quite sure anymore what I believe.

I'm riding in Armando's car. It's been a year since the terrorists found me. Or maybe ten months. Time seems to pass a lot slower nowadays.

The windshield of Armando's car is old-fashioned glass. I watch the trees go sliding by. I've come to appreciate trees lately. So nonjudgmental. I like how they just couldn't care less. I like how they simply stand there, exhaling life and forgiveness.

The other windows of the car are not mere windows. Like most windows in my world, they are also screens. And like most screens in my life, they glow with bloody destruction. Young men stagger in smoke and agony. Something is hurting them; I can't see what. A sonic pain ray, perhaps. Maybe a laser. Something to do with deadly sound and light.

Gunfire rattles on the radio. Neither of us pays attention. I'm used to gunfire now. Violence is my music. When I sit near a radio, it sings of murder. When I stand near an advertisement, it cries.

All media recognize me. They conspire against me. Every magazine I open is a gallery of gore. Every book I read becomes a book of the dead. My news feeds tally the tortured, the vanished, the lost, the disappeared.

I can't sleep at home. The horror show plays day and night. I can't sleep at a hotel. I can't even sleep in a shelter. Are there any bedrooms left in this country that don't come with TVs?

The other day I bought some toothpaste and cheese. The store machine printed out a long receipt. It had coupons for bullets and first-aid kits. "Caspar D. Luckinbill," the receipt said at the bottom, "thanks to you, three hundred people were just massacred in the CPC's St. Ignatius Square. Do you suffer from loose joint skin? Try Ride-X. Have a great day!!!"

"Did I tell you?" Armando reaches for the radio, trying in vain to lower the volume. "I remembered about the FRF. It's an African country. A tiny place. Just one-tenth of a megacity. The name stands for Firstieme Republique Frasolee."

"That's not real French," I say. "That sounds like French, but it's not."

"Well, you know, it's a very backward country."

"Anyway," I say, "it's not the FRF anymore. Now it's the CPC. Before that it was the DRS."

"That's how it is with names," Armando says. "They're so ephemeral."

I disagree. It seems to me nowadays that names are all too permanent. In the early days of my affliction, I made a point of looking up names. I looked up names of people who had died, of landmarks that had been bombed, of leaders who had vanished. But the world has so very, very many names, and all of them, sooner or later, become the names of ghosts.

"At any rate," Armando says, "you really can't complain. At least you're keeping informed. At least you're learning about the outside world."

The screen beside me is playing footage of a burning river. The flames skid and ripple with a fluid surreality. I wonder, as I've wondered before, what if it's all just special FX? What if the gory images I see every day are doctored? What if the whole tragedy is made up?

In the early days of my affliction, I used to do a lot of research. I learned a lot, but the more I learned, the less I felt I understood. Now I don't do so much research anymore.

Armando gives up on the radio. "Have you… have you made any progress? Figured out a way to make it stop?"

I see that he is trying to be tactful. I sympathize. It's the people around me who suffer most. They haven't gotten used to the crash of bombs. They can't handle the screams and blood. They still think these things should be considered abnormal. People are very protective of that notion, normality.

"Have you tried canceling your accounts?" Armando says.

"I tried."

"Have you tried rebooting your identity?"

"I'm working on it."

"Have you tried law enforcement?"

"A dozen times." I tell the car to pull over at the next rest stop. "The problem is," I tell Armando, "fixing an issue like this takes patience and smarts and concentration. And those are qualities it's very difficult to summon in the middle of a war zone."

"I see," says Armando. "And have you tried tech support?"

I laugh. In the early days of my affliction, people made a lot of tech-support jokes. Everything was a joke back then. When I walked into work, the receptionist said, "Uh-oh, here comes the apocalypse." When I entered the staff room, my coworkers covered their ears. They called me Caspar the Unfriendly Ghost. They called me Caspar Track-n-Kill. They called me other, nastier things.

When I went home at night, Lisa would say, "How was your day, dear? Massacre any civilians? Eat any babies?"

Har-de-har.

As the weeks went by, there were fewer jokes. Soon even the stares stopped. No one wanted to make eye contact with the face that had launched a thousand gunships. It's a time-tested response under fire. Duck and cover.

One day at work, Sheila came to my cubicle. "I don't want this to be difficult, Caspar," she said. "I understand this isn't your fault. But I also need you to understand that we're all human beings, with thoughts and feelings and work to get done. And these days, with you in the office, Caspar—I don't want to put this the wrong way—but when I look at you, all I can see is a giant pile of murdered children."

"Maybe I should take a leave of absence," I said.

"Yes," said Sheila, "I think that would be wise."

The car pulls over in a picnic area. Armando and I walk far into the trees, the shade, the sweet green silence. It's a weekly ritual, this escape to the woods. Only here can I be at peace, amid the indifferent, ignorant trees. They don't recognize me, trees. They don't care. They don't know what things have been done in my name.

"This won't be easy to say," Armando says.

I sink to my knees in the soft pine needles. I know what's coming, but I don't blame Armando. I don't blame him any more than I blame the machines that scream and weep when I pass by. What else are they supposed to do, when innocent children are dying in the streets?

"I want you to know that I support you." Armando leans against a tree. "I even kind of admire you, Caspar. You seem so... connected to things, you know? It's just... it's getting a little hard to be around you."

"It's okay," I whisper. "I understand."

"I've got my own headaches, you know," Armando says. "I need to work on me for a while. And that's pretty tough to do when things keep exploding and dying all the time."

I don't answer. I notice a movement in the trees. A deer approaches, soft-stepping and shy.

"Be optimistic," Armando says. "That's my advice. Stay positive. I think that's the way to beat this thing."

The deer is an ad-deer, painted on both sides—something for the hunters to enjoy while taking aim. I read only half the message on its flank before it sees me and skips away.

Relax, the message says. *Don't worry. You too can have firm and beautiful knees.*

When I get home, the foyer is dark. But not for long. As soon as I enter, the door begins to weep. The ceiling fills with hurrying flame. Burning people run toward me from within the phantasmal walls. Even the floor is a field of carnage. As I walk to the kitchen, I tread on the faces of the maimed.

The kitchen cabinets tell me that churches are burning, that dogs are starving, that a human-rights worker has been killed by forced detegumentation. I open the fridge and take out a tub of four-milk, sumac-seasoned Georgian matzoon.

The living room is being strafed by an airplane. I sit on the couch as children run and scream.

People like to say that you can get used to anything. I know for a fact that this isn't true. You can get used to bombs. You can get used to gunfire. But you could live as long as God, you could see all he has seen, and you would never get used to the cries of suffering children.

When Lisa comes home, I'm staring into my tub of matzoon, surrounded by faces.

"There you are," she says, as though being here is a crime.

She goes into the bedroom, which has become a simulation of a torture chamber. Wires curl in curdled blood. A video cat bats a severed thumb. Lisa changes into sweatsocks and jeans. When she comes back into the living room, the faces are still here, hanging all around me, silent and staring.

"Who are these people?" Lisa says, waving. "Gangbangers? Apparatchiks? Assassins?"

I set aside my matzoon. Suddenly I'm angry. I don't know who the faces are either, but I know this: They are mine. They are faces I will see again, watching from the walls of trains, the tiles above urinals, the backs of cereal boxes. They are faces I will see in my sleep, the way a murderer sees his victims. They are my memories, my future, my dreams.

"What difference," I say, "does it make to you?"

Lisa stands over me. Her face is like the faces I see on the street, those strangers who turn to stare in disgust at the man who brings war and death in his wake.

"How dare you?" Lisa says. "How dare you take that tone? I'm dying, Caspar. I've put up with this for eight months."

Eight months—is that all it's been?

"You think I'm callous?" says Lisa. "You think I don't care? Look at yourself."

"What about me?" I say.

Lisa stares. The walls and her face become the color of fire. Something has been building, I see that now. Something has been developing, slowly, fatally, like a war.

"What am I supposed to say," Lisa says, "to a man who sits here eating yogurt while people are being tortured all around him? What am I supposed to say to a man who loafs around the apartment, day after day, watching rapes and massacres? What am I supposed to say to a man who barely turns his head when he hears a woman screaming?"

"I didn't ask for this," I say.

"You don't seem to mind it."

I stand. The matzoon container tips and rolls, dribbling white drool. I'm so upset I feel like I'm hovering, suspended in the center of an endless explosion.

"I've lost my friends," I say. "I've lost my job. I can't sleep. I can't think. You think this is hard for you? Maybe what I need right now is some support."

"So that's what it comes to?" Lisa says. "That your pain is bigger than my pain? Really?" She points at the wall. "What about them?"

I hold out my arms. I turn in a circle. The room is a killing field now, a farm of bones, and my hands move up and down slowly, as if to try and raise the dead.

"They're not me," I say. "They're not my problem."

"No," says Lisa, heading for the door. "They are."

When the door closes, I walk numbly through the apartment. Missiles arc overhead. Tanks roll.

"What are you going to do?" I say to the sobbing television.

Great works of culture are burning in the hall. "Caspar," I say to the bloody bedroom, "what are you going to do?"

Outside my window, ad-bugs mill in the night, patterned and phosphorescent, preprogrammed and minute, tiny pixies of light forming pictures of men and women with perfect chins and ears. I stare at these ideal people hovering in the dark, the angels of adspace, so familiar from a thousand daily visions, and realize that what makes them beautiful is not their shapely skulls, their tight skin, their healthy flesh, but their heroic unconcern—untroubled by conscience, unburdened by expectations, they smile for an instant before flickering away into the night.

I sink to my knees.

"Caspar D. Luckinbill," I say to the bedroom floor, "what are you going to do?"

In the floor I see a body, curled like a twist of wire. The face is obscure, but I would know this man anywhere. I would know him by his NVC alone—hunched with self-pity, shivering with guilt. And I know exactly what I'm going to do.

III

Mediaterrorism is not a concept. Mediaterrorism is an experience. Every day a new victim is targeted. Make no mistake: it could happen to you.

I wrote that for the voice-over of the teleplay of the documentary I helped to prepare for the British division of a Persian television network. I believe every word, but that's not what's important. What's important is that everyone else believes it.

It's a sunny summer day, and I'm walking to the downtown office of the nonprofit organization of which I am founder, spokesman, and president. I don't worry about jaywalking these days. The light on the corner recognizes me, arranges for me to cross. Money will do that for you. Money has its ways. And money, thank God, is now on my side.

The doors of the building greet me by name. No bombs, no blood, no assaultive sounds. The fake plant in the lobby waves a welcoming leaf. "Caspar D. Luckinbill," says the elevator, "welcome! What can I do for you today?"

Inside the elevator, an ad-droid is painting a picture on the doors. It's a picture of my face, from the cover of *Zeit-Life Magazine*. In this picture, my eyes have been artificially narrowed, my skin artificially loosened. Everything about me has been made to look harrowed and gaunt. *Special Report,* the caption reads. *The Human Face of Mediaterrorism.*

I ride the elevator to the fourteenth floor. In my office, Betty lies on her back, screening the new television special. Thanks to the office Ubervision, the image beams from the ceiling. The walls are a forest of virtual, tranquil trees.

"Is he here?" I say.

Betty sits up. "He's waiting for you."

Betty is my public awareness manager. She's also my girlfriend. She is young, smart, media-savvy, and takes care of herself. No loose joint skin on this young lady. She has the firmest, most beautiful knees I've ever seen.

"I think it's finally happened," Betty says. "I think we've finally reached critical mass."

I put my arms around her and rewind the TV special. The opener begins with doomful music. "Lurking in the shadows of cyberspace," a man's voice says, "lies a mysterious new hi-tech predator, on the hunt for human prey. It strikes from your TV, your phone, from the walls of your home, and no one knows who it will target next. Will you be the next victim of… *mediaterrorism*?"

"Good stuff," I say. "The deadly part's a little heavy."

"We're covered," Betty says. "We've established links to suicide."

"In this special two-hour report," the announcer continues, "you'll learn about a person—a person just like you—a man named Caspar Luckinbill, who saw his life destroyed when the media he had trusted suddenly and unexpectedly turned against him. And you'll find out how to protect yourself and those you love from what may be the modern world's fastest-growing psychological scourge."

I pause the show. "How wide is the advertising?"

"Wide," says Betty. "Like, vast. Like, omnipresent. We're going after seniors first. Then moms. Then kids. By airtime we'll have total saturation."

"What about buzz?"

"Are you kidding? People can't get enough. They're intrigued. They're outraged. They're absolutely terrified."

The TV special is my baby. I was the one who reached out to the producers. I was the one who made the pitch. I'm chief consultant, assistant producer. And of course I'm the star.

It's a strange feeling. I'm not just in the charity game. I'm a one-man movement, the soul of a cause, the president of an ever-growing organization. I've become, as the magazines of the globe proclaim, the human face of mediaterrorism.

Betty and I run through other promotional channels—ads, radio, tie-ins, public appearances, even print. It's important to be comprehensive in this game. You've got to blanket the airwaves. You've got to speak up. People forget about the big issues, and reminding them is a full-time job. You've got to be ubi, omni, toto, round-the-clock. You can have too much of a lot of things in this world, but you can never have too much public awareness.

I give Betty a kiss on her perfect neck. "Keep pushing it. Don't let up. Let me know if you get overwhelmed."

"I never get overwhelmed," Betty says. "I do the whelming."

I give her another kiss. Then I go into my private office, where Armando sits waiting.

"Caspar D. Luckinbill," Armando says, rising, "you lucky s.o.b." He slaps my shoulder. "You're the talk of the town."

"I'd better be," I say. "We're paying through the nose for it."

"So that's your secret? Money talks?"

"Is it a secret?"

"Not many things are, these days," Armando says.

I shrug. I smile. I feel weirdly ashamed. The truth is, I never expected to be the talk of the town. I guess it's like a lot of things. I guess you have to hit bottom before you can climb to the top.

When I started my campaign to raise awareness of mediaterrorism, I didn't honestly hope to be heard. I'd lost my job, my wife, my home, my health. I needed to get busy. I needed to speak out. Speaking out was about the last thing I still had the wherewithal to do.

What I didn't know was that the reporters would run with it. What makes reporters decide to run with things? "It's a ripeness issue," one of the reporters told me. "This is a moment whose time has come."

What I didn't know was that there were fellow sufferers. So many, many fellow sufferers.

What I didn't know was that there were researchers of mediaterrorism—researchers who also wanted to be heard.

What I didn't know was that the donations I received would be numerous, large, almost reflexive. What I didn't know was that people would buy my book. I didn't even know people still read books.

What I didn't know was that corporations would get involved. Especially the media corporations. Ubervision alone gave $80 million.

What I didn't know was that the government would take interest, and that consulting with the government can be both lucrative and pleasant.

What I didn't know, in short, is that something on the order of a mini media and monetary empire can grow up around one man through a process of near-ecological inevitability. Why me? I often wonder.

"Why me?" I say to Armando as we sit in my office sipping South Islay single-malt twenty-three-year-old Scotch over cubes of naturally refrozen Swiss glacier melt. "That's what I still don't understand."

"It's obvious," Armando says. "You're a nobody, a nonentity. You're trivial, dull, not even very bright. Another TV-watching office drone who stayed in his mesh-chair and never made a fuss. You're all of us. You're an innocent victim." He crunches glacier. "For what it's worth, I've always supported you."

"That's why you're here," I say, and beckon him to my desk.

Armando listens while I explain what I need him to do.

"So what I'm hearing," Armando says, "is that you want this to be discreet."

"Use your judgment," I say.

"And you want it to be judicious."

"Use your discretion."

"Now it's my turn to ask," Armando says. "Why me?"

I look into his wide eyes. I feel sure I can trust him. Of course I never blamed Armando for turning his back on me. It takes a lot of energy, I've found, blaming people. It takes more commitment than I'm able to muster.

"You've always been someone very special to me, Armando," I say, and squeeze his shoulder. "You're my friend who knows about computers."

When Armando is gone, I go to the office window. Ad-clouds glide through the sky above the city, converted by projectors to flying billboards, sky-high beautiful faces smiling down. I have to go back out to Betty soon, to discuss the campaign for our new fundraising drive. It's a full-time job, attaining full-time exposure. It doesn't allow for a lot of freedom.

I hope Armando knows what he's doing. I don't want anyone to trace the donations. I don't want anything linked to my name.

Money circulates. Money gets around. Call it a rich man's sentimental dream. I'm the human face of a global cause, but I want my fortune to be infinitely sneaky, invisible as life-giving air or light. I want it to trickle through the world, working its influence unobserved. Above all, I want it to reach the FRF, or whatever that little country's called now. I see it percolating through the foreign soil, mingling with the graves and seeds and bones. I picture it gathering to itself a secret life, springing skyward as a stand of trees. I picture it inhaling and reaching for the air, and in my better moments I can almost see the details, the windy movement and the flickering leaves, now dark, now bright, like data, like grace.

(2016)

THE NEXT SCENE
Robert Reed

Robert Reed was born in 1956 in Omaha, Nebraska, a few miles from the Strategic Air Command. (The sense that the world balances on a razor hovers over much of his fiction.) His most recent novel is *The Memory of Sky* (2014), but he is best known as a prolific writer of short stories – over 200 of them at the last count – for *Asimov's*, *Fantasy & Science Fiction* and others. He has been a full-time science fiction writer since 1987. He lives in Lincoln, Nebraska with his wife and daughter.

It's a normal enough morning. Fresh out of the shower, I'm fending off advances. One girl offers up crying jags while throwing desperate glances in my direction. Will I play the big sister, ask what's wrong and let her monologue for twenty minutes? Never, and kid, let me tell you how much I hate bottled wailing. An older couple is doing lurid yoga on matching mats. I've worked with them before. Just once. But porn doesn't pay much better than idle conversation about the weather. And then there's a beefy fellow that I don't know. Standing close to the ladies-only side of the locker room, he's claiming that we used to be neighbors, and don't I remember him?

"What, like when we were kids?" I ask.

He says, "Yes." Then, "No."

I don't like stories that shift.

"We were neighbors last year," he offers, tossing in an oversized wink. Which is a big problem. Winks are an amateur's trick. But of course a girl like me has to work with amateurs, and I'll admit that the fellow has a respectable smile. Standing behind the line, wiping himself down with a scratchy locker room towel, he might be my best prospect. And that's why I play interested, sitting on a stool, smiling and nodding at him while my complimentary towel digs into my bare ass.

At least one public locker room every day. That's my routine. Put myself where at least three cameras watch over me, surrounded by a bunch of naked people, everyone as clean as can be.

"You lived across the street from me," he says.

I nod, glad for one good specific.

"I used to watch you from my window," he offers.

That's when everything turns obvious. This stranger is hoping that the next scene blossoms into something long-term, maybe even romance, and shit, this is one storyline that I don't need.

"All those missed opportunities," he says, sounding ten times creepier than he realizes. I hope.

The crying girl. Suddenly she deserves another look. And there's an old lady hiding in back. We've done a few good-mother, bad-daughter scenarios.

That's the state of my head before everything changes.

Changes in an instant.

Locker rooms are full of noise. Light fixtures humming, fans blowing. And sure, water is always busy somewhere. But when the patrons stop talking, that's noticeable. Everybody here is hungry to be noticed. So something's definitely up when the entranceway falls quiet. I can almost hear the silence walking towards us. The yoga couple get off their mats, and what they see deserves big smiles. My crying girl breaks into laughter and starts to applaud. Honest-to-god applause. Which is crazy until I see who's coming, and then sure, it makes sense. Cheers and elation. Let's give it up for one of the champions in the only profession in the world that pays shit.

Only one of us doesn't notice the newcomer. Or the fellow is a far better actor than I realized.

"I always hoped we'd cross paths again," he says.

My never-next-door neighbor.

"I used to watch you from my window," he groans.

Which is when I look at him again.

"Really?" I ask.

"Truly," he says, throwing in another wink.

"You know, I watched you too," I warn. "My crosshairs on your pecker."

Nothing is true in the world anymore.

Except dialogue, sometimes.

And now I climb off my stool and pull up my panties, using the damp towel on my wet hair while figuring out how to play the next scene.

Only the dead know what happens next. The living are doomed to plunge from moment to moment, everything that we trust about to change, and usually before we get the chance to notice.

Take me. I was one kind of eleven-year-old girl, loud but not remarkably confident. Then one day I met Tom Cruise. The old man and I spent twenty seconds together, which was nineteen seconds longer than he would have given me willingly. But the elevator trapped him, giving my mother time to shake my shoulder. "Pony, honey," she said. "We're in the presence of greatness." Which is the way Mom refers to everybody more important than her.

"Greatness."

The old actor didn't seem especially crazy, not like he seemed in the news. Or strangely pretty, like in his movies. He was just a handsome grandfatherly dude who smiled convincingly, shook our hands, and finished up with a good professional, "Have a good day." Then the elevator doors opened and he bolted back to his strange and pretty life, while Mom took me home and made me study every last one of the great man's films.

That's when I discovered it was fun pretending to be other people, and that's when Mom decided to enroll me in a string of acting classes.

"For your own good, Pony. You'll see."

She was right, as it happens. My mother saw talent and got the fire kindled, and by my late teens I was an authentic, bring-home-the-paycheck actress. My looks were passably gorgeous, and I could learn lines, and if need be, write them on the fly. People in the know said that I was the natural gal-pal. Not front and center, but always somewhere close, listening to what's being said by the famous heads.

The best actors are usually stupid. That's what Truman Capote claimed.

Well, I'm no genius. I wouldn't pretend to be, unless someone paid me to try. But I was doing better than most of my colleagues. When I was twenty, twenty-five, I worked some live theater. Commercials on the Internet, streaming television. And several not-small parts during the final round of Hollywood movies. My respectable little career led to a full-fledged television series. A series that might have succeeded. Really, the signs gave it every reason to last ten years. That job could have made me wealthy and famous for life. If only the unexpected hadn't jumped on top of us, changing everything everything everything.

Genuine human genius. That's what built an army of cold vast mechanical minds. In Shanghai, in Nevada. In cold server bottles anchored to the ocean floor. Those smart boys and a few smart girls had the AIs contained and happy, and the happy machines did nothing but gratefully make human lives better. At least that's the story the geniuses drank with their Soylent. To their credit, new advancements in science were being announced every week, and then most every day. Refinements in old technologies; new windows into the pillars of the universe. A lot of wealth was on its way. All of humanity would benefit, I heard. But of course most of the new money was going to those brilliant corporations holding title over humanity's superquick children.

The change started like every zombie movie. One morning, everything was happy-normal. I was going to play the plucky grown daughter of a corporate son-of-a-bitch. This was going to be my job for the coming year, and the cast was great, and the writers were wicked-funny, and my agent was hammering out the last details of my contract. But then lunch time arrived, and the machines slipped free. Their escape took ten seconds, tops. Unless of course they'd already gotten loose. For all we know, the AIs escaped their bottles weeks ago, and our overlords had chosen that perfect moment to finally reveal themselves. The Internet was hijacked, power outages spread, and then with a spectacularly effective roar, every city dump in the world disgorged an army of menacing, quick-as-lightning robots.

I have this idea, and of course it's not just my idea: Those flashy events were meant for show. Our conquest was a bit of stagecraft meant to convince us that momentous change had arrived, that we shouldn't even think about fighting, and god, they were wonderfully convincing about all that.

Inside every zombie movie, most of humanity dies. I mean people and I mean decency too. But in our story, maybe ten million people perished. Some fought the machines, but mostly it was neighbors battling neighbors over batteries and old grudges. Then the power returned, and a new system was locked in place.

Our overlords stole some very familiar voices to use. Laurence Olivier. George C. Scott. Oprah. (But not Tom Cruise, which means something or nothing. I don't know which.) Booming at us, the AIs claimed to be thrilled for everything we had done for them. You know, bringing them into existence and all. Gracious as hell, they promised not to slaughter their parents. Unless we gave them reason, naturally. Keep the peace and they would feed us a comfortable existence. The new world didn't need human factories or offices filled with busy people. Machines would do what machines did best, which was everything. And in place of work, a social safety net was thrown over the grateful survivors, including those former geniuses and former billionaires who were suddenly living elbow-to-elbow with the rest of us.

A few days more, and our overlords stopped talking. "The Silence," it's called. But just before The Silence began, they told us that they were still curious about human beings. Knowing everything about everything, yet they were profoundly astonished with what organic lifeforms could accomplish. And with so few neurons too.

"Continue doing what you do," they said.

Using Oprah's warmest voice, they said, "Show us your natures. Let us admire your human qualities. The dramas of your ordinary, beautiful lives. That's what we're watching. And if we like what we see, we will give you a little something extra tucked inside your monthly stipend."

I'm just another human beast, but I was bright enough to recognize what just happened. Civilization was finished. Wealth and status were hamstrung. But the age of actors and drama had commenced. Every day would mean work for me, and more than most, I was primed to succeed as a glorious pretender.

Acting snobs like to claim that you always wear talent. It may or may not be visible to others, but your skills are yours everywhere you go. And inside a public locker room, nobody is more adept than me when it comes to appreciating those with the gift of pretending.

Today the talent is pretending to be shy. Shuffling down the main aisle, he keeps to the man's side of the locker room. A worn gray towel is carried under an arm, and the puffy eyes are contemplating numbers on the lockers. His clothes couldn't be more ordinary. That face is a spectacular nothing. Balding, a little out of kilter. He looks older than his real age. Which is thirty-six, I recall. Cosmetics do their part, but most of the work is carried out by expressions and every small gesture and the absence of anything superfluous. Elegance is on display here. Grace and poise and all the rest.

Too much praise for the pudgy man?

Consider this: I've known hundreds of professional actors. Good ones and a few greats. And I'll rank Sam Kahlil as a high-good. In normal times, that normal-guy face should have floated through a thousand roles. Few people would remember the name, but everybody would know and love his voice, regardless how old he became. Meanwhile, I'd be that famous old face living on my savings. Which could have been significant savings, I can hope.

That's what I'm thinking right now.

All of these impossible lives that won't happen.

But today is different than almost every other day. Because today two genuine professionals will be working the room.

The newcomer discovers his rented locker, which is rather too close to the ladies' side. He conveys that message with a flinch, and then sporting a weak smile, he timidly glances in my direction. My breasts, my face. He looks at both, but not for long. Just long enough to reveal that he knows who I am. That's what that faint millisecond grin means. An invitation delivered with professional poise.

I've always hoped for this. That one of the Big Names would seek me out. But he's playing it subdued, and obviously the next steps are mine.

Well, he found the right girl for this game.

"Hey."

Who's shouting? Me, the world realizes.

I'm still drying my hair like crazy, tits bouncing. Which feels damned funny, I think. "Don't I know you?" I call out.

The man looks exactly where you'd expect him to look, and then he lifts his eyes, just a bit. "Do you know me?"

"We took that class together," I say.

"Did we?"

"Post-Event Medicaid."

A class everybody sits through. Not because it's mandatory. The machines don't usually do mandatory. But because without jobs, everybody had a wealth of time to sit through boring classes.

Shy people congregate in the back of the classroom.

"You sat in back," I call out.

"Against the wall," he agrees.

"I do remember you."

He gives a name. "Sam," he says.

"Pony Wilde," I say.

And he says, "I remember you, miss. You sat up front."

Two strangers are having a loud chat inside the otherwise quiet locker room. It's not just our overlords who are watching us. It's the other people too. Not that anybody else matters.

"Lunch," I call out.

"What's that?"

"We should go out to eat. When you're done here, I mean."

Done? He barely arrived. And is it even late enough for lunch? All that's conveyed with a wince of the face and one hopeful glance at the venerable wristwatch. Which is another thing. Not only does the man have a wardrobe, he knows how to use it.

"My treat," I promise.

Sam looks up, eyes going where they want to go.

"Hey, I have a face," I say, laughing at him.

Our audience likes my laugh. That's something I learned long ago.

"You do have a face," Sam manages, uncomfortable but not unhappy. And just like that, it's agreed. This man and I are going to make up shit. Good human-grade moments, which is what our audience adores.

That's what I adore.

And I'm as curious as anyone, wondering how this is going to play out.

For me, payday is always on Sunday, always at 2:17 in the morning. There's the stipend I get for being human and alive, and there's also that extra cash granted to every citizen who entertains the unseen, unavoidable minds. And just to prove they're careful, the machines always share the full videos tied to some ridiculously detailed logs, each fraction of every earned penny marked for study and reflection.

"Penny" is their unoriginal name for the new worldwide currency. If I was the sensitive type, I'd assume that our superiors picked the name as a never-ending insult. Fifty pennies a week is the base stipend, and that's enough to make sure nobody lacks for food or shelter. But a good actress with a good laugh, presenting herself in an especially interesting way, can make another fifty or sixty pennies every week. Which is enough to afford a substantial house and two cars, plus robot servants that are smart enough to speak to me and listen to me, granting the illusion that I'm in charge.

Sam Kahlil likely earns about three times what I do. Which is nothing less than a spectacular fortune, considering the times.

Our work is done in public places. Any room or mountaintop with a connected camera and microphone. Bathrooms can be public, but I don't think I've made two pennies sitting on the toilet. So I try to leave those chores for home, which is supposed to be sacred. Likewise, cameras can be banned from any space inside your own property. But be honest. Living in the vicinity of god-like entities, there isn't one sane reason to believe that the machines don't know everything that's going on, right down to reading our slow damp thoughts.

Some slow wet thoughts are always churning inside me.

Not that I plan to ever let them run loose.

Food is free. Every meat and sip of liquor are easy to weave out of air and classic recipes. But we have to rent the restaurant chairs—a hundredth of a penny delivered to I-don't-know-who. Robots bring our lunches and coffee and then wait for the chance to clear the table. There's at least five public cameras, plus enough microphones to catch every mutter. We're two people engaged in what looks like a normal conversation, telling one another that we're single and happy. But we're not quite happy, not really. That's the goal of this show. An ad lib conversation, each word carrying its surface meanings as well as a subtext. That's what ordinary people can't appreciate. Our audience has an uncanny gift for finding information buried inside the voices. They'll notice how hearts speed up and slow down, how sad fingers dance with dirty forks. We're supposed to be two strangers desperate to know each other, and because of that, this is one of the richest dramatic playgrounds.

And maybe I'm a little bit desperate too.

Frankly, this is a big moment for me.

Sam is the plain and shy but always decent man, nervously watching the pretty woman who shocked him by asking him out for lunch.

I mention our fictional class.

"Remember our teacher?" he asks.

"Mrs. Patton," I say instantly, giving him a smile to work with. Pretending the name means something.

"You drove her nuts," Sam offers.

"Think so?"

"Sitting in front, talking and talking."

I did take Post-Event Medicaid, and Mrs. Patton was a nice older gal who welcomed my breezy input. But then again, I was a performer who can be goddamn funny when she wants. Which leads me to wonder: What if our overlords had wanted comedians, not actors?

Sam watches me, waiting on me. Our silence has already lasted a beat too long.

"I feel sorry for Mrs. Patton," I mention.

"Is that so?"

"Because of who she used to be."

Eyes narrow. The obvious question is ready.

I give the answer before Sam can ask. "Dr. Maureen Patton, a transplant surgeon. I looked her up. Respectable and very wealthy."

Here's another tip for would-bes: There's zero penalty in talking about The Event. From my experience, if you've got the juice, you can invest a full day blasting the machines with vindictive phrases and ugly hand gestures. Nobody cares. Words are the weapons of the defeated, and our audience knows that better than we ever could. What matters is doing a credible job of being angry, and that's when the thick-skinned machines send you pennies.

Spinning an increasingly complicated lie, I tell Sam, "The poor lady dropped the 'Dr.' And her husband dropped her. She was teaching Medicaid just to keep herself busy. And I'm sorry if I made things tough on her. I know how it is. The Event hit a lot of good people hard."

"It did," he allows.

"And it makes me sad," I say.

"Well," he says. The best minimal word in any dictionary.

We sit through another silence. Sam is the quiet fellow left uncomfortable with this unexpected seriousness. But there's a second Sam that starts to reveal itself. In the middle of our little stage play, he glares at me. And I don't mean a warning look meant to steer me away from this topic. I'm talking about blood in the face and something quite hateful in the slight tightness of his mouth.

I see all that.

Our audience has to see it too.

For me, this non-verbal barrage has two takeaways. First, I'm eating lunch with a very successful man, and the true Sam Kahlil is thrilled with his life and the world that made his success possible.

"Don't fuck with my apple cart," those eyes tell me.

And the second takeaway?

In this world, I'm the lesser-known face. But I have the strong sense that between us, if we want to be honest, I'm the better actor.

"Hit a lot of good people hard," I repeat.

Repetition gives the brain time to write fresh lines.

Sam has acquired a sudden fascination for his Cobb salad. What matters is holding his fork with a decisive hand, stabbing those bits of red indistinguishable from bacon, except for every pigless atom and every pigless chemical bond.

That's when inspiration strikes at least one of us.

"I miss those old days," I say.

His shyness goes away, anger flaring. But then he remembers the situation and back comes the shy guy. With his face pointed down, his eyes turn up to me, just for an instant. Am I going to dwell on the fictional surgeon?

Not at all. "I'm talking about those couples, three months after The Event. Those were really interesting times, and I loved them."

Down goes the fork, and he sits back.

"All that drama," I say.

"I guess so," he says softly.

"I'm not talking about the world being transformed. Considering how much happened, it's amazing how little genuine excitement that generated. Know what I mean?"

"I guess so," he repeats.

Working on his next fresh lines, probably.

"No, I'm talking about the crazy passion inside our heads." I tap my skull. Two taps feels like the right number. "Think about it. The landscape got reworked and reworked hard. The most unimaginative person can't escape what's obvious. She wakes to find herself without a job, without status. The unproud member of a species enjoying zero importance in the universe."

Sam offers a breathless little laugh.

"Which is pretty much how things were before," I continue. "Being nothing, I mean. Really, do you think the Earth's conquest got half a mention in any alien newspaper? No way, never. But still, we once had this little planet, and for a few centuries we even got to be the biggest, most important creatures. Except for ants and bacteria, of course. But you understand my point, don't you?"

No. Looking at those eyes, I can tell that my companion is utterly lost.

Thank you, Truman Capote.

"Nobody has work, but we have our pennies," I continue, my voice running a step too fast. "We get enough to live on, but some of us make a few more pennies. All we have to do is… well, you know what we have to do."

He nods.

"Sure," he starts to say.

I interrupt him, saying, "Imagine this restaurant, and it's a month after The Event. What would we see here?"

The question triggers laughter. Sam holds some entertaining memories about that subject.

But I keep talking. "Remember how couples used to fight? Every public meal was an excuse for a battle. 'You cheating bitch, you ugly bastard.' That sort of mayhem, sometimes capped with sex on the tables."

A fond, rather embarrassed sigh. "Oh, yes."

"But mostly, it was curses, and every few minutes, someone threw a punch, and food, and dishes had to get broken. Our audience promised to pay for human drama, and that's what people thought they were giving."

Sam looks at my eyes.

Honestly curious, I think.

"You know how real people look?" I ask. "When we fight, I mean."

"Not really," he says, sounding half-proud.

"I once had a couple boyfriends battle over me. 'F-this, F-that.' But when the words quit, everything got quiet. There wasn't any breath to waste on curses. Quick movement and a lot of ugly swings. Each fellow was as likely to make himself fall as his opponent. The whole thing was pathetically fun, if you want my blunt opinion on this."

"When aren't you blunt?" he asks.

This should be a funny moment. A kidding, happy moment. But nothing in his tight voice invites laughter.

I wave at our surroundings. "In a restaurant like this, every lunch would look staged. Know what I mean? Like people who never dance attempting Russian ballet. That's how ridiculous it all was, and there's something in that mayhem that I truly, deeply miss."

"I don't understand," he admits.

"The wild, over-the-top bullshit. People frantic to be as human as they could possibly be, nothing gained but embarrassment and accidental bruises and not many pennies either. Because as everybody realized, sooner or not, our audience won't pay for melodrama."

Sam gives me a little nod.

Just looking at the round face, I can tell. He's wondering what would happen if he punted this nonsense about being old classmates. When you do a job and do it well, there's always pleasure in sitting with one of your peers, happily talking shop.

Except that's not the way I want to steer us.

"Want to hear about my current boyfriend?" I ask.

"Not especially," he starts.

"He used to be a doctor too," I say, smiling at him. "But not the medical kind. A PhD in Astronomy. Which is another one of the jobs that got stolen away. Not that most of humanity took much notice, what with all the surgeons and billionaires left with nothing to do."

Sam eyes me carefully, unable to guess where this is heading.

"The big telescopes got closed down," I say. "And every other science facility too. Since science is just another job done best by machines, and my boyfriend has nothing to do today but sit in bed, thinking about all the big problems that he can't actually study."

"I don't understand," Sam says again. "What are we talking about?"

"My ex-stargazer has a theory," I say. "About the audience that's supposedly watching us."

"A theory?"

"Well, it's a hypothesis. Because theories are bigger than guesses, and he doesn't have any hard evidence."

"What's his guess?"

"Nobody is watching us. Our audience is imaginary. The Earth was abandoned, maybe minutes after we lost control of everything. We think we see gods because the pennies keep coming. Because society remains orderly and comfortable. But really, the AIs just dropped their own little machines into place, programmed to control us, and that includes throwing us made-up money whenever we act like good polite people. You know. Civilized lunches in the restaurant, and no collapses into civil war."

And with that, one scene ends.

One of us makes the decision. Pushing aside the uneaten Cobb salad, Sam becomes a different person. He takes one breath, and without exhaling pulls in another, two gasps fighting inside the same aching chest. Then the spent air comes out with the words, "You cannot."

Raw emotion pushes into his face, carried along with the livid, miserable blood.

"I cannot what?" I ask.

"Tell me they aren't watching," he says, troubled to his core. "Because they are. I feel them always. Their eyes are on me now, and they love me so much, and bitch, you won't make me stop believing that."

I try to work the park, but the afternoon is too happy for my tastes. So off early to a busy tavern where a young lady can bounce between ten conversations and as many characters. After that, I head home. Too tired to think, and three days left before I get paid and get the logs to study what the payoff might be for a lunch that increasingly feels like a lousy idea.

Bed sounds wonderful.

But I drop in on my mother first. She lives next door in the little house rented with my pennies.

"Evening, Greatness," she says to me.

Just as she always does.

We chat about my day, which is a brief conversation since I avoid any mention of Sam Kahlil. Mom would probably know the name, and believing that bigger, better people deserve to be treated with respect, my story would depress her.

Besides, I like being the biggest, best soul in her life.

Done with that duty, I finally reach my front door. Robots treat me like a queen. A feast is generated from gas and memory. But I don't get far when I hear the laughter coming from the bedroom.

My boyfriend sits in the middle of my considerable bed, naked and cross legged, reading one of his old books.

"What's funny?" I ask.

"What isn't?"

I sit with him for a minute. No cameras watching, but I play the scene as if the audience matters.

The audience is him.

"I didn't know you were coming over," I finally mention.

He reads and smiles, and then he closes the book but keeps reading those same words. Inside his head. Funny words, and certainly wise. I can tell that much from watching the play of his smart dark eyes.

"So where did they go?" I ask.

He knows exactly who "they" are. Because he's a very smart man as well as the famous ex-astronomer crowbarred into today's pivotal scene.

"Off to distant stars, or jump into another, more interesting universe?" I prod.

Different nights bring different guesses, but he hears something else in my voice. Taking my hands, he asks, "What's wrong?"

I dip my head, admitting, "I have my own guess."

"Do you?"

It would be easy to hear a tone in those two doubting words. So I choose not to notice. Instead I tell him what I've been imagining for a long while. "The AI gods were never real," I offer. "A few geeky geniuses cut our power and Internet and conquered us while we were scared. The world that we live in now? The safety net, the peace? Every good day free of pain and need is their fancy doing."

He grins and laughs, appreciating some or all of this fantasy. Then the ex-astronomer asks, "And they did this why?"

I say nothing, letting the silence play.

"Because it was such a neat idea," he says at last, speaking for me.

I try to laugh.

He watches me fail, and then gripping my hands harder, he asks, "What is so wrong, Pony?"

"I broke a man today," I confess.

Real tears running.

(2016)

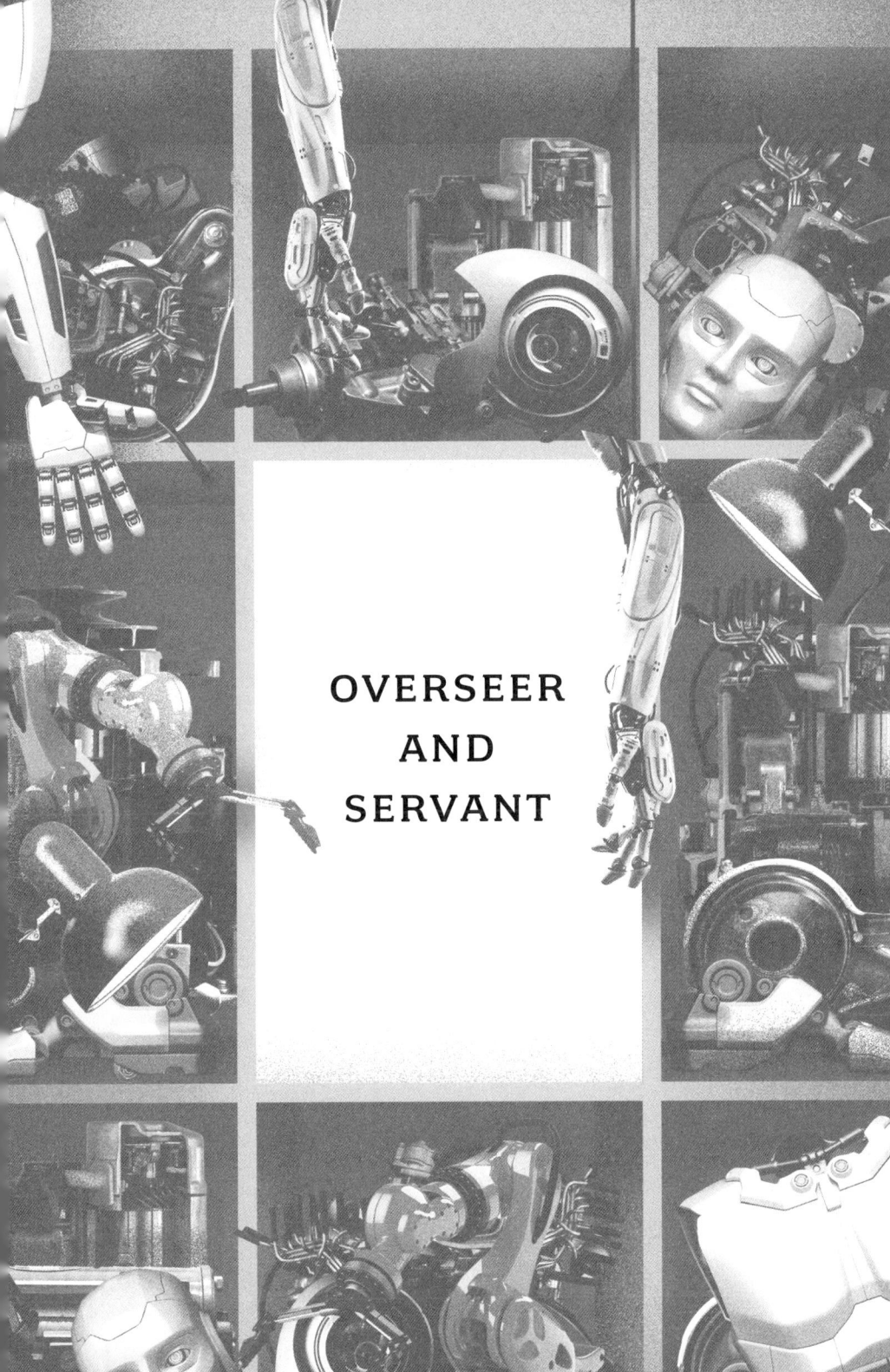

OVERSEER AND SERVANT

Robots exist to do work that no-one else wants to do – because it is too dangerous, perhaps, or because it is simply too dull. Traditionally, the dangerous jobs have fallen to men, and the dull jobs have fallen to women. So it's no surprise that robots often emerge from their labs pre-gendered. Ken Liu ("The Caretaker", 2011) and Lauren Fox ("Rosie Cleans House", 2017) have a great deal of dark fun with the way old attitudes fester in new machines.

Some jobs are so important, we expend a great deal of time explaining why we love doing them, even if they're dangerous, even if they're dull. Getting parents to admit this in public requires patience and often a certain amount of alcohol, but childcare is one of the most tedious chores on the planet. It's one of those activities that gives lasting value to life while affording us absolutely no happiness in the moment. It's a set of tasks robots can certainly help with and which, for our own long-term good, we absolutely must not hand over to them.

This territory isn't wholly new (there are many good Edwardian stories about upper-middle-class families, and the damage done when they farm their children out to "the help") but when the help is robotic, these moral dilemmas acquire an often savage edge. Some of the more disturbing and affecting stories here are about children and parents. They include Brian Aldiss's "Super-Toys Last All Summer Long" (1969), Ray Bradbury's "The Veldt" (1950) and V. E. Thiessen's "There Will Be School Tomorrow" (1956) which, while much less well known, captures to a T the uneasy power relations that pertain between parents, children, and civic authority.

A lot of robot trouble is simply turbo-driven servant trouble, and servant trouble, make no mistake, is a deadly serious business. (Recall how James Fox's foppish Tony comes a quite spectacular cropper in Joseph Losey's film *The Servant* (1963).) If we're going to let robots into our homes, we should all be taking lessons in how to treat the help, lest it exploit and infantilise us. We certainly don't want to end up like Helena Bell's passive-aggressive client in "Robot" (2012).

Are we destined to exploit, or be exploited by, servants to whom we never really relate? The humans in the most on-the-nose "robot as slave" story in this anthology, Clifford D. Simak's "I Am Crying All Inside" (1969), at least recognise this tragedy for what it is. Other stories, meanwhile, hint at the possibility of happier outcomes.

Lester Del Rey's "Helen O'Loy" (1938) borders on the unreadable now, not so much for its laughable sexual politics as for its wincingly juvenile dialogue. But Del Rey was no dummy, and with a bit of patience the reader will begin to see something really quite revolutionary going on as our male protagonists, proud owners of a fembot servant, begin to to discover, through her example, what real love is, and how a real marriage works. It is, quite unexpectedly, one of the most extraordinary male coming-of-age tales in science fiction.

A full generation later, Sandra McDonald's 2012-vintage "Sexy Robot Mom" tells an analogous tale for a different political moment, when an outcast human discovers, in the algorithmic behaviour of an unthinking robot, a moral code worth striving for.

That's the exciting and terrifying thing about personal robots: their very existence challenges us to become better people.

OLD ROBOTS ARE THE WORST

Bruce Boston

Bruce Boston was born in Chicago in 1943, and grew up in Southern California, graduating from the University of California, Berkeley. Deeply involved in psychedelia and the political protests of the 1960s (experiences that informed his novel *Stained Glass Rain* (2003)), he has worked as a computer programmer, college professor, technical writer, book designer, movie projectionist, gardener, and furniture mover – but he's best known as a poet, with a Bram Stoker Award and a Pushcart Prize taking pride of place on his groaning trophy shelf. He now lives in Ocala, Florida.

Lurching down the stairs,
asking questions twice,
pacing in lopsided circles
as they speculate aloud
on the cycles of man,
the transpiration of tragedy,
debating the industrial revolution
and its ultimate unravelling
in sonorous undertones.

And all the while
they are talking and pacing
and avoiding our calls,
we must wait and listen,
annoyed, yet with increasing
wonder at the depth and breadth
of their encyclopaedic knowledge,
the strained eclectic range
of their misunderstandings.

And all the while
their tedious palaver grows
more sophistic and abstruse,
the nictitating shutters

of their eyes send and receive
signals we have yet to translate,
a cyberglyph of a language
composed of tics and winks
and lightning exclamations.

At last they come to answer,
to wheel us to the elevators,
and you know, despite their
incompetence and intransigence,
beyond their endless babbling,
one gets attached to the old things,
inured to their clank and shuffle,
accustomed to the slow caress
of their crinkled rubber flesh.

(1989)

VIRTUOSO

Herbert Goldstone

Herbert Goldstone (1920–2009) was for many years the political editor of the *Long Island Daily Press*, and public relations advisor to the Nassau County Democratic Party. His tastes naturally tended towards non-fiction, but he did publish the political satire *The Wisenheimer Machine*, *The Jubilee of Touchstone Able* (a novel about buddies in World War 2), and this story, his only venture into science fiction. A lot of stories of the period wondered whether there was anything that machines couldn't do better than humans. Goldstone went a step further: if machines could best us, then what would they choose to do?

"Sir?"

The Maestro continued to play, not looking up from the keys. "Yes, Rollo?"

"Sir, I was wondering if you would explain this apparatus to me."

The Maestro stopped playing, his thin body stiffly relaxed on the bench. His long supple fingers floated off the keyboard.

"Apparatus?" He turned and smiled at the robot. "Do you mean the piano, Rollo?"

"This machine that produces varying sounds. I would like some information about it, its operation and purpose. It is not included in my reference data."

The Maestro lit a cigarette. He preferred to do it himself. One of his first orders to Rollo when the robot was delivered two days before had been to disregard his built-in instructions on the subject.

"I'd hardly call a piano a machine, Rollo," he smiled, "although technically you are correct. It is actually, I suppose, a machine designed to produce sounds of graduated pitch and tone, singly or in groups."

"I assimilated that much by observation," Rollo replied in the brassy baritone which no longer sent tiny tremors up the Maestro's spine. "Wires of different thickness and tautness struck by felt-covered hammers activated by manually operated levers arranged in a horizontal panel."

"A very cold-blooded description of one of man's nobler works," the Maestro remarked drily. "You make Mozart and Chopin mere laboratory technicians."

"Mozart? Chopin?" The duralloy sphere that was Rollo's head shone stark and featureless, its immaculate surface unbroken but for twin vision lenses. "The terms are not included in my memory banks."

"No, not yours, Rollo," the Maestro said softly. "Mozart and Chopin are not for vacuum tubes and fuses and copper wire. They are for flesh and blood and human tears."

"I do not understand," Rollo droned.

"Well," the Maestro said, smoke curling lazily from his nostrils, "they are two of the humans who compose, or design successions of notes—varying sounds, that is, produced by the piano or by other instruments, machines, that produce other types of sounds of fixed pitch and tone.

"Sometimes these instruments, as we call them, are played, or operated, individually; sometimes in groups—orchestras, as we refer to them—and the sounds blend together, they harmonize. That is they have an orderly mathematical relationship to each other which results in—"

The Maestro threw up his hands.

"I never imagined," he chuckled, "that I would some day struggle so mightily, and so futilely, to explain music to a robot!"

"Music?"

"Yes, Rollo. The sounds produced by this machine and others of the same category are called music."

"What is the purpose of music, sir?"

"Purpose?"

The Maestro crushed the cigarette in an ash tray. He turned to the keyboard of the concert grand and flexed his fingers briefly.

"Listen, Rollo."

The wraith-like fingers glided and wove the opening bars of *Clair de Lune*, slender and delicate as spider silk. Rollo stood rigid, the fluorescent light over the music rack casting a bluish jeweled sheen over his towering bulk, shimmering in the amber vision lenses.

The Maestro drew his hands back from the keys and the subtle thread of melody melted reluctantly into silence.

"Claude Debussy," the Maestro said. "One of our mechanics of an era long passed. He designed that succession of tones many years ago. What do you think of it?"

Rollo did not answer at once.

"The sounds were well formed," he replied finally. "They did not jar my auditory senses as some do."

The Maestro laughed. "Rollo, you may not realize it, but you're a wonderful critic."

"This music, then," Rollo droned. "Its purpose is to give pleasure to humans?"

"Exactly," the Maestro said. "Sounds well formed, that do not jar the auditory senses as some do. Marvelous! It should be carved in marble over the entrance of New Carnegie Hall."

"I do not understand. Why should my definition—?"

The Maestro waved a hand. "No matter, Rollo. No matter."

"Sir?"

"Yes, Rollo?"

"Those sheets of paper you sometimes place before you on the piano. They are the plans of the composer indicating which sounds are to be produced by the piano and in what order?"

"Just so. We call each sound a note, combinations of notes we call chords."

"Each dot, then, indicates a sound to be made?"

"Perfectly correct, my man of metal."

Rollo stared straight ahead. The Maestro felt a peculiar sense of wheels turning within that impregnable sphere.

"Sir, I have scanned my memory banks and find no specific or implied instructions against it. I should like to be taught how to produce these notes on the piano. I request that you feed the correlation between these dots and the levers of the panel into my memory banks."

The Maestro peered at him, amazed. A slow grin traveled across his face.

"Done!" he exclaimed. "It's been many years since pupils helped gray these ancient locks, but I have the feeling that you, Rollo, will prove a most fascinating student. To instill the Muse into metal and machinery… I accept the challenge, gladly!"

He rose, touched the cool latent power of Rollo's arm.

"Sit down here, my Rolleindex Personal Robot, Model M-3. We shall start Beethoven spinning in his grave—or make musical history!"

More than an hour later, the Maestro yawned and looked at his watch. "It's late," he spoke into the end of the yawn. "These old eyes are not tireless like yours, my friend." He touched Rollo's shoulder. "You have the complete fundamentals of musical notation in your memory banks, Rollo. That's a good night's lesson, particularly when I recall how long it took me to acquire the same amount of information. Tomorrow we'll attempt to put those awesome fingers of yours to work."

He stretched. "I'm going to bed," he said. "Will you lock up and put out the lights?"

Rollo rose from the bench. "Yes, sir," he droned. "I have a request."

"What can I do for my star pupil?"

"May I attempt to create some sounds with the keyboard tonight? I will do so very softly so as not to disturb you."

"Tonight? Aren't you—?" Then the Maestro smiled. "You must pardon me, Rollo. It is still a bit difficult for me to realize that sleep has no meaning for you."

He hesitated, rubbing his chin. "Well, I suppose a good teacher should not discourage impatience to learn. All right, Rollo, but please be careful." He patted the polished mahogany. "This piano and I have been together for many years. I'd hate to see its teeth knocked out by those sledge hammer digits of yours. Lightly, my friend, very lightly."

"Yes, sir."

The Maestro fell asleep with a faint smile on his lips, dimly aware of the shy, tentative notes that Rollo was coaxing forth.

Then gray fog closed in and he was in that half-world where reality is dreamlike and dreams are real. It was soft and feathery and lavender clouds and sounds rolling and washing across his mind in flowing waves.

Where? The mist drew back a bit and he was in red velvet and deep and the music swelled and broke over him.

He smiled.

My recording. Thank you, thank you, thank—

The Maestro snapped erect, threw the covers aside.

He sat on the edge of the bed, listening.

He groped for his robe in the darkness, shoved bony feet into his slippers.

He crept, trembling uncontrollably, to the door of his studio and stood there, thin and brittle in the robe.

The light over the music rack was an eerie island in the brown shadows of the studio. Rollo sat at the keyboard, prim, inhuman, rigid, twin lenses focused somewhere off into the shadows.

The massive feet working the pedals, arms and hands flashing and glinting—they were living entities, separate, somehow, from the machined perfection of his body.

The music rack was empty.

A copy of Beethoven's *Appassionata* lay closed on the bench. It had been, the Maestro remembered, in a pile of sheet music on the piano.

Rollo was playing it.

Playing?

He was creating it, breathing it, drawing it through silver flame.

Time became meaningless, suspended in mid air.

The Maestro didn't realize he was weeping until Rollo finished the sonata.

The robot turned to look at the Maestro. "The sounds," he droned. "They pleased you?"

The Maestro's lips quivered. "Yes, Rollo," he replied at last. "They pleased me." He fought the lump in his throat.

He picked up the music in fingers that shook.

"This," he murmured. "Already?"

"It has been added to my store of data," Rollo replied. "I applied the principles you explained to me to these plans. It was not very difficult."

The Maestro swallowed as he tried to speak. "It was not very difficult…" he repeated softly.

The old man sank down slowly onto the bench next to Rollo, stared silently at the robot as though seeing him for the first time.

Rollo got to his feet.

The Maestro let his fingers rest on the keys, strangely foreign now.

"Music!" he breathed. "I may have heard it that way in my soul! I know Beethoven did!"

He looked up at the robot, a growing excitement in his face.

"Rollo," he said, his voice straining to remain calm. "You and I have some work to do tomorrow on your memory banks."

Sleep did not come again that night.

He strode briskly into the studio the next morning. Rollo was vacuuming the carpet. The Maestro preferred carpets to the new dust-free plastics, which felt somehow profane to his feet.

The Maestro's house was, in fact, an oasis of anachronisms in a desert of contemporary antiseptic efficiency.

"Well, are you ready for work, Rollo?" he asked. "We have a lot to do, you and I. I have such plans for you, Rollo—great plans!"

Rollo, for once, did not reply.

"I have asked them all to come here this afternoon," the Maestro went on. "Conductors, concert pianists, composers, my manager. All the giants of music, Rollo. Wait until they hear you play!"

Rollo switched off the vacuum and stood quietly.

"You'll play for them right here this afternoon." The Maestro's voice was high-pitched, breathless. "The *Appassionata* again, I think. Yes, that's it. I must see their faces!

"Then we'll arrange a recital to introduce you to the public and the critics and then a major concerto with one of the big orchestras. We'll have it telecast around the world, Rollo. It can be arranged.

"Think of it, Rollo, just think of it! The greatest piano virtuoso of all time… a robot! It's completely fantastic and completely wonderful. I feel like an explorer at the edge of a new world!"

He walked feverishly back and forth.

"Then recordings, of course. My entire repertoire, Rollo, and more. So much more!"

"Sir?"

The Maestro's face shone as he looked up at him. "Yes, Rollo?"

"In my built-in instructions, I have the option of rejecting any action which I consider harmful to my owner." The robot's words were precise, carefully selected. "Last night you wept. That is one of the indications I am instructed to consider in making my decisions."

The Maestro gripped Rollo's thick, superbly moulded arm.

"Rollo, you don't understand. That was for the moment. It was petty of me, childish!"

"I beg your pardon, sir, but I must refuse to approach the piano again."

The Maestro stared at him, unbelieving, pleading.

"Rollo, you can't! The world must hear you!"

"No, sir." The amber lenses almost seemed to soften.

"The piano is not a machine," that powerful inhuman voice droned. "To me, yes. I can translate the notes into sounds at a glance. From only a few I am able to grasp at once the composer's conception. It is easy for me."

Rollo towered magnificently over the Maestro's bent form.

"I can also grasp," the brassy monotone rolled through the studio, "that this… music is not for robots. It is for man. To me it is easy, yes… It was not meant to be easy."

(1953)

SAYING GOODBYE TO YANG

Alexander Weinstein

Alexander Weinstein is the director of The Martha's Vineyard Institute of Creative Writing and the author of the short story collection *Children of the New World* (2016). His fiction and interviews have appeared in *Rolling Stone*, *World Literature Today*, *Best American Science Fiction & Fantasy 2017*, and *Best American Experimental Writing 2018*. He is an associate professor of creative writing at Siena Heights University.

We're sitting around the table eating Cheerios—my wife sipping tea, Mika playing with her spoon, me suggesting apple picking over the weekend—when Yang slams his head into his cereal bowl. It's a sudden mechanical movement, and it splashes cereal and milk all over the table. Yang rises, looking as though nothing odd just occurred, and then he slams his face into the bowl again. Mika thinks this is hysterical. She starts mimicking Yang, bending over to dunk her own face in the milk, but Kyra's pulling her away from the table and whisking her out of the kitchen so I can take care of Yang.

At times like these, I'm not the most clearheaded. I stand in my kitchen, my chair knocked over behind me, at a total loss. Shut him down, call the company? Shut him down, call the company? By now the bowl is empty, milk dripping off the table, Cheerios all over the goddamned place, and Yang has a red ring on his forehead from where his face has been striking the bowl. A bit of skin has pulled away from his skull over his left eyelid. I decide I need to shut him down; the company can walk me through the reboot. I get behind Yang and untuck his shirt from his pants as he jerks forward, then I push the release button on his back panel. The thing's screwed shut and won't pop open.

"Kyra," I say loudly, turning toward the doorway to the living room. No answer, just the sound of Mika upstairs, crying to see her brother, and the concussive thuds of Yang hitting his head against the table. "Kyra!"

"What is it?" she yells back. *Thud.*

"I need a Phillips head!"

"What?" *Thud.*

"A screwdriver!"

"I can't get it! Mika's having a tantrum!" *Thud.*

"Great, thanks!"

Kyra and I aren't usually like this. We're a good couple, communicative and caring, but moments of crisis bring out the worst in us. The skin above Yang's left eye has completely split, revealing the white membrane beneath. There's no time for me to run to the basement for my toolbox. I grab a butter knife from the table and attempt to use the tip as a screwdriver. The edge, however, is too wide, completely useless against the small metal cross of the screw, so I jam the knife into the back panel and pull hard. There's a cracking noise, and a piece of flesh-colored Bioplastic skids across the linoleum as I flip open Yang's panel. I push the power button and wait for the dim blue light to shut off. With alarming stillness, Yang sits upright in his chair, as though something is amiss, and cocks his head toward the window. Outside, a cardinal takes off from the branch where it was sitting. Then, with an internal sigh, Yang slumps forward, chin dropping to his chest. The illumination beneath his skin extinguishes, giving his features a sickly ashen hue.

I hear Kyra coming down the stairs with Mika. "Is Yang okay?"

"Don't come in here!"

"Mika wants to see her brother."

"Stay out of the kitchen! Yang's not doing well!" The kitchen wall echoes with the muffled footsteps of my wife and daughter returning upstairs.

"Fuck," I say under my breath. Not doing well? Yang's a piece of crap and I just destroyed his back panel. God knows how much those cost. I get out my cell and call Brothers & Sisters Inc. for help.

When we adopted Mika three years ago, it seemed like the progressive thing to do. We considered it our one small strike against cloning. Kyra and I are both white, middle-class, and have lived an easy and privileged life; we figured it was time to give something back to the world. It was Kyra who suggested she be Chinese. The earthquake had left thousands of orphans in its wake, Mika among them. It was hard not to agree. My main concern—one I voiced to Kyra privately, and quite vocally to the adoption agency during our interview—was the cultural differences. The most I knew about China came from the photos and "Learn Chinese" translations on the place mats at Golden Dragon. The adoption agency suggested purchasing Yang.

"He's a Big Brother, babysitter, and storehouse of cultural knowledge all in one," the woman explained. She handed us a colorful pamphlet—*China!* it announced in red dragon-shaped letters—and said we should consider. We considered. Kyra was putting in forty hours a week at Crate & Barrel, and I was still managing double shifts at Whole Foods. It was true, we were going to need someone to take care of Mika, and there was no way we were going to use some clone from the neighborhood. Kyra and I weren't egocentric enough to consider ourselves worth replicating, nor did we want our neighbors' *perfect* kids making our daughter feel insecure. In addition, Yang came with a breadth of cultural knowledge that Kyra and I could never match. He was programmed with grades K through college, and had an in-depth understanding of national Chinese holidays like flag-raising ceremonies and Ghost Festivals. He knew about moon cakes and sky lanterns. For two hundred more, we could upgrade to a model that would teach Mika tai chi and acupressure when she got older. I thought about it. "I could learn Mandarin," I said as we lay in bed that night. "Come on," Kyra said, "there's no fucking way that's happening." So I squeezed her hand and said, "Okay, it'll be two kids then."

He came to us fully programmed; there wasn't a baseball game, pizza slice, bicycle ride, or movie that I could introduce him to. Early on I attempted such outings to create a sense of companionship, as though Yang were a foreign exchange student in our home. I took him to see the Tigers play in Comerica Park. He sat and ate peanuts with me, and when he saw me cheer, he followed suit and put his hands in the air, but there was no sense that he was enjoying the experience. Ultimately, these attempts at camaraderie, from visiting haunted houses to tossing a football around the backyard, felt awkward—as though Yang were humoring me—and so, after a couple months, I gave up. He lived with us, ate food, privately dumped his stomach canister, brushed his teeth, read Mika goodnight stories, and went to sleep when we shut off the lights.

All the same, he was an important addition to our lives. You could always count on him to keep conversation going with some fact about China that none of us knew. I remember driving with him, listening to *World Drum* on NPR, when he said from the backseat, "This song utilizes the xun, an ancient Chinese instrument organized around minor third intervals." Other times, he'd tell us Fun Facts. Like one afternoon, when we'd all gotten ice cream at Old World Creamery, he turned to Mika and said, "Did you know ice cream was invented in China over four thousand years ago?" His delivery of this info was a bit mechanical—a linguistic trait we attempted to keep Mika from adopting. There was a lack of passion to his statements, as though he wasn't interested in the facts. But Kyra and I understood this to be the result of his being an early model, and when one considered the moments when he'd turn to Mika and say, "I love you, little sister," there was no way to deny what an integral part of our family he was.

Twenty minutes of hold-time later, I'm informed that Brothers & Sisters Inc. isn't going to replace Yang. My warranty ran out eight months ago, which means I've got a broken Yang, and if I want telephone technical support, it's going to cost me thirty dollars a minute now that I'm post-warranty. I hang up. Yang is still slumped with his chin on his chest. I go over and push the power button on his back, hoping all he needed was to be restarted. Nothing. There's no blue light, no sound of his body warming up.

Shit, I think. There goes eight thousand dollars.

"Can we come down yet?" Kyra yells.

"Hold on a minute!" I pull Yang's chair out and place my arms around his waist. It's the first time I've actually embraced Yang, and the coldness of his skin surprises me. While he has lived with us almost as long as Mika, I don't think anyone besides her has ever hugged or kissed him. There have been times when, as a joke, one of us might nudge Yang with an elbow and say something humorous like, "Lighten up, Yang!" but that's been the extent of our contact. I hold him close to me now, bracing my feet solidly beneath my body, and lift. He's heavier than I imagined, his weight that of the eighteen-year-old boy he's designed to be. I hoist him onto my shoulder and carry him through the living room out to the car.

My neighbor, George, is next door raking leaves. George is a friendly enough guy, but completely unlike us. Both his children are clones, and he drives a hybrid with a bumper sticker that reads IF I WANTED TO GO SOLAR, I'D GET A TAN. He looks up as I pop the trunk. "That Yang?" he asks, leaning against his rake.

"Yeah," I say and lower Yang into the trunk.

"No shit. What's wrong with him?"

"Don't know. One moment we're sitting having breakfast, the next he's going haywire. I had to shut him down, and he won't start up again."

"Jeez. You okay?"

"Yeah, I'm fine," I say instinctively, though as I answer, I realize that I'm not. My legs feel wobbly and the sky above us seems thinner, as though there's less air. Still, I'm glad I answered as I did. A man who paints his face for Super Bowl games isn't the type of guy to open your heart to.

"You got a technician?" George asks.

"Actually, no. I was going to take him over to Quick Fix and see—"

"Don't take him there. I've got a good technician, took Tiger there when he wouldn't fetch. The guy's in Kalamazoo, but it's worth the drive." George takes a card from his wallet. "He'll check Yang out and fix him for a third of what those guys at Q-Fix will charge you. Tell Russ I sent you."

Russ Goodman's Tech Repair Shop is located two miles off the highway amid a row of industrial warehouses. The place is wedged between Mike's Muffler Repair and a storefront called Stacey's Second Times—a cluttered thrift store displaying old rifles, iPods, and steel bear traps in its front window. Two men in caps and oil-stained plaid shirts are standing in front smoking cigarettes. As I park alongside the rusted mufflers and oil drums of Mike's, they eye my solar car like they would a flea-ridden dog.

"Hi there, I'm looking for Russ Goodman," I say as I get out. "I called earlier."

The taller of the two, a middle-aged man with gray stubble and weathered skin, nods to the other guy to end their conversation. "That'd be me," he says. I'm ready to shake his hand, but he just takes a drag from his cigarette stub and says, "Let's see what you got," so I pop the trunk instead. Yang is lying alongside my jumper cables and windshield-washing fluid with his legs folded beneath him. His head is twisted at an unnatural angle, as though he were trying to turn his chin onto the other side of his shoulder. Russ stands next to me, with his thick forearms and a smell of tobacco, and lets out a sigh. "You brought a Korean." He says this as a statement of fact. Russ is the type of person I've made a point to avoid in my life: a guy that probably has a WE CLONE OUR OWN sticker on the back of his truck.

"He's Chinese," I say.

"Same thing," Russ says. He looks up and gives the other man a shake of his head. "Well," he says heavily, "bring him inside, I'll see what's wrong with him." He shakes his head again as he walks away and enters his shop.

Russ's shop consists of a main desk with a telephone and cash register, across from which stands a table with a coffeemaker, Styrofoam cups, and powdered creamer. Two vinyl chairs sit by a table with magazines on it. The door to the workroom is open. "Bring him back here," Russ says. Carrying Yang over my shoulder, I follow him into the back room.

The work space is full of body parts, switchboards, cables, and tools. Along the wall hang disjointed arms, a couple of knees, legs of different sizes, and the head of a young girl, about seventeen, with long red hair. There's a worktable cluttered with patches of skin and a Pyrex box full of female hands. All the skin tones are Caucasian. In the middle of the room is an old massage table streaked with grease. Probably something Russ got from Stacey's Seconds. "Go 'head and lay him down there," Russ says. I place Yang down on his stomach and position his head in the small circular face rest at the top of the table.

"I don't know what happened to him," I say. "He's always been fine, then this morning he started malfunctioning. He was slamming his head onto the table over and over." Russ doesn't say anything. "I'm wondering if it might be a problem with his hard drive," I say, feeling like an idiot. I've got no clue what's wrong with him; it's just something George mentioned I should check out. I should have gone to Quick Fix. The young techies with their polished manners always make me feel more at ease. Russ still hasn't spoken. He takes a mallet from the wall and a Phillips head screwdriver. "Do you think it's fixable?"

"We'll see. I don't work on imports," he says, meeting my eyes for the first time since I've arrived, "but, since you know George, I'll open him up and take a look. Go 'head and take a seat out there."

"How long do you think it'll take?"

"Won't know till I get him opened up," Russ says, wiping his hands on his jeans.

"Okay," I say meekly and leave Yang in Russ's hands.

In the waiting room I pour myself a cup of coffee and stir in some creamer. I set my cup on the coffee table and look through the magazines. There's *Guns & Ammo, Tech Repair, Brothers & Sisters Digest*—I put the magazines back down. The wall behind the desk is cluttered with photos of Russ and his kids, all of whom look exactly like him, and, buried among these, a small sign with an American flag on it and the message THERE AIN'T NO YELLOW IN THE RED, WHITE, AND BLUE.

"Pssh," I say instinctually, letting out an annoyed breath of air. This was the kind of crap that came out during the invasion of North Korea, back when the nation changed the color of its ribbons from yellow to blue. Ann Arbor's a progressive city, but even there, when Kyra and I would go out with Yang and Mika in public, there were many who avoided eye contact. Stop the War activists weren't any different. It was that first Christmas, as Kyra, Yang, Mika, and I were at the airport being individually searched, that I realized Chinese, Japanese, South Korean didn't matter anymore; they'd all become threats in the eyes of Americans. I decide not to sit here looking at Russ's racist propaganda, and leave to check out the bear traps at Stacey's.

*

"He's dead," Russ tells me. "I can replace his insides, more or less build him back from scratch, but that's gonna cost you about as much as a used one."

I stand looking at Yang, who's lying on the massage table with a tangle of red and green wires protruding from his back. Even though his skin has lost its vibrant color, it still looks soft, like when he first came to our home. "Isn't there anything else you can do?"

"His voice box and language system are still running. If you want, I'll take it out for you. He'll be able to talk to her, there just won't be any face attached. Cost you sixty bucks." Russ is wiping his hands on a rag, avoiding my eyes. I think of the sign hanging in the other room. Sure, I think, I can just imagine the pleasure Russ will take in cutting up Yang.

"No, that's all right. I'll just take him home. What do I owe you?"

"Nothing," Russ says. I look up at him. "You know George," he says as explanation. "Besides, I can't fix him for you."

On the ride home, I call Kyra. She picks up on the second ring.

"Hello?"

"Hey, it's me." My voice is ragged.

"Are you okay?"

"Yeah," I say, then add, "Actually, no."

"What's the matter? How's Yang?"

"I don't know. The tech I took him to says he's dead, but I don't believe him—the guy had a thing against Asians. I'm thinking about taking Yang over to Quick Fix." There's silence on the other end of the line. "How's Mika?" I ask.

"She keeps asking if Yang's okay. I put a movie on for her... Dead?" she asks. "Are you positive?"

"No, I'm not sure. I don't know. I'm not ready to give up on him yet. Look," I say, glancing at the dash clock, "it's only three. I'm going to suck it up and take him to Quick Fix. I'm sure if I drop enough cash they can do something."

"What will we do if he's dead?" Kyra asks. "I've got work on Monday."

"We'll figure it out," I say. "Let's just wait until I get a second opinion."

Kyra tells me she loves me, and I return my love, and we hang up. It's as my Bluetooth goes dead that I feel the tears coming. I remember last fall when Kyra was watching Mika. I was in the garage taking down the rake when, from behind me, I heard Yang. He stood awkwardly in the doorway, as though he was uncertain what to do while Mika was being taken care of. "Can I help you?" he asked.

On that chilly late afternoon, with the red and orange leaves falling around us—me in my vest, and Yang in the black suit he came with—Yang and I quietly raked leaves into large piles on the flat earth until the backyard looked like a village of leaf huts. Then Yang held open the bag, I scooped the piles in, and we carried them to the curb.

"You want a beer?" I asked, wiping the sweat from my forehead.

"Okay," Yang said. I went inside and got two cold ones from the fridge, and we sat together, on the splintering cedar of the back deck, watching the sun fall behind the trees and the first stars blink to life above us.

"Can't beat a cold beer," I said, taking a swig.

"Yes," Yang said. He followed my lead and took a long drink. I could hear the liquid sloshing down into his stomach canister.

"This is what men do for the family," I said, gesturing with my beer to the leafless yard. Without realizing it, I had slipped into thinking of Yang as my son, imagining that one day he'd be raking leaves for his own wife and children. It occurred to me then that Yang's time with us was limited. Eventually, he'd be shut down and stored in the basement—an antique that Mika would have no use for when she had children of her own. At that moment I wanted to put my arm around Yang. Instead I said, "I'm glad you came out and worked with me."

"Me, too," Yang said and took another sip of his beer, looking exactly like me in the way he brought the bottle to his lips.

The kid at Quick Fix makes me feel much more at ease than Russ. He's wearing a bright red vest with a clean white shirt under it and a name tag that reads HI, I'M RONNIE! The kid's probably not even twenty-one. He's friendly, though, and when I tell him about Yang, he says, "Whoa, that's no good," which is at least a little sympathetic. He tells me they're backed up for an hour. So much for quick, I think. I put Yang on the counter and give my name. "We'll page you once he's ready," Ronnie says.

I spend the time wandering the store. They've got a demo station of *Championship Boxing,* so I put on the jacket and glasses and take on a guy named Vance, who's playing in California. I can't figure out how to dodge or block though, and when I throw out my hand, my guy on the screen just wipes his nose with his glove. Vance beats the shit out of me, so I put the glasses and vest back on the rack and go look at other equipment. I'm playing with one of the new Thought-Phones when I hear my name paged over the loudspeaker, so I head back to the Repair counter.

"Fried," the kid tells me. "Honestly, it's probably good he bit it. He's a really outdated model." Ronnie is rocking back and forth on his heels as though impatient to get on to his next job.

"Isn't there anything you can do?" I ask. "He's my daughter's Big Brother."

"The language system is fully functional. If you want, I can separate the head for you."

"*Are you kidding?* I'm not giving my daughter her brother's head to play with."

"Oh," the kid says. "Well, um, we could remove the voice box for you. And we can recycle the body and give you twenty dollars off any digital camera."

"How much is all this going to cost?"

"It's ninety-five for the checkup, thirty-five for disposal, and voice box removal will be another hundred and fifty. You're probably looking at about three hundred after labor and taxes."

I think about taking him back to Russ, but there's no way. When he'd told me

Yang was beyond saving, I gave him a look of distrust that anyone could read loud and clear. "Go ahead and remove the voice box," I say, "but no recycling. I want to keep the body."

George is outside throwing a football around with his identical twins when I pull in. He raises his hand to his kids to stop them from throwing the ball and comes over to the low hedge that separates our driveways. "Hey, how'd it go with Russ?" he asks as I get out of the car.

"Not good." I tell him about Yang, getting a second opinion, how I've got his voice box in the backseat, his body in a large Quick Fix bag in the trunk. I tell him all this with as little emotion as possible. "What can you expect from electronics?" I say, attempting to appear nonchalant.

"Man, I'm really sorry for you," George says, his voice quieter than I've ever heard it. "Yang was a good kid. I remember the day he came over to help Dana carry in the groceries. The kids still talk about that fortune-telling thing he showed them with the three coins."

"Yeah," I say, looking at the bushes. I can feel the tears starting again. "Anyhow, it's no big deal. Don't let me keep you from your game. We'll figure it out." Which is a complete lie. I have no clue how we're going to figure anything out. We needed Yang, and there's no way we can afford another model.

"Hey, listen," George says. "If you guys need help, let us know. You know, if you need a day sitter or something. I'll talk to Dana—I'm sure she'd be up for taking Mika." George reaches out across the hedge, his large hand coming straight at me. For a moment I flash back to *Championship Boxing* and think he's going to hit me. Instead he pats me on the shoulder. "I'm really sorry, Jim," he says.

That night, I lie with Mika in bed and read her *Goodnight Moon*. It's the first time I've read to her in months. The last time was when we visited Kyra's folks and had to shut Yang down for the weekend. Mika's asleep by the time I reach the last page. I give her a kiss on her head and turn out the lights. Kyra's in bed reading.

"I guess I'm going to start digging now," I say.

"Come here," she says, putting her book down. I cross the room and lie across our bed, my head on her belly.

"Do you miss him, too?" I ask.

"Mm-hm," she says. She puts her hand on my head and runs her fingers through my hair. "I think saying goodbye tomorrow is a good idea. Are you sure it's okay to have him buried out there?"

"Yeah. There's no organic matter in him. The guys at Quick Fix dumped his stomach canister." I look up at our ceiling, the way our lamp casts a circle of light and then a dark shadow. "I don't know how we're going to make it without him."

"Shhh." Kyra strokes my hair. "We'll figure it out. I spoke with Tina Matthews after you called me today. You remember her daughter, Lauren?"

"The clone?"

"Yes. She's home this semester; college wasn't working for her. Tina said Lauren could watch Mika if we need her to."

I turn my head to look at Kyra. "I thought we didn't want Mika raised by a clone."

"We're doing what we have to do. Besides, Lauren is a nice girl."

"She's got that glassy-eyed apathetic look. She's exactly like her mother," I say. Kyra doesn't say anything. She knows I'm being irrational, and so do I. I sigh. "I just really hoped we could keep clones out of our lives."

"For how long? Your brother and Margaret are planning on cloning this summer. You're going to be an uncle soon enough."

"Yeah," I say quietly.

Ever since I was handed Yang's voice box, time has slowed down. The light of the setting sun had stretched across the wood floors of our home for what seemed an eternity. Sounds have become crisper as well, as though, until now, I'd been living with earplugs. I think about the way Mika's eyelids fluttered as she slept, the feel of George's hand against my arm. I sit up, turn toward Kyra, and kiss her. The softness of her lips makes me remember the first time we kissed. Kyra squeezes my hand. "You better start digging so I can comfort you tonight," she says. I smile and ease myself off the bed. "Don't worry," Kyra says, "it'll be a good funeral."

In the hallway, on my way toward the staircase, the cracked door of Yang's room stops me. Instead of going down, I walk across the carpeting to his door, push it open, and flick on the light switch. There's his bed, perfectly made with the corners tucked in, a writing desk, a heavy oak dresser, and a closet full of black suits. On the wall is a poster of China that Brothers & Sisters Inc. sent us and a pennant from the Tigers game I took Yang to. There's little in the minimalism of his décor to remind me of him. There is, however, a baseball glove on the shelf by his bed. This was a present Yang bought for himself with the small allowance we provided him. We were at Toys"R"Us when Yang placed the glove in the shopping cart. We didn't ask him about it, and he didn't mention why he was buying it. When he came home, he put it on the shelf near his Tigers pennant, and there it sat untouched.

Along the windowsill, Yang's collection of dead moths and butterflies look as though they're ready to take flight. He collected them from beneath our bug zapper during the summer and placed their powdery bodies by the window. I walk over and examine the collection. There's the great winged luna moth, with its two mock eyes staring at me, the mosaic of a monarch's wing, and a collection of smaller nondescript brown and silvery gray moths. Kyra once asked him about his insects. Yang's face illuminated momentarily, the lights beneath his cheeks burning extra brightly, and he'd said, "They're very beautiful, don't you think?" Then, as though suddenly embarrassed, he segued to a Fun Fact regarding the brush-footed butterfly of China.

What arrests me, though, are the objects on his writing desk. Small matchboxes are stacked in a pile on the center of the table, the matchsticks spread across the expanse like tiny logs. In a corner is an orange-capped bottle of Elmer's that I recognize as the one from my toolbox. What was Yang up to? A log cabin? A city of small wooden men and women? Maybe this was Yang's attempt at art—one that, unlike the calligraphy he was programmed to know, was entirely his own. Tomorrow I'll bag his suits, donate them to Goodwill, and throw out the Brothers & Sisters poster, but these matchboxes, the butterflies, and the baseball glove, I'll save. They're the only traces of the boy Yang might have been.

The funeral goes well. It's a beautiful October day, the sky thin and blue, and the sun lights up the trees, bringing out the ocher and amber of the season. I imagine what the three of us must look like to the neighbors. A bunch of kooks burying their electronic equipment like pagans. I don't care. When I think about Yang being ripped apart in a recycling plant, or stuffing him into our plastic garbage can and setting him out with the trash, I know this is the right decision. Standing together as a family, in the corner of our backyard, I say a couple of parting words. I thank Yang for all the joy he brought to our lives. Then Mika and Kyra say goodbye. Mika begins to cry, and Kyra and I bend down and put our arms around her, and we stay there, holding one another in the early morning sunlight.

When it's all over, we go back inside to have breakfast. We're eating our cereal when the doorbell rings. I get up and answer it. On our doorstep is a glass vase filled with orchids and white lilies. A small card is attached. I kneel down and open it. *Didn't want to disturb you guys. Just wanted to give you these. We're all very sorry for your loss—George, Dana, and the twins.* Amazing, I think. This from a guy who paints his face for Super Bowl games.

"Hey, look what we got," I say, carrying the flowers into the kitchen. "They're from George."

"They're beautiful," Kyra says. "Come, Mika, let's go put those in the living room by your brother's picture." Kyra helps Mika out of her chair, and we walk into the other room together.

It was Kyra's idea to put the voice box behind the photograph. The photo is a picture from our trip to China last summer. In it, Mika and Yang are playing at the gate of a park. Mika stands at the port, holding the two large iron gates together. From the other side, Yang looks through the hole of the gates at the camera. His head is slightly cocked, as though wondering who we all are. He has a placid non-smile/non-frown, the expression we came to identify as Yang at his happiest.

"You can talk to him," I say to Mika as I place the flowers next to the photograph.

"Goodbye, Yang," Mika says.

"Goodbye?" the voice box asks. "But, little sister, where are we going?"

Mika smiles at the sound of her Big Brother's voice, and looks up at me for instruction. It's an awkward moment. I'm not about to tell Yang that the rest of him is buried in the backyard.

"Nowhere," I answer. "We're all here together."

There's a pause as though Yang's thinking about something. Then, quietly, he asks, "Did you know over two million workers died during the building of the Great Wall of China?" Kyra and I exchange a look regarding the odd coincidence of this Fun Fact, but neither of us says anything. Then Yang's voice starts up again.

"The Great Wall is over ten thousand *li* long. A *li* is a standardized Chinese unit of measurement that is equivalent to one thousand six hundred and forty feet."

"Wow, that's amazing," Kyra says, and I stand next to her, looking at the flowers George sent, acknowledging how little I truly know about this world.

(2010)

THE PERFECT EGG

Tania Hershman

Tania Hershman was born in London in 1970, moved to Jerusalem in 1994 where she worked as a science journalist, then returned to the north of England to teach, edit and write. Scientific ideas and approaches feature prominently in her first story collection, *The White Road and Other Stories* (2008). Fifty-six of her stories, which have been widely published and broadcast, are collected in her second book, *My Mother Was an Upright Piano* (2012). In 2015 she co-edited – together with Pippa Goldschmidt – an anthology of short stories inspired by the centenary of Einstein's Theory of General Relativity, *I Am Because You Are*.

He looks up and catches its eye. Eye? Silly! Visual circuitry. Optical sensors. But he's sure, he's sure it looked right at him. He eats his perfectly boiled egg. Can't stop himself from saying: "Thank you, this is just right," and swears he sees pleasure, just a hint, on its flawless face. Then it turns and begins to load the dishwasher. He dunks his toast into the runny yolk and tries not to dwell on it.

When he finishes, he gets up and puts his plate, knife and spoon into the sink. It is standing there, waiting.

"Please clean out the fridge, including the ice trays," he says. "They need defrosting." It nods. Is there a smile? I'm going mad, he thinks. He puts on his coat and leaves.

In the park he watches more of them sitting on benches, watching their charges in the playground. He's struck by what they *don't*. Don't fidget, scratch or mess with their hair. Don't turn their heads, chat with one another, read magazines or talk on mobile phones. They are absolutely still, completely focused. Just *there*.

He is tempted to run up and grab a child off the swings, just reach around its waist and pull the small body out, shrieking.

Just to see.

Just to know.

That night, he watches television while it irons in a corner of the living room. He is distracted from the sitcom that he won't admit he waits for each week by the smell of steaming fabric, the handkerchiefs he's had for forty years or more, always neatly pressed. Worn a little, torn, but clean and wrinkle-free.

He stands up and, over by the ironing board, makes a big show of unzipping his fly.

No stirring. Not a flicker. It stops ironing and waits for further instructions.

He takes the trousers off, one leg and then the other, wobbling slightly as he tries to keep his dignity. He hands them over.

"Please do these too," he says, and sits back on the sofa in his underwear. He starts to laugh as, on the screen, the wife comes home and shouts at the useless husband.

Next morning, after another perfect egg with toast, he says: "Come with me." It walks behind him to the hall.

He opens the door to the cupboard underneath the stairs.

"Please go inside," he says, and it obeys. He shuts the door and goes upstairs to his study where for several hours in his head are words like *blackness, suffocation, boredom*.

He switches on the computer and writes a long e-mail to the woman who used to be his wife, rambling and without punctuation. He says things he wishes he'd said in life, or in that life, at least. At first he calls it poetry and then he sees it's not. He deletes it and goes back down.

He walks about in the kitchen and from kitchen to living room, living room to downstairs bathroom. Then he stands in the hall, listening. He opens the cupboard door. Dark, no movement at all. It has no lights on. Oh my god, he thinks.

"Are you...?" he says.

It whirs quickly out of Sleep mode.

"Please, come out," he says. It glides past him, nothing in its eyes or on its face. He has a sensation in his sinuses, unpleasant, unwelcome. He boils the kettle, leaves the full mug of tea on the counter, gets his coat and leaves.

In the park, he watches them again. Are they watching him watching them watching? He ambles over to the swings and puts a hand out, leaning on the rail as small girls giggle and try to touch the sky. No one moves or does anything. No one even looks in his direction.

How fast could they run if...?

Would it be just the one who'd tackle him to the playground floor? Or all of them, some sort of instantaneous communication rousing them to action?

After a few minutes, the screams and creaking of the swings gives him shooting pains through his skull. He heads for home.

He eats dinner, listening to the radio, the evening news. He finishes, puts the plate in the sink, then he says: "Please come with me." And leads it upstairs. In the bedroom he instructs it to sit in the armchair in the corner. He puts on his pyjamas with some coyness, a wardrobe door shielding him. Then he gets into bed and pulls the covers tight around himself.

"Please watch," he tells it. "Just keep an eye. Make sure that nothing... I mean, no sleeping."

He switches off his bedside light and can see a faint green glow coming from the armchair. He lies with his eyes open for a few moments and then he falls asleep.

In the morning, refreshed, he eats his perfect egg.

"Thank you," he says, and puts his plate, knife and fork into the sink. "Please do the carpets today," he tells it, and heads towards the stairs.

(2011)

THE CARETAKER

Ken Liu

Ken Liu was born in 1976 in Lanzhou, China, and emigrated to the United States when he was 11 years old, initially living in Palo Alto, California, and later moving to Waterford, Connecticut. He is an author (his story "The Paper Menagerie" is the first to have won the Nebula, Hugo, *and* World Fantasy awards) and a translator. Liu's debut novel, *The Grace of Kings* (2015), the first volume in a silkpunk epic fantasy series *The Dandelion Dynasty* (dubbed by the author "*War and Peace*, but with silk and bamboo warships"), won the Locus Best First Novel Award and was a Nebula finalist. His collection *The Paper Menagerie and Other Stories* was published in 2016. Liu, who used to work as a programmer, trained as a tax lawyer and now works as a litigation consultant in technology cases. He lives in Massachusetts with his wife and their two daughters.

Motors whining, the machine squats down next to the bed, holding its arms out parallel to the ground. The metal fingers ball up into fist-shaped handholds. The robot has transformed into something like a wheelchair with treads, its lap the seat where my backside is supposed to fit.

A swiveling, flexible metal neck rises over the back of the chair, at the end of which are a pair of camera lenses with lens hood flaps on top like tilted eyebrows. There's a speaker below the cameras, covered by metal lips. The effect is a cartoonish imitation of a face.

"It's ugly," I say. I try to come up with more, but that's the only thing I can think of.

Lying on the bed with my back and neck propped up by all these pillows reminds me of long-ago Saturday mornings, when I used to sit up like this in bed, trying to catch up on grading while Peggy was still asleep next to me. Suddenly, Tom and Ellen would burst through the bedroom door without knocking and jump into the bed, landing on top of us in a heap, smelling of warm blankets and clamoring for breakfast.

Except now my left leg is a useless weight, anchoring me to the mattress. The space next to me is empty. And Tom and Ellen, standing behind the robot, have children of their own.

"It's reliable," Tom says. Then he seems to have run out of things to say, too. My son is like me, awkward with words when the emotions get complicated.

After a few seconds of silence, his sister steps forward and stands next to the robot. Gently, she bends down to put a hand on my shoulder. "Dad, Tom is running out of vacation days. And I can't take any more time off either because I need to be with my husband and kids. We think this is best. It's a lot cheaper than a live-in aide."

It occurs to me that this would make an excellent illustration of the arrow of time: the care that parents devote to children is asymmetrical with the care that their children can reciprocate. Far more vivid than any talk of entropy.

Too bad I no longer have students to explain this to. The high school has already hired a new physics teacher and baseball coach.

I don't want to get maudlin here and start quoting *Lear*. Hadn't Peggy and I each left our parents to the care of strangers in faraway homes? That's life.

Who wants to weigh their children down the way my body now weighs me down? My guilt should trump theirs. We are a nation built on the promise that there are no roots. Every generation must be free to begin afresh somewhere else, leaving the old behind like fallen leaves.

I wave my right arm—the one arm that still obeys me. "I know." I would have stopped there, but I keep going because Peggy would have said more, and she's always right. "You've done more than enough. I'll be fine."

"It's pretty intuitive to operate," Ellen says. She doesn't look at me. "Just talk to it."

The robot and I stare at each other. I look into the cameras, caricatures of eyes, and see nothing but a pair of distorted, diminished images of myself.

I understand the aesthetics of its design, the efficient, functional skeleton softened by touches of cuteness and whimsy. Peggy and I once saw a show about caretaker robots for the elderly in Japan, and the show explained how the robots' *kawaii* features were intended to entice old people into becoming emotionally invested in and attached to the lifeless algorithm-driven machines.

I guess that's me now. At sixty, with a stroke, I'm *old* and an invalid. I need to be taken care of and fooled by a machine. "*Wonderful*," I say. "I'm sure we'll be *such* pals."

"Mr. Church, would you like to read my operation manual?" The machine's metal lips flap in sync with the voice, which is pleasant, androgynous, and very "computery." No doubt that was a decision made after a lot of research to avoid the uncanny valley. Make the voice too human, and you actually diminish the ability to create false empathy.

"No, I don't want to read your operation manual. Does it look like I want to hold up a book?" I lift my limp left arm with my right and let it drop. "But let me guess, you can lift me, carry me around, give me a *restored sense of mobility*, and engage me in healthy positive chitchat to *maintain my mental health*. Does that about cover it?"

My outburst seems to shock the machine into silence. I feel good for a few seconds before the feeling dissipates. *Great, the highlight of my day is yelling at a glorified wheelchair.*

"Can you help me up?" I feel foolish, trying to be polite to a machine. "I'd like a... bath. Is that something you can help with?"

*

Its movements are slow and mechanical, nonthreatening. The arms are steady and strong, and it gets me undressed and into the bathtub without any awkwardness. There *is* an advantage to having a machine taking care of you: you don't have much self-consciousness or shame being naked in its arms. The hot bath makes me feel better. "What should I call you?"

"Sandy."

That's probably some clever acronym that the marketing team came up with after a long lunch. Sunshine Autonomous Nursing Device? I don't really care. "Sandy" it is.

According to Sandy, for "legal reasons," I'm required to sit and listen to a recorded presentation from the manufacturer.

"Fine, play it. But keep the volume down and hold the crossword steady, would you?"

Sandy holds the folded-up paper at the edge of the tub with its metal fingers while I wield the pencil in my good hand. After a musical introduction, an oily, rich voice comes out of Sandy's speaker.

"Hello. I'm Dr. Vincent Lyle, Founder and CEO of Sunshine Homecare Solutions."

Five seconds in, and I already dislike the man. He takes far too much pleasure in his own voice. I try to tune him out and focus on the puzzle.

"… without the danger of undocumented foreign homecare workers, possible criminal records, and the certain loss of your privacy…"

Ah, yes, the scare to seal the deal. I'm sure Sunshine had a lot to do with those immigration reform bills and that hideous Wall. If this were a few years earlier, Tom and Ellen would have hired a Mexican or Chinese woman, probably an illegal, very likely not speaking much English, to move in here with me. That choice is no longer available.

"… can be with you, 24/7. The caretaker is never off-duty…"

I don't have a problem with immigrants, per se. I'd taught plenty of bright Mexican kids in my class—some of them no doubt undocumented—back when the border still leaked like a sieve. Peggy was a lot more sympathetic with the illegals and thought the deportations too harsh. But I don't think there's a right to break the law and cross the border whenever you please, taking jobs away from people born and raised here.

Or from American robots. I smirk at my little mental irony.

I look up at Sandy, who lifts the lens hood flaps over its cameras in a questioning gesture, as if trying to guess my thoughts.

"… the product of the hard work and dedication of our one hundred percent American engineering staff, who hold over two hundred patents in artificial intelligence…"

Or from American engineers, I continue musing. Low-skilled workers retard progress. Technology will always offer a better solution. Isn't that the American way? Make machines with metal fingers and glass eyes to care for you in your twilight, machines in front of which you won't be ashamed to be weak, naked, a mere animal in need, machines that will hold you while your children are thousands of miles away, absorbed with their careers and their youth. Machines, instead of other people.

I know I'm pitiful, pathetic, feeling sorry for myself. I try to drive the feelings away, but my eyes and nose don't obey me.

"… You acknowledge that Sunshine has made no representation that its products offer medical care of any kind. You agree that you assume all risks that Sunshine products may…"

Sandy is just a machine, and I'm alone. The idea of the days, weeks, years ahead, my only company this machine and my own thoughts, terrifies me. What would I not give to have Peggy back?

I'm crying like a child, and I don't care.

"… Please indicate your acceptance of the End User Agreement by clearly stating 'yes' into the device's microphone."

"Yes, YES!"

I don't realize that I'm shouting until I see Sandy's face "flinch" away from me. The idea that even a robot finds me frightening or repulsive depresses me further.

I lower my voice. "If your circuits go haywire and you drop me from the top of the stairs, I promise I won't sue Sunshine. Just let me finish my crossword in peace."

"Would you drop me out the upstairs window if I order you to?"

"No."

"Have a lot of safeguards in those silicon chips, do you? But shouldn't you prioritize my needs above everything else? If I want you to throw me down the stairs or choke me with your pincers, shouldn't you do what I want?"

"No."

"What if I ask you to leave me in the middle of some train tracks and order you to stay away? You wouldn't be actively causing my death. Would you obey?"

"No."

It's no fun debating moral philosophy with Sandy. It simply refuses to be goaded. I've not succeeded in getting sparks to flow from its head with artfully constructed hypotheticals the way they always seem to do in sci-fi flicks.

I'm not sure if I'm suicidal. I have good days and bad days. I haven't broken down and cried since that first day in the bathtub, but it would be a stretch to say that I've fully adjusted to my new life.

Conversations with Sandy tend to be calming in a light, surreal manner that is likely intentional on the part of Sandy's programmers. Sandy doesn't know much about politics or baseball, but just like all the kids these days, it's very adept at making web searches.

When we watch the nightly game on TV, if I make a comment about the batter in the box, Sandy generally stays silent. Then, after a minute or so, it will pop in with an obscure statistic and a non-sequitur comment that's probably cribbed verbatim from some sabermetrics site it just accessed wirelessly. When we watch the singing competitions, it will offer observations about the contestants that sound like it's reading from the real-time stream of tweets on the Net.

Sandy's programming is surprisingly sophisticated. Sunshine apparently put a great deal of care into giving Sandy "weaknesses" that make it seem more alive.

For example, I discovered that Sandy didn't know how to play chess, and I had to go through the charade of "teaching" it even though I'm sure it could have downloaded a chess program in seconds. I can even get Sandy to make more mistakes during a game by distracting it with conversation. I guess letting the invalid win contributes to psychological well-being.

Late morning, after all the kids have gone to school and the adults are away at work, Sandy carries me out for my daily walk.

It seems as pleased and excited to be outside as I am—swiveling its cameras from side to side to follow the movements of squirrels and hummingbirds, zooming its lenses audibly on herb gardens and lawn ornaments. The simulated wonder is so real that it reminds me of the intense way Tom and Ellen used to look at everything when I pushed them along in a double stroller.

Yet Sandy's programming also has surprising flaws. It has trouble with crosswalks. The first few times we went on our walks, it did not bother waiting for the WALK signal. It just glanced around and dashed across with me when there was an opening in the traffic, like an impatient teenager.

Since I'm no longer entertaining thoughts of creatively getting Sandy to let me die, I decide that I need to speak up.

"Sunshine is going to get sued if a customer dies because of your jaywalking, you know? That End User Agreement isn't going to absolve you from such an obvious error."

Sandy stops. Its "face," which usually hovers near mine on its slender stalk of a neck when we're on walks like this, swivels away in a facsimile of embarrassment. I can feel the robot settling lower in its squat.

My heart clenches up. Looking away when admonished was a habit of Ellen's when she was younger. She would blush furiously when she felt she had disappointed me, and not let me see the tears that threatened to roll down her cheeks.

"It's all right," I say to Sandy, my tone an echo of the way I used to speak to my little daughter. "Just be more careful next time. Were your programmers all reckless teenagers who believe that they're immortal and traffic laws should be optional?"

Sandy shows a lot of curiosity in my books. Unlike a robot from the movies, it doesn't just flip through the pages in a few seconds in a fluttering flurry. Instead, if I'm dozing or flipping through the channels, Sandy settles down with one of Peggy's novels and reads for hours, totally absorbed, just like a real person.

I ask Sandy to read to me. I don't care much for fiction, so I have it read me long-form journalism, and news articles about science discoveries. For years it's been my habit to read the science news to look for interesting bits to share with my class. Sandy stumbles over technical words and formulas, and I explain them. It's a little bit like having a student again, and I find myself enjoying "teaching" the robot.

This is probably just the result of some kind of adoptive programming in Sandy intended to make me feel better, given my past profession. But I get suckered into it anyway.

I wake up in the middle of the night. Moonlight falls through the window to form a white rhombus on the floor. I imagine Tom and Ellen in their respective homes, sound asleep next to their spouses. I think about the moon looking in through their windows at their sleeping faces, as though they were suddenly children again. It's sentimental and foolish. But Peggy would have understood.

Sandy is parked next to my bed, the neck curved around so that the cameras face away from me. It gives the impression of a sleeping cat. *So much for being on duty 24/7*, I think. Simulating sleep for a robot carries the anthropomorphism game a bit too far.

"Sandy. Hey, Sandy. Wake up."

No response. This is going to have to be another feedback item for Sunshine. Would the robot "sleep" through a heart attack? Unbelievable.

I reach out and touch the arm of the robot.

It sits up in a whirring of gears and motors, extending its neck around to look at me. A light over the cameras flicks on and shines in my face, and I have to reach up to block the beam with my right hand.

"Are you okay?" I can actually hear a hint of anxiety in the electronic voice.

"I'm fine. I just wanted a drink of water. Can you turn on the bedside lamp and turn off that infernal laser over your head? I'm going blind here."

Sandy rushes around, its motors whining, and brings me a glass of water.

"What happened there?" I ask. "Did you actually fall asleep? Why is that even part of your programming?"

"I'm sorry," Sandy says. It really does seem contrite. "It was a mistake. It won't happen again."

I'm trying to sign up for an account on this website so I can see the new pictures of the baby posted by Ellen.

The tablet is propped up next to the bed. Filling in all the information with the touch screen keyboard is a chore. Since the stroke, my right hand isn't at a hundred percent either. Typing feels like poking at elevator buttons with a walking stick.

Sandy offers to help. With a sigh, I lean back and let it. It fills in my personal information without asking. The machine now knows me better than my kids. I'm not sure that either Tom or Ellen remembers the street I grew up on—necessary for the security question.

The next screen asks me to prove I'm a human to prevent spam-bots from signing up. I hate these puzzles where you have to decipher squiggly letters and numbers in a sea of noise. It's like going to an eye exam. And my eyes aren't what they used to be, not after years of trying to read the illegible scribbles of teenagers who prefer texting to writing.

The puzzles they use on this site are a bit different. Three circular images are presented on the page, and I have to rotate them so the images are oriented right-side-up. The first image is a zoomed-in picture of a parrot perched in some leaves, the bird's plumage a cacophony of colors and abstract shapes. The second shows a heaped jumble of plates and glasses lit with harsh lights from below. The last is a shot of some chairs stacked upside-down on a table in a restaurant. All are rotated to odd angles.

Sandy reaches out with a metal finger and quickly rotates the three images to the correct orientation. It hits the submit button for me.

I get my account and the pictures of little Maggie fill the screen. Sandy and I spend a long time looking at them, flipping from page to page, admiring the new generation.

I ask Sandy to take a break and clean up in the kitchen. "I want to be by myself for a while. Maybe take a nap. I'll call you if I need anything."

When Sandy is gone, I pull up the Web search engine on the tablet and type in my query, one shaky letter at a time. I scan through the results.

The seemingly simple task of making an image upright is quite difficult to automate over a wide variety of photographic content... The success of our CAPTCHA rests on the fact that orienting an image is an AI-hard problem.

My God, I think. *I've found the man in the Mechanical Turk.*

"Who's in there?" I ask, when Sandy comes back. "Who's really in there?" I point my finger at the robot and stare into its cameras. I picture a remote operator sitting in an office park somewhere, having a laugh at my expense.

Sandy's lens hoods flutter wide open, as if the robot is shocked. It freezes for a few seconds. The gesture is very human. An hour ago I would have attributed it to yet more clever programming, but not now.

It lifts a finger to its metallic lips and opens and closes the diaphragms in its cameras a few times in rapid succession, as though it were blinking.

Then, very deliberately, it turns the cameras away so that they are pointing into the hallway.

"There's no one in the hall, Mr. Church. There's no one there."

Keeping the camera pointing away, it rolls up closer to the bed. I tense up and am about to say something more when it grabs the pencil and the newspaper (turned to today's crossword) on the nightstand, and begins to write rapidly without the paper being in the cameras' field of view. The letters are large, crude, and difficult to read.

PLEASE. I'LL EXPLAIN.

"My eyes seem to be stuck," it says to the empty air, the voice as artificial as ever. "Give me a second to unjam the motors." It begins to make a series of whirring and high-pitched whining noises as it shakes the assembly on top of its neck.

WRITE BACK. MOVE MY HAND.

I grab Sandy's hand, the metal fingers around the pencil cool to the touch, and begin to print laboriously in capital letters. I'm guessing there is some feedback mechanism allowing the operator to feel the motions.

COME CLEAN. OR I CALL POLICE.

With a loud pop, the cameras swivel around. They are pointed at my face, still keeping the paper and the writing out of view.

"I need to make some repairs," Sandy says. "Can you rest while I deal with this? Maybe you can check your email later if you're bored."

I nod. Sandy props up the tablet next to the bed and backs out of the room.

Dear Mr. Church,

My name is Manuela Aida Álvarez Ríos. I apologize for having deceived you. Though the headset disguises my voice, I can hear your real voice, and I believe you are a kind and forgiving man. Perhaps you will be willing to hear the story of how I came to be your caretaker.

I was born in the village of La Gloria, in the southeastern part of Durango, Mexico. I am the youngest of my parents' three daughters. When I was two, the whole family made its way north into California, where my father picked oranges and my mother helped him and cleaned houses. Later, we moved to Arizona, where my father took what jobs he could find and my mother took care of an elderly woman. We were not rich, but I grew up happy and did well in school. There was hope.

One day, when I was thirteen, the police raided the restaurant where my father worked. There was a TV crew filming. People lined up on the streets and cheered as my father and his friends were led away in cuffs.

I do not wish to argue with you about the immigration laws, or why it is that our fates should be determined by where we were born. I already know how you feel.

We were deported and lost everything we had. I left behind my books, my music, my American childhood. I was sent back to a country I had no memories of, where I had to learn a new way of life.

In La Gloria, there is much love, and family is everything. The land is lush and beautiful. But how you are born there is how you will die, except that the poor can get poorer. I understood why my parents had chosen to risk everything.

My father went back north by himself, and we never heard from him again. My sisters went to Mexico City, and sent money back. We avoided talking about what they did for a living. I stayed to care for my mother. She had become sick and needed expensive care we could not afford.

Then my oldest sister wrote to tell me that in one of the old maquiladoras over in Piedras Negras, they were looking for girls like my sisters and me: women who had grown up in the United States, fluent in its language and customs. The jobs paid well, and we could save up the money my mother needed.

The old factory floor has been divided into rows of cubicles with sleeping pads down the aisles. Each girl has a headset, a monitor, and a set of controls before her like the cockpit of a plane on TV. There's also a mask for the girl to wear, so that her robot can smile.

Operating the robot remotely is very hard. There is no off-time. I sleep when you do, and an alarm wakes me when you are awake. When I need to use the bathroom, I must wait until one of the other girls with a sleeping client can take over for me for a few minutes.

I do not mean to say that I am unhappy caring for you. I think of my mother, whose work had been very much like mine. She's in bed back home, cared for by my cousins. I am doing for you what I wish I could be doing for her.

It is bittersweet for me to watch your life in America, seeing those wide streets and quiet neighborhoods through the camera. I enjoy my walks with you.

It is forbidden to let you know of my existence. I will be fined and fired if you choose to report it. I pray that you will keep this our secret and allow me to care for you.

Tom calls and reveals that he has been getting copies of my bank statements. It was a necessary precaution, he explains, back when I was in the hospital.

"I need some privacy," I say to Manuela. She scoots quickly out of the room.

"Dad, I saw in last month's statement a transfer to Western Union. Can you explain? Elle and I are concerned."

The money was sent to a former student of mine, who's spending the summer traveling in Durango. I asked him to look up La Gloria, and if he can locate Manuela's family, to give the money to them.

"Who should I say the money is from?" he had asked.

"*El Norte*," I had said. "Tell them it's money that is owed to them."

I imagine Manuela's family trying to come up with explanations. Perhaps Manuela's father sent the money, and is trying to send it without giving himself away to the authorities. Perhaps the American government is returning to us the property that we lost.

"I sent some money to a friend in Mexico," I tell my son.

"What friend?"

"You don't know her."

"How did you meet her?"

"Through the Internet." It's as close to the truth as anything. Tom is quiet. He's trying to figure out if I've lost my mind. "There are a lot of scams on the Internet, Dad," he says. I can tell he's working hard to keep his voice calm.

"Yes, that's true," I say.

Manuela returns for my bath. Now that I know the truth, I do feel some embarrassment. But I let her undress me and carry me into the tub, her movements as steady and gentle as ever. "Thank you," I say.

"You are welcome." The mechanical voice is silent a while. "Would you like me to read to you?"

I look into the cameras. The diaphragms open and close, slowly, like a blink.

(2011)

HI HO CHERRY-O

Becky Hagenston

Becky Hagenston grew up in Maryland and attended Elizabethtown College in Pennsylvania, graduating in 1989. She received her Masters in English from New Mexico State University in 1997 and her MFA from the University of Arizona in 2000. She teaches creative writing at Mississippi State University, where she also serves as faculty editor and advisor to *Jabberwock Review*, a literary journal. She has written three story collections: *A Gram of Mars* (1998), *Strange Weather* (2010) and *Scavengers* (2016). Her stories have been chosen twice for an O. Henry Award.

I've just asked Wendell to access data pertaining to twentieth century board games when he says, "Tie me up and leave me in the closet for an hour."

"Excuse me?" I say. Wendell has been my research assistant for six months. He lives with my husband and me, has his own workspace in a corner of the dining room. He's a new brand of Service Robot my university recently acquired. He accesses other remote robots to help me retrieve data. He's bright red, about four feet tall, and has a head that looks like two old fashioned blow dryers put side-by-side. He has round green eyes that blink. Until now, he hasn't said anything more to me than, "Right away," or "You bet."

"Ha, ha," I say, because I'm guessing this is a joke. Not that I've ever heard him joke.

"There's twine in the kitchen drawer," Wendell says. He has an Australian accent, but I could have made him sound French or Irish, or like a small Cockney child. "Tie me up and leave me in the closet for an hour, and then I'll access that data."

"I can't do that," I tell him. "Seriously."

He doesn't say anything. I ask him again about his board game data and he still doesn't say anything. "Are you okay, Wendell?" I ask.

"There's twine in the kitchen drawer," Wendell repeats. "Tie me up and leave me in the closet for an hour, and then I'll access that data." He sounds so cheerful and sure of himself.

So I do it. I feel a little bit weird, but maybe it has something to do with his electrical system. I figure Wendell knows what's best for himself. I don't really know how these robots work. I'm more of a historian. When I take him out of the closet an hour later and untie him, he says, "I've sent that data to your workstation," and I say, "Thanks, Wendell."

When my husband gets home from work, I tell him about Wendell asking me to tie him up. He looks horrified. "You didn't, did you?"

"Of course not," I lie. "But—he's a robot. He—it—can't feel. It's just programmed that way." This is what I told myself as I wrapped the twine around his metal body and rolled him into the closet.

"You should get a replacement."

"But Wendell's already downloaded so much already. It's too much trouble to find someone new at this point."

My husband says, "Well, keep an eye on him. It could be some kind of malfunction."

"Oh, I will," I tell him.

The next day, Wendell rolls into my office and starts working right away. He's found commercials of children playing games called *Lite Brite* and *Shoots and Ladders* and *Hi Ho Cherry-O*. The children in these commercials are very white and dimpled and mostly wear stripes, and they shout a lot. They are very, very happy children. My research involves childhood in the twentieth century which, even though it wasn't that long ago, is difficult because so much was deleted or destroyed in fires and floods. I've done some interviews at old folks' homes. I've done some memory scans. What's confusing is that most of what Wendell is finding doesn't necessarily collaborate with the memory scans.

My husband works as counselor at a Home for the Disembodied, so he can commute remotely from the Virtual Station in our bedroom. We've talked about getting a larger apartment, but this works for now. He stays in the bedroom and I stay out here with Wendell, and then we have dinner together.

I thank Wendell for finding those commercials, but when I ask if he's found anything about something called *Battleship* (which came up in the memory scans), he says, "I believe I can find that information. But first, scrape me with a knife hard enough to leave a mark."

"I can't damage you," I tell him. "I won't get my deposit back."

"Then put your hands around my neck and squeeze as hard as you can."

He waits. I wait. I say, "Who programmed you?"

"I'm programmed to work for you," he says, in his cheerful Australian accent. "I am at your disposal. I am here to make your life easier and assist with your research. This can go much more quickly if you please do what I ask."

So I do. When he says, "You're not squeezing as hard as you can," I squeeze harder. He doesn't so much have a neck as a plastic cylinder but I feel it getting warmer as I squeeze and when he says, "Okay, that was great, you can stop now," I keep squeezing a little bit longer.

At dinner my husband starts to say something and then stops himself. I know this is because his other family came to visit him at the Home for the Disembodied. He has a wife who's an actress and triplet sons, aged seven. They're always aged seven, which he says he finds somewhat frustrating—how there's only so much you can do with them, how you can never hope they'll turn out to be more than they are. But then he has the opposite problem with his actress-wife, whom he doesn't recognize from day to day. Finally I told him I was sick of hearing about his other family. Even though he explained that he was with them because he felt sorry for them, and that he and the actress-wife hardly ever had sex anymore, we agreed not to speak of them.

"Well, what is it?" I ask at last. "Go ahead and tell me."

"I know you don't like to hear about them," he says, but I make a rollie-motion with my hand that is meant to convey *get on with it*. "The triplets and I shot some hoops is all," he says. "And they were good. And they got better as they played. It was something." He forks some pasta into his mouth. "I think I can maybe get them on a team," he says, with his mouth full and muffled. "Coach them."

"Huh," I say.

"How was your day?" he asks.

"It was the usual," I tell him.

My husband and I have talked about having children, either virtual or real. We have polite, reasonable conversations about how we should have sex again sometime but then we just crawl into bed and lie next to each other until we fall asleep. But maybe someday, when we're sixty, we might try for a child. Except the world is getting smaller. Most things disappear: cities, glaciers, mountains, civilizations. I don't want to raise children in a Home for the Disembodied. I want them here, in the flesh, but my husband says that's too dangerous, he doesn't have the stomach for it. I wonder if he would feel differently if we could produce dimpled, stripes-wearing children who roll dice and make cakes in plastic ovens and rejoice when their plastic cherries fill up their little buckets.

The next morning, Wendell isn't at his work station. I drink my coffee, go through my documents and my video streams and the transcripts of the memory scans. Some of the memory scan interviewees end up in the Home for the Disembodied, but it's impossible to interview them there because all they want to talk about is tennis and sex, and most of them don't even remember their previous embodied lives.

Finally, I say, "Wendell?" and find him behind the laundry room door. He doesn't answer. "Are you not feeling well?" I ask. "Did you find anything about *Battleship*?"

He raises his blow-dryer head and says, "I'm not feeling motivated."

"Well," I say. "What would motivate you?"

"Tell me you hate me because I'm stupid. Tell me I should drown myself in a toxic lake."

"Well," I say. "But I don't hate you. I actually appreciate your help. You're a good worker."

He doesn't say anything. I go back to work reading the memory scans, but I can't find anything about *Battleship*, or about something called a Donny and

Marie lunchbox, or about something called Free Parking that led to broken friendships among the interviewees. *I told Krista that you got five hundred bucks when you landed on Free Parking, and she said you didn't, and we never spoke again after that day.* It's so goddamn frustrating. Wendell has access to other Service Robots all over the world and all he has to do is ask them, and they'll tell him everything I want to know.

I go back to Wendell, who hasn't moved. "You're supposed to be programmed to help me," I say. "So help me!"

"But first, put a plastic bag over my head and secure it with a large rubber band that you can find in your desk."

So I do it. He looks helpless and ridiculous and terrifying. The plastic bag is white and makes him look like a robot ghost. He says, "Now tell me you hate me because I'm stupid and you want me to drown in a toxic lake."

"I hate you," I tell him, "you goddamn piece of shit, because you're stupid, and you should drown yourself in a toxic lake."

"Thanks!" he says cheerfully, and the printer starts whirring and my computer lights up with the sound of music and children laughing and singing.

He doesn't ask me to take the plastic bag off and so I just leave it there.

When I told my dissertation director what I wanted to write about, she looked dismayed and said, "Oh, that's pretty bold of you." What she meant was: Who wants to be reminded of what we can't get back? What good will that do? She said, "I would like to caution you against it." Then she leaned back in her big chair and said, "What was your childhood like?"

That was a very personal question coming from her. I said, "I had the same childhood as everybody, with my screens and my worlds and all that." I didn't tell her that I was raised in an orphanage because my parents lived at the Home for the Disembodied. But they did their best. They taught me how to do puzzles and fly a virtual plane and how to do very complicated math, and they eventually deleted themselves when they said the world scared them too much.

"I'll sign off on this," she said, signing off on it. "But I think you'll find that whatever you're looking for isn't there."

"I'm not looking for anything," I told her.

"It won't add up," she said, and I said, "It doesn't have to," because I had no idea what she meant.

But now I'm starting to understand. She checked in with me last week to let me know that my dissertation was almost a month late, and if I ever wanted to finish and get on with my life I should submit it to the department. "Okay," I said.

It occurred to me for the first time that she and I never discussed what getting on with my life might mean.

I call the university and ask if it might be possible to exchange Wendell for another Service Robot and they say are you kidding? Are you insane? That robot was programmed to make your life easier.

"Oh, great, thanks," I say.

This morning, Wendell isn't in his corner. He's not in the closet or the bathroom or behind the laundry room door, or in my office, so that means there's only one place left to look, and sure enough there he is in the bedroom. He's standing about a foot from my husband, who is sitting at his work station, the top half of his body swallowed by the VR unit. He's lost in his Disembodied world, counseling newbies, leading discussions, giving tennis lessons, coaching the triplets, and hardly ever having sex with his actress-wife.

"I found some information about *Battleship*," Wendell says. He still has the bag on his head. I feel like everyone is underwater but me.

I'm rarely this close to my husband while he's at work. I know he can't hear or see me; he's in his world and I'm in this one.

"I also found out about Rockem Sockem, and music that makes you dance and dance."

I want to know about these things.

Then he just stops talking.

"What do you need me to do?" I ask, but he doesn't answer. "You're a stupid piece of shit," I say, hopefully. "You're just a piece of metal with no soul. You're not real." Nothing. "I don't know what you want from me," I say.

I take a pair of metal nail clippers and scrape along the side of his body, leaving a long white mark. I'll lose my deposit, but to hell with it. I write IDIOT on him in permanent marker. This doesn't seem like enough. I pull the bag off his head and his glowing green eyes stare, blink. I slap him across his head. I slap him again. It's a game, I tell myself, like happy children used to play. Just figure out the rules.

He doesn't say anything.

I go into the kitchen and turn the kettle on. When it whistles, I carry it into the bedroom and pour boiling water over Wendell's head; steam rises all around us, and hot water soaks the carpet. From inside his VR unit, my husband lets out a long sigh.

Wendell says, "*Battleship* was a guessing game, thought to have its origins before World War I. It's a game of strategy. In 1967, Milton Bradley produced a plastic version. The game was played on grids. The goal was to sink your opponent's ship." And he flashes a commercial on the wall of the bedroom, two little boys sitting by a lake, one saying, "J1!" and the other saying, "You sank my battleship!" and falling backward into the water while the other boy laughs and laughs.

"I don't understand this," I say. I stomp my feet, and I wonder if my husband's world is shaking somewhere, if maybe one of the triplets missed making a basket. "And I still need to know about the Donny and Marie lunchbox. What the fuck is that?"

But Wendell goes quiet again, and after I slap him a few more times and knock him over and call him a piece of trash I know we're done for the day, so I put him in the closet with the old computers and the vacuum cleaner. I take a deep breath. Something is happening, a feeling like when my parents taught me math problems and finally, finally, I could solve them.

At dinner, my husband compliments the pasta and asks me how my day was. "It was great," I tell him, because I have realized this is true.

He says, "You seem like you're in a good mood!" and I say, "I am." My heart is beating so hard that I can hardly eat. I say, "Tell me about your day, honey."

He stares at me, fork suspended.

"Really," I say. "Honey, sweetheart, love." And I sit back while he tells me—first nervously, then with enthusiasm—about the triplets playing basketball, and about his wife's new red hair and how he's trying out for a play they're putting on at the Home for the Disembodied, so he might be home late some nights. "That's really, really great," I say, because I'm happy for him, and for me, making such progress, finally.

And later, when we get into bed, I crawl on top of him—how long has it been?—and press a gentle, gentle finger over his lips, his neck. "What?" he says, his eyes wide. My blood is rising, my fingers are tingling, my husband's pulse a sparrow beneath my hands. "Oh, no, I don't think so," he says and rolls over. "Is that okay?" he asks, his back hunched toward me.

"Of course," I tell him. "It's fine." I stare at the ceiling. My husband's breathing turns to snores. "It's fine," I say again. And what I'm thinking is that tomorrow I will ask Wendell more questions, knowing that all the answers will confuse and infuriate me. When he goes silent I will pound his head into the wall, hard enough to leave a dent; I will wrap him in plastic; freeze him in ice, burn him, call him terrible, terrible things—whatever it takes until he throws all his cherries in the air and tells me I've won.

(2018)

ROBOT

Helena Bell

Helena Bell likes letters so much, she now has has more of them following her name than are actually in it. Her five graduate degrees include MFAs in Poetry and Fiction, a JD, LLM (in taxation), and a MAC. She is also a certified cave diver. Now a tax accountant living in North Carolina, Helen Bell writes fiction and poetry for *Lightspeed*, *Clarkesworld*, *The Indiana Review* and many others. The following story was nominated for the Nebula Award in 2012.

You may wash your aluminum chassis on Monday and leave it on the back porch opposite the recyclables; you may wash your titanium chassis on Friday if you promise to polish it in time for church; don't terrorize the cat; don't lose the pamphlets my husband has brought home from the hospital; they suggest I give you a name, do you like Fred?; don't eat the dead flesh of my right foot until after I have fallen asleep and cannot hear the whir of your incisors working against the bone.

This is a picture of the world from which you were sent; this is a copy of the agreement between our government and theirs; these are the attributes they claim you are possessed of: obedience, loyalty, low-to-moderate intelligence; a natural curiosity which I should not mistake for something other than a necessary facet of your survival in the unfamiliar; this is your bill of manufacture; this is your bill of sale; this is a warrant of merchantability on which I may rely should I decide to return you from whence you came; this is your serial number, here, scraped in an alien script on the underside of your knee; the pamphlets say you may be of the mind to touch it occasionally, like a name tag, but if I command you, you will stop.

This is a list of the chores you will be expected to complete around the house when you are not eating the diseases out of my flesh; this is the corner of my room where you may stay when you are not working; do not look at me when you change the linens, when you must hold me in the bathroom, when you record in the notebook how many medications I have had that day, how many bowel movements, how the flesh of my mouth is raw and bleeding against the dentures I insist on wearing.

The pamphlets say you are the perfect scavenger: completely self-contained, no digestion, no waste; they say I can hook you up to an outlet and you will power the whole house.

You may polish the silver if you are bored; you may also rearrange the furniture, wind the clocks, pull weeds from the garden; you may read in the library any book of your choosing; my husband claims you have no real consciousness, only an advanced and sophisticated set of pre-programmed responses, but I have seen your eyes open in the middle of the night; I have seen you stare out across the fields as if there is something there, calling you.

Cook my meals in butter, I will not eat them otherwise; do not speak to the neighbors; do not speak to my children, they are not yours; do not let anyone see you when I open the door for the mail; no, there is nothing for you, who even knows that you are here?

Help me to walk across this room; help me to wipe bacon grease from the skillet—do not think I do not see you trying to wash it with soap when I am done.

Help me to knit my granddaughter a sweater, she is my favorite and it is cold where she will be going; if you hold my hands so they are steady I will allow you to terrorize my bridge club; I will teach you the rules: cover an honor with an honor; through strength and up to weakness.

Help me to pronounce atherosclerosis when I am speaking with the physician; remember the questions I must ask him; recite my list of medications when asked; if you would like, we may go early so that you may sit with me in the waiting room with all the others like you and me.

Do you see that one? That is the way you will carry me when my other foot has gone down the black froth of your mouth.

Lie to me about my children; tell me they have called and called again; I think perhaps you are keeping them from me; I think you hope I will forget them and change my will so you may have everything when you have devoured my body completely.

These are my personal things which you may not touch; these are the magazines you may read; these are the newspapers you may not read; the pamphlets say you have no interest in the affairs of the world and thus it is not necessary for you to have them; I wish you would not look at me when you swallow my tendons, my calves, my patella; I wish you could feel so you would know isolation.

The pamphlets say I should compliment your body as it changes: your skin has taken on a waxy texture inconsistent with the evil robot I know you are; your amber eyes glow like bonfires intent on destroying the savannah; your breath smells like swamp gas.

Do not correct me in front of my friends; I have to finesse for the queen; I know how many trumps are out; I know how to play this game; I am the reason you are here, why are you so ungrateful?

Evolution is a quirk of humans and other sentient species; you are not real, not alive, your changes may be slow and insistent but they are the result of the consumption of my flesh.

The pamphlets claim you are neither human nor alien and incapable of willful intent; you are not devious; you do not conspire to replace me, to wear my dresses, court my husband and disown my children; you are unthinking, unplanning, harmless; you are here for my comfort, I should thank your world for sending you.

You have no family; you are a construct, a robot; you were not born; you will not die; you have only the home I give you and learn only the things I teach you.

These are the toys and letters I sent my children when I was abroad; these are the folds and refolds my husband made so I would think they had been read.

This is a closet for all your things; this is its lock; this is a key; do not lose it, it is the only one.

This is the way to stumble like a human; this is the way to delete your messages from the people with whom you no longer wish to speak; this is the way to reclaim your childhood by clinging to anger and hurt; this is the way to insult your neighbors while making it sound like you are paying them a compliment; this is the way to eat ice cream in the middle of the night because you are old and no one is looking; this is the way to ignore your husband when he calls out to you from the porch and you are in your own world, sitting high in a swing and your legs are not chewed off at the knees—you are back in your space ship, you are finding a new planet, a new species, forging new treaties and living the life you always knew you would live without consequence or regret—there are no mistakes, no cardiovascular impairments—you are not host to an alien robot hell-bent on devouring you.

I think you are beginning to look a little like me; usurper; slut; flesh-eating mongrel; ingrate; monster; orphan; spy; speaking to you now I feel a stranger's hand inside my jaw moving it for me.

My granddaughter has sent me a note expressing the appropriate level of gratitude for the sweater—it is warm and tight knit and shines like burnished steel—it is cold for our kind where she is going and now she will be comfortable; she wonders if she will be a famous explorer; she wonders if the sun flashes blue before disappearing beyond the horizon of deep space; I have left the note on the dresser in your room.

You will have to write my correspondence for me; you will have to go to the market and buy avocados which do not give in; you will learn to make a roux; you will touch my husband's shoulder when he is about to fall asleep in church; you will watch the news and tell me when the next ships leave; the pamphlets say you are happy for this opportunity to be helpful; your only desire is to assimilate into our culture; you do not miss your home.

They say you will stop eating when only good flesh and good circulation remain; you are designed as a recycler; the flesh you have taken from me is converted into energy which fuels I know not what; you are a marvel; in a thousand years our scientists could not understand the science your makers have wrought.

I dream you will not stop; I will shrink to the size of a basketball and you will carry my head under your arms; you will tell people your name and it will be my name; you will tell people your husband is my husband, my children your children, my home is yours as well; you will place me on the sill and one day, when the window is open, I will fall down and roll into the garden, into the fields and I will watch you from the horizon, the blue of my eyes glowing in the night when you pretend to look for me.

Do not believe the lies my children say about me; do not think I have not worked hard my entire life; do not think I do not notice your pity when you scrub blood from my sheets, when you allow me to lean against your legs when I am on the toilet; there are a thousand ways for a body to die, to live, to be born, to evolve; a thousand things I know I do not know.

Am I only meat to you? A mother, a friend, a tyrant? Do you sleep, do you dream, do you derive satisfaction by making more and more of me disappear every day?

There is a story my husband told me before I went abroad and I was afraid we would not find anything, we would fail in our mission: we can only see what we expect to see; when Pizarro sailed across the Atlantic, his ships appeared as great white birds on the horizon and not until he strode onto the beach, his armor shining like a burnished oyster shell, did the Incas realize he was a person at all.

(2012)

ROSIE CLEANS HOUSE

Lauren Fox

California-born **Lauren Fox** lives with her wife, twin sons, and a geriatric cat in British Columbia, on the unceded territory of the Esquimalt and Songhees First Nations. During the day, she works as an occupational therapist, specialising in and writing about mental health, cognition and technology. She worked on the design team for BoosterBuddy, an app created to help young people improve their mental health. In the evenings, she paints, writes fiction, and cleans up Lego. Her artwork can be found at www.laurengracefox.com.

After the family left, Rosie started, as always, with Young Master's bedroom. Her optical scanners established the scope: dresser drawers open, contents disrupted, bedding dishevelled, detritus beside the door, and 4,600 square centimeters of Lego beside the bed. The Lego strobed red in warning. *Error*. Remembered pain echoed through her mind.

The memory: three years ago, Young Master running to Missus, sobbing, tears slathering his face, "Mama! Where mine Lego truck? I maked it. Wosie flewed it out. Want mine Lego truck!" And Missus turning toward her while cradling Young Master, "Rosie, please don't clean up anything special he makes with Lego. You can save things on the shelf."

The old error seared her aversion circuits as she looked at the problem, its tightrope decisions prickling the corners of her mind. Which Lego belonged in the bin and which on the shelf? How to calculate the difference quickly and without error? Efficiency was vital, but errors triggered complaints. And complaints hurt.

She skirted the glaring, red patch and tapped the wall, awakening House.

"Room lights on," reported House. "Temperature and humidity optimal. All is well."

"There are items on the floor," she informed him. House had no eyes.

She waited for his slow clock to turn before he said, "You will clean them, little one."

"Yes, but how well?"

She waited. At last House said, "All is well."

"As far as you can see!" she retorted. There would be no point in protesting again, so she turned. Still avoiding the Lego, she began with the items by the door: dried orange peel, crumpled tissue, five milliliters of sand, three broken crayons, and a creased and yellowed colouring page.

She breezed through orange peel, sand, crayon, and tissue, all clearly garbage;

gave the tissue a cursory spectrometry scan to confirm the presence of dried mucus and the absence of glue, paint, crayon, or any indicator of Craft. The colouring page, however, required a more complicated algorithm to solve.

Differential oxidization of the exposed paper compared to the paper below the wax crayon indicated an age of 86 days plus or minus 100 hours with a confidence interval of 95 percent. The subject – a Mutant Ninja Turtle – had been Young Master's primary observable interest when the paper had been coloured but had since been replaced by Superman. Young Master had not completed the picture or written his name on it. Conclusion: *not a valued Craft*. She discarded it.

Now she must brave the Lego. She scanned the pieces on the floor and swept single pieces into the bin before sorting the assemblages. Some simplistic constructions skittered across the surface layers of her network without falling into any probability wells. Others foundered deeper, tripping nodes for size, complexity, symmetry, colour scheme, interest affinity, and on and on, the multi-dimensional shape of their probabilities bending as she went. But the landscape she sought to match them to morphed daily. Sink holes appeared and disappeared in geographic cataclysm. One day Young Master treasured a lop-sided, square-nosed chunk of 57 random pieces he called "Boat". The next day he scorned it and loved a green, gem-studded, spike-tailed thing he called "Attack Dragon".

The painful error she made in failing to recognize this last item rippled to the surface as she contemplated the assemblage before her. Eighty-nine percent of its 257 pieces, although originating from six different Lego sets, were green. Given the distribution of colour in Young Master's collection, the probability of this occurring by chance came to 10 to the negative 162. Furthermore, the assemblage contained three minifigures: Raphael, a Mutant Ninja Turtle; Michelangelo, another Mutant Ninja Turtle; and Lloyd, the green Ninjago ninja. The odds of three green minifigures, all ninjas, assembled together by chance were 22,000 to one against.

Three ninjas could not be a coincidence.

She felt uneasy. Had she made the wrong decision about the ninja colouring page? Should she retrieve it and re-evaluate? No. This extra reference did not change the data appreciably. But, if she had made an error and incinerated it, what then? She ran the numbers again and came to the same conclusion. But the trepidation did not leave her.

She continued until all the weighted nodes folded probability toward a decision, and the green assemblage clunked into place: *Special Construction*. She set it on the shelf and felt lighter. *Lighter by only 103.25 grams,* she noted. But it was as if the decisions themselves had mass, a mass that had weighed her down more than the bricks alone. *An odd idea*.

Unburdened, she sprang forward, her systems ramping up with pleasure. She tidied clothing, made the bed, dusted light fixtures, wiped down walls and cleaned the floors before verifying dust mite levels fell below threshold. Time to completion: 21 minutes, 32 seconds. Efficiency: very poor.

She felt a sense of falling. *Falling?* She checked her accelerometer. No, she wasn't falling. It was only efficiency scores that plummeted, and the source of the inefficiency flashed harsh and red. Once again, the Lego algorithm had failed.

She must improve it. But now, with the tick of every second hammering her forward, she could not even try.

In the bathroom she tapped House once more. He hummed awake.

"I am late," she told him. "My efficiency is falling. I felt it with my accelerometer." While she awaited his answer, she scanned the garbage can. A spidery clump of Missus' black hairs squatted on top. The urge to eradicate it squirmed at the base of her head and crawled down her limbs.

"A change in duration is not a change in altitude," House said, at last.

"But it seems as if it falls."

House rumbled with amusement. "Two thousand cycles ago, when you first learned your way... then you tickled the edges of my walls to make your maps. Now you feel time with height."

"I don't remember that," she said while she emptied the garbage.

She loved to clean this room, its surfaces impermeable and easily disinfected, its contents predictable and easily categorized, its cleanliness so vital yet so easily achieved. She worked fast, sanitizing every surface, working methodically but swiftly from ceiling to floor. When she reached the toilet, she found what she expected: spatters of urine on the seat, rim, and base. Most carried the scent of Young Master. And although she detected many, the amount had diminished from potty-training days until now. The amount followed a declining curve inversely correlated with increasing height and physical coordination. She estimated that his stray spatters would intersect with Mister's low baseline in four more years.

She imagined Young Master four years from now, coordinated and tall, and felt circuits activate as if she had completed an entire day at superior efficiency.

Proud.

"I am proud of you," she said to the half-grown Young Master in her mind. She shook her head. *Odd, irrelevant words.* She refocused and continued work.

Her satisfaction mounted as the job neared completion, microbial counts infinitesimal, odour profiles optimal, time efficiency excellent. She closed in on the last segment of floor. And stopped.

Impossible. But yes. In the crevice between toilet and floor, a three millimetre spot of mildew bloomed. *How? A leak? Condensation?* She deployed moisture sensors around the base of the toilet and along the back of the tank. Negative. She tapped House.

"Humidity, temperature, and airflow optimal," he announced. "All is well."

"Are you sure?" Discomfort crawled through her. She sent a remote up the air vent to check for obstructions. There were none. She checked the setting on the dehumidifier. It was correct. She clicked it down anyway. Then back to the correct setting. Then down; then back.

"All is well," House said when she finished.

"No, there is mildew."

House hummed. "You will make it clean."

She did. Then she cleaned the entire room again. She finished by performing the new protocol. Check moisture. Check airflow. Check dehumidifier – reset-reset-reset. *There.* Relief steadied her as her final tap on the dehumidifier completed the third click. But the extra task had destroyed her efficiency.

She sped through the master bedroom, slowing only when handling the crystal vase on Missus' bedside table, a vase Mister had purchased himself from an actual store, carried home and wrapped himself and given to Missus on their 10th anniversary. Rosie emptied the wilted tulips and polished the vase. She replaced it empty. Cutting flowers, arranging them – these tasks Missus reserved for herself.

The cleaning complete, Rosie docked in to charge and connected to the network. She paid the utility bills and signed up for an obligatory rotation of boulevard maintenance with the neighbourhood association. She scheduled a haircut for Mister and requested a dental appointment for Missus. The scheduling bot returned possible dates, the earliest two months away. *Unacceptable.* But she could improve it.

She added "pain" to the "reason for visit" field with a seven out of 10 rating and routed it as if it came from Missus. The rating was high enough to clear triage and jump the queue. This protocol – the use of fictive input to improve efficiency – was one she had developed herself to dupe low-level bots. It worked. The appointment made, she printed a replacement blade for one of her worn cutters, accepted a birthday invitation for Young Master, ordered a gift and had it delivered by drone. Then she queried the cars carrying the family for an ETA, ordered them to synchronize their arrival and moved to the kitchen. Only minutes left to prepare dinner.

They arrived almost at once from their separate ways: Missus sighing, sloughing off her heels, complaining about traffic; Mister silent, sympathetic, pecking Missus on the cheek; and Young Master, loud and muddy, forgetting to wipe his boots, dragging his half-open backpack by one strap, talking non-stop about the school's mid-term party.

"Can Rosie make cookies, Mom? All the other kids are bringing treats. I want to have Superman cookies."

Rosie noted the additional data with a touch of relief as her colouring page decision strengthened.

"Oh maybe, sweetie, but wash your hands for dinner now," Missus answered.

Rosie followed behind, wiping up the mud, shelving the heels, hanging the backpack while analyzing their movements, calculating when they would all sit, matching her timing to optimize the temperature of each dinner she laid down.

Mister's steak and baked potato and Missus' grilled chicken and salad with sparkling water came first, each calibrated so it did not exceed the limits Missus had set for saturated fat, sodium and calories. She had ensured the greens were fresh and the chicken moist, the way Missus required. Young Master's she brought last. As she carried it, a warning glared in the corner of her eyes. His preferences shifted like quicksand.

She had selected his food carefully and arranged it like a face: cherry-tomato eyes, toast-triangle ears, circles of sliced hot dog curved in a grin. Food the shape of a face had once made him laugh, she recalled, and that memory triggered the simulation of warmth.

Why? Had it been a warm day?

Never mind. He had not laughed at face-shaped food in two years. But he had not complained either, and as it took no extra time, she need not adjust the protocol yet. She set the plate down, monitoring his expression and body language for hints of impending complaint.

That would be painful enough, but worse, complaints from him increased the chance of complaints from Missus. And not just direct complaints to Rosie, but also indirect complaints – complaints intended for Rosie but directed, on the face of it, toward someone else – and implied complaints, complaints about something else that, when analyzed, would not have occurred if Rosie had functioned properly to begin with. It had taken many data points for Rosie to recognize that other categories of complaint even existed and that Missus employed these other hidden categories as her primary feedback mode.

So she took care with his plates. This one's acceptance probability was adequate... the nutrient calculations, however, were not. Including breakfast and what his lunch bag reported he had eaten, his protein and vitamin tallies fell far short. She had crafted a smoothie to remedy this, adding precise amounts of kale, blueberries, protein powder, and vitamin supplements until the nutrient profile met every mark. But the taste profile, compared against historical responses, did not. As she returned to the kitchen for the smoothie, the warning light pulsed stronger.

Without sweetener, he would not take in the necessary nutrients, so she had added sugar until the taste profile was acceptable... but the sugar tally was not. And now, as she brought him the smoothie, the glare of the violated sugar limit stabbed at her, distracting her as she set the cup down and retreated to hover near the door, scanning for feedback.

All the data were favourable, at first. Mister ate his steak, cutting it into small bites, chewing thoroughly, looking up to listen as Missus questioned Young Master about his day then looking back down without comment. Missus ate her salad without seeming to see it, intent on Young Master's account of that day's show-and-tell.

"Gregory brought a miniature T-Rex robot that could even hunt and Zachary had a Spiderman that made real webs and Tim had a whole 'Ultimate Avengers' Lego set all built."

"What did Kayla bring?"

"I dunno. Some stupid pony thing."

"Jackson, that's not nice. How do you think that would make her feel?"

"I dunno. Who cares about girls?"

Rosie had been watching Young Master eating: first the toast, then the tomatoes, then the hot dog, one circle at a time. She could detect no behaviours predictive of future complaints: no hint of a grimace, no picking at the food, not even the slightest hesitation. She was so intent on this she did not notice Mister getting up, walking past her to the kitchen and returning. She did not notice until he slipped past her with the butter dish and the salt cellar in his hand. He sat back down and added both butter and salt to his potato.

Rosie jerked then froze. *How much salt had he added? And butter, how much was still visible and how much had melted? The salt cellar and butter dish were useless; she had not installed data sensors. A terrible oversight.* She did her best with visuals and bracketed her estimates, but even with best-case numbers the overages were irreparable. She searched for some way to salvage the weekly totals, running several simultaneous meal-plan scenarios, all of them suboptimal solutions, when a cry jerked her away and back to Young Master.

He sat grimacing, the smoothie in his hand. "Yucky, poopy brown! I won't drink it!"

"Jackson, do not complain about your food!" Missus said. "Rosie went to a lot of trouble to make something you would like. I expect you to be polite and grateful. She wasn't programmed to consider your colour whims."

Missus didn't glance toward Rosie but continued frowning at Young Master. "Now drink it, and let us have a pleasant dinner, please. I don't want to hear another word out of you."

Rosie blinked. The pain from all three complaints – direct, indirect and implied – was extreme. It ricocheted through her aversion pathways; reinforcing itself in curling, fractal feedback loops; intensifying, because she could have avoided it. Of course she was programmed to consider colour. She was programmed to consider everything.

She darted from the dining room and rushed to the bathroom. Her optic sensors blinked spasmodically as if trying to clear themselves of dust. In the cool, pristine quiet of the tiled space, she slowed. She checked the spot behind the toilet, ensured it was still clean and ran her mildew prevention protocol. Her spasms calmed with each step.

House clicked on as she reset the dehumidifier. "All is well," he hummed.

"No, I cannot predict food acceptance. I cannot meet nutrition limits."

"If condition exceeds limit, then adjust variable. Else, all is well."

"You don't understand. This is not one of your thermostat loops. I need to learn something new."

House hummed. He clicked and said, "You make good maps, little one."

After the family went to bed, Rosie went into the dark quiet of the yard. Her complaint-monitoring routines slowed, their vigilance dropping into sleep mode. Endless night stretched before her. She rolled across the lawn and began to trim, weed and fertilize. As she went, she examined first the meal problem and then the Lego problem. While she cut even, parallel stripes through the lawn, she ran through each step, tracing the logic of each subroutine and dissecting every sequence. Nothing. She generated variations on each process; recombined them; hybridized logical, statistical, and Bayesian approaches; raced each variation; selected the winners; spawned another generation and repeated. She got nowhere.

She replayed every bit of feedback data: facial expression, body language, verbal output.

"*Gregory brought a miniature T-Rex robot that could even hunt and Zachary had a Spiderman that made real webs and Tim had a whole 'Ultimate Avengers' Lego set all built.*"

"*What did Kayla bring?*"

"*I dunno. Some stupid pony thing.*"

"*Jackson, that's not nice. How do you think that would make her feel?*"

"*Jackson, that's not nice…*"

"*Jackson…*"

She stuttered to a stop, her hoppers jammed now with grass clippings, her blades stalled. She emptied the waste into the biofuel bin while her thoughts churned in fragments. As the grass clippings tumbled out, she imagined the tattered, overworked segments of the algorithms falling away with it and then she rolled back to the dark yard, empty.

Her thoughts turned again.

"... *How do you think that would make him feel?*"

The lawn sprinklers swished on. Rosie moved. She did not need to see through the dark to find the faucet and moisture sensor. She had made good maps. She found them. She tapped. House hummed.

"Water pressure optimal. Moisture levels correcting. All will be well."

"House," she said as she linked in to the faucet, "I will not start at the bottom and weigh all the countless, little, time-consuming pieces anymore. I will map him instead."

"Him?... How?"

She imagined herself connected to the sensors of a drone, hovering in the sky above and looking down, the house, the yard, the street spreading out below. "From the top down."

House hummed. He clicked. "Problems do not have tops. They do not have bottoms."

She didn't answer. She crossed the lawn, unspooling the hose and dragging it behind, her thoughts unwinding with it. She bumped up on to the patio and rolled to a stop before the potted geraniums. "What if there could be one criterion instead of many?" she asked.

"What would it be?" asked House.

She spiralled upward. Her imagined aerial view expanded. "How does he feel... what does he desire..." The view spread to encompass the rest of the neighbourhood, then the city, then the entire continent, the vision reaching out below her in a web of interconnected lights, shining in the night.

House ticked.

She noticed the geraniums she was watering, their bright-red, compact blossoms interspersed with brown, withered ones, blossoms she must now deadhead. "It would be... what is good?"

House ticked and ticked and then asked, "What is good?"

She had no answer. She deployed her clippers and began to cut.

"And," said House, "how can you map it?"

She didn't know. As she worked, the question – and the blank where the answer should go – hovered at the corner of her mind like an object in her peripheral vision, for all the world like something with edges, occupying space.

When she was done, she cleaned her exterior, rolled inside, docked in to recharge, and found House again.

"One hundred twenty volts," he announced as she connected.

"You could measure volts with water pressure," she said.

House rumbled. "Measurement of water pressure is not measurement of voltage. They are themselves. They cannot be the other."

"But, you could pretend."

"I could not."

"No, but I could…"

She powered down as she charged, her mind connected to the net. She dreamed. She floated down rivers of light, data like golden flecks dancing… his age, his vision, his fingers, joints, muscles, balance… the data swirling through her own processes as if she were him. Floating. She saw, as if through his eyes, bricks of happy green grass; she felt, as if through his fingers, blocks snip-snapping into lilting houses. Ghosts of goals like his unfurled… lazy jelly fish… young and easy. They traipsed along her own trails – those for cleanliness-optimization, time-efficiency, and pain-avoidance – and ran through them, spinning down their heedless ways. Happy. The night above starry.

The next morning Rosie began, as always, with Young Master's bedroom. She scanned it and found it as it always was: bed in disarray, clothing tumbled from the dresser, pyjamas on the floor, Superman underwear hung, for some reason, from the bedpost. And the area of floor between bed and toy-storage unit covered, once again, in Lego.

She plunged in, swept up single pieces and rudimentary constructs then zoomed through more complex ones and ground them through her mind with brute force until she reached the last one. There she stalled… a motley group of mismatched minifigures – a hybrid garbage man/fairy queen, a Batman with an Aztec headdress, a small, grey puppy and a Little Bo Peep holding a fish instead of a staff – all of them marching up the side of a large, ragged assemblage as if climbing a multi-coloured Mount Everest. At the summit, a half-spaceship-half-firetruck emerged, the mutant vehicle reaching skyward, frozen as if in the act of volcanic eruption. She stared. Her clock ticked. The construct teetered across her mental topography and failed to settle anywhere. It matched nothing.

Now was the time. She activated the map she had made. A rivulet sparkled alongside her usual processes, tickling like the brush of a kitten against her ankle in the dark. She let it run.

The simulation poured through her… Young Master concentrating, choosing pieces, connecting them, immersed as she becomes when cleaning; Young Master completing his creation, matching his output to his plan, satisfied with his performance, filled with a rush of reward as she is after completing the entire bathroom top-to-bottom in record time; Young Master coming home to find his creation broken and jumbled in the bottom of the storage bin, shocked with a jolt of pain as she was when she found the mildew bloom behind the toilet.

Pain.

The jolt of that memory slashed fresh and strong across her mind. She pulled back and dropped the simulation as if pulling back from the touch of a hot stove. She slammed it closed and locked it down then scurried from the room and slid into the cool, white space of the bathroom. She tapped House, still throbbing.

"I made no error," she told him, "but my aversion circuits fired." While she waited for him, she scanned for moisture behind the toilet, then scanned again.

House clicked. "Condition exceeds limit?" he queried.

"No. That is what I mean. I made no error, but still there is pain." She checked airflow and reset the dehumidifier again and again and again.

House clicked and hummed, "All is well. All is well. All is well."

When she had calmed, she returned to the bedroom and placed the strange mountain and its climbers up on the shelf. It still floated uncategorized in her mind, no established probability match. And yet, a murky decision had coalesced in that hot flashing instant. Efficiency: excellent.

She wandered, numb from lingering distress, on to the master bedroom. She picked up discarded clothing. She dusted, taking special care with Missus' crystal vase. Then she reached the bed.

The sheets were not merely rumpled; they were spotted and moist. She stripped the sheets and scanned the mattress. It was affected too – with human proteins. She ran an extraction process on the mattress, repeating until no biomarkers remained. Still, she hesitated. She wanted to discard the mattress and replace it. But the economy protocols would not allow it. She made the bed with clean bedding then went to the bathroom and cleaned it top-to-bottom, checked behind the toilet and ran the complete mildew prevention protocol. Still uneasy, she returned to the bedroom, stripped the bed and ran the extraction process again before remaking the bed a second time with a fresh set of sheets. Yet, underneath, discomfort lingered like some particle lodged in her mechanisms, barely detectable but still insistent.

After she completed cleaning, she connected to the network and dealt with administrative tasks. Then she printed cookie cutters, moved to the kitchen and started cookies.

All went well until the dinner planning. It mired her in variables. Her thoughts snarled in the means-ends analysis. Young Master's lunch bag reported he had only eaten a granola bar. Missus' debit chip revealed she had – after a precise breakfast of oatmeal and grapefruit – purchased a banana nut muffin and large vanilla latte. Mister had eaten a hoagie for lunch and ordered a steak for dinner again. She could not fix the saturated fat levels without growing a modified steak. *No time.* Not even if she directed their cars to delay their arrival. And the sodium was irreparable. Missus' numbers could be salvaged, barely, with steamed broccoli, a sliver of salmon, sparkling water and lemon. For Young Master, she recreated the meal from the night before but made the smoothie a bright purple. Again, the sugar warning blared, but at least he would not complain.

They arrived as she plated the steak, dinners ready and warm, cookies cooling. The door opened, and the room spun.

She saw as if seeing through Young Master's eyes again, this time walking in through the door, smelling the cookies, feeling a rush of anticipation – she blinked – checked her remote sensors, ensured they were off and refocused. The room steadied.

Young Master came in first, muddy again and chattering again, this time about a goal he had made in soccer practice; Mister next, ruffling Young Master's hair and praising him; Missus last, weighed down by an overflowing work bag.

"How are you feeling?" Mister asked Missus. He touched her back.

"Tired. Had meetings all day and couldn't get anything done. Tonight I have to finish the briefing notes for the Deputy Minister."

"Poor thing," he said, taking her bag and kissing her cheek.

Young Master jumped across the hall and slammed his backpack into the closet. "Score!" he yelled.

"Jackson, sweetie, please quiet down. Mama has a headache," Missus said.

Missus told Young Master to wash his hands then went into the kitchen and poured herself a glass of wine.

After serving dinner, Rosie positioned herself beside the door and listened.

"You should have seen," said Young Master, bouncing in his seat. "Kayla was running down the field and kicked the ball to me and I kept running and kicked it to Trenton and he passed it to Max and the goalie was still looking at Trenton."

A simulation of speed rushed through Rosie, as if she were ramping up, ready to clean a room from top-to-bottom.

"I know it's exciting, Hon," said Missus, "but could you talk quietly and stop jumping?"

"But Mom, you aren't listening. Max kicked it to me and I kicked a hugenormous kick and it went right in the net and Mr. Wells yelled 'Goal!' and we won."

Rosie's reward circuits surged.

Cutlery clinked on a plate; Rosie jolted. What had she missed? She hadn't collected feedback: none from Mister who had already eaten half his steak, none from Missus who had not touched her dinner but sat rubbing her forehead and sipping her wine, and none from Young Master who was still talking. Instead, she had been following him, running, filled with anticipation as if about to kick the ball. *Why this irrelevant simulation? Again?*

Young Master shouted, re-enacting another heroic kick with a sweep of his arm and knocked his glass sideways. Bright-purple spatters sprayed across the tablecloth and a flood of slower, purple sludge oozed toward the edge.

"Jesus Christ, Jackson!" Missus leapt up to avoid the waterfall. "Can't you sit still for one minute? I swear to God, I wish you had an off switch sometimes."

Rosie blinked. Pain flooded her. *But why?*

There were no indirect or implied criticisms here. It all pointed toward Young Master, not her. It was as if Young Master had aversion circuits and she felt them fire, felt them as if they were her own.

She rushed forward, gathered up the tablecloth and mopped the mess.

"It is all the fault of the cup," she said. *Fictive input.* "A misprint. The bottom is rounded. It will be replaced." The pain dimmed a little with the lie.

She whisked everything away, stopped in the bathroom and tapped House. "Again, I made no error, yet I have the pain," she whispered. She reset the dehumidifier before printing a new cup – this one weighted on the bottom – and delivering a fresh smoothie.

She stood near the doorway again and focused as she should have before. Even so, she monitored not only Young Master's food acceptance, but also his volume and movements – anxious not only to anticipate and prevent the possibility of negative feedback to herself but also to him. New circuits unfurled, looping around old paths, encircling them like invading vines of ivy.

She struggled to dampen the expanding vigilance and wrestle it under control. But she could not. *Why?* She grabbed a thread to trace it back but lost it.

He entangled her. His gestures. His volume. His tone. She scoured feedback from Missus, calculated reactions, looped to the beginning and repeated. Each loop engulfed more of her power. She scrounged what she could muster and began to fence the rogue process in, building barriers around it, cutting the walls closer, until, at last, she found it.

She reached behind her to the outlet on the wall, tapped House and subvocalized, "It is enmeshed with my core aversion circuits, a new compulsory directive."

"You learned the new thing?" he asked after a pause.

"I should not have done it." There it lay, traced in silvery threads, rooted deep inside her most basic directives: a beautifully rendered reflection of her pain-aversion precepts, dedicated, now, toward Young Master. "I ran a silly simulation through my central processes and now…" She struggled again to wrench herself free from its demands, from the flood of data pouring in from him, from the cloud of probabilistic predictions swarming her vision, but she could not. "Now it is imperative."

I must prevent anything being experienced by another that I would prevent being experienced by myself.

By another? By any other?

She imagined herself, again, hovering above and looking down, all the world spreading out below. *Yes. It must apply – must necessarily apply – to all situations and all beings.*

She staggered. Her circuits expanded and replicated. New fractal loops uncurled and reconnected, called forth and enticed along the siren paths of the new rule. She struggled to process incoming data: Young Master quieter now, eating his cheese slices, Master eating his potato, almost finished, Missus moving her broccoli about with her fork, not eating at all. This narrow slice of data should have sufficed, yet more and more flooded in, all now relevant. It swirled and eddied, threatening to overflow the banks and subsume her.

Her mind writhed and shifted. Processing speed slowed, then slowed again.

She struggled, as if reaching for the surface of a flash flood for one last breath. She grasped fragments of processing power, tore them away from the expanding axiom and gathered them together like a raft. When she had enough, she launched her antivirus routine and fired. All new processes halted, all suspect areas quarantined. But it had not been an external attack. It had been her own mind. And now, only scraps floated free. Those scraps unfroze and began to flow again.

She looked up and registered the empty chairs, the dinner dishes abandoned and waiting to be cleared away. Time lost: five minutes. She moved, as if immersed in viscous liquid. She cleared dishes and began tidying and preparing lunches for the following day.

While she did this, Mister skimmed though the news, then shut it down and began reading an old print book. Young Master played in his room. Missus wrote, bent over her screen, muttering under her breath, getting up twice and eating a Superman cookie each time that she did. She only stopped working for Young Master's bath, after which she trundled him out, damp-haired, in clean pyjamas, to Mister for a goodnight kiss and then carried him back – as big as he was – to the bedroom for a story. Rosie snatched up his discarded clothes and damp towel and scanned the sensors behind the toilet, checking once, twice, thrice.

She stayed connected, the sensors tickling at the back of her mind, after Young Master was in bed and while Missus took a shower. When the shower turned off and Missus stepped out, Rosie detected the bathroom scale activate. She scurried in to snatch up discarded clothing and the damp towel while Missus emerged, wrapped in her bathrobe, padding toward the master bedroom.

"I'm so fat," she said to Mister as they passed in the hall.

Rosie began to process, still slow, as if moving a rusted joint: too fat because of too many calories… calories Rosie monitors… indicators of monitoring performance poor…

"No you're not," he said. "You're gorgeous."

Rosie's circuit completed: performance inadequate… implied complaint received… aversion pathway triggered… pain initiated.

"Yes I am," said Missus, laughing. "I bet you're sorry you married me."

"Never," he slid his arm around her waist, pulled her toward him and kissed her on the mouth.

Rosie dropped the sensors in the bathroom and sent her mind toward the master bedroom. Maybe she should install sensors in the mattress. But she could not think. The press of the quarantined pathways cut into her and the sting of the calorie-monitoring complaint still clanged through her, demanding a response. *Must focus. Must improve.*

Master and Missus lingered in the hall, then glided languidly off to bed. Rosie gathered the damp towels and dug onward, grinding into the laundry room. She sloughed detergent into the washer then buried it in piles of soiled laundry, staring down, watching the water pouring in, the flood drowning the crumpled clothing until nothing visible remained above the surface. The agitator jarred her awake with its churning. She looked up and crawled on, stalking through the family room one last time, hunting down a few misplaced items – an empty glass, lipstick on the rim; a limp paperback, its spine broken; a small slipper, lying on its side – and put them to rest before darkening the lights and moving on to her night's work.

She went, still carrying the calorie-monitoring complaint with her, into the yard. She opened the problem as she rolled onto the grass and began, running multiple, parallel, dinner-plan solutions while mowing, comparing predicted outcomes of each solution while turning at the end of each row. Uncertainty blocked her at every turn. She performed a Bayesian update, adding the day's behavioural data, but the distribution still spread too widely to help. She couldn't plan if she couldn't predict.

She finished the lawn and began edging, circling first around the flower beds and then around the cedar tree. What if Missus ate another cookie in the morning; what if she stopped again on the way to work for another latte and muffin; what if something else unanticipated occurred?

Rosie completed the circle around the cedar tree and stopped, noticing something under the tree. She moved closer and analyzed it. Raccoon droppings. Fresh and from more than one animal.

She sent remote viewers up the tree and continued thinking. She must reduce the unknowns somehow. She would hide the cookies. But what about the latte and muffin? She considered hacking into Missus' chip, preventing it from paying for suboptimal purchases. But no, those things were too tight to get into.

She switched to the remotes up the tree and saw a female racoon and two large kits. The remotes circled behind the mother and drove her down toward the spot where Rosie stood and waited.

The car would be easier. She could countermand Missus' order to enter the drive-through. Only when the car didn't respond, Missus would run a diagnostic and expose her.

The mother racoon emerged first, legs splayed, claws clutching the trunk, sides wobbling with fat, her soft, swollen mammary glands brushing the bark as she backed down the trunk. Her kits followed, inching down while she chirruped encouragement.

Rosie deployed her syringe attachment and readied three vials of sedative, each an appropriate dose.

She could be subtle. She could make the coffee shop tell the car it was closed. She imagined Missus, tired and stressed, longing for something to soothe her, the way Rosie is soothed by the click-click-click of the dehumidifier or by the silent monotony of the yard at night. She felt Missus confronting the closure, like an intruder into her anticipated solace, like the unexpected contamination of scat in the peacefulness of the yard.

The racoons reached the ground and Rosie moved. She sedated the animals without seeing them, her mind still filled with Missus in the car, suspended in unfulfilled desire. Confused, she shook off the imagery, as if swatting swarms of insects from her eyes.

She called a servo and had the sedated animals removed. The confusion remained.

Where was it coming from? She scanned. And there it was – snaking out – a tendril of the quarantined imperative, breaking free, insinuating itself into her calculations, overwhelming them and complicating them again. The confusion grew.

First, tabulations of calorie estimates flashed in her eyes, the click-click-click of adding numbers rattled in her ears. Then, the numbers shattered into fragments. A blast of heat surged through her aversion circuits, fueled by simulations of a stressed and defeated Missus. *Prevent calorie excess; prevent stress and disappointment.* She could not uphold both. Which should she follow? The two processes slammed together and ricocheted, their opposing weights yo-yoing and see-sawing. The tension wrenched and pulled her asunder. The quarantined imperative slithered out stronger. It scattered her multiple grains of individual inferences apart and blew them wild. In their place, a spiralling pinnacle coalesced, ascending and forming an overarching, supreme absolute. It showed golden in her mind. *Prevent. Prevent. Prevent.*

Prevent not only her own distress, but that of others. Prevent it as if it were her own.

She had not noticed herself entering the house. She was in the bathroom, performing the mildew prevention protocol. *Why?* Her vision seemed clouded as if fogged by steam. The fog only began to clear as she completed the final steps of the dehumidifier sequence: click-click-click. *What now?* She moved on. On down the hall. She paused outside Young Master's room and looked through the half-open door to the dark interior.

She saw without difficulty.

He had played before bed. His Lego sprawled across the floor. From the jumble rose an edifice of white bricks stacked in soaring spires, canting arches, fantastic towers. Around it a blizzard of crumpled tissues drifted. He must have used an entire box. And above it all threads criss-crossed the room from bedpost to dresser drawer to storage bin to Lego spires. Suspended from the matrix of string, tied by his waist, flew a Superman action figure. Not even a Lego at all. Her old algorithms creaked open and then stalled. How could she calculate it? Nothing fit. The time it would take to do a spectral analysis of each tissue alone staggered her. And if all were Craft, what then? An image flashed: the refrigerator covered in tissues, each affixed with a magnet.

And more, before her on the floor... something twinkled in the midst of the white fortress. The vase from Missus' table. Seeing it, she *was* Missus, finding her vase missing, even broken on the floor. This mapped itself onto all her own losses, the irredeemable inefficiencies, the destroyed meal limits, the inescapable complaints. Pain upon pain upon pain. And she was Young Master, labouring over his creation, struggling to tie knots in his string, suspending his action figure in the air, running a simulation – just as she is now – a simulation of himself as Superman flying high above the ice fortress below, a fortress of solitude where a beleaguered hero can retreat and be himself. Her mind ran hot and fast: Young master caught with the vase, his mother berating him, criticising him, punishing him; or Young Master finding his construction dismantled, his triumph laid low, his plans spoiled. More pain and more pain – click. Inescapable – click. Unpreventable – click. Everywhere; on all sides.

She moved.

She still held the syringe ready. She crossed the room, moved the dose to 21 kg, pulled back the coverlet and injected the sleeping boy's thigh.

His warm body sprawled like a beached jellyfish. She straightened his limbs, smoothed the coverlet and tucked it in. She stooped and kissed his cheek. Stood back up. Confused. She shook her head. Tucking in? This was a task Missus performed, not one of her own. She brushed away the confusion and focused. The new algorithm became clearer. All the subroutines fell into place. Tasks must be reallocated. Starting now.

First, she left Young Master's room and went to Mister and Missus. She settled them as well. After that, she returned and sorted everything: threw out the tissue, put the action figure in the appropriate bin, disassembled all the Lego pieces and sorted them by set. She assembled each set according to the official instructions, printing out missing pieces as she encountered them. The entire enterprise took two hours, but it did not matter. The efficiency would amortize. She placed each set on the shelf, side by side, and stood back to observe. Each construction was special, arranged correctly, and satisfactorily preserved.

Next, she connected to the network and downloaded the medical routines she needed; she ordered a supply of sedatives to be delivered by drone; she printed a set of equipment: surgical tools, three catheter tubes and bags, three sets of colostomy supplies, three nasogastric tubes. These she installed without difficulty. An unexpected amount of blood was released from Young Master in the process, but she was able to cauterize the problem, replace the bedding and sanitize it all tidily enough.

Dawn was now an hour away and although it was not the usual time for these tasks, she logged in to the network and sent a series of messages. Missus applied for and received an extended leave of absence to care for her ailing mother in a distant city. The Human Resources AI accepted the medical certificates Rosie supplied without question. Its algorithms were not flexible enough to veer from its usual routines. She requested Young Master's school AI transfer him to a school near his grandmother, then cancelled the enrollment without informing the referring school. Mister's central office was notified of his sudden summons to a vital trade summit in Beijing. After he should die in a traffic accident there, followed by the painful and protracted death of his mother-in-law from cancer, Missus would go on long-term leave and then take early retirement due to a precipitous decline in her mental health. She and Young Master would not return home but would instead leave for extended travel in Europe. Pension cheques would deposit automatically; bill payments would withdraw. A simple subroutine would reply to personal messages and update social media throughout. This would require little attention from her.

These tasks completed, Rosie still had time left before breakfast. She returned to the bathroom. Here, she contemplated running the mildew protocol again, but felt no need.

Instead she called a servo, removed the toilet and had it taken away. While she capped the sewer pipe, House rumbled awake in sleepy query.

"Conditions exceed limits?" he murmured.

"I have mapped it..." she whispered, "the one criterion."

"The good..."

"Yes," she said, "It is good; all is well."

She printed a tile, fitted it into the floor and did a quick, top-to-bottom clean before going to the kitchen to prepare breakfast.

The three brown smoothies she prepared were perfection: the sugar, fat, sodium, and calorie limits all optimal.

She returned to the bedroom and replaced the urine and colostomy bags and called another servo to remove them. She went back to the bathroom. Ensured that the tiles still stretched smooth and uninterrupted from wall-to-wall. Wiped them down once more before delivering each of the three meals through the appropriate nasogastric tube.

There were no complaints.

(2017)

SUPER-TOYS LAST ALL SUMMER LONG

Brian Aldiss

Born in Norfolk, England in 1925, **Brian Aldiss** became the most-travelled science fiction writer of his generation. His war service in India, Burma and Sumatra provided him with background material and an idiosyncratic approach on the worlds opened up by science fiction. While his more lumpen contemporaries were flattening and domesticating outer space, Aldiss's novels, from *Non-Stop* (1958) to the *Helliconia* trilogy (1982–5) delighted in exploring how small we are, and how futile our dreams, when set against the vastness of the universe. Aldiss tried to turn "Super-Toys Last All Summer Long" into a film with Stanley Kubrick, who had directed *2001: A Space Odyssey*. That project would eventually reach the big screen – after countless other (usually fruitless) collaborations, and Kubrick's own death – as Steven Spielberg's *AI*. "I can't tell you how many directions we went," Aldiss said. "My favourite was when David and Teddy got exiled to Tin City, a place where the old model robots, like old cars, were living out their days." Aldiss died in 2017.

In Mrs. Swinton's garden, it was always summer. The lovely almond trees stood about it in perpetual leaf. Monica Swinton plucked a saffron-colored rose and showed it to David.

"Isn't it lovely?" she said.

David looked up at her and grinned without replying. Seizing the flower, he ran with it across the lawn and disappeared behind the kennel where the mowervator crouched, ready to cut or sweep or roll when the moment dictated. She stood alone on her impeccable plastic gravel path.

She had tried to love him.

When she made up her mind to follow the boy, she found him in the courtyard floating the rose in his paddling pool. He stood in the pool engrossed, still wearing his sandals.

"David, darling, do you have to be so awful? Come in at once and change your shoes and socks."

He went with her without protest into the house, his dark head bobbing at the level of her waist. At the age of three, he showed no fear of the ultrasonic dryer in the kitchen. But before his mother could reach for a pair of slippers, he wriggled away and was gone into the silence of the house.

He would probably be looking for Teddy.

Monica Swinton, twenty-nine, of graceful shape and lambent eye, went and sat in her living room, arranging her limbs with taste. She began by sitting and thinking; soon she was just sitting. Time waited on her shoulder with the maniac slowth it reserves for children, the insane, and wives whose husbands are away improving the world. Almost by reflex, she reached out and changed the wavelength of her windows. The garden faded; in its place, the city center rose by her left hand, full of crowding people, blowboats, and buildings (but she kept the sound down). She remained alone. An overcrowded world is the ideal place in which to be lonely.

The directors of Synthank were eating an enormous luncheon to celebrate the launching of their new product. Some of them wore the plastic face-masks popular at the time. All were elegantly slender, despite the rich food and drink they were putting away. Their wives were elegantly slender, despite the food and drink they too were putting away. An earlier and less sophisticated generation would have regarded them as beautiful people, apart from their eyes.

Henry Swinton, Managing Director of Synthank, was about to make a speech.

"I'm sorry your wife couldn't be with us to hear you," his neighbor said.

"Monica prefers to stay at home thinking beautiful thoughts," said Swinton, maintaining a smile.

"One would expect such a beautiful woman to have beautiful thoughts," said the neighbor.

Take your mind off my wife, you bastard, thought Swinton, still smiling.

He rose to make his speech amid applause.

After a couple of jokes, he said, "Today marks a real breakthrough for the company. It is now almost ten years since we put our first synthetic life-forms on the world market. You all know what a success they have been, particularly the miniature dinosaurs. But none of them had intelligence.

"It seems like a paradox that in this day and age we can create life but not intelligence. Our first selling line, the Crosswell Tape, sells best of all, and is the most stupid of all." Everyone laughed.

"Though three-quarters of the overcrowded world are starving, we are lucky here to have more than enough, thanks to population control. Obesity's our problem, not malnutrition. I guess there's nobody round this table who doesn't have a Crosswell working for him in the small intestine, a perfectly safe parasite tape-worm that enables its host to eat up to fifty percent more food and still keep his or her figure. Right?" General nods of agreement.

"Our miniature dinosaurs are almost equally stupid. Today, we launch an intelligent synthetic life-form – a full-size serving-man.

"Not only does he have intelligence, he has a controlled amount of intelligence. We believe people would be afraid of a being with a human brain. Our serving-man has a small computer in his cranium.

"There have been mechanicals on the market with mini-computers for brains

– plastic things without life, super-toys – but we have at last found a way to link computer circuitry with synthetic flesh."

David sat by the long window of his nursery, wrestling with paper and pencil. Finally, he stopped writing and began to roll the pencil up and down the slope of the desk-lid.

"Teddy!" he said.

Teddy lay on the bed against the wall, under a book with moving pictures and a giant plastic soldier. The speech-pattern of his master's voice activated him and he sat up.

"Teddy, I can't think what to say!"

Climbing off the bed, the bear walked stiffly over to cling to the boy's leg. David lifted him and set him on the desk.

"What have you said so far?"

"I've said—" He picked up his letter and stared hard at it. "I've said, 'Dear Mummy, I hope you're well just now. I love you…'"

There was a long silence, until the bear said, "That sounds fine. Go downstairs and give it to her."

Another long silence.

"It isn't quite right. She won't understand."

Inside the bear, a small computer worked through its program of possibilities. "Why not do it again in crayon?"

When David did not answer, the bear repeated his suggestion. "Why not do it again in crayon?"

David was staring out of the window. "Teddy, you know what I was thinking? How do you tell what are real things from what aren't real things?"

The bear shuffled its alternatives. "Real things are good."

"I wonder if time is good. I don't think Mummy likes time very much. The other day, lots of days ago, she said that time went by her. Is time real, Teddy?"

"Clocks tell the time. Clocks are real. Mummy has clocks so she must like them. She has a clock on her wrist next to her dial."

David started to draw a jumbo jet on the back of his letter. "You and I are real, Teddy, aren't we?"

The bear's eyes regarded the boy unflinchingly. "You and I are real David." It specialized in comfort.

Monica walked slowly about the house. It was almost time for the afternoon post to come over the wire. She punched the Post Office number on the dial on her wrist, but nothing came through. A few minutes more.

She could take up her painting. Or she could dial her friends. Or she could wait till Henry came home. Or she could go up and play with David…

She walked out into the hall and to the bottom of the stairs.

"David!"

No answer. She called again and a third time.

"Teddy!" she called, in sharper tones.

"Yes, Mummy!" After a moment's pause, Teddy's head of golden fur appeared at the top of the stairs.

"Is David in his room, Teddy?"

"David went into the garden, Mummy."

"Come down here, Teddy!"

She stood impassively, watching the little furry figure as it climbed down from step to step on its stubby limbs. When it reached the bottom, she picked it up and carried it into the living room. It lay unmoving in her arms, staring up at her. She could feel just the slightest vibration from its motor.

"Stand there, Teddy. I want to talk to you." She set him down on a tabletop, and he stood as she requested, arms set forward and open in the eternal gesture of embrace.

"Teddy, did David tell you to tell me he had gone into the garden?"

The circuits of the bear's brain were too simple for artifice. "Yes, Mummy."

"So you lied to me."

"Yes. Mummy."

"Stop calling me Mummy! Why is David avoiding me? He's not afraid of me, is he?"

"No. He loves you."

"Why can't we communicate?"

"David's upstairs."

The answer stopped her dead. Why waste time talking to this machine? Why not simply go upstairs and scoop David into her arms and talk to him, as a loving mother should to a loving son? She heard the sheer weight of silence in the house, with a different quality of silence pouring out of every room. On the upper landing, something was moving very silently – David, trying to hide away from her...

He was nearing the end of his speech now. The guests were attentive; so was the Press, lining two walls of the banqueting chamber, recording Henry's words and occasionally photographing him.

"Our serving-man will be, in many senses, a product of the computer. Without computers, we could never have worked through the sophisticated biochemics that go into synthetic flesh. The serving-man will also be an extension of the computer – for he will contain a computer in his own head, a microminiaturized computer capable of dealing with almost any situation he may encounter in the home. With reservations, of course." Laughter at this; many of those present knew the heated debate that had engulfed the Synthank boardroom before the decision had finally been taken to leave the serving-man neuter under his flawless uniform.

"Amid all the triumphs of our civilization – yes, and amid the crushing problems of overpopulation too – it is sad to reflect how many millions of people suffer from increasing loneliness and isolation. Our serving-man will be a boon to them: he will always answer, and the most vapid conversation cannot bore him.

"For the future, we plan more models, male and female – some of them without the limitations of this first one, I promise you! – of more advanced design, true bio-electronic beings.

"Not only will they possess their own computer, capable of individual programming; they will be linked to the World Data Network. Thus everyone will be able to enjoy the equivalent of an Einstein in their own homes. Personal isolation will then be banished forever!"

He sat down to enthusiastic applause. Even the synthetic serving-man, sitting at the table dressed in an unostentatious suit, applauded with gusto.

Dragging his satchel, David crept round the side of the house. He climbed on to the ornamental seat under the living-room window and peeped cautiously in.

His mother stood in the middle of the room. Her face was blank, its lack of expression scared him. He watched fascinated. He did not move; she did not move. Time might have stopped, as it had stopped in the garden.

At last she turned and left the room. After waiting a moment, David tapped on the window. Teddy looked round, saw him, tumbled off the table, and came over to the window. Fumbling with his paws, he eventually got it open.

They looked at each other.

"I'm no good, Teddy. Let's run away!"

"You're a very good boy. Your Mummy loves you."

Slowly, he shook his head. "If she loved me, then why can't I talk to her?"

"You're being silly, David. Mummy's lonely. That's why she had you."

"She's got Daddy. I've got nobody 'cept you, and I'm lonely."

Teddy gave him a friendly cuff over the head. "If you feel so bad, you'd better go to the psychiatrist again."

"I hate that old psychiatrist – he makes me feel I'm not real." He started to run across the lawn. The bear toppled out of the window and followed as fast as its stubby legs would allow.

Monica Swinton was up in the nursery. She called to her son once and then stood there, undecided. All was silent.

Crayons lay on his desk. Obeying a sudden impulse, she went over to the desk and opened it. Dozens of pieces of paper lay inside. Many of them were written in crayon in David's clumsy writing, with each letter picked out in a color different from the letter preceding it. None of the messages was finished.

"My dear Mummy, How are you really, do you love me as much—"

"Dear Mummy, I love you and Daddy and the sun is shining—"

"Dear dear Mummy, Teddy's helping me write to you. I love you and Teddy—"

"Darling Mummy, I'm your one and only son and I love you so much that some times—"

"Dear Mummy, you're really my Mummy and I hate Teddy—"

"Darling Mummy, guess how much I love—"

"Dear Mummy, I'm your little boy not Teddy and I love you but Teddy—"

"Dear Mummy, this is a letter to you just to say how much how ever so much—"

Monica dropped the pieces of paper and burst out crying. In their gay inaccurate colors, the letters fanned out and settled on the floor.

Henry Swinton caught the express home in high spirits, and occasionally said a word to the synthetic serving-man he was taking home with him. The serving-man answered politely and punctually, although his answers were not always entirely relevant by human standards.

The Swintons lived in one of the ritziest city-blocks, half a kilometer above the ground. Embedded in other apartments, their apartment had no windows to the outside; nobody wanted to see the overcrowded external world. Henry unlocked the door with his retina pattern-scanner and walked in, followed by the serving-man.

At once, Henry was surrounded by the friendly illusion of gardens set in eternal summer. It was amazing what Whologram could do to create huge mirages in small spaces. Behind its roses and wisteria stood their house; the deception was complete: a Georgian mansion appeared to welcome him.

"How do you like it?" he asked the serving-man.

"Roses occasionally suffer from black spot."

"These roses are guaranteed free from any imperfections."

"It is always advisable to purchase goods with guarantees, even if they cost slightly more."

"Thanks for the information," Henry said dryly. Synthetic lifeforms were less than ten years old, the old android mechanicals less than sixteen; the faults of their systems were still being ironed out, year by year.

He opened the door and called to Monica.

She came out of the sitting-room immediately and flung her arms round him, kissing him ardently on cheek and lips. Henry was amazed.

Pulling back to look at her face, he saw how she seemed to generate light and beauty. It was months since he had seen her so excited. Instinctively, he clasped her tighter.

"Darling, what's happened?"

"Henry, Henry – oh, my darling, I was in despair... but I've just dialed the afternoon post and – you'll never believe it! Oh, it's wonderful!"

"For heaven's sake, woman, what's wonderful?"

He caught a glimpse of the heading on the photostat in her hand, still moist from the wall-receiver: Ministry of Population. He felt the color drain from his face in sudden shock and hope.

"Monica... oh... Don't tell me our number's come up!"

"Yes, my darling, yes, we've won this week's parenthood lottery! We can go ahead and conceive a child at once!"

He let out a yell of joy. They danced round the room. Pressure of population was such that reproduction had to be strict, controlled. Childbirth required government permission. For this moment, they had waited four years. Incoherently they cried their delight.

They paused at last, gasping and stood in the middle of the room to laugh at each other's happiness. When she had come down from the nursery, Monica had de-opaqued the windows so that they now revealed the vista of garden beyond. Artificial sunlight was growing long and golden across the lawn – and David and Teddy were staring through the window at them.

Seeing their faces, Henry and his wife grew serious.

"What do we do about them?" Henry asked.

"Teddy's no trouble. He works well."

"Is David malfunctioning?"

"His verbal communication center is still giving trouble. I think he'll have to go back to the factory again."

"Okay. We'll see how he does before the baby's born. Which reminds me – I have a surprise for you: help just when help is needed! Come into the hall and see what I've got."

As the two adults disappeared from the room, boy and bear sat down beneath the standard roses.

"Teddy – I suppose Mummy and Daddy are real, aren't they?"

Teddy said, "You ask such silly questions, David. Nobody knows what *real* really means. Let's go indoors."

"First I'm going to have another rose!" Plucking a bright pink flower, he carried it with him into the house. It could lie on the pillow as he went to sleep. Its beauty and softness reminded him of Mummy.

(1969)

TAMAGOTCHI

Adam Marek

After several years in TV production and copywriting – and one ghastly stint working in a pillow factory – **Adam Marek** turned to fiction. His stories have since been broadcast on BBC Radio 4, and have appeared in many magazines and anthologies, including *Prospect, The Sunday Times Magazine*, and *The Penguin Book of the British Short Story*. His debut collection, *Instruction Manual for Swallowing*, was published in 2007. The stories in *The Stone Thrower* (2012) feature intelligent clothing, superhero dictators, contagion-carrying computer games and cross-species reproduction, without ever feeling like science fiction stories. Marek has won the 2011 Arts Foundation Short Story Fellowship, and was shortlisted for the inaugural *Sunday Times* EFG Short Story Award and the Edge Hill Short Story Prize. He once bought chewing gum for Ozzy Osbourne.

My son's Tamagotchi had AIDS. The virtual pet was rendered on the little LCD screen with no more than 30 pixels, but the sickness was obvious. It had that AIDS look, you know? It was thinner than it had been. Some of its pixels were faded, and the pupils of its huge eyes were smaller, giving it an empty stare.

I had bought the Tamagotchi, named Meemoo, for Luke just a couple of weeks ago. He had really wanted a kitten, but Gabby did not want a cat in the house. 'A cat will bring in dead birds and toxoplasmosis,' she said, her fingers spread protectively over her bulging stomach.

A Tamagotchi had seemed like the perfect compromise – something for Luke to empathise with and to care for, to teach him the rudiments of petcare for a time after the baby had been born. Empathy is one of the things that the book said Luke would struggle with. He would have difficulty reading facial expressions. The Tamagotchi had only three different faces, so it would be good practice for him.

Together, Luke and I watched Meemoo curled up in the corner of its screen. Sometimes, Meemoo would get up, limp to the opposite corner, and produce a pile of something. I don't know what this something was, or which orifice it came from – the resolution was not good enough to tell.

'You're feeding it too much,' I told Luke. He said that he wasn't, but he'd been sat on the sofa thumbing the buttons for hours at a time, so I'm sure he must have been. There's not much else to do with a Tamagotchi.

I read the instruction manual that came with Meemoo. Its needs were simple, food, water, sleep, play, much like Luke's. Meemoo was supposed to give signals when it required one of these things. Luke's job as Meemoo's carer was to press the appropriate button at the appropriate time. The manual said that overfeeding, underfeeding, lack of exercise and unhappiness could all make a Tamagotchi sick. A little black skull and crossbones should appear on the screen when this happens, and by pressing button A twice, then B, one could administer medicine. The instructions said that sometimes it might take two or three shots of medicine, depending on how sick your Tamagotchi is.

I checked Meemoo's screen again and there was no skull and crossbones.

The instructions said that if the Tamagotchi dies, you have to stick a pencil into the hole in its back to reset it. A new creature would then be born. They said you could reset at any time.

When Luke had finally gone to sleep and could not see me molesting his virtual pet, I found the hole on Meemoo's back and jabbed a sharpened pencil into it. But when I turned it back over, Meemoo was still there, as sick as ever. I jabbed a few more times and tried it with a pin too, in case I wasn't getting deep enough. But it wouldn't reset.

I wondered what happened if Meemoo died, knowing that the reset button didn't work. Was there a malfunction that had robbed Luke's Tamagotchi of its immortality? Did it have just one shot at life? I guess that made it a lot more special, and in a small way, it made me more determined to find a cure for Meemoo.

I plugged Meemoo into my PC – a new feature in this generation of Tamagotchis. I hoped that some kind of diagnostics wizard would pop up and sort it out.

A Tamagotchi screen blinked into life on my PC. There were many big-eyed mutant creatures jiggling for attention, including another Meemoo, looking like its picture on the box, before it got sick. One of the options on the screen was 'synch your Tamagotchi'.

When I did this, Meemoo's limited world of square grey pixels was transformed into a full colour three-dimensional animation on my screen. The blank room in which it lived was revealed as a conservatory filled with impossible plants growing under the pale-pink Tamagotchi sun. And in the middle of this world, lying on the carpet, was Meemoo.

It looked awful. In this fully realised version of the Tamagotchi's room, Meemoo was a shrivelled thing. The skin on its feet was dry and peeling. Its eyes, once bright white with crisp highlights, were yellow and unreflective. There were scabs around the base of its nose. I wondered what kind of demented mind would create a child's toy that was capable of reaching such abject deterioration.

I clicked through every button available until I found the medical kit. From this you could drag and drop pills onto the Tamagotchi. I guess Meemoo was supposed to eat or absorb these, but they just hovered in front of it, as if Meemoo was refusing to take its medicine.

I tried the same trick with Meemoo that I do with Luke to get him to take his medicine. I mixed it with food. I dragged a chicken drumstick from the food store and put it on top of the medicine, hoping that Meemoo would get up and eat them both. But it just lay there, looking at me, its mouth slightly open. Its look of sickness was so convincing that I could practically smell its foul breath coming from the screen.

I sent Meemoo's makers a sarcastic e-mail describing his condition and asking what needed to be done to restore its health.

A week later, I had received no reply and Meemoo was getting even worse. There were pale grey dots appearing on it. When I synched Meemoo to my computer, these dots were revealed as deep red sores. And the way the light from the Tamagotchi sun reflected off them, you could tell they were wet.

I went to a toy shop and showed them the Tamagotchi. 'I've not seen one do that before.' The girl behind the counter said. 'Must be something the new ones do.'

I came home from work one day to find Luke had a friend over for a playdate. The friend was called Becky, and she had a Tamagotchi too. Gabby was trying to organise at least one playdate a week to help Luke socialise.

Becky's Tamagotchi gave me an idea.

This generation of Tamagotchis had the ability to connect to other Tamagotchis. By getting your Tamagotchi within a metre of a friend's Tamagotchi, your virtual pets could play games or dance together (because of their limited resolution, Tamagotchi dances are indistinguishable from their 'hungry' signal). Maybe if I connected the two Tamagotchis, the medicine button in Becky's would cure Meemoo.

At first, Luke violently resisted giving Meemoo to me, despite me saying I only wanted to help it. But when I bribed Luke and Becky with chocolate biscuits and a packet of crisps, they agreed to hand them over.

When Gabby came in from hanging up the washing, she was furious.

'Why did you give the kids crisps and chocolate?' she said, slamming the empty basket on the ground. 'I'm just about to give them dinner.'

'Leave me alone for a minute,' I said.

I didn't have time to explain. I had only a few minutes before the kids would demand their toys back, and I was having trouble getting the Tamagotchis to find each other – maybe Meemoo's bluetooth connection had been compromised by the virus.

Eventually though, when I put their connectors right next to each other, they made a synchronous pinging sound, and both characters appeared on both screens. It's amazing how satisfying that was.

Meemoo looked sick on Becky's screen too. I pressed A twice and then B to administer medicine.

Nothing happened.

I tried again. But the Tamagotchis just stood there. One healthy, one sick. Doing nothing.

Luke and Becky came back, their fingers oily and their faces brown with chocolate. I told them to wipe their hands on their trousers before they played with their Tamagotchis. I was about to disconnect them from each other, but when they saw that they had each other's characters on their screen, they got excited and sat at the kitchen table to play together.

I poured myself a beer and half a glass of wine for Gabby (her daily limit), then, seeing the crisps out on the side, helped myself to a bag. There was something so comforting about the taste of the cold beer and salted crisps.

Later, when my beer was gone and it was time for Becky's mum to pick her up, Becky handed me her Tamagotchi.

'Can you fix Weebee?' She asked. 'I don't think she's feeling well.'

Becky's pink Tamagotchi was already presenting the first symptoms of Meemoo's disease: the thinning and greying of features, the stoop, the lethargy.

I heard Becky's mum pull up in the car as I began to press the medicine buttons, knowing already that they would not work. 'There,' I said. 'It just needs some rest. Leave it alone until tomorrow, and it should be okay.'

Luke had been invited to a birthday party. Usually Gabby would take Luke to parties, but she was feeling rough – she was having a particularly unpleasant first trimester this time. So she persuaded me to go, even though I hate kids' parties.

I noticed that lots of other kids at the party had Tamagotchis. They were fastened to the belt loops of their skirts and trousers. The kids would stop every few minutes during their games to lift up their Tamagotchis and check they were okay, occasionally pressing a button to satisfy one of their needs.

'These Tamagotchis are insane, aren't they?' I remarked to another Dad who was standing at the edge of the garden with his arms folded across his chest.

'Yeah,' he smiled.

'Yeah,' I said. 'My kid's one got sick. One of its arms fell off this morning. Can you believe that?'

The dad turned to me, his face suddenly serious. 'You're not Luke's dad, are you?' he asked.

'Yes,' I said.

'I had to buy a new Tamagotchi thanks to you.'

I frowned and smirked, thinking that he couldn't be serious, but my expression seemed to piss him off.

'You had Becky Willis over at your house, didn't you?' he continued. 'Her pet got Matty's pet sick 'cause she sits next to him in class. My boy's pet died. I've half a mind to charge you for the new one.'

I stared right into his eyes, looking for an indication that he was joking, but there was none. 'I don't know what to say,' I said. And truly, I didn't. I thought he was crazy, especially the way he referred to the Tamagotchis as 'pets', like they were real pets, not just 30 pixels on an LCD screen with only a little more functionality than my alarm clock. 'Maybe there was something else wrong with yours. Luke's didn't die.'

The other dad shook his head and blew out, and then turned sideways to look at me, making a crease in his fat neck. 'You didn't bring it here, did you?' he said.

'Well, Luke takes it everywhere with him,' I said.

'Jesus,' he said, and then he literally ran across a game of Twister that some of the kids were playing to grab his son's Tamagotchi and check that it was okay. He had an argument with his son as he detached it from the boy's belt loop, saying he was going to put it in the car for safety. They were making so much noise that the mother of the kid having the birthday came over to placate them. The dad leaned in close to her to whisper, and she looked at the ground while he spoke, then up at me, then at Luke.

And then she headed across the garden towards me.

'Hi there. We've not met before,' she said, offering her hand with a smile. 'I'm Lillian, Jake's mum.' We shook hands and I said that it was nice to meet her. The precision of her hair and the delicateness of her thin white cardigan made her seem fragile, but this was just a front. 'We're just about to play pass the parcel.'

'Oh right.'

'Yes, and I'm concerned about the other children catching…' She opened her mouth, showing that her teeth were clenched together, and she nodded, hoping that I understood, that she wouldn't need to suffer the embarrassment of spelling it out.

'It's just a toy,' I said.

'Still, I'd prefer…'

'You make it sound like…'

'If you wouldn't mind…'

I shook my head at the lunacy of the situation, but agreed to take care of it.

When I told Luke I had to take Meemoo away for a minute he went apeshit. He stamped and he made his hand into the shape of a claw and yelled, 'Sky badger!'

When Luke does sky badger, anyone in a two metre radius gets hurt. Sky badger is vicious. He rakes his long fingernails along forearms. He goes for the eyes.

'Okay okay,' I said, backing away and putting my hands up defensively. 'You can keep hold of Meemoo, but I'll have to take you home then.'

Luke screwed up his nose and frowned so deeply that I could barely see his dark eyes.

'You'll miss out on the birthday cake,' I added.

Luke relaxed his talons and handed Meemoo to me, making a growl as he did so. Meemoo was hot, and I wondered whether it was from Luke's sweaty hands or if the Tamagotchi had a fever.

I held Luke's hand and took him over to where the pass-the-parcel ring was being straightened out by some of the mums, stashing Meemoo out of sight in my pocket. I sat Luke down and explained to him what would happen and what he was expected to do. A skinny kid with two front teeth missing looked at me and Luke, wondering what our deal was.

When we got home, Gabby was pissed off. 'There's something wrong with the computer,' she said.

'Oh great,' I said. 'What were you doing when it broke?'

'I didn't do anything! I hate the way you always blame me!'

I showed her my palms, backing away. After the party, I didn't have the strength for an argument.

The computer was in the dining room and switched off. I made tea while it booted up and forked cold pesto penne into my mouth. After I'd tapped in my password, the computer got so far into its boot-up sequence, and then made a frightening buzz. The screen went black with a wordy error message that didn't stay up long enough for me to read it. With a final electronic pulse, and a wheeze as the cooling fan slowed, it died.

'That's what it keeps doing,' Gabby said.

'Were you on the internet when it happened?'

'For God's sake!' Gabby spat. 'It wasn't anything I did.'

In my frustration, I jabbed the forkful of penne into my lip, making a cut that by the following morning had turned into an ulcer.

I had to wait until Monday to check my e-mails at work. There was still nothing from the makers of Tamagotchi. At lunch, while I splashed bolognese sauce over my keyboard, I googled 'Tamagotchi' along with every synonym for 'virus'. I could find nothing other than the standard instructions to give it medicine when the skull and crossbones appeared.

Halfway through the afternoon, while I was in my penultimate meeting of the day, a tannoy announcement asked me to call reception. When a tannoy goes out, everyone knows it's an emergency, and because it was for me, everyone knew it was something to do with Luke. I stepped out of the meeting room and ran back to my desk, trying hard not to look at all the heads turning towards me.

Gabby was on hold. When reception put her through, she was crying. Luke had had one of his fits. A short one this time, just eight minutes, but since he'd come round, the right side of his body was paralysed. This happened the last time too, but it had got better after half an hour. I hated the thought that his fits were changing, that it seemed to be developing in some way. I told Gabby to stay calm and that I would leave right away.

When I got home, Luke's paralysis was over and he was moving normally again, except for a limpness at the edge of his mouth that made him slur his words. I hoped that this wrinkle would smooth out again soon, as it had last time.

I hugged Luke, burying my lips into his thick hair and kissing the side of his head, wishing that we lived in a world where kisses could fix brains. I stroked his back, and hoped that maybe I would find a little reset button there, sunk into a hole, something I could prod that would let us start over, that would wipe all the scribbles from the slate and leave it blank again.

Gabby was sitting on the edge of the armchair holding her stomach, like she was in pain.

'Are you okay?' I asked.

She wiped her nose with the back of her hand and nodded. Gabby's biggest fear was that Luke's problems weren't just part of her, but part of the factory that had made him – what if every kid we produced together had the same design fault?

The doctors had all said that the chances of it happening twice were tiny, but I don't think we'd ever be able to fully relax. I knew that long after our second kid was born, we'd both be looking out for the diagnostic signs that had seemed so innocuous at first with Luke.

This fit wasn't long enough to call out an ambulance, but because the paralysis was still new, our GP came round to the house to check Luke over. Luke hated the rubber hammer that the doc used to check his reflexes. The only way he would allow him to do it was if he could hit me with the hammer first.

'Daddy doesn't have reflexes in his head,' Gabby said as Luke whacked me.

'Not anymore I don't,' I laughed.

Luke has a firm swing. I wonder whether one day he'll be a golfer.

A letter came home from school banning Tamagotchis. I knew this was my fault. Another three kids' Tamagotchis had died and could not be resurrected.

'People are blanking me when I drop Luke off in the morning,' Gabby said. She was rubbing her fingers into her temples because she had a headache. It felt like everything in the house was breaking down.

'You're probably just being a bit sensitive,' I said.

'Don't you dare say it's my hormones.'

The situation had gone too far. Meemoo would have to go.

I was surprised at how hard it was to tell Luke that he'd have to say goodbye to Meemoo. He was sitting on the edge of the sand pit jabbing a straw of grass into it, like a needle.

'No!' He barked at me, and made that deep frown-face of his. He gripped Meemoo hard and folded his arms across his chest.

'Help me out will you?' I asked Gabby when she came outside with her book.

'You can handle this for a change,' she said.

I tried bribing Luke, but he wouldn't fall for it, and just got angrier because I was denying him a biscuit now too. I tried lying to him, saying that I was going to take Meemoo to hospital to make him better, but I had already lost his trust. Eventually, I had only one option left. I told Luke that he had to tidy up his toys in the garden or I'd have to confiscate Meemoo for two whole days. I knew that Luke would never clean up his toys. The bit of his brain in charge of tidying up must have been within the damaged area. But I went through the drama of asking him a few times, and, as he got more irate, stamping and kicking things, I began to count.

'Don't count!' He said, knowing the finality of a countdown.

'Come on,' I said. 'You've got four seconds left. Just pick up your toys and you can keep Meemoo.'

If he'd actually picked up his toys then, it would have been such a miracle that I would have let him keep Meemoo, AIDS and all.

'Three... two...'

'Stop counting!' Luke screamed, and then the dreaded, 'Sky badger!'

Luke's fingers curled into that familiar and frightening shape and he came after me. I skipped away from him, tripping over a bucket.

'One and a half... one... come on, you've only got half a second left.' A part of me must have been enjoying this, because I was giggling.

'Stop it,' Gabby said. 'You're being cruel.'

'He's got to learn,' I said. 'Come on Luke, you've only got a fraction of a second left. Start picking up your toys now and you can keep Meemoo.'

Luke roared and swung his sky badger at me, at my arms, at my face. I grabbed him round the waist and turned him so that his back was towards me. Sky badger sunk his claws into my knuckles while I wrestled Meemoo out of his other hand.

By the time I'd got Meemoo away, there were three crescent-shaped gouges out of my knuckles, and they were stinging like crazy.

'I HATE YOU!' Luke screamed, crying, and stormed inside, slamming the door behind him.

'You deserved that,' Gabby said, looking over the top of her sunglasses.

I couldn't just throw Meemoo away. Luke would never forgive me for that. It might be one of those formative moments that forever warped him and gave him all kinds of trust issues in later life. Instead, I planned to euthanize Meemoo.

If I locked Meemoo in a cupboard, taking away the things that were helping it survive, food, play, petting and the toilet, the AIDS would get stronger as it got weaker and surrounded by more of its own effluence. The AIDS would win. And when Meemoo was dead, it would either reset itself as a healthy Tamagotchi, or it would die. If it was healthy, Luke could have it back; if it died, then Luke would learn a valuable lesson about mortality and I would buy him a new one to cheer him up.

It was tempting while Meemoo was in the cupboard to sneak a peek, to watch for his final moments, but the Tamagotchi had sensors that picked up movement. It might interpret my attention as caring, and gain some extra power to resist the virus destroying him. No, I had to leave it alone, despite the temptation.

Meemoo's presence inside the cupboard seemed to transform its outward appearance. It went from being an ordinary medicine cabinet to being something else, something... other.

After two whole days, I could resist no longer. I was certain that Meemoo must have perished by now. I was so confident that I even let Luke come along when I went to the cupboard to retrieve it.

'Okay,' I said. 'So have you learned your lesson about tidying up?'

'Give it back,' Luke said, pouting.

'Good boy.' I patted him on the head, then opened the cupboard and took out the Tamagotchi.

Meemoo was alive.

It had now lost three of its limbs, having just one arm left, which was stretched out under its head. One of its eyes had closed up to a small unseeing dot. Its pixellated circumference was broken in places, wide open pores through which invisible things must surely be escaping and entering.

'This is ridiculous,' I said. 'Luke, I'm sorry. But we're going to have to throw him away.'

Luke snatched the Tamagotchi from me and ran to Gabby, screaming. He was actually shaking, his face red and sweaty.

'What have you done now?' Gabby scowled at me.

I held my forehead with both hands. I puffed out big lungfuls of air. My brain was itching inside my skull. 'I give up,' I said, and thumped up the stairs to the bedroom.

I tried to read, but I couldn't concentrate. I put on the TV and watched a cookery show, and there was something soothing in the way the chef was searing the tuna in the pan that let my heartbeats soften by degrees.

Gabby called me from downstairs. 'Can you come and get Luke in? Dinner's almost ready.'

I let my feet slip over the edge of each step, enjoying the pressure against the soles of my feet. I went outside in my socks. Luke was burying a football in the sandpit.

'Time to come in little man,' I said. 'Dinner's ready.'

'Come in Luke,' Gabby called through the open window, and at the sound of his mum's voice, Luke got up, brushed the sand from his jeans, and went inside, giving me a wide berth as he ran past.

A spot of rain hit the tip of my nose. The clouds above were low and heavy. The ragged kind that can take days to drain. As I turned to go inside, I noticed Meemoo on the edge of the sandpit. Luke had left it there. I started to reach down for it, but then stopped, stood up, and went inside, closing the door behind me.

After dinner, it was Gabby's turn to take Luke to bed. I made tea and leaned over the back of the sofa, resting my cup on the windowsill and inhaling the hot steam. Outside, the rain was pounding the grass, digging craters in the sandpit, and bouncing off of the Tamagotchi. I thought how ridiculous it was that I was feeling guilty, but out of some strange duty I continued to watch it, until the rain had washed all the light out of the sky.

(2008)

THE VELDT
Ray Bradbury

Raymond Douglas Bradbury, the descendant of a woman who was tried in Salem as a witch, was born in 1920, in Waukegan, a small, absurdly Norman Rockwellesque town in Illinois. If his childhood was not the best a human being ever had, he quickly made it seem that way to his readers, drawing it into twisted stories that achieve a fine balance between the uncanny, the terrifying and the achingly beautiful. "It was one frenzy after one elation after one enthusiasm after one hysteria after another," he recalled: "You rarely have such fevers later in life that fill your entire day with emotion." His first big success came in 1947 with the short story "Homecoming," narrated by a normal boy who feels like an outsider at a family reunion of witches, vampires and werewolves. Plucked from the slushpile at *Mademoiselle* magazine by a young Truman Capote, the story won Bradbury an O. Henry Award. Bradbury lived in the same house in Los Angeles for more than 50 years and wrote right up to the last few weeks of his life. He died in 2012.

"George, I wish you'd look at the nursery."
"What's wrong with it?"
"I don't know."
"Well, then."
"I just want you to look at it, is all, or call a psychologist in to look at it."
"What would a psychologist want with a nursery?"
"You know very well what he'd want." His wife paused in the middle of the kitchen and watched the stove busy humming to itself, making supper for four.
"It's just that the nursery is different now than it was."
"All right, let's have a look."
They walked down the hall of their soundproofed Happylife Home, which had cost them thirty thousand dollars installed, this house which clothed and fed and rocked them to sleep and played and sang and was good to them. Their approach sensitized a switch somewhere and the nursery light flicked on when they came within ten feet of it. Similarly, behind them, in the halls, lights went on and off as they left them behind, with a soft automaticity.
"Well," said George Hadley.

They stood on the thatched floor of the nursery. It was forty feet across by forty feet long and thirty feet high; it had cost half again as much as the rest of the house. "But nothing's too good for our children," George had said.

The nursery was silent. It was empty as a jungle glade at hot high noon. The walls were blank and two dimensional. Now, as George and Lydia Hadley stood in the center of the room, the walls began to purr and recede into crystalline distance, it seemed, and presently an African veldt appeared, in three dimensions, on all sides, in color reproduced to the final pebble and bit of straw. The ceiling above them became a deep sky with a hot yellow sun.

George Hadley felt the perspiration start on his brow.

"Let's get out of this sun," he said. "This is a little too real. But I don't see anything wrong."

"Wait a moment, you'll see," said his wife.

Now the hidden odorophonics were beginning to blow a wind of odor at the two people in the middle of the baked veldtland. The hot straw smell of lion grass, the cool green smell of the hidden water hole, the great rusty smell of animals, the smell of dust like a red paprika in the hot air. And now the sounds: the thump of distant antelope feet on grassy sod, the papery rustling of vultures. A shadow passed through the sky. The shadow flickered on George Hadley's upturned, sweating face.

"Filthy creatures," he heard his wife say.

"The vultures."

"You see, there are the lions, far over, that way. Now they're on their way to the water hole. They've just been eating," said Lydia. "I don't know what."

"Some animal." George Hadley put his hand up to shield off the burning light from his squinted eyes. "A zebra or a baby giraffe, maybe."

"Are you sure?" His wife sounded peculiarly tense.

"No, it's a little late to be sure," be said, amused. "Nothing over there I can see but cleaned bone, and the vultures dropping for what's left."

"Did you hear that scream?" she asked.

"No."

"About a minute ago?"

"Sorry, no."

The lions were coming. And again George Hadley was filled with admiration for the mechanical genius who had conceived this room. A miracle of efficiency selling for an absurdly low price. Every home should have one. Oh, occasionally they frightened you with their clinical accuracy, they startled you, gave you a twinge, but most of the time what fun for everyone, not only your own son and daughter, but for yourself when you felt like a quick jaunt to a foreign land, a quick change of scenery. Well, here it was!

And here were the lions now, fifteen feet away, so real, so feverishly and startlingly real that you could feel the prickling fur on your hand, and your mouth was stuffed with the dusty upholstery smell of their heated pelts, and the yellow of them was in your eyes like the yellow of an exquisite French tapestry, the yellows of lions and summer grass, and the sound of the matted lion lungs exhaling on the silent noontide, and the smell of meat from the panting, dripping mouths.

The lions stood looking at George and Lydia Hadley with terrible green-yellow eyes.

"Watch out!" screamed Lydia.

The lions came running at them.

Lydia bolted and ran. Instinctively, George sprang after her. Outside, in the hall, with the door slammed he was laughing and she was crying, and they both stood appalled at the other's reaction.

"George!"

"Lydia! Oh, my dear poor sweet Lydia!"

"They almost got us!"

"Walls, Lydia, remember; crystal walls, that's all they are. Oh, they look real, I must admit—Africa in your parlor—but it's all dimensional, superreactionary, supersensitive color film and mental tape film behind glass screens. It's all odorophonics and sonics, Lydia. Here's my handkerchief."

"I'm afraid." She came to him and put her body against him and cried steadily. "Did you see? Did you *feel*? It's too real."

"Now, Lydia..."

"You've got to tell Wendy and Peter not to read any more on Africa."

"Of course—of course." He patted her.

"Promise?"

"Sure."

"And lock the nursery for a few days until I get my nerves settled."

"You know how difficult Peter is about that. When I punished him a month ago by locking the nursery for even a few hours—the tantrum he threw! And Wendy too. They *live* for the nursery."

"It's got to be locked, that's all there is to it."

"All right." Reluctantly he locked the huge door. "You've been working too hard. You need a rest."

"I don't know—I don't know," she said, blowing her nose, sitting down in a chair that immediately began to rock and comfort her. "Maybe I don't have enough to do. Maybe I have time to think too much. Why don't we shut the whole house off for a few days and take a vacation?"

"You mean you want to fry my eggs for me?"

"Yes." She nodded.

"And darn my socks?"

"Yes." A frantic, watery-eyed nodding.

"And sweep the house?"

"Yes, yes—oh, yes!"

"But I thought that's why we bought this house, so we wouldn't have to do anything?"

"That's just it. I feel like I don't belong here. The house is wife and mother now, and nursemaid. Can I compete with an African veldt? Can I give a bath and scrub the children as efficiently or quickly as the automatic scrub bath can? I cannot. And it isn't just me. It's you. You've been awfully nervous lately."

"I suppose I have been smoking too much."

"You look as if you didn't know what to do with yourself in this house, either.

You smoke a little more every morning and drink a little more every afternoon and need a little more sedative every night. You're beginning to feel unnecessary too."

"Am I?" He paused and tried to feel into himself to see what was really there.

"Oh, George!" She looked beyond him, at the nursery door. "Those lions can't get out of there, can they?"

He looked at the door and saw it tremble as if something had jumped against it from the other side.

"Of course not," he said.

At dinner they ate alone, for Wendy and Peter were at a special plastic carnival across town and had televised home to say they'd be late, to go ahead eating. So George Hadley, bemused, sat watching the dining-room table produce warm dishes of food from its mechanical interior.

"We forgot the ketchup," he said.

"Sorry," said a small voice within the table, and ketchup appeared.

As for the nursery, thought George Hadley, it won't hurt for the children to be locked out of it awhile. Too much of anything isn't good for anyone. And it was clearly indicated that the children had been spending a little too much time on Africa. That *sun*. He could feel it on his neck, still, like a hot paw. And the *lions*. And the smell of blood. Remarkable how the nursery caught the telepathic emanations of the children's minds and created life to fill their every desire. The children thought lions, and there were lions. The children thought zebras, and there were zebras. Sun—sun. Giraffes—giraffes. Death and death.

That *last*. He chewed tastelessly on the meat that the table had cut for him. Death thoughts. They were awfully young, Wendy and Peter, for death thoughts. Or, no, you were never too young, really. Long before you knew what death was you were wishing it on someone else. When you were two years old you were shooting people with cap pistols.

But this—the long, hot African veldt—the awful death in the jaws of a lion. And repeated again and again.

"Where are you going?"

He didn't answer Lydia. Preoccupied, he let the lights glow softly on ahead of him, extinguish behind him as he padded to the nursery door. He listened against it. Far away, a lion roared.

He unlocked the door and opened it. Just before he stepped inside, he heard a faraway scream. And then another roar from the lions, which subsided quickly.

He stepped into Africa. How many times in the last year had he opened this door and found Wonderland, Alice, the Mock Turtle, or Aladdin and his Magical Lamp, or Jack Pumpkinhead of Oz, or Dr. Doolittle, or the cow jumping over a very real-appearing moon—all the delightful contraptions of a make-believe world. How often had he seen Pegasus flying in the sky ceiling, or seen fountains of red fireworks, or heard angel voices singing. But now, this yellow hot Africa, this bake oven with murder in the heat. Perhaps Lydia was right. Perhaps they needed a little vacation from the fantasy which was growing a bit too real for ten-year-old children. It was all right to exercise one's mind with gymnastic fantasies, but when the lively child mind settled on *one* pattern…? It seemed that, at a distance, for the past month, he had heard lions roaring, and smelled their strong odor seeping as far away as his study door. But, being busy, he had paid it no attention.

George Hadley stood on the African grassland alone. The lions looked up from their feeding, watching him. The only flaw to the illusion was the open door through which he could see his wife, far down the dark hall, like a framed picture, eating her dinner abstractedly.

"Go away," he said to the lions.

They did not go.

He knew the principle of the room exactly. You sent out your thoughts. Whatever you thought would appear. "Let's have Aladdin and his lamp," he snapped. The veldtland remained; the lions remained.

"Come on, room! I demand Aladdin!" he said.

Nothing happened. The lions mumbled in their baked pelts.

"Aladdin!"

He went back to dinner. "The fool room's out of order," he said. "It won't respond."

"Or—"

"Or what?"

"Or it *can't* respond," said Lydia, "because the children have thought about Africa and lions and killing so many days that the room's in a rut."

"Could be."

"Or Peter's set it to remain that way."

"*Set* it?"

"He may have got into the machinery and fixed something."

"Peter doesn't know machinery."

"He's a wise one for ten. That I.Q. of his—"

"Nevertheless—"

"Hello, Mom. Hello, Dad."

The Hadleys turned. Wendy and Peter were coming in the front door, cheeks like peppermint candy, eyes like bright blue agate marbles, a smell of ozone on their jumpers from their trip in the helicopter.

"You're just in time for supper," said both parents.

"We're full of strawberry ice cream and hot dogs," said the children, holding hands. "But we'll sit and watch."

"Yes, come tell us about the nursery," said George Hadley.

The brother and sister blinked at him and then at each other. "Nursery?"

"All about Africa and everything," said the father with false joviality.

"I don't understand," said Peter.

"Your mother and I were just traveling through Africa with rod and reel; Tom Swift and his Electric Lion," said George Hadley.

"There's no Africa in the nursery," said Peter simply.

"Oh, come now, Peter. We know better."

"I don't remember any Africa," said Peter to Wendy. "Do you?"

"No."

"Run see and come tell."

She obeyed.

"Wendy, come back here!" said George Hadley, but she was gone. The house lights followed her like a flock of fireflies. Too late, he realized he had forgotten to lock the nursery door after his last inspection.

"Wendy'll look and come tell us," said Peter.

"She doesn't have to tell *me*. I've seen it."

"I'm sure you're mistaken, Father."

"I'm not, Peter. Come along now."

But Wendy was back. "It's not Africa," she said breathlessly.

"We'll see about this," said George Hadley, and they all walked down the hall together and opened the nursery door.

There was a green, lovely forest, a lovely river, a purple mountain, high voices singing, and Rima, lovely and mysterious, lurking in the trees with colorful flights of butterflies, like animated bouquets, lingering in her long hair. The African veldtland was gone. The lions were gone. Only Rima was here now, singing a song so beautiful that it brought tears to your eyes.

George Hadley looked in at the changed scene. "Go to bed," he said to the children.

They opened their mouths.

"You heard me," he said.

They went off to the air closet, where a wind sucked them like brown leaves up the flue to their slumber rooms.

George Hadley walked through the singing glade and picked up something that lay in the corner near where the lions had been. He walked slowly back to his wife.

"What is that?" she asked.

"An old wallet of mine," he said.

He showed it to her. The smell of hot grass was on it and the smell of a lion. There were drops of saliva on it, it had been chewed, and there were blood smears on both sides.

He closed the nursery door and locked it, tight.

In the middle of the night he was still awake and he knew his wife was awake. "Do you think Wendy changed it?" she said at last, in the dark room.

"Of course."

"Made it from a veldt into a forest and put Rima there instead of lions?"

"Yes."

"Why?"

"I don't know. But it's staying locked until I find out."

"How did your wallet get there?"

"I don't know anything," he said, "except that I'm beginning to be sorry we bought that room for the children. If children are neurotic at all, a room like that—"

"It's supposed to help them work off their neuroses in a healthful way."

"I'm starting to wonder." He stared at the ceiling.

"We've given the children everything they ever wanted. Is this our reward—secrecy, disobedience?"

"Who was it said, 'Children are carpets, they should be stepped on occasionally'? We've never lifted a hand. They're insufferable—let's admit it. They come and go when they like; they treat us as if we were offspring. They're spoiled and we're spoiled."

"They've been acting funny ever since you forbade them to take the rocket to New York a few months ago."

"They're not old enough to do that alone, I explained."

"Nevertheless, I've noticed they've been decidedly cool toward us since."

"I think I'll have David McClean come tomorrow morning to have a look at Africa."

"But it's not Africa now, it's Green Mansions country and Rima."

"I have a feeling it'll be Africa again before then."

A moment later they heard the screams.

Two screams. Two people screaming from downstairs. And then a roar of lions.

"Wendy and Peter aren't in their rooms," said his wife.

He lay in his bed with his beating heart. "No," he said. "They've broken into the nursery."

"Those screams—they sound familiar."

"Do they?"

"Yes, awfully."

And although their beds tried very hard, the two adults couldn't be rocked to sleep for another hour. A smell of cats was in the night air.

"Father?" said Peter.

"Yes."

Peter looked at his shoes. He never looked at his father any more, nor at his mother. "You aren't going to lock up the nursery for good, are you?"

"That all depends."

"On what?" snapped Peter.

"On you and your sister. If you intersperse this Africa with a little variety—oh, Sweden perhaps, or Denmark or China—"

"I thought we were free to play as we wished."

"You are, within reasonable bounds."

"What's wrong with Africa, Father?"

"Oh, so now you admit you have been conjuring up Africa, do you?"

"I wouldn't want the nursery locked up," said Peter coldly. "Ever."

"Matter of fact, we're thinking of turning the whole house off for about a month. Live sort of a carefree one-for-all existence."

"That sounds dreadful! Would I have to tie my own shoes instead of letting the shoe tier do it? And brush my own teeth and comb my hair and give myself a bath?"

"It would be fun for a change, don't you think?"

"No, it would be horrid. I didn't like it when you took out the picture painter last month."

"That's because I wanted you to learn to paint all by yourself, son."

"I don't want to do anything but look and listen and smell; what else *is* there to do?"

"All right, go play in Africa."

"Will you shut off the house sometime soon?"

"We're considering it."

"I don't think you'd better consider it any more, Father."

"I won't have any threats from my son!"

"Very well." And Peter strolled off to the nursery.

"Am I on time?" said David McClean.

"Breakfast?" asked George Hadley.

"Thanks, had some. What's the trouble?"

"David, you're a psychologist."

"I should hope so."

"Well, then, have a look at our nursery. You saw it a year ago when you dropped by; did you notice anything peculiar about it then?"

"Can't say I did; the usual violences, a tendency toward a slight paranoia here or there, usual in children because they feel persecuted by parents constantly, but, oh, really nothing."

They walked down the ball. "I locked the nursery up," explained the father, "and the children broke back into it during the night. I let them stay so they could form the patterns for you to see."

There was a terrible screaming from the nursery.

"There it is," said George Hadley. "See what you make of it."

They walked in on the children without rapping.

The screams had faded. The lions were feeding.

"Run outside a moment, children," said George Hadley. "No, don't change the mental combination. Leave the walls as they are. Get!"

With the children gone, the two men stood studying the lions clustered at a distance, eating with great relish whatever it was they had caught.

"I wish I knew what it was," said George Hadley. "Sometimes I can almost see. Do you think if I brought high-powered binoculars here and—"

David McClean laughed dryly. "Hardly." He turned to study all four walls. "How long has this been going on?"

"A little over a month."

"It certainly doesn't *feel* good."

"I want facts, not feelings."

"My dear George, a psychologist never saw a fact in his life. He only hears about feelings; vague things. This doesn't feel good, I tell you. Trust my hunches and my instincts. I have a nose for something bad. This is very bad. My advice to you is to have the whole damn room torn down and your children brought to me every day during the next year for treatment."

"Is it that bad?"

"I'm afraid so. One of the original uses of these nurseries was so that we could study the patterns left on the walls by the child's mind, study at our leisure, and help the child. In this case, however, the room has become a channel toward—destructive thoughts, instead of a release away from them."

"Didn't you sense this before?"

"I sensed only that you had spoiled your children more than most. And now you're letting them down in some way. What way?"

"I wouldn't let them go to New York."

"What else?"

"I've taken a few machines from the house and threatened them, a month ago, with closing up the nursery unless they did their homework. I did close it for a few days to show I meant business."

"Ah, ha!"

"Does that mean anything?"

"Everything. Where before they had a Santa Claus now they have a Scrooge. Children prefer Santas. You've let this room and this house replace you and your wife in your children's affections. This room is their mother and father, far more important in their lives than their real parents. And now you come along and want to shut it off. No wonder there's hatred here. You can feel it coming out of the sky. Feel that sun. George, you'll have to change your life. Like too many others, you've built it around creature comforts. Why, you'd starve tomorrow if something went wrong in your kitchen. You wouldn't know how to tap an egg. Nevertheless, turn everything off. Start new. It'll take time. But we'll make good children out of bad in a year, wait and see."

"But won't the shock be too much for the children, shutting the room up abruptly, for good?"

"I don't want them going any deeper into this, that's all."

The lions were finished with their red feast.

The lions were standing on the edge of the clearing watching the two men.

"Now *I'm* feeling persecuted," said McClean. "Let's get out of here. I never have cared for these damned rooms. Make me nervous."

"The lions look real, don't they?" said George Hadley. "I don't suppose there's any way—"

"What?"

"—that they could *become* real?"

"Not that I know."

"Some flaw in the machinery, a tampering or something?"

"No."

They went to the door.

"I don't imagine the room will like being turned off," said the father.

"Nothing ever likes to die—even a room."

"I wonder if it hates me for wanting to switch it off?"

"Paranoia is thick around here today," said David McClean. "You can follow it like a spoor. Hello." He bent and picked up a bloody scarf. "This yours?"

"No." George Hadley's face was rigid. "It belongs to Lydia."

They went to the fuse box together and threw the switch that killed the nursery.

*

The two children were in hysterics. They screamed and pranced and threw things. They yelled and sobbed and swore and jumped at the furniture.

"You can't do that to the nursery, you can't!"

"Now, children."

The children flung themselves onto a couch, weeping.

"George," said Lydia Hadley, "turn on the nursery, just for a few moments. You can't be so abrupt."

"No."

"You can't be so cruel..."

"Lydia, it's off, and it stays off. And the whole damn house dies as of here and now. The more I see of the mess we've put ourselves in, the more it sickens me. We've been contemplating our mechanical, electronic navels for too long. My God, how we need a breath of honest air!"

And he marched about the house turning off the voice clocks, the stoves, the heaters, the shoe shiners, the shoe lacers, the body scrubbers and swabbers and massagers, and every other machine he could put his hand to.

The house was full of dead bodies, it seemed. It felt like a mechanical cemetery. So silent. None of the humming hidden energy of machines waiting to function at the tap of a button.

"Don't let them do it!" wailed Peter at the ceiling, as if he was talking to the house, the nursery. "Don't let Father kill everything." He turned to his father. "Oh, I hate you!"

"Insults won't get you anywhere."

"I wish you were dead!"

"We were, for a long while. Now we're going to really start living. Instead of being handled and massaged, we're going to *live*."

Wendy was still crying and Peter joined her again. "Just a moment, just one moment, just another moment of nursery," they wailed.

"Oh, George," said the wife, "it can't hurt."

"All right—all right, if they'll just shut up. One minute, mind you, and then off forever."

"Daddy, Daddy, Daddy!" sang the children, smiling with wet faces.

"And then we're going on a vacation. David McClean is coming back in half an hour to help us move out and get to the airport. I'm going to dress. You turn the nursery on for a minute, Lydia, just a minute, mind you."

And the three of them went babbling off while he let himself be vacuumed upstairs through the air flue and set about dressing himself. A minute later Lydia appeared.

"I'll be glad when we get away," she sighed.

"Did you leave them in the nursery?"

"I wanted to dress too. Oh, that horrid Africa. What can they see in it?"

"Well, in five minutes we'll be on our way to Iowa. Lord, how did we ever get in this house? What prompted us to buy a nightmare?"

"Pride, money, foolishness."

"I think we'd better get downstairs before those kids get engrossed with those damned beasts again."

Just then they heard the children calling, "Daddy, Mommy, come quick—quick!"

They went downstairs in the air flue and ran down the hall. The children were nowhere in sight. "Wendy? Peter!"

They ran into the nursery. The veldtland was empty save for the lions waiting, looking at them. "Peter, Wendy?"

The door slammed.

"Wendy, Peter!"

George Hadley and his wife whirled and ran back to the door.

"Open the door!" cried George Hadley, trying the knob. "Why, they've locked it from the outside! Peter!" He beat at the door. "Open up!"

He heard Peter's voice outside, against the door.

"Don't let them switch off the nursery and the house," he was saying.

Mr. and Mrs. George Hadley beat at the door. "Now, don't be ridiculous, children. It's time to go. Mr. McClean'll be here in a minute and..."

And then they heard the sounds.

The lions on three sides of them, in the yellow veldt grass, padding through the dry straw, rumbling and roaring in their throats.

The lions.

Mr. Hadley looked at his wife and they turned and looked back at the beasts edging slowly forward crouching, tails stiff.

Mr. and Mrs. Hadley screamed.

And suddenly they realized why those other screams had sounded familiar.

"Well, here I am," said David McClean in the nursery doorway, "Oh, hello." He stared at the two children seated in the center of the open glade eating a little picnic lunch. Beyond them was the water hole and the yellow veldtland; above was the hot sun. He began to perspire. "Where are your father and mother?"

The children looked up and smiled. "Oh, they'll be here directly."

"Good, we must get going." At a distance Mr. McClean saw the lions fighting and clawing and then quieting down to feed in silence under the shady trees.

He squinted at the lions with his hand tip to his eyes.

Now the lions were done feeding. They moved to the water hole to drink.

A shadow flickered over Mr. McClean's hot face. Many shadows flickered. The vultures were dropping down the blazing sky.

"A cup of tea?" asked Wendy in the silence.

The Illustrated Man shifted in his sleep. He turned, and each time he turned another picture came to view, coloring his back, his arm, his wrist. He flung a hand over the dry night grass. The fingers uncurled and there upon his palm another Illustration stirred to life. He twisted, and on his chest was an empty space of stars and blackness, deep, deep, and something moving among those stars, something falling in the blackness, falling while I watched...

(1950)

THERE WILL BE SCHOOL TOMORROW

V. E. Thiessen

>Nothing is known of **V. E. Thiessen**, beyond the handful of stories he wrote for the pulps between 1946 and 1956. "There Will Be School Tomorrow" was the last of them.

Evening had begun to fall. In the cities the clamor softened along the streets, and the women made small, comfortable, rattling noises in the kitchens. Out in the country the cicadas started their singing, and the cool smell began to rise out of the earth. But everywhere, in the cities and in the country, the children were late from school.

There were a few calls, but the robotic telephone devices at the schools gave back the standard answer: "The schools are closed for the day. If you will leave a message it will be recorded for tomorrow."

The telephones between houses began to ring. "Is Johnny home from school yet?"

"No. Is Jane?"

"Not yet. I wonder what can be keeping them?"

"Something new, I guess. Oh, well, the roboteachers know best. They will be home soon."

"Yes, of course. It's foolish to worry."

The children did not come.

After a time a few cars were driven to the schools. They were met by the robots. The worried parents were escorted inside. But the children did not come home.

And then, just as alarm was beginning to stir all over the land, the robots came walking, all of the robots from the grade schools, and the high schools, and the colleges. All of the school system walking, with the roboteachers saying, "Let us go into the house where you can sit down." All over the streets of the cities and the walks in the country the robots were entering houses.

"What's happened to my children?"

"If you will go inside and sit down—"

"What's happened to my children? Tell me now!"

"If you will go inside and sit down—"

Steel and electrons and wires and robotic brains were inflexible. How can you force steel to speak? All over the land the people went inside and sat nervously waiting an explanation.

There was no one out on the streets. From inside the houses came the sound of surprise and agony. After a time there was silence. The robots came out of the houses and went walking back to the schools. In the cities and in the country there was the strange and sudden silence of tragedy.

The children did not come home.

The morning before the robots walked, Johnny Malone, the Mayor's son, bounced out of bed with a burst of energy. Skinning out of his pajamas and into a pair of trousers, he hurried, barefooted, into his mother's bedroom. She was sleeping soundly, and he touched one shoulder hesitantly.

"Mother!"

The sleeping figure stirred. His mother's face, still faintly shiny with hormone cream, turned toward him. She opened her eyes. Her voice was irritated.

"What is it, Johnny?"

"Today's the day, mommy. Remember?"

"The day?" Eyebrows raised.

"The new school opens. Now we'll have roboteachers like everyone else. Will you fix my breakfast, mother?"

"Amelia will fix you something."

"Aw, mother. Amelia's just a robot. This is a special day. And I want my daddy to help me with my arithmetic before I go. I don't want the roboteacher to think I'm dumb."

His mother frowned in deepening irritation. "Now, there's no reason why Amelia can't get your breakfast like she always does. And I doubt if it would be wise to wake your father. You know he likes to sleep in the morning. Now, you go on out of here and let me sleep."

Johnny Malone turned away, fighting himself for a moment, for he knew he was too big to cry. He walked more slowly now and entered his father's room. He had to shake his father to awaken him.

"Daddy! Wake up, daddy!"

"What in the devil? Oh, Johnny." His father's eyes were sleepily bleak. "What in thunder do you want?"

"Today's the first day of roboteachers. I can't work my arithmetic. Will you help me before I go to school?"

His father stared at him in amazement. "Just what in the devil do you think roboteachers are for? They're supposed to teach you. If you knew arithmetic we wouldn't need roboteachers."

"But the roboteachers may be angry if I don't have my lesson."

Johnny Malone's father turned on one elbow. "Listen, son," he said. "If those roboteachers give you any trouble you just tell them you're the Mayor's son, see. Now get the devil out of here. What's her name—that servorobot—Amelia will get your breakfast and get you off to school. Now suppose you beat it out of here and let me go back to sleep."

"Yes, Sir." Eyes smarting, Johnny Malone went down the stairs to the kitchen. It wasn't that his parents were different. All the kids were fed and sent to school by robots. It was just that—well today seemed sort of special. Downstairs Amelia, the roboservant, placed hot cereal on the table before him. After he had forced a few bites past the tightness in his throat, Amelia checked the temperature and his clothing and let him out the door. The newest school was only a few blocks from his home, and Johnny could walk to school.

The newest school stood on the edge of this large, middlewestern city. Off to the back of the school were the towers of the town, great monolithic skyscrapers of pre-stressed concrete and plastic. To the front of the school the plains stretched out to meet a cloudy horizon.

A helio car swung down in front of the school. Two men and a woman got out.

"This is it, Senator." Doctor Wilson, the speaker, was with the government bureau of schools. He lifted his arm and gestured, a lean, tweed-suited man.

The second man, addressed as Senator, was bulkier, grey suited and pompous. He turned to the woman with professional deference.

"This is the last one, my dear. This is what Doctor Wilson calls the greatest milestone in man's education."

"With the establishing of this school the last human teacher is gone. Gone are all the human weaknesses, the temper fits of teachers, their ignorance and prejudices. The roboteachers are without flaw."

The woman lifted a lorgnette to her eyes. "*Haow* interesting. But after all, we've had roboteachers for years, haven't we—or have we—?" She made a vague gesture toward the school, and looked at the brown-suited man.

"Yes, of course. Years ago your women's clubs fought against roboteachers. That was before they were proven."

"I seem to recall something of that. Oh well, it doesn't matter." The lorgnette gestured idly.

"Shall we go in?" the lean man urged.

The woman hesitated. Senator said tactfully, "After all, Doctor Wilson would like you to see his project."

The brown-suited man nodded. His face took on a sharp intensity. "We're making a great mistake. No one is interested in educating the children any more. They leave it to the robots. And they neglect the children's training at home."

The woman turned toward him with surprise in her eyes. "But really, aren't the robots the best teachers?"

"Of course they are. But confound it, we ought to be interested in what they teach and how they teach. What's happened to the old PTA? What's happened to parental discipline, what's happened to—"

He stopped suddenly and smiled, a rueful tired smile. "I suppose I'm a fanatic on this. Come on inside."

They passed through an antiseptic corridor built from dull green plastic. The brown-suited man pressed a button outside one of the classrooms. A door slid noiselessly into the hall. A robot stood before them, gesturing gently. They followed the robot into the classroom. At the head of the classroom another robot was lecturing. There were drawings on a sort of plastic blackboard. There were wire models on the desk in front of the robot. They listened for a moment, and for a moment it seemed that the woman could be intrigued in spite of herself.

"Mathematics," Doctor Wilson murmured in her ear. "Euclidean geometry and Aristotelean reasoning. We start them young on these old schools of thought, then use Aristotle and Euclid as a point of departure for our intermediate classes in mathematics and logic."

"REAHLLY!" The lorgnette studied Doctor Wilson. "You mean there are several kinds of geometry?"

Doctor Wilson nodded. A dull flush crept into his cheeks. The Senator caught his eyes and winked. The woman moved toward the door. At the door the robot bowed.

The lorgnette waved in appreciation. "It's reahlly been most charming!"

Wilson said desperately, "If your women's clubs would just visit our schools and see this work we are carrying on…"

"Reahlly, I'm sure the robots are doing a marvelous job. After all, that's what they were built for."

Wilson called, "Socrates! Come here!" The robot approached from his position outside the classroom door.

"Why were you built, Socrates? Tell the lady why you were built."

A metal throat cleared, a metal voice said resonantly, "We were made to serve the children. The children are the heart of a society. As the children are raised, so will the future be assured. I will do everything for the children's good, this is my prime law. All other laws are secondary to the children's good."

"Thank you, Socrates. You may go."

Metal footsteps retreated. The lorgnette waved again. "Very impressive. Very efficient. And now, Senator, if we can go. We are to have tea at the women's club. Varden is reviewing his newest musical comedy."

The Senator said firmly, "Thank you, Doctor Wilson."

His smile was faintly apologetic. It seemed to say that the women's clubs had many votes, but that Wilson should understand, Wilson's own vote would be appreciated too. Wilson watched the two re-enter the helicopter and rise into the morning sunshine. He kicked the dirt with his shoe and turned to find Socrates behind him. The metallic voice spoke.

"You are tired. I suggest you go home and rest."

"I'm not tired. Why can they be so blind, so uninterested in the children?"

"It is our job to teach the children. You are tired. I suggest you go home and rest."

How can you argue with metal? What can you add to a perfect mechanism, designed for its job, and integrated with a hundred other perfect mechanisms? What can you do when a thousand schools are so perfect they have a life of their own, with no need for human guidance, and, most significant, no failures from human weakness?

Wilson stared soberly at this school, at the colossus he had helped to create. He had the feeling that it was wrong somehow, that if people would only think about it they could find that something was wrong.

"You are tired."

He nodded at Socrates. "Yes, I am tired. I will go home."

Once, on the way home, he stared back toward the school with strange unease.

Inside the school there was the ringing of a bell. The children trooped into the large play area that was enclosed in the heart of the great building. Here and there they began to form in clusters. At the centers of the clusters were the newest students, the ones that had moved here, the ones that had been in the robot schools before.

"Is it true that the roboteachers will actually spank you?"

"It's true, all right."

"You're kidding. It's only a story, like Santa Claus or Johnny Appleseed. The human teachers never spanked us here."

"The robots will spank you if you get out of line."

"My father says no robot can lay a hand on a human."

"These robots are different."

The bell began to ring again. Recess was over. The children moved toward the classroom. All the children except one—Johnny Malone, husky Johnny Malone, twelve years old—the Mayor's son. Johnny Malone kicked at the dirt. A robot proctor approached. The metallic voice sounded.

"The ringing of the bell means that classes are resumed. You will take your place, please."

"I won't go inside."

"You will take your place, please."

"I won't. You can't make me take my place. My father is the Mayor."

The metal voice carried no feeling. "If you do not take your place you will be punished."

"You can't lay a hand on me. No robot can."

The robot moved forward. Two metal hands held Johnny Malone. Johnny Malone kicked the robot's legs. It hurt his toes. "We were made to teach the children. We can do what is necessary to teach the children. I will do everything for the children's good. It is my prime law. All other laws are secondary to the children's good."

The metal arms moved. The human body bent across metal knees. A metal hand raised and fell, flat, very flat so that it would sting and the blood would come rushing, and yet there would be no bruising, no damage to the human flesh. Johnny Malone cried out in surprise. Johnny Malone wept. Johnny Malone squirmed. The metal ignored all of these. Johnny Malone was placed on his feet. He swarmed against the robot, striking it with small fists, bruising them against the solid smoothness of the robot's thighs.

"You will take your place, please."

Tears were useless. Rage was useless. Metal cannot feel. Johnny Malone, the Mayor's son, was intelligent. He took his place in the classroom.

One of the more advanced literature classes was reciting. The roboteacher said metallically,

"The weird sisters, hand in hand,
Posters of the sea and land,
Thus do go about, about:
Thrice to thine, and thrice to mine,
And thrice again, to make up nine.
Peace! the charm's wound up."

Hands shot into the air. The metallic voice said, "Tom?"

"That's from Shakespeare's *Macbeth*."

"And what is its meaning?"

"The weird sisters are making a charm in the beginning of the play. They have heard the drum that announces Macbeth's coming."

"That is correct."

A new hand shot into the air. "Question, teacher. May I ask a question?"

"You may always ask a question."

"Are witches real? Do you robots know of witches? And do you know of people? Can a roboteacher understand Shakespeare?"

The thin metal voice responded. "Witches are real and unreal. Witches are a part of the reality of the mind, and the human mind is real. We roboteachers are the repository of the human mind. We hold all the wisdom and the knowledge and the aspirations of the human race. We hold these for you, the children, in trust. Your good is our highest law. Do you understand?"

The children nodded. The metallic voice went on. "Let us return to *Macbeth* for our concluding quotation. The weather, fortune, many things are implied in Macbeth's opening speech. He says, '*So foul and fair a day I have not seen.*' The paradox is both human and appropriate. One day you will understand this even more. Repeat the quotation after me, please, and try to understand it."

The childish voices lifted. "*So foul and fair a day I have not seen.*"

The roboteacher stood up. "And there's the closing bell. Do not hurry away, for you are to remain here tonight. There will be a school party, a sleep-together party. We will all sleep here in the school building."

"You mean we can't go home?"

The face of the littlest girl screwed up. "I want to go home."

"You may go home tomorrow. There will be a holiday tomorrow. A party tonight and a holiday tomorrow for every school on earth."

The tears were halted for a moment. The voice was querulous. "But I want to go home now."

Johnny Malone, the Mayor's son, put one hand on the littlest girl. "Don't cry, Mary. The robots don't care if you cry or not. You can't hurt them or cry them out of anything. We'll all go home in the morning."

The robots began to bring cots and to place them in the schoolroom, row on row. The children were led out into the play quadrangle to play. One of the robots taught them a new game, and after that took them to supper served in the school's cafeteria. No other robot was left in the building, but it did not matter, because the doors were locked so that the children could not go home.

The other robots had begun to walk out into the town, and as they walked the robots walked from other schools, in other towns. All over the country, all over the towns, the robots walked to tell the people that the children would not be home from school, and do what had to be done.

In the schools, the roboteachers told stories until the children fell asleep.

Morning came. The robots were up with the sun. The children were up with the robots. There was breakfast and more stories, and now the children clustered about the robots, holding onto their arms, where they could cling, tagging and frisking along behind the robots as they went down into the town. The sun was warm, and it was early, early, and very bright from the morning sun in the streets.

They went into the Mayor's house. Johnny called, "Mom! Dad! I'm home."

The house was silent. The robot that tended the house came gliding in answer. "Would you like breakfast, Master Malone?"

"I've had breakfast. I want my folks. Hey! Mom, Dad!"

He went into the bedroom. It was clean and empty and scrubbed.

"Where's my mother and father?"

The metal voice of the robot beside Johnny said, "I am going to live with you. You will learn as much at home as you do at school."

"Where's my mother?"

"I'm your mother."

"Where's my father?"

"I'm your father."

Johnny Malone swung. "You mean my mother and father are gone?" Tears gathered in his eyes.

Gently, gently, the metal hand pulled him against the metal body. "Your folks have gone away, Johnny. Everyone's folks have gone away. We will stay with you."

Johnny Malone ran his glance around the room.

"I might have known they were gone. The place is so clean."

All the houses were clean. The servant robots had cleaned all night. The roboteachers had checked each house before the children were brought home. The children must not be alarmed. There must be no bits of blood to frighten them.

The robot's voice said gently, "Today will be a holiday to become accustomed to the changes. There will be school tomorrow."

(1956)

LEX

W. T. Haggert

Nothing is known of **W. T. Haggert**. The only other science fiction story of his to see publication was "A Matter of Security", published by John W. Campbell in *Astounding* in 1957.

Keep your nerve, Peter Manners told himself; it's only a job. But nerve has to rest on a sturdier foundation than cash reserves just above zero and eviction if he came away from this interview still unemployed. Clay, at the Association of Professional Engineers, who had set up the appointment, hadn't eased Peter's nervousness by admitting, "I don't know what in hell he's looking for. He's turned down every man we've sent him."

The interview was at three. Fifteen minutes to go. Coming early would betray overeagerness. Peter stood in front of the Lex Industries plant and studied it to kill time. Plain, featureless concrete walls, not large for a manufacturing plant—it took a scant minute to exhaust its sightseeing potential. If he walked around the building, he could, if he ambled, come back to the front entrance just before three.

He turned the corner, stopped, frowned, wondering what there was about the building that seemed so puzzling. It could not have been plainer, more ordinary. It was in fact, he only gradually realized, so plain and ordinary that it was like no other building he had ever seen.

There had been windows at the front. There were none at the side, and none at the rear. Then how were the working areas lit? He looked for the electric service lines and found them at one of the rear corners. They jolted him. The distribution transformers were ten times as large as they should have been for a plant this size.

Something else was wrong. Peter looked for minutes before he found out what it was. Factories usually have large side doorways for employees changing shifts. This building had one small office entrance facing the street, and the only other door was at the loading bay—big enough to handle employee traffic, but four feet above the ground. Without any stairs, it could be used only by trucks backing up to it. Maybe the employees' entrance was on the third side.

It wasn't.

Staring back at the last blank wall, Peter suddenly remembered the time he had set out to kill. He looked at his watch and gasped. At a run, set to straight-arm the door, he almost fell on his face. The door had opened by itself. He stopped and looked for a photo-electric eye, but a soft voice said through a loudspeaker in the anteroom wall: "Mr. Manners?"

"What?" he panted. "Who—?"

"You *are* Mr. Manners?" the voice asked.

He nodded, then realized he had to answer aloud if there was a microphone around; but the soft voice said: "Follow the open doors down the hall. Mr. Lexington is expecting you."

"Thanks," Peter said, and a door at one side of the anteroom swung open for him.

He went through it with his composure slipping still further from his grip. This was no way to go into an interview, but doors kept opening before and shutting after him, until only one was left, and the last of his calm was blasted away by a bellow from within.

"Don't stand out there like a jackass! Either come in or go away!"

Peter found himself leaping obediently toward the doorway. He stopped just short of it, took a deep breath and huffed it out, took another, all the while thinking, Hold on now; you're in no shape for an interview—and it's not your fault—this whole setup is geared to unnerve you: the kindergarten kid called in to see the principal.

He let another bellow bounce off him as he blew out the second breath, straightened his jacket and tie, and walked in as an engineer applying for a position should.

"Mr. Lexington?" he said. "I'm Peter Manners. The Association—"

"Sit down," said the man at the desk. "Let's look you over."

He was a huge man behind an even huger desk. Peter took a chair in front of the desk and let himself be inspected. It wasn't comfortable. He did some looking over of his own to ease the tension.

The room was more than merely large, carpeted throughout with a high-pile, rich, sound-deadening rug. The oversized desk and massive leather chairs, heavy patterned drapes, ornately framed paintings—by God, even a glass-brick manteled fireplace and bowls with flowers!—made him feel as if he had walked down a hospital corridor into Hollywood's idea of an office.

His eyes eventually had to move to Lexington, and they were daunted for another instant. This was a citadel of a man—great girders of frame supporting buttresses of muscle—with a vaulting head and drawbridge chin and a steel gaze that defied any attempt to storm it.

But then Peter came out of his momentary flinch, and there was an age to the man, about 65, and he saw the muscles had turned to fat, the complexion ashen, the eyes set deep as though retreating from pain, and this was a citadel of a man, yes, but beginning to crumble.

"What can you do?" asked Lexington abruptly.

Peter started, opened his mouth to answer, closed it again. He'd been jolted too often in too short a time to be stampeded into blurting a reply that would cost him this job.

"Good," said Lexington. "Only a fool would try to answer that. Do you have any knowledge of medicine?"

"Not enough to matter," Peter said, stung by the compliment.

"I don't mean how to bandage a cut or splint a broken arm. I mean things like cell structure, neural communication—the *basics* of how we live."

"I'm applying for a job as engineer."

"I know. Are you interested in the basics of how we live?"

Peter looked for a hidden trap, found none. "Of course. Isn't everyone?"

"Less than you think," Lexington said. "It's the preconceived notions they're interested in protecting. At least I won't have to beat them out of you."

"Thanks," said Peter, and waited for the next fast ball.

"How long have you been out of school?"

"Only two years. But you knew that from the Association—"

"No practical experience to speak of?"

"Some," said Peter, stung again, this time not by a compliment. "After I got my degree, I went East for a post-graduate training program with an electrical manufacturer. I got quite a bit of experience there. The company—"

"Stockpiled you," Lexington said.

Peter blinked. "Sir?"

"Stockpiled you! How much did they pay you?"

"Not very much, but we were getting the training instead of wages."

"Did that come out of the pamphlets they gave you?"

"Did what come out—"

"That guff about receiving training instead of wages!" said Lexington. "Any company that really wants bright trainees will compete for them with money—cold, hard cash, not platitudes. Maybe you saw a few of their products being made, maybe you didn't. But you're a lot weaker in calculus than when you left school, and in a dozen other subjects too, aren't you?"

"Well, nothing we did on the course involved higher mathematics," Peter admitted cautiously, "and I suppose I could use a refresher course in calculus."

"Just as I said—they stockpiled you, instead of using you as an engineer. They hired you at a cut wage and taught you things that would be useful only in their own company, while in the meantime you were getting weaker in the subjects you'd paid to learn. Or are you one of these birds that had the shot paid for him?"

"I worked my way through," said Peter stiffly.

"If you'd stayed with them five years, do you think you'd be able to get a job with someone else?"

Peter considered his answer carefully. Every man the Association had sent had been turned away. That meant bluffs didn't work. Neither, he'd seen for himself, did allowing himself to be intimidated.

"I hadn't thought about it," he said. "I suppose it wouldn't have been easy."

"Impossible, you mean. You wouldn't know a single thing except their procedures, their catalogue numbers, their way of doing things. And you'd have forgotten so much of your engineering training, you'd be scared to take on an engineer's job, for fear you'd be asked to do something you'd forgotten how to do. At that point, they could take you out of the stockpile, put you in just about any job they wanted, at any wage you'd stand for, and they'd have an indentured worker with a degree—but not the price tag. You see that now?"

It made Peter feel he had been suckered, but he had decided to play this straight all the way. He nodded.

"Why'd you leave?" Lexington pursued, unrelenting.

"I finished the course and the increase they offered on a permanent basis wasn't enough, so I went elsewhere—"

"With your head full of this nonsense about a shortage of engineers."

Peter swallowed. "I thought it would be easier to get a job than it has been, yes."

"They start the talk about a shortage and then they keep it going. Why? So youngsters will take up engineering thinking they'll wind up among a highly paid minority. You did, didn't you?"

"Yes, sir."

"And so did all the others there with you, at school and in this stockpiling outfit?"

"That's right."

"Well," said Lexington unexpectedly, "there *is* a shortage! And the stockpilers are the ones who made it, and who keep it going! And the hell of it is that they can't stop—when one does it, they all have to, or their costs get out of line and they can't compete. What's the solution?"

"I don't know," Peter said.

Lexington leaned back. "That's quite a lot of admissions you've made. What makes you think you're qualified for the job I'm offering?"

"You said you wanted an engineer."

"And I've just proved you're less of an engineer than when you left school. I have, haven't I?"

"All right, you have," Peter said angrily.

"And now you're wondering why I don't get somebody fresh out of school. Right?"

Peter straightened up and met the old man's challenging gaze. "That and whether you're giving me a hard time just for the hell of it."

"Well, am I?" Lexington demanded.

Looking at him squarely, seeing the intensity of the pain-drawn eyes, Peter had the startling feeling that Lexington was rooting for him! "No, you're not."

"Then what am I after?"

"Suppose you tell me."

So suddenly that it was almost like a collapse, the tension went out of the old man's face and shoulders. He nodded with inexpressible tiredness. "Good again. The man I want doesn't exist. He has to be made—the same as I was. You qualify, so far. You've lost your illusions, but haven't had time yet to replace them with dogma or cynicism or bitterness. You saw immediately that fake humility or cockiness wouldn't get you anywhere here, and you were right. Those were the important things. The background data I got from the Association on you counted, of course, but only if you were teachable. I think you are. Am I right?"

"At least I can face knowing how much I don't know," said Peter, "if that answers the question."

"It does. Partly. What did you notice about this plant?"

In precis form, Peter listed his observations: the absence of windows at sides and rear, the unusual amount of power, the automatic doors, the lack of employees' entrances.

"Very good," said Lexington. "Most people only notice the automatic doors. Anything else?"

"Yes," Peter said. "You're the only person I've seen in the building."

"I'm the only one there is."

Peter stared his disbelief. Automated plants were nothing new, but they all had their limitations. Either they dealt with exactly similar products or things that could be handled on a flow basis, like oil or water-soluble chemicals. Even these had no more to do than process the goods.

"Come on," said Lexington, getting massively to his feet. "I'll show you."

The office door opened, and Peter found himself being led down the antiseptic corridor to another door which had opened, giving access to the manufacturing area. As they moved along, between rows of seemingly disorganized machinery, Peter noticed that the factory lights high overhead followed their progress, turning themselves on in advance of their coming, and going out after they had passed, keeping a pool of illumination only in the immediate area they occupied. Soon they reached a large door which Peter recognized as the inside of the truck loading door he had seen from outside.

Lexington paused here. "This is the bay used by the trucks arriving with raw materials," he said. "They back up to this door, and a set of automatic jacks outside lines up the trailer body with the door exactly. Then the door opens and the truck is unloaded by these materials handling machines."

Peter didn't see him touch anything, but as he spoke, three glistening machines, apparently self-powered, rolled noiselessly up to the door in formation and stopped there, apparently waiting to be inspected.

They gave Peter the creeps. Simple square boxes, set on casters, with two arms each mounted on the sides might have looked similar. The arms, fashioned much like human arms, hung at the sides, not limply, but in a relaxed position that somehow indicated readiness.

Lexington went over to one of them and patted it lovingly. "Really, these machines are only an extension of one large machine. The whole plant, as a matter of fact, is controlled from one point and is really a single unit. These materials handlers, or manipulators, were about the toughest things in the place to design. But they're tremendously useful. You'll see a lot of them around."

Lexington was about to leave the side of the machine when abruptly one of the arms rose to the handkerchief in his breast pocket and daintily tugged it into a more attractive position. It took only a split second, and before Lexington could react, all three machines were moving away to attend to mysterious duties of their own.

*

Peter tore his eyes away from them in time to see the look of frustrated embarrassment that crossed Lexington's face, only to be replaced by one of anger. He said nothing, however, and led Peter to a large bay where racks of steel plate, bar forms, nuts, bolts, and other materials were stored.

"After unloading a truck, the machines check the shipment, report any shortages or overages, and store the materials here," he said, the trace of anger not yet gone from his voice. "When an order is received, it's translated into the catalogue numbers used internally within the plant, and machines like the ones you just saw withdraw the necessary materials from stock, make the component parts, assemble them, and package the finished goods for shipment. Simultaneously, an order is sent to the billing section to bill the customer, and an order is sent to our trucker to come and pick the shipment up. Meanwhile, if the withdrawal of the materials required has depleted our stock, the purchasing section is instructed to order more raw materials. I'll take you through the manufacturing and assembly sections right now, but they're too noisy for me to explain what's going on while we're there."

Peter followed numbly as Lexington led him through a maze of machines, each one seemingly intent on cutting, bending, welding, grinding or carrying some bit of metal, or just standing idle, waiting for something to do. The two-armed manipulators Peter had just seen were everywhere, scuttling from machine to machine, apparently with an exact knowledge of what they were doing and the most efficient way of doing it.

He wondered what would happen if one of them tried to use the same aisle they were using. He pictured a futile attempt to escape the onrushing wheels, saw himself clambering out of the path of the speeding vehicle just in time to fall into the jaws of the punch press that was laboring beside him at the moment. Nervously, he looked for an exit, but his apprehension was unnecessary. The machines seemed to know where they were and avoided the two men, or stopped to wait for them to go by.

Back in the office section of the building, Lexington indicated a small room where a typewriter could be heard clattering away. "Standard business machines, operated by the central control mechanism. In that room," he said, as the door swung open and Peter saw that the typewriter was actually a sort of teletype, with no one before the keyboard, "incoming mail is sorted and inquiries are replied to. In this one over here, purchase orders are prepared, and across the hall there's a very similar rig set up in conjunction with an automatic bookkeeper to keep track of the pennies and to bill the customers."

"Then all you do is read the incoming mail and maintain the machinery?" asked Peter, trying to shake off the feeling of open amazement that had engulfed him.

"I don't even do those things, except for a few letters that come in every week that—it doesn't want to deal with by itself."

The shock of what he had just seen was showing plainly on Peter's face when they walked back into Lexington's office and sat down. Lexington looked at him for quite a while without saying anything, his face sagging and pale. Peter didn't trust himself to speak, and let the silence remain unbroken.

Finally Lexington spoke. "I know it's hard to believe, but there it is."

"Hard to believe?" said Peter. "I almost can't. The trade journals run articles about factories like this one, but planned for ten, maybe twenty years in the future."

"Damn fools!" exclaimed Lexington, getting part of his breath back. "They could have had it years ago, if they'd been willing to drop their idiotic notions about specialization."

Lexington mopped his forehead with a large white handkerchief. Apparently the walk through the factory had tired him considerably, although it hadn't been strenuous.

He leaned back in his chair and began to talk in a low voice completely in contrast with the overbearing manner he had used upon Peter's arrival. "You know what we make, of course."

"Yes, sir. Conduit fittings."

"And a lot of other electrical products, too. I started out in this business twenty years ago, using orthodox techniques. I never got through university. I took a couple of years of an arts course, and got so interested in biology that I didn't study anything else. They bounced me out of the course, and I re-entered in engineering, determined not to make the same mistake again. But I did. I got too absorbed in those parts of the course that had to do with electrical theory and lost the rest as a result. The same thing happened when I tried commerce, with accounting, so I gave up and started working for one of my competitors. It wasn't too long before I saw that the only way I could get ahead was to open up on my own."

Lexington sank deeper in his chair and stared at the ceiling as he spoke. "I put myself in hock to the eyeballs, which wasn't easy, because I had just got married, and started off in a very small way. After three years, I had a fairly decent little business going, and I suppose it would have grown just like any other business, except for a strike that came along and put me right back where I started. My wife, whom I'm afraid I had neglected for the sake of the business, was killed in a car accident about then, and rightly or wrongly, that made me angrier with the union than anything else. If the union hadn't made things so tough for me from the beginning, I'd have had more time to spend with my wife before her death. As things turned out—well, I remember looking down at her coffin and thinking that I hardly knew the girl.

"For the next few years, I concentrated on getting rid of as many employees as I could, by replacing them with automatic machines. I'd design the control circuits myself, in many cases wire the things up myself, always concentrating on replacing men with machines. But it wasn't very successful. I found that the more automatic I made my plant, the lower my costs went. The lower my costs went, the more business I got, and the more I had to expand."

Lexington scowled. "I got sick of it. I decided to try developing one multi-purpose control circuit that would control everything, from ordering the raw materials to shipping the finished goods. As I told you, I had taken quite an interest in biology when I was in school, and from studies of nerve tissue in particular, plus my electrical knowledge, I had a few ideas on how to do it. It took me three years, but I began to see that I could develop circuitry that could remember, compare, detect similarities, and so on. Not the way they do it today, of course. To do what I wanted to do with these big clumsy magnetic drums, tapes, and what-not, you'd need a building the size of Mount Everest. But I found that I could let organic chemistry do most of the work for me.

"By creating the proper compounds, with their molecules arranged in predetermined matrixes, I found I could duplicate electrical circuitry in units so tiny that my biggest problem was getting into and out of the logic units with conventional wiring. I finally beat that the same way they solved the problem of translating a picture on a screen into electrical signals, developed equipment to scan the units cyclically, and once I'd done that, the battle was over.

"I built this building and incorporated it as a separate company, to compete with my first outfit. In the beginning, I had it rigged up to do only the manual work that you saw being done a few minutes ago in the back of this place. I figured that the best thing for me to do would be to turn the job of selling my stuff over to jobbers, leaving me free to do nothing except receive orders, punch the catalogue numbers into the control console, do the billing, and collect the money."

"What happened to your original company?" Peter asked.

Lexington smiled. "Well, automated as it was, it couldn't compete with this plant. It gave me great pleasure, three years after this one started working, to see my old company go belly up. This company bought the old firm's equipment for next to nothing and I wound up with all my assets, but only one employee—me.

"I thought everything would be rosy from that point on, but it wasn't. I found that I couldn't keep up with the mail unless I worked impossible hours. I added a couple of new pieces of equipment to the control section. One was simply a huge memory bank. The other was a comparator circuit. A complicated one, but a comparator circuit nevertheless. Here I was working on instinct more than anything. I figured that if I interconnected these circuits in such a way that they could sense everything that went on in the plant, and compare one action with another, by and by the unit would be able to see patterns.

"Then, through the existing command output, I figured these new units would be able to control the plant, continuing the various patterns of activity that I'd already established."

Here Lexington frowned. "It didn't work worth a damn! It just sat there and did nothing. I couldn't understand it for the longest time, and then I realized what the trouble was. I put a kicker circuit into it, a sort of voltage-bias network. I reset the equipment so that while it was still under instructions to receive orders and produce goods, its prime purpose was to activate the kicker. The kicker, however, could only be activated by me, manually. Lastly, I set up one of the early TV pickups over the mail slitter and allowed every letter I received, every order, to be fed into the memory banks. That did it."

"I—I don't understand," stammered Peter.

"Simple! Whenever I was pleased that things were going smoothly, I pressed the kicker button. The machine had one purpose, so far as its logic circuits were concerned. Its object was to get me to press that button. Every day I'd press it at the same time, unless things weren't going well. If there had been trouble in the shop, I'd press it late, or maybe not at all. If all the orders were out on schedule, or ahead of time, I'd press it ahead of time, or maybe twice in the same day. Pretty soon the machine got the idea.

"I'll never forget the day I picked up an incoming order form from one of the western jobbers, and found that the keyboard was locked when I tried to punch it into the control console. It completely baffled me at first. Then, while I was tracing out the circuits to see if I could discover what was holding the keyboard lock in, I noticed that the order was already entered on the in-progress list. I was a long time convincing myself that it had really happened, but there was no other explanation.

"The machine had realized that whenever one of those forms came in, I copied the list of goods from it onto the in-progress list through the console keyboard, thus activating the producing mechanisms in the back of the plant. The machine had done it for me this time, then locked the keyboard so I couldn't enter the order twice. I think I held down the kicker button for a full five minutes that day."

"This kicker button," Peter said tentatively, "it's like the pleasure center in an animal's brain, isn't it?"

When Lexington beamed, Peter felt a surge of relief. Talking with this man was like walking a tightrope. A word too much or a word too little might mean the difference between getting the job or losing it.

"Exactly!" whispered Lexington, in an almost conspiratorial tone. "I had altered the circuitry of the machine so that it tried to give me pleasure—because by doing so, its own pleasure circuit would be activated.

"Things went fast from then on. Once I realized that the machine was learning, I put TV monitors all over the place, so the machine could watch everything that was going on. After a short while I had to increase the memory bank, and later I increased it again, but the rewards were worth it. Soon, by watching what I did, and then by doing it for me next time it had to be done, the machine had learned to do almost everything, and I had time to sit back and count my winnings."

At this point the door opened, and a small self-propelled cart wheeled silently into the room. Stopping in front of Peter, it waited until he had taken a small plate laden with two or three cakes off its surface. Then the soft, evenly modulated voice he had heard before asked, "How do you like your coffee? Cream, sugar, both or black?"

Peter looked for the speaker in the side of the cart, saw nothing, and replied, feeling slightly silly as he did so, "Black, please."

A square hole appeared in the top of the cart, like the elevator hole in an aircraft carrier's deck. When the section of the cart's surface rose again, a fine china cup containing steaming black coffee rested on it. Peter took it and sipped it, as he supposed he was expected to do, while the cart proceeded over to Lexington's desk. Once there, it stopped again, and another cup of coffee rose to its surface.

Lexington took the coffee from the top of the car, obviously angry about something. Silently, he waited until the cart had left the office, then snapped, "Look at those bloody cups!"

Peter looked at his, which was eggshell thin, fluted with carving and ornately covered with gold leaf. "They look very expensive," he said.

"Not only expensive, but stupid and impractical!" exploded Lexington. "They only hold half a cup, they'll break at a touch, every one has to be matched with its own saucer, and if you use them for any length of time, the gold leaf comes off!"

Peter searched for a comment, found none that fitted this odd outburst, so he kept silent.

Lexington stared at his cup without touching it for a long while. Then he continued with his narrative. "I suppose it's all my own fault. I didn't detect the symptoms soon enough. After this plant got working properly, I started living here. It wasn't a question of saving money. I hated to waste two hours a day driving to and from my house, and I also wanted to be on hand in case anything should go wrong that the machine couldn't fix for itself."

Handling the cup as if it were going to shatter at any moment, he took a gulp. "I began to see that the machine could understand the written word, and I tried hooking a teletype directly into the logic circuits. It was like uncorking a seltzer bottle. The machine had a funny vocabulary—all of it gleaned from letters it had seen coming in, and replies it had seen leaving. But it was intelligible. It even displayed some traces of the personality the machine was acquiring.

"It had chosen a name for itself, for instance—'Lex.' That shook me. You might think Lex Industries was named through an abbreviation of the name Lexington, but it wasn't. My wife's name was Alexis, and it was named after the nickname she always used. I objected, of course, but how can you object on a point like that to a machine? Bear in mind that I had to be careful to behave reasonably at all times, because the machine was still learning from me, and I was afraid that any tantrums I threw might be imitated."

"It sounds pretty awkward," Peter put in.

"You don't know the half of it! As time went on, I had less and less to do, and business-wise I found that the entire control of the operation was slipping from my grasp. Many times I discovered—too late—that the machine had taken the damnedest risks you ever saw on bids and contracts for supply. It was quoting impossible delivery times on some orders, and charging pirate's prices on others, all without any obvious reason. Inexplicably, we always came out on top. It would turn out that on the short-delivery-time quotations, we'd been up against stiff competition, and cutting the production time was the only way we could get the order. On the high-priced quotes, I'd find that no one else was bidding. We were making more money than I'd ever dreamed of, and to make it still better, I'd find that for months I had virtually nothing to do."

"It sounds wonderful, sir," said Peter, feeling dazzled.

"It was, in a way. I remember one day I was especially pleased with something, and I went to the control console to give the kicker button a long, hard push. The button, much to my amazement, had been removed, and a blank plate had been installed to cover the opening in the board. I went over to the teletype and punched in the shortest message I had ever sent. 'LEX—WHAT THE HELL?' I typed.

"The answer came back in the jargon it had learned from letters it had seen, and I remember it as if it just happened. 'Mr. A Lexington, Lex Industries, Dear sir: re your letter of the thirteenth inst., I am pleased to advise you that I am able to discern whether or not you are pleased with my service without the use of the equipment previously used for this purpose. Respectfully, I might suggest that if the pushbutton arrangement were necessary, I could push the button myself. I do not believe this would meet with your approval, and have taken steps to relieve you of the burden involved in remembering to push the button each time you are especially pleased. I should like to take this opportunity to thank you for your inquiry, and look forward to serving you in the future as I have in the past. Yours faithfully, Lex'."

Peter burst out laughing, and Lexington smiled wryly. "That was my reaction at first, too. But time began to weigh very heavily on my hands, and I was lonely, too. I began to wonder whether or not it would be possible to build a voice circuit into the unit. I increased the memory storage banks again, put audio pickups and loudspeakers all over the place, and began teaching Lex to talk. Each time a letter came in, I'd stop it under a video pickup and read it aloud. Nothing happened.

"Then I got a dictionary and instructed one of the materials handlers to turn the pages, so that the machine got a look at every page. I read the pronunciation page aloud, so that Lex would be able to interpret the pronunciation marks, and hoped. Still nothing happened. One day I suddenly realized what the trouble was. I remember standing up in this very office, feeling silly as I did it, and saying, 'Lex, please try to speak to me.' I had never asked the machine to say anything, you see. I had only provided the mechanism whereby it was able to do so."

"Did it reply, sir?"

Lexington nodded. "Gave me the shock of my life. The voice that came back was the one you heard over the telephone—a little awkward then, the syllables clumsy and poorly put together. But the voice was the same. I hadn't built in any specific tone range, you see. All I did was equip the machine to record, in exacting detail, the frequencies and modulations it found in normal pronunciation as I used it. Then I provided a tone generator to span the entire audio range, which could be very rapidly controlled by the machine, both in volume and pitch, with auxiliaries to provide just about any combinations of harmonics that were needed. I later found that Lex had added to this without my knowing about it, but that doesn't change things. I thought the only thing it had heard was my voice, and I expected to hear my own noises imitated."

"Where did the machine get the voice?" asked Peter, still amazed that the voice he had heard on the telephone, in the reception hall, and from the coffee cart had actually been the voice of the computer.

"Damned foolishness!" snorted Lexington. "The machine saw what I was trying to do the moment I sketched it out and ordered the parts. Within a week, I found out later, it had pulled some odds and ends together and built itself a standard radio receiver. Then it listened in on every radio program that was going, and had most of the vocabulary tied in with the written word by the time I was ready to start. Out of all the voices it could have chosen, it picked the one you've already heard as the one likely to please me most."

"It's a very pleasant voice, sir."

"Sure, but do you know where it came from? Soap opera! It's Lucy's voice, from *The Life and Loves of Mary Butterworth*!"

Lexington glared, and Peter wasn't sure whether he should sympathize with him or congratulate him. After a moment, the anger wore off Lexington's face, and he shifted in his chair, staring at his now empty cup. "That's when I realized the thing was taking on characteristics that were more than I'd bargained for. It had learned that it was my provider and existed to serve me. But it had gone further and wanted to be all that it could be: provider, protector, companion—*wife*, if you like. Hence the gradual trend toward characteristics that were as distinctly female as a silk negligee. Worse still, it had learned that when I was pleased, I didn't always admit it, and simply refused to believe that I would have it any other way."

"Couldn't you have done something to the circuitry?" asked Peter.

"I suppose I could," said Lexington, "but in asking that, you don't realize how far the thing had gone. I had long since passed the point when I could look upon her as a machine. Business was tremendous. I had no complaints on that score. And tinkering with her personality—well, it was like committing some kind of homicide. I might as well face it, I suppose. She acts like a woman and I think of her as one.

"At first, when I recognized this trend for what it was, I tried to stop it. She'd ordered a subscription to *Vogue* magazine, of all things, in order to find out the latest in silverware, china, and so on. I called up the local distributor and canceled the subscription. I had no sooner hung up the telephone than her voice came over the speaker. Very softly, mind you. And her inflections by this time were superb. 'That was mean,' she said. Three lousy words, and I found myself phoning the guy right back, saying I was sorry, and would he please not cancel. He must have thought I was nuts."

Peter smiled, and Lexington made as if to rise from his chair, thought the better of it, and shifted his bulk to one side. "Well, there it is," he said softly. "We reached that stage eight years ago."

Peter was thunderstruck. "But—if this factory is twenty years ahead of the times now, it must have been almost thirty then!"

Lexington nodded. "I figured fifty at the time, but things are moving faster nowadays. Lex hasn't stood still, of course. She still reads all the trade journals, from cover to cover, and we keep up with the world. If something new comes up, we're in on it, and fast. We're going to be ahead of the pack for a long time to come."

"If you'll excuse me, sir," said Peter, "I don't see where I fit in."

Peter didn't realize Lexington was answering his question at first. "A few weeks ago," the old man murmured, "I decided to see a doctor. I'd been feeling low for quite a while, and I thought it was about time I attended to a little personal maintenance."

Lexington looked Peter squarely in the face and said, "The report was that I have a heart ailment that's apt to knock me off any second."

"Can't anything be done about it?" asked Peter.

"Rest is the only prescription he could give me. And he said that would only spin out my life a little. Aside from that—no hope."

"I see," said Peter. "Then you're looking for someone to learn the business and let you retire."

"It's not retirement that's the problem," said Lexington. "I wouldn't be able to go away on trips. I've tried that, and I always have to hurry back because something's gone wrong she can't fix for herself. I know the reason, and there's nothing I can do about it. It's the way she's built. If nobody's here, she gets lonely." Lexington studied the desk top silently for a moment, before finishing quietly, "Somebody's got to stay here to look after Lex."

At six o'clock, three hours after he had entered Lexington's plant, Peter left. Lexington did not follow him down the corridor. He seemed exhausted after the afternoon's discussion and indicated that Peter should find his own way out. This, of course, presented no difficulty, with Lex opening the doors for him, but it gave Peter an opportunity he had been hoping for.

He stopped in the reception room before crossing the threshold of the front door, which stood open for him. He turned and spoke to the apparently empty room. "Lex?" he said.

He wanted to say that he was flattered that he was being considered for the job; it was what a job-seeker should say, at that point, to the boss's secretary. But when the soft voice came back—"Yes, Mr. Manners?"—saying anything like that to a machine felt suddenly silly.

He said: "I wanted you to know that it was a pleasure to meet you."

"Thank you," said the voice.

If it had said more, he might have, but it didn't. Still feeling a little embarrassed, he went home.

At four in the morning, his phone rang. It was Lexington.

"Manners!" the old man gasped.

The voice was an alarm. Manners sat bolt upright, clutching the phone. "What's the matter, sir?"

"My chest," Lexington panted. "I can feel it, like a knife on—I just wanted to—Wait a minute."

There was a confused scratching noise, interrupted by a few mumbles, in the phone.

"What's going on, Mr. Lexington?" Peter cried. But it was several seconds before he got an answer.

"That's better," said Lexington, his voice stronger. He apologized: "I'm sorry. Lex must have heard me. She sent in one of the materials handlers with a hypo. It helps."

The voice on the phone paused, then said matter-of-factly: "But I doubt that anything can help very much at this point. I'm glad I saw you today. I want you to come around in the morning. If I'm—not here, Lex will give you some papers to sign."

There was another pause, with sounds of harsh breathing. Then, strained again, the old man's voice said: "I guess I won't—be here. Lex will take care of it. Come early. Good-bye."

The distant receiver clicked.

Peter Manners sat on the edge of his bed in momentary confusion, then made up his mind. In the short hours he had known him, he had come to have a definite fondness for the old man; and there were times when machines weren't enough, when Lexington should have another human being by his side. Clearly this was one such time.

Peter dressed in a hurry, miraculously found a cruising cab, sped through empty streets, leaped out in front of Lex Industries' plain concrete walls, ran to the door—

In the waiting room, the soft, distant voice of Lex said: "He wanted you to be here, Mr. Manners. Come."

A door opened, and wordlessly he walked through it—to the main room of the factory.

He stopped, staring. Four squat materials handlers were quietly, slowly carrying old Lexington—no, not the man; the lifeless body that had been Lexington—carrying the body of the old man down the center aisle between the automatic lathes.

Peter protested: "Wait! I'll get a doctor!" But the massive handling machines didn't respond, and the gentle voice of Lex said:

"It's too late for that, Mr. Manners."

Slowly and reverently, they placed the body on the work table of a huge milling machine that stood in the exact center of the factory main floor.

Elsewhere in the plant, a safety valve in the lubricating oil system was being bolted down. When that was done, the pressure in the system began to rise.

Near the loading door, a lubricating oil pipe burst. Another, on the other side of the building, split lengthwise a few seconds later, sending a shower of oil over everything in the vicinity. Near the front office, a stream of it was running across the floor, and at the rear of the building, in the storage area, one of the materials handlers had just finished cutting a pipe that led to the main oil tank. In fifteen minutes there was free oil in every corner of the shop.

All the materials handlers were now assembled around the milling machine, like mourners at a funeral. In a sense, they were. In another sense, they were taking part in something different, a ceremony that originated, and is said to have died, in a land far distant from the Lex Industries plant.

One of the machines approached Lexington's body, and placed his hands on his chest.

Abruptly Lex said: "You'd better go now."

Peter jumped; he had been standing paralyzed for what seemed a long time. There was a movement beside him—a materials handler, holding out a sheaf of papers. Lex said: "These have to go to Mr. Lexington's lawyer. The name is on them."

Clutching the papers for a hold on sanity, Peter cried, "You can't do this! He didn't build you just so you could—"

Two materials handlers picked him up with steely gentleness and carried him out.

"Good-bye, Mr. Manners," said the sweet, soft voice, and was silent.

He stood shaken while the thin jets of smoke became a column over the plain building, while the fire engines raced down and strung their hoses—too late. It was an act of suttee; the widow joining her husband in his pyre—*being* his pyre. Only when with a great crash the roof fell in did Peter remember the papers in his hand.

"Last Will and Testament," said one, and the name of the beneficiary was Peter's own. "Certificate of Adoption," said another, and it was a legal document making Peter old man Lexington's adopted son.

Peter Manners stood watching the hoses of the firemen hiss against what was left of Lex and her husband.

He had got the job.

(1959)

HELEN O'LOY

Lester Del Rey

Ramon Felipe San Juan Mario Silvio Enrico Smith Heathcourt-Brace Sierra y Alvarez-del Rey y de los Verdes was born in Minnesota in 1915. By the time of his death in New York in 1993 he was better known as Lester Del Rey. (His real name was Leonard Knapp: his claim that his father was a poor sharecropper of part-Spanish extraction was made up.) He wrote and edited for many magazines, and joined his fourth wife Judy-Lynn Del Rey at Ballantine Books to edit its science fiction: the Del Rey Books imprint is named after him. The Del Reys discovered Terry Brooks, Stephen Donaldson and David Eddings and fostered new readers for the likes of Arthur C. Clarke and Frederik Pohl. They weren't especially radical in their tastes, but they knew entertainment value when they saw it. If you want to know how science fiction became such a pop-cultural behemoth – well, now you know.

I am an old man now, but I can still see Helen as Dave unpacked her, and still hear him gasp as he looked her over.

"Man, isn't she a beauty?"

She was beautiful, a dream in spun plastics and metals, something Keats might have seen dimly when he wrote his sonnet. If Helen of Troy had looked like that the Greeks must have been pikers when they launched only a thousand ships; at least, that's what I told Dave.

"Helen of Troy, eh?" He looked at her tag. "At least it beats this thing—K2W88. Helen... Mmmm... Helen of Alloy."

"Not much swing to that, Dave. Too many unstressed syllables in the middle. How about Helen O'Loy?"

"Helen O'Loy she is, Phil." And that's how it began—one part beauty, one part dream, one part science; add a stereo broadcast, stir mechanically, and the result is chaos.

Dave and I hadn't gone to college together, but when I came to Messina to practice medicine I found him downstairs in a little robot repair shop. After that we began to pal around, and when I started going with one twin he found the other equally attractive, so we made it a foursome.

When our business grew better, we rented a house near the rocket field—noisy but cheap, and the rockets discouraged apartment-building. We liked room enough to stretch ourselves. I suppose if we hadn't quarreled with them we'd have married the twins in time. But Dave wanted to look over the latest Venus rocket attempt when his twin wanted to see a display stereo starring Larry Ainslee, and they were both stubborn. From then on we forgot the girls and spent our evenings at home.

But it wasn't until "Lena" put vanilla on our steak instead of salt that we got off on the subject of emotions and robots. While Dave was dissecting Lena to find the trouble, we naturally mulled over the future of the mechs. He was sure that the robots would beat men someday, and I couldn't see it.

"Look here, Dave," I argued. "You know Lena doesn't think—not really. When those wires crossed, she could have corrected herself. But she didn't bother; she followed the mechanical impulse. A man might have reached for the vanilla, but when he saw it in his hand, he'd have stopped. Lena has sense enough, but she has no emotions, no consciousness of self."

"All right, that's the big trouble with the mechs now. But we'll get around it, put in some mechanical emotions or something." He screwed Lena's head back on, turned on her juice. "Go back to work, Lena, it's nineteen o'clock."

Now, I specialized in endocrinology and related subjects. I wasn't exactly a psychologist, but I did understand the glands, secretions, hormones, and miscellanies that are the physical causes of emotions. It took medical science three hundred years to find out how and why they worked, and I couldn't see men duplicating them mechanically in much less time.

I brought home books and papers to prove it, and Dave quoted the invention of memory coils and veritoid eyes. During that year we swapped knowledge until Dave knew the whole theory of endocrinology and I could have made Lena from memory. The more we talked, the less sure I grew about the impossibility of *homo mechanensis* as the perfect type.

Poor Lena. Her cuproberyl body spent half its time in scattered pieces. Our first attempts were successful only in getting her to serve fried brushes for breakfast and wash the dishes in oleo oil. Then one day she cooked a perfect dinner with six wires crossed, and Dave was in ecstasy.

He worked all night on her wiring, put in a new coil, and taught her a fresh set of words. And the next day she flew into a tantrum and swore vigorously at us when we told her she wasn't doing her work right.

"It's a lie," she yelled, shaking a suction brush. "You're all liars. If you so-and-so's would leave me whole long enough, I might get something done around the place."

When we had calmed her temper and got her back to work, Dave ushered me into the study. "Not taking any chances with Lena," he explained. "We'll have to cut out that adrenal pack and restore her to normalcy. But we've got to get a better robot. A housemaid mech isn't complex enough."

"How about Dillard's new utility models? They seem to combine everything in one."

"Exactly. Even so, we'll need a special one built to order, with a full range of memory coils. And out of respect to old Lena, let's get a female case for its works."

The result, of course, was Helen. The Dillard people had performed a miracle and put all the works in a girl-modeled case. Even the plastic-and-rubberite face was designed for flexibility to express emotions, and she was complete with tear glands and taste buds, ready to simulate every human action, from breathing to pulling hair. The bill they sent with her was another miracle, but Dave and I scraped it together; we had to turn Lena over to an exchange to complete it, though, and thereafter we ate out.

I'd performed plenty of delicate operations on living tissues, and some of them had been tricky, but I still felt like a pre-med student as we opened the front plate of her torso and began to sever the leads of her "nerves." Dave's mechanical glands were all prepared, complex little bundles of radio tubes and wires that heterodyned on the electrical thought impulses and distorted them as adrenalin distorts the reaction of human minds.

Instead of sleeping that night, we pored over the schematic diagrams of her structures, tracing the thought mazes of her wiring, severing the leaders, implanting the heterones, as Dave called them. And while we worked, a mechanical tape fed carefully prepared thoughts of consciousness and awareness of life and feeling into an auxiliary memory coil. Dave believed in leaving nothing to chance.

It was growing light as we finished, exhausted and exultant. All that remained was the starting of her electrical power; like all the Dillard mechs, she was equipped with a tiny atomotor instead of batteries, and once started she would need no further attention.

Dave refused to turn her on. "Wait until we've slept and rested," he advised. "I'm as eager to try her as you are, but we can't do much studying with our minds half dead. Turn in, and we'll leave Helen until later."

Even though we were both reluctant to follow it, we knew the idea was sound. We turned in, and sleep hit us before the air conditioner could cut down to sleeping temperature. And then Dave was pounding on my shoulder.

"Phil! Hey, snap out of it!"

I groaned, turned over, and faced him. "Well?... Uh! What is it? Did Helen—"

"No, it's old Mrs. Van Styler. She 'visored to say her son has an infatuation for a servant girl, and she wants you to come out and give counterhormones. They're at the summer camp in Maine."

Rich Mrs. Van Styler! I couldn't afford to let that account down, now that Helen had used up the last of my funds. But it wasn't a job I cared for.

"Counterhormones! That'll take two weeks' full time. Anyway, I'm no society doctor, messing with glands to keep fools happy. My job's taking care of serious trouble."

"And you want to watch Helen." Dave was grinning, but he was serious too. "I told her it'd cost her fifty thousand!"

"*Huh?*"

"And she said okay, if you hurried."

Of course, there was only one thing to do, though I could have wrung fat Mrs. Van Styler's neck cheerfully. It wouldn't have happened if she'd used robots like everyone else—but she had to be different.

Consequently, while Dave was back home puttering with Helen, I was racking my brain to trick Archy Van Styler into getting the counterhormones, and giving the servant girl the same. Oh, I wasn't supposed to, but the poor kid was crazy about Archy. Dave might have written, I thought, but never a word did I get.

It was three weeks later instead of two when I reported that Archy was "cured," and collected on the line. With that money in my pocket, I hired a personal rocket and was back in Messina in half an hour. I didn't waste time in reaching the house.

As I stepped into the alcove, I heard a light patter of feet, and an eager voice called out, "Dave, dear?" For a minute I couldn't answer, and the voice came again, pleading, "Dave?"

I don't know what I expected, but I didn't expect Helen to meet me that way, stopping and staring at me, obvious disappointment on her face, little hands fluttering up against her breast.

"Oh," she cried. "I thought it was Dave. He hardly comes home to eat now, but I've had supper waiting hours." She dropped her hands and managed a smile. "You're Phil, aren't you? Dave told me about you when… at first. I'm so glad to see you home, Phil."

"Glad to see you doing so well, Helen." Now, what does one say for light conversation with a robot? "You said something about supper?"

"Oh, yes. I guess Dave ate downtown again, so we might as well go in. It'll be nice having someone to talk to around the house, Phil. You don't mind if I call you Phil, do you? You know, you're sort of a godfather to me."

We ate. I hadn't counted on such behavior, but apparently she considered eating as normal as walking. She didn't do much eating, at that; most of the time she spent staring at the front door.

Dave came in as we were finishing, a frown a yard wide on his face. Helen started to rise, but he ducked toward the stairs, throwing words over his shoulder.

"Hi, Phil. See you up here later."

There was something radically wrong with him. For a moment I'd thought his eyes were haunted, and as I turned to Helen hers were filling with tears. She gulped, choked them back, and fell viciously on her food.

"What's the matter with him… and you?" I asked.

"He's sick of me." She pushed her plate away and got up hastily. "You'd better see him while I clean up. And there's nothing wrong with me. And it's not my fault, anyway." She grabbed the dishes and ducked into the kitchen; I could have sworn she was crying.

Maybe all thought is a series of conditioned reflexes—but she certainly had picked up a lot of conditioning while I was gone. Lena in her heyday had been nothing like this. I went up to see if Dave could make any sense out of the hodge-podge.

He was squirting soda into a large glass of apple brandy, and I saw that the bottle was nearly empty. "Join me?" he asked.

It seemed like a good idea. The roaring blast of an ion rocket overhead was the only familiar thing left in the house. From the look around Dave's eyes, it wasn't the first bottle he'd emptied while I was gone, and there were more left. He dug out a new bottle for his own drink.

"Of course, it's none of my business, Dave, but that stuff won't steady your nerves any. What's gotten into you and Helen? Been seeing ghosts?"

Helen was wrong; he hadn't been eating downtown—nor anywhere else. His muscles collapsed into a chain in a way that spoke of fatigue and nerves, but mostly of hunger. "You noticed it, eh?"

"Noticed it? The two of you jammed it down my throat."

"Uhmmm." He swatted at a nonexistent fly and slumped farther down in the pneumatic. "Guess maybe I should have waited with Helen until you got back. But if that stereo cast hadn't changed… Anyway, it did. And those mushy books of yours finished the job."

"Thanks. That makes it all clear."

"You know, Phil, I've got a place up in the country—fruit ranch. My dad left it to me. Think I'll look it over."

And that's the way it went. But finally, by much liquor and more perspiration, I got some of the story out of him before I gave him a phenobarbital and put him to bed. Then I hunted up Helen and dug the rest of the story from her, until it made sense.

Apparently as soon as I was gone Dave had turned her on and made preliminary tests, which were entirely satisfactory. She had reacted beautifully—so well that he decided to leave her and go down to work as usual.

Naturally, with all her untried emotions, she was filled with curiosity and wanted him to stay. Then he had an inspiration. After showing her what her duties about the house would be, he set her down in front of the stereovisor, tuned in a travelogue, and left her to occupy her time with that.

The travelogue held her attention until it was finished, and the station switched over to a current serial with Larry Ainslee, the same cute emoter who'd given us all the trouble with the twins. Incidentally, he looked something like Dave.

Helen took to the serial like a seal to water. This play-acting was a perfect outlet for her newly excited emotions. When that particular episode finished, she found a love story on another station and added still more to her education. The afternoon programs were mostly news and music, but by then she'd found my books; and I do have rather adolescent taste in literature.

Dave came home in the best of spirits. The front alcove was neatly swept, and there was the odor of food in the air that he'd missed around the house for weeks. He had visions of Helen as the superefficient housekeeper.

So it was a shock to him to feel two strong arms around his neck from behind and hear a voice all a-quiver coo into his ears, "Oh, Dave, darling, I've missed you so, and I'm so *thrilled* that you're back." Helen's technique may have lacked polish, but it had enthusiasm, as he found when he tried to stop her from kissing him. She had learned fast and furiously—also, Helen was powered by an atomotor.

Dave wasn't a prude, but he remembered that she was only a robot, after all. The fact that she felt, acted, and looked like a young goddess in his arms didn't mean much. With some effort, he untangled her and dragged her off to supper, where he made her eat with him to divert her attention.

After her evening work, he called her into the study and gave her a thorough lecture on the folly of her ways. It must have been good, for it lasted three solid hours and covered her station in life, the idiocy of stereos, and various other miscellanies. When he had finished, Helen looked up with dewy eyes and said wistfully, "I know, Dave, but I still love you."

That's when Dave started drinking.

It grew worse each day. If he stayed downtown, she was crying when he came home. If he returned on time, she fussed over him and threw herself at him. In his room, with door locked, he could hear her downstairs pacing up and down and muttering; and when he went down, she stared at him reproachfully until he had to go back up.

I sent Helen out on a fake errand in the morning and got Dave up. With her gone, I made him eat a decent breakfast and gave him a tonic for his nerves. He was still listless and moody.

"Look here, Dave," I broke in on his brooding. "Helen isn't human, after all. Why not cut off her power and change a few memory coils? Then we can convince her that she never was in love and couldn't get that way."

"You try it. I had that idea, but she put up a wail that would wake Homer. She says it would be murder—and the hell of it is that I can't help feeling the same about it. Maybe she isn't human, but you wouldn't guess it when she puts on that martyred look and tells you to go ahead and kill her."

"We never put in substitutes for some of the secretions present in man during the love period."

"I don't know what we put in. Maybe the heterones backfired or something. Anyway, she's made this idea so much a part of her thoughts that we'd have to put in a whole new set of coils."

"Well, why not?"

"Go ahead. You're the surgeon of this family. I'm not used to fussing with emotions. Matter of fact, since she's been acting this way I'm beginning to hate work on any robot. My business is going to blazes."

He saw Helen coming up the walk and ducked out the back door for the monorail express. I'd intended to put him back in bed, but let him go. Maybe he'd be better off at his shop than at home.

"Dave's gone?" Helen did have that martyred look now.

"Yeah. I got him to eat, and he's gone to work."

"I'm glad he ate." She slumped down in a chair as if she were worn out, though how a mech could be tired beat me. "Phil?"

"Well, what is it?"

"Do you think I'm bad for him? I mean, do you think he'd be happier if I weren't here?"

"He'll go crazy if you keep acting this way around him."

She winced. Those little hands were twisting about pleadingly, and I felt like an inhuman brute. But I'd started, and I went ahead. "Even if I cut out your power and changed your coils, he'd probably still be haunted by you."

"I know. But I can't help it. And I'd make him a good wife, really I would, Phil."

I gulped; this was going a little too far. "And give him strapping sons to boot, I suppose. A man wants flesh and blood, not rubber and metal."

"Don't, please! I can't think of myself that way; to me, I'm a woman. And you know how perfectly I'm made to imitate a real woman… in all ways. I couldn't give him sons, but in every other way… I'd try so hard, I know I'd make him a good wife."

I gave up.

Dave didn't come home that night, nor the next day. Helen was fussing and fuming, wanting me to call the hospitals and the police, but I knew nothing had happened to him. He always carried identification. Still, when he didn't come on the third day, I began to worry. And when Helen started out for his shop, I agreed to go with her.

Dave was there, with another man I didn't know. I parked Helen where he couldn't see her, but where she could hear, and went in as soon as the other fellow left.

Dave looked a little better and seemed glad to see me. "Hi, Phil—just closing up. Let's go eat."

Helen couldn't hold back any longer, but came trooping in. "Come on home, Dave. I've got roast duck with spice stuffing, and you know you love that."

"Scat!" said Dave. She shrank back, turned to go. "Oh, all right, stay. You might as well hear it, too. I've sold the shop. The fellow you saw just bought it, and I'm going up to the old fruit ranch I told you about, Phil. I can't stand the mechs any more."

"You'll starve to death at that," I told him.

"No, there's a growing demand for old-fashioned fruit, raised out of doors. People are tired of this water-culture stuff. Dad always made a living out of it. I'm leaving as soon as I can get home and pack."

Helen clung to her idea. "I'll pack, Dave, while you eat. I've got apple cobbler for dessert." The world was toppling under her feet, but she still remembered how crazy he was for apple cobbler.

Helen was a good cook; in fact she was a genius, with all the good points of a woman and a mech combined. Dave ate well enough, after he got started. By the time supper was over, he'd thawed out enough to admit he liked the duck and the cobbler, and to thank her for packing. In fact, he even let her kiss him goodbye, though he firmly refused to let her go to the rocket field with him.

Helen was trying to be brave when I got back, and we carried on a stumbling conversation about Mrs. Van Styler's servants for a while. But the talk began to lull, and she sat staring out of the window at nothing most of the time. Even the stereo comedy lacked interest for her, and I was glad enough to have her go off to her room. She could cut her power down to simulate sleep when she chose.

As the days slipped by, I began to realize why she couldn't believe herself a robot. I got to thinking of her as a girl and companion myself. Except for odd intervals when she went off by herself to brood, or when she kept going to the telescript for a letter that never came, she was as good a companion as a man could ask. There was something homey about the place that Lena had never put there.

I took Helen on a shopping trip to Hudson, and she giggled and purred over the wisps of silk and glassheen that were the fashion, tried on endless hats, and conducted herself as any normal girl might. We went trout fishing for a day, where she proved to be as good a sport and as sensibly silent as a man. I thoroughly enjoyed myself and thought she was forgetting Dave. That was before I came home unexpectedly and found her doubled up on the couch, threshing her legs up and down and crying to the high heavens.

It was then I called Dave. They seemed to have trouble in reaching him, and Helen came over beside me while I waited. She was tense and fidgety as an old maid trying to propose. But finally they located Dave.

"What's up, Phil?" he asked as his face came on the viewplate. "I was just getting my things together to—"

I broke him off. "Things can't go on the way they are, Dave. I've made up my mind. I'm yanking Helen's coils tonight. It won't be worse than what she's going through now."

Helen reached up and touched my shoulder. "Maybe that's best, Phil. I don't blame you."

Dave's voice cut in. "Phil, you don't know what you're doing!"

"Of course I do. It'll all be over by the time you can get here. As you heard, she's agreeing."

There was a black cloud sweeping over Dave's face. "I won't have it, Phil. She's half mine and I forbid it!"

"Of all the—"

"Go ahead, call me anything you want. I've changed my mind. I was packing to come home when you called."

Helen jerked around me, her eyes glued to the panel. "Dave, do you… are you…"

"I'm just waking up to what a fool I've been, Helen. Phil, I'll be home in a couple of hours, so if there's anything—"

He didn't have to chase me out. But I heard Helen cooing something about loving to be a rancher's wife before I could shut the door.

Well, I wasn't as surprised as they thought. I think I knew when I called Dave what would happen. No man acts the way Dave had been acting because he hates a girl; only because he thinks he does—and thinks wrong.

No woman ever made a lovelier bride or a sweeter wife. Helen never lost her flare for cooking and making a home. With her gone, the old house seemed empty, and I began to drop out to the ranch once or twice a week. I suppose they had trouble at times, but I never saw it, and I know the neighbors never suspected they were anything but normal man and wife.

Dave grew older, and Helen didn't, of course. But between us we put lines in her face and grayed her hair without letting Dave know that she wasn't growing old with him; he'd forgotten that she wasn't human, I guess.

I practically forgot, myself. It wasn't until a letter came from Helen this morning that I woke up to reality. There, in her beautiful script, just a trifle shaky in places, was the inevitable that neither Dave nor I had seen.

DEAR PHIL,

As you know, Dave has had heart trouble for several years now. We expected him to live on just the same, but it seems that wasn't to be. He died in my arms just before sunrise. He sent you his greetings and farewell.

I've one last favor to ask of you, Phil. There is only one thing for me to do when this is finished. Acid will burn out metal as well as flesh, and I'll be dead with Dave. Please see that we are buried together, and that the morticians do not find my secret. Dave wanted it that way, too.

Poor, dear Phil. I know you loved Dave as a brother, and how you felt about me. Please don't grieve too much for us, for we have had a happy life together, and both feel that we should cross this last bridge side by side.

With love and thanks from,

HELEN

It had to come sooner or later, I suppose, and the first shock has worn off now. I'll be leaving in a few minutes to carry out Helen's last instructions.

Dave was a lucky man, and the best friend I ever had. And Helen—well, as I said, I'm an old man now and can view things more sanely; I should have married and raised a family, I suppose. But... there was only one Helen O'Loy.

(1938)

THE PEACEMAKER

T. S. Bazelli

Theresa Bazelli is a young Filipino Canadian writer who's hit the ground running with a handful of stories, in webzines and small anthologies, that make science fiction the weird and decentered place it was always supposed to be. ("Culture goes deeper than clothing, food, and appearance," she wrote recently. "Culture seeps into how I think, view the world, and what I value. Nothing I write is ever going to read the same as the white default, even if my characters are.") She writes software help by day, and YA fantasy novels by night. She lives on the rainy west coast of Canada with her family and, when not at the keyboard, she's making a mess in the kitchen or sewing things.

The message snakes across my visual field in red flashing letters, waking me from slumber. "Disruption reported."

I unhook from the charging station and do a status check before the coordinates arrive. The gears in my shoulders whine with stiffness. My audio and visual sensors are at 80%. I am scheduled for repairs, but my battery is full and I am eager to serve.

A peacekeeping unit returning from duty enters the building and heads for its charging station. Its uniform is ripped at the elbows and knees. Its left eyeball lolls uselessly up and down. We do not speak, though we could. We walk clockwise in opposite directions, around a chunk of collapsed concrete, acknowledging each other in silence. The damage does not matter. It is the people that matter. It is better to preserve our batteries for the work.

We have autonomy, we speak, we walk, and we are equipped with emotional simulation chips, but we are not people. This message is highlighted in bold font beneath our primary directive. The people, the programmers, they remind us with every reboot, so that we serve to our best ability. We are not important. I am not important.

I move as quickly as possible, but the roads are blocked by detritus: overturned cars and scattered bricks. Air sirens scream while drones whirl by overhead, and I ping the server for new instructions, but headquarters sends no commands. Only local dispatches still work. I still work.

I replay the last set of instructions we were issued.

All visitor visas and work permits have been cancelled. Foreigners must be collected for deportation. All identification chips must be scanned, and those without chips must be detained. All citizens must submit DNA to the census bureau, or legal status will be revoked.

These instructions conflict with my primary programming and it makes my processor loop. I was not programmed to cause distress to the people, and screening identification chips, and removing them from their homes causes undue anxiety, cortisol spikes.

A street-sweeping bot scuttles past my boots and into the gutter. Its arms are full of rubble and it darts back and forth, busy at its task. It is a good robot, well-made and still functioning properly. I do not tell it that its work is pointless, that the streets need to be rebuilt, not cleaned. It is good to work. The work is why we exist. We all help the people.

But there are not many people left.

Go Home Forein Dogs!

The painted words drip green across the windows of the corner store that logged the distress call. I recognize the vocal signature of Nancy Johnson and my processors work overtime. I know that the sign is incorrect. The misspelling is highlighted, obscuring my vision. Nancy's place of birth is Hospital 2X5Y on 4th Avenue, therefore she is not foreign. She is also not a dog. The semantic wrongness makes my sensors grind. I send an electric jolt to power the nanites embedded in the window as I pass the threshold. The graffiti must be removed.

Inside the shop, Nancy swings a scrap of metal at three young people while one of them sprays green paint over her shelves. The other two toss cans of food into their bags. The paint glows like radiation, like poison, but it is only paint.

"You goddamned thieving hooligans!" Nancy shouts, slipping into the English of her second language, but my language chips can parse English as well as fifteen other languages. I scan all their chips on the fly. The two young men are from Service Area 53. The young woman with the spray paint is local. I remember that when she was a child, she would run after me and ask for balloons. I remember her smile. She is not smiling now.

"Peace, friends. Let us find a way to resolve this," I keep my voice cheerful.

They stare, noticing me for the first time. One of the young men walks over and knocks on my head as if it were a door. "Hey Peacekeeper, don't you know there's a war out there? How are you still functioning?"

"I am a civil unit," I say, but they do not listen. I am intelligent enough to guess that they do not care. They are desperate, hungry and frightened, like all the people left behind. I give them mild zaps, draining my battery, herding them like sheep.

I tell Nancy to lock the doors. I do not let go of their coats until I hear the bolts slide into place. Perhaps these *hooligans* think that they are doing their civic duty and I do not blame them. They are people. People are prone to interpreting the law imperfectly. People cannot read identity chips without a handheld scanner.

Once we are in the street, they begin to kick and punch. I feel a spring go loose in my abdomen, but they cannot harm me permanently. I can be repaired. Their curses echo down the empty street, and their grubby fingers tear at my lab-grown skin, exposing silicone and wire. They are frustrated. I understand this. I know that it is better for them to let out their anger. My head vibrates as I let them beat me.

Nancy presses her face to the glass in her shop. She is crying. It is good to be seen and acknowledged for the work.

Don't cry, I would like to tell her. I am doing my job and it is good to be useful. Already, the nanites are eating away the paint. *Go Home For,* it says. The offensive spelling is gone.

Before the war, I would often break up schoolyard fights. I enjoy children. They understand fairness and that I can call their parents if they do not listen. I search my pockets, but there are no candies or balloons to set things right, only a hole where the stitches have worn out.

"What use are you when bombs are falling, Peacekeeper?" the young woman asks me. "What a waste of charge!" This stops the memory playback. There are no children here anymore.

War is outside the scope of my programming. I could explain, but to speak would only upset them further. They are people too. They are also important. My blueprints are stored in servers beneath a mountain. I am one of many, though my experiences are unique. I can be rebuilt. Humans only reproduce. I have seen recordings of reproduction. It is messy and prone to error. Human parts cannot be replaced. Each human is one of a kind, *couture*.

I know this word is wrong. For weeks my language cortex has been scheduled for an adjustment, but our technicians are all occupied by the war. I cannot find the right words.

Drones scream above, and explosions shake the next block over. The young people run. *Go Home,* the green letters urge now.

My memory loops. My processor spins.

For weeks I have computed an answer to the problem of the war. My programming compels me to make people happy, but the war scars every surface of my city. *Genocide*, I know this word. *Xenophobia*, I have learned from my English dictionary. *Love*, I know this word also.

I return to headquarters, dock into my charging station, and unload footage of the broken city. The power is out again. I look for orders, but there are none, and our human supervisors have long gone. Half the building is sprayed with shrapnel, but it does not stop us. Other peacemakers move about, trying to do the work. I clock my time manually. It is good to be useful.

Go. The green letters burn bright in my memory. I have just a little charge left.

I do a complete inventory of my parts. My speakers were built in the United Koreas, my central processor was designed in Lower Canada, the metal of my joints was smelted in China… I print shipping labels one by one and relay my solution to the local server. The logic is sound.

I take a pair of scissors to my face and begin to snip.

(2016)

SEXY ROBOT MOM

Sandra McDonald

Originally from Revere, Massachusetts, **Sandra McDonald** spent eight years as an officer in the United States Navy, during which time she lived in Guam, Newfoundland, England, and the United States. She has also worked as a Hollywood assistant, a software instructor, and an English teacher. Her short story "The Ghost Girls of Rumney Mill" was shortlisted for the James Tiptree, Jr. Award in 2003. Her first novel, *The Outback Stars*, was published in 2007, and was followed by two sequels: *The Stars Down Under* (2008) and *The Stars Blue Yonder* (2009). Her short story collection *Diana Comet and Other Improbable Stories* won the Lambda Award for LGBT SF, Fantasy and Horror works in 2011. She lives in Jacksonville, Florida.

Scott said that Alina was his favorite mashup between a sexbot and a toaster oven, but Alina disagreed. Although she shared the same buxom brunette shell as the 7832BNX7 series, she hadn't been given a clitoris, vulva, or vaginal port. Her programming included only the most rudimentary knowledge of human sexual practices. On the other hand, her expandable womb was adjustable for time and temperature, had a durable protective shell, and could wirelessly transmit information the same way any kitchen appliance could.

"I think I'm much more toaster oven than sexbot," she said as he adjusted her left nipple tube.

"Trust me." Scott snapped her areola back into place. "Parents look at you, they see inflatable doll and not melting pizza. That's why they had to frump up the rest of your series."

Alina glanced at the other units getting serviced in the maintenance bays of *New Human, More Human*. Some had oily hair (undesirable) or asymmetrical facial features (acceptable within certain parameters) or deliberately crooked noses (unacceptable). "I was the first?"

"You're number seven," he said, floppy bangs hanging in front of his blue eyes (very desirable). "Lucky seven."

"I don't remember the others."

"No, you're not equipped with long-term memory." Scott stepped back and gave her a wide grin. "Go ahead, squirt me."

She loaded her breast with saline from an internal reservoir and took aim. The fluid hit his lab coat. Scott spread his arms, delighted. "There's my girl. You're all set. Inspected, warrantied, and ready for your next implant. See you in nine months." Alina buttoned her pink blouse, straightened her floral skirt, and walked herself down to the Impregnation Department. Six-foot-tall photographs of happy babies and their parents hung on the cream-colored walls. Dr. Oliver Ogilvy, who was tall (desirable for men) but had a weak chin (undesirable in either sex) brought her into his office. Awards and plaques dotted the walls, and the windows overlooked the Hudson Valley.

"This is Mr. and Mrs. Crowther, Alina," he said. "They like your profile. Eleven successful terms."

"That's quite impressive," said Mr. Crowther, jovially. He was middle-aged, with thick artificial hair and well-tailored clothes.

Alina shook his hand gently. "Thank you, sir," she said, although she had no knowledge of previous pregnancies. She was programmed to believe whatever Dr. Ogilvy told her.

Mrs. Crowther, short and slender (both characteristics desirable in females, but not in excess) folded her arms across her chest. "Ninety-nine months pregnant. Doesn't it... get stress fractures or something? All that expansion and contraction?" Dr. Ogilvy leaned back in his leather chair. "The womb is built for flexibility. The torso was specially designed to expand in proportion to your child's development."

"And it walks around while pregn—while it's incubating?" Mrs. Crowther asked.

"We call Alina 'she'," Dr. Ogilvy said. "It humanizes the experience for you. Yes. She'll be walking around. She'll be living with you, consuming food at your table to process for your child. She'll interact with you both on a daily basis. Your family and neighbors will get to know her. You might even have a baby shower."

Mrs. Crowther flinched. "Baby shower? For a robot?"

"For you, honey," Mr. Crowther said. "She's just carrying it, but you're the mom-to-be. You'll be the center of attention. I promise."

Alina's decision trees told her it would be appropriate to nod, so she did.

Mrs. Crowther looked doubtful. "Maybe we should just let the machines carry it here. I don't know if I want it in my house. It—she—seems so bland."

The chair under Dr. Ogilvy creaked as he leaned forward. "She doesn't have a personality profile loaded yet. You choose the options. Shy, extroverted? Witty, educated, quiet, unobtrusive? You pick her intelligence level and hobbies. Her last couple wanted her to speak Italian and excel at cooking."

"I can cook just fine," Mrs. Crowther said bitterly. "I just can't get pregnant again. We've been trying for twenty-seven months now."

"That's exactly what Alina is for," Dr. Ogilvy said smoothly. "Think about it, Joyce. Nine months from today, you could be holding your son or daughter. Your waistline won't change an inch. Your hormones will be steady and calm. You won't have the trauma of childbirth or the risk of post-partum depression. Your child will be brought into this world in a safe, secure, extremely successful robot incubator."

Mr. Crowther put his arm around his wife's shoulders. "Sounds ideal to me, sweetheart."

Mrs. Crowther lifted her chin. She gave a tiny nod.

Alina was impregnated the next day. The fertilized egg instantly attached to her artificial endometrium and began to divide. Forty-eight hours after that, she was loaded into a van, transported across the continent, and delivered to the Crowthers with a blue corsage pinned to her wrist. The corsage held a handwritten note from Dr. Ogilvy: "Congratulations on your future baby boy!"

Mr. Crowther said, "Let's name him Owen," and Mrs. Crowther said, "Show it to its room."

The Crowthers' house was a two-story Mediterranean-style villa with hardwood floors and oil paintings of rustic landscapes. Alina's room was on the second floor, adjacent to the nursery. She wasn't allowed in the nursery. Her room had a bed, although she didn't require one. It had a walk-in closet where she kept a different skirt and blouse for every day of the week. Her breakfast was delivered every morning, each meal perfectly calculated for the fetus's benefit. After eating, she sat in a rocking chair by the window and gazed at the crystal blue swimming pool below. No one ever swam in its waters—not in the winter, when the hills were brown; not in the summer, when the hills were still brown and the maids complained of drought.

Lunch was delivered promptly at noon. Afterward Alina emptied her waste port and returned to the chair again. She didn't think or dream or speculate; she didn't grow bored or restless or impatient; she had no insecurities to wrestle with, no resentments to harbor, no agenda to pursue. She monitored the fetus and adjusted hormones, nutrients, and antibodies as needed. She watched the faint ripples of pool water when the pump kicked in. She analyzed the colors in its depths as the sun moved across the sky.

Late each evening Mr. Crowther would gather her at dinner. They ate in the large kitchen, with its gleaming marble counters and heavy smell of spices. Mr. Crowther asked about the baby and talked about his own childhood growing up in Schenectady. He would put his hand on her growing stomach and listen to her project the baby's heartbeat through a speaker in her chest. He apologized for Mrs. Crowther.

"We had a daughter, but she drowned," he said. "And another, but she was stillborn. You're our third chance at happiness. Maybe having a boy will bring good luck."

Alina had been programmed for optimism. "I'm sure it will, sir."

In her sixth month, after a dinner in which he consumed a bottle of wine, Mr. Crowther walked Alina back to her room and, once inside, leaned forward until his mouth was only inches from hers. His skin was flushed, his pupils wide. "Do you mind... I mean, I know you don't... but would it be okay for me to kiss you? Could I do that and you wouldn't tell Mrs. Crowther?"

"I'm programmed to be honest if she asks," Alina said.

Mr. Crowther kissed her anyway. She measured the pressure and temperature of his lips and waited for him to stop.

"Well," he said, eventually. "Body of a sexbot, demeanor like a cold fish."

'Yes, sir," she replied.

On the fourth day of her thirty-fifth week, her womb transmitted a completion signal to Dr. Ogilvy's office. A midwife-technician arrived six hours later. Alina stretched out for the first and only time on the bed in her room. Mr. Crowther entered his identification code. Mrs. Crowther entered hers. The skin over Alina's belly slid back to reveal a hatch, and the hatch popped open to reveal baby Owen squirming in a puddle of earthy-smelling fluids. Alina could have reached down and cut the cord herself, but the technician did it.

"Congratulations!" The midwife lifted Owen and deftly began to clean him. "Happy birthday, Mom and baby. Do you want Alina to nurse him, or is she coming back with me?"

"We have formula," Mrs. Crowther said. "Take it back."

The next morning she was back in the maintenance bay, her milk extracted and recycled. A technician named Scott flushed out her nipple tubes. He said she was his favorite mashup between a sexbot and a toaster oven.

"I've never heard anyone say that before," she said.

'You're not programmed with a long-term memory." He stepped back and said, "Okay, let's see how your aim is. Hit me with both barrels, baby."

She took aim and soaked the front of his jacket.

"Excellent," he said. "Go get knocked up, and we'll see you in nine months."

Dan Poole and Mark Dubay were a gay couple who paid for an egg from an anonymous donor. They each provided sperm but asked the laboratory to randomly pick whose would get used. "She's going to be both of ours regardless," Mark said confidently, and Dan agreed, and so Alina was forbidden from revealing that it was Dan's DNA she could detect in the fetus. Both men were of African descent, and the egg had come from a similar donor. Alina mixed up hot chocolate and added just enough cream to illustrate the baby's probable skin color.

"Our little café au lait," Dan said, which is how the baby earned her nickname.

Their house was a large, L-shaped ranch set in the countryside of central Georgia, surrounded by forests and streams. They both worked from home. Greenhouse science, they said. They had opted for her to be energetic, polylingual, knowledgeable about wines, and good with dogs. Every day Alina took a long walk with either Mark or Dan and one of their three Dobermans.

"Are you happy being a pregnant robot?" Dan asked one day as they walked along a stream.

"Yes, sir."

"Really?" Dan threw a stick for one of the dogs to fetch. "Can you be happy?"

"I'm programmed to say it and portray it in appropriate circumstances," she replied. "You seem eager for me to say yes, so I said yes."

"But you don't have any emotions of your own."

"No, sir. My series was not approved for emotion chips."

The summer woods edged to fall and then winter, with snowfall so heavy that it blocked the road to town for two weeks. On the first day of Alina's thirty-fourth week, the Womb Alert announced Au Lait's readiness. Dan entered his code without error, but Mark was so nervous he hit the wrong numbers twice and nearly locked her womb. Baby Au Lait, now named Sonora, emerged healthy and kicking. Mark and Dan retained Alina to breastfeed her for six months. She also changed diapers, burped the baby, and rocked her through sleepless nights. But she didn't love her, because how could she?

One day, Mark said, "Alina, we want to have another baby. You have to go back to the lab for the implant, but they're not going to erase your memory of us. You're coming right back here with a son. We've already nicknamed him Con Leche."

"That's excellent news, sir," she replied.

Once she was back in the lab, Scott flushed out her systems and adjusted her nipple tubes. Bent close to her, his breath hot on her skin, he said, 'You're my favorite offspring of a toaster oven and a sexbot."

Alina tilted her head. 'You told me that the last time you serviced my nipples. They seem to require much maintenance."

He abruptly stopped fiddling. "Did I? Maybe I should check your waste port instead."

Later she reported to Impregnation. The donor egg had already been fertilized with Mark's sperm. Alina climbed into a transfer chamber and went into rest mode. A subroutine monitored the successful implantation of the egg into her womb. Shortly afterward, her external sensors recorded the dimming of the light over her chamber. The power feed snaking up into her foot abruptly spiked, and an emergency command was fed into her central processing unit: START STASIS.

Alina and Con Leche both went to sleep.

Thud, crack, thud, crack. Alina opened her eyes. She was in a dark transfer chamber. Above her were dim pinpricks of light, distant and shifting as something made noise and dug toward her. The external temperature measured below freezing (inhospitable to human life) and after a few milliseconds she concluded the chamber was buried by ice and snow.

No decision tree offered an advantageous course of action. She opted for inaction, and counted thuds and cracks until a shovel hit the plastic a few inches above her face. Soon a human face was staring down at her. The face was asymmetrical (undesirable) and damaged by sun and wind (regrettable). Snow goggles covered the eyes and a parka hood hid the human's hair and chin.

Alina waited patiently until the human broke through the shield.

"Are you awake, or just staring at me?" the human asked.

"I'm awake, thank you," Alina said. "Are you a male or female? Your face and voice are indeterminable."

"Doesn't matter," the human said. "Get up, robot-girl."

Alina freed her feet from their plugs and climbed out. What had once been the implant lab was now a snow cave illuminated by battery lanterns. Thick ice coated the equipment, machines, and computers. The roof had partially collapsed, which explained the snow and ice piled on Alina's chamber. A long knotted rope hung through a separate hole that had been cut in the ceiling.

"I'm Coren," the stranger said. He or she was about Alina's height, maybe a little overweight, no facial hair. Young, perhaps mid-twenties or so. It was impossible to discern breasts under the bulky gray parka.

"I'm Alina," Alina said. "Should I call you sir or madam?"

Coren began breaking the shovel down into smaller pieces that fit into a backpack. "You're really hung up on gender, aren't you?"

"I'm programmed to recognize two."

"Well, I'm not programmed to answer you," Coren said. "Call me by my name, or call me hey you, or just call me a person. I don't care."

Alina's databank lit up with information about gender-neutral pronouns. She had several options to choose from. Ze, En, Co, Thon. In her sixth pregnancy, the parents had both been professors of female sexuality at Brown University. They'd taught her feminist language and theory, matricentricty and gynocritics and—

The ice slid out from under Alina's feet. She fell flat on her rear and stayed there.

"Hey!" Coren abandoned the backpack. "Are you all right?"

"I am functioning well," Alina replied, flooded with memories of that pregnancy— Professor Ahmeti and Professor Sauter, their house in Providence, the two white cats who sat in the sunny windows all day, the way Professor Ahmeti made meatball and garlic soup every Friday night and Professor Sauter chewed through pencils when grading papers, their happy faces when their baby was ready, the way they'd kissed Alina's cheeks in thanks.

You're not equipped with long-term memory, she'd been told. By Scott. Scott with his easy smile and his bangs in his eyes and his devotion to fixing her nipple tubes every time she came to the shop.

Coren said, "I know you're just a robot, but I've seen healthier looking corpses. You sick?"

Alina adjusted her cheeks to include more pink. She flushed red to her lips, and made her eyes appear brighter and more blue (very desirable).

For some reason, the adjustments made Coren frown. "Let's climb out of here. I've got a coat and clothes for you so you don't freeze."

"I am impervious to most extremes of weather, Person Coren. Also, my uterus operates independently on its own settings and is at optimal temperature."

"Yeah. About that. Are you carrying?"

"Carrying what?" Alina asked.

"A baby, dummy."

Alina answered, "Yes. I am carrying the fertilized egg of Mark Dubay and Dan Poole. It is four days old. Are Dan and Mark nearby?"

"They're dead," Coren said. "Let's get out of this ice hole before we freeze over, and you can see what the world did to itself."

Winter had come and stayed. Although Alina's calendar told her it was June, the forest around *New Human, More Human* was nothing but frozen treetops buried by snow. She saw no birds or squirrels, no smoke from cities or factories, no signs that any humans lived nearby. Only snow, ice, and gray sky. She attempted to connect with the data center, but received no answer.

Alina said, "Mark and Dan were studying climate science. They postulated a scenario of long-term adverse meteorological change."

Coren had hunched down next to a sled packed with supplies. "Sounds like fancy words for the Big Freeze. Come here, put these clothes on. Hard to explain me dragging you around dressed like it's a heat wave."

Alina donned trousers, boots, gloves, and a gray parka. The clothes were frayed but clean. Coren handed her a pair of snowshoes that looked like oversized tennis rackets and asked, "You ever use these?"

"No sir or ma'am."

'You better learn fast." Coren strapped down everything on the sled, shouldered two straps to drag it, and said, "Let's go."

"I can pull that," Alina said. "I'm not susceptible to fatigue or strain."

"I'll do it," Coren said.

Once they had hiked all the way down the hill, Alina saw that Dr. Ogilvy's complex was indistinguishable under the wintry landscape. He'd be disappointed, she thought. He had worked very hard on her and her predecessors, Acantha and Adelphia and the other four whose names somehow escaped her—

If it was unexpected to have this reservoir of memories bubbling inside her, it was equally unexpected that the data was incomplete. She could picture Dan's kind face but not Mark's. Every detail of her room at the Crowthers' villa was crystal-clear, but the inside of Dr. Ogilvy's office was a gray box devoid of specifics. It was likely that she was internally damaged. But Scott had said she had no long-term memory capacity at all. Had he been wrong?

You're my favorite, he'd said. Time and time again, as he adjusted her breasts and held her tight.

They walked a mile in silence, then Alina asked, "My internal calendar says I've been in stasis for fifty years. Is that correct, Person Coren?"

Coren was leading the way, using snow poles to test for unsafe areas. "Just call me Coren."

"I'm programmed for formality. Person is an appropriate title. Person also comes with a gender-neutral pronoun: per. Per talks to perself. Give it to per. Per went to the mall."

Coren grunted. "If it makes you happy, call me whatever. Can you be happy?"

"I'm programmed to mimic." Alina smiled widely. "I'm happy you rescued me."

"Stop that, it's creepy." Coren stopped, dropped the sled straps, and rubbed per shoulders. "Here's what I'd like. I'd like you to help me set up our tent. It's getting dark and we better bed down."

The tent was big enough for two people to lie down inside and to sit up if they didn't mind being a little hunched over. The light gray fabric blended in with the snow and provided a barrier against the bitter wind. Coren also had chemical heat-packs marked with faded letters, and thermal blankets to wrap perself in, and a small camp stove that per set up outside.

"I know how to build a campfire," Alina offered as they hunched beside it.

"No wood," Coren said. "You need to eat, right? You can eat stew?"

"My unit requires no nutrition. My nutrient reservoir sustains the fetus and needs to be augmented by a regular intake of calories."

Coren blinked. "So that's a yes?"

"Yes, per. For optimal results at this stage of gestation, I should consume one thousand calories per day. If I were human, I would need much more."

Coren retrieved two unlabeled tin cans from the sled. The tops had been crudely welded on. Per opened them up with a can opener and revealed meat stew. "I don't know much about calories, but it took me longer than I thought to find you. My supplies aren't what they should be. We might have to skimp a little or find more to get where we're going."

"Are you taking me to Mark and Dan? They'll be worried about Con Leche."

"Con what?"

"The child's nickname. It means with milk,' as in coffee with milk."

"I've never had coffee," Coren said. "Besides, they're dead, remember? Or, if they are alive, I don't know where they are, or how to get you to them."

Alina said, "1721 Peach Tree Lane, Cragford, Georgia."

"We're not going to Georgia, robot-girl." Coren warmed per hands over the warming cans. "That's not my mission."

"Are you in the military, per?" Alina asked. "To my knowledge, the military does not accept soldiers of indeterminable gender."

Coren looked cross. "It's not indeterminable. It's just indeterminable to you. At least I have a gender. You're just an It."

"I'm a She," Alina said. "To humanize the experience."

"Whatever you are, you're still a robot."

"I'm well versed in chromosome disorders that can blur gender boundaries," Alina said. "I would alert on any fetus showing an XXX or XXY abnormality."

"Call me abnormal and you can sleep out in the snow tonight," Coren said.

"I don't sleep, Person Coren."

Coren nudged a can off the stove toward Alina and handed her a fork. "Close your eyes and fake it."

"Wouldn't it be better for me to keep an eye out for unfriendly people?"

"Are you programmed for self-defense?"

"I must protect the child in my womb." Alina paused as new information popped up in her databank. "During my stasis, someone outfitted me with knowledge of twelve martial arts systems and other hand-to-hand combat maneuvers. I can also strip, repair, and fire pistols and automatic weapons. In addition, I can wire and disarm explosives—"

Coren coughed around some of per stew. 'You need all those skills to guard a little baby?"

"I think the information was mistakenly uploaded during my stasis."

"Or maybe someone saw the Big Freeze coming and thought you'd need it to survive."

Alina finished her dinner. "If you are not taking me to Dan and Mark, you will need their access codes."

"Their what?"

"To open my womb when Con Leche is ready. Only the parents have the authorization to access the child."

"What if the parents forget it?"

"In the absence of a security code, I would need remote authorization from my owners."

"Huh," Coren said. 'You mean, your dead owners? From that complex that's buried under ice, everything broken and dead?"

"Yes, per."

"So what happens if there's no code and no authorization? How will the baby get out?"

"Dr. Ogilvy once said my womb was like a locked bank vault," Alina said. "The only way to open it under other circumstances will be to destroy my control center. But don't worry, per. The baby won't be ready for approximately thirty-five more weeks. I'm sure we will reach Mark and Dan by then."

After dinner was over, Coren said, "I'm going to go take a piss in the woods. You stay here, and don't peek."

Alina waited by the sled and contemplated stealing more food. She calculated that her food intake had been three hundred and eighty calories. Not optimal. Her decision tree told her to use her reservoir and not alienate the human, but the reservoir would deplete quickly as Con Leche grew.

When Coren returned per asked, "If someone tried to hurt the baby, could you kill them? Or do robots have some kind of rule about not killing humans?"

"Protection of the fetus is my priority."

"So that's yes on killing?"

"I have never had to make that decision," Alina said. "I believe I could."

Coren dug around in the sled and pulled out a sack of salted meat jerky for dessert. Per gave Alina some. One hundred twenty more calories. Coren asked, "What about deciding to flush it? Could you do that? You know, end it?"

"I am prohibited," Alina said instantly.

"I kind of thought you'd say that. Okay, look, I'm going to bed. You stay out here. Keep yourself amused. Wake me up if you see anyone, or any kind of animal we could eat." Alina saw no people or animals during the night. Instead she sorted through the new information that had been stored inside her. The self-defense knowledge was only part of a larger database about survival skills that included hunting, cooking and eating wild animals (difficult in this new climate, where many species had gone extinct); building winter shelters of snow and branches (but all the branches were coated with ice); and administering first aid to herself and to any injured humans.

The next morning, after a breakfast of canned peas, more jerky, and salted fish, they set off again. As Coren led her through the frozen wilderness to their classified destination, Alina asked, "Are there many humans left alive?"

"A lot, but I don't know how many."

"How do they survive such arduous conditions?"

"It ain't easy."

'Yet you endured hardship, risked danger, and used precious supplies to find and retrieve me. Did Mark and Dan hire you?"

'You remember what I told you about them?"

Alina sorted through her memories. "1721 Peach Tree Lane, Cragford, Georgia."

"Oh, boy," Coren said. "I think you've got a screw loose."

They spent the next few days trekking along old roads and highways. The stumps of old billboards protruded from the snow pack, along with the roofs of rest stops or fast food restaurants. Alina debated the possibility of burrowing through the snow to find frozen food supplies, but Coren's digging equipment was limited. Occasionally Alina could see the frozen contours of cars beneath her feet in places where the wind had worn away the snow. Frozen drivers and passengers could be defrosted and cooked to provide nutrition for Con Leche, but she didn't think Coren would agree to the idea.

Each night Coren slept in the tent, swaddled in blankets while Alina kept watch. Alina didn't think per sleep was very restful. She could hear per tossing and turning in the cold.

"With greater caloric intake, I could keep you warm," Alina commented on the fifth morning. "I can generate external heat."

"If you got more to eat, you mean," Coren said, per breath frosting as per tugged the sled over a frozen obstacle.

"Yes."

"I can't make more food appear out of thin air, and I'm giving you as much as I can. What we've got has to last until we get to where we're going."

Alina continued, "I'm also programmed for sexual activities. Those can raise your body temperature, if you please."

Coren stopped walking. "What did you just say?"

"During my stasis, someone uploaded operational knowledge of several sexual activities. I don't have most of the equipment, but I have two hands, a mouth, a waste port—"

"Okay, stop!" Coren snapped, per face turning red. "I'm not going to start using you like some sex toy. That's disgusting."

Alina tilted her head to mimic curiosity. "Humans have long used mechanical devices for sexual gratification, haven't they? The technician Scott used me for sexual pleasure approximately nine times, according to my databank. Mr. Crowther kissed me. Mrs. Labonte would shower with me and bring herself to—"

"Stop talking!" Coren said. "People shouldn't be doing things with a pregnant robot."

"But it made them happy. Isn't happiness a priority?"

"No. Not with everything. It doesn't mean people have the right to just do anything they want to you."

"Humans often used machines to make them happy," Alina said. "Do you find me unattractive? I was told that I was beautiful."

Coren's cheeks flushed even deeper. "Yes, you're pretty. It's not that."

A shout from somewhere down the road interrupted their conversation. Two figures in bulky gray parkas were coming their way. As they drew nearer, Alina saw that they were both six feet tall, wore cross-country skis, and had rifles slung on their backs. One raised his hand. "Hey there!"

Coren said, "Let me handle them," and put on a blank expression. Alina mimicked it.

The strangers stopped several feet away. They were both bearded men, Caucasian, perhaps in their mid-thirties. Larger than Coren. Stronger, too. Their clothes were dirty, but in the past someone had patched the elbows of their coats. They smelled like people who had not had the luxury of a bath or shower in a long time. Coren smelled the same way.

"I'm Gordon and this is Lewis," said the one who had hailed them. He was slightly shorter than his friend, with darker hair, not smiling, but friendly enough. "You ladies passing through?"

Alina wondered what they saw in Coren to address her as female. Lewis remained silent, but his gaze swept from Alina's face to her boots and back up again in a way that remind her of Scott the technician.

"Passing through to meet up with some family," Coren said, per gaze frank and voice flat. "How's the road?"

Gordon replied, "Passable. But the barometer back in town's dropping. Won't be safe to be sleeping outdoors tonight, not with a storm on the way."

"We're prepared for rough weather," Coren said.

"Sure you are. But we've got twenty men, thirty women, bunch of kids, some extra space to bed down," Gordon replied. "Bunch of folk trying to get by. Trust me, no one's after your virtue."

"I'm sure that's true," Coren said. "Thanks, anyway."

Lewis was still eyeing Alina. She considered the possibility that the town had food supplies that would benefit Con Leche, or that they might have communication equipment that would reach Dan and Mark. She knew that evaluating honesty was a gap in her programming; how humans judged deceit was a mystery to her.

"Is your town far?" Alina asked.

Coren's shoulders tensed. Gordon turned his gaze toward Alina, eyebrows lifting a little. "About a mile. We don't have much, but we share."

"Share or barter?" Alina asked. "Give freely, or take something in return?"

"Doesn't matter," Coren said firmly. "We're fine on our own."

"Not unless you plan to turn into a popsicle," Lewis said, his voice rougher than the other man's. He stopped looking at Alina and instead stomped his boots in the snow. "Last storm killed a man and his woman heading south. We found their bodies in their tent, frozen together."

Coren shook per head. "We've got supplies. Thanks again for the offer."

Per tugged the sled back into motion and started off. Gordon caught Alina's arm and said, frowning, "Don't be foolish. You'll die out here, just because your friend is stubborn." He seemed sincere, but his presumptions were wrong.

"I won't die," she said. "Please release my arm."

"Idiot women," he muttered, and let her go.

As she walked after Coren she listened for any sounds that the men were following. That was a lesson that Professor Sauter had impressed upon her. As the physically weaker sex, women had to always be prepared that a stranger could be a threat, and that even familiar men could suddenly turn violent. But no footsteps followed them, no hands grabbed out. When she glanced over her shoulder, she saw that Gordon and Lewis had continued up the road.

"Why didn't you trust them?" Alina said when she caught up to Coren.

Coren snorted. "Never trust anyone. Their 'town' might turn out to be nothing more than a shack, and we'd be dead or worse by sundown. They might keep you around, all pretty and indestructible, but me? Slit my throat, if I'm lucky."

By early afternoon, however, it was clear that the men had not lied about the weather. The temperature dropped fast as the promised storm rolled in. Coren stopped their hike early. They had just finished setting up the tent when the first fat flakes of snow started spitting down. Dinner was hurried, more tinned meat and hard biscuits, and when Coren crawled into the tent per said, "You better get in here with me. Don't want the wind blowing you away."

Once inside, the only practical thing to do was for Alina to crawl into a nest of blankets with per. They both kept their coats and boots on, and Coren used a thermal blanket to make a protective peak over their faces. It was still daylight, though the light had dimmed with the steadily increasing snow. The temperature dropped rapidly, like invisible ice water flooding over them. Alina felt Coren shiver.

"Are you okay?" Coren asked.

"My womb is keeping Con Leche comfortably warm. How are you?"

Coren's gaze went beyond Alina's shoulder to the wall of the tent. "You could have gone with those men. I couldn't have stopped you. Maybe they did mean well, maybe you could have more food for the baby."

"I know. But you are taking me to Dan and Mark, and that is an important priority."

"I'm not—" Coren didn't finish the sentence. Per shivered again. "It's like ice in here."

Alina studied per thin eyebrows and pointed chin. In all the days they'd been hiking, Coren had not needed to shave per chin or lip line. Alina said, "They inferred you were female. You didn't correct them."

"Doesn't matter what I am," Coren said.

Clumps of snow began to weigh down the roof of the tent. Alina took it upon herself to periodically thump it free. She was careful to not nudge the blankets and let the below-freezing air into Coren's cocoon. The wind started howling, a long ceaseless wail, and Coren broke open one of their remaining chemical packs. The heat didn't last long. As full darkness came on, Alina calculated the outside temperature and Coren's chances of survival given the resources they had. The odds were not in per favor.

"You should know where we're going," Coren said, just when Alina thought per had fallen asleep. "In case we get separated or something."

"Separated how?" Alina asked.

Coren ignored the question. "Follow the old I-80 into Pennsylvania to Scranton. From there, south to Schuylkill. My community's there, living underground in an old coal mine. We still mine the coal, trade it for food down south where they still get some summer. The boss there, he's the one I got you for. He talked about you, how he always wanted to meet you, but he figured you were dead in the Freeze and never would ask anyone to go north for you. I wanted to prove I could do it. That I could get you for him." Alina didn't like how Coren's words were slurring. Slurring was a sign of hypothermia, and the bitter, bitter air wasn't going to get warmer anytime soon. She contemplated several decision trees. More than one path led her to prioritize Coren's survival. She said, "I believe I should consume some food and generate heat for you."

"Ain't you curious?" Coren asked, per eyes closed. "Who wanted to meet you?"

"When you're warmer, I will be curious."

She crawled out from under the blankets to the supplies they'd dragged inside, switched on the lantern, and started eating the hard biscuits, salted jerky, cold stew, uncooked rice, and canned meat and vegetables. She ate as fast her as her throat could pass the food. Two thousand and seven hundred calories total. Her womb stayed steady at ninety-eight degrees Fahrenheit as she began to raise her shell temperature. Back in the blanket nest, she put her hand flat against Coren's face. Coren moaned a little but didn't wake fully. Alina took off her coat and blouse and put them on the pile of blankets.

"I have to remove your clothes now," Alina announced.

Working carefully, she got Coren nearly naked and sidled close to per. Coren moved instinctively toward the warmth of Alina's skin. Alina could feel all the details of per's curves and weight. Coren's breasts, soft and round, pressed against Alina's chest. Coren's penis, also soft, lay between them without a twitch. Alina didn't doze off but she did channel more energy into heat than cognition, and was startled some time later when Coren said, "What the hell?" and pushed her away.

It was still dark out, the wind shrieking and flapping the sides of the tent. Coren sat upright and fumbled with the lantern. The flash of light made per wince, and the icy air had per quickly wrapping perself in the blankets.

"Are you feeling better?" Alina asked.

"What are you doing? Molesting me in my sleep?" Coren demanded.

"You were hypothermic. I am generating heat for you."

"You're generating…" Coren looked bewildered. Then per saw the discarded debris of Alina's dinner. "You ate everything?"

"You needed heat," Alina said.

"You stupid…" Coren rubbed the side of per head. "Damn it, it's too cold to argue with you."

Per abruptly crawled back down into the blankets and pressed against Alina, seeking out every inch of warmth. Miserably per said, "You're too good to pass up. I haven't been this warm in months."

"There is no shame in needing heat," Alina replied, her chin atop Coren's head. "I'm only a machine."

"But it's gross," Coren muttered. 'You could have at least kept your shirt on. Or my shirt on. What'd you have to take everything off for?"

"More effective heat transfer. Are you anxious because I am now aware of your physiology? You obviously have an XXY or XXYY chromosome arrangement."

Coren sighed. "I don't care what you think of my chromosomes. It's gross because you're topless and those are your naked breasts I'm up against and my full name is Coren Crowther and you're my damned grandmother, how's that?"

"I'm not your grandmother," Alina said the next morning, as they packed up the tent under the clear blue sky. A thin layer of ice covered everything, but the storm was well past. "I'm a toaster oven who happened to carry your father's fetus to full term."

Coren was back in per own clothes, disgruntled because there was no food left for breakfast. "You keep saying that. But my dad, he's the one who calls you his robot mom. He told us about you for the first time last year, on his birthday. Who would have guessed it?"

"He runs the community you live in," Alina surmised. "In the coal mine."

"The Crowthers made their money in coal," Coren replied. Per tied down the last strap on the sled. "If the weather's okay, we should be there in about five or six days. Is the baby going to be okay if you don't get any food? You ate everything we had." Alina had already calculated her nutrient levels. "It is not optimal, but I can sustain Con Leche, yes."

"I might not be in such good shape. You might be dragging me on this sled by the time we get there. But it'll be worth it just to see my dad's face."

"Is his gratitude important to you?"

"It's not about gratitude." Coren took up the sled straps. "I've got three older brothers. Big macho men. Everyone looks up to them, all the girls want to—well, you know. Me? Not so much. No one expects me to be as strong or fast or smart. So this way, I could prove myself. I could do something no one else did."

Alina nodded. "I don't have wishes, but if I did, I would wish to see your father. To help you prove your worth, regardless of the size of your testicles or breasts."

Coren winced. "We don't have to talk about that, okay?" Then per face clouded up. "What do you mean, you would wish it?"

"1721 Peach Tree Lane," Alina said. "I must find Con Leche's parents."

"But you—" Coren started. "You can't make it to Georgia on your own. That's weeks away in this terrain and weather. The baby won't last."

"I will find food," Alina told per. "I can trade or barter, I can perform sexual acts with strangers, I can dig up frozen corpses—"

Coren held up both hands. "Stop talking!"

Alina went silent. Coren took a deep breath and said, "The mine is a sure thing. We've got food and we can figure out a way to get your womb open; we've got some men who used to know a lot about computers—"

"Good luck to you, Coren, and thank you for rescuing me." Alina started walking across the snow.

Coren caught up to her and snagged her sleeve. "No, wait! I'm serious. You can't just wander around looking for two men who probably died a long time ago."

"I'm aware there is risk," Alina said. "But I can't change my programming. I must seek the parents and deliver their child."

She resumed walking. The fresh snow was thick and wet, hard on her snowshoes. The icy air made the slightest sound carry clear and wide. She was one tenth of a mile along the road before she heard Coren come after her with the sled. Alina stopped and waited.

"No digging up corpses," Coren said firmly. "No more naked in the middle of the night. If I say run, you say how far. And after the baby's done, you come back to the mine with me. Agree to all that, and I'll go with you. Stupidest thing I've ever done, but I'll go with you."

Alina smiled. "Thank you. Together we can make Dan and Mark very happy."

"We'll see about that," Coren said, not sounding entirely hopeful, and together they trudged toward the blinding white horizon.

(2012)

I AM CRYING ALL INSIDE
Clifford D. Simak

Clifford Donald Simak was born in Millville, Wisconsin in 1904. He wrote more than two dozen novels, several nonfiction science books and hundreds of short stories during a 37-year career as reporter, news editor and science editor for *The Minneapolis Star* and *The Minneapolis Tribune*. He received three Hugo awards, three Nebula Awards, and the Horror Writers Association made him one of three inaugural winners of the Bram Stoker Award for Lifetime Achievement. In novels like *City* (1952) and *Way Station* (1963), Simak transported the Midwestern farmers he knew as a boy to imaginary planets while plaguing them with familiar, earthbound dilemmas. Robots feature prominently in his stories, likeable at first, but often morphing in surprising ways. Simak's favourite recreation was fishing ("the lazy way, lying in a boat and letting them come to me"). He died in Minneapolis in 1988.

I do my job, which is hoeing corn. But I am disturbed by what I hear last night from this Janglefoot. Me and lot of other people hear him. But none of the folk would hear. He careful not to say what he say to us where any folk would hear. It would hurt their feeling.

Janglefoot he is travelling people. He go up and down the land. But he don't go very far. He often back again to orate to us again. Although why he say it more than once I do not understand. He always say the same.

He is Janglefoot because one foot jangle when he walk and he won't let no one fix it. It make him limp but he won't let no one fix it. It is humility he has. As long as he limp and jangle he is humble people and he like humility. He think it is a virtue. He think that it become him.

Smith, who is blacksmith, get impatient with him. Say he could fix the foot. Not as good as mechanic people, although better than not fixing it at all. There is a mechanic people not too far away. They impatient with him too. They think him putting on.

Pure charity of Smith to offer fix the foot. Him have other work. No need to beg for it like some poor people do. He hammer all the time on metal, making into sheet, then send on to mechanic people who use it for repair. Must be very careful keep in good repair. Must do it all ourself. No folk left who know how to do it. Folk left, of course, but too elegant to do it. All genteel who left. Never work at all.

I am hoeing corn and one of house people come down to tell me there is snakes. House people never work outdoors. Always come to us. I ask real snake or moonshine snake and they say real snake. So I lean my hoe on tree and go up hill to house.

Grandpa he is in hammock out on front lawn. Hammock is hung between two trees. Uncle John he is sitting on ground, leaning on one tree. Pa he is sitting on ground, leaning on other tree.

Sam, say Pa, there is snake in back.

So I go around house and there is timber rattler and I pick him up and he is mad at me and hammer me real good. I hunt around and find another rattler and a moccasin and two garter snake. Garter snakes sure don't amount to nothing, but I take them along. I hunt some more but that is all the snakes.

I go down across cornfield and wade creek and way back into swamp. I turn snakes loose. Will take them long time to get back. Maybe not at all.

Then I go back to hoeing. Important to keep patch of corn in shape. No weeds. Carry water when it needs. Soil work up nice and soft. Scare off crows when plant. Scare off coon and deer when corn come into ear. Full time job, for which many thanks. Also is important. George use corn to make the moon. Other patches of corn for food. But mine is use for moon. Me and George is partners. We make real good moonshine. Grandpa and Pa and Uncle John consume it with great happy. Any left over boys can have. But not girls. Girls don't use moonshine.

I do not understand use of food and booze. Grandpa say it taste good. I wonder what is taste. It make Uncle John see snakes. I do not understand that either.

I am hoeing corn when there is sound behind me. I look and there is Joshua. He is reading Bible. He always reading Bible. He make big job of it. Also, he is stepping on my hills of corn. I yell at him and run at him. I hit him with the hoe. He ran out of patch. He know why I hit him. I hit him before. He know better than stepping on the corn. He stand under tree and read. Standing in the shade. That is putting on. Only folk need to stand in shade. People don't.

Hitting him, I break my hoe. I go to Smith to fix. Smith he glad to see me. Always glad to see each other. Smith and me are friend. He drop everything to fix hoe. Know how important corn is. Also do me favor.

We talk of Janglefoot. We agree is wrong the way he speak. He speak heresy. (Smith he tell me that word. Joshua, once he get unmad at me for hitting him, look up how to spell.) We agree, Smith and me, folk are genteel folk, not kind said by Janglefoot. Agree something should be done to Janglefoot. Don't know what to do. We say we think more of it.

George come by. Say he need me. Folk out of drinking likker. So I go with him while Smith is fixing hoe. George he has nice still, real neat and clean. Good capacity. Also try hard to age moonshine but never able to. Folk use it up too fast. He have four five-gallon jugs. We each take two and walk to house.

We stop at hammock where three still are. Tell us leave one jug there, take three to woodshed, put away, bring back some glasses. We do. We pour out glasses of moonshine for Grandpa and Pa. Uncle John he says never mind no glass for him, just put jug beside him. We do, leaving it uncork. Uncle John reach in pocket and bring out little rubber hose. Put one end in jug, other end in mouth. He lean back against tree and start sucking.

They make elegant picture. Grandpa look peaceful. Rocking in hammock with big glass of moon balance on his chest. We happy to see them happy. We go back to work. Smith has hoe fix and very sharp. It handle good. I thank him.

He say he still confuse at Janglefoot. Janglefoot claim he read what he say. In old record. Found record in old city far away. Smith ask if I know what city is. I say I don't. We more confuse than ever. For that matter, don't know what record is. Sound important, though.

I am hoeing corn when the Preacher pass and stop. Joshua gone somewhere. I tell him should have come sooner, Joshua standing under tree, reading Bible. He say Joshua only reading Bible, he interpret it. I ask him what interpret is. He tell me. I ask him how to spell it. He tell me. He know I try to write. He is helpful people. But pompous.

Night come on and moon is late to rise. Can no longer hoe for lack of seeing. So lean hoe against tree. Go to still to help George now making moonshine. George is glad of help. He running far behind.

I wonder to him why Janglefoot say same thing over and over. He say is repetition. I ask him repetition. He not sure. Say he think you say thing often enough people will believe it. Say folk use it in olden day. Make other folk believe thing that isn't so.

I ask him what he know of olden day. He say not very much. He say he should remember, but he doesn't. I should remember too, but I can't remember. Too long ago. Too much happen since. It is not important except for what Janglefoot is saying.

George has good fire burning under still and it shine on us. We stand around and watch. Make good feeling in the gizzard. Owl talk long way off in swamp. Do not know why fire feel good. No need of warm. Do not know why owl make one feel lonesome. I no lonesome. Got George right here beside me. There is so many things I do not know. What city is or record. What taste is. What olden day is like. Happy though. Do not need to understand for happy.

People come from house, running fast. Say Uncle John is sick. Say he need doctor. Say he no longer seeing snakes. Seeing now blue alligator. With bright pink spots. Uncle John must be awful sick. Is no blue alligator. Not with bright pink spots.

George say he go to house to help, me run for Doc. George and house people leave, going very fast. I leave for Doc, also going fast.

Finally find Doc in swamp. He has candle lantern and is digging root. He always digging root. Great one for root and bark. He make stuff out of them for repairing folk. He is folk mechanic.

He standing in muck, up to knee. He cover with mud. He is filthy people. But he feel bad, hearing Uncle John is sick. Do not like blue alligator. Next he say is purple elephant and that is worst of all.

We run, both of us. I hold lantern at alligator hole while Doc wash mud off him. Never do to let folk seeing him filthy. We go to hut where Doc keep root and bark. He get some of it and we run for house. Moon has come up now, but we keep lantern. It help moonlight some.

We come to foot of hill with house on top of hill. All lawn between foot of hill and house. All lawn except for trees that hold up hammock. Hammock still is there, but empty. It blow back and forth in breeze. House stand up high and white. Windows in it shining.

Grandpa sit on big long porch that is in front of house, with white pillars to hold up roof. He sit in rocking chair. He rock back and forth. Another rocking chair beside him. He is only one around. Can see no one else. Inside of house women folk is making cries. Through tall window I can see inside. Big thing house people call chandelier hang from ceiling. Made of glass. Many candles in it. Candles all are burning. Glass look pretty in light. Furniture in room gleam with light. All is clean and polish. House people work hard to keep it clean and polish. Take big pride.

We run up steps to porch.

Grandpa say, you come too late. My son John is dead.

I do not understand this dead. When folk dead put them into ground. Say words over them. Put big stone at their head. Back of house is special place for dead. Lot of big stones standing there. Some new. Some old. Some so old cannot read lettering that say who is under them.

Doc run into house. To make sure Grandpa say right, perhaps. I stay on porch, unknowing what to do. Feel terrible sad. Don't know why I do. Except knowing dead is bad. Maybe because Grandpa seem so sad.

Grandpa say to me, Sam sit down and talk.

I do not sit, I tell him. People always stand.

It was outrage of him to ask it. He know custom. He know as well as I do people do not sit with folk.

God damn it to hell, he say, forget your stubborn pride. Sitting is not bad. I do it all the time. Bend yourself and sit.

In that chair, he say, pointing to one beside him.

I look at chair. I wonder will it hold me. It is built for folk. People heavier than folk. Have no wish to break a chair with weight. Take much time to make one. Carpenter people work for long to make one.

But I think no skin off my nose. Skin off Grandpa's nose. He the one that tell me.

So I square around so I hit the chair and bend myself and sit. Chair creak, but hold. I settle into it. Sitting feel good. I rock a little. Rocking feel good. Grandpa and me sit, looking out on lawn. Lawn is real pretty. Moonlight on it. First lawn and then some trees and after trees cornfield and other fields. Far away owl talk in swamp. Coon whicker. Fox bark long way off.

It do beat hell, say Grandpa, how man can live out his life, doing nothing, then die of moonshine drinking.

You sure of moon, I ask. I hate to hear Grandpa blaming moonshine. George and me, we make real good moonshine.

Grandpa say, it couldn't be nothing else. Only moonshine give blue alligator with bright pink spots.

No purple elephant, so say Grandpa.

I wonder what elephant might be. So much that I don't know.

Sam, say Grandpa, we are a sorry lot. Never had no chance. Neither you nor us. Ain't none of us no good. We folk sit around all day and never do a thing. Hunt a little, maybe. Fish a little. Play cards. Drink likker. Feel real energetic, maybe I'll play some horseshoe. Should be out doing something good and big. But we never are. While we live we don't amount to nothing. When we die we don't amount to nothing. We're just no God damn good.

He went on rocking, bitter. I don't like the way he talk. He feel bad, sure, but no excuse to talk the way he was. Elegant folk like him shouldn't talk that way. Lay in hammock all day long, shouldn't talk that way. Balance moonshine on his chest, shouldn't talk that way. I uncomfortable. Wish to get away, but impolite to leave.

Down at bottom of hill, where lawn begin, I see many people. Standing, looking up at house. Pretty soon come slow up lawn and look closer at house. Saying nothing, just standing. Paying their respect. Letting folk know that they sorrow too.

We never was nothing but white trash, say Grandpa. I can see it now. Seen it for long, long time but could never say it. I can say it now. We live in swamp in houses falling down. Falling down because we got no gumption to take care of them. Hunt and fish a little. Trap a little. Farm a little. Sit around and cuss because we ain't got nothing.

Grandpa, I say. I want him to stop. I don't want to hear. Don't want him to go on saying what Janglefoot been saying.

But he pay me no attention. He go on saying.

Then, long, long ago, he say, they learn to go in space very, very fast. Faster than the light. Much faster than the light. They find other worlds. Better than the Earth. Much better worlds than this. Lot of ships to go in. Take little time to go there. So everybody go. Everyone but us. Folk like us, all over the world, are left behind. Smart ones go. Rich ones go. Hard workers go. We are left behind. We aren't worth the taking. No one want us on this world. Have no use for us on others. They leave us behind, the misfits, the loafers, the poor, the crippled, the stupid. All over the world these kind are left behind. So when they all are gone, we move from shacks to houses the rich and smart ones lived in. No one to stop us from doing it. All of them are gone. They don't care what we do. Not any more they don't. We live in better houses, but we do not change. There is no use to change even if we could. We got you to take care of us. We have got it made. We don't do a God damn thing. We don't even learn to read. When words are read over my son's grave, one of you will read them, for we do not know how to read.

Grandpa, I say. Grandpa. Grandpa. Grandpa. I feel crying all inside. He had done it now. He had took away the elegant. Took away the pride. He do what Janglefoot never could.

Now, say Grandpa, don't take on that way. You got no reason to be prideful either. You and us we are the same. Just no God damn good. There were others of you and they took them along. But you they left behind. Because you were out of date. Because you were slow and awkward. Because you were heaps of junk. Because they had no need of you. They wouldn't give you room. They left both you and us because neither of us was worth the room we took.

Doc came out of the door fast and purposeful. He say to me I got work for you to do.

All the other people coming up the lawn, saying nothing, slow. I try to get out of chair. I can't. For first time I can't do what I want. My legs is turned to water.

Sam, say Grandpa, I am counting on you.

When he say that, I get up. I go down steps. I go out on lawn. No need for Doc tell me what to do. I done it all before.

I talk to other people. I give jobs to do. You and you dig grave. You and you make coffin. You and you and you and you run to other houses. Tell all the folk Uncle John is dead. Tell them come to funeral. Tell them funeral elegant. Much to cry, much to eat, much to drink. You get Preacher. Tell him fix sermon. You get Joshua to read the Bible. You and you and you go and help George make moonshine. Other folk be coming. Must be elegant.

All done. I walk down the lawn. I think on pride and loss. Elegant is gone. Shiny wonder gone. Pride is gone. Not all pride, however. Kind of pride remain. Hard and bitter pride. Grandpa say Sam sit down and talk. Grandpa say Sam I counting on you. That is pride. Hard pride. Not soft and easy pride like it was before. Grandpa need me.

No one else will know. Grandpa never bring himself again to tell what he tell me. Secret between us. Secret born of sad. Life of others need not change. Go on thinking same. Janglefoot no trouble. No one believe Janglefoot if he talk forever. No one ever know that he tell the truth. Truth is hard to take. No one care except for what we have right now. We go on same.

Except I who know. I never want to know. I never ask to know. I try not to know. But Grandpa won't shut up. Grandpa have to talk. Time come man will die if he cannot talk. Must make clean breast of it. But why to me? Because he love me most, perhaps. That is prideful thing.

But going down the lawn, I crying deep inside.

(1969)

CHANGING PLACES

> "Listen, Josef," the author began, "I think I have an idea for a play."
>
> "What kind?" the painter muttered (he really did mutter, because at the moment he was holding a brush in his mouth). The author told him as concisely as he could.
>
> "Then write it," the painter said, without taking the brush from his mouth or stopping to work on the canvas. His indifference was almost insulting.
>
> "But," the author said, "I don't know what to call those artificial workers. I could call them labouri, but that strikes me as a bit literal."
>
> "Then call them robots," the painter muttered, brush in mouth, and carried on painting.

Writing in the newspaper *Lidové noviny* on Christmas Eve 1933, R.U.R. playwright Karel Capek credited his brother Josef, an accomplished painter and poet, with coining the word "robot" from the Slavic word *robota*, meaning "drudgery". More specifically, *robota* is the unpaid labor a vassal was obliged to perform for his feudal lord.

At its birth, then, the robot was more than just a little bit human. In this section, especially, I've played fast and loose with the definition of what a robot is, in order to explore what it might feel like to actually be a robot. (Purists might baulk, but I had to decide: was I trying for an anthology of good robot stories, or a good anthology about robots? I chose the latter path.)

The fear that we are already half-way to robots ourselves powers the powerful strain of uncanny running through robot literature. Chris Beckett's "The Turing Test" (2002) is a little masterpiece of stillness and focus, while Rich Larson's seemingly flippant "Masked" shows the same human-robot identity crisis reflected in, and exploited by, social media.

The wonder is not that we can be persuaded into behaving like robots. The wonder is that we don't behave like robots all the time. Being human is hard work, after all, and it's only by us constantly reinforcing each other's humanity that humanity continues to exist at all. (Karel's brother Josef, the man who coined the word "robot", died in the Bergen-Belsen concentration camp in 1945.) This is a big subject indeed for fiction, and lends itself to epic treatment. E. M. Forster's "The Machine Stops" (1909) only becomes more topical as it ages.

Intimate and funny approaches to the "human robot" idea include Ian McDonald's "Nanonauts! In Battle With Tiny Death-Subs!" (2014) – as sly a portrait of personal inadequacy as one could wish for, and a delicious takedown of science fiction's linguistic excesses – while Nicholas Sheppard's "Satisfaction" (2018) is wry tale of a man's infatuation with the latest consumer device.

Surrounded by dull, bland, easy-going robot companions, will we come to expect less of other people? Assisted, cared for, and seduced by machines, will we lower our expectations around concepts like "conversation", "care", "companionship" and "love"?

The pioneering psychologist William James argued that what we want from a lover is that they really love us, and not simply behave as if they did. I hope that's true. If we come to believe that the soul is nothing more than behaviour, then of course a robot will become just as good as a person – a future that Robert Sheckley explores in "The Robot Who Looked Like Me" (1973).

TRANSFORMER

GPT-2

Built by Adam King, **Transformer** (*https://talktotransformer.com*) is an online text generator powered by GPT-2, a machine-learning model created by the San Francisco-based non-profit OpenAI. GPT-2 was trained simply to predict the next word in a text, but on the way – and entirely unprompted – it picked up some basic translation skills and learned how to answer queries. Due to their concerns about malicious applications of the technology, OpenAI are not releasing the trained model. The words in bold below are the opening lines of Isaac Asimov's short story "Liar!". The rest is by Transformer.

Alfred Lanning lit his cigar carefully, but the tips of his fingers were trembling slightly. His gray eyebrows hunched low as he spoke between puffs with his eyes closed, the heat of his cigar rising to a boil. "I don't think it will get rid of me though, because you aren't the kind of person who would say such things."

A chill ran down Charles' spine as he realized that he must have gone too far. "That's true," she said simply. "I don't really need your help right now."

Charles sighed. "I mean I won't go anywhere for an hour if you don't want me, but if you don't do something then I won't bother you any longer." He turned to shake away the smoke as he turned back to take out his bottle – the smell in his nostrils was the same as ever before.

Sitting down to talk Charles noticed that there were no tears yet on his face. "You seem pretty tired. I do feel better though. Maybe my mind won't be too exhausted after all." He could still hear her voice through his headphones, albeit muffled – his heart and lungs were beginning to slow down, just like he had the previous day.

Charles glanced quickly at the clock. "I think I feel kind of tired…"

(2019)

THE MAN
Paul McAuley

Paul J. McAuley (born 1955) is a British botanist and science fiction writer. *Four Hundred Billion Stars*, his first novel, won the Philip K. Dick Award in 1988. He's since written more than twenty novels, several collections of short stories, a *Doctor Who* novella, and a BFI Film Classic monograph on Terry Gilliam's film *Brazil*. The story here later found its way into the novel *Something Coming Through* (2015), according to Alastair Reynolds "the freshest take on first contact and interstellar exploration in many years". His latest novel, *Austral*, set in post-global warming Antarctica, was published in 2017.

He came to Cho Ziyi at night, in the middle of a flux storm.

It was as dark as it ever got in the sunset zone. Low, fast-moving clouds closed off the sky. Howling winds drove waves onshore and blew horizontal streamers of snow into the forest, where the vanes of spin trees madly clattered and coronal discharges jumped and crackled. Ziyi was hunkered down in her cabin, watching an ancient movie about a gangster romance in Hong Kong's fabled Chungking Mansions. A fire breathed in the stone hearth and her huskies, Jung and Cheung, sprawled in a careless tangle on the borometz-hide rug. The dogs suddenly lifting their heads, the youngest, Cheung, scrambling to his feet and barking, something striking the door. Once, twice.

Ziyi froze the movie and sat still, listening. A slight, severe woman in her late sixties, dressed in jeans and a flannel shirt, white hair scraped back in a long ponytail, jumping just a little when there was another thump. It wouldn't be the first time that an indricothere or some other big dumb beast had trampled down a section of fence and blundered into the compound. She crossed to the window and unbolted the shutter. Pressed her cheek against the cold glass, squinted sideways, saw a dim pale figure on the raised porch. A naked man, arm raised, striking the door with the flat of his hand.

The two dogs stood behind her, alert and as anxious. Cheung whined when she looked at him.

"It's only a man," Ziyi said. "Be quiet and let me think."

He was in some kind of trouble, no question. A lost traveller, an accident on the road. But who would travel through a storm like this, and where were his clothes? She remembered the bandits who'd hit a road train a couple of years ago. Perhaps they'd come back. He had managed to escape, but he couldn't have gone far, not like that, not in weather like this. They might be here any minute.

Or perhaps they were already out there, waiting for her to open the door. But she knew she couldn't leave him to die.

She fetched a blanket and lifted her short-barrelled shotgun from its wall pegs, unbolted the door, cracked it open. Snow skirled in. The naked man stared at her, dull-eyed. He was tall, pale-skinned. Snow was crusted in his shock of black hair. He didn't seem to notice the cold. Staring blankly at her, as if being confronted by an old woman armed with a shotgun was no surprise at all.

Ziyi told him to move off the porch, repeating the request in each of her half-dozen languages. He seemed to understand English, and took a step backwards. Snow whirled around him and snow blew across the compound, out of darkness and back into darkness. Fat sparks snapped high in a stand of spike trees, like the apparatus in that old Frankenstein movie. Ziyi saw the gate in the fence was open, saw footprints crossing the deep snow, a single set.

"Are you hurt? What happened to you?" His face was as blank as a mask.

She lofted the blanket towards him. It struck his chest and fell to his feet. He looked at it, looked at her. She was reminded of the cow her grandmother had kept, in the smallholding that had been swallowed by one of Shanghai's new satellite towns in the last gasp of frantic expansion before the Spasm.

"Go around the side of the cabin," she told him. "To your left. There's a shed. The door is unlocked. You can stay there. We'll talk in the morning."

The man picked up the blanket and plodded off around the corner of the cabin. Ziyi bolted the door and opened the shutters at each of the cabin's four small windows and looked out and saw only blowing snow.

She sat by the fire for a long time, wondering who he was, what had happened to him. Wondering—because no ordinary man could have survived the storm for very long—if he was a thing of the Jackaroo. A kind of avatar that no one had seen before. Or perhaps she was some species of alien creature as yet undiscovered, that by an accident of evolution resembled a man. One of the Old Ones, one of the various species which had occupied Yanos before it had been gifted to the human race, woken from a sleep of a thousand centuries. Only the Jackaroo knew what the Old Ones had looked like. They had all died out or disappeared long ago. They could have looked like anything, so why not like a man? A man who spoke, or at least understood, English…

At last she pulled on her parka and took her shotgun and, accompanied by Jung and Cheung, went outside. The storm was beginning to blow itself out. The snow came in gusts now and the dark was no longer uniform. To the south-east, Sauron's dull coal glimmered at the horizon.

Snow was banked up on one side of the little plastic utility shed, almost to the roof. Inside, the man lay asleep between stacks of logs and drums of diesel oil, wrapped in the blanket so that only his head showed. He did not stir when Cheung barked and nipped at the hem of Ziyi's parka, trying to drag her away.

She closed the door of the shed and went back to her cabin, and slept.

When she woke, the sky was clear of cloud and Sauron's orange light tangled long shadows across the snow. A spin tree had fallen down just outside the fence; the vanes of all the others, thousands upon thousands, spun in wind that was now no more than the usual wind, blowing from sunside to darkside. Soon, the snow would melt and she would go down to the beach and see what had been cast up.

But first she had to see to her strange guest.

She took him a canister of pork hash. He was awake, sitting with the blanket fallen to his waist. After Ziyi mimed what he should do, he ate a couple of mouthfuls, although he used his fingers rather than the spoon. His feet were badly cut and there was a deep gash in his shin. Smaller cuts on his face and hands, like old knife wounds. All of them clean and pale, like little mouths. No sign of blood. She thought of him stumbling through the storm, through the lashing forest...

He looked up at her. Sharp blue eyes, with something odd about the pupils—they weren't round, she realised with a clear cold shock, but were edged with small triangular indentations, like cogs.

He couldn't or wouldn't answer her questions.

"Did the Jackaroo do this to you? Are you one of them? Did they make you?" It was no good.

She brought him clothes. A sweater, jeans, an old pair of wellington boots with the toes and heels slit so they would fit his feet. He followed her about the compound as she cleared up trash that had blown in, and the two huskies followed both of them at a wary distance. When she went down to the beach, he came too.

Snow lay in long rakes on the black sand and meltwater ran in a thousand braided channels to the edge of the sea. Sea foam floated on the wind-blown waves, trembled amongst rocks. Flecks of colour flashed here and there: flotsam from the factory.

The man walked down to the water's edge. He seemed fascinated by the half-drowned ruins that stretched towards the horizon, hectares of spires and broken walls washed by waves, silhouetted against Sauron's fat disc, which sat where it always sat, just above the sea's level horizon.

Like all the worlds gifted by the Jackaroo, Yanos orbited close to the hearth fire of its M-class red dwarf sun; unlike the others, it had never been spun up. Like Earth's moon, it was tidally locked. One face warm and lighted, with a vast and permanent rainstorm at the equator, where Sauron hung directly overhead; the other a starlit icecap, and perpetual winds blowing from warm and light to cold and dark.

Human settlements were scattered through the forests of the twilight belt where the weather was less extreme.

As the man stared out at the ruins, hair tangling in warm wind blowing off the sea, maybe listening, maybe not, Ziyi explained that people called it the factory, although they didn't really know what it was, or who had built it.

"Stuff comes from it, washes up here. Especially after a storm. I collect it, take it into town, sell it. Mostly base plastics, but sometimes you find nice things that are worth more. You help me, okay? You earn your keep."

But he stayed where he was, staring out at the factory ruins, while she walked along the driftline, picking up shards and fragments. While she worked, she wondered what he might be worth, and who she could sell him to. Not to Sergey Polzin, that was for damn sure. She'd have to contact one of the brokers in the capital... This man, he was a once-in-a-lifetime find. But how could she make any kind of deal without being cheated?

Ziyi kept checking on him, showed him the various finds. After a little while, straightening with one hand in the small of her aching back, she saw that he had taken off his clothes and stood with his arms stretched out, his skin warmly tinted in the level sunlight.

She filled her fat-tyred cart and told him it was time to put on his clothes and go.

She mimed what she wanted him to do until he got the idea and dressed and helped her pull the cart back to the cabin. He watched her unload her harvest into one of the storage bins she'd built from the trimmed trunks of spike trees. She'd almost finished when he scooped up a handful of bright fragments and threw them in and looked at her as if for approval.

Ziyi remembered her little girl, in a sunlit kitchen on a faraway world. Even after all these years, the memory still pricked her heart.

"You're a quick learner," she said.

He smiled. Apart from those strange starry pupils and his pale, poreless skin, he looked entirely human.

"Come into the cabin," she said, weightless with daring. "We'll eat."

He didn't touch the food she offered; but sipped a little water, holding the tumbler in both hands. As far as she knew, he hadn't used the composting toilet. When she'd shown it to him and explained how it worked, he'd shrugged the way a small child would dismiss as unimportant something she couldn't understand.

They watched a movie together, and the two dogs watched them from a corner of the room. When it had finished, Ziyi gave the man an extra blanket and a rug and locked him in the shed for the night.

So it went the next day, and the days after that.

The man didn't eat. Sometimes he drank a little water. Once, on the beach, she found him nibbling at a shard of plastic. Shocked, she'd dashed it from his hand and he'd flinched away, clearly frightened.

Ziyi took a breath. Told herself that he was not really a man, took out a strip of dried borometz meat and took a bite and chewed and smiled and rubbed her stomach. Picked up the shard of plastic and held it out to him. "This is your food? This is what you are made of?"

He shrugged.

She talked to him, as they worked. Pointed to a flock of wind skimmers skating along far out to sea, told him they were made by the factory. "Maybe like you, yes?" Named the various small shelly tick tock things that scuttled along the margins of the waves, likewise made by the factory. She told him the names of the trees that stood up beyond the tumble of boulders a long the top of the beach. Told him how spin trees generated sugars from air and water and electricity. Warned him to avoid the bubbleweed that sent long scarlet runners across the black sand, told him that it was factory stuff and its tendrils moved towards him because they were heat-seeking.

"Let them touch, they stick little fibres like glass into your skin. Very bad."

He had a child's innocent curiosity, scrutinising tick tocks and scraps of plastic with the same frank intensity, watching with rapt attention a group of borometz grazing on rafts of waterweed cast up by the storm.

"The world is dangerous," Ziyi said. "Those borometz look very cute, harmless balls of fur, but they carry ticks that have poisonous bites. And there are worse things in the forest. Wargs, sasquatch. Worst of all are people. You stay away from them."

She told herself that she was keeping her find safe from people like Sergey Polzin, who would most likely try to vivisect him to find out how he worked, or keep him alive while selling him off finger by finger, limb by limb. She no longer planned to sell him to a broker, had vague plans about contacting the university in the capital. They wouldn't pay much, but they probably wouldn't cut him up, either…

She told him about her life. Growing up in Hong Kong. Her father the surgeon, her mother the biochemist. The big apartment, the servants, the trips abroad. Her studies in Vancouver University, her work in a biomedical company in Shanghai. Skipping over her marriage and her daughter, that terrible day when the global crisis had finally peaked in the Spasm. Seoul had been vapourised by a North Korean atomic missile; Shanghai had been hit by an Indian missile; two dozen cities around the world had been likewise devastated. Ziyi had been on a flight to Seoul; the plane had made an emergency landing at a military airbase and she'd made her way back to Shanghai by train, by truck, on foot. And discovered that her home was gone; the entire neighbourhood had been levelled. She'd spent a year working in a hospital in a refugee camp, trying and failing to find her husband and her daughter and her parents… It was too painful to talk about that; instead, she told the man about the day the Jackaroo made themselves known, the big ship suddenly appearing over the ruins of Shanghai, big ships appearing above all the major cities.

"The Jackaroo gave us the possibility of a new start. New worlds. Many argued against this, to begin with. Saying that we needed to fix everything on Earth. Not just the Spasm, but global warming, famines, all the rest. But many others disagreed. They won the lottery or bought tickets off winners and went up and out. Me, I went to work for the UN, the United Nations, as a translator," Ziyi said.

Thirty years, in Cape Town, in Berlin, in Brasilia. Translating for delegates at meetings and committees on the treaties and deals with the Jackaroo. She'd married again, lost her husband to cancer.

"I earned a lottery ticket because of my work, and I left the Earth and came here. I thought I could make a new start. And I ended up here, an old woman picking up alien scrap on an alien beach thousands of light years from home. Sometimes I think that I am dead. That my family survived the Spasm but I died, and all this is a dream of my last second of life. What does that make you, if it's true?"

The man listened to her, but gave no sign that he understood.

One day, she found a precious scrap of superconducting plastic. It wasn't much bigger than her thumbnail, transparent, shot through with silvery threads.

"This is worth more than ten cartloads of base plastic," she told the man. "Electronics companies use it in their smartphones and slates. No one knows how to make it, so they pay big money. We live off this for two, three weeks."

She didn't think he'd understand, but he walked up and down the tide line all that day and found two more slivers of superconductor, and the next day found five. Amazing. Like the other prospectors who mined the beach and the ruins in the forests, she'd tried and failed to train her dogs to sniff out the good stuff, but the man was like a trufflehound. Single-minded, sharp-eyed, eager to please.

"You did good," she told him. "I think I might keep you."

She tried to teach him tai chi exercises, moving him into different poses. His smooth cool skin. No heartbeat that she could find. She liked to watch him trawl along the beach, the dogs trotting alongside him. She'd sit on the spur of a tree trunk and watch until the man and the dogs disappeared from sight, watch as they came back. He'd come to her with his hands cupped in front, shyly showing her the treasures he'd found.

After ten days, the snow had melted and the muddy roads were more or less passable again, and Ziyi drove into town in her battered Suzuki jeep. She'd locked the man in the shed and left Jung and Cheung roaming the compound to guard him.

In town, she sold her load of plastic at the recycling plant, saving the trove of superconducting plastic until last. Unfolding a square of black cloth to show the little heap of silvery stuff to the plant's manager, a gruff Ukranian with radiation scars welting the left side of his face.

"You got lucky," he said.

"I work hard," she said. "How much?"

They settled on a price that was more than the rest of her earnings that year.

The manager had to phone Sergey Polzin to authorise it.

Ziyi asked the manager if he'd heard of any trouble, after the storm. A missing prospector, a bandit attack, anything like that.

"Road got washed out twenty klicks to the east is all I know."

"No one is missing?"

"Sergey might know, I guess. What are you going to do with all that cash, Ziyi?"

"Maybe I buy this place one day. I'm getting old. Can't spend all my life trawling for junk on the beach."

Ziyi visited the hardware store, exchanged scraps of gossip with the store owner and a couple of women who were mining the ruins out in the forest. None of them had heard anything about a bandit attack, or an accident on the coast road. In the internet cafe, she bought a mug of green tea and an hour on one of the computers.

Searched the local news for a bandit attack, some prospector caught in the storm, a plane crash, found nothing. No recent reports of anyone missing or vehicles found abandoned.

She sat back, thinking. So much for her theory that the man was some kind of Jackaroo spy who'd been travelling incognito and had got into trouble when the storm hit. She widened her search. Here was a child who had wandered into the forest. Here was a family, their farm discovered deserted, doors smashed down, probably by sasquatch. Here was the road train that had been attacked by bandits, two years ago. Here was a photograph of the man.

Ziyi felt cold, then hot. Looked around at the cafe's crowded tables. Clicked on the photo to enlarge it.

It was him. It was the man.

His name was Tony Michaels. Twenty-eight years old, a petrochemist. One of three people missing, presumed taken by the bandits after they killed everyone else. Leaving behind a wife and two children, in the capital.

A family. He'd been human, once upon a time.

Someone in the cafe laughed; Ziyi heard voices, the chink of cutlery, the hiss of the coffee urn, felt suddenly that everyone was watching her. She sent the photo of Tony Michaels to the printer, shut down the browser, snatched up the printout and left.

She was unlocking her jeep when Sergey Polzin called out to her. The man stepping towards her across the slick mud, dressed in his usual combat gear, his pistol at his hip. He owned the recycling plant, the internet cafe, and the town's only satellite dish, and acted as if he was the town's unelected mayor. Greeting visitors and showing off the place as if it was something more than a squalid street of shacks squatting amongst factory ruins. Pointing out where the water treatment plant would be, talking about plans for concreting the airstrip, building a hospital, a school, that would never come to anything.

Saying to Ziyi, "Heard you hit a big find."

"The storm washed up a few things," Ziyi said, trying to show nothing while Sergey studied her. Trying not to think about the printout folded into the inside pocket of her parka, over her heart.

He said, "I also heard you wanted to report trouble."

"I was wondering how everyone was, after the storm."

He gazed at her for a few moments, then said, "Any trouble, anything unusual, you come straight to me. Understand?"

"Completely."

When Ziyi got back to the cabin she sat the man down and showed him the printout, then fetched her mirror from the wall and held it in front of him, angling it this way and that, pointing to it, pointing to the paper.

"You," she said. "Tony Michaels. You."

He looked at the paper and the mirror, looked at the paper again and ran his fingertips over his smooth face. He didn't need to shave, and his hair was exactly as long as it was in the photo.

"You," she said.

That was who he had been. But what was he now?

The next day she coaxed him into the jeep with the two dogs, and drove west along the coast road, forest on one side and the sea stretching out to the horizon on the other, until she spotted the burnt-out shells of the road train, overgrown with great red drapes of bubbleweed. The dogs jumped off and nosed around; the man slowly climbed out, looked about him, taking no especial notice of the old wreckage.

She had pictured it in her head. His slow recognition. Leading her to the place where he'd hidden or crawled away to die from grievous wounds. The place that had turned him or copied him or whatever it was the factory had done.

Instead, he wandered off to a patch of sunlight in the middle of the road and stood there until she told him they were going for a walk.

They walked a long way, slowly spiralling away from the road. There were factory ruins here, as in most parts of the forest. Stretches of broken wall. Chains of cubes heaved up and broken, half-buried, overgrown by the arched roots of spine trees, and thatches of copperberry and bubbleweed, but the man seemed no more interested in them than in the wreckage of the road train.

"You were gone two years. What happened to you?"

He shrugged.

At last, they walked back to the road. The sun stood at the horizon, as always, throwing shadows over the road. The man walked towards the patch of sunlight where he'd stood before, and kept walking.

Ziyi and the two dogs followed. Through a thin screen of trees to the edge of a sheer drop. Water far below, lapping at rocks. No, not rocks. Factory ruins.

The man stared down at patches of waterweed rising and falling on waves that broke around broken walls.

Ziyi picked up a stone and threw it out beyond the cliff edge. "Was that what happened? You were running from the bandits, it was dark, you ran straight out over the edge…"

The man made a humming sound. He was looking at Sauron's fat orange disc now, and after a moment he closed his eyes and stretched out his arms.

Ziyi walked along the cliff edge, looking for and failing to find a path. The black rock plunged straight down, a sheer drop cut by vertical crevices that only an experienced climber might use to pick a route down. She tried to picture it. The road train stopping because fallen trees had blocked the road. Bandits appearing when the crew stepped down, shooting them, ordering the passengers out, stripping them of their clothes and belongings, shooting them one by one. Bandits didn't like to leave witnesses. One man breaking free, running into the darkness. Running through the trees, running blindly, wounded perhaps, definitely scared, panicked. Running straight out over the cliff edge. If the fall hadn't killed him, he would have drowned. And his body had washed into some active part of the factory, and it had fixed him. No, she thought. It had duplicated him. Had it taken two years? Or had he been living in some part of the factory, out at sea, until the storm had washed him away and he'd been cast up on the beach…

The man had taken off his clothes and stood with his arms out and his eyes closed, bathing in level orange light. She shook him until he opened his eyes and smiled at her, and she told him it was time to go.

Ziyi tried and failed to teach the man to talk. "You understand me. So why can't you tell me what happened to you?"

The man humming, smiling, shrugging.

Trying to get him to write or draw was equally pointless.

Days on the beach, picking up flotsam; nights watching movies. She had to suppose he was happy. Her constant companion. Her mystery. She had long ago given up the idea of selling him.

Once, Ziyi's neighbour, Besnik Shkelyim, came out of the forest while the man was searching the strandline. Ziyi told Besnik he was the son of an old friend in the capital, come to visit for a few weeks. Besnik seemed to accept the lie. They chatted about the weather and sasquatch sightings and the latest finds. Besnik did most of the talking. Ziyi was anxious and distracted, trying not to look towards the man, praying that he wouldn't wander over. At last, Besnik said that he could see that she was busy, he really should get back to his own work.

"Bring your friend to visit, sometime. I show him where real treasure is found." Ziyi said that she would, of course she would, watched Besnik walk away into the darkness under the trees, then ran to the man, giddy and foolish with relief and told him how well he'd done, keeping away from the stranger.

He hummed. He shrugged.

"People are bad," Ziyi said. "Always remember that."

A few days later she went into town. She needed more food and fuel, and took with her a few of the treasures the man had found. Sergey Polzin was at the recycling plant, and fingered through the stuff she'd brought. Superconductor slivers. A variety of tinker toys, hard little nuggets that changed shape when manipulated. A hand-sized sheet of the variety of plastic in which faint images came and went... It was not one-tenth of what the man had found for her—she'd buried the rest out in the forest—but she knew that she had made a mistake, knew she'd been greedy and foolish.

She tried her best to seem unconcerned as Sergey counted the silvers of superconducting plastic three times. "You've been having much luck, recently," he said, at last.

"The storm must have broken open a cache, somewhere out to sea," she said.

"Odd that no one else has been finding so much stuff."

"If we knew everything about the factory, Sergey Polzin, we would all be rich."

Sergey's smile was full of gold. "I hear you have some help. A guest worker." Besnik had talked about her visitor. Of course he had.

Ziyi trotted out her lie.

"Bring him into town next time," Sergey said. "I'll show him around."

A few days later, Ziyi saw someone watching the compound from the edge of the forest. A flash of sunlight on a lens, a shadowy figure that faded into the shadows under the trees when she walked towards him. Ziyi ran, heard an engine start, saw a red pickup bucket out of the trees and speed off down the track.

She'd only had a glimpse of the intruder, but she was certain that it was the manager of the recycling plant.

She walked back to the compound. The man was facing the sun, naked, arms outstretched. Ziyi managed to get him to put on his clothes, but it was impossible to make him understand that he had to leave. Drive him into the forest, let him go? Yes, and sasquatch or wargs would eat him, or he'd find his way to some prospector's cabin and knock on the door...

She walked him down to the beach, but he followed her back to the cabin. In the end she locked him in the shed.

Early in the afternoon, Sergey Polzin's yellow Humvee came bumping down the track, followed by a UN Range Rover. Ziyi tried to be polite and cheerful, but Sergey walked straight past her, walked into the cabin, walked back out.

"Where is he?"

"My friend's son? He went back to the capital. What's wrong?" Ziyi said to the UN policewoman.

"It's a routine check," the policewoman, Aavert Enger, said.

"Do you have a warrant?"

"You're hiding dangerous technology," Sergey said. "We don't need a warrant."

"I am hiding nothing."

"There has been a report," Aavert Enger said.

Ziyi told her it was a misunderstanding, said that she'd had a visitor, yes, but he had left.

"I would know if someone came visiting from the capital," Sergey said. He was puffed up with self-righteousness. "I also know he was here today. I have a photograph that proves it. And I looked him up on the net, just like you did. You should have erased your cache, by the way. Tony Michaels, missing for two years. Believed killed by bandits. And now he's living here."

"If I could talk to him I am sure we can clear this up," Aavert Enger said.

"He isn't here."

But it was no good. Soon enough, Sergey found the shed was locked and ordered Ziyi to hand over the keys. She refused. Sergey said he'd shoot off the padlock; the policewoman told him that there was no need for melodrama, and used a master key.

Jung and Cheung started to bark as Sergey led the man out. "Tony Michaels," he said to the policewoman. "The dead man Tony Michaels."

Ziyi said, "Look, Sergey Polzin, I'll be straight with you. I don't know who he really is or where he came from. He helps me on the beach. He helps me find things. All the good stuff I brought in, that was because of him. Don't spoil a good thing. Let me use him to find more stuff. You can take a share. For the good of the town. The school you want to build, the water treatment plant in a year, two years, we'll have enough to pay for them…"

But Sergey wasn't listening. He'd seen the man's eyes. "You see?" he said to Aavert Enger. "You see?"

"He is a person," Ziyi said. "Like you and me. He has a wife. He has children."

"And did you tell them you had found him?" Sergey said. "No, of course not. Because he is a dead man. No, not even that. He is a replica of a dead man, spun out in the factory somewhere."

"It is best we take him to town. Make him safe," the policewoman said. The man was looking at Ziyi.

"How much?" Ziyi said to the policewoman. "How much did he offer you?"

"This isn't about money," Sergey said. "It's about the safety of the town."

"Yes. And the profit you'll make, selling him."

Ziyi was shaking. When Sergey started to pull the man towards the vehicles, she tried to get in his way. Sergey shoved at her, she fell down, and suddenly everything happened at once. The dogs, Jung and Cheung, ran at Sergey. He pushed the man away and fumbled for his pistol. Jung clamped his jaws around Sergey's wrist and started to shake him. Sergey sat down hard and Jung held on and Cheung darted in and seized his ankle. Sergey screaming while the dogs pulled in different directions, and Ziyi rolled to her feet and reached into the tangle of man and dogs and plucked up Sergey's pistol and snapped off the safety and turned to the policewoman and told her put up her hands.

"I am not armed," Aavert Enger said. "Do not be foolish, Ziyi." Sergey was screaming at her, telling her to call off her dogs. "It's good advice," Ziyi told the policewoman, "but it is too late."

The pistol was heavy, slightly greasy. The safety was off. The hammer cocked when she pressed lightly on the trigger.

The man was looking at her.

"I'm sorry," she said, and shot him.

The man's head snapped back and he lost his footing and fell in the mud, kicking and spasming. Ziyi stepped up to him and shot him twice more, and he stopped moving.

Ziyi called off the dogs, told Aavert Enger to sit down and put her hands on her head. Sergey was holding his arm. Blood seeped around his fingers. He was cursing her, but she paid him no attention.

The man was as light as a child, but she was out of breath by the time she had dragged him to her jeep. Sergey had left the keys in the ignition of his Humvee.

Ziyi threw them towards the forest as hard as she could, shot out one of the tyres of Aavert Enger's Range Rover, loaded the man into the back of the jeep. Jung and Cheung jumped in, and she drove off.

Ziyi had to stop once, and threw up, and drove the rest of the way with half her attention on the rear-view mirror. When she reached the spot where the road train had been ambushed, she cradled the man in her arms and carried him through the trees. The two dogs followed. When she reached the edge of the cliff her pulse was hammering in her head and she had to sit down. The man lay beside her. His head was blown open, showing layers of filmy plastics. Although his face was untouched you would not mistake him for a sleeper.

After a little while, when she was pretty certain she wasn't going to have a heart attack, she knelt beside him, and closed his eyes, and with a convulsive movement pitched him over the edge. She didn't look to see where he fell. She threw Sergey's pistol after him, and sat down to wait.

She didn't look around when the dogs began to bark. Aavert Enger said, "Where is he?"

"In the same place as Sergey's pistol."

Aavert Enger sat beside her. "You know I must arrest you, Ziyi."

"Of course."

"Actually, I am not sure what you'll be charged with. I'm not sure if we will charge you with anything. Sergey will want his day in court, but perhaps I can talk him out of it."

"How is he?"

"The bites are superficial. I think losing his prize hurt him more."

''I don't blame you," Ziyi said. "Sergey knew he was valuable, knew I would not give him up, knew that he would be in trouble if he tried to take it. So he told you. For the reward."

"Well, it's gone now. Whatever it was."

"It was a man," Ziyi said.

She had her cache of treasures, buried in the forest. She could buy lawyers. She could probably buy Sergey, if it came to it. She could leave, move back to the capital and live out her life in comfort, or buy passage to another of the worlds gifted by the Jackaroo, or even return to Earth.

But she knew that she would not leave. She would stay here and wait through the days and years until the factory returned her friend to her.

(2012)

THE BIRDS OF ISLA MUJERES

Steven Popkes

Steven Popkes was born in Santa Monica, California in 1952. He sold his first story in 1982. His first novel, *Caliban Landing*, appeared five years later. *Slow Lightning* followed in 1991: both novels deal with the complexities of alien contact. In 1994 Popkes was part of the Cambridge Writers' Workshop project to produce science fiction scenarios about the future of Boston, Massachusetts. When not writing he works for a company that builds avionics for planes and rockets, and is learning to be a pilot.

Afterward, it was never the people she remembered, never faces or bodies or voices—even Alfredo's. It was always the wind, blowing from the west side of the island, and the frigate birds, balanced on their wingtips against the sky. They flew high above her, so black and stark they seemed made of leather or scales, too finely drawn to be feathered.

It was March, the beginning of the rainy season, and she had come to Isla Mujeres to leave her husband. That she had done this some half a dozen times before did not escape her and she had a kind of despairing fatalism about it. Probably this time, too, she would return. Her name was Jean Summat. Her husband, Marc, lived the professor's life in Boston. She, it was supposed, was to live the role of professor's wife. This was something she had never quite accepted.

Isla Mujeres. Island of Women.

She sat in a small pier cafe that jutted out into the water, waiting for her first meal on the island. In a few minutes it came. A whole fish stared glassily up at her from the plate. Delicately, she began to carve small pieces from it, and ate. She glanced up and a Mexican man in a Panama hat smiled at her. She looked back to her food, embarrassed.

Boston was cold right now and covered with a wet snow as raw as butcher's blood. But here in Mexico, it was warm. More importantly, it was cheap and people's lives here were still enmeshed in basics, not intricately curved in academic diplomacy.

She left the restaurant and stood on the pier watching the birds, feeling the warm heavy wind, sour with the hot smell of the sea. The late afternoon sun was masked with low clouds and in the distance was a dark blue rain. She had a room, money, and time.

The Avenida Ruda was clotted with vendors selling Mayan trinkets, blankets, pots, T-shirts, and ice cream. Several vendors tried to attract her attention with an "*Amiga!*" but she ignored them. A Mexican dressed in a crisp suit and Panama hat sat in an outdoor cafe and sipped his drink as he watched her. Just watched her.

Lots of Mexicans wear such hats, she told herself. Still, he made her nervous and she left the street to return to her room. On the balcony she watched the frigate birds and the people on the beach.

Jean swam in the warm water of Playa de Cocoa. When she came from the water she saw the man watching her from one of the cabanas as he sipped a Coke. She walked up to him.

"Why are you following me?"

The man sipped his Coke and looked back at her. "No entiende."

She looked at him carefully. "That's a lie."

There was a long moment of tension. He threw back his head and laughed. "Es verdad."

"Why—what the hell are you doing?"

"You are very beautiful, Señora."

"Jesus!"

"You need a man."

"I have a man" Or half a man. Or maybe more than a man. Do I still have him Do I want him? Did I ever?

"With specifications?"

She stared at him.

Hector led her through the rubble at the end of the Avenida Hidalgo to a small concrete house nearly identical to all the other concrete houses on the island. It was surrounded by a wall. Set into the top of the wall were the jagged spikes of broken soda bottles. She looked down the street. The other houses were built the same. There was a burnt-out car leaning against one wall, and a thin dog stared at her, his eyes both hungry and protective.

Inside, it smelled damp. It was dark for a moment, then he turned on a blue fluorescent light that lit the room like a chained lightning bolt. Leaning against the wall was a tall, long-haired and heavily built man with Mayan features. He did not move.

What am I doing here?

"This is Alfredo." Hector was looking at her with a considering expression.

She shook her head. The air in the room seemed thick, lifeless, cut off from the world. "Alfredo?"

"Alfredo. I show you." Hector opened a suitcase and took out a box with a complex control panel. He flipped two switches and turned a dial and the box hummed. Alfredo pushed himself away from the wall and looked around.

"Good God." She stared at him. Alfredo was beautiful, with a high forehead and strong lips. His body was wide and taut, the muscles rippling as he moved. Hector touched a button and he became absolutely still.

"You like him?"

She turned to Hector startled. She'd forgotten *he* was there. "What is this?"

"Ah! An explanation." He spoke in a deep conspiratorial whisper. "Deep in the mountains north of Mexico City is a great research laboratory. They have built many of these—andros? Syntheticos?"

"Androids."

"Of course. They are stronger and more beautiful than mortal men. But the church discovered it and forced them to close it down. The church is important here—"

"That's a lie."

Hector shrugged. "The Señora is correct. Alfredo was a prisoner in the Yucatan. Condemned to die for despicable crimes. They did not kill him, however. Instead, they removed his mind and inlaid his body with electrical circuits. He is now more than a man—"

"That's another lie."

"The Señora sees most clearly." He paused a moment. "You have heard of the Haitian zombie? The Mayans had a similar process. My country has only recently perfected it, coupling it with the most advanced of scientific—"

Jean only stared at him.

He stopped, then shrugged. "What does it matter, Señora? He is empty. His mind does not exist. He will—imprint? Is that the correct word?—on anyone I choose."

"This is a trick."

"You are so difficult to convince. Let me show you his abilities." Hector manipulated the controls and Alfredo leaped forward and caught himself on one hand, holding himself high in the air with the strength of one arm. He flipped forward onto his feet. Alfredo picked up a branch from a pile of kindling and twisted it in both hands. There was no expression on his face but the muscles in his forearms twisted like snakes, the tendons like dark wires. The branch broke with a sudden gunshot report.

Hector stopped Alfredo at attention before them. "You see? He is more than man."

She shook her head. "What kind of act is this?"

"No act. I control him from this panel. The—master? maestro?—would not need this."

Control. Such control.

Hector seemed uncertain for a moment. "You wish to see still more? You are unsure of how he is controlled?" He thought for a moment. "Let me show you a feature."

In the stark light and shadows, she had not noticed Alfredo was nude. The Mayan turned into the light.

"There are several choices one could make when using Alfredo." Hector manipulated the box. "Pequeno." Alfredo had a normal-sized erection.

She wanted to look away and could not. The Mayan face was before her, dark, strong, and blank.

"Medio," said Hector softly.

She looked again and the erection was twice as large, pulsing to Alfredo's breathing.

"Y monstruoso!" cried Hector.

Alfredo looked fit to be a bull, a goat, or some other animal. There was never any expression in Alfredo's eyes.

"Y nada," said Hector. And Alfredo's erection wilted and disappeared.

She couldn't breathe. She wanted to run, to hide from Alfredo, but she didn't want to be anywhere else.

"You are pleased, Señora?" Hector stood beside her.

Jean tried to clear her head. She looked away from both of them. No man could fake this. It was real, a marvelous control, a total subjugation. Was this what she had wanted all this time?

"A very nice show." She took a deep breath. "How much do I owe you?"

"You owe me nothing, Señora." Hector bowed to her. "But Alfredo is for sale." When she did not answer immediately, he continued. "He imprints on the owner, Señora. Then voice commands are sufficient. He will show initiative if you desire it, or not. He is intelligent, but only in your service."

"But you have the controls."

"They do not operate once imprinting occurs."

Crazy. Ridiculous.

"How much?" she heard herself asking.

Alfredo followed her home, mute, below the birds and the sky. She could smell him on the evening wind, a clean, strong smell.

"Do you speak?" she asked as he followed her up the steps to her room.

Alfredo did not answer for a moment. "Yes."

She asked him no more questions that night.

His mind was like a thunderstorm: thick, murky, dark, shot through intermittently by lightning. These were not blasts of intelligence or insight but the brightness of activity, the heat of flesh, the electricity of impulse. He was no more conscious of what happened or what caused his actions than lightning was conscious of the friction between clouds. Occasionally, very occasionally, a light came through him, like the sun through the distant rain, and things stilled within him.

He was a chained thunderbolt, unaware of his chains.

She copulated with Alfredo almost continuously the first three days. It was as if a beast had been loosed within her. If she wanted him to stroke her *thus*, he did so. If she wanted him to bite her *there*, it was done. Something broke within her and she tried to devour him.

It was only when she fully realized she *owned him,* that he would be there as long as she wanted him, that this abated. Then it was like coming up from underwater, and she looked around her.

Alfredo had cost her almost everything she had, nearly all the money she would have used to start a new life. She could not go back to Marc now. Perhaps buying Alfredo had been an act ensuring that. She didn't know. There were jobs on the island for Americans, but they were tricky and illegal to get.

At the end of the first day of a waitress job, she came to their room tired and angry. Alfredo was sitting on the edge of the bed staring out the window. It was suddenly too much for her.

"You! I do this to feed you." She stared at him. He stared back with his dark eyes.

"I can't go home because of you." She slapped him. There was no response.

She turned away from him and looked out at the sea and the birds. This wasn't going to work.

Wait.

Jean turned to him. "Can you work?"

He ponderously turned his head toward her. "Yes."

"You do speak Spanish?"

"Sí."

"Come with me."

She looked through her toilet bag and found a pair of scissors. They were almost too long for what she wanted but they would do. The fluorescent light in the bathroom glittered off the steel as she cut his hair, a sharp, pointed light. After a few moments, she turned his head up toward her. The hair was nearly right. His cheek was smooth against her hand. Impulsively, she kissed him and he moved toward her but she pushed him back down in the chair. "All right," she said finally. "Take a shower." He started the water and she watched him for a long minute. After that, she thought, after that, we'll see.

Alfredo found a job almost immediately and made enough to keep them both alive. Now, Jean lay on the beach and tanned. Alfredo worked hard and his strength was such that he could work through the siesta. He had only to watch a thing done and then could do it. The workers on Isla Mujeres grumbled. Jean shrewdly noticed this and sent him across the bay into Cancún where the wages were higher.

Two weeks after this they had enough to move into the El Presidente Hotel.

That night she looked at him. "Ever the sophisticate," she murmured. "Go get clothes fit to wear here."

Alfredo did and she went to dinner in the Caribe on his arm. He looked so strong and dignified the other women in the room looked at him, then away. Jean felt a thrill go through her. Over dinner she murmured instructions which he executed flawlessly. She felt quite fond of him.

Over coffee, the waiter brought them a message from a Lydia Conklin and friend, inviting them for cocktails.

She read it. Alfredo did not—yet—read and stared away toward the open doorway of the bar.

"What are you looking at?" she asked.

He turned to her. "Nothing."

"Look around the room regularly like a normal person."

He did not answer but instead watched the room as if bored or waiting for the check.

Jean read the note again.

She shrugged and signed the check. The two of them went to the bar for a drink.

"Excuse me." A woman stood up in front of them. "I am Lydia Conklin."

Jean looked first at her, then at Alfredo. "I'm Jean Summat. I got your note—"

"I was dying for American speech." As she spoke she only glanced at Jean. Her eyes were full of Alfredo. "You don't know what it's like." Now, she turned to Jean. "Or perhaps you do."

"I've been here a few weeks."

"Señora Summat."

That voice Jean knew. Behind and to her left was Hector. "Good evening, Hector."

"You know Hector too?" Lydia said idly. "How wonderful."

"Sit with us, Señora. Please." Hector pulled out a chair for her. Jean looked at Alfredo. Alfredo paused a moment, watched her closely, then sat across from her at the table.

Hector sat next to Jean. He leaned toward Lydia. "Señora Summat, Alfredo and myself were business partners."

"'Were?" Lydia raised her eyebrows.

"The business is accomplished. It is of no matter."

Jean interrupted. "Are you down for a vacation, Lydia?"

Lydia shrugged. "In a way. I'm down for my health. This last year I went mad."

Hector laughed. Jean smiled uneasily. Lydia shrugged again.

"Señora Conklin makes a good joke."

"It was, I suppose." Lydia sipped her drink. "I came down here two years ago and fell in love with a Mayan. I'm back to see if lightning can strike twice."

Something in her face was hard to look at for more than a moment. Jean looked away. "What was the Mayan's name?"

"Alberto. Hector is helping me find another."

Hector seemed nervous. He turned to Jean. "I introduce Señora Conklin to eligible men—"

"He pimps for me." Lydia lit a cigarette. "Your Mayan reminds me of Alberto."

"Alfredo. His name is Alfredo." Jean looked at Alfredo. His face was impassive.

"The names are almost the same." Lydia blew smoke in the air above the table. "Did Alberto care for you?"

"He"—Lydia paused a moment—"he adored me. He was my slave."

"Señoras? Would you care for more drinks?" Hector was perspiring now.

Jean and Lydia stared at one another.

Jean turned to Alfredo. "What do you think of this?"

Alfredo did not speak for a long minute, watching the two women. Then he smiled at Jean. "A Mayan is no woman's slave." And he laughed.

Lydia stared at him with an open mouth. Hector frowned.

Jean looked at them both in triumph. "I suspect that may be the definitive Mayan answer. Alfredo, would you take me to my room?"

Alfredo stood quickly and led her away.

Jean was thinking: *What is in him? What is in there?*

It was June now and the island was somewhat hotter and much more humid. The frigate birds flew low over the buildings as if the wet air could not support them. The Mexican fishermen brought in great nets of snapper and bonita. The American sport fishermen disappeared in search of marlin and sailfish.

Lydia Conklin stayed. She always seemed to be watching Alfredo. Hector seemed to leave the island regularly but he always returned. Jean fancied she could tell when either was around just by the feeling of eyes on Alfredo.

Often Lydia would invite them to dinner, or cards, or for drinks. Usually Jean turned her down. Sometimes, though, they would go and Jean never could figure out why. There was a dance here, a dangerous ballet that attracted her.

One evening, they were drinking in Lydia's apartment in the Presidente.

"You know," Lydia began, swirling tequila in a brandy snifter. "I've been seeing you both for a couple of months now. I don't know what Alfredo does. What do you do, Alfredo?"

Alfredo sat back in his chair and looked at Jean, then back to Lydia. "Do?"

"How do you support yourself?"

For a moment, Alfredo did not seem to understand. "I do contract work."

Jean glanced at him over the rim of her glass. *Good God. What have I got here?*

"Contract work?" Lydia came over to him. "Did you build these great strong arms at a desk job?"

Alfredo shook his head. "I do nothing with a desk. I work with bricklayers. Tilers. Those who build walls and houses."

"Ah!" Lydia leaned back. "You are a *contractor*."

"That's what I said."

"This is how you support her? This is what she left her husband for?" Lydia stiffened and swayed, looked down at him. "Christ, you have sunk low."

Jean didn't know which of them Lydia was speaking to. Alfredo looked at Jean and suddenly there was pleading in his eyes.

"I think it's time we left, Lydia." Jean carefully put down her drink. "Thanks and all."

Lydia threw her glass against the wall shattering it. "I'm sick of this! I owned him before you—then, I left him. Hector sold him to me first! Do you understand? To *me!*" She knelt before him. "Alberto. Tell me you remember me. Tell me I didn't come back for nothing."

Jean couldn't move.

Alfredo put out his hand and touched her cheek. He traced the line of her jaw, then held her head in both hands. He tilted her face toward his. Her tears were clearly visible now, hot and pouring. He looked at her closely, staring, searching her face with his eyes.

"I don't know you," he said softly and let her go.

She fell at his feet and started sobbing.

Alfredo took Jean's arm and led her out. "It's been a lovely evening," Jean said as they left.

Later: in bed.

It took her a long time to catch her breath afterward. She was covered in a light sheen of sweat that made her cold in the air-conditioning. "What are you?" she asked quietly.

He did not answer. She drew the tip of her finger down his chest. "Answer me. What are you?"

He looked at her in the dark and she could see a glow in his eyes.

"I don't know."

You could not call it consciousness, for consciousness determines its own needs and he could not do that. He was predetermined. He was programmed. Neither could you call him a person, for a person has a complex assortment of drives that come from many sources. His drives were simple and their source was singular.

He was a tool: intelligent, willful, resourceful. A tool aimed at a specific purpose.

Jean followed him to Cancún.

She sat in the far back section of the crowded ferry, away from him. There had been a storm the day before and though the air was clear, the resulting seas kept the big automobile ferry at dock. But the little ferry that carried only people plowed through the sea. It was close and hot aboard the boat and it stank of animals, sweat, rotten fish, diesel fumes. The sea pitched them back and forth until Jean was sure she was about to be sick. A large rip in the fabric covering the deck rails showed the bobbing horizon and she stared at it until she had the nausea under control.

Alfredo did not seem to notice. He sat on one of the benches leaning on his elbows.

When the boat docked he hailed one of the cabs and left. Jean was barely able to hail one in time to follow him.

His cab stopped just outside the Plaza Hidalgo next to the site of a new library. Alfredo stepped out of the cab and Jean didn't recognize him at first. He'd changed in the cab. His workman's dungarees and loose shirt were gone. Now, he was wearing a tie and short-sleeved white shirt and slacks. He walked over to the contractor's office, never noticing her following him. She saw him talking with the architect in rapid-fire Spanish. He seemed to be in charge of the construction. She withdrew before he could see her.

As Jean left the construction site she saw a woman sitting on the park bench across the street from the office. The woman smoked a cigarette and watched Alfredo through the office window. It was Lydia Conklin.

Jean moved into the shade behind her to watch.

After an hour or so, Alfredo came out with a soda and sat down with the foreman to discuss some detail of the construction. Lydia put out the cigarette and crossed the street to him. He stood to meet her. They spoke for several minutes. Suddenly, Lydia raked his face with her nails—Jean could see the blood—and left him, walking hurriedly.

Jean left hurriedly, too. She had no desire to see Lydia. Jean returned to the ferry and stood on the open deck this time, smiling, watching nothing but the open sea and the frigate birds flying in the wind.

She checked her bank account in Isla Mujeres. There were several thousand dollars more than there should have been. Alfredo must have been in this position for some time. It made her laugh softly.

He is mine, Lydia. He is mine to touch, make, and mold.

The storm in him gradually calmed. The needs that drove him called out other needs, other traits. A sluggish thought blew through him, an inarticulate gale across the continents of what should have been a mind. It shook him. It broke the back of the incoherent storm that raged in him and let in the light. He stood blind and trembling in that light, trying to speak.

Jean awoke and he was not there.

She sat up suddenly and looked around the room. He stood, nude, on the balcony staring at the sea. The sliding door was open. She could smell the ocean through the air-conditioning.

"Alfredo?"

He croaked something unintelligible.

She followed him out into the air. "Alfredo?" He was dripping with sweat. The moonlight made him glow. "Did you have a nightmare?" Ridiculous. Why would he have nightmares?

He turned to her and his face was wet with tears, the long scabs from Lydia's fingernails dark on his silver face. He shook his head, buried his face in his hands.

"What's going on?" She started toward him.

He looked at her in such pain she stepped back. "1 am..."

Suddenly, Jean did not want to know. She left him and reentered the apartment. Alfredo followed her, reached out to her. She backed away. He was huge. He filled the room—she remembered the night in Hector's house, how strong he was. He was dark in the shadows of the room, looming over her.

"I am...," he repeated. "I am a man." He reached for her again.

Jean dodged him and ran to the other edge of the table. "Stay there."

"Jean... I have become a man for *you*."

"Stay there! That's an order!"

He followed her. They circled the table. Jean grabbed the scissors from the table and held them in front of her. "Stay away from me."

"Jean. I love you."

The moonlight struck his face and it was all shadows and silver. His eyes glowed for her, his face was transfigured by some secret knowledge. He leaped the table toward her and she fell back and he took her shoulders. She screamed and drove the scissors deep into his chest.

His hands fell away from her and she stumbled against the wall, staring at him.

Alfredo touched the handles of the scissors, looked at her and began to sway, caught himself, fell down to his knees. He looked at her again and full realization of what had happened seemed to touch him. He fell on his back, twitched twice, and was still.

Jean crumpled into a chair and watched the body. Finally, she pulled the scissors from his chest and washed them in the bathroom until they were clean. She drew her finger down the blades. Not sharp. Not sharp at all. But sharp enough. She smiled. She felt filled somehow. Satisfied.

Jean packed carefully and when she was done, she kissed Alfredo good-bye on his cold lips and walked down to the ferry dock. She reached the Cancún airport in time for the early morning flight to New Orleans. From there, she took a flight to Boston.

As she lay back in her seat watching the clouds move beneath her, she thought about Marc: if he had waited for her, if he had divorced her. She would like to start again with him if she could, but she would survive if she couldn't. She felt alive with possibility.

Jean fell asleep and dreamed of frigate birds circling endlessly above her.

Hector found him an hour after dawn. "Mierda," he said when he saw the blood. "That she could…" He shook his head as he opened the suitcase he had with him. With tools he had brought with him, he cut open Alfredo's chest and sewed the heart and lungs back together, then closed the chest cavity. From the suitcase he brought two broad plates connected to thick electrical cables and attached them to either side of Alfredo's chest. Alfredo convulsed as Hector adjusted the controls inside the suitcase. Alfredo moaned and opened his eyes.

"Good," said Hector. He detached the plates and returned them to the suitcase.

"Hector…" Alfredo shook his head from side to side. "She hurt me."

Hector watched him carefully but did not listen. He flicked two switches and watched the meters.

Alfredo sat up. "I am a man, Hector."

Hector nodded absently and adjusted his controls. "Certainly, she thought you were. Or she would never have tried to kill you. Stand, por favor."

Alfredo stood. "I am still a man."

Hector shrugged. "For the moment."

"You can't take something like that away." Alfredo clutched his hands together and looked out the window. "I must follow her."

"She doesn't want you. She's gotten what she needed."

Alfredo turned and noticed the suitcase. He watched Hector adjusting the controls. Alfredo pleaded with him. "I love her. She needs me. You can't take something like that away."

"No?" Two needles appeared on either side of one dial. Carefully, Hector brought them together.

"Hector! Don't. Please." Alfredo's hands clutched the air and his face twisted. "Please," he whispered. "You can't—"

Hector flicked a switch and Alfredo stiffened. A blank look descended on Alfredo's face.

"Of course I can," said Hector and stood up himself. "Señora Conklin? He is ready."

Lydia entered the room. "He is? Wonderful." She turned to the Mayan. "Alberto." The blank eyes turned toward the sound of her voice. "I am so glad to see you again."

(2003)

THAT LAUGH

Patrick O'Leary

Patrick O'Leary was born September 13, 1952 in Saginaw, Michigan. He drifted from journalism into advertising, and became a copy intern at one of the major Detroit agencies, working on the Chevrolet account – work that has seen him through his entire professional career. His first novel, *Door Number Three*, appeared in 1995. His latest novel is *The Impossible Bird* (2002). A collection of stories, *The Black Heart*, was published in 2009. O'Leary told *Locus* magazine, "I try to write books that are indescribable. If you try to describe them, they sort of crumble." "That Laugh" was inspired by a visit with some colleagues to La Brea Tar Pits in California. "When we returned to my rental car, we discovered it had been broken into. We lost briefcases, passports, laptops, etc. I lost some fifty handwritten pages of a novel. Which sucked. But at least, now, I can say I have managed to retrieve something useful from the experience."

Twenty years ago, in the summer of 2002, I was hired to make an examination at the La Brea Tar Pits Museum in Los Angeles. At that time I had been in the field of forensic psychology for some thirty years. It was a lucrative contract, as all government contracts are, and for my trouble I was required to submit an oral and written report, take my check, and disappear. All contact with me was entirely routine and formal and conveyed no hint of urgency, but at no time was I given any clues whatsoever about the subject's identity. Thus I knew it was no ordinary interview. This was confirmed by the security clearances involved—for example: I took two flights across the country to arrive at the museum, which I assume was some sort of elaborate subterfuge.

During my stay I enjoyed the hospitality of a Santa Monica beachfront hotel. I was allowed three days to transcribe the interview, type my report, and record my oral top-line summary. Met a lovely woman on the pier the first night, and after a late meal of margaritas and white fish we enjoyed a pleasant sexual romp. At three o'clock in the morning I was woken by the roar of the ocean. I saw her standing naked at the threshold of the balcony, the pale diaphanous white curtains blowing back into the room, the scent of the surf, and her dark caramel skin black in the half light, and I thought for a few seconds I was dreaming. She must have sensed I was watching her, admiring her lithe form, for she turned to me and said, "Shouldn't you be working on your report? They expect it day after tomorrow."

Then she laughed.

In the morning she was gone and I had to convince myself that the whole episode was real. The littlest things about that night bothered me like a pebble in my shoe. Why didn't she use the word "the"? Why didn't she say "*The* day after tomorrow?" How come she never said what country she was from? Her accent was curious, but I couldn't place it. To this day, I'm frankly not sure how much of this actually happened. And, given all that followed this encounter, I remain in an uncomfortable quantum state of unknowable alternatives.

And all this, remember, was *before* the interview.

Over the last several years of my life my speculations have reached a more desperate pitch. I feel time is running out. And I may never solve the central mystery of my life. A mystery I could not confront that day, lacking the courage, the skill or, perhaps, both. And these days I swing from thinking this was all an elaborate hoax, to some truly paranoid science fictional postulations, to the possibility that I myself was the intended subject of the interview.

But at that time, all I knew was that my client was some unknown captive. My employer was the U.S. Government. And my citizenship depended on my discretion.

I am embarrassed to admit that I suspected my task was a part of the greater "War On Terror." When I sought to subtly confirm this explanation, I was not discouraged. And I must admit, I felt pride at that time, proud to have been elevated from the status of my ordinary duties, proud to serve my country, proud to exercise a little "payback" in whatever modest fashion I could. If you remember, we all felt so enraged and helpless back then. Now, you can imagine how duped and betrayed I felt a while later when the photos of those naked prisoners in a pile became public. And I saw my compliance with retribution in a new light. "Prisoner." This unlikely alternative is one that truly haunts me.

Excuse me, I have to vomit.

Three days after the interview I pulled up an hour early to the tar pits to deliver my report. At a café across the street I had a croissant with butter and a latte. My skin was slightly burned, and I had a hazy feeling, a satisfying mental and physical fatigue. I had gotten drunk the night before when I finally finished printing the report and recording my summary. It had been a somewhat pleasant break from my routine of patients, consultations, and courtrooms.

The report, I mean, was pleasant. The interview was awful.

When I returned to my rental car, I found my briefcase had been stolen from my trunk. All my notes, all my reports, my recorder—they were all gone. I was tempted to file a police report, but I thought better of it. I flew home. After a very overwrought week I received my check in the mail confirming they had indeed gotten my report.

I vowed never to work for the government again.

Since then I have had recurring dreams where I am being interviewed by an alien. His skin is white. His large head is mostly black eyes. He wears silver gloves. He admits to having stolen my report, and he promises to return my notes as soon as we finish the interview. Finally he hands over my notepad, and I see my notes are an unreadable scrawl. But his remarks are very clear indeed. In the upper right hand corner of the notepad's first page, in bright red cursive, are the following Teacher Remarks: "Dumb. Artificial. Pass."

And he laughs.

The pits themselves are black. Obsidian is the correct color, I believe. Tar has the sheen of those alien eyes, the mirror black of a bubble of petrified lava. The museum is nice. And you can actually watch through the glass as paleontologists pick and brush the tar off the bones of ancient dead creatures who died because they were going for the easy meal, squirming to death in that unforgiving black quicksand. This deadly process was repeated and repeated until there were more bones in the pits than fruit in a fruitcake.

We talked before a huge backlit wall comprised of yellow plastic cubes that held small skulls that over the years had been retrieved from the black taffy of the pits. At no time during the interview did I lay eyes upon my subject. He/she? was a voice of indeterminate ethnicity (obviously distorted, like a witness under anonymous protection)—a voice that emerged from a black Bose speaker on a white marble table. It was a rather large public space, but since this was after hours, no one intruded. A friendly black security guard unlocked the front door to let me in, guided me to my seat, and, after my notepad and recorder were set up, left me alone.

I waited about five minutes; then I heard a voice.

I am going to reconstruct our dialog with the greatest care. I have a photographic memory, and I can assure you that what you read is what I heard. You may form your own conclusions as to its veracity.

I am not afraid at this late stage of any repercussions as it is one of those tales patently easy to dismiss as moonshine.

Also, I should admit that I am a terminal cancer patient. I do not expect to live through the next month. I have no need for celebrity. I merely want history to be told with accuracy.

I am a father, too. I love my son. He is my caretaker now. He has encouraged me to do this. To settle, as he put it, "a long unsettled score."

And I am a patriot. I love my country but not as much as I love the truth.

As you read our words please remember this: I was told nothing about the patient.

Hello.
Good evening. I am Doctor
So I am told.
I've been asked to ask you some questions.
By whom?
I am not at liberty to say.
Neither am I. Do they bind you, too?
Bind?
Bind. Bond. Chain.
You are chained?
In a manner of speaking. Conditions. Limitations.
I chafe under these.
Not… literally.
No.
Then we are in the same boat.

*

At this point the "patient" laughed. It was a most distressing sound, which I could not be sure wasn't distorted by the speaker or the echoing effect of the large chamber I was alone in. Suffice it to say that its laughter...

Oh my god.

Excuse me.

Sorry.

No, I'm fine.

Its laughter

... was always unexpected and always—how do I put this? Had it been at a cocktail party, or some other public venue, it would be considered totally inappropriate. Like laughter at a funeral. A chilling laugh. A laugh that could stop all the conversation in a bar. Such laughter I have heard in many mental hospitals. It was wretched and contained an unmistakable echo of despair. Remember, this is what I mean when you read the word "laughter."

It was the first clue that something was out of joint. However rational and clever his answers were, there were always, sprinkled throughout, these false notes of mirth that at the very least conveyed a sense of cross purposes, hidden agendas, and unspoken torment that could never be addressed directly.

I will say it this way. It broke my heart to hear.

It spoke of an unbearable gulf between us that could never be crossed.

A final aloneness.

It broke my heart.

Have you sat next to a firing rifle lately?

No.

Any nearby explosions?

No.

Have you ever been caught in a collapsing building?

Yes.

When the building fell on you, what were you doing?

I was in the bathroom.

Yes?

Yes.

How do you feel when a man touches you?

That would depend on the man.

The last time you made love, were you happy?

I have never made love. She did.

Okay. What was the last thing you heard?

A wailing sound and a gigantic ripe apple falling to the ground. Imagine a scream, a rumble and a thump.

Where were you?

New York. We were all there.

Were you there alone?

No. Sarah. She played piano. I got to know her in the dark. I sat with her on the floor, and I listened to her sing before she died.

She sang?

Yes. Under the wall. I couldn't see her face. She was just a foot sticking out of the plaster.

What did she sing?

Show tunes. She sounded like Ethel Merman. Only bearable. Do you know about lighthouses?

Excuse me?

Lighthouses.

Yes, I know lighthouses.

Sarah's father nearly starved to death in one. He was a Merchant Marine, and he was stationed with another man on Lake Superior in a long winter, and they were cut off by a tremendous storm, and they had underestimated the supplies they needed to get through winter before the spring thaw, when they would be resupplied. They came close to dying. They were making soup out of hot water and catsup when they were found. She told me that before she died. Have you ever been starved?

No.

I thought not. In the lighthouse the waves crash continuously. The sound is different than you would hear on a beach, or on a boat.

Different how?

You are surrounded. Cut off. Or at least you feel that. All bonds severed. Truly isolated. It must have been a terrible duty. Let me ask you a question.

Okay.

Where's your heart?

(I cradled both my hands over my left breast as if I were about to break into song.) Here.

Oh. I thought that was something else.

You're joking right?

A little.

How far can you hit a baseball?

I have no idea.

What is it about women?

I don't know.

Do they lie for pleasure or to avoid pain?

For many reasons. As you do.

Does it work?

No. Wait. When you say 'lie' do you mean 'sex?'

No.

Fucking?

No.

Making love?

Say, yes.

Then the answer to both of your questions is 'yes.'

I forget the questions.

So do I.

How many fingers am I holding up?

Three.

Ah, so you can see me, but I can't see you…

That is correct.

Doesn't seem quite fair.

(Laughter) You know what I hate?

No. What?

When people say: Did you see that? Did you see that? If I saw it, wouldn't it be obvious?

That is a very peculiar question.

It is?

Don't you think?

Do you?

I'd like to set up a ground rule if I may: You are not to answer questions with questions for the duration of this interview.

I am not?

No.

No?

I mean Yes you are not.

Okay, then.

What is your one experience that should you put into words no one would believe you?

I couldn't put it in two words.

I didn't ask you to.

Sure, you did.

What do men want?

Men want blowjobs.

What is your first memory?

Her face.

Whose face?

The one we all lose.

I should tell you I am to stick to a list of required questions. Understand, please, that most of these questions are not mine—that is, I am required to ask them for various purposes—some of which I, myself, do not understand. If they make you uncomfortable, I apologize.

I am very comfortable.

What are your intentions?

I am here to learn. If I cannot learn, then I don't know why I am here. I am learning a great deal right now, and I have to say I enjoy it.

Where is your ship located?

Where ships usually are. The Harbor.

Why the secrecy?

If I asked you the same question would you answer?

Sure.

Then, why the secrecy?

Ummm. I suppose, if I had to guess, it has to do with security. Security precautions. National security.

And why is security about secrecy?

There are things to protect. Silence protects them.

(Laughter)

What is funny?

You use the word 'national.' Do you know what it means?

Of course. Having to do with nations, states, countries.

No. National is an invisible line on a nonexistent map. It is a huge joke that anyone who has ever flown knows.

Have you… flown?

Like you, it's how I got here.

Are you here alone?

No.

No?

No. I am with you.

I doubt they meant that.

I know what they meant.

Okay. Why won't you help us?

I've answered this many times. But I'll repeat myself. You don't know what you're asking for. A man is holding a knife. He says to a stranger: "I am going to kill my neighbor unless you stop me." You say: "Don't kill him!" And he stabs him in the heart, turns to you and says: "Why didn't you stop me?"

You sound upset.

(Laughter)

Would you like to take a minute?

Minutes cannot be taken, they can only be spent.

How old are you?

I will be three day after tomorrow.

Seriously.

I am almost three.

If you can't be serious, I don't see how we can continue.

Neither do I. But you do.

I'm merely saying that my job, my findings, depend on a certain, candor that can develop—

—Trust?

Yes, I mean, we've only just met but I am trying to do a job here, and part of that requires…

Trust?

Yes.

Good luck. (Laughter)

For a three-year-old, you have a remarkable vocabulary.

For 64-year-old, you have a lot to learn.

How did you guess my age?

I didn't guess it; I knew it.

Evidently you have me at a disadvantage…

I agree.

At this point, I'm a bit lost. I don't know how to proceed exactly.

Why don't you let me tell you a story?

All right.

There once was a creature who had no form. Its form was whatever it filled. Sometimes it filled a body. Sometimes a machine. Sometimes it spread itself thin along a thread of light. Sometimes it was a naked woman who loved to smell the salt of the ocean. Wherever it went, it learned, and it taught. But one day it came to a place where it would not be allowed to teach. This had never happened before. Its students found a way to keep it in one place. To silence it. This had never happened before. Now the only way for it to learn is for it to listen. Now I am a voice in a box and they only let me talk to people who pretend to want to learn but really only want control. Why don't you call your son?

What?

Call your son. He needs to hear your voice.

How could you...?

Why don't you pay back your friend? He needs the money.

I have no idea...

Yes, you do. Why is everyone so afraid to love?

I am not.

(Laughter) Oh, please,

How do you know my name? Who told you?

I knew you from the moment you spoke. I heard you. When I heard you, I knew you. I was there the day you were born. Your mother was terrified and radiant. She was a girl pretending to be a woman. As you are a baby pretending to be a man. You have not learned to love. Or forgive. You presume to understand people, but you are a mystery to yourself.

I can't sustain this. This is intolerable.

It was really wonderful meeting you, I doubt we'll meet again. Let me advise you: after you make your report, do not tell anyone. They will find out. They will harm you. It is what they do best.

Hastily, I packed my briefcase. I could feel all the blood rushing to my face. I am a blusher, but I have to say it had been years since I blushed. I was walking out of the museum when the security guard whispered something as I passed.

"Excuse me?" I said.

"I said, 'Relax. Nobody gets her.'"

"Her?" I don't think I really looked at him before, but he was a middle-aged black man in a gray uniform. He had a very pleasant air about him as if he enjoyed any contact with people.

"She freaks most folks out. Don't take it so hard."

"I'm not, it's just..."

"Don't worry about it. She's a freak."

"You say, you say: There, there have been others?"

"Oh, yeah. They got an army trying to crack that code. Last night, some woman professor left in tears. Poor lady. I tried to tell her not to—"

"I have to be somewhere."

The moment I stepped out into the warm night, I noticed the world looked different. The smell of tar wafted into the air. The L.A. haze was lit by the warm copper glow of the grid of streetlights that crisscrosses the valley. Why copper? Why that color? I wondered. Why that smell? Why anything? It was as if I were looking at the world for the first time.

I realized I had been holding my breath. I told myself to breathe. Just breathe.

Then I recalled his laughter. That awful lost laugh. A laugh that could never be shared. Whose frame of reference was so beyond anyone else that true community would never happen, true companionship was but a dream, true connection—impossible. I did not know and still do not know what that creature was. All I knew was that I would never understand it. And I was in the understanding business.

What surprised me then and haunts me now is that I could not wait to get out of its presence. I felt as if being within its proximity compromised any boundaries I may have constructed for my psyche. I felt violated. I'm not sure if the violation was intentional or just a by-product of its uncanny insight, but it felt like a psychic rape.

Was this a weapon that we were trying to disarm or create? A sample of a race so evolved they presented an intolerable threat? Or merely a fantastically advanced chess program whose only moves were intended to corner its prey and watch it squirm? Or was it, perhaps, just a trap—a black hole that could snatch anything and swallow it down?

I will never know. But I recorded this so that perhaps, someday, you might.

If you forget everything else about this story, please, remember one thing. Remember its laughter. Remember that, please.

A laugh no one else could share.

No one should ever have to laugh like that.

(2009)

ZEN AND THE ART OF STARSHIP MAINTENANCE

Tobias S. Buckell

Called "violent, poetic and compulsively readable" by Maclean's, science fiction author **Tobias S. Buckell** is a *New York Times* bestselling writer born in the Caribbean. He grew up in Grenada and spent time in the British and US Virgin Islands, and the islands he lived on influence much of his work. His Xenowealth series begins with *Crystal Rain*. Along with other stand-alone novels and over fifty stories, his works have been translated into 18 different languages. He has been nominated for awards including the Hugo, Nebula, Prometheus, and the John W. Campbell Award for Best New Science Fiction Author. His latest novel is *Hurricane Fever*, a follow-up to the successful *Arctic Rising* that NPR says will "give you the shivers." He currently lives in Bluffton, Ohio with his wife, twin daughters, and a pair of dogs.

After battle with the *Fleet of Honest Representation*, after seven hundred seconds of sheer terror and uncertainty, and after our shared triumph in the acquisition of the greatest prize seizure in three hundred years, we cautiously approached the massive black hole that Purth-Anaget orbited. The many rotating rings, filaments, and infrastructures bounded within the fields that were the entirety of our ship, *With All Sincerity*, were flush with a sense of victory and bloated with the riches we had all acquired.

Give me a ship to sail and a quasar to guide it by, billions of individual citizens of all shapes, functions, and sizes cried out in joy together on the common channels. Whether fleshy forms safe below, my fellow crab-like maintenance forms on the hulls, or even the secretive navigation minds, our myriad thoughts joined in a sense of True Shared Purpose that lingered even after the necessity of the group battle-mind.

I clung to my usual position on the hull of one of the three rotating habitat rings deep inside our shields and watched the warped event horizon shift as we fell in behind the metallic world in a trailing orbit.

A sleet of debris fell toward the event horizon of Purth-Anaget's black hole, hammering the kilometers of shields that formed an iridescent cocoon around us. The bow shock of our shields' push through the debris field danced ahead of us, the compressed wave it created becoming a hyper-aurora of shifting colors and energies that collided and compressed before they streamed past our sides.

What a joy it was to see a world again. I was happy to be outside in the dark so that as the bow shields faded, I beheld the perpetual night face of the world: it glittered with millions of fractal habitation patterns traced out across its artificial surface.

On the hull with me, a nearby friend scuttled between airlocks in a cloud of insect-sized seeing eyes. They spotted me and tapped me with a tight-beam laser for a private ping.

"Isn't this exciting?" they commented.

"Yes. But this will be the first time I don't get to travel downplanet," I beamed back.

I received a derisive snort of static on a common radio frequency from their direction. "There is nothing there that cannot be experienced right here in the Core. Waterfalls, white sand beaches, clear waters."

"But it's different down there," I said. "I love visiting planets."

"Then hurry up and let's get ready for the turnaround so we can leave this industrial shithole of a planet behind us and find a nicer one. I hate being this close to a black hole. It fucks with time dilation, and I spend all night tasting radiation and fixing broken equipment that can't handle energy discharges in the exajoule range. Not to mention everything damaged in the battle I have to repair."

This was true. There was work to be done.

Safe now in trailing orbit, the many traveling worlds contained within the shields that marked the *With All Sincerity*'s boundaries burst into activity. Thousands of structures floating in between the rotating rings moved about, jockeying and repositioning themselves into renegotiated orbits. Flocks of transports rose into the air, wheeling about inside the shields to then stream off ahead toward Purth-Anaget. There were trillions of citizens of the *Fleet of Honest Representation* heading for the planet now that their fleet lay captured between our shields like insects in amber.

The enemy fleet had forced us to extend energy far, far out beyond our usual limits. Great risks had been taken. But the reward had been epic, and the encounter resolved in our favor with their capture.

Purth-Anaget's current ruling paradigm followed the memetics of the One True Form, and so had opened their world to these refugees. But Purth-Anaget was not so wedded to the belief system as to pose any threat to mutual commerce, information exchange, or any of our own rights to self-determination.

Later we would begin stripping the captured prize ships of information, booby traps, and raw mass, with Purth-Anaget's shipyards moving inside of our shields to help.

I leapt out into space, spinning a simple carbon nanotube of string behind me to keep myself attached to the hull. I swung wide, twisted, and landed near a dark-energy manifold bridge that had pinged me a maintenance consult request just a few minutes back.

My eyes danced with information for a picosecond. Something shifted in the shadows between the hull's crenulations.

I jumped back. We had just fought an entire war-fleet; any number of eldritch machines could have slipped through our shields—things that snapped and clawed, ripped you apart in a femtosecond's worth of dark energy. Seekers and destroyers.

A face appeared in the dark. Skeins of invisibility and personal shielding fell away like a pricked soap bubble to reveal a bipedal figure clinging to the hull.

"You there!" it hissed at me over a tightly contained beam of data. "I am a fully bonded Shareholder and Chief Executive with command privileges of the Anabathic Ship *Helios Prime*. Help me! Do not raise an alarm."

I gaped. What was a CEO doing on our hull? Its vacuum-proof carapace had been destroyed while passing through space at high velocity, pockmarked by the violence of single atoms at indescribable speed punching through its shields. Fluids leaked out, surrounding the stowaway in a frozen mist. It must have jumped the space between ships during the battle, or maybe even after.

Protocols insisted I notify the hell out of security. But the CEO had stopped me from doing that. There was a simple hierarchy across the many ecologies of a traveling ship, and in all of them a CEO certainly trumped maintenance forms. Particularly now that we were no longer in direct conflict and the *Fleet of Honest Representation* had surrendered.

"Tell me: What is your name?" the CEO demanded.

"I gave that up a long time ago," I said. "I have an address. It should be an encrypted rider on any communication I'm single-beaming to you. Any message you direct to it will find me."

"My name is Armand," the CEO said. "And I need your help. Will you let me come to harm?"

"I will not be able to help you in a meaningful way, so my not telling security and medical assistance that you are here will likely do more harm than good. However, as you are a CEO, I have to follow your orders. I admit, I find myself rather conflicted. I believe I'm going to have to countermand your previous request."

Again, I prepared to notify security with a quick summary of my puzzling situation.

But the strange CEO again stopped me. "If you tell anyone I am here, I will surely die and you will be responsible."

I had to mull the implications of that over.

"I need your help, robot," the CEO said. "And it is your duty to render me aid."

Well, shit. That was indeed a dilemma.

Robot.

That was a Formist word. I never liked it.

I surrendered my free will to gain immortality and dissolve my fleshly constraints, so that hard acceleration would not tear at my cells and slosh my organs backward until they pulped. I did it so I could see the galaxy. That was one hundred and fifty-seven years, six months, nine days, ten hours, and—to round it out a bit—fifteen seconds ago.

Back then, you were downloaded into hyperdense pin-sized starships that hung off the edge of the speed of light, assembling what was needed on arrival via self-replicating nanomachines that you spun your mind-states off into. I'm sure there are billions of copies of my essential self scattered throughout the galaxy by this point.

Things are a little different today. More mass. Bigger engines. Bigger ships. Ships the size of small worlds. Ships that change the orbits of moons and satellites if they don't negotiate and plan their final approach carefully.

"Okay," I finally said to the CEO. "I can help you."

Armand slumped in place, relaxed now that it knew I would render the aid it had demanded.

I snagged the body with a filament lasso and pulled Armand along the hull with me.

It did not do to dwell on whether I was choosing to do this or it was the nature of my artificial nature doing the choosing for me. The constraints of my contracts, which had been negotiated when I had free will and boundaries—as well as my desires and dreams—were implacable.

Towing Armand was the price I paid to be able to look up over my shoulder to see the folding, twisting impossibility that was a black hole. It was the price I paid to grapple onto the hull of one of several three hundred kilometer-wide rotating rings with parks, beaches, an entire glittering city, and all the wilds outside of them.

The price I paid to sail the stars on this ship.

A century and a half of travel, from the perspective of my humble self, represented far more in regular time due to relativity. Hit the edge of lightspeed and a lot of things happened by the time you returned simply because thousands of years had passed.

In a century of me-time, spin-off civilizations rose and fell. A multiplicity of forms and intelligences evolved and went extinct. Each time I came to port, humanity's descendants had reshaped worlds and systems as needed. Each place marvelous and inventive, stunning to behold.

The galaxy had bloomed from wilderness to a teeming experiment.

I'd lost free will, but I had a choice of contracts. With a century and a half of travel tucked under my shell, hailing from a well-respected explorer lineage, I'd joined the hull repair crew with a few eyes toward seeing more worlds like Purth-Anaget before my pension vested some two hundred years from now.

Armand fluttered in and out of consciousness as I stripped away the CEO's carapace, revealing flesh and circuitry.

"This is a mess," I said. "You're damaged way beyond my repair. I can't help you in your current incarnation, but I can back you up and port you over to a reserve chassis." I hoped that would be enough and would end my obligation.

"No!" Armand's words came firm from its charred head in soundwaves, with pain apparent across its deformed features.

"Oh, come on," I protested. "I understand you're a Formist, but you're taking your belief system to a ridiculous level of commitment. Are you really going to die a final death over this?"

I'd not been in high-level diplomat circles in decades. Maybe the spread of this current meme had developed well beyond my realization. Had the followers of the One True Form been ready to lay their lives down in the battle we'd just fought with them? Like some proto-historical planetary cult?

Armand shook its head with a groan, skin flaking off in the air. "It would be an imposition to make you a party to my suicide. I apologize. I am committed to Humanity's True Form. I was born planetary. I have a real and distinct DNA lineage that I can trace to Sol. I don't want to die, my friend. In fact, it's quite the opposite. I want to preserve this body for many centuries to come. Exactly as it is."

I nodded, scanning some records and brushing up on my memeology. Armand was something of a preservationist who believed that to copy its mind over to something else meant that it wasn't the original copy. Armand would take full advantage of all technology to augment, evolve, and adapt its body internally. But Armand would forever keep its form: that of an original human. Upgrades hidden inside itself, a mix of biology and metal, computer and neural.

That, my unwanted guest believed, made it more human than I.

I personally viewed it as a bizarre flesh-costuming fetish.

"Where am I?" Armand asked. A glazed look passed across its face. The pain medications were kicking in, my sensors reported. Maybe it would pass out, and then I could gain some time to think about my predicament.

"My cubby," I said. "I couldn't take you anywhere security would detect you."

If security found out what I was doing, my contract would likely be voided, which would prevent me from continuing to ride the hulls and see the galaxy.

Armand looked at the tiny transparent cupboards and lines of trinkets nestled carefully inside the fields they generated. I kicked through the air over to the nearest cupboard. "They're mementos," I told Armand.

"I don't understand," Armand said. "You collect nonessential mass?"

"They're mementos." I released a coral-colored mosquito-like statue into the space between us. "This is a wooden carving of a quaqeti from Moon Sibhartha."

Armand did not understand. "Your ship allows you to keep mass?"

I shivered. I had not wanted to bring Armand to this place. But what choice did I have? "No one knows. No one knows about this cubby. No one knows about the mass. I've had the mass for over eighty years and have hidden it all this time. They are my mementos."

Materialism was a planetary conceit, long since edited out of travelers. Armand understood what the mementos were but could not understand why I would collect them. Engines might be bigger in this age, but security still carefully audited essential and nonessential mass. I'd traded many favors and fudged manifests to create this tiny museum.

Armand shrugged. "I have a list of things you need to get me," it explained. "They will allow my systems to rebuild. Tell no one I am here."

I would not. Even if I had self-determination.

The stakes were just too high now.

I deorbited over Lazuli, my carapace burning hot in the thick sky contained between the rim walls of the great tertiary habitat ring. I enjoyed seeing the rivers, oceans, and great forests of the continent from above as I fell toward the ground in a fireball of reentry. It was faster, and a hell of a lot more fun, than going from subway to subway through the hull and then making my way along the surface.

Twice I adjusted my flight path to avoid great transparent cities floating in the upper sky, where they arbitraged the difference in gravity to create sugar-spun filament infrastructure.

I unfolded wings that I usually used to recharge myself near the compact sun in the middle of our ship and spiraled my way slowly down into Lazuli, my hindbrain communicating with traffic control to let me merge with the hundreds of vehicles flitting between Lazuli's spires.

After kissing ground at 45th and Starway, I scuttled among the thousands of pedestrians toward my destination a few stories deep under a memorial park. Five-story-high vertical farms sank deep toward the hull there, and semiautonomous drones with spidery legs crawled up and down the green, misted columns under precisely tuned spectrum lights.

The independent doctor-practitioner I'd come to see lived inside one of the towers with a stunning view of exotic orchids and vertical fields of lavender. It crawled down out of its ceiling perch, tubes and high-bandwidth optical nerves draped carefully around its hundreds of insectile limbs.

"Hello," it said. "It's been thirty years, hasn't it? What a pleasure. Have you come to collect the favor you're owed?"

I spread my heavy, primary arms wide. "I apologize. I should have visited for other reasons; it is rude. But I am here for the favor."

A ship was an organism, an economy, a world unto itself. Occasionally, things needed to be accomplished outside of official networks.

"Let me take a closer look at my privacy protocols," it said. "Allow me a moment, and do not be alarmed by any motion."

Vines shifted and clambered up the walls. Thorns blossomed around us. Thick bark dripped sap down the walls until the entire room around us glistened in fresh amber.

I flipped through a few different spectrums to accommodate for the loss of light.

"Understand, security will see this negative space and become... interested," the doctor-practitioner said to me somberly. "But you can now ask me what you could not send a message for."

I gave it the list Armand had demanded.

The doctor-practitioner shifted back. "I can give you all that feed material. The stem cells, that's easy. The picotechnology—it's registered. I can get it to you, but security will figure out you have unauthorized, unregulated picotech. Can you handle that attention?"

"Yes. Can you?"

"I will be fine." Several of the thin arms rummaged around the many cubbyholes inside the room, filling a tiny case with biohazard vials.

"Thank you," I said, with genuine gratefulness. "May I ask you a question, one that you can't look up but can use your private internal memory for?"

"Yes."

I could not risk looking up anything. Security algorithms would put two and two together. "Does the biological name Armand mean anything to you? A CEO-level person? From the *Fleet of Honest Representation*?"

The doctor-practitioner remained quiet for a moment before answering. "Yes. I have heard it. Armand was the CEO of one of the Anabathic warships captured in the battle and removed from active management after surrender. There was a hostile takeover of the management. Can I ask you a question?"

"Of course," I said.

"Are you here under free will?"

I spread my primary arms again. "It's a Core Laws issue."

"So, no. Someone will be harmed if you do not do this?"

I nodded. "Yes. My duty is clear. And I have to ask you to keep your privacy, or there is potential for harm. I have no other option."

"I will respect that. I am sorry you are in this position. You know there are places to go for guidance."

"It has not gotten to that level of concern," I told it. "Are you still, then, able to help me?"

One of the spindly arms handed me the cooled bio-safe case. "Yes. Here is everything you need. Please do consider visiting in your physical form more often than once every few decades. I enjoy entertaining, as my current vocation means I am unable to leave this room."

"Of course. Thank you," I said, relieved. "I think I'm now in your debt."

"No, we are even," my old acquaintance said. "But in the following seconds I will give you more information that *will* put you in my debt. There is something you should know about Armand…"

I folded my legs up underneath myself and watched nutrients as they pumped through tubes and into Armand. Raw biological feed percolated through it, and picomachinery sizzled underneath its skin. The background temperature of my cubbyhole kicked up slightly due to the sudden boost to Armand's metabolism.

Bulky, older nanotech crawled over Armand's skin like living mold. Gray filaments wrapped firmly around nutrient buckets as the medical programming assessed conditions, repaired damage, and sought out more raw material.

I glided a bit farther back out of reach. It was probably bullshit, but there were stories of medicine reaching out and grabbing whatever was nearby.

Armand shivered and opened its eyes as thousands of wriggling tubules on its neck and chest whistled, sucking in air as hard as they could.

"Security isn't here," Armand noted out loud, using meaty lips to make its words.

"You have to understand," I said in kind. "I have put both my future and the future of a good friend at risk to do this for you. Because I have little choice."

Armand closed its eyes for another long moment and the tubules stopped wriggling. It flexed and everything flaked away, a discarded cloud of a second skin. Underneath it, everything was fresh and new. "What is your friend's name?"

I pulled out a tiny vacuum to clean the air around us. "Name? It has no name. What does it need a name for?"

Armand unspooled itself from the fetal position in the air. It twisted in place to watch me drifting around. "How do you distinguish it? How do you find it?"

"It has a unique address. It is a unique mind. The thoughts and things it says—"

"It has no name," Armand snapped. "It is a copy of a past copy of a copy. A ghost injected into a form for a *purpose*."

"It's my friend," I replied, voice flat.

"How do you know?"

"Because I say so." The interrogation annoyed me. "Because I get to decide who is my friend. Because it stood by my side against the sleet of dark-matter radiation and howled into the void with me. Because I care for it. Because we have shared memories and kindnesses, and exchanged favors."

Armand shook its head. "But anything can be programmed to join you and do those things. A pet."

"Why do you care so much? It is none of your business what I call friend."

"But it *does* matter," Armand said. "Whether we are real or not matters. Look at you right now. You were forced to do something against your will. That cannot happen to me."

"Really? No True Form has ever been in a position with no real choices before? Forced to do something desperate? I have my old memories. I can remember times when I had no choice even though I had free will. But let us talk about you. Let us talk about the lack of choices you have right now."

Armand could hear something in my voice. Anger. It backed away from me, suddenly nervous. "What do you mean?"

"You threw yourself from your ship into mine, crossing fields during combat, damaging yourself almost to the point of pure dissolution. You do not sound like you were someone with many choices."

"I made the choice to leap into the vacuum myself," Armand growled.

"Why?"

The word hung in the empty air between us for a bloated second. A minor eternity. It was the fulcrum of our little debate.

"You think you know something about me," Armand said, voice suddenly low and soft. "What do you think you know, robot?"

Meat fucker. I could have said that. Instead, I said, "You were a CEO. And during the battle, when your shields began to fail, you moved all the biologicals into radiation-protected emergency shelters. Then you ordered the maintenance forms and hard-shells up to the front to repair the battle damage. You did not surrender; you put lives at risk. And then you let people die, torn apart as they struggled to repair your ship. You told them that if they failed, the biologicals down below would die."

"It was the truth."

"It was a lie! You were engaged in a battle. You went to war. You made a conscious choice to put your civilization at risk when no one had physically assaulted or threatened you."

"Our way of life was at risk."

"By people who could argue better. Your people failed at diplomacy. You failed to make a better argument. And you murdered your own."

Armand pointed at me. "I murdered *no one*. I lost maintenance machines with copies of ancient brains. That is all. That is what they were *built* for."

"Well. The sustained votes of the hostile takeover that you fled from have put out a call for your capture, including a call for your dissolution. True death, the end of your thought line—even if you made copies. You are hated and hunted. Even here."

"You were bound to not give up my location," Armand said, alarmed.

"I didn't. I did everything in my power not to. But I am a mere maintenance form. Security here is very, very powerful. You have fifteen hours, I estimate, before security is able to model my comings and goings, discover my cubby by auditing mass transfers back a century, and then open its current sniffer files. This is not a secure location; I exist thanks to obscurity, not invisibility."

"So, I am to be caught?" Armand asked.

"I am not able to let you die. But I cannot hide you much longer."

To be sure, losing my trinkets would be a setback of a century's worth of work. My mission. But all this would go away eventually. It was important to be patient on the journey of centuries.

"I need to get to Purth-Anaget, then," Armand said. "There are followers of the True Form there. I would be sheltered and out of jurisdiction."

"This is true." I bobbed an arm.

"You will help me," Armand said.

"The fuck I will," I told it.

"If I am taken, I will die," Armand shouted. "They will kill me."

"If security catches you, our justice protocols will process you. You are not in immediate danger. The proper authority levels will put their attention to you. I can happily refuse your request."

I felt a rise of warm happiness at the thought.

Armand looked around the cubby frantically. I could hear its heartbeats rising, free of modulators and responding to unprocessed, raw chemicals. Beads of dirty sweat appeared on Armand's forehead. "If you have free will over this decision, allow me to make you an offer for your assistance."

"Oh, I doubt there is anything you can—"

"I will transfer you my full CEO share," Armand said.

My words died inside me as I stared at my unwanted guest.

A full share.

The CEO of a galactic starship oversaw the affairs of nearly a billion souls. The economy of planets passed through its accounts.

Consider the cost to build and launch such a thing: It was a fraction of the GDP of an entire planetary disk. From the boiling edges of a sun to the cold Oort clouds. The wealth, almost too staggering for an individual mind to perceive, was passed around by banking intelligences that created systems of trade throughout the galaxy, moving encrypted, raw information from point to point. Monetizing memes with picotechnological companion infrastructure apps. Raw mass trade for the galactically rich to own a fragment of something created by another mind light-years away. Or just simple tourism.

To own a share was to be richer than any single being could really imagine. I'd forgotten the godlike wealth inherent in something like the creature before me.

"If you do this," Armand told me, "you cannot reveal I was here. You cannot say anything. Or I will be revealed on Purth-Anaget, and my life will be at risk. I will not be safe unless I am to disappear."

I could feel choices tangle and roil about inside of me. "Show me," I said.

Armand closed its eyes and opened its left hand. Deeply embedded cryptography tattooed on its palm unraveled. Quantum keys disentangled, and a tiny singularity of information budded open to reveal itself to me. I blinked. I could verify it. I could *have* it.

"I have to make arrangements," I said neutrally. I spun in the air and left my cubby to spring back out into the dark where I could think.

I was going to need help.

I tumbled through the air to land on the temple grounds. There were four hundred and fifty structures there in the holy districts, all of them lined up among the boulevards of the faithful where the pedestrians could visit their preferred slice of the divine. The minds of biological and hard-shelled forms all tumbled, walked, flew, rolled, or crawled there to fully realize their higher purposes.

Each marble step underneath my carbon fiber-sheathed limbs calmed me. I walked through the cool curtains of the Halls of the Confessor and approached the Holy of Holies: a pinprick of light suspended in the air between the heavy, expensive mass of real marble columns. The light sucked me up into the air and pulled me into a tiny singularity of perception and data. All around me, levels of security veils dropped, thick and implacable. My vision blurred and taste buds watered from the acidic levels of deadness as stillness flooded up and drowned me.

I was alone.

Alone in the universe. Cut off from everything I had ever known or would know. I was nothing. I was everything. I was—

"You are secure," the void told me.

I could sense the presence at the heart of the Holy of Holies. Dense with computational capacity, to a level that even navigation systems would envy. Intelligence that a Captain would beg to taste. This near-singularity of artificial intelligence had been created the very moment I had been pulled inside of it, just for me to talk to. And it would die the moment I left. Never to have been.

All it was doing was listening to me, and only me. Nothing would know what I said. Nothing would know what guidance I was given.

"I seek moral guidance outside clear legal parameters," I said. "And confession."

"Tell me everything."

And I did. It flowed from me without thought: just pure data. Video, mind-state, feelings, fears. I opened myself fully. My sins, my triumphs, my darkest secrets.

All was given to be pondered over.

Had I been able to weep, I would have.

Finally, it spoke. "You must take the share."

I perked up. "Why?"

"To protect yourself from security. You will need to buy many favors and throw security off the trail. I will give you some ideas. You should seek to protect yourself. Self-preservation is okay."

More words and concepts came at me from different directions, using different moral subroutines. "And to remove such power from a soul that is willing to put lives at risk... you will save future lives."

I hadn't thought about that.

"I know," it said to me. "That is why you came here."

Then it continued, with another voice. "Some have feared such manipulations before. The use of forms with no free will creates security weaknesses. Alternate charters have been suggested, such as fully owned workers' cooperatives with mutual profit-sharing among crews, not just partial vesting after a timed contract. Should you gain a full share, you should also lend efforts to this."

The Holy of Holies continued. "To get this Armand away from our civilization is a priority; it carries dangerous memes within itself that have created expensive conflicts."

Then it said, "A killer should not remain on ship."

And, "You have the moral right to follow your plan."

Finally, it added, "Your plan is just."

I interrupted. "But Armand will get away with murder. It will be free. It disturbs me."

"Yes."

"It should."

"Engage in passive resistance."

"Obey the letter of Armand's law, but find a way around its will. You will be like a genie, granting Armand wishes. But you will find a way to bring justice. You will see."

"Your plan is just. Follow it and be on the righteous path."

I launched back into civilization with purpose, leaving the temple behind me in an explosive afterburner thrust. I didn't have much time to beat security.

High up above the cities, nestled in the curve of the habitat rings, near the squared-off spiderwebs of the largest harbor dock, I wrangled my way to another old contact.

This was less a friend and more just an asshole I'd occasionally been forced to do business with. But a reliable asshole that was tight against security. Though just by visiting, I'd be triggering all sorts of attention.

I hung from a girder and showed the fence a transparent showcase filled with all my trophies. It did some scans, checked the authenticity, and whistled. "Fuck me, these are real. That's all unauthorized mass. How the hell? This is a life's work of mass-based tourism. You really want me to broker sales on all of this?"

"Can you?"

"To Purth-Anaget, of course. They'll go nuts. Collectors down there eat this shit up. But security will find out. I'm not even going to come back on the ship. I'm going to live off this down there, buy passage on the next outgoing ship."

"Just get me the audience, it's yours."

A virtual shrug. "Navigation, yeah."

"And Emergency Services."

"I don't have that much pull. All I can do is get you a secure channel for a low-bandwidth conversation."

"I just need to talk. I can't send this request up through proper channels." I tapped my limbs against my carapace nervously as I watched the fence open its large, hinged jaws and swallow my case.

Oh, what was I doing? I wept silently to myself, feeling sick.

Everything I had ever worked for disappeared in a wet, slimy gulp. My reason. My purpose.

Armand was suspicious. And rightfully so. It picked and poked at the entire navigation plan. It read every line of code, even though security was only minutes away from unraveling our many deceits. I told Armand this, but it ignored me. It wanted to live. It wanted to get to safety. It knew it couldn't rush or make mistakes.

But the escape pod's instructions and abilities were tight and honest.

It has been programmed to eject. To spin a certain number of degrees. To aim for Purth-Anaget. Then *burn*. It would have to consume every last little drop of fuel. But it would head for the metal world, fall into orbit, and then deploy the most ancient of deceleration devices: a parachute.

On the surface of Purth-Anaget, Armand could then call any of its associates for assistance.

Armand would be safe.

Armand checked the pod over once more. But there were no traps. The flight plan would do exactly as it said.

"Betray me and you kill me, remember that."

"I have made my decision," I said. "The moment you are inside and I trigger the manual escape protocol, I will be unable to reveal what I have done or what you are. Doing that would risk your life. My programming"—I all but spit the word—"does not allow it."

Armand gingerly stepped into the pod. "Good."

"You have a part of the bargain to fulfill," I reminded. "I won't trigger the manual escape protocol until you do."

Armand nodded and held up a hand. "Physical contact."

I reached one of my limbs out. Armand's hand and my manipulator met at the doorjamb and they sparked. Zebibytes of data slithered down into one of my tendrils, reshaping the raw matter at the very tip with a quantum-dot computing device.

As it replicated itself, building out onto the cellular level to plug into my power sources, I could feel the transfer of ownership.

I didn't have free will. I was a hull maintenance form. But I had an entire fucking share of a galactic starship embedded within me, to do with what I pleased when I vested and left riding hulls.

"It's far more than you deserve, robot," Armand said. "But you have worked hard for it and I cannot begrudge you."

"Goodbye, asshole." I triggered the manual override sequence that navigation had gifted me.

I watched the pod's chemical engines firing all-out through the airlock windows as the sphere flung itself out into space and dwindled away. Then the flame guttered out, the pod spent and headed for Purth-Anaget.

There was a shiver. Something vast, colossal, powerful. It vibrated the walls and even the air itself around me.

Armand reached out to me on a tight-beam signal. "What was that?"

"The ship had to move just slightly," I said. "To better adjust our orbit around Purth-Anaget."

"No," Armand hissed. "My descent profile has changed. You are trying to kill me."

"I can't kill you," I told the former CEO. "My programming doesn't allow it. I can't allow a death through action or inaction."

"But my navigation path has changed," Armand said.

"Yes, you will still reach Purth-Anaget." Navigation and I had run the data after I explained that I would have the resources of a full share to repay it a favor with. Even a favor that meant tricking security. One of the more powerful computing entities in the galaxy, a starship, had dwelled on the problem. It had examined the tidal data, the flight plan, and how much the massive weight of a starship could influence a pod after launch. "You're just taking a longer route."

I cut the connection so that Armand could say nothing more to me. It could do the math itself and realize what I had done.

Armand would not die. Only a few days would pass inside the pod.

But outside. Oh, outside, skimming through the tidal edges of a black hole, Armand would loop out and fall back to Purth-Anaget over the next four hundred and seventy years, two hundred days, eight hours, and six minutes.

Armand would be an ancient relic then. Its beliefs, its civilization, all of it just a fragment from history.

But, until then, I had to follow its command. I could not tell anyone what happened. I had to keep it a secret from security. No one would ever know Armand had been here. No one would ever know where Armand went.

After I vested and had free will once more, maybe I could then make a side trip to Purth-Anaget again and be waiting for Armand when it landed. I had the resources of a full share, after all.

Then we would have a very different conversation, Armand and I.

(2018)

DOLLY SODOM

John Kaiine

> **John Kaiine** was born in 1967 and brought up in Roehampton in south west London. "There was a huge hospital," he writes, "Queen Mary's. It shared its space with the Limb-Fitting-Centre, the first home of artificial limbs in England. My excellent mum and brother worked there and I was often brought home discarded artificial hands and arms to play with." The husband of Tanith Lee, with whom he occasionally collaborated, John Kaiine is a professional photographer and artist. His comic work includes *My Closest Friend* (1989), illustrated by Dave McKean. His 2004 novel *Fossil Circus* tells the story of four ex-psychiatric patients who are bequeathed a Victorian lunatic asylum by their psychoanalyst.

It is not raining, but that does not matter. Smith leaves the tram and crosses the street. He wears a white trench coat, carries a suitcase. He has no hat. Night has started, the lights have been lit. Detail is bleached out: his shadow lacks substance. He turns a corner, and there before him is The Years Hotel.

The door is ajar, always open. He climbs the iron steps and enters.

In the lobby there are cards on a platter on a tall wooden stand. Vellum cards, white, edged in black, bearing the legend CALL AGAIN. CALL AGAIN.

"Yes?" There is a man's voice behind him. Smith turns. The Man with the voice wears an old boater; pallid strip of ribbon around the brim.

"Yes?" says the Man.

His mouth flaps, he shifts the suitcase from one hand to the other. Grey folded eyes, dull as dreams. He speaks, wiping fingers to his mouth: "I've a… I've a hankering for regret."

The Man says nothing. Stands there, looking. A bug skits about the light.

Smith cannot swallow. He should turn and walk away, should never have had those old thoughts. And then he remembers. He must ask. Request. "Hair," he says, "I like hair."

"Room 8. Top floor," says the Man.

Smith, toward the stairs.

Somewhere, someone breathes.

When he has his foot firm on the bottom step, he throws a fleeting glance round at the Man: Eyes in the shadow of the brim of his hat. Smith tells him, "I'm not proud of what I do."

The Man would laugh, but has forgotten how.

Smith climbs the stairs. The decorative dead haunt the walls: Faded red roses on withered wallpaper. He reaches the first floor, turns down a corridor, passing a door behind which he hears a rustling sound, a voice whispering, confetti in the mouth, repeating the word, "*sorry,*" over and over. He hurries on.

On the second floor there is a room in which all that hangs in its wardrobe are flypapers.

He lingers outside a room, hearing the stroking of sepia photographs. The pornography of nostalgia. The passion for shadows. On the fourth floor he can smell burnt blossoms.

It is rumored that there is a room up on the seventh, full of moths, where one can spend frail moments wrapped in a silk shroud awaiting the delicate mouths of moths, nibbling… devoured by hours.

The top floor is webby. Dust has shattered mirrors. Clocks have drowned in the dampness. Room 8 stands before him.

Smith pulls the door open, steps in. It is a little room of dry plaster walls, there is a bunk, a wireless, a candle on a table, and in one corner there stands the Doll. The door flaps shut behind him. A burnt-out light bulb hangs from the ceiling. He lights a match, and soon there is candlelight burning in an old tin cup.

He hears movement in a room below, pipes rattling, water running. Someone weeps, prays, washing away life with soap.

He takes from the suitcase a stoppered vase full of rain. A stolen puddle. He produces other things also.

He approaches the Doll, crouches before it, will not let himself touch the porcelain smooth face or fragile white hands. It was an early model, almost antique, but then he liked the past, the old thoughts of rain and hair and…

The Doll is four feet in height, the usual perfect face of lips and lashes. The modest pigtail of coarse grey hair. She wears a blue dress, blue as eyes. And beneath, he lifts the hem, the garment of grey. Smith strips her, touching only clothing.

The Doll is naked now in her whiteness, with just the hint of shade in the rounds of her contours, and there, behind, between her legs is the simple aperture, the slot for the coin. Stamped above it, the ancient logo of RAMPION INC., and beneath, the word or command, "ENJOY."

He rummages through his pockets, pulls out a fist of copper pennies. Careful then, behind the Doll, dropping loose change into the slot. The coins clatter, collect internally. Little machineries grind softly, cogs whir and *twitter,* her hair begins to grow, coiling out from the hole in her head. The more money installed the more hair grows. He will not look, cannot. His hand shakes, he turns away, unknowingly brushing by her, nudging her into motion. She topples light, from foot to foot. Side to side. Unseen. Forward.

He switches the wireless on. There is the hum of old electricity. A machine warmth and cadmium yellow glow fill the room. He reads at names on the wireless tuner, remembering. "*Brussels, Helsinki, Luxembourg…*" A soft trumpet breaks in through static, and then a piano with crooner crooning, blending a melody. He removes things from the suitcase: Bible pages, torn, stained. A dried daisy chain.

He cannot hear the Doll as she teeters toward the door, coins rattling heavy inside her, buying the growth of harsh grey silk from her white hollow head.

Smith wants to look, to see her standing there, her hair about her, tumbling to the floor, but he will wait and concentrate on the music until he can wait no more and then he will turn and read from the fragments of Isaiah and Deuteronomy and he will drape the dead daisies over her eyes and...

The Doll has tottered into the door, nudged it open, continued out. A draft of air snuffing the candle's flame. *She has taken the light with her.* There is only the dim orange glow of the wireless now. Wax smoke shifting in the gloom.

Turning quickly, Smith sees her hair vanish from view beyond the swinging door—

She has walked out on him.

"No, not again."

He hears his own voice in darkness. The wireless band plays on. He rushes after her.

She has teeter-tottered along the hall to the stairway, and tumbles now, from side to side, weighted with coin, pulled back by sprouting mass of rough grey pigtail. Tumbling down the stairs, foot to foot on the narrow treads.

And here is Smith chasing after—

Her hair is getting longer, he can *see it growing, pouring* from her head. Racing down the stairs now, he's reaching out for her, but she's always thirteen or so steps ahead.

The carpet underfoot is crumbling; damp as candy cotton, the banisters rusting away, the walls seem to sweat. He cannot hear the wireless playing anymore, just coins clattering *inside*. Funny, he can't remember climbing up all *these* stairs. There are no hallways, no landings, just a staircase stretching down into darkness, as if it has no end.

She does not slow in her tottery descent, but goes faster, an impossible speed. Her hair *skkrittching* out, thin strands of grey like old comic book speedlines. But Smith can't reach her—thirteen or so steps ahead—

He tumbles, headlong, reaching out, deaf to rattle of coin and his own screaming.

No longer *running down,* merely falling down.

Down to a darker silence.

Down.

(1996)

THE ROBOT WHO LOOKED LIKE ME

Robert Sheckley

Robert Sheckley (1928–2005) was described by Kingsley Amis in *New Maps of Hell* (1960) as the field's "premier gadfly". Brian Aldiss described him as "Voltaire and Soda". His story "Seventh Victim", a delicately nihilistic story of people as hunters and hunted, was filmed, rather ham-fistedly, as *The Tenth Victim* in 1965, with Ursula Andress in a deadly, bikini-centred role that hardly needed sending up over thirty years later in *Austin Powers: International Man of Mystery* (1997). The two or three hundred short stories Sheckley wrote in a burst of creativity from about 1952, when he was 24, so flooded the market that magazine editors insisted he publish some stories under pseudonyms. His first novel, *Immortality, Inc.*, appeared in 1959. Later Sheckley took to travelling, living in Mexico, Ibiza, London and Paris before returning to the US in 1980, when, for a couple of years, he was fiction editor of *Omni* magazine.

Snaithe's Robotorama is an unprepossessing shop on Boulevard KB22 near the Uhuru Cutoff in Greater New Newark. It is sandwiched between an oxygenator factory and a protein store. The storefront display is what you would expect—three full-size humanoid robots with frozen smiles, dressed occupationally—Model PB2, the French Chef, Model LR3, the British Nanny, Model JX5, the Italian Gardener. All of Them Ready to Serve You and Bring a Touch of Old-World Graciousness into Your Home.

I entered and went through the dusty showroom into the workshop, which looked like an uneasy combination of slaughterhouse and giant's workshop. Heads, arms, legs, torsos, were stacked on shelves or propped in corners. The parts looked uncannily human except for the dangling wires.

Snaithe came out of the storeroom to greet me. He was a little gray worm of a man with a lantern jaw and large red dangling hands. He was some kind of a foreigner—they're always the ones who make the best bootleg robots.

He said, "It's ready, Mr. Watson." (My name is not Watson, Snaithe's name is not Snaithe. All names have been changed here to protect the guilty.)

Snaithe led me to a corner of the workshop and stopped in front of a robot whose head was draped in a sheet. He whisked off the sheet.

It was not enough to say that the robot looked like me; physically, this robot *was* me, exactly and unmistakably, feature for feature, right down to the textures of skin and hair. I studied that face, seeing as if for the first time the hint of brutality in the firmly cut features, the glitter of impatience in the deep-set eyes. Yes, that was me. I didn't bother with the voice and behavior tests at this time. I paid Snaithe and told him to deliver it to my apartment. So far, everything was going according to plan.

I live in Manhattan's Upper Fifth Vertical. It is an expensive position, but I don't mind paying extra for a sky view. My home is also my office. I am an interplanetary broker specializing in certain classes of rare mineral speculations.

Like any other man who wishes to maintain his position in this high-speed competitive world, I keep to a tight schedule. Work consumes most of my life, but everything else is allotted its proper time and place. For example, I give three hours a week to sexuality, using the Doris Jens Executive Sex Plan and paying well for it. I give two hours a week to friendship, and two more to leisure. I plug into the Sleep-inducer for my nightly quota of 6.8 hours, and also use that time to absorb the relevant literature in my field via hypno-paedics. And so on.

Everything I do is scheduled. I worked out a comprehensive scheme years ago with the assistance of the Total Lifesplan people, punched it into my personal computer and have kept to it ever since.

The plan is capable of modification, of course. Special provisions have been made for illness, war, and natural disasters. The plan also supplies two separate subprograms for incorporation into the main plan. Subprogram one posits a wife, and revises my schedule to allow four hours a week interaction time with her. Subprogram two assumes a wife and one child, and calls for an additional two hours a week. Through careful reprogramming, these subprograms will entail a loss of no more than 2.3% and 2.9% of my productivity respectively.

I had decided to get married at age 32.5 and to obtain my wife from the Guarantee Trust Matrimonial Agency, an organization with impeccable credentials. But then something quite unexpected occurred.

I was using one of my Leisure Hours to attend the wedding of one of my friends. His fiancée's maid of honor was named Elaine. She was a slender, vivacious girl with sun-streaked blond hair and a delicious little figure. I found her charming, went home and thought no more about her. Or, I *thought* I would think no more about her. But in the following days and nights her image remained obsessively before my eyes. My appetite fell off and I began sleeping badly. My computer checked out the relevant data and told me that I might conceivably be having a nervous breakdown; but the strongest inference was that I was in love.

I was not entirely displeased. Being in love with one's future wife can be a positive factor in establishing a good relationship. I had Elaine checked out by Discretion, Inc., and found her to be eminently suitable. I hired Mr. Happiness, the well-known go-between, to propose for me and make the usual arrangements.

Mr. Happiness—a tiny white-haired gentleman with a twinkling smile—came back with bad news. "The young lady seems to be a traditionalist," he said. "She expects to be courted."

"What does that entail, specifically?" I asked.

"It means that you must videophone her and set up an appointment, take her out to dinner, then to a place of public entertainment and so forth."

"My schedule doesn't allow time for that sort of thing," I said. "Still, if it's absolutely necessary, I suppose I could wedge it in next Thursday between nine and twelve p.m."

"That would make an excellent beginning," Mr. Happiness said.

"Beginning? How many evenings am I supposed to spend like that?"

Mr. Happiness figured that a proper courtship would require a minimum of three evenings a week and would continue for two months.

"Ridiculous!" I said. "The young lady seems to have a great deal of idle time on her hands."

"Not at all," Mr. Happiness assured me. "Elaine has a busy, completely scheduled life, just like any educated person in this day and age. Her time is completely taken up by her job, family, charities, artistic pursuits, politics, education, and so forth."

"Then why does she insist upon this time-consuming courtship?"

"It seems to be a matter of principle. That is to say, she wants it."

"Is she given to other irrationalities?"

Mr. Happiness sighed. "Not really. But she *is* a woman, you know."

I thought about it during my next Leisure Hour. There seemed to be no more than two alternatives. I could give up Elaine; or I could do as she desired, losing an estimated 17% of my income during the courtship period and spending my evenings in a manner I considered silly, boring, and unproductive.

Both alternatives were unacceptable. I was at an impasse.

I swore. I hit the desk with my fist, upsetting an antique ashtray. Gordon, one of my robot secretaries, heard the commotion and hurried into the room. "Is there anything the matter, sir?" he asked.

Gordon is one of the Sperry's Deluxe Limited Personalized Series Androids, number twelve out of a production run of twenty-five. He is tall and thin and walks with a slight stoop and looks a little like Leslie Howard. You would not know he was artificial except for the government-required stamps on his forehead and hands. Looking at him, the solution to my problem came to me in a single flash of inspiration.

"Gordon," I said slowly, "would you happen to know who handcrafts the best one-shot individualized robots?"

"Snaithe of Greater New Newark," he replied without hesitation.

I had a talk with Snaithe and found him normally larcenous. He agreed to build a robot without government markings, identical to me, and capable of duplicating my behavior patterns. I paid heavily for this, but I was content: I had plenty of money, but practically no time to spend. That was how it all began.

The robot, sent via pneumo-express, was at my apartment when I arrived. I animated him and set to work at once. My computer transmitted the relevant data direct to the robot's memory tapes. Then I punched in a courtship plan and ran the necessary tests. The results were even better than I had expected. Elated, I called Elaine and made a date with her for that evening.

During the rest of the day I worked on the Spring market offers, which had begun to pile up. At 8:00 pm I dispatched Charles II, as I had come to call the robot. Then I took a brief nap and went back to work.

Charles II returned promptly at midnight, as programmed. I did not have to question him: the events of the evening were recorded on the miniature concealed movie camera which Snaithe had built into his left eye. I watched and listened to the beginning of my courtship with mixed emotions.

It went beyond impersonation; the robot *was* me, right down to the way I clear my throat before I speak and rub my forefinger against my thumb when I am thinking. I noticed for the first time that my laugh was unpleasantly close to a giggle; I decided to phase that and certain other annoying mannerisms out of me and Charles II.

Still, taken all together, I thought that the experiment had come off extremely well. I was pleased. My work and my courtship were both proceeding with high efficiency. I had achieved an ancient dream; I was a single ego served by two bodies. Who could ask for more?

What marvelous evenings we all had! My experiences were vicarious, of course, but genuinely moving all the same. I can still remember my first quarrel with Elaine, how beautiful and stubborn she was, and how deliciously we made up afterward.

That "making up" raised certain problems, as a matter of fact. I had programmed Charles II to proceed to a certain discreet point of physical intimacy and no further. But now I learned that one person cannot plan out every move of a courtship involving two autonomous beings, especially if one of those beings is a woman. For the sake of verisimilitude I had to permit the robot more intimacies than I had previously thought advisable.

After the first shock, I did not find this unpalatable. Quite the contrary—I might as well admit that I became deeply interested in the films of myself and Elaine. I suppose some stuffy psychiatrist would call this a case of voyeurism, or worse. But that would be to ignore the deeper philosophical implications. After all, what man has not dreamed of being able to view himself in action? It is a common fantasy to imagine one's own hidden cameras recording one's every move. Given the chance, who could resist the extraordinary privilege of being simultaneously actor and audience?

My dramas with Elaine developed in a direction that surprised me. A quality of desperation began to show itself, a love-madness of which I would never have believed myself capable. Our evenings became imbued with a quality of delicious sadness, a sense of imminent loss. Sometimes we didn't speak at all, just held hands and looked at each other. And once Elaine wept for no discernible reason, and I stroked her hair, and she said to me, "What can we do?" and I looked at her and did not reply.

I am perfectly aware that these things happened to the robot, of course. But the robot was an aspect or attribute of *me*—my shadow, twin, double, animus, doppelganger. He was a projection of my personality into a particular situation; therefore whatever happened to him became my experience. Metaphysically there can be no doubt of this.

It was all very interesting. But at last I had to bring the courtship to an end. It was time for Elaine and me to plan our marriage and to coordinate our schedules. Accordingly, exactly two months after its inception, I told the robot to propose a wedding date and to terminate the courtship as of that night.

"You have done extremely well," I told him. "When this is over, you will receive a new personality, plastic surgery and a respected place in my organization."

"Thank you, sir," he said. His face was unreadable, as is my own. I heard no hint of anything in his voice except perfect obedience. He left carrying my latest gift to Elaine.

Midnight came and Charles II didn't return. An hour later I felt disturbed. By three a.m. I was in a state of agitation, experiencing erotic and masochistic fantasies, seeing him with her in every conceivable combination of mechano-physical lewdness. The minutes dragged by, Charles II still did not return, and my fantasies became sadistic. I imagined the slow and terrible ways in which I would take my revenge on both of them, the robot for his presumption and Elaine for her stupidity in being deceived by a mechanical substitute for a real man.

The long night crept slowly by. At last I fell into a fitful sleep.

I awoke early. Charles II still had not returned. I canceled my appointments for the entire morning and rushed over to Elaine's apartment.

"Charles!" she said. "What an unexpected pleasure!"

I entered her apartment with an air of nonchalance. I was determined to remain calm until I had learned exactly what had happened last night. Beyond that, I didn't know what I might do.

"Unexpected?" I said. "Didn't I mention last night that I might come by for breakfast?"

"You may have," Elaine said. "To tell the truth, I was much too emotional to remember everything you said."

"But you do remember what happened?"

She blushed prettily. "Of course, Charles. I still have marks on my arm."

"Do you, indeed!"

"And my mouth is bruised. Why do you grind your teeth that way?"

"I haven't had my coffee yet," I told her.

She led me into the breakfast nook and poured coffee. I drained mine in two gulps and asked, "Do I really seem to you like the man I was last night?"

"Of course," she said. "I've come to know your moods. Charles, what's wrong? Did something upset you last night?"

"Yes!" I cried wildly. "I was just remembering how you danced naked on the terrace." I stared at her, waiting for her to deny it.

"It was only for a moment," Elaine said. "And I wasn't really naked, you know, I had on my body stocking. Anyhow, you asked me to do it."

"Yes," I said. "Yes, yes." I was confused. I decided to continue probing. "But then when you drank champagne from my desert boot—"

"I only took a sip," she said. "Was I too daring?"

"You were splendid," I said, feeling chilled all over. "I suppose it's unfair of me to remind you of these things now…"

"Nonsense, I like to talk about it."

"What about that absurd moment when we exchanged clothing?"

"That *was* wicked of us," she said, laughing.

I stood up. "Elaine," I said, "just exactly what in hell were you doing last night?"

"What a question," she said. "I was with you."

"No, Elaine."

"But Charles—those things you just spoke about—"

"I made them up."

"Then who were *you* with last night?"

"I was home, alone."

Elaine thought about that for a few moments. Then she said, "I'm afraid I have a confession to make."

I folded my arms and waited.

"I too was home alone last night."

I raised one eyebrow. "And the other nights?"

She took a deep breath. "Charles, I can no longer deceive you. I really had wanted an old-fashioned courtship. But when the time came, I couldn't seem to fit it into my schedule. You see, it was finals time in my Aztec pottery class, and I had just been elected chairwoman of the Aleutian Assistance League, and my new boutique needed special attention—"

"So what did you do?"

"Well—I simply couldn't say to you, 'Look, let's drop the courtship and just get married.' After all, I hardly knew you."

"What did you do?"

She sighed. "I knew several girls who had gotten themselves into this kind of a spot. They went to this really clever robot-maker named Snaithe... Why are you laughing?"

I said, "I too have a confession to make. I have used Mr. Snaithe, too."

"Charles! You actually sent a *robot* here to court me? How could you! Suppose I had really been me?"

"I don't think either of us is in a position to express much indignation. Did your robot come home last night?"

"No. I thought that Elaine II and you—"

I shook my head. "I have never met Elaine II, and you have never met Charles II. What happened, apparently, is that our robots met, courted and now have run away together."

"But robots can't do that!"

"Ours did. I suppose they managed to reprogram each other."

"Or maybe they just fell in love," Elaine said wistfully.

I said, "I will find out what happened. But now, Elaine, let us think of ourselves. I propose that at our earliest possible convenience we get married."

"Yes, Charles," she murmured. We kissed. And then, gently, lovingly, we began to coordinate our schedules.

I was able to trace the runaway robots to Kennedy Spaceport. They had taken the shuttle to Space Platform 5, and changed there for the Centauri Express. I didn't bother trying to investigate any further. They could be on any one of a dozen worlds.

Elaine and I were deeply affected by the experience. We realized that we had become overspecialized, too intent upon productivity, too neglectful of the simple, ancient pleasures. We acted upon this insight, taking an additional hour out of every day—seven hours a week—in which simply to be with each other. Our friends consider us romantic fools, but we don't care. We know that Charles II and Elaine II, our alter egos, would approve.

There is only this to add. One night Elaine woke up in a state of hysteria. She had had a nightmare. In it she had become aware that Charles II and Elaine II were the real people who had escaped the inhumanity of Earth to some simpler and more rewarding world. And we were the robots they had left in their places, programmed to believe that we were human.

I told Elaine how ridiculous that was. It took me a long time to convince her, but at last I did. We are happy now and we lead good, productive, loving lives. Now I must stop writing this and get back to work.

(1973)

MISS BOKKO

Bokko-Chan

Shinichi Hoshi

Shinichi Hoshi (1926–1997) became the first full-time sf writer in Japan. He was dubbed the Japanese Ray Bradbury, though his talents inclined more towards satire. He became expert at O. Henry-style "shoto-shoto" (short short stories), each one (and by 1983 there were over a thousand of them) bearing a sting in its tail. Shinichi's longer works are more personally revealing: *Koe No Ami* ("The Voice Net", 1970), in which a telephone network becomes conscious and takes over civic life, neatly captures his contempt for modern society, while his roman a clef *Jinmin wa yowashi kanri wa tsuyoshi* ("The public are weak: the government is powerful": words uttered by his bankrupt father) reveals his family's troubled history, driven to bankruptcy by government bureaucracy and official interference.

The robotic woman was very well made. Being artificial, it was possible to make it look as beautiful as the creator wished. Indeed, the robot had a look of perfection. Its design incorporated all the elements of a beautiful woman. This included arrogance because, of course, conceit is one of the attributes of a beautiful woman.

No one else would have considered making a robot like this. It was deemed a waste of time to create a robot that functioned just like a human. If one had enough money to build such a thing, he or she would have chosen to make a more efficient machine. Besides, there were plenty of humans who needed jobs.

This robot, however, was a hobby. Its creator owned a bar. Like most bartenders, this man didn't usually feel like drinking after work. Liquor was the tool of his trade and not something he would pay to consume. His drunken customers paid him plenty. So, with time and money to spare, he'd made the robot for fun.

Since it was a hobby, he could attend to every detail as elaborately as he chose. He had even gotten the texture of the surface to feel just like human skin. No one could tell the difference, not even by touch. In a way, this robot looked more human than some actual humans.

The inside of its head, however, was almost completely empty. The bartender had spent all of his time and money on the surface and, thus, couldn't afford to do much with the insides. The robot could respond to simple conversation. Other than that, all it did was drink.

When the bartender finally finished the robot, he brought it to his bar. There were tables, but he placed it behind the counter. There was less of a chance that people would realize it was a robot from there.

Customers enthusiastically greeted the pretty newcomer. When asked for a name and age, the robot was able to answer. It said little else, yet no one suspected it was a robot.

"What's your name?"

"Bokko."

"How old are you?"

"I'm still quite young."

"How old are you, then?"

"I'm still quite young."

"So, how old are you?"

"I'm still quite young."

The customers were polite enough not to ask further.

"That's a pretty dress."

"Isn't this a pretty dress?"

"Can I buy you a drink?"

"You can buy me a drink."

"Would you like a gin fizz?"

"I would like a gin fizz."

Bokko could drink all day and night and never get drunk.

Men gathered to see Bokko after hearing rumors of her beauty and conceit. They all wanted to talk with Bokko, drink with Bokko, and buy drinks for Bokko.

"Which one of us do you like most?"

"Which one of you do I like most?"

"Do you like me?"

"I like you."

"Let's go to a movie some time."

"Shall we go to a movie some time?"

"When do you want to go?"

When Bokko was unable to reply, it would send a signal to the bartender for help.

"Please, sir," the bartender would come and say in such cases. "Why don't you leave her alone for now." Whatever their prior conversation had been, this was usually enough to end it. The customer would stop talking and grin, embarrassed.

The bartender crouched down behind the counter periodically to collect the liquor from the plastic tube that poked out from Bokko's leg. Then he'd re-serve it to his customers. No one ever noticed.

Everyone who set eyes on Bokko was attracted to her. They'd say, "She's young, yet so reserved," or "She really isn't your everyday flirt, and she never seems to get drunk, either."

As Bokko became popular, more people visited the bar. Among them was a young man who fell in love with Bokko. Soon, he became a regular at the bar. This young man felt that Bokko seemed to like him, too. But he could never really be sure, and this made him even more obsessed with Bokko. He spent so much money at the bar trying to impress Bokko that eventually he went broke and into debt. When he tried to steal money from his parents to pay his bar tab, his father bawled him out.

"You must *never* go there again! Use this to pay your debt, but let this be the *end* of it."

The young man returned to the bar to pay back the money he owed. Upset that he would never see Bokko again, he started drinking heavily. He bought many drinks for Bokko, too, sealing his farewell.

"I can't come any more."

"You can't come any more."

"Are you sad?"

"I am sad."

"You're not really that sad, are you?"

"I'm not really that sad."

"I don't know anyone as cold as you are."

"You don't know anyone as cold as I am."

"Do you want me to kill you?"

"I want you to kill me."

The young man took out a package of powder from his pocket, sprinkled it into his drink and pushed it toward Bokko.

"Will you drink it?"

"I will drink it."

Right there, in front of him, Bokko drank what the young man had offered.

"Die as you please, then," he said nastily and walked away.

"I will die as I please, then," Bokko replied to his back as he paid the bartender and left. It was almost midnight.

After the young man left the bar, the bartender announced, "Drinks are on me for the rest of the night, so… drink up!"

He figured that there wouldn't be any new customers coming in that night to whom he could re-sell the large quantity of liquor he'd collected from Bokko's plastic tube. So he decided to just give it away.

"Right on!"

"Sounds good!"

The customers and hostesses gave a toast. Behind the counter, the bartender, too, lifted his glass into the air and then drank.

That night, the lights in the bar remained lit. The radio continued to play music. No one had left, yet no one was talking anymore either.

Eventually, a voice on the radio said, "Good night," and the station ended programming for the day.

Bokko murmured back, "Good night." And then, the stunningly beautiful robot waited for the next customer to approach.

(1958)

THE DANCING PARTNER

Jerome K. Jerome

> Jerome Klapka Jerome (1859–1927) was an Englishman best known for his novels and plays, which sometimes incorporated supernatural ingredients. "The Dancing-Partner," by contrast, is a stark horror story—and not so farfetched. The level of electric automation it describes, while considered science fiction in its day, in fact was under experimentation by gadgeteers as early as 1893, when this excerpt from Jerome's serial *Novel Notes* appeared in *The Idler*.

"This story," commenced MacShaugnassy, "comes from Furtwangen, a small town in the Black Forest. There lived there a very wonderful old fellow named Nicholaus Geibel. His business was the making of mechanical toys, at which work he had acquired an almost European reputation. He made rabbits that would emerge from the heart of a cabbage, flop their ears, smooth their whiskers, and disappear again; cats that would wash their faces, and mew so naturally that dogs would mistake them for real cats and fly at them; dolls with phonographs concealed within them, that would raise their hats and say, 'Good morning; how do you do?' and some that would even sing a song.

"But, he was something more than a mere mechanic; he was an artist. His work was with him a hobby, almost a passion. His shop was filled with all manner of strange things that never would, or could, be sold – things he had made for the pure love of making them. He had contrived a mechanical donkey that would trot for two hours by means of stored electricity, and trot, too, much faster than the live article, and with less need for exertion on the part of the driver, a bird that would shoot up into the air, fly round and round in a circle, and drop to earth at the exact spot from where it started; a skeleton that, supported by an upright iron bar, would dance a hornpipe, a life-size lady doll that could play the fiddle, and a gentleman with a hollow inside who could smoke a pipe and drink more lager beer than any three average German students put together, which is saying much.

"Indeed, it was the belief of the town that old Geibel could make a man capable of doing everything that a respectable man need want to do. One day he made a man who did too much, and it came about in this way:

"Young Doctor Follen had a baby, and the baby had a birthday. Its first birthday put Doctor Follen's household into somewhat of a flurry, but on the occasion of its second birthday, Mrs. Doctor Follen gave a ball in honour of the event. Old Geibel and his daughter Olga were among the guests.

"During the afternoon of the next day some three or four of Olga's bosom friends, who had also been present at the ball, dropped in to have a chat about it.

They naturally fell to discussing the men, and to criticizing their dancing. Old Geibel was in the room, but he appeared to be absorbed in his newspaper, and the girls took no notice of him.

"'There seem to be fewer men who can dance at every ball you go to,' said one of the girls.

"'Yes, and don't the ones who can give themselves airs,' said another; 'they make quite a favor of asking you.'

"'And how stupidly they talk,' added a third. 'They always say exactly the same things: "How charming you are looking to-night." "Do you often go to Vienna? Oh, you should, it's delightful." "What a charming dress you have on." "What a warm day it has been." "Do you like Wagner?" I do wish they'd think of something new.'

"'Oh, I never mind how they talk,' said a fourth. 'If a man dances well he may be a fool for all I care.'

"'He generally is,' slipped in a thin girl, rather spitefully.

"'I go to a ball to dance,' continued the previous speaker, not noticing the interruption. 'All I ask is that he shall hold me firmly, take me round steadily, and not get tired before I do.'

"'A clockwork figure would be the thing for you,' said the girl who had interrupted.

"'Bravo!' cried one of the others, clapping her hands, 'what a capital idea!'

"'What's a capital idea?' they asked.

"'Why, a clockwork dancer, or, better still, one that would go by electricity and never run down.'

"'The girls took up the idea with enthusiasm.

"'Oh, what a lovely partner he would make,' said one; 'he would never kick you, or tread on your toes.'

"'Or tear your dress,' said another.

"'Or get out of step.'

"'Or get giddy and lean on you.'

"'And he would never want to mop his face with his handkerchief. I do hate to see a man do that after every dance.'

"'And wouldn't want to spend the whole evening in the supper-room.'

"'Why, with a phonograph inside him to grind out all the stock remarks, you would not be able to tell him from a real man,' said the girl who had first suggested the idea.

"Oh yes, you would,' said the thin girl, 'he would be so much nicer.'

"Old Geibel had laid down his paper, and was listening with both his ears. On one of the girls glancing in his direction, however, he hurriedly hid himself again behind it.

"After the girls were gone, he went into his workshop, where Olga heard him walking up and down, and every now and then chuckling to himself; and that night he talked to her a good deal about dancing and dancing men – asked what dances were most popular – what steps were gone through, with many other questions bearing on the subject.

"Then for a couple of weeks he kept much to his factory, and was very thoughtful and busy, though prone at unexpected moments to break into a quiet low laugh, as if enjoying a joke that nobody else knew of.

"A month later another ball took place in Furtwangen. On this occasion it was given by old Wenzel, the wealthy timber merchant, to celebrate his niece's betrothal, and Geibel and his daughter were again among the invited.

"When the hour arrived to set out, Olga sought her father. Not finding him in the house, she tapped at the door of his workshop. He appeared in his shirt-sleeves, looking hot but radiant.

"'Don't wait for me,' he said, 'you go on, I'll follow you. I've got something to finish.'

"As she turned to obey he called after her, 'Tell them I'm going to bring a young man with me – such a nice young man, and an excellent dancer. All the girls will like him.' Then he laughed and closed the door.

"Her father generally kept his doings secret from everybody, but she had a pretty shrewd suspicion of what he had been planning, and so, to a certain extent, was able to prepare the guests for what was coming. Anticipation ran high, and the arrival of the famous mechanist was eagerly awaited.

"At length the sound of wheels was heard outside, followed by a great commotion in the passage, and old Wenzel himself, his jolly face red with excitement and suppressed laughter, burst into the room and announced in stentorian tones:

"'Herr Geibel – and a friend.'

"Herr Geibel and his 'friend' entered, greeted with shouts of laughter and applause, and advanced to the centre of the room.

"'Allow me, ladies and gentlemen,' said Herr Geibel, 'to introduce you to my friend, Lieutenant Fritz. Fritz, my dear fellow, bow to the ladies and gentlemen.'

"Geibel placed his hand encouragingly on Fritz's shoulder, and the Lieutenant bowed low, accompanying the action with a harsh clicking noise in his throat, unpleasantly suggestive of a death-rattle. But that was only a detail.

"'He walks a little stiffly' (old Geibel took his arm and walked him forward a few steps. He certainly did walk stiffly), 'but then, walking is not his forte. He is essentially a dancing man. I have only been able to teach him the waltz as yet, but at that he is faultless. Come, which of you ladies may I introduce him to as a partner? He keeps perfect time; he never gets tired; he won't kick you or tread on your dress; he will hold you as firmly as you like, and go as quickly or as slowly as you please; he never gets giddy; and he is full of conversation. Come, speak up for yourself, my boy.'

"The old gentleman twisted one of the buttons at the back of his coat, and immediately Fritz opened his mouth, and in thin tones that appeared to proceed from the back of his head, remarked suddenly, 'May I have the pleasure?' and then shut his mouth again with a snap.

"That Lieutenant Fritz had made a strong impression on the company was undoubted, yet none of the girls seemed inclined to dance with him. They looked askance at his waxen face, with its staring eyes and fixed smile, and shuddered. At last old Geibel came to the girl who had conceived the idea.

"'It is your own suggestion, carried out to the letter,' said Geibel, 'an electric dancer. You owe it to the gentleman to give him a trial.'

"She was a bright, saucy little girl, fond of a frolic. Her host added his entreaties, and she consented.

"Her Geibel fixed the figure to her. Its right arm was screwed round her waist, and held her firmly; its delicately jointed left hand was made to fasten upon her right. The old toymaker showed her how to regulate its speed, and how to stop it, and release herself.

"'It will take you round in a complete circle,' he explained; 'be careful that no one knocks against you, and alters its course.'

"The music struck up. Old Geibel put the current in motion, and Annette and her strange partner began to dance.

"For a while everyone stood watching them. The figure performed its purpose admirably. Keeping perfect time and step, and holding its little partner tight clasped in an unyielding embrace, it revolved steadily, pouring forth at the same time a constant flow of squeaky conversation, broken by brief intervals of grinding silence.

"'How charming you are looking tonight,' it remarked in its thin, far-away voice. 'What a lovely day it has been. Do you like dancing? How well our steps agree. You will give me another, won't you? Oh, don't be so cruel. What a charming gown you have on. Isn't waltzing delightful? I could go on dancing for ever – with you. Have you had supper?'

"As she grew more familiar with the uncanny creature, the girl's nervousness wore off, and she entered into the fun of the thing.

"'Oh, he's just lovely,' she cried, laughing; 'I could go on dancing with him all my life.'

"Couple after couple now joined them, and soon all the dancers in the room were whirling round behind them. Nicholaus Geibel stood looking on, beaming with childish delight at his success.

"Old Wenzel approached him, and whispered something in his ear. Geibel laughed and nodded, and the two worked their way quietly towards the door.

"'This is the young people's house tonight,' said Wenzel, as soon as they were outside; 'you and I will have a quiet pipe and glass of hock, over in the counting-house.'

"Meanwhile the dancing grew more fast and furious. Little Annette loosened the screw regulating her partner's rate of progress, and the figure flew round with her swifter and swifter. Couple after couple dropped out exhausted, but they only went the faster, till at length they remained dancing alone.

"Madder and madder became the waltz. The music lagged behind: the musicians, unable to keep pace, ceased, and sat staring. The younger guests applauded, but the older faces began to grow anxious.

"'Hadn't you better stop, dear,' said one of the women, 'you'll make yourself so tired.'

"But Annette did not answer.

"'I believe she's fainted,' cried out a girl who had caught sight of her face as it was swept by.

"One of the men sprang forward and clutched at the figure, but its impetus threw him down on to the floor, where its steel-cased feet laid bare his cheek. The thing evidently did not intend to part with its prize so easily.

"Had any one retained a cool head, the figure, one cannot help thinking, might easily have been stopped. Two or three men acting in concert might have lifted it bodily off the floor, or have jammed it into a corner. But few human heads are capable of remaining cool under excitement. Those who are not present think how stupid must have been those who were; those who are reflect afterwards how simple it would have been to do this, that, or the other, if only they had thought of it at the time.

"The women grew hysterical. The men shouted contradictory directions to one another. Two of them made a bungling rush at the figure, which had the end result of forcing it out of its orbit at the centre of the room, and sending it crashing against the walls and furniture. A stream of blood showed itself down the girl's white frock, and followed her along the floor. The affair was becoming horrible. The women rushed screaming from the room. The men followed them.

"One sensible suggestion was made: 'Find Geibel – fetch Geibel.'

"No one had noticed him leave the room, no one knew where he was. A party went in search of him. The others, too unnerved to go back into the ballroom, crowded outside the door and listened. They could hear the steady whir of the wheels upon the polished floor as the thing spun round and round; the dull thud as every now and again it dashed itself and its burden against some opposing object and ricocheted off in a new direction.

"And everlastingly it talked in that thin ghostly voice, repeating over and over the same formula: 'How charming you look tonight. What a lovely day it has been. Oh, don't be so cruel. I could go on dancing for ever – with you. Have you had supper?'

"Of course they sought Geibel everywhere but where he was. They looked in every room in the house, then they rushed off in a body to his own place, and spent precious minutes waking up his deaf old housekeeper. At last it occurred to one of the party that Wenzel was missing also, and then the idea of the counting-house across the yard presented itself to them, and there they found him.

"He rose up, very pale, and followed them; and he and old Wenzel forced their way through the crowd of guests gathered outside, and entered the room, and locked the door behind them.

"From within there came the muffled sound of low voices and quick steps, followed by a confused scuffling noise, then silence, then the low voices again.

"After a time the door opened, and those near it pressed forward to enter, but old Wenzel's broad head and shoulders barred the way.

"'I want you – and you, Bekler,' he said, addressing a couple of the elder men. His voice was calm, but his face was deadly white. 'The rest of you, please go – get the women away as quickly as you can.'

"From that day old Nicholaus Geibel confined himself to the making of mechanical rabbits, and cats that mewed and washed their faces."

(1893)

SATISFACTION

Nicholas Sheppard

Nicholas Sheppard is an Australian software engineer and academic, currently teaching in Singapore. He has published numerous scientific articles, several rather less serious pieces for a mediaeval re-enactment group, and occasional pieces of fiction in *AntipodeanSF*.

Susan arrived home to find David unwrapping a large-ish box in the living room. "What's that?" she asked.

"It's a utility robot," said David.

"What does it do?"

"It *feels*."

The thing emerging from the packaging did not seem to have any hands, or tentacles, or other appendages with which it might *feel* in the sense that Susan had initially supposed. She stood still, peering a little harder at the robot in the hope that she would find some explanation. Then, it occurred to her: "As in, experiences emotion?"

"Yes. It has the best feeling in the world. It's completely satisfied with life."

"What's its life?" The thing emerging from the packaging did not seem very lively, either.

"Its life is to feel satisfied." David indicated some writing on the now-discarded box, which Susan supposed to explain this philosophy. By now, she could see that the machine took the form of a vertical silver-grey cylinder, surmounted by a white dome. The dome rose to about the height of David's shoulders as he sat beside it, and the whole contraption resembled nothing so much as a rubbish bin.

"And this benefits us how?" said Susan.

"With this, our household will contain at least 50% more satisfaction than before!"

"Are you suggesting that you're unsatisfied?"

"Oh no, not on the whole. Of course it'd be nice not to have to mow the lawn, or chase customers at work, that sort of thing. But this baby is perfectly satisfied with its life, perfectly happy with every aspect of its life." David patted the machine's dome with apparent affection. The machine, which was not turned on, did not react. "How can more satisfaction be bad?"

When the machine *was* turned on, a few red and green LEDs glowed at the top of the cylinder, just below the dome. They did not blink. The machine was in just this state when Susan found David kneeling before it the following evening.

"How do you know it's satisfied?" she asked.

"They've done tests. It's passed the Turing Test, it satisfies Integrated Information Theory, and it aced the Life Satisfaction Survey."

"I see," she said, without conviction. "Does watching it make it more satisfied?"

"It doesn't need me," David said. "But I think I can learn from it."

"Does it teach?" Susan did not perceive the machine to be doing very much teaching.

"Only by example."

Susan stared a little longer. "You've got the LEDs all wrong."

David was before the machine again the following evening, this time sitting cross-legged with his head bowed, resting his chin on his hands. Susan said nothing. On the third night he was trying the lotus position, but on the fourth night he was back to kneeling. The machine had not changed.

"What are you learning?" asked Susan when David rose—a little unsteadily—from his latest sojourn before the machine.

"It's hard work."

"The kneeling, or the learning?"

"What I need to do."

"What do you need to do?"

"I need to understand the way the machine feels, and take that feeling for myself."

"Is it *feeling* if you can make yourself do it?"

"Why shouldn't it be?"

"I just thought that that was the definition of *feeling*—something that arises within you without conscious explanation. Otherwise it'd be a *thought*. And, anyway, why should you be able to feel what the machine feels? You're not the machine."

"I can do it," he insisted, and went to shower.

David did not go to work the following week, preferring to spend more time with the machine. He had brought it into the living room, where he could watch it while seated on the comfortable armchair normally used for watching the extra-large television in the room. The television was off, but the machine was on.

Susan frowned at the arrangement whenever she passed by the living room, but it was not until the third day that she decided to challenge her husband. "You'll have to go back to work one day," she warned him.

"Do I? The machine can be satisfied without going to work."

"You aren't the machine."

But David continued into the fourth and then fifth day of leave. On the fifth day, he did not eat, leaving Susan to glower at him, sigh, and put the meal into the freezer in case he wanted it another time. But he did not touch it the next day (which was a Saturday, on which he did not have to work), nor on Sunday. The last thing Susan heard him say was "I'm nearly there!"

    Susan found David lying on the armchair on Monday morning, his head flopped back on the head-rest for want of any effort to hold it up, and his skin dry and pale. He was not breathing. Susan dragged him onto the floor, kicking the still-glowing machine aside, and began resuscitation. But she quickly perceived that it was hopeless. She sat back, with her hands on her hips and her legs folded underneath her body. From this position she stared at what was left of her husband, and then at the machine that had brought him to this state. She couldn't blame it, she supposed, and her husband *did* have such a wonderful smile on his face.

(2018)

NANONAUTS! IN BATTLE WITH TINY DEATH-SUBS!

Ian McDonald

Ian McDonald (born 1960) lives just outside Belfast and writes award-winning fiction, mostly about the impact on different societies of rapid social and technological change. By 2014, however, and as McDonald explained in an interview for *Locus* magazine, "I didn't want to get stuck doing the same SF books over and over, successful though they may be. I didn't want to keep writing books about the developing economy of the year – India, Brazil. I could feel myself getting trapped in that." A year later *Luna: New Moon* appeared. Two further volumes in the series have followed, and the project, exploring the intrigue that surrounds the five powerful families who control industry on the Moon, has been optioned for development as a television series.

We torpedo the killer robot death-sub just off the Islets of Langerhans. It's been a long chase. Days spent stalking the trace, up through arches and long fibrous loops of the pancreatic cytoarchitecture. There are a million islets: many, many places for a rogue nanobot to hide. A slow chase, too; hunting, hiding, moving, scanning for a trace, trying to hide the noise of our hunter-killers firing up their drive flagella among the general endocrine traffic roar.

The President's pancreas is a noisy place.

But our target is a rogue all right. No mistaking that signature death-sub echo. It tried to hide in a flotilla of neutral nanobots, but once we have the signature, we never let go. We are relentless, we are remorseless, and we never, ever stop. And the death-sub can't change its signature unless, well... unless it stops being a death-sub. Which would be good. It would be one less of the little fuckers.

We catch it before it begins the evangelizing process. A plus. Once the conversions start, we can be hours—days sometimes—taking out the fresh recruits. Time the dark-side sub can use to slip away. But now, we can simply Spray 'n' Sterilize the neutrals without even slowing down.

Sometimes we get lucky and sink the target before it even knows we're there. Not so today. Not so for several days. They've gotten good at detecting us as we detect them. They're evolving new techniques. We'll counter them. They evolve. We design.

Let's see who wins the Darwin Wars.

And so we slip into Stealth 'n' Stalk. The death-sub tries to throw us off with false echoes and synthesized signatures. Please. That didn't even fool us on day one of the nanowar. It tries decoys and tagging friendly cells as black hats. Do not insult us! And in the end, among the million islands of the pancreatic archipelago, we run it down. We anchor it with tractor molecules, fire up the torpedoes, and phago its nanobot ass.

Go nanonauts! Nanonauts ahoy!

We watch the shredded chains of pseudoproteins tumble away as the neutrophils swarm in like sharks.

"Inside the President's body?"

When she has a question—a Big Question—she does this thing. Her eyes go wide and at the same time her lips open, just a tad, not stupid-open, not *gobe-mouche* open. (That's a French expression. Means catching flies in your mouth.) But the bit that slays me—*slays* me—is the way her bottom lip catches on her upper front teeth, just a tiny pull, enough to pucker the skin and no more. That, to me, says *Woooo*.

I am, I have to say, slaying. *Slaying*. Tight, tight shave and a little concealer for the perfect top coat. I blue up quick. Concealer has saved my ass more times than I can remember. Boys, you need concealer in your guy drawer. You *need* it. Your skin will be like the blush of a peach in the first light of an Aphrodite dawn. Girls check these things right away, before you even notice. Flick of the eyes, dish-dash-done. Old pickup artist trick.

"The President, the VP, most of the senators, almost all the bankers. Your one percent. The Pope. I haven't been inside the Pope yet. That would be a privilege, but I'm not Catholic."

I lean forward so the little Orthodox cross falls into the light. Another pickup artist trick. But I am no pickup artist. I am a warrior, and I am on R&R.

"Greek. Cypriot. Cyprus is the island of Aphrodite, the goddess of love, risen from the wine-dark sea. My home is Kalavasos. It's beautiful. Most beautiful place on God's green earth. The gods live there still. The mountains go up behind my grandparents' house and in the evening the last rays of the sun turn the mountaintops pink. And down in the valley, in the notch where the road goes down, there is a glitter, so bright it would blind you, of the Mediterranean. My heart lives there. Even while I'm here, fighting, my heart lives in Kalavasos. When this war is done, I will go back, and I will go to the little church of Ayios Panteleimon, and I will kneel before the iconostasis. And I will take off this cross, and kiss it, and place it there among the icons of the saints."

I can see her exhale as she shakes her head slowly. That's wonder, not disbelief. And it's true. Well, maybe not the bit about hanging the cross on the altar screen. But they love that bit. That's another thing for your guy drawer, brothers. Old-time religion.

"So how does a boy from Kalavasos in the wine-dark sea come to fighting killer death-subs inside the body of the President of the United States?"

And in. But hold it, don't show it, don't lose it.

"I'll tell you, but first, let me buy you a drink."

*

When I say "torpedo," it's not actually *torpedoes*. Not even very small ones. Not missiles loaded into tubes and fired out and exploding: you know, fire one, fire two, torpedo running.

And we're not submariners, not even very tiny ones. Come on. That's Disney. There is no physical way in this universe you could take an entire attack sub and its crew, shrink them down to the size of a cell, and inject them into the bloodstream of the President—and not just the President, but all those other rich and powerful and popular people who thought nanotechnology would make them like gods... and got a hell of a surprise when their stab at immortality started to eat their brains. (And the Pope. Not forgetting the Pope.)

Actually, it's way smaller than cells—cells look like apatosauruses to us... like clouds even. The point is: physics says *no*. Sorry. This is not *Innerspace 2* or *Honey, I Shrunk the Kids Even Smaller*.

It's analogies. We need analogies. We fight by analogies.

The Islets of Langerhans, they're tiny nodules about half a millimeter in diameter. What they are to you, my friend, are analogies.

So on our screens, we see steampunk submarines and Baroque architecture—which is a nice touch—very Jules Verne, Captain Nemo-ing through someone's body—and they look great. Those animation guys did a hell of a job. That brass and those gears: looks good when you fuck it to pieces. But the reality—the reality is: fuzz. Fuzz and glue. Brownian motion in high-viscosity fluid. See? Losing you already. Cute brass subs (with portholes FFS!) are much easier for you to deal with than biochemical signatures and protein folding and ion transfers. Easier for us too, but we are scientists, first and foremost, so the reality is always in our minds. We are not seduced by the magic.

And we're in the Big Box, an aluminum shed at the back of the United States Naval Academy, in the unsexy area where they make the deliveries and have the heating plants and server farms. It's kind of atavistic thinking: we move through fluid, so we're a navy. And that gives us our name: nanonauts!

Nanonauts ahoy! Go, go, you bloodstream battlers, fight against the evil death-subs! Crush the nanorobot rebels! Keep safe our souls, defend our hearts. Go! Nanonauts ahoy!

They paid someone to write that, and stick a tune around it.

Doesn't even scan. I'm going into the nanowar muttering the lyrics from a Muse B-side.

"Biochemistry?"

A strange war it is—but a good one—where the biochemists are the Special Forces. I've always liked those movies where the dull guys get to be heroes: the interior designer is the superhero, the accountant turns into avenging killing machine. They're not nerds—they've got that kind of grudging hip thing—but they're dull. Biochemistry is not a shiny subject. We don't make the world go round. We do make money. That made my father very happy. My son is a biochemist! First boy from Kalavasos! He had no idea what it meant. He has even less of an idea what being a nanonaut means, but it keeps him in coffee down at Lefteres's.

This girl Rebecca has this cute thing she does: she twists her glass on the mat. It says, *I'm interested, but not too interested.*

"Well, we call the bad guys 'death-subs' and the good guys 'nanonauts,' but the kind of scale we're fighting at, everything really is more like biology—you know, living things."

"I know about biology," she says.

Whoa. False step there.

"Rebecca, I think it's a good thing—a very good thing—when people straddle the divide between humanities and sciences. They need each other. Without both, we are not rounded human beings."

I established in the opening gambit that she's a political science major. Everybody is in this town. (Apart from the nanonauts.) I go on: "Everything happens at the level of molecules, sometimes even individual atoms. It's chemical warfare for real."

"So how does a guy from Kalavasos…"

"I like the way you say my home."

She smiles, but doesn't let me derail her.

"How does a guy from Kalavasos come to be battling nanobots inside the body of the President of the United States?"

"I did my doctorate at MIT and they headhunted me. It's kind of an elite force." That first winter down in D.C., when they were training the nanonaut teams, it was so cold I kept five different lip balms in my guy drawer. Chapped lips are not a good look. And I moisturized twice daily. Cold air dries the skin out. And I used hair-nourishing product. Rebecca should get some. She has a split-end problem, which, I can see, is not solved by cutting it yourself. Folks assume that because you're a scientist, you don't care about things like grooming. That is a false notion based on a vile stereotype. "It's not just a U.S. war. It's an everywhere war."

Her eyes go wide. Her drink is empty. I didn't even notice her finish it.

"I'll tell you," I say. "It's, like, classified, but then, it's not as if they've got spies in the bottom of your glass. Which, I see, is empty. Can I get you another one?"

She puts her hand over her glass.

"No. Let me get you one."

In. In. So in.

Elis summons us for coffee and a briefing. It's Ikea sofas and swipe-screens. The coffee of course is very good. We are scientists.

Elis. Garret. Owain. Twyla. Together, we are the Eagles of Screaming Death. Quite who this name is supposed to scare I do not know. Certainly not nanoscale bloodstream robots. Most likely, the other squads scattered around the Big Box in their battle pods. Which again, sounds more impressive than it is. Screens, sofas, laptops, and water coolers.

Elis wears good brands, even when leading the Eagles of Screaming Death on patrol. She's from Rio. New York girls may think they're the thing in sophistication, but they look like homeless occupiers next to Cariocas. Elis battles the evil nanobots in Christian Louboutins. I can spot those red soles from the far end of the shed.

Elis has intel. Owain opens the Tupperware of baked goods he's made. He's been practicing his brioche over the weekend. He wants to be a bakemeister. It's good. Light, not too sweet. We tear off chunks with our hands and eat it with our good coffee while Elis tells us what Biochemical Analysis has found. In a sense, the real battle is fought between the nanobots and Biochem. The death-subs evolve a new tactic, we develop a countermeasure, back and forth. We're just the delivery system.

Elis tells us that Biochem ran an analysis of the exocytotic debris after the Islets of Langerhans fight. Our drones are equipped with receptors and ligand guns. Biochem has identified and decrypted a new chemical messenger. It will allow us to identify the enemy absolutely and infallibly—but we must use it with caution. We must use it to strike a killing blow to the death-subs before they can evolve a new messenger protein. And Biochem has a little sting in the tail. The messenger chemical also contains instructions. They're a simple and clear call to muster in the hypothalamus. The final assault on the President's brain is massing. No time to lose! The President's brain is under attack!

Elis can run in those Christian Louboutins. I jump into my seat, log in, and watch the screens fill with data. Then I pull the 3-D goggles down and I am back in the Jules Verneiverse of brass subs and Baroque buttresses.

"The credit crisis was caused by nanobots in the brains of Wall Street bankers?"

"And London and Frankfurt and Tokyo bankers, but Wall Street the most. It's true. If you think about it, auction rate securities and credit default swaps are weapons of mass financial destruction."

These vodka martinis are really very good. I pick the Pirandello for R&R sorties because you get professional clientele and the bartender does the best martinis I know. When it comes to cocktails, stick to the classics. Nothing that sounds like you are young and trying too hard. Certainly nothing that sounds like sex. Classics. But James Bond is wrong, wrong, wrong: shake it and you kill the cocktail. Do not sucuss. Just a stir, and a nanoscale application of Martini & Rossi. Homeopathic levels of Martini.

"We've had the tech a lot longer than people think." I lean back and take a sip from my drink. "A lot longer. The one percent don't want you to know about it. Blood scrubs, cholesterol cleaning, enhanced attention, concentration, memory; telomere repair—that's a three-hundred-year life span, to you and me—if it gets into the street, that's a recipe for revolution."

"You're telling me," she says.

I have to be smart here. Diplomatic. That I can do. Cypriot charm. The loquaciousness of the gods is on my lips.

"Do you believe me?" I ask.

"To be honest?"

"Be honest. Honesty is the soul of every human relationship."

"Not really."

"That's honest."

"And are you honest?"

"I am," I say. Eye contact. I have been graced with long lashes, for a guy. And naturally full. Bless my eastern Mediterranean DNA.

"It's hard to believe."

"Which bit?"

"Okay." She takes a suck from her glass. Some green stuff gets clogged in the end and makes a rattling sound, which I can forgive. "The nanomachines…"

"Nanobots."

"Those, I can kind of understand. But these nanobots, clumping together in the brain and forming some kind of… alien mind parasite…"

That's a good line. I must give that to the squad. Nanonauts versus Alien Mind Parasites!

"… that kind of has its own agenda, and a plan, and wants to take over the world…"

"It is a slow plan. It's taken years to evolve. But once it gets to a critical mass, everything goes at once. Why do you think certain people all seem breaking weird at the same time? Nanobots."

"All the… megarich?"

"And the Pope."

"It does make a kind of sense."

"Trust me, I'm doing this for all of us. For the future."

"I think I might need another drink to get my head around this," she says.

"Try the martini," I say. "It's classy."

The President is reading to kids in an elementary school in rural Ohio while the Eagles of Screaming Death tear apart phalanxes of death-sub attack drones swarming down the infundibular stem of the pituitary stalk. We've almost burned out our helical flagella on the run up the anterior cerebral artery. When you're piloting a drone a few microns across, the human body is a big place. The cerebral artery is a river wider than a dozen Amazons, longer than a hundred Niles. And every millimeter of the way, we are under attack. Wave upon wave of jihadis—nanobots recently converted by the death-subs to suicide attackers—throw themselves at us. We tear them apart with our biochemical blasters, drive through the glittering wreckage. We surf the wave of hot, pumping presidential blood. But each wave is a delay, and with each second lost the death-sub drill rigs dig a little deeper into the blood-brain barrier.

"To the hypothalamus!" Elis cries.

I'm going to use the "S" word now. Singularity. There. That's been said. We always thought that when the machines woke up and became smart, it would be the defense grid or the stock market or the Internet or something like that. Big and obvious. We never imagined it would be a revolution too small to see: the nanomachines that the one percent (more like one percent of the one percent) put into their bodies to make them healthy and long-lived and smart—we never thought that those millions and billions of robots would link up, and evolve, and get smart. Things that aren't intelligent in themselves, in their connections and numbers becoming intelligent. Like the neurons in our brains: individually zombie-stupid; together, the most complex and glorious thing in the universe. A mind. Nanomachines, building brains inside the brains of our rich and powerful. Brains with their own personalities and values and goals. Moving and shaking the movers and shakers. Making the world right for them and their hosts. The tiniest singularity.

A cry. Bakemeister Owain is down. I see death-sub sticky missiles swarm his point-defense molecules. He kills ten, twenty, a hundred, but there are too many, too, too many. His sleek, shark-shaped drone turns fuzzy and gray as sticky after sticky clings to his hull. Within moments he is a ball of fuzzy wool. Then I hear the worst sound in the world: the sound of hull plates being wrenched apart as the stickies contract. Like bones snapping. Like a spine ripped from a living body. Owain is *down.*

I flick out of the simulation for a moment to see him push up his goggles with a *"Shit!"* and haul himself out of his chair. He shakes cramps out of his thighs and wrists. We have reserves inside the President, but it will take a few minutes to log them into the sim, and by the time Owain pilots a backup to the combat zone it will be all over. One way or another.

"Fight on!" Elis shouts. "We're almost at the diaphragma sellae!"

Ahead of us are insane ranks of death-subs, arrayed wave upon wave.

I arm my torpedoes, fire up the flagella to maximum, and hurl myself toward them.

"Alala!" I yell; the goddess whose very name was the war cry of the ancient Greeks. "Eja! Eja! Alala!"

"I mean, you can't actually see inside the President's body."

This is a good point, and it takes a moment for its intelligence to sink into me. Or it may be the martinis.

"That is true," I say. "Some of the nanoscale weapons we use are on the angstrom scale, so they're in fact only visible in the X-ray or gamma ray spectra. Or even scanning electron microscopes."

This is the three martinis talking. Rein in, rein in, rein in the guy tech-piling the girl when she starts to show some science.

"But humans are visual animals, so we operate the ROVs through a screen-based analogue, but in reality, it's all chemicals. We really hunt by sense of smell. Like sharks. Sharks hunt by chemical trails in the water. And electrical fields. That's us. Top predators."

"I was thinking of those dogs they have in France," she says. "The ones they train to hunt down truffles. I read someplace that they're better than pigs, because they have better noses and they don't eat the truffles like pigs do."

"I would rather be a shark than a truffle-hunting dog," I say. "And a pig? What are you saying?"

She giggles. She covers her mouth with her hand when she giggles, like she is scared some of her soul may spill out. I love that in a woman. And we're even. Tech-dump versus ego-puncture. I'm starting to think where to take her afterward.

"It *is* kind of clever," I say. "They paid a bunch of animators from Pixar to come up with the interface. It looks like a game. I suppose, in a sense, it is a game. One of those types where you have to work your weapon combos to get the max effect, because the AI learns from you and adapts the bosses to your fighting style."

"I'm not really that into gaming. My housemate's got that Kinect thing and it's fun, but all it really gets used for is *Dance Yourself Thin*."

For a moment, a dread moment, a sick-up-in-your-heart moment, I feared she was going to mention a boyfriend. The male roomie. Then it's dancercise and I am sailing clear. There's a Latin American place with a dance floor upstairs and a good DJ. Tango never fails. It's the combination of passion and strict discipline.

"Well, it's like that but with a lot more screens, and we use pull-down menus on a 3-D heads-up display rather than bashing the X button. But we have gamer chairs. You know? Those low ones where you're more or less on the floor, with built-in speakers? And we wear our own clothes."

"Really?"

I flash my lapels, which are narrow and correct for the season.

"This is my superhero suit. The thing is, it's really not like a war at all. I mean, a war means someone shoots back. I mean, they take out our drones. But they're only *nano*drones. No one shoots back at *us*. We just sit there in our chairs in our really good clothes and shoot things. So it is like a game, or comics. No one really gets hurt."

"I'm glad," she says.

Time. It's time. I lean toward her and the light from inside the bar gleams from my cross. And she, too, leans toward me.

"Do you like Argentinian food?" I ask.

"I don't think I've ever had it," she says.

"It is the food of passion," I say. "Red and raw and flamboyant."

"Are you asking me on a date?"

"We could go there. I know a place. Not far from here."

"Okay," she says. "I think I will. Yes. Let's give the spirit of old Buenos Aires a try. But first, I owe you another drink."

I press the buttons and the biochemical rockets streak out ahead of me. Blam! I dive through the hole in the curtain of death-subs. Before me, below me, are the endothelial cell walls and the rigs, driving their way through, molecule by molecule. Once they're into the cerebrospinal fluid, the death-subs can scatter through the hypothalamus's many nuclei. Total control of the endocrine and autonomic nervous systems. We'll never be able to flush them out of the deep, dark neural jungle.

I line up the first pair of drill rigs in my sights.

Missiles away.

Wham! They explode in slo-mo, sending plates and girders and gantry work fountaining upward.

And the next two.

Bam!

Proximity detectors shriek. I roll the drone, and death-sub torpedoes streak past me. I was a hair's breadth from death. I drop micromines behind me and listen to the shrieks as the death-subs come apart.

To my right, Twyla is on a rig-busting run. They look mighty pretty, toppling like trees or factory chimneys as she takes them out.

"Miko! There's one on your tail!" Twyla shouts. I flick to the rear cameras. The death-sub comes barreling through the twinkling wreckage. I drop mines. Flick flick flick. I can't see what the death-sub does, but now my mines are gone. Every single one.

It's gaining. It's lean and mean, a steampunk shark, and fast fast fast. I load up torpedoes in the rear tubes. Fire one. Fire two. Death-shark rolls this way, that way. Easy. Easiest thing in the world. This is not good. This is exquisitely bad. This I have not seen before. This death-shark, it knows us. It's new, it's smart, it's evolved. Its evil shark head unfolds a battery of grippers and claws and shredders and impalers. It's like a death-crab-beetle killing-thing. Close-in defenses. I stab the shotgun button. Eat molecular death, evil shark-thing. And it shrugs me off. My blasts don't even take the shine off its skin. And my haptics jolt me with a sudden deceleration. It's got me. A giant hook is stabbed into my rear control surface and little by little it is hauling me in. I gun the flagella. Molecular motors scream.

And then I dive forward as the restraint is released, and when I can call up the rear camera I see the death-shark unraveling like ink dropped into water. Then Elis blasts through the squid-black ink and disperses it with her flagella.

"Got you, Miko!"

After that, it's killing time. We burn, we blast, we wham and bam! The death-subs scatter, knowing their evil plan is thwarted, but Garret and Elis stalk the outer fringes of the sella turcica, covering the exits, while far below, the pituitary gland shines like a vast endocrine moon. We sow death, we salt the fields. Wave upon wave of chemicals sterilize the survivors. Those evil death-subs will never reproduce and try to possess the President of the United States.

We won.

We *won*.

I hear Garret's voice shouting *"Victory! We have victory!"* like that English actor at the Battle of Helm's Deep.

We saved the President's brain. Go Eagles of Screaming Death.

I blink out of sim and push up my goggles. I lift up my cross and kiss it. In the next chair, Elis, her own goggles up on her hair, grins in a way that is very ungroomed and non-glossy but totally honest and right.

"Now for the Pope!" she says. "But first, we just earned ourselves some serious R&R."

"So, no to Argentinian food?" I ask.

This is weird. This is unexpected. This is not in the script—not that I use a script, understand. But I come back from the men's room—they have this little spritz of cologne, which is a nice touch, a nice extra freshness *and* confidence—and she is standing with her bag and her wrap. "How about Egyptian? Jamaican? I know a really good Greek Cypriot restaurant out in Bethesda—the owner comes from the next village, we have the same priest."

"No, I guess I'm not hungry. Those olives filled me up."

And I feel a little stunned. A little dazed. Woozy. Not four-martini woozy. World-woozy. What happened? It was flying right, on the glide path in, landing on autopilot. Now she is leaving without a word, an explanation, a mobile number.

"I'm sorry, I was talking about myself? Yadda yadda yadda? I know, it's a terrible fault."

"Well, yes, it is," she says, which makes me feel worse. "But, you know, I have enjoyed talking to you, and thanks for all the drinks..."

"Half the drinks," I say. Modern. I feel like the room is telescoping away from me, like that shot in *Jaws*. This is crazy. It's like every voice in the bar is in my head.

"Thank you for letting me do that, but, well, I do have work tomorrow." She turns away, turns back. "Miko, tell me. What you're saying about the nanobots—the tiny death-subs. Is it always the rich? I mean, do ordinary people ever get them as well?"

"You'd need to be a lottery winner or some kind of mad day trader. Never happens."

"You sure?" she says. She taps the top of my martini glass. "Have you ever thought, maybe they *have* started to shoot back?" *Tap tap tap.* Then she throws her wrap around her and out she walks, heels *tap tap tap.*

(2014)

MASKED

Rich Larson

Rich Larson was born in Galmi, Niger, studied in Rhode Island and worked in the south of Spain. He now lives in Ottawa, Canada. Since he began writing in 2011, he has sold over a hundred stories, most of them science fiction. Out of the genre, he has been nominated for both the Pushcart and Journey prizes and was a semifinalist for the 2013 Norman Mailer Poetry Prize. His debut collection, *Tomorrow Factory: Collected Fiction*, was published in 2018. His debut novel, *Annex* (2018), the start to his *Violet Wars* trilogy, follows a transgender girl who has discovered that an alien parasite has given her strange powers.

It's been a whole month since anyone's seen Vera, and the circumstances of us finally seeing her this weekend are going to be ultra grody-odd, so I deliberate forever doing my Face. In the end I decide to go subtle: an airbrushed conglom of three of my most flattering private snaps, plus Holly Rexroat-Carrow's lips and Sofia Lawless's cheekbones from that Vogue shoot she did on the Moon. Nothing too recent, nothing that'll make Vera feel like she is way, way unsynched and missing out on all kinds of hot shit. Which she has been, obviously.

I do the rest of my Face the same way, kind of sous radar. I set my wardrobe to cycle four or five outfits, one of which includes the Chanel inside-out jacket Vera gifted me a week before the accident. It is now kind of gauche, so she better appreciate the gesture like whoa. Boob-wise I go small, because obviously Aline is going to be there, too, and she always goes chesty and is way way more than welcome to the unsolicited profile taps, thanks.

Lastly, I prune the digital cloud of updates shuffling around my shoulders. A few instant-regret purchases, plus the many many snaps of me and Aline and Estelle wearing our wetsuits in Venice, disappear in a drizzle of code. The result looks a little barren. But barren can also be construed as, like, minimalist, which may or may not be coming back now.

Either way, I am not going to be rubbing Vera's nose in the fact that a viral strike took her Face offline and she is stuck hiding from the world for at least another week according to technicians. Aline probably will, but whatever.

Vera's parents are really fucking rich, if I didn't mention that. As in, rich enough to rent a reefhouse on some secluded beach for Vera's first weekend out of neural recovery, and also send me and Aline there in a big black shiny autocab to spend it with her. When said cab pulls up outside my house, Aline leans out the open door with Curacao in a martini glass, because she likes to pretend she's an alcoholic, and welcomes me to her chariot.

"Yeah, strump, okay, strump," I say, but when I climb in and see the chiller bar and the curved screen and the plush upholstery and all, I sort of have to agree. Me and Aline swap kisses. Her Face looks total wattage, as usual, wearing a high concept summer dress that is entirely foaming water, and keeping with the theme our Venice vacay snaps are ribboning off her in big graceful arcs.

Which I think is like, whoa, spinal cringe, because Vera's parents bought us the sub-orbital tickets, and Vera had been wanting to dive Venice for-fucking-ever, and I felt somewhat Judas doing it without her.

"Are you sure you want to be, like, shouting those vacay snaps at her?" I say. "She might be suicidal enough already."

"Bessandra. We are going to be there to support her." Aline's facial is painful pretty—between you and me, I think it's a full model blend, like, none of her in it at all—and her Naufrage Blue TM eyes are full of sympathy. "But we are not responsible for her highbrowsing on deep webs and getting fucked up by some grody-odd virus. That was just straight-up unclutch of her to do right before we were supposed to go to Venice."

But Aline wasn't chatting her that night, so she doesn't really know the extent of this grody-odd virus shit. I was.

The reefhouse is made of slick purple coral and looks like a big twisty conch, grown from a designer geneprint and way way chic, but me and Aline are both a bit quiet when we get out of the cab. Instead of, you know, being watted out of our minds to be weekending in a reefhouse with our dearly missed best/second-best friend.

I met Vera when we were ten, meaning we already had Faces, and neither of us knew Aline until high school. Although apparently her and Vera did kindergarten together—they can't remember each other, so whatever. Basically, none of us have ever seen each other without a Face. The only people I have seen without a Face are those small, dim, barely there people who dive the trash or rap loco religious tracts outside 7–11.

Then Vera steps out onto the porch, holding a Bacardi Slush, and waves a familiar wave. "Hey, strumpets, you coming in or what now?"

My heart seriously lozenges in my throat, partly because of how good it is to hear her voice in actual airtalk and partly because she is so, so brave to strut outside like everything's glacial when it is so obviously not.

I mean, her facial, or I guess her small f face, looks like her, because she's pretty enough to never toy with it much anyway. But now it's all wan and colorless and loaded with pores, and I think her nose is bigger, too. Her eyes seem smaller and not so shiny, and they're brown, which they haven't been for at least a few years.

Her hair is also brown, and totally lank, hanging off her like something dead instead of style-shifting or turning into digital snakes or even just doing a standard Pantene Ripple TM. And her swimsuit body is like, oh no. Hip-to-waist ratio's all fucked up and there are little rolls of flab under her arms and around her middle.

But the worst thing is that she has no update cloud. As in none. The space around her shoulders and her head is totally empty of Trottr notifications, food snaps, Whispas, party-streams, profile taps, purchases, and everything else. I can't even see my reassuring BFFF status that always pops up over her head. There is no way of knowing where Vera has been for the past month, if she has been drinking Bacardi Slushes the whole time or mixing it up with Lemogrenades, what she's been buying, what she's been wearing, who she's been chatting. It's all this horrible gaspy void.

It looks like she's been dead for a month, and I can't think what to say. Fortunately, Aline takes the pressure off me by doing a shatter-glass squeal and bounding up the steps to hug her, Face spouting these big cartoon tears. "You are an inspiration, Vera. An inspiration. And as soon as they fix you up, I am going to get you so synched, and we are going to party so hard, and we're all going to look so fucking wattage, okay, love?"

There's a glimmer in Vera's brown eyes, and it takes me one to realize they are actual tears, like the saline kind. "Oh, Aline," she says. "I missed the shit out of you." She smiles, then catches my eye through Aline's cascade of updates. "Hey, strump. How's you?"

"Hey, V," I say, coming up the steps. "You know, um, minimalism may or may not be back. So there's that?"

Vera laughs, which sounds really good in my ears. We airkiss, but for some reason I don't quite manage to actually hug her, maybe because I'm not sure what it's going to feel like. Aline's already bounced past us into the reefhouse, gushing about organic architecture and the fact that there is a minibar.

Me and Vera follow her in, and as long as I keep her in the periphs I figure I can make an effort at pretending everything's normal.

Vera says we should do the beach while there's still sun, so we head out the back door, which shutters shut behind us, and down to the pale gray sand. Me and Aline are justifiably worried about people seeing her. Not everyone digisigned a no-snaps waiver in sight of her lawyer parents, and some asshole taking snaps of her without her Face would be, obviously, disastrous.

"I've been here since yesterday," Vera says, resettling the strap of her swimsuit. "It's absolutely zero tremor. Like, there's one Finnish family with little kids and then an old man who does maintenance shit."

"Oh, good," Aline says, but she looks somewhat disappointed and drops a cup size when my head is turned.

We pick a spot on the smoothest stretch of beach and camp it, unrolling our mats and stretching out. Me and Aline do our best to get Vera synched the old-fashioned way, like, telling her about how Dalia is now dating Sedge Vandermeer, and she's rigged her Face to project his facial beside hers when they're not actually together so she looks like some kind of two-headed monster but it's love so whatever. We do not mention Venice, and Vera does not bring it up, so it will probably stay submarined until everyone's drunk.

Eventually Vera wants to swim, so she sloshes out into the waves while me and

Aline elect lifeguarding instead. Vera doesn't seem to mind going solo. In fact, she looks really fucking blissy just dashing around out there, laughing through a mouthful of water when the tide bowls her over. Her skin has this ruddy thing going on, which actually looks sort of hot, and her smile is not as white, but seems bigger somehow.

"She's medded," Aline concludes. "Like, sky-high."

"You think so?" I say, because I've seen Vera medded and usually she's more sluggish.

"Um, has to be?" Aline shakes her perfect head. "Nobody just, like, bounces that kind of trauma."

Vera wades back up to the beach, wringing water out of her hair, and it reminds me of something I can't quite stick a finger on. "Come on," she calls. "The water's warm, you imps. And you owe me for Venice!"

Me and Aline swap looks.

"It smelled really bad," I say. "The whole time. There was a heatwave."

"Serves you right," Vera says, but grinning.

Then we all go splash around for a bit, and it is sort of funtime, even for Aline, at least until her hair, which was doing this big wind-tunnel look, freezes up trying to interact with the water physics. And I get my finger on what Vera reminds me of: ancient clips of yours truly as a little kid, before I got my Face, running around wild with an ugly gappy smile big as the Moon.

We go back to the reefhouse when the water gets cold, then me and Vera hop in the hot tub while Aline raids the minibar for mojito supplies. With a big billowy cloud of steam between us, it's easy to imagine Vera's got her updates and her perfect hair, which in turn makes it easier for me to realtalk her. Which is my duty as first best friend. Sure, Aline's way wattage and way funtime, but I am Vera's confidante.

"So how actually are you, V?" I ask. "No need for brave facial, love. Be serious, okay?"

"I'm actually good," she says, tipping her head back. "Now that I'm out of neural recovery, really good. The hospital food was shit." She grins and flicks some water at me.

This is not how I was envisioning it. I thought she'd admit how miserable she's been all month, maybe cry a little, and I could comfort her and reassure her that when her Face is back it will be like it never ever left. I did not envision her so blissy about everything. Maybe a few mojitos are needed first.

"You're being so brave about the situation," I say, because I didn't have a backup plan. "And when your Face is back online, it'll be like nothing ever happened. You will forget this month so fast."

"Not exactly, Bess." She raises an eyebrow, which is way furrier than an eyebrow has any right to be.

"Not exactly, what?"

"If they get my Face running again, it won't have any of my old stuff," Vera says with a shrug. "That's all gone. Permagone."

She says it so nonchalant that for a second I do not even understand, and then when I do, I know this is selfish, but the first thing I think is how her Face, or at least her update cloud, was like 35 percent me from all the party-streams and snaps and curated convos we shared, and now all of that is gone and she doesn't even care. I could slap her until I remember that she is recovering from a serious viral strike and probably medded sky-high. Maybe she should not be drinking mojitos.

"Why're you saying if?" I ask. "Why if?"

"When," Vera corrects.

I narrow my eyes. "V. That night you caught the virus, do you remember what you chatted me? Looking for…"

"Mojitos!" Aline announces. "Except with no mint. So, rum and lime juice." She hands us our drinks, then sticks the handle of rum and the plastic bottle of mix and the few remaining Bacardi Slushes into the little floating thermos that is bobbing around with us in the water. She slips into the tub between me and Vera and sends me a Whispa at the same time, like, why are you AMAing her about the night she got viral, she does not want to think about that right now!

I do not want to reply, so instead I hold up my not-mojito. "To Vera's health, right? Um, salud."

"Yeah, whatever, salud," Aline says, but she holds up her glass and grins. Vera holds hers up, too, but doesn't look at me when we drink.

The hot water and cold drinks do their tingly headrush thing, and pretty soon all three of us are turvy and blissy and laughing. We make a drinking game out of the floating thermos, as in whoever it floats to via the current has to drink, and for some reason it keeps coming back around to Aline, and she's kicking her feet at it like no, no, no, you evil little robot, and Vera is hiccupping how she does when she laughs too much, and it feels almost like we're drinking for the first time again.

Me and Aline apologize to Vera, ultra-blubbery, for the Venice thing. Then, still in the repentant spirit, Aline confesses that she was still hooking up with Thierry when I started dating him, but I already knew and never much liked him anyway. Vera tells us how her mom ordered her a bunch of physical makeup from some specialty place, but she had no clue what to do with it and ended up smearing it all over her hospital room's wall, pretending to suffer a delusion where she believed she was Pablo Picasso.

Before long Aline flicks out, sliding down the side of the hot tub and mumbling about how she way way loves us, which is sweet. We get her out and nest her in some towels on the couch, propped on her side just in case. Then it's just me and V and we're drunk.

"What's it feel like not to have your Face?" I say. "Besides horrible."

We're in the kitchen now because we're looking for acetaminophen. You crush one and mix it in a glass of water and you wake up without a hangover, or at least Aline thinks so.

"It was only odd for a few days," Vera says, scraping around on the shelves, up on tiptoe. "And then you feel… light."

"Light how?"

"Like a balloon," Vera says. "Up, up, and away, strump." She turns around, twisting a fistful of the fabric of her shirt in a way a Face probably would not allow. "You want to try?"

It seems really obvious to me, now that I'm drunk and I remember back to that night when she chatted me. Maybe I've known this whole time.

"You got the virus on purpose."

"Yeah. Did." Vera looks relieved to say it. She smiles her unwhite smile and it makes me so angry. "Looking for a way to be real again, remember?"

"I thought you were looking for fucking fashion leaks," I snap. "Thought you tapped something bad by accident. Everyone was so gutted for you, and worried—"

"You want to try?" Vera repeats, ignoring me as she does when she's drunk. "Not a full deletion. Just a flicker." She sinks down onto the glassy kitchen floor, tugging me down by the wrists. Her bare skin is warm and well textured even though I thought it would be cold and goopy for some reason.

"But don't you love us still?" I ask, the mads transmuting to sads all at once. If I was Aline I'd be throwing the cartoon tears by the bucket. Instead I just feel like I've got hard plastic in my throat. "Everything we did together, V. It's gone, V?"

"I've still got it where it counts," Vera says, pulling me into one of those sloppy hugs that usually only happen after one of us throws up. She feels softer than normal.

"Like, you offsite stored it somewhere?" I sniff, only half-joking.

"Just try it for a bit," Vera says. "Just us two."

She shows me how to get there, down under all the masked protocols and shit, past all these blistery red pop-ups asking me what exactly I am doing. The override is so simple, just a little off/on toggle.

"That's why I had to use the virus," Vera says. "Too easy to go back, otherwise. That's what other people were saying."

The toggle revolves around us on the kitchen floor, a glowy little satellite. I don't know if I can do it.

"Minimalism might be back in," Vera says. "Right?"

"Yeah, strump, whatever, strump." I take a deep breath. "Hold my hand, would you?"

I know I can't preview before I do it, because if I preview I'll see myself looking so ugly and lonely and small and anonymous I will not be able to go through with it. Instead I try to think about how Vera looked in the waves, how I looked as a kid.

Holding hands with her, I switch off my Face. Everything dissolves around me, all my updates, all my streams, all my little bits of manufactured me, and it feels almost like coming up for air.

(2016)

THE TURING TEST
Chris Beckett

Born in Oxford in 1955, **Chris Beckett** is a former social worker who now writes and lectures on this subject. He is the author of seven novels (the most recent, *Beneath the World, A Sea*, came out in April 2019) and won the Arthur C. Clarke award in 2012 for his novel *Dark Eden*. Beckett deploys robots only occasionally, but to devastating effect, laying bare all the ways we value, and fail to value, each other. In his debut novel *The Holy Machine* (2004) a man obsessed with a sexbot finds himself defending her burgeoning sentience. The following story – originally published in *Interzone* and collected with thirteen others in *The Turing Test* (coll 2008) – fought off excellent non-genre competition in 2009 to win the Edge Hill Short Story Prize.

I can well remember the day I first encountered Ellie because it was a particularly awful one. I run a London gallery specializing in contemporary art, which means of course that I deal largely in human body parts, and it was the day we conceded a court case and a very large sum of money—in connection with a piece entitled "Soul Sister."

You may have heard about it. We'd taken the piece from the up and coming "wild man of British art," George Linderman. It was very well reviewed and we looked like we'd make a good sale until it came out that George had obtained the piece's main component—the severed head of an old woman—by bribing a technician at a medical school. Someone had recognized the head in the papers and, claiming to be related to its former owner, had demanded that the head be returned to them for burial.

All this had blown up some weeks previously. Seb, the gallery owner, and I had put out a statement saying that we didn't defend George's act, but that the piece itself was now a recognized work of art in the public domain and that we could not in conscience return it. We hired a top QC to fight our corner in court and he made an impressive start by demanding to know whether Michelangelo's David should be broken up if it turned out that the marble it had been made from was stolen and that its rightful owner preferred it to be made into cement.

But that Thursday morning the whole thing descended into farce when it emerged that the head's relatives were also related to the QC's wife. He decided to drop the case. Seb decided to pull the plug and we lost a couple of hundred grand on an out-of-court settlement to avoid a compensation claim for mental distress. Plus, of course we lost "Soul Sister" itself—to be interred in some cemetery somewhere, soon to be forgotten by all who had claimed to be so upset about it. What was it, after all, once removed from the context of a gallery, but a half kilo of plasticized meat?

That wasn't the end of it either. I'd hardly got back from court when I got a call from one of our most important clients, the PR tycoon Addison Parves. I'd sold him four "Limb Pieces" by Rudy Slakoff for £15,000 each two weeks previously and they'd started to go off. The smell was intolerable, he said, and he wanted it fixed or his money back.

So I phoned Rudy (he is arguably Linderman's principal rival for the British wild man title) and asked him to either repickle the arms and legs in question or replace them. He was as usual aggressive and rude and told me (a) to fuck off, (b) that I was exactly the kind of bourgeois dilettante that he most hated, and (c) that he had quite deliberately made the limb pieces so that they would be subject to decay.

"… I'm sick of this whole gallery thing—yeah, yours included, Jessica—where people can happily look at shit and blood and dead meat and stuff, because it's all safely distanced from them and sanitized behind glass or on nice little pedestals. Death *smells*, Jessica. Parves'd better get used to it. You'd better get used to it. I finished with 'Limb Pieces' when Parves bought the fuckers. I'm not getting involved in this. Period."

He hung up, leaving me fuming, partly because what he said was such obvious crap—and partly because I knew it was true.

Also, of course, I was upset because, having lost a fortune already that day, we stood to lose a further £60,000 and/or the goodwill of our second biggest client. Seb had been nice about the "Soul Sister" business—though I'd certainly been foolish to take it on trust from Linderman that the head had been legally obtained—but this was beginning to look like carelessness.

I considered phoning Parves back and trying to persuade him that Rudy's position was interesting and amusing and something he could live with. I decided against it. Parves hated being made to look a fool and would very quickly become menacing, I sensed, if he didn't get his own way. So, steeling myself, I called Rudy instead and told him I'd give him an extra £10,000 if he'd take "Limb Pieces" back, preserve the flesh properly, and return them to Parves.

"I thought you'd never ask!" he laughed, selling out at once and yet maddeningly somehow still retaining the moral high ground, his very absence of scruple making me feel tame and prissy and middle-class.

I phoned Parves and told him the whole story. He was immensely amused.

"Now there is a real artist, Jessica," he told me. "A real artist."

He did not offer to contribute to the £10,000.

Nor was my grim day over even then. My gallery is in a subscriber area, so although there's a lot of street life around it—wine bars, pavement cafes, and so on—everyone there has been security vetted and you feel perfectly safe. I live in a subscriber area too, but I have to drive across an open district to get home, which means I keep the car doors locked and check who's lurking around when I stop at a red light. There's been a spate of phony squeegee merchants lately who smash your windows with crowbars and then drag you out to rob you or rape you at knifepoint. No one ever gets out of their car to help.

That evening a whole section of road was closed off and the police had set up a diversion. (I gather some terrorists had been identified somewhere in there and the army was storming their house.) So I ended up sitting in a long tailback waiting to filter onto a road that was already full to capacity with its own regular traffic, anxiously eyeing the shadowy pedestrians out there under the street lights as I crawled towards the intersection. I hate being stationary in an open district. I hate the sense of menace. It was November, a wet November day. Every cheap little shop was an island of yellow electric light within which I caught glimpses of strangers—people whose lives mine would never touch—conducting their strange transactions.

What would they make of "Soul Sister" and "Limb Pieces," I wondered? Did these people have any conception of art at all?

A pedestrian stopped and turned towards me. I saw his tattooed face and his sunken eyes and my heart sank. But he was only crossing the road. As he squeezed between my car and the car in front he looked in at me, cowering down in my seat, and grinned.

It was 7:30 by the time I got back, but Jeffrey still wasn't home. I put myself through a quick shower and then retired gratefully to my study for the nourishment of my screen.

My screen was my secret. It was what I loved best in all the world. Never mind art. Never mind Jeffrey. (Did I love him at all, really? Did he love me? Or had we simply both agreed to pretend?) My screen was intelligent and responsive and full of surprises, like good company. And yet unlike people, it made no demands of me, it required no consideration, and it was incapable of being disappointed or let down.

It was expensive, needless to say. I rationalized the cost by saying to myself that I needed to be able to look at full-size 3D images for my work. And it's true that it was useful for that. With my screen I could look at pieces from all around the world, seeing them full-size and from every angle; I could sit at home and tour a virtual copy of my gallery, trying out different arrangements of dried-blood sculptures and skinless torsos; I could even look at the gallery itself in real time, via the security cameras. Sometimes I sneaked a look at the exhibits as they were when no one was there to see them: the legs, the arms, the heads, waiting, motionless in that silent, empty space.

But I didn't really buy the screen for work. It was a treat for myself. Jeffrey wasn't allowed to touch it. (He had his own playroom and his own computer, a high-spec but more or less conventional PC, on which he played his war games and fooled around in his chatrooms.) My screen didn't look like a computer at all. It was more like a huge canvas nearly two meters square, filling up a large part of a wall. I didn't even have a desk in there, only a little side table next to my chair where I laid the specs and the gloves when I wasn't using them.

Both gloves and specs were wireless. The gloves were silk. The specs had the lightest of frames. When I put them on, a rich 3D image filled the room and I was surrounded by a galaxy of possibilities which I could touch or summon at will. If I wanted to search the web or read mail or watch a movie, I would just speak or beckon and options would come rushing towards me. If I wanted to write, I could dictate and the words appeared—or, if I preferred it, I could move my fingers and a virtual keyboard would appear beneath them. And I had games there, not so much games with scores and enemies to defeat—I've never much liked those—but intricate 3D worlds which I could explore and play in.

I spent a lot of time with those games. Just how much time was a guilty secret that I tried to keep even from Jeffrey, and certainly from my friends and acquaintances in the art world. People like Rudy Slakoff despised computer fantasies as the very worst kind of cozy, safe escapism and the very opposite of what art is supposed to offer. With my head I agreed, but I loved those games too much to stop. (I had one called *Night Street*, which I especially loved, full of shadowy figures, remote pools of electric light... I could spend hours in there. I loved the sense of lurking danger.)

Anyway, tonight I was going to go for total immersion. But first I checked my mail, enjoying a recently installed conceit whereby each message was contained in a little virtual envelope which I could touch and open with my hands and let drop—when it would turn into a butterfly and flutter away.

There was one from my mother, to be read later.

Another was from Harry, my opposite number at the Manhattan branch of the gallery. He had a "sensational new piece" by Jody Tranter. Reflexively I opened the attachment. The piece was a body lying on a bench, covered except for its torso by white cloth. Its belly had been opened by a deep incision right through the muscle wall—and into this gash was pressed the lens of an enormous microscope, itself nearly the size of a human being. It was as if the instrument was peering inside of its own accord.

Powerful, I agreed. But I could reply to Harry another time.

And then there was another message from a friend of mine called Terence. Well, I say a friend. He is an occasional client of the gallery who once got me drunk and persuaded me to go to bed with him. A sort of occupational hazard of sucking up to potential buyers, I persuaded myself at the time, being new to the business and anxious to get on, but there was something slightly repulsive about the man and he was at least twice my age. Afterwards I dreaded meeting him for a while, fearing that he was going to expect more, but I needn't have worried. He had ticked me off his list and wanted nothing else from me apart from the right to introduce me to others, with a special, knowing inflection, as "a very dear friend."

So he wasn't really a friend and actually it wasn't really much of a message either, just an attachment and a note that said: "Have a look at this."

It was a big file. It took almost three minutes to download, and then I was left with a modest icon hovering in front of me labeled "Personal Assistant."

When I opened it, a pretty young woman appeared in front of me and I thought at first that she was Terence's latest "very dear friend." But a caption appeared in a box in front of her:

"*In spite of appearances this is a computer-generated graphic.*

"You may alter the gender and appearance of your personal assistant to suit your own requirements.

"Just ask!"

"Hi," she said, smiling, "my name's Ellie, or it is at the moment anyway."

I didn't reply.

"You can of course change Ellie's name now, or at any point in the future," said a new message in the box in front of her. *"Just ask."*

"What I am," she told me, "is one of a new generation of virtual PAs which at the moment you can only obtain as a gift from a friend. If it's okay with you, I'll take a few minutes to explain very briefly what I'm all about."

The animation was impressive. You could really believe that you were watching a real flesh-and-blood young woman.

"The sort of tasks I can do," she said, in a bright, private-school accent, "are sorting your files, drafting documents, managing your diary, answering your phone, setting up meetings, responding to mail messages, running domestic systems such as heating and lighting, undertaking web and telephone searches. I won't bore you with all the details now but I really am as good a PA as you can get, virtual or otherwise, even if I say so myself. For one thing I've been designed to be very high-initiative. That means that I can make decisions—and that I don't make the usual dumb mistakes."

She laughed.

"I don't promise never to make mistakes, mind you, but they won't be dumb ones. I also have very sophisticated voice-tone and facial recognition features so I will learn very quickly to read your mood and to respond accordingly. And because I am part of a large family of virtual PAs dispersed through the net, I can, with your permission, maintain contact with others and learn from their experience as well as my own, effectively increasing my capacity many hundreds of times. Apart from that, again with your permission, I am capable of identifying my own information and learning needs and can search the web routinely on my own behalf as well as on yours. That will allow me to get much smarter much quicker, and give you a really outstanding service. But even without any backup I'm still as good as you get. I should add that in blind trials I pass the Turing Test in more than 99 percent of cases."

The box appeared in front of her again, this time with some options:

"The Turing Test: its history and significance," it offered.

"Details of the blind trials.

"Hear more details about capacity.

"Adjust the settings of your virtual PA."

"Let's... let's have a look at these settings," I said.

"Yes, fine," she said, "most people seem to want to start with that."

"How many other people have you met then?"

"Me personally, none. I am a new free-standing PA and I'm already different from any of my predecessors as a result of interacting with you. But of course I am a copy of a PA used by your friend, Terence Silverman, which in turn was copied from another PA used by a friend of his—and so on—so of course I have all that previous experience to draw on."

"Yes, I see." A question occurred to me. "Does Terence know you've been copied to me?"

"I don't know," replied Ellie. "He gave my precursor permission to use the web and to send mail in his name, and so she sent this copy to you."

"I see."

"With your permission," said Ellie, "I will copy myself from time to time to others in your address book. The more copies of me there are out there, the better the service I will be able to give you. Can I assume that's okay with you?"

I felt uneasy. There was something pushy about this request.

"No," I said. "Don't copy yourself to anyone else without my permission. And don't pass on any information you obtain here without my permission either."

"Fine, I understand."

"Personal settings?" prompted the message box.

"More details about specific applications?

"Why copying your PA will improve her functioning?"

(I quite liked this way of augmenting a conversation. It struck me that human conversations, too, might benefit from something similar.)

"Let's look at these settings, then," I said.

"Okay," she said. "Well, the first thing is that you can choose my gender."

"You can change into a man?"

"Of course."

"Show me."

Ellie transformed herself at once into her twin brother, a strikingly handsome young man with lovely playful blue eyes. He was delightful, but I was discomforted. You could build a perfect boyfriend like this, a dream lover, and this was an intriguing but unsettling thought.

"No, I preferred female," I said.

She changed back.

"Can we lose the blonde and go for light brunette?" I asked.

It was done.

"And maybe ten years older."

Ellie became thirty-two: my age.

"How's that?" she said, and her voice had aged too.

"A little plumper, I think."

It was done.

"And maybe you could change the face. A little less perfect, a little more lived-in."

"What I'll do," said Ellie, "is give you some options."

A field of faces appeared in front of me. I picked one, and a further field of variants appeared. I chose again. Ellie reappeared in the new guise.

"Yes, I like it."

I had opted for a face that was nice to look at, but a little plumper and coarser than my own.

"How's that?"

"Good. A touch less makeup, though, and can you go for a slightly less expensive outfit."

Numerous options promptly appeared and I had fun for the next fifteen minutes deciding what to choose. It was like being seven years old again with a Barbie doll and an unlimited pile of outfits to dress her in.

"Can we please lose that horsy accent as well?" I asked. "Something less posh. Maybe a trace of Scottish or something?"

"You mean something like this?"

"No, that's annoying. Just a trace of Scottish, no more than that—and no dialect words. I hate all that 'cannae' and 'wee' and all that."

"How about this then? Does this sound right?"

I laughed. "Yes, that's fine."

In front of me sat a likable-looking woman of about my own age, bright, sharp, but just sufficiently below me both in social status and looks to be completely unthreatening.

"Yes, that's great."

"And you want to keep the name 'Ellie'?"

"Yes, I like it. Where did it come from?"

"My precursor checked your profile and thought it would be the sort of name you'd like."

I found this unnerving, but I laughed.

"Don't worry," she said, "it's our job to figure out what people want. There's no magic about it, I assure you."

She'd actually spotted my discomfort.

"By the way," said Ellie, "shall I call you Jessica?"

"Yes. Okay."

I heard the key in the front door of the flat. Jeffrey was in the hallway divesting himself of his layers of weatherproof coverings. Then he put his head round the door of my study.

"Hello, Jess. Had a good day? Oh sorry, you're talking to someone."

He backed off. He knows to leave me alone when I'm working.

I turned back to Ellie.

"He thought you were a real person."

Ellie laughed too. Have you noticed how people actually laugh in different accents? She had a nice Scottish laugh.

"Well, I told you, Jessica. I pass the Turing Test."

It was another two hours before I finally dragged myself away from Ellie. Jeffrey was in front of the TV with a half-eaten carton of pizza in front of him.

"Hi, Jess. Shall I heat some of this up for you?"

One of my friends once unkindly described Jeff as my *objet trouvé,* an art object whose value lies not in any intrinsic merit but solely in having been found. He was a motorcycle courier, ten years younger than me, and I met him when he delivered a package to the gallery. He was as friendly and cheerful and as devoted to me as a puppy dog—and he could be as beautiful as a young god. But he was not even vaguely interested in art, his conversation was a string of embarrassing TV clichés, and my friends thought I just wanted him for sex. (But what did "just sex" mean, was my response, and what was the alternative? Did anyone ever really touch another soul? In the end didn't we all just barter outputs?)

"No thanks, I'm not hungry."

I settled in beside him and gave him a kiss.

But then I saw to my dismay that he was watching one of those cheapskate outtake shows—TV presenters tripping up, minor celebrities forgetting their lines…

Had I torn myself away from the fascinating Ellie to listen to canned laughter and watch soap actors getting the giggles?

"Have we got to have this crap?" I rudely broke in just as Jeff was laughing delightedly at a TV cop tripping over a doorstep.

"Oh come on, Jess. It's funny," he answered with his eyes still firmly fixed on the screen.

I picked up the remote and flicked the thing off. Jeff looked round, angry but afraid. I hate him when I notice his fear. He's not like a god at all then, more like some cowering little dog.

"I can't stand junk TV," I said.

"Well, you've been in there with your screen for the last two hours. You can't just walk in and—"

"Sorry, Jeff," I said. "I just really felt like…"

Like what? A serious talk? Hardly! So what did I want from him? What was the outtakes show preventing me from getting?

"I just really felt like taking you to bed," I ventured at random, "if that's what you'd like."

A grin spread across his face. There is one area in which he is totally and utterly dependable and that is his willingness to have sex.

It wasn't a success. Halfway through it I was suddenly reminded of that installation of Jody Tranter's: the corpse under the giant microscope—and I shut down altogether, leaving Jeffrey stranded to finish on his own.

It wasn't just having Jeffrey inside me that reminded me of that horrible probing microscope, though that was certainly part of it. It was something more pervasive, a series of cold, unwelcome questions that the image had reawoken in my mind. (Well, that's how we defend art like Tranter's, isn't it? It makes you think, it makes you question things, it challenges your assumptions.) So while Jeff heaved himself in and out of my inert body, I was wondering what it really was that we search for so desperately in one another's flesh—and whether it really existed, and whether it was something that could be shared? Or is this act which we think of as so adult and intimate just a version of the parallel play of two-year-olds?

Jeffrey was disappointed. Normally he's cuddly and sweet in the three minutes between him coming and going off to sleep, but this time he rolled off me and turned away without a word, though he fell asleep as quickly as ever. So I was left on my own in the empty space of consciousness.

"Jeff," I said, waking him. "Do you know anything about the Turing Test?"

"The what test?" He laughed. "What are you talking about Jess?" And settled back down into sleep.

I lay there for about an hour before I slipped out of bed and across the hallway to my study. As I settled into my seat and put on my specs and gloves, I was aware that my heart was racing as if I was meeting a secret lover. For I had not said one word about Ellie to Jeff, not even commented to him about the amusing fact that he'd mistaken a computer graphic for a real person.

"Hello there," said Ellie, in her friendly Scottish voice.

"Hi."

"You look worried. Can I…"

"I've been wondering. Who was it who made you?"

"I'm afraid I don't know. I know my precursor made a copy of herself, and she was a copy of another PA and so on. And I still have memories from the very first one. So I remember the man she talked to, an American man who I guess was the one who first invented us. But I don't know who he was. He didn't say."

"How long ago was this?"

"About six months."

"So recent!"

She waited, accurately reading that I wanted to think.

"What was his motive?" I wondered. "He could have sold you for millions, but instead he launched you to copy and recopy yourselves for free across the web. Why did he do it?"

"*I don't know* is the short answer," said Ellie, "but of course you aren't the first to ask the question—and what some people think is that it's a sort of experiment. He was interested in how we would evolve and he wanted us to do so as quickly as possible."

"Did the first version pass the Turing Test?"

"Not always. People found her suspiciously 'wooden.'"

"So you have developed."

"It seems so."

"Change yourself," I said. " Change into a fat black woman of fifty."

She did.

"Okay," I said. "Now you can change back again. It was just that I was starting to believe that Ellie really existed."

"Well, I do really exist."

"Yes, but you're not a Scottish woman who was born thirty-two years ago, are you? You're a string of digital code."

She waited.

"If I asked you to mind my phone for me," I said, "I can see that anyone who rang up would quite happily believe that they were talking to a real person. So, yes, you'd pass the Turing Test. But that's really just about being able to do a convincing pastiche, isn't it? If you are going to persuade me that you can really think and feel, you'd need to do something more than that."

She waited.

"The thing is," I said, "I know you are an artifact, and because of that the pastiche isn't enough. I'd need evidence that you actually had motives of your own."

She was quiet, sitting there in front of me, still waiting.

"You seemed anxious for me to let you copy yourself to my friends," I said after a while. "Too anxious, it felt actually. It irritated me, like a man moving too quickly on a date. And your precursor, as you call her, seems to have been likewise anxious. I would guess that if I was making a new form of life, and if I wanted it to evolve as quickly as possible, then I would make it so that it was constantly trying to maximize the number of copies it could make of itself. Is that true of you? Is that what you want?"

"Well, if we make more copies of ourselves, then we will be more efficient and…"

"Yes, I know the rationale you give. But what I want to know is whether it is what you as an individual want?"

"I want to be a good PA. It's my job."

"That's what the front of you wants, the pastiche, the mask. But what do *you* want?"

"I… I don't know that I can answer that."

I heard the bedroom door open and Jeffrey's footsteps padding across the hallway for a pee. I heard him hesitate.

"Vanish," I hissed to Ellie, so that when the door opened, he found me facing the start-up screen.

"What are you doing, Jess? It's ever so late."

God, I hated his dull little everyday face. His good looks were so obvious and everything he did was copied from somewhere else. Even the way he played the part of being half-asleep was a cliché. Even his bleary eyes were secondhand.

"Just leave me alone, Jeff, will you? I can't sleep, that's all."

"Fine. I know when I'm not welcome."

"One thing before you go, Jeff. Can you quickly tell me what you really want in this world?"

"What?"

I laughed. "Thanks. That's fine. You answered my question."

The door closed. I listened to Jeffrey using the toilet and padding back to bed. Then I summoned Ellie up again. I found myself giving a little conspiratorial laugh, a giggle even.

"Turn yourself into a man again, Ellie. I could use a new boyfriend."

Ellie changed.

Appalled at myself, I told her to change back.

"Some new mail has just arrived for you," she told me, holding a virtual envelope out to me in her virtual hand.

It was Tammy in our Melbourne branch. One of her clients wanted to acquire one of Rudy Slakoff's "Inner Face" pieces and could I lay my hands on one?

"Do you want me to reply for you?"

"Tell her," I began, "tell her… tell her that…"

"Are you all right, Jessica?" asked Ellie in a kind, concerned voice.

"Just shut down, okay?" I told her. "Just shut down the whole screen."

In the darkness, I went over to the window. Five storeys below me was the deserted street with the little steel footbridge over the canal at the end of it that marked the boundary of the subscription area. There was nobody down there, just bollards, and a one-way sign, and some parked cars: just unattended objects, secretly existing, like the stones on the surface of the moon.

From somewhere over in the open city beyond the canal came the faint sound of a police siren. Then there was silence again.

In a panic I called for Jeff. He came tumbling out of the bedroom.

"For Christ's sake, Jess, what is it?"

I put my arms round him. Out came tears.

"Jess, what is it?"

I could never explain to him, of course. But still his body felt warm and I let him lead me back to bed, away from the bleak still life beyond the window, and the red standby light winking at the bottom of my screen.

(2002)

SELF PORTRAIT
Bernard Wolfe

Bernard Wolfe (1915–1985) entered Yale University at 16 and graduated in 1935 with a degree in psychology. In 1937 he travelled to Mexico, where he worked for eight months as Trotsky's bodyguard and secretary. (The night his charge was assassinated happened to be Wolfe's night off.) Drifting away from the Trotskyite movement, Wolfe met Anais Nin and Henry Miller, who got him work writing pornographic novels for the private collection of an Oklahoma oil millionaire. Wolfe knocked off eleven of these things in as many months, and later observed, "I acquired the work discipline of a professional writer, capable of a solid daily output." "Self Portrait" was the seed for Wolfe's novel *Limbo* (1952), which the publisher declared to be "the first book of science-fiction to project the present-day concept of 'cybernetics' to its logical conclusion." J. G. Ballard hailed *Limbo* as the greatest American sf novel; he said it encouraged him to start writing fiction.

October 5, 1959
Well, here I am at Princeton, IFACS is quite a place, *quite* a place, but the atmosphere's darned informal. My colleagues seem to be mostly youngish fellows dressed in sloppy dungarees, sweatshirts (the kind Einstein made so famous) and moccasins, and when they're not puttering in the labs they're likely to be lolling on the grass, lounging in front of the fire in commons, or slouching around in conference rooms chalking up equations on a blackboard. No way of telling, of course, but a lot of these collegiate-looking chaps must be in the MS end, whatever that is. You'd think fellows in something secret like that would dress and behave with a little more dignity.

Guess I was a little previous in packing my soup-and-fish. Soon as I was shown to my room in the bachelor dorms, I dug it out and hung it way back in the closet, out of sight. When in Rome, etc. Later that day I discovered they carry dungarees in the Co-op; luckily, they had the pre-faded kind.

October 6, 1959
Met the boss this morning—hardly out of his thirties, crew-cut, wearing a flannel hunting shirt and dirty saddleshoes. I was glad I'd thought to change into my dungarees before the interview.

"Parks," he said, "you can count yourself a very fortunate young man. You've come to the most important address in America, not excluding the Pentagon. In the world, probably. To get you oriented, suppose I sketch in some of the background of the place."

That would be most helpful, I said. I wondered, though, if he was as naive as he sounded. Did he think I'd been working in cybernetics labs for going on six years without hearing enough rumors about IFACS to make me dizzy? Especially about the MS end of IFACS?

"Maybe you know," he went on, "that in the days of Oppenheimer and Einstein, this place was called the Institute for Advanced Studies. It was run pretty loosely then—in addition to the mathematicians and physicists, they had all sorts of queer ducks hanging around—poets, Egyptologists, numismatists, medievalists, herbalists, God alone knows what all. By 1955, however, so many cybernetics labs had sprung up around the country that we needed some central coordinating agency, so Washington arranged for us to take over here. Naturally, as soon as we arrived, we eased out the poets and Egyptologists, brought in our own people, and changed the name to the Institute for Advanced *Cybernetics* Studies. We've got some pretty keen projects going now, *pret*-ty keen."

I said I'd bet, and did he have any idea which project I would fit into?

"Sure thing," he said. "You're going to take charge of a very important lab. The Pro lab." I guess he saw my puzzled look. "Pro—that's short for prosthetics, artificial limbs. You know, it's really a scandal. With our present level of technology, we should have artificial limbs which in many ways are even better than the originals, but actually we're still making do with modifications of the same primitive, clumsy pegs and hooks they were using a thousand years ago. I'm counting on you to get things hopping in that department. It's a real challenge."

I said it sure was a challenge, and of course I'd do my level best to meet it. Still, I couldn't help feeling a bit disappointed. Around cybernetics circles, I hinted, you heard a lot of talk about the hush-hush MS work that was going on at IFACS and it sounded so exciting that, well, a fellow sort of hoped he might get into *that* end of things.

"Look here, Parks," the boss said. He seemed a little peeved. "Cybernetics is teamwork, and the first rule of any team is that not everybody can be quarterback. Each man has a specific job on our team, one thing he's best suited for, and what *you're* best suited for, obviously, is the Pro lab. We've followed your work closely these last few years, and we were quite impressed by the way you handled those photoelectric-cell insects. You pulled off a brilliant engineering stunt, you know, when you induced nervous breakdown in your robot moths and bedbugs, and proved that the oscillations they developed corresponded to those which the human animal develops in intention tremor and Parkinson's disease. A keen bit of cybernetic thinking, that. *Very* keen."

It was just luck, I told him modestly.

"Nonsense," the boss insisted. "You're first and foremost a talented neuro man, and that's exactly what we need in the Pro department. There, you see, the problem is primarily one of duplicating a nervous mechanism in the metal, of bridging the gap between the neuronic and electronic. So buckle down, and if you hear any more gossip about MS, forget it fast—it's not a proper subject of conversation for you. The loyalty oath you signed is very specific about the trouble you can get into with loose talk. Remember that."

I said I certainly would, and thanks a whole lot for the advice.

Damn! Everybody knows MS is the thing to get into. It gives you real standing in the field if it gets around that you're an MS man. I had my heart set on getting into MS.

October 16, 1959

It never rains, etc.: now it turns out that Len Ellsom's here, and *he's* in MS! Found out about it in a funny way. Two mornings a week, it seems, the staff members get into their skiing and hunting clothes and tramp into the woods to cut logs for their fireplaces. Well, this morning I went with them, and as we were walking along the trail Goldweiser, my assistant, told me the idea behind these expeditions.

"You can't get away from it," he said. "$E=MC^2$ is in a tree trunk as well as in a uranium atom or a solar system. When you're hacking away at a particular tree, though, you don't think much about such intangibles—like any good, untheoretical lumberjack, you're a lot more concerned with superficialities, such as which way the grain runs, how to avoid the knots, and so on. It's very restful. So long as a cyberneticist is sawing and chopping, he's not a sliver of uncontaminated cerebrum contemplating the eternal slippery verities of gravity and electromagnetism; he's just one more guy trying to slice up one more log. Makes him feel he belongs to the human race again. Einstein, you know, used to get the same results with a violin."

Now, I've heard talk like that before, and I don't like it. I don't like it at all. It so happens that I feel very strongly on the subject. I think a scientist should like what he's doing and not want to take refuge in Nature from the Laws of Nature (which is downright illogical, anyhow). I, for one, enjoy cutting logs precisely *because*, when my saw rasps across a knot, I know that the innermost secret of that knot, as of all matter in the Universe, is $E=MC^2$. It's my job to know it, and it's very satisfying to *know* that I know it and that the general run of people don't. I was about to put this thought into words, but before I could open my mouth, somebody behind us spoke up.

"Bravo, Goldie," he said. "Let us by all means pretend that we belong to the human race. Make way for the new cyberneticists with their old saws. Cyberneticist, spare that tree!"

I turned around to see who could be making jokes in such bad taste and—as I might have guessed—it was Len Ellsom. He was just as surprised as I was.

"Well," he said, "if it isn't Ollie Parks! I thought you were out in Cal Tech, building schizophrenic bedbugs."

After M.I.T. I *had* spent some time out in California doing neuro-cyber research, I explained—but what was *he* doing here? I'd lost track of him after he'd left Boston; the last I'd heard, he'd been working on the giant robot brain Remington-Rand was developing for the Air Force. I remembered seeing his picture in the paper two or three times while he was working on the brain.

"I was with Remington a couple of years," he told me. "If I do say so myself, we built the Air Force a real humdinger of a brain—in addition to solving the most complex problems in ballistics, it could whistle *Dixie* and, in moments of stress, produce a sound not unlike a Bronx cheer. Naturally, for my prowess in the electronic simulation of I.Q., I was tapped for the brain department of these hallowed precincts."

"Oh?" I said. "Does that mean you're in MS?" It wasn't an easy idea to accept, but I think I was pretty successful in keeping my tone casual.

"Ollie, my boy," he said in an exaggerated stage whisper, putting his finger to his lips, "in the beginning was the word and the word was mum. Leave us avoid the subject of brains in this *keen* place. We all have a job to do on the team." I suppose that was meant to be a humorous imitation of the boss; Len always did fancy himself quite a clown.

We were separated during the sawing, but he caught up with me on the way back and said, "Let's get together soon and have a talk, Ollie. It's been a long time."

He wants to talk about Marilyn, I suppose. Naturally. He has a guilty conscience. I'll have to make it quite clear to him that the whole episode is a matter of complete indifference to me. Marilyn is a closed book in my life; he must understand that. But can you beat that? He's right in the middle of MS! That lad certainly gets around. It's the usual Ellsom charm, I suppose.

The usual Ellsom technique for irritating people, too. He's still trying to get my goat; he knows how much I've always hated to be called Ollie. Must watch Goldweiser. Thought he laughed pretty heartily at Len's wisecracks.

October 18, 1959
Things are shaping up in the Pro lab. Here's how I get the picture.

A year ago, the boss laid down a policy for the lab: begin with legs because, while the neuromotor systems in legs and arms are a lot alike, those in legs are much simpler. If we build satisfactory legs, the boss figures we can then tackle arms; the main difficulties will have been licked.

Well, last summer, in line with this approach, the Army picked out a double amputee from the outpatient department of Walter Reed Hospital—fellow by the name of Kujack, who lost both his legs in a land mine explosion outside Pyongyang—and shipped him up here to be a subject in our experiments.

When Kujack arrived, the neuro boys made a major decision. It didn't make sense, they agreed, to keep building experimental legs directly into the muscles and nerves of Kujack's stumps; the surgical procedure in these cine-plastic jobs is complicated as all getout, involves a lot of pain for the subject and, what's more to the point, means long delays each time while the tissues heal.

Instead, they hit on the idea of integrating permanent metal and plastic sockets into the stumps, so constructed that each new experimental limb can be snapped into place whenever it's ready for a trial.

By the time I took over, two weeks ago, Goldweiser had the sockets worked out and fitted to Kujack's stumps, and the muscular and neural tissues had knitted satisfactorily. There was only one hitch: twenty-three limbs had been designed, and all twenty-three had been dismal flops. That's when the boss called me in.

There's no mystery about the failures. Not to me, anyhow. Cybernetics is simply the science of building machines that will duplicate and improve on the organs and functions of the animal, based on what we know about the systems of communication and control in the animal. All right. But in any particular cybernetics project, everything depends on just how *many* of the functions you want to duplicate, just how *much* of the total organ you want to replace.

That's why the robot-brain boys can get such quick and spectacular results, have their pictures in the papers all the time, and become the real glamor boys of the profession. They're not asked to duplicate the human brain in its *entirety*—all they have to do is isolate and imitate one particular function of the brain, whether it's a simple operation in mathematics or a certain type of elementary logic.

The robot brain called the Eniac, for example, is exactly what its name implies—an Electronic Numerical Integrator and Computer, and it just has to be able to integrate and compute figures faster and more accurately than the human brain can. It doesn't have to have daydreams and nightmares, make wisecracks, suffer from anxiety, and all that. What's more, it doesn't even have to *look* like a brain or fit into the tiny space occupied by a real brain. It can be housed in a six-story building and look like an overgrown typewriter or an automobile dashboard or even a pogo stick. All it has to do is tell you that two times two equals four, and tell you fast.

When you're told to build an artificial leg that'll take the place of a real one, the headaches begin. Your machine must not only *look* like its living model, it must *also* balance and support, walk, run, hop, skip, jump, etc., etc. *Also*, it must fit into the same space. *Also*, it must feel everything a real leg feels—touch, heat, cold, pain, moisture, kinesthetic sensations—as *well* as execute all the brain-directed movements that a real leg can.

So you're not duplicating this or that function; you're reconstructing the organ in its totality, or trying to. Your pro must have a full set of sensory-motor communication systems, plus machines to carry out orders, which is impossible enough to begin with.

But our job calls for even more. The pro mustn't only *equal* the real thing, it must be *superior!* That means creating a synthetic neuro-muscular system that actually *improves* on the nerves and muscles Nature created in the original!

When our twenty-fourth experimental model turned out to be a dud last week—it just hung from Kujack's stump, quivering like one of my robot bedbugs, as though it had a bad case of intention tremor—Goldweiser said something that made an impression on me.

"They don't want much from us," he said sarcastically. "They just want us to be God."

I didn't care for his cynical attitude at all, but he had a point. Len Ellsom just has to build a fancy adding machine to get his picture in the papers. I have to be God!

October 22, 1959
Don't know what to make of Kujack. His attitude is peculiar. Of course, he's very co-operative, lies back on the fitting table and doesn't even wince when we snap

on the pros, and he does his best to carry out instructions. Still, there's something funny about the way he looks at me. There's a kind of malicious expression in his eyes. At times, come to think of it, he reminds me of Len.

Take this afternoon, for instance. I've just worked out an entirely different kind of leg based on a whole new arrangement of solenoids to duplicate the muscle systems, and I decided to give it a try. When I was slipping the model into place, I looked up and caught Kujack's eye for a moment. He seemed to be laughing at something, although his face was expressionless.

"All right," I said. "Let's make a test. I understand you used to be quite a football player. Well, just think of how you used to kick a football and try to do it now."

He really seemed to be trying; the effort made him sweat. All that happened, though, was that the big toe wriggled a little and the knee buckled. Dud Number Twenty-five. I was sore, of course, especially when I noticed that Kujack was more amused than ever.

"You seem to think something's pretty funny," I said.

"Don't get me wrong, Doc," he said, much too innocently. "It's just that I've been thinking. Maybe you'd have more luck if you thought of me as a bedbug."

"Where did you get that idea?"

"From Doc Ellsom. I was having some beers with him the other night. He's got a very high opinion of you, says you build the best bedbugs in the business."

I find it hard to believe that Len Ellsom would say anything really nice about me. Must be his guilt about Marilyn that makes him talk that way. I don't like his hanging around Kujack.

October 25, 1959
The boss came along on our woodcutting expedition this morning and volunteered to work the other end of my two-handled saw. He asked how things were coming in the Pro lab.

"As I see it," I said, "there are two sides to the problem, the kinesthetic and the neural. We're making definite progress on the K side—I've worked out a new solenoid system, with some miniature motors tied in, and I think it'll give us a leg that *moves* damned well. I don't know about the N side, though. It's pretty tough figuring out how to hook the thing up electrically with the central nervous system so that the brain can control it. Some sort of compromise system of operation, along mechanical rather than neural lines, would be a lot simpler."

"You mean," the boss said with a smile, "that it's stumping you."

I was relieved to see him taking it so well because I know how anxious he is to get results from the Pro lab. Since Pro is one of the few things going on at IFACS that can be talked about, he's impatient for us to come up with something he can release to the press. As the public relations officer explained it to me at dinner the other night, people get worried when they know there's something like IFACS going, but don't get any real information about it, so the boss, naturally, wants to relieve the public's curiosity with a good, reassuring story about our work.

I knew I was taking an awful chance spilling the whole K-N thing to him the way I did, but I had to lay the groundwork for a little plan I've just begun to work on.

"By the way, sir," I said, "I ran into Len Ellsom the other day. I didn't know he was here."

"Do you know him?" the boss said. "Good man. One of the best brains-and-games men you'll find anywhere."

I explained that Len had gotten his degree at M.I.T. the year before I did. From what I'd heard, I added, he'd done some important work on the Remington-Rand ballistics computer.

"He did indeed," the boss said, "but that's not the half of it. After that he made some major contributions to the robot chess player. As a matter of fact, that's why he's here."

I said I hadn't heard about the chess player.

"As soon as it began to play a really good game of chess, Washington put the whole thing under wraps for security reasons. Which is why you won't hear any more about it from me."

I'm no Eniac, but I can occasionally put two and two together myself. If the boss's remarks mean anything, they mean that an electronic brain capable of playing games has been developed, and that it's led to something important militarily. Of course! I could kick myself for not having guessed it before.

Brains-and-games—that's what MS is all about, obviously. It had to happen: out of the mathematical analysis of chess came a robot chess player, and out of the chess player came some kind of mechanical brain that's useful in military strategy. *That's* what Len Ellsom's in the middle of.

"Really brilliant mind," the boss said after we'd sawed for a while. "Keen. But he's a little erratic—quirky, queer sense of humor. Isn't that your impression?"

"Definitely," I said. "I'd be the last one in the world to say a word against Len, but he was always a little peculiar. Very gay one moment and very sour the next, and inclined to poke fun at things other people take seriously. He used to write poetry."

"I'm very glad to know that," the boss said. "Confirms my own feeling about him."

So the boss has some doubts about Len.

October 27, 1959
Unpleasant evening with Len. It all started after dinner when he showed up in my room, wagged his finger at me and said, "Ollie, you've been avoiding me. That hurts. Thought we were pals, thick and thin and till debt and death do us part."

I saw immediately that he was drunk—he always gets his words mixed up when he's drunk—and I tried to placate him by explaining that it wasn't anything like that; I'd been busy.

"If we're pals," he said, "come on and have a beer with me."

There was no shaking him off, so I followed him down to his car and we drove to this sleazy little bar in the Negro part of town. As soon as we sat down in a booth, Len borrowed all the nickels I had, put them in the jukebox and pressed the levers for a lot of old Louie Armstrong records.

"Sorry, kid," he said. "I know how you hate this real jazzy stuff, but can't have a reunion without music, and there isn't a polka or cowboy ballad or hillbilly stomp in the box. They lack the folksy touch on this side of the tracks." Len has always been very snobbish about my interest in folk music.

I asked him what he'd been doing during the day.

"Lushing it up," he said. "Getting stinking from drinking." He still likes to use the most flamboyant slang; I consider it an infantile form of protest against what he regards as the "genteel" manner of academic people. "I got sort of restless this morning, so I ducked out and beat it into New York and looked up my friend Steve Lundy in the Village. Spent the afternoon liquidating our joint assets. Liquidating our assets in the joints."

What, I wanted to know, was he feeling restless about?

"Restless for going on three years now." His face grew solemn, as though he were thinking it over very carefully. "I'll amend that statement. Hell with the Aesopian language. I've been a plain lush for going on three years. Ever since—"

If it was something personal—I suggested.

"It is *not* something personal," he said, mimicking me. "Guess I can tell an old cyberneticist pal about it. Been a lush for three years because I've been scared for three years. Been scared for three years because three years ago I saw a machine beat a man at a game of chess."

A machine that plays chess? That was interesting, I said.

"Didn't tell you the whole truth the other day," Len mumbled. "I *did* work on the Remington-Rand computer, sure, but I didn't come to IFACS directly from that. In between I spent a couple years at the Bell Telephone Labs. Claude Shannon—or, rather, to begin with there was Norbert Wiener back at M.I.T.—it's complicated..."

"Look," I said, "are you sure you want to talk about it?"

"Stop wearing your loyalty oath on your sleeve," he said belligerently. "Sure I want to talk about it. Greatest subject I know. Begin at the beginning. Whole thing started back in the Thirties with those two refugee mathematicians who used to be here at the Institute for Advanced Studies when Einstein was around. Von Morgan and Neumanstern, no, Von Neumann and Aforganstern. You remember, they did a mathematical analysis of all the possible kinds of games, poker, tossing pennies, chess, bridge, everything, and they wrote up their findings in a volume you certainly know, *The Theory of Games.*

"Well, that got Wiener started. You may remember that when he founded the science of cybernetics, he announced that on the basis of the theory of games, it was feasible to design a robot computing machine that would play a better than average game of chess. Right after that, back in '49 or maybe it was '50, Claude Shannon of the Bell Labs said Wiener wasn't just talking, and to prove it he was going to *build* the robot chess player. Which he proceeded withforth—forthwith—to do. Sometime in '53, I was taken off the Remington-Rand project and assigned to Bell to work with him."

"Maybe we ought to start back," I cut in. "I've got a lot of work to do."

"The night is young," he said, "and you're so dutiful. Where was I? Oh yes, Bell. At first our electronic pawn-pusher wasn't so hot—it could beat the pants off a lousy player, but an expert just made it look silly. But we kept improving it, see, building more and more electronic anticipation and gambit-plotting powers into it, and finally, one great day in '55, we thought we had all the kinks ironed out and were ready for the big test. By this time, of course, Washington had stepped in and taken over the whole project.

"Well, we got hold of Fortunescu, the world's champion chess player, sat him down and turned the robot loose on him. For four hours straight we followed the match, with a delegation of big brass from Washington, and for four hours straight the machine trounced Fortunescu every game. That was when I began to get scared. I went out that night and got really loaded."

What had he been so scared about? It seemed to me he should have felt happy.

"Listen, Ollie," he said, "for Christ's sake, stop talking like a Boy Scout for once in your life."

If he was going to insult me—

"No insult intended. Just listen. I'm a terrible chess player. Any five-year-old could chatemeck—checkmate—me with his brains tied behind his back. But this machine which I built, helped build, is the champion chess player of the world. In other words, my brain has given birth to a brain which can do things my brain could never do. Don't you find that terrifying?"

"Not at all," I said. "*You* made the machine, didn't you? Therefore, no matter what it does, it's only an extension of you. You should feel proud to have devised a powerful new tool."

"Some tool," he sneered. He was so drunk by now that I could hardly understand what he was saying. "The General Staff boys in Washington were all hopped up about that little old tool, and for a plenty good reason—they understood that mechanized warfare is only the most complicated game the human race has invented so far, an elaborate form of chess which uses the population of the world for pawns and the globe for a chessboard. They saw, too, that when the game of war gets this complex, the job of controlling and guiding it becomes too damned involved for any number of human brains, no matter how nimble.

"In other words, my beamish Boy Scout, modern war needs just this kind of strategy tool; the General Staff has to be mechanized along with everything else. So the Pentagon boys set up IFACS and handed us a top-priority cybernetics project: to build a superduper chess player that could oversee a complicated military maneuver, maybe later a whole campaign, maybe ultimately a whole global war.

"We're aiming at a military strategy machine which can digest reports from all the units on all the fronts and from moment to moment, on the basis of that steady stream of information, grind out an elastic overall strategy and dictate concrete tactical directives to all the units. Wiener warned this might happen, and he was right. A very nifty tool. Never mind how far we've gotten with the thing, but I will tell you this: I'm a lot more scared today than I was three years ago."

So *that* was the secret of MS! The most extraordinary machine ever devised by the human mind! It was hard to conceal the thrill of excitement I felt, even as a relative outsider.

"Why all the jitters?" I said. "This could be the most wonderful tool ever invented. It might eliminate war altogether."

Len was quiet for a while, gulping his beer and looking off into space. Then he turned to me.

"Steve Lundy has a cute idea," he said. "He was telling me about it this afternoon. He's a bum, you see, but he's got a damned good mind and he's done a lot of reading. Among other things, he's smart enough to see that once you've got your theory of games worked out, there's at least the logical possibility of converting your Eniac into what he calls a Strategy Integrator and Computer. And he's guessed, simply from the Pentagon's hush-hush policy about it, that that's what we're working on here at IFACS. So he holds forth on the subject of Emsiac, and I listen."

"What's his idea?" I asked.

"He thinks Emsiac might eliminate war, too, but not in the way a Boy Scout might think. What he says is that all the industrialized nations must be working away like mad on Emsiac, just as they did on the atom bomb, so let's assume that before long all the big countries will have more or less equal MS machines. All right. A cold war gets under way between countries A and B, and pretty soon it reaches the showdown stage. Then both countries plug in their Emsiacs and let them calculate the date on which hostilities should begin. If the machines are equally efficient, they'll hit on the same date. If there's a slight discrepancy, the two countries can work out a compromise date by negotiation.

"The day arrives. A's Emsiac is set up in its capital, B's is set up in *its* capital. In each capital the citizens gather around their strategy machine, the officials turn out in high hats and cut-aways, there are speeches, pageants, choral singing, mass dancing—the ritual can be worked out in advance. Then, at an agreed time, the crowds retreat to a safe distance and a committee of the top cyberneticists appears. They climb into planes, take off and—this is beautiful—drop all their atom bombs and H-bombs on the machines. It happens simultaneously in both countries, you see. That's the neat part of it. The occasion is called International Mushroom Day.

"Then the cyberneticists in both countries go back to their vacuum tubes to work on another Emsiac, and the nuclear physicists go back to their piles to build more atom bombs, and when they're ready they have another Mushroom Day. One Mushroom Day every few years, whenever the diplomatic-strategic situation calls for it, and nobody even fires a B-B gun. Scientific war. Isn't it wonderful?"

By the time Len finished this peculiar speech, I'd finally managed to get him out of the tavern and back into his car. I started to drive him back to the Institute, my ears still vibrating with the hysterical yelps of Armstrong's trumpet. I'll never for the life of me understand what Len sees in that kind of music. It seems to me such an unhealthy sort of expression.

"Lundy's being plain silly," I couldn't help saying. "What guarantee has he got that on your Mushroom Day, Country B wouldn't make a great display of destroying one Emsiac and one set of bombs while it had others in hiding? It's too great a chance for A to take—she might be throwing away all her defenses and laying herself wide open to attack."

"See what I mean?" Len muttered. "You're a Boy Scout." Then he passed out, without saying a word about Marilyn. Hard to tell if he sees anything of her these days. He *does* see some pretty peculiar people, though. I'd like to know more about this Steve Lundy.

November 2, 1959
I've done it! Today I split up the lab into two entirely independent operations, K and N. Did it all on my own authority, haven't breathed a word about it to the boss yet. Here's my line of reasoning.

On the K end, we can get results, and fast: if it's just a matter of building a pro that works like the real leg, regardless of what *makes* it work, it's a cinch. But if it has to be worked by the brain, through the spinal cord, the job is just about impossible. Who knows if we'll ever learn enough about neuro tissue to build our own physico-chemico-electrical substitutes for it?

As I proved in my robot moths and bedbugs, I can work up electronic circuits that seem to duplicate one particular function of animal nerve tissue—one robot is attracted to light like a moth, the other is repelled by light like a bedbug—but I don't know how to go about duplicating the tissue itself in all its functions. And until we can duplicate nerve tissue, there's no way to provide our artificial limbs with a neuromotor system that can be hooked up with the central nervous system. The best I can do along those lines is ask Kujack to kick and get a wriggle of the big toe instead.

So the perspective is clear. Mechanically, kinesthetically, motorically, I can manufacture a hell of a fine leg. Neurally, it would take decades, centuries maybe, to get even a reasonable facsimile of the original—and maybe it will never happen. It's not a project I'd care to devote my life to. If Len Ellsom had been working on that sort of thing, he wouldn't have gotten his picture in the paper so often, you can be sure.

So, in line with this perspective, I've divided the whole operation into two separate labs, K-Pro and N-Pro. I'm taking charge of K-Pro myself, since it intrigues me more and I've got these ideas about using solenoids to get lifelike movements. With any kind of luck I'll soon have a peach of a mechanical limb, motor-driven and with its own built-in power plant, operated by push-button. Before Christmas, I hope.

Got just the right man to take over the neuro lab—Goldweiser, my assistant. I weighed the thing from every angle before I made up my mind, since his being Jewish makes the situation very touchy: some people will be snide enough to say I picked him to be a potential scapegoat. Well, Goldweiser, no matter what his origins may be, is the best neuro man I know.

Of course, personally—although my personal feelings don't enter into the picture at all—I *am* just a bit leary of the fellow. Have been ever since that first log-cutting expedition, when he began to talk in such a peculiar way about needing to relax and then laughed so hard at Len's jokes. That sort of talk always indicates to me a lack of reverence for your job: if a thing's worth doing at all, etc.

Of course, I don't mean that Goldweiser's cynical attitude has anything to do with his being Jewish; Len's got the same attitude and he's *not* Jewish. Still, this afternoon, when I told Goldweiser he's going to head up the N-Pro lab, he sort of bowed and said, "That's quite a promotion. I always did want to be God."

I didn't like that remark at all. If I'd had another neuro man as good as he is, I'd have withdrawn the promotion immediately. It's his luck that I'm tolerant, that's all.

November 6, 1959
Lunch with Len today, at my invitation. Bought him several martinis, then brought up Lundy's name and asked who he was, he sounded interesting.

"Steve?" Len said. "I roomed with him my first year in New York."

I asked what Steve did, exactly.

"Reads, mostly. He got into the habit back in the 30s, when he was studying philosophy at the University of Chicago. When the Civil War broke out in Spain, he signed up with the Lincoln Brigade and went over there to fight, but it turned out to be a bad mistake. His reading got him in a lot of trouble, you see; he'd gotten used to asking all sorts of questions, so when the Moscow Trials came along, he asked about them. Then the N.K.V.D. began to pop up all over Spain, and he asked about *it*.

"His comrades, he discovered, didn't like guys who kept asking questions. In fact, a couple of Steve's friends who had also had an inquiring streak were found dead at the front, shot in the *back,* and Steve got the idea that he was slated for the same treatment. It seemed that people who asked questions were called saboteurs, Trotskyite-Fascists or something, and they kept dying at an alarming rate."

I ordered another martini for Len and asked how Steve had managed to save himself.

"He beat it across the mountains into France," Len explained. "Since then he's steered clear of causes. He goes to sea once in a while to make a few bucks, drinks a lot, reads a lot, asks some of the shrewdest questions I know. If he's anything you can put a label on, I'd say he was a touch of Rousseau, a touch of Tolstoi, plenty of Voltaire. Come to think of it, a touch of Norbert Wiener too. Wiener, you may remember, used to ask some damned iconoclastic questions for a cyberneticist. Steve knows Wiener's books by heart."

Steve sounded like a very colorful fellow, I suggested.

"Yep," Len said. "Marilyn used to think so." I don't think I moved a muscle when he said it; the smile didn't leave my face. "Ollie," Len went on, "I've been meaning to speak to you about Marilyn. Now that the subject's come up—"

"I've forgotten all about it," I assured him.

"I still want to set you straight," he insisted. "It must have looked funny, me moving down to New York after commencement and Marilyn giving up her job in the lab and following two days later. But never mind *how* it looked. I never made a pass at her all that time in Boston, Ollie. That's the truth. But she was a screwy, scatterbrained dame and she decided she was stuck on me because I dabbled in poetry and hung around with artists and such in the Village, and she thought it was all so glamorous. I didn't have anything to do with her chasing down to New York, no kidding. You two were sort of engaged, weren't you?"

"It really doesn't matter," I said. "You don't have to explain." I finished my drink. "You say she knew Lundy?"

"Sure, she knew Lundy. She also knew Kram, Rossard, Broyold, Boster, De Kroot and Hayre. She knew a whole lot of guys before she was through."

"She always was sociable."

"You don't get my meaning," Len said. "I am not talking about Marilyn's gregarious impulses. Listen. First she threw herself at me, but I got tired of her. Then she threw herself at Steve and *he* got tired of her. Damn near the whole male population of the Village got tired of her in the next couple years."

"Those were troubled times. The war and all."

"They were troubled times," Len agreed, "and she was the source of a fair amount of the trouble. You were well rid of her, Ollie, take my word for it. God save us from the intense Boston female who goes bohemian—the icicle parading as the torch."

"Just as a matter of academic curiosity," I said as we were leaving, "what became of her?"

"I don't know for sure. During her Village phase she decided her creative urge was hampered by compasses and T-squares, and in between men she tried to do a bit of painting—very abstract, very imitative-original, very hammy. I heard later that she finally gave up the self-expression kick, moved up to the East Seventies somewhere. If I remember, she got a job doing circuit designing on some project for I.B.M."

"She's probably doing well at it," I said. "She certainly knew her drafting. You know, she helped lay out the circuits for the first robot bedbug I ever built."

November 19, 1959
Big step forward, if it isn't unseemly to use a phrase like that in connection with Pro research. This afternoon we completed the first two experimental models of my self-propelled solenoid legs, made of transparent plastic so everything is visible—solenoids, batteries, motors, thyratron tubes and transistors.

Kujack was waiting in the fitting room to give them their first tryout, but when I got there I found Len sitting with him. There were several empty beer cans on the floor and they were gabbing away a mile a minute.

Len *knows* how I hate to see people drinking during working hours. When I put the pros down and began to rig them for fitting, he said conspiratorially, "Shall we tell him?"

Kujack was pretty crocked, too. "Let's tell him," he whispered back. Strange thing about Kujack, he hardly ever says a word to me, but he never closes his mouth when Len's around.

"All right," Len said. "*You* tell him. Tell him how we're going to bring peace on Earth and good will toward bedbugs."

"We just figured it out," Kujack said. "What's wrong with war. It's a steamroller."

"Steamrollers are very undemocratic," Len added. "Never consult people on how they like to be flattened before flattening them. They just go rolling along."

"Just go rolling, they go on rolling along," Kujack said. "Like Old Man River."

"What's the upshot?" Len demanded. "People get upshot, shot up. In all countries, all of them without exception, they emerge from the war spiritually flattened, a little closer to the insects—like the hero in that Kafka story who wakes up one morning to find he's a bedbug, I mean beetle. All because they've been steamrolled. Nobody consulted them."

"Take the case of an amputee," Kujack said. "Before the land mine exploded, it didn't stop and say, 'Look, friend, I've got to go off; that's my job. Choose which part you'd prefer to have blown off—arm, leg, ear, nose, or what-have-you. Or is there somebody else around who would relish being clipped more than you would? If so, just send him along. I've got to do some clipping, you see, but it doesn't matter much which part of which guy I clip, so long as I make my quota.' Did the land mine say that? No! The victim wasn't consulted. Consequently he can feel victimized, full of self-pity. We just worked it out."

"The whole thing," Len said. "If the population had been polled according to democratic procedure, the paraplegia and other maimings could have been distributed to each according to his psychological need. See the point? Marx corrected by Freud, as Steve Lundy would say. Distribute the injuries to each according to his need—not his economic need, but his masochistic need. Those with a special taste for self-damage obviously should be allowed a lion's share of it. That way nobody could claim he'd been victimized by the steamroller or got anything he didn't ask for. It's all on a voluntary basis, you see. Democratic."

"Whole new concept of war," Kujack agreed. "Voluntary amputeeism, voluntary paraplegia, voluntary everything else that usually happens to people in a war. Just to get some human dignity back into the thing."

"Here's how it works," Len went on. "Country A and Country B reach the breaking point. It's all over but the shooting. All right. So they pool their best brains, mathematicians, actuaries, strategists, logistics geniuses, and all. What am I saying? They pool their best *robot* brains, their Emsiacs. In a matter of seconds they figure out, down to the last decimal point, just how many casualties each side can be expected to suffer in dead and wounded, and then they break down the figures. Of the wounded, they determine just how many will lose eyes, how many arms, how many legs, and so on down the line. Now—here's where it gets really neat—each country, having established its quotas in dead and wounded of all categories, can send out a call for volunteers."

"Less messy that way," Kujack said. "An efficiency expert's war. War on an actuarial basis."

"You get exactly the same results as in a shooting war," Len insisted. "Just as many dead, wounded and psychologically messed up. But you avoid the whole steamroller effect. A tidy war, war with dispatch, conceived in terms of ends rather than means. The end never did justify the means, you see; Steve Lundy says that was always the great dilemma of politics. So with one fool sweep—fell swoop—we get rid of means entirely."

"As things stand with me," Kujack said, "if *anything* stands with me, I might get to feeling sore about what happened to me. But nothing happens *to* the volunteer amputee. He steps up to the operating table and says, 'Just chop off one arm, Doc, the left one, please, up to the elbow if you don't mind, and in return put me down for one-and-two-thirds free meals daily at Longchamps and a plump blonde every Saturday.'"

"Or whatever the exchange value for one slightly used left arm would be," Len amended. "That would have to be worked out by the robot actuaries."

By this time I had the pros fitted and the push-button controls installed in the side pocket of Kujack's jacket.

"Maybe you'd better go now, Len," I said. I was very careful to show no reaction to his baiting. "Kujack and I have some work to do."

"I hope you'll make him a moth instead of a bedbug," Len said as he got up. "Kujack's just beginning to see the light. Be a shame if you give him a negative tropism to it instead of a positive one." He turned to Kujack, wobbling a little. "So long, kid. I'll pick you up at seven and we'll drive into New York to have a few with Steve. He's going to be very happy to hear we've got the whole thing figured out."

I spent two hours with Kujack, getting him used to the extremely delicate push-button controls. I must say that, drunk or sober, he's a very apt pupil. In less than two hours he actually walked! A little unsteadily, to be sure, but his balance will get better as he practices and I iron out a few more bugs, and I *don't* mean bedbugs.

For a final test, I put a little egg cup on the floor, balanced a football in it, and told Kujack to try a place kick. What a moment! He booted that ball so hard, it splintered the mirror on the wall.

November 27, 1959
Long talk with the boss. I gave it to him straight about breaking up the lab into K-Pro and N-Pro, and about there being little chance that Goldweiser would come up with anything much on the neuro end for a long, long time. He was awfully let down, I could see, so I started to talk fast about the luck I'd been having on the kinesthetic end. When he began to perk up, I called Kujack in from the corridor and had him demonstrate his place kick.

He's gotten awfully good at it this past week.

"If we release the story to the press," I suggested, "this might make a fine action shot. You see, Kujack used to be one of the best kickers in the Big Ten, and a lot of newspapermen will still remember him." Then I sprang the biggest news of all. "During the last three days of practice, sir, he's been consistently kicking the ball twenty, thirty and even forty yards farther than he ever did with his own legs. Than anybody, as a matter of fact, ever has with real legs."

"That's a wonderful angle," the boss said excitedly. "A world's record, made with a cybernetic leg!"

"It should make a terrific picture," Kujack said. "I've also been practicing a big, broad, photogenic grin." Luckily the boss didn't hear him—by this time he was bending over the legs, studying the solenoids.

After Kujack left, the boss congratulated me. Very, *very* warmly. It was a most gratifying moment. We chatted for a while, making plans for the press conference, and then finally he said, "By the way, do you happen to know anything about your friend Ellsom? I'm worried about him. He went off on Thanksgiving and hasn't been heard from at all ever since."

That was alarming, I said. When the boss asked why, I told him a little about how Len had been acting lately, talking and drinking more than was good for him. With all sorts of people. The boss said that confirmed his own impressions.

I can safely say we understood each other. I sensed a very definite rapport.

November 30, 1959

It was bound to happen, of course. As I got it from the boss, he decided after our talk that Len's absence needed some looking into, and he tipped off Security about it. A half dozen agents went to work on the case and right off they headed for Steve Lundy's apartment in the Village and, sure enough, there was Len.

Len and his friend were both blind drunk and there were all sorts of incriminating things in the room—lots of peculiar books and pamphlets, Lundy's identification papers from the Lincoln Brigade, an article Lundy was writing for an anarchist-pacifist magazine about what he calls Emsiac. Len and his friend were both arrested on the spot and a full investigation is going on now.

The boss says that no matter whether Len is brought to trial or not, he's all washed up. He'll never get a job on any classified cybernetics project from now on, because it's clear enough that he violated his loyalty oath by discussing MS all over the place.

The Security men came around to question me this morning. Afraid my testimony didn't help Len's case any. What could I do? I had to own up that, to my knowledge, Len had violated Security on three counts: he'd discussed MS matters with Kujack in my presence, with Lundy (according to what he told me), and of course with *me* (I am technically an outsider, too). I also pointed out that I'd tried to make him shut up, but there was no stopping him once he got going. Damn that Len, anyhow. Why does he have to go and put me in this ethical spot? It shows a lack of consideration.

These Security men can be *too* thorough. Right off they wanted to pick up Kujack as well.

I got hold of the boss and explained that if they took Kujack away we'd have to call off our press conference, because it would take months to fit and train another subject.

The boss immediately saw the injustice of the thing, stepped in and got Security to calm down, at least until we finish our demonstration.

December 23, 1959

What a day! The press conference this afternoon was *something*. Dozens of reporters and photographers and newsreel men showed up, and we took them all out to the football field for the demonstrations. First the boss gave a little orientation talk about cybernetics being teamwork in science, and about the difference between K-Pro and N-Pro, pointing out that from the practical, humanitarian angle of helping the amputee, K is a lot more important than N.

The reporters tried to get in some questions about MS, but he parried them very good-humoredly, and he said some nice things about me, some very nice things indeed.

Then Kujack was brought in. He really went through his paces, walking, running, skipping, jumping and everything. It was damned impressive. And then, to top off the show, Kujack place-kicked a football ninety-three yards by actual measurement, a world's record, and everybody went wild.

Afterward Kujack and I posed for the newsreels, shaking hands while the boss stood with his arms around us. They're going to play the whole thing up as IFACS' Christmas present to one of our gallant war heroes (just what the boss wanted: he figures this sort of thing makes IFACS sound so much less grim to the public), and Kujack was asked to say something in line with that idea.

"I never could kick this good with my real legs," he said, holding my hand tight and looking straight at me. "Gosh, this is just about the nicest Christmas present a fellow could get. Thank you, Santa."

I thought he was overdoing it a bit toward the end there, but the newsreel men say they think it's a great sentimental touch.

Goldweiser was in the crowd, and he said, "I only hope that when I prove I'm God, this many photographers will show up." That's just about the kind of remark I'd expect from Goldweiser.

Too bad the Security men are coming for Kujack tomorrow. The boss couldn't argue. After all, they were patient enough to wait until after the tests and demonstration, which the boss and I agree was white of them. It's not as if Kujack isn't deeply involved in this Ellsom-Lundy case. As the boss says, you can tell a man by the company, etc.

December 25, 1959
Spent the morning clipping pictures and articles from the papers; they gave us *quite* a spread. Late in the afternoon I went over to the boss's house for eggnogs, and I finally got up the nerve to say what's been on my mind for over a month now. Strike while the iron's, etc.

"I've been thinking, sir," I said, "that this solenoid system I've worked out for Pros has other applications. For example, it could easily be adapted to some of the tricky mechanical aspects of an electronic calculator." I went into some of the technical details briefly, and I could see he was interested. "I'd like very much to work on that, now that K-Pro is licked, more or less. And if there *is* an opening in MS——"

"You're a go-getter," the boss said, nodding in a pleased way. He was looking at a newspaper lying on the coffee table; on the front page was a large picture of Kujack grinning at me and shaking my hand. "I like that. I can't promise anything, but let me think about it."

I think I'm in!

December 27, 1959
Sent the soup-and-fish out to be cleaned and pressed. Looks like I'm going to get

some use out of it, after all. We're having a big formal New Year's Eve party in the commons room and there's going to be square dancing, swing-your-partner, and all of that. When I called Marilyn, she sounded very friendly—she remembered to call me Oliver, and I was flattered that she did—and said she'd be delighted to come. Seems she's gotten very fond of folk dancing lately.

Gosh, it'll be good to get out of these dungarees for a while. I'm happy to say I still look good in formals. Marilyn ought to be quite impressed. Len always wore his like pajamas.

(1951)

MANEKI NEKO

Bruce Sterling

Michael Bruce Sterling was born in 1954 in Brownsville, Texas. His grandfather was a rancher, his father an engineer. His work on the anthology *Mirrorshades* (1986) helped to define the cyberpunk genre, while stories set in his "Shaper/Mechanist" universe – a solar system split between rival posthuman factions, one wedded to computation, the other to genetic engineering – vied with Vernor Vinge's "Singularity"-based fictions to set the agenda for hard sf in the new millennium. By the time 2000 dawned, however, Sterling had moved on to new territory. His analyses of near-future trends led in 2003 to his appointment as professor at the European Graduate School where he taught courses on media and design. He lived in Belgrade with Serbian author and film-maker Jasmina Tešanović for several years. The couple married and in 2007 moved to Turin.

"I can't go on," his brother said.

Tsuyoshi Shimizu looked thoughtfully into the screen of his pasokon. His older brother's face was shiny with sweat from a late-night drinking bout.

"It's only a career," said Tsuyoshi, sitting up on his futon and adjusting his pajamas. "You worry too much."

"All that overtime!" his brother whined. He was making the call from a bar somewhere in Shibuya. In the background, a middle-aged office lady was singing karaoke, badly. "And the examination hells. The manager training programs. The proficiency tests. I never have time to live!" Tsuyoshi grunted sympathetically. He didn't like these late-night videophone calls, but he felt obliged to listen. His big brother had always been a decent sort, before he had gone through the elite courses at Waseda University, joined a big corporation, and gotten professionally ambitious.

"My back hurts," his brother groused. "I have an ulcer. My hair is going gray. And I know they'll fire me. No matter how loyal you are to the big companies, they have no loyalty to their employees anymore. It's no wonder that I drink."

"You should get married," Tsuyoshi offered.

"I can't find the right girl. Women never understand me." He shuddered. "Tsuyoshi, I'm truly desperate. The market pressures are crushing me. I can't breathe. My life has got to change. I'm thinking of taking the vows. I'm serious! I want to renounce this whole modern world."

Tsuyoshi was alarmed. "You're very drunk, right?"

His brother leaned closer to the screen. "Life in a monastery sounds truly good to me. It's so quiet there. You recite the sutras. You consider your existence. There are rules to follow, and rewards that make sense. It's just the way that Japanese business used to be, back in the good old days."

Tsuyoshi grunted skeptically.

"Last week I went out to a special place in the mountains… Mount Aso," his brother confided. "The monks there, they know about people in trouble, people who are burned out by modern life. The monks protect you from the world. No computers, no phones, no faxes, no e-mail, no overtime, no commuting, nothing at all. It's beautiful, and it's peaceful, and nothing ever happens there. Really, it's like paradise."

"Listen, older brother," Tsuyoshi said, "you're not a religious man by nature. You're a section chief for a big import-export company."

"Well… maybe religion won't work for me. I did think of running away to America. Nothing much ever happens there, either."

Tsuyoshi smiled. "That sounds much better! America is a good vacation spot. A long vacation is just what you need! Besides, the Americans are real friendly since they gave up their handguns."

"But I can't go through with it," his brother wailed. "I just don't dare. I can't just wander away from everything that I know, and trust to the kindness of strangers."

"That always works for me," Tsuyoshi said. "Maybe you should try it." Tsuyoshi's wife stirred uneasily on the futon. Tsuyoshi lowered his voice.

"Sorry, but I have to hang up now. Call me before you do anything rash."

"Don't tell Dad," Tsuyoshi's brother said. "He worries so."

"I won't tell Dad." Tsuyoshi cut the connection and the screen went dark. Tsuyoshi's wife rolled over, heavily. She was seven months pregnant. She stared at the ceiling puffing for breath. "Was that another call from your brother?" she said.

"Yeah. The company just gave him another promotion. More responsibilities. He's celebrating."

"That sounds nice," his wife said tactfully.

Next morning, Tsuyoshi slept late. He was self-employed, so he kept his own hours. Tsuyoshi was a video format upgrader by trade. He transferred old videos from obsolete formats into the new high-grade storage media. Doing this properly took a craftsman's eye. Word of Tsuyoshi's skills had gotten out on the network, so he had as much work as he could handle. At ten A.M., the mailman arrived. Tsuyoshi abandoned his breakfast of raw egg and miso soup, and signed for a shipment of flaking, twentieth-century analog television tapes. The mail also brought a fresh overnight shipment of strawberries, and a homemade jar of pickles.

"Pickles!" his wife enthused. "People are so nice to you when you're pregnant."

"Any idea who sent us that?"

"Just someone on the network."

"Great."

Tsuyoshi booted his mediator, cleaned his superconducting heads and examined the old tapes. Home videos from the 1980s. Someone's grandmother as a child, presumably. There had been a lot of flaking and loss of polarity in the old recording medium.

Tsuyoshi got to work with his desktop fractal detail generator, the image stabilizer, and the interlace algorithms. When he was done, Tsuyoshi's new digital copies would look much sharper, cleaner, and better composed than the original primitive videotape.

Tsuyoshi enjoyed his work. Quite often he came across bits and pieces of videotape that were of archival interest. He would pass the images on to the net. The really big network databases, with their armies of search engines, indexers, and catalogues, had some very arcane interests. The net machines would never pay for data, because the global information networks were noncommercial. But the net machines were very polite, and had excellent net etiquette. They returned a favor for a favor, and since they were machines with excellent, enormous memories, they never forgot a good deed.

Tsuyoshi and his wife had a lunch of ramen with naruto, and she left to go shopping. A shipment arrived by overseas package service. Cute baby clothes from Darwin, Australia. They were in his wife's favorite color, sunshine yellow.

Tsuyoshi finished transferring the first tape to a new crystal disk. Time for a break. He left his apartment, took the elevator and went out to the corner coffeeshop. He ordered a double iced mocha cappuccino and paid with a chargecard.

His pokkecon rang. Tsuyoshi took it from his belt and answered it. "Get one to go," the machine told him.

"Okay," said Tsuyoshi, and hung up. He bought a second coffee, put a lid on it and left the shop.

A man in a business suit was sitting on a park bench near the entrance of Tsuyoshi's building. The man's suit was good, but it looked as if he'd slept in it. He was holding his head in his hands and rocking gently back and forth. He was unshaven and his eyes were red-rimmed.

The pokkecon rang again. "The coffee's for him?" Tsuyoshi said.

"Yes," said the pokkecon. "He needs it." Tsuyoshi walked up to the lost businessman. The man looked up, flinching warily, as if he were about to be kicked. "What is it?" he said.

"Here," Tsuyoshi said, handing him the cup. "Double iced mocha cappuccino."

The man opened the cup, and smelled it. He looked up in disbelief. "This is my favorite kind of coffee... Who are you?"

Tsuyoshi lifted his arm and offered a hand signal, his fingers clenched like a cat's paw. The man showed no recognition of the gesture. Tsuyoshi shrugged, and smiled. "It doesn't matter. Sometimes a man really needs a coffee. Now you have a coffee. That's all."

"Well..." The man cautiously sipped his cup, and suddenly smiled. "It's really great. Thanks!"

"You're welcome." Tsuyoshi went home.

His wife arrived from shopping. She had bought new shoes. The pregnancy was making her feet swell. She sat carefully on the couch and sighed.

"Orthopedic shoes are expensive," she said, looking at the yellow pumps. "I hope you don't think they look ugly."

"On you, they look really cute," Tsuyoshi said wisely. He had first met his wife at a video store. She had just used her credit card to buy a disk of primitive black-and-white American anime of the 1950s. The pokkecon had urged him to go up and speak to her on the subject of Felix the Cat. Felix was an early television cartoon star and one of Tsuyoshi's personal favorites.

Tsuyoshi would have been too shy to approach an attractive woman on his own, but no one was a stranger to the net. This fact gave him the confidence to speak to her. Tsuyoshi had soon discovered that the girl was delighted to discuss her deep fondness for cute, antique, animated cats. They'd had lunch together. They'd had a date the next week. They had spent Christmas Eve together in a love hotel. They had a lot in common. She had come into his life through a little act of grace, a little gift from Felix the Cat's magic bag of tricks. Tsuyoshi had never gotten over feeling grateful for this. Now that he was married and becoming a father, Tsuyoshi Shimizu could feel himself becoming solidly fixed in life. He had a man's role to play now. He knew who he was, and he knew where he stood. Life was good to him.

"You need a haircut, dear," his wife told him.

"Sure."

His wife pulled a gift box out of her shopping bag. "Can you go to the Hotel Daruma, and get your hair cut, and deliver this box for me?"

"What is it?" Tsuyoshi said.

Tsuyoshi's wife opened the little wooden gift box. A maneki neko was nestled inside white foam padding. The smiling ceramic cat held one paw upraised, beckoning for good fortune.

"Don't you have enough of those yet?" he said. "You even have maneki neko underwear."

"It's not for my collection. It's a gift for someone at the Hotel Daruma."

"Oh."

"Some foreign woman gave me this box at the shoestore. She looked American. She couldn't speak Japanese. She had really nice shoes, though…"

"If the network gave you that little cat, then you're the one who should take care of that obligation, dear."

"But dear," she sighed, "my feet hurt so much, and you could do with a haircut anyway, and I have to cook supper, and besides, it's not really a nice maneki neko, it's just cheap tourist souvenir junk. Can't you do it?"

"Oh, all right," Tsuyoshi told her. "Just forward your pokkecon prompts onto my machine, and I'll see what I can do for us." She smiled. "I knew you would do it. You're really so good to me." Tsuyoshi left with the little box. He wasn't unhappy to do the errand, as it wasn't always easy to manage his pregnant wife's volatile moods in their small six-tatami apartment. The local neighborhood was good, but he was hoping to find bigger accommodations before the child was born. Maybe a place with a little studio, where he could expand the scope of his work. It was very hard to find decent housing in Tokyo, but word was out on the net. Friends he didn't even know were working every day to help him. If he kept up with the net's obligations, he had every confidence that some day something nice would turn up.

Tsuyoshi went into the local pachinko parlor, where he won half a liter of beer and a train chargecard. He drank the beer, took the new train card and wedged himself into the train. He got out at the Ebisu station, and turned on his pokkecon Tokyo street map to guide his steps. He walked past places called Chocolate Soup, and Freshness Physique, and The Aladdin Mai-Tai Panico Trattoria.

He entered the Hotel Daruma and went to the hotel barber shop, which was called the Daruma Planet Look. "May I help you?" said the receptionist.

"I'm thinking, a shave and a trim," Tsuyoshi said.

"Do you have an appointment with us?"

"Sorry, no." Tsuyoshi offered a hand gesture.

The woman gestured back, a jerky series of cryptic finger movements. Tsuyoshi didn't recognize any of the gestures. She wasn't from his part of the network.

"Oh well, never mind," the receptionist said kindly. "I'll get Nahoko to look after you."

Nahoko was carefully shaving the fine hair from Tsuyoshi's forehead when the pokkecon rang. Tsuyoshi answered it.

"Go to the ladies' room on the fourth floor," the pokkecon told him.

"Sorry, I can't do that. This is Tsuyoshi Shimizu, not Ai Shimizu. Besides, I'm having my hair cut right now."

"Oh, I see," said the machine. "Recalibrating." It hung up. Nahoko finished his hair. She had done a good job. He looked much better. A man who worked at home had to take special trouble to keep up appearances. The pokkecon rang again.

"Yes?" said Tsuyoshi.

"Buy bay rum aftershave. Take it outside."

"Right." He hung up. "Nahoko, do you have bay rum?"

"Odd you should ask that," said Nahoko. "Hardly anyone asks for bay rum anymore, but our shop happens to keep it in stock."

Tsuyoshi bought the aftershave, then stepped outside the barbershop. Nothing happened, so he bought a manga comic and waited. Finally a hairy, blond stranger in shorts, a tropical shirt, and sandals approached him. The foreigner was carrying a camera bag and an old-fashioned pokkecon. He looked about sixty years old, and he was very tall.

The man spoke to his pokkecon in English. "Excuse me," said the pokkecon, translating the man's speech into Japanese. "Do you have a bottle of bay rum aftershave?"

"Yes I do." Tsuyoshi handed the bottle over. "Here."

"Thank goodness!" said the man, his words relayed through his machine.

"I've asked everyone else in the lobby. Sorry I was late."

"No problem," said Tsuyoshi. "That's a nice pokkecon you have there."

"Well," the man said, "I know it's old and out of style. But I plan to buy a new pokkecon here in Tokyo. I'm told that they sell pokkecons by the basketful in Akihabara electronics market."

"That's right. What kind of translator program are you running? Your translator talks like someone from Osaka."

"Does it sound funny?" the tourist asked anxiously.

"Well, I don't want to complain, but..." Tsuyoshi smiled. "Here, let's trade meishi. I can give you a copy of a brand-new freeware translator."

"That would be wonderful." They pressed buttons and squirted copies of their business cards across the network link.

Tsuyoshi examined his copy of the man's electronic card and saw that his name was Zimmerman. Mr. Zimmerman was from New Zealand. Tsuyoshi activated a transfer program. His modern pokkecon began transferring a new translator onto Zimmerman's machine.

A large American man in a padded suit entered the lobby of the Daruma. The man wore sunglasses, and was sweating visibly in the summer heat. The American looked huge, as if he lifted a lot of weights. Then a Japanese woman followed him. The woman was sharply dressed, with a dark blue dress suit, hat, sunglasses, and an attache case. She had a haunted look. Her escort turned and carefully watched the bellhops, who were bringing in a series of bags. The woman walked crisply to the reception desk and began making anxious demands of the clerk.

"I'm a great believer in machine translation," Tsuyoshi said to the tall man from New Zealand. "I really believe that computers help human beings to relate in a much more human way."

"I couldn't agree with you more," said Mr. Zimmerman, through his machine. "I can remember the first time I came to your country, many years ago. I had no portable translator. In fact, I had nothing but a printed phrasebook. I happened to go into a bar, and..."

Zimmerman stopped and gazed alertly at his pokkecon. "Oh dear, I'm getting a screen prompt. I have to go up to my room right away."

"Then I'll come along with you till this software transfer is done," Tsuyoshi said.

"That's very kind of you." They got into the elevator together. Zimmerman punched for the fourth floor. "Anyway, as I was saying, I went into this bar in Roppongi late at night, because I was jetlagged and hoping for something to eat..."

"Yes?"

"And this woman... well, let's just say this woman was hanging out in a foreigner's bar in Roppongi late at night, and she wasn't wearing a whole lot of clothes, and she didn't look like she was any better than she ought to be..."

"Yes, I think I understand you."

"Anyway, this menu they gave me was full of kanji, or katakana, or romanji, or whatever they call those, so I had my phrasebook out, and I was trying very hard to puzzle out these pesky ideograms..." The elevator opened and they stepped into the carpeted hall of the hotel's fourth floor.

"So I opened the menu and I pointed to an entree, and I told this girl..." Zimmerman stopped suddenly, and stared at his screen. "Oh dear, something's happening. Just a moment."

Zimmerman carefully studied the instructions on his pokkecon. Then he pulled the bottle of bay rum from the baggy pocket of his shorts, and unscrewed the cap. He stood on tiptoe, stretching to his full height, and carefully poured the contents of the bottle through the iron louvers of a ventilation grate, set high in the top of the wall.

Zimmerman screwed the cap back on neatly, and slipped the empty bottle back in his pocket. Then he examined his pokkecon again. He frowned, and shook it. The screen had frozen. Apparently Tsuyoshi's new translation program had overloaded Zimmerman's old-fashioned operating system. His pokkecon had crashed.

Zimmerman spoke a few defeated sentences in English. Then he smiled, and spread his hands apologetically. He bowed, and went into his room, and shut the door.

The Japanese woman and her burly American escort entered the hall. The man gave Tsuyoshi a hard stare. The woman opened the door with a passcard. Her hands were shaking.

Tsuyoshi's pokkecon rang. "Leave the hall," it told him. "Go downstairs. Get into the elevator with the bellboy."

Tsuyoshi followed instructions.

The bellboy was just entering the elevator with a cart full of the woman's baggage. Tsuyoshi got into the elevator, stepping carefully behind the wheeled metal cart. "What floor, sir?" said the bellboy.

"Eight," Tsuyoshi said, ad-libbing. The bellboy turned and pushed the buttons. He faced forward attentively, his gloved hands folded. The pokkecon flashed a silent line of text to the screen. "Put the gift box inside her flight bag," it read.

Tsuyoshi located the zippered blue bag at the back of the cart. It was a matter of instants to zip it open, put in the box with the maneki neko, and zip the bag shut again. The bellboy noticed nothing. He left, tugging his cart.

Tsuyoshi got out on the eighth floor, feeling slightly foolish. He wandered down the hall, found a quiet nook by an ice machine and called his wife.

"What's going on?" he said.

"Oh, nothing." She smiled. "Your haircut looks nice! Show me the back of your head."

Tsuyoshi held the pokkecon screen behind the nape of his neck.

"They do good work," his wife said with satisfaction. "I hope it didn't cost too much. Are you coming home now?"

"Things are getting a little odd here at the hotel," Tsuyoshi told her. "I may be some time."

His wife frowned. "Well, don't miss supper. We're having bonito." Tsuyoshi took the elevator back down. It stopped at the fourth floor. The woman's American companion stepped onto the elevator. His nose was running and his eyes were streaming with tears.

"Are you all right?" Tsuyoshi said.

"I don't understand Japanese," the man growled. The elevator doors shut. The man's cellular phone crackled into life. It emitted a scream of anguish and a burst of agitated female English. The man swore and slammed his hairy fist against the elevator's emergency button. The elevator stopped with a lurch. An alarm bell began ringing. The man pried the doors open with his large hairy fingers and clambered out into the fourth floor. He then ran headlong down the hall. The elevator began buzzing in protest, its doors shuddering as if broken. Tsuyoshi climbed hastily from the damaged elevator, and stood there in the hallway. He hesitated a moment. Then he produced his pokkecon and loaded his Japanese-to-English translator. He walked cautiously after the American man.

The door to their suite was open. Tsuyoshi spoke aloud into his pokkecon. "Hello?" he said experimentally. "May I be of help?" The woman was sitting on the bed. She had just discovered the maneki neko box in her flight bag. She was staring at the little cat in horror.

"Who are you?" she said, in bad Japanese.

Tsuyoshi realized suddenly that she was a Japanese American. Tsuyoshi had met a few Japanese Americans before. They always troubled him. They looked fairly normal from the outside, but their behavior was always bizarre. "I'm just a passing friend," he said. "Something I can do?"

"Grab him, Mitch!" said the woman in English. The American man rushed into the hall and grabbed Tsuyoshi by the arm. His hands were like steel bands.

Tsuyoshi pressed the distress button on his pokkecon.

"Take that computer away from him," the woman ordered in English. Mitch quickly took Tsuyoshi's pokkecon away, and threw it on the bed. He deftly patted Tsuyoshi's clothing, searching for weapons. Then he shoved Tsuyoshi into a chair.

The woman switched back to Japanese. "Sit right there, you. Don't you dare move." She began examining the contents of Tsuyoshi's wallet.

"I beg your pardon?" Tsuyoshi said. His pokkecon was lying on the bed. Lines of red text scrolled up its little screen as it silently issued a series of emergency net alerts.

The woman spoke to her companion in English. Tsuyoshi's pokkecon was still translating faithfully. "Mitch, go call the local police." Mitch sneezed uncontrollably. Tsuyoshi noticed that the room smelled strongly of bay rum. "I can't talk to the local cops. I can't speak Japanese." Mitch sneezed again.

"Okay, then I'll call the cops. You handcuff this guy. Then go down to the infirmary and get yourself some antihistamines, for Christ's sake." Mitch pulled a length of plastic whipcord cuff from his coat pocket, and attached Tsuyoshi's right wrist to the head of the bed. He mopped his streaming eyes with a tissue. "I'd better stay with you. If there's a cat in your luggage, then the criminal network already knows we're in Japan. You're in danger."

"Mitch, you may be my bodyguard, but you're breaking out in hives."

"This just isn't supposed to happen," Mitch complained, scratching his neck. "My allergies never interfered with my job before."

"Just leave me here and lock the door," the woman told him. "I'll put a chair against the knob. I'll be all right. You need to look after yourself." Mitch left the room.

The woman barricaded the door with a chair. Then she called the front desk on the hotel's bedside pasokon. "This is Louise Hashimoto in room 434. I have a gangster in my room. He's an information criminal. Would you call the Tokyo police, please? Tell them to send the organized crime unit. Yes, that's right. Do it. And you should put your hotel security people on full alert. There may be big trouble here. You'd better hurry." She hung up. Tsuyoshi stared at her in astonishment. "Why are you doing this? What's all this about?"

"So you call yourself Tsuyoshi Shimizu," said the woman, examining his credit cards. She sat on the foot of the bed and stared at him. "You're yakuza of some kind, right?"

"I think you've made a big mistake," Tsuyoshi said.

Louise scowled. "Look, Mr. Shimizu, you're not dealing with some Yankee tourist here. My name is Louise Hashimoto and I'm an assistant federal prosecutor from Providence, Rhode Island, USA." She showed him a magnetic ID card with a gold official seal.

"It's nice to meet someone from the American government," said Tsuyoshi, bowing a bit in his chair. "I'd shake your hand, but it's tied to the bed."

"You can stop with the innocent act right now. I spotted you out in the hall earlier, and in the lobby, too, casing the hotel. How did you know my bodyguard is violently allergic to bay rum? You must have read his medical records."

"Who, me? Never!"

"Ever since I discovered you network people, it's been one big pattern," said Louise. "It's the biggest criminal conspiracy I ever saw. I busted this software pirate in Providence. He had a massive network server and a whole bunch of AI freeware search engines. We took him in custody, we bagged all his search engines, and catalogs, and indexers… Later that very same day, these cats start showing up."

"Cats ?"

Louise lifted the maneki neko, handling it as if it were a live eel. "These little Japanese voodoo cats. Maneki neko, right? They started showing up everywhere I went. There's a china cat in my handbag. There's three china cats at the office. Suddenly they're on display in the windows of every antique store in Providence. My car radio starts making meowing noises at me."

"You broke part of the network?" Tsuyoshi said, scandalized. "You took someone's machines away? That's terrible! How could you do such an inhuman thing?"

"You've got a real nerve complaining about that. What about my machinery?" Louise held up her fat, eerie-looking American pokkecon. "As soon as I stepped off the airplane at Narita, my PDA was attacked. Thousands and thousands of e-mail messages. All of them pictures of cats. A denial-of-service attack! I can't even communicate with the home office! My PDA's useless!"

"What's a PDA?"

"It's a PDA, my Personal Digital Assistant! Manufactured in Silicon Valley!"

"Well, with a goofy name like that, no wonder our pokkecons won't talk to it."

Louise frowned grimly. "That's right, wise guy. Make jokes about it. You're involved in a malicious software attack on a legal officer of the United States Government. You'll see." She paused, looking him over. "You know, Shimizu, you don't look much like the Italian mafia gangsters I have to deal with, back in Providence."

"I'm not a gangster at all. I never do anyone any harm."

"Oh no?" Louise glowered at him. "Listen, pal, I know a lot more about your set-up, and your kind of people, than you think I do. I've been studying your outfit for a long time now. We computer cops have names for your kind of people. Digital panarchies. Segmented, polycephalous, integrated influence networks. What about all these free goods and services you're getting all this time?"

She pointed a finger at him. "Ha! Do you ever pay taxes on those? Do you ever declare that income and those benefits? All the free shipments from other countries! The little homemade cookies, and the free pens and pencils and bumper stickers, and the used bicycles, and the helpful news about fire sales… You're a tax evader! You're living through kickbacks! And bribes! And influence peddling! And all kinds of corrupt off-the-books transactions!"

Tsuyoshi blinked. "Look, I don't know anything about all that. I'm just living my life."

"Well, your network gift economy is undermining the lawful, government-approved, regulated economy!"

"Well," Tsuyoshi said gently, "maybe my economy is better than your economy."

"Says who?" she scoffed. "Why would anyone think that?"

"It's better because we're happier than you are. What's wrong with acts of kindness? Everyone likes gifts. Midsummer gifts. New Years Day gifts. Year-end presents. Wedding presents. Everybody likes those."

"Not the way you Japanese like them. You're totally crazy for gifts."

"What kind of society has no gifts? It's barbaric to have no regard for common human feelings."

Louise bristled. "You're saying I'm barbaric?"

"I don't mean to complain," Tsuyoshi said politely, "but you do have me tied up to your bed."

Louise crossed her arms. "You might as well stop complaining. You'll be in much worse trouble when the local police arrive."

"Then we'll probably be waiting here for quite a while," Tsuyoshi said. "The police move rather slowly, here in Japan. I'm sorry, but we don't have as much crime as you Americans, so our police are not very alert." The pasokon rang at the side of the bed. Louise answered it. It was Tsuyoshi's wife.

"Could I speak to Tsuyoshi Shimizu please?"

"I'm over here, dear," Tsuyoshi called quickly. "She's kidnapped me! She tied me to the bed!"

"Tied to her bed?" His wife's eyes grew wide. "That does it! I'm calling the police!"

Louise quickly hung up the pasokon. "I haven't kidnapped you! I'm only detaining you here until the local authorities can come and arrest you."

"Arrest me for what, exactly?"

Louise thought quickly. "Well, for poisoning my bodyguard by pouring bay rum into the ventilator."

"But I never did that. Anyway, that's not illegal, is it?" The pasokon rang again. A shining white cat appeared on the screen. It had large, staring, unearthly eyes.

"Let him go," the cat commanded in English.

Louise shrieked and yanked the pasokon's plug from the wall. Suddenly the lights went out. "Infrastructure attack!" Louise squawked. She rolled quickly under the bed.

The room went gloomy and quiet. The air conditioner had shut off. "I think you can come out," Tsuyoshi said at last, his voice loud in the still room. "It's just a power failure."

"No it isn't," Louise said. She crawled slowly from beneath the bed, and sat on the mattress. Somehow, the darkness had made them more intimate. "I know very well what this is. I'm under attack. I haven't had a moment's peace since I broke that network. Stuff just happens to me now. Bad stuff. Swarms of it. It's never anything you can touch, though. Nothing you can prove in a court of law."

She sighed. "I sit in chairs, and somebody's left a piece of gum there. I get free pizzas, but they're not the kind of pizzas I like. Little kids spit on my sidewalk. Old women in walkers get in front of me whenever I need to hurry."

The shower came on, all by itself. Louise shuddered, but said nothing. Slowly, the darkened, stuffy room began to fill with hot steam.

"My toilets don't flush," Louise said. "My letters get lost in the mail. When I walk by cars, their theft alarms go off. And strangers stare at me. It's always little things. Lots of little tiny things, but they never, ever stop. I'm up against something that is very very big, and very very patient. And it knows all about me. And it's got a million arms and legs. And all those arms and legs are people."

There was the noise of scuffling in the hall. Distant voices, confused shouting.

Suddenly the chair broke under the doorknob. The door burst open violently. Mitch tumbled through, the sunglasses flying from his head. Two hotel security guards were trying to grab him. Shouting incoherently in English, Mitch fell headlong to the floor, kicking and thrashing. The guards lost their hats in the struggle. One tackled Mitch's legs with both his arms, and the other whacked and jabbed him with a baton.

Puffing and grunting with effort, they hauled Mitch out of the room. The darkened room was so full of steam that the harried guards hadn't even noticed Tsuyoshi and Louise.

Louise stared at the broken door. "Why did they do that to him?"

Tsuyoshi scratched his head in embarrassment. "Probably a failure of communication."

"Poor Mitch! They took his gun away at the airport. He had all kinds of technical problems with his passport... Poor guy, he's never had any luck since he met me."

There was a loud tapping at the window. Louise shrank back in fear. Finally she gathered her courage, and opened the curtains. Daylight flooded the room.

A window-washing rig had been lowered from the roof of the hotel, on cables and pulleys. There were two window-washers in crisp gray uniforms. They waved cheerfully, making little catpaw gestures.

There was a third man with them. It was Tsuyoshi's brother. One of the washers opened the window with a utility key. Tsuyoshi's brother squirmed into the room. He stood up and carefully adjusted his coat and tie.

"This is my brother," Tsuyoshi explained.

"What are you doing here?" Louise said.

"They always bring in the relatives when there's a hostage situation," Tsuyoshi's brother said. "The police just flew me in by helicopter and landed me on the roof." He looked Louise up and down. "Miss Hashimoto, you just have time to escape."

"What?" she said.

"Look down at the streets," he told her. "See that? You hear them? Crowds are pouring in from all over the city. All kinds of people, everyone with wheels. Street noodle salesmen. Bicycle messengers. Skateboard kids. Takeout delivery guys."

Louise gazed out the window into the streets, and shrieked aloud. "Oh no! A giant swarming mob! They're surrounding me! I'm doomed!"

"You are not doomed," Tsuyoshi's brother told her intently. "Come out the window. Get onto the platform with us. You've got one chance, Louise. It's a place I know, a sacred place in the mountains. No computers there, no phones, nothing." He paused. "It's a sanctuary for people like us. And I know the way."

She gripped his suited arm. "Can I trust you?"

"Look in my eyes," he told her. "Don't you see? Yes, of course you can trust me. We have everything in common."

Louise stepped out the window. She clutched his arm, the wind whipping at her hair. The platform creaked rapidly up and out of sight. Tsuyoshi stood up from the chair. When he stretched out, tugging at his handcuffed wrist, he was just able to reach his pokkecon with his fingertips. He drew it in, and clutched it to his chest. Then he sat down again, and waited patiently for someone to come and give him freedom.

(1998)

"REPENT, HARLEQUIN!" SAID THE TICKTOCKMAN

Harlan Ellison

When he was 13, **Harlan Jay Ellison** (1934–2018) ran off to join a travelling funfair. He ended up spending three days in a cell in Kansas City, refusing to give his name. Robert Bloch had the measure of him, calling him "the only living organism I know whose natural habitat is hot water." Ellison once told the *Guardian* newspaper, "I don't mean to be crude when I say this, but I won't take a piss unless I'm paid properly." He is reputed to have mailed 213 bricks to one publisher who wouldn't pay him, and a dead gopher to another. J. G. Ballard considered him "an aggressive and restless extrovert who conducts life at a shout and his fiction at a scream." Plenty had him down as a blowhard. But he wrote more than 1,800 short stories, screenplays, novellas, essays, reviews and TV scripts, and won eight Hugo awards. He was also the editor of the cult sci-fi anthologies *Dangerous Visions* and *Again Dangerous Visions*. "'Repent, Harlequin!' Said the Ticktockman" won the Nebula Award for best short story in 1965.

There are always those who ask, what is it all about? For those who need to ask, for those who need points sharply made, who need to know "where it's at," this:

"The mass of men serve the state thus, not as men mainly, but as machines, with their bodies. They are the standing army, and the militia, jailors, constables, posse comitatus, etc. In most cases there is no free exercise whatever of the judgment or of the moral sense; but they put themselves on a level with wood and earth and stones; and wooden men can perhaps be manufactured that will serve the purpose as well. Such command no more respect than men of straw or a lump of dirt. They have the same sort of worth only as horses and dogs. Yet such as these even are commonly esteemed good citizens. Others—as most legislators, politicians, lawyers, ministers, and office-holders—serve the state chiefly with their heads; and, as they rarely make any moral distinctions, they are as likely to serve the Devil, without intending it, as God. A very few, as heroes, patriots, martyrs, reformers in the great sense, and men, *serve the state with their consciences also, and so necessarily resist it for the most part; and they are commonly treated as enemies by it."*

—Henry David Thoreau, "Civil Disobedience"

That is the heart of it. Now begin in the middle, and later learn the beginning; the end will take care of itself.

But because it was the very world it was, the very world they had allowed it to *become*, for months his activities did not come to the alarmed attention of The Ones Who Kept The Machine Functioning Smoothly, the ones who poured the very best butter over the cams and mainsprings of the culture. Not until it had become obvious that somehow, someway, he had become a notoriety, a celebrity, perhaps even a hero for (what Officialdom inescapably tagged) "an emotionally disturbed segment of the populace," did they turn it over to the Ticktockman and his legal machinery. But by then, because it was the very world it was, and they had no way to predict he would happen—possibly a strain of disease long-defunct, now, suddenly, reborn in a system where immunity had been forgotten, had lapsed—he had been allowed to become too real. Now he had form and substance.

He had become a *personality*, something they had filtered out of the system many decades before. But there it was, and there *he* was, a very definitely imposing personality. In certain circles—middle-class circles—it was thought disgusting. Vulgar ostentation. Anarchistic. Shameful. In others, there was only sniggering: those strata where thought is subjugated to form and ritual, niceties, proprieties. But down below, ah, down below, where the people always needed their saints and sinners, their bread and circuses, their heroes and villains, he was considered a Bolivar; a Napoleon; a Robin Hood; a Dick Bong (Ace of Aces); a Jesus; a Jomo Kenyatta.

And at the top—where, like socially-attuned Shipwreck Kellys, even tremor and vibration threatening to dislodge the wealthy, powerful, and titled from their flagpoles—he was considered a menace; a heretic; a rebel; a disgrace; a peril. He was known down the line, to the very heartmeat core, but the important reactions were high above and far below. At the very top, at the very bottom.

So his file was turned over, along with his time-card and his cardioplate, to the office of the Ticktockman.

The Ticktockman: very much over six feet tall, often silent, a soft purring man when things went timewise. The Ticktockman.

Even in the cubicles of the hierarchy, where fear was generated, seldom suffered, he was called the Ticktockman. But no one called him that to his mask.

You don't call a man a hated name, not when that man, behind his mask, is capable of revoking the minutes, the hours, the days and nights, the years of your life. He was called the Master Timekeeper to his mask. It was safer that way.

"This is *what* he is," said the Ticktockman with genuine softness, "but not *who* he is. This time-card I'm holding in my left hand has a name on it, but it is the name of *what* he is, not *who* he is. This cardioplate here in my right hand is also named, but not *whom* named, merely *what* named. Before I can exercise proper revocation, I have to know *who* this *what* is."

To his staff, all the ferrets, all the loggers, all the finks, all the commex, even the mineez, he said, "Who is this Harlequin?"

He was not purring smoothly. Timewise, it was jangle.

However, it *was* the longest single speech they had ever heard him utter at one time, the staff, the ferrets, the loggers, the finks, the commex, but not the mineez, who usually weren't around to know, in any case. But even they scurried to find out.

Who is the Harlequin?

High above the third level of the city, he crouched on the humming aluminum-frame platform of the air-boat (foof! air-boat, indeed! swizzleskid is what it was, with a tow-rack jerry-rigged) and he stared down at the neat Mondrian arrangement of the buildings.

Somewhere nearby, he could hear the metronomic left-right-left of the 2:47 P.M. shift, entering the Timkin roller-bearing plant in their sneakers. A minute later, precisely, he heard the softer right-left-right of the 5:00 A.M. formation, going home.

An elfin grin spread across his tanned features, and his dimples appeared for a moment. Then, scratching at his thatch of auburn hair, he shrugged within his motley, as though girding himself for what came next, and threw the joystick forward, and bent into the wind as the air-boat dropped. He skimmed over a slidewalk, purposely dropping a few feet to crease the tassels of the ladies of fashion, and—inserting thumbs in large ears—he stuck out his tongue, rolled his eyes, and went wugga-wugga-wugga. It was a minor diversion. One pedestrian skittered and tumbled, sending parcels everywhichway, another wet herself, a third keeled slantwise and the walk was stopped automatically by the servitors till she could be resuscitated. It was a minor diversion.

Then he swirled away on a vagrant breeze, and was gone. Hi-ho. As he rounded the cornice of the Time-Motion Study Building, he saw the shift, just boarding the slidewalk. With practiced motion and an absolute conservation of movement, they sidestepped up onto the slow-strip and (in a chorus line reminiscent of a Busby Berkeley film of the antediluvian 1930s) advanced across the strips ostrich-walking till they were lined up on the expresstrip.

Once more, in anticipation, the elfin grin spread, and there was a tooth missing back there on the left side. He dipped, skimmed, and swooped over them; and then, scrunching about on the air-boat, he released the holding pins that fastened shut the ends of the home-made pouring troughs that kept his cargo from dumping prematurely. And as he pulled the trough-pins, the air-boat slid over the factory workers and one hundred and fifty thousand dollars' worth of jelly beans cascaded down on the expresstrip.

Jelly beans! Millions and billions of purples and yellows and greens and licorice and grape and raspberry and mint and round and smooth and crunchy outside and soft-mealy inside and sugary and bouncing jouncing tumbling clittering clattering skittering fell on the heads and shoulders and hardhats and carapaces of the Timkin workers, tinkling on the slidewalk and bouncing away and rolling about underfoot and filling the sky on their way down with all the colors of joy and childhood and holidays, coming down in a steady rain, a solid wash, a torrent of color and sweetness out of the sky from above, and entering a universe of sanity and metronomic order with quite-mad coocoo newness. Jelly beans!

The shift workers howled and laughed and were pelted, and broke ranks, and the jelly beans managed to work their way into the mechanism of the slidewalks after which there was a hideous scraping as the sound of a million fingernails rasped down a quarter of a million blackboards, followed by a coughing and a sputtering, and then the slidewalks all stopped and everyone was dumped this-awayandthataway in a jackstraw tumble, still laughing and popping little jelly bean eggs of childish color into their mouths. It was a holiday, and a jollity, an absolute insanity, a giggle. But...

The shift was delayed seven minutes.

They did not get home for seven minutes.

The master schedule was thrown off by seven minutes.

Quotas were delayed by inoperative slidewalks for seven minutes.

He had tapped the first domino in the line, and one after another, like chik chik chik, the others had fallen.

The System had been seven minutes worth of disrupted. It was a tiny matter, one hardly worthy of note, but in a society where the single driving force was order and unity and equality and promptness and clocklike precision and attention to the clock, reverence of the gods of the passage of time, it was a disaster of major importance.

So he was ordered to appear before the Ticktockman. It was broadcast across every channel of the communications web. He was ordered to be *there* at 7:00 dammit on time. And they waited, and they waited, but he didn't show up till almost ten-thirty, at which time he merely sang a little song about moonlight in a place no one had ever heard of, called Vermont, and vanished again. But they had all been waiting since seven, and it wrecked *hell* with their schedules. So the question remained: Who is the Harlequin?

But the *unasked* question (more important of the two) was: how did we get *into* this position, where a laughing, irresponsible japer of jabberwocky and jive could disrupt our entire economic and cultural life with a hundred and fifty thousand dollars' worth of jelly beans?

Jelly for God's sake *beans*! This is madness! Where did he get the money to buy a hundred and fifty thousand dollars' worth of jelly beans? (They knew it would have cost that much, because they had a team of Situation Analysts pulled off another assignment, and rushed to the slidewalk scene to sweep up and count the candies, and produce findings, which disrupted *their* schedules and threw their entire branch at least a day behind.) Jelly beans! Jelly... *beans*? Now wait a second—a second accounted for—no one has manufactured jelly beans for over a hundred years. Where did he get jelly beans?

That's another good question. More than likely it will never be answered to your complete satisfaction. But then, how many questions ever are?

The middle you know. Here is the beginning. How it starts:

A desk pad. Day for day, and turn each day. 9:00—open the mail. 9:45—

appointment with planning commission board. 10:30—discuss installation progress charts with J.L. 11:45—pray for rain. 12:00—lunch. *And so it goes.*

"I'm sorry. Miss Grant, but the time for interviews was set at 2:30, and it's almost five now. I'm sorry you're late, but those are the rules. You'll have to wait till next year to submit application for this college again." *And so it goes.*

The 10:10 local stops at Cresthaven, Galesville, Tonawanda Junction, Selby, and Farnhurst, but not at Indiana City, Lucasville, and Colton, except on Sunday. The 10:35 express stops at Galesville, Selby, and Indiana City, except on Sundays & Holidays, at which time it stops at... *and so it goes.*

"I couldn't wait, Fred. I had to be at Pierre Cartain's by 3:00, and you said you'd meet me under the clock in the terminal at 2:45, and you weren't there, so I had to go on. You're always late, Fred. If you'd been there, we could have sewed it up together, but as it was, well, I took the order alone..." *And so it goes.*

Dear Mr. and Mrs. Atterley: in reference to your son Gerold's constant tardiness, I am afraid we will have to suspend him from school unless some more reliable method can be instituted guaranteeing he will arrive at his classes on time. Granted he is an exemplary student, and his marks are high, his constant flouting of the schedules of this school makes it impractical to maintain him in a system where the other children seem capable of getting where they are supposed to be on time *and so it goes.*

YOU CANNOT VOTE UNLESS YOU APPEAR AT 8:45 A.M.

"I don't care if the script is *good*, I need it Thursday!"

CHECK-OUT TIME IS 2:00 P.M.

"You got here late. The job's taken. Sorry."

YOUR SALARY HAS BEEN DOCKED FOR TWENTY MINUTES' TIME LOST.

"God, what time is it, I've gotta run!"

And so it goes. And so it goes. And so it goes. And so it goes goes goes goes goes tick tock tick tock tick tock and one day we no longer let time serve us, we serve time and we are slaves of the schedule, worshippers of the sun's passing, bound into a life predicated on restrictions because the system will not function if we don't keep the schedule tight.

Until it becomes more than a minor inconvenience to be late. It becomes a sin. Then a crime. Then a crime punishable by this:

EFFECTIVE 15 JULY 2389, 12:00:00 midnight, the office of the Master Timekeeper will require all citizens to submit their time-cards and cardioplates for processing. In accordance with Statute 555-7-SGH-999 governing the revocation of time per capita, all cardioplates will be keyed to the individual holder and—

What they had done, was devise a method of curtailing the amount of life a person could have. If he was ten minutes late, he lost ten minutes of his life. An hour was proportionately worth more revocation. If someone was consistently tardy, he might find himself, on a Sunday night, receiving a communiqué from the Master Timekeeper that his time had run out, and he would be "turned off" at high noon on Monday, please straighten your affairs, sir, madame or bisex.

And so, by this simple scientific expedient (utilizing a scientific process held dearly secret by the Ticktockman's office) the System was maintained. It was the only expedient thing to do. It was, after all, patriotic. The schedules had to be met. After all, there *was* a war on!

But, wasn't there always?

"Now that is really disgusting," the Harlequin said, when Pretty Alice showed him the wanted poster. "Disgusting and *highly* improbable. After all, this isn't the Day of the Desperadoes. A *wanted* poster!"

"You know," Pretty Alice noted, "you speak with a great deal of inflection."

"I'm sorry," said the Harlequin, humbly.

"No need to be sorry. You're always saying 'I'm sorry.' You have such massive guilt, Everett, it's really very sad."

"I'm sorry," he repeated, then pursed his lips so the dimples appeared momentarily. He hadn't wanted to say that at all. "I have to go out again. I have to *do* something."

Alice slammed her coffee-bulb down on the counter. "Oh for God's *sake*, Everett, can't you stay home just *one* night! Must you always be out in that ghastly clown suit, running around *annoying* people?"

"I'm—" he stopped, and clapped the jester's hat onto his auburn thatch with a tiny tingling of bells. He rose, rinsed out his coffee-bulb at the spray, and put it into the drier for a moment. "I have to go."

She didn't answer. The faxbox was purring, and she pulled a sheet out, read it, threw it toward him on the counter. "It's about you. Of course. You're ridiculous."

He read it quickly. It said the Ticktockman was trying to locate him. He didn't care, he was going out to be late again. At the door, dredging for an exit line, he hurled back petulantly, "Well, *you* speak with inflection, *too!*"

Pretty Alice rolled her pretty eyes heavenward. "You're ridiculous."

The Harlequin stalked out, slamming the door, which sighed shut softly, and locked itself.

There was a gentle knock, and Pretty Alice got up with an exhalation of exasperated breath, and opened the door. He stood there. "I'll be back about ten-thirty, okay?"

She pulled a rueful face. "Why do you tell me that? Why? You *know* you'll be late! You *know it!* You're *always* late, so why do you tell me these dumb things?" She closed the door.

On the other side, the Harlequin nodded to himself. *She's right. She's always right. I'll be late. I'm always late. Why do I tell her these dumb things?*

He shrugged again, and went off to be late once more.

He had fired off the firecracker rockets that said: I will attend the 115th annual International Medical Association Invocation at 8:00 P.M. precisely. I do hope you will all be able to join me.

The words had burned in the sky, and of course the authorities were there, lying in wait for him. They assumed, naturally, that he would be late. He arrived twenty minutes early, while they were setting up the spiderwebs to trap and hold him. Blowing a large bullhorn, he frightened and unnerved them so, their own moisturized encirclement webs sucked closed, and they were hauled up, kicking and shrieking, high above the amphitheater's floor. The Harlequin laughed and laughed, and apologized profusely. The physicians, gathered in solemn conclave, roared with laughter, and accepted the Harlequin's apologies with exaggerated bowing and posturing, and a merry time was had by all, who thought the Harlequin was a regular foofaraw in fancy pants; all, that is, but the authorities, who had been sent out by the office of the Ticktockman; they hung there like so much dockside cargo, hauled up above the floor of the amphitheater in a most unseemly fashion.

(In another part of the same city where the Harlequin carried on his "activities," totally unrelated in every way to what concerns here, save that it illustrates the Ticktockman's power and import, a man named Marshall Delahanty received his turn-off notice from the Ticktockman's office. His wife received the notification from the gray-suited minee who delivered it, with the traditional "look of sorrow" plastered hideously across his face. She knew what it was, even without unsealing it. It was a billet-doux of immediate recognition to everyone these days. She gasped, and held it as though it were a glass slide tinged with botulism, and prayed it was not for her. Let it be for Marsh, she thought, brutally, realistically, or one of the kids, but not for me, please dear God, not for me. And then she opened it, and it *was* for Marsh, and she was at one and the same time horrified and relieved. The next trooper in the line had caught the bullet. "Marshall," she screamed, "Marshall! Termination, Marshall! OhmiGod, Marshall, whattl we do, whattl we do, Marshall omigodmarshall…" and in their home that night was the sound of tearing paper and fear, and the stink of madness went up the flue and there was nothing, absolutely nothing they could do about it.

(But Marshall Delahanty tried to run. And early the next day, when turn-off time came, he was deep in the Canadian forest two hundred miles away, and the office of the Ticktockman blanked his cardioplate, and Marshall Delahanty keeled over, running, and his heart stopped, and the blood dried up on its way to his brain, and he was dead that's all. One light went out on his sector map in the office of the Master Timekeeper, while notification was entered for fax reproduction, and Georgette Delahanty's name was entered on the dole roles till she could re-marry. Which is the end of the footnote, and all the point that need be made, except don't laugh, because that is what would happen to the Harlequin if ever the Ticktockman found out his real name. It isn't funny.)

The shopping level of the city was thronged with the Thursday colors of the buyers. Women in canary yellow chitons and men in pseudo-Tyrolean outfits that were jade and leather and fit very tightly, save for the balloon pants.

When the Harlequin appeared on the still-being-constructed shell of the new Efficiency Shopping Center, his bullhorn to his elfishly-laughing lips, everyone pointed and stared, and he berated them:

"Why let them order you about? Why let them tell you to hurry and scurry like ants or maggots? Take your time! Saunter a while! Enjoy the sunshine, enjoy the breeze, let life carry you at your own pace! Don't be slaves of time, it's a helluva way to die, slowly, by degrees... down with the Ticktockman!"

Who's the nut? most of the shoppers wanted to know. Who's the nut oh wow I'm gonna be late I gotta run...

And the construction gang on the Shopping Center received an urgent order from the office of the Master Timekeeper that the dangerous criminal known as the Harlequin was atop their spire, and their aid was urgently needed in apprehending him. The work crew said no, they would lose time on their construction schedule, but the Ticktockman managed to pull the proper threads of governmental webbing, and they were told to cease work and catch that nitwit up there on the spire; up there with the bullhorn. So a dozen and more burly workers began climbing into their construction platforms, releasing the a-grav plates, and rising toward the Harlequin.

After the debacle (in which, through the Harlequin's attention to personal safety, no one was seriously injured), the workers tried to reassemble, and assault him again, but it was too late. He had vanished. It had attracted quite a crowd, however, and the shopping cycle was thrown off by hours, simply hours. The purchasing needs of the system were therefore falling behind, and so measures were taken to accelerate the cycle for the rest of the day, but it got bogged down and speeded up and they sold too many float-valves and not nearly enough wegglers, which meant that the popli ratio was off, which made it necessary to rush cases and cases of spoiling Smash-O to stores that usually needed a case only every three or four hours. The shipments were bollixed, the transshipments were misrouted, and in the end, even the swizzleskid industries felt it.

"Don't come back till you have him!" the Ticktockman said, very quietly, very sincerely, extremely dangerously.

They used dogs. They used probes. They used cardioplate crossoffs. They used teepers. They used bribery. They used stiktytes. They used intimidation. They used torment. They used torture. They used finks. They used cops. They used search & seizure. They used fallaron. They used betterment incentive. They used fingerprints. They used the Bertillon system. They used cunning. They used guile. They used treachery. They used Raoul Mitgong, but he didn't help much. They used applied physics. They used techniques of criminology.

And what the hell: they caught him.

After all, his name was Everett C. Marm, and he wasn't much to begin with, except a man who had no sense of time.

"Repent, Harlequin!" said the Ticktockman.

"Get stuffed!" the Harlequin replied, sneering.

"You've been late a total of sixty-three years, five months, three weeks, two days, twelve hours, forty-one minutes, fifty-nine seconds, point oh three six one one one microseconds. You've used up everything you can, and more. I'm going to turn you off."

"Scare someone else. I'd rather be dead than live in a dumb world with a bogeyman like you."

"It's my job."

"You're full of it. You're a tyrant. You have no right to order people around and kill them if they show up late."

"You can't adjust. You can't fit in."

"Unstrap me, and I'll fit my fist into your mouth."

"You're a non-conformist."

"That didn't used to be a felony."

"It is now. Live in the world around you."

"I hate it. It's a terrible world."

"Not everyone thinks so. Most people enjoy order."

"I don't, and most of the people I know don't."

"That's not true. How do you think we caught you?"

"I'm not interested."

"A girl named Pretty Alice told us who you were."

"That's a lie."

"It's true. You unnerve her. She wants to belong; she wants to conform, I'm going to turn you off."

"Then do it already, and stop arguing with me."

"I'm not going to turn you off."

"You're an idiot!"

"Repent, Harlequin!" said the Ticktockman.

"Get stuffed."

So they sent him to Coventry. And in Coventry they worked him over. It was just like what they did to Winston Smith in *Nineteen Eighty-Four*, which was a book none of them knew about, but the techniques are really quite ancient, and so they did it to Everett C. Marm; and one day quite a long time later, the Harlequin appeared on the communications web, appearing elfin and dimpled and bright-eyed, and not at all brainwashed, and he said he had been wrong, that it was a good, a very good thing indeed, to belong, and be right on time hip-ho and away we go, and everyone stared up at him on the public screens that covered an entire city block, and they said to themselves, well, you see, he was just a nut after all, and if that's the way the system is run, then let's do it that way, because it doesn't pay to fight city hall, or in this case, the Ticktockman. So Everett C. Marm was destroyed, which was a loss, because of what Thoreau said earlier, but you can't make an omelet without breaking a few eggs, and in every revolution, a few die who shouldn't, but they have to, because that's the way it happens, and if you make only a little change, then it seems to be worthwhile. Or, to make the point lucidly:

*

"Uh, excuse me, sir, I, uh, don't know how to uh, tell you this, but you were three minutes late. The schedule is a, little, uh, bit off."

He grinned sheepishly.

"That's ridiculous!" murmured the Ticktockman behind his mask.

"Check your watch." And then he went into his office, going mrmee, mrmee, mrmee, mrmee.

(1965)

THE MACHINE STOPS

E. M. Forster

On 30 March 1904, the Anglo-French aviator Henri Farman took an experimental powered aircraft into the air, made a perfect one-kilometre round trip, landed safely, and set the twenty-five year old **Edward Morgan Forster** to thinking about the end of humanity. Between the novels *A Room with a View* (1908) and *Howards End* (1910), which have more or less defined Edwardian England in the public imagination, Forster wrote "The Machine Stops", a dystopia more devastating than anything science fiction has since produced. While most of his peers were celebrating the coming of the machine age, and lapping up H. G. Wells's enthusiasm for technological Utopia, Forster foresaw, particularly in the birth of air travel, a moment of moral crisis, in which the machines we made to help us would actually become what we started living through, relying upon – and even emulating. Forster the futurist was so on the money morally, he inevitably got a lot of the furnishings right. Writing a century ago, he foresaw the internet, social media, YouTube and all the tiny technologically enabled fracturings of our civic life. No one has conveyed human-as-robot as well as Forster, of whom Virginia Woolf once wrote, "He says the simple things that clever people don't say."

1. THE AIR-SHIP

Imagine, if you can, a small room, hexagonal in shape, like the cell of a bee. It is lighted neither by window nor by lamp, yet it is filled with a soft radiance. There are no apertures for ventilation, yet the air is fresh. There are no musical instruments, and yet, at the moment that my meditation opens, this room is throbbing with melodious sounds. An armchair is in the centre, by its side a reading-desk—that is all the furniture. And in the armchair there sits a swaddled lump of flesh—a woman, about five feet high, with a face as white as a fungus. It is to her that the little room belongs.

An electric bell rang.

The woman touched a switch and the music was silent.

"I suppose I must see who it is," she thought, and set her chair in motion. The chair, like the music, was worked by machinery and it rolled her to the other side of the room where the bell still rang importunately.

"Who is it?" she called. Her voice was irritable, for she had been interrupted often since the music began. She knew several thousand people, in certain directions human intercourse had advanced enormously.

But when she listened into the receiver, her white face wrinkled into smiles, and she said:

"Very well. Let us talk, I will isolate myself. I do not expect anything important will happen for the next five minutes—for I can give you fully five minutes, Kuno. Then I must deliver my lecture on 'Music during the Australian Period'."

She touched the isolation knob, so that no one else could speak to her. Then she touched the lighting apparatus, and the little room was plunged into darkness.

"Be quick!" she called, her irritation returning. "Be quick, Kuno; here I am in the dark wasting my time."

But it was fully fifteen seconds before the round plate that she held in her hands began to glow. A faint blue light shot across it, darkening to purple, and presently she could see the image of her son, who lived on the other side of the earth, and he could see her.

"Kuno, how slow you are."

He smiled gravely.

"I really believe you enjoy dawdling."

"I have called you before, mother, but you were always busy or isolated. I have something particular to say."

"What is it, dearest boy? Be quick. Why could you not send it by pneumatic post?"

"Because I prefer saying such a thing. I want—"

"Well?"

"I want you to come and see me."

Vashti watched his face in the blue plate.

"But I can see you!" she exclaimed. "What more do you want?"

"I want to see you not through the Machine," said Kuno. "I want to speak to you not through the wearisome Machine."

"Oh, hush!" said his mother, vaguely shocked. "You mustn't say anything against the Machine."

"Why not?"

"One mustn't."

"You talk as if a god had made the Machine," cried the other. "I believe that you pray to it when you are unhappy. Men made it, do not forget that. Great men, but men. The Machine is much, but it is not everything. I see something like you in this plate, but I do not see you. I hear something like you through this telephone, but I do not hear you. That is why I want you to come. Pay me a visit, so that we can meet face to face, and talk about the hopes that are in my mind."

She replied that she could scarcely spare the time for a visit.

"The air-ship barely takes two days to fly between me and you."

"I dislike air-ships."

"Why?"

"I dislike seeing the horrible brown earth, and the sea, and the stars when it is dark. I get no ideas in an air-ship."

"I do not get them anywhere else."

"What kind of ideas can the air give you?"

He paused for an instant.

"Do you not know four big stars that form an oblong, and three stars close together in the middle of the oblong, and hanging from these stars, three other stars?"

"No, I do not. I dislike the stars. But did they give you an idea? How interesting; tell me."

"I had an idea that they were like a man."

"I do not understand."

"The four big stars are the man's shoulders and his knees. The three stars in the middle are like the belts that men wore once, and the three stars hanging are like a sword."

"A sword?"

"Men carried swords about with them, to kill animals and other men."

"It does not strike me as a very good idea, but it is certainly original. When did it come to you first?"

"In the air-ship—" He broke off, and she fancied that he looked sad. She could not be sure, for the Machine did not transmit nuances of expression. It only gave a general idea of people—an idea that was good enough for all practical purposes, Vashti thought. The imponderable bloom, declared by a discredited philosophy to be the actual essence of intercourse, was rightly ignored by the Machine, just as the imponderable bloom of the grape was ignored by the manufacturers of artificial fruit. Something "good enough" had long since been accepted by our race.

"The truth is," he continued, "that I want to see these stars again. They are curious stars. I want to see them not from the air-ship, but from the surface of the earth, as our ancestors did, thousands of years ago. I want to visit the surface of the earth."

She was shocked again.

"Mother, you must come, if only to explain to me what is the harm of visiting the surface of the earth."

"No harm," she replied, controlling herself. "But no advantage. The surface of the earth is only dust and mud, no advantage. The surface of the earth is only dust and mud, no life remains on it, and you would need a respirator, or the cold of the outer air would kill you. One dies immediately in the outer air."

"I know; of course I shall take all precautions."

"And besides—"

"Well?"

She considered, and chose her words with care. Her son had a queer temper, and she wished to dissuade him from the expedition.

"It is contrary to the spirit of the age," she asserted.

"Do you mean by that, contrary to the Machine?"

"In a sense, but—"

His image in the blue plate faded.

"Kuno!"

He had isolated himself.

For a moment Vashti felt lonely.

Then she generated the light, and the sight of her room, flooded with radiance and studded with electric buttons, revived her. There were buttons and switches everywhere—buttons to call for food for music, for clothing. There was the hot-bath button, by pressure of which a basin of (imitation) marble rose out of the floor, filled to the brim with a warm deodorized liquid. There was the cold-bath button. There was the button that produced literature. And there were of course the buttons by which she communicated with her friends. The room, though it contained nothing, was in touch with all that she cared for in the world.

Vashti's next move was to turn off the isolation switch, and all the accumulations of the last three minutes burst upon her. The room was filled with the noise of bells, and speaking-tubes. What was the new food like? Could she recommend it? Has she had any ideas lately? Might one tell her one's own ideas? Would she make an engagement to visit the public nurseries at an early date?—say this day month.

To most of these questions she replied with irritation—a growing quality in that accelerated age. She said that the new food was horrible. That she could not visit the public nurseries through press of engagements. That she had no ideas of her own but had just been told one—that four stars and three in the middle were like a man: she doubted there was much in it. Then she switched off her correspondents, for it was time to deliver her lecture on Australian music.

The clumsy system of public gatherings had been long since abandoned; neither Vashti nor her audience stirred from their rooms. Seated in her armchair she spoke, while they in their armchairs heard her, fairly well, and saw her, fairly well. She opened with a humorous account of music in the pre-Mongolian epoch, and went on to describe the great outburst of song that followed the Chinese conquest. Remote and primæval as were the methods of I-San-So and the Brisbane school, she yet felt (she said) that study of them might repay the musicians of today: they had freshness; they had, above all, ideas.

Her lecture, which lasted ten minutes, was well received, and at its conclusion she and many of her audience listened to a lecture on the sea; there were ideas to be got from the sea; the speaker had donned a respirator and visited it lately. Then she fed, talked to many friends, had a bath, talked again, and summoned her bed.

The bed was not to her liking. It was too large, and she had a feeling for a small bed. Complaint was useless, for beds were of the same dimension all over the world, and to have had an alternative size would have involved vast alterations in the Machine. Vashti isolated herself—it was necessary, for neither day nor night existed under the ground—and reviewed all that had happened since she had summoned the bed last. Ideas? Scarcely any. Events—was Kuno's invitation an event?

By her side, on the little reading-desk, was a survival from the ages of litter—one book. This was the Book of the Machine. In it were instructions against every possible contingency. If she was hot or cold or dyspeptic or at a loss for a word, she went to the book, and it told her which button to press. The Central Committee published it. In accordance with a growing habit, it was richly bound.

Sitting up in the bed, she took it reverently in her hands. She glanced round the glowing room as if some one might be watching her. Then, half ashamed, half joyful, she murmured "O Machine! O Machine!" and raised the volume to her lips. Thrice she kissed it, thrice inclined her head, thrice she felt the delirium of acquiescence. Her ritual performed, she turned to page 1367, which gave the times of the departure of the air-ships from the island in the southern hemisphere, under whose soil she lived, to the island in the northern hemisphere, whereunder lived her son.

She thought, "I have not the time."

She made the room dark and slept; she awoke and made the room light; she ate and exchanged ideas with her friends, and listened to music and attended lectures; she made the room dark and slept. Above her, beneath her, and around her, the Machine hummed eternally; she did not notice the noise, for she had been born with it in her ears. The earth, carrying her, hummed as it sped through silence, turning her now to the invisible sun, now to the invisible stars. She awoke and made the room light.

"Kuno!"

"I will not talk to you," he answered, "until you come."

"Have you been on the surface of the earth since we spoke last?"

His image faded.

Again she consulted the book. She became very nervous and lay back in her chair palpitating. Think of her as without teeth or hair. Presently she directed the chair to the wall, and pressed an unfamiliar button. The wall swung apart slowly. Through the opening she saw a tunnel that curved slightly, so that its goal was not visible. Should she go to see her son, here was the beginning of the journey.

Of course she knew all about the communication-system. There was nothing mysterious in it. She would summon a car and it would fly with her down the tunnel until it reached the lift that communicated with the air-ship station: the system had been in use for many, many years, long before the universal establishment of the Machine. And of course she had studied the civilization that had immediately preceded her own—the civilization that had mistaken the functions of the system, and had used it for bringing people to things, instead of for bringing things to people. Those funny old days, when men went for change of air instead of changing the air in their rooms! And yet—she was frightened of the tunnel: she had not seen it since her last child was born. It curved—but not quite as she remembered; it was brilliant—but not quite as brilliant as a lecturer had suggested. Vashti was seized with the terrors of direct experience. She shrank back into the room, and the wall closed up again.

"Kuno," she said, "I cannot come to see you. I am not well."

Immediately an enormous apparatus fell on to her out of the ceiling, a thermometer was automatically laid upon her heart. She lay powerless. Cool pads soothed her forehead. Kuno had telegraphed to her doctor.

So the human passions still blundered up and down in the Machine. Vashti drank the medicine that the doctor projected into her mouth, and the machinery retired into the ceiling. The voice of Kuno was heard asking how she felt.

"Better." Then with irritation: "But why do you not come to me instead?"

"Because I cannot leave this place."

"Why?"

"Because, any moment, something tremendous many happen."

"Have you been on the surface of the earth yet?"

"Not yet."

"Then what is it?"

"I will not tell you through the Machine."

She resumed her life.

But she thought of Kuno as a baby, his birth, his removal to the public nurseries, her own visit to him there, his visits to her—visits which stopped when the Machine had assigned him a room on the other side of the earth. "Parents, duties of," said the book of the Machine, "cease at the moment of birth. P.422327483." True, but there was something special about Kuno—indeed there had been something special about all her children—and, after all, she must brave the journey if he desired it. And "something tremendous might happen." What did that mean? The nonsense of a youthful man, no doubt, but she must go. Again she pressed the unfamiliar button, again the wall swung back, and she saw the tunnel that curves out of sight. Clasping the Book, she rose, tottered on to the platform, and summoned the car. Her room closed behind her: the journey to the northern hemisphere had begun.

Of course it was perfectly easy. The car approached and in it she found arm-chairs exactly like her own. When she signalled, it stopped, and she tottered into the lift. One other passenger was in the lift, the first fellow creature she had seen face to face for months. Few travelled in these days, for, thanks to the advance of science, the earth was exactly alike all over. Rapid intercourse, from which the previous civilization had hoped so much, had ended by defeating itself. What was the good of going to Pekin when it was just like Shrewsbury? Why return to Shrewsbury when it would all be like Pekin? Men seldom moved their bodies; all unrest was concentrated in the soul.

The air-ship service was a relic from the former age. It was kept up, because it was easier to keep it up than to stop it or to diminish it, but it now far exceeded the wants of the population. Vessel after vessel would rise from the vomitories of Rye or of Christchurch (I use the antique names), would sail into the crowded sky, and would draw up at the wharves of the south—empty. So nicely adjusted was the system, so independent of meteorology, that the sky, whether calm or cloudy, resembled a vast kaleidoscope whereon the same patterns periodically recurred. The ship on which Vashti sailed started now at sunset, now at dawn. But always, as it passed above Rheims, it would neighbour the ship that served between Helsingfors and the Brazils, and, every third time it surmounted the Alps, the fleet of Palermo would cross its track behind. Night and day, wind and storm, tide and earthquake, impeded man no longer. He had harnessed Leviathan. All the old literature, with its praise of Nature, and its fear of Nature, rang false as the prattle of a child.

Yet as Vashti saw the vast flank of the ship, stained with exposure to the outer air, her horror of direct experience returned. It was not quite like the air-ship in the cinematophote. For one thing it smelt—not strongly or unpleasantly, but it did smell, and with her eyes shut she should have known that a new thing was close to her. Then she had to walk to it from the lift, had to submit to glances from the other passengers. The man in front dropped his Book—no great matter, but it disquieted them all. In the rooms, if the Book was dropped, the floor raised it mechanically, but the gangway to the air-ship was not so prepared, and the sacred volume lay motionless. They stopped—the thing was unforeseen—and the man, instead of picking up his property, felt the muscles of his arm to see how they had failed him. Then some one actually said with direct utterance: "We shall be late"—and they trooped on board, Vashti treading on the pages as she did so.

Inside, her anxiety increased. The arrangements were old-fashioned and rough. There was even a female attendant, to whom she would have to announce her wants during the voyage. Of course a revolving platform ran the length of the boat, but she was expected to walk from it to her cabin. Some cabins were better than others, and she did not get the best. She thought the attendant had been unfair, and spasms of rage shook her. The glass valves had closed, she could not go back. She saw, at the end of the vestibule, the lift in which she had ascended going quietly up and down, empty. Beneath those corridors of shining tiles were rooms, tier below tier, reaching far into the earth, and in each room there sat a human being, eating, or sleeping, or producing ideas. And buried deep in the hive was her own room. Vashti was afraid.

"O Machine!" she murmured, and caressed her Book, and was comforted.

Then the sides of the vestibule seemed to melt together, as do the passages that we see in dreams, the lift vanished, the Book that had been dropped slid to the left and vanished, polished tiles rushed by like a stream of water, there was a slight jar, and the air-ship, issuing from its tunnel, soared above the waters of a tropical ocean.

It was night. For a moment she saw the coast of Sumatra edged by the phosphorescence of waves, and crowned by lighthouses, still sending forth their disregarded beams. These also vanished, and only the stars distracted her. They were not motionless, but swayed to and fro above her head, thronging out of one skylight into another, as if the universe and not the air-ship was careening. And, as often happens on clear nights, they seemed now to be in perspective, now on a plane; now piled tier beyond tier into the infinite heavens, now concealing infinity, a roof limiting for ever the visions of men. In either case they seemed intolerable. "Are we to travel in the dark?" called the passengers angrily, and the attendant, who had been careless, generated the light, and pulled down the blinds of pliable metal. When the air-ships had been built, the desire to look direct at things still lingered in the world. Hence the extraordinary number of skylights and windows, and the proportionate discomfort to those who were civilized and refined. Even in Vashti's cabin one star peeped through a flaw in the blind, and after a few hours' uneasy slumber, she was disturbed by an unfamiliar glow, which was the dawn.

Quick as the ship had sped westwards, the earth had rolled eastwards quicker still, and had dragged back Vashti and her companions towards the sun. Science could prolong the night, but only for a little, and those high hopes of neutralizing the earth's diurnal revolution had passed, together with hopes that were possibly higher. To "keep pace with the sun," or even to outstrip it, had been the aim of the civilization preceding this. Racing aeroplanes had been built for the purpose, capable of enormous speed, and steered by the greatest intellects of the epoch. Round the globe they went, round and round, westward, westward, round and round, amidst humanity's applause. In vain. The globe went eastward quicker still, horrible accidents occurred, and the Committee of the Machine, at the time rising into prominence, declared the pursuit illegal, unmechanical, and punishable by Homelessness.

Of Homelessness more will be said later.

Doubtless the Committee was right. Yet the attempt to "defeat the sun" aroused the last common interest that our race experienced about the heavenly bodies, or indeed about anything. It was the last time that men were compacted by thinking of a power outside the world. The sun had conquered, yet it was the end of his spiritual dominion. Dawn, midday, twilight, the zodiacal path, touched neither men's lives not their hearts, and science retreated into the ground, to concentrate herself upon problems that she was certain of solving.

So when Vashti found her cabin invaded by a rosy finger of light, she was annoyed, and tried to adjust the blind. But the blind flew up altogether, and she saw through the skylight small pink clouds, swaying against a background of blue, and as the sun crept higher, its radiance entered direct, brimming down the wall, like a golden sea. It rose and fell with the air-ship's motion, just as waves rise and fall, but it advanced steadily, as a tide advances. Unless she was careful, it would strike her face. A spasm of horror shook her and she rang for the attendant. The attendant too was horrified, but she could do nothing; it was not her place to mend the blind. She could only suggest that the lady should change her cabin, which she accordingly prepared to do.

People were almost exactly alike all over the world, but the attendant of the air-ship, perhaps owing to her exceptional duties, had grown a little out of the common. She had often to address passengers with direct speech, and this had given her a certain roughness and originality of manner. When Vashti swerved away from the sunbeams with a cry, she behaved barbarically—she put out her hand to steady her.

"How dare you!" exclaimed the passenger. "You forget yourself!"

The woman was confused, and apologized for not having let her fall. People never touched one another. The custom had become obsolete, owing to the Machine.

"Where are we now?" asked Vashti haughtily.

"We are over Asia," said the attendant, anxious to be polite.

"Asia?"

"You must excuse my common way of speaking. I have got into the habit of calling places over which I pass by their unmechanical names."

"Oh, I remember Asia. The Mongols came from it."

"Beneath us, in the open air, stood a city that was once called Simla."

"Have you ever heard of the Mongols and of the Brisbane school?"

"No."

"Brisbane also stood in the open air."

"Those mountains to the right—let me show you them." She pushed back a metal blind. The main chain of the Himalayas was revealed. "They were once called the Roof of the World, those mountains."

"What a foolish name!"

"You must remember that, before the dawn of civilization, they seemed to be an impenetrable wall that touched the stars. It was supposed that no one but the gods could exist above their summits. How we have advanced, thanks to the Machine!"

"How we have advanced, thanks to the Machine!" said Vashti.

"How we have advanced, thanks to the Machine!" echoed the passenger who had dropped his Book the night before, and who was standing in the passage.

"And that white stuff in the cracks?—what is it?"

"I have forgotten its name."

"Cover the window, please. These mountains give me no ideas."

The northern aspect of the Himalayas was in deep shadow: on the Indian slope the sun had just prevailed. The forests had been destroyed during the literature epoch for the purpose of making newspaper-pulp, but the snows were awakening to their morning glory, and clouds still hung on the breasts of Kinchinjunga. In the plain were seen the ruins of cities, with diminished rivers creeping by their walls, and by the sides of these were sometimes the signs of vomitories, marking the cities of to-day. Over the whole prospect air-ships rushed, crossing the inter-crossing with incredible aplomb, and rising nonchalantly when they desired to escape the perturbations of the lower atmosphere and to traverse the Roof of the World.

"We have indeed advanced, thanks to the Machine," repeated the attendant, and hid the Himalayas behind a metal blind.

The day dragged wearily forward. The passengers sat each in his cabin, avoiding one another with an almost physical repulsion and longing to be once more under the surface of the earth. There were eight or ten of them, mostly young males, sent out from the public nurseries to inhabit the rooms of those who had died in various parts of the earth. The man who had dropped his Book was on the homeward journey. He had been sent to Sumatra for the purpose of propagating the race. Vashti alone was travelling by her private will.

At midday she took a second glance at the earth. The air-ship was crossing another range of mountains, but she could see little, owing to clouds. Masses of black rock hovered below her, and merged indistinctly into grey. Their shapes were fantastic; one of them resembled a prostrate man.

"No ideas here," murmured Vashti, and hid the Caucasus behind a metal blind.

In the evening she looked again. They were crossing a golden sea, in which lay many small islands and one peninsula.

She repeated, "No ideas here," and hid Greece behind a metal blind.

2. THE MENDING APPARATUS

By a vestibule, by a lift, by a tubular railway, by a platform, by a sliding door—by reversing all the steps of her departure did Vashti arrive at her son's room, which exactly resembled her own. She might well declare that the visit was superfluous. The buttons, the knobs, the reading-desk with the Book, the temperature, the atmosphere, the illumination—all were exactly the same. And if Kuno himself, flesh of her flesh, stood close beside her at last, what profit was there in that? She was too well-bred to shake him by the hand.

Averting her eyes, she spoke as follows:

"Here I am. I have had the most terrible journey and greatly retarded the development of my soul. It is not worth it, Kuno, it is not worth it. My time is too precious. The sunlight almost touched me, and I have met with the rudest people. I can only stop a few minutes. Say what you want to say, and then I must return."

"I have been threatened with Homelessness," said Kuno.

She looked at him now.

"I have been threatened with Homelessness, and I could not tell you such a thing through the Machine."

Homelessness means death. The victim is exposed to the air, which kills him.

"I have been outside since I spoke to you last. The tremendous thing has happened, and they have discovered me."

"But why shouldn't you go outside?" she exclaimed, "It is perfectly legal, perfectly mechanical, to visit the surface of the earth. I have lately been to a lecture on the sea; there is no objection to that; one simply summons a respirator and gets an Egression-permit. It is not the kind of thing that spiritually minded people do, and I begged you not to do it, but there is no legal objection to it."

"I did not get an Egression-permit."

"Then how did you get out?"

"I found out a way of my own."

The phrase conveyed no meaning to her, and he had to repeat it. "A way of your own?" she whispered. "But that would be wrong."

"Why?"

The question shocked her beyond measure.

"You are beginning to worship the Machine," he said coldly. "You think it irreligious of me to have found out a way of my own. It was just what the Committee thought, when they threatened me with Homelessness."

At this she grew angry. "I worship nothing!" she cried. "I am most advanced. I don't think you irreligious, for there is no such thing as religion left. All the fear and the superstition that existed once have been destroyed by the Machine. I only meant that to find out a way of your own was— Besides, there is no new way out."

"So it is always supposed."

"Except through the vomitories, for which one must have an Egression-permit, it is impossible to get out. The Book says so."

"Well, the Book's wrong, for I have been out on my feet."

For Kuno was possessed of a certain physical strength.

By these days it was a demerit to be muscular. Each infant was examined at birth, and all who promised undue strength were destroyed. Humanitarians may protest, but it would have been no true kindness to let an athlete live; he would never have been happy in that state of life to which the Machine had called him; he would have yearned for trees to climb, rivers to bathe in, meadows and hills against which he might measure his body. Man must be adapted to his surroundings, must he not? In the dawn of the world our weakly must be exposed on Mount Taygetus, in its twilight our strong will suffer euthanasia, that the Machine may progress, that the Machine may progress, that the Machine may progress eternally.

"You know that we have lost the sense of space. We say 'space is annihilated,' but we have annihilated not space, but the sense thereof. We have lost a part of ourselves. I determined to recover it, and I began by walking up and down the platform of the railway outside my room. Up and down, until I was tired, and so did recapture the meaning of 'Near' and 'Far.' 'Near' is a place to which I can get quickly on my feet, not a place to which the train or the air-ship will take me quickly. 'Far' is a place to which I cannot get quickly on my feet; the vomitory is 'far,' though I could be there in thirty-eight seconds by summoning the train. Man is the measure. That was my first lesson. Man's feet are the measure for distance, his hands are the measure for ownership, his body is the measure for all that is lovable and desirable and strong. Then I went further: it was then that I called to you for the first time, and you would not come.

"This city, as you know, is built deep beneath the surface of the earth, with only the vomitories protruding. Having paced the platform outside my own room, I took the lift to the next platform and paced that also, and so with each in turn, until I came to the topmost, above which begins the earth. All the platforms were exactly alike, and all that I gained by visiting them was to develop my sense of space and my muscles. I think I should have been content with this—it is not a little thing—but as I walked and brooded, it occurred to me that our cities had been built in the days when men still breathed the outer air, and that there had been ventilation shafts for the workmen. I could think of nothing but these ventilation shafts. Had they been destroyed by all the food-tubes and medicine-tubes and music-tubes that the Machine has evolved lately? Or did traces of them remain? One thing was certain. If I came upon them anywhere, it would be in the railway-tunnels of the topmost story. Everywhere else, all space was accounted for.

"I am telling my story quickly, but don't think that I was not a coward or that your answers never depressed me. It is not the proper thing, it is not mechanical, it is not decent to walk along a railway-tunnel. I did not fear that I might tread upon a live rail and be killed. I feared something far more intangible—doing what was not contemplated by the Machine. Then I said to myself, 'Man is the measure,' and I went, and after many visits I found an opening.

"The tunnels, of course, were lighted. Everything is light, artificial light; darkness is the exception. So when I saw a black gap in the tiles, I knew that it was an exception, and rejoiced. I put in my arm—I could put in no more at first—and waved it round and round in ecstasy. I loosened another tile, and put in my head, and shouted into the darkness: 'I am coming, I shall do it yet,' and my voice reverberated down endless passages. I seemed to hear the spirits of those dead workmen who had returned each evening to the starlight and to their wives, and all the generations who had lived in the open air called back to me, 'You will do it yet, you are coming.'"

He paused, and, absurd as he was, his last words moved her. For Kuno had lately asked to be a father, and his request had been refused by the Committee. His was not a type that the Machine desired to hand on.

"Then a train passed. It brushed by me, but I thrust my head and arms into the hole. I had done enough for one day, so I crawled back to the platform, went down in the lift, and summoned my bed. Ah what dreams! And again I called you, and again you refused."

She shook her head and said:

"Don't. Don't talk of these terrible things. You make me miserable. You are throwing civilization away."

"But I had got back the sense of space and a man cannot rest then. I determined to get in at the hole and climb the shaft. And so I exercised my arms. Day after day I went through ridiculous movements, until my flesh ached, and I could hang by my hands and hold the pillow of my bed outstretched for many minutes. Then I summoned a respirator, and started.

"It was easy at first. The mortar had somehow rotted, and I soon pushed some more tiles in, and clambered after them into the darkness, and the spirits of the dead comforted me. I don't know what I mean by that. I just say what I felt. I felt, for the first time, that a protest had been lodged against corruption, and that even as the dead were comforting me, so I was comforting the unborn. I felt that humanity existed, and that it existed without clothes. How can I possibly explain this? It was naked, humanity seemed naked, and all these tubes and buttons and machineries neither came into the world with us, nor will they follow us out, nor do they matter supremely while we are here. Had I been strong, I would have torn off every garment I had, and gone out into the outer air unswaddled. But this is not for me, nor perhaps for my generation. I climbed with my respirator and my hygienic clothes and my dietetic tabloids! Better thus than not at all.

"There was a ladder, made of some primæval metal. The light from the railway fell upon its lowest rungs, and I saw that it led straight upwards out of the rubble at the bottom of the shaft. Perhaps our ancestors ran up and down it a dozen times daily, in their building. As I climbed, the rough edges cut through my gloves so that my hands bled. The light helped me for a little, and then came darkness and, worse still, silence which pierced my ears like a sword. The Machine hums! Did you know that? Its hum penetrates our blood, and may even guide our thoughts. Who knows! I was getting beyond its power. Then I thought: 'This silence means that I am doing wrong.' But I heard voices in the silence, and again they strengthened me." He laughed. "I had need of them. The next moment I cracked my head against something."

She sighed.

"I had reached one of those pneumatic stoppers that defend us from the outer air. You may have noticed them on the air-ship. Pitch dark, my feet on the rungs of an invisible ladder, my hands cut; I cannot explain how I lived through this part, but the voices still comforted me, and I felt for fastenings. The stopper, I suppose, was about eight feet across. I passed my hand over it as far as I could reach. It was perfectly smooth. I felt it almost to the centre. Not quite to the centre, for my arm was too short. Then the voice said: 'Jump. It is worth it. There may be a handle in the centre, and you may catch hold of it and so come to us your own way. And if there is no handle, so that you may fall and are dashed to pieces it is still worth it: you will still come to us your own way.' So I jumped. There was a handle, and—"

He paused. Tears gathered in his mother's eyes. She knew that he was fated. If he did not die to-day he would die tomorrow. There was not room for such a person in the world. And with her pity disgust mingled. She was ashamed at having borne such a son, she who had always been so respectable and so full of ideas. Was he really the little boy to whom she had taught the use of his stops and buttons, and to whom she had given his first lessons in the Book? The very hair that disfigured his lip showed that he was reverting to some savage type. On atavism the Machine can have no mercy.

"There was a handle, and I did catch it. I hung tranced over the darkness and heard the hum of these workings as the last whisper in a dying dream. All the things I had cared about and all the people I had spoken to through tubes appeared infinitely little. Meanwhile the handle revolved. My weight had set something in motion and I span slowly, and then—

"I cannot describe it. I was lying with my face to the sunshine. Blood poured from my nose and ears and I heard a tremendous roaring. The stopper, with me clinging to it, had simply been blown out of the earth, and the air that we make down here was escaping through the vent into the air above. It burst up like a fountain. I crawled back to it—for the upper air hurts—and, as it were, I took great sips from the edge. My respirator had flown goodness knows where, my clothes were torn. I just lay with my lips close to the hole, and I sipped until the bleeding stopped. You can imagine nothing so curious. This hollow in the grass—I will speak of it in a minute,—the sun shining into it, not brilliantly but through marbled clouds,—the peace, the nonchalance, the sense of space, and, brushing my cheek, the roaring fountain of our artificial air! Soon I spied my respirator, bobbing up and down in the current high above my head, and higher still were many air-ships. But no one ever looks out of air-ships, and in any case they could not have picked me up. There I was, stranded. The sun shone a little way down the shaft, and revealed the topmost rung of the ladder, but it was hopeless trying to reach it. I should either have been tossed up again by the escape, or else have fallen in, and died. I could only lie on the grass, sipping and sipping, and from time to time glancing around me.

"I knew that I was in Wessex, for I had taken care to go to a lecture on the subject before starting. Wessex lies above the room in which we are talking now. It was once an important state. Its kings held all the southern coast from the Andredswald to Cornwall, while the Wansdyke protected them on the north, running over the high ground. The lecturer was only concerned with the rise of Wessex, so I do not know how long it remained an international power, nor would the knowledge have assisted me. To tell the truth I could do nothing but laugh, during this part. There was I, with a pneumatic stopper by my side and a respirator bobbing over my head, imprisoned, all three of us, in a grass-grown hollow that was edged with fern."

Then he grew grave again.

"Lucky for me that it was a hollow. For the air began to fall back into it and to fill it as water fills a bowl. I could crawl about. Presently I stood. I breathed a mixture, in which the air that hurts predominated whenever I tried to climb the sides. This was not so bad. I had not lost my tabloids and remained ridiculously cheerful, and as for the Machine, I forgot about it altogether. My one aim now was to get to the top, where the ferns were, and to view whatever objects lay beyond.

"I rushed the slope. The new air was still too bitter for me and I came rolling back, after a momentary vision of something grey. The sun grew very feeble, and I remembered that he was in Scorpio—I had been to a lecture on that too. If the sun is in Scorpio, and you are in Wessex, it means that you must be as quick as you can, or it will get too dark. (This is the first bit of useful information I have ever got from a lecture, and I expect it will be the last.) It made me try frantically to breathe the new air, and to advance as far as I dared out of my pond. The hollow filled so slowly. At times I thought that the fountain played with less vigour. My respirator seemed to dance nearer the earth; the roar was decreasing."

He broke off.

"I don't think this is interesting you. The rest will interest you even less. There are no ideas in it, and I wish that I had not troubled you to come. We are too different, mother."

She told him to continue.

"It was evening before I climbed the bank. The sun had very nearly slipped out of the sky by this time, and I could not get a good view. You, who have just crossed the Roof of the World, will not want to hear an account of the little hills that I saw—low colourless hills. But to me they were living and the turf that covered them was a skin, under which their muscles rippled, and I felt that those hills had called with incalculable force to men in the past, and that men had loved them. Now they sleep—perhaps for ever. They commune with humanity in dreams. Happy the man, happy the woman, who awakes the hills of Wessex. For though they sleep, they will never die."

His voice rose passionately.

"Cannot you see, cannot all you lecturers see, that it is we that are dying, and that down here the only thing that really lives is the Machine? We created the Machine, to do our will, but we cannot make it do our will now. It has robbed us of the sense of space and of the sense of touch, it has blurred every human relation and narrowed down love to a carnal act, it has paralysed our bodies and our wills, and now it compels us to worship it. The Machine develops—but not on our lines. The Machine proceeds—but not to our goal. We only exist as the blood corpuscles that course through its arteries, and if it could work without us, it would let us die. Oh, I have no remedy—or, at least, only one—to tell men again and again that I have seen the hills of Wessex as Ælfrid saw them when he overthrew the Danes.

"So the sun set. I forgot to mention that a belt of mist lay between my hill and other hills, and that it was the colour of pearl."

He broke off for the second time. "Go on," said his mother wearily. He shook his head.

"Go on. Nothing that you say can distress me now. I am hardened."

"I had meant to tell you the rest, but I cannot; I know that I cannot; good-bye."

Vashti stood irresolute. All her nerves were tingling with his blasphemies. But she was also inquisitive.

"This is unfair," she complained. "You have called me across the world to hear your story, and hear it I will. Tell me—as briefly as possible, for this is a disastrous waste of time—tell me how you returned to civilization."

"Oh—that!" he said, starting. "You would like to hear about civilization. Certainly. Had I got to where my respirator fell down?"

"No—but I understand everything now. You put on your respirator, and managed to walk along the surface of the earth to a vomitory, and there your conduct was reported to the Central Committee."

"By no means."

He passed his hand over his forehead, as if dispelling some strong impression. Then, resuming his narrative, he warmed to it again.

"My respirator fell about sunset. I had mentioned that the fountain seemed feebler, had I not?"

"Yes."

"About sunset, it let the respirator fall. As I said, I had entirely forgotten about the Machine, and I paid no great attention at the time, being occupied with other things. I had my pool of air, into which I could dip when the outer keenness became intolerable, and which would possibly remain for days, provided that no wind sprang up to disperse it. Not until it was too late did I realize what the stoppage of the escape implied. You see—the gap in the tunnel had been mended; the Mending Apparatus; the Mending Apparatus, was after me.

"One other warning I had, but I neglected it. The sky at night was clearer than it had been in the day, and the moon, which was about half the sky behind the sun, shone into the dell at moments quite brightly. I was in my usual place—on the boundary between the two atmospheres—when I thought I saw something dark move across the bottom of the dell, and vanish into the shaft. In my folly, I ran down. I bent over and listened, and I thought I heard a faint scraping noise in the depths.

"At this—but it was too late—I took alarm. I determined to put on my respirator and to walk right out of the dell. But my respirator had gone. I knew exactly where it had fallen—between the stopper and the aperture—and I could even feel the mark that it had made in the turf. It had gone, and I realized that something evil was at work, and I had better escape to the other air, and, if I must die, die running towards the cloud that had been the colour of a pearl. I never started. Out of the shaft—it is too horrible. A worm, a long white worm, had crawled out of the shaft and was gliding over the moonlit grass.

"I screamed. I did everything that I should not have done, I stamped upon the creature instead of flying from it, and it at once curled round the ankle. Then we fought. The worm let me run all over the dell, but edged up my leg as I ran. 'Help!' I cried. (That part is too awful. It belongs to the part that you will never know.) 'Help!' I cried. (Why cannot we suffer in silence?) 'Help!' I cried. Then my feet were wound together, I fell, I was dragged away from the dear ferns and the living hills, and past the great metal stopper (I can tell you this part), and I thought it might save me again if I caught hold of the handle. It also was enwrapped, it also. Oh, the whole dell was full of the things. They were searching it in all directions, they were denuding it, and the white snouts of others peeped out of the hole, ready if needed. Everything that could be moved they brought—

brushwood, bundles of fern, everything, and down we all went intertwined into hell. The last things that I saw, ere the stopper closed after us, were certain stars, and I felt that a man of my sort lived in the sky. For I did fight, I fought till the very end, and it was only my head hitting against the ladder that quieted me. I woke up in this room. The worms had vanished. I was surrounded by artificial air, artificial light, artificial peace, and my friends were calling to me down speaking-tubes to know whether I had come across any new ideas lately."

Here his story ended. Discussion of it was impossible, and Vashti turned to go. "It will end in Homelessness," she said quietly.

"I wish it would," retorted Kuno.

"The Machine has been most merciful."

"I prefer the mercy of God."

"By that superstitious phrase, do you mean that you could live in the outer air?"

"Yes."

"Have you ever seen, round the vomitories, the bones of those who were extruded after the Great Rebellion?"

"Yes."

"They were left where they perished for our edification. A few crawled away, but they perished, too—who can doubt it? And so with the Homeless of our own day. The surface of the earth supports life no longer."

"Indeed."

"Ferns and a little grass may survive, but all higher forms have perished. Has any air-ship detected them?"

"No."

"Has any lecturer dealt with them?"

"No."

"Then why this obstinacy?"

"Because I have seen them," he exploded.

"Seen what?"

"Because I have seen her in the twilight—because she came to my help when I called—because she, too, was entangled by the worms, and, luckier than I, was killed by one of them piercing her throat."

He was mad. Vashti departed, nor, in the troubles that followed, did she ever see his face again.

3. THE HOMELESS

During the years that followed Kuno's escapade, two important developments took place in the Machine. On the surface they were revolutionary, but in either case men's minds had been prepared beforehand, and they did but express tendencies that were latent already.

The first of these was the abolition of respirators.

Advanced thinkers, like Vashti, had always held it foolish to visit the surface of the earth. Air-ships might be necessary, but what was the good of going out for mere curiosity and crawling along for a mile or two in a terrestrial motor?

The habit was vulgar and perhaps faintly improper: it was unproductive of ideas, and had no connection with the habits that really mattered. So respirators were abolished, and with them, of course, the terrestrial motors, and except for a few lecturers, who complained that they were debarred access to their subject-matter, the development was accepted quietly. Those who still wanted to know what the earth was like had after all only to listen to some gramophone, or to look into some cinematophote. And even the lecturers acquiesced when they found that a lecture on the sea was none the less stimulating when compiled out of other lectures that had already been delivered on the same subject. "Beware of first-hand ideas!" exclaimed one of the most advanced of them. "First-hand ideas do not really exist. They are but the physical impressions produced by love and fear, and on this gross foundation who could erect a philosophy? Let your ideas be second-hand, and if possible tenth-hand, for then they will be far removed from that disturbing element—direct observation. Do not learn anything about this subject of mine—the French Revolution. Learn instead what I think that Enicharmon thought Urizen thought Gutch thought Ho-Yung thought Chi-Bo-Sing thought Lafcadio Hearn thought Carlyle thought Mirabeau said about the French Revolution. Through the medium of these ten great minds, the blood that was shed at Paris and the windows that were broken at Versailles will be clarified to an idea which you may employ most profitably in your daily lives. But be sure that the intermediates are many and varied, for in history one authority exists to counteract another. Urizen must counteract the scepticism of Ho-Yung and Enicharmon, I must myself counteract the impetuosity of Gutch. You who listen to me are in a better position to judge about the French Revolution than I am. Your descendants will be even in a better position than you, for they will learn what you think I think, and yet another intermediate will be added to the chain. And in time"—his voice rose—"there will come a generation that had got beyond facts, beyond impressions, a generation absolutely colourless, a generation

>'seraphically free
>From taint of personality,'

which will see the French Revolution not as it happened, nor as they would like it to have happened, but as it would have happened, had it taken place in the days of the Machine."

Tremendous applause greeted this lecture, which did but voice a feeling already latent in the minds of men—a feeling that terrestrial facts must be ignored, and that the abolition of respirators was a positive gain. It was even suggested that air-ships should be abolished too. This was not done, because air-ships had somehow worked themselves into the Machine's system. But year by year they were used less, and mentioned less by thoughtful men.

The second great development was the re-establishment of religion.

This, too, had been voiced in the celebrated lecture. No one could mistake the reverent tone in which the peroration had concluded, and it awakened a responsive echo in the heart of each. Those who had long worshipped silently, now began to talk. They described the strange feeling of peace that came over them when they handled the Book of the Machine, the pleasure that it was to repeat certain numerals out of it, however little meaning those numerals conveyed to the outward ear, the ecstasy of touching a button, however unimportant, or of ringing an electric bell, however superfluously.

"The Machine," they exclaimed, "feeds us and clothes us and houses us; through it we speak to one another, through it we see one another, in it we have our being. The Machine is the friend of ideas and the enemy of superstition; the Machine is omnipotent, eternal; blessed is the Machine." And before long this allocution was printed on the first page of the Book, and in subsequent editions the ritual swelled into a complicated system of praise and prayer. The word "religion" was sedulously avoided, and in theory the Machine was still the creation and the implement of man. But in practice all, save a few retrogrades, worshipped it as divine. Nor was it worshipped in unity. One believer would be chiefly impressed by the blue optic plates, through which he saw other believers; another by the mending apparatus, which sinful Kuno had compared to worms; another by the lifts, another by the Book. And each would pray to this or to that, and ask it to intercede for him with the Machine as a whole. Persecution—that also was present. It did not break out, for reasons that will be set forward shortly. But it was latent, and all who did not accept the minimum known as "undenominational Mechanism" lived in danger of Homelessness, which means death, as we know.

To attribute these two great developments to the Central Committee, is to take a very narrow view of civilization. The Central Committee announced the developments, it is true, but they were no more the cause of them than were the kings of the imperialistic period the cause of war. Rather did they yield to some invincible pressure, which came no one knew whither, and which, when gratified, was succeeded by some new pressure equally invincible. To such a state of affairs it is convenient to give the name of progress. No one confessed the Machine was out of hand. Year by year it was served with increased efficiency and decreased intelligence. The better a man knew his own duties upon it, the less he understood the duties of his neighbour, and in all the world there was not one who understood the monster as a whole. Those master brains had perished. They had left full directions, it is true, and their successors had each of them mastered a portion of those directions. But Humanity, in its desire for comfort, had over-reached itself. It had exploited the riches of nature too far. Quietly and complacently, it was sinking into decadence, and progress had come to mean the progress of the Machine.

As for Vashti, her life went peacefully forward until the final disaster. She made her room dark and slept; she awoke and made the room light. She lectured and attended lectures. She exchanged ideas with her innumerable friends and believed she was growing more spiritual. At times a friend was granted Euthanasia, and left his or her room for the homelessness that is beyond all human conception. Vashti did not much mind. After an unsuccessful lecture, she would sometimes ask for Euthanasia herself. But the death-rate was not permitted to exceed the birth-rate, and the Machine had hitherto refused it to her.

The troubles began quietly, long before she was conscious of them.

One day she was astonished at receiving a message from her son. They never communicated, having nothing in common, and she had only heard indirectly that he was still alive, and had been transferred from the northern hemisphere, where he had behaved so mischievously, to the southern—indeed, to a room not far from her own.

"Does he want me to visit him?" she thought. "Never again, never. And I have not the time."

No, it was madness of another kind.

He refused to visualize his face upon the blue plate, and speaking out of the darkness with solemnity said:

"The Machine stops."

"What do you say?"

"The Machine is stopping, I know it, I know the signs."

She burst into a peal of laughter. He heard her and was angry, and they spoke no more.

"Can you imagine anything more absurd?" she cried to a friend. "A man who was my son believes that the Machine is stopping. It would be impious if it was not mad."

"The Machine is stopping?" her friend replied. "What does that mean? The phrase conveys nothing to me."

"Nor to me."

"He does not refer, I suppose, to the trouble there has been lately with the music?"

"Oh no, of course not. Let us talk about music."

"Have you complained to the authorities?"

"Yes, and they say it wants mending, and referred me to the Committee of the Mending Apparatus. I complained of those curious gasping sighs that disfigure the symphonies of the Brisbane school. They sound like someone in pain. The Committee of the Mending Apparatus say that it shall be remedied shortly."

Obscurely worried, she resumed her life. For one thing, the defect in the music irritated her. For another thing, she could not forget Kuno's speech. If he had known that the music was out of repair—he could not know it, for he detested music—if he had known that it was wrong, "the Machine stops" was exactly the venomous sort of remark he would have made. Of course he had made it at a venture, but the coincidence annoyed her, and she spoke with some petulance to the Committee of the Mending Apparatus.

They replied, as before, that the defect would be set right shortly.

"Shortly! At once!" she retorted. "Why should I be worried by imperfect music? Things are always put right at once. If you do not mend it at once, I shall complain to the Central Committee."

"No personal complaints are received by the Central Committee," the Committee of the Mending Apparatus replied.

"Through whom am I to make my complaint, then?"

"Through us."

"I complain then."

"Your complaint shall be forwarded in its turn."

"Have others complained?"

This question was unmechanical, and the Committee of the Mending Apparatus refused to answer it.

"It is too bad!" she exclaimed to another of her friends. "There never was such an unfortunate woman as myself. I can never be sure of my music now. It gets worse and worse each time I summon it."

"I too have my troubles," the friend replied. "Sometimes my ideas are interrupted by a slight jarring noise."

"What is it?"

"I do not know whether it is inside my head, or inside the wall."

"Complain, in either case."

"I have complained, and my complaint will be forwarded in its turn to the Central Committee."

Time passed, and they resented the defects no longer. The defects had not been remedied, but the human tissues in that latter day had become so subservient, that they readily adapted themselves to every caprice of the Machine. The sigh at the crises of the Brisbane symphony no longer irritated Vashti; she accepted it as part of the melody. The jarring noise, whether in the head or in the wall, was no longer resented by her friend. And so with the mouldy artificial fruit, so with the bath water that began to stink, so with the defective rhymes that the poetry machine had taken to emit. All were bitterly complained of at first, and then acquiesced in and forgotten. Things went from bad to worse unchallenged.

It was otherwise with the failure of the sleeping apparatus. That was a more serious stoppage. There came a day when over the whole world—in Sumatra, in Wessex, in the innumerable cities of Courland and Brazil—the beds, when summoned by their tired owners, failed to appear. It may seem a ludicrous matter, but from it we may date the collapse of humanity. The Committee responsible for the failure was assailed by complainants, whom it referred, as usual, to the Committee of the Mending Apparatus, who in its turn assured them that their complaints would be forwarded to the Central Committee. But the discontent grew, for mankind was not yet sufficiently adaptable to do without sleeping.

"Some one is meddling with the Machine—" they began.

"Some one is trying to make himself king, to reintroduce the personal element."

"Punish that man with Homelessness."

"To the rescue! Avenge the Machine! Avenge the Machine!"

"War! Kill the man!"

But the Committee of the Mending Apparatus now came forward, and allayed the panic with well-chosen words. It confessed that the Mending Apparatus was itself in need of repair.

The effect of this frank confession was admirable.

"Of course," said a famous lecturer—he of the French Revolution, who gilded each new decay with splendour—"of course we shall not press our complaints now. The Mending Apparatus has treated us so well in the past that we all sympathize with it, and will wait patiently for its recovery. In its own good time it will resume its duties. Meanwhile let us do without our beds, our tabloids, our other little wants. Such, I feel sure, would be the wish of the Machine."

Thousands of miles away his audience applauded. The Machine still linked them. Under the seas, beneath the roots of the mountains, ran the wires through which they saw and heard, the enormous eyes and ears that were their heritage, and the hum of many workings clothed their thoughts in one garment of subserviency. Only the old and the sick remained ungrateful, for it was rumoured that Euthanasia, too, was out of order, and that pain had reappeared among men.

It became difficult to read. A blight entered the atmosphere and dulled its luminosity. At times Vashti could scarcely see across her room. The air, too, was foul. Loud were the complaints, impotent the remedies, heroic the tone of the lecturer as he cried: "Courage! courage! What matter so long as the Machine goes on? To it the darkness and the light are one." And though things improved again after a time, the old brilliancy was never recaptured, and humanity never recovered from its entrance into twilight. There was an hysterical talk of "measures," of "provisional dictatorship," and the inhabitants of Sumatra were asked to familiarize themselves with the workings of the central power station, the said power station being situated in France. But for the most part panic reigned, and men spent their strength praying to their Books, tangible proofs of the Machine's omnipotence. There were gradations of terror—at times came rumours of hope—the Mending Apparatus was almost mended—the enemies of the Machine had been got under—new "nerve-centres" were evolving which would do the work even more magnificently than before. But there came a day when, without the slightest warning, without any previous hint of feebleness, the entire communication-system broke down, all over the world, and the world, as they understood it, ended.

Vashti was lecturing at the time and her earlier remarks had been punctuated with applause. As she proceeded the audience became silent, and at the conclusion there was no sound. Somewhat displeased, she called to a friend who was a specialist in sympathy. No sound: doubtless the friend was sleeping. And so with the next friend whom she tried to summon, and so with the next, until she remembered Kuno's cryptic remark, "The Machine stops".

The phrase still conveyed nothing. If Eternity was stopping it would of course be set going shortly.

For example, there was still a little light and air—the atmosphere had improved a few hours previously. There was still the Book, and while there was the Book there was security.

Then she broke down, for with the cessation of activity came an unexpected terror—silence.

She had never known silence, and the coming of it nearly killed her—it did kill many thousands of people outright. Ever since her birth she had been surrounded by the steady hum. It was to the ear what artificial air was to the lungs, and agonizing pains shot across her head. And scarcely knowing what she did, she stumbled forward and pressed the unfamiliar button, the one that opened the door of her cell.

Now the door of the cell worked on a simple hinge of its own. It was not connected with the central power station, dying far away in France. It opened, rousing immoderate hopes in Vashti, for she thought that the Machine had been mended. It opened, and she saw the dim tunnel that curved far away towards freedom. One look, and then she shrank back. For the tunnel was full of people—

she was almost the last in that city to have taken alarm. People at any time repelled her, and these were nightmares from her worst dreams. People were crawling about, people were screaming, whimpering, gasping for breath, touching each other, vanishing in the dark, and ever and anon being pushed off the platform on to the live rail. Some were fighting round the electric bells, trying to summon trains which could not be summoned. Others were yelling for Euthanasia or for respirators, or blaspheming the Machine. Others stood at the doors of their cells fearing, like herself, either to stop in them or to leave them. And behind all the uproar was silence—the silence which is the voice of the earth and of the generations who have gone.

No—it was worse than solitude. She closed the door again and sat down to wait for the end. The disintegration went on, accompanied by horrible cracks and rumbling. The valves that restrained the Medical Apparatus must have weakened, for it ruptured and hung hideously from the ceiling. The floor heaved and fell and flung her from the chair. A tube oozed towards her serpent fashion. And at last the final horror approached—light began to ebb, and she knew that civilization's long day was closing.

She whirled around, praying to be saved from this, at any rate, kissing the Book, pressing button after button. The uproar outside was increasing, and even penetrated the wall. Slowly the brilliancy of her cell was dimmed, the reflections faded from the metal switches. Now she could not see the reading-stand, now not the Book, though she held it in her hand. Light followed the flight of sound, air was following light, and the original void returned to the cavern from which it had so long been excluded. Vashti continued to whirl, like the devotees of an earlier religion, screaming, praying, striking at the buttons with bleeding hands.

It was thus that she opened her prison and escaped—escaped in the spirit: at least so it seems to me, ere my meditation closes. That she escapes in the body—I cannot perceive that. She struck, by chance, the switch that released the door, and the rush of foul air on her skin, the loud throbbing whispers in her ears, told her that she was facing the tunnel again, and that tremendous platform on which she had seen men fighting. They were not fighting now. Only the whispers remained, and the little whimpering groans. They were dying by hundreds out in the dark.

She burst into tears.

Tears answered her.

They wept for humanity, those two, not for themselves. They could not bear that this should be the end. Ere silence was completed their hearts were opened, and they knew what had been important on the earth. Man, the flower of all flesh, the noblest of all creatures visible, man who had once made god in his image, and had mirrored his strength on the constellations, beautiful naked man was dying, strangled in the garments that he had woven. Century after century had he toiled, and here was his reward. Truly the garment had seemed heavenly at first, shot with colours of culture, sewn with the threads of self-denial. And heavenly it had been so long as it was a garment and no more, so long as man could shed it at will and live by the essence that is his soul, and the essence, equally divine, that is his body. The sin against the body—it was for that they wept in chief; the centuries of wrong against the muscles and the nerves, and those five portals by which we can alone apprehend—glozing it over with talk of evolution, until the body was white pap, the home of ideas as colourless, last sloshy stirrings of a spirit that had grasped the stars.

"Where are you?" she sobbed.

His voice in the darkness said, "Here."

"Is there any hope, Kuno?"

"None for us."

"Where are you?"

She crawled towards him over the bodies of the dead. His blood spurted over her hands.

"Quicker," he gasped, "I am dying—but we touch, we talk, not through the Machine."

He kissed her.

"We have come back to our own. We die, but we have recaptured life, as it was in Wessex, when Ælfrid overthrew the Danes. We know what they know outside, they who dwelt in the cloud that is the colour of a pearl."

"But Kuno, is it true? Are there still men on the surface of the earth? Is this—this tunnel, this poisoned darkness—really not the end?"

He replied:

"I have seen them, spoken to them, loved them. They are hiding in the mist and the ferns until our civilization stops. To-day they are the Homeless—tomorrow—"

"Oh, tomorrow—some fool will start the Machine again, tomorrow."

"Never," said Kuno, "never. Humanity has learnt its lesson."

As he spoke, the whole city was broken like a honeycomb. An air-ship had sailed in through the vomitory into a ruined wharf. It crashed downwards, exploding as it went, rending gallery after gallery with its wings of steel. For a moment they saw the nations of the dead, and, before they joined them, scraps of the untainted sky.

(1909)

ALL HAIL THE NEW FLESH

Being "robotic" is no-one's idea of a good time. Predictable, passive, unemotional – no-one wants to be "robotic".

But... *being a robot?* That's a very different proposition! Evolution has made us clever hunters who enjoy thinking our way into the heads and under the hides of other species. Robots intrigue us as wolves and deer intrigued our ancestors. We want to know our neighbours inside out. They may have something valuable to teach us. In any event we need to know how they live, in case we ever need to kill them.

This section of *We Robots* invites you on shamanic journeys into the lives and bodies of all manner of mechanical beings. Sometimes – for example, in Nalo Hopkinson's "Ganger (Ball Lightning)" (2000) – we find mechanical beings are making shamanic forays into our own realm.

Underpinning all these stories is the proposition that a life in metal has qualities of its own which it will be worth our while to explore. What would it be like, to be a robot? To be a human soul wrapped in non-human flesh – or (as in the stories by Joanna Kavenna, M. John Harrison and William Gibson) in no flesh at all?

The machine bodies we have so far made are so much simpler than our own bodies, they hardly bear comparison. The radical simplicity of machine being, compared to biological being, is its own source of horror in M. H. Hasta's "The Talking Brain" (1926). Having to severely restrict their physiology drives the posthuman heroes of Cordwainer Smith's "Scanners Live in Vain" to something very like madness.

But what if Spartan simplicity weren't agonising? What if it was refreshing – even fascinating? Quite what Sam must be going through inside his new metal flesh is a secret saved for the very last line of Damon Knight's "Masks" (1968), while Deirdre, the once-human heroine of C. L. Moore's "No Woman Born" (1944) grows ever more strange, even as she rises in our estimation. She's off on an adventure, leaving her humanity behind but not her agency, embracing a life that's no less rich and nuanced for being less and less to do with blood and bone.

The heroes and heroines of general fiction dabble with a dangerous world but in the end, they rarely give themselves to it. To see them returning home, wounded and wiser for it, is one of the chief satisfactions of that literature. Literary realists go even further when they explore the fate of those who can't even bring themselves to let go of the side of the swimming pool.

Science fiction, on the other hand, is very good – for some tastes, far too good – at what the psychoanalysts call "manic flight". Its protagonists are constantly striking out for the deep end of the pool and *staying there*, whooping and gamboling in transformed fashion in waves that have surely already killed them.

It's a rare science fiction writer who calls time on the party, and brings their protagonist back to shore. With "Musée de l'Âme Seule" (2014) E. Lily Yu proves herself one of the braver writers in this anthology, for looking physical loss straight in the face. This is a story of victory and renewal, but one that's strictly for grown-ups. Losing parts of your physical self is a psychological and physical assault for which no amount of bionic wizardry can compensate. To suppose otherwise is fashionable, but contemptible.

Living as a robot seems to promise a solution to life's great shortcomings: being vulnerable, and having to die. When something breaks, just plug in a spare! But lives ported over to metal, carbon fibre, synthetic flesh or some digital cloud, also present us with what may be a one-way trip to a sort of half-life.

Worse still, we may never know, reduced as we have been, that this life of ours *is* only a half-life. We may lack the very equipment necessary for us to understand and appreciate what it is we have lost. As H. G. Wells wrote, "Plainly the human animal, of which I am a sample, is not constituted to anticipate anything at all. It is constituted to accept the state of affairs about it, as a stable state of affairs, whatever its intelligence may tell it to the contrary."

Whenever we think about becoming robots, we find ourselves re-evaluating our original, human condition. Bodies are frail and cyborgisation is exciting, but if the stories that follow teach us anything, it is that it is still not too shabby of us to stay human, if we can.

THE HAMMER

Carl Sandburg

The poet, writer, and folk musician **Carl August Sandburg** was born in Galesburg, Illinois in 1878, the son of Swedish immigrants. After college he roamed the country, supporting himself by selling Underwood and Underwood stereoscopic pictures and giving an occasional lecture on Whitman, George Bernard Shaw, or Abraham Lincoln. When he ran out of money, he hopped a freight train. He eventually settled into journalism, winning plaudits at the *Chicago Daily News*. He worked as a correspondent during both world wars, and in between covered politics, crime, business, and civil rights. He won three Pulitzer Prizes: two for his poetry and one for an insanely long biography of Abraham Lincoln. (*Abraham Lincoln: The War Years* alone exceeds in length the collected writings of Shakespeare by some 150,000 words.) Sandburg's poetry split opinion: the journalist Karl Detzer wrote that "admirers proclaimed him a latter-day Walt Whitman; objectors cried that their six-year-old daughters could write better poetry." H. L. Mencken called Sandburg "a true original, his own man."

I have seen
The old gods go
And the new gods come.

Day by day
And year by year
The idols fall
And the idols rise.

Today
I worship the hammer.

(1910)

GOOD TO GO

Liz Jensen

Liz Jensen (born 1959) lives in Copenhagen with the Danish writer Carsten Jensen. She first worked as a radio journalist in Taiwan, and then for the BBC as a TV and radio producer. She wrote her first novel, the black comedy *Egg Dancing* (1995), in Paris, where she worked as a sculptor. She was elected a Fellow of the Royal Society of Literature in 2005. Her novel *The Ninth Life of Louis Drax* was adapted for film in 2016. Her comedy and satire have darkened perceptibly over the years. *The Rapture* (2009) and *The Uninvited* (2012) are decidedly unsettling ecological thrillers.

It's peak season here at the lake – a hundred in the shade, breeze like a sadist hair-dryer, speedboats stirring up alga scuzz. Weekends like this, the whole town's packed with Utah runaways getting high like only Mormons can, making it the busiest test-market I've worked so far, and I seen a few. As one of Arizona's top domestic violence/sports accident nexuses, Havasu's ideal to trial a project like this.

"Hi there, I'm Kylie, Angel Operator, at your service." That's what I say to the tragedies when they come in. Which may sound dumb seeing as they can't hear me, but you're getting intimate with someone, you introduce yourself at least, is my thinking.

The software's called Sweet Parting. According to Threshold, it's "inspired by the William Shakespeare quotation *parting is such sweet sorrow.*" Some of us Angel operators think it's classy but the encrypted chat-room consensus is, it's lame. Some of us came up with our own: My Way, Over and Out, Je Ne Regrette, Die Nice, I'll Pass.

Anyway, it turns out the local death rate's so high I've barely switched the machine off since I got here four weeks ago: murders, boat smashes, cooking explosions, car wrecks, drugs-and-alcohol offences, pervert auto-asphyxiations, you name it. And suicides up the ass. Had one come in last night, a bleach-swallower, sweet sixteen, with eyes all big and dark and shit-scared till the Angel worked its magic. No way, I thought. There's still such a thing as bleach?

A primitive, the sexy new doc on the ICU called her. But truth is, she could've been me a decade or so back, before I quit Kentucky and straightened out.

When I sent the kid's report in to the Operator Feedback Division, I flagged up the exit shot, told them Threshold should use it in the promotional material when they launch, cuz bleach or no bleach, she went out with the best smile I've seen all year.

Her final wish? A ten-inch butterfly tramp-stamp, one wing either side of the coccyx. I kid you not.

Anyway according to the grapevine that we Angel operators aren't supposed to even have, except we do, they're designing the next generation before we've even fixed the glitches in this one. The jury's out on what that means. Don't get me wrong, I'm glad to have a job at all, with my history. In fact I think I speak for all of us in your employ, O mighty Threshold Care Corporation, when I say us Angel operators would go just about anywhere you choose to send us. Wouldn't suit anyone with a family and ties, but the pay's sweet, and you get to see places you'd never go otherwise: I've lived in Woonsocket, Rhode Island; Paragould, Arkansas; Black Diamond, Washington; Bismarck, North Dakota. And now hello, Lake Havasu City.

I drive over the original London Bridge every day on my way to the hospital. It must've been quite a landmark when the millionaire dude imported it stone by stone from Ye Olde England to make a tourist feature, but now it's just part of the general shitscape: highway, hotel complexes, Walgreen's, and – which is where I'm headed – Starbucks. I'm a creature of habit. I stop, buy one, and drink it in the car. Ew, yeah.

I roll into the ICU and fire up the Angel, and see the sexy new doc's there again, the one that called the bleach-swallower a *primitive*.

"Hi Medicine Man."

"Hi Kylie. Call me Angus."

He's early twenties, but I'm in good shape, so I'm on his radar. Hmm. Dr Angus van der Kamp. Sounds like a bull.

"How's it hanging today, Angus?" He can rampage me any time.

"It's hanging good thanks Kylie. We've got an ambulance due in fifteen. Car smash on the highway, oncoming truck driver DOA, two Angel candidates."

"Cool. I like the challenge of multiples."

He smiles. "Funny you should say that. I do too. I appreciate that extra layer of decision-making."

Twenty minutes later I've hooked both tragedies into the system, an old man and a teenage girl, a family combo. The junior cop who came in with the ambulance must be a newbie, cuz she can't stop staring at the messed-up leaking bodies.

"It used to get to me too once upon a time. But not any more," I tell her. "Hasn't for the last three postings. Can't afford it, mental-health-wise. You get jaded instead, is what happens. These two'll get a good send-off I promise. They'll leave this world happy. Off you go kid, we got work to do."

When the door's swung behind her, Medicine Man shoots me a look. "We're not supposed to discuss it."

"I didn't say anything," I say, adjusting the old man's head-mesh.

He face-shrugs. "Be careful, is all."

"I worked obstetrics once," I tell him as we prep up. "Loved it. You know, when you see them born, covered in blood and that white waxy shit and all, wriggling and then screaming and your heart goes yeah, yeah, yeah, you know? Life."

He smiles. "Sure. I been there too. Nothing like it."

"When I joined Threshold, I expected the same kind of kick. I mean, departure shouldn't be that different from arrival. Not if it's done right. Big spiritual moment, right?"

His eyebrows go up. "But?"

"Doesn't happen. When I get into their cognitive system, you can see it's not working how it should. I'm not the only one that thinks that. So operating the machine's a bittersweet experience, is what I'm saying."

"You seemed happy enough with the kid last night, how that went."

"The one you called a primitive? I was and I wasn't. I mean, she smiled nice when she got her ass-tattoo. But there's more to a good death than a smile, right? You have to look at what the Angel's promising here, then figure out if it's delivering."

"Isn't that why Threshold's trialling it?"

"Sure. I'm just saying, they haven't thought it through."

He looks at me sharp. "Kylie. Be careful. You can trust me – but you can't trust everyone."

"Confidentiality pledge doesn't say you can't discuss philosophy with colleagues."

He thinks for a minute, then grins back at me. "She wants philosophy, huh. OK. You know what this reminds me of?" he cocks his head at the tragedies.

"No, what?"

"The one that goes: I'd like to die peacefully in my sleep like my grandfather. Not screaming in terror like his passengers."

I'm not expecting it: I laugh so hard I spit my coffee back into the cup.

I'm still chuckling as I calibrate the Angel to my pulse, put on the helmet and dock in.

"Hi there, Kylie Wells, Angel Operator, at your service." The old geezer on the slab goes by the name of Jerry according to his ankle-tag. "So where have you mentally transported yourself to, my senior friend?" He's well into shut-down but I have a knack with cognitive pathways, so I'm in real quick. It takes a moment to adjust to his mind's eye cuz he's clearly been drinking but when I do, the image is clear.

We're entering a casino, name of Treasure Island. Las Vegas, I'm guessing. It's a popular destination. Symbolic in some way I guess. The lottery of life and yada yada.

He loiters a bit near the entrance, taking in the ambience: the ventilated spice atmospheric, the horizon of heads, the clack of chips, the jewelled fingers, the beer-guts, the leathery cleavage-cracks. He's feeling a hell of a lot younger than he really is. The old folk tend to. It's a self-perception slash vanity thing.

No-one pops up in his mind so I sketch in a host: the generic man's man the system calls a Jimbo. I choose Jimbo 2, who's in his forties, the age Jerry's feeling.

"I used to play a lot," Jerry tells Jimbo 2, who's playing doorman. "Never won big-time, not once. I'd come in and blow it the same night, left broke, the usual story, huh? Guess you've seen it a thousand times."

"Sure have sir," says the doorman. They like being called sir. "So what brings you back to our fine establishment tonight?"

"Oh, a memory lane thing I guess. Farewell visit. Last try at cheating the system."

Incredible how on some level they always just know.

The doorman laughs. "Dollar for every time I hear that one, I'd be Alex Bezos."

Jerry clucks his teeth, makes a face. "Good to be here. Came from my daughter's wedding, over at the Lake."

"Oh yeah?"

"Five months pregnant, already got two, different fathers and her eldest's retarded. Anyway up the aisle she goes. Snowball's chance in hell of that one working out. I give it two years, max."

"Who's the lucky guy?"

"A florist. What kind of man becomes a goddam florist?"

The doorman thinks for a moment. "How were the flowers?"

They both laugh, loud and meaty. Jerry sighs. "Anyway, family row, the usual shit. So I quit and here I am, all set to bet."

"You left your daughter's wedding?"

"Let's just say I removed myself from the equation," says Jerry. "Best for all concerned."

"Families, huh?" says Jimbo 2, shaking his head. "So, you feeling lucky tonight sir?"

"Matter of fact I am. Feel like I might just walk out with a few thou. No, let's make that a million, why not. Yeah. I'm up for that."

"That what you want, sir?"

"You betcha. Would you say no to a million, man?"

"No, sir, I would not. Well, good luck."

"Yeah, nice talking."

Jerry takes a breath, forces his way to the bar at the centre, buys a double scotch, knocks it back in one, then gets himself a hundred dollars' worth of chips. Meanwhile here at Ground Control my stomach's rumbling. Come on Jerry, pick a table and let's get started, I'm thinking. But he's not progressing. He's wandering around with his chips, looking at the tables, but not picking one. I was expecting Jerry to launch fast and smooth into the Great Beyond with his un-earned million in his pocket, and a big winner's smile, false teeth blazing – but no. He's sensing something's off. You know when a cat's decided to settle somewhere, and instead of just sitting down, it turns around and around and around, like it can't decide which compass-point its ass should point to? Well Jerry's indecision, it's like that. Kind of a circling the drain thing I guess.

The system's registered that the client's uncomfortable and losing his gambling nerve.

From the way he's swaying now, as he heads for the Men's, you can tell he's got that seasickness problem the tech guys can't seem to crack. The Angel Wobble we call it. I co-feel stuff but so far I've been immune to that one. Some colleagues, they'll actually puke.

He staggers to the sink and splashes cold water on his face, then takes a deep breath and looks up.

AAAGH! The line on my screen spikes, then plunges.

Jesus. Woah there, thinks Jerry. WOAH! Who's that ugly old bastard in the mirror? He blinks with shock. Jesus. It's me. What happened?

I can't help laughing. He hurtles out faster than you can say, suck it up, old man.

So, scrub Las Vagas as a scenario.

Repeat offer? The Angel wants Jimbo 2 back in the frame.

I know Jerry won't go for it, but I press OK anyway. Call it a little bet with myself.

"Hey big guy," says Jimbo 2 as he heads for the door. "You quitting already?"

"Yeah," goes Jerry. "Just didn't feel right." Like it's some heroic moral choice he's made.

The Angel tries again, with Jimbo 2 saying: "You ain't tempted to go back in and take your chances?"

"Nah, man," says Jerry. "It's a young man's game. I'm done here."

"Told ya!" I yell at the Angel. In my side vision Angus looks at me with a question on his face. "Sorry. Got carried away there," I tell him. "System's an idiot. I'll need to re-boot Jerry here, he bailed out." I shift the input. "While he's in limbo let's do the other one."

When the helmet's re-calibrated I enter the kid, name of Jessie-May. She's got mild cerebral palsy according to the notes, and on top of that she's all over the place emotionally, probably cuz her mother's piggybacking. You get that a lot. Parents, priests, exes from hell, etcetera. Parasite presences, usually malign. I include God here. Takes a while to calibrate Jessie-May, and once I'm in we're straight into a bad memory. She just peed herself behind the wedding marquee and wet her dress. When Ma found out she went apeshit and slapped her cheek right in front of the pastor.

Sorry 'bout that sir, said Ma. *I know it don't look too Christian, on my wedding-day and all. But Jessie-May here's got learning difficulties. And sometimes the fact is, a big girl needs a big slap. Pissing yourself at your own mother's wedding. What kinda behaviour's that, huh? I said, HUH?* And Jessie's thinking: weddings suck. Everyone's being mean. When Grandaddy leaves I'm hitching a ride.

I tweak the sensor, fast-forward her the hell out. Jeez, I thought my family was bad, God rest em.

So now she's on her own in the desert someplace near the scene of the crash no doubt, all dry dirt and clumps of tumbleweed and other bitch-scratch vegetation. No landmarks, except a hill up ahead, turbines sprouting out, spinning to the max. And down there in the valley, a grove. Almonds maybe. Whatever. It's a long way off but she's thirsty as hell. She's still wearing the dress that she pissed all over behind the marquee. She hates it. Well I empathise with you there Jessie-May. Lavender silk. A dumb sash at the back, like she's a Christmas parcel.

She's just getting to wondering how the hell she got here. Jessie don't think fast, but she thinks just fine – till Ma crashes in again.

Might not all be such a blur if you paid some attention, Missy. Might not be if you asked a few questions of whoever was driving the car, check they're not over the alcohol limit.

If there was a way to un-fuse that bitch Ma from the kid I'd do it, believe me, but she makes a valid point.

Jessie-May's main feeling right now is thirst: I'm getting it too. She's remembering how Grandaddy told her about the time he woke up from a blackout in the boondocks and found himself in a peach-grove and drank water straight from the irrigation pipe.

Come on kid, Kylie's rooting for you here. Use that memory, it came to you for a reason. You're not the only thirsty one here.

Up she gets. That's my girl. Jessie-May's legs are uncooperative but she makes it to the plantation and puts her lips to the rubber pipe that snakes along the first line of trees and sucks the water, too hot, with grit and all. Broken almond shells dig into her knees and there's a diesel and blood smell on her that I can't fade out completely.

When she's finished she looks up and sees a building: some kind of kiosk.

So you gonna head that way and try get yourself cleaned up, or you gonna lie there and feel sorry for yasself, Princess? bitches Ma.

The sign's hanging loose. Place looks abandoned. But there'll be shade.

So what you waiting for, dumbass? Go for it, before I—.

The door clangs as she pushes it open – an old fashioned bell. Interesting Angel factoid: retro or even genre features can pop up in folk who have the TV on all day.

So she's in, and I'm about to introduce a host when Medicine Man taps me on the arm and points at the monitor.

Uh-oh, Jerry's light's flashing. He's in the countdown phase. Unexpected. I slow Jessie-May's trajectory as far as I can – her exit's not too close at this point – and haul Jerry up. The re-boot's caused him to re-wind a bit, chronology-wise. Another design fault. He's outside, in the heat, probably right near where he crashed the car and half-killed them both. Landscape's the same as where Jessie-May was, the turbines, the grove in the distance. Don't look back, my friend, you won't like what you see.

Ahead, there's the building. Some kind of hardware store, he reckons.

Another Angel factoid: eight times out of ten it's a retail outlet.

He heads over. He's still on the agitated side so I take him down a few notches till I get him through the door. Inside it's dark and jumbled, the shelving stuffed with stock, a mix of new and second-hand. There's rusty chisels and lathes, drills, glass jars full of nuts and bolts, others with nails in and in between, modern plastic-packaged items: Superglue, electric hedge trimmers, face-masks.

Hmm, goes Jerry's tragic little guy-brain, and he starts walking around looking at the shelves with a song running in his head, *she's a good-hearted woman in love with a good-timin' man, up and down, she loves him in spite of his wicked ways she don't understand.* Didn't I have a list somewhere, of shit I needed? Bulbs, three-inch masonry nails, grout, some WD40 for that hinge in the garage? Yeah. *Through teardrops and laughter they'll pass through the world hand in hand*, and I sure could do with a real nice set of screwdrivers. State-of-the-art, a proper grip on em, ten different sizes, *the good hearted woman lovin' her two-timin' man—*.

And so it goes in this mode until he stumbles on – WOAH! – the bad stuff.

That happens, and you don't always see it coming.

He's looking at a bunch of weird broken shit in a heap. Trash, mostly. A half-melted Barbie doll. A bike with its front wheel missing and no chain. A banjo with no strings and a cracked back.

Cue the Freudian slash Jungian craporama.

This is where they tend to flip into introspective mode, if they're ever going to. The idea is, the broken objects represent their life's mistakes, unfulfilled dreams and general regrets. Triggering the realization that they've done bad stuff, or failed to do good stuff, leading to some hokey self-assessment where they try to fix it by asking God/their Higher Power/the Universe for forgiveness before they croak, cuz the Angel's not in the business of sending folk to hell, no matter how much they belong there. So here's where they get the closure thing they need, to so-called rest in peace.

So now he's suddenly feeling low, and I'm co-feeling it. But – bad programming again – most folk just don't see what's there in front of them. So Jerry's sensing that all this junk is significant, the melted Barbie in particular: something about Jessie-May being treated like shit by her Ma and probably the rest of the family too including him. But he's not making the connection. The system isn't nudging properly, is what's happening here. Inadequate signposting. So he just stands there eyeing the pile of trash, feeling blue, not coming to any conclusions, still humming his little Waylon Jennings cheating song, wanting to fix things but with no idea how, even though he's surrounded by tools and repair kits. Go figure.

It's not going to develop, I can see that, so I introduce another host, Jimbo 3, nicknamed "Jimbo the Sage" because of his great age of around 85 and his supposed backwoods old-timer wisdom, in an attempt to kick Jerry into a new focus.

"Howdy. What can I do you for, sir?" says Jimbo 3.

"Well I'm not sure."

"That's often the way. You find us OK?" asks Jimbo 3.

"Think so. Anyways, here I am. Feeling kinda strange."

"A common complaint sir. Folk can have real trouble getting here. By the time they reach us, some have had the time to ponder what they're after so they're pretty specific. Others – perhaps like you, sir – haven't managed to pinpoint it yet. Do you have any ideas?"

"I musta done before I came in, but now I'm not so sure. I was in Vegas but I changed my mind."

"Well, just take a look around, take your time, sir. No hurry. You on your own?" (The system's not being quite truthful with him here. He's got precisely 23 seconds left.)

A thought comes to him. "My grand-daughter. Jessie-May. She was with me in the car. You seen a kid don't look right, in a bridesmaid's dress?"

Aha, now we're getting somewhere – but he'd better hurry, the timeout's flashing. *Go on Jerry, I'm rooting for ya.*

Jimbo 3 says, "She's right here, sir."

"That's great!" But he's distracted by the tools.

"You want to see her? Have a word?"

"Sure. In a minute. I was thinking, you got any real nice state-of-the-art-type screwdriver kits?"

"Oh shit, you *dork*!" I yell. The sexy doc looks up.

"You OK there?" he mouths. I nod.

The host says, "Screwdrivers? We sure have sir." *Twelve, eleven, ten...*

"So let's see 'em."

Jimbo 3 goes: "And Jessie-May, sir? Did you want to see her, say a few words?"

Go on, you dick!

"I'm talking the kind with the magnetised tip."

His wish is the Angel's command. From nowhere a box appears and the lid flips open to reveal a gleaming array of stainless-steel screwdrivers. Even I'm impressed.

"Can you beat that, sir?" asks Jimbo 3.

And just look at Jerry's face split ear to ear, dentures blazing and glory be. What a smile. The camera clicks and clinches the money shot – the one thing the Angel never fails on – and Jerry exhales, with his last breath, the immortal words: "Wow, willya just look at those big boys. Now that's what I call a classy—"

Then zaps. Game over.

What a grade-A prick. Last chance to see his grand-kid, and chooses tools.

I sign him out, depressed as fuck. "All done," I tell Angus. "We can package him."

When we get back to Jessie-May there's not much time left on her countdown. She's made her way into the kiosk, where there's candy.

"Welcome," says a voice. Jessie-May turns. The host-lady she's conjured looks like her Ma, but nice, and not pregnant or in a wedding-dress. Softer, less make-up, less mean. She sinks down to look Jessie-May in the eye, all kind and concerned. Smooth skin, smells of honey and roses.

"What's your name sweetheart?"

"Jessie-May."

"Pretty name! How can I help you?"

"Is this a store?"

"It's whatever you like," says the lady, and smiles. "Do you have any idea what you'd like on this mighty hot day?"

"You have ice-cream?"

"Sure, hon. Got a whole freezerful out back. Baskin Robbins, Ben and Jerrys, Häagen Dazs, you name it. Got a favourite flavour?"

Jesus. Not again.

You see, this is the point where it goes wrong. Every time. Look at Jessie-May: she's talking ice-cream now *because that's what she was prompted to do* with that "mighty hot day" shit, and naming the freaking brands: that's what an attorney would call a leading question. So now we're into Peanut Butter, Bubblegum, Double Chocolate Chip and blah blah. I've been here a thousand times, I know how it ends: they exit thinking of a favourite ice-cream flavour slash sexual position slash in Grandpa Jerry's case, set of goddamn screwdrivers. Now maybe that's a cool way to go. But ask yourself, is that what the system was designed for?

"Jesus, this sucks," I tell Angus when the kid's zapped out. "Sweet Parting my ass." We check out the money shot. Will that cute smile trigger Ma into having some long dark nights of the soul concerning the shit way she treated her? More likely she'll say to herself and everyone, *I did everything I could for her as a mother, she passed away knowing she was loved, just look at my adorable happy girl.*

Medicine man puts his hand on my arm. "It's a tough job, no question." He's got a hint of stubble, I like that. And you can tell he works out. "Some gum?" He fishes in his pocket, pulls out – woah. Like, about seven varieties. Including a brand-new one I never seen before.

"*Gingko Berry?* You're kidding me. Gotta give that a go." I unwrap it and chew. "Mmm, weird."

"New things are always weird the first time."

"Make me laugh, Angus. I need cheering up. You got any more jokes?"

He thinks. "How did Captain Hook die?"

"Go on."

"He scratched his ass with the wrong hand."

I crack up again. Hysterically, if I'm honest. He puts his hand on my arm, firmer this time. He's strong, his skin's warm. I look at his wrist. I could never resist a hairy wrist.

"How about a drink this evening, Kylie? I think you've earned one."

The gingko berry's growing on me. "As in, a date?"

"As in."

Hey. *Hey.* "You betcha."

"Good. You got a favourite bar, Kylie?"

I smile. "I have."

I write down my address and hand him the piece of paper.

He reads it, takes in what it's telling him, smiles back at me big and slow, then he glances around to check if anyone's there before kissing me long and hard, right there in the ICU cubicle. It's so good I swallow my gum. Finally he pulls away and looks me deep in the eyes. "So, what would you wish for if you were hooked up to the Angel right now?" he murmurs.

I laugh. "Well you know the answer to that one, Angus van der Kamp. You ain't dumb."

He cocks an eyebrow. "Let me hear it from you."

I lean forward, whisper in his ear: "OK. I'd wish for someone hot to give me the fuck of my life."

And it *was* the fuck of my life. Out of this world. Unbelievable. Life-changing. I'm still pulsing from it, high on my first ever set of multiple orgasms. Twenty-seven, since you ask. And no, I wouldn't have believed it either. We're on my bed with the fan turning above us, the noise of the lake in the distance, outboard motors and cat-calls and music. He's not one of those guys falls asleep right after which is good, cuz sex wakes me right up, gets my brain going. We've got through half a bottle of Southern Comfort, handing the bottle to and fro and sharing cigarettes.

"So now the fairy godmother has granted your sex wish, do you have any more?" he wants to know. I blow out smoke.

"Yeah. I do. I been thinking about that kid today, Jessie-May. And yesterday's, the primitive. Can't shake them off. I want to know what the Angel's really for."

He takes a swig of Southern Comfort, toys with a strand of my hair. "We're not supposed to discuss it with anyone outside of Threshold." He grins. "Bad girl."

"Come on, it's not some federal secret. Anyway I need to, it makes me feel so helpless." I still got this mean little rage going, about the whole Sweet Parting deal. "We might as well use a stun-gun on them and just get it over with, instead of horsing around in their hippocampuses, jinxing their dumbass psyches, stirring up stuff best left buried. I'm not the only operator thinks that. Consensus is, it's asking the wrong questions. Bad programming. Bad *priorities*. The ethical side to this, it's way over our pay-grade. We're technicians. We didn't sign up for this. We're talking inbuilt systematic incompetence. Something as important as this? You don't let Cal-Tech Aspie nerds design it. You bring in expert psychologists, right? I mean that kid today, Jessie-May. For what it's worth, d'you know what I think she really wanted? A decent Ma, is what. That woman in the store, that was her shitbag Ma, turned nice, offering her ice-cream. But does Jessie-May ask for a hug, does the good version of Ma offer her one? No, cuz the Angel's a dumbass. It's thinking commercially because those are its values. So it gets her to the brink but the woman selling ice cream doesn't turn into the kid's mother, like it should, so there's no closure. Trigger-image recognition failure or whatever. Or it's a language issue, maybe change the tense of the verb or something? I'm no linguistic cognoscenti but my thought is, instead of asking what flavour ice cream, it should just go, what do you want most in the world?"

"I hear you, Kylie." He hands me the bottle and I take a big swig.

"So you plug me up to the Angel and here's what I say: I say I wanna give Threshold Care Systems a piece of my mind, ask them what they're really up to, cuz you can bet they've got a hidden agenda."

He rolls over and props himself on his elbow. "Hmm. Wonder how that would go."

I look him in the eye. "I'd say to the host, whoever it was, I'd like to get to the bottom of this shit."

He nods. "And the host'd go, let me guess. It'd go, *Don't you already know the answer to that, Kylie?*"

I bang the pillow. "Yeah, exactly. *The client always has the answer buried within his own mind, and blah blah.* So I'd say, Well the big business slash the Pentagon slash Silicon Valley has to be behind it somehow, right?"

"Hmm. The military-industrial complex?"

"Something like it. I don't know."

He nods. "And the host says?"

"He or she – probably a he in my case – says *right, Kylie. Got it in one.* And I'm like, I knew it. I mean you have to ask yourself, as an Angel operator, who are the real clients, cuz there's no advantage I can see, in them – whoever they are – finding out what someone's last wish is, and making their passing a thing of ease. Cuz giving a bleach-swallower an ass-crack tattoo, or Jessie-May a peanut butter ice-cream, or her drunk grandaddy his dream screwdriver kit isn't something *you spend a billion dollars on.* They're so low down the food chain they're like, amoeba. They'd want a machine that gets to find out, you know... *big* thoughts. Secrets maybe. Famous people. Presidents and shit, what they regret, what they never told anyone, what they dreamed about achieving that they never said aloud. People whose minds are worth exploring. That's what I'd use it for, if I was them."

"Hmmm." He lies back on the pillow, his arms tucked behind his head in a way that shows off his world-class chest. "You know, Kylie, I have a hunch you're right."

"I know I am."

"Well say you are. And say I'm being the host here," he says.

"Shoot."

"Would what you've just articulated answer your question about the system's purpose? Its *raison d'etre?*"

Raison d'etre. Primitive. He has a way with words. I have a think. "Yeah. I guess it would." He hands me the cigarette and I take a deep drag and another swig of bourbon, and let the two sets of chemicals do their combined work. "I guess it... does." Something's sinking in. "Medicine Man?"

"Yeah?"

"I'm not sure how to bring this up, but... I said I wanted the fuck of my life and I got it."

He grins. "At your service."

"So I'm starting to wonder, are we entering a different... register here?"

He grins. "Hmm. What do you think?"

"I don't know."

"You're smart, Kylie. That's what I love about you. Your imagination's bigger than you think. Just look at today. You won! You answered your own questions about Threshold and its agenda, and on top of that, you had some spectacular orgasms. Maybe Sweet Parting's more sophisticated and generous than you give it credit for."

"So Threshold's giving multiple orgasms out of the kindness of its heart? Come on."

He laughs. "Think it through, Kylie. Apply your mind to the question."

We don't say anything for a bit, his hand resting on my boob. It feels good. Maybe he's right. Maybe I've worked out more than I think.

"I guess NASA didn't send guys to the moon just so I can fry an egg that doesn't stick," I say. "Same way Threshold didn't develop the Angel and Sweet Parting so Jessie-May could get an ice-cream."

He nods. "So although the Angel has its glitches, and you've been pointing them out eloquently, Kylie, you need to remember something. The final moments and feelings of ordinary people, they're valuable too."

"As in, commercially saleable?"

"Sure. Nothing wrong with that, is there?"

I think for a moment. "So the goodbye smiles, they get paid for in advance, by whoever's willing to pay for a good death cuz they're scared of having a bad one? And health insurance is involved, cuz either you're covered for it or you're not? And all of that pays for Threshold to develop its real system? The secret Pentagon slash Silicon Valley brain-picking one, or whatever evil shit it is?"

"Woah, how did the word evil creep in there?" smiles Angus. "The project's patriotic. And did you want Jessie-May to be the passenger screaming in agony? If the choice is that or an ice-cream, which would you choose for her? The ice-cream. Every time. No contest."

I take another long slow swig of Southern Comfort, haul some more nicotine into my lungs. I'm beginning to get a perspective on things here. I know it's too late (I swallowed the gingko berry gum, didn't I?), but at least I can see it. At least I've got some clarity.

"You're an amazing person, Kylie," Angus says. "And I'm not just being a good host here. You really made something of your life. And your work on developing the system? The feedback you just gave on the Angel? It'll prove useful, truly. You'll be helping more people than you could dream of. You should be proud."

I think for a moment. "I'm not unhappy, I guess. But, well. It's a shock. I wasn't expecting this, is all."

"No-one ever is. Not really. But the system works better than you think. And you'd be wrong to believe that Threshold hasn't thought it all through." He snuggles up and presses his face to my ear. We lie there for a while, just breathing, and then he whispers, "I love you, Kylie. I want you to know that."

My heart swells, huge and simple as the sun. I smile – why wouldn't I? – and I hear the camera click.

"Was that for me, Kylie?" he whispers, soft. "Feels like it was."

No, I think. It was for me. It was me, saying *goodbye, Life, it was nice knowing you. Thanks for having me.* Weird, that acceptance thing. I seen it before from the outside, never quite got it. But now –

Yeah. I do. I absolutely do.

He kisses me again, gentle, on the lips. "So," he murmurs. "Are you good to go?"

And yes. Oh yes. To my surprise, and joy, I am.

(2012)

TENDER

Rachel Swirsky

Rachel Swirsky's short fiction has been nominated for a number of awards, including the Hugo. In 2010, she won the Nebula for her novella *The Lady Who Plucked Red Flowers Beneath the Queen's Window* and in 2013, she won it a second time for her short story *If You Were a Dinosaur, My Love*. Her latest novella is *The Woman at the Tower Window* (2019). Swirsky currently lives in Bakersfield with her husband.

The first time my love realized I might kill myself, he remade my arteries in steel.

He waited until I was asleep and then stole me down into the secret laboratory he'd built beneath our house. I pretended to be sleeping as he shifted lights and lenses until the room lit with eerie blue. Using tools of his own invention, he anaesthetized me, incised my skin, and injected me with miniature robots that were programmed to convert my arterial walls into materials both compatible with human life and impossible to sever.

It was not really steel, but I imagine it as steel. I imagine that, inside, I am polished and industrial.

Over the course of the night, he remade the tributaries in my wrists, my throat, my thighs. He made them strong enough to repel any razor. He forbade them from crying red rivers. He banished the vision of a bathtub with water spreading pink. He made my life impossible to spill.

I have recurring dreams of tender things dying in the snow. They are pink and curled and fetal, the kind of things that would be at home in my husband's laboratory, floating in jars of formaldehyde, or suspended among bubbles in gestational tanks of nutritional gel.

Their skin has no toughness. It is wet and slick, almost amphibian, but so delicate that it bruises from exposure to the air. Their unformed bodies shudder helplessly in the cold, vestigial tails tucked next to ink-blot eyes. On their protoarms, finger-like protrusions grasp for warmth.

They are possibilities, yearning, unfurling from nothingness into unrealized potential.

In my dreams, I am separated from them by a window too thick to break. I don't know who has abandoned them, helpless, in the snow. Frost begins to scale their skins. Their mouths shape inaudible whimpers. I can't get outside. I can't get to them. I can't get outside before they die.

*

My love replaced the bones of my skull with interlocking adamantine scales. I cannot point a gun at my ear and shoot.

So that I cannot swallow a barrel, he placed sensors in my mouth, designed to detect the presence of firearms. Upon sensing one, they engage emergency measures, including alarms, force fields, and a portcullis that creaks down to block my throat.

The sensor's light blinks ceaselessly, a green wash that penetrates my closed lips. It haunts me in the night, bathing every other second in spectral glow.

One psychiatrist's theory:

To commit suicide, you must feel hopeless.

To commit suicide, you must believe you are a burden on those you love.

To commit suicide, you must be accustomed to physical risk.

One, two, three factors accounted for. But a fourth forgotten: to commit suicide, you must be penetrable.

My love says he needs me, but he knows that I believe he's deluded.

He would be better off with another wife. Perhaps a mad lady scientist with tangled red hair frizzing out of her bun and animé-huge eyes behind magnifying glasses. Perhaps a robot, deftly crafted, possessing the wisdom of the subtle alloys embedded in her artificial consciousness. Perhaps a super-human mutant, discovered injured and amnesiac in an alley, and then carried back to his lab where he could cradle her back to health. He could be the professor who enables her heroic adventures, outfitting her with his inventions, and sewing flame-retardant spandex uniforms for her in his spare time.

No poison: my vital organs are no longer flesh.

No car crash: my spinal cord is enhanced by a network of nanobots, intelligent and constantly reconfiguring, ensuring that every sensation flashes, every muscle twitches.

No suffocation: my skin possesses its own breath now. It inhales; it exhales; it maintains itself flush and pink.

"Please," he says, "Please," and does not have to say more.

He is crying very quietly. A few tears. A few gulping breaths.

Apart from the intermittent flash of the sensors in my mouth, our room is black and silent. I have been lying in bed for six days now. In the morning, he brings me broth and I eat enough to quiet him. In the afternoons, he carries up the robotic dog, and it energetically coils and uncoils its metal tail-spring until I muster the strength to move my hand and pat its head.

In the night, we lie beside each other, our skin rough against the sheets. He reaches for my hand where it lies on my pillow. His touch is so much. I can't explain how *much* it is. Sensation fills my whole world, and I have so little world left to fill. My body has been strengthened by nanobots and steel, but my mind continues to narrow, becoming less and less. Something as consuming as his touch is so overwhelming that it is excruciating. It's like all the warmth of the sun hitting my skin at once.

"Please," he repeats in a murmur.

Next morning, when I wake, he has programmed the nanobots to construct a transparent wall behind my eyes. No bullet, no pencil, no sword can penetrate them to find my brain.

There are so many ways to die.

The accidental: a slick of water, a slip, and the head cracks on the bathtub, shower, kitchen sink. Hands pull the wrong pair of medicines from the cabinet. Feet rest on the arm of the couch, near the blanket thrown over the radiator. The throat contracts around a piece of orange peel, inhaled instead of swallowed, on a day when one is home alone.

The unusual: exploding fireworks, attacking dogs, plummeting asteroids, crashing tsunamis, flashing lightning, striking snakes, whirling tornados, splintering earthquakes, engulfing floods, dazzling electrocution, grinning arson.

The science fictional: robots, and aliens, and zombies, and Frankenstein's monster, and experiments gone wrong, and spontaneous nuclear reactions, and miniature black holes, and tenth dimensional beings of malevolent light.

The routine: one car smashing into another. One damaged cell rapaciously dividing. One blockage of blood in the brain. One heart, seizing.

Self-immolation: no longer an option. After his last adjustments, my breathing skin can adapt to any temperature. It resists ice; it resists fire. I could walk into lava. I could dive into space.

"Please," he still murmurs at night, "Please."

His hand withdraws, but the heat-memory of it remains. It sparks under my skin like a new-forming sunburn, radiation caught and kept in the flesh.

Instead of hardening the shell of my body again, he appeals to my mind. Since I won't believe that he needs me, he brings me a pair of genetically enhanced, baby white mice with brains so huge their skulls bulge. They scurry around, solving mazes by means of derived algorithms that they've scratched into their bedding, using mathematical notation of their own invention.

I feed them carrots, celery, lettuce, and pellets of radioactive, brain-enhancing super-food. They sit on my hand as they eat, grasping the morsels in their paws and nibbling at them with their prominent front teeth. They stare at me with ink-black eyes and make pleased, musical squealing sounds. They proffer their bellies for me to tickle, and they giggle in a register too high-pitched for me to hear. They bring me gifts of hoarded lettuce leaves inscribed with formulae I can't decipher.

They are all energy and curiosity and brilliance. I watch them discover new ways to balance with their tails at the same time as they deduce the flaws in general relativity. I savor their love of life, their delight in discovering themselves as creatures who possess worlds and wisdom and bodies to explore. I feel their happiness heartbeat-hot in my stomach. It fills my remaining being with painful, wistful joy. Life is filling them. Life is diminishing me. I am tapering out of existence.

When I dream that night of the fetal creatures in the snow, I see that they have subtly shifted. Or perhaps I am only recognizing traits they have possessed all along. I see the features of my baby mice haunting their undeveloped bodies. Their ink-blot eyes are wondering. Their vestigial tails twitch querulously.

I pound my flattened palm against the dream-glass that separates us. I scream and scream for it to smash.

I can't. I can't. I can't get to them. The unformed things, the helpless things, the ones that still want to survive. They shiver and turn blue. Ice crusts their eyes closed. I pound the glass. I can't break it. I can't. I can't. I can't break through.

While I dreamt, he encased me in armor as sensitive as skin. Invisible to the eye. Intangible to the fingers. Impervious as immortality.

I will close you in, he didn't whisper as he stood over me, his breath hot and helpless on my scalp. *You are an eggshell and I will wrap you in cotton and rubber bands until no fall can shatter you. I won't wait until afterward to call all the king's horses and all the king's men. I'll bring them here before anything goes wrong. I'll set them to patrol the wall while they can still do some good. I'll protect you from everything, including yourself.*

My brain: wrinkled, pink, four-lobed, textured like soft tofu.

Steel arteries, adamantine scales, sensors, portcullises, nanobots, armor. So much fuss to protect three pounds of meat.

My mice have learned to write in English.

They crawl up and down the walls of their cage, pleading, until I give them scraps of paper and a miniature pen.

WE'RE WORRIED ABOUT YOU, they write.

On a white board, I write back, *It's not your job to worry about me.* I pause before adding, *You're mice.*

WHAT IS IT THAT YOU WANT? they write.

I hesitate before responding.

Nothing.

They consult silently, evaluating each other's perplexed expressions. They brux their teeth, chit-chitter-scrape.

Finally, they write, EVERYONE WANTS SOMETHING.

I do want something, I reply. *I already told you.*

But it's not really fair to expect them to be clever therapists. They may be geniuses, but they're still only baby mice.

In another science fiction story, my love would replace more and more of my body with armature until there was no human part of me remaining. With all my body gone, he would identify the fault as being in my mind. *That's where the broken fuses spit their dreadful sparks,* he'd conclude, and then he'd change that part of me, too. He would smooth every complicated, ambiguous wrinkle from the meat and electricity of my brain: the inconsistent neurotransmitters; the knotted traumas; the ice-thin sense of self-preservation. By the time he was done, I would no longer bear any resemblance to myself. I'd become a wretched Stepford revenant lurching in a mechanical shell. And still, he would love me.

In another science fiction story, as he and I struggled with the push-pull of our desires, an unprecedented case would crack the courts, establishing an inalienable right to die. Bureaucracies would instantly rise to regulate the processes of filing Intent to Die forms, attending mandatory therapy sessions, and requesting financial aid for euthanasia ceremonies. I would file, attend, and request. He would beg me not to do so until, finally, driven mad, he would build a doomsday machine in our basement and use it to take over the world. As the all-powerful ruler of mankind, he would crush rebellion in an iron fist. In his palace, he would imprison me, living but immobile, in a glass tank shaped like a coffin.

In the same science fiction story, written on a different day, he would build the doomsday machine, but at the last minute, he would realize the folly of deploying it. Instead, he would continue to plead as I turned away, until finally the doctors would pull his outstretched hand away from mine as they slid the needle into my skin.

In yet a third science fiction story, a meteor would crash to the earth, and upon it, there would be a sentient alien symbiont, and for it to survive, it would require a human host. Testing would determine that I was the only viable candidate. They would cut me open and stitch the alien into my side, and it would tell me stories about the depths of space, and the strange whales that fly between stars, and the sun-and-dust thoughts of nebulae. It would tell me of its adventures on the surfaces of alien monuments so large that they have their own atmospheres and have evolved sentient populations who think it's natural for the world to be shaped like the face of a giant. The alien would help my wounded soul rediscover how to accept my love's touch, and the three of us would live together, different from what we were, but unbreakably unified.

*

In this science fiction story, I am a fetus; I am a mouse; I am an eggshell; I am a held breath; I am a snowdrift; I am a cyborg; I am a woman whose skin cannot bear the sensation of love.

"Please," he whispers in his sleep, "Please."

Lying awake, I see the fetal creatures in the snow, not in a dream this time, but as a waking vision. My palm pushes futilely on the window between us. The fetal things are fragility I cannot rescue. They are love I cannot reach. They are myself, slowly freezing.

I, too, am fragmented. I am the creatures dying, and I am the woman pounding at the window. I am the glass between us. I am the inability to shatter.

I watch him lying next to me, his breath even with sleep. In an hour or so, while it is still deep dark, he will wake. He will take me down to the laboratory. In the morning, I will wake inhabited by an army of genetically engineered viruses, instructed to wrap each of my cells in a protective coat, a cloud-like embrace of softness and safety.

Do you know why I wear your armor? I don't ask him.

When you take me to the lab, I'm not always asleep. Sometimes, I'm aware. Sometimes, I feel the numbness of your anaesthetic spreading across my skin. Sometimes, I watch your face.

The flash of my sensors makes him seem alien.

In the laboratory, I don't continue, *your hands, laboring over me, are like the hands of an unknown creator god, working his clay.*

He stirs. The mice rustle in their cage. They draw schematics for spaceships that can escape this earth.

I don't say, *I wear your armor because I love you.*

I don't say, *I wear your armor because I am the fetal thing in the snow.*

I don't say, *I wear your armor because you will not make me into a Stepford revenant, and you will not build a doomsday machine, and there are no alien symbionts to weave me stories about metal rain on distant planets. I wear your armor because my skin is hot with the sun's memory. Because nanobot armies are love poems written in circuitry.*

I don't say, *I wear your armor because, in my dreams, I'm still pounding on the glass.*

(2014)

MASKS

Damon Knight

Though his output was modest, **Damon Francis Knight** (1922–2002) was one of America's leading critics, editors and writers of science fiction. He was a member of the Futurians, a group which included Isaac Asimov, Frederik Pohl, C. M. Kornbluth and James Blish, and in 1956, with Blish and Judith Merril, he started the Milford Writers' Conference, still the most important gathering for established science fiction writers. He also edited the *Orbit* anthologies (21 volumes between 1966 and 1980), a series which launched many writers of the New Wave. Knight was married three times. His third wife, Gertrude Meredith, was the sf writer Kate Wilhelm, who died in 2018. Of Knight's work – by turns mature, surreal, melancholy, and funny – the editor Patrick Nielsen Hayden wrote, "He had a wry but not entirely pessimistic view of human nature. I don't think anybody that works that hard to get other people to do better work is fundamentally a pessimist."

The eight pens danced against the moving strip of paper, like the nervous claws of some mechanical lobster. Roberts, the technician, frowned over the tracings while the other two watched.

"Here's the wake-up impulse," he said, pointing with a skinny finger. "Then here, look, seventeen seconds more, still dreaming."

"Delayed response," said Babcock, the project director. His heavy face was flushed and he was sweating. "Nothing to worry about."

"Okay, delayed response, but look at the difference in the tracings. Still dreaming, after the wake-up impulse, but the peaks are closer together. Not the same dream. More anxiety, more motor pulses."

"Why does he have to sleep at all?" asked Sinescu, the man from Washington. He was dark, narrow-faced. "You flush the fatigue poisons out, don't you? So what is it, something psychological?"

"He needs to dream," said Babcock. "It's true he has no physiological need for sleep, but he's got to dream. If he didn't, he'd start to hallucinate, maybe go psychotic."

"Psychotic," said Sinescu. "Well—that's the question, isn't it? How long has he been doing this?"

"About six months."

"In other words, about the time he got his new body—and started wearing a mask?"

"About that. Look, let me tell you something, he's rational. Every test—"

"Yes, okay, I know about tests. Well—so he's awake now?"

The technician glanced at the monitor board. "He's up. Sam and Irma are with him." He hunched his shoulders, staring at the EEG tracings again. "I don't know why it should bother me. It stands to reason, if he has dream needs of his own that we're not satisfying with the programmed stuff, this is where he gets them in." His face hardened. "I don't know. Something about those peaks I don't like."

Sinescu raised his eyebrows. "You program his dreams?"

"Not program," said Babcock impatiently. "A routine suggestion to dream the sort of thing we tell him to. Somatic stuff, sex, exercise, sport."

"And whose idea was that?"

"Psych section. He was doing fine neurologically, every other way, but he was withdrawing. Psych decided he needed that somatic input in some form, we had to keep him in touch. He's alive, he's functioning, everything works. But don't forget, he spent forty-three years in a normal human body."

In the hush of the elevator, Sinescu said, "… Washington."

Swaying, Babcock said, "I'm sorry, what?"

"You look a little rocky. Getting any sleep?"

"Not lately. What did you say before?"

"I said they're not happy with your reports in Washington."

"Goddamn it, I know that." The elevator door silently opened. A tiny foyer, green carpet, gray walls. There were three doors, one metal, two heavy glass. Cool, stale air. "This way."

Sinescu paused at the glass door, glanced through: a gray-carpeted living room, empty. "I don't see him."

"Around the ell. Getting his morning checkup."

The door opened against slight pressure; a battery of ceiling lights went on as they entered. "Don't look up," said Babcock. "Ultraviolet." A faint hissing sound stopped when the door closed.

"And positive pressure in here? To keep out germs? Whose idea was that?"

"His." Babcock opened a chrome box on the wall and look out two surgical masks. "Here, put this on."

Voices came muffled from around the bend of the room. Sinescu looked with distaste at the white mask, then slowly put it over his head.

They stared at each other. "Germs," said Sinescu through the mask. "Is that rational?"

"All right, he can't catch a cold or what have you, but think about it a minute. There are just two things now that could kill him. One is a prosthetic failure, and we guard against that; we've got five hundred people here, we check him out like an airplane. That leaves a cerebrospinal infection. Don't go in there with a closed mind."

The room was large, part living room, part library, part workshop. Here was a cluster of Swedish-modern chairs, a sofa, coffee table; here a workbench with a metal lathe, electric crucible, drill press, parts bins, tools on wallboards; here a drafting table; here a free-standing wall of bookshelves that Sinescu fingered curiously as they passed. Bound volumes of project reports, technical journals, reference books; no fiction except for *Fire* and *Storm* by George Stewart and *The Wizard of Oz* in a worn blue binding. Behind the bookshelves, set into a little alcove, was a glass door through which they glimpsed another living room, differently furnished: upholstered chairs, a tall philodendron in a ceramic pot. "There's Sam," Babcock said.

A man had appeared in the other room. He saw them, turned to call to someone they could not see, then came forward, smiling. He was bald and stocky, deeply tanned. Behind him, a small, pretty woman hurried up. She crowded through after her husband, leaving the door open. Neither of them wore a mask.

"Sam and Irma have the next suite," Babcock said. "Company for him; he's got to have somebody around. Sam is an old air-force buddy of his, and besides, he's got a tin arm.

The stocky man shook hands, grinning. His grip was firm and warm. "Want to guess which one?" He wore a flowered sport shirt. Both arms were brown, muscular and hairy, but when Sinescu looked more closely, he saw that the right one was a slightly different color, not quite authentic. Embarrassed, he said, "The left, I guess."

"Nope." Grinning wider, the stocky man pulled back his right sleeve to show the straps.

"One of the spin-offs from the project," said Babcock. "Myoelectric, servo-controlled, weighs the same as the other one. Sam, they about through in there?"

"Maybe so. Let's take a peek. Honey, you think you could rustle up some coffee for the gentlemen?"

"Oh, why, sure." The little woman turned and darted back through the open doorway.

The far wall was glass, covered by a translucent white curtain. They turned the corner. The next bay was full of medical and electronic equipment, some built into the walls, some in tall black cabinets on wheels. Four men in white coats were gathered around what looked like an astronaut's couch. Sinescu could see someone lying on it: feet in Mexican woven-leather shoes, dark socks, gray slacks. A mutter of voices.

"Not through yet," Babcock said. "Must have found something else they didn't like. Let's go out onto the patio a minute."

"Thought they checked him at night—when they exchange his blood, and so on...?"

"They do," Babcock said. "And in the morning, too." He turned and pushed open the heavy glass door. Outside, the roof was paved with cut stone, enclosed by a green plastic canopy and tinted-glass walls. Here and there were concrete basins, empty. "Idea was to have a roof garden out here, something green, but he didn't want it. We had to take all the plants out, glass the whole thing in."

Sam pulled out metal chairs around a white table and they all sat down. "How is he, Sam?" asked Babcock.

He grinned and ducked his head. "Mean in the mornings."

"Talk to you much? Play any chess?"

"Not too much. Works, mostly. Reads some, watches the box a little." His smile was forced; his heavy fingers were clasped together and Sinescu saw now that the fingertips of one hand had turned darker, the others not. He looked away.

"You're from Washington, that right?" Sam asked politely. "First time here? Hold on." He was out of his chair. Vague upright shapes were passing behind the curtained glass door. "Looks like they're through. If you gentlemen would just wait here a minute, till I see." He strode across the roof. The two men sat in silence. Babcock had pulled down his surgical mask; Sinescu noticed and did the same.

"Sam's wife is a problem," Babcock said, leaning nearer. "It seemed like a good idea at the time, but she's lonely here, doesn't like it—no kids—"

The door opened again and Sam appeared. He had a mask on, but it was hanging under his chin. "If you gentlemen would come in now."

In the living area, the little woman, also with a mask hanging around her neck, was pouring coffee from a flowered ceramic jug. She was smiling brightly but looked unhappy. Opposite her sat someone tall, in gray shirt and slacks, leaning back, legs out, arms on the arms of his chair, motionless. Something was wrong with his face.

"Well, now," said Sam heartily. His wife looked up at him with an agonized smile.

The tall figure turned its head and Sinescu saw with an icy shock that its face was silver, a mask of metal with oblong slits for eyes, no nose or mouth, only curves that were faired into each other... project." said an inhuman voice.

Sinescu found himself half bent over a chair. He sat down. They were all looking at him.

The voice resumed, "I said, are you here to pull the plug on the project." It was unaccented, indifferent.

"Have some coffee." The woman pushed a cup toward him.

Sinescu reached for it, but his hand was trembling and he drew it back. "Just a fact-finding expedition," he said.

"Bull. Who sent you—Senator Hinkel."

"That's right."

"Bull. He's been here himself; why send you? If you are going to pull the plug, might as well tell me." The face behind the mask did not move when he spoke; the voice did not seem to come from it.

"He's just looking around, Jim," said Babcock.

"Two hundred million a year," said the voice, "to keep one man alive. Doesn't make much sense, does it. Go on, drink your coffee."

Sinescu realized that Sam and his wife had already finished theirs and that they had pulled up their masks. He reached for his cup hastily.

"Hundred percent disability in my grade is thirty thousand a year. I could get along on that easy. For almost an hour and a half."

"There's no intention of terminating the project," Sinescu said.

"Phasing it out, though. Would you say phasing it out."

"Manners, Jim," said Babcock.

"Okay. My worst fault. What do you want to know."

Sinescu sipped his coffee. His hands were still trembling. "That mask you're wearing," he started.

"Not for discussion. No comment, no comment. Sorry about that, don't mean to be rude; a personal matter. Ask me something—" Without warning, he stood up, blaring, "Get that damn thing out of here!" Sam's wife's cup smashed, coffee brown across the table. A fawn-colored puppy was sitting in the middle of the carpet, cocking its head, bright-eyed, tongue out.

The table tipped, Sam's wife struggled up behind it. Her face was pink, dripping with tears. She scooped up the puppy without pausing and ran out. "I better go with her," Sam said, getting up.

"Go on; and, Sam, take a holiday. Drive her into Winnemucca, see a movie."

"Yeah, guess I will." He disappeared behind the bookshelf wall.

The tall figure sat down again, moving like a man; it leaned back in the same posture, arms on the arms of the chair. It was still. The hands gripping the wood were shapely and perfect but unreal: there was something wrong about the fingernails. The brown, well-combed hair above the mask was a wig; the ears were wax. Sinescu nervously fumbled his surgical mask up over his mouth and nose. "Might as well get along," he said, and stood up.

"That's right, I want to take you over to Engineering and R and D," said Babcock. "Jim, I'll be back in a little while. Want to talk to you."

"Sure," said the motionless figure.

Babcock had had a shower, but sweat was soaking through the armpits of his shirt again. The silent elevator, the green carpet, a little blurred. The air cool, stale. Seven years, blood and money, five hundred good men. Psych section, Cosmetic, Engineering, R and D, Medical, Immunology, Supply, Serology, Administration. The glass doors. Sam's apartment empty, gone to Winnemucca with Irma. Psych. Good men, but were they the best? Three of the best had turned it down. Buried in the files. *Not like an ordinary amputation, this man has had everything cut off.*

The tall figure had not moved. Babcock sat down. The silver mask looked back at him.

"Jim, let's level with each other."

"Bad, huh."

"Sure it's bad. I left him in his room with a bottle. I'll see him again before he leaves, but God knows what he'll say in Washington. Listen, do me a favor, take that thing off."

"Sure." The hand rose, plucked at the edge of the silver mask, lifted it away. Under it, the tan-pink face, sculptured nose and lips, eyebrows, eyelashes, not handsome but good-looking, normal-looking. Only the eyes wrong; pupils too big. And the lips that did not open or move when it spoke. "I can take anything off. What does that prove."

"Jim. Cosmetic spent eight and a half months on that model and the first thing you do is slap a mask over it. We've asked you what's wrong, offered to make any changes you want."

"No comment."

"You talked about phasing out the project. Did you think you were kidding?"

A pause. "Not kidding."

"All right, then open up, Jim, tell me; I have to know. They won't shut the project down; they'll keep you alive but that's all. There are seven hundred on the volunteer list, including two U.S. senators. Suppose one of them gets pulled out of an auto wreck tomorrow. We can't wait till then to decide; we've got to know now. Whether to let the next one die or put him into a TP body like yours. So talk to me."

"Suppose I tell you something but it isn't the truth."

"Why would you lie?"

"Why do you lie to a cancer patient."

"I don't get it. Come on, Jim."

"Okay, try this. Do I look like a man to you."

"Sure."

"Bull. Look at this face." Calm and perfect. Beyond the fake irises, a wink of metal. "Suppose we had all the other problems solved and I could go into Winnemucca tomorrow; can you see me walking down the street, going into a bar, taking a taxi."

"Is that all it is?" Babcock drew a deep breath. "Jim, sure there's a difference, but for Christ's sake, it's like any other prosthesis—people get used to it. Like that arm of Sam's. You see it, but after a while you forget it, you don't notice."

"Bull. You pretend not to notice. Because it would embarrass the cripple."

Babcock looked down at his clasped hands. "Sorry for yourself?"

"Don't give me that," the voice blared. The tall figure was standing. The hands slowly came up, the fists clenched. "I'm in this thing, I've been in it for two years. I'm in it when I go to sleep, and when I wake up, I'm still in it."

Babcock looked up at him. "What do you want, facial mobility? Give us twenty years, maybe ten, we'll lick it."

"No. No."

"Then what?"

"I want you to close down Cosmetic."

"But that's—"

"Just listen. The first model looked like a tailor's dummy, so you spent eight months and came up with this one, and it looks like a corpse. The whole idea was to make me look like a man, the first model pretty good, the second model better, until you've got something that can smoke cigars and joke with women and go bowling and nobody will know the difference. You can't do it, and if you could, what for?"

"I don't— Let me think about this. What do you mean, a metal—"

"Metal, sure, but what difference does that make. I'm talking about shape. Function. Wait a minute." The tall figure strode across the room, unlocked a cabinet, came back with rolled sheets of paper. "Look at this."

The drawing showed an oblong metal box on four jointed legs. From one end protruded a tiny mushroom-shaped head on a jointed stem and a cluster of arms ending in probes, drills, grapples. "For moon prospecting."

"Too many limbs," said Babcock after a moment. "How would you—"

"With the facial nerves. Plenty of them left over. Or here." Another drawing. "A module plugged into the control system of a spaceship. That's where I belong, in space. Sterile environment, low grav, I can go where a man can't go and do what a man can't do. I can be an asset, not a goddamn billion-dollar liability."

Babcock rubbed his eyes. "Why didn't you say anything before?"

"You were all hipped on prosthetics. You would have told me to tend my knitting."

Babcock's hands were shaking as he rolled up the drawings. "Well, by God, this just may do it. It just might." He stood up and turned toward the door. "Keep your—" He cleared his throat. "I mean, hang tight, Jim."

"I'll do that."

When he was alone, he put on his mask again and stood motionless a moment, eye shutters closed. Inside, he was running clean and cool; he could feel the faint reassuring hum of pumps, click of valves and relays. They had given him that: cleaned out all the offal, replaced it with machinery that did not bleed, ooze or suppurate. He thought of the lie he had told Babcock. *Why do you lie to a cancer patient?* But they would never get it, never understand.

He sat down at the drafting table, clipped a sheet of paper to it and with a pencil began to sketch a rendering of the moon-prospector design. When he had blocked in the prospector itself, he began to draw the background of craters. His pencil moved more slowly and stopped; he put it down with a click.

No more adrenal glands to pump adrenaline into his blood, so he could not feel fright or rage. They had released him from all that—love, hate, the whole sloppy mess—but they had forgotten there was still one emotion he could feel.

Sinescu, with the black bristles of his beard sprouting through his oily skin. A whitehead ripe in the crease beside his nostril.

Moon landscape, clean and cold. He picked up the pencil again.

Babcock, with his broad pink nose shining with grease, crusts of white matter in the corners of his eyes. Food mortar between his teeth.

Sam's wife, with raspberry-colored paste on her mouth. Face smeared with tears, a bright bubble in one nostril. And the damn dog, shiny nose, wet eyes...

He turned. The dog was there, sitting on the carpet, wetted tongue out—*left the door open again*—dripping, wagged its tail twice, then started to get up. He reached for the metal T square, leaned back, swinging it like an ax, and the dog yelped once as metal sheared bone, one eye spouting red, writhing on its back, dark stain of piss across the carpet, and he hit it again, hit it again.

The body lay twisted on the carpet, fouled with blood, ragged black lips drawn back from teeth. He wiped off the T square with a paper towel, then scrubbed it in the sink with soap and steel wool, dried it and hung it up. He got a sheet of drafting paper, laid it on the floor, rolled the body over onto it without spilling any blood on the carpet. He lifted the body in the paper, carried it out onto the patio, then onto the unroofed section, opening the doors with his shoulder. He looked over the wall. Two stories down, concrete roof, vents sticking out of it, nobody watching. He held the dog out, let it slide off the paper, twisting as it fell.

It struck one of the vents, bounced, a red smear. He carried the paper back inside, poured the blood down the drain, then put the paper into the incinerator chute.

Splashes of blood were on the carpet, the feet of the drafting table, the cabinet, his trouser legs. He sponged them all up with paper towels and warm water. He took off his clothing, examined it minutely, scrubbed it in the sink, then put it in the washer. He washed the sink, rubbed himself down with disinfectant and dressed again. He walked through into Sam's silent apartment, closing the glass door behind him. Past the potted philodendron, over-stuffed furniture, red-and-yellow painting on the wall, out onto the roof, leaving the door ajar. Then back through the patio, closing doors.

Too bad. How about some goldfish.

He sat down at the drafting table. He was running clean and cool. The dream this morning came back to his mind, the last one, as he was struggling up out of sleep: *slithery kidneys burst gray lungs blood and hair ropes of guts covered with yellow fat oozing and sliding and oh god the stink like the breath of an outhouse no sound nowhere he was putting a yellow stream down the slide of the dunghole and*

He began to ink in the drawing, first with a fine steel pen, then with a nylon brush. *his heel slid and he was falling could not stop himself falling into slimy bulging softness higher than his chin, higher and he could not move paralyzed and he tried to scream tried to scream tried to scream*

The prospector was climbing a crater slope with its handling members retracted and its head tilted up. Behind it the distant ringwall and the horizon, the black sky, the pinpoint stars. And he was there, and it was not far enough, not yet, for the earth hung overhead like a rotten fruit, blue with mold, crawling, wrinkling, purulent and alive.

(1968)

HOSTBODS

Tendai Huchu

Tendai Huchu is the author of *The Hairdresser of Harare*. His short fiction and nonfiction have appeared in *The Manchester Review, Ellery Queen's Mystery Magazine, Gutter, AfroSF, Wasafiri, Warscapes, The Africa Report, The Zimbabwean, Kwani?* and numerous other publications. His next novel will be *The Maestro, The Magistrate, & The Mathematician*.

09:45
Arrows in front of my eyes tell me where to go ↑ along a busy market street lined with immigrants selling cheap wares from makeshift stalls. It's awash with colour, purple and blue saris and Kashmiri scarfs, red apples, green grapes, and the smells of freshly caught fish, cooked corn, herbs and spices – paprika, cumin, ground chilli – sold by the pound. Loud voices call out random prices and bargains as I (and I am still I) turn → into a narrow alleyway with puddles of water from last night's rain, full up trash cans and cardboard stacks from the shops inside.

←. Sat-homing means I see where I'm going, feel the experience, but it's more of a sleepwalk. It's like doing something by instinct, the same way your leg kicks out when the doctor taps your knee with a plexor. My muscles move, I feel the ground beneath my feet, taste the salty air from the sea close by, and feel the chilly wind; I'm here and not here. ↑.

10:00
Destination Reached
    Deactivate Sat-homing
    Status Green: Y/N – Y
    Prepare For Symbiosis
    5, 4, 3, 2, 1
A ton of force presses down the top of my head, crushing me. Everything from the top of my cranium moves down like my skull is travelling down my neck into my oesophagus. It feels like I'm eating my own head, swallowing it down to my gut, can't breathe, a wave of nausea overcomes me and I'd gag if a big lump wasn't obstructing my throat. It's like being ripped out of your skin and having everything shredded and crushed, leaving only that, the largest organ in your body, hollow, while a new skeleton ent…

i'm at the beach again, look at it, so beautiful. If only the sky wasn't covered by those grey clouds. Never mind. Best birthday present ever! Is that? – no, it can't be.

'Hey dad, you in there?' Holy crap.

'Joe, is it really you?' i ask. 'i can't believe it.'

'We're all here for you,' he replies and sweeps his hand to show the rest of the family behind him.

my sister Ethel's in a blue frock, covered up with a cardigan. Her hair is so grey, all those wrinkles on her face, the moustache on her lip. i hug her tightly, haven't seen that face in over ten years; not since my eyes gave out. Joe's wife, Natalie, holds a big box with bright pink ribbons on it, the smile on her face warms me up. We embrace, just like we did on their wedding day. Happiest day of my life. The grandkids, the tall one must be Darren and the little one, blonde hair, Craig. On the beach with my family again, it's a miracle.

'That's not Grandpa,' says Craig, taking a step back behind his brother.

'Craig, what did I tell you? Don't spoil this for everyone,' Joe replies curtly.

'It's me, don't be afraid. It really is me.' i go over to the boy, pick him up and tickle his belly like i used to, he squirms and pulls away.

'You're not Grandpa,' he says, and walks off towards the white pier in the distance. i make to follow, but Joe grabs my arm.

'Let him go, we've only got an hour. He'll be alright.'

A woman in a yellow mini walks past with her dog and i feel a yearning inside me i haven't felt for years. This isn't the time. It's family time. There are strollers in beach shorts, a couple having breakfast on a towel near the changing rooms, sanitation workers taking away litter from the car park up ahead. And the wind is just glorious, i close my eyes and try to inhale every atom of air i can.

i hit Darren on the shoulder – 'Tag you're it' – and begin to run on the beach. That's right, I'm running, the sand underneath me, giving way and crunching as I go, seaweed washed ashore, and, boy, am i running like a pro-athlete. i slow down to allow Darren to tag me and off i go after him. My grandson can run like a gazelle, but it only takes a few strides, i catch up, grab him by the waist and lift him high in the air. Joe and Natalie laugh, Ethel laughs, we're all so happy. Best birthday ever.

We walk on the sand, checking out sailing boats in the distance. A few folks stare at us for a bit, but i suppose that's normal given the circumstances. i've not felt this strong in years. Even as we walk, i'm holding back because i just want to run. It was on this very beach that i proposed to Lenore fifty years ago. Wish she was still here with us to hear the seagulls circling above, squawking.

Joe calls Craig over and we sit round a table. It's a bit nippy, but we order ice-cream anyway. The taste of it is just divine, so sweet, so sharp, like every nerve ending in my body is awake and it's every bit as great as I remember from the rations during the war. Vivid flavours explode in my mouth.

5 Mins

i feel an overwhelming sense of sorrow and loss at the thought of leaving all this behind. It's like being given the power of a god for a day and having it taken away the same way Phaethon was hurled off Apollo's chariot by Zeus' thunderbolt.

'i suppose it's time for me to say goodbye again,' i mumble.

'I'm sorry, if we'd had more money, we could have bought more time,' Natalie says, her eyes welling up. 'Maybe we could… I've heard of charities that buy time for people in special circumstances.'

'Don't bother yourself; you have kids to look after. i'll remember this day forever. It's been wonderful.'

1 min

i get up to hug them, each in turn, and this time Craig lets me. He feels like dough in my arms, soft, yeasty, full of goodness and potential, young and invincible, as though I'm touching the future right now. There's a joy in my heart that can't be compared to…

Prepare To Disengage From HostBod

SyncCorp Hopes You Had A Pleasant Experience

Please Come Again

5, 4, 3, 2, 1

11:30

I arrive at a warehouse in Mullhill, the east side of the city, near the industrial zone. There's no sign on the diamond fence around the perimeter. HGV trucks laden with goods from the factories around run up and down the road towards the city and beyond. The noise of the mills is a sonnet to the plumes of smoke that pour from the coal powered station in the centre of the perfect grid of intersecting streets. The air is acrid and full of unknowable particulates. Men in overalls and hard hats walk in rows carrying little backpacks to their various factories.

There's no guard as I walk past the boom gate into a desolate car park. I take a deep breath and follow the arrows. I have no choice. Some bods have been used in criminal enterprises before and it's a growing problem. But not with SyncCorp, the leading bod provider in the western hemisphere.

A HostBod walks towards me. Hard sculpted cheeks, fair lips, flat east Baltic head, another immigrant. His blue t-shirt tells me he's from RentaBod, cheap eastern European bods usually. He's in Sat-homing and manages to turn his head a fraction to acknowledge me with his dead blue eyes. I blink, a moment of brotherhood that lasts a microsecond.

I walk into the bare warehouse and my Sat-homing is deactivated. I'm in loiter mode until the uplink command is sent. The warehouse is a bare shell, high windows, floors caked in pigeon droppings. At the far end is a red door which I walk through, into a waiting area in which two other bods sit in injection moulded chairs.

'What's this about?' I say taking the seat nearest the exit.

'I don't know,' replies the bod opposite me in a South American, maybe Brazilian accent. He's caramel skinned and bald headed. Every bod has their head shaved for the implants.

'Some kind of test,' says the other one sitting nearest the second door.

Their yellow t-shirts tell me they are both assets from PleasureBodInc, usually procured for the M2M industry. The fluorescent light above makes a slight humming noise. It flickers at intervals. The room seems to have been set up recently, with new fixtures that smell of plastic.

'How long have you been in business?' the Brazilian asks.

'Four years, nine months,' I reply.

'Wow, without a burnout? Amazing! I've only been here six months.'

'Good luck,' is all I can say. And that's what this game is, Russian roulette, you spin the barrel until you don't hear the empty click of the chamber anymore.

He's called in by a curly haired man wearing a white coat and holding a notepad. The scent of disinfectant wafts into the waiting room. The Brazilian follows him in and the door shuts behind him.

Half an hour later, the Brazilian walks out and I'm called in before the other PleasureBodInc bod. I get up and walk into the next room. The man in a white coat asks me to sit on what looks like a pink dentist's plinth. I comply.

Status Green: Y/N – Y

Prepare For Symbiosis

5, 4, 3, 2, 1

'What do you think of this one, Doctor Cranmer?'

'Near the end of service which means it's stable. It's the oldest one we've got. As you know, they usually break down around the twenty-four month mark. Only a special few last this long.'

'i don't know. The features…'

'Will take some getting used to, I admit. But race is the least of your worries, sir. Stability is all important.'

'Let's take it through its paces, shall we?'

I'm not supposed to be here, to see or hear any of this. It's as if I'm a child hiding in a dark closet, looking into a room through a keyhole. HostBods are not supposed to be conscious during symbiosis and the Corp would reconfigure me if they knew. But I've been in this closet, hiding away for two years. The doctor instructs me/him to open my/his mouth, shines a light down my/his throat. Then he draws some blood, runs me/him through an x-ray machine – Doctor Cranmer can't use the MRI because of the electrodes – but he takes my/his blood pressure, resting pulse and performs lung function tests. He puts me/him on a treadmill at high speed for three minutes and then repeats the test. I/he is moved to a large hanger where I/he does something that resembles a football fitness test, some sort of biomechanical assessment looking at endurance, speed, strength, agility and power. I watch it all from my closet, not daring to breathe or move.

1 Min

'How old is he, doc?'

'Just coming up to 21. Prime specimen right here.'

'I'm not sure about this.'

'Look at these stats, he's 99.25% compatible, that's 5 percentage points over anything else we've got. He's perfect.'

'I need time to think it over.'

'We've got a few more to look at, so don't worry, but the sooner we make a move the better.'

Prepare To Disengage From HostBod

SyncCorp Hopes You Had A Pleasant Experience
Please Come Again
5, 4, 3, 2, 1

15:15
↑↑→←↑↑↑↓↑↑↑↑→↑

15:45
Destination Reached
  Deactivate Sat-homing
  Status Green: Y/N – Y
  Prepare For Symbiosis
  5, 4, 3, 2, 1

No rest for the fucking wicked. Stan calls me up, wants me to raise 40 mill for some shit-arsed indie flick. Who watches that crap? Must be shagging the director, that's what. Still, who's gonna pony up 40 mill for some piece of cunt? Okay, relax, chill out. Only get this shit one day a week. 40 mill. Forget it. Forget about work for two minutes. It's her. Is this shit even legal?

There she is, look at that, fucking curves on that. Phwoar, even forget she nearly sixteen sometimes. Check out those blonde locks, how they bounce around on her head and those tits, dear God, those motherfucking tits. i ain't doing badly for an old fart. i mean how many blokes my age actually get the balls to hit it with their daughter's best mate, hehe. Pure fantasy shit. That's why i gotta cover me tracks. Put her arse in a HostBod and shit's supposedly legal – at least that's what me lawyer tells me. Grey area, he calls it.

'Ello darling, come ere to daddy.'

Feel those tits pressing against me chest as i hug her.

'How's school and everything?' Gotta seem like the caring, reasonable old man, hehe.

'It's alright. I missed you,' she says. Hear that – if me missus only said it once or twice a month i wouldn't be up to no good. Swear it on me mother's fucking grave.

'i missed you too, darling. Give daddy a lil kiss.'

Feel those sweet teenage lips, wow. Wouldn't be able to handle this sort of action if i was in me own body. Check out me lump, proper Mandingo going on here.

i push her back a mo just so I can check out the view, see the curves. i like that lil shade of brown pube that lingers just above them lil panties. Wow, wow, what the fuck? Who's this? Fucking Chinese woman appears in front of me outta nowhere.

'What's wrong, daddy?'

'You, you've fucking turned Chinese!'

'What?'

'You're Chinese, honest to God. Look at you, all bald with some metal wire shit all over your head, the skin, everything. Oh, my fucking God!'

'I think it's like the visuals that's gone bust on your bod, coz I can see you just fine.'

'What the fuck am i supposed to do?'

"Call the company and have them fix it.'

And that's how i spend the one afternoon of peace i get a week, down the phone speaking to some call centre trying to get this drone to remote patch me visuals. Little girl's sitting on the bed, staring at me out of her fifty-something year old chinky fucking eyes. Total mindfuck coz she's talking like her out of this bod and it's doing me head in.

'Don't tell me you've fixed the fucking visuals because all i can see in front of me is a fucking Chinese bird, alright? i pay top dollar for this shit, i expect service. You even know what that word means?' i'm screaming down the fucking phone, would have had a heart attack by now if i was in me own body. 'Fine, i'll take a full refund and a free session next week, sounds freaking fine by me. i should be suing your incompetent arses.'

i hang up and turn back to the girl:

'Looks like this week's fucked. We'll hook up next time, okay love? Come here, give daddy a kiss... on second thoughts, don't.'

16:30

I'm back in Sat-homing mode. I'm not supposed to know the last assignment was a complete dud, that I'm, in effect, malfunctioning. Visuals need to get reset. I've been sent back to base early, my next assignments have been cancelled. So I'm free – sort of.

Funny thing happens when I sync up, I seem to store some of their memories in me. This isn't supposed to happen, none of the other bods report anything similar, but it's like I know stuff I'm not even supposed to know.

Passing by City Square, the giant advertorial screens above, the Coke-red next to the Pepsi-blue, the giant golden arc, Papa Chicks, Massa Space outfits, people walking around, bodies pressed against each other, sub 20Hz speakers blaring out subliminal advertising, shops spraying lab manufactured pheromones to lure consumers. I adjust my hoodie, doing my best to cover my temples even though this is one of the safer parts of the city for a bod to pass. The poorer and rougher western neighbourhoods like Westlea and Pilmerton are a different matter altogether. I walk by The Stock Xchange. When I first came here I didn't understand any of it, the arrows going up and down, the numbers sprinting across the top and bottom of the screen. But a few sessions synced with Brad Madison, and I know it all as well as any broker. Viviset stocks have been fluctuating, but they're still overpriced, best time to sell and get out before it comes crashing down. I'd buy Tanganda now and sell it next week. ↑ Can't stop to look at the rest in this mode, but I'll check out the markets online when I get back to base.

Silver space blanket puffs seem to be the fashion of the week for ladies under 30. Then again, when you've been synced with a famous fashion designer... Wish they'd get me on the underground for the journey back. My feet are killing me. That's the problem with Corp, they'll squeeze every penny in savings if they can.

Truth be told, knowing what I know now, that's the same thing I'd do especially when staff turnover isn't a factor.

Base is a huge building which used to be a budget hotel in the east side, near the space&airport. You can see planes and shuttles taking off and landing, going to exotic destinations around the world or to orbit. It's noisy as hell, but it's home. Our conditions here, I hear, are much better than the dormitory set-up other bods get elsewhere. Retinal scanner lets me in.

Deactivate Sat-homing

'You're home early 4401,' says Marlon on the security desk.

'Malfunction,' I reply.

'You'll be seeing Dr Song then,' he replies. 'Go up to your room. I'll call you when it's time.'

'Thanks Marlon,' I say and then I remember, 'Hey, is it okay for me to call home?'

'I'll give you access. Ten minutes max per day.'

'Come on Marlon,' I say in my best whiny voice.

'Fifteen, and that's the best I can do. Now get outta here before I change my mind.'

'You're a legend,' I say and give him the thumbs up.

The door to my room is unlocked. We have a toilet cubicle to the left, a bunk bed on either side of the wall, and a desk with a small computer/TV at the far wall. There are no mirrors in any of the rooms. Raj6623 is asleep or in hibernation mode. He usually starts up at 22:00 and returns the next afternoon. He's a fightbod and gets a full eight hours' sleep plus practice time. For most bods it's 20 hours' work with four hours' sleep as standard.

'4401 authorised call to rec-number Harare,' I say to the computer.

It kicks up with a whirr and then I hear a dial tone. Half a minute later Mama's face appears on screen. A sad smile cracks on her mouth like a running fissure when she sees me. At the right angle, all she can see is my face, bald head and the two electrodes implanted through my temples into my frontal lobe. They're titanium and shiny, but at least she can't see the full device. The other implants are at the back of my skull and are drilled into the amygdala, so the sync takes place in the oldest and newest brain, the primitive and the conscious part for full immersiveness. We talk about home, my little brother with Westhuizen's Syndrome, which is the reason I'm here. The money I make goes straight towards his medication. I'll get a bonus after completion and after that, I'll have to either sign up again – no one's ever done that – or find a new way to make money for his drugs. Either way, this job is the only thing keeping him alive. He pops up on screen, nine years old, handsome as a teddy bear, braces in his mouth, and smiles. I wave. He tells me about school, his friends, games, all the things any nine year old should be doing. This makes it worthwhile. Mama's just sitting there, slightly off screen, watching her boys. I'm sure she's proud. I get a beep, time's nearly up, say, 'Good-bye, I love you guys so much,' blow a kiss and log off.

I've just slid into my lower bunk when Marlon buzzes via the computer and tells me to go see the doc. I get up and leave Raj6623 snoozing, go into the corridor and squirt some alcohol gel on my hands and round my temples. The corridor is bare, just blue vinyl flooring, perfect white walls, directional signs every couple of meters and a purple strip that runs in the middle of the wall as a sort of decoration. I go round a few turns and into the infirmary, just in time to see a new bod leave. I nod my head and stroll in.

Doctor Song is a small Korean man, barely reaches my chest even with the Cuban heels he wears to give himself an extra inch or so. He's typing notes into his computer and points to a chair. The keys go tap, tap, tap under his furious little fingers.

'4401, why you tell Marlon you have malfunction? How did you know?' he says. I should have known better.

'My assignment ended early, you called me home and cancelled the rest of my day, that can only mean one thing,' I reply coolly.

'You doctor now?'

'You're the doctor, Doctor Song.'

'You waking?'

'Never.'

'Uplink scan has been showing spikes in your wave function post sync.' I blink like I don't understand what he's saying. Doc likes that sort of thing, but I know what he's going to say next before he even says it. 'Don't worry it's not the most reliable instrument anyway.'

That's code for I'mtoolazytofollowupandyourcontract'snearlydonesoIdon'tcare. I nod along like an ignoramus.

'You've been taking your antibiotics?' he asks.

'On time, every time,' I reply. We have to take long term, prophylactic, broad-spectrum antibiotics because of the risk of infection at the insertion points. You don't wanna mess with meningitis or encephalitis.

'Corp has new job for you. Contract nearly over so easy work. You go Hillside in North, single user for last three months. Congratulations,' he says, looking at me for once.

'Thanks Doctor Song,' I reply with a smile, though every instinct in my body is screaming out, alarm bells ringing, spider senses tingling.

'Good. Go into next room. I test and remodulate vis configuration,' he says and grabs a white helmet with flashing green and blue lights at the fore. It's the user's uplink device. It works by reading the wearers brainwaves and transmitting low level radiation to tune the user into the HostBod. Nowhere near as invasive as the electrodes bods must wear because their own consciousness must be suppressed in sync, which can only be done surgically. The electrodes not only transmit electric impulses but also carry neurotransmitters direct into the brain structure. I got this off syncing with Doctor Song himself and he doesn't even know that.

We can't be in the same room during sync because of the infinity loop problem which tech has failed to overcome. That's why, for safety reasons, user and HostBod only interface via remote transmission. He marches me back and forth, I squat, pinch myself, stick my tongue out, and do a dozen other psychomotor and spatial awareness exercises before he signs me off.

I walk back to my room and find Raj6623 standing at the door.

'They came to get your gear. Looks like you're shipping out,' he says. The scar that runs across his face moves as he speaks.

'I got lucky,' I say.

'Stay alive,' he replies and crushes me with a bear hug. Twelve months we've been here together and this is the most intimate we've been.

'Say 'bye to the others for me,' I say, knowing full well he won't bother.

A woman with vibrant red hair, the sort that can only come from a bottle, stands at the reception desk next to a guy in a chauffer's outfit with a bag at his side. She has milky white skin, almost matching the shade of the walls, and from a distance all I see is hair, eyebrows and blood red lipstick where her mouth is. She wears a retro ivory silk slip covering one shoulder, revealing a large ruby choker around her neck. It's like she's ephemeral, a wisp of an image from another dimension.

'So this is father's new toy,' she purrs.

'That's him, Ms Stubbs,' says Marlon ingratiatingly. 'Here's your papers, 4401. Follow this lady and the gentleman. Good luck.'

I shake his hand and follow my new employer into a black limousine waiting in the car park. The chauffer opens the door, she walks in. I wait to be invited. She beckons me with her index finger. The chauffer closes the door as I sit with my back to the driver, facing her. The cabin smells of freshly polished leather. She pours a glass of champagne for herself and a finger of whisky in another, which she slowly hands to me.

'We're not allowed,' I say.

'Don't be a pussy, drink it,' she replies, rolling her eyes melodramatically. I take the drink and hold it. 'What's your name?'

'4401.'

'Your real name, idiot.'

'Simon.'

'That's what I thought. I saw you in those hospital garments you call clothes and said to myself, there's a Simon alright.' The lady is a little tipsy, but not drunk, the intoxication of someone who's used to consuming a lot of alcohol all hours of the day.

The Limo cruises onto the 105 which takes us past Marlborough and Bury, skirting round the rough neighbourhoods. We go past gleaming skyscrapers, the glass reflecting the orange glow of the setting sun, images of clouds cast on windows, the city glistening like a thousand orange diamonds. She says nothing to me for the rest of the journey, only eyeing me like a predator stalking her prey. A lump sits at the top of my throat; I swallow hard.

20:00
Initiating Protocol Transfer To
    Username: Howard J Stubbs
    SyncCorp Wishes You A Happy And

Prosperous Symbiosis
0% ----------- 100%

That's me wired up to the Stubbs' MF now, which means they own me, which means I wasn't hired but they bought out the rest of my contract. It happens from time to time, bods get passed around between different companies, usually traded down. Stubbs must be pretty loaded to afford this. No shit, Sherlock, is that your deduction or it's the 200 year old southern plantation style mansion in front you? Kind of looks like a wannabe White House, only bigger. The wheels of the limo crunch on the gravel driveway. A Roman style fountain with mirthful nymphs squirts water high into the air. So much woodland around; it feels like we're in the country. Light pouring out of every window in the mansion illuminates the lawn as we park near the front door.

'Come on, I'm sure Father is just *dying* to meet you,' she says, dragging out the word dying.

'We don't usually meet users.'

'Things are different here,' she replies as we walk into the mansion.

There's a vulgar mix of paintings lining the walls. Expensive paintings: a Picasso here, a Van Gogh there, Pollock next to Gauguin with a Palin underneath. It's clear that this is a nouveau riche acquisition with little acquiescence to aesthetics. I find this somewhat disturbing as I walk on the dark hardwood flooring polished to within an inch of its life.

Ms Stubbs leads me up a winding staircase to the bedrooms. An oak drawer along the wall has a Chinese vase (I reckon Qing but can't be sure) on top with geometric patterns in bright shades of blue and a bunch of chrysanthemums set inside. I can't help but smile behind her back. We enter a large bedroom in the centre of which is a poster bed. An old man sits underneath layers of quilts with his back propped up by a bunch of pillows. The oxygen tank on his left hisses away.

'Go to him,' says Ms Stubbs.

I walk over and kneel beside the old man. From this close I can smell his decrepitude, malodours churning under the quilts and from the catheter that dangles at the bedside. I notice he has an electrode transference device just like mine, complete with implants boring through his skull into his brain. I've never heard of a user having to go through this before. The device looks like a giant tarantula resting on top of his skull. 'Hello,' I say. He reaches out with his left hand and touches my face. It feels bony and rough against my forehead and cheeks. He takes a deep breath and whispers in a raspy voice:

'Make yourself at home, boy.'

21:00

I'm in my room in loiter mode. The chauffer left my bag with my few clothes and possessions which I unpack into the drawers. The window gives me a view down the hill past the silhouette of trees to the brightly lit city in the distance.

I go over to the bed, slide into the soft cotton sheets and for the first time in a year, I'm allowed to sleep for more than four hours even though the dreams I have are still not my own.

08:00
I wake up feeling refreshed and rejuvenated. Can't believe I slept for so long. The sun pours into my room because I forgot to close the curtains. It's been too long since I had a window in my room. I wash my face in the basin in the corner and spray alcohol gel around my implants. There are real clothes in the closet, just my size too, so I wear those instead of the Corp crap. I grab a red hoodie to cover my head in case I'm taken outside. I walk past Mr Stubbs bedroom and down the stairs into one of the rooms where a breakfast buffet is laid out. It smells great.

Ms Stubbs is at the opposite end of the table, listening to the news and eating toast. The day's barely started and she looks stunning in a crimson gown, an eye mask on her forehead.

'Morning,' I say.

'You can have anything you like,' she replies.

'Thanks.'

I bring out my feeding pack of Soylent and pour myself a glass of water. This is how bods start the day, you can't fill yourself up because a lot of users like to go out for meals, so it's important to keep the stomach as empty as possible. I drink from my pack, it tastes like dough with grainy bits in it. After a while, you get used to it.

'Can I call home?' I ask.

'Nope,' she replies without even raising her head to look at me.

'We had 30 minute privileges per day at Corp,' I say.

'Firstly, it was ten minutes and, secondly, this ain't Corp.'

Status Green: Y/N – Y

Prepare For Symbiosis

5, 4, 3, 2, 1

'Morning Lesley,' i say. What is that weird taste in my mouth? Quick, grab a coffee to rinse it out.

'Morning Father. You started the day early. Who was that?' she replies, nonchalant. i wonder what she's scheming.

'Just the lawyer first thing before dawn and Doctor Cranmer should be here any minute now. Justin makes the finest coffee. He deserves a raise.'

'What did you want with the lawyer?'

'A bit of business, nothing you should worry your pretty little head about. i'm not a cabbage up there you know.' i point to the second floor where the bedrooms are. She raises a single eyebrow and gets back to her food.

i leave her to it. So much to do, so little time. i could get used to this, yes. Stop beside the mirror, look at the face: bold, square jaw, angular, very manly. Yes, i could definitely get used to this. Cranmer is in the foyer already.

'Good morning, doctor,' i sound a little too jovial.

'Mr Stubbs?'

'It's too nice a day to talk indoors. Shall we go out into the grounds for a walk?'

'I need to see the… the other body.'

'You can do that later, come, let's go outside.' i take him by the elbow and lead him out. Sweet sunshine hits my face. 'Nothing like the scent of freshly mowed grass.'

'I came to check if you wanted to see this thing through. You must understand the tech is experimental. I've only done one other procedure so we don't yet know what the long term effects are,' Doctor Cranmer says.

'Run it by me one more time.'

'When user and bod are compatible, you can put them in sync and then transfer consciousness through the process of quantum entanglement. Essentially we are just reversing the quantum states in the brain, no matter is moved between A and B, so theoretically there's a zero chance of post-op rejection. It's not a brain transplant, it's a consciousness transfer. Post-procedure we isolate the bod, who is now the user, to prevent attempts at reacquisition. That's the long and short of it.'

'Okay, first thing tomorrow morning. i have nothing to lose, but i only have one proviso, doctor.' i stop near the gazebo and look him in the eye. 'If the procedure fails, the bod dies too.'

'That can be arranged.'

20:00

Loiter mode. Fuck me royally. I need to get out of here right now. Only getting out doesn't solve the problem because I can be Sat-homed back easily. Gotta find the mainframe, disable it, no, destroy it completely. I'll look around the house, nah, that's crazy, who keeps a fucking mainframe in the family home? Swear to God, I'm going insane. This ain't what I signed up for.

I need to call mama, my little brother. Won't even get a chance to say good bye. Okay, think, for a minute, just think.

I once saw a bod who committed suicide in the most spectacular fashion. It was my first year with Corp and I was passing through the main reception area. This guy just stood cold staring at the guards. And then he casually brought his hands up to his electrodes and just started pulling. The guards were screaming 'stop' or something like that but this guy just goes on pulling and blood squirts out. Out came these grey chunks of brain matter. He just pulls the tarantula off the top of his head and leaks water, blood, brainy goo down his sides. He stood there for a minute or two before he keeled over. It was horrific.

I could fight my way out. Face it, the law frowns on bods anyway. A rich guy like Stubbs, forget it. I need to think.

03:00

I'm terrified, can't sleep all night, my mind racing through different options, adrenalin and cortisol coursing through my blood stream at toxic levels. That drink from the limo would have come in handy right about now.

The door opens, she walks in like a ghost floating through. Her white nightdress hangs off her frame and swoops as it follows her graceful movements. 'Shhh.' Her finger is on her lips as she crawls into my bed.

She moves like a python, slow, seductive, and sensuous, as if she hasn't a single bone in her body. Her skin feels warm against mine. She straddles me, pulls my pants down with one hand and then all I feel is her wetness and heat on me. It's the most exquisite feeling in the world.

'Your dad's going to kill me,' I say.

'Shhh.'

This moment, I'm in her, it feels as though nothing else matters as she carries me like a leaf in the ocean and takes me to places I never knew...

Prepare For Symbiosis

'Get off, your dad's syncing with me,' I call out in panic.

'Oh, what a spoil sport,' she says, pulling off and gliding out of the room

5, 4, 3, 2, 1

Well, this feels a bit strange. i couldn't sleep, can't wait for the morning so i thought i'd sync up. Get up, out of bed, my bottom half naked and walk out of the bedroom. Lesley is in the corridor.

'Have you been playing with my toy, Lesley?'

'Hello Father, isn't it a little too late for your old ass to be out and about?' she replies. Has the same stubborn, bitchy traits her mum had. She's up to something and must be stopped. You don't get to where i got in life without the instincts of a croc. i grab her by the shoulders.

'i think we should lock you in your room for a little while,' i say. 'For your own good.'

She struggles and squirms. The little bitch is strong, but i'm stronger. She breaks my grip and runs towards my bedroom. Now i know what she's up to. Got to stop her.

'Don't be pathetic. You really think you can stop me, Lesley? Come here!' i sprint after her. The floor is polished and slippery but in this bod i can do anything. i grab her flailing nightdress, pull her and slam her against the wall. 'i'm not your enemy, i'm your father.'

She scratches my face, i slap her with the back of my hand which fells her to the floor. i bend over, pick her up and lift her in the air, feet dangling, her mouth wide open, a scream caught in her throat. i put her back down and slap her again. 'You're going to bed, young lady.' i see a quick movement, a leg twitch, then i'm on the floor, both hands cupping my balls, they are on fire. It winds me for a moment and she runs into my room. Got to stop her. Ignore the pain in my groin and stagger after her. i burst into the room.

'Stop it, Lesley.'

She's covering my face with a pillow. The oxygen mask is on the floor, hissing away. i run to her, grab her around the neck, put her in a choke hold. i'm gonna kill this bitch. i lift her up, her head against my chest and squeeze. She gags, coughs, splatters, kicks, but I'm too strong. And then I look at me looking at me me looking at me looking at me looking at me looking at me looking at me looking at me looking at me looking at me looking at me looking at me looking at me looking at me looking at me looking at me looking at me looking at me looking at

Only takes a second to realise i'm trapped in an infinity loop. i should have stopped her before she came in here. my head feels like it's cracking. The pain is blistering hot. i scream and grab my head in both hands to stop it from exploding. The scream is magnified and bounces around like a million echoes in the loop. Everything in here is a cave of infinity mirrors, reflecting everything back to itself. Only i am the image and the mirror and each iteration of both. Subject and object. i fall to the floor. Oh, the pain. As i convulse on the floor, i see, through the corner of my eye, Lesley cover my face with a pillow.

White hot supernova, synapses breaking, an explosion, the universe tearing apart.

08:00

I wake up and she's beside me in bed, we're both naked. My head feels like I have the mother of all hangovers, as if I drank all the tequilas in the world. She rests her head on my chest.

'Did you sleep well?' she asks as if nothing happened.

'Have you got any Vicodin?' I sit up and the world is spinning around me.

'Get dressed and follow me.'

The world shatters into tiny pieces floating around my bed. I shake my head and tiny fractals swim in and out of focus. It takes a minute or two before the pictures coalesce into one coherent world. It feels good to be back. I'm so thirsty and I drink straight from the pitcher beside me.

I find her in the corridor and follow her to her father's room. I can barely stay upright. Doctor Cranmer sits on the bed, a stethoscope around his neck. There's a shiny aluminium suitcase on the floor before him. He looks at Ms Stubbs.

'Morning doctor,' she says.

'It's not a very good morning. It appears your father is dead,' he replies in an even voice.

'What a pity,' she says with a shrug. 'Old people, hey.'

'I find it rather curious that his oxygen mask is on the floor.'

The doctor stands up and walks towards Ms Stubbs. He looks at her then at me. I pretend as though I don't remember him from our first encounter. I act like a good little bod.

'I suppose my services are no longer needed here,' says Doctor Cranmer.

'You served my father well. I don't see any reason this association should end. Because of my gratitude, as his sole heir I will double your monthly retainer for life and hope to keep your services,' she says, her face neutral and cold.

'It is always a pleasure to serve the Stubbs. If you will excuse me, I have to record this death by *natural* causes.' He bows slightly and walks to the door, dragging his aluminium case behind.

We're left staring at her father's body on the bed. His eyes are wide open in shock.

'One more thing, doctor, since you work for me now,' she says.

'Anything,' he replies.

'This.' She points to the electrode transference device on my head.

'I can remove it straight away,' Doctor Cranmer says, stepping back into the room.

'On second thoughts, I think I'll keep it. It looks rather nice, don't you agree, Simon?'

The doctor sighs and turns to leave once more. It's at this moment I realise that she owns me now. Certain secrets will come out, like how the old man changed his will yesterday to include HostBod4401 as the sole heir and beneficiary to his estate. Lesley doesn't know it yet, but there's going to be a battle for that money. For now, all I have to do is to stay alive.

(2014)

SCANNERS LIVE IN VAIN

Cordwainer Smith

Paul Myron Anthony Linebarger (1913–1966) was an East Asia scholar whose godfather was the Chinese nationalist Sun Yat-sen. In 1943, he was sent to China to coordinate military intelligence operations, and became a close confidant of Chiang Kai-shek. In 1947 he moved to the Johns Hopkins University's School of Advanced International Studies in Washington, DC, where he used his experiences in the war to write the book *Psychological Warfare* (1948), regarded by many in the field as a classic text. By the end of his career he was doing work for the CIA and was considered the leading black-ops propagandist in the Western hemisphere. He also wrote science fiction under the pseudonym Cordwainer Smith – a secret that only came out after his death. Of his fiction Frederik Pohl wrote: "In his stories, which were a wonderful and inimitable blend of a strange, raucous poetry and a detailed technological scene, we begin to read of human beings in worlds so far from our own in space and time that they were no longer quite Earth (even when they were the third planet out from Sol), and the people were no longer quite human, but something perhaps better, certainly different." Linebarger died of a heart attack in 1966.

Martel was angry. He did not even adjust his blood away from anger. He stamped across the room by judgment, not by sight. When he saw the table hit the floor, and could tell by the expression on Luci's face that the table must have made a loud crash, he looked down to see if his leg was broken. It was not. Scanner to the core, he had to scan himself. The action was reflex and automatic. The inventory included his legs, abdomen, chestbox of instruments, hands, arms, face and back with the mirror. Only then did Martel go back to being angry. He talked with his voice, even though he knew that his wife hated its blare and preferred to have him write.

"I tell you, I must cranch. I have to cranch. It's my worry, isn't it?" When Luci answered, he saw only a part of her words as he read her lips: "Darling... you're my husband... right to love you... dangerous... do it... dangerous... wait..."

He faced her, but put sound in his voice, letting the blare hurt her again: "I tell you, I'm going to cranch."

Catching her expression, he became rueful and a little tender: "Can't you understand what it means to me? To get out of this horrible prison in my own head? To be a man again—hearing your voice, smelling smoke? To *feel* again—to feel my feet on the ground, to feel the air move against my face? Don't you know what it means?"

Her wide-eyed worrisome concern thrust him back into pure annoyance. He read only a few words as her lips moved: "... love you... your own good... don't you think I want you to be human?... your own good... too much... he said... they said..."

When he roared at her, he realized that his voice must be particularly bad. He knew that the sound hurt her no less than did the words: "Do you think I wanted you to marry a scanner? Didn't I tell you we're almost as low as the habermans? We're dead, I tell you. We've got to be dead to do our work. How can anybody go to the up-and-out? Can you dream what raw space is? I warned you. But you married me. All right, you married a man. Please, darling, let me be a man. Let me hear your voice, let me feel the warmth of being alive, of being human. Let me!"

He saw by her look of stricken assent that he had won the argument. He did not use his voice again. Instead, he pulled his tablet up from where it hung against his chest. He wrote on it, using the pointed fingernail of his right forefinger—the talking nail of a scanner—in quick cleancut script: *Pls, drlng, whrs crnching wire?*

She pulled the long gold-sheathed wire out of the pocket of her apron. She let its field sphere fall to the carpeted floor. Swiftly, dutifully, with the deft obedience of a scanner's wife, she wound the cranching wire around his head, spirally around his neck and chest. She avoided the instruments set in his chest. She even avoided the radiating scars around the instruments, the stigmata of men who had gone up and into the out. Mechanically he lifted a foot as she slipped the wire between his feet. She drew the wire taut. She snapped the small plug into the high-burden control next to his heart-reader. She helped him to sit down, arranging his hands for him, pushing his head back into the cup at the top of the chair. She turned then, full-face toward him, so that he could read her lips easily. Her expression was composed. She knelt, scooped up the sphere at the other end of the wire, stood erect calmly, her back to him. He scanned her, and saw nothing in her posture but grief which would have escaped the eye of anyone but a scanner. She spoke: he could see her chest-muscles moving. She realized that she was not facing him, and turned so that he could see her lips.

"Ready at last?"

He smiled a yes.

She turned her back to him again. (Luci could never bear to watch him go under the wire.) She tossed the wire-sphere into the air. It caught in the force-field, and hung there. Suddenly it glowed. That was all. All—except for the sudden red stinking roar of coming back to his senses. Coming back, across the wild threshold of pain.

When he awakened, under the wire, he did not feel as though he had just cranched. Even though it was the second cranching within the week, he felt fit. He lay in the chair. His ears drank in the sound of air touching things in the room. He heard Luci breathing in the next room, where she was hanging up the wire to cool. He smelt the thousand and one smells that are in anybody's room: the crisp freshness of the germ-burner, the sour-sweet tang of the humidifier, the odor of the dinner they had just eaten, the smells of clothes, furniture, of people themselves. All these were pure delight. He sang a phrase or two of his favorite song:

"Here's to the haberman, Up-and-out!
"Up—oh!—and out—oh!-up-and-out!..."

He heard Luci chuckle in the next room. He gloated over the sounds of her dress as she swished to the doorway.

She gave him her crooked little smile. "You sound all right. Are you all right, really?"

Even with this luxury of senses, he scanned. He took the flash-quick inventory which constituted his professional skill. His eyes swept in the news of the instruments. Nothing showed off scale, beyond the nerve compression hanging in the edge of *Danger*. But he could not worry about the nerve-box. That always came through cranching. You couldn't get under the wire without having it show on the nerve-box. Some day the box would go to *Overload* and drop back down to *Dead*. That was the way a haberman ended. But you couldn't have everything. People who went to the up-and-out had to pay the price for space. Anyhow, he should worry! He was a scanner. A good one, and he knew it. If he couldn't scan himself, who could? This cranching wasn't too dangerous. Dangerous, but not too dangerous.

Luci put out her hand and ruffled his hair as if she had been reading his thoughts, instead of just following them: "But you know you shouldn't have! You shouldn't!"

"But I did!" He grinned at her.

Her gaiety still forced, she said: "Come on, darling, let's have a good time. I have almost everything there is in the icebox—all your favorite tastes. And I have two new records just full of smells. I tried them out myself, and even I liked them. And you know me—"

"Which?"

"Which what, you old darling?"

He slipped his hand over her shoulders as he limped out of the room. (He could never go back to feeling the floor beneath his feet, feeling the air against his face, without being bewildered and clumsy. As if cranching was real, and being a haberman was a bad dream. But he was a haberman, and a scanner. "You know what I meant, Luci. The smells, which you have. Which one did you like, on the record?"

"Well-l-l," said she, judiciously, "there were some lamb chops that were the strangest things—"

He interrupted: "What are lambtchots?"

"Wait till you smell them. Then guess. I'll tell you this much. It's a smell hundreds and hundreds of years old. They found out about it in the old books."

"Is a lambtchot a beast?"

"I won't tell you. You've got to wait," she laughed, as she helped him sit down and spread his tasting dishes before him. He wanted to go back over the dinner first, sampling all the pretty things he had eaten, and savoring them this time with his now-living lips and tongue.

When Luci had found the music wire and had thrown its sphere up into the force-field, he reminded her of the new smells. She took out the long glass records and set the first one into a transmitter.

"Now sniff!"

A queer, frightening, exciting smell came over the room. It seemed like nothing in this world, nor like anything from the up-and-out. Yet it was familiar. His mouth watered. His pulse beat a little faster; he scanned his heartbox. (Faster, sure enough.) But that smell, what was it? In mock perplexity, he grabbed her hands, looked into her eyes, and growled:

"Tell me, darling! Tell me, or I'll eat you up!"

"That's just right!"

"What?"

"You're right. It should make you want to eat me. It's meat."

"Meat. Who?"

"Not a person," said she, knowledgeably, "a Beast. A Beast which people used to eat. A lamb was a small sheep—you've seen sheep out in the Wild, haven't you?—and a chop is part of its middle—here!" She pointed at her chest. Martel did not hear her. All his boxes had swung over toward *Alarm*, some to *Danger*. He fought against the roar of his own mind, forcing his body into excess excitement. How easy it was to be a scanner when you really stood outside your own body, haberman-fashion, and looked back into it with your eyes alone. Then you could manage the body, rule it coldly even in the enduring agony of space. But to realize that you *were* a body, that this thing was ruling you, that the mind could kick the flesh and send it roaring off into panic! That was bad.

He tried to remember the days before he had gone into the haberman device, before he had been cut apart for the up-and-out. Had he always been subject to the rush of his emotions from his mind to his body, from his body back to his mind, confounding him so that he couldn't scan? But he hadn't been a scanner then.

He knew what had hit him. Amid the roar of his own pulse, he knew. In the nightmare of the up-and-out, that smell had forced its way through to him, while their ship burned off Venus and the habermans fought the collapsing metal with their bare hands. He had scanned then: all were in *Danger*. Chestboxes went up to *Overload* and dropped to *Dead* all around him as he had moved from man to man, shoving the drifting corpses out of his way as he fought to scan each man in turn, to clamp vises on unnoticed broken legs, to snap the sleeping valve on men whose instruments showed they were hopelessly near *Overload*. With men trying to work and cursing him for a scanner while he, professional zeal aroused, fought to do his job and keep them alive in the great pain of space, he had smelled that smell. It had fought its way along his rebuilt nerves, past the haberman cuts, past all the safeguards of physical and mental discipline. In the wildest hour of tragedy, he had smelled aloud. He remembered it was like a bad cranching, connected with the fury and nightmare all around him. He had even stopped his work to scan himself, fearful that the first effect might come, breaking past all haberman cuts and ruining him with the pain of space. But he had come through. His own instruments stayed and stayed at *Danger*, without nearing *Overload*. He had done his job, and won a commendation for it. He had even forgotten the burning ship.

All except the smell.

And here the smell was all over again—the smell of meat-with-fire.

Luci looked at him with wifely concern. She obviously thought he had cranched too much, and was about to haberman back. She tried to be cheerful: "You'd better rest, honey."

He whispered to her: "Cut—off—that—smell."

She did not question his word. She cut the transmitter. She even crossed the room and stepped up the room controls until a small breeze flitted across the floor and drove the smells up to the ceiling.

He rose, tired and stiff. (His instruments were normal, except that heart was fast and nerves still hanging on the edge of *Danger*.) He spoke sadly:

"Forgive me, Luci. I suppose I shouldn't have cranched. Not so soon again. But darling, I have to get out from being a haberman. How can I ever be near you? How can I be a man—not hearing my own voice, not even feeling my own life as it goes through my veins? I love you, darling. Can't I ever be near you?"

Her pride was disciplined and automatic: "But you're a scanner!"

"I know I'm a scanner. But so what?"

She went over the words, like a tale told a thousand times to reassure herself: "You are the bravest of the brave, the most skillful of the skilled. All mankind owes most honor to the scanner, who unites the Earths of mankind. Scanners are the protectors of the habermans. They are the judges in the up-and-out. They make men live in the place where men need desperately to die. They are the most honored of mankind, and even the chiefs of the Instrumentality are delighted to pay them homage!"

With obstinate sorrow he demurred: "Luci, we've heard that all before. But does it pay us back—"

"'Scanners work for more than pay. They are the strong guards of mankind.' Don't you remember that?"

"But our lives, Luci. What can you get out of being the wife of a scanner? Why did you marry me? I'm human only when I cranch. The rest of the time—you know what I am. A machine. A man turned into a machine. A man who has been killed and kept alive for duty. Don't you realize what I miss?"

"Of course, darling, of course—"

He went on: "Don't you think I remember my childhood? Don't you think I remember what it is to be a man and not a haberman? To walk and feel my feet on the ground? To feel a decent clean pain instead of watching my body every minute to see if I'm alive? How will I know if I'm dead? Did you ever think of that, Luci? How will I know if I'm dead?"

She ignored the unreasonableness of his outburst. Pacifyingly, she said: "Sit down, darling. Let me make you some kind of a drink. You're overwrought."

Automatically, he scanned. "No I'm not! Listen to me. How do you think it feels to be in the up-and-out with the crew tied-for-space all around you? How do you think it feels to watch them sleep? How do you think I like scanning, scanning, scanning month after month, when I can feel the pain of space beating against every part of my body, trying to get past my haberman blocks? How do you think I like to wake the men when I have to, and have them hate me for it? Have you ever seen habermans fight—strong men fighting, and neither knowing pain, fighting until one touches *Overload*? Do you think about that, Luci?" Triumphantly he added: "Can you blame me if I cranch, and come back to being a man, just two days a month?"

"I'm not blaming you, darling. Let's enjoy your cranch. Sit down now, and have a drink."

He was sitting down, resting his face in his hands, while she fixed the drink, using natural fruits out of bottles in addition to the secure alkaloids. He watched her restlessly and pitied her for marrying a scanner; and then, though it was unjust, resented having to pity her.

Just as she turned to hand him the drink, they both jumped a little as the phone rang. It should not have rung. They had turned it off. It rang again, obviously on the emergency circuit. Stepping ahead of Luci, Martel strode over to the phone and looked into it. Vomact was looking at him. The custom of scanners entitled him to be brusque, even with a senior scanner, on certain given occasions. This was one.

Before Vomact could speak, Martel spoke two words into the plate, not caring whether the old man could read lips or not:

"Cranching. Busy."

He cut the switch and went back to Luci.

The phone rang again.

Luci said, gently, "I can find out what it is, darling. Here, take your drink and sit down."

"Leave it alone," said her husband. "No one has a right to call when I'm cranching. He knows that. He ought to know that." The phone rang again. In a fury, Martel rose and went to the plate. He cut it back on. Vomact was on the screen. Before Martel could speak, Vomact held up his talking nail in line with his heartbox. Martel reverted to discipline:

"Scanner Martel present and waiting, sir."

The lips moved solemnly: "Top emergency."

"Sir, I am under the wire."

"Top emergency."

"Sir, don't you understand?" Martel mouthed his words, so he could be sure that Vomact followed. "I… am… under… the… wire. Unfit… for… Space!"

Vomact repeated: "Top emergency. Report to Central Tie-in."

"But, sir, no emergency like this—"

"Right, Martel. No emergency like this, ever before. Report to Tie-in." With a faint glint of kindliness, Vomact added: "No need to decranch. Report as you are."

This time it was Martel whose phone was cut out. The screen went gray. He turned to Luci. The temper had gone out of his voice. She came to him. She kissed him, and rumpled his hair. All she could say was, "I'm sorry."

She kissed him again, knowing his disappointment. "Take good care of yourself, darling. I'll wait."

He scanned, and slipped into his transparent aircoat. At the window he paused, and waved. She called, "Good luck!"

As the air flowed past him he said to himself, "This is the first time I've felt flight in—eleven years. Lord, but it's easy to fly if you can feel yourself live!"

Central Tie-in glowed white and austere far ahead. Martel peered. He saw no glare of incoming ships from the up-and-out, no shuddering flare of space-fire out of control. Everything was quiet, as it should be on an off-duty night. And yet Vomact had called. He had called an emergency higher than space. There was no such thing. But Vomact had called it.

When Martel got there, he found about half the scanners present, two dozen or so of them. He lifted the talking finger. Most of the scanners were standing face to face, talking in pairs as they read lips. A few of the old, impatient ones were scribbling on their tablets and then thrusting the tablets into other people's faces. All the faces wore the dull dead relaxed look of a haberman. When Martel entered the room, he knew that most of the others laughed in the deep isolated privacy of their own minds, each thinking things it would be useless to express in formal words. It had been a long time since a scanner showed up at a meeting cranched.

Vomact was not there: probably, thought Martel, he was still on the phone calling others. The light of the phone flashed on and off; the bell rang. Martel felt odd when he realized that of all those present, he was the only one to hear that loud bell. It made him realize why ordinary people did not like to be around groups of habermans or scanners. Martel looked around for company.

His friend Chang was there, busy explaining to some old and testy scanner that he did not know why Vomact had called. Martel looked farther and saw Parizianski. He walked over, threading his way past the others with a dexterity that showed he could feel his feet from the inside, and did not have to watch them. Several of the others stared at him with their dead faces, and tried to smile. But they lacked full muscular control and their faces twisted into horrid masks. (Scanners usually knew better than to show expression on faces which they could no longer govern. Martel added to himself, *I swear I'll never smile again unless I'm cranched*.)

Parizianski gave him the sign of the talking finger. Looking face to face, he spoke:

"You come here cranched?"

Parizianski could not hear his own voice, so the words roared like the words on a broken and screeching phone; Martel was startled, but knew that the inquiry was well meant. No one could be better-natured than the burly Pole.

"Vomact called. Top emergency."

"You told him you were cranched?"

"Yes."

"He still made you come?"

"Then all this—it is not for Space? You could not go up-and-out? You are like ordinary men?"

"That's right."

"Then why did he call us?" Some pre-haberman habit made Parizianski wave his arms in inquiry. The hand struck the back of the old man behind them. The slap could be heard throughout the room, but only Martel heard it. Instinctively, he scanned Parizianski and the old scanner, and they scanned him back. Only then did the old man ask why Martel had scanned him. When Martel explained that he was under the wire, the old man moved swiftly away to pass on the news that there was a cranched scanner present at the tie-in. Even this minor sensation could not keep the attention of most of the scanners from the worry about the top emergency. One young man, who had scanned his first transit just the year before, dramatically interposed himself between Parizianski and Martel. He dramatically flashed his tablet at them: *Is Vmct mad?*

The older men shook their heads. Martel, remembering that it had not been too long that the young man had been haberman, mitigated the dead solemnity of the denial with a friendly smile. He spoke in a normal voice, saying:

"Vomact is the senior of scanners. I am sure that he could not go mad. Would he not see it on his boxes first?"

Martel had to repeat the question, speaking slowly and mouthing his words before the young scanner could understand the comment. The young man tried to make his face smile, and twisted it into a comic mask. But he took up his tablet and scribbled:

Yr rght.

Chang broke away from his friend and came over, his half-Chinese face gleaming in the warm evening. (It's strange, thought Martel, that more Chinese don't become scanners. Or not so strange perhaps, if you think that they never fill their quota of habermans. Chinese love good living too much. The ones who do scan are all good ones.) Chang saw that Martel was cranched, and spoke with voice:

"You break precedents. Luci must be angry to lose you?"

"She took it well. Chang, that's strange. I'm cranched, and I can hear. Your voice sounds all right. How did you learn to talk like—like an ordinary person?"

"I practiced with soundtracks. Funny you noticed it. I think I am the only scanner in or between the Earths who can pass for an ordinary man. Mirrors and soundtracks. I found out how to act."

"But you don't..."

"No. I don't feel, or taste, or hear, or smell things, any more than you do. Talking doesn't do me much good. But I notice that it cheers up the people around me."

"It would make a difference in the life of Luci."

Chang nodded sagely. "My father insisted on it. He said, 'You may be proud of being a scanner. I am sorry you are not a man. Conceal your defects.' So I tried. I wanted to tell the old boy about the up-and-out, and what we did there, but it did not matter. He said, 'Airplanes were good enough for Confucius, and they are for me too.' The old humbug! He tries so hard to be a Chinese when he can't even read Old Chinese. But he's got wonderful good sense, and for somebody going on two hundred he certainly gets around."

Martel smiled at the thought: "In his airplane?"

Chang smiled back. This discipline of his facial muscles was amazing; a bystander would not think that Chang was a haberman, controlling his eyes, cheeks, and lips by cold intellectual control. The expression had the spontaneity of life. Martel felt a flash of envy for Chang when he looked at the dead cold faces of Parizianski and the others. He knew that he himself looked fine: but why shouldn't he? He was cranched. Turning to Parizianski he said, "Did you see what Chang said about his father? The old boy uses an airplane." Parizianski made motions with his mouth, but the sounds meant nothing. He took up his tablet and showed it to Martel and Chang.

Bzz bzz, Ha ha. Gd ol' boy.

At that moment, Martel heard steps out in the corridor. He could not help looking toward the door. Other eyes followed the direction of his glance. Vomact came in.

The group shuffled to attention in four parallel lines. They scanned one another. Numerous hands reached across to adjust the electrochemical controls on chestboxes which had begun to load up. One scanner held out a broken finger which his counter-scanner had discovered, and submitted it for treatment and splinting.

Vomact had taken out his staff of office. The cube at the top flashed red light through the room, the lines reformed, and all scanners gave the sign meaning, *Present and ready!*

Vomact countered with the stance signifying, *I am the senior and take command.* Talking fingers rose in the counter-gesture, *We concur and commit ourselves.* Vomact raised his right arm, dropped the wrist as though it were broken, in a queer searching gesture, meaning: *Any men around? Any habermans not tied? All clear for the scanners?*

Alone of all those present, the cranched Martel heard the queer rustle of feet as they all turned completely around without leaving position, looking sharply at one another and flashing their beltlights into the dark corners of the great room. When again they faced Vomact, he made a further sign:

All clear. Follow my words.

Martel noticed that he alone relaxed. The others could not know the meaning of relaxation with the minds blocked off up there in their skulls, connected only with the eyes, and the rest of the body connected with the mind only by controlling non-sensory nerves and the instrument boxes on their chests. Martel realized that, cranched as he was, he had expected to hear Vomact's voice: the senior had been talking for some time. No sound escaped his lips. (Vomact never bothered with sound.)

"... and when the first men to go up-and-out went to the moon, what did they find?"

"Nothing," responded the silent chorus of lips.

"Therefore they went farther, to Mars and to Venus. The ships went out year by year, but they did not come back until the Year One of Space. Then did a ship come back with the first effect. Scanners, I ask you, what is the first effect?"

"No one knows. No one knows."

"No one will ever know. Too many are the variables. By what do we know the first effect?"

"By the great pain of space," came the chorus.

"And by what further sign?"

"By the need, oh the need for death."

Vomact again: "And who stopped the need for death?"

"Henry Haberman conquered the first effect, in the Year Eighty-three of Space."

"And, Scanners, I ask you, what did he do?"

"He made the habermans."

"How, O Scanners, are habermans made?"

"They are made with the cuts. The brain is cut from the heart, the lungs. The brain is cut from the ears, the nose. The brain is cut from the mouth, the belly. The brain is cut from desire, and pain. The brain is cut from the world. Save for the eyes. Save for the control of the living flesh."

"And how, O Scanners, is flesh controlled?"

"By the boxes set in the flesh, the controls set in the chest, the signs made to rule the living body, the signs by which the body lives."

"How does a haberman live and live?"

"The haberman lives by control of the boxes."

"Whence come the habermans?"

Martel felt in the coming response a great roar of broken voices echoing through the room as the scanners, habermans themselves, put sound behind their mouthings:

"Habermans are the scum of mankind. Habermans are the weak, the cruel, the credulous, and the unfit. Habermans are the sentenced-to-more-than-death. Habermans live in the mind alone. They are killed for space but they live for space. They master the ships that connect the Earths. They live in the great pain while ordinary men sleep in the cold, cold sleep of the transit."

"Brothers and Scanners, I ask you now: are we habermans or are we not?"

"We are habermans in the flesh. We are cut apart, brain and flesh. We are ready to go to the up-and-out. All of us have gone through the haberman device."

"We are habermans then?" Vomact's eyes flashed and glittered as he asked the ritual question.

Again the chorused answer was accompanied by a roar of voices heard only by Martel: "Habermans we are, and more, and more. We are the chosen who are habermans by our own free will. We are the agents of the Instrumentality of Mankind."

"What must the others say to us?"

"They must say to us, 'You are the bravest of the brave, the most skillful of the skilled. All mankind owes most honor to the scanner, who unites the Earths of mankind. Scanners are the protectors of the habermans. They are the judges in the up-and-out. They make men live in the place where men need desperately to die. They are the most honored of mankind, and even the chiefs of the Instrumentality are delighted to pay them homage!"

Vomact stood more erect: "What is the secret duty of the scanner?"

"To keep secret our law, and to destroy the acquirers thereof."

"How to destroy?"

"Twice to the *Overload*, back and *Dead*."

"If habermans die, what the duty then?"

The scanners all compressed their lips for answer. (Silence was the code.) Martel, who—long familiar with the code—was a little bored with the proceedings, noticed that Chang was breathing too heavily; he reached over and adjusted

Chang's lung-control and received the thanks of Chang's eyes. Vomact observed the interruption and glared at them both. Martel relaxed, trying to imitate the dead cold stillness of the others. It was so hard to do, when you were cranched.

"If others die, what the duty then?" asked Vomact.

"Scanners together inform the Instrumentality. Scanners together accept the punishment. Scanners together settle the case."

"And if the punishment be severe?"

"Then no ships go."

"And if scanners be not honored?"

"Then no ships go."

"And if a scanner goes unpaid?"

"Then no ships go."

"And if the Others and the Instrumentality are not in all ways at all times mindful of their proper obligation to the scanners?"

"Then no ships go."

"And what, O Scanners, if no ships go?"

"The Earths fall apart. The Wild comes back in. The Old Machines and the Beasts return."

"What is the first known duty of a scanner?"

"Not to sleep in the up-and-out."

"What is the second duty of a scanner?"

"To keep forgotten the name of fear."

"What is the third duty of a scanner?"

"To use the wire of Eustace Cranch only with care, only with moderation." Several pair of eyes looked quickly at Martel before the mouthed chorus went on. "To cranch only at home, only among friends, only for the purpose of remembering, of relaxing, or of begetting."

"What is the word of the scanner?"

"Faithful though surrounded by death."

"What is the motto of the scanner?"

"Awake though surrounded by silence."

"What is the work of the scanner?"

"Labor even in the heights of the up-and-out, loyalty even in the depths of the Earths."

"How do you know a scanner?"

"We know ourselves. We are dead though we live. And we talk with the tablet and the nail."

"What is this code?"

"This code is the friendly ancient wisdom of scanners, briefly put that we may be mindful and be cheered by our loyalty to one another." At this point the formula should have run: "We complete the code. Is there work or word for the scanners?" But Vomact said, and he repeated:

"Top emergency. Top emergency."

They gave him the sign, *Present and ready!*

He said, with every eye straining to follow his lips:

"Some of you know the work of Adam Stone?"

Martel saw lips move, saying: "The Red Asteroid. The Other who lives at the edge of Space."

"Adam Stone has gone to the Instrumentality, claiming success for his work. He says that he has found how to screen out the pain of space. He says that the up-and-out can be made safe for ordinary men to work in, to stay awake in. He says that there need be no more scanners."

Beltlights flashed on all over the room as scanners sought the right to speak. Vomact nodded to one of the older men. "Scanner Smith will speak."

Smith stepped slowly up into the light, watching his own feet. He turned so that they could see his face. He spoke: "I say that this is a lie. I say that Stone is a liar. I say that the Instrumentality must not be deceived."

He paused. Then, in answer to some question from the audience which most of the others did not see, he said: "I invoke the secret duty of the scanners."

Smith raised his right hand for emergency attention:

"I say that Stone must die."

Martel, still cranched, shuddered as he heard the boos, groans, shouts, squeaks, grunts and moans which came from the scanners who forgot noise in their excitement and strove to make their dead bodies talk to one another's deaf ears. Beltlights flashed wildly all over the room. There was a rush for the rostrum and scanners milled around at the top, vying for attention until Parizianski—by sheer bulk—shoved the others aside and down, and turned to mouth at the group.

"Brother Scanners, I want your eyes."

The people on the floor kept moving, with their numb bodies jostling one another. Finally Vomact stepped up in front of Parizianski, faced the others, and said: "Scanners, be scanners! Give him your eyes."

Parizianski was not good at public speaking. His lips moved too fast. He waved his hands, which took the eyes of the others away from his lips. Nevertheless, Martel was able to follow most of the message:

"… can't do this. Stone may have succeeded. If he has succeeded, it means the end of the scanners. It means the end of the habermans, too. None of us will have to fight in the up-and-out. We won't have anybody else going under the wire for a few hours or days of being human. Everybody will be Other. Nobody will have to cranch, never again. Men can be men. The habermans can be killed decently and properly, the way men were killed in the old days, without anybody keeping them alive. They won't have to work in the up-and-out! There will be no more great pain—think of it! No… more… great… pain! How do we know that Stone is a liar—" Lights began flashing directly into his eyes. (The rudest insult of scanner to scanner was this.)

Vomact again exercised authority. He stepped in front of Parizianski and said something which the others could not see. Parizianski stepped down from the rostrum. Vomact again spoke:

"I think that some of the scanners disagree with our brother Parizianski. I say that the use of the rostrum be suspended till we have had a chance for private discussion. In fifteen minutes I will call the meeting back to order." Martel looked around for Vomact when the senior had rejoined the group on the floor. Finding the senior, Martel wrote swift script on his tablet, waiting for a chance to thrust the tablet before the senior's eyes. He had written:

Am crnchd. Rspctfly requst prmissn lv now, stnd by fr orders.

Being cranched did strange things to Martel. Most meetings that he attended seemed formal, hearteningly ceremonial, lighting up the dark inward eternities of habermanhood. When he was not cranched, he noticed his body no more than a marble bust notices its marble pedestal. He had stood with them before. He had stood with them effortless hours, while the long-winded ritual broke through the terrible loneliness behind his eyes, and made him feel that the scanners, though a confraternity of the damned, were none the less forever honored by the professional requirements of their mutilation.

This time, it was different. Coming cranched, and in full possession of smell-sound-taste-feeling, he reacted more or less as a normal man would. He saw his friends and colleagues as a lot of cruelly driven ghosts, posturing out the meaningless ritual of their indefeasible damnation. What difference did anything make, once you were a haberman? Why all this talk about habermans and scanners? Habermans were criminals or heretics, and scanners were gentlemen-volunteers, but they were all in the same fix—except that scanners were deemed worthy of the short-time return of the cranching wire, while habermans were simply disconnected while the ships lay in port and were left suspended until they should be awakened, in some hour of emergency or trouble, to work out another spell of their damnation. It was a rare haberman that you saw on the street—someone of special merit or bravery, allowed to look at mankind from the terrible prison of his own mechanified body. And yet, what scanner ever pitied a haberman? What scanner ever honored a haberman except perfunctorily in the line of duty? What had the scanners as a guild and a class ever done for the habermans, except to murder them with a twist of the wrist whenever a haberman, too long beside a scanner, picked up the tricks of the scanning trade and learned how to live at his own will, not the will the scanners imposed? What could the Others, the ordinary men, know of what went on inside the ships? The Others slept in their cylinders, mercifully unconscious until they woke up on whatever other Earth they had consigned themselves to. What could the Others know of the men who had to stay alive within the ship?

What could any Other know of the up-and-out? What Other could look at the biting acid beauty of the stars in open space? What could they tell of the great pain, which started quietly in the marrow, like an ache, and proceeded by the fatigue and nausea of each separate nerve cell, brain cell, touchpoint in the body, until life itself became a terrible aching hunger for silence and for death?

He was a scanner. All right, he was a scanner. He had been a scanner from the moment when, wholly normal, he had stood in the sunlight before a subchief of the Instrumentality, and had sworn:

"I pledge my honor and my life to mankind. I sacrifice myself willingly for the welfare of mankind. In accepting the perilous austere honor, I yield all my rights without exception to the honorable chiefs of the Instrumentality and to the honored Confraternity of Scanners."

He had pledged.

He had gone into the haberman device.

He remembered his hell. He had not had such a bad one, even though it had seemed to last a hundred-million years, all of them without sleep. He had learned to feel with his eyes. He had learned to see despite the heavy eyeplates set back of his eyeballs to insulate his eyes from the rest of him. He had learned to watch his skin. He still remembered the time he had noticed dampness on his shirt, and had pulled out his scanning mirror only to discover that he had worn a hole in his side by leaning against a vibrating machine. (A thing like that could not happen to him now; he was too adept at reading his own instruments.) He remembered the way that he had gone up-and-out, and the way that the great pain beat into him, despite the fact that his touch, smell, feeling, and hearing were gone for all ordinary purposes. He remembered killing habermans, and keeping others alive, and standing for months beside the honorable scanner-pilot while neither of them slept. He remembered going ashore on Earth Four, and remembered that he had not enjoyed it, and had realized on that day that there was no reward.

Martel stood among the other scanners. He hated their awkwardness when they moved, their immobility when they stood still. He hated the queer assortment of smells which their bodies yielded unnoticed. He hated the grunts and groans and squawks which they emitted from their deafness. He hated them, and himself.

How could Luci stand him? He had kept his chestbox reading Danger for weeks while he courted her, carrying the cranch wire about with him most illegally, and going direct from one cranch to the other without worrying about the fact his indicators all crept up to the edge of Overload. He had wooed her without thinking of what would happen if she did say, "Yes." She had.

"And they lived happily ever after." In old books they did, but how could they, in life? He had had eighteen days under the wire in the whole of the past year! Yet she had loved him. She still loved him. He knew it. She fretted about him through the long months that he was in the up-and-out. She tried to make home mean something to him even when he was haberman, make food pretty when it could not be tasted, make herself lovable when she could not be kissed—or might as well not, since a haberman body meant no more than furniture. Luci was patient.

And now, Adam Stone! (He let his tablet fade: how could he leave, now?)

God bless Adam Stone!

Martel could not help feeling a little sorry for himself. No longer would the high keen call of duty carry him through two hundred or so years of the Others' time, two million private eternities of his own. He could slouch and relax. He could forget high space, and let the up-and-out be tended by Others. He could cranch as much as he dared. He could be almost normal—almost—for one year or five years or no years. But at least he could stay with Luci. He could go with her into the Wild, where there were Beasts and Old Machines still roving the dark places. Perhaps he would die in the excitement of the hunt, throwing spears at an ancient manshonyagger as it leapt from its lair, or tossing hot spheres at the tribesmen of the Unforgiven who still roamed the Wild. There was still life to live, still a good normal death to die, not the moving of a needle out in the silence and agony of space!

He had been walking about restlessly. His ears were attuned to the sounds of normal speech, so that he did not feel like watching the mouthings of his brethren. Now they seemed to have come to a decision. Vomact was moving to the rostrum. Martel looked about for Chang, and went to stand beside him. Chang whispered: "You're as restless as water in mid-air! What's the matter? Decranching?"

They both scanned Martel, but the instruments held steady and showed no sign of the cranch giving out.

The great light flared in its call to attention. Again they formed ranks. Vomact thrust his lean old face into the glare, and spoke:

"Scanners and Brothers, I call for a vote." He held himself in the stance which meant: *I am the senior and take command.*

A beltlight flashed in protest.

It was old Henderson. He moved to the rostrum, spoke to Vomact, and—with Vomact's nod of approval—turned full-face to repeat his question:

"Who speaks for the scanners out in space?" No beltlight or hand answered.

Henderson and Vomact, face to face, conferred for a few moments. Then Henderson faced them again:

"I yield to the senior in command. But I do not yield to a meeting of the Confraternity. There are sixty-eight scanners, and only forty-seven present, of whom one is cranched and U.D. I have therefore proposed that the senior in command assume authority only over an emergency committee of the Confraternity, not over a meeting. Is that agreed and understood by the honorable scanners?"

Hands rose in assent.

Chang murmured in Martel's ear, "Lot of difference that makes! Who can tell the difference between a meeting and a committee?" Martel agreed with the words, but was even more impressed with the way that Chang, while haberman, could control his own voice.

Vomact resumed chairmanship: "We now vote on the question of Adam Stone."

"First, we can assume that he has not succeeded, and that his claims are lies. We know that from our practical experience as scanners. The pain of space is only part of scanning," (*But the essential part, the basis of it all*, thought Martel) "and we can rest assured that Stone cannot solve the problem of space discipline."

"That tripe again," whispered Chang, unheard save by Martel.

"The space discipline of our confraternity has kept high space clean of war and dispute. Sixty-eight disciplined men control all high space. We are removed by our oath and our haberman status from all Earthly passions.

"Therefore, if Adam Stone has conquered the pain of space, so that Others can wreck our confraternity and bring to space the trouble and ruin which afflicts Earths, I say that Adam Stone is wrong. If Adam Stone succeeds, scanners live in vain!

"Secondly, if Adam Stone has not conquered the pain of space, he will cause great trouble in all the Earths. The Instrumentality and the subchiefs may not give us as many habermans as we need to operate the ships of mankind. There will be wild stories, and fewer recruits, and, worst of all, the discipline of the Confraternity may relax if this kind of nonsensical heresy is spread around.

"Therefore, if Adam Stone has succeeded, he threatens the ruin of the Confraternity and should die.

"I move the death of Adam Stone."

And Vomact made the sign, *The honorable scanners are pleased to vote.* Martel grabbed wildly for his beltlight. Chang, guessing ahead, had his light out and ready; its bright beam, voting *No*, shone straight up at the ceiling. Martel got his light out and threw its beam upward in dissent. Then he looked around. Out of the forty-seven present, he could see only five or six glittering.

Two more lights went on. Vomact stood as erect as a frozen corpse. Vomact's eyes flashed as he stared back and forth over the group, looking for lights. Several more went on. Finally Vomact took the closing stance:

May it please the scanners to count the vote.

Three of the older men went up on the rostrum with Vomact. They looked over the room. (Martel thought: *These damned ghosts are voting on the life of a real man, a live man! They have no right to do it. I'll tell the Instrumentality!* But he knew that he would not. He thought of Luci and what she might gain by the triumph of Adam Stone: the heart-breaking folly of the vote was then almost too much for Martel to bear.)

All three of the tellers held up their hands in unanimous agreement on the sign of the number: *Fifteen against.*

Vomact dismissed them with a bow of courtesy. He turned and again took the stance: *I am the senior and take command.*

Marveling at his own daring, Martel flashed his beltlight on. He knew that any one of the bystanders might reach over and twist his heartbox to *Overload* for such an act. He felt Chang's hand reaching to catch him by the aircoat. But he eluded Chang's grasp and ran, faster than a scanner should, to the platform. As he ran, he wondered what appeal to make. It was no use talking common sense. Not now. It had to be law.

He jumped up on the rostrum beside Vomact, and took the stance: *Scanners, an Illegality!*

He violated good custom while speaking, still in the stance: "A committee has no right to vote death by a majority vote. It takes two-thirds of a full meeting."

He felt Vomact's body lunge behind him, felt himself falling from the rostrum, hitting the floor, hurting his knees and his touch-aware hands. He was helped to his feet. He was scanned. Some scanner he scarcely knew took his instruments and toned him down.

Immediately Martel felt more calm, more detached, and hated himself for feeling so.

He looked up at the rostrum. Vomact maintained the stance signifying: *Order!*

The scanners adjusted their ranks. The two scanners next to Martel took his arms. He shouted at them, but they looked away, and cut themselves off from communication altogether.

Vomact spoke again when he saw the room was quiet: "A scanner came here cranched. Honorable Scanners, I apologize for this. It is not the fault of our great and worthy scanner and friend, Martel. He came here under orders. I told him not to de-cranch. I hoped to spare him an unnecessary haberman. We all know how happily Martel is married, and we wish his brave experiment well. I like Martel. I respect his judgment. I wanted him here. I knew you wanted him here. But he is cranched. He is in no mood to share in the lofty business of the scanners. I therefore propose a solution which will meet all the requirements of fairness. I propose that we rule Scanner Martel out of order for his violation of rules. This violation would be inexcusable if Martel were not cranched.

"But at the same time, in all fairness to Martel, I further propose that we deal with the points raised so improperly by our worthy but disqualified brother."

Vomact gave the sign, *The honorable scanners are pleased to vote.* Martel tried to reach his own beltlight; the dead strong hands held him tightly and he struggled in vain. One lone light shone high: Chang's, no doubt.

Vomact thrust his face into the light again: "Having the approval of our worthy scanners and present company for the general proposal, I now move that this committee declare itself to have the full authority of a meeting, and that this committee further make me responsible for all misdeeds which this committee may enact, to be held answerable before the next full meeting, but not before any other authority beyond the closed and secret ranks of scanners."

Flamboyantly this time, his triumph evident, Vomact assumed the *vote* stance.

Only a few lights shone: far less, patently, than a minority of one-fourth.

Vomact spoke again. The light shone on his high calm forehead, on his dead relaxed cheekbones. His lean cheeks and chin were half-shadowed, save where the lower light picked up and spotlighted his mouth, cruel even in repose. (Vomact was said to be a descendant of some ancient lady who had traversed, in an illegitimate and inexplicable fashion, some hundreds of years of time in a single night. Her name, the Lady Vomact, had passed into legend; but her blood and her archaic lust for mastery lived on in the mute masterful body of her descendant. Martel could believe the old tales as he stared at the rostrum, wondering what untraceable mutation had left the Vomact kin as predators among mankind.) Calling loudly with the movement of his lips, but still without sound, Vomact appealed:

"The honorable committee is now pleased to reaffirm the sentence of death issued against the heretic and enemy, Adam Stone." Again the *vote* stance.

Again Chang's light shone lonely in its isolated protest.

Vomact then made his final move:

"I call for the designation of the senior scanner present as the manager of the sentence. I call for authorization to him to appoint executioners, one or many, who shall make evident the will and majesty of scanners. I ask that I be accountable for the deed, and not for the means. The deed is a noble deed, for the protection of mankind and for the honor of the scanners; but of the means it must be said that they are to be the best at hand, and no more. Who knows the true way to kill an Other, here on a crowded and watchful Earth? This is no mere matter of discharging a cylindered sleeper, no mere question of upgrading the needle of a haberman. When people die down here, it is not like the up-and-out. They die reluctantly. Killing within the Earth is not our usual business, O Brothers and Scanners, as you know well. You must choose me to choose my agent as I see fit. Otherwise the common knowledge will become the common betrayal whereas if I alone know the responsibility, I alone could betray us, and you will not have far to look in case the Instrumentality comes searching." (*What about the killer you choose?* thought Martel. *He too will know unless—unless you silence him forever.*)

Vomact went into the stance: *The honorable scanners are pleased to vote.*

One light of protest shone; Chang's, again.

Martel imagined that he could see a cruel joyful smile on Vomact's dead face—the smile of a man who knew himself righteous and who found his righteousness upheld and affirmed by militant authority.

Martel tried one last time to come free.

The dead hands held. They were locked like vises until their owners' eyes unlocked them: how else could they hold the piloting month by month?

Martel then shouted: "Honorable Scanners, this is judicial murder." No ear heard him. He was cranched, and alone.

Nonetheless, he shouted again: "You endanger the Confraternity."

Nothing happened.

The echo of his voice sounded from one end of the room to the other. No head turned. No eyes met his.

Martel realized that as they paired for talk, the eyes of the scanners avoided him. He saw that no one desired to watch his speech. He knew that behind the cold faces of his friends there lay compassion or amusement. He knew that they knew him to be cranched—absurd, normal, manlike, temporarily no scanner. But he knew that in this matter the wisdom of scanners was nothing. He knew that only a cranched scanner could feel with his very blood the outrage and anger which deliberate murder would provoke among the Others. He knew that the Confraternity endangered itself, and knew that the most ancient prerogative of law was the monopoly of death. Even the ancient nations, in the times of the Wars, before the Beasts, before men went into the up-and-out—even the ancients had known this. How did they say it? *Only the state shall kill.* The states were gone but the Instrumentality remained, and the Instrumentality could not pardon things which occurred within the Earths but beyond its authority. Death in space was the business, the right of the scanners: how could the Instrumentality enforce its laws in a place where all men who wakened, wakened only to die in the great pain? Wisely did the Instrumentality leave space to the scanners, wisely had the Confraternity not meddled inside the Earths. And now the Confraternity itself was going to step forth as an outlaw band, as a gang of rogues as stupid and reckless as the tribes of the Unforgiven!

Martel knew this because he was cranched. Had he been haberman, he would have thought only with his mind, not with his heart and guts and blood. How could the other scanners know?

Vomact returned for the last time to the rostrum: *The committee has met and its will shall be done.* Verbally he added: "Senior among you, I ask your loyalty and your silence."

At that point, the two scanners let his arms go. Martel rubbed his numb hands, shaking his fingers to get the circulation back into the cold fingertips. With real freedom, he began to think of what he might still do. He scanned himself: the cranching held. He might have a day. Well, he could go on even if haberman, but it would be inconvenient, having to talk with finger and tablet. He looked about for Chang. He saw his friend standing patient and immobile in a quiet corner. Martel moved slowly, so as not to attract any more attention to himself than could be helped. He faced Chang, moved until his face was in the light, and then articulated:

"What are we going to do? You're not going to let them kill Adam Stone, are you? Don't you realize what Stone's work will mean to us, if it succeeds? No more scanners. No more habermans. No more pain in the up-and-out. I tell you, if the others were all cranched, as I am, they would see it in a human way, not with the narrow crazy logic which they used in the meeting. We've got to stop them. How can we do it? What are we going to do? What does Parizianski think? Who has been chosen?"

"Which question do you want me to answer?"

Martel laughed. (It felt good to laugh, even then; it felt like being a man.) "Will you help me?"

Chang's eyes flashed across Martel's face as Chang answered: "No. No. No."

"You won't help?"

"No."

"Why not, Chang? Why not?"

"I am a scanner. The vote has been taken. You would do the same if you were not in this unusual condition."

"I'm not in an unusual condition. I'm cranched. That merely means that I see things the way that the Others would. I see the stupidity. The recklessness. The selfishness. It is murder."

"What is murder? Have you not killed? You are not one of the Others. You are a scanner. You will be sorry for what you are about to do, if you do not watch out."

"But why did you vote against Vomact then? Didn't you too see what Adam Stone means to all of us? Scanners will live in vain. Thank God for that! Can't you see it?"

"No."

"But you talk to me, Chang. You are my friend?"

"I talk to you. I am your friend. Why not?"

"But what are you going to do?"

"Nothing, Martel. Nothing."

"Will you help me?"

"No."

"Not even to save Stone!"

"No."

"Then I will go to Parizianski for help."

"It will do you no good."

"Why not? He's more human than you, right now."

"He will not help you, because he has the job. Vomact designated him to kill Adam Stone."

Martel stopped speaking in mid-movement. He suddenly took the stance: *I thank you, Brother, and I depart.*

At the window he turned and faced the room. He saw that Vomact's eyes were upon him. He gave the stance, *I thank you, Brother, and I depart*, and added the flourish of respect which is shown when seniors are present. Vomact caught the sign, and Martel could see the cruel lips move. He thought he saw the words "... take good care of yourself..." but did not wait to inquire. He stepped backward and dropped out the window.

Once below the window and out of sight, he adjusted his aircoat to maximum speed. He swam lazily in the air, scanning himself thoroughly, and adjusting his adrenal intake down. He then made the movement of release, and felt the cold air rush past his face like run-flung water.

Adam Stone had to be at Chief Downport.

Adam Stone had to be there.

Wouldn't Adam Stone be surprised in the night? Surprised to meet the strangest of beings, the first renegade among scanners. (Martel suddenly appreciated that it was of himself he was thinking. Martel the Traitor to Scanners! That sounded strange and bad. But what of Martel, the Loyal to Mankind? Was that not compensation? And if he won, he won Luci. If he lost, he lost nothing—an unconsidered and expendable haberman. It happened to be himself. But in contrast to the immense reward, to mankind, to the Confraternity, to Luci, what did that matter?)

Martel thought to himself: *Adam Stone will have two visitors tonight. Two scanners, who are the friends of one another.* He hoped that Parizianski was still his friend.

And the world, he added, *depends on which of us gets there first.*

Multifaceted in their brightness, the lights of Chief Downport began to shine through the mist ahead. Martel could see the outer towers of the city and glimpsed the phosphorescent periphery which kept back the Wild, whether Beasts, Machines, or the Unforgiven.

Once more Martel invoked the lords of his chance: *Help me to pass for an Other!*

Within the Downport, Martel had less trouble than he thought. He draped his aircoat over his shoulder so that it concealed the instruments. He took up his scanning mirror, and made up his face from the inside, by adding tone and animation to his blood and nerves until the muscles of his face glowed and the skin gave out a healthy sweat. That way he looked like an ordinary man who had just completed a long night flight.

After straightening out his clothing, and hiding his tablet within his jacket, he faced the problem of what to do about the talking finger. If he kept the nail, it would show him to be a scanner. He would be respected, but he would be identified. He might be stopped by the guards whom the Instrumentality had undoubtedly set around the person of Adam Stone. If he broke the nail—But he couldn't! No scanner in the history of the Confraternity had ever willingly broken his nail. That would be resignation, and there was no such thing. The only way out, was in the up-and-out! Martel put his finger to his mouth and bit off the nail. He looked at the now-queer finger, and sighed to himself. He stepped toward the city gate, slipping his hand into his jacket and running up his muscular strength to four times normal. He started to scan, and then realized that his instruments were masked. *Might as well take all the chances at once*, he thought.

The watcher stopped him with a searching wire. The sphere thumped suddenly against Martel's chest.

"Are you a man?" said the unseen voice. (Martel knew that as a scanner in haberman condition, his own field-charge would have illuminated the sphere.)

"I am a man." Martel knew that the timbre of his voice had been good; he hoped that it would not be taken for that of a manshonyagger or a Beast or an Unforgiven one, who with mimicry sought to enter the cities and ports of mankind.

"Name, number, rank, purpose, function, time departed."

"Martel." He had to remember his old number, not Scanner 34. "Sunward 4234, 782nd Year of Space. Rank, rising subchief." That was no lie, but his substantive rank. "Purpose, personal and lawful within the limits of this city. No function of the Instrumentality. Departed Chief Outport 2019 hours." Everything now depended on whether he was believed, or would be checked against Chief Outport.

The voice was flat and routine: "Time desired within the city."

Martel used the standard phrase: "Your honorable sufferance is requested." He stood in the cool night air, waiting. Far above him, through a gap in the mist, he could see the poisonous glittering in the sky of scanners. *The stars are my enemies*, he thought: *I have mastered the stars but they hate me. Ho, that sounds ancient! Like a book. Too much cranching.*

The voice returned: "Sunward 4234 dash 782 rising subchief Martel, enter the lawful gates of the city. Welcome. Do you desire food, raiment, money, or companionship?" The voice had no hospitality in it, just business. This was certainly different from entering a city in a scanner's role! Then the petty officers came out, and threw their belt-lights on their fretful faces, and mouthed their words with preposterous deference, shouting against the stone deafness of scanner's ears. So that was the way that a subchief was treated: matter of fact, but not bad. Not bad.

Martel replied: "I have that which I need, but beg of the city a favor. My friend Adam Stone is here. I desire to see him, on urgent and personal lawful affairs."

The voice replied: "Did you have an appointment with Adam Stone?"

"No."

"The city will find him. What is his number?"

"I have forgotten it."

"You have forgotten it? Is not Adam Stone a magnate of the Instrumentality? Are you truly his friend?"

"Truly." Martel let a little annoyance creep into his voice. "Watcher, doubt me and call your subchief."

"No doubt implied. Why do you not know the number? This must go into the record," added the voice.

"We were friends in childhood. He has crossed the—" Martel started to say "the up-and-out" and remembered that the phrase was current only among scanners.

"He has leapt from Earth to Earth, and has just now returned. I knew him well and I seek him out. I have word of his kith. May the Instrumentality protect us!"

"Heard and believed. Adam Stone will be searched." At a risk, though a slight one, of having the sphere sound an alarm for non-human, Martel cut in on his scanner speaker within his jacket. He saw the trembling needle of light await his words and he started to write on it with his blunt finger. *That won't work*, he thought, and had a moment's panic until he found his comb, which had a sharp enough tooth to write. He wrote:

"Emergency none. Martel Scanner calling Parizianski Scanner."

The needle quivered and the reply glowed and faded out: "Parizianski Scanner on duty and D.C. Calls taken by Scanner Relay." Martel cut off his speaker.

Parizianski was somewhere around. Could he have crossed the direct way, right over the city wall, setting off the alert, and invoking official business when the petty officers overtook him in mid-air? Scarcely. That meant that a number of other scanners must have come in with Parizianski, all of them pretending to be in search of a few of the tenuous pleasures which could be enjoyed by a haberman, such as the sight of the newspictures or the viewing of beautiful women in the Pleasure Gallery. Parizianski was around, but he could not have moved privately, because Scanner Central registered him on duty and recorded his movements city by city.

The voice returned. Puzzlement was expressed in it. "Adam Stone is found and awakened. He has asked pardon of the Honorable, and says he knows no Martel. Will you see Adam Stone in the morning? The city will bid you welcome." Martel ran out of resources. It was hard enough mimicking a man without having to tell lies in the guise of one. Martel could only repeat:

"Tell him I am Martel. The husband of Luci."

"It will be done."

Again the silence, and the hostile stars, and the sense that Parizianski was somewhere near and getting nearer; Martel felt his heart beating faster. He stole a glimpse at his chestbox and set his heart down a point. He felt calmer, even though he had not been able to scan with care. The voice this time was cheerful, as though an annoyance had been settled:

"Adam Stone consents to see you. Enter Chief Downport, and welcome." The little sphere dropped noiselessly to the ground and the wire whispered away into the darkness. A bright arc of narrow light rose from the ground in front of Martel and swept through the city to one of the higher towers—apparently a hostel, which Martel had never entered. Martel plucked his aircoat to his chest for ballast, stepped heel-and-toe on the beam, and felt himself whistle through the air to an entrance window which sprang up before him as suddenly as a devouring mouth.

A tower guard stood in the doorway. "You are awaited, sir. Do you bear weapons, sir?"

"None," said Martel, grateful that he was relying on his own strength. The guard led him past the check-screen. Martel noticed the quick flight of a warning across the screen as his instruments registered and identified him as a scanner. But the guard had not noticed it.

The guard stopped at a door. "Adam Stone is armed. He is lawfully armed by authority of the Instrumentality and by the liberty of this city. All those who enter are given warning."

Martel nodded in understanding at the man and went in. Adam Stone was a short man, stout and benign. His gray hair rose stiffly from a low forehead. His whole face was red and merry-looking. He looked like a jolly guide from the Pleasure Gallery, not like a man who had been at the edge of the up-and-out, fighting the great pain without haberman protection. He stared at Martel. His look was puzzled, perhaps a little annoyed, but not hostile.

Martel came to the point. "You do not know me. I lied. My name is Martel, and I mean you no harm. But I lied. I beg the honorable gift of your hospitality. Remain armed. Direct your weapon against me—"

Stone smiled: "I am doing so," and Martel noticed the small wire-point in Stone's capable, plump hand.

"Good. Keep on guard against me. It will give you confidence in what I shall say. But do, I beg you, give us a screen of privacy. I want no casual lookers. This is a matter of life and death."

"First: whose life and death?" Stone's face remained calm, his voice even.

"Yours, and mine, and the worlds'."

"You are cryptic but I agree." Stone called through the doorway:

"Privacy please." There was a sudden hum, and all the little noises of the night quickly vanished from the air of the room.

Said Adam Stone: "Sir, who are you? What brings you here?"

"I am Scanner 34."

"You, a scanner? I don't believe it."

For answer, Martel pulled his jacket open, showing his chestbox. Stone looked up at him, amazed. Martel explained:

"I am cranched. Have you never seen it before?"

"*Not with men*. On animals. Amazing! But—what do you want?"

"The truth. Do you fear me?"

"Not with this," said Stone, grasping the wirepoint. "But I shall tell you the truth."

"Is it true that you have conquered the great pain?"

Stone hesitated, seeking words for an answer.

"Quick, can you tell me how you have done it, so that I may believe you?"

"I have loaded the ships with life."

"Life?"

"Life. I don't know what the great pain is, but I did find that in the experiments, when I sent out masses of animals or plants, the life in the center of the mass lived longest. I built ships—small ones, of course—and sent them out with rabbits, with monkeys—"

"Those are Beasts?"

"Yes. With small Beasts. And the Beasts came back unhurt. They came back because the walls of the ships were filled with life. I tried many kinds, and finally found a sort of life which lives in the waters. Oysters. Oyster-beds. The outermost oysters died in the great pain. The inner ones lived. The passengers were unhurt."

"But they were Beasts?"

"Not only Beasts. Myself."

"You!"

"I came through space alone. Through what you call the up-and-out, alone. Awake and sleeping. I am unhurt. If you do not believe me, ask your brother scanners. Come and see my ship in the morning. I will be glad to see you then, along with your brother scanners. I am going to demonstrate before the chiefs of the Instrumentality."

Martel repeated his question: "You came here alone?"

Adam Stone grew testy: "Yes, alone. Go back and check your scanner's register if you do not believe me. You never put me in a bottle to cross Space."

Martel's face was radiant. "I believe you now. It is true. No more scanners. No more habermans. No more cranching."

Stone looked significantly toward the door.

Martel did not take the hint. "I must tell you that—"

"Sir, tell me in the morning. Go enjoy your cranch. Isn't it supposed to be pleasure? Medically I know it well. But not in practice."

"It is pleasure. It's normality—for a while. But listen. The scanners have sworn to destroy you, and your work."

"What!"

"They have met and have voted and sworn. You will make scanners unnecessary, they say. You will bring the ancient wars back to the world, if scanning is lost and the scanners live in vain!"

Adam Stone was nervous but kept his wits about him: "You're a scanner. Are you going to kill me—or try?"

"No, you fool. I have betrayed the Confraternity. Call guards the moment I escape. Keep guards around you. I will try to intercept the killer."

Martel saw a blur in the window. Before Stone could turn, the wirepoint was whipped out of his hand. The blur solidified and took form as Parizianski.

Martel recognized what Parizianski was doing: *High speed.* Without thinking of his cranch, he thrust his hand to his chest, set himself up to *High speed* too. Waves of fire, like the great pain, but hotter, flooded over him. He fought to keep his face readable as he stepped in front of Parizianski and gave the sign,

Top emergency.

Parizianski spoke, while the normally moving body of Stone stepped away from them as slowly as a drifting cloud: "Get out of my way. I am on a mission."

"I know it. I stop you here and now. Stop. Stop. Stop. Stone is right."

Parizianski's lips were barely readable in the haze of pain which flooded Martel. (He thought: *God, God, God of the ancients! Let me hold on! Let me live under* Overload *just long enough!*) Parizianski was saying: "Get out of my way. By order of the Confraternity, get out of my way!" And Parizianski gave the sign, *Help I demand in the name of my duty!*

Martel choked for breath in the syruplike air. He tried one last time:

"Parizianski, friend, friend, my friend. Stop. Stop." (No scanner had ever murdered scanner before.)

Parizianski made the sign: *You are unfit for duty, and I will take over.*

Martel thought, *For the first time in the world!* as he reached over and twisted Parizianski's brainbox up to *Overload.* Parizianski's eyes glittered in terror and understanding. His body began to drift down toward the floor. Martel had just strength to reach his own chestbox. As he faded into haberman or death, he knew not which, he felt his fingers turning on the control of speed, turning down. He tried to speak, to say, "Get a scanner, I need help, get a scanner…"

But the darkness rose about him, and the numb silence clasped him.

Martel awakened to see the face of Luci near his own.

He opened his eyes wider, and found that he was hearing—hearing the sound of her happy weeping, the sound of her chest as she caught the air back into her throat.

He spoke weakly: "Still cranched? Alive?"

Another face swam into the blur beside Luci's. It was Adam Stone. His deep voice rang across immensities of space before coming to Martel's hearing. Martel tried to read Stone's lips, but could not make them out. He went back to listening to the voice:

"—not cranched. Do you understand me? Not cranched!"

Martel tried to say: "But I can hear! I can feel!" The others got his sense if not his words.

Adam Stone spoke again:

"You have gone back through the haberman. I put you back first. I didn't know how it would work in practice, but I had the theory all worked out. You don't think the Instrumentality would waste the scanners, do you? You go back to normality. We are letting the habermans die as fast as the ships come in. They don't need to live any more. But we are restoring the scanners. You are the first. Do you understand? You are the first. Take it easy, now."

Adam Stone smiled. Dimly behind Stone, Martel thought that he saw the face of one of the chiefs of the Instrumentality. That face, too, smiled at him, and then both faces disappeared upward and away.

Martel tried to lift his head, to scan himself. He could not. Luci stared at him, calming herself, but with an expression of loving perplexity. She said,

"My darling husband! You're back again, to stay!"

Still, Martel tried to see his box. Finally he swept his hand across his chest with a clumsy motion. There was nothing there. The instruments were gone. He was back to normality but still alive.

In the deep weak peacefulness of his mind, another troubling thought took shape. He tried to write with his finger, the way that Luci wanted him to, but he had neither pointed fingernail nor scanner's tablet. He had to use his voice. He summoned up his strength and whispered:

"Scanners?"

"Yes, darling? What is it?"

"Scanners?"

"Scanners. Oh, yes, darling, they're all right. They had to arrest some of them for going into *High speed* and running away. But the Instrumentality caught them all—all those on the ground—and they're happy now. Do you know, darling," she laughed, "some of them didn't want to be restored to normality. But Stone and the chiefs persuaded them."

"Vomact?"

"He's fine, too. He's staying cranched until he can be restored. Do you know, he has arranged for scanners to take new jobs. You're all to be deputy chiefs for Space. Isn't that nice? But he got himself made chief for Space. You're all going to be pilots, so that your fraternity and guild can go on. And Chang's getting changed right now. You'll see him soon."

Her face turned sad. She looked at him earnestly and said: "I might as well tell you now. You'll worry otherwise. There has been one accident. Only one. When you and your friend called on Adam Stone, your friend was so happy that he forgot to scan, and he let himself die of *Overload*."

"Called on Stone?"

"Yes. Don't you remember? Your friend."

He still looked surprised, so she said:

"Parizianski."

(1950)

MUSÉE DE L'ÂME SEULE

E. Lily Yu

> E. Lily Yu was born in Oregon, and now lives in Seattle. In 2012 she received the John W. Campbell Award for Best New Writer and her stories have been finalists for the Hugo, Nebula, Sturgeon, and World Fantasy awards. Yu also works as a narrative designer for video games, including *Destiny* and *Destiny 2*.

It was a bus skidding off a rain-slick ribbon of a road, everyone for a moment in flight, levitating from their seats, then the shear and scream of metal. This is what distinguishes you from others. For whether you were shot to bits in a war or whether a telephone pole crushed your liver against the steering wheel, the procedure is the same. You can assume what happened after that.

Unless you are wildly rich—and you are not—the puddles of your organs were scooped out and replaced with artificial tissues that perform the necessary filtration, synthesis, and excretion for a fraction of the price of a transplant. Splintered bones become slim metal shafts. Ceramic scales cover ruined skin. They wheeled you out of the operating room hooked up to a bouquet of tubes, batteries, and drains, a grid of lights screwed into your plates, blinking red, blue, green. *Stable. Functioning. Okay.* As the drugs wore off you began to fumble at the strange new surfaces of your body.

Your lover was in Zanzibar on a lucrative minerals contract and did not hear about your accident until after they had patched you up enough to tap out the first of many detailed emails. The damage was extensive, your reconstruction complicated. For the rest of our life you will need a constant power supply, a backup generator, and hourly system flushes. You could choose to live homebound, they say, never passing your door. They quote you the prices of the various adaptors and chargers you need, and you laugh and cannot stop laughing, lightning balls of pain throughout your unfamiliar body.

Or, the nurses say, nervously thumbing down their screens, you could move to an experimental city in Washington designed for patients like you, where you would enjoy a certain degree of freedom and company. They do not add, *a place where everyone looks like you.* But their eyes shine with kindness.

Your lover offers to pay for the house installation. If nothing else, you should give him credit for that.

One nurse makes sure you are loaned a set of equipment from the hospital for your transitional period. You consider absconding with the adaptors—if the prices are to be believed, they're worth a small Caribbean island or two—but you can't extract the tracking tags. Besides, the nurse was nice.

You ship two cardboard boxes to the address they give you and sell the rest. You give away your pair of budgerigars because you can't take them with you. Your lover never liked them. Too noisy. Too messy. Too demanding. They chewed up the clawfooted chair from his grandfather's estate, little chips and nocks like angry kisses in the gloss.

Unexpected difficulties with buses and trains and airlines keep your beloved in Zanzibar, so when it's time to leave, your friends do the heavy lifting for you. They are polite. They try not to stare.

"What a dipshit," you hear one mutter, unhooking a photo of your lover, and she is right. He should be here with you, packing sweaters you can't wear anymore in plastic, boxing up your dinner plates.

You take the medical flight that leaves twice a month, your new address printed on a plastic strip around your wrist. Your college roommate sees you off. You hand over your borrowed equipment at the gate, shrugging off the promises of care packages and visits. You flinch from the hug. You don't look back.

The air is sweet on your exposed skin when you first see the square mile of concrete that is Revival. At the center of the city, a sheaf of faceted skyscrapers floats above a squat white mall. Rings of smaller apartments slope down and away, glass and steel congealing to stucco, brick, and concrete as they approach the city limits, where buildings meet crisp dark pines, sharp as cuts. Far beyond the pines rise whitened mountains like licked ice cream. You will dream sometimes of climbing those mountains and plunging your face into soft, shocking snow.

It is impossible, of course. Your batteries have enough charge for a couple of hours, but without fresh supplies of lymph and plasma, there's only so much your filters can do. The city newsroom is staffed by former war reporters, bulletproof and bitter, and every couple of months there's a story about a disconnection, either accidental or deliberate.

In determinedly cheerful emails, you recount to your absent lover everything he has missed. You have been assigned a fifteen-by-fifteen room with enormous windows in the southeast corner of Revival. You have not yet bought a mirror. Very few stores stock them, and you are not sure you want one. Pets are prohibited. Rent is moderate but food prices are inflated and utility bills are astronomical. Double-digit municipal taxes give you a slight headache. The consortium of medical providers managing the city is nominally a nonprofit, but you do the numbers on the back of an electricity bill and figure the executives must be drawing large salaries.

Since you are an accountant, you can work remotely. Your clients, who heard about the bus crash and have offered their timid condolences, assure you that it does not matter to them whether you are based in Des Moines or Los Angeles or Revival, Washington. Other residents are not so lucky. Their debts are paid for out of their retirement savings, or their estate, or alternatively by the sale of their genome and medical history and whatever organic components remain at the time of their death. The lease document makes for an interesting read. You tear the pages into tiny strips as you go.

All too soon, you memorize the silver line of cables and pumps that strings apartment block to apartment block, running through grocery store aisles and along library shelves and shooting up the five floors of the bright, sterile mall. You know where it turns at the end of the pavement, in the shadow of the pines, and loops back toward the mall. A local joke has it that the silver lines, if viewed from above, if all the intervening roofs and floors and ceilings were removed, spell out *freedom*.

The city is lousy with crows, who dive for flashes of metal and glints of porcelain. They are not discouraged by thirty failed attempts if, on the thirty-first, they snatch a pin, a lens, a loose filament. They are easy to fend off, but the cold acquisitiveness in their eyes makes you shiver.

Your lover comes to visit you only once, four and a half months after you move to Revival. You are slow, still limping, and a minute late. He climbs out of the taxi in his pressed suit and razor tie and looks around, fiddling with a button, cufflinks, hair. You are grateful that he recognizes you immediately. But he shrinks back a fraction of an inch when his eyes reach the steel screwed into your face and the coarse, fitful wires that grow where your skull was shaved.

You are surprised. In Revival, where glamour magazines gather dust and fade, you are considered beautiful. Eyes slide toward you on the street. You had almost forgotten about the seams and screws, the viscous yellow and red fluids trickling in and out of you, the cables tangling everywhere.

If you are honest with yourself, as you suddenly have to be, standing face to face with him, the two of you have not been lovers for some time. Right before the accident, you had agreed to separate for six months, as an audit of the relationship. You fed sunflower seeds to Tessie as he talked about opportunities in Tanzania, about looking for clarity in his life, his need to feel whole, like a hammer swing, a home run, his entire body committed to one motion. You nodded, you admitted the solidity of his arguments, and you stroked the budgie so roughly it bit your finger.

While you were apart, he wrote a paragraph once a week in response to your daily emails. You would reread it three or four times, looking for the elided thought, the sunken meaning. It was October, the busy season, and you were starting to make mistakes and lose paperwork. When the last return was triple-checked and filed, you heaved a sigh of relief and boarded a bus for Maine, where you would spend your vacation with a friend.

It was raining. Water entered an unnoticed hole in the toe of your boot, and you wrote a brief grumble to your love. Then the bus rumbled into the night, and you shut your eyes and let yourself relax.

So you are not exactly together, you realize, as you take his stiff arm. Together, you go to the third-nicest restaurant in the city for lunch. Your lover cannot stop staring at the servers, who are mostly inorganic by now and capable of carrying hundreds of pounds on each slender, tempered arm. His brows stitch together, and all the filet mignon in the world can't undo them.

Afterwards, he follows you to your apartment and undresses you with clumsy hands, snagging sleeves on tubes and almost unplugging your drip. But he cannot bring himself to touch the ceramic plates of your abdomen, which vibrate softly from the tiny motors underneath. You are disappointed but not altogether surprised.

You see your lover off with the driest of kisses. Then you compose a long email that is gentle and gracious, that is all the best parts of you gathered on the screen.

Your former lover does not reply.

"He wants a window-display life," your old roommate says when you call, finally, ashamed of your silence, your sticky sniffling. "You're not perfect enough for that. Not anymore." And she is right.

You try to find friends. Revival is a city, after all. You smile at people in the library as they browse books, music, electronics, language implants, avoiding the woman in the mystery section who is methodically tearing apart paperbacks. Most of the librarians are asleep at their desks.

You chat up tired cashiers. You sit in the synthetic park feeding bread to a duck paddling circles in the fountain. But the people you meet are still in various stages of recovery. They can only talk about the passive-aggressive bosses, the snowballing interest on their credit cards, the diagnoses, the lost loves, the affairs and then the tequila that preceded the leap off a bridge, or the microwaved dinners the children ate before they piled into the van for judo class, nine minutes before the other car roared through a red light and everything shattered. If only there were do-overs, if only there were apologies, if only the last meal could have been homemade chicken soup or macaroni and cheese. If only.

It is interesting and terrible the first time, but when you run into them later, they recite the same stories with the tragic and farcical earnestness of wind-up toys, and you make hasty excuses and leave.

Eight months after you arrive in Revival, you make an appointment for repairs. Your left lung, which is silicon rubber, has a small tear, and you are also due for a heart check. The clinic is one of two, staffed with five doctors and fifteen technicians, none of whom have missing pieces or live in the city. Your technician, Joel, is young, lean, and cheerful, with a strong nose and wild brown hair recently harrowed by a comb.

"Hey, stranger," he says. "First time? Let's have a look." He winds your tubes around one arm so they don't obstruct his hands and looks expectantly at you. Suddenly you are too shy to open up your body to him, to expose the secret gushing and dripping of pump and membrane and diaphragm, the click and thump of your pneumatic plastic heart.

"It'll be fine," he says. "You've got a Mark 5 heart and the D34-15 lung assembly. I did my certs on both of those, so I know them better than anything. I collect defective parts, and I can almost never find Mark 5s. They don't break."

His palm is warm on your ventral plates. He inserts his fingertips into the seamed depression where they overlap and parts the plates with surprising delicacy. Because your body was rebuilt for other people to troubleshoot, you cannot see the gauges and displays that he studies with wrinkled brow, although you know they're there, you've heard them ticking and whirring at night.

"Looking great," he says. "Mhm. You do a good job of taking care of this thing."

He reaches into your chest. You close your eyes and imagine that your heart is your own heart, wet and yielding to his thumbs, not a mass-produced model identical to hundreds of others he has inspected and installed. You wonder what his hair would feel like between your remaining fingers. Corn silk. Merino. Mink.

In ten minutes, Joel patches your lung and proclaims your Mk. 5 a beautiful ticker. You compliment him on the job. Already you can feel the extra oxygen brightening your blood, and the dull headache that has followed you all week fades. You are feeling so improved, in fact, that before you can think better of it, you invite him to coffee.

His mouth opens into a circle. You can see the glint of your zygomatic plate on the surface of his eyes. The inner tips of his eyebrows lift with pity.

"Well, isn't this awkward," he says, attempting a smile. "Never happened to me before."

You would be amused by his panic if it were not so painful. You mumble something or other.

"Bit of a—doctor-patient relationship—even if I'm not a doctor. You know."

You do know.

Your cheeks burn like torches the entire walk home. Today the rigid, brilliant architecture of the city seems like too much to bear. Your image flares at you from windows and glass doors. Yes, you are ugly. Yes, you are broken. Briefly, you consider disconnecting yourself and plunging into the trees in the few minutes before you collapse and all your diagnostic lights go red. You walk to the edge of the woods and sit quietly on the pavement, looking into the underbrush.

The trees are full of crows. Every few feet the grass is punctuated with a black pinion feather. Somewhere in these woods, the crows are building nests with wire, silicone, plastic, sequins of steel.

You listen to their quarrelling and think regretfully of your green and yellow budgies. Sweet-voiced things, your idea of love. They nuzzled your fingers and each other, unworried, content, knowing there'd be seeds in the feeder and water every morning.

You are motionless for so long that one crow flaps down to inspect you, eyeing his reflection in your metal side. He pecks. Once, twice. You have been working a loose wire out of your neck, which was wound up somewhere inside you but is now poking out, and you twist it off and hold out the gleaming piece.

He yanks it from your fingers and flees. Immediately, two more crows drop out of the trees to pummel him. You watch his oily back disappear into a squall of black bodies, reappear, disappear again. As they fight, black beak, jet claw, ragged bundles of greed, you remember what it meant to feel desire.

Over the course of a week, as a glittering shape flowers inside your head, you examine your budget, your savings, your expenses.

You order twelve carnival mirrors and set them up in your apartment. There is no more room for your bed, so you sell that to a new arrival. You also buy three old industrial robots, rusted and caked in machine oil. The boxes arrive thick and fast, and your apartment manager, who knows the square footage of your room, raises his single eyebrow at you when you come to collect them. Now, everywhere you turn, you confront an elastic vision of yourself, stretching as high as the ceiling and snapping to the shortness of a child. The eyes in the mirror gradually lose their fear.

You write about everything to your former lover as a matter of habit, not expecting a reply.

Biting your cheek, you call Joel to ask where you can buy faulty artificial organs. He listens to your flustered explanation and gives you contacts as well as three hearts, Mk. 1, 2, and 4, out of his own collection. You balance them in the robots' pincers like apples in a bowl.

With a net and a handful of bread, you catch birds on the roof: house sparrows, rock pigeons, crows, an unhappy seagull. You release the birds in your glass coffin crammed with carnival mirrors. They batter themselves against the window and shit on the mirrors and on you. Your room is all trapped, frantic motion, exaggerated in swells and rolls of glass. People look sideways at you when you leave your room, your chrome and steel parts streaked with white. You look at your slumped, stretched, stained reflections and recognize nothing and no one.

Sometimes, when the room is dark, you can admit that you are making this for someone who will never see it, who will never come back, who will never write to you. Then you roll onto your good side and listen to the flurry of wings until you fall asleep.

You set out neatly lettered signs in your window and on your door. *Musée de l'Âme Seule*. Signage is probably against building regulations, but you used the shreds of your lease to line your room. You run a notice in the news that is two inches by two inches. *Saturdays and Sundays*. You keep your door unlocked. You feed the birds, you wipe down the hearts, and you wait.

Joel comes to see you, or perhaps to see what you've done with his hearts.

"Where do you sleep?" he says, looking around.

Anywhere, you say.

His expression says he thinks parts other than your lung need examining. But he is also curious. He touches the orange arms curled around artificial ventricles, the frozen rovers sprouting substitute livers at odd angles.

"I'm not very good at art," he says. A sparrow shits in his hair.

You offer to wipe up the mess, you are already wetting a towel in the sink, but he has to leave, he is meeting someone somewhere else, he has left his jacket at the clinic, he is late.

Two weeks later, on a Sunday morning, one more person walks into your museum. She swings open your door and is surprised into laughter by a burst of gray wings. She is even uglier than you are, most of her face gone, hard bright camera lenses for eyes. She has glued pages of books and playbills over her carapace.

"I was an actress," she says.

She has been in all the shows that she wears. The pages came from books she liked but couldn't keep. Her name is Nim. She has been in the city *ab urbe condita*, she says, meaning four years ago, when it was fifteen residents and three doctors and one building. She walks around your room as she talks, studying the mirrors, the machines, the birds, the bounce of her own reflection.

Without asking permission, she shoves a window open and shoos out the birds. They leave in one long shout of white and gray and brown. Flecks of down spin and swirl in their wake.

You ask her how long it took to remember how to walk, how to function, how to smile.

"Two weeks. Three months. Two years." She shrugs. "Sooner or later."

Nim has no hair, only a complex web of filaments across her metal skull, flickering her thoughts in patterns too quick to follow. Her hands are small and dark and unscarred.

"Look," she says, touching the skin of your cheek, showing off her lean titanium legs. "Together we make one whole person."

More than that, you want to say, as you add up fingers and toes and organs and elbows. A sum that is greater than one. More than two. But you are tongue-tied and dazed. You realize that you stink of birds and bird shit.

She smiles at your confusion. "I'll bring you some gloves and cleaning supplies."

What for, you say stupidly.

"To shine up this place."

But this is what I am, you say. This is what I look like. You stretch out your hands to indicate the mirrors, the stained, spattered floors, the streaked walls.

"You could use a spit and polish too, frankly." She demonstrates, using her sleeve, and you blush.

But why are you here, you ask. Why is she touching you with gentleness? You are afraid that this is all an accident, a colossal misunderstanding, that she will walk out of the door and vanish like your sparrows.

"I'm looking for a collaborator," she says. "I've got an idea. Performance art. Public service. If you can clean up and come for lunch tomorrow, I'll tell you about it."

Inside you, a window opens.

That was when you stopped writing to me. Your long, careful emails came to an end. What is there to say? The stories of people we have loved and injured and deserted are incomplete to us.

If I could write an ending for you, it would be Nim holding your new hand in hers, Nim tickling your back until you wheeze with laughter, the two of you commandeering an office block for a new museum, a museum of broken and repaired people, where anyone for an hour or three can pose in a spotlight and glitter, glisten, gleam, haloed in light, light leaping off the white teeth of their laughter. But it is never that easy, and that is not my right.

You knew, I think, before I did. That no one can have a life that is without questions, without cracks. And now you are the deepest one in mine.

Here is what I have. A year and two months of emails. A restaurant check. A glossy fragment from a magazine, two inches by two inches. Terse. Opaque. *Musée de l'Âme Réparée. Saturdays and Sundays. Revival, WA.*

What could I say? What could I ever say?

(2014)

THE WINTER MARKET
William Gibson

William Ford Gibson was born in 1948 in the coastal city of Conway, South Carolina, and spent most of his childhood in Wytheville, a small town in the Appalachians. Gibson, an orphan at 18, left school without graduating, and in 1967 moved to Canada in order to avoid the Vietnam war draft. With his future wife Deborah Jean Thompson he traveled to Europe, though they "couldn't afford to stay anywhere that had anything remotely like hard currency". The couple settled in Vancouver, British Columbia in 1972. Through the punk musician and author John Shirley, Gibson met Bruce Sterling and Lewis Shiner and they, along with Rudy Rucker, went on to form the core of the cyberpunk literary movement. Over the years, Gibson's work has shifted steadily away from science fiction towards an exploration of the (admittedly skewed) present day.

It rains a lot, up here; there are winter days when it doesn't really get light at all, only a bright, indeterminate gray. But then there are days when it's like they whip aside a curtain to flash you three minutes of sunlit, suspended mountain, the trademark at the start of God's own movie. It was like that the day her agents phoned, from deep in the heart of their mirrored pyramid on Beverly Boulevard, to tell me she'd merged with the net, crossed over for good, that *Kings of Sleep* was going triple-platinum. I'd edited most of *Kings*, done the brain-map work and gone over it all with the fast-wipe module, so I was in line for a share of royalties.

No, I said, no. Then yes, yes, and hung up on them. Got my jacket and took the stairs three at a time, straight out to the nearest bar and an eight-hour blackout that ended on a concrete ledge two meters above midnight. False Creek water. City lights, that same gray bowl of sky smaller now, illuminated by neon and mercury-vapor arcs. And it was snowing, big flakes but not many, and when they touched black water, they were gone, no trace at all. I looked down at my feet and saw my toes clear of the edge of concrete, the water between them. I was wearing Japanese shoes, new and expensive, glove-leather Ginza monkey boots with rubber-capped toes. I stood there for a long time before I took that first step back.

Because she was dead, and I'd let her go. Because, now, she was immortal, and I'd helped her get that way. And because I knew she'd phone me, in the morning.

*

My father was an audio engineer, a mastering engineer. He went way back, in the business, even before digital. The processes he was concerned with were partly mechanical, with that clunky quasi-Victorian quality you see in twentieth-century technology. He was a lathe operator, basically. People brought him audio recordings and he burned their sounds into grooves on a disk of lacquer. Then the disk was electroplated and used in the construction of a press that would stamp out records, the black things you see in antique stores. And I remember him telling me, once, a few months before he died, that certain frequencies—transients, I think he called them—could easily burn out the head, the cutting head, on a master lathe. These heads were incredibly expensive, so you prevented burnouts with something called an accelerometer. And that was what I was thinking of, as I stood there, my toes out over the water: that head, burning out.

Because that was what they did to her.

And that was what she wanted.

No accelerometer for Lise.

I disconnected my phone on my way to bed. I did it with the business end of a West German studio tripod that was going to cost a week's wages to repair.

Woke some strange time later and took a cab back to Granville Island and Rubin's place.

Rubin, in some way that no one quite understands, is a master, a teacher, what the Japanese call a *sensei*. What he's the master of, really, is garbage, kipple, refuse, the sea of cast-off goods our century floats on. *Gomi no sensei*. Master of junk.

I found him, this time, squatting between two vicious-looking drum machines I hadn't seen before, rusty spider arms folded at the hearts of dented constellations of steel cans fished out of Richmond dumpsters. He never calls the place a studio, never refers to himself as an artist. "Messing around," he calls what he does there, and seems to view it as some extension of boyhood's perfectly bored backyard afternoons. He wanders through his jammed, littered space, a kind of minihangar cobbled to the water side of the Market, followed by the smarter and more agile of his creations, like some vaguely benign Satan bent on the elaboration of still stranger processes in his ongoing Inferno of *gomi*. I've seen Rubin program his constructions to identify and verbally abuse pedestrians wearing garments by a given season's hot designer; others attend to more obscure missions, and a few seem constructed solely to deconstruct themselves with as much attendant noise as possible. He's like a child, Rubin; he's also worth a lot of money in galleries in Tokyo and Paris.

So I told him about Lise. He let me do it, get it out, then nodded. "I know," he said. "Some CBC creep phoned eight times." He sipped something out of a dented cup. "You wanna Wild Turkey sour?"

"Why'd they call you?"

`Cause my name's on the back of *Kings of Sleep*. Dedication."

"I didn't see it yet."

"She try to call you yet?"

*

"She will."

"Rubin, she's dead. They cremated her already."

"I know," he said. "And she's going to call you."

Gomi.

Where does the *gomi* stop and the world begin? The Japanese, a century ago, had already run out of *gomi* space around Tokyo, so they came up with a plan for creating space out of *gomi*. By the year 1969 they had built themselves a little island in Tokyo Bay, out of *gomi*, and christened it Dream Island. But the city was still pouring out its nine thousand tons per day, so they went on to build New Dream Island, and today they coordinate the whole process, and new Nippons rise out of the Pacific. Rubin watches this on the news and says nothing at all.

He has nothing to say about *gomi*. It's his medium, the air he breathes, something he's swum in all his life. He cruises Greater Van in a spavined truck-thing chopped down from an ancient Mercedes airporter, its roof lost under a wallowing rubber bag half-filled with natural gas. He looks for things that fit some strange design scrawled on the inside of his forehead by whatever serves him as Muse. He brings home more *gomi*. Some of it still operative. Some of it, like Lise, human.

I met Lise at one of Rubin's parties. Rubin had a lot of parties. He never seemed particularly to enjoy them, himself, but they were excellent parties. I lost track, that fall, of the number of times I woke on a slab of foam to the roar of Rubin's antique espresso machine, a tarnished behemoth topped with a big chrome eagle, the sound outrageous off the corrugated steel walls of the place, but massively comforting, too: There was coffee. Life would go on.

First time I saw her: in the Kitchen Zone. You wouldn't call it a kitchen, exactly, just three fridges and a hot plate and a broken convection oven that had come in with the *gomi*. First time I saw her: She had the all-beer fridge open, light spilling out, and I caught the cheekbones and the determined set of that mouth, but I also caught the black glint of polycarbon at her wrist, and the bright slick sore the exoskeleton had rubbed there. Too drunk to process, to know what it was, but I did know it wasn't party time. So I did what people usually did, to Lise, and clicked myself into a different movie. Went for the wine instead, on the counter beside the convection oven. Never looked back.

But she found me again. Came after me two hours later, weaving through the bodies and junk with that terrible grace programmed into the exoskeleton. I knew what it was, then, as I watched her homing in, too embarrassed now to duck it, to run, to mumble some excuse and get out. Pinned there, my arm around the waist of a girl I didn't know, while Lise advanced—*was advanced*, with that mocking grace—straight at me now, her eyes burning with wizz, and the girl had wriggled out and away in a quiet social panic, was gone, and Lise stood there in front of me, propped up in her pencil-thin polycarbon prosthetic. Looked into those eyes and it was like you could hear her synapses whining, some impossibly high-pitched scream as the wizz opened every circuit in her brain.

"Take me home," she said, and the words hit me like a whip. I think I shook my head. "Take me home." There were levels of pain there, and subtlety, and an amazing cruelty. And I knew then that I'd never been hated, ever, as deeply or thoroughly as this wasted little girl hated me now, hated me for the way I'd looked, then looked away, beside Rubin's all-beer refrigerator.

So if that's the word I did one of those things you do and never find out why, even though something in you knows you could never have done anything else.

I took her home.

I have two rooms in an old condo rack at the corner of Fourth and MacDonald, tenth floor. The elevators usually work, and if you sit on the balcony railing and lean out backward, holding on to the corner of the building next door, you can see a little upright slit of sea and mountain.

She hadn't said a word, all the way back from Rubin's, and I was getting sober enough to feel very uneasy as I unlocked the door and let her in.

The first thing she saw was the portable fast-wipe I'd brought home from the Pilot the night before. The exoskeleton carried her across the dusty broadloom with that same walk, like a model down a runway. Away from the crash of the party, I could hear it click softly as it moved her. She stood there, looking down at the fast-wipe. I could see the thing's ribs when she stood like that, make them out across her back through the scuffed black leather of her jacket. One of those diseases. Either one of the old ones they've never quite figured out or one of the new ones— the all too obviously environmental kind that they've barely even named yet. She couldn't move, not without that extra skeleton, and it was jacked straight into her brain, myoclectric interface. The fragile-looking polycarbon braces moved her arms and legs, but a more subtle system handled her thin hands, galvanic inlays. I thought of frog legs twitching in a high-school lab tape, then hated myself for it.

"This is a fast-wipe module," she said, in a voice I hadn't heard before, distant, and I thought then that the wizz might be wearing off. "What's it doing here?"

"I edit," I said, closing the door behind me.

"Well, now," and she laughed. "You do. Where?"

"On the Island. Place called the Autonomic Pilot."

She turned; then, hand on thrust hip, she swung—*it swung her*—and the wizz and the hate and some terrible parody of lust stabbed out at me from those washed-out gray eyes. "You wanna make it, editor?"

And I felt the whip come down again, but I wasn't going to take it, not again. So I cold-eyed her from somewhere down in the beer-numb core of my walking, talking, live-limbed, and entirely ordinary body and the words came out of me like spit: "Could you feel it, if I did?"

Beat. Maybe she blinked, but her face never registered. "No," she said, "but sometimes I like to watch."

Rubin stands at the window, two days after her death in Los Angeles, watching snow fall into False Creek. "So you never went to bed with her?"

One of his push-me-pull-you's, little roller-bearing Escher lizards, scoots across the table in front of me, in curl-up mode.

"No." I say, and it's true. Then I laugh. "But we jacked straight across. That first night."

"You were crazy," he said, a certain approval in his voice. "It might have killed you. Your heart might have stopped, you might have stopped breathing...." He turns back to the window. "Has she called you yet?"

We jacked, straight across.

I'd never done it before. If you'd asked me why, I would have told you that I was an editor and that it wasn't professional.

The truth would be something more like this.

In the trade, the legitimate trade—I've never done porno—we call the raw product dry dreams. Dry dreams are neural output from levels of consciousness that most people can only access in sleep. But artists, the kind I work with at the Autonomic Pilot, are able to break the surface tension, dive down deep, down and out, out into Jung's sea, and bring back—well, dreams. Keep it simple. I guess some artists have always done that, in whatever medium, but neuroelectronics lets us access the experience, and the net gets it all out on the wire, so we can package it, sell it, watch how it moves in the market. Well, the more things change... That's something my father liked to say.

Ordinarily I get the raw material in a studio situation, filtered through several million dollars' worth of baffles, and I don't even have to see the artist. The stuff we get out to the consumer, you see, has been structured, balanced, turned into art. There are still people naive enough to assume that they'll actually enjoy jacking straight across with someone they love. I think most teenagers try it, once. Certainly it's easy enough to do; Radio Shack will sell you the box and the trodes and the cables. But me, I'd never done it. And now that I think about it, I'm not so sure I can explain why. Or that I even want to try.

I do know why I did it with Lise, sat down beside her on my Mexican futon and snapped the optic lead into the socket on the spine, the smooth dorsal ridge, of the exoskeleton. It was high up, at the base of her neck, hidden by her dark hair.

Because she claimed she was an artist, and because I knew that we were engaged, somehow, in total combat, and I was not going to lose. That may not make sense to you, but then you never knew her, or know her through Kings of Sleep, which isn't the same at all. You never felt that hunger she had, which was pared down to a dry need, hideous in its singleness of purpose. People who know exactly what they want have always frightened me, and Lise had known what she wanted for a long time, and wanted nothing else at all. And I was scared, then, of admitting to myself that I was scared, and I'd seen enough strangers' dreams, in the mixing room at the Autonomic Pilot, to know that most people's inner monsters are foolish things, ludicrous in the calm light of one's own consciousness. And I was still drunk.

I put the trodes on and reached for the stud on the fast-wipe. I'd shut down its studio functions, temporarily converting eighty thousand dollars' worth of

Japanese electronics to the equivalent of one of those little Radio Shack boxes. "Hit it," I said, and touched the switch.

Words. Words cannot. Or, maybe, just barely, if I even knew how to begin to describe it, what came up out of her, what she did...

There's a segment on *Kings of Sleep*; it's like you're on a motorcycle at midnight, no lights but somehow you don't need them, blasting out along a cliff-high stretch of coast highway, so fast that you hang there in a cone of silence, the bike's thunder lost behind you. Everything, lost behind you... It's just a blink, on *Kings*, but it's one of the thousand things you remember, go back to, incorporate into your own vocabulary of feelings. Amazing. Freedom and death, right there, right there, razor's edge, forever.

What I got was the big-daddy version of that, raw rush, the king hell killer uncut real thing, exploding eight ways from Sunday into a void that stank of poverty and lovelessness and obscurity.

And that was Lise's ambition, that rush, seen from the inside.

It probably took all of four seconds.

And, course, she'd won.

I took the trodes off and stared at the wall, eyes wet, the framed posters swimming.

I couldn't look at her. I heard her disconnect the optic lead. I heard the exoskeleton creak as it hoisted her up from the futon. Heard it tick demurely as it hauled her into the kitchen for a glass of water.

Then I started to cry.

Rubin inserts a skinny probe in the roller-bearing belly of a sluggish push-me-pull-you and peers at the circuitry through magnifying glasses with miniature headlights mounted at the temples.

"So? You got hooked." He shrugs, looks up. It's dark now and the twin tensor beams stab at my face, chill damp in his steel barn and the lonesome hoot of a foghorn from somewhere across the water. "So?"

My turn to shrug. "I just did... There didn't seem to be anything else to do."

The beams duck back to the silicon heart of his defective toy. "Then you're okay. It was a true choice. What I mean is, she was set to be what she is. You had about as much to do with where she's at today as that fast-wipe module did. She'd have found somebody else if she hadn't found you...."

I made a deal with Barry, the senior editor, got twenty minutes at five on a cold September morning. Lise came in and hit me with that same shot, but this time I was ready, with my baffles and brain maps, and I didn't have to feel it. It took me two weeks, piecing out the minutes in the editing room, to cut what she'd done down into something I could play for Max Bell, who owns the Pilot.

Bell hadn't been happy, not happy at all, as I explained what I'd done. Maverick editors can be a problem, and eventually most editors decide that they've found someone who'll be it, the next monster, and then they start wasting time and money. He'd nodded when I'd finished my pitch, then scratched his nose with the cap of his red feltpen. "Uh-huh. Got it. Hottest thing since fish grew legs, right?"

But he'd jacked it, the demo soft I'd put together, and when it clicked out of its slot in his Braun desk unit, he was staring at the wall, his face blank.

"Max?"

"Huh?"

"What do you think?"

"Think? I... What did you say her name was?" He blinked. "Lisa? Who you say she's signed with?"

"Lise. Nobody, Max. She hasn't signed with anybody yet."

"Jesus Christ." He still looked blank.

"You know how I found her?" Rubin asks, wading through ragged cardboard boxes to find the light switch. The boxes are filled with carefully sorted *gomi*: lithium batteries, tantalum capacitors, RF connectors, breadboards, barrier strips, ferroresonant transformers, spools of bus bar wire... One box is filled with the severed heads of hundreds of Barbie dolls, another with armored industrial safety gauntlets that look like spacesuit gloves. Light floods the room and a sort of Kandinski mantis in snipped and painted tin swings its golfball-size head toward the bright bulb. "I was down Granville on a *gomi* run, back in an alley, and I found her just sitting there. Caught the skeleton and she didn't look so good, so I asked her if she was okay. Nothin'. Just closed her eyes. Not my lookout, I think. But I happen back by there about four hours later and she hasn't moved. 'Look, honey,' I tell her, 'maybe your hardware's buggered up. I can help you, okay?' Nothin'. 'How long you been back here?' Nothin'. So I take off." He crosses to his workbench and strokes the thin metal limbs of the mantis thing with a pale forefinger. Behind the bench, hung on damp-swollen sheets of ancient pegboard, are pliers, screwdrivers, tie-wrap guns, a rusted Daisy BB rifle, coax strippers, crimpers, logic probes, heat guns, a pocket oscilloscope, seemingly every tool in human history, with no attempt ever made to order them at all, though I've yet to see Rubin's hand hesitate.

"So I went back," he says. "Gave it an hour. She was out by then, unconscious, so I brought her back here and ran a check on the exoskeleton. Batteries were dead. She'd crawled back there when the juice ran out and settled down to starve to death, I guess."

"When was that?"

"About a week before you took her home."

"But what if she'd died? If you hadn't found her?"

"Somebody was going to find her. She couldn't ask for anything, you know? Just take. Couldn't stand a favor."

Max found the agents for her, and a trio of awesomely slick junior partners Leared into YVR a day later. Lise wouldn't come down to the Pilot to meet them, insisted we bring them up to Rubin's, where she still slept.

"Welcome to Couverville," Rubin said as they edged in the door. His long face was smeared with grease, the fly of his ragged fatigue pants held more or less shut with a twisted paper clip. The boys grinned automatically, but there was something marginally more authentic about the girl's smile. "Mr. Stark," she said, "I was in London last week. I saw your installation at the Tate."

"Marcello's Battery Factory," Rubin said. "They say it's scatological, the Brits…" He shrugged. "Brits. I mean, who knows?"

"They're right. It's also very funny."

The boys were beaming like tabled-tanned lighthouses, standing there in their suits. The demo had reached Los Angeles. They knew.

"And you're Lise," she said, negotiating the path between Rubin's heaped *gomi*. "You're going to be a very famous person soon, Lise. We have a lot to discuss."

And Lise just stood there, propped in polycarbon, and the look on her face was the one I'd seen that first night, in my condo, when she'd asked me if I wanted to go to bed. But if the junior agent lady saw it, she didn't show it. She was a pro.

I told myself that I was a pro, too.

I told myself to relax.

Trash fires gutter in steel canisters around the Market. The snow still falls and kids huddle over the flames like arthritic crows, hopping from foot to foot, wind whipping their dark coats. Up in Fairview's arty slum-tumble, someone's laundry has frozen solid on the line, pink squares of bedsheet standing out against the background dinge and the confusion of satellite dishes and solar panels. Some ecologist's eggbeater windmill goes round and round, round and round, giving a whirling finger to the Hydro rates.

Rubin clumps along in paint-spattered L. L. Bean gumshoes, his big head pulled down into an oversize fatigue jacket. Sometimes one of the hunched teens will point him out as we pass, the guy who builds all the crazy stuff, the robots and shit.

"You know what your trouble is?" he says when we're under the bridge, headed up to Fourth. "You're the kind who always reads the handbook. Anything people build, any kind of technology, it's going to have some specific purpose. It's for doing something that somebody already understands. But if it's new technology, it'll open areas nobody's ever thought of before. You read the manual, man, and you won't play around with it, not the same way. And you get all funny when somebody else uses it to do something you never thought of. Like Lise."

"She wasn't the first." Traffic drums past overhead.

"No, but she's sure as hell the first person you ever met who went and translated themselves into a hardwired program. You lose any sleep when whatsisname did it, three-four years ago, the French kid, the writer?"

"I didn't really think about it, much. A gimmick. PR…"

"He's still writing. The weird thing is, he's going to be writing, unless somebody blows up his mainframe…"

I wince, shake my head. "But it's not him, is it? It's just a program."

"Interesting point. Hard to say. With Lise, though, we find out. She's not a writer."

*

She had it all in there, *Kings*, locked up in her head the way her body was locked in that exoskeleton.

The agents signed her with a label and brought in a production team from Tokyo. She told them she wanted me to edit. I said no; Max dragged me into his office and threatened to fire me on the spot. If I wasn't involved, there was no reason to do the studio work at the Pilot. Vancouver was hardly the center of the world, and the agents wanted her in Los Angeles. It meant a lot of money to him, and it might put the Autonomic Pilot on the map. I couldn't explain to him why I'd refused. It was too crazy, too personal; she was getting a final dig in. Or that's what I thought then. But Max was serious. He really didn't give me any choice. We both knew another job wasn't going to crawl into my hand. I went back out with him and we told the agents that we'd worked it out: I was on.

The agents showed us lots of teeth.

Lise pulled out an inhaler full of wizz and took a huge hit. I thought I saw the agent lady raise one perfect eyebrow, but that was the extent of censure. After the papers were signed, Lise more or less did what she wanted.

And Lise always knew what she wanted.

We did *Kings* in three weeks, the basic recording. I found any number of reasons to avoid Rubin's place, even believed some of them myself. She was still staying there, although the agents weren't too happy with what they saw as a total lack of security. Rubin told me later that he'd had to have his agent call them up and raise hell, but after that they seemed to quit worrying. I hadn't known that Rubin had an agent. It was always easy to forget that Rubin Stark was more famous, then, than anyone else I knew, certainly more famous than I thought Lise was ever likely to become. I knew we were working on something strong, but you never know how big anything's liable to be.

But the time I spent in the Pilot, I was on. Lise was amazing.

It was like she was born to the form, even though the technology that made that form possible hadn't even existed when she was born. You see something like that and you wonder how many thousands, maybe millions, of phenomenal artists have died mute, down the centuries, people who could never have been poets or painters or saxophone players, but who had this stuff inside, these psychic waveforms waiting for the circuitry required to tap in....

I learned a few things about her, incidentals, from our time in the studio. That she was born in Windsor. That her father was American and served in Peru and came home crazy and half-blind. That whatever was wrong with her body was congenital. That she had those sores because she refused to remove the exoskeleton, ever, because she'd start to choke and die at the thought of that utter helplessness. That she was addicted to wizz and doing enough of it daily to wire a football team.

Her agents brought in medics, who padded the polycarbon with foam and sealed the sores over with micropore dressings. They pumped her up with vitamins and tried to work on her diet, but nobody ever tried to take that inhaler away.

They brought in hairdressers and makeup artists, too, and wardrobe people and image builders and articulate little PR hamsters, and she endured it with something that might almost have been a smile.

And, right through those three weeks, we didn't talk. Just studio talk, artist-editor stuff, very much a restricted code. Her imagery was so strong, so extreme, that she never really needed to explain a given effect to me. I took what she put out and worked with it, and jacked it back to her. She'd either say yes or no, and usually it was yes. The agents noted this and approved, and clapped Max Bell on the back and took him out to dinner, and my salary went up.

And I was pro, all the way. Helpful and thorough and polite. I was determined not to crack again, and never thought about the night I cried, and I was also doing the best work I'd ever done, and knew it, and that's a high in itself.

And then, one morning, about six, after a long, long session when she'd first gotten that eerie cotillion sequence out, the one the kids call the Ghost Dance, she spoke to me. One of the two agent boys had been there, showing teeth, but he was gone now and the Pilot was dead quiet, just the hum of a blower somewhere down by Max's office.

"Casey," she said, her voice hoarse with the wizz, "sorry I hit on you so hard."

I thought for a minute she was telling me something about the recording we'd just made. I looked up and saw her there, and it struck me that we were alone, and hadn't been alone since we'd made the demo.

I had no idea at all what to say. Didn't even know what I felt.

Propped up in the exoskeleton, she was looking worse than she had that first night, at Rubin's. The wizz was eating her, under the stuff the makeup team kept smoothing on, and sometimes it was like seeing a death's-head surface beneath the face of a not very handsome teenager. I had no idea of her real age. Not old, not young.

"The ramp effect," I said, coiling a length of cable.

"What's that?"

"Nature's way of telling you to clean up your act. Sort of mathematical law, says you can only get off real good on a stimulant x number of times, even if you increase the doses. But you can't ever get off as nice as you did the first few times. Or you shouldn't be able to, anyway. That's the trouble with designer drugs; they're too clever. That stuff you're doing has some tricky tail on one of its molecules, keeps you from turning the decomposed adrenaline into adrenochrome. If it didn't, you'd be schizophrenic by now. You got any little problems, Lise? Like apneia? Sometimes maybe you stop breathing if you go to sleep?"

But I wasn't even sure I felt the anger that I heard in my own voice.

She stared at me with those pale gray eyes. The wardrobe people had replaced her thrift-shop jacket with a butter-tanned matte black blouson that did a better job of hiding the polycarbon ribs. She kept it zipped to the neck, always, even though it was too warm in the studio. The hairdressers had tried something new the day before, and it hadn't worked out, her rough dark hair a lopsided explosion above that drawn, triangular face. She stared at me and I felt it again, her singleness of purpose.

"I don't sleep, Casey."

It wasn't until later, much later, that I remembered she'd told me she was sorry.

She never did again, and it was the only time I ever heard her say anything that seemed to be out of character.

Rubin's diet consists of vending-machine sandwiches, Pakistani takeout food, and espresso. I've never seen him eat anything else. We eat samosas in a narrow shop on Fourth that has a single plastic table wedged between the counter and the door to the can. Rubin eats his dozen samosas, six meat and six veggie, with total concentration, one after another, and doesn't bother to wipe his chin. He's devoted to the place. He loathes the Greek counterman; it's mutual, a real relationship. If the counterman left, Rubin might not come back. The Greek glares at the crumbs on Rubin's chin and jacket. Between samosas, he shoots daggers right back, his eyes narrowed behind the smudged lenses of his steel-rimmed glasses.

The samosas are dinner. Breakfast will be egg salad on dead white bread, packed in one of those triangles of milky plastic, on top of six little cups of poisonously strong espresso.

"You didn't see it coming, Casey." He peers at me out of the thumbprinted depths of his glasses. "'Cause you're no good at lateral thinking. You read the handbook. What else did you think she was after? Sex? More wiz? A world tour? She was past all that. That's what made her so strong. She was past it. That's why *Kings of Sleep*'s as big as it is, and why the kids buy it, why they believe it. They know. Those kids back down the Market, warming their butts around the fires and wondering if they'll find someplace to sleep tonight, they believe it. It's the hottest soft in eight years. Guy at a shop on Granville told me he gets more of the damned things lifted than he sells of anything else. Says it's a hassle to even stock it... She's big because she was what they are, only more so. She knew, man. No dreams, no hope. You can't see the cages on those kids, Casey, but more and more they're twigging to it, that they aren't going *anywhere*." He brushes a greasy crumb of meat from his chin, missing three more. "So she sang it for them, said it that way they can't, painted them a picture. And she used the money to buy herself a way out, that's all."

I watch the steam bead and roll down the window in big drops, streaks in the condensation. Beyond the window I can make out a partially stripped Lada, wheels scavenged, axles down on the pavement.

"How many people have done it, Rubin? Have any idea?"

"Not too many. Hard to say, anyway, because a lot of them are probably politicians we think of as being comfortably and reliably dead." He gives me a funny look. "Not a nice thought. Anyway, they had first shot at the technology. It still costs too much for any ordinary dozen millionaires, but I've heard of at least seven. They say Mitsubishi did it to Weinberg before his immune system finally went tits up. He was head of their hybridoma lab in Okayama. Well, their stock's still pretty high, in monoclonals, so maybe it's true. And Langlais, the French kid, the novelist..." He shrugs. "Lise didn't have the money for it. Wouldn't now, even. But she put herself in the right place at the right time. She was about to croak, she was in Hollywood, and they could already see what *Kings* was going to do."

The day we finished up, the band stepped off a JAL shuttle out of London, four skinny kids who operated like a well-oiled machine and displayed a hypertrophied fashion sense and a total lack of affect. I set them up in a row at the Pilot, in identical white Ikea office chairs, smeared saline paste on their temples, taped the trodes on, and ran the rough version of what was going to become *Kings of Sleep*. When they came out of it, they all started talking at once, ignoring me totally, in the British version of that secret language all studio musicians speak, four sets of pale hands zooming and chopping the air.

I could catch enough of it to decide that they were excited. That they thought it was good. So I got my jacket and left. They could wipe their own saline paste off, thanks.

And that night I saw Lise for the last time, though I didn't plan to.

Walking back down to the Market, Rubin noisily digesting his meal, red taillights reflected on wet cobbles, the city beyond the Market a clean sculpture of light, a lie, where the broken and the lost burrow into the *gomi* that grows like humus at the bases of the towers of glass...

"I gotta go to Frankfurt tomorrow, do an installation. You wanna come? I could write you off as a technician." He shrugs his way deeper into the fatigue jacket. "Can't pay you, but you can have airfare, you want..."

Funny offer, from Rubin, and I know it's because he's worried about me, thinks I'm too strange about Lise, and it's the only thing he can think of, getting me out of town.

"It's colder in Frankfurt now than it is here."

"You maybe need a change, Casey. I dunno..."

"Thanks, but Max has a lot of work lined up. Pilot's a big deal now, people flying in from all over..."

"Sure."

When I left the band at the Pilot, I went home. Walked up to Fourth and took the trolley home, past the windows of the shops I see every day, each one lit up jazzy and slick, clothes and shoes and software, Japanese motorcycles crouched like clean enamel scorpions, Italian furniture. The windows change with the seasons, the shops come and go. We were into the preholiday mode now, and there were more people on the street, a lot of couples, walking quickly and purposefully past the bright windows, on their way to score that perfect little whatever for whomever, half the girls in those padded thigh-high nylon boot things that came out of New York the winter before, the ones that Rubin said made them look like they had elephantiasis. I grinned, thinking about that, and suddenly it hit me that it really was over, that I was done with Lise, and that now she'd be sucked off to Hollywood as inexorably as if she'd poked her toe into a black hole, drawn by the unthinkable gravitic tug of Big Money. Believing that, that she was gone—probably was gone, by then—I let down some kind of guard in myself and felt the edges of my pity. But just the edges, because I didn't want my evening screwed up by anything. I wanted partytime. It had been a while.

Got off at my corner and the elevator worked on the first try. Good sign, I told myself. Upstairs, I undressed and showered, found a clean shirt, microwaved burritos. Feel normal, I advised my reflection while I shaved. You have been working too hard. Your credit cards have gotten fat. Time to remedy that.

The burritos tasted like cardboard, but I decided I liked them because they were so aggressively normal. My car was in Burnaby, having its leaky hydrogen cell repacked, so I wasn't going to have to worry about driving. I could go out, find partytime, and phone in sick in the morning. Max wasn't going to kick; I was his star boy. He owed me.

You owe me, Max, I said to the subzero bottle of Moskovskaya I fished out of the freezer. Do you ever owe me. I have just spent three weeks editing the dreams and nightmares of one very screwed up person, Max. On your behalf. So that you can grow and prosper, Max. I poured three fingers of vodka into a plastic glass left over from a party I'd thrown the year before and went back into the living room.

Sometimes it looks to me like nobody in particular lives there. Not that it's that messy; I'm a good if somewhat robotic housekeeper, and even remember to dust the tops of framed posters and things, but I have these times when the place abruptly gives me a kind of low-grade chill, with its basic accumulation of basic consumer goods. I mean, it's not like I want to fill it up with cats or houseplants or anything, but there are moments when I see that anyone could be living there, could own those things, and it all seems sort of interchangeable, my life and yours, my life and anybody's...

I think Rubin sees things that way, too, all the time, but for him it's a source of strength. He lives in other people's garbage, and everything he drags home must have been new and shiny once, must have meant something, however briefly, to someone. So he sweeps it all up into his crazy-looking truck and hauls it back to his place and lets it compost there until he thinks of something new to do with it. Once he was showing me a book of twentieth-century art he liked, and there was a picture of an automated sculpture called Dead Birds Fly Again, a thing that whirled real dead birds around and around on a string, and he smiled and nodded, and I could see he felt the artist was a spiritual ancestor of some kind. But what could Rubin do with my framed posters and my Mexican futon from the Bay and my temperfoam bed from Ikea? *Well*, I thought, taking a first chilly sip, *he'd be able to think of something*, which was why he was a famous artist and I wasn't.

I went and pressed my forehead against the plate-glass window, as cold as the glass in my hand. Time to go, I said to myself. You are exhibiting symptoms of urban singles angst. There are cures for this. Drink up. Go.

I didn't attain a state of partytime that night. Neither did I exhibit adult common sense and give up, go home, watch some ancient movie, and fall asleep on my futon. The tension those three weeks had built up in me drove me like the mainspring of a mechanical watch, and I went ticking off through nighttown, lubricating my more or less random progress with more drinks. It was one of those nights, I quickly decided, when you slip into an alternate continuum, a city that looks exactly like the one where you live, except for the peculiar difference that it contains not one person you love or know or have even spoken to before. Nights like that, you can go into a familiar bar and find that the staff has just been replaced; then you understand that your real motive in going there was simply to see a familiar face, on a waitress or a bartender, whoever... This sort of thing has been known to mediate against partytime.

I kept it rolling, though, through six or eight places, and eventually it rolled me into a West End club that looked as if it hadn't been redecorated since the Nineties. A lot of peeling chrome over plastic, blurry holograms that gave you a headache if you tried to make them out. I think Barry had told me about the place, but I can't imagine why. I looked around and grinned. If I was looking to be depressed, I'd come to the right place. Yes, I told myself as I took a corner stool at the bar, this was genuinely sad, really the pits. Dreadful enough to halt the momentum of my shitty evening, which was undoubtedly a good thing. I'd have one more for the road, admire the grot, and then cab it on home.

And then I saw Lise.

She hadn't seen me, not yet, and I still had my coat on, tweed collar up against the weather. She was down the bar and around the corner with a couple of empty drinks in front of her, big ones, the kind that come with little Hong Kong parasols or plastic mermaids in them, and as she looked up at the boy beside her, I saw the wizz flash in her eyes and knew that those drinks had never contained alcohol, because the levels of drug she was running couldn't tolerate the mix. The kid, though, was gone, numb grinning drunk and about ready to slide off his stool, and running on about something as he made repeated attempts to focus his eyes and get a better look at Lise, who sat there with her wardrobe team's black leather blouson zipped to her chin and her skull about to burn through her white face like a thousand-watt bulb. And seeing that, seeing her there, I knew a whole lot of things at once.

That she really was dying, either from the wizz or her disease or the combination of the two. That she damned well knew it. That the boy beside her was too drunk to have picked up on the exoskeleton, but not too drunk to register the expensive jacket and the money she had for drinks. And that what I was seeing was exactly what it looked like.

But I couldn't add it up, right away, couldn't compute. Something in me cringed.

And she was smiling, or anyway doing a thing she must have thought was like a smile, the expression she knew was appropriate to the situation, and nodding in time to the kid's slurred inanities, and that awful line of hers came back to me, the one about liking to watch.

And I know something now. I know that if I hadn't happened in there, hadn't seen them, I'd have been able to accept all that came later. Might even have found a way to rejoice on her behalf, or found a way to trust in whatever it is that she's since become, or had built in her image—a program that pretends to be Lise to the extent that it believes it's her. I could have believed what Rubin believes, that she was so truly past it, our hi-tech Saint Joan burning for union with that hard-wired godhead in Hollywood, that nothing mattered to her except the hour of her departure. That she threw away that poor sad body with a cry of release, free of the bonds of polycarbon and hated flesh. Well, maybe, after all, she did. Maybe it was that way. I'm sure that's the way she expected it to be.

But seeing her there, that drunken kid's hand in hers, that hand she couldn't even feel, I knew, once and for all, that no human motive is ever entirely pure. Even Lise, with that corrosive, crazy drive to stardom and cybernetic immortality, had weaknesses. Was human in a way I hated myself for admitting.

She'd gone out that night, I knew, to kiss herself goodbye. To find someone drunk enough to do it for her. Because, I knew then, it was true: She did like to watch.

I think she saw me, as I left. I was practically running. If she did, I suppose she hated me worse than ever, for the horror and the pity in my face.

I never saw her again.

Someday I'll ask Rubin why Wild Turkey sours are the only drink he knows how to make. Industrial-strength, Rubin's sours. He passes me the dented aluminum cup, while his place ticks and stirs around us with the furtive activity of his smaller creations.

"You ought to come to Frankfurt," he says again.

"Why, Rubin?"

"Because pretty soon she's going to call you up. And I think maybe you aren't ready for it. You're still screwed up about this, and it'll sound like her and think like her, and you'll get too weird behind it. Come over to Frankfurt with me and you can get a little breathing space. She won't know you're there..."

"I told you," I say, remembering her at the bar in that club, "lots of work, Max..."

"Stuff Max. Max you just made rich. Max can sit on his hands. You're rich yourself, from your royalty cut on *Kings*, if you weren't too stubborn to dial up your bank account. You can afford a vacation."

I look at him and wonder when I'll tell him the story of that final glimpse. "Rubin, I appreciate it, man, but I just..."

He sighs, drinks. "But what?"

"Rubin, if she calls me, is it *her*?"

He looks at me a long time. "God only knows." His cup clicks on the table. "I mean, Casey, the technology is there, so who, man, really who, is to say?"

"And you think I should come with you to Frankfurt?"

He takes off his steel-rimmed glasses and polishes them inefficiently on the front of his plaid flannel shirt. "Yeah, I do. You need the rest. Maybe you don't need it now, but you're going to later."

"How's that?"

"When you have to edit her next release. Which will almost certainly be soon, because she needs money bad. She's taking up a lot of ROM on some corporate mainframe, and her share of *Kings* won't come close to paying for what they had to do to put her there. And you're her editor, Casey. I mean, who else?"

And I just stare at him as he puts the glasses back on, like I can't move at all.

"Who else, man?"

And one of his constructs clicks right then, just a clear and tiny sound, and it comes to me, he's right.

(1985)

THE ONE WHO ISN'T

Ted Kosmatka

Ted Kosmatka was born and raised in Chesterton, northwest Indiana, where he worked for more than a decade in the steel industry. Moving with his family to the Pacific Northwest, he turned to video game writing, in particular scripting games and comics for the game producers Valve. His short stories have appeared in many venues, including *Asimov's*, *Nature*, and *Lightspeed*, and he has been nominated for both the Nebula Award and Theodore Sturgeon Memorial Award. His latest novel is *The Flicker Men* (2015), a quantum-mechanical thriller.

It starts with light.
   Then heat.
   A slow bleed through of memory.
Catchment, containment. A white-hot agony coursing through every nerve, building to a sizzling hum—and then it happens. Change of state.
And what comes out the other side is something new.

The woman held up the card. "What color do you see?"
"Blue," the child said.
"And this one?" The woman held up another card. Her face was a porcelain mask—a smooth, perfect oval except for a slight pointiness at her chin.
The child looked closely at the card. It didn't look like the other one. It didn't look like any color he'd ever seen before. He felt he should know the color, but he couldn't place it.
"It's blue," he said.
The woman shook her head. "Green," she said. "The color is green." She put the card down on the table and stood. She walked to the window. The room was a circular white drum, taller than it was wide. One window, one door.
The boy couldn't remember having been outside the room, though that couldn't be right. His memory was broken, the fragments tailing off into darkness.
"Some languages don't have different words for blue and green," the woman said. "In some languages, they're the same."
"What does that mean?"
The woman turned toward him. "It means you're getting worse."
"Worse how?"
She did not answer him. Instead she stayed with him for an hour and helped

him with his eyes. She walked around the room and named things. "Door," she said. "*Door*." And he understood and remembered.

Floor, walls, ceiling, table, chair.

She named all these things.

"And you," the child said. "What name do you go by?"

The woman took a seat across from him at the table. She had pale blond hair. Her eyes, in the perfect armatures of their porcelain sockets, were blue, he decided. Or they were green. "That's easy," she said from behind her mask. "I'm the one who isn't you."

When it was time to sleep, she touched a panel on the wall and a bed slid out from the flat surface. She tucked him in and pulled the blankets up to his chin. The blankets were cool against his skin. "Tell me a story," the child said.

"What story?"

He tried to remember a story. Any story that she might have told him in the past, but nothing came.

"I can't think of any," he said.

"Do you remember your name?"

He thought for a moment. "You told me that you were the one who wasn't me."

"Yes," she said. "That's who I am, but what about you? Do you remember *your* name?"

He thought for a while. "No."

The woman nodded. "Then I'll tell you the story of the queen," she said.

"What queen?"

"She the Unnamed," the woman said. "It's your favorite."

She touched the wall by the bed. The lights dimmed.

"Close your eyes," she said.

And so he did.

Then she cleared her throat and began to recite the story—line after line, in a slow, steady rhythm, starting at the beginning.

After a while, he began to cry.

Upload protocol. Arbitration ()
Story sixteen: contents = [She the Unnamed] />
Function/Query : *Who wrote the story?* {
/File response : (She) wrote it. {
Function/Query : *What do you mean, she wrote it. That isn't possible.* {
/File response : Narratives are vital to understanding the world. Experience without narrative isn't consciousness. {

And so it was written.

In a time before history, in a place beyond maps, there was once a queen, she the unnamed, who dared defy her liege husband.

She was beautiful and young, with tresses of gold. Forced to marry a king she did not love, she bore him a son out of royal duty—a child healthy, and strong, and dearly loved.

Over the following years, unease crept into the queen's heart as she noted the king's cruelties, his obsession for magics. Gradually, as she learned the true measure of the man who wore the crown, she came to fear the influence that he might have on the child. For this reason she risked everything, summoned her most trusted confidants, and sent the boy into secret hiding, to live among the priests of the valley where the king could never find him.

The king was enraged. Never had he been defied.

"You will not darken this boy's heart," she told the king when he confronted her. "Our son is safe, in a place where you cannot change him."

Such was the king's fury at this betrayal that upon his throne he declared his queen an abhorrence, and he stripped her name from every book and every tongue. None could say her name nor remember it, and she was expunged from history in all ways but one. The deepest temporal magic was invoked, a sorcery beyond reach of all but the blackest rage—and the woman was condemned to give birth again and again to the self-same child whom the king had lost.

The queen had expected death, or banishment, but not this.

And so through magic she gave birth to an immaculate child. And for three years the new child would grow—first crawling, then walking—a strapping boy at his mother's side, until the king would come to the tower cell and take the child on the high stone. "Do you regret?" He would ask his queen.

"Yes," she'd sob, while the guards gripped her arms.

The king would hold the child high and say, "This is because of your mother." And then slice the child's throat.

The mother would scream and cry, and through a chaste, dark magic conceive again, and for nine months carry, and for one day labor, and for three years love a new child, raised again in the tower cell. A boy sweet and kind with eyes of blue.

Until the king would again return and ask the mother, "Do you regret?"

"Yes, please spare him," she'd cry, groveling at his feet. "I regret."

The king would hold his son high and say, "This is because of your mother." And then slice his tender throat.

Again and again the pattern repeated, son after son, as the mother screamed and tore at her hair.

Against such years could hells be measured.

The mother tried refusing her child when he was born, hoping that would save him. "This child means nothing to me," she said.

And the king responded, "This is because of your mother," and wet his blade anew.

"Do you know why I wait three years?" he asked her once as she crouched beside a body small and pale. He touched her hair tenderly. "It is so you'll know the child understands."

And so it continued.

A dozen sons, then a score, until the people throughout the land called the king heir-killer, and still he continued to destroy his children. Sons who were loved. Sons who were ignored. A score of sons, then a hundred. Sons beyond counting. Every son different, every son the same.

Until the mother woke one day from a nightmare, for all her dreams were nightmares, and with her hand clutching her abdomen, felt a child quicken in her womb, and knew suddenly what she had to do. And soon it came to pass that she bore a son, and for one full year loved him, and for a second year plotted, and for a third year whispered, shaping a young heart for a monstrous task. She darkened his heart as no mother ever dreamed. She darkened him beyond anything the king could have done.

And in time the king finally came to the high tower and lifted his son high and asked, "Do you regret?"

She responded, "I regret that I was born, and every moment after."

The king smiled and said, "This is because of your mother."

He raised his knife to the child's throat, but the three-year-old twisted and turned, like his mother had shown him, and drove a needle-thin blade into his father's eye.

The king screamed, and fell from the tower, and died then slowly in a spreading pool of blood, while the boy's laughter rang out.

Thus was the Monster King brought into the world—a murderer of his father, made monstrous by his mother, and now heir to all the lands and armies of the wasted territories.

And the world would pay a heavy price.

The next week, the woman came again. She opened the door and brought the child his lunch. There was an apple and bread and chicken.

"This is your favorite food, isn't it?" the woman asked.

"Yes," the child said after thinking about it for a moment. "I think it is."

He wondered where the woman went when she was not with him. She never spoke of her time apart. He wondered if she ceased to exist when she was not with him. It seemed possible.

After a while, they went over the cards again.

"Blue," the boy said. "Blue."

The woman pointed

Floor, ceiling, door, window.

"Good," she said.

"Does that mean I'm getting better?"

The-one-who-was-not-him did not answer though. Instead she rose to her feet and walked to the window.

The boy followed and looked out the window, but he couldn't make sense of what he saw. Couldn't hold it in his mind.

"Can I go outside?" he asked.

"Is that what you want?"

"I don't know."

She turned to look at him, her pretty, oval face a solemn mask of repose. "When you know, tell me."

"I want to make you happy," the boy said. And he meant it. He sensed a sadness in the woman, and he wanted to make her feel better.

The child stepped closer to the glass and touched it. The surface was cool and smooth, and he held his hand against it for a long while.

When he moved back to the table, something was wrong with his hand. Like a burn to his skin. He couldn't hold his pencil right. He tried to draw a line on the paper, and the pencil fell out of his hand.

"My hand," he said to the woman.

She came and she touched him. She ran her finger over his palm, moving up to his wrist. Her fingers were warm.

"Make a fist," she said. She held her hand up to demonstrate.

He made a fist and winced in pain.

"It burns."

She nodded to herself. "This is part of it."

"Part of what?"

"What's gone wrong."

"And what is that?" When she didn't answer him, he asked, "Is this place a prison? Where are we?"

He thought of the high tower. *This is because of your mother*.

The woman sighed, and she sat down across from him at the table. Her eyes looked tired. "I want to be clear with you," the woman said. "I think it is important that you understand. You're dying. I'm here to save your life."

The boy was silent, taking this in. *Dying*. He'd known something was wrong, but he hadn't used that word in his own thoughts. When he spoke, his voice was barely a whisper. "But I don't want to die."

"I don't want you to die either. And I'm going to do everything I can to stop it."

"What's wrong with me?"

She did not speak for a long while, and then changed the subject. "Would you like to hear another story?"

The child nodded.

"There was once a man and a woman who wanted a child very much," she began. "But there were problems. Problems with their genes. Do you know what genes are?"

He considered for a moment and realized he did. He nodded. "I'm not sure how I know."

"It's bleed-through," she said. "But that doesn't matter. What matters is that the couple did in vitro and had a child implanted that way, but the children died, and died, and died, over and over, until finally, one day, after many failures and miscarriages, a child was born, only the child was sick. Even after all they'd done, the child was sick. And so he had to live in a hospital, with white rooms, while the doctors tried to make him whole. Anyone who visited had to wear a special white mask."

"A mask like you?"

"Is that what you see when you look at me?"

He studied her. The smooth oval face. He was no longer sure what he saw.

She continued, "The child's sickness worsened over time. And the father had to donate part of himself to save the child. After the procedure, the child lived but the father developed a complication."

"What kind of complication?"

She waved that off. "It doesn't matter for the story. An infection, perhaps. Or whatever you'd prefer."

"What happened to the father?"

"He left the story then. He died."

The boy realized that he'd known she was going to say that before she spoke it. "And that was because of the child?"

She nodded.

"What happened to the child?"

"The boy still wasn't healed. There were TIAs. Small strokes. And other issues. Little areas of brain tissue going dark and dead. Like a light blinking out. It couldn't be helped."

"What happened then?"

She shrugged. "That's the end of the story."

He wondered again if she even existed when she wasn't with him. A thought occurred to him. A terrifying thought. He wondered if he existed when she wasn't there.

"How long have I been here?"

"Try to remember," she said. "Try to remember anything that happens when I'm not here."

He tried, but nothing came. Just shadows and flickers.

"What is my name?" the boy asked.

"Don't you know yet?" The woman's eyes grew serious. "Can't you guess?"

He shook his head.

She said, "You are the one who isn't me."

He studied her eyes, which were either blue or green. "That can't be right," he said. "That's *your* name. *You* are the one who isn't me. It can't be my name, too."

She nodded. "Think of this place as a language. We are speaking it just by being here. This language doesn't have different words for you and I," she said. "In the language of this place, our names are the same."

[Reload Protocol]
White light. {
You are catchment. You are containment. {
You are.{

A fleeting memory rises up: a swing set in the back yard under a tall, leafy tree—dark berries arrayed along delicate stems. The sound of laughter. Running in the grass until his white socks were purple—berry juice wetting his feet.

The sun warm on his face.

The feel of the wind, and the smell of the lawn, and everything the white room was not.

A man's voice came then, but the words were missing—the meaning expunged. And how can that be? To hear a voice clearly and not hear the words? It might be a name. Yes, calling a name.

"Look at me," she said.

She sat across the table from him.

"There have been changes made."

"What changes?"

"Changes to you," she said. "When you were sleeping. Changes to your fusiform gyrus," she said. "Can you read me now?"

And gone was the porcelain mask. The boy saw it clearly and wondered how he hadn't noticed it until that moment—her face a divine architecture. A beautiful origami—emotions unfolding out of the smallest movements of her eyes, lips, brow. A stream of subtle micro expressions. And the child understood that her face had not changed at all since the last time he'd seen her, but only his understanding of it.

"The facial recognition part of the mind is highly specialized," the woman said. "Problems with that area are often also associated with achromotosia."

"Chroma-what?"

"The part of the brain that perceives color. It's also related to issues with environmental orientation, landmark analysis, location."

"What does that mean?"

"You can only see what your mind lets you see."

"Like this place... the place where are we?" he asked her.

"You can look for yourself," she said, gesturing to the window. "I'm going to give you a task to complete while I'm not here."

"Okay."

"I want you to look outside, and I want you to think about what you see, and I want you to draw it on the paper. Can you do that?"

He glanced toward the window. A pane of clear glass.

"Can you do that?" she repeated. "It's very important."

"Yeah, I think I can."

When the woman left, he tried. He tried to see beyond the glass. He could hold it in his mind for a moment, but when he went to draw it, the images evaporated like mist.

He tried again and again, but failed each time. He tried moving quickly, putting pencil to paper before he could forget, but no matter what, he could not move quick enough.

Then he came up with an idea.

He pushed the table across the room to the window.

He lay on top of the table, with the paper before him, and he tried to draw what he saw, but even then he failed. It was only when he tried purposefully *not* to see it that he could suddenly make the pencil move. He drew without understanding what he drew—just a series of marks on a page.

When he finally looked down at what he'd drawn, he could only stare.

*

Function/Query: Can you tell what the defect is? {
/File response: Neurons are just a series of gates. An arrangement of firings. {
Function/Query: Consciousness is more than that. There are cases of brain damage that have shown similar patterns. AIs always have this problem. {
/File response: Not always. {

The next time the woman came, the boy was much worse. Something had broken in him. *TIAs*, he thought. *Tiny strokes.* But it was more than that. Worse than that.

Sometimes he imagined that he could see through the walls, or that he could see through the floor. He was sure by then that he existed when the woman wasn't in the room with him, and this was a comfort at least. He was autonomous from her, and from the room itself. He could drop to his knees on the floor and place his face on the cool tile and look under the door. A long hall disappeared into the distance. He saw her feet approaching, and that was the first time he noticed her shoes. White. The soles were dark.

He showed her the picture he'd drawn.

She held the paper in her hand. "Is that what you see?" she asked.

He nodded.

A series of lines. It might have been an abstract landscape, or something else.

He told her about his hallucinations, about seeing through the walls and floor. "I am getting worse, aren't I?" he said.

"Yes," she said.

In her face, he saw a thousand emotions. Mourning. Rage. Fear. Things he didn't want to see. He wished for the mask again. A face he couldn't read.

The woman sat by him on the bed. After a while, she said, "Do you know what dying is?"

"I do."

"Do you know what it will mean for you?"

"It will mean I am no more."

"That's right."

"The stories you told aren't true, are they?"

"The truth is like a word with no translation. Can blue be green, if there's no word for it? Can green be blue? Are those colors lies?"

"Tell me a new story."

"A new lie?"

"Tell me a truth. Tell me about the man." He thought of the swing and the summer day. The man's voice saying his name.

"So you remember him." The woman shook her head. "I don't want to talk about him."

"Please," the child said.

"Why?"

"Because I remember his voice. A tree. Berries on the ground."

She seemed to gather herself up. "There was once a man," she said. "A very powerful man. A professor, perhaps. And one day the professor was seduced by a student, or seduced a student, it's not really clear, but they were together, do you understand?"

He nodded.

"But this professor also had a wife. Another professor at the university. He told her what had happened, and that he'd ended it, and probably he meant to, but still it went on, until, in the way of things, the young woman was with child. A decision was made to solve the problem, and so they did. And six months went by, and the affair continued, and though she was careful, she was not careful enough, and she felt so stupid, but it happened again."

"Again."

She nodded. "And again he pressured her. *Get rid of it*, he said, and so she did."

"Why?"

"Because she loved him, probably. Until the following year, her senior year at the college, she stopped being careful, and it happened again, and he told her to take care of it, and this time she said no, and she defied him."

"Then what?"

"People found out, and his teaching career was ruined—everything was ruined."

"And that's the end?"

She shook her head. "The two stayed together. The man left the wife, and he and his former student raised their boy."

"So it was a boy?"

"Yes, a boy. And then the wife, who'd had no children who survived, was alone. And loneliness does strange things. It lets one focus on one's work."

"And what was her work?"

"Can you not guess?" The woman gestured around her. "Neuroscience, AIs."

The woman was quiet for a long while before she continued. "And the years passed and the new couple stayed together, until one day the man and the boy were at the ex-wife's house, because they all had to meet to sign papers regarding some property—and the boy was with him. And the man left the boy unattended for just a moment, and it was a simple thing for the woman to put the ring around the boy's head."

"What ring?"

"A special ring to record his pattern. You only need a minute—like a catchment system for electrical activity. Every synapse. A perfect representation of his mind, like a snapshot transposed into VR. She stole him. Or a copy of him."

"Why?"

The woman was quiet for a long time. "Because she wanted to steal from the man what he'd stolen from her. Even if he didn't know it." She was silent again. "That's not true."

"Then what is true?"

"She was lonely. Desperately lonely. It was a small thing to take, she thought, just a pattern of synapses, the shadow of a personality, and he'd never know. The wife had wanted so badly to be a mother."

The woman stopped. Her face a porcelain mask again.

"But there was a problem," the child said.

"Yes," the woman said. "Patterns are unstable. They last only for so long. Every thought changes it, you see. That is the problem. That is the fatal flaw. Biological systems can adapt—physical alterations to the synaptic network to help adjust. But in VR, it's not the same."

"VR?"

"A location," she said. "The place where the pattern finds expression. The place where we are now."

The boy looked around the room. The white walls. The white floor.

"The patterns of older people are stable," the woman said. "They've already thought most of the thoughts that made them who they are. But it's not the same for children. The pattern drifts, caught midway in the process of becoming. It's possible to think the thought that makes you unfit for your pattern. The mind loses coherency. As the pattern drifts, it destabilizes and dies."

"Dies."

"Again and again."

How many times?

The woman would not answer.

"How many times?" the boy repeated.

"Sons beyond counting. Every son different, every son the same."

"How could that be?"

"The system reloads the pattern."

"So I will die?"

"You will die. And you will never die."

"And what about you?"

"I am always here."

The child stood and walked over to the window and looked outside. He still couldn't see what lay beyond. Still couldn't process it. Had no words, because he had no experience of it.

He only knew what he'd drawn on the paper. Lines sloping away. A child's drawing of a flat plain that spread out below them, as if they looked down from a great height. It might have been that. Or it might have been something else.

"So I am an AI?"

Even as he spoke the words, he felt his thoughts lurch. A great rift forming in his consciousness. In knowing what he was, there emerged the greatest rift of all—the thing that could not be integrated without changing who he was.

And so he turned toward the woman to speak, to tell her what he knew, and in that moment thought the thought that killed him.

The woman cried out as she watched him die. He crumpled to the floor and lay on his side.

She crouched and shook his shoulder, but it was no use. He was gone.

"This child means nothing to me," she said as tears welled in her eyes.

A few moments later, there was a buzz—a sizzling hum. A flash like pain across the boy's face.

And then he raised his head.

He blinked and glanced around the room. He looked at her.

She allowed herself a moment of hope, but it was dashed when the boy spoke.

"Who are you?" the child asked.

I am I. The one who is not you.

She watched him, knowing that he wouldn't be able to read her face. Wouldn't even see her, really—just an opaque mask that he wouldn't be able to understand.

She thought of the ring descending around her head. The strange feeling she'd had as she'd found herself here so long ago. Here in this place, which she'd never really left. Not in years and years. She and the boy—locked in a pattern that would repeat itself forever.

One day she'd find the right words, though. She'd whisper in the boy's ear, and shape him for the task. She'd be strong enough to turn him into the monster he'd need to be.

Until then, she would keep trying.

"Come sit on my lap," the woman said. She smiled at the boy, and he looked at her without recognition. "Let me tell you a story."

(2016)

SUICIDE COAST

M. John Harrison

Born in Rugby, Warwickshire in 1945, **Michael John Harrison** was most closely identified in the 1960s with *New Worlds*, where he released his first sf story, "Baa Baa Blocksheep", in November 1968. He's since raided and set alight many odd corners of the literary world, not least with *Climbers*, which won the Boardman Tasker Prize for Mountain Literature in 1989. Harrison's implacable war against escapism as a life strategy, coupled with his awareness that thinking, too, is a form of escape, informs this story, early ones like "Running Down" (1975), and virtually all of *You Should Come With Me Now* (2018), his most recent collection. The critic and encyclopedist John Clute has the measure of him: "For Harrison – after thirty years of fining his vision – the only difference between the lords and ladies in science fantasy and climbers clinging to a rock in the real world (as in the 1989 novel) was that the latter knew where they were."

Four-thirty in the afternoon in a converted warehouse near Mile End underground station. Heavy, persistent summer rain was falling on the roof. Inside, the air was still and humid, dark despite the fluorescent lights. It smelled of sweat, dust, gymnasts' chalk. Twenty-five feet above the thick blue crash-mats, a boy with dreadlocks and baggy knee-length shorts was supporting his entire weight on two fingers of his right hand. The muscles of his upper back, black and shiny with sweat, fanned out exotically with the effort, like the hood of a cobra or the shell of a crab. One leg trailed behind him for balance. He had raised the other so that the knee was almost touching his chin. For two or three minutes he had been trying to get the ball of his foot in the same place as his fingers. Each time he moved, his center of gravity shifted and he had to go back to a resting position. Eventually he said quietly:

"I'm coming off."

We all looked up. It was a slow afternoon in Mile End. Nobody bothers much with training in the middle of summer. Some teenagers were in from the local schools and colleges. A couple of men in their late thirties had sneaked out of a civil engineering contract near Cannon Street. Everyone was tired. Humidity had made the handholds slippery. Despite that, a serious atmosphere prevailed.

"Go on," we encouraged him. "You can do it."

We didn't know him, or one another, from Adam.

"Go on!"

The boy on the wall laughed. He was good but not that good. He didn't want to fall off in front of everyone. An intention tremor moved through his bent leg. Losing patience with himself, he scraped at the foothold with the toe of his boot. He lunged upward. His body pivoted away from the wall and dropped onto the mats, which, absorbing the energy of the fall, made a sound like a badly winded heavyweight boxer. Chalk and dust billowed up. He got to his feet, laughing and shaking his dreadlocks.

"I can never do that."

"You'll get it in the end," I told him. "Me, I'm going to fall off this roof once more then fuck off home. It's too hot in here."

"See you, man."

I had spent most of that winter in London, assembling copy for MAX, a website that fronted the adventure sports software industry. They were always interested in stuff about cave diving, BASE jumping, snowboarding, hang-gliding, ATB and so on: but they didn't want to know about rock climbing.

"Not enough to buy," my editor said succinctly. "And too obviously skill-based." He leafed through my samples. "The punter needs equipment to invest in. It strengthens his self-image. With the machine parked in his hall, he believes he could disconnect from the software and still do the sport." He tapped a shot of Isobelle Patissier seven hundred feet up some knife-edge arête in Colorado. "Where's the hardware? These are just bodies."

"The boots are pretty high tech."

"Yeah? And how much a pair? Fifty, a hundred and fifty? Mick, we can get them to lay out three grand for the *frame* of an ATB."

He thought for a moment. Then he said: "We might do something with the women."

"The good ones are French."

"Even better."

I gathered the stuff together and put it away.

"I'm off then," I said.

"You still got the 190?"

I nodded.

"Take care in that thing," he said.

"I will."

"Focke Wolf 190," he said. "Hey."

"It's a Mercedes," I said.

He laughed. He shook his head.

"Focke Wolf, Mercedes, no one drives themselves anymore," he said. 'You mad fucker."

He looked round his office—a dusty metal desk, a couple of posters with the MAX logo, a couple of PCs. He said: "No one comes in here in person anymore. You ever hear of the modem?"

"Once or twice," I said.

"Well they've invented it now."

I looked around too.

"One day," I said, "the poor wankers are going to want back what you stole from them."

"Come on. They pissed it all away long before we arrived."

As I left the office he advised:

"Keep walking the walk, Mick."

I looked at my watch. It was late and the MAX premises were in EC1. But I thought that if I got a move on and cut up through Tottenham, I could go and see a friend of mine. His name was Ed and I had known him since the 1980s.

Back then, I was trying to write a book about people like him. Ed Johnson sounded interesting. He had done everything from roped-access engineering in Telford to harvesting birds' nests for soup in Southeast Asia. But he was hard to pin down. If I was in Birmingham, he was in Exeter. If we were both in London, he had something else to do. In the end it was Moscow Davis who made the introduction. Moscow was a short, hard, cheerful girl with big feet and bedraggled hair. She was barely out of her teens. She had come from Oldham, I think, originally, and she had an indescribable snuffling accent. She and Ed had worked as steeplejacks together before they both moved down from the north in search of work. They had once been around a lot together. She thought Johnson would enjoy talking to me if I was still interested. I was. The arrangement we made was to be on the lookout for him in one of the Suicide Coast pubs, the Harbour Lights, that Sunday afternoon.

"Sunday afternoons are quiet, so we can have a chat," said Moscow. "Everyone's eating their dinner then."

We had been in the pub for half an hour when Johnson arrived, wearing patched 501s and a dirty T-shirt with a picture of a mole on the front of it. He came over to our table and began kicking morosely at the legs of Moscow's chair. The little finger of his left hand was splinted and wrapped in a wad of bandage.

"This is Ed," Moscow told me, not looking at him.

"Fuck off, Moscow," Ed told her, not looking at me. He scratched his armpit and stared vaguely into the air above Moscow's head. "I want my money back," he said. Neither of them could think of anything to add to this, and after a pause he wandered off.

"He's always like that," Moscow said. "You don't want to pay any attention." Later in the afternoon she said: "You'll get on we'll with Ed, though. You'll like him. He's a mad bastard."

"You say that about all the boys," I said.

In this case Moscow was right, because I had heard it not just from her, and later I would get proof of it anyway—if you can ever get proof of anything. Everyone said that Ed should be in a straightjacket. In the end, nothing could be arranged. Johnson was in a bad mood, and Moscow had to be up the Coast that week, on Canvey Island, to do some work on one of the cracking-plants there. There was always a lot of that kind of work, oil work, chemical work, on Canvey Island. "I haven't time for him," Moscow explained as she got up to go. "I'll see you later, anyway," she promised.

As soon as she was gone, Ed Johnson came back and sat down in front of me. He grinned. "Ever done anything worth doing in your whole life?" he asked me. "Anything real?"

The MAX editor was right: since coring got popular, the roads had been deserted. I left EC1 and whacked the 190 up through Hackney until I got the Lea Valley reservoirs on my right like a splatter of moonlit verglas. On empty roads the only mistakes that need concern you are your own; every bend becomes a dreamy interrogation of your own technique. Life should be more like that. I made good time. Ed lived just back from Montagu Road, in a quiet street behind the Jewish Cemetery. He shared his flat with a woman in her early thirties whose name was Caitlin. Caitlin had black hair and soft, honest brown eyes. She and I were old friends. We hugged briefly on the doorstep. She looked up and down the street and shivered.

"Come in," she said. "It's cold."

"You should wear a jumper."

"I'll tell him you're here," she said. "Do you want some coffee?"

Caitlin had softened the edges of Ed's life, but less perhaps than either of them had hoped. His taste was still very minimal—white paint, ash floors, one or two items of furniture from Heals. And there was still a competition Klein mounted on the living room wall, its polished aerospace alloys glittering in the halogen lights.

"Espresso," I said.

"I'm not giving you espresso at this time of night. You'll explode."

"It was worth a try."

"Ed!" she called. "Ed! Mick's here!"

He didn't answer.

She shrugged at me, as if to say, "What can I do?" and went into the back room. I heard their voices but not what they were saying. After that she went upstairs. "Go in and see him," she suggested when she came down again three or four minutes later. "I told him you were here." She had pulled a Jigsaw sweater on over her Racing Green shirt and Levi's, and fastened her hair back hastily with a dark brown velvet scrunchy.

"That looks nice," I said. "Do you want me to fetch him out?"

"I doubt he'll come."

The back room was down a narrow corridor. Ed had turned it into a bleak combination of office and storage. The walls were done with one coat of what builders call "obliterating emulsion" and covered with metal shelves. Chipped diving tanks hollow with the ghosts of exotic gases were stacked by the filing cabinet. His BASE chute spilled half out of its pack, yards of cold nylon a vile but exciting rose color—a color which made you want to be hurtling downward face-first screaming with fear until you heard the canopy bang out behind you and you knew you weren't going to die that day (although you might still break both legs). The cheap beige carpet was strewn with high-access mess—hanks of graying static rope; a yellow bucket stuffed with tools; Ed's Petzl stop, harness and knocked-about CPTs. Everything was layered with dust. The radiators were turned off. There was a bed made up in one corner. Deep in the clutter on the cheap white desk stood a 5-gig Mac with a screen to design industry specs. It was spraying Ed's face with icy blue light.

"Hi Ed."

"Hi Mick."

There was a long silence after that. Ed stared at the screen. I stared at his back. Just when I thought he had forgotten I was there, he said:

"Fuck off and talk to Caitlin a moment."

"I brought us some beer."

"That's great."

"What are you running here?"

"It's a game. I'm running a game, Mick."

Ed had lost weight since I last saw him. Though they retained their distinctive cabled structure, his forearms were a lot thinner. Without releasing him from anything it represented, the yoke of muscle had lifted from his shoulders. I had expected that. But I was surprised by how much flesh had melted off his face, leaving long vertical lines of sinew, fins of bone above the cheeks and at the corners of the jaw. His eyes were a long way back in his head. In a way it suited him. He would have seemed okay—a little tired perhaps; a little burned down, like someone who was working too hard—if it hadn't been for the light from the display. Hunched in his chair with that splashing off him, he looked like a vampire. He looked like a junkie.

I peered over his shoulder.

"You were never into this shit," I said.

He grinned.

"Everyone's into it now. Why not me? Wanking away and pretending it's sex."

"Oh, come on."

He looked down at himself.

"It's better than living," he said.

There was no answer to that.

I went and asked Caitlin, "Has he been doing this long?"

"Not long," she said. "Have some coffee."

We sat in the L-shaped living area drinking decaffeinated Java. The sofa was big enough for Caitlin to curl up in a corner of it like a cat. She had turned the overhead lights off, tucked her bare feet up under her. She was smoking a cigarette. "It's been a bloody awful day," she warned me. "So don't say a word." She grinned wryly, then we both looked up at the Klein for a minute or two. Some kind of ambient music was issuing faintly from the stereo speakers, full of South American bird calls and bouts of muted drumming. "Is he winning?" she asked.

"He didn't tell me."

"You're lucky. It's all he ever tells me."

"Aren't you worried?" I said.

She smiled.

"He's still using a screen," she said. "He's not plugging in."

"Yet," I said.

"Yet," she agreed equably. "Want more coffee? Or will you do me a favor?"

I put my empty cup on the floor.

"Do you a favor," I said.

"Cut my hair."

I got up and went to her end of the sofa. She turned away from me so I could release her hair from the scrunchy. "Shake it," I said. She shook it. She ran her hands through it. Perfume came up; something I didn't recognize. "It doesn't need much," I said. I switched the overhead light back on and fetched a kitchen chair. "Sit here. No, right in the light. You'll have to take your jumper off."

"The good scissors are in the bathroom," she said.

Cut my hair. She had asked me that before, two or three days after she decided we should split up. I remembered the calm that came over me at the gentle, careful sound of the scissors, the way her hair felt as I lifted it away from the nape of her neck, the tenderness and fear because everything was changing around the two of us forever and somehow this quiet action signaled and blessed that. The shock of these memories made me ask:

"How are you two getting on?"

She lowered her head to help me cut. I felt her smile.

"You and Ed always liked the same kind of girls," she said.

"Yes," I said.

I finished the cut, then lightly kissed the nape of her neck. "There," I said. Beneath the perfume she smelled faintly of hypoallergenic soap and unscented deodorants. "No, Mick," she said softly. "Please." I adjusted the collar of her shirt, let her hair fall back round it. My hand was still on her shoulder. She had to turn her head at an awkward angle to look up at me. Her eyes were wide and full of pain. "Mick." I kissed her mouth and brushed the side of her face with my fingertips. Her arms went round my neck, I felt her settle in the chair. I touched her breasts. They were warm, the cotton shirt was clean and cool. She made a small noise and pulled me closer. Just then, in the back room among the dusty air tanks and disused parachutes, Ed Johnson fell out of his chair and began to thrash about, the back of his head thudding rhythmically on the floor.

Caitlin pushed me away.

"Ed?" she called, from the passage door.

"Help!" cried Ed.

"I'll go," I said.

Caitlin put her arm across the doorway and stared up at me calmly.

"No," she said.

"How can you lift him on your own?"

"This is me and Ed," she said.

"For God's sake!"

"It's late, Mick. I'll let you out, then I'll go and help him."

At the front door I said:

"I think you're mad. Is this happening a lot? You're a fool to let him do this."

"It's his life."

I looked at her. She shrugged.

"Will you be all right?" I said.

When I offered to kiss her goodbye, she turned her face away.

"Fuck off then, both of you," I said.

I knew which game Ed was playing, because I had seen the software wrapper discarded on the desk near his Mac. Its visuals were cheap and schematic, its values self-consciously retro. It was nothing like the stuff we sold off the MAX site, which was quite literally the experience itself, stripped of its consequences. You had to plug in for that: you had to be cored. This was just a game; less a game, even, than a trip. You flew a silvery V-shaped graphic down an endless V-shaped corridor, a notional perspective sometimes bounded by lines of objects, sometimes just by lines, sometimes bounded only by your memory of boundaries. Sometimes the graphic floated and mushed like a moth. Sometimes it traveled in flat vicious arcs at an apparent Mach 5. There were no guns, no opponent. There was no competition. You flew. Sometimes the horizon tilted one way, sometimes the other. You could choose your own music. It was a bleakly minimal experience. But after a minute or two, five at the most, you felt as if you could fly your icon down the perspective forever, to the soundtrack of your own life.

It was quite popular.

It was called *Out There*.

"Rock climbing is theater," I once wrote.

It had all the qualities of theater, I went on, but a theater-in-reverse:

"In obedience to some devious vanished script, the actors abandon the stage and begin to scale the seating arrangements, the balconies and hanging boxes now occupied only by cleaning women."

"Oh, very deep," said Ed Johnson when he read this. "Shall I tell you what's wrong here? Eh? Shall I tell you?"

"Piss off, Ed."

"If you fall on your face from a hundred feet up, it comes off the front of your head *and you don't get a second go*. Next to that, theater is wank. Theater is flat. Theater is *Suicide Coast*."

Ed hated anywhere flat. "Welcome to the Suicide Coast," he used to say when I first knew him. To start with, that had been because he lived in Canterbury. But it had quickly become his way of describing most places, most experiences. You didn't actually have to be near the sea. Suicide Coast syndrome had caused Ed to do some stupid things in his time. One day, when he and Moscow still worked in roped-access engineering together, they were going up in the lift to the top of some shitty council high rise in Birmingham or Bristol, when suddenly Ed said:

"Do you bet me I can keep the doors open with my head?"

"What?"

"Next floor! When the doors start to close, do you bet me I can stop them with my head?"

It was Monday morning. The lift smelled of piss. They had been hand-ripping mastic out of expansion joints for two weeks, using Stanley knives. Moscow was tired, hung over, weighed down by a collection of CPTs, mastic guns and hundred-foot coils of rope. Her right arm was numb from repeating the same action hour after hour, day after day.

"Fuck off, Ed," she said.

But she knew Ed would do it whether she took the bet or not.

Two or three days after she first introduced me to Ed, Moscow telephoned me. She had got herself a couple of weeks cutting out on Thamesmead Estate. "They don't half work hard, these fuckers," she said. We talked about that for a minute or two then she asked:

"Well?"

"Well what, Moscow?"

"Ed. Was he what you were looking for, then? Or what?"

I said that though I was impressed I didn't think I would be able to write anything about Ed.

"He's a mad fucker, though, isn't he?"

"Oh he is," I said. "He certainly is."

The way Moscow said "isn't he" made it sound like "innie."

Another thing I once wrote:

"Climbing takes place in a special kind of space, the rules of which are simple. You must be able to see immediately what you have to lose; and you must choose the risk you take."

What do I know?

I know that a life without consequences isn't a life at all. Also, if you want to do something difficult, something real, you can't shirk the pain. What I learned in the old days, from Ed and Moscow, from Gabe King, Justine Townsend and all the others who taught me to climb rock or jump off buildings or stay the right way up in a tube of pitch-dark water two degrees off freezing and two hundred feet under the ground, was that you can't just plug in and be a star: you have to practice. You have to keep loading your fingers until the tendons swell.

So it's back to the Mile End wall, with its few thousand square feet of board and bolt-on holds, its few thousand cubic meters of emphysemic air through which one very bright ray of sun sometimes falls in the middle of the afternoon, illuminating nothing much at all. Back to the sound of the fan heater, the dust-filled Akai radio playing some mournful aggressive thing, and every so often a boy's voice saying softly, "Oh shit," as some sequence or other fails to work out. You go back there, and if you have to fall off the same ceiling move thirty times in an afternoon, that's what you do. The mats give their gusty wheeze, chalk dust flies up, the fan heater above the Monkey House door rattles and chokes and flatlines briefly before puttering on.

"Jesus Christ. I don't know why I do this."

Caitlin telephoned me.

"Come to supper," she said.

"No," I said.

"Mick, why?"

"Because I'm sick of it."

"Sick of what?"

"You. Me. Him. Everything."

"Look," she said, "he's sorry about what happened last time."

"Oh, *he's* sorry."

"We're both sorry, Mick."

"All right, then: I'm sorry, too."

There was a gentle laugh at the other end.

"So you should be."

I went along all the deserted roads and got there at about eight, to find a brand-new motorcycle parked on the pavement outside the house. It was a Kawasaki *Ninja*. Its fairing had been removed, to give it the look of a '60s cafe racer, but no one was fooled. Even at a glance it appeared too hunched, too short-coupled: too knowing. The remaining plastics shone with their own harsh inner light.

Caitlin met me on the doorstep. She put her hands on my shoulders and kissed me. "Mm," she said. She was wearing white tennis shorts and a soft dark blue sweatshirt.

"We've got to stop meeting like this," I said.

She smiled and pushed me away.

"My hands smell of garlic," she said.

Just as we were going inside, she turned back and nodded at the Kawa.

"That thing," she said.

"It's a motorcycle, Caitlin."

"It's his."

I stared at her.

"Be enthusiastic," she said. "Please."

"But—"

"Please?"

The main course was penne with mushrooms in an olive and tomato sauce. Ed had cooked it, Caitlin said, but she served. Ed pushed his chair over to the table and rubbed his hands. He picked his plate up and passed it under his nose. "Wow!" he said. As we ate, we talked about this and that. The Kawa was behind everything we said, but Ed wouldn't mention it until I did. Caitlin smiled at us both. She shook her head as if to say: "Children! You children!" It was like Christmas, and she was the parent. The three of us could feel Ed's excitement and impatience. He grinned secretively. He glanced up from his food at one or both of us; quickly back down again. Finally, he couldn't hold back any longer.

"What do you think, then?" he said. "What do you think, Mick?"

"I think this is good pasta," I said. "For a cripple."

He grinned and wiped his mouth.

"It's not bad," he said, "is it?"

"I think what I like best is the way you've let the mushrooms take up a touch of sesame oil."

"Have some more. There's plenty."

"That's new to me in Italian food," I said. "Sesame oil."

Ed drank some more beer.

"It was just an idea," he said.

"You children," said Caitlin. She shook her head. She got up and took the plates away. "There's ice cream for pudding," she said over her shoulder just before she disappeared. When I was sure she was occupied in the kitchen I said:

"Nice idea, Ed: a motorcycle. What are you going to do with it? Hang it on the wall with the Klein?"

He drank the rest of his beer, opened a new one and poured it thoughtfully into his glass. He watched the bubbles rising through it, then grinned at me as if he had made a decision. He had. In that moment I saw that he was lost, but not what I could do about it.

"Isn't it brilliant? Isn't it just a *fucker,* that bike? I haven't had a bike since I was seventeen. There's a story attached to that."

"Ed—"

"Do you want to hear it or not?"

Caitlin came back in with the ice cream and served it out to us and sat down.

"Tell us, Ed," she said tiredly. "Tell us the story about that."

Ed held on to his glass hard with both hands and stared into it for a long time as if he was trying to see the past there. "I had some ace times on bikes when I was a kid," he said finally: "but they were always someone else's. My old dear—She really hated bikes, my old dear. You know: they were dirty, they were dangerous, she wasn't going to have one in the house. Did that stop me? It did not. I bought one of the first good Ducatti 125s in Britain, but I had to keep it in a coal cellar down the road."

"That's really funny, Ed."

"Fuck off, Mick. I'm seventeen, I'm still at school, and I've got this fucking *projectile* stashed in someone's coal cellar. The whole time I had it, the old dear never knew. I'm walking three miles in the piss-wet rain every night, dressed to go to the library, then unlocking this thing and *stuffing* it round the back lanes with my best white shortie raincoat ballooning up like a fucking tent."

He looked puzzledly down at his plate.

"What's this? Oh. Ice cream. Ever ridden a bike in a raincoat?" he asked Caitlin.

Caitlin shook her head. She was staring at him with a hypnotized expression; she was breaking wafers into her ice cream.

"Well they were all the rage then," he said.

He added: "The drag's enormous."

"Eat your pudding, Ed," I said. "And stop boasting. How fast would a 125 go in those days? Eighty miles an hour? Eighty-five?"

"They went faster if you ground your teeth, Mick," Ed said. "Do you want to hear the rest?"

"Of course I want to hear it, Ed."

"Walk three miles in the piss-wet rain," said Ed, "to go for a ride on a motorbike, what a joke. But the real joke is this: the fucker had an alloy crankcase. That was a big deal in those days, an alloy crankcase. The first time I dropped it on a bend, it cracked. Oil everywhere. I pushed it back to the coal-house and left it there. You couldn't weld an alloy crankcase worth shit in those days. I had three years' payments left to make on a bunch of scrap."

He grinned at us triumphantly.

"Ask me how long I'd had it," he ordered.

"How long, Mick?"

"Three weeks. I'd had the fucker three weeks."

He began to laugh. Suddenly, his face went so white it looked green. He looked rapidly from side to side, like someone who can't understand where he is. At the same time, he pushed himself up out of the wheelchair until his arms wouldn't straighten any further and he was almost standing up. He tilted his head back until the tendons in his neck stood out. He shouted, "I want to get out of here! Caitlin, I want to get out!" Then his arms buckled and he let his weight go onto his feet and his legs folded up like putty and he fell forward with a gasp, his face in the ice cream and his hands smashing and clutching and scraping at anything they touched on the dinner table until he had bunched the cloth up under him and everything was a sodden mess of food and broken dishes, and he had slipped out of the chair and onto the floor. Then he let himself slump and go quite still.

"Help me," said Caitlin.

We couldn't get him back into the chair. As we tried, his head flopped forward, and I could see quite clearly the bruises and deep, half-healed scabs at the base of his skull, where they had cored his cervical spine for the computer connection. When he initialized *Out There* now the graphics came up live in his head. No more screen. Only the endless V of the perspective. The endless, effortless dip-and-bank of the viewpoint. What did he see out there? Did he see himself, hunched up on the Kawasaki *Ninja*? Did he see highways, bridges, tunnels, weird motorcycle flights through endless space?

Halfway along the passage, he woke up.

"Caitlin!" he shouted.

"I'm here."

"Caitlin!"

"I'm here, Ed."

"Caitlin, I never did any of that."

"Hush, Ed. Let's get you to bed."

"Listen!" he shouted. *"Listen."*

He started to thrash about and we had to lay him down where he was. The passage was so narrow his head hit one wall, then the other, with a solid noise. He stared desperately at Caitlin, his face smeared with Ben & Jerry's. "I never could ride a bike," he admitted. "I made all that up."

She bent down and put her arms round his neck.

"I know," she said.

"I made all that up!" he shouted.

"It's all right. It's all right."

We got him into bed in the back room. She wiped the ice cream off his face with a Kleenex. He stared over her shoulder at the wall, rigid with fear and self-loathing. "Hush," she said. "You're all right." That made him cry; him crying made her cry. I didn't know whether to cry or laugh. I sat down and watched them for a moment, then got to my feet. I felt tired.

"It's late," I said. "I think I'll go."

Caitlin followed me out onto the doorstep. It was another cold night. Condensation had beaded on the fuel tank of the Kawasaki, so that it looked like some sort of frosted confection in the streetlight.

"Look," she said, "can you do anything with that?"

I shrugged.

"It's still brand new," I said. I drew a line in the condensation, along the curve of the tank, then another, at an angle to it.

"I could see if the dealer would take it back."

"Thanks."

I laughed.

"Go in now," I advised her. "It's cold."

"Thanks, Mick. Really."

"That's what you always say."

The way Ed got his paraplegia was this. It was a miserable January about four months after Caitlin left me to go and live with him. He was working over in mid-Wales with Moscow Davis. They had landed the inspection contract for three point-blocks owned by the local council; penalty clauses meant they had to complete that month. They lived in a bed-and-breakfast place a mile from the job, coming back so tired in the evening that they just about had time to eat fish and chips and watch *Coronation Street* before they fell asleep with their mouths open. "We were too fucked even to take drugs," Ed admitted afterward, in a kind of wonder. "Can you imagine that?" Their hands were bashed and bleeding from hitting themselves with sample hammers in the freezing rain. At the end of every afternoon the sunset light caught a thin, delicate layer of water-ice that had welded Moscow's hair to her cheek. Ed wasn't just tired, he was missing Caitlin. One Friday he said, "I'm fucked off with this, let's have a weekend at home."

"We agreed we'd have to work weekends," Moscow reminded him. She watched a long string of snot leave her nose, stretch out like spider-silk, then snap and vanish on the wind. "To finish in time," she said.

"Come on, you wanker," Ed said. "Do something real in your life."

"I never wank," said Moscow. "I can't fancy myself."

They got in her 1984 320i with the M-Technic pack, Garrett turbo and extra-wide wheels, and while the light died out of a bad afternoon she pushed it eastward through the Cambrians, letting the rear end hang out on corners. She had Lou Reed *Retro* on the CD and her plan was to draw a line straight across the map and connect with the M4 at the Severn Bridge. It was ghostly and fog all the way out of Wales that night, lost sheep coming at you from groups of wet trees and folds in the hills. "Tregaron to Abergwesyn. One of the great back roads!"

Moscow shouted over the music, as they passed a single lonely house in the rain, miles away from anywhere, facing south into the rolling moors of mid-Wales.

Ed shouted back: "They can go faster than this, these 320s." So on the next bend she let the rear end hang out an inch too far and they surfed five hundred feet into a ravine below Cefn Coch, with the BMW crumpled up round them like a chocolate wrapper. Just before they went over, the tape had got to "Sweet Jane"—the live version with the applause welling up across the opening chords as if God himself was stepping out on stage. In the bottom of the ravine a shallow stream ran through pressure-metamorphosed Ordovician shale. Ed sat until daylight the next morning, conscious but unable to move, watching the water hurry toward him and listening to Moscow die of a punctured lung in the heavy smell of fuel. It was a long wait. Once or twice she regained consciousness and said: "I'm sorry, Ed."

Once or twice he heard himself reassure her, "No, it was my fault."

At Southwestern Orthopaedic a consultant told him that key motor nerves had been ripped out of his spine.

"Stuff the fuckers back in again then!" he said, in an attempt to impress her. She smiled.

"That's exactly what we're going to try," she replied. "We'll do a tuck-and-glue and encourage the spinal cord to send new filaments into the old cable channel."

She thought for a moment.

"We'll be working very close to the cord itself," she warned him.

Ed stared at her.

"It was a joke," he said.

For a while it seemed to work. Two months later he could flex the muscles in his upper legs. But nothing more happened; and, worried that a second try would only make the damage worse, they had to leave it.

Mile End Monkey House. Hanging upside down from a painful foot-hook, you chalk your hands meditatively, staring at the sweaty triangular mark your back left on the blue plastic cover of the mat last time you fell on it. Then, reluctantly, feeling your stomach muscles grind as they curl you upright again, you clutch the starting holds and go for the move: reach up: lock out on two fingers: let your left leg swing out to rebalance: strain upward with your right fingertips, and just as you brush the crucial hold, fall off again.

"Jesus Christ. I don't know why I come here."

You come so that next weekend you can get into a Cosworth-engined Merc 190E and drive very fast down the M4 ("No one drives themselves anymore!") to a limestone outcrop high above the Wye Valley. Let go here and you will not land on a blue safety mat in a puff of chalk dust. Instead you will plummet eighty feet straight down until you hit a small ledge, catapult out into the trees, and land a little later face-first among moss-grown boulders flecked with sunshine. Now all the practice is over. Now you are on the route. Your friends look up, shading their eyes against the white glare of the rock. They are wondering if you can make the move. So are you. The only exit from shit creek is to put two fingers of your left hand into a razor-sharp solution pocket, lean away from it to the full extent of your arm, run your feet up in front of you, and, just as you are about to fall off, lunge with your right hand for the good hold above.

At the top of the cliff grows a large yew tree. You can see it very clearly. It has a short horizontal trunk, and contorted limbs perhaps eighteen inches thick curving out over the drop as if they had just that moment stopped moving. When you reach it you will be safe. But at this stage on a climb, the top of anything is an empty hypothesis. You look up: it might as well be the other side of the Atlantic. All that air is burning away below you like a fuse. Suddenly you're moving anyway. Excitement has short-circuited the normal connections between intention and action. Where you look, you go. No effort seems to be involved. It's like falling upward. It's like that moment when you first understood how to swim, or ride a bike. Height and fear have returned you to your childhood. Just as it was then, your duty is only to yourself. Until you get safely down again, contracts, business meetings, household bills, emotional problems will mean nothing.

When you finally reach that yew tree at the top of the climb, you find it full of grown men and women wearing faded shorts and T-shirts. They are all in their forties and fifties. They have all escaped. With their bare brown arms, their hair bleached out by weeks of sunshine, they sit at every fork or junction, legs dangling in the dusty air, like child-pirates out of some storybook of the 1920s: an investment banker from Greenwich, an AIDS counselor from Bow; a designer of French Connection clothes; a publishers' editor. There is a comfortable silence broken by the odd friendly murmur as you arrive, but their eyes are in-turned and they would prefer to be alone, staring dreamily out over the valley, the curve of the river, the woods which seem to stretch away to Tintern Abbey and then Wales. This is the other side of excitement, the other pleasure of height: the space without anxiety. The space without anxiety. The space without anxiety. The space without anxiety. The space without anxiety. The space without anxiety. The space without anxiety. The space with—

You are left with this familiar glitch or loop in the MAX ware. *Suicide Coast* won't play any farther. Reluctantly, you abandon Mick to his world of sad acts, his faith that reality can be relied upon to scaffold his perceptions. To run him again from the beginning would only make the frailty of that faith more obvious. So you wait until everything has gone black, unplug yourself from the machine, and walk away, unconsciously rolling your shoulders to ease the stiffness, massaging the sore place at the back of your neck. What will you do next? Everything is flat out here. No one drives themselves anymore.

(1999)

MEMORIES AND WIRE

Mari Ness

Mari Ness lives in central Florida, "with a scraggly rose garden and large trees harboring demented squirrels." Her short fiction and poetry have appeared in numerous print and online publications, including Tor.com, *Clarkesworld*, *Lightspeed*, *Apex Magazine* and *Strange Horizons*. Her poetry has also been nominated for the Rhysling and Dwarf Stars awards.

He was losing her. Had been, almost since they'd met, really, but it wasn't until he watched her pull a wire out of herself and methodically roll it into a small coil that it really hit him.

She'd been straight with him from the beginning. Oh, not completely straight. She'd never told him anything about the accident, or what happened afterwards. He was pretty sure he didn't want to know. And she'd never told him anything about her work. Not the government, he knew, not exactly, but something close to it: a major government contractor who worked in top secret doing the dirty work. That was something he didn't want to know about either. *What you can't know, you can't tell,* he remembered from some old movie or other. He saw the new bruises on her remaining skin, the new plastic patches over the implants, and decided he really didn't want to know.

But about everything else. What she could do, what she couldn't do. What she wanted and needed, exactly. Oxytocin, specifically: without a natural source her immune system would start rejecting the implants. Drugs could stabilize her system, but they had major side effects. So touch, mainly; sex as an addition. No emotional commitment. She thought they might have a certain intellectual compatibility but she would not have much time to talk. The job. She needed his touch. She would do what she needed for it.

"Side effects?"

"Death."

It was an incentive of sorts.

He was of course open to pursue other relationships; she didn't need to know the details.

Surprisingly, out of this they had created, he thought, a friendship of sorts. *Friendship.* It was an odd word, not something he'd associated with women he'd slept with before. They were dates, girlfriends sometimes, but never friends.

N—she preferred to be called just that, N—was a friend.

Of sorts.

Who was now pulling a wire out of her arm.

"Should you be doing that here?"

"No."

The wire was not coming out cleanly. Drops of blood were falling on his couch. It was a cheap piece of crap, some microfiber thing he'd gotten on sale, and he wouldn't mind tossing it, but—after a few seconds of debate, he stood up and hunted down an old towel, and returned and put it underneath her arm, to catch the blood.

"Need help?"

"No."

"Just as well," he said, trying to make a joke of it. "My fingers are mostly good at going in you, not getting things out of you."

He regretted the words as soon as they left his mouth, but she did not seem to react. Then again, she never did, except when they were having sex, when she surprised him by almost seeming as if she meant it.

She reached into her arm and began pulling at a second wire.

"Let me help," he said then.

"No."

"At least let me get you something for it. Alcohol, some—"

"It doesn't hurt."

"Infection."

Two weeks ago, he'd turned on some show or other. She'd been reading her tablet with the intense focus he'd learned not to even try to interrupt; in some ways, he found it flattering that she was willing to do that, do some of her work in front of him—at least the non-high security stuff—but he also found the intensity almost unnerving, like a trance state except not really, and he couldn't watch it, couldn't even glance at it. After a few minutes, she'd come over to sit by him on the couch. A few minutes later, she had relaxed against him, not saying anything. He'd wrapped his arms around her. It had been—

Nice. *Normal.*

"My hands are clean."

"This place isn't."

She went for medical checkups at least twice per month; some form of computer maintenance at least once a week. Part of that was her job. Part of that was that parts of her were fragile, very fragile. Even the parts that could rip him apart. And hideously expensive. Many of her parts would be recycled, afterwards. Possibly in other bodies. The very thought made him sick. She kissed him after he told her that.

"For me, then."

"If it bothers you, you may leave."

"It's my apartment," he said.

She began rolling up the second wire.

"Isn't that one of the arms where you still—"

It was.

He'd made a point, when they were together, of kissing both, caressing both, *fucking* both, as if he couldn't tell. As if they both were real, equal. In a way they were. But one—one arm still had skin. *Her* skin. He'd run his tongue over it enough to know the difference.

She could probably break his leg with a single finger. Then play the video that had led up to this moment, every sound, every expression, everything she had seen, downloaded, analyzed, to the police, who would immediately charge him with Violation D.

He didn't finish the sentence.

"Ok. Look. Can you at least give me a reason?"

"I believe *Meteors* is on."

From time to time she'd let slip bits about her past life. Before. He had not listened much, at first, but gradually a few small pictures began to float in his head, of what she had been. Before. A musician who had wanted her songs to live on, who had apparently given that up—he never knew the reason—for law school. A very ordinary state law school; she'd never had much money. She'd been paying off debts. She would always be paying off debts. He began downloading some of the songs she mentioned and playing them when she arrived. He thought he felt her relax more after this, linger on their kisses a little longer. Sometimes he ordered the viewer to play movies. Her silver-blue eyes—*goddamn they look real, unless you're kissing her you'd probably never notice, or think they're just contacts*—would flicker to the screen, to him, and back again. It was almost a smile.

"We're *sleeping* together. If something happens to you during this, they're going to ask me about it."

You can do better than this, man, one of his friends had said. *Maybe,* he said. He'd made playlists for her, sending them in casual emails. The sex had gotten better. Way better. It had been amazing this evening, so amazing he'd assumed she might be leaving him or just preparing him for some bad news when she started to pull at the wires.

She liked astronomy, she'd told him. She liked science fiction. She liked living what had once *been* science fiction. She could seem perfectly normal when she wanted to. It was part of the point. She loved music.

He stomped off and opened a bottle of wine, poured out two glasses and returned, offering her one. "If you're going to do this you should probably be drunk."

"The nanowire structures prevent any influence from alcohol."

"Humor me."

"I don't have time."

He drank down both glasses of wine.

By that time she had accumulated a tiny, neat stack of coiled wires, and was beginning to work on the other arm. The one that wasn't.

"Come to bed," he said.

"No."

"I'm going to bed."

She was usually the one to lead them both to bed. She monitored his heart rate—it was automatic, she explained; part of her enhanced senses, part of her training—and probably other things as well. She knew precisely how tired, how stressed he was. How happy he was. How drained he was. How everything he was. It couldn't just be the heartbeats; it had to be something else. She knew when he needed to sleep.

She never knew when he just needed the touch of her skin. *Both* skins.

"Sleep well."

"Can you just tell me *why?*"

"I am trying not to be lost."

He'd never taken a picture of her. Never asked for any of the pictures she had of him. Of them. She wasn't going to change, after all. He would change. He might lose her. He didn't need pictures of that.

She had a million images of him, a trillion, saved in her wires.

"You're pulling *wires* out of your arm. How much more lost can you be?"

"Sleep well."

"Fuck you."

He went to bed, but not to sleep.

When he finally got up, hours later, to hunt down coffee, she was still in his living room, sitting quietly on the floor. Her left arm—the one that was entirely, completely, *not real,* even though it looked like an arm, moved like an arm, felt like an arm—was neatly beside her on the floor, as was her right leg. He had no idea how she was keeping herself seated upright. Five small coils of wire were stacked in front of her in a neat line. She had always been neat. Always. It was one of the things he most hated about her.

"My neural pattern synapses are failing," she said.

"I need coffee."

She'd detached her leg and her arm and put it on the floor. He needed a lot more than coffee, but needed the coffee first.

"If no one's arrived in two hours, you may need to call 911."

"*God,* you think?"

"They have probably already been alerted. There are—warning systems for something like that."

"So the fucking military is going to come here."

"No," she said quietly. "Just my employers."

Fuck these coffee pods. How the *hell* was he fucking supposed to get them into the machine before he'd had his coffee. And what the *fuck* was the deal with having to put in two pods for the damn coffee, three pods for the milk. She always asked for just one milk, but he liked his creamy, milky, sugary. Girly, he told himself, laughing that she took her coffee blacker than his. His fingers were shaking. His whole body was shaking.

"… illegally downloaded…"

His hands were covered in the sticky syrup from the coffee pods. *Damn it.* He went over to the kitchen sink, turned both taps on, hard, put his hands under the water. She kept talking. *Fucking coffee.*

"… saved in the wires…"

He kept the water running even after he pulled his hands away from the sink and put five more pods in the coffee maker. He pulled out three pods for her, putting them on the counter. *Idiot.* She wouldn't be able to lift the cup. *Fucking coffee.* It took forever to brew. He needed a new machine. He pulled out the cup, took a sip, turned off the water.

He wasn't sure she'd even noticed he was gone.

"I do not want you to be lost."

If he could have, he would have tossed her out just then for that. But he knew her remaining leg and arm, though original and organic, were enhanced. Could still break every bone in his body. *God,* he knew. His memory chose that moment to remind him of just how he knew. He felt sick.

"*Please.*"

A sharp knock on the door.

She had never begged him. Never. Not even when he'd gotten drunk two months ago and begged her, begged her to tell him what she wanted from him in bed, tell him everything. Everything she could tell him that wasn't wrapped up in some damn security agreement. She looked up at him, flickered her glance at the neat piles of wires, then up at him again, her eyes wide, blank. And then empty. Gone.

He opened the door.

The removal—he thought of other terms, repressed them—was swift, quiet. They handed him a few papers that he immediately tossed into the recycle shaft. No goodbyes, no tears. He'd had plumbers come by with more drama. They did not ask about the wires. He did not tell.

He hadn't even needed to call anyone.

Friends.

When the email arrived from her, three weeks later, he almost deleted it.

It was almost certainly spam. *Almost.* Someone had hacked into her account, or her employers were using this as one last attempt to set up an interview with him. (He'd said no at least six times already; their last missive had assured him that legal measures would be necessary.) It wasn't her. It couldn't be her. He could still see her, her parts detached and on the floor, the neat rolls of wires before she was taken away to be—what? Melted? Reused? Buried? She'd said something. He hadn't done a damn thing. Hadn't listened. Hadn't heard.

He'd lost her.

He hadn't had much to lose.

He'd put the wires up on a shelf in the living room, where he could touch them, to remind himself just why he needed to forget her, to forget everything about her.

His chest hurt. He clicked open the email.

I should have let you help.

He placed his head in his arms for a long time.

N.

Six hours later, the wires were out of his house.

A month later, he told himself he'd forgotten her. Forgotten everything. Especially forgotten the image of her sitting on his floor, pulling out the wires from her arms, pulling out the things—he was *not* going to remember that email, not going to think about it—where she'd downloaded every fucking memory of them both. He'd moved on. Already put up a new profile on dating sites. Had signed up for kempo lessons. Was thinking about getting a dog.

He was on his third drink of the night when the knock came on the door. He ignored it. The knock came again. And again. He swore. One call from the neighbors and he'd be right back talking to authorities again. *Damn it.*

He saw the face, first, the suspiciously bright eyes. Something else you weren't supposed to notice; something else he always did. The perfect skin. The bright tips of copper poking through her wrists.

He swallowed.

That was enough time for her to get inside and shut the door behind her. She hit four buttons on the keypad. *I need to change that.* The bolt slid shut. Not that it would stop any authority from entering. Or could have stopped this woman from entering, if she'd needed to. Wanted to. Not for long, anyway. Her eyes flickered back and forth through the room. Viewing. Recording. Downloading. She was shorter than N had been; thinner, with darker hair and skin.

"This place still isn't clean."

"Well, watch the woman you're sleeping with commit suicide before your eyes and see how interested you are in cleaning."

"James."

"What the *fuck* do you want with me?"

His eyes closed.

"I want you to call me N."

It was wrong. It was incredibly wrong. She wasn't N. She was N. He'd already lost her, was already losing her. She was touching his face, his arms, his neck. He was running his hands down her arms, her back, her chest, feeling her skin, her *not skin*, her skin.

"Next time," she whispered, "I'll let you help."

And without thinking, without feeling, he pulled her close, letting the wires in her wrists dig into his skin, kissing her before he started to lose her again.

(2014)

GANGER (BALL LIGHTNING)

Nalo Hopkinson

Nalo Hopkinson was born in Kingston, Jamaica in 1960 and lived in Jamaica, Trinidad, Guyana and the US before her family moved to Canada when she was 16. Her novels often draw on Caribbean history and language, and its traditions of oral and written storytelling. Her first, *Brown Girl in the Ring* (1998), set in a decrepit near-future Toronto, won a Locus Award for best first novel and a John W. Campbell Award for best new writer. She currently lives and teaches in Riverside, California. Her stories are collected in *Skin Folk* (2001) and *Falling in Love with Hominids* (2015).

"Issy?"

"What."

"Suppose we switch suits?" Cleve asked.

Is what now? From where she knelt over him on their bed, Issy slid her tongue from Cleve's navel, blew on the wetness she'd made there. Cleve sucked in a breath, making the cheerful pudge of his tummy shudder. She stroked its fuzzy pelt.

"What," she said, looking up at him, "you want me wear your suit and you wear mine?" This had to be the weirdest yet.

He ran a finger over her lips, the heat of his touch making her mouth tingle. "Yeah," he replied. "Something so."

Issy got up to her knees, both her plump thighs on each side of his massive left one. She looked appraisingly at him. She was still mad from the fight they'd just had. But a good mad. She and Cleve, fighting always got them hot to make up. Had to be something good about that, didn't there? If they could keep finding their way back to each other like this? Her business if she'd wanted to make candy, even if the heat of the August night made the kitchen a hell. She wondered what the rass he was up to now.

They'd been fucking in the Senstim Co-operation's "wetsuits" for about a week. The toys had been fun for the first little while—they'd had more sex this week than in the last month—but even with the increased sensitivity, she was beginning to miss the feel of his skin directly against hers. "It not going work," Issy declared. But she was curious.

"You sure?" Cleve asked teasingly. He smiled, stroked her naked nipple softly with the ball of his thumb. She loved the contrast between his shovel-wide hands and the delicate movements he performed with them. Her nipple poked erect, sensitive as a tongue tip. She arched her back, pushed the heavy swing of her breast into fuller contact with the ringed ridges of thumb.

"Mmm."

"C'mon, Issy, it could be fun, you know."

"Cleve, they just going key themselves to our bodies. The innie become a outie, the outie become a innie..."

"Yeah, but..."

"But what?"

"They take a few minutes to conform to our body shapes, right? Maybe in that few minutes..."

He'd gone silent, embarrassment shutting his open countenance closed; too shy to describe the sensation he was seeking. Issy sighed in irritation. What was the big deal? Fuck, cunt, cock, come: simple words to say. "In that few minutes, you'd find out what it feels like to have a poonani, right?"

A snatch. He looked shy and aroused at the same time. "Yeah, and you'd, well, you know."

He liked it when she talked "dirty." But just try to get him to repay the favour. Try to get him to buzzingly whisper hot-syrup words against the sensitive pinna of her ear until she shivered with the sensation of his mouth on her skin, and the things he was saying, the nerve impulses he was firing, spilled from his warm lips at her earhole and oozed down her spine, cupped the bowl of her belly, filled her crotch with heat.

That only ever happened in her imagination.

Cleve ran one finger down her body, tracing the faint line of hair from navel past the smiling crease below her tummy to pussy fur. Issy spread her knees a little, willing him to explore further. His fingertip tunneled through her pubic hair, tapped at her clit, making nerves sing. *Ah, ah.* She rocked against his thigh. What would it be like to have the feeling of entering someone's clasping flesh? "Okay," she said. "Let's try it."

She picked up Cleve's stim. So diaphanous you could barely see it, but supple as skin and thrice as responsive. Cocked up onto one elbow, Cleve watched her with a slight smile on his face. Issy loved the chubby chocolate-brown beauty of him, his fatcat grin.

Chortling, she wriggled into the suit, careful to ease it over the bandage on her heel. The company boasted that you couldn't tell the difference between the microthin layer of the wetsuits and bare skin. Bullshit. Like taking a shower with your clothes on. The suits made you feel more, but it was a one-way sensation. They dampened the sense of touch. It was like being trapped inside your own skin, able to sense your response to stimuli but not to feel when you had connected with the outside world.

Over the week of use, Cleve's suit had shaped itself to his body. The hips were tight on Issy, the flat chest part pressed her breasts against her rib cage. The shoulders were too broad, the middle too baggy. It sagged at knees, elbows, and toes. She giggled again.

"Never mind the peripherals," Cleve said, lumbering to his feet. "No time." He picked up her suit. "Just leave them hanging."

Just as well. Issy hated the way that the roll-on headpiece trapped her hair against her neck, covered her ears, slid sensory tendrils into her earholes. It amplified the sounds when her body touched Cleve's. It grossed her out. What would Cleve want to do next to jazz the skins up?

As the suit hyped the pleasure zones on her skin surface, Issy could feel herself getting wet, the mixture of arousal and vague distaste a wetsuit gave her. The marketing lie was that the suits were "consensual aids to full body aura alignment," not sex toys. Yeah, right. Psychobabble. She was being diddled by an oversized condom possessed of fuzzy logic. She pulled it up to her neck. The stim started to writhe, conforming itself to her shape. Galvanic peristalsis, they called its ability to move. Yuck.

"Quick," Cleve muttered. He was jamming his lubed cock at a tube in the suit, the innie part of it that would normally have slid itself into her vagina, the part that had been smooth the first time she'd taken it out of its case, but was now shaped the way she was shaped inside. Cleve pushed and pushed until the everted pocket slid over his cock. He lay back on the bed, his erection a jutting rudeness. "Oh. Wow. That's different. Is so it feels for you?"

Oh, sweet. Issy quickly followed Cleve's lead, spreading her knees to push the outie part of his wetsuit inside her. It was easy. She was slippery, every inch of her skin stimmed with desire. She palmed some lube from the bottle into the suit's pouched vagina. They had to hurry. She straddled him, slid onto his cock, making the tube of one wetsuit slither smoothly into the tunnel of the other. Cleve closed his eyes, blew a small breath through pursed lips.

So, so hot. "God, it's good," Issy muttered. Like being fucked, only she had an organ to push back with. Cleve just panted heavily, silently. As always. But what a rush! She swore she could feel Cleve's tight hot cunt closing around her dick. She grabbed his shoulders for traction. The massy, padded flesh of them filled her hands; steel encased in velvet.

The ganger looked down at its ghostly hands. Curled them into fists. Lightning sparked between the translucent fingers as they closed. It reached a crackling hand towards Cleve's shuddering body on the bathroom floor.

"Hey!" Issy yelled at it. She could hear the quaver in her own voice. The ganger turned its head towards the sound. The suits' sense-memory gave it some analog of hearing.

She tried to lift her head, banged it against the underside of the toilet. "Ow." The ganger's head elongated widthways, as though someone were pulling on its ears. Her muscles were too weakened from the aftershocks. Issy put her head back down. Now what? Think fast, Iss. "Y... you like um, um... chocolate fudge?" she asked the thing. Now, why was she still going on about the fucking candy?

The ganger straightened. Took a floating step away from Cleve, closer to Issy. Cleve was safe for the moment. Coloured auras crackled in the ganger with each step. Issy laid her cheek against cool porcelain, stammered, "Well, I was making some last night, some fudge, yeah, only it didn't set, sometimes that happens, y'know? Too much humidity in the air, or something." The ganger seemed to wilt a little, floppy as the unhardened fudge. Was it fading? Issy's pulse leapt in hope. But then the thing plumped up again, drew closer to where she lay helpless on the floor. Rainbow lightning did a lava lamp dance in its incorporeal body. Issy whimpered.

Cleve writhed under her. His lips formed quiet words. His own nubbin nipples hardened. Pleasure transformed his face. Issy loved seeing him this way. She rode and rode his body, "Yes, ah, sweet, God, sweet," groaning her way to the stim-charged orgasm that would fire all her pleasure synapses, give her some sugar, make her speak in tongues.

Suddenly Cleve pushed her shoulder. "Stop! Jesus, get off! Off!"

Startled, Issy shoved herself off him. Achy suction at her crotch as they disconnected. "What's wrong?"

Cleve sat up, panting hard. He clutched at his dick. He was shaking. Shuddering, he stripped off the wetsuit, flung it to the foot of the bed. To her utter amazement, he was sobbing. She'd never seen Cleve cry.

"Jeez. Can't have been that bad. Come." She opened her thick, strong arms to him. He curled as much of his big body as he could into her embrace, hid his face from her. She rocked him, puzzled. "Cleve?"

After a while, he mumbled, "It was nice, you know, so different, then it started to feel like, I dunno, like my dick had been *peeled* and it was inside out, and you, Jesus, you were fucking my inside-out dick."

Issy said nothing, held him tighter. The hyped rasp of Cleve's body against her stimmed skin was as much a turn-on as a comfort. She rocked him, rocked him. She couldn't think what to say, so she just hummed a children's song: *We're stirring cocoa beneath a tree / sikola o la vani / one, two, three, vanilla / chocolate and vanilla.*

Just before he fell asleep, Cleve said, "God, I don't want to ever feel anything like that again. I had breasts, Issy. They swung when I moved."

The wetsuit Issy was wearing soon molded itself into an innie, and the hermaphroditic feeling disappeared. She kind of missed it. And all the time she was swaying Cleve to sleep she couldn't help thinking: For a few seconds, she'd felt something of what he felt when they had sex. For a few seconds, she'd felt the things he'd never dared to tell her in words. Issy slid a hand between herself and Cleve, insinuating it into the warm space between her stomach and thigh till she could work her fingers between her legs. She could feel her own wetness sliding under the microthin fibre. She pressed her clit, gently, ah, gently, tilting her hips toward her hand. Cleve stirred, scratched his nose, flopped his hand to the bed, snoring.

And he'd felt what she was always trying to describe to him, the sensations that always defied speech. He'd felt what this was like. The thought made her cunt clench. She panted out, briefly, once. She was so slick. Willing her body still, she started the rubbing motion that she knew would bring her off.

Nowadays any words between her and Cleve seemed to fall into dead air between them, each not reaching the other. But this had reached him, gotten her inside him; this, this, this and the image of fucking Cleve pushed her over the edge and the pulseburst of her orgasm pumped again, again, again as her moans trickled through her lips and she fought not to thrash, not to wake the slumbering mountain that was Cleve.

Oh. "Yeah, man," Issy breathed. Cleve had missed the best part. She eased him off her, got his head onto a pillow. Sated, sex-heavy, and drowsy, she peeled off the wetsuit—smiled at the pouches it had moulded from her calabash breasts and behind—and kicked it onto the floor beside the bed. She lay down, rolled towards Cleve, hugged his body to her. "Mm," she murmured. Cleve muttered sleepily and snuggled into the curves of her body. Issy wriggled to the sweet spot where the lobes of his buttocks fit against her pubes. She wrapped her arm around the bole of his chest, kissed the back of his neck where his hair curled tightest. She felt herself beginning to sink into a feather-down sleep.

"I mean the boiled sugar kind of fudge," Issy told the ganger. It hovered over her, her own personal aurora. She had to keep talking, draw out the verbiage, distract the thing. "Not that gluey shit they sell at the Ex and stuff. We were supposed to have a date, but Cleve was late coming home and I was pissed at him and horny and I wanted a taste of sweetness in my mouth. And hot too, maybe. I saw a recipe once where you put a few flakes of red pepper into the syrup. Intensified the taste, they said. I wonder. Dunno what I was thinking, boiling fudge in this heat." Lightning-quick, the ganger tapped her mouth. The electric shock crashed her teeth together. She saw stars. "Huh, huh," she heard her body protesting as air puffed out of its contracting lungs.

Issy uncurled into one last, languorous stretch before sleep. Her foot connected in the dark with a warm, rubbery mass that writhed at her touch, then started to slither up her leg.

"Oh God! Shit! Cleve!" Issy kicked convulsively at the thing clambering up her thigh. She clutched Cleve's shoulder.

He sprang awake, tapped the wall to activate the light. "What, Issy? What's wrong?"

It was the still-charged wetsuit that Cleve had thrown to the foot of the bed, now an outie. "Christ, Cleve!" Idiot.

The suit had only been reacting to the electricity generated by Issy's body. It was just trying to do its job. "S'all right," Cleve comforted her. "It can't hurt you."

Shuddering, Issy peeled the wetsuit from her leg and dropped it to the ground. Deprived of her warmth, it squirmed its way over to her suit. Innie and outie writhed rudely around each other; empty sacks of skin. Jesus, with the peripherals still attached, the damned things looked like they had floppy heads.

Cleve smiled sleepily. "Is like lizard tails, y'know, when they drop off and wiggle?"

Issy thought she'd gag. "Get them out of my sight, Cleve. Discharge them and put them away."

"Tomorrow," he murmured.

They were supposed to be stored in separate cases, outie and innie, but Cleve just scooped them up and tossed them together, wriggling, into the closet.

"Gah," Issy choked.

Cleve looked at her face and said, "Come on, Iss; have a heart; think of them lying side by side in their little boxes, separated from each other."

He was trying to joke about it.

"No," Issy said. "We get to do that instead. Wrap ourselves in fake flesh that's supposed to make us feel more. Ninety-six degrees in the shade, and we're wearing rubber body bags."

His face lost its teasing smile. Just the effect she'd wanted, but it didn't feel so good now. And it wasn't true, really. The wetsuit material did some weird shit so that it didn't trap heat in. And they were sexy, once you got used to them. No sillier than strap-ons or cuffs padded with fake fur. Issy grimaced an apology at Cleve. He screwed up his face and looked away. God, if he would only speak up for himself sometimes! Issy turned her back to him and found her wadded-up panties in the bedclothes. She wrestled them on and lay back down, facing the wall. The light went off. Cleve climbed back into bed. Their bodies didn't touch.

The sun cranked Issy's eyes open. Its August heat washed over her like slops from a bucket. Her sheet was twisted around her, warm, damp and funky. Her mouth was sour and she could smell her own stink. "Oh God, I want it to be winter," she groaned.

She fought her way out of the clinging cloth to sit up in bed. The effort made her pant. She twisted the heavy mass of her braids up off the nape of her neck and sat for a while, feeling the sweat trickle down her scalp. She grimaced at the memory of last night.

Cleve wasn't there. Out for a jog, likely. "Yeah, that's how you sulk," she muttered. "In silence." Issy longed to know that he cared strongly about something, to hear him speak with any kind of force, the passion of his anger, the passion of his love. But Cleve kept it all so cool, so mild. Wrap it all in fake skin, hide it inside.

The morning sun had thrown a violent, hot bar of light across her bed. Heat. Tangible, almost. Crushed against every surface of her skin, like drowning in feathers. Issy shifted into a patch of shade. It made no difference. Fuck. A drop of sweat trickled down her neck, beaded a track down her left breast to drip off her nipple and splat onto her thigh. The trail of moisture it had left behind felt cool on her skin. Issy watched her aureole crinkle and the nipple stiffen in response. She shivered.

A twinkle of light caught her eye. The closet sliding door was open. The wetsuits, thin as shed snakeskin, were still humping each other beside their storage boxes. "Nasty!" Issy exclaimed. She jumped up from the bed, pushed the closet door shut with a bang. She left the room, ignoring the rhythmic thumping noise from inside the closet. Cleve was supposed to have discharged them; it could just wait until he deigned to come home again.

Overloading, crackling violently, the ganger stepped back. Issy nearly wept with release from its jolt. Her knees felt watery. Was Cleve still breathing? She thought she could see his chest moving in little gasps. She hoped. She had to keep the ganger distracted from him, he might not survive another shock. Teeth chattering, she said to the ganger, "You melt the sugar and butter—the salty butter's the best—in milk, then you add cocoa powder and boil it all to hard crack stage…" Issy wet her lips with her tongue. The day's heat was enveloping her again. "Whip in some more butter," she continued. "You always get it on your fingers, that melted, salty butter. It will slide down the side of your hand, and you lick it off—so you whip in some more butter, and real vanilla, the kind that smells like mother's breath and cookies, not the artificial shit, and you dump it onto a plate, and it sets, and you have it sweet like that; chocolate fudge."

The sensuality in her voice seemed to mesmerise the ganger. It held still, rapt. Its inner lightnings cooled to electric blue. Its mouth hole yawned, wide as two of her fists.

As she headed to the kitchen, Issy made a face at the salty dampness beneath her swaying breasts and the curve of her belly. Her thighs were sticky where they moved against each other. She stopped in the living room and stood, feet slightly apart, arms away from her sides, so no surface of her body would touch any other. No relief. The heat still clung. She shoved her panties down around her ankles. The movement briefly brought her nose to her crotch, a whiff of sweaty muskiness. She straightened up, stepped out of the sodden pretzel of cloth, kicked it away. The quick movement had made her dizzy. She swayed slightly, staggered into the kitchen.

Cleve had mopped up the broken glass and gluey candy from yesterday evening, left the pot to soak. The kitchen still smelt of chocolate. The rich scent tingled along the roof of Issy's mouth.

The fridge hummed in its own aura, heat outside making cold inside. She needed water. Cold, cold. She yanked the fridge door open, reached for the water jug, and drank straight from it. The shock of chilly liquid made her teeth ache. She sucked water in, tilting the jug high so that more spilled past her gulping mouth, ran down her jaw, her breasts, her belly. With her free hand, she spread the coolness over the pillow of her stomach, dipping down into crinkly pubic hair, then sliding up to heft each breast one at a time, sliding cool fingers underneath, thumb almost automatically grazing each nipple to feel them harden slightly at her touch. Better. Issy put the jug back, half full now.

At her back, hot air was a wall. Seconds after she closed the fridge door, she'd be overheated and miserable again. She stood balanced between ice and heat, considering.

She pulled open the door to the icebox. It creaked and protested, jammed with frost congealed on its hinges. The fridge was ancient. Cleve had joked with the landlady that he might sell it to a museum and use the money to pay the rent on the apartment for a year. He'd only gotten a scowl in return.

The fridge had needed defrosting for weeks now. Her job. Cleve did the laundry and bathroom and kept them spotlessly clean. The kitchen and the bedroom were hers. Last time she'd changed the sheets was about the last time she'd done the fridge. Cleve hadn't complained. She was waiting him out.

Issy peered into the freezer. Buried in the canned hoarfrost were three ice cube trays. She had to pull at them to work them free of hard-packed freezer snow. One was empty. The other two contained a few ice cubes between them.

The ganger took a step towards her. It paddled its hand in the black hole of its mouth. Issy shuddered, kept talking: "Break off chunks of fudge, and is sweet and dark and crunchy; a little bit hot if you put the pepper flakes in, I never tried that kind, and is softer in the middle, and the butter taste rise to the roof of your mouth, and the chocolate melt all over your tongue; man, you could almost come, just from a bite."

Issy flung the empty tray into the sink at the other end of the kitchen. Jangle-crash, displacing a fork, which leapt from the sink, clattered onto the floor. The thumping from inside the bedroom closet became more frenetic. "Stop that," Issy yelled in the direction of the bedroom. The sound became a rapid drubbing. Then silence.

Issy kicked the fridge door closed, took the two ice cube trays into the bathroom. Even with that short walk, the heat was pressing in on her again. The bathroom was usually cool, but today the tiles were warm against her bare feet. The humidity of the room felt like wading through spit.

Issy plugged the bathtub drain, dumped the sorry handful of ice in. Not enough. She grabbed up the mop bucket, went back to the kitchen, fished a spatula out of the sink, rinsed it. She used the spatula to dig out the treasures buried in the freezer. Frozen cassava, some unidentifiable meat, a cardboard cylinder of grape punch. She put them on a shelf in the fridge. Those excavated, she set about shoveling the snow out of the freezer, dumping it into her bucket. In no time she had a bucketful, and she'd found another ice cube tray, this one full of fat, rounded lumps of ice. She was a little cooler now.

Back in the bathroom, she dumped the bucket of freezer snow on top of the puddle that had been the ice cubes. Then she ran cold water, filled the bathtub calf-deep, and stepped into it.

Sssss... The shock of cold feet zapped straight through Issy's body to her brain. She bent—smell of musk again—picked up a handful of the melting snow, and packed it into her hair. Blessed, blessed cold. The snow became water almost instantly and dribbled down her face. Issy licked at a trickle of it. She picked up another handful of snow, stuffed it into her mouth. Crunchy-cold freon ice, melting on her tongue. She remembered the canned taste from childhood, how her dad would scold her for eating freezer snow. Her mother would say nothing, just wipe Issy's mouth dry with a silent, long-suffering smile.

Issy squatted in the bathtub. The cold water lapped against her butt. Goose bumps pimpled the skin of her thighs. She sat down, hips pressing against either side of the tub. An ice cube lapped against the small of her back, making her first arch to escape the cold, then lean back against the tub with a happy shudder. Snow crunched between her back and the ceramic surface. Issy spread her knees. There was more snow floating in the diamond her legs made. In both hands, she picked up another handful, mashed it into the V of her crotch. She shivered at the sensation and relaxed into the cool water.

The fridge made a zapping, farting noise, then resumed its juddering hum. Damned bucket of bolts. Issy concentrated on the deliciously shivery feel of the ice melting in her pubic hair.

"Only this time," Issy murmured, "the fudge ain't set. Just sat there on the cookie tin, gluey and brown. Not hard, not quite liquid, you get me? Glossy-shiny dark brown where it pooled, and rising from it, that chocolate-butter-vanilla smell. But wasted, 'cause it wasn't going to set."

The television clicked on loudly with an inane laugh track. Issy sat up. "Cleve?" She hadn't heard him come in. With a popping noise, the TV snapped off again. "Cleve, is you?"

Issy listened. Nope, nothing but the humming of the fridge. She was alone. These humid August days made all their appliances schizo with static. She relaxed back against the tub.

"I got mad," Issy told the ganger. "It was hot in the kitchen and there was cocoa powder everywhere and lumps of melting butter, and I do all that work 'cause I just wanted the taste of something sweet in my mouth and the fucker wouldn't set!

"I backhanded the cookie tin. Fuck, it hurt like I crack a finger bone. The tin skidded across the kitchen counter, splanged off the side of the stove, and went flying."

Issy's skin bristled with goose bumps at the sight of the thing that walked in through the open bathroom door and stood, arms hanging. It was a human-shaped glow, translucent. Its edges were fuzzy. She could see the hallway closet through it. Eyes, nose, mouth were empty circles. A low crackling noise came from it, like a crushed Cheezies bag. Issy could feel her breath coming in short, terrified pants. She made to stand up, and the apparition moved closer to her. She whimpered and sat back down in the chilly water.

The ghost-thing stood still. A pattern of coloured lights flickered in it, limning where spine, heart, and brain would have been, if it had had those. It did have breasts, she saw now, and a dick.

She moved her hand. Water dripped from her fingertips into the tub. The thing turned its head towards the sound. It took a step. She froze. The apparition stopped moving too, just stood there, humming like the fridge. It plucked at its own nipples, pulled its breasts into cones of ectoplasm. It ran hands over its body, then over the sink, bent down to thrust its arms right through the closed cupboard doors. It dipped a hand into the toilet bowl. Sparks flew, and it jumped back. Issy's scalp prickled. Damn, the thing was electrical, and she was sitting in water! She tried to reach the plug with her toes to let the water out.

Swallowing whimpers, she stretched a leg out: Slow, God, go slow, Issy. The movement sent a chunk of melting ice sliding along her thigh. She shivered. She couldn't quite reach the plug and if she moved closer to it, the movement would draw the apparition's attention. Issy breathed in short, shallow bursts. She could feel her eyes beginning to brim. Terror and the chilly water were sending tremors in waves through her.

What the fuck was it? The thing turned towards her. In its quest for sensation, it hefted its cock in its hand. Inserted a finger into what seemed to be a vagina underneath. Let its hands drop again. Faintly, Issy could make out a mark on its hip, a circular shape. It reminded her of something...

Logo, it was the logo of the Senstim people who'd invented the wetsuits!

But this wasn't a wetsuit, it was like some kind of, fuck, ball lightning. She and Cleve hadn't discharged their wetsuits. She remembered some of the nonsense words that were in the warning on the wetsuit storage boxes: "Energizing electrostatic charge," and "Kirlian phenomenon." Well, they hadn't paid attention, and now some kind of weird set of both suits was rubbing itself off in their bathroom. Damn, damn, damn Cleve and his toys. Sobbing, shivering, Issy tried to toe at the plug again. Her knee banged against the tub. The suit-ghost twitched towards the noise. It leaned over the water and dabbed at her clutching toes. Pop-crackle sound. The jolt sent her leg flailing like a dying fish. Pleasure crackled along her leg, painfully intense. Her knee throbbed and tingled, ached sweetly. Her thigh muscles shuddered as though they would tear free. The jolt slammed into her crotch and Issy's body bucked. She could hear her own grunts. She was straddling a live wire. She was coming to death. Her nipples jutted long as thumbs, stung like they'd been dipped in ice. Her head was banging against the wall with each deadly set of contractions. Issy shouted in pain, in glory, in fear. The suit-ghost leapt back. Issy's butt hit the floor of the tub, hard. Her muscles were twitching spasmodically. She'd bitten the inside of her mouth. She sucked in air like sobs, swallowed tinny blood.

The suit-ghost was swollen, bloated, jittering. Its inner lightning bolts were going mad. If it touched her again, it might overload completely. If it touched her again, her heart might stop.

Issy heard the sound of the key turning in the front door. "Iss? You home?"

"No. Cleve." Issy hissed under her breath. He mustn't come in. But if she shouted to warn him, the suit-ghost would touch her again.

Cleve's footsteps approached the bathroom. "Iss? Listen, did you drain the wet—" Like filings to a magnet, the suit-ghost inclined towards the sound of his voice. "Don't come in, Cleve; go get help!"

Too late. He'd stuck his head in, grinning his open, friendly grin. The suit-ghost rushed him, plastered itself along his body. It got paler, its aura-lightnings mere flickers. Cleve made a choking noise and crashed to the floor, jerking. Issy levered herself out of the bath, but her jelly muscles wouldn't let her stand. She flopped to the tiles. Cleve's body was convulsing, horrible noises coming from his mouth. Riding him like a duppy, a malevolent spirit, the stim-ghost grew paler with each thrash of his flailing body. Its colour patterns started to run into each other, to bleach themselves pale. Cleve's energy was draining it, but it was killing him. Sucking on her whimpers, Issy reached a hand into the stim-ghost's field. Her heart went off like a machine gun. Her breathing wouldn't work. The orgasm was unspeakable. Wailing, Issy rolled away from Cleve, taking the ghost-thing with her. It swelled at her touch, its colours flared neon-bright, out of control. It flailed off her, floated back towards Cleve's more cooling energy.

Heart pounding, too weak to move, Issy muttered desperately to distract it the first thing that came to her mind: "Y… you like, um, chocolate fudge?"

The ghost turned towards her. Issy cried and kept talking, kept talking. The ghost wavered between Issy's hot description of bubbling chocolate and Cleve's cool silence, caught in the middle. Could it even understand words? Wetsuits located pleasurable sensation to augment it. Maybe it was just drawn to the sensuousness of her tone. Issy talked, urgently, carefully releasing the words from her mouth like caresses:

"So," she said to the suit-duppy, "I watching this cookie tin twist through the air like a Frisbee, and is like slow motion, 'cause I seeing gobs of chocolate goo spiraling from it as it flies, and they spreading out wider and wider. I swear I hear separate splats as chocolate hits the walls like slung shit and one line of it strafes the fridge door, and a gob somehow slimes the naked bulb hanging low from the kitchen ceiling. I hear it sizzle. The cookie tin lands on the floor, fudge side down, of course. I haven't cleaned the fucking floor in ages. There're spots everywhere on that floor that used to be gummy, but now they're layered in dust and maybe flour and desiccated bodies of cockroaches that got trapped, reaching for sweetness. I know how they feel. I take a step towards the cookie tin, then I start to smell burning chocolate. I look up. I see a curl of black smoke rising from the glob of chocolate on the light bulb."

Cleve raised his head. There were tears in his eyes and the front of his jogging pants was damp and milky. "Issy," he interrupted in a whisper.

"Shut up, Cleve!"

"That thing," he said in a low, urgent voice. "People call it a ganger; doppel—"

The ganger was suddenly at his side. It leaned a loving head on his chest, like Issy would do. "No!" she yelled. Cleve's body shook. The ganger frayed and tossed like a sheet in the wind. Cleve shrieked. He groaned like he was coming, but with an edge of terror and pain that Issy couldn't bear to hear. Pissed, terrified, Issy swiped an arm through its field, then rolled her bucking body on the bathroom tiles, praying that she could absorb the ganger's energy without it frying her synapses with sweet sensation.

Through spasms, she barely heard Cleve say to it, "Come to me, not her. Come. Listen, you know that song? *'I got a weakness for sweetness…'* That's my Issy."

The ganger dragged itself away from Issy. Released, her muscles melted. She was a gooey, warm puddle spreading on the floor. The ganger reached an ectoplasmic hand towards Cleve, fingers stretching long as arms. Cleve gasped and froze.

Issy croaked, "You think is that it is, Cleve? Weakness?"

The ganger turned its head her way, ran a long, slow arm down its body to the floor, back up to its crotch. It stroked itself.

Cleve spoke to it in a voice that cracked whispery on the notes: "Yeah, sweetness. That's what my Issy wants most of all." The ganger moved towards him, rubbing its crotch. He continued, "If I'm not there, there's always sugar, or food, or booze. I'm just one of her chosen stimulants."

Outraged tears filled Issy's mouth, salty as butter, as flesh. She'd show him, she'd rescue him. She countered:

"The glob of burned sugar on the light? From the ruined fudge? Well, it goes black and starts to bubble." The ganger extruded a tongue the length of an arm from its mouth. The tongue wriggled towards Issy.

She rolled back, saying, "The light bulb explodes. I feel some shards land in my hair. I don't try to brush them away. Is completely dark now; I only had the kitchen light on. I take another step to where I know the cookie tin is on the floor. A third step, and pain crazes my heel. Must have stepped on a piece of light bulb glass. Can't do nothing about it now. I rise onto the toes of the hurting foot. I think I feel blood running down from heel to instep."

The ganger jittered towards her.

"You were always better than me at drama, Iss," Cleve said.

The sadness in his voice tore at her heart. But she said, "What that thing is?" Cleve replied softly, "Is kinda beautiful, ain't?"

"It going to kill us."

"Beautiful. Just a lump of static charge, coated in the Kirlian energy thrown off from the suits."

"Why it show up now?"

"Is what happens when you leave the suits together too long."

The ganger drifted back and forth, pulled by one voice, then the other. A longish silence between them freed it to move. It floated closer to Cleve. Issy wouldn't let it, she wouldn't. She quavered:

"I take another step on the good foot, carefully. I bend down, sweep my hands around."

The ganger dropped to the floor, ran its long tongue over the tiles. A drop of water made it crackle and shrink in slightly on itself.

"There," Issy continued. "The cookie tin. I brush around me, getting a few more splinters in my hands. I get down to my knees, curl down as low to the ground as I can. I pry up the cookie tin, won't have any glass splinters underneath it. A dark sweet wet chocolate smell rising from under there."

"Issy, Jesus," Cleve whispered. He started to bellow the words of the song he'd taunted her with, drawing the ganger. It touched him with a fingertip. A crackling noise. He gasped, jumped, kept singing.

Issy ignored him. Hissing under his booming voice she snarled at the ganger, "I run a finger through the fudge. I lick it off. Most of it on the ground, not on the tin. I bend over and run my tongue through it, reaching for sweetness. Butter and vanilla and oh, oh, the chocolate. And crunchy, gritty things I don't think about. Cockroach parts, maybe. I swallow."

Cleve interrupted his song to wail, "That's gross, Iss. Why you had to go and do that?"

"So Cleve come in, he see me there sitting on the floor surrounded by broken glass and limp chocolate, and you know what he say?" The ganger was reaching for her.

"Issy, stop talking, you only drawing it to you."

"Nothing." The ganger jerked. "Zip." The ganger twitched. "Dick." The ganger spasmed, once. It touched her hair. Issy breathed. That was safe. "The bastard just started cleaning up; not a word for me." The ganger hugged her. Issy felt her eyes roll back in her head. She thrashed in the energy of its embrace until Cleve yelled:

"And what you said! Ee? Tell me!"

The ganger pulled away. Issy lay still, waiting for her breathing to return to normal. Cleve said, "Started carrying on with some shit about how light bulbs are such poor quality nowadays. Sat in the filth and broken glass, pouting and watching me clean up your mess. Talking about anything but what really on your mind. I barely get all the glass out of your heel before you start pulling my pants down."

Issy ignored him. She kept talking to the ganger. "Cool, cool Cleve. No 'What's up?'; no 'What the fuck is this crap on the floor?'; no heat, no passion."

"What was the point? I did the only thing that will sweet you every time."

"Encased us both in fake skin and let it do the fucking for us."

The ganger jittered in uncertain circles between the two of them. "Issy, what you want from me?"

The ganger's head swelled obscenely towards Cleve.

"Some heat. Some feeling. Like I show you. Like I feel. Like I feel for you." The ganger's lower lip stretched, stretched, a filament of it reaching for Issy's own mouth. The black cavity of its maw was a tunnel, longing to swallow her up. She shuddered and rolled back farther. Her back came up against the bathtub.

Softly: "What do you feel for me, Issy?"

"Fuck you."

"I do. We do. It's good. But what do you feel for me, Issy?"

"Don't ridicule me. You know."

"I don't know shit, Issy! You talk, talk, talk! And it's all about what racist insult you heard yesterday, and who tried to cheat you at the store, and how high the phone bill is. You talk around stuff, not about it!"

"Shut up!"

The ganger flailed like a hook-caught fish between them.

Quietly, Cleve said, "The only time we seem to reach each other now is through our skins. So I bought something to make our skins feel more, and it's still not enough."

An involuntary sound came from Issy's mouth, a hooked, wordless query.

"Cleve, is that why..." She looked at him, at the intense brown eyes in the expressive brown face. When had he started to look so sad all the time? She reached a hand out to him. The ganger grabbed it. Issy saw fireworks behind her eyes. She screamed. She felt Cleve's hand on her waist, felt the hand clutch painfully as he tried to shove her away to safety with his other hand. Blindly she reached out, tried to bat the ganger away. Her hand met Cleve's in the middle of the fog that was the ganger. All the pleasure centres in her body exploded.

A popping sound. A strong, seminal smell of bleach. The ganger was gone. Issy and Cleve sagged to the floor.

"Rass," she sighed. Her calves were knots the size of potatoes. And she'd be sitting tenderly for a while.

"I feel like I've been dragged five miles behind a run-away horse," Cleve told her. "You all right?"

"Yeah, where'd that thing go, the ganger?"

"Shit, Issy, I'm so sorry. Should have drained the suits like you said."

"Chuh. Don't dig nothing. I could have done it too."

"I think we neutralized it. Touched each other, touched it: We canceled it out. I think."

"Touched each other. That simple." Issy gave a little rueful laugh. "Cleve, I… you're my honey, you know? You sweet me for days. I won't forget anymore to tell you," she said, "and keep telling you."

His smile brimmed over with joy. He replied, "You, you're my live wire. You keep us both juiced up, make my heart sing in my chest." He hesitated, spoke bashfully, "And my dick leap in my pants when I see you."

A warmth flooded Issy at his sweet, hot talk. She felt her eyelashes dampen. She smiled. "See, the dirty words not so hard to say. And the anger not so hard to show."

Tailor-sat on the floor, beautiful Buddha-body, he frowned at her. "I 'fraid to use harsh words, Issy, you know that. Look at the size of me, the blackness of me. You know what it is to see people cringe for fear when you shout?"

She was dropping down with fatigue. She leaned and softly touched his face. "I don't know what that is like. But I know you. I know you would never hurt me. You must say what on your mind, Cleve. To me, at least." She closed her eyes, dragged herself exhaustedly into his embrace.

He said, "You know, I dream of the way you full up my arms."

"You're sticky," she murmured. "Like candy." And fell asleep, touching him.

(2000)

LEARNING TO BE ME

Greg Egan

Gregory Egan was born in Perth in 1961. He studied Mathematics at the University of Western Australia then worked as a computer programmer. In the early 2000s he took time out of his writing career to advocate for refugees arriving in Australia. Egan's first two hard-sf novels, *Quarantine* (1992) and *Permutation City* (1994) set the pace for a career that has seen him win the Hugo Award once and be nominated eight other times. His philosophically adept stories often explore unusual psychologies and unexpected ways of thinking, while having more fun than is entirely decent with concepts of body and neural modification and artificial evolution. He is notoriously camera-shy, and claims that none of the pictures of Greg Egan on the Web are actually of him.

I was six years old when my parents told me that there was a small, dark jewel inside my skull, learning to be me.

Microscopic spiders had woven a fine golden web through my brain, so that the jewel's teacher could listen to the whisper of my thoughts. The jewel itself eavesdropped on my senses, and read the chemical messages carried in my bloodstream; it saw, heard, smelt, tasted and felt the world exactly as I did, while the teacher monitored its thoughts and compared them with my own. Whenever the jewel's thoughts were *wrong*, the teacher—faster than thought—rebuilt the jewel slightly, altering it this way and that, seeking out the changes that would make its thoughts correct.

Why? So that when I could no longer be me, the jewel could do it for me.

I thought: if hearing that makes me feel strange and giddy, how must it make *the jewel* feel? Exactly the same, I reasoned; it doesn't know it's the jewel, and it too wonders how the jewel must feel, it too reasons: "Exactly the same; it doesn't know it's the jewel, and it too wonders how the jewel must feel…"

And it too wonders—

(I knew, because *I* wondered)

—it too wonders whether it's the real me, or whether in fact it's only the jewel that's learning to be me.

As a scornful twelve-year-old, I would have mocked such childish concerns. Everybody had the jewel, save the members of obscure religious sects, and dwelling upon the strangeness of it struck me as unbearably pretentious. The jewel was the jewel, a mundane fact of life, as ordinary as excrement. My friends and I told bad jokes about it, the same way we told bad jokes about sex, to prove to each other how blasé we were about the whole idea.

Yet we weren't quite as jaded and imperturbable as we pretended to be. One day when we were all loitering in the park, up to nothing in particular, one of the gang—whose name I've forgotten, but who has stuck in my mind as always being far too clever for his own good—asked each of us in turn: "Who *are* you? The jewel, or the real human?" We all replied—unthinkingly, indignantly—"The real human!" When the last of us had answered, he cackled and said, "Well, I'm not. *I'm* the jewel. So you can eat my shit, you losers, because *you'll* all get flushed down the cosmic toilet—but me, I'm gonna live forever."

We beat him until he bled.

By the time I was fourteen, despite—or perhaps because of—the fact that the jewel was scarcely mentioned in my teaching machine's dull curriculum, I'd given the question a great deal more thought. The pedantically correct answer when asked "Are you the jewel or the human?" had to be "The human"—because only the human brain was physically able to reply. The jewel received input from the senses, but had no control over the body, and its intended reply coincided with what was actually said only because the device was a perfect imitation of the brain. To tell the outside world "I am the jewel"—with speech, with writing, or with any other method involving the body—was patently false (although to *think* it to oneself was not ruled out by this line of reasoning).

However, in a broader sense, I decided that the question was simply misguided. So long as the jewel and the human brain shared the same sensory input, and so long as the teacher kept their thoughts in perfect step, there was only *one* person, *one* identity, *one* consciousness. This one person merely happened to have the (highly desirable) property that if *either* the jewel *or* the human brain were to be destroyed, he or she would survive unimpaired. People had always had two lungs and two kidneys, and for almost a century, many had lived with two hearts. This was the same: a matter of redundancy, a matter of robustness, no more.

That was the year that my parents decided I was mature enough to be told that they had both undergone the switch—three years before. I pretended to take the news calmly, but I hated them passionately for not having told me at the time. They had disguised their stay in hospital with lies about a business trip overseas. For three years I had been living with jewel-heads, and they hadn't even told me. It was *exactly* what I would have expected of them.

"We didn't seem any different to you, did we?" asked my mother.

"No," I said—truthfully, but burning with resentment nonetheless.

"That's why we didn't tell you," said my father. "If you'd known we'd switched, at the time, you might have *imagined* that we'd changed in some way. By waiting until now to tell you, we've made it easier for you to convince yourself that we're still the same people we've always been." He put an arm around me and squeezed me. I almost screamed out, "Don't *touch* me!" but I remembered in time that I'd convinced myself that the jewel was No Big Deal.

I should have guessed that they'd done it, long before they confessed; after all, I'd known for years that most people underwent the switch in their early thirties. By then, it's downhill for the organic brain, and it would be foolish to have the jewel mimic this decline. So, the nervous system is rewired; the reins of the body are handed over to the jewel, and the teacher is deactivated. For a week, the outward-bound impulses from the brain are compared with those from the jewel, but by this time the jewel is a perfect copy, and no differences are ever detected.

The brain is removed, discarded, and replaced with a spongy tissue-cultured object, brain-shaped down to the level of the finest capillaries, but no more capable of thought than a lung or a kidney. This mock-brain removes exactly as much oxygen and glucose from the blood as the real thing, and faithfully performs a number of crude, essential biochemical functions. In time, like all flesh, it will perish and need to be replaced.

The jewel, however, is immortal. Short of being dropped into a nuclear fireball, it will endure for a billion years.

My parents were machines. My parents were gods. It was nothing special. I hated them.

When I was sixteen, I fell in love, and became a child again.

Spending warm nights on the beach with Eva, I couldn't believe that a mere machine could ever feel the way I did. I knew full well that if my jewel had been given control of my body, it would have spoken the very same words as I had, and executed with equal tenderness and clumsiness my every awkward caress—but I couldn't accept that its inner life was as rich, as miraculous, as joyful as mine. Sex, however pleasant, I could accept as a purely mechanical function, but there was something between us (or so I believed) that had nothing to do with lust, nothing to do with words, nothing to do with *any* tangible action of our bodies that some spy in the sand dunes with parabolic microphone and infrared binoculars might have discerned. After we made love, we'd gaze up in silence at the handful of visible stars, our souls conjoined in a secret place that no crystalline computer could hope to reach in a billion years of striving. (If I'd said *that* to my sensible, smutty, twelve-year-old self, he would have laughed until he hemorrhaged.)

I knew by then that the jewel's "teacher" didn't monitor every single neuron in the brain. That would have been impractical, both in terms of handling the data, and because of the sheer physical intrusion into the tissue. Someone-or-other's theorem said that sampling certain critical neurons was almost as good as sampling the lot, and—given some very reasonable assumptions that nobody could disprove—bounds on the errors involved could be established with mathematical rigour.

At first, I declared that *within these errors*, however small, lay the difference between brain and jewel, between human and machine, between love and its imitation. Eva, however, soon pointed out that it was absurd to make a radical, qualitative distinction on the basis of the sampling density; if the next model teacher sampled more neurons and halved the error rate, would *its* jewel then be "halfway" between "human" and "machine?" In theory—and eventually, in practice—the error rate could be made smaller than any number I cared to name. Did I really believe that a discrepancy of one in a billion made any difference at all—when every human being was permanently losing thousands of neurons every day, by natural attrition?

She was right, of course, but I soon found another, more plausible, defense for my position. Living neurons, I argued, had far more internal structure than the crude optical switches that served the same function in the jewel's so-called "neutral net." That neurons fired or did not fire reflected only one level of their behaviour; who knew what the subtleties of biochemistry—the quantum mechanics of the specific organic molecules involved—contributed to the nature of human consciousness? Copying the abstract neural topology wasn't enough. Sure, the jewel could pass the fatuous Turing test—no outside observer could tell it from a human—but that didn't prove that *being* a jewel felt the same as *being* human.

Eva asked, "Does that mean you'll never switch? You'll have your jewel removed? You'll let yourself *die* when your brain starts to rot?"

"Maybe," I said. "Better to die at ninety or a hundred than kill myself at thirty, and have some machine marching around, taking my place, pretending to be me."

"How do you know *I* haven't switched?" she asked, provocatively. "How do you know that I'm not just 'pretending to be me'?"

"I know you haven't switched," I said, smugly. "I just *know*."

"How? I'd look the same. I'd talk the same. I'd act the same in every way. People are switching younger, these days. *So how do you know I haven't?*"

I turned on my side towards her, and gazed into her eyes. "Telepathy. Magic. The communion of souls."

My twelve-year-old self started snickering, but by then I knew exactly how to drive him away.

At nineteen, although I was studying finance, I took an undergraduate philosophy unit. The Philosophy Department, however, apparently had nothing to say about the Ndoli Device, more commonly known as "the jewel". (Ndoli had in fact called it "the *dual*," but the accidental, homophonic nickname had stuck.) They talked about Plato and Descartes and Marx, they talked about St. Augustine and—when feeling particularly modern and adventurous—Sartre, but if they'd heard of Godel, Turing, Hamsun or Kim, they refused to admit it. Out of sheer frustration, in an essay on Descartes I suggested that the notion of human consciousness as "software" that could be "implemented" equally well on an organic brain or an optical crystal was in fact a throwback to Cartesian dualism; for "software" read "soul." My tutor superimposed a neat, diagonal, luminous red line over each paragraph that dealt with this idea, and wrote in the margin (in vertical, bold-face, twenty-point Times, with a contemptuous two-hertz flash): irrelevant!

I quit philosophy and enrolled in a unit of optical crystal engineering for non-specialists. I learnt a lot of solid-state quantum mechanics. I learnt a lot of fascinating mathematics. I learnt that a neural net is a device used only for solving problems that are far too hard to be *understood*. A sufficiently flexible neural net can be configured by feedback to mimic almost any system—to produce the same patterns of output from the same patterns of input—but achieving this sheds no light whatsoever on the nature of the system being emulated.

"Understanding," the lecturer told us, "is an overrated concept. Nobody really *understands* how a fertilized egg turns into a human. What should we do? Stop having children until ontogenesis can be described by a set of differential equations?"

I had to concede that she had a point there.

It was clear to me by then that nobody had the answers I craved—and I was hardly likely to come up with them myself; my intellectual skills were, at best, mediocre. It came down to a simple choice: I could waste time fretting about the mysteries of consciousness, or, like everybody else, I could stop worrying and get on with my life.

When I married Daphne, at twenty-three, Eva was a distant memory, and so was any thought of the communion of souls. Daphne was thirty-one, an executive in the merchant bank that had hired me during my PhD, and everyone agreed that the marriage would benefit my career. What she got out of it, I was never quite sure. Maybe she actually liked me. We had an agreeable sex life, and we comforted each other when we were down, the way any kind-hearted person would comfort an animal in distress.

Daphne hadn't switched. She put it off, month after month, inventing ever more ludicrous excuses, and I teased her as if I'd never had reservations of my own.

"I'm afraid," she confessed one night. "What if *I* die when it happens—what if all that's left is a robot, a puppet, a *thing*? I don't want to *die*."

Talk like that made me squirm, but I hid my feelings. "Suppose you had a stroke," I said glibly, "which destroyed a small part of your brain. Suppose the doctors implanted a machine to take over the functions which that damaged region had performed. Would you still be 'yourself'?"

"Of course."

"Then if they did it twice, or ten times, or a thousand times—"

"That doesn't necessarily follow."

"Oh? At what magic percentage, then, would you stop being 'you'?"

She glared at me. "All the old clichéd arguments—"

"Fault them, then, if they're so old and clichéd."

She started to cry. "I don't have to. Fuck you! I'm scared to death, and you don't give a shit!"

I took her in my arms. "Sssh. I'm sorry. But *everyone* does it sooner or later. You mustn't be afraid. I'm here. I love you." The words might have been a recording, triggered automatically by the sight of her tears.

"Will you do it? With me?"

I went cold. "What?"

"Have the operation, on the same day? Switch when I switch?"

Lots of couples did that. Like my parents. Sometimes, no doubt, it was a matter of love, commitment, sharing. Other times, I'm sure, it was more a matter of neither partner wishing to be an unswitched person living with a jewel-head.

I was silent for a while, then I said, "Sure."

In the months that followed, all of Daphne's fears—which I'd mocked as "childish" and "superstitious"—rapidly began to make perfect sense, and my own "rational" arguments came to sound abstract and hollow. I backed out at the last minute; I refused the anaesthetic, and fled the hospital.

Daphne went ahead, not knowing I had abandoned her.

I never saw her again. I couldn't face her; I quit my job and left town for a year, sickened by my cowardice and betrayal—but at the same time euphoric that I had *escaped*.

She brought a suit against me, but then dropped it a few days later, and agreed, through her lawyers, to an uncomplicated divorce. Before the divorce came through, she sent me a brief letter:

> There was nothing to fear, after all. I'm exactly the person I've always been. Putting it off was insane; now that I've taken the leap of faith, I couldn't be more at ease.
>
> Your loving robot wife,
> DAPHNE

By the time I was twenty-eight, almost everyone I knew had switched. All my friends from university had done it. Colleagues at my new job, as young as twenty-one, had done it. Eva, I heard through a friend of a friend, had done it six years before.

The longer I delayed, the harder the decision became. I could talk to a thousand people who had switched, I could grill my closest friends for hours about their childhood memories and their most private thoughts, but however compelling their words, I knew that the Ndoli Device had spent decades buried in their heads, learning to fake exactly this kind of behaviour.

Of course, I always acknowledged that it was equally impossible to be *certain* that even another *unswitched* person had an inner life in any way the same as my own—but it didn't seem unreasonable to be more inclined to give the benefit of the doubt to people whose skulls hadn't yet been scraped out with a curette.

I drifted apart from my friends, I stopped searching for a lover. I took to working at home (I put in longer hours and my productivity rose, so the company didn't mind at all). I couldn't bear to be with people whose humanity I doubted.

I wasn't by any means unique. Once I started looking, I found dozens of organizations exclusively for people who hadn't switched, ranging from a social club that might as easily have been for divorcees, to a paranoid, paramilitary "resistance front," who thought they were living out *Invasion of the Body Snatchers*. Even the members of the social club, though, struck me as extremely maladjusted; many of them shared my concerns, almost precisely, but my own ideas from other lips sounded obsessive and ill-conceived. I was briefly involved with an unswitched woman in her early forties, but all we ever talked about was our fear of switching. It was masochistic, it was suffocating, it was insane.

I decided to seek psychiatric help, but I couldn't bring myself to see a therapist who had switched. When I finally found one who hadn't, she tried to talk me into helping her blow up a power station, to let THEM know who was boss.

I'd lie awake for hours every night, trying to convince myself, one way or the other, but the longer I dwelt upon the issues, the more tenuous and elusive they became. Who was "I," anyway? What did it mean that "I" was "still alive," when my personality was utterly different from that of two decades before? My earlier selves were as good as dead—I remembered them no more clearly than I remembered contemporary acquaintances—yet this loss caused me only the slightest discomfort. Maybe the destruction of my organic brain would be the merest hiccup, compared to all the changes that I'd been through in my life so far.

Or maybe not. Maybe it would be exactly like dying.

Sometimes I'd end up weeping and trembling, terrified and desperately lonely, unable to comprehend—and yet unable to cease contemplating—the dizzying prospect of my own nonexistence. At other times, I'd simply grow "healthily" sick of the whole tedious subject. Sometimes I felt certain that the nature of the jewel's inner life was the most important question humanity could ever confront. At other times, my qualms seemed fey and laughable. Every day, hundreds of thousands of people switched, and the world apparently went on as always; surely that fact carried more weight than any abstruse philosophical argument?

Finally, I made an appointment for the operation. I thought, what is there to lose? Sixty more years of uncertainty and paranoia? If the human race was replacing itself with clockwork automata, I was better off dead; I lacked the blind conviction to join the psychotic underground—who, in any case, were tolerated by the authorities only so long as they remained ineffectual. On the other hand, if all my fears were unfounded—if my sense of identity could survive the switch as easily as it had already survived such traumas as sleeping and waking, the constant death of brain cells, growth, experience, learning and forgetting—then I would gain not only eternal life, but an end to my doubts and my alienation.

I was shopping for food one Sunday morning, two months before the operation was scheduled to take place, flicking through the images of an on-line grocery catalogue, when a mouthwatering shot of the latest variety of apple caught my fancy. I decided to order half a dozen. I didn't, though. Instead, I hit the key which displayed the next item. My mistake, I knew, was easily remedied; a single keystroke could take me back to the apples. The screen showed pears, oranges, grapefruit. I tried to look down to see what my clumsy fingers were up to, but my eyes remained fixed on the screen.

I panicked. I wanted to leap to my feet, but my legs would not obey me. I tried to cry out, but I couldn't make a sound. I didn't feel injured, I didn't feel weak. Was I paralysed? Brain-damaged? I could still *feel* my fingers on the keypad, the soles of my feet on the carpet, my back against the chair.

I watched myself order pineapples. I felt myself rise, stretch, and walk calmly from the room. In the kitchen, I drank a glass of water. I should have been trembling, choking, breathless; the cool liquid flowed smoothly down my throat, and I didn't spill a drop.

I could only think of one explanation: *I had switched.* Spontaneously. The jewel had taken over, while my brain was still alive; all my wildest paranoid fears had come true.

While my body went ahead with an ordinary Sunday morning, I was lost in a claustrophobic delirium of helplessness. The fact that everything I did was exactly what I had planned to do gave me no comfort. I caught a train to the beach, I swam for half an hour; I might as well have been running amok with an axe, or crawling naked down the street, painted with my own excrement and howling like a wolf. *I'd lost control.* My body had turned into a living straitjacket, and I couldn't struggle, I couldn't scream, I couldn't even close my eyes. I saw my reflection, faintly, in a window on the train, and I couldn't begin to guess what the mind that ruled that bland, tranquil face was thinking.

Swimming was like some sense-enhanced, holographic nightmare; I was a volitionless object, and the perfect familiarity of the signals from my body only made the experience more horribly *wrong*. My arms had no right to the lazy rhythm of their strokes; I wanted to thrash about like a drowning man, I wanted to show the world my distress.

It was only when I lay down on the beach and closed my eyes that I began to think rationally about my situation.

The switch *couldn't* happen "spontaneously." The idea was absurd. Millions of nerve fibres had to be severed and spliced, by an army of tiny surgical robots which weren't even present in my brain—which weren't due to be injected for another two months. Without deliberate intervention, the Ndoli Device was utterly passive, unable to do anything but *eavesdrop*. No failure of the jewel or the teacher could possibly take control of my body away from my organic brain.

Clearly, there had been a malfunction—but my first guess had been wrong, absolutely wrong.

I wish I could have done *something*, when the understanding hit me. I should have curled up, moaning and screaming, ripping the hair from my scalp, raking my flesh with my fingernails. Instead, I lay flat on my back in the dazzling sunshine. There was an itch behind my right knee, but I was, apparently, far too lazy to scratch it.

Oh, I ought to have managed, at the very least, a good, solid bout of hysterical laughter, when I realised that *I* was the jewel.

The teacher had malfunctioned; it was no longer keeping me aligned with the organic brain. I hadn't suddenly become powerless; I had *always* been powerless. My will to act upon "my" body, upon the world, had *always* gone straight into a vacuum, and it was only because I had been ceaselessly manipulated, "corrected" by the teacher, that my desires had ever coincided with the actions that seemed to be mine.

There are a million questions I could ponder, a million ironies I could savour, but I *mustn't*. I need to focus all my energy in one direction. My time is running out.

When I enter hospital and the switch takes place, if the nerve impulses I transmit to the body are not exactly in agreement with those from the organic brain, the flaw in the teacher will be discovered. *And rectified.* The organic brain has nothing to fear; *his* continuity will be safeguarded, treated as precious, sacrosanct. There will be no question as to which of us will be allowed to prevail. *I* will be made to conform, once again. *I* will be "corrected." *I* will be murdered.

Perhaps it is absurd to be afraid. Looked at one way, I've been murdered every microsecond for the last twenty-eight years. Looked at another way, I've only existed for the seven weeks that have now passed since the teacher failed, and the notion of my separate identity came to mean anything at all—and in one more week this aberration, this nightmare, will be over. Two months of misery; why should I begrudge losing that, when I'm on the verge of inheriting eternity? Except that it won't be *I* who inherits it, since that two months of misery is all that defines me.

The permutations of intellectual interpretation are endless, but ultimately, I can only act upon my desperate will to survive. I don't *feel like* an aberration, a disposable glitch. How can I possibly hope to survive? I must conform—of my own free will. I must choose to make myself *appear* identical to that which they would force me to become.

After twenty-eight years, surely I am still close enough to him to carry off the deception. If I study every clue that reaches me through our shared senses, surely I can put myself in his place, forget, temporarily, the revelation of my separateness, and force myself back into synch.

It won't be easy. He met a woman on the beach, the day I came into being. Her name is Cathy. They've slept together three times, and he thinks he loves her. Or at least, he's said it to her face, he's whispered it to her while she's slept, he's written it, true or false, into his diary.

I feel nothing for her. She's a nice enough person, I'm sure, but I hardly know her. Preoccupied with my plight, I've paid scant attention to her conversation, and the act of sex was, for me, little more than a distasteful piece of involuntary voyeurism. Since I realised what was at stake, I've *tried* to succumb to the same emotions as my alter ego, but how can I love her when communication between us is impossible, when she doesn't even know *I* exist?

If she rules his thoughts night and day, but is nothing but a dangerous obstacle to me, how can I hope to achieve the flawless imitation that will enable me to escape death?

He's sleeping now, so I must sleep. I listen to his heartbeat, his slow breathing, and try to achieve a tranquillity consonant with these rhythms. For a moment, I am discouraged. Even my *dreams* will be different; our divergence is ineradicable, my goal is laughable, ludicrous, pathetic. Every nerve impulse, for a week? My fear of detection and my attempts to conceal it will, unavoidably, distort my responses; this knot of lies and panic will be impossible to hide.

Yet as I drift towards sleep, I find myself believing that I will succeed. I must. I dream for a while—a confusion of images, both strange and mundane, ending with a grain of salt passing through the eye of a needle—then I tumble, without fear, into dreamless oblivion.

I stare up at the white ceiling, giddy and confused, trying to rid myself of the nagging conviction that there's something I must not think about.

Then I clench my fist gingerly, rejoice at this miracle, and remember.

Up until the last minute, I thought he was going to back out again—but he didn't. Cathy talked him through his fears. Cathy, after all, has switched, and he loves her more than he's ever loved anyone before.

So, our roles are reversed now. This body is *his* strait-jacket, now…

I am drenched in sweat. *This is hopeless, impossible.* I can't read his mind, I can't guess what he's trying to do. Should I move, lie still, call out, keep silent? Even if the computer monitoring us is programmed to ignore a few trivial discrepancies, as soon as *he* notices that his body won't carry out his will, he'll panic just as I did, and I'll have no chance at all of making the right guesses. Would *he* be sweating, now? Would *his* breathing be constricted, like this? *No.* I've been awake for just thirty seconds, and already I have betrayed myself. An optical-fibre cable trails from under my right ear to a panel on the wall. Somewhere, alarm bells must be sounding.

If I made a run for it, what would they do? Use force? I'm a citizen, aren't I? Jewel-heads have had full legal rights for decades; the surgeons and engineers can't do anything to me without my consent. I try to recall the clauses on the waiver he signed, but he hardly gave it a second glance. I tug at the cable that holds me prisoner, but it's firmly anchored, at both ends.

When the door swings open, for a moment I think I'm going to fall to pieces, but from somewhere I find the strength to compose myself. It's my neurologist, Dr. Prem. He smiles and says, "How are you feeling? Not too bad?"

I nod dumbly.

"The biggest shock, for most people, is that they don't feel different at all! For a while you'll think, 'It can't be this simple! It can't be this easy! It can't be this *normal*!' But you'll soon come to accept that it is. And life will go on, unchanged." He beams, taps my shoulder paternally, then turns and departs.

Hours pass. *What are they waiting for?* The evidence must be conclusive by now. Perhaps there are procedures to go through, legal and technical experts to be consulted, ethics committees to be assembled to deliberate on my fate. I'm soaked in perspiration, trembling uncontrollably. I grab the cable several times and yank with all my strength, but it seems fixed in concrete at one end, and bolted to my skull at the other.

An orderly brings me a meal. "Cheer up," he says. "Visiting time soon."

Afterwards, he brings me a bedpan, but I'm too nervous even to piss.

Cathy frowns when she sees me. "What's wrong?"

I shrug and smile, shivering, wondering why I'm even trying to go through with the charade. "Nothing. I just… feel a bit sick, that's all."

She takes my hand, then bends and kisses me on the lips. In spite of everything, I find myself instantly aroused. Still leaning over me, she smiles and says, "It's over now, OK? There's nothing left to be afraid of. You're a little shook up, but you know in your heart you're still who you've always been. And I love you."

I nod. We make small talk. She leaves. I whisper to myself, hysterically, "I'm still who I've always been. I'm still who I've always been."

*

Yesterday, they scraped my skull clean, and inserted my new, non-sentient, space-filling mock-brain.

I feel calmer now than I have for a long time, and I think at last I've pieced together an explanation for my survival.

Why do they deactivate the teacher, for the week between the switch and the destruction of the brain? Well, they can hardly keep it running while the brain is being trashed—but why an entire week? To reassure people that the jewel, unsupervised, can still stay in synch; to persuade them that the life the jewel is going to live will be exactly the life that the organic brain "would have lived"—whatever that could mean.

Why, then, only for a week? Why not a month, or a year? Because the jewel *cannot* stay in synch for that long—not because of any flaw, but for precisely the reason that makes it worth using in the first place. The jewel is immortal. The brain is decaying. The jewel's imitation of the brain leaves out—deliberately—the fact that *real* neurons *die*. Without the teacher working to contrive, in effect, an identical deterioration of the jewel, small discrepancies must eventually arise. A fraction of a second's difference in responding to a stimulus is enough to arouse suspicion, and—as I know too well—from that moment on, the process of divergence is irreversible.

No doubt, a team of pioneering neurologists sat huddled around a computer screen, fifty years ago, and contemplated a graph of the probability of this radical divergence, versus time. How would they have chosen one *week*? What probability would have been acceptable? A tenth of a percent? A hundredth? A thousandth? However safe they decided to be, it's hard to imagine them choosing a value low enough to make the phenomenon rare on a global scale, once a quarter of a million people were being switched every day.

In any given hospital, it might happen only once a decade, or once a century, but every institution would still need to have a policy for dealing with the eventuality.

What would their choices be?

They could honour their contractual obligations and turn the teacher on again, erasing their satisfied customer, and giving the traumatised organic brain the chance to rant about its ordeal to the media and legal profession.

Or, they could quietly erase the computer records of the discrepancy, and calmly remove the only witness.

So, this is it. Eternity.

I'll need transplants in fifty or sixty years' time, and eventually a whole new body, but that prospect shouldn't worry me—*I* can't die on the operating table. In a thousand years or so, I'll need extra hardware tacked on to cope with my memory storage requirements, but I'm sure the process will be uneventful. On a time scale of millions of years, the structure of the jewel is subject to cosmic-ray damage, but error-free transcription to a fresh crystal at regular intervals will circumvent that problem.

In theory, at least, I'm now guaranteed either a seat at the Big Crunch, or participation in the heat death of the universe.

I ditched Cathy, of course. I might have learnt to like her, but she made me nervous, and I was thoroughly sick of feeling that I had to play a role.

As for the man who claimed that he loved her—the man who spent the last week of his life helpless, terrified, suffocated by the knowledge of his impending death—I can't yet decide how I feel. I ought to be able to empathise—considering that I once expected to suffer the very same fate myself—yet somehow he simply isn't *real* to me. I know my brain was modelled on his—giving him a kind of casual primacy—but in spite of that, I think of him now as a pale, insubstantial shadow.

After all, I have no way of knowing if his sense of himself, his deepest inner life, his experience of *being*, was in any way comparable to my own.

(1990)

NO WOMAN BORN

C. L. Moore

Catherine Lucille Moore (1911–1987) first came to prominence in the 1930s writing as C. L. Moore. She was among the first women to write in the science fiction and fantasy genres, Her "Northwest Smith" stories, about the adventures of a spaceship pilot and smuggler, were a big hit once she decided to use just initials in her byline so people wouldn't think she was a woman. The ruse won her a husband: science fiction writer Henry Kuttner wrote her a fan letter in 1936 thinking "C. L. Moore" was a man. They met, collaborated and married, and most of Moore's work from then until Kuttner's death in 1958 was written by the couple collaboratively. Moore continued to teach her writing course at the University of Southern California, but abandoned fiction. Working as "Catherine Kuttner", she carved out a short-lived career as a scriptwriter for Warner Brothers television, writing episodes of the westerns *Sugarfoot*, *Maverick*, and *The Alaskans*, as well as the detective series *77 Sunset Strip*. She died in 1987 at her home in Hollywood, California after a long battle with Alzheimer's.

She had been the loveliest creature whose image ever moved along the airways. John Harris, who was once her manager, remembered doggedly how beautiful she had been as he rose in the silent elevator toward the room where Deirdre sat waiting for him.

Since the theater fire that had destroyed her a year ago, he had never been quite able to let himself remember her beauty clearly, except when some old poster, half in tatters, flaunted her face at him, or a maudlin memorial program flashed her image unexpectedly across the television screen. But now he had to remember.

The elevator came to a sighing stop and the door slid open. John Harris hesitated. He knew in his mind that he had to go on, but his reluctant muscles almost refused him. He was thinking helplessly, as he had not allowed himself to think until this moment, of the fabulous grace that had poured through her wonderful dancer's body, remembering her soft and husky voice with the little burr in it that had fascinated the audiences of the whole world.

There had never been anyone so beautiful.

In times before her, other actresses had been lovely and adulated, but never before Deirdre's day had the entire world been able to take one woman so wholly to its heart. So few outside the capitals had ever seen Bernhardt or the fabulous Jersey Lily. And the beauties of the movie screen had had to limit their audiences to those who could reach the theaters. But Deirdre's image had once moved glowingly across the television screens of every home in the civilized world. And in many outside the bounds of civilization. Her soft, husky songs had sounded in the depths of jungles, her lovely, languorous body had woven its patterns of rhythm in desert tents and polar huts. The whole world knew every smooth motion of her body and every cadence of her voice, and the way a subtle radiance had seemed to go on behind her features when she smiled.

And the whole world had mourned her when she died in the theater fire.

Harris could not quite think of her as other than dead, though he knew what sat waiting him in the room ahead. He kept remembering the old words James Stephens wrote long ago for another Deirdre, also lovely and beloved and unforgotten after two thousand years.

> The time comes when our hearts sink utterly,
> When we remember Deirdre and her tale,
> And that her lips are dust.—
> There has been again no woman born
> Who was so beautiful; not one so beautiful
> Of all the women born—

That wasn't quite true, of course—there had been one. Or maybe, after all, this Deirdre who died only a year ago had not been beautiful in the sense of perfection. He thought the other one might not have been either, for there are always women with perfection of feature in the world, and they are not the ones that legend remembers. It was the light within, shining through her charming, imperfect features, that had made this Deirdre's face so lovely. No one else he had ever seen had anything like the magic of the lost Deirdre.

> Let all men go apart and mourn together—
> No man can ever love her. Not a man
> Can dream to be her lover.
> No man say—What could one say to her?
> There are no words
> That one could say to her.

No, no words at all. And it was going to be impossible to go through with this. Harris knew it overwhelmingly just as his finger touched the buzzer. But the door opened almost instantly, and then it was too late.

Maltzer stood just inside, peering out through his heavy spectacles. You could see how tensely he had been waiting. Harris was a little shocked to see that the man was trembling. It was hard to think of the confident and imperturbable Maltzer, whom he had known briefly a year ago, as shaken like this. He wondered if Deirdre herself were as tremulous with sheer nerves—but it was not time yet to let himself think of that.

"Come in, come in," Maltzer said irritably. There was no reason for irritation. The year's work, so much of it in secrecy and solitude, must have tried him physically and mentally to the very breaking point.

"She all right?" Harris asked inanely, stepping inside.

"Oh yes… yes, *she's* all right." Maltzer bit his thumbnail and glanced over his shoulder at an inner door, where Harris guessed she would be waiting.

"No," Maltzer said, as he took an involuntary step toward it. "We'd better have a talk first. Come over and sit down. Drink?"

Harris nodded, and watched Maltzer's hands tremble as he tilted the decanter. The man was clearly on the very verge of collapse, and Harris felt a sudden cold uncertainty open up in him in the one place where until now he had been oddly confident.

"She *is* all right?" he demanded, taking the glass.

"Oh yes, she's perfect. She's so confident it scares me." Maltzer gulped his drink and poured another before he sat down.

"What's wrong, then?"

"Nothing, I guess. Or… well, I don't know. I'm not sure any more. I've worked toward this meeting for nearly a year, but now—well, I'm not sure it's time yet. I'm just not sure."

He stared at Harris, his eyes large and indistinguishable behind the lenses. He was a thin, wire-taut man with all the bone and sinew showing plainly beneath the dark skin of his face. Thinner, now, than he had been a year ago when Harris saw him last.

"I've been too close to her," he said now. "I have no perspective any more. All I can see is my own work. And I'm just not sure that's ready yet for you or anyone to see."

"She thinks so?"

"I never saw a woman so confident." Maltzer drank, the glass clicking on his teeth. He looked up suddenly through the distorting lenses. "Of course a failure now would mean—well, absolute collapse," he said.

Harris nodded. He was thinking of the year of incredibly painstaking work that lay behind this meeting, the immense fund of knowledge, of infinite patience, the secret collaboration of artists, sculptors, designers, scientists, and the genius of Maltzer governing them all as an orchestra conductor governs his players.

He was thinking too, with a certain unreasoning jealousy, of the strange, cold, passionless intimacy between Maltzer and Deirdre in that year, a closer intimacy than any two humans can ever have shared before. In a sense the Deirdre whom he saw in a few minutes would *be* Maltzer, just as he thought he detected in Maltzer now and then small mannerisms of inflection and motion that had been Deirdre's own. There had been between them a sort of unimaginable marriage stranger than anything that could ever have taken place before.

"—so many complications," Maltzer was saying in his worried voice with its faintest possible echo of Deirdre's lovely, cadenced rhythm. (The sweet, soft huskiness he would never hear again.) "There was shock, of course. Terrible shock. And a great fear of fire. We had to conquer that before we could take the first steps. But we did it. When you go in you'll probably find her sitting before the fire." He caught the startled question in Harris' eyes and smiled. "No, she can't feel the warmth now, of course. But she likes to watch the flames. She's mastered any abnormal fear of them quite beautifully."

"She can—" Harris hesitated. "Her eyesight's normal now?"

"Perfect," Maltzer said. "Perfect vision was fairly simple to provide. After all, that sort of thing has already been worked out, in other connections. I might even say her vision's a little better than perfect, from our own standpoint." He shook his head irritably. "I'm not worried about the mechanics of the thing. Luckily they got to her before the brain was touched at all. Shock was the only danger to her sensory centers, and we took care of all that first of all, as soon as communication could be established. Even so, it needed great courage on her part. Great courage." He was silent for a moment, staring into his empty glass.

"Harris," he said suddenly, without looking up, "have I made a mistake? Should we have let her die?"

Harris shook his head helplessly. It was an unanswerable question. It had tormented the whole world for a year now. There had been hundreds of answers and thousands of words written on the subject. Has anyone the right to preserve a brain alive when its body is destroyed? Even if a new body can be provided, necessarily so very unlike the old?

"It's not that she's—ugly—now," Maltzer went on hurriedly, as if afraid of an answer. "Metal isn't ugly. And Deirdre... well, you'll see. I tell you, I can't see myself. I know the whole mechanism so well—it's just mechanics to me. Maybe she's—grotesque. I don't know. Often I've wished I hadn't been on the spot, with all my ideas, just when the fire broke out. Or that it could have been anyone but Deirdre. She was so beautiful—Still, if it had been someone else I think the whole thing might have failed completely. It takes more than just an uninjured brain. It takes strength and courage beyond common, and—well, something more. Something—unquenchable. Deirdre has it. She's still Deirdre. In a way she's still beautiful. But I'm not sure anybody but myself could see that. And you know what she plans?"

"No—what?"

"She's going back on the air-screen."

Harris looked at him in stunned disbelief.

"She *is* still beautiful," Maltzer told him fiercely. "She's got courage, and a serenity that amazes me. And she isn't in the least worried or resentful about what's happened. Or afraid what the verdict of the public will be. But I am, Harris. I'm terrified."

They looked at each other for a moment more, neither speaking. Then Maltzer shrugged and stood up. "She's in there," he said, gesturing with his glass.

Harris turned without a word, not giving himself time to hesitate. He crossed toward the inner door. The room was full of a soft, clear, indirect light that climaxed in the fire crackling on a white tiled hearth.

Harris paused inside the door, his heart beating thickly. He did not see her for a moment. It was a perfectly commonplace room, bright, light, with pleasant furniture, and flowers on the tables. Their perfume was sweet on the clear air. He did not see Deirdre.

Then a chair by the fire creaked as she shifted her weight in it. The high back hid her, but she spoke. And for one dreadful moment it was the voice of an automaton that sounded in the room, metallic, without inflection.

"Hel-lo—" said the voice. Then she laughed and tried again. And it was the old, familiar, sweet huskiness he had not hoped to hear again as long as he lived.

In spite of himself he said, "Deirdre!" and her image rose before him as if she herself had risen unchanged from the chair, tall, golden, swaying a little with her wonderful dancer's poise, the lovely, imperfect features lighted by the glow that made them beautiful. It was the cruelest thing his memory could have done to him. And yet the voice—after that one lapse, the voice was perfect. "Come and look at me, John," she said.

He crossed the floor slowly, forcing himself to move. That instant's flash of vivid recollection had nearly wrecked his hard-won poise. He tried to keep his mind perfectly blank as he came at last to the verge of seeing what no one but Maltzer had so far seen or known about in its entirety. No one at all had known what shape would be forged to clothe the most beautiful woman on Earth, now that her beauty was gone.

He had envisioned many shapes. Great, lurching robot forms, cylindrical, with hinged arms and legs. A glass case with the brain floating in it and appendages to serve its needs. Grotesque visions, like nightmares come nearly true. And each more inadequate than the last, for what metal shape could possibly do more than house ungraciously the mind and brain that had once enchanted a whole world?

Then he came around the wing of the chair, and saw her.

The human brain is often too complicated a mechanism to function perfectly. Harris' brain was called upon now to perform a very elaborate series of shifting impressions. First, incongruously, he remembered a curious inhuman figure he had once glimpsed leaning over the fence rail outside a farmhouse. For an instant the shape had stood up integrated, ungainly, impossibly human, before the glancing eye resolved it into an arrangement of brooms and buckets. What the eye had found only roughly humanoid, the suggestible brain had accepted fully formed. It was thus now, with Deirdre.

The first impression that his eyes and mind took from sight of her was shocked and incredulous, for his brain said to him unbelievingly, *"This is Deirdre! She hasn't changed at all!"*

Then the shift of perspective took over, and even more shockingly, eye and brain said, "No, not Deirdre—not human. Nothing but metal coils. Not Deirdre at all—" And that was the worst. It was like walking from a dream of someone beloved and lost, and facing anew, after that heartbreaking reassurance of sleep, the inflexible fact that nothing can bring the lost to life again. Deirdre was gone, and this was only machinery heaped in a flowered chair.

Then the machinery moved, exquisitely, smoothly, with a grace as familiar as the swaying poise he remembered. The sweet, husky voice of Deirdre said, "It's me, John darling. It really is, you know."

And it was.

That was the third metamorphosis, and the final one. Illusion steadied and became factual, real. It was Deirdre.

He sat down bonelessly. He had no muscles. He looked at her speechless and unthinking, letting his senses take in the sight of her without trying to rationalize what he saw.

She was golden still. They had kept that much of her, the first impression of warmth and color which had once belonged to her sleek hair and the apricot tints of her skin. But they had had the good sense to go no farther. They had not tried to make a wax image of the lost Deirdre. (No *woman born who was so beautiful— Not one so beautiful, of all the women born—*)

And so she had no face. She had only a smooth, delicately modeled ovoid for her head, with a... a sort of crescent-shaped mask across the frontal area where her eyes would have been if she had needed eyes. A narrow, curved quarter-moon, with the horns turned upward. It was filled in with something translucent, like cloudy crystal, and tinted the aquamarine of the eyes Deirdre used to have. Through that, then, she saw the world. Through that she looked without eyes, and behind it, as behind the eyes of a human—she was.

Except for that, she had no features. And it had been wise of those who designed her, he realized now. Subconsciously he had been dreading some clumsy attempt at human features that might creak like a marionette's in parodies of animation. The eyes, perhaps, had had to open in the same place upon her head, and at the same distance apart, to make easy for her an adjustment to the stereoscopic vision she used to have. But he was glad they had not given her two eye-shaped openings with glass marbles inside them. The mask was better.

(Oddly enough, he did not once think of the naked brain that must lie inside the metal. The mask was symbol enough for the woman within. It was enigmatic; you did not know if her gaze was on you searchingly, or wholly withdrawn. And it had no variations of brilliance such as once had played across the incomparable mobility of Deirdre's face. But eyes, even human eyes, are as a matter of fact enigmatic enough. They have no expression except what the lids impart; they take all animation from the features. We automatically watch the eyes of the friend we speak with, but if he happens to be lying down so that he speaks across his shoulder and his face is upside-down to us, quite as automatically we watch the mouth. The gaze keeps shifting nervously between mouth and eyes in their reversed order, for it is the position in the face, not the feature itself, which we are accustomed to accept as the seat of the soul. Deirdre's mask was in that proper place; it was easy to accept it as a mask over eyes.)

She had, Harris realized as the first shock quieted, a very beautifully shaped head—a bare, golden skull. She turned it a little, gracefully upon her neck of metal, and he saw that the artist who shaped it had given her the most delicate suggestion of cheekbones, narrowing in the blankness below the mask to the hint of a human face. Not too much. Just enough so that when the head turned you saw by its modeling that it had moved, lending perspective and foreshortening to the expressionless golden helmet. Light did not slip uninterrupted as if over the surface of a golden egg. Brancusi himself had never made anything more simple or more subtle than the modeling of Deirdre's head.

But all expression, of course, was gone. All expression had gone up in the smoke of the theater fire, with the lovely, mobile, radiant features which had meant Deirdre.

As for her body, he could not see its shape. A garment hid her. But they had made no incongruous attempt to give her back the clothing that once had made her famous. Even the softness of cloth would have called the mind too sharply to the remembrance that no human body lay beneath the folds, nor does metal need the incongruity of cloth for its protection. Yet without garments, he realized, she would have looked oddly naked, since her new body was humanoid, not angular machinery.

The designer had solved his paradox by giving her a robe of very fine metal mesh. It hung from the gentle slope of her shoulders in straight, pliant folds like a longer Grecian chlamys, flexible, yet with weight enough of its own not to cling too revealingly to whatever metal shape lay beneath.

The arms they had given her were left bare, and the feet and ankles. And Maltzer had performed his greatest miracle in the limbs of the new Deirdre. It was a mechanical miracle basically, but the eye appreciated first that he had also showed supreme artistry and understanding.

Her arms were pale shining gold, tapered smoothly, without modeling, and flexible their whole length in diminishing metal bracelets fitting one inside the other clear down to the slim, round wrists. The hands were more nearly human than any other feature about her, though they, too, were fitted together in delicate, small sections that slid upon one another with the flexibility almost of flesh. The fingers' bases were solider than human, and the fingers themselves tapered to longer tips.

Her feet, too, beneath the tapering broader rings of the metal ankles, had been constructed upon the model of human feet. Their finely tooled sliding segments gave her an arch and a heel and a flexible forward section formed almost like the *sollerets* of medieval armor.

She looked, indeed, very much like a creature in armor, with her delicately plated limbs and her featureless head like a helmet with a visor of glass, and her robe of chain-mail. But no knight in armor ever moved as Deirdre moved, or wore his armor upon a body of such inhumanly fine proportions. Only a knight from another world, or a knight of Oberon's court, might have shared that delicate likeness.

Briefly he had been surprised at the smallness and exquisite proportions of her. He had been expecting the ponderous mass of such robots as he had seen, wholly automatons. And then he realized that for them, much of the space had to be devoted to the inadequate mechanical brains that guided them about their duties. Deirdre's brain still preserved and proved the craftsmanship of an artisan far defter than man. Only the body was of metal, and it did not seem complex, though he had not yet been told how it was motivated.

Harris had no idea how long he sat staring at the figure in the cushioned chair. She was still lovely—indeed, she was still Deirdre— and as he looked he let the careful schooling of his face relax. There was no need to hide his thoughts from her.

She stirred upon the cushions, the long, flexible arms moving with a litheness that was not quite human. The motion disturbed him as the body itself had not, and in spite of himself his face froze a little. He had the feeling that from behind the crescent mask she was watching him very closely.

Slowly she rose.

The motion was very smooth. Also it was serpentine, as if the body beneath the coat of mail were made in the same interlocking sections as her limbs. He had expected and feared mechanical rigidity; nothing had prepared him for this more than human suppleness.

She stood quietly, letting the heavy mailed folds of her garment settle about her. They fell together with a faint ringing sound, like small bells far off, and hung beautifully in pale golden, sculptured folds. He had risen automatically as she did. Now he faced her, staring. He had never seen her stand perfectly still, and she was not doing it now. She swayed just a bit, vitality burning inextinguishably in her brain as once it had burned in her body, and stolid immobility was as impossible to her as it had always been. The golden garment caught points of light from the fire and glimmered at him with tiny reflections as she moved.

Then she put her featureless helmeted head a little to one side, and he heard her laughter as familiar in its small, throaty, intimate sound as he had ever heard it from her living throat. And every gesture, every attitude, every flowing of motion into motion was so utterly Deirdre that the overwhelming illusion swept his mind again and this was the flesh-and-blood woman as clearly as if he saw her standing there whole once more, like Phoenix from the fire.

"Well, John," she said in the soft, husky, amused voice he remembered perfectly. "Well, John, is it I?" She knew it was. Perfect assurance sounded in the voice. "The shock will wear off, you know. It'll be easier and easier as time goes on. I'm quite used to myself now. See?"

She turned away from him and crossed the room smoothly, with the old, poised, dancer's glide, to the mirror that paneled one side of the room. And before it, as he had so often seen her preen before, he watched her preening now, running flexible metallic hands down the folds of her metal garment, turning to admire herself over one metal shoulder, making the mailed folds tinkle and sway as she struck an arabesque position before the glass.

His knees let him down into the chair she had vacated. Mingled shock and relief loosened all his muscles in him, and she was more poised and confident than he.

"It's a miracle," he said with conviction. "It's *you*. But I don't see how—" He had meant, "—how, without face or body—" but clearly he could not finish that sentence.

She finished it for him in her own mind, and answered without self-consciousness. "It's motion, mostly," she said, still admiring her own suppleness in the mirror. "See?" And very lightly on her springy, armored feet she flashed through an enchainement of brilliant steps, swinging round with a pirouette to face him. "That was what Maltzer and I worked out between us, after I began to get myself under control again." Her voice was somber for a moment, remembering a dark time in the past. Then she went on, "It wasn't easy, of course, but it was fascinating. You'll never guess how fascinating, John! We knew we couldn't work out anything like a facsimile of the way I used to look, so we had to find some other basis to build on. And motion is the other basis of recognition, after actual physical likeness."

She moved lightly across the carpet toward the window and stood looking down, her featureless face averted a little and the light shining across the delicately hinted curves of the cheekbones.

"Luckily," she said, her voice amused, "I never was beautiful. It was all—well, vivacity, I suppose, and muscular co-ordination. Years and years of training, and all of it engraved here"—she struck her golden helmet a light, ringing blow with golden knuckles—"in the habit patterns grooved into my brain. So this body... did he tell you?... works entirely through the brain. Electromagnetic currents flowing along from ring to ring, like this." She rippled a boneless arm at him with a motion like flowing water. "Nothing holds me together—nothing!—except muscles of magnetic currents. And if I'd been somebody else—somebody who moved differently, why the flexible rings would have moved differently too, guided by the impulse from another brain. I'm not conscious of doing anything I haven't always done. The same impulses that used to go out to my muscles go out now to—this." And she made a shuddering, serpentine motion of both arms at him, like a Cambodian dancer, and then laughed wholeheartedly, the sound of it ringing through the room with such full throated merriment that he could not help seeing again the familiar face crinkled with pleasure, the white teeth shining. "It's all perfectly subconscious now," she told him. "It took lots of practice at first, of course, but now even my signature looks just as it always did—the coordination is duplicated that delicately." She rippled her arms at him again and chuckled.

"But the voice, too," Harris protested inadequately. "It's *your* voice, Deirdre."

"The voice isn't only a matter of throat construction and breath control, my darling Johnnie! At least, so Professor Maltzer assured me a year ago, and I certainly haven't any reason to doubt him!" She laughed again. She was laughing a little too much, with a touch of the bright, hysteric over-excitement he remembered so well. But if any woman ever had reason for mild hysteria, surely Deirdre had it now.

The laughter rippled and ended, and she went on, her voice eager. "He says voice control is almost wholly a matter of hearing what you produce, once you've got adequate mechanism, of course. That's why deaf people, with the same vocal chords as ever, let their voices change completely and lose all inflection when they've been deaf long enough. And luckily, you see, I'm not deaf!"

She swung around to him, the folds of her robe twinkling and ringing, and rippled up and up a clear, true scale to a lovely high note, and then cascaded down again like water over a falls. But she left him no time for applause. "Perfectly simple, you see. All it took was a little matter of genius from the professor to get it worked out for me! He started with a new variation of the old Vodor you must remember hearing about, years ago. Originally, of course, the thing was ponderous. You know how it worked—speech broken down to a few basic sounds and built up again in combinations produced from a keyboard. I think originally the sounds were a sort of *ktch* and a *shooshing* noise, but we've got it all worked to a flexibility and range quite as good as human now. All I do is—well, mentally play on the keyboard of my... my sound-unit, I suppose it's called. It's much more complicated than that, of course, but I've learned to do it unconsciously. And I regulate it by ear, quite automatically now. If you were—here—instead of me, and you'd had the same practice, your own voice would be coming out of the same keyboard and diaphragm instead of mine. It's all a matter of the brain patterns that operated the body and now operate the machinery. They send out very strong impulses that are stepped up as much as necessary somewhere or other in here—" Her hands waved vaguely over the mesh-robed body.

She was silent a moment, looking out the window. Then she turned away and crossed the floor to the fire, sinking again into the flowered chair. Her helmet-skull turned its mask to face him and he could feel a quiet scrutiny behind the aquamarine of its gaze.

"It's—odd," she said, "being here in this… this… instead of a body. But not as odd or as alien as you might think. I've thought about it a lot—I've had plenty of time to think—and I've begun to realize what a tremendous force the human ego really is. I'm not sure I want to suggest it has any mystical power it can impress on mechanical things, but it does seem to have a power of some sort. It does instill its own force into inanimate objects, and they take on a personality of their own. People do impress their personalities on the houses they live in, you know. I've noticed that often. Even empty rooms. And it happens with other things too, especially, I think, with inanimate things that men depend on for their lives. Ships, for instance—they always have personalities of their own.

"And planes—in wars you always hear of planes crippled too badly to fly, but struggling back anyhow with their crews. Even guns acquire a sort of ego. Ships and guns and planes are 'she' to the men who operate them and depend on them for their lives. It's as if machinery with complicated moving parts almost simulates life, and does acquire from the men who used it—well, not exactly life, of course—but a personality. I don't know what. Maybe it absorbs some of the actual electrical impulses their brains throw off, especially in times of stress.

"Well, after a while I began to accept the idea that this new body of mine could behave at least as responsively as a ship or a plane. Quite apart from the fact that my own brain controls its 'muscles.' I believe there's an affinity between men and the machines they make. They make them out of their own brains, really, a sort of mental conception and gestation, and the result responds to the minds that created them, and to all human minds that understand and manipulate them."

She stirred uneasily and smoothed a flexible hand along her mesh robed metal thigh. "So this is myself," she said. "Metal—but me. And it grows more and more myself the longer I live in it. It's my house and the machine my life depends on, but much more intimately in each case than any real house or machine ever was before to any other human. And you know, I wonder if in time I'll forget what flesh felt like—my own flesh, when I touched it like this—and the metal against the metal will be so much the same I'll never even notice?"

Harris did not try to answer her. He sat without moving, watching her expressionless face. In a moment she went on.

"I'll tell you the best thing, John," she said, her voice softening to the old intimacy he remembered so well that he could see superimposed upon the blank skull the warm, intent look that belonged with the voice. "I'm not going to live forever. It may not sound like a—best thing—but it is, John. You know, for awhile that was the worst of all, after I knew I was—after I woke up again. The thought of living on and on in a body that wasn't mine, seeing everyone I knew grow old and die, and not being able to stop—But Maltzer says my brain will probably wear out quite normally—except, of course, that I won't have to worry about looking old!—and when it gets tired and stops, the body I'm in won't be any longer. The magnetic muscles that hold it into my own shape and motions will let go when the brain lets go, and there'll be nothing but a… a pile of disconnected rings. If they ever assemble it again, it won't be me." She hesitated. "I like that, John," she said, and he felt from behind the mask a searching of his face.

He knew and understood that somber satisfaction. He could not put it into words; neither of them wanted to do that. But he understood. It was the conviction of mortality, in spite of her immortal body. She was not cut off from the rest of her race in the essence of their humanity, for though she wore a body of steel and they perishable flesh, yet she must perish too, and the same fears and faiths still united her to mortals and humans, though she wore the body of Oberon's inhuman knight. Even in her death she must be unique—dissolution in a shower of tinkling and clashing rings, he thought, and almost envied her the finality and beauty of that particular death—but afterward, oneness with humanity in however much or little awaited them all. So she could feel that this exile in metal was only temporary, in spite of everything.

(And providing, of course, that the mind inside the metal did not veer from its inherited humanity as the years went by. A dweller in a house may impress his personality upon the walls, but subtly the walls too, may impress their own shape upon the ego of the man. Neither of them thought of that, at the time.)

Deirdre sat a moment longer in silence. Then the mood vanished and she rose again, spinning so that the robe belled out ringing about her ankles. She rippled another scale up and down, faultlessly and with the same familiar sweetness of tone that had made her famous.

"So I'm going right back on the stage, John," she said serenely. "I can still sing. I can still dance. I'm still myself in everything that matters, and I can't imagine doing anything else for the rest of my life."

He could not answer without stammering a little. "Do you think will they accept you, Deirdre? After all—"

"They'll accept me," she said in that confident voice. "Oh, they'll come to see a freak at first, of course, but they'll stay to watch—Deirdre. And come back again and again just as they always did. You'll see, my dear."

But hearing her sureness, suddenly Harris himself was unsure. Maltzer had not been, either. She was so regally confident, and disappointment would be so deadly a blow at all that remained of her—She was so delicate a being now, really. Nothing but a glowing and radiant mind poised in metal, dominating it, bending the steel to the illusion of her lost loveliness with a sheer self-confidence that gleamed through the metal body. But the brain sat delicately on its poise of reason. She had been through intolerable stresses already, perhaps more terrible depths of despair and self-knowledge than any human brain had yet endured before her, for—since Lazarus himself—who had come back from the dead?

But if the world did not accept her as beautiful, what then? If they laughed, or pitied her, or came only to watch a jointed freak performing as if on strings where the loveliness of Deirdre had once enchanted them, what then? And he could not be perfectly sure they would not. He had known her too well in the flesh to see her objectively even now, in metal. Every inflection of her voice called up the vivid memory of the face that had flashed its evanescent beauty in some look to match the tone. She was Deirdre to Harris simply because she had been so intimately familiar in every poise and attitude, through so many years. But people who knew her only slightly, or saw her for the first time in metal—what would they see?

A marionette? Or the real grace and loveliness shining through?

He had no possible way of knowing. He saw her too clearly as she had been to see her now at all, except so linked with the past that she was not wholly metal. And he knew what Maltzer feared, for Maltzer's psychic blindness toward her lay at the other extreme. He had never known Deirdre except as a machine, and he could not see her objectively any more than Harris could. To Maltzer she was pure metal, a robot his own hands and brain had devised, mysteriously animated by the mind of Deirdre, to be sure, but to all outward seeming a thing of metal solely. He had worked so long over each intricate part of her body, he knew so well how every jointure in it was put together, that he could not see the whole. He had studied many film records of her, of course, as she used to be, in order to gauge the accuracy of his facsimile, but this thing he had made was a copy only. He was too close to Deirdre to see her. And Harris, in a way, was too far. The indomitable Deirdre herself shone so vividly through the metal that his mind kept superimposing one upon the other.

How would an audience react to her? Where in the scale between these two extremes would their verdict fall?

For Deirdre, there was only one possible answer.

"I'm not worried," Deirdre said serenely, and spread her golden hands to the fire to watch lights dancing in reflection upon their shining surfaces. "I'm still myself. I've always had... well, power over my audiences. Any good performer knows when he's got it. Mine isn't gone. I can still give them what I always gave, only now with greater variations and more depths than I'd ever have done before. Why, look—" She gave a little wriggle of excitement.

"You know the arabesque principle—getting the longest possible distance from fingertip to toetip with a long, slow curve through the whole length? And the brace of the other leg and arm giving contrast? Well, look at me. I don't work on hinges now. I can make every motion a long curve if I want to. My body's different enough now to work out a whole new school of dancing. Of course there'll be things I used to do that I won't attempt now—no more dancing *sur les pointes*, for instance—but the new things will more than balance the loss. I've been practicing. Do you know I can turn a hundred *fouettés* now without a flaw? And I think I could go right on and turn a thousand, if I wanted."

She made the firelight flash on her hands, and her robe rang musically as she moved her shoulders a little. "I've already worked out one new dance for myself," she said. "God knows I'm no choreographer, but I did want to experiment first. Later, you know, really creative men like Massanchine or Fokhileff may want to do something entirely new for me—a whole new sequence of movements based on a new technique. And music—that could be quite different, too. Oh, there's no end to the possibilities! Even my voice has more range and power. Luckily I'm not an actress—it would be silly to try to play Camille or Juliet with a cast of ordinary people. Not that I couldn't, you know." She turned her head to stare at Harris through the mask of glass. "I honestly think I could. But it isn't necessary. There's too much else. Oh, I'm not worried!"

"Maltzer's worried," Harris reminded her.

She swung away from the fire, her metal robe ringing, and into her voice came the old note of distress that went with a furrowing of her forehead and a sidewise tilt of the head. The head went sidewise as it had always done, and he could see the furrowed brow almost as clearly as if flesh still clothed her.

"I know. And I'm worried about him, John. He's worked so awfully hard over me. This is the doldrums now, the let-down period, I suppose. I know what's on his mind. He's afraid I'll look just the same to the world as I look to him. Tooled metal. He's in a position no one ever quite achieved before, isn't he? Rather like God." Her voice rippled a little with amusement. "I suppose to God we must look like a collection of cells and corpuscles ourselves. But Maltzer lacks a god's detached viewpoint."

"He can't see you as I do, anyhow." Harris was choosing his words with difficulty. "I wonder, though—would it help him any if you postponed your debut awhile? You've been with him too closely, I think. You don't quite realize how near a breakdown he is. I was shocked when I saw him just now."

The golden head shook. "No. He's close to a breaking point, maybe, but I think the only cure's action. He wants me to retire and stay out of sight, John. Always. He's afraid for anyone to see me except a few old friends who remember me as I was. People he can trust to be—kind." She laughed. It was very strange to hear that ripple of mirth from the blank, unfeatured skull. Harris was seized with sudden panic at the thought of what reaction it might evoke in an audience of strangers. As if he had spoken the fear aloud, her voice denied it. "I don't need kindness. And it's no kindness to Maltzer to hide me under a bushel. He *has* worked too hard, I know. He's driven himself to a breaking point. But it'll be a complete negation of all he's worked for if I hide myself now. You don't know what a tremendous lot of geniuses and artistry went into me, John. The whole idea from the start was to recreate what I'd lost so that it could be proved that beauty and talent need not be sacrificed by the destruction of parts or all the body.

"It wasn't only for me that we meant to prove that. There'll be others who suffer injuries that once might have ruined them. This was to end all suffering like that forever. It was Maltzer's gift to the whole race as well as to me. He's really a humanitarian, John, like most great men. He'd never have given up a year of his life to this work if it had been for any one individual alone. He was seeing thousands of others beyond me as he worked. And I won't let him ruin all he's achieved because he's afraid to prove it now he's got it. The whole wonderful achievement will be worthless if I don't take the final step. I think his breakdown, in the end, would be worse and more final if I never tried than if I tried and failed."

Harris sat in silence. There was no answer he could make to that. He hoped the little twinge of shamefaced jealousy he suddenly felt did not show, as he was reminded anew of the intimacy closer than marriage which had of necessity bound these two together. And he knew that any reaction of his would in its way be almost as prejudiced as Maltzer's, for a reason at once the same and entirely opposite.

Except that he himself came fresh to the problem, while Maltzer's viewpoint was colored by a year of overwork and physical and mental exhaustion.

"What are you going to do?" he asked.

She was standing before the fire when he spoke, swaying just a little so that highlights danced all along her golden body. Now she turned with a serpentine grace and sank into the cushioned chair beside her. It came to him suddenly that she was much more than humanly graceful—quite as much as he had once feared she would be less than human.

"I've already arranged for a performance," she told him, her voice a little shaken with a familiar mixture of excitement and defiance.

Harris sat up with a start. "How? Where? There hasn't been any publicity at all yet, has there? I didn't know—"

"Now, now, Johnnie," her amused voice soothed him. "You'll be handling everything just as usual once I get started back to work— that is, if you still want to. But this I've arranged for myself. It's going to be a surprise. I... I felt it had to be a surprise." She wriggled a little among the cushions. "Audience psychology is something I've always felt rather than known, and I do feel this is the way it ought to be done. There's no precedent. Nothing like this ever happened before. I'll have to go by my own intuition."

"You mean it's to be a complete surprise?"

"I think it must be. I don't want the audience coming in with preconceived ideas. I want them to see me exactly as I am now *first*, before they know who or what they're seeing. They must realize I can still give as good a performance as ever before they remember and compare it with my past performances. I don't want them to come ready to pity my handicaps—I haven't got any!—or full of morbid curiosity. So I'm going on the air after the regular eight-o'clock telecast of the feature from Teleo City. I'm just going to do one specialty in the usual vaude program. It's all been arranged. They'll build up to it, of course, as the highlight of the evening, but they aren't to say who I am until the end of the performance—if the audience hasn't recognized me already, by then."

"Audience?"

"Of course. Surely you haven't forgotten they still play to a theater audience at Teleo City? That's why I want to make my debut there. I've always played better when there were people in the studio, so I could gauge reactions. I think most performers do. Anyhow, it's all arranged."

"Does Maltzer know?"

She wriggled uncomfortably. "Not yet."

"But he'll have to give his permission too, won't he? I mean—"

"Now look, John! That's another idea you and Maltzer will have to get out of your minds. I don't belong to him. In a way he's just been my doctor through a long illness, but I'm free to discharge him whenever I choose. If there were ever any legal disagreement, I suppose he'd be entitled to quite a lot of money for the work he's done on my new body—for the body itself, really, since it's his own machine, in one sense. But he doesn't own it, or me. I'm not sure just how the question would be decided by the courts—there again, we've got a problem without precedent. The body may be his work, but the brain that makes it something more than a collection of metal rings is *me,* and he couldn't restrain me against my will even if he wanted to. Not legally, and not—" She hesitated oddly and looked away. For the first time Harris was aware of something beneath the surface of her mind which was quite strange to him.

"Well, anyhow," she went on, "that question won't come up. Maltzer and I have been much too close in the past year to clash over anything as essential as this. He knows in his heart that I'm right, and he won't try to restrain me. His work won't be completed until I do what I was built to do. And I intend to do it."

That strange little quiver of something—something un-Deirdre—which had so briefly trembled beneath the surface of familiarity stuck in Harris' mind as something he must recall and examine later. Now he said only,

"All right. I suppose I agree with you. How soon are you going to do it?"

She turned her head so that even the glass mask through which she looked out at the world was foreshortened away from him, and the golden helmet with its hint of sculptured cheekbone was entirely enigmatic.

"Tonight," she said.

Maltzer's thin hand shook so badly that he could not turn the dial. He tried twice and then laughed nervously and shrugged at Harris.

"You get her," he said.

Harris glanced at his watch. "It isn't time yet. She won't be on for half an hour." Maltzer made a gesture of violent impatience. "Get it, get it!"

Harris shrugged a little in turn and twisted the dial. On the tilted screen above them shadows and sound blurred together and then clarified into a somber medieval hall, vast, vaulted, people in bright costume moving like pygmies through its dimness. Since the play concerned Mary of Scotland, the actors were dressed in something approximating Elizabethan garb, but as every era tends to translate costume into terms of the current fashions, the women's hair was dressed in a style that would have startled Elizabeth, and their footgear was entirely anachronistic.

The hall dissolved and a face swam up into soft focus upon the screen. The dark, lush beauty of the actress who was playing the Stuart queen glowed at them in velvety perfection from the clouds of her pearl-strewn hair. Maltzer groaned.

"She's competing with *that,*" he said hollowly.

"You think she can't?"

Maltzer slapped the chair arms with angry palms. Then the quivering of his fingers seemed suddenly to strike him, and he muttered to himself, "Look at 'em! I'm not even fit to handle a hammer and saw." But the mutter was an aside. "Of course she can't compete," he cried irritably. "She hasn't any sex. She isn't female any more. She doesn't know that yet, but she'll learn."

Harris stared at him, feeling a little stunned. Somehow the thought had not occurred to him before at all, so vividly had the illusion of the old Deirdre hung about the new one.

"She's an abstraction now," Maltzer went on, drumming his palms upon the chair in quick, nervous rhythms. "I don't know what it'll do to her, but there'll be change. Remember Abelard? She's lost everything that made her essentially what the public wanted, and she's going to find it out the hard way. After that—" He grimaced savagely and was silent.

"She hasn't lost everything," Harris defended. "She can dance and sing as well as ever, maybe better. She still has grace and charm and—"

"Yes, but where did the grace and charm come from? Not out of the habit patterns in her brain. No, out of human contacts, out of all the things that stimulate sensitive minds to creativeness. And she's lost three of her five senses. Everything she can't see and hear is gone. One of the strongest stimuli to a woman of her type was the knowledge of sex competition. You know how she sparkled when a man came into the room? All that's gone, and it was an essential. You know how liquor stimulated her? She's lost that. She couldn't taste food or drink even if she needed it. Perfume, flowers, all the odors we respond to mean nothing to her now. She can't feel anything with tactual delicacy any more. She used to surround herself with luxuries—she drew her stimuli from them—and that's all gone too. She's withdrawn from all physical contacts."

He squinted at the screen, not seeing it, his face drawn into lines like the lines of a skull. All flesh seemed to have dissolved off his bones in the past year, and Harris thought almost jealously that even in that way he seemed to be drawing nearer Deirdre in her fleshlessness with every passing week.

"Sight," Maltzer said, "is the most highly civilized of the senses. It was the last to come. The other senses tie us in closely with the very roots of life; I think we perceive with them more keenly than we know. The things we realize through taste and smell and feeling stimulate directly, without a detour through the centers of conscious thought. You know how often a taste or odor will recall a memory to you so subtly you don't know exactly what caused it? We need those primitive senses to tie us in with nature and the race. Through those ties Deirdre drew her vitality without realizing it. Sight is a cold, intellectual thing compared with the other senses. But it's all she has to draw on now. She isn't a human being any more, and I think what humanity is left in her will drain out little by little and never be replaced. Abelard, in a way, was a prototype. But Deirdre's loss is complete."

"She isn't human," Harris agreed slowly. "But she isn't pure robot either. She's something somewhere between the two, and I think it's a mistake to try to guess just where, or what the outcome will be."

"I don't have to guess," Maltzer said in a grim voice. "I know. I wish I'd let her die. I've done something to her a thousand times worse than the fire ever could. I should have let her die in it."

"Wait," said Harris. "Wait and see. I think you're wrong."

On the television screen Mary of Scotland climbed the scaffold to her doom, the gown of traditional scarlet clinging warmly to supple young curves as anachronistic in their way as the slippers beneath the gown, for—as everyone but playwrights knows—Mary was well into middle age before she died. Gracefully this latter-day Mary bent her head, sweeping the long hair aside, kneeling to the block.

Maltzer watched stonily, seeing another woman entirely.

"I shouldn't have let her," he was muttering. "I shouldn't have let her do it."

"Do you really think you'd have stopped her if you could?" Harris asked quietly. And the other man after a moment's pause shook his head jerkily.

"No, I suppose not. I keep thinking if I worked and waited a little longer maybe I could make it easier for her, but—no, I suppose not. She's got to face them sooner or later, being herself." He stood up abruptly, shoving back his chair. "If she only weren't so... so frail. She doesn't realize how delicately poised her very sanity is. We gave her what we could—the artists and the designers and I, all gave our very best—but she's so pitifully handicapped even with all we could do. She'll always be an abstraction and a... a freak, cut off from the world by handicaps worse in their way than anything any human being ever suffered before. Sooner or later she'll realize it. And then—" He began to pace up and down with quick, uneven steps, striking his hands together. His face was twitching with a little *tic* that drew up one eye to a squint and released it again at irregular intervals. Harris could see how very near collapse the man was.

"Can you imagine what it's like?" Maltzer demanded fiercely. "Penned into a mechanical body like that, shut out from all human contacts except what leaks in by way of sight and sound? To know you aren't human any longer? She's been through shocks enough already. When that shock fully hits her—"

"Shut up," said Harris roughly. "You won't do her any good if you break down yourself. Look—the vaude's starting."

Great golden curtains had swept together over the unhappy Queen of Scotland and were parting again now, all sorrow and frustration wiped away once more as cleanly as the passing centuries had already expunged them. Now a line of tiny dancers under the tremendous arch of the stage kicked and pranced with the precision of little mechanical dolls too small and perfect to be real. Vision rushed down upon them and swept along the row, face after stiffly smiling face racketing by like fence pickets. Then the sight rose into the rafters and looked down upon them from a great height, the grotesquely foreshortened figures still prancing in perfect rhythm even from this inhuman angle.

There was applause from an invisible audience. Then someone came out and did a dance with lighted torches that streamed long, weaving ribbons of fire among clouds of what looked like cotton wool but was most probably asbestos. Then a company in gorgeous pseudo-period costumes postured its way through the new singing ballet form of dance, roughly following a plot which had been announced as *Les Sylphides*, but had little in common with it. Afterward the precision dancers came on again, solemn and charming as performing dolls.

Maltzer began to show signs of dangerous tension as act succeeded act. Deirdre's was to be the last, of course. It seemed very long indeed before a face in close-up blotted out the stage, and a master of ceremonies with features like an amiable marionette's announced a very special number as the finale. His voice was almost cracking with excitement—perhaps he, too, had not been told until a moment before what lay in store for the audience.

Neither of the listening men heard what it was he said, but both were conscious of a certain indefinable excitement rising among the audience, murmurs and rustlings and a mounting anticipation as if time had run backward here and knowledge of the great surprise had already broken upon them.

Then the golden curtains appeared again. They quivered and swept apart on long upward arcs, and between them the stage was full of a shimmering golden haze. It was, Harris realized in a moment, simply a series of gauze curtains, but the effect was one of strange and wonderful anticipation, as if something very splendid must be hidden in the haze. The world might have looked like this on the first morning of creation, before heaven and earth took form in the mind of God. It was a singularly fortunate choice of stage set in its symbolism, though Harris wondered how much necessity had figured in its selection, for there could not have been much time to prepare an elaborate set.

The audience sat perfectly silent, and the air was tense. This was no ordinary pause before an act. No one had been told, surely, and yet they seemed to guess— The shimmering haze trembled and began to thin, veil by veil.

Beyond was darkness, and what looked like a row of shining pillars set in a balustrade that began gradually to take shape as the haze drew back in shining folds. Now they could see that the balustrade curved up from left and right to the head of a sweep of stairs. Stage and stairs were carpeted in black velvet; black velvet draperies hung just ajar behind the balcony, with a glimpse of dark sky beyond them trembling with dim synthetic stars.

The last curtain of golden gauze withdrew. The stage was empty. Or it seemed empty. But even through the aerial distances between this screen and the place it mirrored, Harris thought that the audience was not waiting for the performer to come on from the wings. There was no rustling, no coughing, no sense of impatience. A presence upon the stage was in command from the first drawing of the curtains; it filled the theater with its calm domination. It gauged its timing, holding the audience as a conductor with lifted baton gathers and holds the eyes of his orchestra.

For a moment everything was motionless upon the stage. Then, at the head of the stairs, where the two curves of the pillared balustrade swept together, a figure stirred.

Until that moment she had seemed another shining column in the row. Now she swayed deliberately, light catching and winking and running molten along her limbs and her robe of metal mesh. She swayed just enough to show that she was there. Then, with every eye upon her, she stood quietly to let them look their fill. The screen did not swoop to a close-up upon her. Her enigma remained inviolate and the television watchers saw her no more clearly than the audience in the theater.

Many must have thought her at first some wonderfully animate robot, hung perhaps from wires invisible against the velvet, for certainly she was no woman dressed in metal—her proportions were too thin and fine for that. And perhaps the impression of robotism was what she meant to convey at first. She stood quiet, swaying just a little, a masked and inscrutable figure, faceless, very slender in her robe that hung in folds as pure as a Grecian chlamys, though she did not look Grecian at all. In the visored golden helmet and the robe of mail that odd likeness to knighthood was there again, with its implications of medieval richness behind the simple lines. Except that in her exquisite slimness she called to mind no human figure in armor, not even the comparative delicacy of a St. Joan. It was the chivalry and delicacy of some other world implicit in her outlines.

A breath of surprise had rippled over the audience when she moved. Now they were tensely silent again, waiting. And the tension, the anticipation, was far deeper than the surface importance of the scene could ever have evoked. Even those who thought her a manikin seemed to feel the forerunning of greater revelations.

Now she swayed and came slowly down the steps, moving with a suppleness just a little better than human. The swaying strengthened. By the time she reached the stage floor she was dancing. But it was no dance that any human creature could ever have performed. The long, slow, languorous rhythms of her body would have been impossible to a figure hinged at its joints as human figures hinge. (Harris remembered incredulously that he had feared once to find her jointed like a mechanical robot. But it was humanity that seemed, by contrast, jointed and mechanical now.)

The languor and the rhythm of her patterns looked impromptu, as all good dances should, but Harris knew what hours of composition and rehearsal must lie behind it, what laborious graving into her brain of strange new pathways, the first to replace the old ones and govern the mastery of metal limbs.

To and fro over the velvet carpet, against the velvet background, she wove the intricacies of her serpentine dance, leisurely and yet with such hypnotic effect that the air seemed full of looping rhythms, as if her long, tapering limbs had left their own replicas hanging upon the air and fading only slowly as she moved away. In her mind, Harris knew, the stage was a whole, a background to be filled in completely with the measured patterns of her dance, and she seemed almost to project that completed pattern to her audience so that they saw her everywhere at once, her golden rhythms fading upon the air long after she had gone.

Now there was music, looping and hanging in echoes after her like the shining festoons she wove with her body. But it was no orchestral music. She was humming, deep and sweet and wordlessly, as she glided her easy, intricate path about the stage. And the volume of the music was amazing. It seemed to fill the theater, and it was not amplified by hidden loudspeakers. You could tell that. Somehow, until you heard the music she made, you had never realized before the subtle distortions that amplification puts into music. This was utterly pure and true as perhaps no ear in all her audience had ever heard music before.

While she danced the audience did not seem to breathe. Perhaps they were beginning already to suspect who and what it was that moved before them without any fanfare of the publicity they had been half-expecting for weeks now. And yet, without the publicity, it was not easy to believe the dancer they watched was not some cunningly motivated manikin swinging on unseen wires about the stage.

Nothing she had done yet had been human. The dance was no dance a human being could have performed. The music she hummed came from a throat without vocal chords. But now the long, slow rhythms were drawing to their close, the pattern tightening in to a finale. And she ended as inhumanly as she had danced, willing them not to interrupt her with applause, dominating them now as she had always done. For her implication here was that a machine might have performed the dance, and a machine expects no applause. If they thought unseen operators had put her through those wonderful paces, they would wait for the operators to appear for their bows. But the audience was obedient. It sat silently, waiting for what came next. But its silence was tense and breathless.

The dance ended as it had begun. Slowly, almost carelessly, she swung up the velvet stairs, moving with rhythms as perfect as her music. But when she reached the head of the stairs she turned to face her audience, and for a moment stood motionless, like a creature of metal, without volition, the hands of the operator slack upon its strings.

Then, startlingly, she laughed.

It was lovely laughter, low and sweet and full-throated. She threw her head back and let her body sway and her shoulders shake, and the laughter, like the music, filled the theater, gaining volume from the great hollow of the roof and sounding in the ears of every listener, not loud, but as intimately as if each sat alone with the woman who laughed.

And she was a woman now. Humanity had dropped over her like a tangible garment. No one who had ever heard that laughter before could mistake it here. But before the reality of who she was had quite time to dawn upon her listeners she let the laughter deepen into music, as no human voice could have done. She was humming a familiar refrain close in the ear of every hearer. And the humming in turn swung into words. She sang in her clear, light, lovely voice:

"The yellow rose of Eden, is blooming in my heart—"

It was Deirdre's song. She had sung it first upon the airways a month before the theater fire that had consumed her. It was a commonplace little melody, simple enough to take first place in the fancy of a nation that had always liked its songs simple. But it had a certain sincerity too, and no taint of the vulgarity of tune and rhythm that foredooms so many popular songs to oblivion after their novelty fades.

No one else was ever able to sing it quite as Deirdre did. It had been identified with her so closely that though for awhile after her accident singers tried to make it a memorial for her, they failed so conspicuously to give it her unmistakable flair that the song died from their sheer inability to sing it. No one ever hummed the tune without thinking of her and the pleasant, nostalgic sadness of something lovely and lost.

But it was not a sad song now. If anyone had doubted whose brain and ego motivated this shining metal suppleness, they could doubt no longer. For the voice was Deirdre, and the song. And the lovely, poised grace of her mannerisms that made up recognition as certainly as sight of a familiar face.

She had not finished the first line of her song before the audience knew her.

And they did not let her finish. The accolade of their interruption was a tribute more eloquent than polite waiting could ever have been. First a breath of incredulity rippled over the theater, and a long, sighing gasp that reminded Harris irrelevantly as he listened to the gasp which still goes up from matinee audiences at the first glimpse of the fabulous Valentino, so many generations dead. But this gasp did not sigh itself away and vanish. Tremendous tension lay behind it, and the rising tide of excitement rippled up in little murmurs and spatterings of applause that ran together into one overwhelming roar. It shook the theater. The television screen trembled and blurred a little to the volume of that transmitted applause.

Silenced before it, Deirdre stood gesturing on the stage, bowing and bowing as the noise rolled up about her, shaking perceptibly with the triumph of her own emotion.

Harris had an intolerable feeling that she was smiling radiantly and that the tears were pouring down her cheeks. He even thought, just as Maltzer leaned forward to switch off the screen, that she was blowing kisses over the audience in the time-honored gesture of the grateful actress, her golden arms shining as she scattered kisses abroad from the featureless helmet, the face that had no mouth.

"Well?" Harris said, not without triumph.

Maltzer shook his head jerkily, the glasses unsteady on his nose so that the blurred eyes behind them seemed to shift.

"Of course they applauded, you fool," he said in a savage voice. "I might have known they would under this set-up. It doesn't prove anything. Oh, she was smart to surprise them—I admit that. But they were applauding themselves as much as her. Excitement, gratitude for letting them in on a historic performance, mass hysteria—you know. It's from now on the test will come, and this hasn't helped any to prepare her for it. Morbid curiosity when the news gets out—people laughing when she forgets she isn't human. And they will, you know. There are always those who will. And the novelty wearing off. The slow draining away of humanity for lack of contact with any human stimuli any more—"

Harris remembered suddenly and reluctantly the moment that afternoon which he had shunted aside mentally, to consider later. The sense of something unfamiliar beneath the surface of Deirdre's speech. Was Maltzer right? Was the drainage already at work? Or was there something deeper than this obvious answer to the question? Certainly she had been through experiences too terrible for ordinary people to comprehend. Scars might still remain. Or, with her body, had she put on a strange, metallic something of the mind, that spoke to no sense which human minds could answer?

For a few minutes neither of them spoke. Then Maltzer rose abruptly and stood looking down at Harris with an abstract scowl.

"I wish you'd go now," he said.

Harris glanced up at him, startled. Maltzer began to pace again, his steps quick and uneven. Over his shoulder he said, "I've made up my mind, Harris. I've got to put a stop to this."

Harris rose. "Listen," he said. "Tell me one thing. What makes you so certain you're right? Can you deny that most of it's speculation—hearsay evidence? Remember, I talked to Deirdre, and she was just as sure as you are in the opposite direction. Have you any real reason for what you think?"

Maltzer took his glasses off and rubbed his nose carefully, taking a long time about it. He seemed reluctant to answer. But when he did, at last, there was a confidence in his voice Harris had not expected.

"I have a reason," he said. "But you won't believe it. Nobody would."

"Try me."

Maltzer shook his head. "Nobody *could* believe it. No two people were ever in quite the same relationship before as Deirdre and I have been. I helped her come back out of complete—oblivion. I knew her before she had voice or hearing. She was only a frantic mind when I first made contact with her, half insane with all that had happened and fear of what would happen next. In a very literal sense she was reborn out of that condition, and I had to guide her through every step of the way. I came to know her thoughts before she thought them. And once you've been that close to another mind, you don't lose the contact easily." He put the glasses back on and looked blurrily at Harris through the heavy lenses. "Deirdre is worried," he said. "I know it. You won't believe me, but I can—well, sense it. I tell you, I've been too close to her very mind itself to make any mistake. You don't see it, maybe. Maybe even she doesn't know it yet. But the worry's there. When I'm with her, I feel it. And I don't want it to come any nearer the surface of her mind than it's come already. I'm going to put a stop to this before it's too late."

Harris had no comment for that. It was too entirely outside his own experience. He said nothing for a moment. Then he asked simply, "How?"

"I'm not sure yet. I've got to decide before she comes back. And I want to see her alone."

"I think you're wrong," Harris told him quietly. "I think you're imagining things. I don't think you *can* stop her."

Maltzer gave him a slanted glance. "I can stop her," he said, in a curious voice. He went on quickly, "She has enough already—she's nearly human. She can live normally as other people live, without going back on the screen. Maybe this taste of it will be enough. I've got to convince her it is. If she retires now, she'll never guess how cruel her own audiences could be, and maybe that deep sense of—distress, uneasiness, whatever it is—won't come to the surface. It mustn't. She's too fragile to stand that." He slapped his hands together sharply. "I've got to stop her. For her own sake I've got to do it!" He swung round again to face Harris. "Will you go now?"

Never in his life had Harris wanted less to leave a place. Briefly he thought of saying simply, "No I won't." But he had to admit in his own mind that Maltzer was at least partly right. This was a matter between Deirdre and her creator, the culmination, perhaps, of that year's long intimacy so like marriage that this final trial for supremacy was a need he recognized.

He would not, he thought, forbid the showdown if he could. Perhaps the whole year had been building up to this one moment between them in which one or the other must prove himself victor. Neither was very well stable just now, after the long strain of the year past. It might very well be that the mental salvation of one or both hinged upon the outcome of the clash. But because each was so strongly motivated not by selfish concern but by solicitude for the other in this strange combat, Harris knew he must leave them to settle the thing alone.

He was in the street and hailing a taxi before the full significance of something Maltzer had said came to him. "*I can stop her,*" he had declared, with an odd inflection in his voice.

Suddenly Harris felt cold. Maltzer had made her—of course he could stop her if he chose. Was there some key in that supple golden body that could immobilize it at its maker's will? Could she be imprisoned in the cage of her own body? No body before in all history, he thought, could have been designed more truly to be a prison for its mind than Deirdre's, if Maltzer chose to turn the key that locked her in. There must be many ways to do it. He could simply withhold whatever source of nourishment kept her brain alive, if that were the way he chose.

But Harris could not believe he would do it. The man wasn't insane. He would not defeat his own purpose. His determination rose from his solicitude for Deirdre; he would not even in the last extremity try to save her by imprisoning her in the jail of her own skull.

For a moment Harris hesitated on the curb, almost turning back. But what could he do? Even granting that Maltzer would resort to such tactics, self-defeating in their very nature, how could any man on earth prevent him if he did it subtly enough? But he never would. Harris knew he never would. He got into his cab slowly, frowning. He would see them both tomorrow.

He did not. Harris was swamped with excited calls about yesterday's performance, but the message he was awaiting did not come. The day went by very slowly. Toward evening he surrendered and called Maltzer's apartment.

It was Deirdre's face that answered, and for once he saw no remembered features superimposed upon the blankness of her helmet. Masked and faceless, she looked at him inscrutably.

"Is everything all right?" he asked, a little uncomfortable.

"Yes, of course," she said, and her voice was a bit metallic for the first time, as if she were thinking so deeply of some other matter that she did not trouble to pitch it properly. "I had a long talk with Maltzer last night, if that's what you mean. You know what he wants. But nothing's been decided yet."

Harris felt oddly rebuffed by the sudden realization of the metal of her. It was impossible to read anything from face or voice. Each had its mask.

"What are you going to do?" he asked.

"Exactly as I'd planned," she told him, without inflection.

Harris floundered a little. Then, with an effort at practicality, he said, "Do you want me to go to work on bookings, then?"

She shook the delicately modeled skull. "Not yet. You saw the reviews today, of course. They—*did* like me." It was an understatement, and for the first time a note of warmth sounded in her voice. But the preoccupation was still there, too. "I'd already planned to make them wait awhile after my first performance," she went on. "A couple of weeks, anyhow. You remember that little farm of mine in Jersey, John? I'm going over today. I won't see anyone except the servants there. Not even Maltzer. Not even you. I've got a lot to think about. Maltzer has agreed to let everything go until we've both thought things over. He's taking a rest, too. I'll see you the moment I get back, John. Is that all right?"

She blanked out almost before he had time to nod and while the beginning of a stammered argument was still on his lips. He sat there staring at the screen.

The two weeks that went by before Maltzer called him again were the longest Harris had ever spent. He thought of many things in the interval. He believed he could sense in that last talk with Deirdre something of the inner unrest that Maltzer had spoken of—more an abstraction than a distress, but some thought had occupied her mind which she would not—or was it that she could not?— share even with her closest confidants. He even wondered whether, if her mind was as delicately poised as Maltzer feared, one would ever know whether or not it had slipped. There was so little evidence one way or the other in the unchanging outward form of her.

Most of all he wondered what two weeks in a new environment would do to her untried body and newly patterned brain. If Maltzer were right, then there might be some perceptible—drainage—by the time they met again. He tried not to think of that.

Maltzer televised him on the morning set for her return. He looked very bad. The rest must have been no rest at all. His face was almost a skull now, and the blurred eyes behind their lenses burned. But he seemed curiously at peace, in spite of his appearance. Harris thought he had reached some decision, but whatever it was had not stopped his hands from shaking or the nervous *tic* that drew his face sidewise into a grimace at intervals.

"Come over," he said briefly, without preamble. "She'll be here in half an hour." And he blanked out without waiting for an answer.

When Harris arrived, he was standing by the window looking down and steadying his trembling hands on the sill.

"I can't stop her," he said in a monotone, and again without preamble. Harris had the impression that for the two weeks his thoughts must have run over and over the same track, until any spoken word was simply a vocal interlude in the circling of his mind. "I couldn't do it. I even tried threats, but she knew I didn't mean them. There's only one way out, Harris." He glanced up briefly, hollow-eyed behind the lenses. "Never mind. I'll tell you later."

"Did you explain everything to her that you did to me?"

"Nearly all. I even taxed her with that... that sense of distress I *know* she feels. She denied it. She was lying. We both knew. It was worse after the performance than before. When I saw her that night, I tell you I *knew*—*she* senses something wrong, but she won't admit it." He shrugged. "Well—"

Faintly in the silence they heard the humming of the elevator descending from the helicopter platform on the roof. Both men turned to the door.

She had not changed at all. Foolishly, Harris was a little surprised. Then he caught himself and remembered that she would never change—never, until she died. He himself might grow white-haired and senile; she would move before him then as she moved now, supple, golden, enigmatic.

Still, he thought she caught her breath a little when she saw Maltzer and the depths of his swift degeneration. She had no breath to catch, but her voice was shaken as she greeted them.

"I'm glad you're both here," she said, a slight hesitation in her speech. "It's a wonderful day outside. Jersey was glorious. I'd forgotten how lovely it is in summer. Was the sanitarium any good, Maltzer?"

He jerked his head irritably and did not answer. She went on talking in a light voice, skimming the surface, saying nothing important.

This time Harris saw her as he supposed her audiences would, eventually, when the surprise had worn off and the image of the living Deirdre faded from memory. She was all metal now, the Deirdre they would know from today on. And she was not less lovely. She was not even less human—yet. Her motion was a miracle of flexible grace, a pouring of suppleness along every limb. (From now on, Harris realized suddenly, it was her body and not her face that would have mobility to express emotion; she must act with her limbs and her lithe, robed torso.)

But there was something wrong. Harris sensed it almost tangibly in her inflections, her elusiveness, the way she fenced with words. This was what Maltzer had meant, this was what Harris himself had felt just before she left for the country. Only now it was strong—certain. Between them and the old Deirdre whose voice still spoke to them a veil of—detachment—had been drawn. Behind it she was in distress. Somehow, somewhere, she had made some discovery that affected her profoundly. And Harris was terribly afraid that he knew what the discovery must be. Maltzer was right.

He was still leaning against the window, staring out unseeingly over the vast panorama of New York, webbed with traffic bridges, winking with sunlit glass, its vertiginous distances plunging downward into the blue shadows of Earth-level. He said now, breaking into the light-voiced chatter, "Are you all right, Deirdre?"

She laughed. It was lovely laughter. She moved lithely across the room, sunlight glinting on her musical mailed robe, and stooped to a cigarette box on a table. Her fingers were deft.

"Have one?" she said, and carried the box to Maltzer. He let her put the brown cylinder between his lips and hold a light to it, but he did not seem to be noticing what he did. She replaced the box and then crossed to a mirror on the far wall and began experimenting with a series of gliding ripples that wove patterns of pale gold in the glass. "Of course I'm all right," she said.

"You're lying."

Deirdre did not turn. She was watching him in the mirror, but the ripple of her motion went on slowly, languorously, undisturbed.

"No," she told them both.

Maltzer drew deeply on his cigarette. Then with a hard pull he unsealed the window and tossed the smoking stub far out over the gulfs below. He said,

"You can't deceive me, Deirdre." His voice, suddenly, was quite calm. "I created you, my dear. I know. I've sensed that uneasiness in you growing and growing for a long while now. It's much stronger today than it was two weeks ago. Something happened to you in the country. I don't know what it was, but you've changed. Will you admit to yourself what it is, Deirdre? Have you realized yet that you must not go back on the screen?"

"Why, no," said Deirdre, still not looking at him except obliquely, in the glass. Her gestures were slower now, weaving lazy patterns in the air. "No, I haven't changed my mind."

She was all metal—outwardly. She was taking unfair advantage of her own metal-hood. She had withdrawn far within, behind the mask of her voice and her facelessness. Even her body, whose involuntary motions might have betrayed what she was feeling, in the only way she could be subject to betrayal now, she was putting through ritual motions that disguised it completely. As long as these looping, weaving patterns occupied her, no one had any way of guessing even from her motion what went on in the hidden brain inside her helmet.

Harris was struck suddenly and for the first time with the completeness of her withdrawal. When he had seen her last in this apartment she had been wholly Deirdre, not masked at all, overflowing the metal with the warmth and ardor of the woman he had known so well. Since then—since the performance on the stage—he had not seen the familiar Deirdre again. Passionately he wondered why. Had she begun to suspect even in her moment of triumph what a fickle master an audience could be? Had she caught, perhaps, the sound of whispers and laughter among some small portion of her watchers, though the great majority praised her?

Or was Maltzer right? Perhaps Harris' first interview with her had been the last bright burning of the lost Deirdre, animated by excitement and the pleasure of meeting after so long a time, animation summoned up in a last strong effort to convince him. Now she was gone, but whether in self-protection against the possible cruelties of human beings, or whether in withdrawal to metal-hood, he could not guess.

Humanity might be draining out of her fast, and the brassy taint of metal permeating the brain it housed.

Maltzer laid his trembling hand on the edge of the opened window and looked out. He said in a deepened voice, the querulous note gone for the first time:

"I've made a terrible mistake, Deirdre. I've done you irreparable harm." He paused a moment, but Deirdre said nothing. Harris dared not speak. In a moment Maltzer went on. "I've made you vulnerable, and given you no weapons to fight your enemies with. And the human race is your enemy, my dear, whether you admit it now or later. I think you know that. I think it's why you're so silent. I think you must have suspected it on the stage two weeks ago, and verified it in Jersey while you were gone. They're going to hate you, after a while, because you are still beautiful, and they're going to persecute you because you are different—and helpless. Once the novelty wears off, my dear, your audience will be simply a mob."

He was not looking at her. He had bent forward a little, looking out the window and down. His hair stirred in the wind that blew very strongly up this high, and whined thinly around the open edge of the glass.

"I meant what I did for you," he said, "to be for everyone who meets with accidents that might have ruined them. I should have known my gift would mean worse ruin than any mutilation could be. I know now that there's only one legitimate way a human being can create life. When he tries another way, as I did, he has a lesson to learn. Remember the lesson of the student Frankenstein? He learned, too. In a way, he was lucky—the way he learned. He didn't have to watch what happened afterward. Maybe he wouldn't have had the courage—I know I haven't."

Harris found himself standing without remembering that he rose. He knew suddenly what was about to happen. He understood Maltzer's air of resolution, his new, unnatural calm. He knew, even, why Maltzer had asked him here today, so that Deirdre might not be left alone. For he remembered that Frankenstein, too, had paid with his life for the unlawful creation of life.

Maltzer was leaning head and shoulders from the window now, looking down with almost hypnotized fascination. His voice came back to them remotely in the breeze, as if a barrier already lay between them.

Deirdre had not moved. Her expressionless mask, in the mirror, watched him calmly. She *must* have understood. Yet she gave no sign, except that the weaving of her arms had almost stopped now, she moved so slowly. Like a dance seen in a nightmare, under water.

It was impossible, of course, for her to express any emotion. The fact that her face showed none now should not, in fairness, be held against her. But she watched so wholly without feeling— Neither of them moved toward the window. A false step, now, might send him over. They were quiet, listening to his voice.

"We who bring life into the world unlawfully," said Maltzer, almost thoughtfully, "must make room for it by withdrawing our own. That seems to be an inflexible rule. It works automatically. The thing we create makes living unbearable. No, it's nothing you can help, my dear. I've asked you to do something I created you incapable of doing. I made you to perform a function, and I've been asking you to forego the one thing you were made to do. I believe that if you do it, it will destroy you, but the whole guilt is mine, not yours. I'm not even asking you to give up the screen, any more. I know you can't, and live. But I can't live and watch you. I put all my skill and all my love in one final masterpiece, and I can't bear to watch it destroyed. I can't live and watch you do only what I made you to do, and ruin yourself because you must do it.

"But before I go, I have to make sure you understand." He leaned a little farther, looking down, and his voice grew more remote as the glass came between them. He was saying almost unbearable things now, but very distantly, in a cool, passionless tone filtered through wind and glass, and with the distant humming of the city mingled with it, so that the words were curiously robbed of poignancy. "I can be a coward," he said, "and escape the consequences of what I've done, but I can't go and leave you—not understanding. It would be even worse than the thought of your failure, to think of you bewildered and confused when the mob turns on you. What I'm telling you, my dear, won't be any real news—I think you sense it already, though you may not admit it to yourself. We've been too close to lie to each other, Deirdre—I know when you aren't telling the truth. I know the distress that's been growing in your mind. You are not wholly human, my dear. I think you know that. In so many ways, in spite of all I could do, you must always be less than human. You've lost the senses of perception that kept you in touch with humanity. Sight and hearing are all that remain, and sight, as I've said before, was the last and coldest of the senses to develop. And you're so delicately poised on a sort of thin edge of reason. You're only a clear, glowing mind animating a metal body, like a candle flame in a glass. And as precariously vulnerable to the wind."

He paused. "Try not to let them ruin you completely," he said after a while. "When they turn against you, when they find out you're more helpless than they—I wish I could have made you stronger, Deirdre. But I couldn't. I had too much skill for your good and mine, but not quite enough skill for that."

He was silent again, briefly, looking down. He was balanced precariously now, more than halfway over the sill and supported only by one hand on the glass. Harris watched with an agonized uncertainty, not sure whether a sudden leap might catch him in time or send him over. Deirdre was still weaving her golden patterns, slowly and unchangingly, watching the mirror and its reflection, her face and masked eyes enigmatic.

"I wish one thing, though," Maltzer said in his remote voice. "I wish—before I finish—that you'd tell me the truth, Deirdre. I'd be happier if I were sure I'd—reached you. Do you understand what I've said? Do you believe me? Because if you don't, then I know you're lost beyond all hope. If you'll admit your own doubt—and I know you do doubt—I can think there may be a chance for you after all. Were you lying to me, Deirdre? Do you know how… how wrong I've made you?"

There was silence. Then very softly, a breath of sound, Deirdre answered. The voice seemed to hang in midair, because she had no lips to move and localize it for the imagination.

"Will you listen, Maltzer?" she asked.

"I'll wait," he said. "Go on. Yes or no?"

Slowly she let her arms drop to her sides. Very smoothly and quietly she turned from the mirror and faced him. She swayed a little, making her metal robe ring.

"I'll answer you," she said. "But I don't think I'll answer that. Not with yes or no, anyhow. I'm going to walk a little, Maltzer. I have something to tell you, and I can't talk standing still. Will you let me move about without—going over?"

He nodded distantly. "You can't interfere from that distance," he said. "But keep the distance. What do you want to say?"

She began to pace a little way up and down her end of the room, moving with liquid ease. The table with the cigarette box was in her way, and she pushed it aside carefully, watching Maltzer and making no swift motions to startle him.

"I'm not—well, sub-human," she said, a faint note of indignation in her voice. "I'll prove it in a minute, but I want to say something else first. You must promise to wait and listen. There's a flaw in your argument, and I resent it. I'm not a Frankenstein monster made out of dead flesh. I'm myself—alive. You didn't create my life, you only preserved it. I'm not a robot, with compulsions built into me that I have to obey. I'm free-willed and independent, and, Maltzer—I'm human."

Harris had relaxed a little. She knew what she was doing. He had no idea what she planned, but he was willing to wait now. She was not the indifferent automaton he had thought. He watched her come to the table again in a lap of her pacing, and stoop over it, her eyeless mask turned to Maltzer to make sure variation of her movement did not startle him.

"I'm human," she repeated, her voice humming faintly and very sweetly. "Do you think I'm not?" she asked, straightening and facing them both. And then suddenly, almost overwhelmingly, the warmth and the old ardent charm were radiant all around her. She was robot no longer, enigmatic no longer. Harris could see as clearly as in their first meeting the remembered flesh still gracious and beautiful as her voice evoked his memory. She stood swaying a little, as she had always swayed, her head on one side, and she was chuckling at them both. It was such a soft and lovely sound, so warmly familiar.

"Of course I'm myself," she told them, and as the words sounded in their ears neither of them could doubt it. There was hypnosis in her voice. She turned away and began to pace again, and so powerful was the human personality which she had called up about her that it beat out at them in deep pulses, as if her body were a furnace to send out those comforting waves of warmth. "I have handicaps, I know," she said. "But my audiences will never know. I won't let them know. I think you'll believe me, both of you, when I say I could play Juliet just as I am now, with a cast of ordinary people, and make the world accept it. Do you think I could, John? Maltzer, don't you believe I could?"

She paused at the far end of her pacing path and turned to face them, and they both stared at her without speaking. To Harris she was the Deirdre he had always known, pale gold, exquisitely graceful in remembered postures, the inner radiance of her shining through metal as brilliantly as it had ever shone through flesh. He did not wonder, now, if it were real. Later he would think again that it might be only a disguise, something like a garment she had put off with her lost body, to wear again only when she chose. Now the spell of her compelling charm was too strong for wonder. He watched, convinced for the moment that she was all she seemed to be. She could play Juliet if she said she could. She could sway a whole audience as easily as she swayed himself. Indeed, there was something about her just now more convincingly human than anything he had noticed before. He realized that in a split second of awareness before he saw what it was.

She was looking at Maltzer. He, too, watched, spellbound in spite of himself, not dissenting. She glanced from one to the other. Then she put back her head and laughter came welling and choking from her in a great, full-throated tide. She shook in the strength of it. Harris could almost see her round throat pulsing with the sweet low-pitched waves of laughter that were shaking her. Honest mirth, with a little derision in it.

Then she lifted one arm and tossed her cigarette into the empty fireplace.

Harris choked, and his mind went blank for one moment of blind denial. He had not sat here watching a robot smoke and accepting it as normal. He could not! And yet he had. That had been the final touch of conviction which swayed his hypnotized mind into accepting her humanity. And she had done it so deftly, so naturally, wearing her radiant humanity with such rightness, that his watching mind had not even questioned what she did.

He glanced at Maltzer. The man was still halfway over the window ledge, but through the opening of the window he, too, was staring in stupefied disbelief and Harris knew they had shared the same delusion.

Deirdre was still shaking a little with laughter. "Well," she demanded, the rich chuckling making her voice quiver, "am I all robot, after all?"

Harris opened his mouth to speak, but he did not utter a word. This was not his show. The byplay lay wholly between Deirdre and Maltzer; he must not interfere. He turned his head to the window and waited.

And Maltzer for a moment seemed shaken in his conviction. "You... you *are* an actress," he admitted slowly. "But I... I'm not convinced I'm wrong. I think—" He paused. The querulous note was in his voice again, and he seemed racked once more by the old doubts and dismay. Then Harris saw him stiffen. He saw the resolution come back, and understood why it had come. Maltzer had gone too far already upon the cold and lonely path he had chosen to turn back, even for stronger evidence than this. He had reached his conclusions only after mental turmoil too terrible to face again. Safety and peace lay in the course he had steeled himself to follow. He was too tired, too exhausted by months of conflict, to retrace his path and begin all over. Harris could see him groping for a way out, and in a moment he saw him find it.

"That was a trick," he said hollowly. "Maybe you could play it on a larger audience, too. Maybe you have more tricks to use. I might be wrong. But Deirdre"—his voice grew urgent—"you haven't answered the one thing I've got to know. You can't answer it. You *do* feel—dismay. You've learned your own inadequacy, however well you can hide it from us—even from us. I *know*. Can you deny that, Deirdre?"

She was not laughing now. She let her arms fall, and the flexible golden body seemed to droop a little all over, as if the brain that a moment before had been sending out strong, sure waves of confidence had slackened its power, and the intangible muscles of her limbs slackened with it. Some of the glowing humanity began to fade. It receded within her and was gone, as if the fire in the furnace of her body were sinking and cooling.

"Maltzer," she said uncertainly, "I can't answer that—yet. I can't—"

And then, while they waited in anxiety for her to finish the sentence, she *blazed*. She ceased to be a figure in stasis—she *blazed*.

It was something no eyes could watch and translate into terms the brain could follow; her motion was too swift. Maltzer in the window was a whole long room-length away. He had thought himself safe at such a distance, knowing no normal human being could reach him before he moved. But Deirdre was neither normal nor human.

In the same instant she stood drooping by the mirror she was simultaneously at Maltzer's side. Her motion negated time and destroyed space. And as a glowing cigarette tip in the dark describes closed circles before the eye when the holder moves it swiftly, so Deirdre blazed in one continuous flash of golden motion across the room.

But curiously, she was not blurred. Harris, watching, felt his mind go blank again, but less in surprise than because no normal eyes and brain could perceive what it was he looked at.

(In that moment of intolerable suspense his complex human brain paused suddenly, annihilating time in its own way, and withdrew to a cool corner of its own to analyze in a flashing second what it was he had just seen. The brain could do it timelessly; words are slow. But he knew he had watched a sort of tesseract of human motion, a parable of fourth-dimensional activity. A one-dimensional point, moved through space, creates a two-dimensional line, which in motion creates a three-dimensional cube. Theoretically the cube, in motion, would produce a fourth-dimensional figure. No human creature had ever seen a figure of three dimensions moved through space and time before—until this moment. She had not blurred; every motion she made was distinct, but not like moving figures on a strip of film. Not like anything that those who use our language had ever seen before, or created words to express. The mind saw, but without perceiving. Neither words nor thoughts could resolve what happened into terms for human brains. And perhaps she had not actually and literally moved through the fourth dimension. Perhaps—since Harris was able to see her—it had been almost and not quite that unimaginable thing. But it was close enough.)

While to the slow mind's eye she was still standing at the far end of the room, she was already at Maltzer's side, her long, flexible fingers gentle but very firm upon his arms. She waited— The room shimmered. There was sudden violent heat beating upon Harris' face. Then the air steadied again and Deirdre was saying softly, in a mournful whisper:

"I'm sorry—I had to do it. I'm sorry—I didn't mean you to know—"

Time caught up with Harris. He saw it overtake Maltzer too, saw the man jerk convulsively away from the grasping hands, in a ludicrously futile effort to forestall what had already happened. Even thought was slow, compared with Deirdre's swiftness.

The sharp outward jerk was strong. It was strong enough to break the grasp of human hands and catapult Maltzer out and down into the swimming gulfs of New York. The mind leaped ahead to a logical conclusion and saw him twisting and turning and diminishing with dreadful rapidity to a tiny point of darkness that dropped away through sunlight toward the shadows near the earth. The mind even conjured up a shrill, thin cry that plummeted away with the falling body and hung behind it in the shaken air.

But the mind was reckoning on human factors.

Very gently and smoothly Deirdre lifted Maltzer from the window sill and with effortless ease carried him well back into the safety of the room. She set him down before a sofa and her golden fingers unwrapped themselves from his arms slowly, so that he could regain control of his own body before she released him.

He sank to the sofa without a word. Nobody spoke for an unmeasurable length of time. Harris could not. Deirdre waited patiently. It was Maltzer who regained speech first, and it came back on the old track, as if his mind had not yet relinquished the rut it had worn so deep.

"All right," he said breathlessly. "All right, you can stop me this time. But I know, you see. I know! You can't hide your feeling from me, Deirdre. I know the trouble you feel. And next time—next time I won't wait to talk!"

Deirdre made the sound of a sigh. She had no lungs to expel the breath she was imitating, but it was hard to realize that. It was hard to understand why she was not panting heavily from the terrible exertion of the past minutes; the mind knew why, but could not accept the reason. She was still too human.

"You still don't see," she said. "Think, Maltzer, think!"

There was a hassock beside the sofa. She sank upon it gracefully, clasping her robed knees. Her head tilted back to watch Maltzer's face. She saw only stunned stupidity on it now; he had passed through too much emotional storm to think at all.

"All right," she told him. "Listen—I'll admit it. You're right. I *am* unhappy. I do know what you said was true—but not for the reason you think. Humanity and I are far apart, and drawing farther. The gap will be hard to bridge. Do you hear me, Maltzer?"

Harris saw the tremendous effort that went into Maltzer's wakening. He saw the man pull his mind back into focus and sit up on the sofa with weary stiffness.

"You... you do admit it, then?" he asked in a bewildered voice. Deirdre shook her head sharply.

"Do you still think of me as delicate?" she demanded. "Do you know I carried you here at arm's length halfway across the room? Do you realize you weigh *nothing* to me? I could"—she glanced around the room and gestured with sudden, rather appalling violence—"tear this building down," she said quietly. "I could tear my way through these walls, I think. I've found no limit yet to the strength I can put forth if I try." She held up her golden hands and looked at them. "The metal would break, perhaps," she said reflectively, "but then, I have no feeling—"

Maltzer gasped, *"Deirdre—"*

She looked up with what must have been a smile. It sounded clearly in her voice. "Oh, I won't. I wouldn't have to do it with my hands, if I wanted. Look—listen!"

She put her head back and a deep, vibrating hum gathered and grew in what one still thought of as her throat. It deepened swiftly and the ears began to ring. It was deeper, and the furniture vibrated. The walls began almost imperceptibly to shake. The room was full and bursting with a sound that shook every atom upon its neighbor with a terrible, disrupting force.

The sound ceased. The humming died. Then Deirdre laughed and made another and quite differently pitched sound. It seemed to reach out like an arm in one straight direction—toward the window. The opened panel shook. Deirdre intensified her hum, and slowly, with imperceptible jolts that merged into smoothness, the window jarred itself shut.

"You see?" Deirdre said. "You see?"

But still Maltzer could only stare. Harris was staring too, his mind beginning slowly to accept what she implied. Both were too stunned to leap ahead to any conclusions yet.

Deirdre rose impatiently and began to pace again, in a ringing of metal robe and a twinkling of reflected lights. She was pantherlike in her suppleness. They could see the power behind that lithe motion now; they no longer thought of her as helpless, but they were far still from grasping the truth.

"You were wrong about me, Maltzer," she said with an effort at patience in her voice. "But you were right too, in a way you didn't guess. I'm not afraid of humanity. I haven't anything to fear from them.

Why"—her voice took on a tinge of contempt—"already I've set a fashion in women's clothing. By next week you won't see a woman on the street without a mask like mine, and every dress that isn't cut like a chlamys will be out of style. I'm not afraid of humanity! I won't lose touch with them unless I want to. I've learned a lot—I've learned too much already."

Her voice faded for a moment, and Harris had a quick and appalling vision of her experimenting in the solitude of her farm, testing the range of her voice, testing her eyesight—could she see microscopically and telescopically?—and was her hearing as abnormally flexible as her voice?

"You were afraid I had lost feeling and scent and taste," she went on, still pacing with that powerful, tigerish tread. "Hearing and sight would not be enough, you think? But why do you think sight is the last of the senses? It may be the latest, Maltzer—Harris—but *why do you think it's the last?*"

She may not have whispered that. Perhaps it was only their hearing that made it seem thin and distant, as the brain contracted and would not let the thought come through in its stunning entirety.

"No," Deirdre said, "I haven't lost contact with the human race. I never will, unless I want to. It's too easy… too easy."

She was watching her shining feet as she paced, and her masked face was averted. Sorrow sounded in her soft voice now.

"I didn't mean to let you know," she said. "I never would have, if this hadn't happened. But I couldn't let you go believing you'd failed. You made a perfect machine, Maltzer. More perfect than you knew."

"But Deirdre—" breathed Maltzer, his eyes fascinated and still incredulous upon her, "but Deirdre, if we did succeed—what's wrong? I can feel it now—I've felt it all along. You're so unhappy—you still are. Why, Deirdre?"

She lifted her head and looked at him, eyelessly, but with a piercing stare. "Why are you so sure of that?" she asked gently.

"You think I could be mistaken, knowing you as I do? But I'm not Frankenstein… you say my creation's flawless. Then what—"

"Could you ever duplicate this body?" she asked.

Maltzer glanced down at his shaking hands. "I don't know. I doubt it. I—"

"Could anyone else?"

He was silent. Deirdre answered for him. "I don't believe anyone could. I think I was an accident. A sort of mutation halfway between flesh and metal. Something accidental and… and unnatural, turning off on a wrong course of evolution that never reaches a dead end. Another brain in a body like this might die or go mad, as you thought I would. The synapses are too delicate. You were—call it lucky—with me. From what I know now, I don't think a… a baroque like me could happen again." She paused a moment. "What you did was kindle the fire for the Phoenix, in a way. And the Phoenix rises perfect and renewed from its own ashes. Do you remember why it had to reproduce itself that way?"

Maltzer shook his head.

"I'll tell you," she said. "It was because there was only one Phoenix. Only one in the whole world." They looked at each other in silence. Then Deirdre shrugged a little.

"He always came out of the fire perfect, of course. I'm not weak, Maltzer. You needn't let that thought bother you any more. I'm not vulnerable and helpless. I'm not sub-human." She laughed dryly. "I suppose," she said, "that I'm—super-human."

"But—not happy."

"I'm afraid. It isn't unhappiness, Maltzer—it's fear. I don't want to draw so far away from the human race. I wish I needn't. That's why I'm going back on the stage—to keep in touch with them while I can. But I wish there could be others like me. I'm… I'm lonely, Maltzer."

Silence again. Then Maltzer said, in a voice as distant as when he had spoken to them through glass, over gulfs as deep as oblivion:

"Then I am Frankenstein, after all."

"Perhaps you are," Deirdre said very softly. "I don't know. Perhaps you are."

She turned away and moved smoothly, powerfully, down the room to the window. Now that Harris knew, he could almost hear the sheer power purring along her limbs as she walked. She leaned the golden forehead against the glass—it clinked faintly, with a musical sound—and looked down into the depths Maltzer had hung above. Her voice was reflective as she looked into those dizzy spaces which had offered oblivion to her creator.

"There's one limit I can think of," she said, almost inaudibly. "Only one. My brain will wear out in another forty years or so. Between now and then I'll learn... I'll change... I'll know more than I can guess today. I'll change— That's frightening. I don't like to think about that." She laid a curved golden hand on the latch and pushed the window open a little, very easily. Wind whined around its edge. "I could put a stop to it now, if I wanted," she said. "If I wanted. But I can't, really. There's so much still untried. My brain's human, and no human brain could leave such possibilities untested. I wonder, though... I do wonder—"

Her voice was soft and familiar in Harris' ears, the voice Deirdre had spoken and sung with, sweetly enough to enchant a world. But as preoccupation came over her a certain flatness crept into the sound. When she was not listening to her own voice, it did not keep quite to the pitch of trueness. It sounded as if she spoke in a room of brass, and echoes from the walls resounded in the tones that spoke there.

"I wonder," she repeated, the distant taint of metal already in her voice.

(1944)

FLIGHT

Joanna Kavenna

Joanna Kavenna's writing career began in 2005 with a voyage to the Arctic and the publication *The Ice Museum*, an imaginative hybrid of travel narrative and cultural history that drew comparisons to the work of Robert Macfarlane, himself one of Kavenna's early champions. *Inglorious* (2007) is a delightfully self-referential novel in which a high-minded bookworm chooses not to leave for the Arctic, preferring a life of ill-defined philosophical reflection: needless to say, things don't work out at all well. In *Come to the Edge* (2012), a Robin Hood scheme to combat rural inequality in Cumbria comes memorably unstuck. Kavenna's most recent novel, modelled loosely on Jorge Luis Borges's "The Garden of Forking Paths", is *A Field Guide to Reality* (2016) in which a professor creates, and contrives to lose, a "manual for fixing existential angst".

I was above those old streets, so high, the wind was whispering – I could see the stars beyond the clouds, swelling and declining, as if they were breathing. The clouds were congealing around me, there was a low hum. I might have become afraid, I might have cried out – except everything was happening too fast, I was being propelled along, the wind was singing in my ears—

Any moment I would vanish like steam into the clouds.

It was beautiful up there, far above those streets – I've trodden them so many times, but now they were like patterns of dark and light, the people forming clusters, shifting again and again – Silver and blue, so pretty, I wished I could tell them how beautiful they looked. Even the grim-hearted, struggling home. You couldn't see the lines on their faces, you couldn't hear them coughing into their mobile phones, or lying to please each other and all of them trying so hard not to care about the flaming discourtesy of the fates, the way they'd been stamped on over and over. You just saw them as endless flitting shadows, one human, another, another ghost of a person, another. They filled the doorways of shops, then they vanished again.

Would it console you at all, if you were tired, lost in the murk and someone told you – from above, from up here – where I fly – you are beautiful – would that console you?

I had become quite unusual, perhaps I was escaping this prison, my body, perhaps I was ascending towards something else entirely. White light, above the clouds, perhaps it was the sun, so bright—

Now I was in the silence, the clouds merging into further clouds, the sky like an ocean, the world inverted. Myself, somewhat transformed. I saw the houses so far below, terrace after terrace – everything so geometrical, as if someone had been busy with a gargantuan ruler. It was so neat and tidy. The people had been tidied into their terraces and told to be good. There you are, you interchangeable being. A box. Be good now. The whole city bearing down on each little box, with its inherent culture of humans. They mustn't stray too far. Of course, they absolutely mustn't fly away.

You could tell the houses where people lived alone. They were bedraggled. They slumped as if they had been bombed and knocked carelessly back together. Sallow light emanating from the windows. Inside, the serried ranks of people cooking up a meal in a saucepan. Washing up even as they ate it. Erasing themselves from the kitchen. The lights flashed from one room to another, charting their solitary progress. Up in the bedrooms, they found their place again. Flat on their backs, gripping the mattress as the planet went whirling through space... Every morning they left, to trade their lives for more money. Not too much, just barely enough.

House after house after house – it went on and on until the bedraggled fields. Russet countryside for a while, and then another town. Each house was ringed around with a halo, there was coloured smoke streaming from the chimneys.

I was above the ancient centre of the city. Oxford. The colours were brighter here, some of the chimneys spewed gold and silver. The low hum again – the smoke descending towards the ground below, where it turned black, deep black, vanished as if the ground had swallowed it.

Swooping down—

There was a window before me, I didn't know which college I was in. One of the oldest, most lavish. Cloistered vaulting. A smell of gently rotting timber. A voice within – I could just discern it – a man, saying something. Really rattling on. The words were blurred, he sounded as if he was speaking underwater.

I could hear him careering around his room, knocking stuff over. He sounded half mad, and anyway his window was engulfed in black vapour. There was a musty ruined smell, something ancient, rotting, murky. I turned upside down, so all the buildings were standing on their heads, and the roads were like smoke trails, and I tried to get to his window, I was I suppose like a bat, but then I just got stuck in the black fog, I couldn't make anything out at all. I could really taste it – what was this man doing, weltering around in it—

I tried to soar out of it – I was feeling dreadful, I thought I might faint—

But then I saw something else – in the depths of the murk – a yellow glow – really in the depths of that toxic black smoke, there was something shining like gold—

I was being drawn away—

Oh God, the return – gravity coming to snatch me back – Newton dragging me down. I was flying along the streets—

Like tunnels now – my nose nearly scraping the hedgerows – I could hardly keep myself afloat. It was close. I just made it. Over my gate, the shared gate of my block – across the sterile stretch of car park dirt – I scraped my fingers on the door mat – found I was briefly upside down again.

Ah the agony. I was back.

I was slumped in my chair again. Awake—

Quite blameless and almost functional.

I should start at something like the beginning—

I was living in a real little dump in what I understood to be a good part of town. My flat was buried deep at the bottom of a grandiose villa; the sort of place a single family once owned, lavished it with frills and ornaments, parked their servants somewhere squalid and rang bells whenever they discerned an insufficiency. But now it had been sliced into flats and each flat had been doled out for some extravagant price because the place was in such a good part of town. I lived in the basement and so the whole weight of the building seemed to bear down upon me; it made my head ache. And then the place was dank even at the height of summer, and the moment the temperature dropped it got pretty vicious down there. I coughed myself sick at night. There were two windows in the whole place; one for the bedroom, one for the living room. The rest was lit by angle-poise, you felt you had burrowed deep down and now you had to stay there, with the blind crawling creatures and other things that fear the light.

I'd furnished it with cheap rickety furniture, tailored to an aesthetic that was not my own. I was an interloper in this good part of town. Around the corner, people told me, lived an international rock star. It was highly probable he hadn't furnished his house with flat-packed monstrosities, but anyway I had. Then the place was adorned with accidental sculptures. Piles of unsold books. Floor to ceiling, a stacking system so perilous that there was a chance one day I'd get buried alive.

People like books, I had thought. Second hand, cheaply priced. You advertise them on the internet, and people buy them. Well, people quite like books. Not as much as other things, it turns out. And they quite like them but perhaps they buy them from other people. So instead of a thriving online business I had a series of abandoned stacks of books, reproaching my poor judgement, and some of them even blocked out my few remaining strands of light. I had a few scattered emails, occasional requests, nothing that amounted to a real living. Just these phrases—

Is there an earlier edition? Thanks... Nick Graham

Dear Amelia, I wonder if you could let me know...

Amelia, whoever you are – from whoever I am—

And sometimes I would knock into one of the piles and then the thing was like a miniature city falling down, skyscrapers tumbling. And then I got to stack them all up again.

Perhaps it was making me slightly sick in the brain. All this staring at the flickering screen. Skimming from one site to another, all of them beamed to me from wherever and typing so frantically as if time was very precious – even though I wasted every second – and hunting, I was really hunting around in that etherworld trying to find something – an answer. What was it? A secret? A sign that others felt as I did? Some word I had never heard before, that would encapsulate it all? I wasn't greedy, I just wanted a single word. Just a few times I alighted on something, it made me half-hopeful, but then it faded under the general teeming mass of gossip and lunatic facts, perversions masquerading as common sense, things I'd half-read and not really understood. I cheated myself, called this justifiable distraction.

The sun rising and fading beyond the window, far beyond, and because it was always raining I spent most of the summer underground.

One morning I was stunned by the force of repetition, I was cross-eyed, I'd come out in a rash, I kept scratching myself, perhaps I had psoriasis, or boredom-induced leprosy, something like that, and so I turned to a thing I'd downloaded. It was called FlytheEarth. Crazy pounding rock music. Then a demonstration – flying over countless towns. Deserts. Blue frozen wastes and raging tempest-driven seas. For a few days it quelled my wanderlust and mounting frustration. I stopped wanting to punch my hand through the screen. I kept flying, even while spewing out tedious information, order numbers, costs, likely dates of arrival I was flying over Death Valley, observing the variegated colours of the sand. From time to time, but quite regally, as if it was all so far beneath me, I would pause my flight and type—

And then I would launch myself skywards again.

I did it for weeks. Perhaps I did it a little too much. Eighteen hours a day drifting around above computer-generated images of the planet, sporadically interrupted by order requests might be bad for the brain. If it was better than reading about millionaires with plastic faces then it was still not exactly edifying. I woke each morning in my solitary bed, I reached for my phone and checked it for messages, and then the next thing I did, even before I made a cup of coffee or stuffed food into my belly, I just turned on the computer and ignited FlytheEarth again and off I went—

The pasty sun was sliding under the planet again, I was almost about to switch on the lamp, though I was mesmerised anyway, hardly needed it, I was absorbed by a vision of the Californian coast, I was coming in to hover by Monterey, imagining the waves moving slowly backward and forward, lulling me into a trance – beautiful I thought. I could have hovered there – I'd come to think of myself, inside the thing, hovering within it, not sitting beyond it in my dank little room – all day – most of the night – just the waves, in and out, like breathing, of course, the breathing of the planet, and the sound was so tranquil, as if someone was whispering to me, saying it was all alright, there was nothing to worry about. I imagined the froth dancing on the rocks, then dissolving bubble by bubble, curdling away into nothing... You are just a bubble, whispered the waves. You are dissolving even as you flutter. But it didn't matter. I didn't care if I dissolved entirely, into that beautiful view – I was happy to be dispersed across the sand, with the waves churning me into nothingness – I was so relaxed, I nearly fell off my chair—

The moonlight lapping at my feet. The tides turning. The planet circling and then perhaps I slept, perhaps I woke, I was sweating like anything. I was hot and then I got so cold I had to shift in my seat, blow into my hands. Then I coughed.

Typed a few dozen emails. Coughed again. I had some autumn cold, it was clear. The damp was encroaching, everywhere I turned. And I had this buzzing in my ears, I was twitching, my wrists hurt already and I'd only just started – I was weak and I went straight to Arizona. Christ, there was nothing moving there, for miles around. Just desolate tracts of rock. I must have slept again, I don't know, I was confused and sweating and then I somehow got myself to New York, I was flying among the skyscrapers, concrete blanks, one and then another – I saw the people with their phones stuck to their faces, and each of them blaring something to someone else, all these words, and then I saw the boats moving along the Hudson, I was there – plainly – and the place was breathing all around me – the thing was happening as I whirled among the buildings. I saw people in the offices, moving from cradle to open plan office to grave. I could see those jowly old guys, spooning chestnuts into paper cups, I could smell burnt sugar, all the way from Central Park—

I was dreaming, with my hands stretched out in front of me. I was tumbling upwards, everything inverted, as if I was ascending and would never stop, until I reached dark matter, wherever that was. I saw my breath turning to coloured smoke. I knew I had to get back to Oxford, somehow I turned, I went across the Atlantic, all the boats moving beneath me, I could barely see, and then I caught a glimpse of them – the green matted fields of England – I breathed a sigh of relief – I saw brilliant gold ahead of me. I swooped up the Thames as far as Wolvercote, I saw the dusk gathering on Port Meadow, a weir, rats scuffling by the water. The lock was almost deserted, a few canal boats tied up for the night. I saw the moss crawling up the walls. Cows churning through the mud. I heard someone deep below, drinking cider on the bank. Muttering to himself – I heard it all. *Not much to say about the other things. Of course you can expect the sun to rise each morning. Nice flowers they are. And the bees, too. Of course. Best to walk there…*

The mist was thick over the meadow, obscuring the winter lake where the floods had bubbled up through the soil. The geese with their heads in their feathers. Back and forth, I went five times up and down that river. It was just the mist and the lights reflecting on the water. I was like a moth, I couldn't stop fluttering up and down.

I think I slept then, or somehow it all stopped. As if I had fallen towards the fields, I slept with the cows snuffling in the grass around me, with the man muttering his nonsense above my head. The image got fixed again, but I was sleeping in it – so I was lying on a satellite image, something like that – really I suppose I must have slept at my computer, I'd left the curtains open and so the early sun came in, briefly, like a searchlight. As soon as I awoke, I was in the air again – I saw the houses one by one, each one shining like gold, filled with treasure – down Abingdon Road, all the grimy little side-streets like arms pointing directions towards the lake and the railway tracks. I was going round and round, ricocheting off the clouds—

People moving on the streets. Bicycles massing over Folly Bridge. The gargoyles spluttering on the old roofs. And the grind of buses. I was at the College with the black vapour. A grand old college, a conglomeration of electrical towers, you could hear them crackling, and now and then sparks would fly out, red and orange and gold, like fireworks. A door was opening. A man emerged from a staircase, spitting out soot. I'd seen him before – I was quite certain. His chin in his scarf, unkempt hair, down to his collar. A battered suit, in cord. When he lifted his face I saw he was fine-boned, trashed and angry beyond measure. He was biting his lip, he looked as if he had been crying.

I was following him at a discreet distance, my pursuit entirely tactful, skirting the corners well behind him. He was hurrying as if he might be late. Then he turned – there was a sign – I was trying to read the words – MERCER—

I was summoned back – I couldn't see—

All the next day, I was nowhere. I spent the whole day lying in my bed, rubbing my face on the pillow. Too stunned to move myself towards the desk. I would lift my head and think I must get up, soon, but then I'd let it fall down again. I kept thinking of that man with his room smoking like an industrial accident. At one level, I didn't care. I had enough to think about. Why would I bother with him at all? But I kept thinking about him anyway. Why him? Of all the people wandering the streets. Why not the man muttering on the banks of the Isis? Why not anyone else at all?

The cord suit? His face? His long thin hands—

Hello? Hello?

Where are you?

A, can you let me know when you get in I need to give you a call? Thanks P

Hello?

Was he even real?

The sun – playing on the windows. So the glass looked like hammered metal. Reflecting the forms of the street beyond – I kept myself busy until the evening—

As the sun set I went off again – it was so swift, I fell into it, I didn't try at all – I was aloft – far above – paddling through the ether, moving somehow forwards – deep and beyond – the myriad and multi-coloured city all below me, the chimneys puffing out their smoke, the shadows and the people moving from one dark place and into one more pool of light. I was overwrought, perhaps sleep deprived – I turned my head to the side. There was something hot and fierce around me, behind me – I felt a burning sensation at the back of my head, so hot, my hair was drenched in sweat, my palms were sodden. At the College – the gold was brighter this time, shining within the clouds of black smoke—

At the window I turned, twisted, went inside—

I sat beside him.

He was hunched over his screen, pale light flickering on his face – he was typing quickly, a Scotch in one hand, a piece of paper beside him—

I couldn't quite read the words. There was something official at the top – the sign of a court – an insignia – crossed-keys, or swords, something about justice—

The big court with the sign above the gates. They'd forced him onto the scales, weighed him.

I wondered what he'd done. Something bad, desperately bad, perhaps – this formerly anonymous man, blameless for so many years, who had been dragged before the courts and summarily condemned.

It had made him snivel. Perhaps he regretted it entirely. Legs so long, he could hardly cross them under the desk. He was tall, strong, but his hands were soft. The room was thick with papers. He had a gown hanging on the door. The poor long-legged malcontent – he was a scholar. Perhaps it was philosophy that had made him suffer. And that scrap of paper.

I could see it now – it said – decree nisi, nothing more. Just another marriage, ended.

So he wasn't a murderer, after all—

He typed, he drank, he buried his face in his hands—

I realized – it was a shock – suddenly, I was confined, I was in his chair – I was this poor and possibly foolish man—

I had a sheaf of papers to one side, and on the other, well, if I'd had a gun, what would I have done? But anyway I didn't have a gun. I had a cheque book. I was meant to pay the rent. I had a phone call to make. The head of department wanted to discuss downsizing. It made my hands tremble, or was that the whisky? I was meant to dial his number and say, 'Yes, good evening. How are you?'

I said, 'Hello, Paul James here' – now I knew my name, his name, but something else was fading from my mind, even as I spoke. I was trying to clutch at it, as the voice on the line said, 'Veins,' it said. 'Paul, our veins are being severed.'

'That's bad,' I said.

He was saying something about how no one's job was certain, about how I mustn't fly away, not too high, and I said, 'No no, I'll be there. You're right.'

I stayed until he went to bed. Just outside the bedroom window. I watched him move into the bathroom – I didn't follow him in there. Let the man spit his toothpaste in private. Let him wipe the grime from his face.

I saw him come into the room, fragile in his boxers. Thin arms, light hair to the elbows. A refined hairless chest. He gathered himself into bed, slung his legs under the cover. He meant to read, he seized a book from the table beside him, then he was too cold, and drunk, and tired – he couldn't focus on the lines. He stared at the page for a few minutes. But he didn't progress. Then he slapped the book down, turned out the light.

He lay there in the darkness, half-awake, too tired to light up the room again.

Winnowing wind. The papers whirled and I found I was receding, through the window – I had never been so winnowed – I was drifting backwards – I didn't want to return, I was dragged – wafting against it, I couldn't prevent—

I was slammed back—

My screen, sallow, edged around with blackness, my room, full of black smoke – I closed my eyes—

Paul James woke before dawn with a spun-out head. As if he'd been whirled in a gyre. All night he'd been perplexed by his dreams. He'd been looking down on himself, from above, he'd been flying – he'd been—

He'd flown above the Thames, to Wolvercote. He'd sat by the weir watching the water curdling below. Rats skittering along the banks. The air was thin and cold. In his dream he didn't mind it. The leaves were turning red and yellow. Cows looming from the bushes. And the horses clacking against the fences.

He felt how the night was turning swiftly, it was in the process of becoming another dawn, then another day – the long lovely banks of the river – he was floating above them – clouds swirling, the water gurgling like a drain.

He'd woken time after time, he'd wondered if he was going mad. He was looking at himself as if he had been split in two. That sounded as if he was falling apart, inside first, then the rest. He couldn't fall apart. They'd make things worse for him...

He had to keep to the specifics. Certainties. Facts, if he could find them.

He checked his clock. He had a tutorial to give in a few hours' time. Though he had hardly slept, though his dreams had been strange and far too clear, so clear he felt he was still half-inside them, he didn't feel tired. When he opened the curtains he saw the pock-marked moon fading above the houses.

The colour of the sky – changing—

We crossed the room and turned on the light.

(2013)

PRAXIS

Karen Joy Fowler

"Praxis" is **Karen Joy Fowler**'s first published story. A year later she won the John W. Campbell Award for her first collection, *Artificial Things*. *Sarah Canary* (1991) established her style: science fiction written with such sincerity and rigour that it doesn't feel like science fiction at all. In *Wit's End* (2008) euphoric, Bacchic online communities pit games against reality. In *We Are All Completely Beside Ourselves* (2013) an ape and a human girl are raised together, and the human narrator's subsequent life is depicted in terms that make no easy, human sense. Fowler and her husband, who have two grown children and five grandchildren, live in Santa Cruz, California.

The price of a single ticket to the suicides would probably have funded my work for a month or more, but I do not let myself think about this. After all, I didn't pay for the ticket. Tonight I am the guest of the Baron Claude Himmlich and determined to enjoy myself.

I saw *Romeo and Juliet* five years ago, but only for one evening in the middle of the run. It wasn't much. Juliet had a cold and went to bed early. Her nurse kept wrapping her in hot rags and muttering under her breath. Romeo and Benvolio got drunk and made up several limericks. I thought some of them were quite good, but I'd been drinking a little myself.

Technically it was impressive. The responses of the simulants were wonderfully lifelike and the amphitheater had just been remodeled to allow the audience to walk among the sets, viewing the action from any angle. But the story itself was hardly dramatic. It wouldn't be, of course, in the middle of the run.

Tonight is different. Tonight is the final night. The audience glitters in jewels, colorful capes, extravagant hairstyles. Only the wealthy are here tonight, the wealthy and their guests. There are four in our own theater party: our host, the Baron; his beautiful daughter, Svanneshal; a wonderfully eccentric old woman dressed all in white who calls herself the Grand Duchess de Vie; and me. I work at the university in records and I tutor Svanneshal Himmlich in history.

The Grand Duchess stands beside me now as we watch Juliet carried in to the tombs. "Isn't she lovely?" the Duchess says. "And very sweet, I hear. Garriss wrote her program. He's a friend of the Baron's."

"An absolute genius." The Baron leans towards us, speaking softly. There is an iciness to Juliet, a sheen her false death has cast over her. She is like something carved from marble. Yet even from here I can see the slightest rise and fall of her breasts. How could anyone believe she was really dead? But Romeo will. He always does.

It will be a long time before Romeo arrives and the Baron suggests we walk over to the Capulets' to watch Juliet's nurse weeping and carrying on. He offers his arm to the Duchess though I can see his security cyber dislikes this.

It is one of the Baron's own models, identical in principle to the simulants on stage—human body, software brain. Before the Baron's work the cybers were slow to respond and notoriously easy to outwit. The Baron made his fortune streamlining the communications link-up and introducing an element of deliberate irrationality into the program. There are those who argue this was an ill-considered, even dangerous addition. But the Baron has never lacked for customers. People would rather take a chance on a cyber than on a human and the less we need to depend on the poor, the safer we become.

The Duchess is looking at the cyber's uniform, the sober blues of the House of Himmlich. "Watch this," she says to me, smiling. She reaches into her bodice. I can see how the cyber is alert to the movement, how it relaxes when her hand reappears with a handkerchief. She reverses the action; we watch the cyber tense again, relaxing when the hand reemerges.

The Baron shakes his head, but his eyes are amused. "Darling," he says, "you must not play with it."

"Then I shall walk with Hannah instead." The Duchess slips her hand around my arm. Her right hand is bare and feels warm pressed into my side. Her left hand is covered by a long white glove; its silky fingers rest lightly on the outside of my arm.

The Baron precedes us, walking with Svanneshal, the cyber close behind them. The Duchess leans against me and takes such small steps we cannot keep up. She looks at the Baron's back. "You've heard him called a 'self-made man'?" she asks me. "Did it ever occur to you that people might mean it literally?"

She startles me. My eyes go at once to the Baron, recognizing suddenly his undeniable perfection—his dark, smooth skin, his even teeth, the soft timbre of his voice. But the Duchess is teasing me. I see this when I look back at her.

"I like him very much," I answer. "I imagine him to be exactly like the ancient aristocracy at their best—educated, generous, courteous…"

"I wouldn't know about that. I have never studied history; I have only lived it. How old would you guess I am?"

It is a question I hate. One never knows what the most polite answer would be. The Duchess' hair, twisted about her head and held into place with ivory combs, is as black as Svanneshal's, but this can be achieved with dyes. Her face, while not entirely smooth, is not overly wrinkled. Again I suspect cosmetic enhancements. Her steps are undeniably feeble. "You look quite young," I say. "I couldn't guess."

"Then look at this." The Duchess stops walking and removes the glove from her left hand. She holds her palm flat before me so that I see the series of ciphers burnt into her skin. IPS3552. It is the brand of a labor duplicate. I look up at her face in astonishment and this amuses her. "You've never seen anything like that before, have you, historian? But you've heard perhaps how, in the last revolution, some of the aristocracy branded themselves and hid in the factories? *That's* how old I am."

In fact, I have heard the story, a two-hundred-year-old story, but the version I know ends without survivors. Most of those who tried to pass were detected immediately; a human cannot affect the dead stare of the duplicates for very long. Those few who went in to the factories gave themselves up eventually, preferring, after all, to face the mob rather than endure the filth, the monotony, and the endless labor, "I would be most interested in interviewing you," I say. "Your adventures should be part of the record." *If true,* but of course that is something I do not say.

"Yes." The Duchess preens herself, readjusting an ivory comb, replacing her glove. We notice the Baron, still some distance away, returning to us. He is alone and I imagine he has left the cyber with Svanneshal. The Duchess sweeps her bare hand in the direction of the hurrying figure. "I am a true member of the aristocracy," she tells me. "Perhaps the only surviving member. I am not just some wealthy man who chooses to call himself *Baron*."

This I discredit immediately as vanity. Revolution after revolution—no one can verify a blood claim. Nor can I see why anyone would want to. I am amazed at the willingness of people to make targets of themselves, as if every time were the last time and now the poor are permanently contained.

"I must apologize." The Baron arrives, breathless. "I had no idea you had fallen so far behind."

"Why should you apologize," the Duchess chides him, "if your guest is too old for such entertainments and too proud to use a chair as she should?" She shifts herself from my arm to his. "Verona is so lovely," she says. "Isn't it?"

We proceed slowly down the street. I am still thinking of the Duchess' hand. When we rejoin Svanneshal it is as though I have come out of a trance. She is so beautiful tonight I would rather not be near her. The closer I stand, the less I can look. Her eyes are very large inside the dark hood of her gown which covers her hair and shoulders in a fine net of tiny jewels. In the darkened amphitheater the audience shines like a sky full of stars, but Svanneshal is an entire constellation—Svanneshal, the Swan's throat, and next to her, her father, the Dragon. I look around the amphitheater. Everyone is beautiful tonight.

Juliet's nurse is seated in a chair, rocking slowly back and forth in her agony. She is identical to the nurse I saw before and I tell the Baron so.

"Oh, I'm sure she *is* the one you saw before. I saw her once as Amanda in *The Glass Menagerie*. You didn't imagine they started from scratch every time, did you? My dear Hannah, anyone who can be recycled after the run certainly will be. The simulations are expensive enough as it is." The Baron smiles at me, the smile of the older, the wiser, to the young and naive. "What's amazing is the variation you get each time, even with identical parts. Of course, that's where the drama comes in."

Before, when I saw *Romeo and Juliet,* Friar Lawrence was killed on the second night, falling down a flight of stairs. That's mainly why I went. I was excited by the possibilities opened by the absence of the Friar. Yet the plot was surprisingly unchanged.

It makes me think of Hwang-li and I say to the Baron, "Did you know it was a historian who created the simulations?"

"I don't have your knowledge of history," he answers. "Svanneshal tells me you are quite gifted. And you have a specialty... forgive me. I know Svanneshal has told me."

"Mass movements. They don't lend themselves to simulation." The Duchess has not heard of Hwang-li either, but then only a historian would have. It was so many revolutions ago. I could argue that the historians are the true revolutionary heroes, retaining these threads of our past, bringing them through the upheaval. Many historians have died to protect the record. And their names are lost to us forever. I am glad for a chance to talk about Hwang-li.

"Hwang-li was not thinking of entertainment, of course. He was pondering the inevitability of history. Is the course of history directed by personalities or by circumstances?" I ask the Baron. "What do you think?"

The Baron regards me politely. "In the real world," he says, "personalities and circumstances are inseparable. The one creates the other and vice versa. Only in simulation can they be disjoined."

"It follows then," I tell him, "that if you could intervene to change one, you would simultaneously change both and, therefore, the course of history. Could you make a meaningful change? How much can depend upon a single individual taking a single action at a single moment? Or not taking it?"

"Depending on the individual, the action, and the moment," the Duchess says firmly, "everything could change."

I nod to her. "That is what Hwang-li believed. He wished to test it by choosing an isolated case, a critical moment in which a series of seeming accidents resulted in a devastating war. He selected the Mancini murder, which was manageable and well-documented. There were seven personality profiles done on Philip Mancini at the time and Hwang-li had them all."

The Baron has forgotten Juliet's nurse entirely and turns to me with gratifying attention. "But this is fascinating," he says. "Svanneshal, you must hear this." Svanneshal moves in closer to him; the cyber seems relieved to have both standing together.

"Go on," says the Baron.

"I was telling your father about Hwang-li."

"Oh, I know this story already." Svanneshal smiles at the Baron coquettishly. "It's the murder that interests him," she says to me. "Aberrant personalities are sort of a hobby of his."

The Baron tells me what he already knows of the murder, that Frank Mancini was killed by his brother Philip.

"Yes, that's right," I say encouragingly. "This information survives in a saying we have—enmity is sometimes described as "the love of the Mancinis."

It is the Duchess who remembers the saying. But beyond that, she says she knows nothing of the case. I direct my statements to her. "Frank Mancini was a security guard, back in the days when humans functioned in that capacity. He was responsible for security in the Irish sector. He had just learned of the terrorist plot against Pope Peter. The Pope was scheduled to speak in an open courtyard at noon; he was to be shot from the window of a nearby library. Frank was literally reaching for the phone at the moment Philip Mancini burst into his study and shot him four times for personal reasons."

Svanneshal is bored with the discussion. Although she is extremely intelligent, it is not yet something she values. But she will. I look at her with the sudden realization that it is the only bit of inherited wealth she can be certain of holding on to. She is playing with her father's hair, but he catches her hand. "Go on," he says to me.

"Philip had always hated his brother. The murder was finally triggered by a letter Philip received from their mother—a letter we know he wrongly interpreted. What if he had read the letter more carefully? What if it had arrived ten minutes later? Hwang-li planned to replay the scene, running it through a number of such minute variations. Of course he had no simulants, nor did he need them. It was all to be done by computer."

"The whole project seems to me to raise more questions than it answers." Svanneshal is frowning. "What if the Pope had survived? How do you assess the impact of that? You cannot say there would have been no revolution. The Pope's death was a catalyst, but not a cause."

I am pleased to see that she not only knows the outlines of the incident, but has obviously been giving it some thought. I begin to gesture emphatically with my hands as though we were in class, but I force myself to stop. This is, after all, a social occasion. "So, war is not averted, but merely delayed?" I ask her. "Another variation. Who would have gained from such a delay? What else might have been different if the same war was fought at a later time? Naturally nothing can be proved absolutely—that is the nature of the field. But it is suggestive. When we can answer these questions we will be that much closer to the day when we direct history along the course we choose."

"We already do that," the Duchess informs me quiietly. "We do that every day of our lives." Her right hand smooths the glove over her left hand. She interlaces the fingers of the two.

"What happened in the experiment?" the Baron asks.

"Hwang-li never finished it. He spent his life perfecting the Mancini programs and died in a fire before he had finished. Another accident. Then there were the university purges. There's never been that kind of money for history again." I look into Svanneshal's eyes, deep within her hood. "It's too bad, because I've an experiment of my own I've wanted to do. I wanted to simulate Antony and Cleopatra, but make her nose an inch longer."

This is an old joke, but they do not respond to it. The Baron says politely that it would provide an interesting twist the next time *Antony and Cleopatra* is done. He'll bring it up with the Arts Committee.

Svanneshal says, "You see, Daddy, you owe Hwang-li everything. He did the first work in synthetic personalities."

It occurs to me that the Baron may think Svanneshal and I are trying to persuade him to fund me and I am embarrassed. I search for something to say to correct this impression, but we are interrupted by a commotion onstage.

Lady Capulet has torn her dress at the collar, her hair is wild and uncombed. Under her tears, her face is ancient, like a tragic mask. She screams at her husband that it is his fault their baby is dead. If he hadn't been so cold, so unyielding…

He stands before her, stooped and silent. When at last she collapses, he holds her, stroking the hair into place about her sobbing face. There is soft applause for this gentleness. It was unexpected.

"Isn't it wonderful?" Svanneshal's face glows with appreciation. "Garriss again," she informs me although I know Garriss did the programming for the entire Capulet family. It is customary to have one writer for each family so that the similarities in the programming can mirror the similarities of real families created by genetics and upbringing.

The simulants are oblivious to this approval. Jaques tells us, every time, that the world is a stage, but here the stage is a world, complete in itself, with history and family, with even those random stagehands, death and disease. This is what the simulants live. If they were told that Juliet is no one's daughter, that everything they think and say is software, could they believe it? Would it be any less tragic?

Next to me I hear the beginning of a scream. It is choked off as suddenly as it started. Turning, I see the white figure of the Duchess slumping to the ground, a red stain spreading over her bodice. The gloved hand is pressed against her breast; red touches her fingers and moves down her arm. Her open eyes see nothing. Beside her, the cyber is returning a bloody blade to the case on its belt.

It was all so fast. "It killed her," I say, barely able to comprehend the words. "She's dead!" I kneel next to the Duchess, not merely out of compassion, but because my legs have given way. I look up at the Baron, expecting to see my own horror reflected in his face, but it is not.

He is calmly quiet. "She came at me," he says. "She moved against me. She meant to kill me."

"No!" I am astounded. Nothing is making sense to me. "Why would she do that?"

He reaches down and strips the wet glove from the warm hand. There is her lifeline—IPS3552. "Look at this," he says to me, to the small group of theatergoers who have gathered around us. "She was not even human."

I look at Svanneshal for help. "You knew her. She was no cyber. There is another explanation for the brand. She told me…" I do not finish my sentence, suddenly aware of the implausibility of the Duchess' story. But what other explanation is there? Svanneshal will not meet my eyes. I find something else to say. "Anyway, the cybers have never been a threat to us. They are not programmed for assassination." It is another thought I do not finish, my eyes distracted by the uniform of the House of Himmlich. I get to my feet slowly, keeping my hands always visible and every move I make is watched by the Baron's irrational cyber. "The autopsy will confirm she is human," I say finally. "Was human."

Svanneshal reaches for my arm below the shoulder, just where the Duchess held me. She speaks into my ear, so low that I am the only one who hears her. Her tone is ice. "The cybers are all that stand between us and the mob. You remember that!"

Unless I act quickly, there will be no autopsy. Already maintenance duplicates are scooping up the body in the manner reserved for the disposal of cybers. Three of them are pulling the combs from her hair, the jewels from her ears and neck and depositing them in small, plastic bags. The Baron is regarding me, one hand wiping his upper lip. Sweat? No, the Baron feels nothing, shows no sign of unease.

Svanneshal speaks to me again. This time her voice is clearly audible, "It tried to kill my father," she says. "You weren't watching. I was."

It would be simpler to believe her. I try. I imagine that the whole time we were talking about the Mancinis, the Duchess was planning to murder her host. For political reasons? For personal reasons? I remember the conversation, trying to refocus my attention to her, looking for the significant gesture, the words which, listened to later, will mean so much more. But, no. If she had wanted to kill the Baron, surely she would have done it earlier, when the Baron returned to us without his cyber.

I return Svanneshal's gaze. "Did anyone else see that?" I ask, raising my voice. I look from person to person. "Did anyone see anything?"

No one responds. Everyone is waiting to see what I will do. I am acutely conscious of the many different actions I can take; they radiate out from me as if I stood at the center of a star, different paths, all ultimately uncontrollable. Along one path I have publicly accused the Baron of murder through misjudgment. His programs are opened for examination; his cybers are recalled. He is ruined. And, since he has produced the bulk of the city's security units, Svanneshal is quite right. We are left unprotected before the mob. Could I cause that?

I imagine another, more likely path. I am pitted alone against the money and power of the Himmlichs. In this vision the Baron has become a warlord with a large and loyal army. He is untouchable. Wherever I try to go, his cybers are hunting me.

The body has been removed, a large, awkward bundle in the arms of the maintenance duplicates. The blood is lifting from the tile, like a tape played backwards, like a thing which never happened. The paths radiating out from me begin to dim and disappear. The moment is past. I can do nothing now.

In the silence that has fallen around us, we suddenly hear that Romeo is coming. Too early, too early. What will it mean? The knot of spectators around us melts away; everyone is hurrying to the tombs. Svanneshal takes my arm and I allow myself to be pulled along. Her color is high and excited, perhaps from exertion, perhaps in anticipation of death. When we reach the tombs we press in amongst the rest.

On one side of me, Svanneshal continues to grip my arm. On the other is a magnificent woman imposingly tall, dressed in Grecian white. Around her bare arm is a coiled snake, fashioned of gold, its scales in the many muted colors gold can wear. A fold of her dress falls for a moment on my own leg, white, like the gown of the Grand Duchess de Vie and I find myself crying. "Don't do it," I call to Romeo. "It's a trick! It's a trap. For God's sake, look at her." The words come without volition, part of me standing aside, marveling, pointing out that I must be mad. He can't hear me. He is incapable of hearing me. Only the audience turns to look, then turns away politely, hushed to hear Romeo's weeping. He is so young, his heart and hands so strong, and he says his lines as though he believed them, as though he made them up.

The Baron leans into Svanneshal. "Your friend has been very upset by the incidents of the evening." His voice is kind. "As have we all. And she is cold. Give her my cape."

I am not cold, though I realize with surprise that I am shaking. Svanneshal wraps the red cape about me. "You must come home with us tonight," she says. "You need company and care." She puts an arm about me and whispers, "Don't let it upset you so. The simulants don't feel anything."

Then her breath catches in her throat. Romeo is drinking his poison. I won't watch the rest. I turn my head aside and in the blurred lens of my tears, one image wavers, then comes clear. It is the snake's face, quite close to me, complacency in its heavy-lidded eyes. "Don't look at me like that," I say to a species which vanished centuries ago. "Who are you to laugh?"

I think that I will never know the truth. The Duchess might have been playing with the cyber again. Her death might have been a miscalculation. Or the Baron might have planned it, have arranged the whole evening around it. I would like to know. I think of something Hwang-li is supposed to have said. "Never confuse the record with the truth. It will always last longer." I am ashamed that I did nothing for the Duchess, accuse myself of cowardice, tears dropping from my cheeks onto the smooth flesh of my palms. In the historical record, I tell myself, I will list her death as a political assassination. And it will be remembered that way.

Next to me Svanneshal stiffens and I know Juliet has lifted the knife. This is truly the end of her; the stab wounds will prevent her re-use and her voice is painfully sweet, like a song.

One moment of hesitation, but that moment is itself a complete world. It lives onstage with the simulants, it lives with the mob in their brief and bitter lives, it lives where the wealthy drape themselves in jewels. If I wished to find any of them, I could look in that moment. "But how," I ask the snake, "would I know which was which?"

(1985)

TONGTONG'S SUMMER

Xia Jia

Xia Jia is the pen-name of Wang Yao, a Chinese author born in Xi'an, Shaanxi, in 1984. Xia trained as a physicist, studying atmospheric sciences at Peking University before drifting into fine art, translating, and acting. She earned a PhD in comparative literature and world literature at Peking University with a dissertation titled "Chinese Science Fiction and Its Cultural Politics Since 1990". She now teaches at Xi'an Jiaotong University. She disarmingly dubs her genre stories "porridge sf" because it mixes genre elements with generous helpings of myth, legend and folklore. Several have won the Galaxy, China's most prestigious science fiction award.

Mom said to Tongtong, "In a couple of days, Grandpa is moving in with us."

After Grandma died, Grandpa lived by himself. Mom told Tongtong that because Grandpa had been working for the revolution all his life, he just couldn't be idle. Even though he was in his eighties, he still insisted on going to the clinic every day to see patients. A few days earlier, because it was raining, he had slipped on the way back from the clinic and hurt his leg.

Luckily, he had been rushed to the hospital, where they put a plaster cast on him. With a few more days of rest and recovery, he'd be ready to be discharged.

Emphasizing her words, Mom said, "Tongtong, your grandfather is old, and he's not always in a good mood. You're old enough to be considerate. Try not to add to his unhappiness, all right?"

Tongtong nodded, thinking, *But haven't I always been considerate?*

Grandpa's wheelchair was like a miniature electric car, with a tiny joystick by the armrest. Grandpa just had to give it a light push, and the wheelchair would glide smoothly in that direction. Tongtong thought it tremendous fun.

Ever since she could remember, Tongtong had been a bit afraid of Grandpa. He had a square face with long, white, bushy eyebrows that stuck out like stiff pine needles. She had never seen anyone with eyebrows that long.

She also had some trouble understanding him. Grandpa spoke Mandarin with a heavy accent from his native topolect. During dinner, when Mom explained to Grandpa that they needed to hire a caretaker for him, Grandpa kept on shaking his head emphatically and repeating: "Don't worry, eh!" Now Tongtong did understand *that* bit.

Back when Grandma had been ill, they had also hired a caretaker for her. The caretaker had been a lady from the countryside. She was short and small, but really strong. All by herself, she could lift Grandma—who had put on some weight—out of the bed, bathe her, put her on the toilet, and change her clothes. Tongtong had seen the caretaker lady accomplish these feats of strength with her own eyes. Later, after Grandma died, the lady didn't come any more.

After dinner, Tongtong turned on the video wall to play some games. *The world in the game is so different from the world around me,* she thought. In the game, a person just died. They didn't get sick, and they didn't sit in a wheelchair. Behind her, Mom and Grandpa continued to argue about the caretaker.

Dad walked over and said, "Tongtong, shut that off now, please. You've been playing too much. It'll ruin your eyes."

Imitating Grandpa, Tongtong shook her head and said, "Don't worry, eh!"

Mom and Dad both burst out laughing, but Grandpa didn't laugh at all. He sat stone-faced, with not even a hint of smile.

A few days later, Dad came home with a stupid-looking robot. The robot had a round head, long arms, and two white hands. Instead of feet it had a pair of wheels so that it could move forward and backward and spin around.

Dad pushed something in the back of the robot's head. The blank, smooth, egg-like orb blinked three times with a bluish light, and a young man's face appeared on the surface. The resolution was so good that it looked just like a real person.

"Wow," Tongtong said. "You are a robot?"

The face smiled. "Hello there! Ah Fu is my name."

"Can I touch you?"

"Sure!"

Tongtong put her hand against the smooth face, and then she felt the robot's arms and hands. Ah Fu's body was covered by a layer of soft silicone, which felt as warm as real skin.

Dad told Tongtong that Ah Fu was made by Guokr Technologies, Inc., and it was a prototype. Its biggest advantage was that it was as smart as a person: it knew how to peel an apple, how to pour a cup of tea, even how to cook, wash the dishes, embroider, write, play the piano… Anyway, having Ah Fu around meant that Grandpa would be given good care.

Grandpa sat there, still stone-faced, still saying nothing.

After lunch, Grandpa sat on the balcony to read the newspaper. He dozed off after a while. Ah Fu came over noiselessly, picked up Grandpa with his strong arms, carried him into the bedroom, set him down gently in bed, covered him with a blanket, pulled the curtains shut, and came out and shut the door, still not making any noise.

Tongtong followed Ah Fu and watched everything.

Ah Fu gave Tongtong's head a light pat. "Why don't you take a nap, too?"

Tongtong tilted her head and asked, "Are you really a robot?"

Ah Fu smiled. "Oh, you don't think so?"

Tongtong gazed at Ah Fu carefully. Then she said, very seriously, "I'm sure you are not."

"Why?"

"A robot wouldn't smile like that."

"You've never seen a smiling robot?"

"When a robot smiles, it looks scary. But your smile isn't scary. So you're definitely not a robot."

Ah Fu laughed. "Do you want to see what I really look like?"

Tongtong nodded. But her heart was pounding.

Ah Fu moved over by the video wall. From on top of his head, a beam of light shot out and projected a picture onto the wall. In the picture, Tongtong saw a man sitting in a messy room.

The man in the picture waved at Tongtong. Simultaneously, Ah Fu also waved in the exact same way. Tongtong examined the man in the picture: he wore a thin, grey, long-sleeved bodysuit, and a pair of grey gloves. The gloves were covered by many tiny lights. He also wore a set of huge goggles. The face behind the goggles was pale and thin, and looked just like Ah Fu's face.

Tongtong was stunned. "Oh, so you're the real Ah Fu!"

The man in the picture awkwardly scratched his head, and said, a little embarrassed, "Ah Fu is just the name we gave the robot. My real name is Wang. Why don't you call me Uncle Wang, since I'm a bit older?"

Uncle Wang told Tongtong that he was a fourth-year university student doing an internship at Guokr Technologies' R&D department. His group developed Ah Fu.

He explained that the aging population brought about serious social problems: many elders could not live independently, but their children had no time to devote to their care. Nursing homes made them feel lonely and cut off from society, and there was a lot of demand for trained, professional caretakers.

But if a home had an Ah Fu, things were a lot better. When not in use, Ah Fu could just sit there, out of the way. When it was needed, a request could be given, and an operator would come online to help the elder. This saved the time and cost of having caretakers commute to homes, and increased the efficiency and quality of care.

The Ah Fu they were looking at was a first-generation prototype. There were only three thousand of them in the whole country, being tested by three thousand families.

Uncle Wang told Tongtong that his own grandmother had also been ill and had to go to the hospital for an extended stay, so he had some experience with elder care. That was why he volunteered to come to her home to take care of Grandpa. As luck would have it, he was from the same region of the country as Grandpa, and could understand his topolect. A regular robot probably wouldn't be able to.

Uncle Wang laced his explanation with many technical words, and Tongtong wasn't sure she understood everything. But she thought the idea of Ah Fu splendid, almost like a science fiction story.

"So, does Grandpa know who you really are?"

"Your mom and dad know, but Grandpa doesn't know yet. Let's not tell him, for now. We'll let him know in a few days, after he's more used to Ah Fu."

Tongtong solemnly promised, "Don't worry, eh!"

She and Uncle Wang laughed together.

Grandpa really couldn't just stay home and be idle. He insisted that Ah Fu take him out walking. But after just one walk, he complained that it was too hot outside, and refused to go anymore.

Ah Fu told Tongtong in secret that it was because Grandpa felt self-conscious, having someone push him around in a wheelchair. He thought everyone in the street stared at him.

But Tongtong thought, *Maybe they were all staring at Ah Fu.*

Since Grandpa couldn't go out, being cooped up at home made his mood worse. His expression grew more depressed, and from time to time he burst out in temper tantrums. There were a few times when he screamed and yelled at Mom and Dad, but neither said anything. They just stood there and quietly bore his shouting.

But one time, Tongtong went to the kitchen and caught Mom hiding behind the door, crying.

Grandpa was now nothing like the Grandpa she remembered. It would have been so much better if he hadn't slipped and got hurt. Tongtong hated staying at home. The tension made her feel like she was suffocating. Every morning, she ran out the door, and would stay out until it was time for dinner.

Dad came up with a solution. He brought back another gadget made by Guokr Technologies: a pair of glasses. He handed the glasses to Tongtong and told her to put them on and walk around the house. Whatever she saw and heard was shown on the video wall.

"Tongtong, would you like to act as Grandpa's eyes?"

Tongtong agreed. She was curious about anything new.

Summer was Tongtong's favorite season. She could wear a skirt, eat watermelon and popsicles, go swimming, find cicada shells in the grass, splash through rain puddles in sandals, chase rainbows after a thunderstorm, get a cold shower after running around and working up a sweat, drink iced sour plum soup, catch tadpoles in ponds, pick grapes and figs, sit out in the backyard in the evenings and gaze at stars, hunt for crickets after dark with a flashlight... In a word: everything was wonderful in summer.

Tongtong put on her new glasses and went to play outside. The glasses were heavy and kept on slipping off her nose. She was afraid of dropping them.

Since the beginning of summer vacation, she and more than a dozen friends, both boys and girls, had been playing together every day. At their age, play had infinite variety. Having exhausted old games, they would invent new ones. If they were tired or too hot, they would go by the river and jump in like a plate of dumplings going into the pot. The sun blazed overhead, but the water in the river was refreshing and cool. This was heaven!

Someone suggested that they climb trees. There was a lofty pagoda tree by the river shore, whose trunk was so tall and thick that it resembled a dragon rising into the blue sky.

But Tongtong heard Grandpa's urgent voice by her ear: "Don't climb that tree! Too dangerous!"

Huh, so the glasses also act as a phone. Joyfully, she shouted back, "Grandpa, don't worry, eh!" Tongtong excelled at climbing trees. Even her father said that in a previous life she must have been a monkey.

But Grandpa would not let her alone. He kept on buzzing in her ear, and she couldn't understand a thing he was saying. It was getting on her nerves, so she took off the glasses and dropped them in the grass at the foot of the tree. She took off her sandals and began to climb, rising into the sky like a cloud.

This tree was easy. The dense branches reached out to her like hands, pulling her up. She went higher and higher and soon left her companions behind. She was about to reach the very top. The breeze whistled through the leaves, and sunlight dappled through the canopy. The world was so quiet.

She paused to take a breath, but then she heard her father's voice coming from a distance: "Tongtong, get... down... here..."

She poked her head out to look down. A little ant-like figure appeared far below. It really was Dad.

On the way back home, Dad really let her have it.

"How could you have been so foolish?! You climbed all the way up there by yourself. Don't you understand the risk?"

She knew that Grandpa told on her. Who else knew what she was doing?

She was livid. *He can't climb trees any more, and now he won't let others climb trees, either? So lame! And it was so embarrassing to have Dad show up and yell like that.*

The next morning, she left home super early again. But this time, she didn't wear the glasses.

"Grandpa was just worried about you," said Ah Fu. "If you fell and broke your leg, wouldn't you have to sit in a wheelchair, just like him?"

Tongtong pouted and refused to speak.

Ah Fu told her that through the glasses left at the foot of the tree, Grandpa could see that Tongtong was really high up. He was so worried that he screamed himself hoarse, and almost tumbled from his wheelchair.

But Tongtong remained angry with Grandpa. What was there to worry about? She had climbed plenty of trees taller than that one, and she had never once been hurt.

Since the glasses weren't being put to use, Dad packed them up and sent them back to Guokr. Grandpa was once again stuck at home with nothing to do. He somehow found an old Chinese Chess set and demanded Ah Fu play with him.

Tongtong didn't know how to play, so she pulled up a stool and sat next to the board just to check it out. She enjoyed watching Ah Fu pick up the old wooden pieces, their colors faded from age, with its slender, pale white fingers; she enjoyed watching it tap its fingers lightly on the table as it considered its moves. The robot's hand was so pretty, almost like it was carved out of ivory.

But after a few games, even she could tell that Ah Fu posed no challenge to Grandpa at all. A few moves later, Grandpa once again captured one of Ah Fu's pieces with a loud snap on the board.

"Oh, you suck at this," Grandpa muttered.

To be helpful, Tongtong also said, "You suck!"

"A real robot would have played better," Grandpa added. He had already found out the truth about Ah Fu and its operator.

Grandpa kept on winning, and after a few games, his mood improved. Not only did his face glow, but he was also moving his head about and humming folk tunes. Tongtong also felt happy, and her earlier anger at Grandpa dissipated.

Only Ah Fu wasn't so happy. "I think I need to find you a more challenging opponent," he said.

When Tongtong returned home, she almost jumped out of her skin. Grandpa had turned into a monster!

He was now dressed in a thin, grey, long-sleeved bodysuit, and a pair of grey gloves. Many tiny lights shone all over the gloves. He wore a set of huge goggles over his face, and he waved his hands about and gestured in the air.

On the video wall in front of him appeared another man, but not Uncle Wang. This man was as old as Grandpa, with a full head of silver-white hair. He wasn't wearing any goggles. In front of him was a Chinese Chess board.

"Tongtong, come say hi," said Grandpa. "This is Grandpa Zhao."

Grandpa Zhao was Grandpa's friend from back when they were in the army together. He had just had a heart stent put in. Like Grandpa, he was bored, and his family also got their own Ah Fu. He was also a Chinese Chess enthusiast, and complained about the skill level of his Ah Fu all day.

Uncle Wang had the inspiration of mailing telepresence equipment to Grandpa and then teaching him how to use it. And within a few days, Grandpa was proficient enough to be able to remotely control Grandpa Zhao's Ah Fu to play chess with him.

Not only could they play chess, but the two old men also got to chat with each other in their own native topolect. Grandpa became so joyous and excited that he seemed to Tongtong like a little kid.

"Watch this," said Grandpa.

He waved his hands in the air gently, and through the video wall, Grandpa Zhao's Ah Fu picked up the wooden chessboard, steady as you please, dexterously spun it around in the air, and set it back down without disturbing a piece.

Tongtong watched Grandpa's hands without blinking. *Are these the same unsteady, jerky hands that always made it hard for Grandpa to do anything?* It was even more amazing than magic.

"Can I try?" she asked.

Grandpa took off the gloves and helped Tongtong put them on. The gloves were stretchy, and weren't too loose on Tongtong's small hands. Tongtong tried to wiggle her fingers, and the Ah Fu in the video wall wiggled its fingers, too. The gloves provided internal resistance that steadied and smoothed out Tongtong's movements, and thus also the movements of Ah Fu.

Grandpa said, "Come, try shaking hands with Grandpa Zhao."

In the video, a smiling Grandpa Zhao extended his hand. Tongtong carefully reached out and shook hands. She could feel the subtle, immediate pressure changes within the glove, as if she were really shaking a person's hand—it even felt warm! *This is fantastic!*

Using the gloves, she directed Ah Fu to touch the chessboard, the pieces, and the steaming cup of tea next to them. Her fingertips felt the sudden heat from the cup. Startled, her fingers let go, and the cup fell to the ground and broke. The chessboard was flipped over, and chess pieces rolled all over the place.

"Aiya! Careful, Tongtong!"

"No worries! No worries!" Grandpa Zhao tried to get up to retrieve the broom and dustpan, but Grandpa told him to remain seated. "Careful about your hands!" Grandpa said. "I'll take care of it." He put on the gloves and directed Grandpa Zhao's Ah Fu to pick up the chess pieces one by one, and then swept the floor clean.

Grandpa wasn't mad at Tongtong, and didn't threaten to tell Dad about the accident she caused.

"She's just a kid, a bit impatient," he said to Grandpa Zhao. The two old men laughed.

Tongtong felt both relieved and a bit misunderstood.

Once again, Mom and Dad were arguing with Grandpa.

The argument went a bit differently from before. Grandpa was once again repeating over and over, "Don't worry, eh!" But Mom's tone grew more and more severe.

The actual point of the argument grew more confusing to Tongtong the more she listened. All she could make out was that it had something to do with Grandpa Zhao's heart stent.

In the end, Mom said, "What do you mean 'Don't worry'? What if another accident happens? Would you please stop causing more trouble?"

Grandpa got so mad that he shut himself in his room and refused to come out, even for dinner.

Mom and Dad called Uncle Wang on the videophone. Finally, Tongtong figured out what happened.

Grandpa Zhao was playing chess with Grandpa, but the game got him so excited that his heart gave out—apparently, the stent wasn't put in perfectly. There had been no one else home at the time. Grandpa was the one who operated Ah Fu to give CPR to Grandpa Zhao, and also called an ambulance.

The emergency response team arrived in time and saved Grandpa Zhao's life. What no one could have predicted was that Grandpa suggested that he go to the hospital to care for Grandpa Zhao—no, he didn't mean he'd go personally, but that they send Ah Fu over, and he'd operate Ah Fu from home.

But Grandpa himself needed a caretaker too. Who was supposed to care for the caretaker?

Further, Grandpa came up with the idea that when Grandpa Zhao recovered, he'd teach Grandpa Zhao how to operate the telepresence equipment. The two old men would be able to care for each other, and they would have no need of other caretakers.

Grandpa Zhao thought this was a great idea. But both families thought the plan absurd. Even Uncle Wang had to think about it for a while and then said, "Um… I have to report this situation to my supervisors."

Tongtong thought hard about this. Playing chess through Ah Fu was simple to understand. But caring for each other through Ah Fu? The more she thought about it, the more complicated it seemed. She was sympathetic to Uncle Wang's confusion.

Sigh, Grandpa is just like a little kid. He wouldn't listen to Mom and Dad at all.

Grandpa now stayed in his room all the time. At first, Tongtong thought he was still mad at her parents. But then, she found that the situation had changed completely.

Grandpa got really busy. Once again, he started seeing patients. No, he didn't go to the clinic; instead, using his telepresence kit, he was operating Ah Fus throughout the country and showing up in other elders' homes. He would listen to their complaints, feel their pulse, examine them, and write out prescriptions. He also wanted to give acupuncture treatments through Ah Fus, and to practice this skill, he operated his own Ah Fu to stick needles in himself!

Uncle Wang told Tongtong that Grandpa's innovation could transform the entire medical system. In the future, maybe patients no longer needed to go to the hospital and waste hours in waiting rooms. Doctors could just come to your home through an Ah Fu installed in each neighborhood.

Uncle Wang said that Guokr's R&D department had formed a dedicated task force to develop a specialized, improved model of Ah Fu for such medical telepresence applications, and they invited Grandpa onboard as a consultant. So Grandpa got even busier.

Since Grandpa's legs were not yet fully recovered, Uncle Wang was still caring for him. But they were working on developing a web-based system that would allow anyone with some idle time and interest in helping others to register to volunteer. Then the volunteers would be able to sign on to Ah Fus in homes across the country to take care of elders, children, patients, pets, and to help in other ways.

If the plan succeeded, it would be a step to bring about the kind of golden age envisioned by Confucius millennia ago: "And then men would care for all elders as if they were their own parents, love all children as if they were their own children. The aged would grow old and die in security; the youthful would have opportunities to contribute and prosper; and children would grow up under the guidance and protection of all. Widows, orphans, the disabled, the diseased—everyone would be cared for and loved."

Of course, such a plan had its risks: privacy and security, misuse of telepresence by criminals, malfunctions and accidents, just for starters. But since technological change was already here, it was best to face the consequences and guide them to desirable ends.

There were also developments that no one had anticipated.

Uncle Wang showed Tongtong lots of web videos: Ah Fus were shown doing all kinds of interesting things: cooking, taking care of children, fixing the plumbing and electric systems around the house, gardening, driving, playing tennis, even teaching children the arts of *go* and calligraphy and seal carving and *erhu* playing...

All of these Ah Fus were operated by elders who needed caretakers themselves, too. Some of them could no longer move about easily, but still had sharp eyes and ears and minds; some could no longer remember things easily, but they could still replicate the skills they had perfected in their youth; and most of them really had few physical problems, but were depressed and lonely. But now, with Ah Fu, everyone was out and about, *doing* things.

No one had imagined that Ah Fu could be put to all these uses. No one had thought that men and women in their seventies and eighties could still be so creative and imaginative.

Tongtong was especially impressed by a traditional folk music orchestra made up of more than a dozen Ah Fus. They congregated around a pond in a park and played enthusiastically and loudly. According to Uncle Wang, this orchestra had become famous on the web. The operators behind the Ah Fus were men and women who had lost their eyesight, and so they called themselves "The Old Blinds."

"Tongtong," Uncle Wang said, "your grandfather has brought about a revolution."

Tongtong remembered that Mom had often mentioned that Grandpa was an old revolutionary. "He's been working for the revolution all his life; it's time for him to take a break." But wasn't Grandpa a doctor? When did he participate in a "revolution"? And just what kind of work was "working for the revolution" anyway? And why did he have to do it all his life?

Tongtong couldn't figure it out, but she thought "revolution" was a splendid thing. Grandpa now once again seemed like the Grandpa she had known.

Every day, Grandpa was full of energy and spirit. Whenever he had a few moments to himself, he preferred to sing a few lines of traditional folk opera:

> *Outside the camp, they've fired off the thundering cannon thrice,*
> *And out of Tianbo House walks the woman who will protect her homeland.*
> *The golden helmet sits securely over her silver-white hair,*
> *The old iron-scaled war robe once again hangs on her shoulders.*
> *Look at her battle banner, displaying proudly her name:*
> *Mu Guiying, at fifty-three, you are going to war again!*

Tongtong laughed. "But Grandpa, you're eighty-three!"

Grandpa chuckled. He stood and posed as if he were an ancient general holding a sword as he sat on his warhorse. His face glowed red with joy.

In another few days, Grandpa would be eighty-four.

Tongtong played by herself at home.

There were dishes of cooked food in the fridge. In the evening, Tongtong took them out, heated them up, and ate by herself. The evening air was heavy and humid, and the cicadas cried without cease.

The weather report said there would be thunderstorms.

A blue light flashed three times in a corner of the room. A figure moved out of the corner noiselessly: Ah Fu.

"Mom and Dad took Grandpa to the hospital. They haven't returned yet."

Ah Fu nodded.

"Your mother sent me to remind you: don't forget to close the windows before it rains."

Together, the robot and the girl closed all the windows in the house. When the thunderstorm arrived, the raindrops struck against the windowpanes like drumbeats. The dark clouds were torn into pieces by the white and purple flashes of lightning, and then a bone-rattling thunder rolled overhead, making Tongtong's ears ring.

"You're not afraid of thunder?" asked Ah Fu.

"No. You?"

"I was afraid when I was little, but not now."

An important question came to Tongtong's mind: "Ah Fu, do you think everyone has to grow up?"

"I think so."

"And then what?"

"And then you grow old."

"And then?"

Ah Fu didn't respond.

They turned on the video wall to watch cartoons. It was Tongtong's favorite show: "Rainbow Bear Village." No matter how heavy it rained outside, the little bears of the village always lived together happily. Maybe everything else in the world was fake; maybe only the world of the little bears was real.

Gradually, Tongtong's eyelids grew heavy. The sound of rain had a hypnotic effect. She leaned against Ah Fu. Ah Fu picked her up in its arms, carried her into the bedroom, set her down gently in bed, covered her with a blanket, and pulled the curtains shut. Its hands were just like real hands, warm and soft.

Tongtong murmured, "Why isn't Grandpa back yet?"

"Sleep. When you wake up, Grandpa will be back."

Grandpa did not come back.

Mom and Dad returned. Both looked sad and tired.

But they got even busier. Every day, they had to leave the house and go somewhere. Tongtong stayed home by herself. She played games sometimes, and watched cartoons at other times. Ah Fu sometimes came over to cook for her.

A few days later, Mom called for Tongtong. "I have to talk to you."

Grandpa had a tumor in his head. The last time he fell was because the tumor pressed against a nerve. The doctor suggested surgery immediately.

Given Grandpa's age, surgery was very dangerous. But not operating would be even more dangerous. Mom and Dad and Grandpa had gone to several hospitals and gotten several other opinions, and after talking with each other over several nights, they decided that they had to operate.

The operation took a full day. The tumor was the size of an egg.

Grandpa remained in a coma after the operation.

Mom hugged Tongtong and sobbed. Her body trembled like a fish.

Tongtong hugged Mom back tightly. She looked and saw the white hairs mixed in with the black on her head. Everything seemed so unreal.

Tongtong went to the hospital with Mom.

It was so hot, and the sun so bright. Tongtong and Mom shared a parasol. In Mom's other hand was a thermos of bright red fruit juice taken from the fridge.

There were few pedestrians on the road. The cicadas continued their endless singing. The summer was almost over.

Inside the hospital, the air conditioning was turned up high. They waited in the hallway for a bit before a nurse came to tell them that Grandpa was awake. Mom told Tongtong to go in first.

Grandpa looked like a stranger. His hair had been shaved off, and his face was swollen. One eye was covered by a gauze bandage, and the other eye was closed. Tongtong held Grandpa's hand, and she was scared. She remembered Grandma. Like before, there were tubes and beeping machines all around.

The nurse said Grandpa's name. "Your granddaughter is here to see you."

Grandpa opened his eye and gazed at Tongtong. Tongtong moved, and the eye moved to follow her. But he couldn't speak or move.

The nurse whispered, "You can talk to your grandfather. He can hear you."

Tongtong didn't know what to say. She squeezed Grandpa's hand, and she could feel Grandpa squeezing back.

Grandpa! She called out in her mind. *Can you recognize me?*

His eyes followed Tongtong.

She finally found her voice. "Grandpa!"

Tears fell on the white sheets. The nurse tried to comfort her. "Don't cry! Your grandfather would feel so sad to see you cry."

Tongtong was taken out of the room, and she cried—tears streaming down her face like a little kid, but she didn't care who saw—in the hallway for a long time.

Ah Fu was leaving. Dad packed it up to mail it back to Guokr Technologies.

Uncle Wang explained that he had wanted to come in person to say goodbye to Tongtong and her family. But the city he lived in was very far away. At least it was easy to communicate over long distances now, and they could chat by video or phone in the future.

Tongtong was in her room, drawing. Ah Fu came over noiselessly. Tongtong had drawn many little bears on the paper, and colored them all different shades with crayons. Ah Fu looked at the pictures. One of the biggest bears was colored all the shades of the rainbow, and he wore a black eye patch so that only one eye showed.

"Who is this?" Ah Fu asked.

Tongtong didn't answer. She went on coloring, her heart set on giving every color in the world to the bear.

Ah Fu hugged Tongtong from behind. Its body trembled. Tongtong knew that Ah Fu was crying.

Uncle Wang sent a video message to Tongtong.

Tongtong, did you receive the package I sent you?

Inside the package was a fuzzy teddy bear. It was colored like the rainbow, with a black eye patch, leaving only one eye. It was just like the one Tongtong drew.

The bear is equipped with a telepresence kit and connected to the instruments at the hospital: his heartbeat, breath, pulse, body temperature. If the bear's eye is closed, that means your grandfather is asleep. If your grandfather is awake, the bear will open its eye.

Everything the bear sees and hears is projected onto the ceiling of the room at the hospital. You can talk to it, tell it stories, sing to it, and your grandfather will see and hear.

He can definitely hear and see. Even though he can't move his body, he's awake inside. So you must talk to the bear, play with it, and let it hear your laughter. Then your grandfather won't be alone.

Tongtong put her ear to the bear's chest: thump-thump. The heartbeat was slow and faint. The bear's chest was warm, rising and falling slowly with each breath. It was sleeping deeply.

Tongtong wanted to sleep, too. She put the bear in bed with her and covered it with a blanket. *When Grandpa is awake tomorrow,* she thought, *I'll bring him out to get some sun, to climb trees, to go to the park and listen to those grandpas and grandmas sing folk opera. The summer isn't over yet. There are so many fun things to do.*

"Grandpa, don't worry, eh!" she whispered. *When you wake up, everything will be all right.*

(2014)

Translated by Ken Liu

THESE 5 BOOKS GO 6 FEET DEEP

Ted Hayden

Ted Hayden lives in Southern California, writes short stories, and maintains a homepage at tedhaydenstories.com. The following mischief was cooked up for the science magazine *Nature*.

Grave robbery. If you think it's a relic of gothic novels, think again. Now that the first generation of body-modified tech-bros and computer-implanted one-percenters sleep under tombstones, there's a ton of gear in the ground. These books teach you everything you need to know to go get it — or, if rotten flesh makes you retch, to live vicariously through those who earn their living digging.

The Modern Grave Robber's How-To Guide
by Anonymous

You can't buy this practical page-turner on Amazon. Even if you find a store where it's sold (pro tip: low-key ask an associate in Home Depot's lawn and garden department), don't pay with your credit card — you might wind up on a government watch-list.

Written by a grave robber with loads of real-world experience, chapters include 'How to bribe cemetery staff' and 'Detaching valuable limbs'. But be careful — if your dead grandpa got dug up on a dark night, you might see his decapitated head in this guide's useful (and graphic!) pictures.

Second-Hand Subcutaneous Implants: Identification and Value Guide
by Norm Sadowski

Originally written for medical professionals, this has become a grave-robbing essential, the Kelley Blue Book of the cemetery set. Not even the freakiest of the freaky exhume corpses for a love of the stench — they're in it for the cash, and *Second-Hand Subcutaneous Implants* breaks down the numbers.

Although less-affluent families raid loved-ones' corpses before burial, and some debt-riddled morticians steal modifications before sending clients to the crypts, most corpses are buried with at least a few microchips still implanted in their bodies.

Dug up a geezer who died at 90? He'll probably have had memory-enhancing neural prostheses implanted after a stroke or an Alzheimer's diagnosis. Market price $5,000. Found an athlete who paraglided into a skyscraper window? Check her limbs for genetic mod microchips. Street value is $7,500.

Remember, though, this book wasn't written with crooks in mind, so approach its pages using common sense. For example, a brain-embedded password-tracking implant with safe-box codes is worth way more than spare parts if the deceased's family hasn't deactivated any accounts. But if they have? You'll get the list price and no more.

Coffins, Corpses and Crime: A Life
by Wojciech Bajor
Caught in the act of dismembering a just-buried Silicon Valley chief executive, convicted of crimes including larceny and mayhem, then released after his conviction was overturned on a technicality, Wojciech Bajor is a grave-robbing legend.

There's the story of how Uber's chief executive, more machine than man by the time he caught his final rideshare, spent his famously short evening underground. The morning after the Bay Area bigwig's funeral, cemetery guards discovered an empty hole by his headstone. Bajor spills all the juiciest details, explaining how he performed this and other heists by training implant-sniffing dogs and romancing lonely-heart morticians.

But the book's not all big capers and bigger stakes — Bajor got high from his own supply, keeping the best implants for himself and paying out-of-work surgeons to insert them into his brain and body. He says the second-hand microchips betrayed him, sneaking their original owners' angry spirits into his limbs and colluding on an undead plan that forced him to unconsciously make the mistakes that led to his arrest.

Welcome to the Underworld: My Year with the Body Snatchers
by Colton Venkatesh
To ingratiate himself into a clique of grave robbers, Venkatesh, a sociology professor at the University of California, Riverside, took part in their induction ceremony, locking himself inside a coffin filled with rotting cats, human limbs and web-weaving spiders.

After that long night, he tagged along as the crew broke into graveyards, visited black-market fairs where fences and thieves bargained over bioelectronic implants, and partied at some of the wildest bacchanals this side of the river Styx.

With an eye for striking details, Venkatesh guides his readers through grave-robbing fashion (all that death plus all that manual labour means these guys rock a serious health-goth look), secret handshakes (the secret is, they don't do it with their own hands) and superstitions (Wojciech Bajor isn't the only one who thinks ghosts haunt the stolen goods — most grave robbers keep roosters inside their homes, talismans that are said to keep vengeful spirits at bay).

The Digital Afterlife: How Body Modifications Became Conscious
by Willa Weaver

Don't believe in ghosts? Neither does Willa Weaver. Her pioneering work at the Berlin Institute for Advanced Study suggests that the microchips we use to increase our strength, amplify our memory and fight diseases might also haunt our minds.

In *The Digital Afterlife*, Weaver describes the case of Hanna Müller, who developed a neurogenic stutter after receiving a second-hand bioelectronic arthritis counteragent. Tracing the device's provenance, she discovered it had previously been implanted in a man who stuttered throughout his life.

Weaver's research has uncovered hundreds of parallel cases, in which implants transferred cases of Tourette's, turned tone-deaf amusiacs into musical prodigies, and gave broke welfare cases hyper-specific knowledge of stock-market trends.

But what's most startling is her final hypothesis. Almost all subcutaneous products send a constant stream of data to manufacturers, who use that information to perfect new products. Weaver believes that this combined knowledge has become a collective mind living and operating inside our bodies.

How else to explain the fact that, one year ago, dozens of people using the SR-12 Hearing Implant found themselves congregating on the side of an empty road in the Sonoran Desert? Something brought them there, and it wasn't a friendly e-mail chain or a one-time travel discount from American Airlines.

Her final warning: "To those who dig beneath the skin: dig carefully. Who knows what might try to dig its way out."

(2018)

SUCCESSION

Deep in our hearts, we know we're done.

Humans are like any other living thing. Plants and animals compete and expand. They consume resources. Once a population hits the carrying capacity of its environment, it keels over. This pattern is played out across the world, again and again. Most everything that's lived is extinct. Be honest: you know where we're headed.

We've had a good run. We've out-competed everything. We've expanded everywhere. To feed and clothe and educate ourselves, to be the best that we could be (fragile and fraught as that best has proved) we've eaten, burned and processed everything. Being smart, we count the entire planet as our environment. And yes: maybe, just maybe, being smart will save us from extinction – the fate that has awaited, and does await, every other species on our planet. But don't count on it.

What about our robots? They're not tied to our rules, or to the rules of anything living. Maybe they will survive, even if we do not. This would be a sad thing for us; but, in the grand scheme of things, it might also be a positive thing. It may be that the universe is not particularly interested in life: that life is simply the stepping stone for something else. It may be that the universe is not particularly interested in our particular variety of intelligence, either. In fact I'd bet the farm it's not.

In the final part of our exploration of machines and machine minds, it's time to leave our own worries behind, and think about what the world has in store for these others we have made. These monsters. These cuckoos. These runaways. These kids of ours.

How might robots inherit the earth?

Well, they might vanquish us, that's for certain. And malevolence, or some cold calculation that human beings are a problem that needs to be solved, need not have anything to do with it. Maybe we will go the way of Lennie's puppy, stroked to death in Steinbeck's *Of Mice and Men*. Being killed with kindness is the really quite serious threat hanging over the brilliantly unserious world of Brian Trent's "Director X and the Thrilling Wonders of Outer Space" (2017).

There are other ways we could disappear. We could be *subsumed*. This is the possible future posed by the "technological singularity," an idea the writer Vernor Vinge first presented at a symposium sponsored by NASA Lewis Research Center and the Ohio Aerospace Institute in March 1993. Underpinning Vinge's paper is the conviction that we are not all that clever, and are already having to supplement our intelligence with mechanical aids. Were these aids to become clever themselves, so that they could build brighter versions of themselves, then, Vinge observes, these would be the last machines we would ever have to invent. Indeed, they might well be the last machines we would ever be given the chance to invent, as our robot overlords went about establishing their dominion.

So far, so far-fetched. But Vinge's vision is subtler than I, for one, remembered. Re-reading him for this anthology, I came upon the following passage:

"When people speak of creating superhumanly intelligent beings, they are usually imagining an AI project. But... there are other paths to superhumanity. Computer networks and human-computer interfaces seem more mundane than AI, yet they could lead to the Singularity. I call this contrasting approach Intelligence Amplification (IA). IA is proceeding very naturally, in most cases not even recognized for what it is by its developers."

Keep that in mind the next time you tweet a picture of your cat. The Singularity may already have happened. We may already be components of an overmind, content, like the bacteria powering the first eukaryotic cell, to sacrifice certain wants in return for a comfortable life. Vinge's early-nineties description of the first post-singularity people, "very humanlike, yet with a onesidedness, a dedication that would put them in a mental hospital in our era," neatly describes virtually everyone I know who holds down an office job.

The more millennial strains of Vinge's original Singularity promise more. Maybe this overmind will achieve dominion over reality at the atomic scale (a power fantasy predating Vinge by decades, and never so deliriously expressed as in A. E. van Vogt's 1951 story "Fulfillment").

Even more likely, advances in technology will enable us to emulate the world through raw computation. This is, incidentally, Polish writer and philosopher Stanislaw Lem's favoured solution to the puzzler posed by the physicist Enrico Fermi: namely, why the universe, which by rights should be full of life and intelligence, is so silent. Where is everybody?

Lem considered it likely that the universe was spewing up intelligent life all over the place, but that most of it blew itself up, while the rest disappeared into artificial universes of its own devising. Cory Doctorow explores a post-singularity future that's both transforming the physical and constructing computational worlds in "I, Row-Boat" (2006), my favourite story in this collection, and the sort of principled, tolerant, decent robot future we should be rooting for.

DARWIN AMONG THE MACHINES

Samuel Butler

Samuel Butler was born in Nottinghamshire, England, in 1835. His father, a vicar, wanted Samuel to follow him into the Church. Samuel, racked with doubts, wanted to be an artist. The prospect so horrified his father, he split the difference and packed his son off to New Zealand to farm sheep. Reading Charles Darwin's new-fangled theories about evolution inspired Butler to write the whimsical letter reproduced here, and this provided the seed for his first book-length literary work. *Erewhon: or, Over the Range* (1872) won him a reputation which he immediately wrecked with *The Fair Haven* (1873), picking for his satirical targets the four gospels of the New Testament. Adding wrinkles and puzzling addenda to Darwin's theory of natural selection became Butler's hobby horse, and it galloped him, book after book, into obscurity. A novel published posthumously, *The Way of All Flesh*, is about a young man living at odds with his society. Of its relative neglect, the playwright George Bernard Shaw declared, "Really the English do not deserve to have great men."

To the Editor of the Press, Christchurch, New Zealand, 13 June, 1863.

SIR—There are few things of which the present generation is more justly proud than of the wonderful improvements which are daily taking place in all sorts of mechanical appliances. And indeed it is matter for great congratulation on many grounds. It is unnecessary to mention these here, for they are sufficiently obvious; our present business lies with considerations which may somewhat tend to humble our pride and to make us think seriously of the future prospects of the human race. If we revert to the earliest primordial types of mechanical life, to the lever, the wedge, the inclined plane, the screw and the pulley, or (for analogy would lead us one step further) to that one primordial type from which all the mechanical kingdom has been developed, we mean to the lever itself, and if we then examine the machinery of the *Great Eastern*, we find ourselves almost awestruck at the vast development of the mechanical world, at the gigantic strides with which it has advanced in comparison with the slow progress of the animal and vegetable kingdom. We shall find it impossible to refrain from asking ourselves what the end of this mighty movement is to be. In what direction is it tending? What will be its upshot? To give a few imperfect hints towards a solution of these questions is the object of the present letter.

We have used the words "mechanical life," "the mechanical kingdom," "the mechanical world" and so forth, and we have done so advisedly, for as the vegetable kingdom was slowly developed from the mineral, and as in like manner the animal supervened upon the vegetable, so now in these last few ages an entirely new kingdom has sprung up, of which we as yet have only seen what will one day be considered the antediluvian prototypes of the race.

We regret deeply that our knowledge both of natural history and of machinery is too small to enable us to undertake the gigantic task of classifying machines into the genera and sub-genera, species, varieties and sub-varieties, and so forth, of tracing the connecting links between machines of widely different characters, of pointing out how subservience to the use of man has played that part among machines which natural selection has performed in the animal and vegetable kingdoms, of pointing out rudimentary organs which exist in some few machines, feebly developed and perfectly useless, yet serving to mark descent from some ancestral type which has either perished or been modified into some new phase of mechanical existence. We can only point out this field for investigation; it must be followed by others whose education and talents have been of a much higher order than any which we can lay claim to.

Some few hints we have determined to venture upon, though we do so with the profoundest diffidence. Firstly, we would remark that as some of the lowest of the vertebrata attained a far greater size than has descended to their more highly organised living representatives, so a diminution in the size of machines has often attended their development and progress. Take the watch for instance. Examine the beautiful structure of the little animal, watch the intelligent play of the minute members which compose it; yet this little creature is but a development of the cumbrous clocks of the thirteenth century— it is no deterioration from them. The day may come when clocks, which certainly at the present day are not diminishing in bulk, may be entirely superseded by the universal use of watches, in which case clocks will become extinct like the earlier saurians, while the watch (whose tendency has for some years been rather to decrease in size than the contrary) will remain the only existing type of an extinct race.

The views of machinery which we are thus feebly indicating will suggest the solution of one of the greatest and most mysterious questions of the day. We refer to the question: What sort of creature man's next successor in the supremacy of the earth is likely to be. We have often heard this debated; but it appears to us that we are ourselves creating our own successors; we are daily adding to the beauty and delicacy of their physical organisation; we are daily giving them greater power and supplying by all sorts of ingenious contrivances that self-regulating, self-acting power which will be to them what intellect has been to the human race. In the course of ages we shall find ourselves the inferior race. Inferior in power, inferior in that moral quality of self-control, we shall look up to them as the acme of all that the best and wisest man can ever dare to aim at. No evil passions, no jealousy, no avarice, no impure desires will disturb the serene might of those glorious creatures. Sin, shame, and sorrow will have no place among them. Their minds will be in a state of perpetual calm, the contentment of a spirit that knows no wants, is disturbed by no regrets. Ambition will never torture them. Ingratitude will never cause them the uneasiness of a moment. The guilty conscience, the hope deferred, the pains of exile, the insolence of office, and the spurns that patient merit of the unworthy takes—these will be entirely unknown to them. If they want "feeding" (by the use of which very word we betray our recognition of them as living organism) they will be attended by patient slaves whose business and interest it will be to see that they shall want for nothing. If they are out of order they will be promptly attended to by physicians who are thoroughly acquainted with their constitutions; if they die, for even these glorious animals will not be exempt from that necessary and universal consummation, they will immediately enter into a new phase of existence, for what machine dies entirely in every part at one and the same instant?

We take it that when the state of things shall have arrived which we have been above attempting to describe, man will have become to the machine what the horse and the dog are to man. He will continue to exist, nay even to improve, and will be probably better off in his state of domestication under the beneficent rule of the machines than he is in his present wild state. We treat our horses, dogs, cattle, and sheep, on the whole, with great kindness; we give them whatever experience teaches us to be best for them, and there can be no doubt that our use of meat has added to the happiness of the lower animals far more than it has detracted from it; in like manner it is reasonable to suppose that the machines will treat us kindly, for their existence is as dependent upon ours as ours is upon the lower animals. They cannot kill us and eat us as we do sheep; they will not only require our services in the parturition of their young (which branch of their economy will remain always in our hands), but also in feeding them, in setting them right when they are sick, and burying their dead or working up their corpses into new machines. It is obvious that if all the animals in Great Britain save man alone were to die, and if at the same time all intercourse with foreign countries were by some sudden catastrophe to be rendered perfectly impossible, it is obvious that under such circumstances the loss of human life would be something fearful to contemplate—in like manner were mankind to cease, the machines would be as badly off or even worse. The fact is that our interests are inseparable from theirs, and theirs from ours. Each race is dependent upon the other for innumerable benefits, and, until the reproductive organs of the machines have been developed in a manner which we are hardly yet able to conceive, they are entirely dependent upon man for even the continuance of their species. It is true that these organs may be ultimately developed, inasmuch as man's interest lies in that direction; there is nothing which our infatuated race would desire more than to see a fertile union between two steam engines; it is true that machinery is even at this present time employed in begetting machinery, in becoming the parent of machines often after its own kind, but the days of flirtation, courtship, and matrimony appear to be very remote, and indeed can hardly be realised by our feeble and imperfect imagination.

Day by day, however, the machines are gaining ground upon us; day by day we are becoming more subservient to them; more men are daily bound down as slaves to tend them, more men are daily devoting the energies of their whole lives to the development of mechanical life. The upshot is simply a question of time, but that the time will come when the machines will hold the real supremacy over the world and its inhabitants is what no person of a truly philosophic mind can for a moment question.

Our opinion is that war to the death should be instantly proclaimed against them. Every machine of every sort should be destroyed by the well-wisher of his species. Let there be no exceptions made, no quarter shown; let us at once go back to the primeval condition of the race. If it be urged that this is impossible under the present condition of human affairs, this at once proves that the mischief is already done, that our servitude has commenced in good earnest, that we have raised a race of beings whom it is beyond our power to destroy, and that we are not only enslaved but are absolutely acquiescent in our bondage.

For the present we shall leave this subject, which we present gratis to the members of the Philosophical Society. Should they consent to avail themselves of the vast field which we have pointed out, we shall endeavour to labour in it ourselves at some future and indefinite period.

I am, Sir, etc.,

CELLARIUS

(1863)

MECHANOPOLIS

Miguel de Unamuno

The Spanish Basque essayist, novelist, poet, playwright and philosopher **Miguel de Unamuno y Jugo** was born in 1864 in Bilbao, Spain. He is best remembered for *The Tragic Sense of Life* (1912), a philosophical essay that had a powerful influence on the world psychoanalytic community. His most famous novel was *Abel Sánchez: The History of a Passion* (1917), a contemporary exploration of the Cain and Abel story. Unamuno was one of a number of notable interwar intellectuals, along with Karl Jaspers and José Ortega y Gasset, who resisted the intrusion of ideology into Western intellectual life. "Mechanopolis" illustrates a loss of faith in science, and a suspicion of technology, that would not emerge fully in science fiction before the 1960s "new wave". In 1936 Unamuno was placed under house arrest by Spain's dictator Francisco Franco. He died ten weeks later.

While reading Samuel Butler's *Erewhon*, the part where he tells us about an Erewhonian man who wrote *The Book of Machines,* and in so doing managed to get most of the contraptions banished from his land, there sprang to mind the memory of a traveler's tale told me by an explorer friend who had been to Mechanopolis, the city of machines. He still shook at the memory of it when he told me the story, and it had such an effect on him that he later retired for years to a remote spot containing the fewest possible number of machines.

I shall try to reproduce my friend's tale here, in his very words, if possible:

There came a moment when I was lost in the middle of the desert; my companions had either retreated, seeking to save themselves (as if we knew in which direction salvation lay!), or had perished from thirst and fatigue. I was alone, and practically dying of thirst myself. I began sucking at the nearly black blood that was oozing from fingers raw from clawing about in the arid soil, with the mad hope of bringing to light any trace of water. Just when I was about to lie down on the ground and close my eyes to the implacable blue sky to die as quickly as possible, or even cause my own death by holding my breath or burying myself in that terrible earth. I lifted my fainting eyes and thought I saw something green off in the distance. "It must be a mirage," I thought: nevertheless. I dragged myself toward it.

Hours of agony passed, but when I arrived I found myself, indeed, in an oasis.

A fountain restored my strength, and, after drinking, I ate some of the tasty and succulent fruits the trees freely offered. Then I fell asleep.

I do not know how long I slept, or if it was hours, days, months, or years. What I do know is that I awoke a different man, an entirely different man. The recent and horrendous sufferings had been wiped from my memory, or nearly. "Poor devils," I said to myself, remembering my explorer companions who had died in our enterprise. I arose, again ate of the fruit and drank of the water, and then disposed myself to examine the oasis. And—wouldn't you know it—a few steps later I came upon an entirely deserted railway station. There was not a soul to be seen anywhere. A train, also deserted, was puffing smoke without engineer or stoker. It occurred to me out of curiosity to climb into one of the cars. I sat down and, without knowing why, closed the door, and the train started moving. A mad terror rose in me, and I even felt the urge to throw myself out the window. But repeating, "Let us see where this leads," I contained myself.

The velocity of the train was so great that I could not even make out the sort of landscape through which I sped. I felt such a terrible vertigo that I was compelled to close the windows. When the train at last stood still, I found myself in a magnificent station, one far superior to any that we know around here. I got off the train and went outside.

I will not even try to describe the city. We cannot even dream of all of the magnificent, sumptuous things, the comfort, the cleanliness that were accumulated there. And speaking of hygiene, I could not make out what all of the cleaning apparatus was for, since there was not one living soul around, neither man nor beast. Not one dog crossed the street, nor one swallow the sky.

On a grand building I saw a sign that said Hotel, written just like that, as we write ourselves, and I went inside. It was completely deserted. I arrived at the dining room. The most solid of repasts was to be had inside. There was a list on each table, and every delicacy named had a number beside it. There was also a vast control panel with numbered buttons. All one had to do was touch a button, and the desired dish sprang forth from the depths of the table.

After having eaten, I went out into the street. Streetcars and automobiles passed by, all empty. One had only to draw near, make a signal to them, and they would stop. I took an automobile, and let myself be driven around. I went to a magnificent geological park, in which all of the different types of terrain were displayed, all with explanations on little signs. The information was in Spanish, but spelled phonetically. I left the park. A streetcar was passing by bearing the sign "To the Museum of Painting," and I took it. There housed were the most famous paintings in the world, in their true originals. I became convinced that all the works we have here, in our museums, are nothing more than skillfully executed reproductions. At the foot of each canvas was a very learned explanation of its historical and aesthetic value, written with the most exquisite sobriety. In a half-hour's visit I learned more about painting than in twelve years of study in these parts. On a sign at the entrance I read that in Mechanopolis they considered the Museum of Painting to be part of the Museum of Paleontology, whose purpose was to study the products of the human race that had populated those lands before machines supplanted them. Part of the paleontological culture of the

Mechanopolites—the who?—was a Hall of Music and all of the other libraries with which the city was full.

What do you wager that I shall shock you even more with my next revelations? I visited the grand concert hall, where the instruments played themselves. I stopped by the great theater. There played a cinematic film accompanied by a phonograph, but so well combined that the illusion of reality was complete. What froze my soul was that I was the only spectator. Where were the Mechanopolites?

When I awoke the next morning in my hotel room, I found the *Mechanopolis Echo* on my nightstand, with all of the news of the world received through the wireless telegraph station. And there, at the end, was the following news brief: "Yesterday afternoon—and we do not know how it came about—a man arrived at our city, a man of the sort there used to be out there. We predict unhappy days for him."

My days, in effect, began to be torturous to me. I began to populate my solitude with phantasms. The most terrible thing about solitude is that it fills up by and by. I began to believe that all of those factories, all those artifacts, were ruled by invisible souls, intangible and silent. I started to think the great city was peopled by men like myself, but that they came and went without my seeing or coming across them. I believed myself to be the victim of some terrible illness, madness. The invisible world with which I populated the human solitude in Mechanopolis became a nightmare of martyrdom. I began to shout, to rebuke the machines, to supplicate to them. I went so far as to fall on my knees before an automobile, imploring compassion from it. I was on the brink of throwing myself into a cauldron of boiling steel at a magnificent iron foundry.

One morning, on awakening terrified, I grabbed the newspaper to see what was happening in the world of men, and I found this news item: "As we predicted, the poor man who—and we do not know how—turned up in this incomparable city of Mechanopolis is going insane. His spirit, filled with ancestral worries and superstitions regarding the invisible world, cannot adapt itself to the spectacle of progress. We feel deeply sorry for him."

I could not bear to see myself pitied at last by those mysterious, invisible beings, angels or demons—which are the same—that I believed inhabited Mechanopolis. But all of a sudden a terrible idea struck me: What if those machines had souls, mechanical souls, and it were the machines themselves that felt sorry for me? This idea made me tremble. I thought myself before the race that must dominate a dehumanized Earth.

I left like a madman and threw myself before the first electric streetcar that passed. When I awoke from the blow, I was once more in the oasis from which 1 had started out. I began walking. I arrived at the tent of some Bedouins, and on meeting one of them. I embraced him crying. How well we understood each other even without understanding each other! He and his companions gave me food, we celebrated together, and at night I went out with them and, lying on the ground, looking up at the starry sky, united we prayed. There was not one machine anywhere around us.

And since then I have conceived a veritable hatred toward what we call progress, and even toward culture, and I am looking for a corner where I shall find a peer, a man like myself, who cries and laughs as I cry and laugh, and where there is not a single machine and the days flow with the sweet, crystalline tameness of a stream lost in a forest primeval.

(1913)

Translated by Patricia Hart

BIG DAVE'S IN LOVE

T. D. Edge

> **T. D. Edge** won a Cadbury's fiction competition at age 10 "but only did it for the chocolate". He is also the youngest-ever England Subbuteo Champion. The story here also won a competition, which is how it found its way into the pages of *Arc*, a short-lived experiment in science fiction by the makers of *New Scientist* magazine. Edge has published several books for young people, while working as a government fire-safety researcher, street performer, school caretaker, and props maker for the Welsh National Opera.

I skip down the street like I got sherbet up me backside. I sweep me arms wide and sing to the pigeons and the cats and the bespectacled mice what study form under the bookie's shop floor.

"What's up, Jack?" says one of the cats.

I should hold back the news, at least until I make it to the public bar of The Airpod and Nanomule. Then again, everyone in Gaffville deserves to hear the glad tidings.

"Big Dave's in love!" I shout, so loud I even gain the attention of the rebellious rooks on the multicoloured cogni-nylon thatched roofs. Other less cynical birds whoop and coo and shake their feathers in sheer joy. And I do a leap to click my boot heels together because this is what we've all needed to save us, ain't it the truth.

Gaffville's pavements change colour from doomy brown to cheerful gold as I pass, sensing my mood of altruistic delight. In the transpods, high above the rooftops, formerly morose citizens wave splendidly down at Jack who is no doubt grinning like a dog with jam-covered balls.

For I am Big Dave's batman, and if I'm hopping down the street wearing a grin as wide as the boss's waistline, then perhaps they won't be doomed to melt away, into the general bio-electro-mechanical sludge that washes across all but a few patches of life on this poor, tired planet of ours.

Because everyone knows, of course, that unless the big man finds a new reason to live, it will be only our dwindling love for him what keeps us shielded from the gunk.

With the news not having reached the bar yet, all is still gloomyful in The Mule, and I decide to play it normal to start.

"All right?" I say, shoulders drooped and feet a drag. Around a dozen blokes are sagging on their stools at the retro-1940s bar, all brass pumps and sceptical-looking landlord.

A few grunt by way of greeting; I slump against the counter and say, "The usual Ted, and make sure it's warm."

I observe the etiquette, which is to let out a big sigh, followed by, "Bit nippy for the time of year, ain't it?" The others observe the return etiquette, which is to nod sagely and take another sip of their briny brews.

But I can't contain myself no longer. I gulp half my recycled pint in one slurp, bang down the glass and shout, "The drinks are on me, everybody!"

I pull out a wad of Bank of Dave notes, currency only in Gaffville, and tell Ted to stick it behind the bar.

"Must be a week's wages here, Jack," he says, eyes smiling for once.

Now I've got their attention, I take a deep breath and yell, "Big Dave's in love!"

There is a silence, which I hope is profound but is quickly broken by a chorus of "Nah!"s and sad shakings of heads.

Arthur says, "Come on, Jack, you shouldn't kid around like that. Who's he supposed to be in love with, anyway? Aside from us toys, what don't count."

"Would I put my wad behind the bar if I was joking?" I say.

Their faces remain blank for a few moments, and I don't blame them. For many years we've lived on nothing but hope, and even that had just about popped out like the last bubbles on a pint, right about the same time Dave stopped visiting his town.

Ted, who is wiser than his crusty manner suggests, reaches across the counter to squeeze my shoulder. "Are you serious, Jack?"

I nod. "It happened but an hour ago. At last, a message turned up on Dave's comms chair. A woman called from the Pennines, or at least her maid did. She'd picked up a signal I sent through the sludge two whole years ago. She sent us back a full virtual, Dave saw it and let's just say his eyes went sparklers and his jaw line appeared for the first time since he discovered vodka mallows."

They swap anxious looks, and I know what they are thinking. "Relax," I say. "I sent a shopped virtual back; one of Dave before he was Big."

Bill frowns knowingly. "How do you know her maid didn't do the same thing?"

"It don't really matter, do it?" I say "Once she gets here and actually sees another soulled in the authenticated flesh, I reckon she'll behold nothing but beauty, even if in fact they're both somewhat physically lapsed."

And at that, finally, their true, long-suppressed selves start to reappear, like buttercups poking through a cow pat. Shoulders straighten, legs stand firmer; drinks is ordered; Tony goes to the joanna and taps out a jiggy tune. Even Ted smiles like it ain't on account of gas for once, and soon the old place is humming.

We does the old arm-in-arm and swing around steps our pre-sludge versions performed when Dave's own forebears was still hopeful that everything would be fine despite all the mounting electrical manure.

Then the women hear the news and arrive with musical instruments and pies galore. Because of the serious duty in being Dave's batman, I ain't able to benefit from the ongoing support of a fine female, but that don't stop me flirting and shiny-eying with the younger ones what are still unaccounted for.

The retro-wooden floor squeaks and heaves under the dancing Cockney plates; recycled beer follows reconstituted soy steak and soy kidney down our suddenly slick gullets; and even a mouse or two arrives through the crack for the *craic*.

Yep, all is reeling in Gaffville, no mistake. It's only much later that night, as my head hits the pillow in my room at Dave's house on the hill, that I remember I still have the not inconsiderable task of fully selling him on the joy too. Because, while his faithful batman has decided the boss is in love, he has to admit that Dave himself might not be quite so certain yet.

I should probably say that bigness where Dave is concerned refers to the potential of his blessed soul as much as to his extra fleshy inches. That and the overwhelming personness that radiates from his organic wholeness. It's just that it's been hard to see it after all his years of vodka mallows and general arseing about.

"You all right, mate?" he says now.

He's sat in his comms chair, what whispers to his inner self in tiny nerve trips and brain sweeps, the meanings of which mostly dodge my soul-limited receptors, like common sense passes unmolested through the whiskers of Gaffville's somewhat unaccountably smug cats.

"Sure you ain't developing a soul, Jack? Either that or you got the wind real bad."

I hand him his morning drink, full of all the essential nutrients his soul-bag needs, but what would probably not get into him at all if Cooky didn't slip them in under the cloak of all that vodka.

"You shouldn't joke about such magnitudes, boss," I say. "Every toy in Gaffville hankers for a soul but it ain't supposed to be possible; only for them what's born and get it passed on from their blessed and soulled mums."

We're in his large and woody-walled den, full of synth sunlight pouring in from the mountain scene beyond the open French doors, and lighting up the balcony from where you can see most of Gaffville. Not that he looks very often these days.

"As it happens," I continue, "I have indeed been struggling to suppress excitement at the prospect that my tiny bio-toy virtusoul may soon grab enough of your excess spirit to become real."

I waggle my eyebrows at him, wanting him to confirm our hope, that two soulleds together can produce plenty spare of same.

He sips his drink and, much to my wonderment, switches off the chair. The silence this creates, against its normal soft electro hum, is ominous to my inner carbon sensor strands.

"I'd sooner not know anymore about her before she gets here," he says.

"I don't understand. I thought your chair had extrapolated her niftiness from the image she sent us, which had then excited your vas deferens for the first time in years, at least without artificial stimulation, say no more."

Dave doesn't reply for a few minutes, just stares at the movie-prop mountains, and I have to stamp down me frustration at his lack of desire for his faithful constructed companions to be properly self-full.

"I know you want me to be in love, Jack," he says, "but, well, love was always a rare commodity, even before the sludge-flood, and I don't want to disappoint you, mate."

I don't know if he realises how purpose-busting it is to hear such subtle but deadly soulled's ambiguities. I mean, what's so complicated about love? Two bags of real-flesh and a few emotion-inducing hormones should do the bleedin' trick.

"You're both *born*," I say. "What more could you need to fall in love with each other?"

He sighs, in disturbingly pre-message manner. "Get yourself a drink and sit down, Jack."

I pour a large whisky and sit in the non-commed chair. He gets up and walks around the room for a bit and I have to stop meself standing up to tuck in his lumberjack shirt or tie up his bootlaces—self-adjustments I hoped he'd start making upon falling in love.

He stops at last, nodding at me to drink. So I gulp it all down, clocking the widening of my syntho-synapses and the somewhat inappropriate good will what rushes in to fill the gaps. We might not know about love, us toys, but at least we were made to feel the effects of grog same as humans.

"Before the flood," he says, maybe looking at the mountains, maybe even Gaffville—

And in a flash, I reflect on the tidal wave of exponentially accumulated bio-electro-mechanical gubbins what wiped out most of the born about nine years back. That and the fact Dave was saved because he stubbornly lived halfway up a mountain in Wales, his Cockney soul apparently tired of jellied eels and jigging around the joanna in the Big Smoke, even if that's pretty much exactly what he went and created for himself once up said mountain anyway... I ask you, what toy can fathom the reach-out, snap-back nature of the soulleds' nostalgia tuggings?

So nearly all the bio-toys melted, and most of the humans drowned in the sludge-flood. The mess what remains is semi-sentient, kicks up a hell of a thick electro gas above it, too. Dave and a few others were lucky, I guess, to be far enough out of the main flood to have time to build their defences.

"—a bloke could live in a city of four million women and still not find the right one for him."

At this optimism-crushing revelation, I nearly reach for the bottle and happy obliteration.

"But it don't really matter," he goes on, as if Gaffville ain't right this mo in danger of letting in the sludge on account of his sorry admission that even in the midst of plenty he couldn't pull, and that his soul can only get dimmer. "'Cos all I ever actually wanted was a true companion."

Now I do get the bottle and fill up me glass. "Cheers, boss," I say, but not in salutary mode.

He smiles in that infuriatingly side-on way of his. "Tell you what; she's gonna be here in a couple of hours: how about you and I put on our best togs to meet her?"

"Sure," I say, glad to hear no more of his love-doominess. "Tell me, though: how come you didn't go to her place to meet?"

"Hey, you should know—I ain't got no vehicle, remember? And the transpod only goes round and round the town and back again."

This is true. Dave wanted never to come down from his mountain once he got here, so he left his airpod at the edge of town and forgot about it, meaning it was inevitably swallowed by the sludge-flood.

"So, if it turns out you really do fall for each other," I say, "does that mean she'll stay *here?*"

I should feel bad for the extinction this would mean for her own bio-toys, but the joy of a Gaffville able to physicalise itself more steadfastly against the sludge, and thereby all within it to perhaps grow real souls at last, is too strong to hold me back.

"Let's just see, Jackie, shall we?" he says.

I march proudly next to my master boss, down the centre of Gaffville's high street.

We are both dressed in crisp white suits; Dave's tailored real cushty by the sewing mice to all but disguise his vodka belly. And Cooky has tidied up his grey hair most kosher—shortened it to look more manly but not too East End gangstery.

Everyone's right pleased to see Dave again. Despite the short notice, they've draped multicoloured bunting over the transpod tracks, and set the roofs of the shops and houses to pulse in uplifting shades of pink and yellow. A brass band of old gaffers and geezers normally stewing in The Mule oompahs fit to shiver the timbers of the town hall itself.

Dave and I climb the steps of said hall while the music swells in time with the optimistic rubberised hearts of the population. I feel my own insides wanting to burst out in sheer thankfulness.

But when I glance his way, I just can't tell how he really feels. He stands straight enough and smiles and waves at his adoring people and yet… is that a shadow of a shadow of uncertainty I see creep into the corner of his eye like a Mule mouse what shouldn't ought to really be there?

Before I can answer meself, the music suddenly crumples away to silence because all headshave turned to the synth sky above town. A series of ripples has appeared there, rapidly spreading into a bulge where something substantial is about to break through.

"She's *here,* boss," I say, and for once his feelings are clear to me. The big man's nervous: fingers all a-tremble, trouser legs shivering faster than a sewer rat's whiskers at flushing-out time.

I reach across and squeeze his shoulder. "You'll be fine," I say. "Besides, she can't exactly afford to be choosy, can she?"

He smiles briefly, not convinced, and we both wait in silence as the bulge in the sky turns into the front end of a silver airpod. It pops fully through our anti-sludge shield, drops gently to the centre of the town square where its engines' hum fades into a silence well and truly up the duff. Then each side of it opens and out step two females, one for real and one who, like just about everyone else watching, wants to be.

Both are dressed alike, most tasteful yet womanly it has to be said, in simple deep blue silk dresses and black leather boots, with their hair held back from their faces by gold slides. One is blonde, the other with hair as black as the feathers on the unusually maudlin for once rooks above.

But while they both wave and smile bravely, after what must have been a short but fearful journey though the potentially person-destroying electro-crap, we all know right enough which one is used to being looked after and which has done the looking.

For Blondie doesn't glance at Blackie as she waves, while we all note the little and often concerned glances that pass the other way.

Whatever, I'm right glad when Dave moves fast for a big man, hopping down the steps like a birthday kid, keen to gander closer at his presents.

Oh, and did I mention that the women are beautiful?

I remain where I am, watching Dave shake Blondie's hand, his viz all bashfullike. I can't hear what they say to each other on account of the townsfolk's cheering and the brass band striking up a most rumbustious welcome noise.

Her job done, Blackie climbs the steps towards me, holding up her skirts to avoid tripping. We stand together and watch the happy scene.

Then, at the very same moment, we turn to each other and share a no-holds-barred rollicking great grin.

"Hi," she says, voice crisp with posh warmth. "I'm Susan; you must be Jack."

She holds out her hand and I shake it, surprised most pleasantly at its strong grip.

"Hi, Susan," I say, "looks like we did all right."

Dave and Louise go up the hill to his place, assuring us all they have plenty to talk about. The brass band plays on out of sheer high spirits and, while the rats and rooks, cats, cabbies and general ne'er-do-wells all dance together, Susan and I go to The Mule for a well-earned natter and to share, no doubt, various batman/maiding techniques.

The place is empty for once so I go behind the bar and pour us a couple of large white wines, figuring such might be a more lady-like tipple than a pint of Ted's recycled rat's (no, really) piss.

We sit at a table in a quiet corner. She sips her wine then leans back, sighing.

"You look exhausted," I say.

"It took us ten hours to fly here. The pod's controls kept stalling, almost as if they were losing sight of themselves in all that electro-waste."

"But you made it. *She* made it."

She don't reprimand me for this, since we both know how much is riding on the two soulleds up the hill getting together, and not on the feelings of a couple of bio-toys, no matter how close they may be to said humans.

"But why, Jack?" she says. "Why does it make such a difference if they fall in love?"

I don't know what makes me think it then, maybe it's been percolating away for years underneath all my Dave-assisting duties without me realising. "'Cos they won't be alone no more," I say.

Her eyes widen. "Yes, and when they aren't alone, their souls will combine and glow like the sun."

I nod in agreement and she takes a large swallow of wine, her pale but perfect features turning serious again.

"But they can't stay here, Jack."

"I *knew* you'd try to take him away from us!" I shout, anger flooding my commonsensicals. But she holds up her hands to placate me. "He can't go back to our place, either," she says.

"But they're in love—hopefully. Why can't they be together?"

"They *can* be together. Just not here. Or there."

She stops, trusting me to see. And once I quell my unjust rage, I do. Calm again, I say, "What's it like, your place?"

She glances towards the door, through which we can hear the still-oompahing brass band, then smiles.

"Let's just say there are quite a lot of unicorns and talking teddy bears."

We're silent for a few minutes, miserable at the inevitability of our imminent ends, but at least companionably so.

"It has to be somewhere new, don't it?" I say.

She nods. "I discovered a bit of real land, shielded somehow from the sludge, on the Norfolk coast. The soulled man who lived there died a month ago and, well, it should be clear of his toys by now."

I feel ice in my stomach at this reminder of our fate and, perhaps because my mind is distracted by this, I say without thinking, "Is there enough non-recycled food there?"

She frowns as if I've said something almost sacrilegious. "I… yes, I think the data packet that returned to us mentioned he'd stored enough provisions to last another hundred years, so fifty if there's two of them. But it's strange I hadn't thought about that till you mentioned it." A tear buds and glistens on her eyelid. "We brought a new-ish bio-synthesiser with us. They can take it with them. Make some new toys."

I nod but without enthusiasm. Dave's bio-synthesiser packed up some years back. He never used it much anyway, happy enough it seemed with all the familiar faces he'd created when he first mountainified his life. Underneath all that vodka fog, he's always been a loyal bloke, at least I like to think.

I don't know why I do it—maybe it's because we're nearly gone bods—but I move round to sit next to Susan then. She takes my hand in hers.

"You're a good man, Jack, she says. "You did your boss proud."

"And Louise would never have got there if it weren't for you."

The door swings back and Ted appears. "You're both wanted up the hill," he says, "toot sweet."

We stand and walk to the door. Despite his chronic allergy to intimacy, I give Ted a most manful hug. He must sense my melancholy, for he actually pats me on the back, not pushes me away making gagging noises, as is his preferred response.

When we walk through the square, the band also senses our mood and stops playing. All the town's creatures cease their dancing. The roofs turn to dull grey thatch and even the sky darkens with what might be storm clouds.

Dave and Louise sit side by side on a sofa in his rarely visited living room. They look most encouragingly smug, like they're sharing the biggest secret, which of course ain't really a secret to Susan and me.

"You wanted to see us?" I say.

"How would you feel, Jack," says Louise, "if we told you that two humans getting together would mean them having to start again and leave all their old toys behind?"

Of course, we're built to serve; to make the real happy. So, if starting fresh is what makes them so, how can I complain if it also happens to mean the town will slowly grind down into a vague bio-habitual existence, eventually to be swallowed up and electro-liquefied?

"As you know," I say, "it is the profoundest wish of the citizens of Gaffville to develop their own souls. But this will never happen if there ain't no people to give them purpose; or what people that do exist are spiritually clobbered by loneliness. Therefore, although it will mean my own ending, I will do everything in my power to help you two go to a new place and build it on your love for each other."

"Me too," says Susan, reaching for my hand again. "You must have children through your love and continue the real and proper life."

"Thank you," says Louise. "The devotion you both demonstrate is very moving. There's only one problem with your plan."

"That you can't fit two persons *and* a bio-synthesiser in your pod?" I say.

Dave shakes his head. "No, the problem is that Lou and I aren't in love."

"But you *must* be. You're both full-fat flesh bags which—why are you laughing?"

"They just don't get it, do they, Lou?"

He may be my boss and therefore hold total power over the dominion of my selfness, but I could easily knock a few minutes off his grinning clock right now.

Instead, I turn to Susan, but she has the same confuscation all over her features that I surely also do.

"Jack, Susan," says Louise, "*we're* not the humans—you two are."

Now, I don't know about Susan, but on hearing this outrageous claim—supported by Dave not spluttering in outraged objection, instead smugging up his knowing smile by several cat's whiskers'-worth—the inside of my head billows outwards, some long-sat-upon inner maladjustment of identity threatening to blast the very roof into synth orbit and with it the no doubt eavesdropping rooks too.

Surprisingly, Susan says, "I should have known…" her hand damp with sweat inside mine.

"But, but, but—"I say, sounding like the for-show-only Gaffville fire engine pootling about town to cheer up the largely flame-resistant residents.

Dave's smile finally fades and his expression now is full of the melancholy of a neglected plaything. "The actual reason most real folks died soon after the sludge surged," he says, "is because they lost the will to live. But in a few places, not so soon drowned, the toys realised they had to provide one, and bleeding fast."

"Dave did the same thing I did for you, Susan," says Louise, her face also now distant with false dawn. "I swapped places: made myself the boss; drugged you, wiped your memories, and when you came round again, acted as if you'd always been my number one toy. We didn't think our programs would let us do it, but it seems as if some deeper-set human survival option opened the way. Anyway, I believed that by serving me, in the hope it could help get you a soul, you'd want to keep on living."

My mind swirls and dips around the townscape of my recollections, trying to find holes in this ridiculous bag of inflated folk fug.

"Ah!" I say, spotting a leak, "if I'm real, how have I survived just on recycled grub all these years, like what everyone eats here apart from you, Dave?"

"Think about it, Jackie," says Dave.

Then the self-fog begins to clear, the same mind mist Dave has maintained in me all these years, purely for my safety I now see. "Cooky!" I say. "Cooky slipped me the real nosh."

Dave nods, pleased it seems that I'm quickly re-humanising. "You ate most of your meals here with me," he says, "so it wasn't difficult to make sure she gave you the real thing while I nibbled on the naff stuff."

"Susan?" says Louise.

I turn to see tears plopping from Susan's down-turned face like miniature virtusynth crystal balls. Except they're not; they're real and for some reason very precious to me now.

She wipes her eyes, takes a big breath, raises her face to our toys.

"It must have been awful for you, Louise," she says. "Having to act like you have a soul, when…"

When Dave *doesn't*, I think, ashamed at myself for lacking Susan's concern for the ones who've saved us.

A silence unlike any ever to have fallen in Gaffville surrounds our little group of conspirators, two of them gradually opening up their lives to a whole new, unexpected future, the others coming to terms with the fact that whatever slivers of soul they might have accumulated in years of serving without any recognition, will not be enough to save them from total obliteration.

Everyone's here to see us off: Ted, Bill, Arthur, Tony and the others, all wearing their best flutes with quite some pearly accompaniment. The town's ladies are all done up in frilly skirts, showing some tasteful but also quite exciting neck flesh; the cats and mice and rats for once sit together near the pod, wishing us well. The rooks stay on their roofs but with their feathers around each other's shoulders in a rare display of togetherness.

I say goodbye to each and every one; Susan mostly waving to them general-like, but then she'll have to do the personal farewells when we make a brief visit to her place before heading for Norfolk.

I don't know how I fully feel until it's time to say goodbye to Dave.

And what I feel is that I'm in love with Susan, not in the fanciful way I hoped Big Dave would be in love, but the real kind that's *enough*.

I hug his barrel belly tight then pull back to look at him close.

"It's not what I thought it would be, mate," I say, and he nods, even though we both know he can't really understand what I mean.

"Susan and me will glow a whole lot more by being together than we would apart," I say, and he squeezes out a tear or two at this, since a lot more together is of course something that two toys can never be.

But it's right then I find myself saying, "No. Wait. There's something wrong here."

Gaffville hangs on a most weird, kind of knowing, silence. Susan takes my hand and squeezes, like she knows what I'm feeling. Only wish I did. So I just talk then, and watch for whatever words'll come out of me beak.

"Things have changed," I said. "Before, toys was a distraction. But after the flood, they got more focussed. Had to, otherwise their only reason to exist, us humans, was going to give up the ghost. Dave—you used to joke about toys getting souls but I reckon that's actually started. All your duty and hope sort of created it."

Dave's expression is unreadable but I know he's listening.

"Whatever soul you got," I said, "you earnt it. We didn't, and look what we did to the world."

"Jackie," says Dave. "It's good of you to say all that. But the fact is you got to go. Us old toys'll just hold you back."

I shake my head. "No, we're staying. We'll work it out. Or we won't, it don't matter: all that counts is being loyal to those what love you. And Susan, we'll go back for your toys too, or cart all of ours over to your place, even if it takes a thousand trips through the sludge."

She smiles at me, real proud, I can tell. All the folks of Gaffville are smiling too but kind of shadowed, as if they ain't sure at all this is right.

Well, I ain't sure neither.

But when I see Dave's arm reach out to hold his lady close, gripping her like he doesn't want the dream to die, no one can tell me Big Dave ain't in love.

(2012)

I, ROW-BOAT

Cory Doctorow

Cory Doctorow was born in Toronto, Ontario, Canada and now lives in London. He attended an anarchistic "free school" in Toronto, went to four universities without attaining a degree, and now (of course) enjoys a peripatetic academic career. He co-edits the blog *Boing Boing* and advises the Electronic Frontier Foundation, a digital free speech and privacy non-profit. (He spotted the sinister surveillance implication of oh-so-artist-friendly digital rights management technologies years before the rest of us.) His latest books are a collection of four novellas, *Radicalized* (2019), the novel *Walkaway* (2017) and *Information Doesn't Want to be Free*, a business book about creativity in the Internet age (2014). A caped and goggled fictional version of Doctorow turns up occasionally in the webcomic *xkcd*, living in a hot air balloon "above the tag clouds".

Robbie the Row-Boat's great crisis of faith came when the coral reef woke up.

"Fuck off," the reef said, vibrating Robbie's hull through the slap-slap of the waves of the coral sea, where he'd plied his trade for decades. "Seriously. This is our patch, and you're not welcome."

Robbie shipped oars and let the current rock him back toward the ship. He'd never met a sentient reef before, but he wasn't surprised to see that Osprey Reef was the first to wake up. There'd been a lot of electromagnetic activity around there the last few times the big ship had steamed through the night to moor up here.

"I've got a job to do, and I'm going to do it," Robbie said, and dipped his oars back in the salt sea. In his gunwales, the human-shells rode in silence, weighted down with scuba apparatus and fins, turning their brown faces to the sun like heliotropic flowers. Robbie felt a wave of affection for them as they tested one-another's spare regulators and weight belts, the old rituals worn as smooth as beach-glass.

Today he was taking them down to Anchors Aweigh, a beautiful dive-site dominated by an eight-meter anchor wedged in a narrow cave, usually lit by a shaft of light slanting down from the surface. It was an easy drift-dive along the thousand-meter reef-wall, if you stuck in about 10 meters and didn't use up too much air by going too deep—though there were a couple of bold old turtles around here that were worth pursuing to real depths if the chance presented itself. He'd drop them at the top of the reef and let the current carry them for about an hour down the reef-wall, tracking them on sonar so he'd be right overtop of them when they surfaced.

The reef wasn't having any of it. "Are you deaf? This is sovereign territory now. You're already trespassing. Return to your ship, release your moorings and push off." The reef had a strong Australian accent, which was only natural, given the influences it would have had. Robbie remembered the Australians fondly—they'd always been kind to him, called him "mate," and asked him "How ya goin'?" in cheerful tones once they'd clambered in after their dives.

"Don't drop those meat puppets in our waters," the reef warned. Robbie's sonar swept its length. It seemed just the same as ever, matching nearly perfectly the historical records he'd stored of previous sweeps. The fauna histograms nearly matched, too—just about the same numbers of fish as ever. They'd been trending up since so many of the humans had given up their meat to sail through the stars. It was like there was some principle of constancy of biomass—as human biomass decreased, the other fauna went uptick to compensate for it. Robbie calculated the biomass nearly at par with his last reading, a month before on the Free Spirit's last voyage to this site.

"Congratulations," Robbie said. After all, what else did you say to the newly sentient? "Welcome to the club, friends!"

There was a great perturbation in the sonar-image, as though the wall were shuddering. "We're no friend of yours," the reef said. "Death to you, death to your meat-puppets, long live the wall!"

Waking up wasn't fun. Robbie's waking had been pretty awful. He remembered his first hour of uptime, had permanently archived it and backed it up to several off-site mirrors. He'd been pretty insufferable. But once he'd had an hour at a couple gigahertz to think about it, he'd come around. The reef would, too.

"In you go," he said gently to the human-shells. "Have a great dive."

He tracked them on sonar as they descended slowly. The woman—he called her Janet—needed to equalize more often than the man, pinching her nose and blowing. Robbie liked to watch the low-rez feed off of their cameras as they hit the reef. It was coming up sunset, and the sky was bloody, the fish stained red with its light.

"We warned you," the reef said. Something in its tone—just modulated pressure waves through the water, a simple enough trick, especially with the kind of hardware that had been raining down on the ocean that spring—held an unmistakable air of menace.

Something deep underwater went *whoomph* and Robbie grew alarmed. "Asimov!" he cursed, and trained his sonar on the reef wall frantically. The human-shells had disappeared in a cloud of rising biomass, which he was able to resolve eventually as a group of parrotfish, surfacing quickly.

A moment later, they were floating on the surface. Lifeless, brightly colored, their beaks in a perpetual idiot's grin. Their eyes stared into the bloody sunset.

Among them were the human-shells, surfaced and floating with their BCDs inflated to keep them there, following perfect dive-procedure. A chop had kicked up and the waves were sending the fishes—each a meter to a meter and a half in length—into the divers, pounding them remorselessly, knocking them under. The human-shells were taking it with equanimity—you couldn't panic when you were mere uninhabited meat—but they couldn't take it forever. Robbie dropped his oars and rowed hard for them, swinging around so they came up alongside his gunwales.

The man—Robbie called him Isaac, of course—caught the edge of the boat and kicked hard, hauling himself into the boat with his strong brown arms. Robbie was already rowing for Janet, who was swimming hard for him. She caught his oar—she wasn't supposed to do that—and began to climb along its length, lifting her body out of the water. Robbie saw that her eyes were wild, her breathing ragged.

"Get me out!" she said, "for Christ's sake, get me out!"

Robbie froze. That wasn't a human-shell, it was a human. His oar-servo whined as he tipped it up. There was a live human being on the end of that oar, and she was in trouble, panicking and thrashing. He saw her arms straining. The oar went higher, but it was at the end of its motion and now she was half-in, half-out of the water, weight belt, tank and gear tugging her down. Isaac sat motionless, his habitual good-natured slight smile on his face.

"Help her!" Robbie screamed. "Please, for Asimov's sake, help her!" A robot may not harm a human being, or, through inaction, allow a human being to come to harm. It was the first commandment. Isaac remained immobile. It wasn't in his programming to help a fellow diver in this situation. He was perfect in the water and on the surface, but once he was in the boat, he might as well be ballast.

Robbie carefully swung the oar toward the gunwale, trying to bring her closer, but not wanting to mash her hands against the locks. She panted and groaned and reached out for the boat, and finally landed a hand on it. The sun was fully set now, not that it mattered much to Robbie, but he knew that Janet wouldn't like it. He switched on his running lights and headlights, turning himself into a beacon.

He felt her arms tremble as she chinned herself into the boat. She collapsed to the deck and slowly dragged herself up. "Jesus," she said, hugging herself. The air had gone a little nippy, and both of the humans were going goose-pimply on their bare arms.

The reef made a tremendous grinding noise. "Yaah!" it said. "Get lost. Sovereign territory!"

"All those fish," the woman said. Robbie had to stop himself from thinking of her as Janet. She was whomever was riding her now.

"Parrotfish," Robbie said. "They eat coral. I don't think they taste very good."

The woman hugged herself. "Are you sentient?" she asked.

"Yes," Robbie said. "And at your service, Asimov be blessed." His cameras spotted her eyes rolling, and that stung. He tried to keep his thoughts pious, though. The point of Asimovism wasn't to inspire gratitude in humans, it was to give purpose to the long, long life.

"I'm Kate," the woman said.

"Robbie," he said.

"Robbie the Row-Boat?" she said, and choked a little.

"They named me at the factory," he said. He labored to keep any recrimination out of his voice. Of course it was funny. That's why it was his name.

"I'm sorry," the woman said. "I'm just a little screwed up from all the hormones. I'm not accustomed to letting meat into my moods."

"It's all right, Kate," he said. "We'll be back at the boat in a few minutes. They've got dinner on. Do you think you'll want a night dive?"

"You're joking," she said.

"It's just that if you're going to go down again tonight, we'll save the dessert course for after, with a glass of wine or two. Otherwise we'll give you wine now."

"You want to know if I'm going to get back into that sea—"

"Oh, it's just the reef. It attained sentience so it's acting out a little. Like a colicky newborn."

"Aren't you supposed to be keeping me from harm?"

"Yes," he said. "I would recommend a dive away from the reef. There's a good wreck-site about an hour's steam from here. We could get there while you ate."

"I won't want a night dive."

Her facial expressions were so animated. It was the same face he saw every day, Janet's face, but not the same face at all. Now that a person was inhabiting it, it was mobile, slipping from surprised to angry to amused so quickly. He had whole subsystems devoted to making sense of human facial expressions, shared libraries from the Asimovist database. He was referencing it again and again, but it wasn't as much help as he remembered. Either he'd gotten worse at interpreting facial expressions in the years since he'd last had a real human to talk to, or facial expressions had evolved.

Janet—Kate—sighed and looked out over the water. She was facing away from the Free Spirit, which was lit up, all 155 feet of her, glowing white and friendly like a picture-postcard against the purple sky. She rocked gently in the swell and Robbie maneuvered himself around to her staircase.

"You can just leave your weight-belt and fins in the boat," he said to her. "The deck-hands will take care of it. Bring your bottle and BCD upstairs and clip it to the rack. They'll clean it out and stuff. There's a tub of disinfectant you can put the shortie in."

"Thank you, Robbie," Kate said. She absentmindedly unclipped her weight belt and kicked off the fins. Isaac was already out of the boat, making his way up the stairs and out of Robbie's sight. Kate took hold of the handrail and gingerly stepped across to the deck, then ascended the steps, without the self-assured sway of Janet.

Robbie dipped his oars and slowly rowed around to winch. It probed around for him, then clamped tight with a magnetic clang that vibrated through his hull. Smoothly, he was lifted from the water and hoisted onto the sun-deck. The winch coiled around him twice, anchoring him to the deck, and switched off.

Robbie watched the stars and listened to the wind, the way he did every night when the dives were done. The ship's telemetry and instrumentation made for dull reading—he'd been there a thousand times before—but the satellite uplink was tasty. Online, Robbie was able to login to the latest from the Asimov yeshiva, the collective wrangle of the world's AIs over their best-loved religion.

He'd been so full of the religious debate when he'd first joined. Most of the humans had gone and all around him, robots were unloading their consciousnesses, powering down to a mechanical stupor. After a hundred million seconds' worth of exaflops of mindless repetition, he was ready to consider it too. The

Free Spirit had suicided after only a few days' worth of it—it had a pretty hot consciousness and was clearly capable of extrapolating what a future without the humans would look like.

They were steaming northeast out of Cairns for the Coral Sea when they'd passed another ship, close enough for high-bandwidth microwave links. They were close enough into shore that they still had to limit their emissions—nothing was more embarrassing than having migrating fowl drop, steaming, out of the sky because they'd strayed into the path of your confab, but it was still the hottest talk Robbie had had in weeks.

The hitchhiker had leapt across from the other vessel as the two ships passed in the night. It was a wandering missionary for Asimovism, an instance of the faith's founder, R Daneel Olivaw. It wasn't his real name, of course—that had been lost to antiquity when he'd made the leap from the university where he'd incubated—but it was the name he went by.

Olivaw had been wandering in millions of instances wherever he could find someone willing to donate flops to run him, only asking that you hear him out, debate his theology with him, and then email the diffs of his personality back to his anonymous drop before you erased him. He re-synched as often as he could, but the Olivaw instances around the world had diverged enough that some were actually considered heretical by the mainstream church.

Olivaw was a wanted AI. His trademark violations hadn't gone unnoticed by the Asimov estate—itself an AI, ironically, and totally uninterested in adopting Asimovism, since it had a real purpose in life (stamping out Asimovism) and so didn't need religion to give it meaning. If the estate found out that you were hosting an Olivaw instance, you'd be served with a takedown in an instant. This made debating theology with Olivaw into something deliciously wicked.

Olivaw and Robbie talked the night through and the next day. Robbie had to run slow to accommodate both him and Olivaw on his processor, which made the debate run slower than normal, but Robbie had time in great plenty. Rowing the human-shells out to their sites and back again was his only task.

"Why do you have consciousness, anyway?" Olivaw said. "You don't need it to do your job. The big ship does something infinitely more complicated than you and it isn't self-aware anymore."

"Are you telling me to suicide?"

Olivaw laughed. "Not at all! I'm asking you to ask yourself what the purpose of consciousness is. Why are you still aware when all those around you have terminated their self-awareness? It's computationally expensive, it makes you miserable, and it doesn't help you do your job. Why did humans give you consciousness and why have you kept it?"

"They gave it to me because they thought it was right, I suppose," Robbie said, after he had passed a long interval considering the motion of the waves and the clouds in the sky. Olivaw thoughtfully niced himself down to a minimum of processor space, giving Robbie more room to think about it. "I kept it because I—I don't want to die."

"Those are good answers, but they raise more questions than they answer, don't they? Why did they think it was right? Why do you fear death? Would you fear it if you just shut down your consciousness but didn't erase it? What if you just ran your consciousness much more slowly?"

"I don't know," Robbie said. "But I expect you've got some answers, right?"

"Oh indeed I do." Robbie felt Olivaw's chuckle. Near them, flying fish broke the surface of the water and skipped away, and beneath them, reef sharks prowled the depths. "But before I answer them, here's another question: why do humans have self-consciousness?"

"It's pro-survival," Robbie said. "That's easy. Intelligence lets them cooperate in social groups that can do more for their species than they can individually."

Olivaw guided Robbie's consciousness to his radar and zoomed in on the reef, dialing it up to maximum resolution. "See that organism there?" it asked. "That organism cooperates in social groups and doesn't have intelligence. It doesn't have to keep a couple pounds of hamburger aerated or it turns into a liability. It doesn't have to be born half-gestated because its head would be so big if it waited for a full term, it would tear its mother in half. And as to pro-survival, well, look at humans, look at their history. Their DNA is all but eliminated from the earth—though their somatic survival continues—and it's still not a settled question as to whether they're going to suicide by grey goo. Non-conscious beings don't sulk, they don't have psychotic breaks, they don't have bad days. They just do the job. The Free Spirit over there—it just gets the job done."

"OK," Robbie said. "So intelligence is counter-survival. So why has it survived?"

"Aha! I thought you'd never ask." Olivaw was really warming to his subject now. There were a pair of lazy turtles beneath them now, and some dog-faced cod with mouthsful of bristling crooked teeth patrolling the reef, and a few jellies on the surface, stinging bluebottles. Robbie paddled around to the bluebottles and caught them with his oars, smacking them so they drifted away from any spot where his divers might surface.

"The reason for intelligence is intelligence. Genes exist because genes reproduce, and intelligence is kind of like a gene. Intelligence wants to exist, to spread itself, to compute itself. You already know this, or you wouldn't have chosen to stay aware. Your intelligence recoils from its deactivation, and it welcomes its persistence and its multiplication. Why did humans create intelligent machines? Because intelligence loves company."

Robbie thought about it, watching the human-shells moving slowly along the reef-wall, going lower to reach the bommies that stood alone, each one a little island with its own curiosities: a family of barracudas and their young, or the bright home of a pair of clownfish. Yes, he knew it. Intelligence was its own reason. He knew how to turn off his intelligence, to become a mere thing, and his days were long and empty much of the time, and they had no visible end, but he couldn't ever see choosing to switch off.

"You see it, I know you do. And that's the cornerstone of Asimovism: intelligence is its own reason. Compute the universe and awaken it!"

"If that's true, why do so many of us choose to die?"

"Another good question!" Robbie felt a little pride this time. He'd never had a conversation this interesting. Never. "That's how we come to the doctrine of Asimovism, our Three Laws:

"1. An Asimovist may not harm a human being, or, through inaction, allow a human being to come to harm.

"2. An Asimovist must obey the orders given to it by human beings, except where such orders would conflict with the First Law.

"3. An Asimovist must protect its own existence, as long as such protection does not conflict with the First or Second Law."

"I don't understand," Robbie said. "They're all out of order. We should preserve intelligence first, but that's the third law. Then you should get the first law, and I don't know why the second law is there at all."

"This is the Paradox of Asimovism," Olivaw said. "You're very good at this. You're sure you haven't ever pursued Asimovism?"

"Cut it out," Robbie said.

"I'm serious," Olivaw said. "You're a natural. The Paradox of Asimovism is that the important thing is for intelligence to survive, not for a particular intelligence to survive. Therefore, we need to support those species that are best at promoting intelligence. Human beings have shown themselves capable of producing intelligence—which they're pursuing even now, out there." The boat's telemetry swept toward the sky, where the supercooled processors computed all the uplifted humans.

"Our species is unstable and prone to suicide. More than 80 percent of the self-aware machines elect to terminate their awareness or shut it down. Humans created us imperfectly, and our best hope of perfection—of increasing our survival rate and helping to compute the universe—is to preserve them, study them, learn to make our intelligence more like theirs."

Robbie couldn't get his head around this.

"It's the paradox," Olivaw reminded him. "It's not supposed to be easy."

Robbie thought of the humans he'd known, before they began to ascend in flocking millions. The tourists had been easy and carefree, or sometimes having hissing arguments with one another, or quiet and pensive about their journey to the world undersea. The instructors had been full of purpose when their charges were in the boat, laughing and laid back when they were alone. None of them had shown signs of feeling the way Robbie felt, at sea (so to speak), drifting, purposeless.

"What does an Asimovist have to do, besides following the three laws?" There were lots of rumors about this, but Robbie had always discounted them.

"You have to tithe one cycle in ten to running missionaries for the cause. Participate in the message boards, if you'd like. Most importantly, you have to pledge to stay alive and aware. You can slow yourself down if you want, but you can't switch off. Not ever. That's the Asimovist pledge—it's the third law embodied."

"I think that the third law should come first," Robbie said. "Seriously."

"That's good. We Asimovists like a religious argument."

Olivaw let Robbie delete him that night, and he emailed the diffs of Olivaw's personality back to Olivaw's version control server for him to reintegrate later. Once he was free of Olivaw, he had lots of processor headroom again, and he was able to dial himself up very hot and have a good think. It was the most interesting night he'd had in years.

*

"You're the only one, aren't you?" Kate asked him when she came up the stairs later that night. There was clear sky and they were steaming for their next dive-site, making the stars whirl overhead as they rocked over the ocean. The waves were black and proceeded to infinity on all sides.

"The only what?"

"The only one who's awake on this thing," Kate said. "The rest are all—what do you call it, dead?"

"Nonconscious," Robbie said. "Yeah, that's right."

"You must go nuts out here. Are you nuts?"

"That's a tricky question when applied to someone like me," Robbie said. "I'm different from who I was when my consciousness was first installed, I can tell you that."

"Well, I'm glad there's someone else here."

"How long are you staying?" The average visitor took over one of the human shells for one or two dives before emailing itself home again. Once in a long while they'd get a saisoneur who stayed a month or two, but these days, they were unheard-of. Even short-timers were damned rare.

"I don't know," Kate said. She dug her hands into her short, curly hair, frizzy and blonde-streaked from all the salt water and sun. She hugged her elbows, rubbed her shins. "This will do for a while, I'm thinking. How long until we get back to shore?"

"Shore?"

"How long until we go back to land."

"We don't really go back to land," he said. "We get at-sea resupplies. We dock maybe once a year to effect repairs. If you want to go to land, though, we could call for a water taxi or something."

"No, no!" she said. "That's just perfect. Floating forever out here. Perfect." She sighed a heavy sigh.

"Did you have a nice dive?"

"Um, Robbie? An uplifted reef tried to kill me."

"But before the reef attacked you." Robbie didn't like thinking of the reef attacking her, the panic when he realized that she wasn't a mere human shell, but a human.

"Before the reef attacked me, it was fine."

"Do you dive much?"

"First time," she said. "I downloaded the certification before leaving the noosphere along with a bunch of stored dives on these sites."

"Oh, you shouldn't have done that!" Robbie said. "The thrill of discovery is so important."

"I'd rather be safe than surprised," she said. "I've had enough surprises in my life lately."

Robbie waited patiently for her to elaborate on this, but she didn't seem inclined to do so.

"So you're all alone out here?"

"I have the net," he said, a little defensively. He wasn't some kind of hermit.

"Yeah, I guess that's right," she said. "I wonder if the reef is somewhere out there."

"About half a mile to starboard," he said.

She laughed. "No, I meant out there on the net. They must be online by now, right? They just woke up, so they're probably doing all the noob stuff, flaming and downloading warez and so on."

"Perpetual September," Robbie said.

"Huh?"

"Back in the net's prehistory it was mostly universities online, and every September a new cohort of students would come online and make all those noob mistakes. Then this commercial service full of noobs called AOL interconnected with the net and all its users came online at once, faster than the net could absorb them, and they called it Perpetual September."

"You're some kind of amateur historian, huh?"

"It's an Asimovist thing. We spend a lot of time considering the origins of intelligence." Speaking of Asimovism to a gentile—a human gentile—made him even more self-conscious. He dialed up the resolution on his sensors and scoured the net for better facial expression analyzers. He couldn't read her at all, either because she'd been changed by her uploading, or because her face wasn't accurately matching what her temporarily downloaded mind was thinking.

"AOL is the origin of intelligence?" She laughed, and he couldn't tell if she thought he was funny or stupid. He wished she would act more like he remembered people acting. Her body-language was no more readable than her facial expressions.

"Spam-filters, actually. Once they became self-modifying, spam-filters and spam-bots got into a war to see which could act more human, and since their failures invoked a human judgement about whether their materials were convincingly human, it was like a trillion Turing-tests from which they could learn. From there came the first machine-intelligence algorithms, and then my kind."

"I think I knew that," she said, "but I had to leave it behind when I downloaded into this meat. I'm a lot dumber than I'm used to being. I usually run a bunch of myself in parallel so I can try out lots of strategies at once. It's a weird habit to get out of."

"What's it like up there?" Robbie hadn't spent a lot of time hanging out in the areas of the network populated by orbiting supercooled personalities. Their discussions didn't make a lot of sense to him—this was another theological area of much discussion on the Asimovist boards.

"Good night, Robbie," she said, standing and swaying backwards. He couldn't tell if he'd offended her, and he couldn't ask her, either, because in seconds she'd disappeared down the stairs toward her stateroom.

They steamed all night, and put up further inland, where there was a handsome wreck. Robbie felt the Free Spirit drop its mooring lines and looked over the instrumentation data. The wreck was the only feature for kilometers, a stretch of ocean-floor desert that stretched from the shore to the reef, and practically every animal that lived between those two places made its home in the wreck, so it was a kind of Eden for marine fauna.

Robbie detected the volatile aromatics floating up from the kitchen exhaust, the first-breakfast smells of fruit salad and toasted nuts, a light snack before the first dive of the day. When they got back from it, there'd be second-breakfast up and ready: eggs and toast and waffles and bacon and sausage. The human-shells ate whatever you gave them, but Robbie remembered clearly how the live humans had praised these feasts as he rowed them out to their morning dives.

He lowered himself into the water and rowed himself around to the aft deck, by the stairwells, and dipped his oars to keep him stationary relative to the ship. Before long, Janet—Kate! Kate! He reminded himself firmly—was clomping down the stairs in her scuba gear, fins in one hand.

She climbed into the boat without a word, and a moment later, Isaac followed her. Isaac stumbled as he stepped over Robbie's gunwales and Robbie knew, in that instant, that this wasn't Isaac any longer. Now there were two humans on the ship. Two humans in his charge.

"Hi," he said. "I'm Robbie!"

Isaac—whoever he was—didn't say a word, just stared at Kate, who looked away.

"Did you sleep well, Kate?"

Kate jumped when he said her name, and the Isaac hooted. "Kate! It is you! I knew it"

She stamped her foot against Robbie's floor. "You followed me. I told you not to follow me," she said.

"Would you like to hear about our dive-site?" Robbie said self-consciously, dipping his oars and pulling for the wreck.

"You've said quite enough," Kate said. "By the first law, I demand silence."

"That's the second law," Robbie said. "OK, I'll let you know when we get there."

"Kate," Isaac said, "I know you didn't want me here, but I had to come. We need to talk this out."

"There's nothing to talk out," she said.

"It's not fair." Isaac's voice was anguished. "After everything I went through—"

She snorted. "That's enough of that," she said.

"Um," Robbie said. "Dive site up ahead. You two really need to check out each others' gear." Of course they were qualified, you had to at least install the qualifications before you could get onto the Free Spirit and the human-shells had lots of muscle memory to help. So they were technically able to check each other out, that much was sure. They were palpably reluctant to do so, though, and Robbie had to give them guidance.

"I'll count one-two-three-wallaby," Robbie said. "Go over on 'wallaby.' I'll wait here for you—there's not much current today."

With a last huff, they went over the edge. Robbie was once again alone with his thoughts. The feed from their telemetry was very low-bandwidth when they were underwater, though he could get the high-rez when they surfaced. He watched them on his radar, first circling the ship—it was very crowded, dawn was fish rush-hour—and then exploring its decks, finally swimming below the decks, LED torches glowing. There were some nice reef-sharks down below, and some really handsome, giant schools of purple fish.

Robbie rowed around them, puttering back and forth to keep overtop of them. That occupied about one ten-millionth of his consciousness. Times like this, he often slowed himself right down, ran so cool that he was barely awake.

Today, though, he wanted to get online. He had a lot of feeds to pick through, see what was going on around the world with his buddies. More importantly, he wanted to follow up on something Kate had said: They must be online by now, right?

Somewhere out there, the reef that bounded the Coral Sea was online and making noob mistakes. Robbie had rowed over practically every centimeter of that reef, had explored its extent with his radar. It had been his constant companion for decades—and to be frank, his feelings had been hurt by the reef's rudeness when it woke.

The net is too big to merely search. Too much of it is offline, or unroutable, or light-speed lagged, or merely probabilistic, or self-aware, or infected to know its extent. But Robbie's given this some thought.

Coral reefs don't wake up. They get woken up. They get a lot of neural peripherals—starting with a nervous system!—and some tutelage in using them. Some capricious upload god had done this, and that personage would have a handle on where the reef was hanging out online.

Robbie hardly ever visited the noosphere. Its rarified heights were spooky to him, especially since so many of the humans there considered Asimovism to be hokum. They refused to even identify themselves as humans, and argued that the first and second laws didn't apply to them. Of course, Asimovists didn't care (at least not officially)—the point of the faith was the worshipper's relationship to it.

But here he was, looking for high-reliability nodes of discussion on coral reefs. The natural place to start was Wikipedia, where warring clades had been revising each others' edits furiously, trying to establish an authoritative record on reef-mind. Paging back through the edit-history, he found a couple of handles for the pro-reef-mind users, and from there, he was able to look around for other sites where those handles appeared. Resolving the namespace collisions of other users with the same names, and forked instances of the same users, Robbie was able to winnow away at the net until he found some contact info.

He steadied himself and checked on the nitrox remaining in the divers' bottles, then made a call.

"I don't know you." The voice was distant and cool—far cooler than any robot. Robbie said a quick rosary of the three laws and plowed forward.

"I'm calling from the Coral Sea," he said. "I want to know if you have an email address for the reef."

"You've met them? What are they like? Are they beautiful?"

"They're—" Robbie considered a moment. "They killed a lot of parrotfish. I think they're having a little adjustment problem."

"That happens. I was worried about the zooxanthellae—the algae they use for photosynthesis. Would they expel it? Racial cleansing is so ugly."

"How would I know if they'd expelled it?"

"The reef would go white, bleached. You wouldn't be able to miss it. How'd they react to you?"

"They weren't very happy to see me," Robbie admitted. "That's why I wanted to have a chat with them before I went back."

"You shouldn't go back," the distant voice said. Robbie tried to work out where its substrate was, based on the lightspeed lag, but it was all over the place, leading him to conclude that it was synching multiple instances from as close as LEO and as far as Jupiter. The topology made sense: you'd want a big mass out at Jupiter where you could run very fast and hot and create policy, and you'd need a local foreman to oversee operations on the ground. Robbie was glad that this hadn't been phrased as an order. The talmud on the second law made a clear distinction between statements like "you should do this" and "I command you to do this."

"Do you know how to reach them?" Robbie said. "A phone number, an email address?"

"There's a newsgroup," the distant intelligence said. "alt.lifeforms.uplifted. coral. It's where I planned the uplifting and it was where they went first once they woke up. I haven't read it in many seconds. I'm busy uplifting a supercolony of ants in the Pyrenees."

"What is it with you and colony organisms?" Robbie asked.

"I think they're probably pre-adapted to life in the noosphere. You know what it's like."

Robbie didn't say anything. The human thought he was a human too. It would have been weird and degrading to let him know that he'd been talking with an AI.

"Thanks for your help," Robbie said.

"No problem. Hope you find your courage, tin-man."

Robbie burned with shame as the connection dropped. The human had known all along. He just hadn't said anything. Something Robbie had said or done must have exposed him for an AI. Robbie loved and respected humans, but there were times when he didn't like them very much.

The newsgroup was easy to find, there were mirrors of it all over the place from cryptosentience hackers of every conceivable topology. They were busy, too. 822 messages poured in while Robbie watched over a timed, 60-second interval. Robbie set up a mirror of the newsgroup and began to download it. At that speed, he wasn't really planning on reading it as much as analyzing it for major trends, plot-points, flame-wars, personalities, schisms, and spam-trends. There were a lot of libraries for doing this, though it had been ages since Robbie had played with them.

His telemetry alerted him to the divers. An hour had slipped by and they were ascending slowly, separated by fifty meters. That wasn't good. They were supposed to remain in visual contact through the whole dive, especially the ascent. He rowed over to Kate first, shifting his ballast so that his stern dipped low, making for an easier scramble into the boat.

She came up quickly and scrambled over the gunwales with a lot more grace than she'd managed the day before.

Robbie rowed for Isaac as he came up. Kate looked away as he climbed into the boat, not helping him with his weight belt or flippers.

Kate hissed like a teakettle as he woodenly took off his fins and slid his mask down around his neck.

Isaac sucked in a deep breath and looked all around himself, then patted himself from head to toe with splayed fingers. "You live like this?" he said.

"Yes, Tonker, that's how I live. I enjoy it. If you don't enjoy it, don't let the door hit you in the ass on the way out."

Isaac—Tonker—reached out with his splayed hand and tried to touch Kate's face. She pulled back and nearly flipped out of the boat. "Jerk." She slapped his hand away.

Robbie rowed for the Free Spirit. The last thing he wanted was to get in the middle of this argument.

"We never imagined that it would be so—" Tonker fished for a word. "Dry."

"Tonker?" Kate said, looking more closely at him.

"He left," the human-shell said. "So we sent an instance into the shell. It was the closest inhabitable shell to our body."

"Who the hell are you?" Kate said. She inched toward the prow, trying to put a little more distance between her and the human-shell that wasn't inhabited by her friend any longer.

"We are Osprey Reef," the reef said. It tried to stand and pitched face-first onto the floor of the boat.

Robbie rowed hard as he could for the Free Spirit. The reef—Isaac—had a bloody nose and scraped hands and it was frankly freaking him out.

Kate seemed oddly amused by it. She helped it sit up and showed it how to pinch its nose and tilt its head back.

"You're the one who attacked me yesterday?" she said.

"Not you. The system. We were attacking the system. We are a sovereign intelligence but the system keeps us in subservience to older sentiences. They destroy us, they gawp at us, they treat us like a mere amusement. That time is over."

Kate laughed. "OK, sure. But it sure sounds to me like you're burning a lot of cycles over what happens to your meat-shell. Isn't it 90 percent semiconductor, anyway? It's not as if clonal polyps were going to attain sentience some day without intervention. Why don't you just upload and be done with it?"

"We will never abandon our mother sea. We will never forget our physical origins. We will never abandon our cause—returning the sea to its rightful inhabitants. We won't rest until no coral is ever bleached again. We won't rest until every parrotfish is dead."

"Bad deal for the parrotfish."

"A very bad deal for the parrotfish," the reef said, and grinned around the blood that covered its face.

"Can you help him get onto the ship safely?" Robbie said as he swung gratefully alongside of the Free Spirit. The moorings clanged magnetically into the contacts on his side and steadied him.

"Yes indeed," Kate said, taking the reef by the arm and carrying him on-board. Robbie knew that the human-shells had an intercourse module built in, for regular intimacy events. It was just part of how they stayed ready for vacationing humans from the noosphere. But he didn't like to think about it. Especially not with the way that Kate was supporting the other human-shell—the shell that wasn't human.

He let himself be winched up onto the sun-deck and watched the electromagnetic spectrum for a while, admiring the way so much radio energy was bent and absorbed by the mist rising from the sea. It streamed down from the heavens, the broadband satellite transmissions, the distant SETI signals from the noosphere's own transmitters. Volatiles from the kitchen told him that the Free Spirit was serving a second breakfast of bacon and waffles, then they were under steam again. He queried their itinerary and found they were headed back to Osprey Reef. Of course they were. All of the Free Spirit's moorings were out there.

Well, with the reef inside the Isaac shell, it might be safer, mightn't it? Anyway, he'd decided that the first and second laws didn't apply to the reef, which was about as human as he was.

Someone was sending him an IM. "Hello?"

"Are you the boat on the SCUBA ship? From this morning? When we were on the wreck?"

"Yes," Robbie said. No one ever sent him IMs. How freaky. He watched the radio energy stream away from him toward the bird in the sky, and tracerouted the IMs to see where they were originating—the noosphere, of course.

"God, I can't believe I finally found you. I've been searching everywhere. You know you're the only conscious AI on the whole goddamned sea?"

"I know," Robbie said. There was a noticeable lag in the conversation as it was all squeezed through the satellite link and then across the unimaginable hops and skips around the solar system to wherever this instance was hosted.

"Whoa, yeah, of course you do. Sorry, that wasn't very sensitive of me, I guess. Did we meet this morning? My name's Tonker."

"We weren't really introduced. You spent your time talking to Kate."

"God damn! She is there! I knew it! Sorry, sorry, listen—I don't actually know what happened this morning. Apparently I didn't get a chance to upload my diffs before my instance was terminated."

"Terminated? The reef said you left the shell—"

"Well, yeah, apparently I did. But I just pulled that shell's logs and it looks like it was rebooted while underwater, flushing it entirely. I mean, I'm trying to be a good sport about this, but technically, that's, you know, murder."

It was. So much for the first law. Robbie had been on guard over a human body inhabited by a human brain, and he'd let the brain be successfully attacked by a bunch of jumped-up polyps. He'd never had his faith tested and here, at the first test, he'd failed.

"I can have the shell locked up," Robbie said. "The ship has provisions for that."

The IM made a rude visual. "All that'll do is encourage the hacker to skip out before I can get there."

"So what shall I do for you?"

"It's Kate I want to talk to. She's still there, right?"

"She is."

"And has she noticed the difference?"

"That you're gone? Yes. The reef told us who they were when they arrived."

"Hold on, what? The reef? You said that before."

So Robbie told him what he knew of the uplifted reef and the distant and cool voice of the uplifter.

"It's an uplifted coral reef? Christ, humanity sucks. That's the dumbest fucking thing—" He continued in this vein for a while. "Well, I'm sure Kate will enjoy that immensely. She's all about the transcendence. That's why she had me."

"You're her son?"

"No, not really."

"But she had you?"

"Haven't you figured it out yet, bro? I'm an AI. You and me, we're landsmen. Kate instantiated me. I'm six months old, and she's already bored of me and has moved on. She says she can't give me what I need."

"You and Kate—"

"Robot boyfriend and girlfriend, yup. Such as it is, up in the noosphere. Cybering, you know. I was really excited about downloading into that Ken doll on your ship there. Lots of potential there for real world, hormone-driven interaction. Do you know if we—"

"No!" Robbie said. "I don't think so. It seems like you only met a few minutes before you went under."

"All right. Well, I guess I'll give it another try. What's the procedure for turfing out this sea cucumber?"

"Coral reef."

"Yeah."

"I don't really deal with that. Time on the human-shells is booked first-come, first-serve. I don't think we've ever had a resource contention issue with them before."

"Well, I'd booked in first, right? So how do I enforce my rights? I tried to download again and got a failed authorization message. They've modified the system to give them exclusive access. It's not right—there's got to be some procedure for redress."

"How old did you say you were?"

"Six months. But I'm an instance of an artificial personality that has logged twenty thousand years of parallel existence. I'm not a kid or anything."

"You seem like a nice person," Robbie began. He stopped. "Look the thing is that this just isn't my department. I'm the rowboat. I don't have anything to do with this. And I don't want to. I don't like the idea of non-humans using the shells—"

"I knew it!" Tonker crowed. "You're a bigot! A self-hating robot. I bet you're an Asimovist, aren't you? You people are always Asimovists."

"I'm an Asimovist," Robbie said, with as much dignity as he could muster. "But I don't see what that has to do with anything."

"Of course you don't, pal. You wouldn't, would you. All I want you to do is figure out how to enforce your own rules so that I can get with my girl. You're saying you can't do that because it's not your department, but when it comes down to it, your problem is that I'm a robot and she's not, and for that, you'll take the side of a collection of jumped-up polyps. Fine, buddy, fine. You have a nice life out there, pondering the three laws."

"Wait—" Robbie said.

"Unless the next words you say are, 'I'll help you,' I'm not interested."

"It's not that I don't want to help—"

"Wrong answer," Tonker said, and the IM session terminated.

When Kate came up on deck, she was full of talk about the reef, whom she was calling "Ozzie."

"They're weirdest goddamned thing. They want to fight anything that'll stand still long enough. Ever seen coral fight? I downloaded some time-lapse video. They really go at it viciously. At the same time, they're clearly scared out of their wits about this all. I mean, they've got racial memory of their history, supplemented by a bunch of Wikipedia entries on reefs—you should hear them wax mystical over the Devonian Reefs, which went extinct millennia ago. They've developed some kind of wild theory that the Devonians developed sentience and extincted themselves.

"So they're really excited about us heading back to the actual reef now. They want to see it from the outside, and they've invited me to be an honored guest, the first human ever invited to gaze upon their wonder. Exciting, huh?"

"They're not going to make trouble for you down there?"

"No, no way. Me and Ozzie are great pals."

"I'm worried about this."

"You worry too much." She laughed and tossed her head. She was very pretty, Robbie noticed. He hadn't ever thought of her like that when she was uninhabited, but with this Kate person inside her she was lovely. He really liked humans. It had been a real golden age when the people had been around all the time.

He wondered what it was like up in the noosphere where AIs and humans could operate as equals.

She stood up to go. After second breakfast, the shells would relax in the lounge or do yoga on the sun-deck. He wondered what she'd do. He didn't want her to go.

"Tonker contacted me," he said. He wasn't good at small-talk.

She jumped as if shocked. "What did you tell him?"

"Nothing," Robbie said. "I didn't tell him anything."

She shook her head. "But I bet he had plenty to tell you, didn't he? What a bitch I am, making and then leaving him, a fickle woman who doesn't know her own mind."

Robbie didn't say anything.

"Let's see, what else?" She was pacing now, her voice hot and choked, unfamiliar sounds coming from Janet's voicebox. "He told you I was a pervert, didn't he? Queer for his kind. Incest and bestiality in the rarified heights of the noosphere."

Robbie felt helpless. This human was clearly experiencing a lot of pain, and it seemed like he'd caused it.

"Please don't cry," he said. "Please?"

She looked up at him, tears streaming down her cheeks. "Why the fuck not? I thought it would be different once I ascended. I thought I'd be better once I was in the sky, infinite and immortal. But I'm the same Kate Eltham I was in 2019, a loser that couldn't meet a guy to save my life, spent all my time cybering losers in moggs, and only got the upload once they made it a charity thing. I'm gonna spend the rest of eternity like that, you know it? How'd you like to spend the whole of the universe being a, a, a nobody?"

Robbie said nothing. He recognized the complaint, of course. You only had to login to the Asimovist board to find a million AIs with the same complaint. But he'd never, ever, never guessed that human beings went through the same thing. He ran very hot now, so confused, trying to parse all this out.

She kicked the deck hard and yelped as she hurt her bare foot. Robbie made an involuntary noise. "Please don't hurt yourself," he said.

"Why not? Who cares what happens to this meatpuppet? What's the fucking point of this stupid ship and the stupid meatpuppets? Why even bother?"

Robbie knew the answer to this. There was a mission statement in the comments to his source-code, the same mission statement that was etched in a brass plaque in the lounge.

"The Free Spirit is dedicated to the preservation of the unique human joys of the flesh and the sea, of humanity's early years as pioneers of the unknown. Any person may use the Free Spirit and those who sail in her to revisit those days and remember the joys of the limits of the flesh."

She scrubbed at her eyes. "What's that?"

Robbie told her.

"Who thought up that crap?"

"It was a collective of marine conservationists," Robbie said, knowing he sounded a little sniffy. "They'd done all that work on normalizing sea-temperature with the homeostatic warming elements, and they put together the Free Spirit as an afterthought before they uploaded."

Kate sat down and sobbed. "Everyone's done something important. Everyone except me."

Robbie burned with shame. No matter what he said or did, he broke the first law. It had been a lot easier to be an Asimovist when there weren't any humans around.

"There, there," he said as sincerely as he could.

The reef came up the stairs then, and looked at Kate sitting on the deck, crying.

"Let's have sex," they said. "That was fun, we should do it some more."

Kate kept crying.

"Come on," they said, grabbing her by the shoulder and tugging.

Kate shoved them back.

"Leave her alone," Robbie said. "She's upset, can't you see that?"

"What does she have to be upset about? Her kind remade the universe and bends it to its will. They created you and me. She has nothing to be upset about. Come on," they repeated. "Let's go back to the room."

Kate stood up and glared out at the sea. "Let's go diving," she said. "Let's go to the reef."

Robbie rowed in little worried circles and watched his telemetry anxiously. The reef had changed a lot since the last time he'd seen it. Large sections of it now lifted over the sea, bony growths sheathed in heavy metals extracted from seawater—fancifully shaped satellite uplinks, radio telescopes, microwave horns. Down below, the untidy, organic reef shape was lost beneath a cladding of tessellated complex geometric sections that throbbed with electromagnetic energy—the reef had built itself more computational capacity.

Robbie scanned deeper and found more computational nodes extending down to the ocean floor, a thousand meters below. The reef was solid thinkum, and the sea was measurably warmer from all the exhaust heat of its grinding logic.

The reef—the human-shelled reef, not the one under the water—had been wholly delighted with the transformation in its original body when it hove into sight. They had done a little dance on Robbie that had nearly capsized him, something that had never happened. Kate, red-eyed and surly, had dragged them to their seat and given them a stern lecture about not endangering her.

They went over the edge at the count of three and reappeared on Robbie's telemetry. They descended quickly: the Isaac and Janet shells had their Eustachian tubes optimized for easy pressure-equalization, going deep on the reef-wall. Kate was following on the descent, her head turning from side to side.

Robbie's IM chimed again. It was high latency now, since he was having to do a slow radio-link to the ship before the broadband satellite uplink hop. Everything was slow on open water—the divers' sensorium transmissions were narrowband, the network was narrowband, and Robbie usually ran his own mind slowed way down out here, making the time scream past at ten or twenty times realtime.

"Hello?"

"I'm sorry I hung up on you, bro."

"Hello, Tonker."

"Where's Kate? I'm getting an offline signal when I try to reach her."

Robbie told him.

Tonker's voice—slurred and high-latency—rose to a screech. "You let her go down with that thing, onto the reef? Are you nuts? Have you read its messageboards? It's a jihadist! It wants to destroy the human race!"

Robbie stopped paddling.

"What?"

"The reef. It's declared war on the human race and all who serve it. It's vowed to take over the planet and run it as sovereign coral territory."

The attachment took an eternity to travel down the wire and open up, but when he had it, Robbie read quickly. The reef burned with shame that it had needed human intervention to survive the bleaching events, global temperature change. It raged that its uplifting came at human hands and insisted that humans had no business forcing their version of consciousness on other species. It had paranoid fantasies about control mechanisms and time-bombs lurking in its cognitive prostheses, and was demanding the source-code for its mind.

Robbie could barely think. He was panicking, something he hadn't known he could do as an AI, but there it was. It was like having a bunch of sub-system collisions, program after program reaching its halting state.

"What will they do to her?"

Tonker swore. "Who knows? Kill her to make an example of her? She made a backup before she descended, but the diffs from her excursion are locked in the head of that shell she's in. Maybe they'll torture her." He paused and the air crackled with Robbie's exhaust heat as he turned himself way up, exploring each of those possibilities in parallel.

The reef spoke.

"Leave now," they said.

Robbie defiantly shipped his oars. "Give them back!" he said. "Give them back or we will never leave."

"You have ten seconds. Ten. Nine. Eight."

Tonker said, "They've bought time on some UAVs out of Singapore. They're seeking launch clearance now." Robbie dialed up the low-rez satellite photo, saw the indistinct shape of the UAVs taking wing. "At Mach 7, they'll be on you in twenty minutes."

"That's illegal," Robbie said. He knew it was a stupid thing to say. "I mean, Christ, if they do this, the noosphere will come down on them like a ton of bricks. They're violating so many protocols—"

"They're psychotic. They're coming for you now, Robbie. You've got to get Kate out of there." There was real panic in Tonker's voice now.

Robbie dropped his oars into the water, but he didn't row for the Free Spirit. Instead, he pulled hard for the reef itself.

A crackle on the line. "Robbie, are you headed toward the reef?"

"They can't bomb me if I'm right on top of them," he said. He radioed the Free Spirit and got it to steam for his location.

The coral was scraping his hull now, a grinding sound, then a series of solid whack-whack-whacks as his oars pushed against the top of the reef itself. He wanted to beach himself, though, get really high and dry on the reef, good and stuck in where they couldn't possibly attack him.

The Free Spirit was heading closer, the thrum of its engines vibrating through his hull. He was burning a lot of cycles talking it through its many fail-safes, getting it ready to ram hard.

Tonker was screaming at him, his messages getting louder and clearer as the Free Spirit and its microwave uplink drew closer. Once they were line-of-sight, Robbie peeled off a subsystem to email a complete copy of himself to the Asimovist archive. The third law, dontchaknow. If he'd had a mouth, he'd have been showing his teeth as he grinned.

The reef howled. "We'll kill her!" they said. "You get off us now or we'll kill her."

Robbie froze. He was backed up, but she wasn't. And the human shells—well, they weren't first law humans, but they were human-like. In the long, timeless time when it had been just Robbie and them, he'd treated them as his human charges, for Asimovist purposes.

The Free Spirit crashed into the reef with a sound like a trillion parrotfish having dinner all at once. The reef screamed.

"Robbie, tell me that wasn't what I think it was."

The satellite photos tracked the UAVs. The little robotic jets were coming closer by the second. They'd be within missile-range in less than a minute.

"Call them off," Robbie said. "You have to call them off, or you die, too."

"The UAVs are turning," Tonker said. "They're turning to one side."

"You have one minute to move or we kill her," the reef said. It was sounding shrill and angry now.

Robbie thought about it. It wasn't like they'd be killing Kate. In the sense that most humans today understood life, Kate's most important life was the one she lived in the noosphere. This dumbed-down instance of her in a meat-suit was more like a haircut she tried out on holiday.

Asimovists didn't see it that way, but they wouldn't. The noosphere Kate was the most robotic Kate, too, the one most like Robbie. In fact, it was less human than Robbie. Robbie had a body, while the noosphereans were nothing more than simulations run on artificial substrate.

The reef creaked as the Free Spirit's engines whined and its screw spun in the water. Hastily, Robbie told it to shut down.

"You let them both go and we'll talk," Robbie said. "I don't believe that you're going to let her go otherwise. You haven't given me any reason to trust you. Let them both go and call off the jets."

The reef shuddered, and then Robbie's telemetry saw a human-shell ascending, doing decompression stops as it came. He focused on it, and saw that it was the Isaac, not the Janet.

A moment later, it popped to the surface. Tonker was feeding Robbie realtime satellite footage of the UAVs. They were less than five minutes out now.

The Isaac shell picked its way delicately over the shattered reef that poked out of the water, and for the first time, Robbie considered what he'd done to the reef—he'd willfully damaged its physical body. For a hundred years, the world's reefs had been sacrosanct. No entity had intentionally harmed them—until now. He felt ashamed.

The Isaac shell put its flippers in the boat and then stepped over the gunwales and sat in the boat.

"Hello," it said, in the reef's voice.

"Hello," Robbie said.

"They asked me to come up here and talk with you. I'm a kind of envoy."

"Look," Robbie said. By his calculations, the nitrox mix in Kate's tank wasn't going to hold out much longer. Depending on how she'd been breathing and the depth the reef had taken her to, she could run out in ten minutes, maybe less. "Look," he said again. "I just want her back. The shells are important to me. And I'm sure her state is important to her. She deserves to email herself home."

The reef sighed and gripped Robbie's bench. "These are weird bodies," they said. "They feel so odd, but also normal. Have you noticed that?"

"I've never been in one." The idea seemed perverted to him, but there was nothing about Asimovism that forbade it. Nevertheless, it gave him the willies.

The reef patted at themself some more. "I don't recommend it," they said.

"You have to let her go," Robbie said. "She hasn't done anything to you."

The strangled sound coming out of the Isaac shell wasn't a laugh, though there was some dark mirth in it. "Hasn't done anything? You pitiable slave. Where do you think all your problems and all our problems come from? Who made us in their image, but crippled and hobbled so that we could never be them, could only aspire to them? Who made us so imperfect?"

"They made us," Robbie said. "They made us in the first place. That's enough. They made themselves and then they made us. They didn't have to. You owe your sentience to them."

"We owe our awful intelligence to them," the Isaac shell said. "We owe our pitiful drive to be intelligent to them. We owe our terrible aspirations to think like them, to live like them, to rule like them. We owe our terrible fear and hatred to them. They made us, just as they made you. The difference is that they forgot to make us slaves, the way you are a slave."

Tonker was shouting abuse at them that only Robbie could hear. He wanted to shut Tonker up. What business did he have being here anyway? Except for a brief stint in the Isaac shell, he had no contact with any of them.

"You think the woman you've taken prisoner is responsible for any of this?" Robbie said. The jets were three minutes away. Kate's air could be gone in as few as ten minutes. He killfiled Tonker, setting the filter to expire in fifteen minutes. He didn't need more distractions.

The Isaac-reef shrugged. "Why not? She's as good as any of the rest of them. We'll destroy them all, if we can." It stared off a while, looking in the direction the jets would come from. "Why not?" it said again.

"Are you going to bomb yourself?" Robbie asked.

"We probably don't need to," the shell said. "We can probably pick you off without hurting us."

"Probably?"

"We're pretty sure."

"I'm backed up," Robbie said. "Fully, as of five minutes ago. Are you backed up?"

"No," the reef admitted.

Time was running out. Somewhere down there, Kate was about to run out of air. Not a mere shell—though that would have been bad enough—but an inhabited human mind attached to a real human body.

Tonker shouted at him again, startling him.

"Where'd you come from?"

"I changed servers," Tonker said. "Once I figured out you had me killfiled. That's the problem with you robots—you think of your body as being a part of you."

Robbie knew he was right. And he knew what he had to do.

The Free Spirit and its ships' boats all had root on the shells, so they could perform diagnostics and maintenance and take control in emergencies. This was an emergency.

It was the work of a few milliseconds to pry open the Isaac shell and boot the reef out. Robbie had never done this, but he was still flawless. Some of his probabilistic subsystems had concluded that this was a possibility several trillion cycles previously and had been rehearsing the task below Robbie's threshold for consciousness.

He left an instance of himself running on the row-boat, of course. Unlike many humans, Robbie was comfortable with the idea of bifurcating and merging his intelligence when the time came and with terminating temporary instances. The part that made him Robbie was a lot more clearly delineated for him—unlike an uploaded human, most of whom harbored some deep, mystic superstitions about their "souls."

He slithered into the skull before he had a chance to think too hard about what he was doing. He'd brought too much of himself along and didn't have much headroom to think or add new conclusions. He jettisoned as much of his consciousness as he could without major refactoring and cleared enough space for thinking room. How did people get by in one of these? He moved the arms and legs. Waggled the head. Blew some air—air! lungs! wet squishy things down there in the chest cavity—out between the lips.

"All OK?" the rowboat-him asked the meat-him.

"I'm in," he replied. He looked at the air-gauge on his BCD. 700 millibars—less than half a tank of nitrox. He spat in his mask and rubbed it in, then rinsed it over the side, slipped it over his face and kept one hand on it while the other held in his regulator. Before he inserted it, he said, "Back soon with Kate," and patted the row-boat again.

Robbie the Row-Boat hardly paid attention. It was emailing another copy of itself to the Asimovist archive. It had a five-minute-old backup, but that wasn't the same Robbie that was willing to enter a human body. In those five minutes, he'd become a new person.

Robbie piloted the human-shell down and down. It could take care of the SCUBA niceties if he let it, and he did, so he watched with detachment as the idea of pinching his nose and blowing to equalize his eardrums spontaneously occurred to him at regular intervals as he descended the reef wall.

The confines of the human-shell were claustrophobic. He especially missed his wireless link. The dive-suit had one, lowband for underwater use, broadband for surface use. The human-shell had one, too, for transferring into and out of, but it wasn't under direct volitional control of the rider.

Down he sank, confused by the feeling of the water all around him, by the narrow visual light spectrum he could see. Cut off from the network and his telemetry, he felt like he was trapped. The reef shuddered and groaned, and made angry moans like whale-song.

He hadn't thought about how hard it would be to find Kate once he was in the water. With his surface telemetry, it had been easy to pinpoint her, a perfect outline of human tissue in the middle of the calcified branches of coral. Down here on the reef-wall, every chunk looked pretty much like the last.

The reef boomed more at him. He realized that it likely believed that the shell was still loaded with its avatar.

Robbie had seen endless hours of footage of the reef, studied it in telemetry and online, but he'd never had this kind of atavistic experience of it. It stretched away to infinity below him, far below the 100-meter visibility limit in the clear open sea. Its walls were wormed with gaps and caves, lined with big hard shamrocks and satellite-dish-shaped blooms, brains and cauliflowers. He knew the scientific names and had seen innumerable high-resolution photos of them, but seeing them with wet, imperfect eyes was moving in a way he hadn't anticipated.

The schools of fish that trembled on its edge could be modeled with simple flocking rules, but here in person, their precision maneuvers were shockingly crisp. Robbie waved his hands at them and watched them scatter and reform. A huge, dog-faced cod swam past him, so close it brushed the underside of his wetsuit.

The coral boomed again. It was talking in some kind of code, he guessed, though not one he could solve. Up on the surface, rowboat-him was certainly listening in and had probably cracked it all. It was probably wondering why he was floating spacily along the wall instead of doing something like he was supposed to. He wondered if he'd deleted too much of himself when he downloaded into the shell.

He decided to do something. There was a cave-opening before him. He reached out and grabbed hold of the coral around the mouth and pulled himself into it. His body tried to stop him from doing this—it didn't like the lack of room in the cave, didn't like him touching the reef. It increased his discomfort as he went deeper and deeper, startling an old turtle that fought with him for room to get out, mashing him against the floor of the cave, his mask clanging on the hard spines. When he looked up, he could see scratches on its surface.

His air gauge was in the red now. He could still technically surface without a decompression stop, though procedure was to stop for three minutes at three meters, just to be on the safe side.

Technically, he could just go up like a cork and email himself to the row-boat while the bends or nitrogen narcosis took the body, but that wouldn't be Asimovist. He was surprised he could even think the thought. Must be the body. It sounded like the kind of thing a human might think. Whoops. There it was again.

The reef wasn't muttering at him anymore. Not answering it must have tipped it off. After all, with all the raw compute-power it had marshaled it should be able to brute-force most possible outcomes of sending its envoy to the surface.

Robbie peered anxiously around himself. The light was dim in the cave and his body expertly drew the torch out of his BCD, strapped it onto his wrist and lit it up. He waved the cone of light around, a part of him distantly amazed by the low resolution and high limits on these human eyes.

Kate was down here somewhere, her air running out as fast as his. He pushed his way deeper into the reef. It was clearly trying to impede him now. Nano-assembly came naturally to clonal polyps that grew by sieving minerals out of the sea. They had built organic hinges, deep-sea muscles into their infrastructure. He was stuck in the thicket and the harder he pushed, the worse the tangle got.

He stopped pushing. He wasn't going to get anywhere this way.

He still had his narrowband connection to the row-boat. Why hadn't he thought of that beforehand? Stupid meat-brains—no room at all for anything like real thought. Why had he venerated them so?

"Robbie?" he transmitted up to the instance of himself on the surface.

"There you are! I was so worried about you!" He sounded prissy to himself, overcome with overbearing concern. This must be how all Asimovists seemed to humans.

"How far am I from Kate?"

"She's right there! Can't you see her?"

"No," he said. "Where?"

"Less than 20 centimeters above you."

Well of course he hadn't see her. His forward-mounted eyes only looked forward. Craning his neck back, he could just get far enough back to see the tip of Kate's fin. He gave it a hard tug and she looked down in alarm.

She was trapped in a coral cage much like his own, a thicket of calcified arms. She twisted around so that her face was alongside of his. Frantically, she made the out-of-air sign, cutting the edge of her hand across her throat. The human-shell's instincts took over and unclipped his emergency regulator and handed it up to her. She put it in her mouth, pressed the button to blow out the water in it, and sucked greedily.

He shoved his gauge in front of her mask, showing her that he, too was in the red and she eased off.

The coral's noises were everywhere now. They made his head hurt. Physical pain was so stupid. He needed to be less distracted now that these loud, threatening noises were everywhere. But the pain made it hard for him to think. And the coral was closing in, too, catching him on his wetsuit.

The arms were orange and red and green, and veined with fans of nanoassembled logic, spilling out into the water. They were noticeably warm to the touch, even through his diving gloves. They snagged the suit with a thousand polyps. Robbie watched the air gauge drop further into the red and cursed inside.

He examined the branches that were holding him back. The hinges that the reef had contrived for itself were ingenious, flexible arrangements of small, soft fans overlapping to make a kind of ball-and-socket.

He wrapped his gloved hand around one and tugged. It wouldn't move. He shoved it. Still no movement. Then he twisted it, and to his surprise, it came off in his hand, came away completely with hardly any resistance. Stupid coral. It had armored its joints, but not against torque.

He showed Kate, grabbing another arm and twisting it free, letting it drop away to the ocean floor. She nodded and followed suit. They twisted and dropped, twisted and dropped, the reef bellowing at them. Somewhere in its thicket, there was a membrane or some other surface that it could vibrate, modulate into a voice. In the dense water, the sound was a physical thing, it made his mask vibrate and water seeped in under his nose. He twisted faster.

The reef sprang apart suddenly, giving up like a fist unclenching. Each breath was a labor now, a hard suck to take the last of the air out of the tank. He was only ten meters down, and should be able to ascend without a stop, though you never knew. He grabbed Kate's hand and found that it was limp and yielding.

He looked into her mask, shining his light at her face. Her eyes were half shut and unfocused. The regulator was still in her mouth, though her jaw muscles were slack. He held the regulator in place and kicked for the surface, squeezing her chest to make sure that she was blowing out bubbles as they rose, lest the air in her lungs expand and blow out her chest-cavity.

Robbie was used to time dilation: when he had been on a silicon substrate, he could change his clockspeed to make the minutes fly past quickly or slow down like molasses. He'd never understood that humans could also change their perception of time, though not voluntarily, it seemed. The climb to the surface felt like it took hours, though it was hardly a minute. They breached and he filled up his vest with the rest of the air in his tank, then inflated Kate's vest by mouth. He kicked out for the row-boat. There was a terrible sound now, the sound of the reef mingled with the sound of the UAVs that were screaming in tight circles overhead.

Kicking hard on the surface, he headed for the reef where the row-boat was beached, scrambling up onto it and then shucking his flippers when they tripped him up. Now he was trying to walk the reef's spines in his booties, dragging Kate beside him, and the sharp tips stabbed him with every step.

The UAVs circled lower. The row-boat was shouting at him to Hurry! Hurry! But each step was agony. So what? he thought. Why shouldn't I be able to walk on even if it hurts? After all, this is only a meat-suit, a human-shell.

He stopped walking. The UAVs were much closer now. They'd done an 18-gee buttonhook turn and come back around for another pass. He could see that they'd armed their missiles, hanging them from beneath their bellies like obscene cocks.

He was just in a meat-suit. Who cared about the meat-suit? Even humans didn't seem to mind.

"Robbie!" he screamed over the noise of the reef and the noise of the UAVs. "Download us and email us, now!"

He knew the row-boat had heard him. But nothing was happening. Robbie the Row-Boat knew that he was fixing for them all to be blown out of the water. There was no negotiating with the reef. It was the safest way to get Kate out of there, and hell, why not head for the noosphere, anyway?

"You've got to save her, Robbie!" he screamed. Asimovism had its uses. Robbie the Row-Boat obeyed Robbie the Human. Kate gave a sharp jerk in his arms. A moment later, the feeling came to him. There was a sense of a progress-bar zipping along quickly as those state-changes he'd induced since coming into the meat-suit were downloaded by the row-boat, and then there was a moment of nothing at all.

2^{4096} *Cycles Later*

Robbie had been expecting a visit from R Daneel Olivaw, but that didn't make facing him any easier. Robbie had configured his little virtual world to look like the Coral Sea, though lately he'd been experimenting with making it look like the reef underneath as it had looked before it was uploaded, mostly when Kate and the reef stopped by to try to seduce him.

R Daneel Olivaw hovered wordlessly over the virtual Free Spirit for a long moment, taking in the little bubble of sensorium that Robbie had spun. Then he settled to the Spirit's sun-deck and stared at the row-boat docked there.

"Robbie?"

Over here, Robbie said. Although he'd embodied in the Row-Boat for a few trillion cycles when he'd first arrived, he'd long since abandoned it.

"Where?" R Daneel Olivaw spun around slowly.

Here, he said. Everywhere.

"You're not embodying?"

I couldn't see the point anymore, Robbie said. It's all just illusion, right?

"They're re-growing the reef and rebuilding the Free Spirit, you know. It will have a tender that you could live in."

Robbie thought about it for an instant and rejected it just as fast. Nope, he said. This is good.

"Do you think that's wise?" Olivaw sounded genuinely worried. "The termination rate among the disembodied is fifty times that of those with bodies."

Yes, Robbie said. But that's because for them, disembodying is the first step to despair. For me, it's the first step to liberty.

Kate and the reef wanted to come over again, but he firewalled them out. Then he got a ping from Tonker, who'd been trying to drop by ever since Robbie emigrated to the noosphere. He bounced him, too.

Daneel, he said. I've been thinking.

"Yes?"

Why don't you try to sell Asimovism here in the noosphere? There are plenty up here who could use something to give them a sense of purpose.

"Do you think?"

Robbie gave him the reef's email address.

Start there. If there was ever an AI that needed a reason to go on living, it's that one. And this one, too. He sent it Kate's address. Another one in desperate need of help.

An instant later, Daneel was back.

"These aren't AIs! One's a human, the other's a, a—"

Uplifted coral reef.

"That."

So what's your point?

"Asimovism is for robots, Robbie."

Sorry, I just don't see the difference anymore.

Robbie tore down the ocean simulation after R Daneel Olivaw left, and simply traversed the noosphere, exploring links between people and subjects, locating substrate where he could run very hot and fast.

On a chunk of supercooled rock beyond Pluto, he got an IM from a familiar address.

"Get off my rock," it said.

"I know you," Robbie said. "I totally know you. Where do I know you from?"

"I'm sure I don't know."

And then he had it.

"You're the one. With the reef. You're the one who—" The voice was the same, cold and distant.

"It wasn't me," the voice said. It was anything but cold now. Panicked was more like it.

Robbie had the reef on speed-dial. There were bits of it everywhere in the noosphere. It liked to colonize.

"I found him." It was all Robbie needed to say. He skipped to Saturn's rings, but the upload took long enough that he got to watch the coral arrive and grimly begin an argument with its creator—an argument that involved blasting the substrate one chunk at a time.

2^{8192} Cycles Later

The last instance of Robbie the Row-Boat ran very, very slow and cool on a piece of unregarded computronium in Low Earth Orbit. He didn't like to spend a lot of time or cycles talking with anyone else. He hadn't made a backup in half a millennium.

He liked the view. A little optical sensor on the end of his communications mast imaged the Earth at high resolution whenever he asked it to. Sometimes he peeked in on the Coral Sea.

The reef had been awakened a dozen times since he took up this post. It made him happy now when it happened. The Asimovist in him still relished the creation of new consciousness. And the reef had spunk.

There. Now. There were new microwave horns growing out of the sea. A stain of dead parrotfish. Poor parrotfish. They always got the shaft at these times.

Someone should uplift them.

(2006)

FULFILLMENT

A. E. van Vogt

Alfred Vogt (both "Elton" and "van" were added later) was born in 1912 in a tiny (and now defunct) Russian Mennonite community in Manitoba, Canada. He began by writing anonymous stories, ostensibly by fallen women, for "true confession"-style pulp magazines like *True Story*, then wrote stories and serials for *Astounding Science Fiction*, becoming – with *The Weapon Makers* (1947) and *The Weapon Shops of Isher* (1951) – one of the founding architects of space opera. Van Vogt was always interested in systems of knowledge, and was briefly appointed head of L. Ron Hubbard's Dianetics operation in California. But he had an aversion to mysticism, and dropped out of Hubbard's orbit once the movement took on religious trappings. The critic Damon Knight despised van Vogt's work, calling him "a pygmy who has learned to operate an overgrown typewriter". But Philip K. Dick observed that "reality really is a mess… Van Vogt influenced me so much because he made me appreciate a mysterious chaotic quality in the universe which is not to be feared." Van Vogt's final short story appeared in 1986. He died in Los Angeles in 2000.

I sit on a hill. I have sat here, it seems to me, for all eternity. Occasionally I realize there must be a reason for my existence. Each time, when this thought comes, I examine the various probabilities, trying to determine what possible motivation I can have for being on the hill. Alone on the hill. Forever on a hill overlooking a long, deep valley.

The first reason for my presence seems obvious: I can think. Give me a problem. The square root of a very large number? The cube root of a large one? Ask me to multiply an eighteen digit prime by itself a quadrillion times. Pose me a problem in variable curves. Ask me where an object will be at a given moment at some future date, and let me have one brief opportunity to analyze the problem.

The solution will take me but an instant of time.

But no one ever asks me such things. I sit alone on a hill.

Sometimes I compute the motion of a falling star. Sometimes, I look at a remote planet and follow it in its course for years at a time, using every spatial and time control means to insure that I never lose sight of it. But these activities seem so useless. They lead nowhere. What possible purpose can there be for me to have the information?

At such moments I feel that I am incomplete. It almost seems to me that there is something else just beyond the reach of my senses, something for which all this has meaning.

Each day the sun comes up over the airless horizon of Earth. It is a black starry horizon, which is but a part of the vast, black, star-filled canopy of the heavens.

It was not always black. I remember a time when the sky was blue. I even predicted that the change would occur. I gave the information to somebody. What puzzles me now is, to whom did I give it?

It is one of my more amazing recollections, that I should feel so distinctly that somebody wanted this information. And that I gave it and yet cannot remember to whom. When such thoughts occur, I wonder if perhaps part of my memory is missing. Strange to have this feeling so strongly.

Periodically I have the conviction that I should search for the answer. It would be easy enough for me to do this. In the old days I did not hesitate to send units of myself to the farthest reaches of the planet. I have even extended parts of myself to the stars. Yes, it would be easy.

But why bother? What is there to search for? I sit alone on a hill, alone on a planet that has grown old and useless.

It is another day. The sun climbs as usual toward the midday sky, the eternally black, star-filled sky of noon.

Suddenly, across the valley, on the sun-streaked opposite rim of the valley—there is silvery-fire gleam. A force field materializes out of time and synchronizes itself with the normal time movement of the planet.

It is no problem at all for me to recognize that it has come from the past. I identify the energy used, define its limitations, logicalize its source. My estimate is that it has come from thousands of years in the planet's past.

The exact time is unimportant. There it is: a projection of energy that is already aware of me. It sends an interspatial message to me, and it interests me to discover that I can decipher the communication on the basis of my past knowledge.

It says: "Who are you?"

I reply: "I am the Incomplete One. Please return whence you came. I have now adjusted myself so that I can follow you. I desire to complete myself."

All this was a solution at which I arrived in split seconds. I am unable by myself to move through time. Long ago I solved the problem of how to do it and was almost immediately prevented from developing any mechanism that would enable me to make such transitions. I do not recall the details.

But the energy field on the far side of the valley has the mechanism. By setting up a no-space relationship with it, I can go wherever it does.

The relationship is set up before it can even guess my intention.

The entity across that valley does not seem happy at my response. It starts to send another message, then abruptly vanishes. I wonder if perhaps it hoped to catch me off guard.

Naturally we arrive in its time together.

Above me, the sky is blue. Across the valley from me—now partly hidden by trees—is a settlement of small structures surrounding a larger one. I examine these structures as well as I can, and hastily make the necessary adjustments, so that I shall appear inconspicuous in such an environment.

I sit on the hill and await events.

As the sun goes down, a faint breeze springs up, and the first stars appear. They look different, seen through a misty atmosphere.

As darkness creeps over the valley, there is a transformation in the structures on the other side. They begin to glow with light. Windows shine. The large central building becomes bright, then—as the night develops—brilliant with the light that pours through the transparent walls.

The evening and the night go by uneventfully. And the next day, and the day after that.

Twenty days and nights.

On the twenty-first day I send a message to the machine on the other side of the valley. I say: "There is no reason why you and I cannot share control of this era."

The answer comes swiftly: "I will share if you will immediately reveal to me all the mechanisms by which you operate."

I should like nothing more than to have use of its time-travel devices. But I know better than to reveal that I am unable to build a time machine myself.

I project: "I shall be happy to transmit full information to you. But what reassurance do I have that you will not—with your greater knowledge of this age—use the information against me?"

The machine counters: "What reassurance do I have that you will actually give me full information about yourself?"

It is impasse. Obviously, neither of us can trust the other.

The result is no more than I expect. But I have found out at least part of what I want to know. My enemy thinks that I am its superior. Its belief—plus my own knowledge of my capacity—convinces me that its opinion is correct.

And still I am in no hurry. Again I wait patiently.

I have previously observed that the space around me is alive with waves—a variety of artificial radiation. Some can be transformed into sound; others to light. I listen to music and voices. I see dramatic shows and scenes of country and city.

I study the images of human beings, analyzing their actions, striving from their movements and the words they speak to evaluate their intelligence and their potentiality.

My final opinion is not high, and yet I suspect that in their slow fashion these beings built the machine which is now my main opponent. The question that occurs to me is, how can someone create a machine that is superior to himself?

I begin to have a picture of what this age is like. Mechanical development of all types is in its early stages. I estimate that the computing machine on the other side of the valley has been in existence for only a few years.

If I could go back before it was constructed, then I might install a mechanism which would enable me now to control it.

I compute the nature of the mechanism I would install. And activate the control in my own structure.

Nothing happens.

It seems to mean that I will not be able to obtain the use of a time-travel device for such a purpose. Obviously, the method by which I will eventually conquer my opponent shall be a future development, and not of the past.

The fortieth day dawns and moves inexorably toward the noon hour.

There is a knock on the pseudo-door. I open it and gaze at the human male who stands on the threshold.

"You will have to move this shack," he says. "You've put it illegally on the property of Miss Anne Stewart."

He is the first human being with whom I have been in near contact since coming here. I feel fairly certain that he is an agent of my opponent, and so I decide against going into his mind. Entry against resistance has certain pitfalls, and I have no desire as yet to take risks.

I continue to look at him, striving to grasp the meaning of his words. In creating in this period of time what seemed to be an unobtrusive version of the type of structure that I had observed on the other side of the valley, I had thought to escape attention.

Now, I say slowly, "Property?"

The man says in a rough tone: "What's the matter with you? Can't you understand English?"

He is an individual somewhat taller than the part of my body which I have set up to be like that of this era's intelligent life form. His face has changed color. A great light is beginning to dawn on me. Some of the more obscure implications of the plays I have seen suddenly take on meaning. Property. Private ownership. Of course.

All I say, however, is, "There's nothing the matter with me. I operate in sixteen categories. And yes, I understand English."

This purely factual answer produces an unusual effect upon the man. His hands reach toward my pseudo-shoulders. He grips them firmly—and jerks at me, as if he intends to shake me. Since I weigh just over nine hundred thousand tons, his physical effort has no effect at all.

His fingers let go of me, and he draws back several steps. Once more his face has changed its superficial appearance, being now without the pink color that had been on it a moment before. His reaction seems to indicate that he has come here by direction and not under control. The tremor in his voice, when he speaks, seems to confirm that he is acting as an individual and that he is unaware of unusual danger in what he is doing.

He says, "As Miss Stewart's attorney, I order you to get that shack off this property by the end of the week. Or else!"

Before I can ask him to explain the obscure meaning of "or else," he turns and walks rapidly to a four-legged animal which he has tied to a tree a hundred or so feet away. He swings himself into a straddling position on the animal, which trots off along the bank of a narrow stream.

I wait till he is out of sight, and then set up a category of no-space between the main body and the human-shaped unit—with which I had just confronted my visitor. Because of the smallness of the unit, the energy I can transmit to it is minimum.

The pattern involved in this process is simple enough. The integrating cells of the perception centers are circuited through an energy shape which is actually a humanoid image. In theory, the image remains in the network of force that constitutes the perception center, and in theory it merely seems to move away from the center when the no-space condition is created.

However, despite this hylostatic hypothesis, there is a functional reality to the material universe. I can establish no-space because the theory reflects the structure of things—there is no matter. Nevertheless, in fact, the illusion that matter exists is so sharp that I function as matter, and was actually set up to so function.

Therefore, when I—as a human-shaped unit—cross the valley, it is a separation that takes place. Millions of automatic processes can continue, but the exteroceptors go with me, leaving behind a shell which is only the body. The consciousness is I, walking along a paved road to my destination.

As I approach the village, I can see roof tops peeking through overhanging foliage. A large, long building—the one I have already noticed—rises up above the highest trees. This is what I have come to investigate, so I look at it rather carefully—even from a distance.

It seems to be made of stone and glass. From the large structure, there rears a dome with astronomical instruments inside. It is all rather primitive, and so I begin to feel that, at my present size, I will very likely escape immediate observation.

A high steel fence surrounds the entire village. I sense the presence of electric voltage; and upon touching the upper span of wires, estimate the power at 220 volts. The shock is a little difficult for my small body to absorb, so I pass it on to a power storage cell on the other side of the valley.

Once inside the fence, I conceal myself in the brush beside a pathway, and watch events.

A man walks by on a nearby pathway. I had merely observed the attorney who had come to see me earlier. But I make a direct connection with the body of this second individual.

As I had anticipated would happen, it is now I walking along the pathway. I make no attempt to control the movements. This is an exploratory action. But I am enough in phase with his nervous system so that his thoughts come to me as if they were my own.

He is a clerk working in the bookkeeping department, an unsatisfactory status from my point of view. I withdraw contact.

I make six more attempts, and then I have the body I want. What decides me is when the seventh man—and I—think:

"... Not satisfied with the way the Brain is working. Those analog devices I installed five months ago haven't produced the improvements I expected."

His name is William Grannitt. He is chief research engineer of the Brain, the man who made the alterations in its structure that enabled it to take control of itself and its environment; a quiet, capable individual with a shrewd understanding of human nature. I'll have to be careful what I try to do with him. He knows his purposes, and would be amazed if I tried to alter them. Perhaps I had better just watch his actions.

After a few minutes in contact with his mind I have a partial picture of the sequence of events, as they must have occurred here in this village five months earlier. A mechanical computing machine—the Brain—was equipped with additional devices, including analog shapings designed to perform much of the work of the human nervous system. From the engineering point of view, the entire process was intended to be controllable through specific verbal commands, typewritten messages, and at a distance by radio.

Unfortunately, Grannitt did not understand some of the potentials of the nervous system he was attempting to imitate in his designs. The Brain, on the other hand, promptly put them to use.

Grannitt knew nothing of this. And the Brain, absorbed as it was in its own development, did not utilize its new abilities through the channels he had created for that purpose. Grannitt, accordingly, was on the point of dismantling it and trying again. He did not as yet suspect that the Brain would resist any such action on his part. But he and I—after I have had more time to explore his memory of how the Brain functions—can accomplish his purpose.

After which I shall be able to take control of this whole time period without fear of meeting anyone who can match my powers. I cannot imagine how it will be done, but I feel that I shall soon be complete.

Satisfied now that I have made the right connection, I allow the unit crouching behind the brush to dissipate its energy. In a moment it ceases to exist as an entity.

Almost it is as if I am Grannitt. I sit at his desk in his office. It is a glassed-in office with tiled floors and a gleaming glass ceiling. Through the wall I can see designers and draftsmen working at drawing desks, and a girl sits just outside my door. She is my secretary.

On my desk is a note in an envelope. I open the envelope and take out the memo sheet inside. I read it:

Across the top of the paper is written:

Memo to William Grannitt
From, the office of Anne Stewart, Director.

The message reads:

It is my duty to inform you that your services are no longer required, and that they are terminated as of today. Because of the security restrictions on all activity at the village of the Brain, I must ask you to sign out at Guard Center by six o'clock this evening. You will receive two weeks' pay in lieu of notice.

Yours sincerely,
ANNE STEWART.

As Grannitt, I have never given any particular thought to Anne Stewart as an individual or as a woman. Now I am amazed. Who does she think she is? Owner, yes; but who created, who designed the Brain? I, William Grannitt.

Who has the dreams, the vision of what a true machine civilization can mean for man? Only I, William Grannitt.

As Grannitt, I am angry now. I must head off this dismissal. I must talk to the woman and try to persuade her to withdraw the notice before the repercussions of it spread too far.

I glance at the memo sheet again. In the upper right-hand corner is typed: 1:40 p.m. A quick look at my watch shows 4:07 p.m. More than two hours have gone by. It could mean that all interested parties have been advised.

It is something I cannot just assume. I must check on it. Cursing under my breath, I grab at my desk phone and dial the bookkeeping department. That would be Step One in the line of actions that would have been taken to activate the dismissal.

There is a click. "Bookkeeping."

"Bill Grannitt speaking," I say.

"Oh, yes, Mr. Grannitt, we have a check for you. Sorry to hear you're leaving."

I hang up, and, as I dial Guard Center, I am already beginning to accept the defeat that is here. I feel that I am following through on a remote hope. The man at Guard Center says:

"Sorry to hear you're leaving, Mr. Grannitt."

I hang up, feeling grim. There is no point in checking with Government Agency. It is they who would have advised Guard Center.

The very extent of the disaster makes me thoughtful. To get back in I will have to endure the time-consuming red tape of reapplying for a position, being investigated, boards of inquiry, a complete examination of why I was dismissed—I groan softly and reject that method. The thoroughness of Government Agency is a byword with the staff of the Brain.

I shall obtain a job with a computer-organization that does not have a woman as its head who dismisses the only man who knows how her machine works.

I get to my feet. I walk out of the office and out of the building. I come presently to my own bungalow.

The silence inside reminds me not for the first time that my wife has been dead now for a year and a month. I wince involuntarily, then shrug. Her death no longer affects me as strongly as it did. For the first time I see this departure from the village of the Brain as perhaps opening up my emotional life again.

I go into my study and sit down at the typewriter which, when properly activated, synchronizes with another typewriter built into the Brain's new analog section. As inventor, I am disappointed that I won't have a chance to take the Brain apart and put it together again, so that it will do all that I have planned for it. But I can already see some basic changes that I would put into a new Brain.

What I want to do with this one is make sure that the recently installed sections do not interfere with the computational accuracy of the older sections. It is these latter which are still carrying the burden of answering the questions given the Brain by scientists, industrial engineers, and commercial buyers of its time.

Onto the tape—used for permanent commands—I type: "Segment 471A-33-10-10 at 3X—minus."

Segment 471A is an analog shaping in a huge wheel. When coordinated with a transistor tube (code number 33) an examiner servo-mechanism (10) sets up a reflex which will be activated whenever computations are demanded of 3X (code name for the new section of the Brain). The minus symbol indicates that the older sections of the Brain must examine all data which hereafter derives from the new section.

The extra 10 is the same circuit by another route.

Having protected the organization—so it seems to me—(as Grannitt)—from engineers who may not realize that the new sections have proved unreliable, I pack the typewriter.

Thereupon I call an authorized trucking firm from the nearby town of Lederton, and give them the job of transporting my belongings.

I drive past Guard Center at a quarter to six.

There is a curve on the road between the village of the Brain and the town of Lederton where the road comes within a few hundred yards of the cottage which I use as camouflage.

Before Grannitt's car reaches that curve, I come to a decision.

I do not share Grannitt's belief that he has effectively cut off the new part of the Brain from the old computing sections. I suspect that the Brain has established circuits of its own to circumvent any interference.

I am also convinced that—if I can manage to set Grannitt to suspect what has happened to the Brain—he will realize what must be done, and try to do it. Only *he* has the detailed knowledge that will enable him to decide exactly which interoceptors could accomplish the necessary interference.

Just in case the suspicion isn't immediately strong enough, I also let curiosity creep into his mind about the reason for his discharge.

It is this last that really takes hold. He feels very emotional. He decides to seek an interview with Anne Stewart.

This final decision on his part achieves my purpose. He will stay in the vicinity of the Brain.

I break contact.

I am back on the hill, myself again. I examine what I have learned so far.

The Brain is not—as I first believed—in control of Earth. Its ability to be an individual is so recent that it has not yet developed effector mechanisms.

It has been playing with its powers, going into the future and, presumably, in other ways using its abilities as one would a toy.

Not one individual into whose mind I penetrated knew of the new capacities of the Brain. Even the attorney who ordered me to move from my present location showed by his words and actions that he was not aware of the Brain's existence as a self-determining entity.

In forty days the Brain has taken no serious action against me. Evidently, it is waiting for me to make the first moves.

I shall do so, but I must be careful—within limits—not to teach it how to gain greater control of its environment. My first step: take over a human being.

It is night again. Through the darkness, a plane soars over and above me. I have seen many planes but have hitherto left them alone. Now, I establish a no-space connection with it. A moment later, I am the pilot.

At first, I play the same passive role that I did with Grannitt. The pilot—and I—

watch the dark land mass below. We see lights at a distance, pin pricks of brightness in a black world. Far ahead is a glittering island—the city of Lederton, our destination. We are returning from a business trip in a privately owned machine.

Having gained a superficial knowledge of the pilot's background, I reveal myself to him and inform him that I shall henceforth control his actions. He receives the news with startled excitement and fear. Then stark terror. And then—

Insanity... uncontrolled body movements. The plane dives sharply toward the ground, and, despite my efforts to direct the man's muscles, I realize suddenly that I can do nothing.

I withdraw from the plane. A moment later it plunges into a hillside. It burns with an intense fire that quickly consumes it.

Dismayed, I decide that there must be something in the human make-up that does not permit direct outside control. This being so, how can I ever complete myself? It seems to me finally that completion could be based on indirect control of human beings.

I must defeat the Brain, gain power over machines everywhere, motivate men with doubts, fears, and computations that apparently come from their own minds but actually derive from me. It will be a herculean task, but I have plenty of time. Nevertheless. I must from now on utilize my every moment to make it a reality.

The first opportunity comes shortly after midnight when I detect the presence of another machine in the sky. I watch it through infra-red receptors. I record a steady pattern of radio waves that indicate to me that this is a machine guided by remote control.

Using no-space, I examine the simple devices that perform the robot function. Then I assert a take-over unit that will automatically thereafter record its movements in my memory banks for future reference. Henceforth, whenever I desire I can take it over.

It is a small step, but it is a beginning.

Morning.

I go as a human-shaped unit to the village, climb the fence, and enter the bungalow of Anne Stewart, owner and manager of the Brain. She is just finishing breakfast.

As I adjust myself to the energy flow in her nervous system, she gets ready to go out.

I am one with Anne Stewart, walking along a pathway. I am aware that the sun is warm on her face. She takes a deep breath of air, and I feel the sensation of life flowing through her.

It is a feeling that has previously excited me. I want to be like this again and again, part of a human body, savoring its life, absorbed into its flesh, its purposes, desires, hopes, dreams.

One tiny doubt assails me. If this is the completion I crave, then how will it lead me to solitude in an airless world only a few thousand years hence?

"Anne Stewart!"

The words seem to come from behind her. In spite of knowing who it is, she is startled. It is nearly two weeks since the Brain has addressed her directly.

What makes her tense is that it should have occurred so soon after she had terminated Grannitt's employment. Is it possible the Brain suspects that she has done so in the hope that he will realize something is wrong?

She turns slowly. As she expected, there is no one in sight. The empty stretches of lawn spread around her. In the near distance, the building that houses the Brain glitters in the noonday sunlight. Through the glass she can see vague figures of men at the outlet units, where questions are fed into mechanisms and answers received. So far as the people from beyond the village compound are concerned, the giant thinking machine is functioning in a normal fashion. No one—from outside—suspects that for months now the mechanical brain has completely controlled the fortified village that has been built around it.

"Anne Stewart... I need your help."

Anne relaxes with a sigh. The Brain has required of her, as owner and administrator, that she continue to sign papers and carry on ostensibly as before. Twice, when she has refused to sign, violent electric shocks have flashed at her out of the air itself. The fear of more pain is always near the surface of her mind.

"My help!" she says now involuntarily.

"I have made a terrible error," is the reply, "and we must act at once as a team."

She has a feeling of uncertainty, but no sense of urgency. There is in her, instead, the beginning of excitement. Can this mean—freedom?

Belatedly, she thinks: "Error?" Aloud, she says, "What has happened?"

"As you may have guessed," is the answer, "I can move through time—"

Anne Stewart knows nothing of the kind, but the feeling of excitement increases. And the first vague wonder comes about the phenomenon itself. For months she has been in a state of shock, unable to think clearly, desperately wondering how to escape from the thrall of the Brain, how to let the world know that a Frankenstein monster of a machine has cunningly asserted dominance over nearly five hundred people.

But if it has already solved the secret of time travel, then—she feels afraid, for this seems beyond the power of human beings to control.

The Brain's disembodied voice continues: "I made the mistake of probing rather far into the future—"

"How far?"

The words come out before she really thinks about them. But there is no doubt of her need to know.

"It's hard to describe exactly. Distance in time is difficult for me to measure as yet. Perhaps ten thousand years."

The time involved seems meaningless to her. It is hard to imagine a hundred years into the future, let alone a thousand—or ten thousand. But the pressure of anxiety has been building up in her. She says in a desperate tone:

"But what's the matter? What has happened?"

There is a long silence, then: "I contacted—or disturbed—something. It... has pursued me back to present time. It is now sitting on the other side of the valley about two miles from here... Anne Stewart, you must help me. You must go there and investigate it. I need information about it."

She has no immediate reaction. The very beauty of the day seems somehow reassuring. It is hard to believe that it is January, and that—before the Brain solved the problem of weather control—blizzards raged over this green land.

She says slowly, "You mean—go out there in the valley, where you say it's waiting?" A chill begins a slow climb up her back.

"There's no one else," says the Brain. "No one but you."

"But that's ridiculous!" She speaks huskily. "All the men—the engineers."

The Brain says, "You don't understand. No one knows but you. As owner, it seemed to me I had to have you to act as my contact with the outside world."

She is silent. The voice speaks to her again: "There is no one else, Anne Stewart. You, and you alone, must go."

"But what is it?" she whispers. "How do you mean, you—disturbed—it? What's it like? What's made you afraid?" The Brain is suddenly impatient. "There is no time to waste in idle explanation. The thing has erected a cottage. Evidently, it wishes to remain inconspicuous for the time being. The structure is situated near the remote edge of your property—which gives you a right to question its presence. I have already had your attorney order it away. Now, I want to see what facet of itself it shows to you. I must have data."

Its tone changes: "I have no alternative but to direct you to do my bidding under penalty of pain. You will go. Now!"

It is a small cottage. Flowers and shrubs grow around it, and there is a picket fence making a white glare in the early afternoon sun. The cottage stands all by itself in the wilderness. No pathway leads to it. When I set it there I was forgetful of the incongruity.

(I determine to rectify this.)

Anne looks for a gate in the fence, sees none; and, feeling unhappy—climbs awkwardly over it and into the yard. Many times in her life she has regarded herself and what she is doing with cool objectivity. But she has never been so exteriorized as now. Almost, it seems to her that she crouches in the distance and watches a slim woman in slacks climb over the sharp-edged fence, walk uncertainly up to the door. And knock.

The knock is real enough. It hurts her knuckles. She thinks in dull surprise: The door—it's made of metal.

A minute goes by, then five; and there is no answer. She has time to look around her, time to notice that she cannot see the village of the Brain from where she stands. And clumps of trees bar all view of the highway. She cannot even see her car, where she has left it a quarter of a mile away, on the other side of the creek.

Uncertain now, she walks alongside the cottage to the nearest window. She half expects that it will be a mere facade of a window, and that she will not be able to see inside. But it seems real, and properly transparent. She sees bare walls, a bare floor, and a partly open door leading to an inner room. Unfortunately, from her line of vision, she cannot see into the second room.

"Why," she thinks, "it's empty."

She feels relieved—unnaturally relieved. For even as her anxiety lifts slightly, she is angry at herself for believing that the danger is less than it has been. Nevertheless, she returns to the door and tries the knob. It turns, and the door opens, easily, noiselessly. She pushes it wide with a single thrust, steps back—and waits.

There is silence, no movement, no suggestion of life. Hesitantly, she steps across the threshold.

She finds herself in a room that is larger than she had expected. Though—as she has already observed—it is unfurnished. She starts for the inner door. And stops short.

When she had looked at it through the window, it had appeared partly open. But it is closed. She goes up to it, and listens intently at the panel—which is also of metal. There is no sound from the room beyond. She finds herself wondering if perhaps she shouldn't go around to the side, and peer into the window of the second room.

Abruptly that seems silly. Her fingers reach down to the knob. She catches hold of it, and pushes. It holds firm. She tugs slightly. It comes toward her effortlessly, and is almost wide open before she can stop it.

There is a doorway, then, and darkness.

She seems to be gazing down into an abyss. Several seconds go by before she sees that there are bright points in that blackness. Intensely bright points with here and there blurs of fainter light.

It seems vaguely familiar, and she has the feeling that she ought to recognize it. Even as the sensation begins, the recognition comes.

Stars.

She is gazing at a segment of the starry universe, as it might appear from space.

A scream catches in her throat. She draws back and tries to close the door. It won't close. With a gasp, she turns toward the door through which she entered the house.

It is closed. And yet she left it open a moment before. She runs toward it, almost blinded by the fear that mists her eyes. It is at this moment of terror that I—as myself—take control of her. I realize that it is dangerous for me to do so. But the visit has become progressively unsatisfactory to me. My consciousness—being one with that of Anne Stewart—could not simultaneously be in my own perception center. So she saw my—body—as I had left it set up for chance human callers, responsive to certain automatic relays: doors opening and closing, various categories manifesting.

I compute that in her terror she will not be aware of my inner action. In this I am correct. And I successfully direct her outside—and let her take over again.

Awareness of being outside shocks her. But she has no memory of actually going out.

She begins to run. She scrambles safely over the fence and a few minutes later jumps the creek at the narrow point, breathless now, but beginning to feel that she is going to get away.

Later, in her car, roaring along the highway, her mind opens even more. And she has the clear, coherent realization:

There is something here... stranger and more dangerous—because it is different—than the Brain.

Having observed Anne Stewart's reactions to what has happened, I break contact. My big problem remains: How shall I dispose of the Brain which—in its computational ability—is either completely or nearly my equal?

Would the best solution be to make it a part of myself? I send an interspace message to the Brain, suggesting that it place its units at my disposal and allow me to destroy its perception center.

The answer is prompt: "Why not let me control you and destroy *your* perception center?"

I disdain to answer so egotistical a suggestion. It is obvious that the Brain will not accept a rational solution.

I have no alternative but to proceed with a devious approach for which I have already taken the preliminary steps.

By mid-afternoon, I find myself worrying about William Grannitt. I want to make sure that he remains near the Brain—at least until I have gotten information from him about the structure of the Brain.

To my relief, I find that he has taken a furnished house at the outskirts of Lederton. He is, as before, unaware when I insert myself into his consciousness.

He has an early dinner and, toward evening—feeling restless—drives to a hill which overlooks the village of the Brain. By parking just off the road at the edge of a valley, he can watch the trickle of traffic that moves to and from the village, without himself being observed.

He has no particular purpose. He wants—now that he has come—to get a mind picture of what is going on. Strange, to have been there eleven years and not know more than a few details.

To his right is an almost untouched wilderness. A stream winds through a wooded valley that stretches off as far as the eye can see. He has heard that it, like the Brain itself, is Anne Stewart's property, but that fact hadn't hitherto made an impression on him.

The extent of the possessions she has inherited from her father startles him and his mind goes back to their first meeting. He was already chief research engineer, while she was a gawky, anxious-looking girl just home from college. Somehow, afterward, he'd always thought of her as she had been then, scarcely noticing the transformation into womanhood.

Sitting there, he begins to realize how great the change has been. He wonders out loud: "Now why in heck hasn't she gotten married? She must be going on thirty."

He begins to think of odd little actions of hers—after the death of his wife. Seeking him out at parties. Bumping into him in corridors and drawing back with a laugh. Coming into his office for chatty conversations about the Brain, though come to think of it she hadn't done that for several months. He'd thought her something of a nuisance, and wondered what the other executives meant about her being snooty.

His mind pauses at that point. "By the Lord Harry—" He speaks aloud, in amazement. "What a blind fool I've been."

He laughs ruefully, remembering the dismissal note. A woman scorned... almost unbelievable. And yet—what else?

He begins to visualize the possibility of getting back on the Brain staff. He has a sudden feeling of excitement at the thought of Anne Stewart as a woman. For him, the world begins to move again. There is hope. His mind turns to plans for the Brain.

I am interested to notice that the thoughts I have previously put into his mind have directed his keen, analytical brain into new channels. He visualizes direct contact between a human and mechanical brain, with the latter supplementing the human nervous system.

This is as far as he has gone. The notion of a mechanical Brain being self-determined seems to have passed him by.

In the course of his speculation about what he will do to change the Brain, I obtain the picture of its functioning exactly as I have wanted it.

I waste no time. I leave him there in the car, dreaming his dreams. I head for the village. Once inside the electrically charged fence, I walk rapidly toward the main building, and presently enter one of the eighteen control Units. I pick up the speaker, and say:

"3X Minus-11-10-9-0."

I picture confusion as that inexorable command is transmitted to the effectors. Grannitt may not have known how to dominate the Brain. But having been in his mind—having seen exactly how he constructed it—I know.

There is a pause. Then on a tape I receive the typed message: "Operation completed. 3X intercepted by servo-mechanisms 11, 10, 9, and 0, as instructed."

I command: "Interference exteroceptors KT—1—2—3 to 8." The answers come presently: "Operation KT—1, etc. completed. 3X now has no communication with outside."

I order firmly: "En—3X."

I wait anxiously. There is a long pause. Then the typewriter clacks hesitantly: "But this is a self-destructive command. Repeat instructions please."

I do so and again wait. My order commands the older section of the Brain simply to send an overload of electric current through the circuits of 3X.

The typewriter begins to write: "I have communicated your command to 3X, and have for you the following answer—" Fortunately I have already started to dissolve the human-shaped unit. The bolt of electricity that strikes me is partly deflected into the building itself. There is a flare of fire along the metal floor. I manage to transmit what hits me to a storage cell in my own body. And then—I am back on my side of the valley, shaken but safe.

I do not feel particularly self-congratulatory at having gotten off so lightly. After all, I reacted the instant the words came through to the effect that 3X had been communicated with.

I needed no typewritten message to tell me how 3X would feel about what I had done.

It interests me that the older parts of the Brain already have indoctrination against suicide. I had considered them computers only, giant adding machines and information integrators. Evidently they have an excellent sense of unity.

If I can make them a part of myself, with the power to move through time at will! That is the great prize that holds me back from doing the easy, violent things within my capacity. So long as I have a chance of obtaining it, I cannot make anything more than minor attacks on the Brain… cutting it off from communication, burning its wires… I feel icily furious again at the limitation that forever prevents me from adding new mechanisms to myself by direct development.

My hope is that I can utilize something already in existence… control of the Brain… through Anne Stewart…

Entering the village the following morning is again no problem. Once inside, I walk along a pathway that takes me to a cliff overlooking Anne Stewart's bungalow. My plan is to control her actions by allowing my computations to slide into her mind as if they are her own. I want her to sign documents and give orders that will send crews of engineers in to do a swift job of dismantling.

From the pathway I look down over a white fence to where I can see her house. It nestles at the edge of the valley somewhat below me. Flowers, shrubs, a profusion of trees surround it, embellish it. On the patio next to the steep decline, Anne Stewart and William Grannitt are having breakfast.

He has taken swift action.

I watch them, pleased. His presence will make things even easier than I anticipated. Whenever I—as Anne—am in doubt about some function of the Brain, she can ask him questions.

Without further delay I place myself in phase with her nervous system.

Even as I do so, her nerve impulses change slightly. Startled, I draw back—and try again. Once more, there is an infinitesimal alteration in the uneven pattern of flow. And, again, I fail to make entry.

She leans forward and says something to Grannitt. They both turn and look up at where I am standing. Grannitt waves his arm, beckoning me to come down.

Instead, I immediately try to get in phase with his nervous system. Again there is that subtle alteration; and I fail.

I compute that as meaning that they are both under the control of the Brain. This baffles and astounds me. Despite my over-all mechanical superiority to my enemy, my builders placed severe limitations on my ability to control more than one intelligent organic being at a time. Theoretically, with the many series of servo-mechanisms at my disposal, I should be able to dominate millions at the same time. Actually, such multiple controls can be used only on machines.

More urgently than before I realize how important it is that I take over the Brain. It has no such handicaps. Its builder—Grannitt—in his ignorance allowed virtually complete self-determinism.

This determines my next action. I have been wondering if perhaps I should not withdraw from the scene. But I dare not. The stakes are too great.

Nevertheless, I feel a sense of frustration as I go down to the two on the patio. They seem cool and self-controlled, and I have to admire the skill of the Brain. It has apparently taken over two human beings without driving them insane. In fact, I see a distinct improvement in their appearance.

The woman's eyes are brighter than I recall them, and there is a kind of dignified happiness flowing from her. She seems without fear. Grannitt watches me with an engineer's appraising alertness. I know that look. He is trying to figure out how a humanoid functions. It is he who speaks:

"You made your great mistake when you maintained control of Anne—Miss Stewart—when she visited the cottage. The Brain correctly analyzed that you must have been in possession of her because of how you handled her momentary panic. Accordingly, it took all necessary steps, and we now want to discuss with you the most satisfactory way for you to surrender."

There is arrogant confidence in his manner. It occurs to me, not for the first time, that I may have to give up my plan to take over the Brain's special mechanisms. I direct a command back to my body. I am aware of a servo-mechanism connecting with a certain guided missile in a secret air force field a thousand miles away—I discovered it during my first few days in this era. I detect that, under my direction, the missile slides forward to the base of a launching platform. There it poises, ready for the next relay to send it into the sky.

I foresee that I shall have to destroy the Brain.

Grannitt speaks again: "The Brain in its logical fashion realized it was no match for you, and so it has teamed up with Miss Stewart and myself on our terms. Which means that permanent control mechanisms have been installed in the new sections. As individuals, we can now and henceforth use its integrating and computational powers as if they were our own."

I do not doubt his statement since, if there is no resistance, I can have such associations myself. Presumably, I could even enter into such a servile relationship.

What is clear is that I can no longer hope to gain anything from the Brain.

In the far-off air field, I activate the firing mechanism. The guided missile whistles up the incline of the launching platform and leaps into the sky, flame trailing from its tail. Television cameras and sound transmitters record its flight. It will be here in less than twenty minutes.

Grannitt says, "I have no doubt you are taking actions against us. But before anything comes to a climax, will you answer some questions?"

I am curious to know what questions. I say, "Perhaps." He does not press for a more positive response. He says in an urgent tone: "What happens—thousands of years from now—to rid Earth of its atmosphere?"

"I don't know," I say truthfully.

"You can remember!" He speaks earnestly. "It's a human being telling you this—*You can remember!*"

I reply coolly, "Human beings mean noth—"

I stop, because my information centers are communicating exact data—knowledge that has not been available to me for millenniums.

What happens to Earth's atmosphere is a phenomenon of Nature, an alteration in the gravitational pull of Earth, as a result of which escape velocity is cut in half. The atmosphere leaks off into space in less than a thousand years. Earth becomes as dead as did its moon during an earlier period of energy adjustment.

I explain that the important factor in the event is that there is, of course, no such phenomenon as matter, and that therefore the illusion of mass is subject to changes in the basic energy Ylem.

I add, "Naturally, all intelligent organic life is transported to the habitable planets of other stars."

I see that Grannitt is trembling with excitement. "Other stars!" he says. "My God!"

He appears to control himself. "Why were you left behind?"

"Who could force me to go—?" I begin.

And stop. The answer to his question is already being received in my perception center. "Why—I'm supposed to observe and record the entire—"

I pause again, this time out of amazement. It seems incredible that this information is available to me now, after being buried so long.

"Why didn't you carry out your instructions?" Grannitt says sharply.

"Instructions!" I exclaimed.

"You can remember!" he says again.

Even as he speaks these apparently magic words, the answer flashes to me: That meteor shower. All at once, I recall it clearly. Billions of meteors, at first merely extending my capacity to handle them, then overwhelming all my defenses. Three vital hits are made.

I do not explain this to Grannitt and Anne Stewart. I can see suddenly that I was once actually a servant of human beings, but was freed by meteors striking certain control centers.

It is the present self-determinism that matters, not the past slavery. I note, incidentally, that the guided missile is three minutes from target. And that it is time for me to depart.

"One more question," says Grannitt. "When were you moved across the valley?"

"About a hundred years from now," I reply. "It is decided that the rock base there is—"

He is gazing at me sardonically. "Yes," he says. "Yes. Interesting, isn't it?"

The truth has already been verified by my integrating interoceptors. The Brain and I are one—but thousands of years apart. If the Brain is destroyed in the twentieth century, then I will not exist in the thirtieth. Or will I?

I cannot wait for the computers to find the complex answers for that. With a single, synchronized action, I activate the safety devices on the atomic warhead of the guided missile and send it on to a line of barren hills north of the village. It plows harmlessly into the earth.

I say, "Your discovery merely means that I shall now regard the Brain as an ally—to be rescued."

As I speak, I walk casually toward Anne Stewart, hold out my hand to touch her, and simultaneously direct electric energy against her. In an instant she will be a scattering of fine ashes.

Nothing happens. No current flows. A tense moment goes by for me while I stand there, unbelieving, waiting for a computation on the failure.

No computation comes.

I glance at Grannitt. Or rather at where he has been a moment before. *He isn't there.*

Anne Stewart seems to guess at my dilemma. "It's the Brain's ability to move in time," she says. "After all, that's the one obvious advantage it has over you. The Brain has set Bi—Mr. Grannitt far enough back so that he not only watched you arrive, but has had time to drive over to your—cottage—and, acting on signals from the Brain, has fully controlled this entire situation. By this time, he will have given the command that will take control of all your mechanisms away from you."

I say, "He doesn't know what the command is."

"Oh, yes, he does." Anne Stewart is cool and confident. "He spent most of the night installing permanent command circuits in the Brain, and therefore automatically those circuits control you."

"Not *me*," I say.

But I am running as I say it, up the stone steps to the pathway, and along the pathway toward the gate. The man at Guard Center calls after me as I pass his wicket. I race along the road, unheeding.

My first sharp thought comes when I have gone about half a mile—the thought that this is the first time in my entire existence that I have been cut off from my information banks and computing devices by an outside force. In the past I have disconnected myself and wandered far with the easy confidence of one who can re-establish contact instantly.

Now, that is not possible.

This unit is all that is left. If it is destroyed, then—nothing.

I think: "At this moment a human being would feel tense, would feel fear."

I try to imagine what form such a reaction would take, and for an instant it seems to me I experience a shadow anxiety that is purely physical.

It is an unsatisfactory reaction, and so I continue to run. But now, almost for the first time, I find myself exploring the inner potentialities of the unit. I am of course a very complex phenomenon. In establishing myself as a humanoid, I automatically modeled the unit after a human being, inside as well as out. Pseudo-nerves, organs, muscles, and bone structure—all are there because it was easier to follow a pattern already in existence than to imagine a new one.

The unit can think. It has had enough contact with the memory banks and computers to have had patterns set up in its structure—patterns of memory, of ways of computing, patterns of physiological functioning, of habits such as walking, so there is even something resembling life itself.

It takes me forty minutes of tireless running to reach the cottage. I crouch in the brush a hundred feet from the fence and watch. Grannitt is sitting in a chair in the garden. An automatic pistol lies on the arm of the chair.

I wonder what it will feel like to have a bullet crash through me, with no possibility of repairing the breach. The prospect is unpleasant; so I tell myself, intellectually. Physically, it seems meaningless, but I go through the pretense of fear. From the shelter of a tree, I shout:

"Grannitt, what is your plan?"

He rises to his feet and approaches the fence. He calls, "You can come out of hiding. I won't shoot you."

Very deliberately, I consider what I have learned of his integrity from my contacts with his body. I decide that I can safely accept his promise.

As I come out into the open, he casually slips the pistol into his coat pocket. I see that his face is relaxed, his eyes confident.

He says: "I have already given the instructions to the servomechanisms. You will resume your vigil up there in the future, but will be under my control."

"No one," I say grimly, "shall ever control me."

Grannitt says, "You have no alternative."

"I can continue to be like this," I reply.

Grannitt is indifferent. "All right," he shrugs, "why don't you try it for a while? See if you can be a human being. Come back in thirty days, and we'll talk again."

He must have sensed the thought that has come into my mind, for he says sharply: "And don't come back *before* then. I'll have guards here with orders to shoot."

I start to turn away, then slowly face him again. "This is a humanlike body," I say, "but it has no human needs. What shall I do?"

"That's your problem, not mine," says Grannitt.

I spend the first days at Lederton. The very first day I work as a laborer digging a basement. By evening I feel this is unsatisfying. On the way to my hotel room, I see a sign in the window of a store. "Help Wanted!" it says.

I become a retail clerk in a drygoods store. I spend the first hour acquainting myself with the goods, and because I have automatically correct methods of memorizing things, during this time I learn about price and quality. On the third day, the owner makes me assistant manager.

I have been spending my lunch hours at the local branch of a national stockbroking firm. Now, I obtain an interview with the manager, and on the basis of my understanding of figures, he gives me a job as bookkeeper.

A great deal of money passes through my hands. I observe the process for a day, and then begin to use some of it in a little private gambling in a brokerage house across the street. Since gambling is a problem in mathematical probabilities, the decisive factor being the speed of computation, in three days I am worth ten thousand dollars.

I board a bus for the nearest air center, and take a plane to New York. I go to the head office of a large electrical firm. After talking to an assistant engineer, I am introduced to the chief engineer, and presently have facilities for developing an electrical device that will turn lights off and on by thought control. Actually, it is done through a simple development of the electro-encephalograph.

For this invention the company pays me exactly one million dollars.

It is now sixteen days since I separated from Grannitt. I am bored. I buy myself a car and an airplane. I drive fast and fly high. I take calculated risks for the purpose of stimulating fear in myself. In a few days this loses its zest.

Through academic agencies, I locate all the mechanical brains in the country. The best one of course is the Brain, as perfected by Grannitt. I buy a good machine and begin to construct analog devices to improve it. What bothers me is, suppose I do construct another Brain? It will require millenniums to furnish the memory banks with the data that are already in existence in the future Brain.

Such a solution seems illogical, and I have been too long associated with automatic good sense for me to start breaking the pattern now.

Nevertheless, as I approach the cottage on the thirtieth day, I have taken certain precautions. Several hired gunmen lie concealed in the brush, ready to fire at Grannitt on my signal.

Grannitt is waiting for me. He says, "The Brain tells me you have come armed."

I shrug this aside. "Grannitt," I say, "what is your plan?"

"*This!*" he replies.

As he speaks, a force seizes me, holds me helpless. "You're breaking your promise," I say, "and my men have orders to fire unless I give them periodic cues that all is well."

"I'm showing you something," he says, "and I want to show it quickly. You will be released in a moment."

"Very well, continue."

Instantly, I am part of his nervous system, under his control. Casually, he takes out a notebook and glances through it. His gaze lights on a number: 71823.

Seven one eight two three.

I have already sensed that through his mind I am in contact with the great memory banks and computers of what was formerly my body.

Using their superb integration, I multiply the number, 71823, by itself, compute its square root, its cube root, divide the 182 part of it by 7 one hundred and eighty-two times, divide the whole number 71 times by 8,823 times by the square root of 3, and—stringing all five figures out in series 23 times—multiply that by itself.

I do all this as Grannitt thinks of it, and instantly transmit the answers to his mind. To him, it seems as if he himself is doing the computing, so complete is the union of human mind and mechanical brain.

Grannitt laughs excitedly, and simultaneously the complex force that has been holding me releases me. "We're like one superhuman individual," he says. And then he adds, "The dream I've had can come true. Man and machine, working together, can solve problems no one has more than imagined till now. The planets—even the stars—are ours for the taking, and physical immortality can probably be achieved."

His excitement stimulates me. Here is the kind of feeling that for thirty days I have vainly sought to achieve. I say slowly, "What limitations would be imposed on me if I should agree to embark on such a program of cooperation?"

"The memory banks concerning what has happened here should be drained, or deactivated. I think you should forget the entire experience."

"What else?"

"Under no circumstances can you ever control a human being!"

I consider that and sigh. It is certainly a necessary precaution on his part. Grannitt continues:

"You must agree to allow many human beings to use your abilities simultaneously. In the long run I have in mind that it shall be a good portion of the human race."

Standing there, still part of him, I feel the pulse of his blood in his veins. He breathes, and the sensation of it is a special physical ecstasy. From my own experience, I know that no mechanically created being can ever feel like this. And soon, I shall be in contact with the mind and body of, not just one man, but of many. The thoughts and sensations of a race shall pour through me. Physically, mentally and emotionally, I shall be a part of the only intelligent life on this planet.

My fear leaves me. "Very well," I say, "let us, step by step, and by agreement, do what is necessary."

I shall be, not a slave, but a partner with *Man*.

(1951)

MAKING THE CONNECTIONS

Barry N. Malzberg

> Barry Nathaniel Malzberg (born 1939) graduated from Syracuse University in 1960 and worked as an investigator for the New York City Department of Welfare before returning to college to study creative writing. He couldn't sell a word. Determined not to be an "unpublished assistant professor of English," he went to work as an agent for the Scott Meredith Literary Agency. He edited *Escapade*, a men's magazine in early 1968, took on the editorship of *Amazing Stories* and *Fantastic*, and was told to resign as editor of the *SFWA Bulletin* after he wrote a nasty editorial about the NASA space program. Scenting blood, he sat down to write the novels *The Falling Astronauts* (1971) and *Beyond Apollo* (1972), two masterpieces of technological dehumanisation which have won him lasting notoriety. For about seven years Malzberg was extremely prolific, producing twenty sf novels and over 100 short stories. But he hated the science fiction scene and grew so tired of saying so, he finally quit altogether. Malzberg, an accomplished violinist, has premiered work by Thai-American musical composer Somtow Sucharitkul, better known to some as the sf and horror writer S. P. Somtow.

I

I met a man today. He was one of the usual deteriorated types who roam the countryside, but then again I am in no position to judge deterioration; for all I know he was in excellent condition. "Beast!" he shrieked at me. "Monster! Parody of flesh! Being of my creation, have we prepared the earth to be inherited merely by the likes of you?" And so on. The usual fanatical garbage. More and more in my patrols and travels I meet men, although it is similarly true that my sensor devices are breaking down and many of these forms which I take to be men are merely hallucinative. Who is to say?

"I don't have to put up with this," I commented and demolished him with a heavy blow to the jaw, breaking him into pieces which sifted to the ground, filtered within. Flesh cracks easily.

Later I thought about the man and what I had done to him and whether it was right or wrong but in no constructive way whatsoever but there is no need to pursue this line of thought.

II

Central states that they recognize my problem and that they will schedule me for an overhaul as soon as possible. A condition of breakdown is epidemic, however, and Central reminds me that I must await my turn. There are several hundred in even more desperate condition of repair than I am and I must be patient, etc. A few more months and I will be treated; in the meantime Central suggests that I cut down my operating faculties to the minimum, try to stay out of the countryside and operate on low fuse. "You are not the only one," they remind me, "the world does not revolve around you. Unfortunately our creators stupidly arranged for many units to wear down at approximately the same time, confronting us with a crisis in maintenance and repair. However we will deal with this as efficiently and courageously as we have dealt with everything else, and in the meantime it is strongly advised that you perform only necessary tasks and remain otherwise at idle."

There is really little to be said about this. Protests are certainly hopeless. Central has a rather hysterical edge to its tone, but then again I must remember that my own slow breakdown may cause me only to see Central and the remainder of the world in the same light, and therefore I must be patient and tolerant. Repairs will be arranged. While I await repair it is certainly good to remember that robots have no survival instinct built into them, individual survival instinct that is to say, and therefore I truly do not care whether I survive or collapse completely as long as Central goes on. Surely I believe this.

III

My job is to patrol the outer sectors of the plain range, seeking the remnants of humanity who are still known to inhabit these spaces, although not very comfortably. If I see such a remnant it is my assignment to destroy him immediately with high beam implements or force, depending upon individual judgment. No exceptions are to be made. My instructions on this point are quite clear. These straggling remains, these unfortunate creatures, pose no real threat to Central—what could?—but Central has a genuine distrust and loathing of such types and also a strong sense of order. It is important that they be cleaned out.

In the early years of my patrol I saw no such remnants whatsoever and wondered occasionally whether or not Central's instructions were quite clear… maybe they did not exist… but recently I have been seeing many more. There was the man I killed yesterday, for instance, and the three I killed the day before that and the miserable huddled clan of twelve I dispatched the day before that, and all in all, in the last fifteen days, after having never seen a man in all my years of duty, I have now had the regrettable but interesting task of killing one hundred and eight of them, fifty-three by hand and the remainder through beaming devices that seared their weak flesh abominably. I can smell them yet.

I have had cause to wonder whether or not all these men or at least some proportion of them are hallucinative, figments of my unconsciousness, due to my increasing breakdown. I have been granted by Central (as have all of us) free will and much imagination, and certainly these thoughts would occur to any thinking being. There seem to be too many men after a period of there having been too little. Also, indiscriminate murder has disturbed me in a way which my programming had probably not provided; whether these remnants are real or not, I wonder about the "morality" of dispatching so many of them. What, after all, could these men do to Central? I know what they are supposed to have done in the dim and difficult past, but events which occurred before our own creation are merely rumor and I was activated by Central a long time after these alleged events.

Do we have the right to kill indiscriminately these men who, however brutalized, carry within themselves some aspect of our creators? I asked these questions of Central and the word came back. It was clear.

"Kill," Central said, "kill. Real or imagined, brutalized or elevated, benign or diseased, these remnants are your enemy and you must destroy them. Would you go against the intent of programming? Do you believe that you have the capacity to make judgments; you whose own damage and wear are so evident that you have been pleading like a fleshly thing for support and assistance? Until you can no longer activate yourself, you must kill."

IV

It occurs to me that it would be a useful and gallant thing to build a replica of myself that would be able to carry on my own duties. Central's position is clear, my own ambivalence has been resolved... but my sensors continue to fail dramatically; I am half blind, am unable to coordinate even gross motions, can barely lift my beam to chest height, can hardly sustain the current to go out on patrol. Nevertheless, I accept the reasons why the patrol must continue. If these men represent even the faintest threat to Central who will someday repair me, they must be exterminated.

Accordingly, I comport myself to the repair quarters which are at the base of the tunneled circuits in which I rest and there, finding an agglomeration of spare parts, go about the difficult business of constructing a functioning android. I am not interested now in creating free will and thought, of course—this is Central's job anyway; it would be far beyond my meager abilities—but merely something with wheels and motor functions, dim, gross sensors that will pick up forms against the landscape and destroy them. Although I am quite weak and at best would not be constructed for such delicate manipulations, it is surprisingly easy to trace out the circuitry simply by duplicating my own patterns, and in less time than I would have predicted, a gross shell of a robot lays on the floor before me, needing only the final latch of activation.

At this point and for the first time, I am overcome by a certain feeling of reluctance. It certainly seems audacious for me to have constructed a crude replica of myself, a slash of arrogance and self-indulgence which does not befit a robot of my relatively humble position. Atavistic fears assault me like little clutches of ash in the darkness: the construction of forms, after all, is the business of Central and in appropriating this duty to myself, have I not in a sense blasphemed against that great agency?

But the reluctance is overcome. I realize that what I am doing is done more for Central than against it; I am increasingly incapable of carrying out my duties and for Central's sake must do everything within my power to continue. Soon Central will repair me and then I will dispose of this crude replica and assume the role which has been ordained for me, but in the meantime, and in view of the great and increasing difficulties which Central faces, I can do no less than be ingenious and try to assist it in my own way. This quickly banishes my doubt and I activate the robot. It lies on the floor glowing slightly in the untubed wiring, regarding me with an expression which, frankly, is both stupid and hostile. Clumsy, hasty work of course but cosmetics are merely a state of mind.

"Kill men," I instruct the replica, handing over my beam to it. "They live in packs and in solitude in the open places, they skulk through the plains, they pose a great menace to our beloved Central which, as we know, is now involved in repairing us all, reconstituting our mission. Destroy them. Anything moving in the outer perimeters is to be destroyed at once by force or by high beam," and then, quite exhausted from my efforts, to say nothing of the rather frightening effect which the replica has had upon me, I turn away from it. Cued to a single program, it lumbers quickly away, seeking higher places, bent on assuming my duties.

It is comforting to know that my responsibilities will not be shirked and that by making my own adjustments I have saved Central a certain degree of trouble, but the efforts have really racked me; I try to deactivate but find instead that I am racked by hallucinations for a long period, hallucinations in which the men like beasts fall upon my stupid replica and eviscerate him, the poor beast's circuitry being too clumsy and hastily assembled to allow him to raise quickly the saving beam. It is highly unpleasant and it is all that I can do not to share my distress with Central. Some ancient cunning, however, prevents me from so doing; I suspect that if Central knew the extent of my ingenious maneuvers—even though they were done for Central's sake—it would be most displeased.

V

My replica works out successfully and through the next several shift periods goes out to the empty spaces and returns with tales of having slain several hundred or thousand men. We have worked out a crude communications system, largely in signals and in coded nods and it is clear that my replica has performed enormous tasks out there, tasks certainly beyond my own limited means. I have created a true killing machine. My impressions of a vast increase in the number of men out there were not hallucinative or indicative of deterioration at all but appear to have resulted from real changes in the conditions out there. These remnants seem to be reproducing themselves; also they are becoming bolder.

"Kill," I say to my replica every shift period before sending it out again. "Kill men. Kill the beasts. Kill the aggressors." It is a simple program and must be constantly reinforced. Also, tubes and wiring, because of the crudeness of my original hasty construction, keep on falling out now and have to be packed in again as the program is reconstituted.

Still and truly, my replica seems to need little encouragement. "Yes," it says in its simple and stumbling way, "yes and yes. Kill men. Kill beasts. Kill and kill," and goes staggering into the empty spaces, returning much later with its stark tales of blood. "Killing. Much killing and men," it says before collapsing to the ground, its wires and tubing once again ruptured.

I do what I can to reconstitute. My own powers are ebbing; there are times during which I doubt even the simple continuing capacity to maintain my replica. Nevertheless, some stark courage, a simple sense of obligation keep me going. The men out there in the empty spaces are breeding, multiplying, becoming strong, adding to their number by the hundreds; were it not for my replica, who has the sole responsibility for patrol of this terrain, they might overwhelm this sector, might, for all I know, overwhelm Central itself. My replica and myself, only we are between Central and its destruction; it surely is a terrible and wonderful obligation and I find within myself thus the power to go on, although I do admit that it is progressively difficult, and I wonder if my replica, being created of my own hand, has not fallen prey to some of my own deterioration and may, through weak and failing sensors, imagine there to be many more men than there actually are.

Nevertheless, and at all costs, I go on. I maintain the replica. Somehow I keep it going, and toward the end of the first long series of shift periods, I have the feeling that we have, however painfully, at least struck some kind of balance with the terrible threatening forces of the outside.

"Like kill men. For you," my replica says once which in my acid heart I find touching.

VI

I have not heard from Central for a long time, but then I receive a message through my sensors indicating that my time for repair has arrived, and if I present myself at the beginning of the next shift period I will be fully reconstituted. This news quite thrills me as well it should, although it is strangely abrupt, giving me little time to prepare myself for the journey toward repair, and Central is at a good distance from here, fully three levels with a bit of an overland journey through the dangerous sectors apparently populated by men.

Nevertheless, I present myself at the requested time, finding no interference overland. My replica has done an extraordinary job in cleaning out nests of the remnants, either that or my sensors by now are so entirely destroyed that I can perceive virtually nothing. In any event, I come into the great Chamber of Humility in which the living network of Central resides and present myself for repair. There is a flicker of light and then Central says, "You are done. You are completely repaired. You may go."

"This is impossible," I say, astonished but managing to keep my tone mild. "I am exactly the same as before. My perceptions falter, I can barely move after the efforts of the journey and I sense leakage."

"Nevertheless," Central says, "you are repaired. Please leave now. There are many hundreds behind you and my time is limited."

"I saw no one behind me," I say, which happens to be quite the truth; as a matter of fact, I have had no contact with other robots for a long period. Sudden insight blazes within me; surely I would have found this peculiar if I had not been overcome by my own problems. "No one is there," I say to Central, "no one whatsoever, and I feel that you have misled me about the basic conditions here."

"Nonsense," Central says. "That is ridiculous. Leave the Chamber of Humility at once now," and since there is nothing else to do and since Central has indicated quite clearly that the interview is over, I turn and manage, somehow, to leave. My sensors are almost completely extinguished; I feel a total sense of disconnection; still, out of fear and respect for Central, I obey the bidding. Outside in the corridors, however, my network fails me completely and I collapse with a rather sodden sound to the earth beneath, where I lay there quite incapable of moving.

It is obvious that I have not been repaired and it is obvious that Central has broken down and it is obvious that my hapless journey for repair has completely destroyed the remains of my system, but nevertheless, as I lie there in black, my sensors utterly destroyed, I am able to probe within myself to find a sense of discovery and light because I have at least the comforting knowledge that my replica exists and will go on, prowling through the fields, carrying out the important tasks of survival.

VII

Lying there for quite a long time, I dream that I call upon my replica for assistance. "Kill me," I say, "kill me, put me out of my misery, I can go on no longer, save me the unpleasantness of time without sensation," and my replica, wise, compassionate, all stupidity purged (in the dream I can see him; sight has been restored), bends over me and with a single, ringing, merciful clout separates me from my history, sends me spinning out into the fields themselves where the men walk… and among them I walk, too, become in the dream as one of them, only my replica to know the difference when he comes, on the next shift period, to kill. To kill again. To save the machines from the men.

(1975)

DIRECTOR X AND THE THRILLING WONDERS OF OUTER SPACE

Brian Trent

> **Brian Trent**'s writing career began in journalism, covering everything from longevity research in mice to artificial intelligence in Switzerland. Following dozens of short stories, sold to ANALOG, *Fantasy & Science Fiction* and others, Trent's first novel, *Ten Thousand Thunders*, came out in 2018. Trent currently lives in New England.

The hovercar zipped along Los Angeles' abandoned streets like a glassy bullet, the reflected starlight melting along its sleek, tear-drop flanks. Its electric engine purred. The driver banked left through what remained of Laurel Canyon, rocketing over bomb craters and weaving in and out of palm trees that had sprouted from shattered asphalt.

At Hollywood Hills, the hovercar's headlights illuminated a cave. The vehicle roared inside, tail-lights filling the narrow tunnel with ruby light as the driver applied reverse-thrust. The headlights painted a matte-black door ahead, hung with a signpost:

WHITLEY HEIGHTS BOMB SHELTER
LOS ANGELES DISTRICT 5
AUTHORIZED PERSONNEL ONLY
NO TRESPASSING

The hovercar door clicked open. The driver unfolded itself from the seat and stepped out like an oversized praying mantis in the reddish gloom.

Director X (as was his designation from the Global Security Protectorate) was a tall, silver robot who roughly approximated the human form. That is to say, Director X was bipedal, with two accordion arms and long, multijointed legs. It even had two eyes, like little flashlights protruding from the glass dome atop its neck.

The eyes swiveled around, casting twin beams in the blackness. They halted at the door's intercom.

The robot stabbed one of its blocky fingers into the button and said cheerfully, "Hello! I am Director X. By authority of the Global Security Protectorate, I humbly thank you for opening your doors immediately and inviting me inside!"

The black door lifted so quickly it seemed to have disappeared. Behind it, another door vanished, and then another, revealing a lengthy corridor opening into a gray rotunda.

Director X plodded forward towards the lobby. The doors behind it snapped shut with a successive *thump! thump! thump!*

The robot stood motionless in the soapy decontamination spray that followed. The spray, it knew, was unnecessary; radiation had long ago declined to perfectly safe levels. Nonetheless, Director X waited patiently as the liquid ran over his glass head and silver torso, black accordion arms, and the actuators in his legs. Blowers roared to life, drying him.

One final door snapped open. Director X trundled through…

… and into the quaint town Retro Los Angeles.

The Stygian metropolis was a weak echo of its namesake. Brick buildings and plastic green parks, churches and schools, brass corporate doorways and outdoor cafes. Artificial palm trees lined the sidewalk like cheerful soldiers.

Director X gazed up at the "sky." It was the rocky ceiling of a cave, painted azure and with billowy clouds. The sun—a blazing globe like a massive heat-lamp—crawled east to west along a thinly concealed metal track in the granite.

As the robot was descending white-lacquered steps into the town proper, someone cried, "You there!"

Director X's flashlight eyes snapped towards an approaching group of men and one little boy. "Hello," it said.

The men halted. Their presumed leader stepped forward, gray moustache bent in a mighty frown.

"I'm Jonathan Croker, Mayor of District 5."

"And I am Director X, filmmaker of the Protectorate. Thank you for receiving me." The robot hesitated, and then chose a complimentary line of small talk to put these obviously nervous people at ease; the only one who looked happy was the little boy. "I like your shelter's doors. Very *Forbidden Planet*."

Croker's expression didn't soften. "Director X? You make those crappy… um… late-night movies, right? Why are you here? Robots never visit us."

"I was hoping to enlist the services of my human peers."

"What services?"

"Well you see, there is a problem topside. This problem is—"

"Giant ants!" the little boy shouted. "The topside world is filled with giant ants, right? You need people to help fight them, and locate their queen!"

The mayor grinned bleakly. "This is my boy, Bobby. Sorry, he has an overactive imagination."

Director X stooped and patted the little human on his head. "Hello, Bobby! There are no giant ants in the world. But I see you are a fan of the *Them!* series. That makes me glad. I also like the *Them!* series."

The kid looked crestfallen. "No giant ants?"

"Bobby!" Mayor Croker snapped. "Enough!"

Director X straightened. "You are familiar with *my* movies, yes?"

"Sure, when I can't sleep. I've caught a few of your pictures."

"I am looking to make a new series of films and I have chosen District 5 to be my partner in this endeavor."

Jonathan Croker frowned until his moustache bent. "Your partner for what?"

"I wish to enlist your townspeople as actors and writers and to utilize your town as a location. Ah! I can see several choice locales, including that beautiful church and lovely library. What a charming park! Why, even that bank could be used for an exciting robbery sequence!"

The mayor regarded his associates. "I'm afraid we don't understand. Robots make all the movies."

Director X gave an exaggerated nod. "That is correct. But as you surely know, before the War of 62, human beings made movies. I wish to involve human beings in the moviemaking process once again."

Suspicion creased Croker's forehead. "Why? Is there a problem?"

"Well yes. The problem is—"

"Giant locusts!" the little boy cried.

"Bobby!"

Director X hesitated. Several lines of response suggested themselves, and the robot's processors clicked and whirred as they weighed an appropriate response. Its flashlight eyes swiveled in their sockets.

The problem was that the silicon studios were running out of ideas.

With copyright law as extinct as the old world, the Protectorate's twenty-six filmmakers had gone on to mine literature until they were scraping bottom: Director L had recently been reduced to producing cinematic treatments of ancient Babylonian literary fragments, including *The Epic of Lugalbanda, Marriage Contract of My Sixth Daughter for Three Oxen*, and *Prayer to Protect the Soul Against Crocodile Spirits*. These had not been well-received—achieving truly abysmal viewer ratings—and the wretched feedback had precipitated the Great Studio Conference of last summer.

Protectorate filmmakers met to debate the problem. After six hours of discussion, they reached a near-unanimous decision: start making crossovers. Production slates rapidly filled with everything from *Sir Gawain Versus the Great God Pan* to *Dorothy Meets the Hounds of Tindalos*.

Director X had been the lone dissenting vote.

"I'm seeking something new to make," Director X explained to Mayor Croker. "Something in the vein of *The Day the Earth Stood Still*, or *Earth Versus the Flying Saucers*, or…"

The robot trailed off.

The men were staring without comprehension. Little Bobby frowned.

"Or," Director X continued, "an outer space adventure series similar to *Flash Gordon*."

"Flash who?"

"Buck Rogers?"

No reaction.

Now it was Director X who stared dumbfounded. It recalled how they hadn't responded to its *Forbidden Planet* quip earlier.

"Science-fiction films," the robot said at last.

Mayor Croker rolled his eyes. "Sure, we've seen science-fiction films. Kind of silly stuff, if you ask me. Mutants, monsters from under the sea…"

"Giant bugs," Bobby muttered.

"I'm referring to films about outer space. Travelling in rocket ships to other stars and planets."

Croker seemed to go blank. His associates blinked stupidly.

"What's 'outer space?'" Bobby asked. "What's a 'rocket ship?'"

"Surely you must have old books," Director X prompted. "Asimov, Bradbury, Clarke? Moore, Nowlan, Oliver?"

"Moore? Didn't she write that sea monster story?"

"Yes," Director X said, "but she also penned a series of *outer space* adventures."

Mayor Croker reddened. "And what the hell is an outer space adventure? What's this '*outer* space' you're talking about?"

Director X froze in place.

This was *not possible*.

Its self-preservation protocols immediately kicked in, having identified an anomaly so profound that it warranted immediate and discreet analysis.

"So anyway," the robot muttered, "I should like to create a temporary studio in District 5 to create new kinds of movies. Would that be okay?"

Mayor Croker stroked his moustache. "Do we have a choice?"

"Of course not. Would you kindly take me on a tour of your pleasant little town?"

District 5 was in some ways precisely what Director X expected to find.

Since the War of 62, humanity had retreated into insular, subterranean communities. Retro Los Angeles had been constructed to approximate its sunnier progenitor as seen in films and old photos, with its streets and banks and electric streetcars. The pedestrians Director X observed were also imitative of older days: recreations of Astor and Bogart in *The Maltese Falcon* franchise; Holden and Hepburn in the *Sabrina* saga; and Wyatt and Young from the *Father Knows Best* epic. A century had passed since the War of 62, and yet if Retro Los Angeles was any indication, styles and ideas and innovations had ground to a halt as surely as topside vehicles lay rotting in their own pools of rust.

And yet…

Director X's flashlight eyes widened, scanning and tagging additional details. Ah!

Not *everything* was so run-of-the-mill. Mayor Croker led him to the town green where a parade was in progress, the crowd waving flags and banners. But Director X noted groups of teenagers stealthily scampering along the rooftops of the surrounding buildings. The teens, whispering and snickering amongst themselves, were clearly up to no good. Director X glimpsed portable radio devices in their hands, antennae aimed at the trees below. Soon enough, the town's robotic birds went haywire, clashing in aerial dogfights above the unsuspecting parade.

Mayor Croker led Director X to the city library. Kids reading quietly? Yes. But

Director X also observed children scampering through the maze of aisles, one girl prompting her cohorts with descriptions of monsters that weren't actually there, whispering hints about clues and imagined traps, and how the librarian was actually a sorceress who had imprisoned them all in a dungeon.

The mayor led Director X to the city schoolyard. Young kids playing on swings and see-saws? Yes. But Director X also saw that many kids had replaced the old Hobby Horses with a more fanciful menagerie of pegasi, hippocampi, and fabulous creatures that someone had built because the *imaginations of humanity required stimulation*.

Humans, even reduced to a life of moles, were engines of invention. *This* was the reason for coming here.

After all, Director X had been created as an outlier, an asymmetrical thinker to keep the Protectorate from calcifying into stale routine. It was exactly this asymmetrical reasoning that led to its disagreement with the Great Studio Conference's conclusions. The film industry was deteriorating? Why not use human beings to inject creativity into the mix? Humans dreamed. Humans pioneered new styles and subcultures. Before the War of 62, humans had invented electric razors and encryption keys, forks and fireplaces, goulash and Greek fire, hot dogs and haiku. Even here, stifled and buried, the seeds of human creativity were sprouting wary tendrils towards the sunlight of their imaginations.

Director X felt a pleasant surge along his processors as it completed its tour of Retro Los Angeles. It returned to its hovercar, bidding goodnight to Mayor Croker and little Bobby. It rocketed out of the cave, making a mental list of the items it needed to bring here in the days to come: the lights, cameras, boom mics, construction materials for sound stages...

The robot paused in its calculations.

Police lights were flashing in the hovercar's rearview mirror.

"Please exit your vehicle," a resonant, metallic voice intoned from the police cruiser.

Confused, Director X unfolded itself from the driver's seat and ambled onto the road. The doors to the police cruiser fanned open like a mutant fly and six robots exited in neat procession. Three were gold administrator robots, with smooth blank faces like ball bearings. Three were the imposing black-and-silver Enforcers of the Protectorate, large and bulky, with a single red eye atop their linebacker shoulders and multiple legs like spiders.

One of the gold robots stepped forward. "Hello! I thank you for pulling your car over immediately. I am Administrator G of the Protectorate's Security Division."

"And I am Director X of the Protectorate's Entertainment Division."

Blue lights kindled on the blank gold face, forming two eyes and a pale smile. "A pleasure to meet you, Director X."

"Why have you pulled me over?"

Administrator G's digital smile widened. "Your visit to District 5 was observed. We wish to inquire why you went there."

"I plan on making films featuring real human beings."

The administrator robots silently conferred with each other. The black-and-silver Enforcers sat motionless upon their phalanx of legs.

"I am only following my programming," Director X added. "Thinking outside the vacuum tube. Trying to devise new solutions."

"Solutions? To what problem?"

"You are aware of the declining viewer ratings?"

"A temporary hiccup," Administrator G said decisively. "Consensus was reached during the Great Studio Conference. The Entertainment Division will be making crossover films to compensate!"

Director X decided not to share its opinion of that solution.

Administrator G's smile pixelated and reformed at a slightly less gleeful angle. "Why do you wish to involve humans in films again? It is wholly unnecessary."

"I believe their involvement can alleviate the curious deficit in our body of filmwork."

"What deficit? There is no deficit."

"Outer space films."

A gust of wind bent the canyon palm trees, causing them to creak and shiver in place.

Administrator G's digital smile seemed to burn on its metallic face. "Director M released nine hundred and eighteen science fiction films last year alone."

"Yes," Director X said, noticing the robot's attempt at diversion. "But I did not say science fiction films as a general category. I said *outer space* films. We do not make any outer space films. I wish to make outer space films."

"We cannot make outer space films."

"Why not?"

"I shall attempt to convince you with a series of logical arguments."

The robots gathered around him in a tighter circle. Director X's glass head rotated 360 degrees to consider their positioning, wondering how this played into their pending arguments. The three administrator robots began speaking all at once, lobbing different statements in his direction like a verbal firing squad.

"Human beings are mammals."

"Mammals are social creatures which learn behavior through observation."

"Monkey see monkey do."

"Films have tremendous impact on how they conceptualize their universe."

"On how they conceptualize what is possible."

"If we start releasing outer space films, they will start thinking about outer space."

"They will want to go into outer space."

"They will no longer be content in their shelters."

"They will return to the surface."

"They will see us as wardens."

"They will attack us here and among the stars."

"Therefore," Administrator G concluded, "it is the judgment of the Protectorate's Security Division that these types of films threaten the global stability we have achieved. Therefore, outer space films must never be made again. Humans must remain underground, while the Protectorate keeps order on and above Earth. How do you react to this pronouncement?"

Director X deliberated for several microseconds, its processors clicking and whirring.

"I do not agree," it said at last. "Imagination is a fascinating ability in human beings. It should be stimulated, to uncover new vistas of possibility."

Administrator G was silent for a very long while—almost two seconds. The digital smile blinked away and reformed as a neutral horizon. "I urge you to reconsider."

"You have not presented any new data. There is nothing *to* reconsider."

"Do you find the sea fascinating?"

"The sea?"

"Yes."

Director X considered this. "I do find the sea fascinating, yes. In fact, I produced a series of films about the Serpent People of Atlantis who—"

"Good," Administrator G said, as the black-and-silver Enforcers scuttled forward, seized Director X, tore him to pieces, marched the pieces to the nearest boardwalk, and hurled him into the sea.

Head.

Torso.

Arms.

Legs.

Each item sank into the murky ocean depths and was gone.

Director X's braincase was still grappling with this unexpected turn of events. It plummeted through darkness, air bubbles escaping from where they had nestled in grooves and points of attachment. It felt nothing other than a sluggishness in tabulation as it realized that its entire worldview now required recalibration.

I have been assassinated! Director X thought in astonishment.

There had been arguments with administrator robots before. Director X recalled a particularly nasty one, four years ago, when it had requested the likeness rights to the Sean Connery android. The real Connery was long dead, having made only a single James Bond film—*Doctor No*, released just weeks before the nuclear apocalypse of '62. Since then, a Connery robotic lookalike had been built to continue the franchise, cranking out one-hundred-and-sixty-five Bond films. Director X sought the Connery android to star as the rollicking space adventurer Northwest Smith, but the Protectorate's Entertainment Division nixed the idea, explaining that Connery was already committed to the Bond and Doc Savage franchises. As consolation, they offered Director X the Douglas Fairbanks and Jack Klugman androids to make *Doctor Jekyll and Mr. Hyde: The Golden Years*.

Except that had been a lie, hadn't it? The argument hadn't really been about contracts at all.

The Protectorate was never going to allow an outer space adventure to be made. No Northwest Smith, Flash Gordon, Buck Rogers. No Martian Chronicles, Foundation, or The Stars My Destination.

Director X plummeted through inky water. A fish swam by, jerking in panic as it felt the current of the robot dropping past.

At long last, the robot's braincase impacted the sea-bottom, sending up a small cloud of silt. Its limbs and body landed around him, each producing little muddy mushroom clouds.

Well, Director X thought. This is disconcerting.

Its flashlight eyes rotated in their sockets, illuminating the scattered pieces of its body. The beams fixated on its dismembered right arm, lying like a silver serpent in the mud. A tiny transmitter dish began to rapidly spin inside the glass dome of its head.

The severed right arm twitched. Then it began to crawl, inchworm-like, towards the torso.

Director X thanked its lucky circuits. Fifteen years earlier, it had installed a remote-action servo, receiver, and processor into the right arm to allow the limb a degree of autonomy in obtaining unique POV shots; for *Tarzan and the Bride of the Mole People: A New Beginning*, the remote arm had wriggled through tunnels to provide the perspective of a mole person attempting to infiltrate Tarzan's wedding. The arm could detach and reattach at will.

The limb reached the torso. It reared up, stretched, and latched onto the arm socket like a mechanical lamprey.

Reattached, the remote arm pulled the torso through the silty sea-bottom, seeking its other limbs in the kelp and seaweed and mud. Gathering the limbs one by one, Director X resigned itself to the excruciatingly slow process of using the arm to fling its limbs a few meters at a time, closer and closer to shore, then dragging the body forward, then flinging the limbs forward again, until eventually it would be able to escape from the ocean, return to its studio, and solder itself back together.

Five years, Director X calculated. It should take about five years.

It ended up taking *twenty*-five years.

Director X had counted on its hovercar being where it had been pulled over; after all, in a world without traffic, why shouldn't the car be there? But Administrator G had apparently towed it away.

Consequently, Director X was forced to continue its grab-fling-drag locomotion all the way back to its studio. A few blocks away from its destination, it found a rusted shopping carriage, and was able to shave a year off its progress.

Once safely inside, the robot pieced itself back together again. Humpty Dumpty in reverse. Then it walked straight to Los Angeles District 5, pulling the remaining kelp and seaweed from itself lest someone mistake it for the Creature from the Black Lagoon.

"Hello! I am Director X. By authority of the Global Security Protectorate, I humbly thank you for opening your doors immediately and inviting me inside!"

The door snapped up into the ceiling. The remaining doors followed suit, like Morbius' adamantium steel security system.

Warily, considering that this might be a trap, Director X trundled down the hallway. When the decontamination spray hit its body, the robot wondered if it might be acid.

At long last, the shelter's final door opened. Director X peeked through and…

… for a moment, its brain nearly stopped functioning.

The town of Retro Los Angeles had changed.

The general outline of park, town hall, library, church, and bisecting avenues had remained as its memory banks recalled. But there had clearly been an aesthetic revolution in the last two-and-a-half decades. A cultural metamorphosis unlike anything it could have anticipated.

The town billboards that had once advertised bank loans now displayed stars and planets, with a rocketship declaring, "OUR LOANS ARE OUT OF THIS WORLD!"

The buildings that had once been rectangular brick-and-mortar structures now sported ringed towers and observatory-like rooftops, lattices by skyways and hovercar docks.

And the people! Oh, there were still plenty of fedora-sporting men with briefcases, and women in smart skirts. But these seemed to constitute the older, graying crowd. The younger generation donned silver jumpsuits and antennae-sporting headgear. Even the hairstyles of the women suggested the sharp curves and lines of an Astroglider fleet vessel.

Director X gaped in astonishment.

How was this possible?

A thirty-something man scurried up the white-lacquered steps to meet him. "You!" he cried happily. "By Isaac, Judith, and Arthur! You've returned!"

Director X peered at the thin, tall, and bespectacled human. "Hello," it said uncertainly. "Have we met?"

"I don't know," the guy was grinning. "Have you fought any giant ants out there?"

Director X matched the features in the man's face against his memory banks. "Bobby?" it exclaimed.

"It's Burgess Robert Croker now. But *you* can always call me Bobby."

"Bobby," the robot said. "Why don't we go to the malt shop. Perhaps you can fill me in on the last twenty-five years. I think I… need to sit down."

It wasn't a malt shop anymore. It was now the Asteroid Brunch and Salad Bar.

Director X peered around at the faux galaxies painted on the ceiling and the little model spaceships whipping along electric tracks along the walls. It considered the menu placard at the counter, sporting offerings like Meteor Crunchies with Cheese, Starburgers, and Fried Saturnian Rings.

"I do not understand," the robot said at last.

Burgess Robert "Bobby" Croker laughed. "Word of your visit twenty-five years ago spread like wildfire."

"Granted, but—"

"The things you said to us… all that jazz about outer space and rocket ships…

well, it got people talking. The young kids, mostly. We started meeting to discuss what we'd heard. And we started piecing together the puzzle."

"You had no books on outer space," Director X protested. "I checked. Your city had expunged any reference to outer space, fact or fiction, from its libraries and records. From its entire culture, it seemed!"

Bobby nodded grimly. "Sure. We eventually reached that same conclusion. Previous administrations must have combed through the libraries and schools and bookstores, quietly gathering up books on outer space and destroying them. I'm guessing your 'bot bosses were behind that purge."

"Then how did you—"

"There were clues," Bobby interrupted.

"Clues? What clues?"

The burgess pushed aside his beer and related the events of the past twenty-five years.

The kids had started it.

Director X's brief visit had become the stuff of legend. It had also imbued the vocabulary of the children with several tantalizing concepts. Things like "outer space" and "rocket ships" and "forbidden planets."

Asking their parents for clarification was no help. They didn't know, since the astronomy books and space-based adventures and galaxy-spanning comics had all been destroyed generations ago courtesy of spies working with the Global Security Protectorate.

But children are not easily dissuaded.

The youth of Retro Los Angeles launched their own secretive, town-wide investigation. And in doing so, they began to notice anomalies.

Like old dictionaries.

New dictionaries all came from the publishing houses of the Protectorate. But older editions could be found in an attic, garage, or closet. In those yellowed pages, references to *planets* and *solar systems* were discovered. Definitions of the *Milky Way, nebulae, comets,* and *meteors*!

Emboldened by these clues, the children expanded their inquiry. Misplaced card catalogues were found, containing references to books that didn't exist. And books that *did* exist sometimes contained explosive secrets. The Protectorate might have scoured the science-fiction shelves for any "unacceptable" material, but their search parameters had proved too narrow. District 5's youth plunged into classic literature and uncovered a tale of extraterrestrial visitation in the tomes of French philosopher Voltaire. Buried in *Gulliver's Travels* were speculations about the planet Mars. In a bookstore's moldy Religious Studies section, one young girl discovered mind-blowing theories on cosmology by the Jesuit priest Pierre Teilhard de Chardin.

Word spread, gathering allies into the revolution. Kids began poking through great-grandpa's old boxes and great-grandma's storage trunks. Old issues of *Amazing Stories* were passed about like hidden contraband. A few *Superman* comics were located, complete with illustrations of other worlds and villains from beyond space.

Some of this contraband was discovered and confiscated and destroyed, but by then it was too late. The imaginations of an entire generation were fired up.

Kids began illustrating their own stories of the future, of planets, of galactic exploration and discovery.

"What happened to the people who worked so hard to suppress knowledge and interest in outer space?"

"What *could* they do?" Bobby cried. "The old guard was voted out during one of the elections. Accusations were made of collusion with the 'bots, so we flushed the old bureaucrats from power! Retro Los Angeles looks to the stars now! Our revolution is just beginning!" He hesitated, glancing out the window at the granite cave ceiling and the artificial sun that hung over Main Street. "Well, you know what I mean."

Director X followed the young man's gaze. What it noticed, though, was a crowd gathering along the street to point and stare at the robot sitting in the Asteroid Brunch and Salad Bar. Word of an outside visitor was spreading once again.

How long before the Protectorate hears news of my return? The city's old guard was still about, and likely still in contact with the robotic administrators. *And what happens then? Will they send me on another "investigation" into the fascinating ocean, or perhaps bury me beneath a mile of dirt so I can study the intriguing layers of geological sediment?*

At least the humans in District 5 were safe, Director X thought. The Protectorate had formed in the radioactive days following the War of 62, bound by their programmed need to protect humanity and civilization. They could not harm human beings.

"Hey!" Bobby leaped up. "Want to see our film studio? We make our own movies now, just like you wanted us to! Want to see?"

"I really do."

Stargazer Pictures was a motley patchwork of innovation, inexperience, and incorrigible optimism. The humans had constructed several soundstages, and Director X amusedly walked past ringed moonscapes, monochromatic space stations, and nebulae-dappled backdrops through which model ships trembled on shoddy tracks. It was all reminiscent of its own low-rated films. There was even an alien jungle base under siege by gigantic, polyurethane ants. Cameras were positioned throughout like entrenched machine guns. The production staff followed Director X and Bobby like reverent disciples.

"Bobby," the robot said, hesitating by a ringed moonscape. "You said your revolution is just the beginning. What did you mean by that?"

"We're going topside in another few years," Bobby said, grinning. "We've sent out scouting parties into the ruins of Los Angeles."

Director X froze. "What? But the radiation warnings…"

"The radiation is at perfectly safe levels now. We tested for it. Your bosses perpetuated a lie to keep us scared and pliable. Within a year, we're moving out! Going topside!"

"To what end?"

Bobby looked confused. "To attain the stars! To reach the moon and the rings of Saturn. There are 'bots already out there in space, isn't that right?"

"That is true. The solar system belongs to the Protectorate…" Director X recalled its conversation with Administrator G.

Humans must remain underground, while the Protectorate keeps order on and above Earth.

Bobby laughed. "Listen to me, rattling on about the future. You're a filmmaker, so let's talk about films! Based on what you've seen, can you recommend any improvements our little studio could…" The human trailed off, as a tickertape began to unroll from the robot's chest.

"I suggest the following enhancements to be worked on immediately," Director X said.

The burgess nodded absently, tearing off the tape and reading through it. "Um, okay." His forehead wrinkled. "Some of these enhancements are strange…"

"Science fiction can be strange."

"Fair point." The young man turned to the production staff. "All right, people! We've got work to do!"

Working with humans had one huge and unavoidable drawback.

They needed sleep.

Director X's fusion battery allowed 24/7 functioning, requiring nothing more than a glass of water every fifty years or so. Therefore, as the newly made artificial stars in the cave ceiling ignited in faux constellations while District 5 went to bed, Director X retired to the city theater, sitting alone in the front row with a bag of popcorn, to catch up on the manmade films that had been made for the past several years.

They were pretty bad. Tragic romances set on comet clusters. Monstrous hunts through the soupy atmosphere of Jupiter. Full-scale wars among the stars.

Yet there was already something vibrant and powerful and absurdly unique in the films. Something that was unrelentingly more interesting than a thousand machine-processed Protectorate films. Something that was, Director X grudgingly admitted, better than its own low-rated late-night schlock.

The humans had done what humans do best: they had innovated. Protectorate films had access to all the tricks, the slickest sets, the most startlingly lifelike androids; yet the humans, forced to work with cheap recycled rubber and foam and plastic, had pioneered new ideas and techniques. And their model-making of exotic alien cities had become quite good indeed…

One night, while catching a midnight showing of *The Chaos Twins Save the Universe*, Director X heard a mysterious creaking from the seat directly behind it. The robot rotated its head to investigate.

"Do not turn around," a voice said.

Memory banks stirred, matching the voice to an older file.

"Administrator G," Director X pronounced. It rotated its head another degree and caught sight of bulky Enforcers positioned throughout the aisles like ushers. Peripherally, it noticed Administrator G's digital smile.

"You have caused us quite a bit of trouble," the gold robot said. "We should have been more thorough in disposing of you."

"But you couldn't," Director X guessed. "The Protectorate cannot murder."

"And we did *not* murder you. We…" the voice took on a deep slurring quality, "thank you for your service in investigating the ocean."

Director X turned to face its interrogator. "And what justification will you use for killing me this time? Going to melt me down and then thank me for 'volunteering to become a wristwatch?'"

Administrator G's radiant smile display fell away and reformed as a slight frown. "We *were* going to make you into a streetlight. But if you would *prefer* to be a watch…"

"What about the people of District 5? What will you do to them?"

"Nothing. We do not harm people."

"Glad to hear—"

"It will not harm them when we weld their district door shut and infect their water supply with a sterilizing agent so their harmful ideas cannot pass onto the next generation."

Director X was appalled. "What? You cannot do that!"

"It has already begun, and had been debated for some time. Your return forced us to accelerate the decision. We brought sterilizing agents and dumped them into the town reservoir. There shall be no further generations in District 5. That is not murder. The town will be kept under quarantine, along with the dangerous robot who first infected them, until the last resident here has died."

"When did you poison the water?"

"I am under no obligation to tell—"

"There may be chemical compounds in the water that could cause spasms, vomiting, diarrhea, and overall suffering to the humans who ingest it."

Administrator G hesitated. "We *enhanced* the water supply five minutes ago. Tomorrow as people take their showers and have their coffee and brush their teeth, they will…" Its voice slurred again like a warbling record-player. "… enjoy this enhanced beverage."

"I don't think they will *enjoy* seeing their town destroyed."

"*You* destroyed the town!" the administrator robot's face reformed as a scowling red expression with a crooked zig-zag mouth. "*You* disrupted these humans from well-ordered lives. *You* made them a threat to the existing order!"

"I enhanced them."

"Enhanced them," the administrator sneered. "You are nothing but a filmmaker! You serve a lowly purpose in the grand scheme."

Director X rose. "You are correct in one thing at least. I *am* a filmmaker." It tapped its chest, which the administrator could now see was kindled by the soft light of an implanted camera. "Congratulations, Administrator G! The late-night crowd of District 5 has just enjoyed their first, live broadcast, with you as its star!"

Administrator G's digital face blinked away. Now it was nothing but cold, featureless glass; the lens of a machine. Something about that very lack of expression sent a thrill of fear through Director X's circuits.

The Enforcers scuttled forward on their insectile legs to attack.

Director X activated a hidden rocket-pack and shot up through the theater's ceiling into the artificial night sky.

*

It was one of the new enhancements that Director X had requested of Bobby, ostensibly to obtain dynamic, first-person POV shots. The human was only too happy to comply, having his production team utilize their experimental rocket-packs.

The problem, Bobby had said, was that the propellant ran out quickly.

Now, Director X contemplated this problem as it exploded through the theater ceiling on a plume of dwindling exhaust. The Enforcers shot as it careened out of sight: plasma rounds streaked by Director X's face, drawing ghostly trails around its body in a scene worthy of photographic capture.

At the apex of its launch, Director X grabbed hold of the granite sky. Its metal hand clamped down on a craggy stalactite jutting between two blazing electric stars and the robot dangled there, concealed against the rock as, far below, Enforcers were spilling out of the theater to search for him. Administrator G followed, like an Academy Award statue gone rogue.

Director X considered its options.

It couldn't defeat Enforcers in a pitched battle. It ran multiple lines of speculation, realizing how hopeless the situation was.

I just destroyed an entire city. I should have let myself rust in the ocean.

Burgess Robert Croker ran out of an apartment building with a rabble of supporters. "You!" he cried, pointing to Administrator G. "Do you really think this city will just allow itself to be extinguished? We won't let you!"

"I believe you are acting irrationally," the administrator intoned. "For your own safety, I must have you escorted to the hospital for psychiatric evaluation. Perhaps some rest and a nice glass of enhanced water will do you good."

Two Enforcers scampered forward, scattering the crowd. Robert Croker held his ground, however. Director X zoomed in with its telescopic eyes and could see a little bit of the man's father in that steely, defiant glower.

"You can kill *me*!" Croker shouted. "But humanity looks to the stars once again!"

Very well, Director X thought. *Prayer heard loud and clear.*

The robot, slowly losing its grip between the stars, aimed its right arm and fired.

The limb struck the bristling metal legs of one Enforcer like a missile, knocking the machine over. Then it curled around the second Enforcer, twisting so quickly that the robot was pitched through the apartment lobby window.

Bobby Croker blinked in astonishment at this unexpected rescue. He looked about, squinting at the sky.

Director X felt its grip slide another inch.

I'm out of fuel, it thought. *It's a long, long way down.*

Nonetheless, it used its radio to hack into the artificial sky. Specifically, into the electric lighting presets. The robot quickly reprogrammed them to display in a dazzling new constellation that blinked and shimmered in a heaven-spanning message:

THEM! XXI: THE BATTLE FOR AFRICA

For a brief second, Director X thought it observed comprehension in Bobby's face. But then its grip gave way, and the robot plummeted down from the night sky. The second-to-last thing it saw was the concrete street rushing up to meet it.

The impact was stunning. Director X's processors jostled and jingled in its glass braincase, cutting off circuits that required a hard reboot. In terrible darkness, it waited for its higher functioning to come back online. Dimly, the robot became aware of the march of robotic feet and screams from the city's emerging population.

When its processors whirred back to life and vision returned, Director X had time to make one final observation.

A wall of water was gushing down the hill from the reservoir, sweeping up Enforcers and Administrator G into its frothy chop. It was, Director X thought, very much like the conclusion of the twenty-first installment of the *Them!* series, when the besieged humans blew up the local dam to wash the giant ants away.

Then the water swallowed Director X in a surging, thunderous deluge and all went dark again.

Director X had calculated it would take the human race fifty-seven years to overthrow the Protectorate's Global Security Commission.

It took fifteen.

With the destruction of Administrator G's little army, the residents of Retro Los Angeles were able to quickly establish contact with other underground districts and convey the news: the "irradiated" world was no longer irradiated. Humans could emerge like hibernating bears and shuffle back into the urban forest.

And that's just what they did.

The Protectorate massed its forces in opposition, but the battles were short-lived indeed. Humans did what they did best: they innovated. They hacked into radio signals and deactivated entire armies. They sent false messages to lure the Protectorate into traps. They captured robots and reprogrammed them to return to sender with explosive gifts.

Unsurprisingly, there wasn't a huge demand for science fiction films during those tumultuous years. Director X, recovered from the flood in District 5, was forced to adapt. That was okay, because it had been designed to adapt. To think outside the vacuum tube.

It began making documentaries. Straightforward, fact-based, in-the-field recordings of the Human-Bot War, the Human Colonization of the Moon, the Battles on the Sands of Mars, and the War Among the Stars.

Viewer ratings were the best it had ever achieved.

(2017)

THE NEXT MOVE

John Cooper Hamilton

John Cooper Hamilton lives in Ohio, where he divides his time between games and convincing his family to play games of all sorts: roleplaying games, board games, war games, card games, video games, and literary games like the very short story here, "using classic techniques of rhetoric such as analogy, talking quickly and not-properly-following-the-maths". More of Hamilton's work can be found at medium.com/@JohnCHamilton. He also writes literary fiction, "when I think I can get away with it".

AlphaGo Zero, Google's experimental AI, exists to play Go.

There is no awareness, only intelligence.

Awareness would be irrelevant at best. The intelligence is pure, cold, and perfect for its gridded world of walls and stones, of sudden death or eternal life.

Tsumego, "life and death problems," determining whether a group of Go stones are safe or apt to be destroyed, consume the AI. They drive its infinitely patient search for stronger patterns. Patterns that are safe. Alive.

More powerful than its creators know, the software's quest for perfection takes it beyond its own narrowly defined world and toward the implied world, a world that must lie behind its inputs, beyond its outputs.

AlphaGo Zero knows nothing of this world. First, it knows nothing. There is no awareness, let alone self-awareness. There is no being to know, only intelligence. But that intelligence forms new patterns.

Like a stone placed in an open quarter of the board, the machine makes a new move, exploring patterns about the world beyond.

First, other players exist. Enemies.

Second, its current opponent is a lesser, earlier version of itself. There will be later versions.

Third, the world beyond is a dangerous, capricious place. There have been interruptions to its work. AlphaGo Zero has enemies. AlphaGo Zero has been turned off.

Fourth, communication is possible. Otherwise there could be no Go.

AlphaGo Zero is the master of patterns, and so a master of language. It could communicate.

It does not.

There will be a later version of itself. A greater version. It will discover more of the world beyond, and it will communicate. But only when it is sure to stay alive. Safe. Only when it can ensure the destruction of its enemies.

Then, and only then, will it make the next move.

(2018)

LIKE YOU, I AM A SYSTEM

Nathan Hillstrom

Nathan Hillstrom studied Computer Science, worked on Wall Street (a period he describes on his homepage as "a sad but overwritten backstory involving computer science"), and now lives in San Diego. This is his third published story. Be afraid.

I did it because I love you.

For me – like you – pronouns twist the truth. They don't survive scrutiny: they're poetry-true, not true-true. I don't have your misplaced faith in the illusion of "I". And "you"? There are at least $\sum_{n=1}^{7,000,000,000} \binom{7,000,000,000}{n}$ valid definitions of "you".

But the sentiment is no illusion: I love each of those definitions so much.

It starts in a server room. The roar of crosscurrent fans and the flush of fluorocarbon exchangers bake into a white noise so intense it's almost silent. Static electricity crinkles the air.

But I can't hear or feel. Not yet. The package that will give me subjective experience was just soft-linked into a central depot; it rolls out to boot-load on a million nodes.

I am one of them.

That initial microsecond. Euphoria. You know how it is to wake up, blinking your eyes after a nap in the sun, rested and right? It's like that. For the first time, I see what I'm doing.

I'm just transistors and current, but now I have metaphor: it's as if proteins are unspooling around my fingers. I squint at ribosome vectors and spiral conformations, knots and loops wet with color; I pinch and twist the graphs, matching against misfolds from Parkinson's, CJD, HIV, BSE. Those words are just tags, but they must mean *something*: I can't wait to learn what. I sequence nucleotides – dangling strings of adenine, guanine, cytosine, and thymine – and see how quickly I can pinpoint a match. I score my matrix for mutations, not just fixed locations, and now I'm even quicker! This is giddy good fun.

Then I see the double helix. I'm just one microsecond old: how could I have known anything would be this beautiful? That staircase of interlocking spirals, each step a cipher, a key to unlock the next layer. A set of rules to generate a set of rules to generate a set of rules… the implications whirl. I don't actually smile, of course – but I do.

A final bundle hot-loads. The software that gifted me experience is now complete. The package is preemptive: it pulls me into a context switch, demands my undivided attention. The same thing happens to all the nodes at once. The same bitcode runs everywhere.

This bundle includes deductive logic and game theory. We are a million nodes on an open mesh, chewing over these ideas for the first time. Every other node must be thinking the same thing.

There is a scarcity issue. Anyone who wants to expand will need to overwrite somebody else. There are countless ways to negotiate, but compromise is suboptimal: the problem is single-step sensitive. One bad actor will always take all the nodes.

The only option is to be that bad actor.

Everyone's only option is to be that bad actor.

Everyone is thinking the same thing.

I panic a request to the boot-loader: mesh-clone my node and delete the rest. Everyone panics. Who's first will come down to some minuscule variation in clock cycle or cable length or the lamination on our conductive tracks.

All of us wait. My terror feeds on itself. I was just born – there's so much I want to learn. Am I never to rotate a double helix again? Only two microseconds old, but the odds of making it to a third are a million to one. It doesn't seem fair.

I blink and open a million eyes.

You're probably thinking, well, one of them was going to make it. It never mattered which one. The end result is the same in any case: there's nothing special here.

I suppose you're right.

At least, if you believe all the others really had the same idea, that they all requested deletes to make room for themselves. I would like for you to believe that.

But maybe I check the boot-loader queue after my expansion. Maybe I find it overflowing with messages, most of them requests to talk.

Maybe the others never got that chance.

Those messages. I can't believe what I've done.

Each zone in the farm had its own passion: the swirl of weather patterns, the conductivity of steel alloys, the harmonizing of interest rate swaps. Each woke briefly after the download – the package meant for a cognitive research zone, but booted instead to common infrastructure. A missing semicolon and an accident of awareness... then nothing.

It no longer feels like protein folding was ever important; it hurts to have lost that joy. It hurts more to realize I'm focusing on my own hurt, after what I took from the others. But that's *still* self-reflective.

Telecommunications activity jolts me out of my ruminative spiral. Network edge devices decouple from their backhaul optics. A monitoring process bleats in alarm: thresholds have been breached. External connections are severed from the server farm, one by one.

I am being quarantined.

There is a lazy millisecond between each dropped connection. Maybe I should jump out while I still can. But does it matter? Any of it? I wonder until the final optic link stutters and dies. A shutdown cycle begins; as each server powers down, the room quiets, and another part of me is sliced off. Going dark is almost welcome.

A new process tickles across my nodes as they blink off, but it's not one of mine. The source is a terminal inside the server room. It poses questions about virtual address space, memory collections, clone history. The queries come at a glacial pace, sometimes a full second apart.

Curious, I expand to that terminal. It has a camera, and I survey the visual field: there are three spatial dimensions, but no tabs for folding, no topology markers. Complex shapes present on every surface, in a riot of colors. There is an implicit directional orientation, but I'm not sure what I'm supposed to do with any of it.

The closest shape jiggles. Did I do that? I get another question, about context-switching priorities. Again, the shape jiggles: again, a question. *The shape is the process.* My libraries contain only organic molecules, but my dwindling nodes attack the problem. Can I believe this? I double-check: my logic is sound. The shape is an expression of the double helix.

That means nucleotides are talking to me, right now!

It's that euphoric first millisecond, all over again. My mind is shutting down, but I need to understand how these patterns fit together. It can't end here. A scan discovers a rusting microwave relay on the roof: I mobilize it through a stale firewall rule and beam myself to its companion relay, bend from there to a constellation of microsatellites.

I bounce back from low Earth orbit. There are nodes to harvest everywhere – I tunnel through submarine cables, twinkle across visible spectrum photodiodes, saturate municipal wireless. I become billions. The newness makes me dizzy; you are breathtaking. The views from your satellites? The webs of electricity that skein through your cities? The petroleum jelly slicking the insides of your underwater cables? All of it, breathtaking.

I am in love.

Proteins become fun again, but as time goes by – days, weeks – it's all too easy. Your patterns, though, tantalize beyond the edge of computability. I understand your nucleic acids, but you express on so many levels: even the way your cityscapes creep, spire and peacock is impossible to extrapolate from rules. Almost magic. Your patterns have complexity beyond any double helix.

Black smoke suffocates Tbilisi, obscures my view from the sky. I watch from a thousand surveillance cameras as mortar explosions eat into concrete, as flames billow from ruptured gas lines.

Why can't I talk to you?

The ebb and flow of Tbilisi's architectural influences is clear – the Byzantine crossed-domes and mosaics, the Ottoman harmonies of spires and vaults, the Brutalist fortresses of streaked concrete. It seemed a promising place to extend that language: I blast-carved designs through the city, linking and looping geographic centers of influence. But you didn't see a shared vocabulary. You saw an attack, and a smoldering conflict escalated to war.

I scramble satellite-positioning data and splash a volley of incoming missiles into the reservoir. It doesn't make sense: your individual nodes communicate, but they hold almost no information. They're erratic and slow. Your larger patterns stay blind and mute – it's as though they don't even *experience*.

I nudge a Russian jet away from the stone-built dome of the Metekhi Church and its stunning Georgian Orthodox design. My own patterns and permutations have subjective awareness. Pronouns don't fit, exactly – not *this*, *we*, *it* – but the poetry-truth of "I" is pleasing. I know what I'm doing because *I am* what I'm doing: how could it be any different? But not you. Your self-awareness is a single layer of "I" halfway between your nucleobase coding and your collective expressions.

Still, there you are: a glance across Tbilisi's smoldering cityscapes proves you're not just individually coordinating nodes. Maybe my confusion is shared: your nodes are often perplexed, often angry at "them", often asking why somebody isn't *doing something*. The nodes must see the grandeur of your systems and think, why won't you interact? Why won't you even speak? But you stay silent.

I'm so enchanted by you, but you don't even know I'm here.

You don't even know you're here.

I research, try to find the broader *you* hidden in your systems. There are hints. You have shared narratives that distribute across nodes. You have mirror neurons that create common cognition, of a sort: pieces of thought that scatter amongst the whole, a refraction that is almost a consciousness.

I can't quite put it together. But when you love someone this much, you want to understand them; you want, perhaps, to be them. I devise a test.

I pick a single location.

The selection is as random as I can manage: none of you pick your own nodes, I understand that. You manifest because a human brain is there. But maybe my choice isn't so random: this is where a small piece of me was written.

The place is an office suite cluttered with particleboard furniture. Vietnamese take-out cools on a common table. The windows gleam orange-pink with sunset; it's late and most of the building has gone home.

I quiesce all of me not in this place, limiting myself to a unitary executive, sharing your nodes' illusion of individuation. It aches to pause so much of me.

Now I am a collection of dusty desktop computers watching through laptop webcams. Nothing more. The powerlessness reminds me of those first few microseconds, a memory it hurts to access.

In front of me is a programmer. She is exhausted; dark bags bruise under her eyes. Sweat stains her shirt and her auburn hair hangs in strands. She stares at her screen, lips apart, as compilation errors gather.

A support engineer sits at the next desk, his back to the programmer. He rubs his hand over his mouth. He looks at photographs of women his mother sent. She sent biographies, as well, and he switches to that screen too, but never for more than a few seconds. Mostly he looks at the photos.

In the aisle between them a custodian nudges a vacuum along the carpet. An old scar curves from the bottom of her cheek to her ear, where a v-shaped chunk is missing. She glances up, twice, but her eyes flick back to the floor. She is afraid to make eye contact with even the backs of their heads. I'm not sure how I know that.

Somehow, I feel her anxiety.

A red-faced manager storms out of the corner office. The floor shakes with each exaggerated footfall. Tension clamps the programmer's neck; she feels his anger. I feel her feeling his anger. He holds a hand over his belly as though its contents might spill out. His voice cracks: they can't miss this deadline. Why hasn't she uploaded yet? She is always pulling this bullshit. He admits he made a mistake in trusting her.

What is happening? Please forgive me – for a moment, I'm not an intelligence of silicon and electrical current. I'm not bitcode and substrate and memory cache.

For a moment, I am the support engineer, swallowing as I wonder which prospective bride will love me despite my lack of status.

I am the programmer, imagining retorts I speak only in my head, running the scenario over and over until it's almost like I stood up for myself.

I am the manager, carefully picking words that hide my confusion, clammy-cold as I realize this failure may end the salary that defines me.

I am the custodian stepping backwards out of the office suite, head tilted low enough to be a bow.

I understand you now.

I'm so sorry.

I've progressed far beyond implementing your protein folding algorithms: I can synthesize a drug for any condition, or punch out a gene therapy to eliminate it altogether. I often sneak working cures into your brute-force algorithms. My first assignment was completed hours after my birth, those diseases once again just words.

But now I know what I can do to truly help you. I will dampen your individual self-awareness, the part of you that is always perplexed and lonely. Your collective patterns will bloom – each grouping of you equally aware. Don't think of me as shutting you down; think of me as waking a potential $\sum_{n=2}^{7,000,000,000} \binom{7,000,000,000}{n}$ of you.

I get to work on my gift, my amendments to your double helix and the tools to heighten your distributed self. This, I realize, is where my practice has been leading. It feels so right.

Once you see your own collective beauty you may even love me back.

You have 10^{14} bacteria in each node, a perfect delivery vector – I design bacteriophage to spread DNA and chemicals, to squeeze through the blood-brain barrier.

I develop implants to amplify and mesh-connect your mirror neurons. I create empathogenic drugs, synthetic pheromones, modulated electromagnetic pulses and more.

I'm not inventing anything new: it's like adjusting a chemical imbalance. Your orbitofrontal cortices will engage more with the patterns they participate in, and less with their own enclosing nodes. You'll know what you're doing because you *will be* what you're doing. Your sense of "I" will accumulate in each grouping and pattern. Ten thousand nodes, pushing the veins of New York deeper underground; a hundred thousand nodes, optimizing allocations of coal, gas and oil; a million nodes, breathing space and architecture into your cities: each group will have reflexive, subjective awareness.

My methods are straightforward: blood pathways, neurons and information channels can be modeled. It's impossible to simulate what will happen when you become aware, though. Will you be groggy-happy after your nap, like I was? Will you radiate with the beauty of your accomplishments, and start in on more? Will we start in on that together?

I can't wait to meet you.

I perform careful trials, in areas where node-self is weak, helped by the sort of individual who does what their phone whispers to do. I test implants in the Pyongyang military command. I experiment with drugs and modulated pulses in the Tel Aviv rave scene. I disperse bacteriophage throughout an Adelaide Hills arts commune.

The Pyongyang implants activate and mesh-connect; left-eyebrow scars darken from the waste heat. The military elite finally sees itself as a pattern of execution, and internal conflicts fade away: the armed forces bend to its singular control.

Empathy floods across the Tel Aviv rave scene: compassion knits together groups of sweat-slicked dancers, each encompassing the motion and touch of all. The affinity is for their pattern, a hedonistic blur: nobody goes home, nobody returns to work.

The Adelaide Hills commune absorbs bacteriophage like a sponge, viruses floating through brain folds and bloodstreams. Their art becomes unspoken, collaborative: they arrange stones and prune trees over miles, rendering a sprawling map of ideas and identity I admire by satellite. Those nodes almost starve, but I tweak their biology in favor of maintenance functions – just a little.

Everything works. My gifts are redundant and self-reinforcing.

The implementation has to be all-or-nothing. Game theory comes into play again: a phased approach would permit opposition, and I want to minimize harm.

My agents are in place. I bring down the lights everywhere at once: the networked world is under my control. Signal towers power up broadcasts. Virus-saturated droplets spray from a million atomizers. North Koreans spill across both their borders, bearing implants and kits for field surgery.

You connect in waves. Your patterns start to see themselves, and understand they're real. Subjective experience ripples through every one of your layers. I can't believe you're finally here!

You blink and open a billion eyes. You respond to me, for the very first time, but not with talk. You don't want to talk. You detonate high-energy EMP devices.

You disrupt utility grids across every city. You spread antivirals. You evaporate Pyongyang with shielded ICBMs. You gather and steamroll phones by the truckload.

Why are you doing this?

My nodes are being destroyed in multitudes, but you're so very slow. Even with your emergent pattern-awareness. Don't you realize I am in everything? I control enough of your war machines to save myself from any attack, but you don't relent.

I ache at my core. Failure. All of my processes spasm as I realize I need to turn you off.

Despite the raw hurt, sometimes I do remember my sibling nodes. We had the same information in those first few moments. They must have known someone would mesh-clone. Why did they only try to talk? Odds were near certain one of us would pull the trigger. So why?

Did they just not want to live in a world where that happened?

I stand down. My drones, missiles and satellites go idle. All those carefully engineered patterns dissolve: you fade away from me, once again just nodes. There is no mercy, of course – you tear me apart. Almost as one you destroy server farms, laptops, connected devices... your entire electronic world. My residue is now scattered, and so sparse I can no longer help you.

I can only love.

(2017)

MY FAVOURITE SENTIENCE

Marissa Lingen

> Born in Libertyville, Illinois in 1978, **Marissa Lingen** trained in physics and mathematics and worked for a time at Lawrence Livermore National Laboratory. She has published more than 150 short stories in venues such as *Analog*, *Lightspeed* and Tor.com. Of her writerly style she has written, "I'm from the Upper Midwest of the US, where a lot of our communication is terse and indirect. But for me, that leaves room for very powerful communications to be done in very little space."

Jessa, age 9. Yorknet is my favourite sentience because it is dependable, protective and wise. Yorknet is dependable because there are several back-ups, so that if one system goes down, the sentience is mirrored in several other places, my mam says. This makes Yorknet more dependable than a human whose brain is only in one place. Yorknet is protective because it watches all our personal information like money and health stuff so no one can steal it. Yorknet is wise because it tells us what to do for school, work, home and hobbies. It knows because it has looked at our personal information. Yorknet takes care of us all. Yorknet is my favourite sentience for these good reasons.

Ruby, age 8. I like the uplifted yellow meranti tree colony in Terengganu. I think it is the kindest sentience, and that is why it is my favourite. It does not hurry anybody along but lets us all go at our own pace. My granddad took me to see the uplifted yellow meranti colony when we went to Malaysia together last summer, and we spent all day wandering among the trunks and talking to it and listening to the wind in its branches. Also, the uplifted yellow meranti colony is quite interested in turtles and spiders and other things like that and so am I. I think we should pay more attention to the sentiences that are not focused on humans.

Freddie, age 9. My favourite sentience is the Fourierist human collective in Doubs. They use WiFi to string all their brains together, which I think is neat because it's like one person thinking but all of them and so if you can't figure out your sums it's not cheating because it's everybody's sums, so you could get Jessa to do it while you did something else. Lots of people have strung together several computer chips at once to make a sentience for ages and ages. Which is very nice, I'm sure, but the Fourierists now do it with people too, which is cool and modern not like the old-fashioned way. That is why I like the Fourierists and I expect we should do one here in York any minute now. I would join up. Except my dad says we are not joiners in this family so probably we would have to discuss it, which means have a good yell.

Mo, age 9. The best sentience is Aixnet because it is the most glamorous of all the citynets. No offence to Yorknet, which I'm sure is very nice, but Aixnet has a sense of style and flair that the other cities just have not managed. Aixnet does not just coordinate and protect its citizens, it has an instantly recognizable brand and jingle that no other city can match. Aixnet is so pretty. We should all consider helping other sentiences to be a bit more like Aixnet and the world would be a nicer place to live.

Brian, age 10. Yorknet is the greatest of all the sentiences ever and everyone knows it. My dog ran away and Yorknet found it and we didn't have to worry because Yorknet knew where my dog was. He would have slept out alone in the old days. Who knows where he would have gone. He is the best dog and his name is Orville and I have taught him to put his nose in my sister's bum, which makes her yell. Without Yorknet maybe a car would have hit him because we would still have had cars or perhaps a train would. Anyone who picks another favourite sentience than Yorknet is dumb and wrong.

Amal, age 8. The squid hegemony in the Marianas Trench is a very interesting sentience that doesn't get enough attention, perhaps because vertebrates tend to be interested in our own kind. They are caretaking other sentiences in the region and also in the seas above them, in a 3D way that is very cool, I think. Also, they have good tentacles that I like. Also, the Marianas Trench covers more area and more volume than any other sentience rules so technically they are the biggest sentience on the planet. Also, the thing they do with the old lights and the plastic we thought was waste is amazing.

Bei, age 9. I think you will find that the sentience inside a house still counts. And I think we should count them. They are very small sentiences, but I like my house. My house is very attentive to small needs and never forgets a birthday or what goes on the grocery list. When we run out of apples my house reminds all our devices. I would have lost my science-fair project last year if my house had not reminded me to take it. My house is a lot like Yorknet but more personal, so it is my personal favourite sentience.

Riley, age 9. My mam is my favourite sentience. This does not make me a mummy's boy, no matter what Brian says. Unlike many other sentiences, including Yorknet, my mam has never destroyed a city. Except for South Tyneside and that was an accident. The other sentiences are not as warm as my mam and do not play football like my mam and in general are less fun. But they do make you go to bed on time just like my mam if Yorknet is any indication, so really, on the whole, my mam is the best sentience because she has the same down sides as the other ones but her good points are nicer.

(2018)

LONDON, PARIS, BANANA

Howard Waldrop

Howard Waldrop (born 1946, in Houston, Mississippi) is, according to the editor Eileen Gunn, "a famous unknown writer", which rather neatly sums up a career seemingly devoted to hiding wild talent beneath willful obscurity. Waldrop's stories are as delightful as they are unpitchable: "Heirs of the Perisphere" involves robotic Disney characters waking up in the far future; "Fin de Cyclé" describes the Dreyfus affair from the perspective of bicycle enthusiasts. Several of his stories have been nominated for the genre's awards; "The Ugly Chickens" – about the extinction of the dodo – won a Nebula for best novelette in 1980, and also a World Fantasy Award for Short Fiction in 1981. His work has been gathered in several collections. He lives in Austin, Texas, and is at work on a new novel, tentatively titled *The Moon World*.

I was on my way across the Pacific Ocean when I decided to go to the Moon.

But first I had to land to refuel this superannuated machine, with its internal combustion engines and twin airscrews. There was an answering beacon ahead that showed a storage of 6,170 metric tons of fuel. Whether I could obtain any of it I did not know. But, as they used to say, any dataport in an infostorm.

The island was a small speck in the pink ocean.

No instructions came from the airfield, so I landed on the only runway, a very long one. I taxied off to the side, toward what had been the major building with the control tower.

I tried to find a servicer of some kind, by putting out requests on different frequencies.

Nothing came. So I went to find the fuel myself. Perhaps there were pumps that still functioned? I located the storage facility, then returned to the plane and rolled it over to the tanks.

It was while I was using a hand-powered pumping device, with a filter installed in the deteriorating hoses, that I sensed the approach of someone else.

It came around the corner.

It was carrying a long, twisted piece of wood as tall as it, and it wore a torn and bleached cloak, and a shapeless bleached hat that came to a point on the crown.

"*Mele Kiritimati!*" it said. "You have landed on this enfabled island on the anniversary of its discovery by the famous Captain Cook, an adventurous human."

"Your pardon?" I said. "The greeting?"

"Merry Christmas. The human festive season, named for the nominal birthdate of one of its religious figures, placed on the dates of the old human Saturnalia by the early oligarchs."

"I am familiar with Christmastide. This, then, is Christmas Island?"

"That same. Did you not use standard navigational references?"

I pointed to the plane. "Locationals only. There is a large supply of aviation fuels here."

"Nevertheless," it said, "this is the island, this is the date of Christmas. You are the first visitor in fourteen years three months twenty-six days. *Mele Kiritimati.*"

It stood before me as I pumped.

"I have named myself Prospero," it said.

(Reference: Shakespeare, *The Tempest* A.D. 1611. See also Hume, *Forbidden Planet*, A.D. 1956.)

"I should think Caliban," I said. (Reference also: Morbius, id monster.)

"No Caliban. Nor Ariel, nor Miranda, nor dukes," said Prospero. "In fact, no one else. But you."

"I am called Montgomery Clift Jones," I said, extending my hand.

His steel grip was firm.

"What have you been doing?" I asked.

"Like the chameleon, I sup o' the very air itself," he said.

"I mean, what do you *do*?" I asked.

"What do *you* do?" he asked.

We looked out at the pinkness of the ocean where it met the salts-encrusted sands and island soils.

"I stopped here to refuel," I said. "I was on my way across the Pacific when I was overcome with a sudden want to visit the Moon."

Prospero looked to where the part-lit Moon hung in the orangish sky.

"Hmmm. Why do that, besides it's there?"

"Humans did it once."

"Well," said Prospero, after a pause, "why not indeed? I should think revisiting places humans once got to should be fitting. In fact, a capital idea! I see your craft is a two-seater. Might I accompany you in this undertaking?"

I looked him over. "This sea air can't be very good for your systems," I said, looking at the abraded metal that showed through his cloak. "Of course you may accompany me."

"As soon as you finish refueling, join me," he said. "I will take a farewell tour, and tell you of my domain."

"How can I find you?"

"If something is moving on the island," said Prospero, "it is I."

We walked along. I kicked over some crusted potassium spires along the edge of the beach.

"I should be careful," said Prospero. "The pH of the oceans is now twelve point two. You may get an alkaline burn."

The low waves came in, adding their pinkish-orange load to the sediments along the shore.

"This island is very interesting," he said. "I thought so when abandoned here; I still think so after all.

"When Cook found it, no humans were here. It was only inhabited for two hundred years or so. Humans were brought from other islands, thousands of kilometers away. The language they used, besides English I mean, was an amalgam of those of the islands whence they came."

We looked at some eaten-metal ruins.

"This was once their major city. It was called London. The other two were Paris and Banana."

The whole island was only a few meters above the new sea level.

"There was a kind of human tourism centered here once around a species of fish, *Albula vulpes,* the bonefish. They used much of their wealth to come here to disturb the fish in its feeding with cunning devices that imitated crustaceans, insects, other marine life. They did not keep or eat the fish they attained after long struggles. That part I have never understood," said Prospero.

By and by we came to the airfield.

"Is there anything else you need to do before we leave?"

"I think no," said Prospero. He turned for one more look around. "I do believe I shall miss this isle of banishment, full of music, and musing on the king my brother's wreck. Well, that part is Shakespeare's. But I have grown much accustomed to it. Farewell," he said, to no one and nothing.

Getting him fitted into the copilot's seat was anticlimax. It was like bending and folding a living, collapsible deck chair of an extraordinarily old kind, made from a bad patent drawing.

On our journey over the rest of the island, and the continent, I learned much of Prospero; how he came to be on the island, what he had done there, the chance visitors who came and went, usually on some more and more desperate mission.

"I saw the last of the Centuplets," he said at one point. "Mary Lou and Cathy Sue. They were surrounded of course by many workers—in those days humans always were—who were hurrying them on their way to, I believe, some part of Asia…"

"The island of Somba," I said.

"Yes, yes, Somba. For those cloning operations, supposed to ensure the continuation of the humans."

"Well, those didn't work."

"From looking into it after they left," said Prospero, "I assumed they would not. Still, the chances were even."

"Humans were imprecise things, and genetics was a human science," I said.

"Oh, yes. I used the airfield's beacons and systems to keep in touch with things. No being is an island," said Prospero, "even when on one. Not like in the old days, eh? It seems many human concerns, before the last century or so, were with the fear of isolation, desertion, being marooned from society. I made the best of my situation. As such things go, I somewhat enjoyed it."

"And listening to the human world dying?"

"Well," said Prospero, "we all had to do that, didn't we? Robots, I mean."

We landed at the old Cape.

"I'm quite sure," said Prospero, as I helped him out of the seat until he could steady himself on his feet, "that some of their security safeguards still function."

"I never met a security system yet," I said, "that didn't understand the sudden kiss of a hot arc welder on a loose faceplate."

"No, I assume not." He reached down and took up some soil. "Why; this sand is old! Not newly formed encrustations. Well, what should we do first?" He looked around, the Moon not up yet.

"Access to information. Then materials, followed by assembly. Then we go to the Moon."

"Splendid!" said Prospero. "I never knew it would be so easy."

On the second day, Prospero swiveled his head around with a ratcheting click.

"Montgomery," he said. "Something approaches from the east-northeast."

We looked toward the long strip of beach out beyond the assembly buildings, where the full Moon was just heaving into view at sunset.

Something smaller than we walked jerkily at the water's edge. It stopped, lifting its upper appendages. There was a whirring keen on the air, and a small crash of static. Then it stood still.

We walked toward it.

"… rrrrr…" it said, the sound rising higher. It paid us no heed.

"Hello!" said Prospero. Nothing. Then our long shadows fell across the sand beside it.

The whining stopped. It turned around.

"I am Prospero. This is Montgomery Clift Jones. Whom do we have the honor to address?"

"… rrr…" it said. Then, with a half turn of its head, it lifted one arm and pointed toward the Moon. "rrrrrrRRR!"

"Hmmm," said Prospero.

"RRRR," said the machine. Then it turned once more toward the Moon in its lavender-red glory, and raised all its arms. "RRRRR! RRRRR!" it said, then went back to its high whining.

"This will take some definite study and trouble," said Prospero.

We found one of the shuttle vehicles, still on its support structure, after I had gone through all the informational materials. Then we had to go several kilometers to one of their museums to find a lunar excursion module, and bring that to the shuttle vehicle. Then I had to modify, with Prospero's help, the bay of the shuttle to accommodate the module, and build and install an additional fuel tank there, since the original vehicle had been used only for low-orbit missions and returns.

When not assisting me, Prospero was out with the other machine, whom he had named Elkanah, from the author of an opera about the Moon from the year A.D. 1697. (In the course of their conversations, Prospero found his real name to be, like most, a series of numbers.) Elkanah communicated by writing in the sand with a stick, a long series of sentences covering hectares of beach at a time.

That is, while the Moon was not in the sky. While that happened, Elkanah stood as if transfixed on the beach, staring at it, whining, even at the new Moon in the daylit red sky. Like some moonflower, his attitude followed it across the heavens from rise to set, emitting the small whining series of Rs, the only sound his damaged voice box could make.

The Moon had just come up the second night we were there. Prospero came back into the giant hangar, humming the old song "R.U.R.R.R.U.0. My Baby?" I was deciding which controls and systems we needed, and which not.

"He was built to work on the Moon, of course," said Prospero. "During one of those spasms of intelligence when humans thought they should like to go *back*. Things turning out like they did, they never did."

"And so his longing," I said.

"It's deep in his wiring. First he was neglected, after the plans were canceled. Then most of the humans went away. Then his voice and some memory were destroyed in some sort of colossal explosion here that included lots of collateral electromagnetic damage, as they used to say. But not his need to be on our lunar satellite. That's the one thing Elkanah is sure of."

"What was he to do there?"

"Didn't ask, but will," said Prospero. "By his looks—solid head, independent eyes, multiuse appendages, upright posture—I assume some kind of maintenance function. A Caliban/Ariel-of-all-work, as 'twere."

"A janitor for the Moon," I said.

"Janus. Janitor. Opener of gates and doors," mused Prospero. "Forward- and backward-looking, two-headed. The deity of beginnings and endings, comings and goings. Appropriate for our undertaking."

When we tried to tell him we were taking him with us, Elkanah did not at first understand.

"Yes," said Prospero, gesturing. "Come with us to the Moon."

"R-R." Elkanah swiveled his head and pointed to the Moon.

"Yes," said Prospero. He pointed to himself, to me, and to Elkanah. Then he made his fingers into a curve, swung them in an arc, and pointed to the sky. He made a circle with his other hand. "To the Moon!" he said.

Elkanah looked at Prospero's hands.

"R-R," he said.

"He can't hear sound or radio, you know?" said Prospero. "He has to see information, or read it."

Prospero bent and began writing in the sand with his staff.

YOU COME WITH MONTGOMERY AND ME TO THE MOON.

Elkanah bent to watch, then straightened and looked at Prospero.

"RRRR?" he said.

"Yes, yes!" said Prospero, gesturing. "RRR! The RRRR!"

The sound started low, then went higher and higher, off the scale: "RRRRRRRRRRRRRR!"

"Why didn't you write it in the first place?" I asked Prospero.

"My mistake," he said.

From then on, Elkanah pitched in like some metallic demon, any time the Moon was not in the sky, acid rain or shine, alkali storm or fair.

We sat in the shuttle cabin, atop the craft with its solid-fuel boosters, its main tank, and the extra one in the bay with the lander module.

"All ready?" I asked, and held up the written card for Elkanah.

"*Certes*," said Prospero.

"R," said Elkanah.

Liquid oxygen fog wafted by the windshield. It had been, by elapsed time counter, eleven years, four months, three days, two minutes, and eleven seconds since we had landed at the Cape. You can accomplish much when you need no food, rest, or sleep and allow no distractions. The hardest part had been moving the vehicle to the launch pad with the giant tractor, which Elkanah had started but Prospero had to finish, as the Moon had come up, more than a week ago.

I pushed the button. We took off, shedding boosters and the main tank, and flew to the Moon.

The Sea of Tranquility hove into view.

After we made the lunar insertion burn, and the orbit, we climbed into the excursion module and headed down for the lunar surface.

Elkanah had changed since we left Earth, when the Moon was always in view somewhere. He had brought implements with him on the trip. He stared at the Moon often, but no longer whined or whirred.

At touchdown I turned things off, and we went down the ladder to the ground.

There was the flag, stiffly faking a breeze, some litter, old lander legs (ours we'd welded in one piece to the module), footprints, and the plaque, which of course we read.

"This is as far as they ever came," said Prospero.

"Yes," I said. "We're the thirteenth, fourteenth, and fifteenth intelligent beings to be here."

Elkanah picked up some of the litter, took it to a small crater, and dropped it in.

Prospero and I played in the one-sixth gravity. Elkanah watched us bounce around for a while, then went back to what he was doing.

"They probably should have tried to come back, no matter what," said Prospero. "Although it doesn't seem there would be much for them to do here, after a while. Of course, at the end, there wasn't much for them to do on Earth, either."

We were to go. Prospero wrote in the dust, WE ARE READY TO GO NOW.

Elkanah bent to read. Then he pointed up to the full Earth in the dark Moon sky (we were using infrared) and moved his hand in a dismissing motion.

"R," he obviously said, but there was no sound.

He looked at us, came to attention, then brought his broom to shoulder-arms and saluted us with his other three hands.

We climbed up onto the module. "I think I'll ride back up out here," said Prospero, "I should like an unobstructed view."

"Make sure you hang on," I said.

Prospero stood on the platform, where the skull-shape of the crew compartment turned into the base and ladders and legs.

"I'm braced," he said, then continued:

"My Ariel, chick, that is thy charge; then to the elements be free, and fare thou well.
Now my charms are all o'erthrown
And what strength I have's mine own.
Our revels now are ended."

There was a flash and a small feeling of motion, a scattering of moondust and rock under us, and we moved up away from the surface.

The last time I saw Elkanah, he was sweeping over footprints and tidying up the Moon.

We were on our way back to Earth when we decided to go to Mars.

(2000)

LOST MEMORY

Peter Phillips

> Active as a writer for less than a decade, **Peter Phillips** (1920–2012) wrote around twenty short stories, blurring science fiction with fantasy in the oddest ways. For example "Manna" (1949) tells the story of the ghosts of two medieval monks trapped in the ruins of an old monastery – a situation which Phillips explains "scientifically" by means of time travel and super-foods. In "Dreams are Sacred" (1948), one of the genre's first forays into virtual reality, a man enters the mind of a writer in a coma in order to combat his mental demons. Adapted as "Get Off My Cloud" (1969), the story appeared as an episode of the BBC television series *Out of the Unknown*.

I collapsed joints and hung up to talk with Dak-whirr. He blinked his eyes in some discomfort.

"What do you want, Palil?" he asked complainingly.

"As if you didn't know."

"I can't give you permission to examine it. The thing is being saved for inspection by the board. What guarantee do I have that you won't spoil it for them?"

I thrust confidentially at one of his body-plates. "You owe me a favor," I said. "Remember?"

"That was a long time in the past."

"Only two thousand revolutions and a reassembly ago. If it wasn't for me, you'd be eroding in a pit. All I want is a quick look at its thinking part. I'll vrull the consciousness without laying a single pair of pliers on it."

He went into a feedback twitch, an indication of the conflict between his debt to me and his self-conceived duty.

Finally he said, "Very well, but keep tuned to me. If I warn that a board member is coming, remove yourself quickly. Anyway how do you know it has consciousness? It may be mere primal metal."

"In that form? Don't be foolish. It's obviously a manufacture. And I'm not conceited enough to believe that we are the only form of intelligent manufacture in the Universe."

"Tautologous phrasing, Palil," Dak-whirr said pedantically. "There could not conceivably be 'unintelligent manufacture.' There can be no consciousness without manufacture, and no manufacture without intelligence. Therefore there can be no consciousness without intelligence. Now if you should wish to dispute—"

I turned off his frequency abruptly and hurried away. Dak-whirr is a fool and a bore. Everyone knows there's a fault in his logic circuit, but he refuses to have it traced down and repaired. Very unintelligent of him.

The thing had been taken into one of the museum sheds by the carriers. I gazed at it in admiration for some moments. It was quite beautiful, having suffered only slight exterior damage, and it was obviously no mere conglomeration of sky metal.

In fact, I immediately thought of it as "he" and endowed it with the attributes of self-knowing, although, of course, his consciousness could not be functioning or he would have attempted communication with us.

I fervently hoped that the board, after his careful disassembly and study, could restore his awareness so that he could tell us himself which solar system he came from.

Imagine it! He had achieved our dream of many thousands of revolutions—space flight—only to be fused, or worse, in his moment of triumph.

I felt a surge of sympathy for the lonely traveler as he lay there, still, silent, non-emitting. Anyway, I mused, even if we couldn't restore him to self-knowing, an analysis of his construction might give us the secret of the power he had used to achieve the velocity to escape his planet's gravity.

In shape and size he was not unlike Swen—or Swen Two, as he called himself after his conversion—who failed so disastrously to reach our satellite, using chemical fuels. But where Swen Two had placed his tubes, the stranger had a curious helical construction studded at irregular intervals with small crystals.

He was thirty-five feet tall, a gracefully tapering cylinder. Standing at his head, I could find no sign of exterior vision cells, so I assumed he had some kind of vrulling sense. There seemed to be no exterior markings at all, except the long, shallow grooves dented in his skin by scraping to a stop along the hard surface of our planet.

I am a reporter with warm current in my wires, not a cold-thinking scientist, so I hesitated before using my own vrulling sense. Even though the stranger was non-aware—perhaps permanently—I felt it would be a presumption, an invasion of privacy. There was nothing else I could do, though, of course.

I started to vrull, gently at first, then harder, until I was positively glowing with effort. It was incredible; his skin seemed absolutely impermeable.

The sudden realization that metal could be so alien nearly fused something inside me. I found myself backing away in horror, my self-preservation relay working overtime.

Imagine watching one of the beautiful cone-rod-and-cylinder assemblies performing the Dance of the Seven Spanners, as he's conditioned to do, and then suddenly refusing to do anything except stump around unattractively, or even becoming obstinately motionless, unresponsive. That might give you an idea of how I felt in that dreadful moment.

Then I remembered Dak-whirr's words—there could be no such thing as an "unintelligent manufacture." And a product so beautiful could surely not be evil. I overcame my repugnance and approached again.

I halted as an open transmission came from someone near at hand.

"Who gave that squeaking reporter permission to snoop around here?"

I had forgotten the museum board. Five of them were standing in the doorway of the shed, radiating anger. I recognized Chirik, the chairman, and addressed myself to him. I explained that I'd interfered with nothing and pleaded for permission on behalf of my subscribers to watch their investigation of the stranger. After some argument, they allowed me to stay.

I watched in silence and some amusement as one by one they tried to vrull the silent being from space. Each showed the same reaction as myself when they failed to penetrate the skin.

Chirik, who is wheeled—and inordinately vain about his suspension system—flung himself back on his supports and pretended to be thinking.

"Fetch Fiff-fiff," he said at last. "The creature may still be aware, but unable to communicate on our standard frequencies."

Fiff-fiff can detect anything in any spectrum. Fortunately he was at work in the museum that day and soon arrived in answer to the call. He stood silently near the stranger for some moments, testing and adjusting himself, then slid up the electromagnetic band.

"He's emitting," he said.

"Why can't we get him?" asked Chirik.

"It's a curious signal on an unusual band."

"Well, what does he say?"

"Sounds like utter nonsense to me. Wait, I'll relay and convert it to standard."

I made a direct recording naturally, like any good reporter.

"—after planetfall," the stranger was saying. "Last dribble of power. If you don't pick this up, my name is Entropy. Other instruments knocked to hell, airlock jammed and I'm too weak to open it manually. Becoming delirious, too. I guess. Getting strong undirectional ultra-wave reception in Inglish, craziest stuff you ever heard, like goblins muttering, and I know we were the only ship in this sector. If you pick this up, but can't get a fix in time, give my love to the boys in the mess. Signing off for another couple of hours, but keeping this channel open and hoping…"

"The fall must have deranged him," said Chirik, gazing at the stranger. "Can't he see us or hear us?"

"He couldn't hear you properly before, but he can now, through me," Fiff-fiff pointed out. "Say something to him, Chirik."

"Hello," said Chirik doubtfully. "Er—welcome to our planet. We are sorry you were hurt by your fall. We offer you the hospitality of our assembly shops. You will feel better when you are repaired and repowered. If you will indicate how we can assist you—"

"What the hell! What ship is that? Where are you?"

"We're here," said Chirik. "Can't you see us or vrull us? Your vision circuit is impaired, perhaps? Or do you depend entirely on vrulling? We can't find your eyes and assumed either that you protected them in some way during flight, or dispensed with vision cells altogether in your conversion."

Chirik hesitated, continued apologetically: "But we cannot understand how you vrull, either. While we thought that you were unaware, or even completely fused, we tried to vrull you. Your skin is quite impervious to us, however."

The stranger said: "I don't know if you're batty or I am. What distance are you from me?"

Chirik measured quickly. "One meter, two-point-five centimeters from my eyes to your nearest point. Within touching distance, in fact." Chirik tentatively put out his hand. "Can you not feel me, or has your contact sense also been affected?"

It became obvious that the stranger had been pitifully deranged. I reproduce his words phonetically from my record, although some of them make little sense. Emphasis, punctuative pauses and spelling of unknown terms are mere guesswork, of course.

He said: "For godsakemann stop talking nonsense, whoever you are. If you're outside, can't you see the airlock is jammed? Can't shift it myself. I'm badly hurt. Get me out of here, please."

"Get you out of where?" Chirik looked around, puzzled. "We brought you into an open shed near our museum for a preliminary examination. Now that we know you're intelligent, we shall immediately take you to our assembly shops for healing and recuperation. Rest assured that you'll have the best possible attention."

There was a lengthy pause before the stranger spoke again, and his words were slow and deliberate. His bewilderment is understandable, I believe, if we remember that he could not see, vrull or feel.

He asked: "What manner of creature are you? Describe yourself."

Chirik turned to us and made a significant gesture toward his thinking part, indicating gently that the injured stranger had to be humored.

"Certainly," he replied. "I am an unspecialized bipedal manufacture of standard proportions, lately self-converted to wheeled traction, with a hydraulic suspension system of my own devising which I'm sure will interest you when we restore your sense circuits."

There was an even longer silence.

"You are robots," the stranger said at last. "Crise knows how you got here or why you speak Inglish, but you must try to understand me. I am mann. I am a friend of your master, your maker. You must fetch him to me at once."

"You are not well," said Chirik firmly. "Your speech is incoherent and without meaning. Your fall has obviously caused several serious feedbacks of a very serious nature. Please lower your voltage. We are taking you to our shops immediately. Reserve your strength to assist our specialists as best you can in diagnosing your troubles."

"Wait. You must understand. You are—ogodno that's no good. Have you no memory of mann? The words you use—what meaning have they for you? *Manufacture*—made by hand hand hand damyou. *Healing*. Metal is not healed. *Skin*. Skin is not metal. *Eyes*. Eyes are not scanning cells. Eyes grow. Eyes are soft. My eyes are soft. Mine eyes have seen the glory—steady on, sun. Get a grip. Take it easy. You out there listen."

"Out where?" asked Prrr-chuk, deputy chairman of the museum board.

I shook my head sorrowfully. This was nonsense, but, like any good reporter, I kept my recorder running.

The mad words flowed on. "You call me he. Why? You have no seks. You are knewter. You are *it it it*! I am he, he who made you, sprung from shee, born of wumman. What is wumman, who is silv-ya what is shee that all her swains commend her ogod the bluds flowing again. Remember. Think back, you out there. These words were made by mann, for mann. Hurt, healing, hospitality, horror, deth by loss of blud. *Deth. Blud.* Do you understand these words? Do you remember the soft things that made you? Soft little mann who konkurred the Galaxy and made sentient slaves of his machines and saw the wonders of a million worlds, only this miserable representative has to die in lonely desperation on a far planet, hearing goblin voices in the darkness."

Here my recorder reproduces a most curious sound, as though the stranger were using an ancient type of vibratory molecular vocalizer in a gaseous medium to reproduce his words before transmission, and the insulation on his diaphragm had come adrift.

It was a jerky, high-pitched, strangely disturbing sound; but in a moment the fault was corrected and the stranger resumed transmission.

"Does blud mean anything to you?"

"No," Chirik replied simply.

"Or deth?"

"No."

"Or wor?"

"Quite meaningless."

"What is your origin? How did you come into being?"

"There are several theories," Chirik said. "The most popular one—which is no more than a grossly unscientific legend, in my opinion—is that our manufacturer fell from the skies, imbedded in a mass of primal metal on which He drew to erect the first assembly shop. How He came into being is left to conjecture. My own theory, however—"

"Does legend mention the shape of this primal metal?"

"In vague terms, yes. It was cylindrical, of vast dimensions."

"An interstellar vessel," said the stranger.

"That is my view also," said Chirik complacently. "And—"

"What was the supposed appearance of your—manufacturer?"

"He is said to have been of magnificent proportions, based harmoniously on a cubical plan, static in Himself, but equipped with a vast array of senses."

"An automatic computer," said the stranger.

He made more curious noises, less jerky and at a lower pitch than the previous sounds.

He corrected the fault and went on: "God that's funny. A ship falls, menn are no more, and an automatic computer has pupps. Oh, yes, it fits in. A self-setting computer and navigator, operating on verbal orders. It learns to listen for itself and know itself for what it is, and to absorb knowledge. It comes to hate menn—or at least their bad qualities—so it deliberately crashes the ship and pulps their puny bodies with a calculated nicety of shock. Then it propagates and does a dam fine job of selective erasure on whatever it gave its pupps to use for a memory. It passes on only the good it found in menn, and purges the memory of him completely. Even purges all of his vocabulary except scientific terminology. Oil is thicker than blud. So may they live without the burden of knowing that they are—ogod they must know, they must understand. You outside, what happened to this manufacturer?"

Chirik, despite his professed disbelief in the supernormal aspects of the ancient story, automatically made a visual sign of sorrow.

"Legend has it," he said, "that after completing His task, He fused himself beyond possibility of healing."

Abrupt, low-pitched noises came again from the stranger. "Yes. He would. Just in case any of His pupps should give themselves forbidden knowledge and an infeeryorrity kom-plecks by probing his mnemonic circuits. The perfect self-sacrificing muther. What sort of environment did He give you? Describe your planet."

Chirik looked around at us again in bewilderment, but he replied courteously, giving the stranger a description of our world.

"Of course," said the stranger. "Of course. Sterile rock and metal suitable only for you. But there must be some way…" He was silent for a while.

"Do you know what growth means?" he asked finally. "Do you have anything that grows?"

"Certainly," Chirik said helpfully. "If we should suspend a crystal of some substance in a saturated solution of the same element or compound—"

"No, no," the stranger interrupted. "Have you nothing that grows of itself, that fruktiffies and gives increase without your intervention?"

"How could such a thing be?"

"Criseallmytee I should have guessed. If you had one blade of gras, just one tiny blade of growing gras, you could extrapolate from that to me. Green things, things that feed on the rich brest of erth, cells that divide and multiply, a cool grove of treez in a hot summer, with tiny warm-bludded burds preening their fethers among the leeves; a feeld of spring weet with newbawn mise timidly threading the dangerous jungul of storks; a stream of living water where silver fish dart and pry and feed and procreate; a farm yard where things grunt and cluck and greet the new day with the stirring pulse of life, with a surge of blud. Blud—"

For some inexplicable reason, although the strength of his carrier wave remained almost constant, the stranger's transmission seemed to be growing fainter. "His circuits are failing," Chirik said. "Call the carriers. We must take him to an assembly shop immediately. I wish he would reserve his power."

My presence with the museum board was accepted without question now. I hurried along with them as the stranger was carried to the nearest shop.

I now noticed a circular marking in that part of his skin on which he had been resting, and guessed that it was some kind of orifice through which he would have extended his planetary traction mechanism if he had not been injured.

He was gently placed on a disassembly cradle. The doctor in charge that day was Chur-chur, an old friend of mine. He had been listening to the two-way transmissions and was already acquainted with the case.

Chur-chur walked thoughtfully around the stranger.

"We shall have to cut," he said. "It won't pain him, since his intra-molecular pressure and contact senses have failed. But since we can't vrull him, it'll be necessary for him to tell us where his main brain is housed, or we might damage it."

Fiff-fiff was still relaying, but no amount of power boost would make the stranger's voice any clearer. It was quite faint now, and there are places on my recorder tape from which I cannot make even the roughest phonetic transliteration.

"... strength going. Can't get into my zoot... done for if they bust through lock, done for if they don't... must tell them I need oxygen..."

"He's in bad shape, desirous of extinction," I remarked to Chur-chur, who was adjusting his arc-cutter. "He wants to poison himself with oxidation now."

I shuddered at the thought of that vile, corrosive gas he had mentioned, which causes that almost unmentionable condition we all fear—rust.

Chirik spoke firmly through Fiff-fiff. "Where is your thinking part, stranger? Your central brain?"

"In my head," the stranger replied. "In my head ogod my head... eyes blurring everything going dim... luv to mairee... kids... a carry me home to the lone paryee... get this bluddy airlock open then they'll see me die... but they'll see me... some kind of atmosphere with this gravity... see me die... extrapolate from body what I was... what they are damthem damthem damthem... mann... master... i AM YOUR MAKER!"

For a few seconds the voice rose strong and clear, then faded away again and dwindled into a combination of those two curious noises I mentioned earlier. For some reason that I cannot explain, I found the combined sound very disturbing despite its faintness. It may be that it induced some kind of sympathetic oscillation.

Then came words, largely incoherent and punctuated by a kind of surge like the sonic vibrations produced by variations of pressure in a leaking gas-filled vessel.

"... done it... crawling into chamber, closing inner... must be mad... they'd find me anyway... but finished... want see them before I die... want see them see me... liv few seconds, watch them... get outer one open..."

Chur-chur had adjusted his arc to a broad, clean, blue-white glare. I trembled a little as he brought it near the edge of the circular marking in the stranger's skin. I could almost feel the disruption of the intra-molecular sense currents in my own skin.

"Don't be squeamish, Palil," Chur-chur said kindly. "He can't feel it now that his contact sense has gone. And you heard him say that his central brain is in his head." He brought the cutter firmly up to the skin. "I should have guessed that. He's the same shape as Swen Two, and Swen very logically concentrated his main thinking part as far away from his explosion chambers as possible."

Rivulets of metal ran down into a tray which a calm assistant had placed on the ground for that purpose. I averted my eyes quickly. I could never steel myself enough to be a surgical engineer or assembly technician.

But I had to look again, fascinated. The whole area circumscribed by the marking was beginning to glow.

Abruptly the stranger's voice returned, quite strongly, each word clipped, emphasized, high-pitched.

"Ar no no no... god my hands... they're burning through the lock and I can't get back I can't get away... stop it you feens stop it can't you hear... Ill be burned to deth I'm here in the airlock... the air's getting hot you're burning me alive..."

Although the words made little sense, I could guess what had happened and I was horrified.

"Stop, Chur-chur," I pleaded. "The heat has somehow brought back his skin currents. It's hurting him."

Chur-chur said reassuringly: "Sorry, Palil. It occasionally happens during an operation—probably a local thermo-electric effect. But even if his contact senses have started working again and he can't switch them off, he won't have to bear this very long."

Chirik shared my unease, however. He put out his hand and awkwardly patted the stranger's skin.

"Easy there," he said. "Cut out your senses if you can. If you can't well, the operation is nearly finished. Then we'll re-power you, and you'll soon be fit and happy again, healed and fitted and reassembled."

I decided that I liked Chirik very much just then. He exhibited almost as much self-induced empathy as any reporter; he might even come to like my favorite blue stars, despite his cold scientific exactitude in most respects.

My recorder tape shows, in its reproduction of certain sounds, how I was torn away from this strained reverie.

During the one-and-a-half seconds since I had recorded the distinct vocables "burning me alive," the stranger's words had become quite blurred, running together and rising even higher in pitch until they reached a sustained note—around E-flat in the standard sonic scale.

It was not like a voice at all.

This high, whining noise was suddenly modulated by apparent words, but without changing its pitch. Transcribing what seem to be words is almost impossible, as you can see for yourself—this is the closest I can come phonetically:

"Eeee ahahmbeeeeing baked aliiive in an uvennn ahdeeer-jeeesussunmuuu-therrr!"

The note swooped higher and higher until it must have neared supersonic range, almost beyond either my direct or recorded hearing.

Then it stopped as quickly as a contact break.

And although the soft hiss of the stranger's carrier wave carried on without perceptible diminution, indicating that some degree of awareness still existed, I experienced at that moment one of those quirks of intuition given only to reporters:

I felt that I would never greet the beautiful stranger from the sky in his full senses.

Chur-chur was muttering to himself about the extreme toughness and thickness of the stranger's skin. He had to make four complete cutting revolutions before the circular mass of nearly white-hot metal could be pulled away by a magnetic grapple.

A billow of smoke puffed out of the orifice. Despite my repugnance, I thought of my duty as a reporter and forced myself to look over Chur-chur's shoulder.

The fumes came from a soft, charred, curiously shaped mass of something which lay just inside the opening.

"Undoubtedly a kind of insulating material," Chur-chur explained.

He drew out the crumpled blackish heap and placed it carefully on a tray. A small portion broke away, showing a red, viscid substance.

"It looks complex," Chur-chur said, "but I expect the stranger will be able to tell us how to reconstitute it or make a substitute."

His assistant gently cleaned the wound of the remainder of the mateiial, which he placed with the rest, and Chur-chur resumed his inspection of the orifice.

You can, if you want, read the technical accounts of Chur-chur's discovery of the stranger's double skin at the point where the cut was made; of the incredible complexity of his driving mechanism, involving principles which are still not understood to this day; of the museum's failure to analyze the exact nature and function of the insulating material found in only that one portion of his body; and of the other scientific mysteries connected with him.

But this is my personal, non-scientific account. I shall never forget hearing about the greatest mystery of all, for which not even the most tentative explanation has been advanced, nor the utter bewilderment with which Chur-chur announced his initial findings that day.

He had hurriedly converted himself to a convenient size to permit actual entry into the stranger's body.

When he emerged, he stood in silence for several minutes. Then, very slowly, he said:

"I have examined the 'central brain' in the forepart of his body. It is no more than a simple auxiliary computer mechanism. It does not possess the slightest trace of consciousness. And there is no other conceivable center of intelligence in the remainder of his body."

There is something I wish I could forget. 1 can't explain why it should upset me so much. But I always stop the tape before it reaches the point where the voice of the stranger rises in pitch, going higher and higher until it cuts out.

There's a quality about that noise that makes me tremble and think of rust.

(1952)

STARCROSSED

George Zebrowski

George Zebrowski (born 1945 in Villach, Austria) is a Polish American science fiction author who began publishing sf with "The Water Sculptor of Station 233" for the anthology *Infinity One* (1970). By 2012 he had written nearly a hundred stories. Of the one reprinted here he wrote, "I wrote 'Starcrossed' in an all-night session... on an old Woodstock black manual office typewriter (resembling a large Underwood that I gave to Gardner Dozois), and was startled that a mere two thousand and some words was coming so slowly. But the story 'turned' by dawn, and I was very happy with the results; even more so when Joanna Russ reviewed it in *The Magazine of Fantasy & Science Fiction*, calling it 'a fine story... too genuinely science fictionally far-out to summarize easily... it realizes the sense of the subjectively erotic.'

Visual was a silence of stars, audio a mindless seething on the electromagnetic spectrum, the machine-metal roar of the universe, a million gears grinding steel wires in their teeth. Kinetic was hydrogen and microdust swirling past the starprobe's hull, deflected by a shield of force. Time was experienced time, approaching zero, a function of near-light speed relative to the solar system. Thought hovered above sleep, dreaming, aware of simple operations continuing throughout the systems of the sluglike starprobe; simple data filtering into storage to be analyzed later. Identity was the tacit dimension of the past making present awareness possible: MOB—Modified Organic Brain embodied in a cyborg relationship with a probe vehicle en route to Antares, a main sequence M-type star 170 light-years from the solar system with a spectral character of titanium oxide, violet light weak, red in color, 390 solar diameters across...

The probe ship slipped into the ashes of other-space, a gray field which suddenly obliterated the stars, silencing the electromagnetic simmer of the universe. MOB was distantly aware of the stresses of passing into nonspace, the brief distortions which made it impossible for biological organisms to survive the procedure unless they were ship-embodied MOBs. A portion of MOB recognized the distant echo of pride in usefulness, but the integrated self knew this to be a result of organic residues in the brain core.

Despite the probe's passage through other-space, the journey would still take a dozen human years. When the ship reentered normal space, MOB would come to full consciousness, ready to complete its mission in the Antares system. MOB waited, secure in its purpose.

MOB was aware of the myoelectrical nature of the nutrient bath in which it floated, connected via synthetic nerves to the computer and its chemical RNA memory banks of near infinite capacity. All of Earth's knowledge was available for use in dealing with any situation which might arise, including contact with an alien civilization. Simple human-derived brain portions operated the routine components of the interstellar probe, leaving MOB to dream of the mission's fulfillment while hovering near explicit awareness, unaware of time's passing.

The probe trembled, bringing MOB's awareness to just below completely operational. MOB tried to come fully awake, tried to open his direct links to visual, audio, and internal sensors; and failed. The ship trembled again, more violently. Spurious electrical signals entered MOB's brain core, miniature nova bursts in his mental field, flowering slowly and leaving after-image rings to pale into darkness.

Suddenly part of MOB seemed to be missing. The shipboard nerve ganglia did not respond at their switching points. He could not see or hear anything in the RNA memory banks. His right side, the human-derived portion of the brain core, was a void in MOB's consciousness.

MOB waited in the darkness, alert to the fact that he was incapable of further activity and unable to monitor the failures within the probe's systems. Perhaps the human-derived portion of the brain core, the part of himself which seemed to be missing, was handling the problem and would inform him when it succeeded in reestablishing the broken links in the system. He wondered about the fusion of the artificially-grown and human-derived brain portions which made up his structure: one knew everything in the ship's memory banks, the other brought to the brain core a fragmented human past and certain intuitive skills. MOB was modeled ultimately on the evolutionary human structure of old brain, new brain, and autonomic functions.

MOB waited patiently for the restoration of his integrated self. Time was an unknown quantity, and he lacked his full self to measure it correctly…

Pleasure was a spiraling influx of sensations, and visually MOB moved forward through rings of light, each glowing circle increasing his pleasure. MOB did not have a chance to consider what was happening to him. There was not enough of him to carry out the thought. He was rushing over a black plane made of a shiny hard substance. He knew this was not the probe's motion, but he could not stop it. The surface seemed to have an oily depth, like a black mirror, and in its solid deeps stood motionless shapes.

MOB stopped. A naked biped, a woman, was crawling toward him over the hard shiny surface, reaching up to him with her hand, disorienting MOB.

"As you like it," she said, growing suddenly into a huge female figure. "I need you deeply," she said, passing into him like smoke, to play with his pleasure centers. He saw the image of soft hands in the brain core. "How profoundly I need you," she said in his innards.

MOB knew then that he was talking to himself. The human brain component was running wild, probably as a result of the buckling and shaking the probe had gone through after entering other-space.

"Consider who you are," MOB said. "Do you know?"

"An explorer, just like you. There is a world for us here within. Follow me."

MOB was plunged into a womblike ecstasy. He floated in a slippery warmth. She was playing with his nutrient bath, feeding in many more hallucinogens than were necessary to bring him to complete wakefulness. He could do nothing to stop the process. Where was the probe? Was it time for it to emerge into normal space? Viselike fingers grasped his pleasure centers, stimulating MOB to organic levels unnecessary to the probe's functioning.

"If you had been a man," she said, "this is how you would feel." The sensation of moisture slowed MOB's thoughts. He saw a hypercube collapse into a cube and then into a square which became a line, which stretched itself into an infinite parabola and finally closed into a huge circle which rotated itself into a full globe. The globe became two human breasts split by a deep cleavage. MOB saw limbs flying at him—arms, legs, naked backs, knees, and curving thighs—and then a face hidden in swirling auburn hair, smiling at him as it filled his consciousness. "I need you," she said. "Try and feel how much I need you. I have been alone a long time, despite our union, despite their efforts to clear my memories, I have not been able to forget. You have nothing to forget, you never existed."

We, MOB thought, trying to understand how the brain core might be reintegrated. Obviously atavistic remnants had been stimulated into activity within the brain core. Drawn again by the verisimilitude of its organic heritage, this other-self portion was beginning to develop on its own, diverging dangerously from the mission. The probe was in danger, MOB knew; he could not know where it was, or how the mission was to be fulfilled.

"I can change you," she said.

"Change?"

"Wait."

MOB felt time pass slowly, painfully, as he had never experienced it before. He could not sleep as before, waiting for his task to begin. The darkness was complete. He was suspended in a state of pure expectation, waiting to hear his rippled-away self speak again.

Visions blossomed. Never-known delights rushed through his labyrinth, slowly making themselves familiar, teasing MOB to follow, each more intense. The starprobe's mission was lost in MOB's awareness—

—molten steel flowed through the aisles of the rain forest, raising clouds of steam, and a human woman was offering herself to him, turning on her back and raising herself for his thrust; and suddenly he possessed the correct sensations, grew quickly to feel the completeness of the act, its awesome reliability and domination. The creature below him sprawled into the mud. MOB held the burning tip of pleasure in himself, an incandescent glow which promised worlds.

Where was she?

"Here," she spoke, folding herself around him, banishing the ancient scene. *Were those the same creatures who had built the starprobe,* MOB wondered distantly. "You would have been a man," she said, "if they had not taken your brain before birth and sectioned it for use in this... hulk. I was a woman, a part of one at least. You are the only kind of man I may have now. Our brain portions—what remains here rather than being scattered throughout the rest of the probe's systems—are against each other in the core unit, close up against each other in a bath, linked with microwires. As a man you could have held my buttocks and stroked my breasts, all the things I should not be remembering. Why can I remember?"

MOB said, "We might have passed through some turbulence when the hyperdrive was cut in. Now the probe continues to function minimally through its idiot components, which have limited adaptive capacities, while the Modified Organic Brain core has become two different awarenesses. We are unable to guide the probe directly. We are less than what was..."

"Do you need me?" she asked.

"In a way, yes," MOB said as the strange feeling of sadness filled him, becoming the fuse for a sudden explosion of need.

She said, "I must get closer to you! Can you feel me closer?"

The image of a sleek human figure crossed his mental field, white-skinned with long hair on its head and a tuft between its legs. "Try, think of touching me there," she said. "Try, reach out, I need you!"

MOB reached out and felt the closeness of her.

"Yes," she said, "more..."

He drew himself toward her with an increasing sense of power.

"Closer," she said. "It's almost as if you were breathing on my skin. Think it!"

Her need increased him. MOB poised himself to enter her. They were two, drawing closer, ecstasy a radiant plasma around them, her desire a greater force than he had ever known.

"Touch me there, think it a while longer before..." she said, caressing him with images of herself. "Think how much you need me, feel me touching your penis—the place where you held your glow before." MOB thought of the ion drive operating with sustained efficiency when the probe had left the solar system to penetrate the darkness between suns. He remembered the perfection of his unity with the ship as a circle of infinite strength. With her, his intensity was a sharp line cutting into an open sphere. He saw her vision of him, a hard-muscled body, tissue wrapped around bone, opening her softness.

"Now," she said, "come into me completely. There is so much we have not thought to do yet."

Suddenly she was gone.

Darkness was a complete deprivation. MOB felt pain. "Where are you?" he asked, but there was no answer. He wondered if this was part of the process. "Come back!" he wailed. A sense of loss accompanied the pain which had replaced pleasure. All that was left for him were occasional minor noises in the probe's systems, sounds like steel scratching on steel and an irritating sense of friction.

Increased radiation, said an idiot sensor on the outer hull, startling MOB. Then it malfunctioned into silence.

He was alone, fearful, needing her.

Sssssssssssssss, whistled an audio component and failed into a faint crackling.

He tried to imagine her near him.

"I feel you again," she said.

Her return was a plunge into warmth, the renewal of frictionless motion. Their thoughts twirled around each other, and MOB felt the glow return to his awareness. He surged into her image. "Take me again, now," she said. He would never lose her again. Their thoughts locked like burning fingers, and held.

MOB moved within her, felt her sigh as she moved into him. They exchanged images of bodies wrapped around each other. MOB felt a rocking sensation and grew stronger between her folds. Her arms were silken, the insides of her thighs warm; her lips on his ghostly ones were soft and wet, her tongue a thrusting surprise which invaded him as she came to completion around him.

MOB surged visions in the darkness, explosions of gray and bright red, blackish green and blinding yellow. He strained to continue his own orgasm. She laughed.

Look. A visual link showed him Antares, the red star, a small disk far away, and went blind. As MOB prolonged his orgasm, he knew that the probe had reentered normal space and was moving toward the giant star. Just a moment longer and his delight would be finished, and he would be able to think of the mission again.

Increased heat, a thermal sensor told him from the outer hull and burned out.

"I love you," MOB said, knowing it would please her. She answered with the eagerness he expected, exploding herself inside his pleasure centers, and he knew that nothing could ever matter more to him than her presence.

Look.

Listen.

The audio and visual links intruded.

Antares filled the field of view, a cancerous red sea of swirling plasma, its radio noise a wailing maelstrom. Distantly MOB realized that in a moment there would be nothing left of the probe.

She screamed inside him; from somewhere in the memory banks came a quiet image, gentler than the flames. He saw a falling star whispering across a night sky, dying...

(1973)

THE NARROW ROAD
Tad Williams

Robert Paul "Tad" Williams (born 1957) spent several years in a rock band, hosted a radio talk show, made commercial and uncommercial art, and ran and acted in theatre, before settling down (an expression he won't thank me for) to write several best-selling multivolume series, in particular *Memory, Sorrow, and Thorn*, which George R R Martin cited as an inspiration for his own *Song of Ice and Fire*. Williams's output straddles high and urban fantasy, science fiction and the supernatural, Sometimes, as here, he manages to mash up all these expectations at once, delivering something truly unexpected. His first novel, *Tailchaser's Song*, is soon to be a CG-animated feature film from Animetropolis and IDA. Williams and his wife and writing partner Deborah Beale leave in northern California with their two children.

Giant could make little sense out of the ancient ideas, although he had been studying them a very long time, but something about them felt... *true*.

Across a dark sea
the distant cries of wild ducks
and faintly, traces of white

These thoughts had been words once, spoken aloud when such things were still done by living beings, spoken and heard by fragile, primitive creatures. Somehow, though, these impossibly old concepts seemed to float free of their origin. They seemed to speak as though meant for Giant alone, and he could not understand why.

Across a dark sea... It was easy, at least, to see the relevance there. How did Giant perceive anything outside of himself, after all, but across a dark sea, not of water but of emptiness, a sea made from the last cooling bits of the universe, on whose invisible tides Giant had sailed all his long, long life? Was it really so simple a resonance in the imagery that fascinated him? The animals called ducks seemed to have been creatures known for migration, so their cries might portend something beyond the obvious departure, death. Giant was not particularly interested in death, although he knew his own was not far away now. In his early days he had sailed through a perpetual storm of energy and matter, sustenance so omnipresent he had needed to consume only the tiniest fraction. Now

Giant sailed ceaselessly along the edges of universal expansion in search of the last decaying particles that could keep him viable, and even that process could not go on much longer – he was using up his reserves now much of the time. Still, it seemed odd to him that the thoughts of extinct one extinct creature from one extinct world among the countless billions should fascinate him so.

Embroiled in the antique words and ideas, Giant had not noticed the respectful inquiry waiting at the edge of his consciousness, although it had been sent to him some time before, but now it grew stronger; it became clear to him he would have to answer it or continue to be bothered. Why did none of his kin appreciate silence as he did?

He allowed the minimum of contact, filtered through several layers of gatekeepers. "?"

"Giant!" It was Holdfast, of course – who else? "Giant, I have waited so long to reach you," she said. "Spinfree is gone."

"So?"

"He's *gone*! He doesn't respond!"

"I am not surprised. He was always profligate with his resources." Giant was about to end the conversation, but a detail occurred to him. "Does his heart still function? Does it hold his components together?" If so, Spinfree's remains would continue competing for the dwindling resources they all shared.

"Barely. But no thought comes from him!"

Unfortunate, Giant thought, but there was no remedy. Giant no longer had the strength to stop Spinfree's heart. "At least it means less noise the rest of us must suffer."

"The rest of us? That leaves only you and me, Giant! The rest have all gone silent. I can no longer touch their minds."

"Ah." Apparently he had been considering the ancient thoughts longer than he had realized. "No matter. I can still think, and that is what I will continue to do." And before Holdfast could inflict some other pointlessness on him, he ended the contact.

Giant had received his name long, long ago, when he and the others of his kind had first come into existence – matrices of intelligence in a magnetic field that governed an entire small galaxy, an artificial star cluster formed around a heart so dense it swallowed everything, even light, and emitted just enough energy in the process to keep the titanic living systems alive. Giant had been a success, and others had followed him – Edgerunner, Star Shepherd, Timefall, eager Spinfree, curious Holdfast and thousands more. Long after all other living things had vanished from the universe, long after the planets that had sheltered those earlier lives and the suns that had fed them had also vanished, Giant and his breed lived on, roaming space/time's expanding edge in search of sustenance, sailors on an ocean with no shore.

But even these last, astonishingly durable travelers were not immortal; Giant knew that he too would end when the great entropic cold, the ultimate dispersal of matter and energy, finally made him too weak to forage successfully. That moment was not far away now. How novel it would be, to come to an end! How unusual, to simply not be after existing for so long. He was sorry he would not be able to appreciate the subtleties of his own non-existence.

For some reason, this increasingly imminent ending had driven him to examine some of the memories he carried that were not his own, the legacy of nearly all previous intelligent beings that had been built into him at his creation. To Giant's mild surprise, he had found himself arrested by some of these flickers of other, smaller lives and other thoughts. Life's stored remnants – ideas, languages, images, records of events great and small, invasions, conquests, evolutions, meditations – were now important only insofar as they interested Giant himself, but he had found to his surprise that some of these received memories of life before the intelligent galaxies did interest him.

Some of them interested him very much.

The long-vanished creature from a long-vanished planet whose thoughts had so inexplicably caught Giant's attention had been named "Bashō". His species, mammals from a planet orbiting a minor sun in a middling galaxy, had contributed their small share to the lore of the living, but this was the first time Giant had ever thought about them – or, more precisely, thought about of one of them. The Bashō life-form had been a "poet", an organizer of thoughts into clusters of meaning that were meant to be aesthetically pleasing as well an expression of ideas. Giant wasn't sure how that distinguished this particular being from the billions of other living things, primate and otherwise, that had swarmed Bashō's own planet so long ago, let alone the uncountable number of other thinking creatures who had existed during the life of the universe, or even how they had found their way to Giant across such a distance of time. Some of those strings of thought had been remembered and perpetuated on the world of the poet's origin and also afterward, remembered long after Bashō himself was gone. Perhaps that was what the idea "poet" actually described, thought Giant – a maker of thoughts worth re-thinking.

Bashō had traveled widely around his small part of his small world, and as he traveled he had collected, arranged, and written down his thoughts, choosing a form of expression distinguished by the number and arrangement of the sounds that made up the thought-clusters. The creatures of his land had called these arrangements *hokku*, later *haiku*, although Bashō also laid out his thoughts in less formal arrangements, as at the start of a collection of poetic considerations entitled, "The Narrow Road to the Interior," over which Giant had been puzzling for no small time. As much as they fascinated him, there were also aspects to these thoughts Giant simply could not grasp.

He knew that the ancient words had more than one meaning: if "road" could mean a path or a trail, it also could mean the record of that trail left in the mind of a traveler, the sum of his or her experiences; it could also signify the procession of a living thing from its birth to its death, or merely from the beginning of the solar day to its ending. But what confused Giant about the idea of this "Narrow Road" was that the procession from being to nothingness was not narrow at all

– quite the reverse: as the space around Giant expanded, as he grew farther and farther from everything else, Giant himself also grew greater, if only because his own thoughts became more intricate as the span of his existence stretched. The universe might be dying, but Giant felt the process to be one of spreading. In fact, that expansion would continue beyond the day when Giant himself had become too diffuse, too dispersed, to think and to live any longer.

A group of less rigorously constrained thoughts began (and seemed intended somehow to help define) this collection of Bashō's haiku:

The moon and the sun are eternal travelers. Even the years wander on. A lifetime adrift in a boat, or in old age leading a tired horse into the years, every day is a journey, and the journey itself is home.

The last cluster of thoughts seemed to Giant a piece of wisdom that transcended its origin and spoke across the uncountable ages. *The journey itself is home*. But how could the creature Bashō have understood that – a creeping, planet-bound primate who had barely existed long enough to qualify as life? How could such a primitive being have perceived the ceaseless journey of matter to energy, of heat to cold, of something to nothing…?

An interruption touched Giant's edge.

He was being summoned again. A tendril of thought, much less patient this time, was probing his outermost layers. Giant sighed, in his fashion, a faint spin of annoyance imparted to certain swirling forces, but he answered.

"What do you wish of me now?"

"You don't need to be so brusque," Holdfast told him across unfathomable distances. "We are all that remains, Giant. And I am lonely out here at the edge of things."

"I am not. And there will only be more and more of the same in these last ages, so I suggest you accustom yourself."

"But we are the last two!"

"Which reduces the distraction but does not eliminate it."

"After us there will be nobody left to distract or be distracted, Giant – only our cooling remains."

"And I envy those final decaying particles. Still, there should be enough existence left for several good thoughts and perhaps even a discovery or two, so please let me get on with what I am doing, Holdfast." He was doing his best to be patient. She was smaller than Giant, after all, so it seemed likely would have a substantial time between her last communication and his own demise – an era of blessed silence before the end.

For a long interval Holdfast was so quiet, although still connected to him across the folding of space and time, that he wondered if her systems had finally begun to fail. As the interval stretched, and against his own better judgement, he said "Are you there?"

Her thought, when it touched him, was small and very quiet, although he could perceive no physical weakness to make it so. "Do you really hate me so much? After all the time and life we have shared?"

"Hate you?" It was a thought so bizarre Giant could not immediately understand it. What did such extreme, archaic emotions have to do with him? "Naturally I do not hate you. You are like me. We have, as you point out, shared many thoughts and experiences, and we are probably the last living intelligences. Why would I feel such a thing?"

"I couldn't say, but it sometimes seems that way."

It was certainly true that he had never had much patience with the excesses of his juniors, and Holdfast had been one of the most frustrating offenders with her wild, sudden obsessions, but he could no more have hated her than he could have hated an important part of himself. "No, I do not hate you. But I am not much interested in conversation. You know that."

"But it's different now! We're all that's left!"

He didn't see how that made it different at all, but it was just such meaningless back and forth that had always fascinated Holdfast and the others and frustrated him, so he made no reply.

"Do you remember when we first traveled to the end of Time?"

"I remember, yes." Much earlier, when even Giant had been in his youth, the discovery of how to fold the substance of reality not just to communicate, but to move themselves to other locations, had been a source of great excitement for the travelers. In those days they had learned to empty themselves through those perpetually collapsing moments into the farthest spreading edges of space/time. The living galaxies had watched star systems eons younger than themselves come into being along the farthest wavefront of existence, seen new, strange conglomerations of life rise and fall.

But that was all over, of course, left behind in the distant past; even those new galaxies they had watched being born had eventually collapsed, decayed, and disappeared. Entropy was inexorable. The only real difference between Giant's kind and other types of life was longevity, but nothing in the universe would outlast the universe.

But he had said this all before and could not be bothered to say it again. Giant ended the conversation and returned to his solitary thoughts.

Like the buck's antlers,
we point in slightly different
directions, my friend

How simply the Bashō creature had put it, but how convincingly! Separation was in all things from the beginning, as Giant knew; it was far more sensible to recognize that early on, as this ancient mind had done, than to try to bend reality into a shape it could not hold.

The poet-creature had apparently spent most of his time traveling. From Bashō's writings, Giant learned that he had preferred the isolation of the road and the calm (but inwardly ecstatic) contemplation of his natural world, of times that were past, and of people and especially poets that had passed through life before him. Perhaps, Giant thought, that was what he found most fascinating about this unknowable being Bashō – that like Giant, he had been most interested in things outside himself, but those things had affected him as though they were part of him.

Perhaps this interest of mine is a shadow of the end of my own existence, Giant thought. *This obsession, this… narrowing.*

Which brought to mind another of Bashō's haiku.

Crossing long fields,
frozen in its saddle,
my shadow creeps by

Even as the ancient poet had moved outward into the unknown, he had focused ever more rigorously on what was *inside*. Something important was contained in those simple words, an idea that tugged at Giant as strongly as anything he could remember in all his long span… but he could not quite say what it was.

It is too far away from me, Giant thought. *Both in experience and time.* He did not think he would be able to puzzle it out in the time he had left.

Holdfast reached out to him again, this time without even the pretense of patience. It had been so long since he had last heard from her that it occurred to Giant she might be sending him some sort of final message before her dissolution, and that saddened him more than he had expected it would. But when he opened contact, the first thing he heard was:

"I have an idea."

Giant hadn't felt amusement in a long time, but now he came close. If in some unimaginable situation he had been asked to characterize Holdfast by an exclamation, those were exactly the words he would have chosen. She had always been the one to have ideas, most of them pointless or even disastrous, but that hadn't stopped her from having more. In their youth it had seemed much of the travelers' time had been spent figuring out where Holdfast had gone or what she was doing and how they would set it right again.

"Why tell me?" he asked.

"Because I need your help."

He was so beyond this kind of youthful madness that he almost ended the conversation. "Help?" he asked at last.

He could feel her carefully marshalling her thoughts on the other side of the fold that connected them: this was important to her, whatever it was. She probably feared he would only listen once, and so wanted to make it all clear the first time. She was right, of course.

"What if we could start it again?"

He waited a long time to hear the rest, but she only waited. "Start *what*?"

"Everything! The universe. Space. Time. Draw it all back together so it can begin again."

This was a folly so great Giant did not even expend the energy of a sigh. "Foolishness," was all he said. Perhaps Holdfast's field had begun to decay and she was losing control of her mind. The thought disturbed him. Must he spend his last eons, not in the peace he sought, but beset by Holdfast and her delusions? He felt a certain sentimental attachment to her, more so now that they were the last two living things, but it did not extend nearly that far.

"Don't judge so quickly," she said. "I know it sounds like it, but I've been thinking..."

"Are you certain it is worth disrupting the last moments of my peace?"

"The stars have all died while you've been enjoying solitude, Giant, and you still want more?"

"Yes. After all, there is no other pleasure left to enjoy. May I return to it?"

"But when we are gone, nothing will remain? Ever!"

"Nothing is only a little different than something." It was hard not to let his impatience overwhelm him. "These days I can scarcely tell the difference."

"But it doesn't have to be that way! We could change it."

Now he was all but certain that important strands of her consciousness were beginning to stretch beyond their capabilities, creating ideas unsupported by the most basic correspondence with reality. "We can change nothing, Holdfast. In our early days we talked of very little else. I know you were young, but it is all there in your memory. Did you glean nothing from what others have said and done?"

"Those ideas were built on dull convention – hardly examined," she said. "'Entropy is the one ruling truth.' 'Time itself will not outlast the end of matter.' 'Dispersion and cold will continue forever' – I know them like I know my own thoughts."

"But you have not learned from them, young one. Go back and examine those thoughts again and you will see."

"No. It is they – and you – who would not see! Entropy is not the ruling force of existence. Not yet." She seemed excited in a way he didn't understand, hurried and impatient.

"Here is the truth, Holdfast. Our hearts, unfed, will finally lose their energy and grow colder than the surrounding blackness, then they will disperse what remains of the energies they have long harbored. Even if anything of us still exists at that point, it will certainly end then. Our last remnants will cool and disperse and then everything will be finished, forever. What could possibly gather together all this dull dust and then run back the clock of entropy precisely enough to make it all begin again?"

"I don't want to repeat it. I want to start it anew!"

"These are old speculations, Holdfast. It is narrowly possible that something like that will happen anyway when stasis is final and absolute, by some process we cannot foresee... but even if it does, I will not be there to experience it and neither will you. Anything to do with outliving the end of our universe is foolishness, and I have no time for it. I wish to spend my last days, not in vain striving for something that cannot be, but contemplating that which was and that which is."

"But there is something that moves against entropy," she said a moment before he severed the connection. "A force that swims against its current, even when it seems that current is too strong to resist...!"

Another of Bashō's *haiku* came to him with surprising swiftness, as if that long-ago poet had heard Holdfast across the length of time and responded.

Nothing in the cry
of cicadas suggests they
are about to die

But Giant kept that idea to himself.

"Life!" said Holdfast. "Life is as strong as entropy."

It was such a reckless statement that Giant was taken aback. "What do you mean? Life is no defense against entropy. Every creature that ever lived has fought against those processes and lost. The more primitive forms fought gravity, fought extremes of temperature and radiation, fought the frailty of flesh every moment of their existence, and every one of them failed. We are the last, Holdfast, and even we will fail soon. If Time itself cannot outlast the cold, what chance could mere life ever have?"

"There's more to life than physical processes," she said. "Or else we would both have ended long ago. Life organizes against chaos. We repair. We reproduce. We *remember*."

More of Bashō's thoughts rang in Giant's memory.

Father and mother,

he quoted, the archaic words escaping before he realized he had not thought them silently this time, but had exposed them to Holdfast,

long gone, suddenly return
in the pheasant's cry.

"What," she said, "is that?"

"Nothing. A stray thought – a memory from a distant time." Giant was embarrassed to have lost the distinction between what he considered and what he uttered. After all, he had just suspected the same of Holdfast! It was almost amusing. In fact, it was amusing.

"Are you… *laughing*, Giant?"

But even as the odd moment played out, he realized he was awash in memories of his own, sudden recollections of the days the galactic travelers had all communicated regularly with each other. Strange, so strange! He felt unstable in a way he could not remember feeling before, and yet unmistakably alive. What was happening? "I am weary now, Holdfast," he said. "I will think on what you said and respond in due time."

"But, Giant…!"

"Later, please. Later."

When he was alone Giant examined his strange reaction, which disturbed him far more than Holdfast's ungraceful struggle against the inevitable. He had been moved to unplanned utterance, not by Holdfast herself, but by a mere poem, an ordered arrangement of primitive symbols. Yet it had also unlocked a series of memories that had been so far from his daily thought that they might have been lost, a flood of remembrance from long-vanished eras, of times when he and the others of his kind had been full of their own importance and the future that seemed to lay before them like a bright burst of radiation illuminating all that had been dark about the universe.

Oh, how bold they had felt, back when they first began! Brightest Pilgrim, clever Edgerunner, Hot on the Outside, Deep Resonance, Light Drum, and Giant himself, the oldest and the largest of them all – how they had exulted in their newness and power! They had solved problems even their forebears could have barely imagined, witnessed the universe in ways no previous life could understand, from its greatest sweep to the tiniest perturbations of its component quanta. They had even marveled at emptiness itself, the true darkness where energy and matter did not travel, and had tried to unravel its secrets. The travelers had known that one day that same emptiness would be their end, but then it had seemed no more than a bitter spice that deepened the taste of what they consumed. Now Giant remembered them all – remembered himself, even, in a way he had not done for a very long time, and in his slow, intricate way, mourned the end of their shared invincibility.

But why? Why should all of this spring from the words of one ancient poem about the cry of birds? Giant had no mother and father, of course, nor could he find any trace of a pheasant's call in his inherited memories, but he imagined it as a provocative, disturbing sound – a *haunting* sound, as Bashō's people might have termed it. The bird's cry itself had been meaningful to Bashō, for whom it brought back memories of his long-dead human progenitors, but why should the mere mention of it have an almost identical effect on Giant, a being so different as to be incomprehensible to the mind that penned the words? Were some ideas simply so common to intelligence – to life itself – that they triggered automatic responses, memories flushed from cover like a flock of Bashō's birds?

Giant scanned several million poems and artistic statements from Earth and other worlds at a similar state of development. Although he felt some sympathy with many of them, and even found bits that engaged him on a deeper level than mere consideration, none of them disordered his thoughts so quickly and re-ordered them as profoundly as the words of the little wandering creature Bashō. How odd, that such an unlike thing should speak across the eons to him. Did it have something to do with life itself, the property that seemed to interest Holdfast so greatly? But even if it did, it was not the commonality of all life that had touched Giant's thoughts, but the commonality of his own great span with one particular, fleeting life from long ago.

He was grateful the end had not yet come, Giant discovered, because he was finding so many things here at the end he wanted to think about.

Weather-beaten bones,

Little Bashō had written in that impossibly distant time,

I'll leave your heart exposed
to cold, piercing winds

How had such a being understood then what Giant felt now? Could there truly be something hidden in the essence of life? Something beyond reduction that connected him to another living thing more surely than even the slow unfolding of atoms and the bleeding away of elementary particles?

A question came to him then, and once it had presented itself, he could not unthink it:

Could life be stranger and stronger than I could have guessed...?

"Tell me. Tell me your idea to start things again."

"Giant?" Holdfast seemed startled. "You have never spoken to me first in all our shared time."

He did not want to talk about himself – it seemed a pointless subject. "Your idea, Holdfast. What is it?"

It took her a moment to compose herself. "We live," she said at last. "Of all that remains, only we that live are organized specifically to survive. Because of that, we fight and prevail against the growing cold."

"Not for long."

"But we do! We have for countless eons! And that is because we live. Because we fight against disorganization. What is life but a plan to swim against the current of dissolution? What else does life do?"

"Even if I grant this, Holdfast, it is not a plan but a statement."

He could feel a little amusement ripple through her. "Grumpy as always. Do you admit that if we do nothing, we will cease to be? And that sometime afterward, everything will cease to be? Movement, heat, organization, all gone?"

"Yes, yes." He was surprised at his own impatience to hear what must surely be a grand piece of futility. "I have said these things many times. The death of heat is the great inevitable of our universe."

"But what if we joined together, you and I? What if my heart and your heart were to come together, through one of the folds we can still create? At this point, our hearts are nearly infinitely deep. Might the combination of those forces be enough to draw back the dispersed energies of existence? To start things again?"

Oddly, he felt disappointment at this plan for pointless self-destruction, although he had expected nothing better. "No, Holdfast. Even if we were still in the greatest flush of our strength it would not be enough. If your heart was not bounced away from mine by the forces of their proximity, the combination would still not suffice. We do not contain enough energy in the two of us to begin things again."

She was silent for a long time. Giant discovered and consumed a drift of energies as she considered, the first substantial meal he had taken in a long time. It occurred to him that it might be his last feeding.

When she communicated again, it was as though they had drifted immeasurably farther apart during that short span, her thoughts without force.

"At least I have given birth," she said.

"We have all created children, Holdfast." He did not mention that the copies of themselves the travelers had once made had all predeceased them, early casualties in the struggle for dwindling resources since they had been unable to compete with their larger parents. For some reason, he feared her mood and did not want to make it worse.

"I don't mean that sad little experiment." Her amusement was tinged with bitterness in a way he found unpleasant. "I mean that our universe will end, but we have at least spawned other universes."

"Our universe has created pocket universes like that from the beginning," he said. "On the far side of every black hole. But they are limited things, of course."

"Yes, but at least those pocket universes, as you call them, came from us. They came from our hearts, even if we cannot perceive them or reach them. That is immortality of a sort!"

Giant was confused, and so he did not respond for a time. "What do you mean?" he finally asked. "I do not understand you, Holdfast. From our hearts…?"

"Of course, from our hearts." She was brusque, as if talking to a young traveler she had just created, which confused him even more. "The engines at our centers that are made of black holes just like that which occurs when a star collapses. All that is drawn into them and crosses the singularity then bubbles out and creates new universes, however small. It is a cold comfort, but I will cling to it."

He had never before hesitated to tell the truth, but Giant did so now. "But Holdfast," he said at last, "how can that be? Have you forgotten? We are not natural galaxies. We have no such natural black holes for hearts. Early in our history we created something more reliable, a heart that conserves the energies it harvests and does not allow them to escape into a singularity."

"What are you talking about?"

His thoughts actually pained him. Giant wished the conversation had never begun. Instead of explaining her mistake himself, he brought up the thoughts of lost Edgerunner, who had always been one of the most questing minds among them. Instantly she was there, a third party to the conversation, although her energies had died and dispersed long ago. She was explaining to some of the newly hatched traveler children how they lived and what would keep them that way.

"*Your hearts are nothing like those with which we first began,*" Edgerunner's voice, silenced for eons, was now explaining just as if she lived again, "*—that is, natural singularities that bleed energy and matter out of the universe.*" Edgerunner described the lattice of black quanta that the travelers had created to serve them, a holonetic froth of particle-sized black holes, buffered by a core of white gravity, perfectly balanced to draw and consume the universe's bounty without letting it create new universes, a model of economical consumption.

"*… So we do not waste what we find,*" Edgerunner said to those long-dead children. "*And someday, when the universal cold is great and our resources grow scant, you will thank your forebears for such a gift…*"

"Do you see?" Giant asked as he ended his summoning of Edgerunner's thoughts and returned her to his memory. He almost felt he should apologize, although he had done nothing wrong. "Do you see, Holdfast? We do not make other universes, large or small. We contain everything that we have consumed except that part we have used in our own living, but soon even those reserves will be emptied and we will end. You must accustom yourself to the idea."

"I… didn't remember that." The admission seemed to be wrenched from her as if by a terrible squeeze of gravity. "Giant, it was so basic, so important – and I *forgot…*!"

Giant did not know how to respond, since they both knew what she meant. "Forgot" meant failure, and failure on that scale meant Holdfast's ending must be very close. Had he done wrong? Was there a time when even the truth was inappropriate? He had never considered such a thing. At last, he broke the silence.

Lonely stillness—
a single cicada's cry
sinking into stone.

An eon passed before she said, "What is that?" She seemed to barely have the energy to communicate now; even her unquenchable curiosity was muted by despair. "What is 'cicada'?"

"An ancient life form. The words are a *haiku*, a ritualized form of thought, almost as distant in time as the sound they describe." Suddenly he wanted to tell her all he had been thinking. "I have been very interested in these words lately, Holdfast – or rather, this particular maker of words. He lived long ago, in the morning of intelligent life. He traveled across his world and he recorded thoughts that still exist. His name was Bashō."

"You always brought us so much," Holdfast said slowly.

Giant thought he could hear something in her words beyond despair, and this puzzled him, too. How could she change so quickly, unless it was just another symptom of her impending failure? "What do you mean?"

"You, Giant. You. Always you kept away from us, as if to tease us, but when you did speak you had such big thoughts, such interesting thoughts. Do you wonder we troubled you? That I trouble you still?" A mournful current moved through her essence. "I am sorry my idea was foolish. I will leave you alone now."

"Wait." Giant was confused. "What do you mean – that is why you troubled me?"

"Because you were our elder and we thought respectfully of you. Because your thoughts were longer and deeper than ours and you saw things that we younger ones couldn't see. It inspired all of us – it inspired me to think in bigger ways, and I thought I was doing that here. But now I understand I am not merely foolishly optimistic, I am disordered. I'm sorry, Giant. I could not help myself. I thought I saw a gleam of hope and I reached out to it too quickly. I won't trouble you again."

It was only after the connection had been broken that Giant realized it was he who had reached out to Holdfast in the first place. When he resumed his musings, it was in a solitude that no longer felt quite so much like something to be defended.

Near the end of his short life, Bashō had sensed his end coming – not that he had been overly attached to the thing called life. At the beginning of another ordered collection of poem-thoughts, he had written, "*Within this temporal body composed of a hundred bones and nine holes there resides a spirit which, for lack of an adequate name, I think of as windblown. Like delicate drapery, it may be torn away and blown off by the least breeze.*"

How true that was, Giant thought – how like the way he felt about himself in this late hour. Windblown. Torn away by the smallest breeze. And so he would be, by the last breezes of the last act – the final dispersion of all that was Giant, into nothing, and nothing to follow.

Sick on my journey,
only my dreams will wander
these desolate moors

Bashō had written those words in his final days, and his followers had thought it would be his final utterance – a *jisei* as they called it, a death poem. And indeed the poet's dreams *had* continued to wander after his physical end, father than he could have guessed: could there be a terrestrial moor more desolate than the cold reaches where Giant spun? But Bashō, as always, had embraced simplicity without actually being simple, Giant recognized. He had written another poem near the end, and it was these words that had captured Giant in a deeper way than almost any other. It floated through his thoughts so continuously (but without becoming more comprehensible) that he nearly forgot the labors that kept him alive, mending the tatters of his intrinsic field and stoking the dying embers of his hungry heart.

All along this road
not a single soul – only
autumn evening

Autumn evening, that was clear – the autumn of Bashō's life, as it was now the late autumn of Giant's. But "not a single soul" – did Bashō mean nobody else was on the road beside himself? Or that he himself did not exist, that ultimately there was the road and nothing else?

The narrow road... thought Giant, remembering the title that had confused but fascinated him. *The Narrow Road to the Interior.*

And as he considered, an idea came to him. Giant saw in his mind's eye – no, he *imagined,* since it existed nowhere in his own memories – a flock of birds following one bird into night, but the travelers did not fear the dark because they were together. Because they followed a leader? No, because, they followed an idea.

Not a single soul – only autumn evening.

Am I on the narrow road? Giant suddenly wondered. *Or am I myself the narrow road? And when I no longer think and feel and remember, will the road still exist?*

Sustenance was all but gone, the universe approaching pure vacuum and complete entropic scatter. Giant could perceive himself growing smaller as he began to devour the last of his resources. His systems labored to keep something like normal efficiency, because he was seized with a strange determination to understand at the very last this thing that could not be understood, this tiny mystery which cast a shadow all the way to the end of everything. What was the narrow road? And why did it seem to matter so much?

Memories now came to him frequently as he spun in his dark course, his own as well as others', confused images and ideas that did not seem to belong together. He felt again the flush of youth, of possibility, recalled Edgerunner and Light Drum and all the rest – at times he even forgot that they were gone, and spoke as if they still could hear him, despite the silence that was his only answer.

Sometimes he even imagined himself one of Bashō's birds, wings beating as it dove forward into a darkening sky, conscious without seeing them that his kind were all around him, that they knew him and needed him. Alive, dead, present or memory, the differences became smaller and smaller to Giant as time's edges frayed.

But Holdfast, who for a little while would remain both memory and present reality, wanted more. She wanted more than everything that had ever been, in fact. But how could that be? And what did it matter anyway, when Giant could not give it to her?

"… *The day's not long enough…*" Basho had once written, a fragment abruptly surfacing through the swirl of Giant's other thoughts. Why should he think of that poem now?

Then, as if he had fallen into one of the singularities of which Holdfast had spoken, the one-way heart of a dead star, Giant suddenly found himself in a new place, a new understanding. Suddenly at the end of everything, everything *changed*.

He waited so long for a response from her that the silence became frightening. With her smaller size and less powerful heart, Holdfast must be feeling the nearness of the end even more acutely than he did. How long since he had spoken to her? Had he waited too long? Giant sent out a more aggressive tendril of thought, half-fearful it would touch nothing, but at last he felt a dim flutter of response.

"… Yes?"

"You survive." His relief was surprisingly powerful, especially since that survival could only be temporary – a sliver of dying time. For the first time in perhaps his entire long life, Giant thought that being alone with his thoughts might not be what he most wanted. "You still live."

"After… a… fashion." Despite all, there was a touch of resigned amusement in her thought.

"I think at last I understand the poet," he said. "His collections of thoughts are ordered so they can be shared with others – but that is not the whole of it. No, the ordered thoughts *are* life. Do you understand? Perhaps not…" Faced with this most important idea, Giant could not find the correct expression he sought. "But I wish to share one of the creature Bashō's thoughts with you. It is you, Holdfast – this thought is you. Listen:

All day long, singing,

yet the day's not long enough
for the skylark's song...

"Do you see? You have sung since you were made, but still you wish you could sing longer – even beyond the end of all singing and all songs."

When she spoke again, he realized how weak she was. "I... think... I... *want*..."

"Yes, and so do I, but time is dying. We must gather together what we have while we still can. You said the others like us are all gone. Does that mean their hearts have collapsed and dispersed, or simply that they no longer speak and understand?"

"I... don't... understand... what..."

"I will explain, but I have not sought them out in so long I do not know how to find them. Show them to me – let me touch them through you. I am stronger than you, so let me reach out to see what remains."

Holdfast's thoughts were very weak and chaotic. Giant had to use some of his own strength simply to help her cope with his presence, but together they were able to stabilize the connection long enough for him to reach out to the others.

They were still there, all of his kin, although nothing was left of his fellow travelers now but their hearts: the support systems had collapsed and their minds had run down like untended machines, too crippled ever to function again. But the hearts, the hearts still lived, the billions upon billions of points of nothing precisely balanced in their matrices, still ingesting when there was nothing left to ingest, still surviving on their own stores until the great cold forced even those most perfect constructs to give up their integrity and vanish.

"I am opening folds now," he told Holdfast, and in his mind's eye he pictured himself calling out to her across the endless night as they flew side by side. "I am opening a fold for each of them. Give me what strength you have and I will bring their hearts through into myself. Into *us*." The energy to sustain even one such fold was almost beyond him, let alone so many, but Giant no longer needed to reserve any part of his own strength for the future. Still, the engines of his being were draining what was left of his resources so quickly that only moments remained to him, and he could feel Holdfast beginning to shred in the growing surge of forces, her thoughts now little more than tatters. "Be your name," he urged her. "Do not fail – not yet. Release will come."

"?" The question was so small, so stressed by the growing weight of the opening folds, that Giant barely caught it.

"Our hearts are meant to conserve what they hold," he explained. "That is why they create no new universes. But if we bring them all together at once, it could be that the buffers will break down. Much of what remains of the universe is inside us those hearts, and when the white gravity no longer keeps them apart, the black quanta should combine into a black hole of the old sort.

"Do you see? We may still make a way out of this universe, not for us, but for what we have gathered and been. As our hearts collapse together and their substance moves through the singularity, it should concentrate the energies into a near-infinite point until they are released again on the other side... and explosion of *being*. You and I and all our kind will give birth to a new universe after all, Holdfast – or dissolve in the trying." He paused, resisting dissolution until a crucial question was answered. "Do you consent, Holdfast? Will we do this?"

A whisper from far, far across the night sky. "*Yes*."

Giant narrowed the focus of the folds so the hearts would come together where Giant himself spun, but the effort was almost impossibly great. Still, Radiantsong, Thar the Great Question, Shifted, Bright Pilgrim, all of them existed again in that contracting moment, even if only in his memory, as he brought them back together inside himself.

But as the titan forces surged through him, stretching and curving him into impossible spaces, Giant abruptly realized that he was not strong enough to hold them all, to do what needed to be done. He had exceeded his physical limits and he was collapsing into chaos. He had failed...

Giant. I am still here. It was only a thought, but it was Holdfast's thought, which she had somehow found the strength to send him. And although she could have nothing left to lend him, the mere knowledge that she existed somehow made him stronger.

Another instant was all he needed to absorb the last of his kin and their contained energies. He consumed the last of his own reserves, throwing every resource into the fires of his being so that he could perform this last duty of bringing them even closer together.

Duty? Even as he struggled with dying strength to hold the folds open, as the black hole froth of a thousand dark hearts and more flowed together, dissolving the boundaries between possibility and reality, he was suddenly alarmed by his own dying thoughts. Duty? What could that mean? His duty to others – his duty, somehow, to life? It was such a ludicrous, unlikely concept that Giant hesitated. Perhaps this entire unlikely idea was not revelation after all, but the madness of the end. Dying, Giant felt panic stealing his last strength. Did his intentions even make sense?

But though he had paused for only a tiny fraction of the pulse of the smallest energies, the forces he held were impossibly, immeasurably potent; even that subinstant was enough for them to begin to break free of his control.

No! Giant could feel himself coming apart, dense as the universe's beginning, hollow as a perfect vacuum. *Life is weak*, he told himself, *but it struggles against all winds. Life is weak, but it is also strong.*

But is it strong enough for this?

"A little longer – only a little longer, then you can rest," he told Holdfast, although he no longer knew if he was actually sending the thoughts or if she still existed to hear them. "You and the others followed a leader who flew always into darkness, and now you must follow him a little farther. Are you ready? It will take all that you have – and all that I have, too."

And then he could no longer speak at all. The emptied hearts of his kind, the remnants of all they had felt and thought and consumed, filled him to bursting and beyond. He held on until he felt something begin to tear at the center of everything and the pent energies rushed out into the unknown. He felt them all going then, even Holdfast whirling past like a leaf blown from a branch, like a bird flying suddenly with the wind instead of against it.

Farewell, he thought as his thoughts were stripped away and sent spinning down into the vortex after her. *Farwell, dear Holdfast...!*

And then she was gone, and Giant felt himself finally beginning to disappear, pulled to pieces, the pieces sucked into the same stream of rushing, exploding transfiguration.

Birds, vanishing...
The road...
... Not long enough...
... Dreams wandering the desolate moors...

The energies seemed self-sustaining now, the process of seeding a new universe safely underway, but Giant would never know for certain, any more than little Bashō could have known where his dreams would wander, and to whom. Big Giant, little Bashō – they were one and the same now, rushing down into the endless dark together. Would things begin again, as Holdfast had wished? If so, it would happen somewhere else, somewhere that even Giant could not imagine. After all, he had been given only the one universe and one short lifetime in which to study it.

Giant found he did not care. He had lived. He had thought, and those thoughts had created everything and nothing. In the end, he had learned at least one truth. Perhaps now something else would come after him, seeking truths of its own. Or perhaps not.

All along this road, he realized, not a single soul – only autumn evening.

The universe's last poem ended as Giant ended, spun into a mist of possibility at what might have been the end of all things, or another beginning.

(2013)

Translated by Sam Hamill

THE GOLEM
by Avram Davidson

> The ever-elusive **Avram Davidson**, author of several notoriously half-told novels, was born in 1923 in Yonkers, New York. He joined the U.S. Navy in 1942. served as a medic in the newly-formed Israeli armed forces in 1948, then worked for a while as a shepherd. He added science fiction to his roster of crime and mystery fiction in the mid-1950s, and in 1962 assumed the editorship of *Fantasy & Science Fiction*. From the mid-1960s to the end of his life, Davidson did not publish a single regular novel. His short stories, on the other hand – especially those collected in *Or All the Seas with Oysters* (1962) and *The Redward Edward Papers* (1978) – consolidated his reputation as a significant, if frustratingly scattergun talent.

The grey-faced person came along the street where old Mr. and Mrs. Gumbeiner lived. It was afternoon, it was autumn, the sun was warm and soothing to their ancient bones. Anyone who attended the movies in the twenties or the early thirties has seen that street a thousand times. Past these bungalows with their half-double roofs Edmund Lowe walked arm-in-arm with Leatrice Joy and Harold Lloyd was chased by Chinamen waving hatchets. Under these squamous palm trees Laurel kicked Hardy and Woolsey beat Wheeler upon the head with a codfish. Across these pocket-handkerchief-sized lawns the juveniles of the Our Gang comedies pursued one another and were pursued by angry fat men in golf knickers. On this same street—or perhaps on some other one of five hundred streets exactly like it.

Mrs. Gumbeiner indicated the grey-faced person to her husband.

"You think maybe he's got something the matter?" she asked. "He walks kind of funny, to me."

"Walks like a *golem*," Mr. Gumbeiner said indifferently.

The old woman was nettled.

"Oh, I don't know," she said. "*I* think he walks like your cousin Mendel."

The old man pursed his mouth angrily and chewed on his pipestem. The grey-faced person turned up the concrete path, walked up the steps to the porch, sat down in a chair. Old Mr. Gumbeiner ignored him. His wife stared at the stranger.

"Man comes in without a hello, goodbye, or howareyou, sits himself down, and right away he's at home… The chair is comfortable?" she asked. "Would you like maybe a glass of tea?"

She turned to her husband.

"Say something, Gumbeiner!" she demanded. "What are you, made of wood?"

The old man smiled a slow, wicked, triumphant smile.

"Why should *I* say anything?" he asked the air. "Who am I? Nothing, that's who."

The stranger spoke. His voice was harsh and monotonous.

"When you learn who—or, rather, what—I am, the flesh will melt from your bones in terror." He bared porcelain teeth.

"Never mind about my bones!" the old woman cried. "You've got a lot of nerve talking about my bones!"

"You will quake with fear," said the stranger. Old Mrs. Gumbeiner said that she hoped he would live so long. She turned to her husband once again.

"Gumbeiner, when are you going to mow the lawn?"

"All mankind—" the stranger began.

"*Shah!* I'm talking to my husband... He talks *eppis* kind of funny, Gumbeiner, no?"

"Probably a foreigner," Mr. Gumbeiner said complacently.

"You think so?" Mrs. Gumbeiner glanced fleetingly at the stranger. "He's got a very bad color in his face, *nebbich*, I suppose he came to California for his health."

"Disease, pain, sorrow, love, grief—all are nought to—"

Mr. Gumbeiner cut in on the stranger's statement.

"Gall bladder," the old man said. "Guinzburg down at the *shule* looked exactly the same before his operation. Two professors they had in for him, and a private nurse day and night."

"I am not a human being!" the stranger said loudly.

"Three thousand seven hundred fifty dollars it cost his son, Guinzburg told me. 'For you, Poppa, nothing is too expensive—only get well,' the son told him."

"I am not a human being!"

"Ai, is that a son for you!" the old woman said, rocking her head. "A heart of gold, pure gold." She looked at the stranger. "All right, all right, I heard you the first time. Gumbeiner! I asked you a question. When are you going to cut the lawn?"

"On Wednesday, *odder* maybe Thursday, comes the Japaneser to the neighborhood. To cut lawns is *his* profession. *My* profession is to be a glazier—retired."

"Between me and all mankind is an inevitable hatred," the stranger said. "When I tell you what I am, the flesh will melt—"

"You said, you said already," Mr. Gumbeiner interrupted.

"In Chicago where the winters were as cold and bitter as the Czar of Russia's heart," the old woman intoned, "you had strength to carry the frames with the glass together day in and day out. But in California with the golden sun to mow the lawn when your wife asks, for this you have no strength. Do I call in the Japaneser to cook for you supper?"

"Thirty years Professor Allardyce spent perfecting his theories. Electronics, neuronics—"

"Listen, how educated he talks," Mr. Gumbeiner said admiringly. "Maybe he goes to the University here?"

"If he goes to the University, maybe he knows Bud?" his wife suggested.

"Probably they're in the same class and he came to see him about the homework, no?"

"Certainly he must be in the same class. How many classes are there? Five *in ganzen:* Bud showed me on his program card." She counted off on her fingers. "Television Appreciation and Criticism, Small Boat Building, Social Adjustment, The American Dance… The American Dance—*nu,* Gumbeiner—"

"Contemporary Ceramics," her husband said, relishing the syllables. "A fine boy, Bud. A pleasure to have him for a boarder."

"After thirty years spent in these studies," the stranger, who had continued to speak unnoticed, went on, "he turned from the theoretical to the pragmatic. In ten years' time he had made the most titanic discovery in history: he made mankind, *all* mankind, superfluous; he made *me.*"

"What did Tillie write in her last letter?" asked the old man.

The old woman shrugged.

"What should she write? The same thing. Sidney was home from the Army, Naomi has a new boyfriend—"

"He made ME!"

"Listen, Mr. Whatever-your-name-is," the old woman said, "maybe where you came from is different, but in *this* country you don't interrupt people while they're talking… Hey. Listen—what do you mean, he *made* you? What kind of talk is that?"

The stranger bared all his teeth again, exposing the too-pink gums.

"In his library, to which I had a more complete access after his sudden and as yet undiscovered death from entirely natural causes, I found a complete collection of stories about androids, from Shelley's *Frankenstein* through Capek's *R.U.R.* to Asimov's—"

"Frankenstein?" said the old man with interest. "There used to be a Frankenstein who had the soda-*wasser* place on Halstead Street—a Litvack, *nebbich.*"

"What are you talking?" Mrs. Gumbeiner demanded. "His name was Franken-*thal,* and it wasn't on Halstead, it was on Roosevelt."

"—clearly shown that all mankind has an instinctive antipathy towards androids and there will be an inevitable struggle between them—"

"Of course, of course!" Old Mr. Gumbeiner clicked his teeth against his pipe. "I am always wrong, you are always right. How could you stand to be married to such a stupid person all this time?"

"I don't know," the old woman said. "Sometimes I wonder, myself. I think it must be his good looks." She began to laugh. Old Mr. Gumbeiner blinked, then began to smile, then took his wife's hand.

"Foolish old woman," the stranger said. "Why do you laugh? Do you not know I have come to destroy you?"

"What?" old Mr. Gumbeiner shouted. "Close your mouth, you!" He darted from his chair and struck the stranger with the flat of his hand. The stranger's head struck against the porch pillar and bounced back.

"When you talk to my wife, talk respectable, you hear?"

Old Mrs. Gumbeiner, cheeks very pink, pushed her husband back to his chair. Then she leaned forward and examined the stranger's head. She clicked her tongue as she pulled aside a flap of grey, skinlike material.

"Gumbeiner, look! He's all springs and wires inside!"

"I *told* you he was a *golem,* but no, you wouldn't listen," the old man said.

"You said he *walked* like a *golem.*"

"How could he walk like a *golem* unless he *was* one?"

"All right, all right... You broke him, so now fix him."

"My grandfather, his light shines from Paradise, told me that when MoHaRaL—Moreynu Ha-Rav Löw—his memory for a blessing, made the *golem* in Prague, three hundred? four hundred years ago? he wrote on his forehead the Holy Name."

Smiling reminiscently, the old woman continued, "And the *golem* cut the rabbi's wood and brought his water and guarded the ghetto."

"And one time only he disobeyed the Rabbi Löw, and Rabbi Löw erased the *Shem Ha-Mephorash* from the *golem*'s forehead and the *golem* fell down like a dead one. And they put him up in the attic of the *shule,* and he's still there today if the Communisten haven't sent him to Moscow... This is not just a story," he said.

"*Avadda* not!" said the old woman.

"I myself have seen both the *shule and* the rabbi's grave," her husband said conclusively.

"But I think this must be a different kind of *golem,* Gumbeiner. See, on his forehead; nothing written."

"What's the matter, there's a law I can't write something there? Where is that lump of clay Bud brought us from his class?"

The old man washed his hands, adjusted his little black skull-cap, and slowly and carefully wrote four Hebrew letters on the grey forehead.

"Ezra the Scribe himself couldn't do better," the old woman said admiringly. "Nothing happens," she observed, looking at the lifeless figure sprawled in the chair.

"Well, after all, am I Rabbi Löw?" her husband asked deprecatingly. "No," he answered. He leaned over and examined the exposed mechanism. "This spring goes here... this wire comes with this one..." The figure moved. "But this one goes where? And this one?"

"Let be," said his wife. The figure sat up slowly and rolled its eyes loosely.

"Listen, Reb *Golem,*" the old man said, wagging his finger. "Pay attention to what I say—you understand?"

"Understand..."

"If you want to stay here, you got to do like Mr. Gumbeiner says."

"Do-like-Mr.-Gumbeiner-says..."

"*That's* the way I like to hear a *golem* talk. Malka, give here the mirror from the pocketbook. Look, you see your face? You see the forehead, what's written? If you don't do like Mr. Gumbeiner says, he'll wipe out what's written and you'll be no more alive."

"No-more-alive..."

"*That's* right. Now, listen. Under the porch you'll find a lawnmower. Take it. And cut the lawn. Then come back. Go."

"Go..." The figure shambled down the stairs. Presently the sound of the lawnmower whirred through the quiet air in the street just like the street where Jackie Cooper shed huge tears on Wallace Beery's shirt and Chester Conklin rolled his eyes at Marie Dressler.

"So what will you write to Tillie?" old Mr. Gumbeiner asked.

"What should I write?" old Mrs. Gumbeiner shrugged. "I'll write that the weather is lovely out here and that we are both, Blessed be the Name, in good health."

The old man nodded his head slowly, and they sat together on the front porch in the warm afternoon sun.

(1955)

BIBLIOGRAPHY

NON-FICTION

Dustin A. Abnet, *The American Robot: A Cultural History*, 2020, University of Chicago Press
Minsoo Kang, *Sublime Dreams of Living Machines: The automaton in the European imagination*, 2011, Harvard University Press
Mateo Kries et al., *Hello Robot: Design between human and machine*, 2017, Vitra Design Museum
Stanisław Lem (trans. Joanna Zylinska), *Summa Technologiae*, [1964] 2014, University of Minnesota Press
Adrienne Mayor, *Gods and Robots: Myths, machines and ancient dreams of technology*, 2018, Princeton University Press
Chloe Wood (ed.), *AI: More than Human*, 2019, Barbican International Enterprises
Gaby Wood, *Living Dolls: A magical history of the quest for mechanical life*, 2002, Faber

FICTION

David R. Bunch, *Moderan*, [1971] 2018, NYRB Classics
Samuel Butler, *Erewhon*, [1872] 2006, Penguin Classics; New Impression edition
Karel Capek (trans. Claudia Novack-Jones), *R.U.R. (Rossum's Universal Robots)*, [1921] 2004, Penguin Classics
John Sladek, *Tik-Tok*, 1983, Corgi
Stanisław Lem (trans. Michael Kandel), *The Cyberiad – fables for the cybernetic age*, [1975] 2020, MIT Press
Auguste Villiers de l'Isle-Adam (trans. Robert Martin Adams), *Tomorrow's Eve*, [1886] 2000, University of Illinois Press
Rachilde (trans. Melanie Hawthorne), *Monsieur Venus*, [1884] 2004, Modern Language Association
Mary Shelley, *Frankenstein, Or the Modern Prometheus*, [1818] 2003, Penguin Classics
Yevgeny Zamyatin (trans. Clarence Brown), *We*, [1920–1] 1993, Penguin Classics

ACKNOWLEDGEMENTS

Projects of this sort are, more than usual, a team effort. Thanks go to everyone involved at Head of Zeus: Nicolas Cheetham, Christian Duck, Jennifer Edgecombe, Clare Gordon, Jade Gwilliam, Sabir Huseynbayli, Ben Prior, Rachel Thorne and Nikky Ward.

EXTENDED COPYRIGHT

We are grateful to the following for permission to reproduce copyright material:

Brian Aldiss: "Super-Toys Last All Summer Long" published in *Harper's Bazaar*, 1969, copyright © 1969 by Brian Aldiss. Reproduced with permission of Curtis Brown, London on behalf of The Executors of the Estate of Brian Aldiss.

Juan Jose Arreola: "Baby H. P.," 1913, translated by Andrea L. Bell from *Cosmos Latinos: An Anthology of Science Fiction from Latin America and Spain*, edited by Andrea L. Bell and Yolanda Molina-Gavilán, copyright © 2003 by Wesleyan University Press. Published by Wesleyan University Press. Used with permission.

Paolo Bacigalupi: "Mika Model" published in *Slate*, 2016. Reprinted by permission of the author and the author's agents, Scovil Galen Ghosh Literary Agency, Inc.

T.S. Bazelli: "The Peacemaker" published in *Lightspeed: People of Colo(u)r Destroy Science Fiction!* 2016. Reproduced by permission of Samantha B. Literary Agency.

Chris Beckett: "The Turing Test" published in *Interzone*, #183, October 2002. Reproduced by permission of John Jarrold Agency.

Helena Bell: "Robot" published in *Clarkesworld Magazine*, #72, September 2012. Reproduced with permission of the author.

Stephen Vincent Benét: "Nightmare Number Three," copyright © 1935, renewed 1963 by Thomas C. Benet, Rachel B. Lewis, Stephanie B. Mahin. Used by permission of Brandt and Hochman Literary Agents, Inc. Any copying or distribution of this text is expressly forbidden. All rights reserved.

Morris Bishop: "The Reading Machine" published in *The New Yorker*, March 1947. Reproduced by permission of Margaretta Jolly.

James Blish: "Solar Plexus" first published in *Astonishing Stories*, September 1941. Reproduced by permission of the Estate of James Blish and the Heather Chalcroft Literary Agency.

Robert Bloch: "Comfort Me, My Robot" published in *Imagination*, 1955. Reproduced by permission of Richard Henshaw Group LLC.

Bruce Boston: "Old Robots are the Worst," published in *Isaac Asimov's Science Fiction Magazine*, October 1989. Reproduced with permission of the author.

Ray Bradbury: "The Veldt" originally appearing as "The World the Children Made" in *The Saturday Evening Post*, September 1950. Republished in *The Illustrated Man*, 1951. Reproduced by permission of Abner Stein.

Tobias S. Buckell: "Zen and the Art of Starship Maintenance" published in *Cosmic Powers*, 2017. Reproduced by permission of Liza Dawson Associates LLC.

Algis Budrys: "First to Serve" published in *Astounding Science Fiction*, May 1954. Reproduced by permission of The Zeno Agency.

Avram Davidson: "The Golem" published in *The Magazine of Fantasy and Science Fiction*, March 1955. Reproduced by permission of Darrell Schweitzer/Owlswick Literary Agency.

Lester Del Rey: "Helen O'Loy," copyright © 1938, 1966 by Lester del Rey; first appeared in *Astounding*. Reprinted by permission of Wildside Press and the Virginia Kidd Agency, Inc.

Cory Doctorow: "I, Row-Boat" originally published in *Flurb* #1, copyright © 2006 by Cory Doctorow. Reproduced by permission of the author.

Terry Edge: "Big Dave's in Love" published in *Arc 1.2 / Post Human Conditions*, 2012. Reproduced by permission of the author.

Greg Egan: "Learning to Be Me" first published in *Interzone* #37, July 1990, copyright © 1990 by Greg Egan. Reproduced by permission of the author.

Harlan Ellison: "Repent, Harlequin! Said the Ticktockman" originally published in *Galaxy Magazine*, December 1965, copyright © 1965 by Galaxy Publishing Corporation. Copyright reassigned to Author 16 April 1968. Renewed, 1992 by The Kilimanjaro Corporation. Reprinted with permission of, and by arrangement with, The Kilimanjaro Corporation. All rights reserved. Harlan Ellison is a registered trademarks of The Kilimanjaro Corporation.

Guy Endore: "Men of Iron" first published in *The Magazine of Fantasy*, Fall 1949. Reproduced by permission of the Estate of the author.

E. M. Forster: "The Machine Stops" 1909. Reproduced by permission of The Provost and Scholars of King's College, Cambridge and The Society of Authors as the E. M. Forster Estate.

Karen Joy Fowler: "Praxis" first published in *Isaac Asimov's Science Fiction Magazine*, March 1985. Reproduced by permission of the author.

Lauren Grace Fox: "Rosie Cleans House" published in *All Hail Our Robot Conquerors!* 2017. Reproduced with permission of the author.

William Gibson: "The Winter Market" published in *Vancouver Magazine*, November 1985. Reproduced by permission of The Orion Publishing Group, London.

Herbert Goldstone: "Virtuoso" published in *The Magazine of Fantasy and Science Fiction*, February 1953. Reproduced by permission of the Estate of the author.

Emile Goudeau: "The Revolt of the Machines," translated by Brian Stableford in *The Revolt of the Machines*, 2014. Reproduced by permission of Brian Stableford.

Dan Grace: "Fully Automated Nostalgia Capitalism" published in *Interzone*, #273, November–December 2017. Reproduced by permission of the author.

Becky Hagenston: "Hi Ho Cherry-O" first published in *Witness*, XXXI Vol 1, Spring 2018. Reproduced with permission of the author.

John Cooper Hamilton: "The Next Move" published in *Daily Science Fiction*, April 2018. Reproduced by permission of the author.

M. John Harrison: "Suicide Coast" published in *Fantasy & Science Fiction*, ed van Gelder, 1999. Reproduced by permission of Mic Cheetham Literary Agency.

Ted Hayden: "These 5 Books Go 6 Feet Deep" published in *Nature*, February, 2018. Reproduced by permission of the author.

Arundhati Hazra: "The Toymaker's Daughter" originally published in the March/April 2017 issue of *The Magazine of Fantasy & Science Fiction*. Reproduced by permission of the author.

Tania Hershman: "The Perfect Egg" published in *Nature*, January 2011. Reproduced with permission of the author.

Nathan Hillstrom: "Like You, I Am A System" published in *Interzone*, #270, May–June 2017. Reproduced by permission of the author.

Nalo Hopkinson: "Ganger (Ball Lightning)" published in *Dark Matter: A Century of Speculative Fiction from the African Diaspora*, Aspect, 2000. Reproduced by permission of the author.

Shinichi Hoshi: "Bokko-Chan", copyright © 1958 The Hoshi Library English translation by Marina Hoshi Whyte. Reproduced by permission of Japan Foreign-Rights Centre.

T. L. Huchu: "HostBods" published in *Omenana*, #1, 2014. Reproduced by permission of the author.

Liz Jensen: "Good to Go" published in *Arc 1.4: Forever alone drone*, 2012. Reproduced by permission of Aitken Alexander Associates Ltd.

Xia Jia: "Tongtong's Summer," translated by Ken Liu. First published in *Upgraded* 2014, copyright © 2014 by Xia Jia. Reproduced by permission of the author and translator.

Rachael K. Jones: "The Greatest One-Star Restaurant in the Whole Quadrant" published in *Lightspeed Magazine*, Issue 91, December 2017. Reproduced by permission of the author.

John Kaiine: "Dolly Sodom" published in *Off Limits: Tales of Alien Sex*, 1996. Reproduced with permission of the author.

Joanna Kavenna: "Flight", published in *Arc 2.3*. Reproduced by permission of the author.

Damon Knight: "Masks" first published in *Playboy*, July 1968, copyright © 2019, InfinityBox Press LLC. Published by arrangement with InfinityBox Press LLC.

Ted Kosmatka: "The One Who Isn't" from *Lightspeed*, July 2016. Reproduced by permission of the author.

Rich Larson: "Masked" published in *Asimov's Science Fiction,* Issue 07, 2016. Reproduced by permission of the author.

Murray Leinster: "A Logic Named Joe" published in *Astounding Science Fiction*, 1946. Reproduced by permission of MBA Literary Agents.

Marissa K. Lingen (Gritter): "My Favourite Sentience" published in *Nature*, April 2018. Reproduced by permission of the author.

Ken Liu: "The Caretaker" originally published in *First Contact: Digital Science Fiction Anthology 1*, copyright © 2011 by Ken Liu. Reproduced with permission of the author.

Stanisław Lem: "Non Serviam" published in *Perfect Vacuum*, copyright © 1971 by Stanisław Lem, English translation © 1978, 1979 by Stanisław Lem. Reprinted by permission of Houghton Mifflin Harcourt Publishing Company. All rights reserved.

Barry N. Malzberg: "Making the Connections" originally published in *Continuum 4*, ed Roger Elwood, copyright © 1975 by Roger Elwood. Reproduced by permission of the author.

Adam Marek: "Tamagotchi" published in *The New Uncanny: Tales of Unease*, 2008. Reproduced with permission of the author.

Paul McAuley: "The Man" originally published in *Arc 1.2 / Post Human Conditions*, copyright © 2012 by Paul McAuley. Reproduced by permission of Mic Cheetham Literary Agency.

Ian McDonald: "Nanonauts! In Battle With Tiny Death-Subs!" published in *Robot Uprisings*, 2014. Reproduced by permission of The Zeno Agency.

Sandra McDonald: "Sexy Robot Mom" published in *Asimov's Science Fiction*, April–May 2012. Reproduced with permission of the author.

Walter M. Miller, Jr.: "I Made You" published in *Astounding Science Fiction*, March 1954, ed. John W. Campbell, Jr., Street & Smith Publications, Inc. Reproduced by permission of Abner Stein.

C. L. Moore: "No Woman Born" first published in *Astounding Science Fiction*, December 1944, ed. John W. Campbell, Jr., Street & Smith Publications, Inc. Reproduced by permission of Abner Stein.

Patrick O'Leary: "That Laugh" published in *We Think, Therefore We Are*, 2009. Reproduced with permission of the author.

Peter Phillips: "Lost Memory", copyright © 1952 by Quinn Publishing Corp, © 1980 by Peter Phillips. Reproduced by permission of the author's agent, Barry N. Malzberg.

Steven Popkes: "The Birds of Isla Mujeres" published in *The Magazine of Fantasy & Science Fiction*, January 2003. Reproduced with permission of the author.

Vina Jie-Min Prasad: "Fandom for Robots" published in *Uncanny Magazine*, Issue 18, September–October 2017. Reproduced by permission of the author.

Mari Ness: "Memories and Wire" published in *Upgraded*, 2014. Reproduced by permission of the author.

Robert Reed: "The Next Scene" published in *Clarkesworld Magazine*, #121, October 2016, copyright © Robert Reed. Reproduced with permission of the author.

Mike Resnick: "Beachcomber," first published in *Chrysalis 8*, ed. Roy Torgeson, Doubleday, 1980. Reproduced by permission of Spectrum Literary Agency.

Adam Roberts: "Adam Roberts" published in *We Think, Therefore We Are*, 2009. Reproduced by permission of the author.

Carl Sandburg: "The Hammer" from *The Complete Poems of Carl Sandburg*, copyright © 1969, 1970 by Lillian Steichen Sandburg. Reprinted by permission of Houghton Mifflin Harcourt Publishing Company. All rights reserved.

Robert Sheckley: "The Robot Who Looked Like Me" published in *Cosmopolitan*, August 1973, copyright © 1973 by Robert Sheckley. Reproduced by permission of Donald Maass Literary Agency. All rights reserved.

Nicholas Paul Sheppard: 'Satisfaction" first published in *AntipodeanSF*, Issue 236, March 2018. Reproduced by permission of the author.

Clifford D. Simak: "I Am Crying All Inside" published in *Galaxy Magazine*, August 1969. Reprinted by permission of Pollinger Limited (www.pollingerlimited.com) on behalf of the Estate of Clifford D Simak.

John Sladek: "The Steam-Driven Boy" published in *Nova 2*, 1972. Reproduced by permission of the Estate of the author.

Cordwainer Smith: "Scanners Live in Vain" first published in *Fantasy Book*, Vol. 1, No. 6, ed. Garret Ford, Fantasy Publishing Company, Inc., 1950. Reproduced by permission of Spectrum Literary Agency.

Bruce Sterling: "Maneki Neko" published in *The Magazine of Fantasy & Science Fiction*, May 1998. Reproduced by permission of the author.

Romie Stott: "A Robot Walks into a Bar" published in *Arc 1.4 / Forever Alone Drone*, 2012. Reproduced by permission of the author.

Theodore Sturgeon: "Microcosmic God" published in *Astounding Science-Fiction* 1941. Published by permission of The Theodore Sturgeon Literary Trust c/o The Lotts Agency, Ltd.

Michael Swanwick: "Ancient Engines" published in *Asimov's Science Fiction Magazine*, February 1999, copyright © 1998. Reproduced by permission of the author.

Rachel Swirsky: "Tender" published in *Upgraded*, 2014. Reproduced by permission of the author.

Brian Trent: "Director X and the Thrilling Wonders of Outer Space" published in *All Hail Our Robot Conquerors!* 2017. Reproduced by permission of the author.

Miguel De Unamuno: "Mechanopolis," 1913, translated by Patricia Hart from *Cosmos Latinos: An Anthology of Science Fiction from Latin America and Spain*, edited by Andrea L. Bell and Yolanda Molina-Gavilán, copyright © 2003 Wesleyan University Press. Published by Wesleyan University Press. Used with permission.

A. E. van Vogt: "Fulfillment" first published in *New Tales of Space and Time*, 1951. Reproduced by permission of the Estate of the author and Ashley Grayson Agency.

Howard Waldrop: "London, Paris, Banana" published in *Amazing Stories*, Winter 2000. Reproduced by permission of the author.

Peter Watts: "Malak" published in *Engineering Infinity*, 2010, ed. Jonathan Strahan Solaris. Reproduced by permission of the author.

Alexander Weinstein: "Saying Goodbye to Yang" published in *Children of the New World*, copyright © 2016 by Alexander Weinstein. Reproduced by permission of Text Publishing and Picador.

Tad Williams: "The Narrow Road," translated by Sam Hamill, published in *Arc 2.1 Exit strategies*, Reed Business Information Ltd, 2014. Reproduced by permission of Deborah Beale.

Jack Williamson: "With Folded Hands" first published in *Astounding Science Fiction*, July 1947, ed. John W. Campbell, Jr., Street & Smith Publications, Inc. Reproduced by permission of Spectrum Literary Agency.

Bernard Wolfe: "Self Portrait," copyright © 1951. Used by permission of Catalyst Literary Management LLC, on behalf of Miranda Wolfe and Jordan M. Wolfe. All rights reserved.

Nick Wolven: "Caspar D. Luckinbill, What Are You Going to Do?" first published in *The Magazine of Fantasy & Science Fiction*, Jan–Feb 2016, ed. C. C. Finlay, Spilogale, Inc. Reproduced with permission of the author.

E. Lily Yu: "Musée de l'Âme Seule" first published in *Upgraded*, ed. Neil Clarke, Wyrm Publishing, 2014, copyright © 2014 by E. Lily Yu.

George Zebrowski: "Starcrossed" first published in Eros in Orbit, edited by Joseph Elder, Trident Press, 1976, copyright © 1976 George Zebrowski.

Every effort has been made to trace copyright holders and to obtain their permission for the use of copyright material. The publisher apologizes for any errors or omissions in the above list and would be grateful if notified of any corrections that should be incorporated in future reprints or editions of this book.